The Encyclopedia *of* Murder and Mystery

Bruce F. Murphy

palgrave
for St. Martin's Minotaur

ENCYCLOPEDIA OF MURDER AND MYSTERY

First published 1999 by
PALGRAVE™
175 Fifth Avenue, New York, N.Y. 10010.
Companies and representatives throughout the world.

PALGRAVE™ is the new global publishing imprint of St. Martin's Press LLC Scholarly and Reference Division and Palgrave Publishers Ltd (formerly Macmillan Press Ltd).

ISBN 0-312-21554-1 hardback
ISBN 0-312-29414-X paperback

Library of Congress Cataloging-in-Publication Data

Murphy, Bruce F., 1962-
The encyclopedia of murder and mystery / Bruce F. Murphy.
p. cm.
Includes bibliographical references.
ISBN 0-312-21554-1 (cloth) ISBN 0-312-29414-X (paperback)
1. Detective and mystery stories Encyclopedias. 2. Murder in literature Encyclopedias. I. Title.
PN3448.D4M87 1999
809.3'872'03—dc21 99-25316
CIP

Design by planettheo.com

First paperback edition: December 2001
10 9 8 7 6 5 4 3 2 1

Printed in the United States of America.

CONTENTS

ACKNOWLEDGEMENTS

Many people have contributed to this book with their energy, ideas, and patience and I have to thank my family and friends for their help, especially my parents; Kevin D. Murphy and Mary Anne Caton; Patrick Ambrose, who provided many important insights and also assisted in research; Deirdre Murphy, Esq., without whom this book would not have happened; Kathy Iwasaki, who saved the book at a critical stage; and Michael Flamini, my editor. I would also like to thank the West Village Committee, which in addition to saving the West Village from development, operates a used bookstore where I found bushels of treasures. Above all I have to thank Alessandra de Rosa, who enjoyed and endured this project over several years.

BIBLIOGRAPHY

In addition to general works of reference literature, a number of specialized sources were consulted in the writing of this book. They include *A Catalogue of Crime* (1971, rev 1989) by Jacques Barzun and Wendell Hertig Taylor; *Bloody Murder* (1972, rev 1985) by Julian Symons; *Detecting Women* (1994) by Willetta L. Heising; *Murder for Pleasure* (1941) by Howard Haycraft; *Whodunit?* (1982) by H. R. F. Keating; *Encyclopedia Mysteriosa* (1994) by William L. DeAndrea; *The Encyclopedia of Mystery and Detection* (1975) edited by Otto Penzler and Chris Steinbrunner; *Les auteurs de la Série Noir* (1996) by Claude Mesplède and Jean-Jacques Schleret; and *Twentieth Century Crime and Mystery Writers*, edited by Lesley Henderson.

ABOUT THIS BOOK

This book contains entries on authors, characters, individual works, terminology, famous criminal cases, slang, subgenres and plot devices, murder techniques and poisons, all of which are part of the matter and manner and context of crime and murder literature. Entries are also provided for select slang terms that I have come across in my reading. Commonly known terms or those with obvious derivations have not been included, such as the many versions of the verb "to kill" (to chill, to cool, to waste, to rub out, etc.). Mysteries that fall under children's literature (such as the Encyclopedia Brown mysteries) fall outside the scope of this work. In some plot summaries, ambiguities have been deliberately left in so as not to spoil the mystery for the reader.

Cross-references using small capitals have been added to direct the reader to other entries in the book. To make the book as readable as possible, however, not all terms have been cross-referenced, but only those germane to the subject at hand, and where several occur in a single sentence only the most particular has been placed in small capitals (thus, if a book has an entry, the title is in small caps but not the author's name, for example "Dashiell Hammett's RED HARVEST"). Words that appear constantly are also not cross-referenced, such as "p.i." and "short story." Though articles such as "the" and "an" that appear at the beginning of titles have been placed in small capitals they are not used in alphabetizing. In some cases, single words have been cross-referenced to indicate multiple word entries (for example, PULP, in order to direct a reader to the entry on PULP MAGAZINES).

Bibliographies are appended to entries for series characters, listing the books not discussed in the entry itself. Complete bibliographies of all of an author's published works can be found in such sources as *Twentieth Century Crime and Mystery Writers* or *The Dictionary of Literary Biography.* Dates of publication are usually those of publication in the country of origin, i.e. first U.S. publication for an American book, first U.K. publication for British books, etc. In cases where a date is not known or is not available, asterisks (***) or question marks (?) have been inserted instead. Along with dates of publication are abbreviations indicating the type of book: coll: collected, repr: reprinted, ed: edited, tr: translated, retr: retranslated, rev: revised, exp: expanded, pub: published, orig: original.

PREFACE

THE TRIUMPH OF THE MYSTERY STORY

W. Somerset Maugham wrote in a famous essay that when twentieth century literary history came to be written, future critics might "pass somewhat lightly over the compositions of the 'serious' novelists and turn their attention to the immense and varied achievement of the detective writers." This apparent justification of the mystery was seized upon by Ellery Queen and others as proof that the detective story had arrived as a respectable genre. Moreover, Maugham seemed to be saying that the mystery had already surpassed the "serious" novel, which had gotten bogged down in modernism and lost its popular audience, leaving the field wide open for detective fiction. But to see Maugham as the champion of the genre one had to overlook that his essay was actually entitled "The Decline and Fall of the Detective Story" and that in less publicized passages he declared the genre virtually dead. Maugham's equivocal message illustrates one of the ironies of the mystery genre: although the question of whether mystery and detective novels could achieve the same level of craftsmanship and literary significance as the "serious" novel was long ago laid to rest, mystery writers themselves keep digging it up again. Ross Macdonald said that the detective novel was "still available for the highest art"; Julian Symons said that the best writers of mysteries have been artists, not artisans; and the South African writer Wessel Ebersohn wrote that "it is possible for a thriller to be a work of art." Those mystery writers who have gained reputations as "serious" authors are often the staunchest defenders of the genre's past achievements and potential—and the harshest critics of its failures and also-rans.

No author illustrates this phenomenon better than Raymond Chandler. His famous essay "The Simple Art of Murder" has been the touchstone for partisans of the genre for more than fifty years. He credited Dashiell Hammett and the hard-boiled writers with taking murder out of the drawing room and putting it in the street, with restoring the mystery's attachment to life by portraying real people with real emotions who commit murder suddenly with whatever comes to hand—more likely a hammer than curare-tipped darts. Privately, Chandler wondered whether he was not the best writer in the United States and asked whether he would have been more recognized had he written outside of the genre. But Chandler also (like Maugham) criticized the "serious" novel, believing that it had lost the popular audience because of its pretentiousness, stylistic contortionism, obscurity, and political line-toeing. At the same time, he attacked other mystery writers—and not only English ones—for slick products with cardboard characters and feeble motives.

The day that Maugham foresaw has arrived, and Chandler's view has prevailed. Looking back on the twentieth century, we can see that the crime story has progressively displaced the "serious" novel as the center of fiction, so to speak. Not only are the best crime writers taken seriously; but numerous writers who have already established literary reputations have chosen to write crime and mystery novels. Murder is made a basis for plot, for example, in works by Robertson Davies, E. L. Doctorow, Timothy Findley, Rosellyn Brown, Thomas Keneally, William Trevor, and Thomas Berger. Today mystery, detective, and crime literature have a permanent lock on the bestseller lists. One certainly is entitled to ask why, for as Jacques Barzun wrote, "murder and detection in real life can give pleasure to very few. The one evokes anger and misery, the other boredom."

There are many reasons for the inexorable growth of the crime and mystery genre. Some of them are obvious sociological ones: people like to read about what's bothering them. As crime becomes more and more of an international obsession, particularly in the country that has a larger proportion of its population incarcerated than any other industrialized nation (the United States), every novelist who responds to reality must perforce be a crime novelist. It is no accident that the rise of the detective novel parallels that of the industrial revolution; heightened anonymity, social insecurity, and urban poverty are like fertilizer for criminality. As soon as people began clamoring for police forces to protect them from increasing urban violence, writers (Charles Dickens among them) began writing stories about how the detectives went about doing so. In the process, the traditional hero of Western literature was revised in the image of the sleuth. More than one critic has traced the mystery detective back to Arthurian legend and the knight errant. Errancy meant being on an adventure apart from one's group or *comitatus*—in modern terms, without backup. Being essentially alone is as much a part of Philip Marlowe's character as it is Sir Gawain's. On the other side (the side of evil), the figure of the villain has been traced to the original Napoleon of crime, Satan. Dorothy L. Sayers pointed to Biblical passages as the earliest models for the genre; the modern criminal-as-hero is easily seen to be a descendant of the fascinating Satan created by Milton in *Paradise Lost*. Thus, crime and mystery fiction responded to contemporary social developments but merged with the ancient patterns of Western literature. Sin became Crime.

There will always be those who claim that a fascination with the murder story is unhealthy, and that the success of the genre rests on ghoulishness. No doubt there are and always will be some bloodthirsty readers. But the beauty of the mystery story, and what, when well done, gives it its power and raises it to the level of "serious" fiction, is how it reveals human weakness. Tough guys crack wise and entertain, but the emotional center of good mysteries is weakness of character and such failures of courage or surrenders to temptation as can turn reasonably good men or women into criminals and at worst, murderers. (The "psycho," the monster whose motivations are incomprehensible, is for that reason one of the most boring characters in popular literature.) Whether seen as crimes or sins, the acts that drive the plots of mysteries and the emotions behind them rivet our attention. It is possible to view the succumbing to temptation in the mystery novel as a version of the Fall. It has also been seen as Oedipal. What is important is that the well-wrought crime story makes us aware of our intimate knowledge of the archetypal tempter and our horrified fascination with the figure of the fallen, which is well expressed by Leo Perutz in *Master of the Day of Judgement:*

> We are all creatures who have disappointed the Creator's grand design. Without suspecting it we have a terrible enemy inside us. He lies there motionless, asleep, as if he were dead. Woe if he comes back to life.

One reason for the recent explosion of interest in crime fiction is that the moral-psychological territory it explores has been largely abandoned by serious fiction. The criticisms of the modernist novel made by mystery writers at mid-century apply today even more strongly to the postmodern novel. When Chandler's Philip Marlowe tries to read a novel by Hemingway, he asks why the writer keeps saying the same thing over and over. Hemingway, however, wrote about violent and passionate subjects. One wonders what Marlowe/Chandler would have thought of the novel that purports to be about language itself, or fiction that has completely detached itself from the concept of story. Admirers of postmodern writing may find the detective novel hopelessly unsophisticated because of its straight-ahead focus on content, plot, and resolution. The critic Geoffrey Hartman wrote that

> Most popular mysteries are devoted to solving rather than examining a problem. Their reasonings put reason to sleep, abolish darkness by elucidation, and bury the corpse for good. Few detective novels want the reader to exert his intelligence fully, to find gaps in the plot or the reasoning, to worry about the moral question of fixing the blame. They are exorcisms,

> stories with happy endings that could be classified with comedy because they settle the unsettling.

Many mysteries—some of them discussed in this book—focus on precisely those difficult problems (such as fixing blame) that Hartman denies are examined in mysteries. In much of contemporary "literary" fiction, on the other hand, nothing seems to be at stake. It substitutes the nebulous for the precise and the obscure for the profound, and uses "openendedness" as an excuse for shapelessness and lack of technique.

The crime story is about consequences. In the mystery novel, infidelity leads to murder; in the "serious" novel, more often than not it leads merely to divorce and opportunities for characters to feel sorry for themselves. So-called literary fiction frequently deals with the relatively minor disappointments of the overprivileged. By contrast, in *The Ax* Donald Westlake writes a superficially humorous but deeply angry crime novel about corporate downsizing. James Ellroy's *American Tabloid* explodes the myth of America and attacks the cynicism and greed behind state and corporate power. Contemporary crime and mystery fiction are most compelling when they probe the insecurities and fears of those confronted with situations and actions antithetical to the feel-good, sound-byte images sold by politicians and the media, and which we buy at our peril.

The detective story is thus not merely a toy created by Poe; it has become a form of serious fiction. That does not mean, however, that Maugham's and Chandler's criticisms of lesser writers do not still apply. No doubt many readers dismiss the classic and cozy mysteries as representing a fanciful world of impossible people with unbelievable motives. But neither are other subgenres inherently better or more "real." It is not difficult to conceive shocking scenes that hit the reader in the stomach, or to base a novel on newspaper accounts of gruesome crimes. The writer who aims no higher than this will achieve nothing more than mere sensationalism. Similarly, thrillers often create suspense by the crudest method—simply by withholding information from the reader. The techno-thriller depends on technology rather than the detective's intellect, experts and organizations rather than individuals. Mystery novelist Agnes Bushell has written that "mysteries, God bless them, follow the rules. In fact, the mystery may be the only literary genre left with a sense of honor. There's no honor, however, in the thriller-for-film-rights genre books that clunk along like first-draft screenplays, and no honor in substituting 'location' for setting or using 'natives' as stage props." Books that are merely manipulative or in which the hero is a computer or a new kind of jet airplane do not really belong to a genre that has always stressed the possibilities of individual action and (often) the weight of conscience. With the growth in the number of published mystery novels that began in the eighties, there has also been a rush to establish series characters like those Bushell describes, and to somehow distinguish them from the ever-growing pack. What best reveals this eighties mentality is that, to tell us about himself, the detective thinks it is sufficient to tells us about his *things*—as spies in the James Bond mold have special guns and special cars, so detectives have signature weapons, strange quarters (in Dennis Lehane's novels, the steeple of a church), and odd hangers-on. Stephen King has observed that "it has become ever more difficult to create a character with enough individuality to make him (or her) stand out, and as a result, a lot of writers have resorted to caricature rather than character. Put another way, they have resorted to cats of various shapes and colors . . . but all of them, alas, seem gray in the dark."

A genre grows by setting up outposts and then exploring the intervening territory. One recent development, the "ecothriller," deals with crimes against the environment, thus responding to our newly troubled awareness of a kind of violence that was always there. Many of those who come along to settle the outlying areas of an innovation are simply members of King's army of "gray cats." Others, however, set off in new directions. The approach of this book to the now enormous array presented by mystery and detective fiction is to show the genre's depth as well as breadth while singling out the superlative for attention. To give as complete a picture as possible of the genre as a field of literature with its own historical development, factual background, and rich vocabulary, there are entries on the language and terminology of the mystery (including slang, the use of which the genre legitimized), on major and minor characters who are particularly intriguing, on the antecedents of the genre, and on true cases that have sparked debate among historians of crime and have sometimes produced fictional adaptations. Also included is information related to the mechanics of murder—poisons, weapons, and investigative tools such as fingerprinting.

It is hard to say how far the expansion of the mystery genre will go in the future, for it encompasses not only new work but revisions of the canon. For example, the *New Mystery Anthology*, edited by Jerome Charyn, contains several works that are neither new nor mysteries, such as Isaac Babel's "The King" (Ray Carver's excellent story "Cathedral" is the most unlikely selection). Charyn goes so far as to make the unanswerable remark that because of the evil in the world, "one might even argue that God himself is a crime novelist." The mystery and crime genre is changing because, as Charyn's anthology shows, the terms in which we think about it have changed. As the mystery novel shoulders its way even further into the mainstream, or center stage, of contemporary writing (how far we've come from the day when H. L. Mencken dismissed his own mystery magazine, *Black Mask*, as "a louse"), our view of it will no doubt undergo further metamorphosis. I hope that mystery fans who pick up this book will not only find the old friends they are looking for, but will also make some new ones—as I have done over the years of writing it.

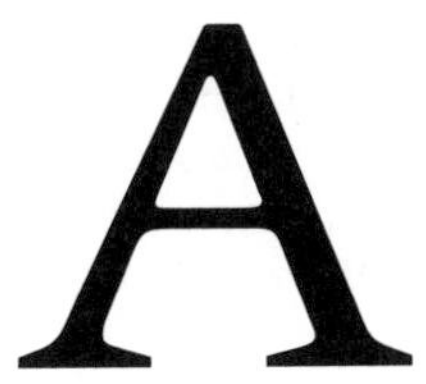

AARONS, EDWARD S[IDNEY] (1916–1975) Edward S. Aarons was one of the most prolific writers in the genre, turning out more than 40 novels about CIA agent Sam DURELL as well as another two hundred stories and novelettes. Aarons was born in Philadelphia and worked as a newspaperman and in a series of odd jobs. His schooling was interrupted by World War II, in which he served in the Coast Guard, and he received his degree from Columbia University after the war. Although he had published his first mystery novel in 1938, *Death in the Lighthouse,* it was in the fifties that he began to turn out books at a great rate. He wrote under the pseudonyms of Edward Ronns and Paul Ayres as well as under his own name. Aarons's work stresses action, adventure, and exoticism. Many of the Durell novels were named for the dangerous ingenues the agent was "assigned" to and usually slept with. Among his non-series novels is *The Catspaw Ordeal* (1950), a tale of espionage and betrayal set on the Connecticut coast. Many of his books have heroes defeating the diabolical forces of communism and foreigners, and the black-and-white attitude to U.S. Cold War foreign policy and hawkishness of the books is somewhat distasteful; however, Aarons's failure to create believable characters and the lack of modulation in his stories are bigger problems. The writing is heavy handed, and Aarons's efforts at description show a feeble grasp of metaphor; for example, a crashing plane is seen "spilling fire like a gutted barnyard animal."

ABBOT, ANTHONY (pseudonym of Charles Fulton Oursler, 1893–1952) Fulton Oursler was once famous for his popular religious works, particularly *The Greatest Story Ever Told* (1949), a retelling of the story of the Bible. It was followed by *The Greatest Book Ever Written* (1951) and *The Greatest Faith Ever Known* (1953), as well as other books of Christian apologetics. But as Anthony Abbot, he wrote a brief series of mysteries about Thatcher COLT, head of the New York City police department.

Abbot began his writing career as a newspaperman with the *Baltimore American,* having previously worked at jobs as various as law clerk and water boy for a construction crew. Although he never finished high school—actually, he never entered it, having dropped out of the eighth grade—he rose to high positions with publishing companies in New York City. While working for MacFadden Publications, he oversaw various PULP MAGAZINES including *True Detective*. Abbot continued his own writing, however, and had a long-running play on Broadway, *The Spider* (1927), co-written with Lowell Brentano. He began the Thatcher Colt series with *About the Murder of Geraldine Foster* (1930), which features an AXE murder, inviting comparisons with the Lizzie BORDEN case. Like S. S. VAN DINE, Abbot sometimes used real cases as inspiration; also like Van Dine, the connection to reality stopped there. Thatcher Colt is the police commissioner of New York City, but he goes about in evening dress and is clearly a GENIUS DETECTIVE of the Philo VANCE school. Although the Colt books are now even harder to find than the Vance mysteries, BARZUN and TAYLOR gave Abbot credit for being more "sensible" than Van Dine.

Oursler became a senior editor at *Reader's Digest* in 1944. He was a broadcaster during World War II. He also lectured on criminology and pursued a wide variety of interests, including psychic phenomena. His autobiography is *Behold This Dreamer* (1964).

ABBOT, SERGEANT FRANK See SILVER, MISS.

ABBOTT, PAT AND JEAN A husband-and-wife team of detectives created by Frances CRANE. Pat and Jean have been forgotten; they were latecomers to the subgenre of detecting couples, and lacked the originality of Nick and Nora CHARLES (who only appeared in one book) and Pam and Jerry NORTH. The Abbott books depended more on the setting, which was often exotic, than on the qualities of the characters themselves. The first book, *The Turquoise Shop* (1941), set the pattern for the series. The shop of the title is in New Mexico and belongs to Jean Holly; Pat Abbott is on vacation when he runs into Jean (the vacation motif would be used throughout the series). Abbott has to investigate the local art colony after a prospector is killed. The second novel in the series, *The Golden Box* (1942), is set in the town of Elm Hill, which is ruled by the domineering Claribel Fabian Lake. No one is sad when she dies, until it is revealed that she was murdered. In *The Yellow Violet* (1943), Pat and Jean get married.

Pat Abbott is from San Francisco and is a typical HARD-BOILED private investigator, except that he is an amateur painter. He also narrates the stories. Jean is a typical heroine of the forties—feisty, energetic, but subordinate to her male counterpart, who is the expert. This male-professional-married-to-female-amateur model goes back to Nick and Nora Charles, and also describes the interaction of Bertha COOL and Donald LAM. The man is the cool and collected one, while the woman is curious and gets things going but doesn't know what to do next. In this pattern, the woman frequently has to be rescued by the male of the series. Like Bertha Cool, Jean Abbott is left on her own when Pat goes off to fight in World War II, and a few books feature her alone.

BIBLIOGRAPHY Novels: *The Pink Umbrella* (1943), *The Applegreen Cat* (1943), *The Amethyst Spectacles* (1944), *The Indigo Necklace* (1945), *The Cinnamon Murder* (1946), *The Shocking Pink Hat* (1946), *Murder on the Purple Water* (1947), *Black Cypress* (1948), *The Flying Red Horse* (1949), *The Daffodil Blonde* (1950), *Murder in Blue Street* (1951; British title: *Death in the Blue Hour*), *The Polkadot Murder* (1951), *Thirteen White Tulips* (1953), *Murder in Bright Red* (1953), *The Coral Princess Murders* (1954), *Death in Lilac Time* (1955), *Horror on the Ruby X* (1956), *The Ultraviolet Widow* (1956), *The Man in Gray* (1958; British title: *The Grey Stranger*), *The Buttercup Case* (1958), *Death-Wish Green* (1960), *The Amber Eyes* (1962), *The Body Beneath a Mandarin Tree* (1965).

ABNER, UNCLE Character created by Melville Davisson POST, a larger-than-life figure who roots out evil with a Biblical enthusiasm. His great size, stern aspect, and thick beard enhance his prophetic quality. Abner is one of the landed gentry in West Virginia; the period is the early nineteenth century. The stories are narrated by Martin, the son of Abner's brother Rufus. Post cleverly has Martin remember stories from his childhood; in a child's eyes, the magnificent and forbidding Abner is almost a god.

When Abner and the magistrate Squire Randolph ride out against the moonshiner Doomdorf in their first adventure, they sound like two paladins. "The Doomdorf Mystery" has the flavor of quest literature, with the two men "crossing the broken spine of the mountains," passing "along the river in the shade of the great chestnut trees," and finally climbing to where, like a castle, Doomdorf's cabin is perched on a sheer rock.

Squire Randolph represents the law, but Abner is a servant of "God's court." He observes clues, but he interprets them in terms of divine justice and with reference to Biblical parallels. A lawyer, Post does not seem to have much confidence in the law. Randolph's efforts to find mundane, secular explanations for events are treated with a knowing reserve by Abner, making Randolph seem hopelessly naive. (Elsewhere he is referred to as "vain, pompous, and proud.") Abner is not a religious crank, however; he is a wonderful character in Old Testament style, who thrashes a tavern-full of men when they laugh at him for reading his Bible by the fire.

Uncle Abner gives his theory of justice in THE TENTH COMMANDMENT, one of many stories with Biblical titles; another is the parable of democracy, NABOTH'S VINEYARD. THE WRONG HAND is a dark fairy tale that also includes disputations on religion between Abner and an evil hunchback.

BIBLIOGRAPHY Short Stories: *Uncle Abner: Master of Mysteries* (1918), *The Methods of Uncle Abner* (pub 1974).

"ABSENT-MINDED COTERIE, THE" A story by Robert BARR about Eugène VALMONT that has several ingenious features. It is set in November 1896, just after William Jennings Bryan had been defeated by William McKinley for the U.S. Presidency. A major issue of the campaign was silver, the price of which had sunk to unheard-of depths compared with gold (hence Bryan's famous "Cross of Gold" speech at the Democratic convention). In Barr's story, clever counterfeiters have found that, instead of making fake coins from base metals, they can now mint silver coins cheaply enough to make a profit. Spenser Hale of Scotland Yard puts Valmont onto the case, and he discovers another swindle of even greater ingenuity (if not plausibility). The twist at the end is delightfully exasperating.

ACK-EMMA A British expression meaning "A.M.," in the morning.

ACKROYD, PETER (1949–) English critic, biographer, and (occasionally) author of mysteries. Ackroyd was educated at Cambridge and Yale, worked for *The Spectator,* and later became the book critic for *The Times* of London. By then, he had already begun writing a series of highly respected critical works. Ackroyd's biographies of Ezra Pound (1980; rev 1987), Charles DICKENS (1990), and particularly T. S. Eliot (1984) have established his scholarly reputation.

As a fiction writer, Ackroyd has written about crime with a particular interest in creating new permutations on the detective and suspense stories. Ackroyd's "mysteries" are also historical; the unconventionally structured THE TRIAL OF ELIZABETH CREE (1995), which blends fact with fiction, was widely acclaimed, even though it is inferior in conception and execution to his first novel, HAWKSMOOR (1985), which won the Prix Goncourt as well as the Whitbread award.

ADAMS, DOC The central character in a series of mysteries by Rick BOYER. When Adams is first introduced, he is a somewhat neurotic oral surgeon who is bored with life. Having started out as a physician, he quit when he failed to save the life of an eight-year-old patient—his nephew. Adams himself has two sons, a wife named Mary, a catboat, and two homes—a house in Concord, Massachusetts and a cottage on Cape Cod overlooking BILLINGSGATE SHOAL (the title of the first book in the series, published in 1982). In the first novel, Charlie's boredom is more than relieved as he is plunged into a series of violent events that transform him into an amateur sleuth. The author gives Adams maximum fortuitous assistance by making his wife a trained nurse (she is also a ceramicist) and his brother-in-law a Massachusetts state policeman. Later in the series, Doc Adams becomes more like Aaron Elkins's Gideon OLIVER.

Unfortunately, the Adams series went rapidly downhill after a promising debut. The mystery in *The Whale's Footprints* (1988) begins on a stormy night on Cape Cod when a friend of Doc's son, Jack, goes out for a walk in the driving rain, comes back in a couple of hours, and then is found dead the next morning. Adams discovers the substitution of a lethal drug (to which his own son had obvious access) for the boy's epilepsy medicine. The suspicion cast on his son allows Doc Adams to pontificate in a tiresome way on the value of family and to beat up a police officer, demonstrating that although he's middle-aged he is still macho. There are many scenes in which he is revealed to be a typical 1980s middle-aged guy trying to convince himself he is still young through obsessive jogging, ogling women, etc. His references to sex are embarrassingly trite and juvenile. In *Yellow Bird* (1991), Adams and his wife are walking past a closed-up beach house when they hear a shot, which they dismiss as a car backfiring until Adams gets called in to identify the victim through his dental work. In that book, Boyer trades in the somewhat brooding, New England flavor of the original for the situation-comedy-of-manners of, for example, Sue GRAFTON, complete with hokey Texan accents and jokes guaranteed to evoke canned laughter.

BIBLIOGRAPHY Novels: *The Penny Ferry* (1984), *The Daisy Duck* (1986), *Moscow Metal* (1987), *Gone to Heaven* (1991), *The Man Who Whispered* (1998).

ADAMS, HERBERT (1874–1958) An English author of mysteries who wrote some fifty books, Herbert Adams's works are now out of print. Adams was born in London; his first literary efforts were not mysteries, but fiction and poetry, and failed to find an audience. It was only fairly late in life that he returned to writing after a business career. Adams is chiefly worth looking up for golfers; Adams used the sport as the basis for several mysteries, most involving an amateur detective named Roger Bennion, whose activities are often in the classic, English village, and COUNTRY HOUSE mold—for example, *Crime Wave at Little Cornford* (1948). *The Crooked Lip* (1926) owes much to Conan DOYLE, starting with its title. In this case, the lip belongs to a woman, who passes the train compartment of a man who is killed soon after. The insipid heroine is the daughter of the victim.

Sometimes, however, Adams moved beyond the conventional and produced truly strange and original stories, such as *The Chief Witness* (1939), about brothers who shoot themselves at the same time on the same night but miles apart. *Oddways* (1929), about a kept woman who is on trial for the murder of her lover, was mildly adventurous for its time. Adams's style is typical of the GOLDEN AGE, and he used typically Golden Age devices, but his writing is fresher and lighter than that of many of his contemporaries. He avoided melodrama and, though not comic, was also not heavy-handed; his virtue as a narrator was his affability.

Adams's golf mysteries include *The Body in the Bunker* (1935), *Death Off the Fairway* (1936), *The Nineteenth Hole Mystery* (1939), and *Death on the First Tee* (1957) (see GOLF MYSTERIES). He also wrote the short story collection, *The Perfect Round: Tales of the Links* (1927).

ADAMS, HILDA A nurse in a series of novels by Mary Roberts RINEHART. Middle-aged and unromantic, Hilda Adams is nicknamed "Miss Pinkerton" because of her sleuthing abilities. In contrast to the young and beautiful heroines in some of Rinehart's other books, Adams's very plainness is her greatest asset: "Sitting there in her nightgown she looked rather like a thirty-eight year old cherub. Her skin was rosy, her eyes clear, almost childish. That appearance of hers was her stock in trade, as Inspector Fuller had said to the new commissioner."

Hilda Adams appeared in only three novels, published at ten-year intervals. *Miss Pinkerton* (1932) was the first; it takes place, as do many Rinehart books, in a house whose appearance indicates something about its inhabitants. In this case, the run-down genteel house complements the status of the socially well-positioned but hard-up Mitchell family. Miss Juliet Mitchell, a bed-ridden old woman, loses her nephew, Herbert Wynne, who is found shot; the question is whether the death was a suicide made to look like a murder (for insurance purposes) or a murder made to look like a suicide. Herbert had been carrying on secret romances and was fearful for his life. Hilda inadvertently kills one of the other characters herself with an injection that had been tampered with. The opening is very HAD-I-BUT-KNOWN: "before me lay the old house, blazing with lights. Always I had been curious about it; now I was to know it well."

In *Haunted Lady* (1942; repr 1962), Adams is dispatched by Fuller to stay with the wealthy, aged widow Eliza Fairbanks, who lives in an old mansion in a once-fashionable part of the city. Someone has tried to poison her with arsenic, and she is alarmed because, though she lives in a sealed-off room, she keeps finding bats, rats, snakes, and other undesirables in her room. Other occupants of the house include Eliza's divorced daughter, Marion Garrison; her granddaughter Janice, who is in love with Eliza's doctor; her unemployed son Carlton and his crude wife, Susie; and some surly old servants. Nurse Hilda installs herself in the house, another creepy old family residence. Hilda does not prevent, but ultimately solves, a series of murders.

Hilda Adams also appeared in several short stories, collected in *Mary Roberts Rinehart's Crime Book* (1933). The last Hilda Adams novel was *The Wandering Knife* (1952). Two Hilda Adams films were made in the thirties and forties.

ADAMS, SAMUEL HOPKINS (1871–1958) American journalist and mystery author. Around the turn of the century, Adams was one of that group of journalists known as "muckrakers" that included Sinclair Lewis and Ida M. Tarbell, who set out to expose corruption in big business and government. Once a household name, Adams wrote for *McClure's* magazine, the leading journal of the movement.

Adams also wrote many books, most of them historical, on such subjects as the westward expansion of the United States and the Erie Canal. His journalistic work included a series of articles on quackery and patent medicines for *Collier's*, contained in *The Great American Fraud* (1905), and a series for the *New York Tribune* on false advertising, collected as *The Adams Articles* (1916). Although his work is out of print and no longer read, one part of it is still seen: Adams wrote the story on which Frank Capra's film *It Happened One Night* was based.

In 1911, Adams put his muckraking experience to use in the mystery genre, creating a detective who is a specialist in spotting false advertising. His name is Average JONES, an independently wealthy member of the Cosmic Club. Jones is a detective who gets his cases by culling newspaper advertisements for unusual or fishy notices. The stories were later praised by Howard HAYCRAFT and Ellery QUEEN.

Adams wrote several other mystery novels, including his first book, *The Mystery* (1907). This novel, co-authored with Stewart Edward White, was based on the mysterious case of the disappearance of the ship MARY CELESTE. Another mystery with a nautical connection is *The Secret of Lonesome Cove* (1912). Adams based it on the real case of a body found in 1909 at the base of the cliffs of Cornwall. Adams moved the story to the New England coast, and introduced another in the then-popular subgenre of scientific detectives, Professor Kent, who works for the Department of Justice on the most baffling cases. He has come to Lonesome Cove to study the tides, but finds a crowd surrounding the body of a well-dressed woman lashed to a grating, with handcuffs and a chain attached to her wrist. Adams dedicated the novel to the unknown person who knew the secret of the Cornwall mystery—presumably the murderer.

Adams also was one of the contributors to *The President's Mystery Story* (1935), a collaborative novel written by several authors and based on a plot supplied by Franklin D. Roosevelt.

ADAMSON, LYDIA See CATS.

AFRICAN POISON MURDERS, THE (1939; orig title *Death of an Aryan;* repub 1988) A novel by Elspeth HUXLEY, the second case of Superintendent VACHELL. The story focuses on the colonial community in East Africa, an uneasy mixture of pro-Nazi German settlers and English. Vachell is originally drawn into the case because he wants to observe the leader of the local Nazi *bund,* Karl Munson. It is not a spy story, however; it is told in continuous close-up, showing the farm life, difficulties, and jealousies of the community. Vachell is invited to stay with the Wests, neighbors of Munson; the powerful attraction Janice West exercises on Vachell is depicted with subtle force, reminiscent of P. M. HUBBARD. In a piteous and horrifying scene, Vachell soon discovers that a deranged person in the neighborhood is brutally maiming animals.

As the original title suggested, Munson is found dead, lying in the shed where pyrethrum flowers are dried before being ground up for insecticide. The cause of death is difficult to determine, but Sir Jolyot ANSTEY suggests OUABAIN. Munson's widow is a woman with the personality of a Cape buffalo, and is only one of several suspicious characters, both English and German. The descriptions of bush life are vivid and sometimes frightening, the appearances of the leopard being especially eerie. (It is unfortunate that Vachell never meets up with the Dorobo mole-catcher who lives in the neighborhood.) Vachell has an uncharacteristic outburst at the end that dissipates the pressure of the story like a balloon suddenly let go; the book could happily be read without the last chapter.

AGATHA AWARDS See MALICE DOMESTIC.

AIRD, CATHERINE (pseudonym of Kinn Hamilton McIntosh, 1930–) It was because of a potentially fatal disease that Catherine Aird became a mystery writer. While recuperating (she was bedridden for years), she wrote her first mystery, the strange and unusual THE RELIGIOUS BODY (1966), set in a nunnery. Aird's novels are in the classic English style, and are set in the town of Berebury in the invented county of "Calleshire." The sleuth is Inspector Christopher Dennis Sloan, head of the Criminal Investigation Department; he is nicknamed "Seedy" after his first initials. Sloan's hobby is roses, and he lives comfortably with his wife, Margaret; domestic scenes are often included in the stories, though they are not integral to the plot. Sloan's assistant, Detective Constable William Crosby, is poorly educated but useful. His boss, Superintendent Leeyes, is by turns competent and comical. Leeyes disparages Crosby as a representative of the younger generation, and Sloan tries to get out of working with him (partly because of Crosby's love of driving fast). The long-suffering Crosby is sometimes addressed as "Defective Constable." Humor, however, is not Aird's forte. There is a religious background in later books as well, such as *A Most Contagious Game* (1967), a HISTORICAL MYSTERY involving a crime a century-and-a-half old, and *His Burial Too* (1973), a variation on the LOCKED ROOM MYSTERY, in which an enormous marble statue falls on a man inside the Saxon tower of a church. Unlike many books in this subgenre, the focus in *His Burial Too* is not on how the murder was accomplished, but why and by whom. The search for the killer is sprinkled with various tantalizing elements, including jewels and industrial espionage, but the weak link is the motive; Aird must have felt so herself, for she deals with it almost as an aside. In *A Late Phoenix* (1971), a young doctor, William Latimer, discovers a skeleton in a bombed-out house left over from the war. It was not a bomb, however, that killed this person, but a bullet (the case shares similarities with OLD BONES [1987], a Gideon OLIVER mystery).

Another book in the Sloan series is *The Complete Steel* (1969; U.S. title *The Stately Home Murder*), about a country house whose owners have had to begin showing it to tourists on certain days to make ends meet.

ALBRAND, MARTHA (pseudonym of Heidi Huberta Freybe, 1912–1981) The German-born author who became known under this pseudonym lived in several European countries during her youth, and published a commercially successful novel in Germany, *Carlotta Torrensani* (1938), while she was still in her twenties. She did not stay there long enough to enjoy her success, however, and fled the NAZIS, first settling in England and then in the United States. She was, in a sense, returning to her roots: her great-grandfather had been a missionary among the Chippewa Indians. Albrand published *No Surrender* in 1942; a novel about Dutch resistance to the Nazis, it was the first of many suspense novels published in English under the Albrand pseudonym. *Without Orders* (1943) was another novel about the war and dealt with an escaped American prisoner.

Even though she settled permanently in the United States, Albrand's books are set in Italy, the Netherlands, and other European nations where she had lived. Most of them are thrillers that involve espionage and murder, but mystery and detection are sometimes present. An American who had worked for the Italian resistance returns to Italy in *After Midnight* (1948) to investigate a wartime murder. In *A Door Fell Shut* (1966), a concert violinist is caught up in a murderous plot in Berlin. One of Albrand's later books, *Manhattan North* (1971), was a POLICE PROCEDURAL. In *Zürich AZ/900* (1974), a new therapy for arteriosclerosis is stolen in order to treat a South American dictator.

In 1950, Albrand won the Grand Prix de Littérature Policière. She also wrote non-mystery novels under the name Christine Lambert.

ALCOHOLISM The whiskey bottle in the desk drawer is one of the most hackneyed images of the HARD-BOILED era of mystery writing (even Perry MASON had one). But detectives who overtly identify themselves as alcoholics are more of a modern invention. Raymond CHANDLER rejected the idea that Philip MARLOWE was an alcoholic, saying that he simply took a drink when he felt like it—which was often. Harry STONER describes himself as a "part-time drunk." Other detectives who have or have had a drinking problem include Lew ARCHER, Matthew SCUDDER, M. PINAUD, Peter DULUTH, Pepe Carvalho, Dashiell HAMMETT's Ned Beaumont, Inspector MORSE, Milo MILODRAGOVITCH, and of course, Nick CHARLES.

ALEXANDER, DAVID (1907–1973) Born in Kentucky, David Alexander had a lifelong interest in horses and horse racing. After graduating from the University of Kentucky he moved to New York. He worked for various newspapers, including the *Morning Telegraph,* a paper that covered show business and horse racing. Alexander was managing editor for ten years; his experience with this paper would later provide the basis for his series of novels about the tough journalist Bart HARDIN. Alexander also worked for the *New York Herald Tribune* and *National Thoroughbred.* His ambition, however, was to be a crime novelist, and so he enrolled at New York's Institute of Criminology. Alexander took to the subject and did so well academically that he was offered several jobs in the field, which he turned down in order to write. During World War II, Alexander served in the tanks corps.

In addition to the Hardin series, Alexander wrote about Tommy Tuthill and Terry Bob Rooke, who are a similar pair to Nero WOLFE and Archie GOODWIN. Tuthill and Rooke appeared in *Most Men Don't Kill* (1951) and *Murder in Black and White* (1951). His non-series work, *The Madhouse in Washington Square* (1958), is a dark crime novel in which Alexander depicted the netherworld of street people, washed-up performers, has-beens, and others on the fringe of society. (Washington Square is in Alexander's own neighborhood, Greenwich Village.) *Hangman's Dozen* (1961) is a collection of Alexander's short fiction; one of his stories won a prize in an *Ellery Queen's Mystery Magazine* contest.

ALIENIST, THE See CARR, CALEB.

ALLAIN, MARCEL (1885–1969) French author, co-writer with Pierre SOUVESTRE of the FANTÔMAS series. Allain was working for Souvestre as a secretary and writing simultaneously for automotive trade magazines and drama reviews when they collaborated on the first Fantômas novel. Following its spectacular success, they went on to write dozens of novels together about the terrifying thief and murderer. After Souvestre's untimely death in 1914, Allain enlisted and fought in World War I. He later wrote eleven Fantômas novels on his own, and also married his partner's widow. As can already be gathered, Allain was a PULP MAGAZINE writer; during a long life, he wrote literally hundreds of sensational and suspense novels, and was as prolific as John CREASEY or Erle Stanley GARDNER. Unlike them, he was lauded by surrealists and literary society as a cult figure of popular culture long before it was fashionable to do so in the English-speaking world. Allain's other work has been forgotten, but the fame of Fantômas endures.

ALLEN, [CHARLES] GRANT [BLAIRFINDIE] (1848–1899) On his circuitous route to fame, Grant Allen began as the author of serious books about science and found notoriety for a scandalous attitude toward sex. Born in Ontario, Allen was the son of a minister. He married at a young age and received his degree from Oxford University, thereafter settling in England. After an abortive attempt at a teaching career, Allen began to write serious works on philosophy and natural science. *Physiological Aesthetics* (1877) and *The Colour Sense* (1879) were well received, earning Allen the praise of Charles Darwin and other noted scientists, but apparently not much money. He then turned to popular literature and journalism. Some of his short stories of this period were collected in *Strange Stories* (1884) and *The Beckoning Hand and Other Stories* (1887). Allen reacted against his North American upbringing, which he made fun of in "The Great Ruby Robbery: A Detective Story" (1892), about an American heiress whose great treasure is a bar rather than a boon to the penniless Irish baronet who wants to marry her. In this story, he also played with the idea of the gentleman thief years before he created Colonel CLAY.

Allen is remembered today for three books written over as many years. *The Woman Who Did* (1895) was a taboo-shattering book about a heroine with a liberal attitude toward sexuality, which shocked Victorian England. This forward-looking viewpoint was only one of several similarities between Allen and H. G. WELLS. In Allen's *The British Barbarians* (1896), a time-travel story, a man from the future looks at the primitiveness of contemporary Britain. In terms of the mystery genre, *An African Millionaire* (1897) was a trend-setting work. It was the first novel to make a charming thief its protagonist (Colonel Clay) and to view him positively, predating RAFFLES by a couple of years.

Allen suffered from poor health and died at a relatively young age. As his death neared, he made provisions for his last novel, *Hilda Wade* (1900), to be completed and published. He discussed the book with his friend, Arthur Conan DOYLE, who wrote the final chapter. In the last year of his life, two more volumes of Allen's short fiction were published, *Twelve Tales* (1899) and *Miss Cayley's Adventures* (1899).

ALLEYN, INSPECTOR Detective character created by Ngaio MARSH. Employed by Scotland Yard, Inspector (and later, Superintendent) Roderick Alleyn is urbane, sophisticated, and upper class—he is the son of a baronet. Marsh named him after Edward Alleyn, who founded Dulwich College in 1617 (which her father, and later, Raymond CHANDLER, attended). Alleyn's brother is in the diplomatic service, in which he himself also served at the end of the First World War before entering the police. Alleyn, typically understated, has a subtle sense of humor (he is not given to wisecracking), and Marsh wisely refrained from giving him eccentricities or other strange tics that might fix him in the reader's mind. Alleyn is clever, however, and sometimes disguises himself or goes undercover, for example in *Colour Scheme* (1943), one of his wartime adventures (see NAZIS), and *Singing in the Shrouds* (1958), an example of MURDER AFLOAT. The third Alleyn novel, *The Nursing Home Murder* (1936), is a medical mystery; Marsh wrote it with the help of Dr. Henry Jellett, much as Dorothy L. SAYERS had chosen a physician collaborator for *The Documents in the Case* (1930).

Alleyn is a family man, and sometimes writes letters to his wife, the artist Agatha Troy. He meets her in ARTISTS IN CRIME (1938) while on a cruise. They marry, and are seen together in a number of the mysteries, in which she is more the muse of his detection than an assistant in it. Alleyn's sidekick is Inspector Fox, whom he addresses by the pet names of "Foxkin" and "Bre'r Fox."

As a fundamentally decent man, without CAMPION's weirdness nor WIMSEY's pride, Alleyn belongs in the same category with Alan GRANT and Henry TIBBETT, being the equal of the former and superior to the latter. His formality and his upper-class connections suit him to investigations among the aristocracy; in some of the books, the social setting looms larger than the mystery itself. This criticism (if, in fact, this is a defect at all) has been aimed at *A Surfeit of Lampreys* (1940; U.S. title DEATH OF A PEER)—though the murder in that book is not at all nice.

Death in a White Tie (1938) is another high society murder. Lord Robert "Bunchy" Gospell had been helping Alleyn investigate a blackmail case involving two society women, Lady Evelyn Carrados (a nod to Ernest BRAMAH) and Mrs. Halcutt-Hackett. The suspected murderer is an Italian caterer with a Russian name, Colombo Dimitri. The case hinges on an interrupted phone call to Alleyn by the victim during the last moments of a party, and determining who left when and other details.

Marsh used all the classic mystery gambits at one time or another, and often repeatedly; the COUNTRY HOUSE mystery, and especially its subset, the SNOWBOUND mystery, were among her favorites. *Death of a Fool* (1956; British title *Off with His Head*) is a case of beheading. A German folklore enthusiast is stranded in a hotel by a snowstorm, where she spies on preparations for an ancient rite, the South Mardian sword dance. The murder happens at the climax of this fertility and resurrection ritual. *Death and the Dancing Footman* (1942) is also a snowbound mystery. As often happens, Alleyn does not come on the scene immediately. The first part of the investigation is carried out by the playwright Aubrey Mandrake.

BIBLIOGRAPHY Novels: *A Man Lay Dead* (1934), *Enter a Murderer (*1935), *Death in Ecstasy* (1936), *Vintage Murder* (1937), *Overture to Death* (1939), *Death at the Bar* (1940), *Died in the Wool* (1945), *Final Curtain* (1947), *Swing, Brother, Swing* (1949; U.S. title *A Wreath for Rivera*), *Opening Night* (1951; U.S. title *Night at the Vulcan*), *Spinsters in Jeopardy* (1953), *Scales of Justice* (1955), *False Scent* (1959), *Hand in Glove* (1962), *Dead Water* (1963), *Killer Dolphin* (1966; British title *Death at the Dolphin*), *Clutch of Constables* (1969), *When in Rome* (1971), *Tied Up in Tinsel* (1972), *Black as He's Painted* (1974).

ALL GRASS ISN'T GREEN (1970) The last novel featuring Bertha COOL and Donald LAM. Bertha, sporting diamond rings but still "stiff as a roll of barbed wire," seems to have gone into semi-retirement, now only responsible for "executive management." The pair are hired to find a missing man, a writer named Colburn Hale who was supposed to be writing a story about marijuana smuggling across the Mexican border. The client is millionaire Milton Carling Calhoun, a nasty man who lies to them about almost everything. Lam does the detection and Bertha hardly appears in the story.

ALLINGHAM, MARGERY [LOUISE] (1904–1966) British mystery author and creator of the detective Albert CAMPION, who first appears in *The Crime at Black Dudley* (1929). She went on to produce a series of books about him that, while relatively few in number compared with the output of some of her contemporaries, are of very high quality.

The Crime at Black Dudley was not Allingham's first published writing; born into a literary family, she published her first story when she was eight years old and her first novel at nineteen (*Blackkerchief Dick,* 1923). The novel, it was rumored, had been communicated to the writer by dead pirates during seances. Allingham's mother and father were cousins, and both had literary backgrounds. Herbert John Allingham edited the *Christian Globe* and later wrote pulp fiction; Emily Allingham wrote for women's magazines—and an aunt founded the film magazine, *Picture Show.*

In her youth, Margery Allingham studied drama and speech as a treatment for her stammering, which was cured. Thereafter she began to write plays. Her first effort in the genre for which she would become famous was *The White Cottage Mystery* (1927), which was serialized in the *Daily Express.* She was married to Philip Youngman Carter, an artist and one-time editor of the *Tatler,* in the same year that her first mystery appeared. Her new husband designed the cover for it, and for most of her later books. Youngman would also complete her last mystery after her death, *Cargo of Eagles* (1968), and then went on to write two more Campion mysteries by himself.

Along with such writers as CHRISTIE, MARSH, and SAYERS, Allingham was one of those who defined the GOLDEN AGE of the mystery in Britain. Allingham's stories are considerably more strange than those of her peers, and her detective is more eccentric than either Lord Peter WIMSEY or Hercule POIROT. Early on he was often perceived to be a parody of the former, but he "matured" into a great detective in his own right. Campion is only a peripheral character (as well as a suspect) in *The Crime at Black Dudley;* in *Mystery Mile* (1929) he becomes the focus. His servant and assistant is Magersfontein LUGG, an ex-convict.

Allingham matured as a writer in the early thirties, and began to lean more on the quality of her writing and less on the ridiculous trappings of Campionism. In *Sweet Danger* (1933; U.S. titles *Kingdom of Death* and *The Fear Sign*), Allingham stresses Campion's "foolish" appearance. In this case, Campion becomes involved in a quasi-spy mission for the government; he has to find the heirlooms of the noble family of Averna, a small but strategically placed Balkan country whose titular rulers, the Pontisbrights of West Sussex, are now extinct. Campion poses as the Paladin of Averna in order to get the artifacts, which include a receipt of sorts from Metternich, showing that the British had paid for this territory. The plot represents the extremity of Allingham's romanticism, which was modulated in her very next book, in which Campion becomes more serious—so much so that in the preface to DEATH OF A GHOST (1934) she felt compelled to explain Campion's personality change.

Allingham's output was lower than that of her contemporaries, and her audience may be smaller because of her idiosyncracy, but her work could be seen as more interesting for the same reasons. She never uses the same formula twice or seems to be merely going through the motions. Some of her finest work was done after World War II, when her production was even slower, though as with Sayers critics disagree rather severely as to which are the best. Allingham's best mystery is THE TIGER IN THE SMOKE (1952), which is more a crime novel than a mystery; among the most curious are THE CASE OF THE LATE PIG (1937), in which a bully from Campion's childhood gets his comeuppance, and *Traitor's Purse* (1941), a case of AMNESIA.

Many of the other characters in Allingham's books are as sensitive and unique as Campion himself. *Death of a Ghost* is largely about the painter, Lafcadio, who supposedly died in 1912; his legacy lives on, however, with interesting results. The book has been both praised and criticized for the many pages devoted to exploring the artistic milieu rather than the mystery. Allingham again focused on artistic personalities in *Dancers in Mourning* (1937), about a persecuted dancer, Jimmy Sutane. It also has a very effective subplot: Campion falls in love with Linda Sutane, Jimmy's wife, a distraction that causes him to make errors in detection. It is interesting that the "romantic subplot" exists entirely in Campion's head, and the book shows to the fullest Allingham's characteristic combination of mystery with portraits of character.

During World War II, the Allingham's home in Essex (an area thought to be a likely site for a German invasion), D'Arcy House, was used to billet two hundred soldiers with their weapons and munitions. Margery Allingham worked in civil defense; her book *The Oaken Heart* (1941) is a fictionalized account of this episode in her life. After the war, her writing continued to develop, and the last book she completed, *The Mind Readers* (1965), included a SCIENCE FICTION element.

After Margery Allingham's death from cancer, her husband wrote *Mr. Campion's Farthing* (1969) and *Mr. Campion's Falcon* (1970; U.S. title *Mr. Campion's Quarry*), which show his deep familiarity with the characters and which have been much better rated than most such continuations.

ALTER, ROBERT EDMOND (1926–1966) At the time of his death in Los Angeles at the age of forty, Robert Edmond Alter had written fourteen children's books and three HARD-BOILED novels. He was born in San Francisco and attended the University of Southern California and Pasadena City College. He worked in various jobs, including as a migratory worker, and served in the army and National Guard. Alter started out writing for PULP MAGAZINES and also published in "slicks" like the *Saturday Evening Post.* His writing is very descriptive for hard-boiled work; his depictions of nature in *Swamp Sister* (1961) have a reality and concern with detail much pulp writing lacks, though he alternates it with the homespun dialogue of a Jim THOMPSON and the occasional tough-guy wisecrack. Alter could write terse, entertaining prose: "Shad tossed his cigarette butt overboard and watched it take a quarter-turn in a sudden surface ripple. It was his last tailor made. He looked up, suddenly sensing his aloneness. The swamp was still, brooding. It made him feel like an intruder in a rehearsal for eternity. 'The thing not to go and do,' he said, as though passing on information to another not-quite-so intelligent him, 'is fer to lose your skiff.'" In *Swamp Sister,* the man named Shad looks for a crashed plane containing a briefcase full of money somewhere in a landscape of silent trees, scurrying, frightened things, and circling alligators. Once he finds it, he tries to keep the discovery quiet, but he can't hide the truth from his lover, the local bombshell. The typical *femme fatale* plot of pulp literature is enlivened by the setting.

Carny Kill (1966) is a more conventional pulp product. It takes place at Neverland, a cheap imitation Disneyland in Florida. Thaxton, an experienced sleight-of-hand man, gets a job there and finds his ex-wife married to the boss. Then he finds the boss with a knife in him, and his ex-wife happens to be a knife thrower. Had Alter lived, he might have been more than a minor artist of the NOIR style. His novels were reprinted twenty years after his death, but because of his small output he remains virtually unknown.

ALVAREZ, INSPECTOR ENRIQUE A Mallorca-based detective in a series of novels by Roderic JEFFRIES. Alvarez is a bon vivant type, a connoisseur of wine and women—the latter interest inhibited by the presence of his wife. He is also chronically sleepy. The strengths of the series are the author's legal expertise, the local color, and the imaginative modi operandi.

The Alvarez mysteries are now closing on the two dozen mark, the point at which any series is likely to become moribund. The plots have become thinner, the props tired. *An Arcadian Death* (1995) is a LOCKED ROOM problem about the death of a spinster living in conditions of poverty but with signs of hidden wealth. *An Artistic Way to Go* (1996) is about Oliver Cooper, a slimy art dealer who has disappeared. His wife had conveniently fallen down the stairs, leaving him free to marry his mistress. There are a variety of unpleasant characters; unfortunately, they are not all murdered. Because of Cooper's dishonest practices, he is now being threatened. His enemies include his adulterous new wife and the restorer/forger whom he has exploited. The book is marred by a half-hearted lewdness and bad dialogue ("Your husband's a creep. . . . divorce him and marry me and learn what life can be like").

In *A Maze of Murders* (1997), a group of English tourists—two men and the two women they had picked up the night before in Mallorca—wake up on a motor yacht with terrible hangovers. They then discover that one of the men is no longer on board. Alvarez's search for the missing man reveals that he is something else than what he seems.

See also TONTINE.

BIBLIOGRAPHY Novels: *Mistakenly in Mallorca* (1974), *Two-Faced Death* (1976), *Troubled Deaths* (1977), *Murder Begets Murder* (1979), *Just Desserts* (1980), *Unseemly End* (1981), *Deadly Petard* (1983), *Three and One Make Five* (1984), *Layers of Deceit* (1985), *Almost Murder* (1986), *Relatively Dangerous* (1987), *Death Trick* (1988), *Dead Clever* (1989), *Too Clever by Half* (1990).

ALWAYS A BODY TO TRADE (1983) A novel by K. C. CONSTANTINE, in the Mario BALZIC series. It is a believable story, HARD-BOILED but without romance. It shows the seamy and sometimes ugly side of police work with no frills and no nonsense. Balzic finds his life about to be made miserable by the election of 34-year old mayor Kenny Strohn, an overbearing, idealistic, and obnoxious man who has no idea of how government (or policing) works but wants to run the town and the Police Department anyway. At this point, Balzic is distracted by a double burglary of two sumptuous and identical apartments owned by a local drug dealer, as well as the murder of a young woman shot in the face at point-blank range. He thinks the two crimes are related. The new mayor, of course, wants instant results; Balzic hopes an informant will come forward. When none does, he is forced to seek the help of the Reverend RUFEE, who presides over a kingdom of vice.

The dialogue between Balzic and Rufee is wonderful, as is the dark humor that pervades the grisly story. Constantine also explores the complicated and ambiguous relationships between the criminal and the police, and between law and "justice"—subjects in which Balzic must teach the mayor a lesson.

AMBLER, ERIC (1909–1999) The English novelist Eric Ambler has had a dominant effect on the development of the spy novel, but his books are not of the 007, tricks and gadgets variety. In fact, some of them, like A COFFIN FOR DIMITRIOS (1939), go back to the style of Childers's RIDDLE OF THE SANDS (1903) and Buchan's THIRTY-NINE STEPS (1915) by not focusing on spies at all, but ordinary people who find themselves in surprising and dangerous situations. The books are finely plotted and make the most of mystery elements such as detection and deduction as well as suspense. The only spy writer still active who is up to Ambler's level is John LE CARRÉ.

Ambler studied engineering at London University and worked in advertising before he became successful writing novels; already, before World War II, he had authored a number of them. During the war he was in the film and photographic unit of the British Army and rose to the rank of lieutenant colonel. He continued writing after the war even after he branched out into screenwriting, and won four Gold Dagger awards from the British CRIME WRITERS' ASSOCIATION as well as an EDGAR for *A Kind of Anger* (1964). The spy novel has now become a fantasy vehicle, but Ambler's books often deal with important contemporary issues, such as revolution in Southeast Asia in *The Night-Comers* (1956; U.S. title *State of Siege*). In this sense, Ambler shares the political quality of Graham GREENE, though to a lesser degree.

Other highly regarded books include *The Schirmer Inheritance* (1953), *The Levanter* (1972), and *Doctor Frigo* (1974). *Here Lies* (1985) is an autobiographical (and Edgar-winning) work, as is *The Story So Far: Memories and Other Fictions* (1993).

AMERICAN TRAGEDY, AN (1925) A novel by Theodore DREISER, based on a real murder case that took place in 1906. Chester Gillette was found guilty of murdering Grace Brown at Big Moose Lake in the Adirondacks. In Dreiser's story, the characters are named Clyde Griffiths and Roberta Alden. Like Dreiser himself, Griffiths comes from a poverty-stricken background. He gets a job at a factory in Upstate New York, where he meets (and seduces) Roberta. Dreiser shows Clyde to be ruthlessly ambitious, but his character is twisted by the values of the society around him, which teaches greed and covetousness—in this case, of Sondra Finchley, a wealthy young woman who symbolizes everything Clyde would like to be. When Roberta becomes pregnant and insists that he own up to his responsibility by marrying her, Clyde decides to do away with Roberta instead. He takes her out on the lake to kill her, but is overcome by cowardice. Then, when an accident occurs, he allows her to drown. Clyde is apprehended and tried.

Dreiser's questioning of the role of socially constructed images of glory and success in the genesis of Clyde's crime is echoed in other crime fiction, including Norman MAILER's *American Dream* (1965).

AMIS, KINGSLEY (1922–1995) Known for his satirical novels in the manner of Evelyn Waugh, particularly *Lucky Jim* (1954), Kingsley Amis was a leader among that group of English writers in the 1950s known as "Angry Young Men." Amis's heroes challenge the legitimacy of the established order of society, which they view as little more than a scam cooked up by snobs, elitists, and the fools who run the establishment. Despite his lasting relationship with the comic novel, Amis wrote in virtually every genre, from poetry to science fiction. His works include two mysteries and a modernized GOTHIC tale.

Born in London and educated at St. John's College, Oxford, Amis taught at several universities, including Princeton; the university formed the background for Jim Dixon's trials and tribulations in *Lucky Jim,* Amis's first novel. *The James Bond Dossier* (1965) is Amis's homage to the works of Ian FLEMING. *Colonel Sun* (1968) is a spy thriller and pastiche of the James BOND novels, which he published under the pseudonym of Robert Markham. In *The Riverside Villa Murders* (1973), Amis employed the framework of the classic English mystery, but added to it some of the racier features of his other books (the seduction of a fourteen-year-old boy by an older woman, for example). His innovations met with only lukewarm approval from critics. *The Green Man* (1969; repr 1986, 1991) is a modern gothic mystery with a supernatural figure out of fable literature, a destructive creature made out of sticks.

Amis's most satisfying mystery is *The Crime of the Century* (book pub 1987). It may be the only novel wherein the detective is a committee. The story was serialized in the *Times* of London in five installments between July and September 1975. Before the final part was published, readers were invited to submit their solutions for a contest. The story concerns a series of murders of young women in London; a task force is set up, its members including not only policemen but such unlikely figures as a rock star, a crime novelist (who finds the crimes following the pattern of his unpublished work), and a motley group of politicians. The story skips along in a series of deft sketches of scenes and conversations, rather than through a detailed investigation; with the committee at odds, the real detective is the reader.

Kingsley Amis's son, Martin Amis (1949–), has also dabbled in detective fiction, with *Night Train* (1998) and an earlier novel about AMNESIA.

AMNESIA Amnesia is a perfect theme for a mystery—almost too perfect. Because mystery is so obviously embedded in the loss of memory, amnesia is something of a cheap trick. (Perhaps it should have been included in the list of items proscribed by FAIR PLAY, just after identical twins.) But, although it smacks of television re-runs and soap operas, some of the most famous writers have worked ably with the idea.

E. C. BENTLEY's *Elephant's Work* (1950) plays on the idea that "elephants never forget." The elephant in question, however, is responsible for the accident that causes the hero, Severn, to lose his memory and to be mistaken for an American gangster named Nick the Chill. (The elephant becomes upset over the quality of the bananas it is fed and reacts indignantly; unfortunately, the elephant is on a train at the time.)

One of the mystery writers who was most fascinated by amnesia was Cornell WOOLRICH. *The Black Curtain* (1941) concerns a man named Frank Townsend who "wakes up" after three years of amnesia to find that he is wearing a hat labeled "D.N."; these happen to be the initials of a murderer sought by the police. Townsend must first find out whether he committed the crime before he can set about clearing himself, which involves investigating his own secret life. Woolrich also used the amnesia theme in short stories such as "C-jag."

In *Traitor's Purse* (1941), Albert CAMPION returns to consciousness to find that he has apparently killed a policeman. Lying in a hospital bed, he doesn't know who he is; Campion's ignorance of his own past—and thus of his own fame and success—allows him to rediscover his character (while uncovering a plot against the nation).

More improbably, in *Pray Silence* (1940), Tommy HAMBLEDON regains consciousness of his identity to find that he has been a kind of shining star of the Nazi Party for over a decade, and has risen to the leadership of the Berlin police. One of the most peculiar aspects of the book is that, even after his awakening and rediscovery of his commitment to English democracy, Hambledon appears to continue to espouse some Nazi ideas, including sympathy with their resentment of Jews and blaming of them for the economic disaster of the interwar years. Another wartime story, written on the other side of the Channel but also involving amnesia, was Léo Malet's 120, RUE DE LA GARE (1943), about the enigmatic P.O.W. known as "the Blob," who has lost his memory.

The year 1948 was a strong one for the amnesia theme. The period after World War II saw intense interest in psychoanalysis and Freudian theory, which no doubt led writers to explore amnesia as a means of questioning the nature of identity and not only as a vehicle for constructing a mysterious blank space at the heart of the novel. In *Ten Days' Wonder* (1948), an acquaintance of Ellery QUEEN from his Paris days turns up at his house. Howard Van Horn has just woken up from one of his periodic amnesia fits, this one lasting nineteen days, to find himself covered with blood. The opening of the novel is striking, but then the authors drag Ellery back to WRIGHTSVILLE, which is coincidentally Howard's hometown. Ellery also engages in much armchair psychology in trying to figure the causes of Howard's amnesia, which is invested with Oedipal and Biblical overtones, building to a drawn-out and preposterous denouement.

Ross MACDONALD's *The Three Roads* (1948) tells the story of Bret Taylor, a Navy lieutenant lying in a mental hospital. The son of a repressive ex-seminarian, Taylor rejected the woman he loved and married a floozy one drunken night before his last voyage. Having had his ship sunk under him, returned home and discovered his wife murdered, Taylor has had a breakdown and lost his memory. After therapy—Macdonald deals with Freudian and Oedipal themes more overtly here than in his later books—he sets out on an obsessive search for the killer and to recover his lost memories. Of Macdonald's early works, this is the finest, and provides a key to themes he later embeds in the Lew ARCHER novels. The exploration of emotion and memory and the surprise ending make it satisfying on the "mysterious" and psychological levels.

The Case of William Smith (1948), by Patricia WENTWORTH, is a case for Miss SILVER, and as in many of her stories she makes a late appearance. "William Smith" has returned from World War II and is a gifted toy maker in the shop of the pious Mr. Tattlecombe. Smith woke up in a German prisoner-of-war camp in 1942 having no memory of his previous existence. He has good reason to believe that he is not Smith. When he falls in love with Katherine Eversley and a series of life-threatening accidents begins, he has a sudden motivation for discovering the truth. The novel is built as a romantic story which some will find dopey but that, in 1948, was a touching example not far removed from the experience of many whose loved ones had not returned from war or had returned virtually as different people. Miss Silver does almost no detection, a little deduction, and a great deal of knitting. But the author makes one care about William Smith, and takes the risk, not usual for the genre, of banking on getting the reader hooked on the story with characterization alone. She also admits one stupendous coincidence. Wentworth had earlier dealt with amnesia in *Outrageous Fortune* (1933), in which the wandering James Randall returns to England after ten years, but soon loses his memory when the coastal steamer he is traveling on capsizes. His mumbling about "Jimmie Riddell" and some green beads has some connection with the shooting of wealthy Elmer Van Berg. Caroline Leigh, James's cousin, is the heroine of this romantic suspense novel.

Also during the late forties, John Franklin BARDIN was writing a series of novels on a much deeper level, beginning with THE DEADLY PERCHERON (1946), in which amnesia was used to probe the meaning of sanity and insanity. Bardin's bizarre plots concern both mentally disturbed characters who are pushed over the brink by episodes of memory loss—or diabolically clever attempts to make them doubt their memories—as well as ordinarily sane people who, bereft of memory, quickly begin to doubt their sanity and even their own identities. Also in 1946, Patrick QUENTIN was responsible for the absurdist *A Puzzle for Fiends*. Peter DULUTH escorts his movie-star wife to the airport and drives away. He wakes up in a luxurious home with his arm and leg in a cast and with no memory of who he is. His "wife" Selena, a lascivious blonde, his mother, his sister, and his doctor all tell him that he is Gordy Friend, a wild, drunken philanderer who has been in a car accident. He is also the potential heir of the millions of dollars of the recently deceased Mr. Friend, a Bible-thumping fanatic and patron of the preposterous temperance association, the Aurora Clean Living League.

Other cases involving amnesia are George BAXT's *The Affair at Royalties* (1971), in which a mystery writer wakes up with a bloody knife in her hand (a classic device, already employed by Henry KANE and others); Richard Neely's SHATTERED (1969); and Sue GRAFTON's *"C" Is for Corpse* (1986). Norman MAILER's novel TOUGH GUYS DON'T DANCE (1984) is about a hard-drinking writer who suffers blackouts and thinks he may have killed two women. Sébastien JAPRISOT's novel, TRAP FOR CINDERELLA (1962), involves the ingenious idea of the survivor of a murder attempt who does not know if she is the killer, who may have succeeded, or the intended victim, who may have escaped. Martin Amis published *Other People: A Mystery Story,* in 1981. A woman wakes up in the hospital with no memory; she gradually learns that the person she is supposed to have been was thought to have been murdered, and she makes other disturbing discoveries about her "self."

In a real—or pretended, as some have speculated—case of amnesia, Agatha CHRISTIE claimed not to remember the details of her famous 1926 disappearance.

AND BE A VILLAIN (1948) A novel by Rex STOUT, in which Nero WOLFE solves a case without any evidence. Having been hit hard by his annual taxes, Wolfe decides to investigate a baffling case in which a radio-show guest has been murdered in front of several witnesses and millions of listeners. The case contains some of Wolfe's best deduction, and also brings him into conflict with Arnold ZECK. It has a good deal of humor, with Wolfe tasting the concoction of the soft drink company that sponsors the program ("Hi Spot") and ejaculating "Good heavens" and other remarks expressive of his disgust with commercialism. The story is based on fact: one of Stout's best friends actually did collapse during a radio show on which they were both appearing, and died shortly afterward.

AND THEN THERE WERE NONE (1940) A novel by Agatha CHRISTIE in which, as in THE MURDER OF ROGER ACKROYD (1926), she plays a trick on the reader but plays fair. The original English title of the book was *Ten Little Niggers,* but this was judged offensive and it was changed to *Ten Little Indians,* and then changed again to the present title. The original title referred to a nursery rhyme about ten little boys who are bumped off one at a time à la Edward Gorey.

A Mr. Owen has invited ten strangers for a weekend on Indian Island, off the Devon coast, with various tantalizing promises including a free vacation for some and a needed job for others. The retired judge, Lawrence Wargrave, is described as "reptilian"; Philip Lombard (one "l," as in Philip Marlowe) is a tough guy with a gun; General Macarthur is commanding. None of them seems particularly worth killing, but that is what begins to happen, precisely according to the nursery rhyme. After dinner on the first evening, a hidden recording indicts each of the guests for murder, and the plan is obviously to make them pay, beginning with the first Indian who "choked his little self," right after the recording is played.

The dwindling survivors are, shall we say, mortified. There are even little china figures of Indians on the dining table, which are removed as the people they stand for are done in. The mutual suspicions and fearful attempts at trust—which come to naught—are well done. The absolute certainty that there is no one else on the island makes the murders more perplexing.

If one can suspend disbelief, the story is amusing. Some people cannot: Raymond CHANDLER called the book "bunk," finding the motivation totally unbelievable.

"ANGELFISH" See MURDER AFLOAT.

ANHOLT, MICI See O'DONNELL, LILLIAN.

ANSTEY, SIR JOLYOT A retired Harley Street doctor who lives on a farm on a mountaintop in THE AFRICAN POISON MURDERS (1939). Anstey's experiments range from the chemistry of local plants to the effect of the variation in the light of stars on plant growth. He doesn't use locks or guns, because "both indicate a distrust of one's fellow men which they then feel impelled to justify."

ANTHONY AWARDS See BOUCHERON.

ANTHROPOMETRICS See BERTILLON SYSTEM.

APPLEBY, SIR JOHN A SCOTLAND YARD inspector created by Michael INNES, Appleby first appeared in *Death at the President's Lodging* (1936; also pub as *Seven Suspects*), which, like many of the books, was set at Oxford. Appleby is an upper-class, well-educated Englishman whose cases take him through the loftier echelons of English society. His career is incredibly long, and he continues to solve cases even after retirement, for example in THE GAY PHOENIX (1976) and DEATH BY WATER (1968). Like Inspector ALLEYN, Appleby has an artist wife, the sculptor Judith Raven; she and their son, Bobby, sometimes participate in the cases. He meets her in *Appleby's End* (1945). At the close of his career, Appleby has been knighted and been made the head of Scotland Yard. His urbane speech and literary references reflect the personality and vocation of Innes himself; Appleby seems more like an Oxford don than a policeman. His knowledge of literature is encyclopedic, and the literary references are thrown in by the fistful. What would be unbearable pretension in another writer is carried off by Innes without the least ponderousness, probably because he keeps the dry and witty conversation trotting along at such a pace that the story does not get mired in its own cleverness.

Over a fifty-year run, Innes presented Appleby in almost every typical mystery situation. Several of the books involve ART, including FROM LONDON FAR (1946), ONE-MAN SHOW (1952), and SILENCE OBSERVED (1961), and the absurd gallery owner Hildebert BRAUNKOPF appears more than once. The Appleby novels are often comic. Innes even went through a period where they became so madcap, and the complications were so ornate, that they were almost parodies of the mystery story. At times, it is evident that Innes is imitating the Gervase FEN novels, though Innes's plots are often too lengthy for such light comedy. Still, Julian SYMONS called Innes the "finest of the Farceurs."

Late in the series, Appleby is paired with another Innes series character, Charles Honeybath.

BIBLIOGRAPHY Novels: *Hamlet, Revenge!* (1937), *Lament for a Maker* (1938), *Stop Press* (1939; U.S. title *The Spider Strikes*), *There Came Both Mist and Snow* (1940; U.S. title *A Comedy of Terrors*), *The Secret Vanguard* (1940), *Appleby on Ararat* (1941), *The Daffodil Affair* (1942), *The Weight of Evidence* (1943), *A Night of Errors* (1947), *Operation Pax* (1951; U.S. title *The Paper Thunderbolt*), *Appleby Plays Chicken* (1957; U.S. title *Death on a Quiet Day*), *The Long Farewell* (1958), *Hare Sitting Up* (1959), *A Connoisseur's Case* (1962; U.S. title *The Crabtree Affair*), *The Bloody Wood* (1966), *A Family Affair* (1969, U.S. title *Picture of Guilt*), *Death at the Chase* (1970), *An Awkward Lie* (1971), *The Open House* (1972), *Appleby's Answer* (1973), *Appleby's Other Story* (1974), *The Ampersand Papers* (1978), *Sheiks and Adders* (1982), *Appleby and Honeybath* (1983), *Carson's Conspiracy* (1984), *Appleby and the Ospreys* (1987).

Short Stories: *Appleby Talking* (1954; stories and one novella; U.S. title *Dead Man's Shoes*), *Appleby Talks Again* (1956), *The Appleby File* (1975).

ARAGON, TOM The young Chicano lawyer in a late series of novels by Margaret MILLAR. Aragon first appears in ASK FOR ME TOMORROW (1976), in which a divorcée hires him to search for her first husband in Mexico. He is the junior employee of Smedler, Downs, Castleberg, McFee, Powell; even Charity Nelson, Smedler's orange-wigged, cryptic and bizarre secretary, treats Aragon like an errand boy. Aragon, who makes simple statements of truth seem like wisecracks, has the "I don't care" exterior of a Philip MARLOWE, masking a deep commitment to what is right. Whether that happens to coincide with what is legal is another matter. While Aragon practices law in Santa Felicia, his wife, Laurie MacGregor, is a pediatrics resident in a hospital in San Francisco. Their relationship is carried on over the telephone but is still interesting and believable. Dialogue in fact is critically important to the series; the people of Aragon's world use wry humor to deflate each other's illusions, while often leaving their own intact. Aragon's own dry-but-sly use of the truth makes up for this deficiency.

In *The Murder of Miranda* (1979), Aragon becomes involved in the case of another middle-aged female client of Smedler's, the widow Miranda Shaw. Miranda is obsessed with appearing youthful, though she is fifty-two, and travels to a quack clinic in Mexico for injections made from goat embryo glands. On her last visit, she takes Grady Keaton, the lifeguard at the prestigious Penguin Club. The club and its odd members are the focus of the novel. The patrons include Frederic Quinn the Third, a nine-year-old practical joker and "smart ass *número uno*," who is amusing rather than irritating; Admiral Cooper Young and his invalid wife, Iris; their two daughters, Cordelia and Juliet, a flighty pair who conduct themselves in public like vaudevillians to cover some mental impairment; and Iris's elderly brother Charles, who writes nasty anonymous letters and plays a very surprising role. As usual, dialogue is central and in this case superb. The characters are believably human and moving in that each succumbs to their own weakness, be it fear, pride, cowardice, or vanity, and contributes their little piece to the tragedy. *Mermaid* (1982) was the last book in the Aragon series.

ARCHAEOLOGY Several classic mystery authors used archaeology as the background for mysteries. Foremost among them was Agatha CHRISTIE, who visited the Middle East many times. Christie's second marriage was to an archaeologist and she made yearly visits with him to archaeological sites. She wrote one of the best archaeological mysteries, *Murder in Mesopotamia* (1936). Amy Leatheran is the English nurse to an American woman, Louise Leidner, wife of an archaeologist leading a dig in Iraq. Mrs. Leidner believes she is going to be killed; she has been receiving threatening letters from her previous husband, who is supposed to be dead. She is in fact killed, and Hercule POIROT, who happens to be in the area, tries to find the murderer from the collection of archaeologists and hangers-on working at the site.

Another Christie story about archaeology is "The Adventure of the Egyptian Tomb" from *Poirot Investigates* (1924). The impetus for the story may have been that the tomb of King Tutankhamen had recently been opened (in 1922) and the archaeologist had died, leading to the legend of King Tut's "curse." In this tale, Sir John Willard opens the tomb of Men-her-Ra and then dies. Soon others die, and Poirot is brought in.

Carter Dickson (John Dickson CARR) also played with the mummy's curse theme. He set *The Curse of the Bronze Lamp* (1945) in England, but it starts in Cairo. A two-year search led by Lord Severn has revealed an important tomb of an Egyptian king, a priest of Hamon. Professor Gilray suddenly dies of a scorpion sting, and a "curse" is blamed. Helen Severn, Lord Severn's daughter, leaves Egypt with a small lamp as a gift. She meets Sir Henry MERRIVALE at the train station, and a seer makes the prophesy that after she returns home she will disappear—if she takes the lamp with her. She does not fear the curse, and she has hardly arrived home when she does in fact vanish. Strangely, the news has almost immediately been leaked to the press, and Scotland Yard's Inspector Masters turns up to discuss a complaint by the Egyptian government against Helen for smuggling. Merrivale, and not the inspector, unravels the case.

The list of series detectives who are archaeologists of one sort or another is long. Tim Mulligan and Elsie Mae Hunt, a husband-and-wife archaeological team created by Aaron Marc STEIN, appeared in almost twenty novels, beginning with *The Sun Is a Witness* (1940). *Days of Misfortune* (1949) was set in Mexico. *The Menorah Men* (1966), by Lionel DAVIDSON, is set in Israel, where the young scholar Caspar Laing is hired to examine a scroll fragment which reveals the location of the True Menorah, the seven-branched candelabra stolen from Solomon's temple in A.D. 70. Laing and the Israeli archaeologists race against a similar Arab team also searching for the sacred object.

Several currently active writers have made archaeology a focus of their mysteries, including Elizabeth Peters, author of the Amelia PEABODY mysteries; Sharyn MCCRUMB, who writes about forensic anthropologist Elizabeth McPherson; and Aaron ELKINS, creator of Gideon OLIVER, who specializes in bones rather than objects or artifacts but in one case goes to Egypt as a consultant. Other recent archaeological mysteries include Alfred Alcorn's *Murder in the Museum of Man* (1997), which takes place in a museum of anthropology and archaeology. It begins with the cannibalistic murder of a dean, but succumbs to its own romantic subplot. Ron FAUST's *Lord of the Dark Lake* (1996) is set on an island in Greece, where a mad billionaire re-enacts the story of the Minotaur. One of the guests at the macabre party is Jay Chandler, an American archaeologist.

Still other books use archaeology as a prop, a source of local color and creepy locations. In MURDER AT THE FLEA CLUB (1955), archaeological works are in progress in the basement of a Parisian discotheque. Similarly, in Ngaio MARSH's *When in Rome* (1971), a body is found in a Mithraic temple buried under a church. G. K. CHESTERTON put archaeology to provocative use in "The Hole in the Wall," in which an archaeologist's research into the meaning of place names leads to murder and also to reflections on how historical crimes have shaped English history.

Richard Herley's *The Stone Arrow* (1978), a thriller set in Sussex, England, during the Paleolithic period, was highly praised for its archaeological details. The story concerns the conflict between hunter-gatherers and settled farmers during the Stone Age. A hunter named Tagart wages a single-handed battle against a fortified village after the farmers wipe out his entire tribe. The book is written in modern English, and though the language is contemporary, the author refrains from imputing modern ideas to the characters, with the exception of Tagart's desire to overturn an order based on slavery.

ARCHER, LEW A private detective created by Ross MACDONALD. Archer is one of the most interesting and enduring characters in mystery fiction. His very name shows how he grew out of the HARD-BOILED tradition: MacDonald named him after the hapless Miles Archer of THE MALTESE FALCON (1928), in which Sam SPADE presents his ex-partner as something of a sap. In fact, Lew Archer is a more sensitive, introverted version of the classic tough guy. We learn that he was on the Long Beach police force beginning in 1935, quit because of a conflict of conscience over the disparity between justice and the workings of the law, and served in Intelligence in World War II. For some time Archer had a bout with alcoholism, and was divorced from his wife Sue a year before the time of *The Drowning Pool* (1950). In the first Archer novel, *The Moving Target* (1948), he has already lost Sue, and describes himself as a "new-type detective"—one who doesn't drink before lunch. This first case takes him to Santa Teresa, the privileged seaside community that is the site for many other investigations. Elaine Sampson, a wealthy and shamming invalid, hires Archer to look for her husband, Ralph, an oil millionaire with a secret life. They have a beautiful daughter, Miranda; Bert Graves, a former District Attorney for whom Archer worked, is in love with her. Sampson's disappearance begins to look like kidnapping, but it remains ambiguous (a frequent Macdonald motif). Another major theme, the corruption of California from the outside, is also introduced; Archer says that "war and inflation always raise a crop of stinkers, and a lot of them have settled in California." The cast of stinkers is long: has-beens in Hollywood, crooks in Las Vegas, and even (in 1947) quack holy men bilking their gullible followers. Archer gets help from his friend Morris Crumm, who is a collector of facts (i.e., dirt) for a newspaper columnist.

The Doomsters (1958), despite having a less complex (or tight) plot than other Archer novels, is interesting because of what Archer reveals about his past. Prior to his police career, he was a "street boy," a "gang-fighter," a "thief," and a "poolroom lawyer," until an older cop finally straightened him out. In the novel, the return of a broken young heroin addict whom he had tried to help reminds Archer of his past, including the still painful loss of his wife: "the thought of Sue fell through me like a feather in a vacuum." Archer's thinking about what he lost through his alcoholism is largely free of self-pity and rarely extended. The expression of his personality is not the major focus of his narrative, except as it helps or hinders him from making choices. The book itself makes many of the innovations that are usually attributed to THE GALTON CASE (1959); the sympathetic young man in *The Doomsters* is also one of Macdonald's best characters.

The Underground Man (1971) was something of a breakthrough for Macdonald, winning him critical acclaim and new readers (like *The Green Ripper* [1979] for John D. MACDONALD). Yet it is not one of the best Archer novels; the detective's searching for a killer during a forest fire, however, made for some exciting scenes. It was in MacDonald's middle period that he found and perfected the kind of novel he wanted to write, a version of the Oedipus legend to which he added different permutations in each book. THE CHILL (1964) and THE FAR SIDE OF THE DOLLAR (1965) are compelling in different ways; one is about a man in search of his past, the other about one running away from it. THE BLUE HAMMER (1976) was the last novel in the series and dealt with ART.

The Archer short stories are relatively few but have been collected twice. One of the stories, "Guilt-Edged Blonde," is frequently anthologized; a pulpier Archer is hired as a bodyguard by a mobster who has settled down to lemon growing. "Gone Girl" is more like the Archer novels. In the opening scene, Archer is almost driven off the road late at night by a half-naked man in a Cadillac.

BIBLIOGRAPHY Novels: *The Way Some People Die* (1951), *The Ivory Grin* (1952), *Find a Victim* (1954), *The Barbarous Coast* (1956), *The Wycherly Woman* (1961), *The Zebra-Striped Hearse* (1962), *Black Money* (1966), *The Instant Enemy* (1968), *The Goodbye Look* (1969), *Sleeping Beauty* (1973).

Short Stories: *The Name Is Archer* (1955), *Lew Archer, Private Investigator: The First Complete Collection of Lew Archer Stories* (1977).

ARD, WILLIAM (1922–1960) In a life cut tragically short by cancer, William Ard made a mark on the genre with one series character, Timothy DANE. Ard was born in Brooklyn, attended Dartmouth College, and served in the Marines during World War II. After the war, Ard was working in advertising and publicity in New York when he published his first fiction. He was active in the fifties, a time when the field was glutted with HARD-BOILED private eyes and imitators of HAMMETT and CHANDLER. Timothy Dane is a more understated character. *Hell Is a City* (1955), Ard's best-known book, is a NOIR novel set in New York City in which a young man is railroaded so that a corrupt cop can appear a hero. Some of the plots in the Dane series were more about suspense than detection. In *The Root of His Evil* (1957), Dane is supposed to deliver a hundred thousand dollars for actor Buddy Lewis to a gambling industry boss in Florida, which allows for many close shaves, last-minute escapes, and a final chase across the sunshine state. Ard wrote other novels under the pseudonyms Ben Kerr and Thomas Wills, including both mysteries and Westerns.

ARLEN, MICHAEL (1895–1956) Michael Arlen was born in Bulgaria, became a British subject, and finally retired to New York City. He had one great success, the novel *The Green Hat* (1924), which captured the spirit of the "lost generation" in London in the early twenties. His major contribution to the mystery genre was THE FALCON, a character who appeared in more than a dozen Hollywood films but was based on a single Arlen short story.

Arlen was born Dikran Kouyoumdjian; his father, an Armenian merchant, escaped with his family to England to avoid Turkish persecution. In his early twenties, Michael Arlen adopted his English name and became a British subject. By that time, he had begun publishing in magazines. He published two collections of short stories before his first novel, *"Piracy,"* appeared in 1922. *The Green Hat* was an international bestseller. The story combined the gaiety of the twenties with a tale of sex and horror; the protagonist kills himself on his wedding night because he has syphilis. Arlen wrote a handful of mysteries and thrillers: *Hell! Said the Duchess* (1934), *The Crooked Coronet* (1937), and *The Flying Dutchman* (1939).

Married to an Italian countess, Arlen lived in southern France for many years. He later went to Hollywood but wrote only one screenplay, *The Heavenly Body* (1944). "Gay Falcon" (1940) was about a tough character who steals from crooks. Another story, "The Gentleman from America," was singled out by Dorothy L. SAYERS as a tale of disease and madness.

ARMCHAIR DETECTIVE An armchair detective, as should be obvious, is one who solves crimes from the comfort of his or her study using deductive reasoning alone. One famous example of the type is Nero WOLFE—though Wolfe cheats a little by employing Archie GOODWIN as his legman.

The Armchair Detective is a magazine devoted to the mystery genre founded by the mystery reviewer and critic Al Hubin (1936–) in 1967. It was subsequently acquired by Otto PENZLER.

ARMSTRONG, CHARLOTTE (1905–1969) The prolific American mystery writer Charlotte Armstrong began her writing career as a playwright and poet. After moving to New York from her native Michigan in the early twenties to attend Barnard College, Armstrong worked as a fashion writer to support herself while publishing poems in *The New Yorker.* Two of her plays, *The Happiest Days* (1939) and *The Ring Around Elizabeth* (1941), had short runs on Broadway. Her first mystery novel (*Lay On, MacDuff,* 1942) had a theatrical theme and featured the professor and amateur detective MacDougal Duff. Duff appeared in two more novels, but Armstrong never developed a long-running series character. Her other novels include *The Unsuspected* (1946), which is similar to an INVERTED MYSTERY in that the killer's identity is revealed early on; A DRAM OF POISON (1956), for which she won an EDGAR award; and *Lemon in the Basket* (1967). *Trouble in Thor* (1953; repr 1971) takes place in a mining town similar to Vulcan ("Thor"), the Michigan town where she grew up.

Armstrong's work depends more on suspense than detection; as in the HAD-I-BUT-KNOWN formula, the characters endure the mystery more than investigate it. But although she often wrote about women in trouble, and children appear in her work with some frequency, Armstrong avoided the worst excesses of romantic suspense. In her books, women are more assertive and able to get themselves out of trouble without the assistance of a man. They are also sometimes depicted as villains, for example in *Mischief* (1950), about a disturbed babysitter who has thoughts of hurting the child she is caring for.

Many of Armstrong's later works were set in California, and some have a flavor reminiscent of Margaret MILLAR's novels—also concerned with odd communities and families and the lives of women. *The Better to Eat You* (1954; repr 1992) is one of the books in which Armstrong depicted the California of the postwar boom. It focuses on Professor David Wakeley and his student, Sarah Shepherd, to whom he is attracted. David is invited by Sarah's grandfather, the old vaudevillian Bertrand Fox, to move in with his entourage—Sarah, the doctor Edgar Parrot, and Fox's adopted daughter, Malvina—so that Sarah can help the professor with the book he is writing. Sarah, however, fears that she is a "jinx": her first husband died, and other friends and relatives have died or contracted terrible diseases. Like Fox's ultra-modern house, everyone is perched on a cliff, and soon things start falling, beginning when Wakeley's car rolls down a hill in San Francisco and kills someone.

The Protégé (1970) was published posthumously, and like some of Armstrong's other work, is about an elderly woman. Mrs. Moffatt, lonely and seventy-four years old, takes in a young man claiming to be the son of a neighbor who had moved away when he was still a boy. Whether the red-haired and bearded stranger really is Simon Warren does not matter to Mrs. Moffatt, but their relationship does, so much so that she will not hear anything said against him by her spinster friends or her granddaughter-in-law, Zan. Warren also claims to have known Tommy Moffatt, a liar and a thief who abandoned Zan when she was pregnant with their child. Armstrong develops the symbiosis between Simon and Mrs. Moffatt with some delicacy, and despite the muddied conclusion, *The Protégé* is one of her most successful novels.

In addition to writing novels, Armstrong was a short-story author. She was twice nominated for an Edgar award for her short fiction, and won a prize from *Ellery Queen's Mystery Magazine* in 1951 for "The Enemy."

ARRAN MYSTERY, THE One of the most spectacular murders of the late nineteenth century occurred on the Scottish island of Arran in July 1889. The story could have been taken from a sensational novel of the day, only it was real. The case has fascinated writers ever since. "The Arran Mystery," as it came to be called, had everything: romantic setting, a mountain climb, bizarre personalities, and a manhunt. Few writers would have dared to invent one of the details, however: the murderer corresponded with newspapers during the manhunt and protested his innocence. As one can imagine, these missives only stirred up the frenzy further.

An English clerk from London named Edwin Robert Rose went on a holiday to Arran, and had the misfortune to strike up a friendship on the ferry with a man calling himself "Annandale." Landing on the island, they decided to take rooms together. There must have been something fishy about Annandale, because Rose's friends warned him to end the friendship. Instead, Rose and Annandale decided to climb the Goatfell, the island's mountain; only Annandale came down, and left the island the next morning. Search parties eventually found Rose's brutally battered body hidden under a pile of heavy rocks. By that time Annandale—resuming his real name of John Watson Laurie—was back in Glasgow, and when news of the crime leaked out, he ran to Liverpool. He was later captured and tried in Edinburgh. The defense claim that Rose had fallen and bashed in his head was not successful. Sentenced to death, Laurie escaped execution when he was judged mentally unsound. He died in prison in 1930. William ROUGHEAD wrote *The Trial of John Watson Laurie* (1932) and shorter pieces about the case.

"ARSÈNE LUPIN IN PRISON" A story by Maurice LEBLANC, in which the thief Lupin writes from his cell to the wealthy baron who lives in the castle of Malaquis, guarding his goods like a miser. Lupin specifies the *objets d'art* he would like delivered to him, and threatens to break in and take everything if his demand is not met. Though the outcome (as usual) is never in doubt, the premise is amusing and Lupin is at his more playful, even if the story is as fantastic as ever. Lupin has previously had himself arrested in America by his foe, Inspector Ganimard. At the end of the story, he receives a telegram hidden in his soft-boiled egg.

ARSENIC Arsenic is an element, not a compound, and is used in a wide variety of industrial processes, from enameling to the manufacture of pesticides and insecticides. Arsenic poisoning can take one of two forms: a single exposure, or poisoning over time in smaller doses. Arsenic poisoning causes severe abdominal pains, vomiting, and burning of the throat.

It is possible for a person, in some cases, to develop a certain tolerance to the poison. As an element, arsenic cannot be broken down, and thus traces remain in hair and fingernails after death—as in the famous case of Napoleon, whose body was exhumed and tested for traces of arsenic. Alan Schom in *Napoleon Bonaparte* (1998) says that there is "no doubt that Napoleon was murdered." Analysis of his hair showed arsenic levels 35 to 640 times normal. However, Schom notes a massive dose would have been "too obvious," and so, though Napoleon was given poisoned wine for months, thus weakening him, he was finished off with hydrocyanic acid—CYANIDE.

ART The art business and art theft are among the most popular sources of mystery plots. From thieves who take art (like John DORTMUNDER) to sleuths who deal in it (like Aaron ELKINS's most recent creation, Chris Norgren), art is an endless source of crime stories.

The writers of the GOLDEN AGE produced some of the best-known art-related mysteries, but two of the most interesting are fairly recent. One is Charles Willeford's THE BURNT ORANGE HERESY (1971), which is more a crime novel than a mystery, less a whodunit than a who-did-what. Ross MacDonald's last novel, THE BLUE HAMMER (1976), deals with a missing painter and the explosive relations between a group of artistic people, which are set off by the discovery of a painting. (Macdonald had dealt with artists earlier, in his story "The Bearded Lady.")

Among the English mystery authors, Michael INNES is perhaps the one who used art most often, sometimes in plots involving the ridiculous gallery owner Hildebert BRAUNKOPF. Michael GILBERT also wrote art mysteries, including *The Etruscan Net* (1969), which is set in Florence and has a gallery owner as its sleuth. THE FIVE RED HERRINGS (1931), by Dorothy L. SAYERS, begins with an artist's plunge to his death while painting *en plein air* in Scotland. In this novel, the artistic material is functional rather than decorative; the same is true of DEATH OF A GHOST (1934), by Margery ALLINGHAM, which portrays a sycophantic clique of has-beens surrounding a great artist; they continue to live off his reputation even years after he is dead. THE MALTESE FALCON (1929), of course, involves an art object, though its aesthetic qualities (as opposed to its value) seem only to be of interest to Caspar GUTMAN, and it is more a story of covetousness than connoisseurship. Other novels with a tangential artistic theme include *Ten Days' Wonder* (1948), an Ellery QUEEN novel; at its center is a sculptor suffering from AMNESIA who uses his art to release violent obsessions. Elliot PAUL's series detective, Homer EVANS, is himself a painter and becomes entangled in wacky art mysteries in Paris. Another painter-detective is Philip TRENT. Freeman Wills CROFTS used a valuable art collection in GOLDEN ASHES (1940). In ARTISTS IN CRIME (1938), a Ngaio MARSH novel, a murder takes place in a London art school.

The Baron and the Missing Old Masters (1968) has John CREASEY's long-running series character being asked to go through a widow's attic and her husband's old oil paintings. The chore escalates into a case of art forgery, theft, and murder. Several other Baron books also involved art or artists. Art smuggling is one of the specialties of Robert L. FISH's series character Kek HUUYGENS. The classic thieves, too, dabbled in art theft, like FOUR SQUARE JANE in "The Stolen Romney," which uses the hide-in-plain-sight motif. Other stories from the early part of the century involving art include one of Victor WHITECHURCH's stories about Thorpe HAZELL ("Sir Gilbert Murrell's Picture") and the THINKING MACHINE story "The Problem of the Stolen Rubens." In Ben HECHT's story "Café Sinister," a dissipated old aristocrat uses the lure of valuable paintings to exact his revenge on an unscrupulous connoisseur.

Art continues to be one of the standard sources of mystery plots. Charlie MORTDECAI, like his creator Kyril BONFIGLIOLI, is an art dealer. He is also a bit of a crook; both roles play a part in his adventures. Douglas Skeggs writes a series that often involves stolen paintings or other art works. *Thus Was Adonis Murdered* (1981), the first Hilary TAMAR mystery, concerns a death in Venice during an art tour. FINAL NOTICE (1980), a Harry STONER mystery, combines BOOKS and art in the case of a disturbed vandal who cuts the genitals and eyes from plates of paintings in library books. John BANVILLE wrote a best-selling novel about a man so in love with a painting that he is driven to a senseless crime. *The Black Moon* (1989), a SERIAL NOVEL, concerns stolen paintings. Michael Gilbert's *Paint, Gold and Blood* (1989) involves painting, among other things. Margaret Truman's *Murder at the National Gallery* (1996) centers around a long-lost Caravaggio. In a departure from his usual horse racing themes, Dick FRANCIS wrote about stolen objects in TO THE HILT (1996).

ARTISTS IN CRIME (1938) Ngaio MARSH's sixth novel about Roderick ALLEYN has the sleuth vacationing in Suva, where he meets Agatha Troy, who later becomes his wife. The story starts aboard ship but the main action is in the art school in England where Troy teaches. An artist's model is stabbed in a studio in front of the entire class, pushed onto a hidden knife. Alleyn investigates the murder in between trying to get Troy to like him despite the revolting circumstances of their meeting. Suspicion fastens upon one of the art students, who turns out to be a blackmailer; however, he turns up dead himself, which sends Alleyn back to the drawing board. In this mystery, Alleyn receives assistance from his mother. The novel also contains a grotesque depiction of death by the swallowing of nitric acid, which is a common ingredient of cleaning solutions.

ASHDOWN, CLIFFORD A pseudonym of R. Austin FREEMAN and J.J. Pitcairn.

ASHENDEN; OR, THE BRITISH AGENT (1928) A series of interlocking stories by Somerset MAUGHAM, based on his own experiences as an agent in World War I. Ashenden, like the author himself, is a successful playwright. He is recruited by a British intelligence officer known as "R"—prefiguring the other code-named bosses of spy fiction, like James BOND's "M." *Ashenden* was the first book to present spying realistically; the spymaster is practical, and wants Ashenden not for his boldness and dash but because he knows a lot of languages and can travel without arousing suspicion. R. is "not a very nice man to get on the wrong side of" because he will sacrifice anyone without a qualm.

Ashenden himself is a complicated person, who sometimes sees other people as mere fodder for his writing. He is a student of human nature, a man who "admired goodness, but was not outraged by wickedness." He goes at spying like a job, or perhaps a game of chess, in which one would not scruple to take a piece as the game demanded simply out of pity for the knight or queen. The word "shabby" appears with some frequency in the book, and best describes some of Ashenden's missions, such as the luring of an Indian nationalist into a trap baited with his lover; undertaking an assassination attempt with "the HAIRLESS MEXICAN"; and helping a weak man to make a bad decision. Yet Ashenden's moral neutrality makes him empathize with people, whether he is destroying them or not. Maugham's characterizations are remarkable. The proper ambassador Sir Herbert Witherspoon's confession to Ashenden of a tragic affair has nothing to do with the plot, but like the Flitcraft story in THE MALTESE FALCON (1929), it makes the surrounding narrative into something more by the questions it raises. It throws a stark light on Ashenden's subsequent decision to flip a coin to determine whether an operation that will kill many people will go forward.

Ashenden appeared again in *Cakes and Ale* (1930), but not as a spy. In this literary satire, he and a fellow writer named Kear probe the life of the Victorian writer Driffield. The latter was thought to be based on Thomas Hardy, a claim Maugham denied.

ASHES OF LODA, THE (1965) A novel by Andrew GARVE, a spy thriller that showcases the author's intimate knowledge of the life of a correspondent in Moscow. The affable Lord Quainton is the reporter for the London *Sunday Recorder* in Moscow. While on leave in England, he meets a beautiful young woman, Marya Raczinski, and falls in love. They are at the point of arranging their marriage when Quainton discovers that Marya's father, the chemist Stefan Raczinski, has been condemned in absentia by a Soviet court for war crimes committed at the Loda camp during World War II. Raczinski claims that he was a fighter with the Polish resistance and that the charges are false. The ingenious working of the plot is that

Quainton believes the case has been cooked up by the Soviets for propaganda purposes, but everything he does to expose the fraud reveals new and disturbing questions about Raczinski's story. Quainton uses his journalist's skills and contacts to become a sleuth, but his investigation takes him to the edge of the law—the brink of death. The scenes of Moscow life and the Russian winter are authentic and grim.

ASIMOV, ISAAC (1920–1992) Known primarily as a scientist and a SCIENCE FICTION writer, the Russian-born and Brooklyn-raised Isaac Asimov also produced a surprisingly large body of mystery fiction. Many of these works were science fiction mysteries; they include his stories about David "Lucky" Starr, which began with *David Starr, Space Ranger* (1952). Other mysteries were futuristic, such as the stories included in *Asimov's Mysteries* (1968) and novels about detective Lije Bailey and his robotic assistant, including *Caves of Steel* (1954) and *The Robots of Dawn* (1983). Asimov's combination of the detection and science fiction genres is on the whole successful, though he is less effective in the development of character.

Asimov also wrote "straight" mysteries, some of them about a group of men known as the Black Widowers, who often discuss problematic crimes. There are six collections of these stories, beginning with *Tales of the Black Widowers* (1974). Another club is featured in a different set of stories, collected in *The Union Club Mysteries* (1983); only the name of the club seems to be changed, and except for the addition of the character of Griswold the two series are of a piece. *The Death Dealers* (1958) is a novel that takes place in a medical school. *Murder at the ABA* (1976), in which Asimov himself is a character, is set at the annual meeting of the American Booksellers' Association.

Asimov is considered by many to have been a genius, and his grasp of ideas and subjects was indeed awesome, as was his output of several hundred books. His emphasis is on the concepts on which his fiction usually turns, explicated in a serviceable prose. He did not, however, achieve anything as startling as Philip K. DICK's lone venture in the sci-fi detection subgenre.

Asimov also once wrote an essay entitled, "How Good a Scientist Was Sherlock Holmes?" (1980), in which he gave the most famous sleuth of all time poor marks for his grasp of scientific concepts.

ASK FOR ME TOMORROW (1976) Margaret MILLAR said of this novel, "It was the only book of mine that was truly made of whole cloth," and that "the plot came to mind in its entirety." Except for the tricky and somewhat abrupt ending, it does have a remarkable unity. The story concerns Gilda Grace ("Gilly") Decker's quest to resolve the fate of her first husband, B. J. Lockwood, who ran off to Mexico with a servant in their "Dreamboat" motor home. Years later, Gilly engages the young Chicano lawyer, Tom ARAGON, to got to Mexico and find out what happened to B. J., whose last message—a desperate cry for money—came from Bahia de Ballenas, the deserted hamlet in Baja where B. J. had become involved in an absurd, doomed real estate venture, a dream in which no one believed but himself.

As Aragon searches through the sleazy, dusty streets of Rio Seco for traces of B. J., one by one his contacts turn into dead ends—literally. The dialogue, particularly between Tom, Gilly, and her sanctimonious born-again maid, is humor with a cutting edge. The evocation of the slow death of Marco, Gilly's second husband, and his mute suffering under the incapacitating effects of a stroke, is sobering and painfully true to life.

ASPERN PAPERS, THE (1888) A novella by Henry JAMES, whose plot—the effort to get hold of valuable papers by hook or by crook—is an early example of a CAPER and has been much copied by later writers. The papers are those belonging to Juliana Bordereau, the now elderly lover of the long-dead romantic poet, Jeffrey Aspern. James based his story on the lover of Lord Byron, Claire Clairmont, who was still living at the time.

An American editor goes to Venice in order to get hold of the Aspern papers under false pretenses. To get the papers from this bitter and imperious woman (a great character), he uses an alias, plays upon her stinginess and gets her to rent him a room, pretends to have a romantic interest in Juliana's niece, and even attempts burglary. His growing desperation brings about a startling and unexpected conclusion.

ASPHALT JUNGLE, THE See BURNETT, W. R.

ASSASSINATION BUREAU, LTD., THE (1916; pub 1963) A novel by the American writer Jack London, completed by Robert L. FISH and published in 1963. Although melodramatic and thoroughly a work of the nineteenth century, it surpasses all later assassination/hit-man books (of which it is the grandfather) in its intricate series of paradoxes. Ivan DRAGOMILOFF runs an organization that commits murder for money, but only if the assassination is "socially justifiable." Dragomiloff is, however, oddly incorruptible, and possesses an iron will. Thus, he looks down on the anarchists and socialists who come to him to contract assassinations that they are too weak to commit themselves. When Winter Hall, the "millionaire socialist," comes to visit him, it seems an ordinary transaction—until Hall tries to demonstrate to him that he himself, Dragomiloff, is a social menace who should be eliminated. Their arguments and counter arguments, lasting for days, are both an occasion for London's examination of various revolutionary philosophies, from meliorism to vanguardism, and a kind of farce. In the flurry of telegrams between the other members of the secret society, "ethical fanatics" to a man, the comedy is played out with aplomb. The entire book is a meditation on the question of right. In London's original notes for the ending, Dragomiloff died like Socrates; Fish substitutes an ending that carries the organization's absolute rectitude to an absurd, ironical conclusion.

ATKEY, BERTRAM (1880–1952) The English writer Bertram Atkey lived during the heyday of the SHORT STORY and created many series characters, but none was as famous as Smiler BUNN. Atkey published his first collection of stories, *Folk of the Wild,* in 1905. Two years later, he began the series of stories about the gentleman thief Bunn, which would eventually amount to many volumes. When the novel began to replace the short story as "the" mystery form during the GOLDEN AGE, Atkey wrote novels about Bunn. His other books include *Winnie O'Wynn and the Wolves* (1921), about a female character as wily as Bunn. *The Pyramid of Lead* (1925) is a bizarre tale of murders that centers on the lead pyramid constructed by an aristocrat in his garden.

Atkey's nephew wrote under the name Barry PEROWNE.

ATKEY, PHILIP See PEROWNE, BARRY.

ATROPINE An alkaloid found in a number of plants, particularly those of the NIGHTSHADE family, atropine is used in many common medical preparations, including some for surgical purposes. But in sufficient doses it can cause death by paralyzing the nervous system, leading to coronary and respiratory failure. Some of the symptoms of atropine poisoning are bizarre, such as mania and psychosis. Among its stranger applications is as an antidote to nerve gas; it can also be used to counteract chloral hydrate, better known as the MICKEY FINN.

AUDEMARS, PIERRE (1909–1989) Born in London of Swiss ancestry, Audemars is a direct descendant of Louis Audemars, a famous watchmaker of the nineteenth century. He also wrote books under the name Peter Hodemart. Audemars actually worked for Louis Audemars and Company before World War II. He served throughout the war and became a lieutenant; afterwards, he managed a London jewelry company, and later became sales manager of a watch company. Even though his first book, *Night without Darkness,* was published in 1936, and he published dozens of novels, Audemars worked in the jewelry and watch industry until he was almost seventy.

Most of Audemars's novels concern the detective M. PINAUD and are set in Paris, France. As the stories are supposed to be memories of past cases chosen from his long career, they do not follow a chronological order. The style is heavy with stock images. All the rich and noble characters seem to have high-bridged and dominant noses, broad and intelligent foreheads, or a look that Pinaud saw on Roman busts of the emperors from whom these people are descended. He makes large use of French words to increase the credibility of the setting, but unfortunately sometimes does so inappropriately and with spelling or grammar mistakes. Pinaud frequently refers to God and religion—a surprising quality as fictional detectives go—but the violence is sometimes a shock. The narratives are over-explanatory, obliging us to share every single thought of Pinaud's, every drink and bit of food—which are invariably out of this world. Sometimes he limits himself to adjectives such as "excellent."

The plots are not bad. The inspector, in spite of his nerdy side, is endearing and one willingly goes on reading new stories because of a feeling of entering a cozy and familiar room. In *And One for the Dead* (1975), Pinaud has to save his boss from a dark conspiracy that wants him out of the way because of politics, drug dealing, and corruption. A maid is killed in the bed of the chief of the Paris Sûreté when he is alone in his isolated country manor. The whole village knows he sleeps with his temporary "maids" when his wife is away. As usual, Pinaud fights alone against the influence of the rich and powerful. In *Now Dead Is Any Man* (1978), Pinaud tries to discover the killer of a senior executive of a large firm who has been found floating in the river with a hole in the back of his head. On the side, Pinaud saves his wife and kids from kidnappers and breaks a large drug-dealing operation. In *The Bitter Path of Death* (1982), passionate crimes occur against a background of precious jewels, skillful master watchmakers, innocent girls, and powerful members of the nobility.

AUDEN, W[YSTAN] H[UGH] (1907–1973) The English poet W. H. Auden wrote about the mystery genre on several occasions. He also served as the model for Nigel STRANGEWAYS, a character created by Auden's friend

C. Day-Lewis. Auden appears as a character in Amanda CROSS's *Poetic Justice* (1970). He also wrote a classic appreciation of the detective genre, "The Guilty Vicarage: Notes on the Detective Story by an Addict."

AUPRÈS DE MA BLONDE (1972; orig title *A Long Silence*) The last novel in the Inspector VAN DER VALK series by Nicholas FREELING. The title of the story is taken from a French march. Van der Valk has been promoted to a pan-European commission studying social problems and has been given the rank of Commissaris. He travels back and forth from Amsterdam to The Hague and looks ruefully at the bourgeois bureaucracy he has fallen into. Perhaps out of boredom, or his own eccentric theories about police work and imagination, he decides to pursue a case on the side and all on his own, in the manner of a fictional private eye. A young man of no experience who was mysteriously taken on in a jewelry and antique business brings van der Valk a valuable watch that he believes was planted in some refuse he was throwing out, either as a bribe or a way to set him up as a thief. Van der Valk begins probing and soon comes upon the suspicious figure of Larry Saint, the manager of the store, who lives above a sex shop and seems to know very little about antiques. But van der Valk has forgotten the saying about curiosity and the cat; in the end, it is his French wife, Arlette, who has to put the pieces of the puzzle together. Stanley ELLIN called *Auprès de ma Blonde* "the strangest and most powerful of all the Van der Valk stories."

AUSTER, PAUL See BASEBALL.

"AVENGING CHANCE, THE" (1925) A story by Anthony BERKELEY, which was later expanded into the novel *The Poisoned Chocolates Case* (1929), thereby illustrating Ellery Queen's point about the mystery novel being a SHORT STORY with a few extra slices of ham thrown in. It is also probably the best-known case of Roger SHERINGHAM who, despite his nasty reputation, is more cocky than obnoxious in this story. The murder method is ingenious: Sir William Anstruther receives a package of chocolates at the Rainbow Club as a free sample from the manufacturer. He does not like chocolates, so he passes them on to a fellow club member, Graham Beresford, with disastrous results. It seems that mere chance has spared Sir William from the vengeance of some jilted woman or jealous husband (Anstruther is a notorious womanizer). The murder has been carefully planned and the package proves to be untraceable by the police. Through a mere chance meeting on the sidewalk, Sheringham is put on the trail of a surprising solution. The plot is brilliantly simple, and Sheringham's deduction satisfyingly clever. His relations with the police are carried on with very little bluster.

AX, THE (1997) A disturbing novel by Donald WESTLAKE that takes on the serious issues of corporate greed, the tearing up of the social contract, and the growing desperation of the American middle class. The central character, Burke Devore, is a victim of corporate "downsizing," having been fired after twenty-five years by the paper company where he was a middle manager. The implicit violence and barbarity of a system devoted to "competitiveness"—a code word for the old laissez faire capitalism of the nineteenth century—becomes explicit in Burke's solution to his apparent unemployability. After a fruitless two-year search, Burke realizes that there is *always* going to be another candidate who is better than he is—younger, more qualified, or simply less tainted as a loser. The black irony that drives this crime novel is that, in his solution to his problem, Devore applies the same ruthlessness and disregard for his competitors as human beings as the corporate bosses who destroy other people's lives by remote control. The irony is that Burke's anger at rich executives who cut back even profitable businesses in order to fatten their bonuses and to please equally greedy shareholders gets directed at other betrayed employees like himself. Bleak, unsettling, and eloquently angry, this novel has a depth and feeling similar to the novels of Thomas BERGER.

AXE The axe murder has become a cliché, if it is possible for a grisly homicide technique to be a cliché. Lizzie BORDEN is the most famous alleged axe murderer of history (she was acquitted). The crime occurred in 1892, and since then the axe has been a popular weapon in crime and mystery stories, including those based on the Borden case itself. Others include: "The Lady with the Hatchet," in which Arsène LUPIN investigates the killings of several women who were found with their skulls cloven; *The After House,* by Mary Roberts RINEHART (1914), based on a real murder (she reused the axe motif in *The Album,* 1933); LET DEAD ENOUGH ALONE, a Captain Heimrich mystery (1955); *Ax* (1964), by Ed MCBAIN, which features a serial axe murderer (as Evan Hunter, McBain also wrote a novel based on the Borden case); *The Bilbao Looking Glass* (1983), by Charlotte MACLEOD; and Richard Hugo's DEATH AND THE GOOD LIFE (1980; repr 1991), set in Montana.

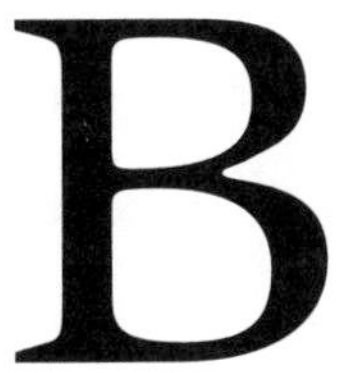

BABSON, MARION See CATS.

"BABY IN THE ICEBOX, THE" (coll in *The Baby in the Icebox,* 1987) A story by James M. CAIN, originally published in *The American Mercury.* Lura and Duke run a combined gas station and lunchroom, much like the couple in THE POSTMAN ALWAYS RINGS TWICE (1934). Duke decides, however, to bring in more trade by having a display of wild cats, eventually including a tiger. Duke is a fool, parading around in a cowboy hat with a whip and a six-gun, and decides to get in the cage with the tiger and play tamer. Lura, on the other hand, has "a way with cats," and can get the tiger to put its head in her lap. The narrator is the third wheel, a hired man at the gas station. Ron is the baby, and how he winds up in the icebox is the central surprise of a surprising mystery. The setup is Cain's most familiar, but with a few twists, including the cats, which would be more at home in a story by Frederic BROWN or Cornell WOOLRICH.

BAD FOR BUSINESS See FOX, TECUMSEH.

BAGBY, GEORGE See STEIN, AARON MARK.

BAILEY, DETECTIVE CHIEF INSPECTOR GEOFFREY See WEST, HELEN.

BAILEY, H[ENRY] C[HRISTOPER] (1878–1961) Born in London, H. C. Bailey took a degree in classics at Oxford before becoming a journalist at the *Daily Telegraph.* He published his first book (*My Lady of Orange,* 1901) while still a student, but it was an historical novel rather than a mystery. He continued to write fiction in the historical genre for the next twenty years. Meanwhile, he also wrote drama criticism and editorials for the newspaper. Bailey was a war correspondent during World War I. Social commentary was to become the hallmark—and to some, the weakness—of his mystery fiction.

In 1920 Bailey introduced Mr. FORTUNE, who was primarily a short story character, though he later appeared in novels. Fortune is a doctor as well as an amateur sleuth, but unlike Dr. THORNDYKE, Fortune is not a scientific detective. He depends more on psychology and the occasional brilliant intuition to help him over the tough spots. These fortuitous insights are one of the aspects of the stories that has been criticized. Another is the frequent appearance of children, who often have to be rescued or protected by Reggie.

Bailey's second series character was Joshua CLUNK, who was not as well liked by readers as the kindly Mr. Fortune for the simple reason that he was not as likeable. Today, however, Mr. Fortune's bonhomie and affectation can be grating, and Clunk's ambiguity—like Melville Davisson Post's Randolph MASON, he is both scoundrel and hero—may be more suited to contemporary tastes. But Clunk is rarely amusing, as Fortune is. The point is almost moot, however, since almost all of Bailey's work is out of print.

BAINBRIDGE, BERYL [MARGARET] (1933–) Born in Liverpool, Beryl Bainbridge worked as an actress and in a bottling factory before becoming a novelist. She is known for her psychological explorations, often of disturbed and violent people. The traumatic household of her own early years is played out in stories of domestic terror; Bainbridge has said that "you never recover from childhood." She has not only written about violence against children (*Another Part of the Wood,* 1968), but also by them: *Harriet Said* (1972) is based on a true story of two teenage girls who killed their mother. The book was actually written in the fifties, but publishers found it too shocking and the subject matter was still taboo.

Bainbridge is not interested in crime in and of itself but as the final outbreak of a violence latent in "ordinary" life. Her domestic scenes are as menacing as a house in which there is a strong smell of gas, and anything can touch off the explosion. *A Weekend With Claude* (1967) is a portrait of a disturbing personality. *Injury Time* (1977) begins as a dinner party, but fugitive bank robbers turn it into a hostage crisis. *Winter Garden* (1980) is a mystery rather than a crime story, in which a British tourist vanishes during a trip to the Soviet Union. The novel WATSON'S APOLOGY (1984) is based on a nineteenth-century murder case.

BAKER STREET IRREGULARS In the stories of Conan DOYLE, the Baker Street Irregulars are a small army of street urchins used by Sherlock HOLMES for the gathering of information. (Holmes, of course, lived at 221B Baker Street.) The boys go everywhere, see everything, and pick up the latest tips from everyone. The name was later adopted by an organization of Holmes devotees, formed by Christopher MORLEY and Vincent STARRETT. The society inaugurated *The Baker Street Journal* in 1946, which publishes Sherlockian scholarship. "Sherlockian" refers to work that pretends that Sherlock Holmes really existed and that the stories are true.

BAKSHEESH (or *buckshee*) This word entered English in the eighteenth century with the meaning "a tip," but baksheesh is now also used generally to mean money. Its etymological roots are said to be Hindu or Persian.

BALL, BRIAN See GOLF MYSTERIES.

BALL, JOHN (1911–1988) Born in Schenectady, New York, John Ball became known for novels that dealt with racism in the United States through the quiet, intense figure of detective Virgil TIBBS. Ball's first mystery, IN THE HEAT OF THE NIGHT (1965), won an EDGAR award, and quickly made Tibbs one of the most famous fictional detectives. The film version of *In the Heat of the Night* starred Sidney Poitier and Rod Steiger; it won five Academy Awards, but Ball's story was significantly altered. A television show based on the book and using its title premiered in the year of Ball's death.

Ball was the son of a scientist, whose career path he followed. He grew up in Milwaukee and attended Carroll College in Wisconsin. Ball had a varied career as a journalist, often specializing in scientific subjects. He was a staff writer for *Fortune*, wrote music criticism and features for the *Brooklyn Eagle*, and had a daily column in the *New York World Telegram & Sun*. At one time Ball was a broadcaster for a radio station in Washington, D.C., where he was also the public relations director of the Institute of Aerospace Sciences. He gave Virgil Tibbs some of his own personal interests, such as music and martial arts.

Ball wrote five other books featuring Tibbs, in which he continued to explore the issue of discrimination. He also published young adult books and a few non-series novels. *The Van* (1989), a novel without Tibbs, was based on an actual series of brutal murders. Ball rode with the Los Angeles County Sheriff's Department on many patrols in order to get background for the story; his other books were similarly researched, including the Tibetan material in *The Eyes of Buddha* (1976).

BALLARD, WILLIS TODHUNTER (1903–1980) The American PULP MAGAZINE writer Willis Todhunter Ballard was a cousin of Rex STOUT's. He began writing for the pulps in the thirties, and published many stories in BLACK MASK. He had several series sleuths, including Bill Lennox, who works in Hollywood straightening out jams for the studios. Ballard also wrote collaborative novels with Norbert DAVIS and Robert Leslie BELLEM.

BALLISTICS *Ballistics* comes from the Latin word for a catapult, *ballista,* which in turn is based on a Greek root meaning "to throw." The first uses in English of "ballistics" did not refer to firearms, but to the art of throwing heavy objects with a "ballistic engine"—a catapult or similar contraption.

In relation to the crime story, of course, "ballistics" means the scientific study of firearms and their projectiles, particularly the matching of recovered bullets with the weapons that fired them using a comparison microscope with a split field. The riflings of pistol and rifle barrels (see CALIBER) leave scorings on the bullet (and often the casings) that are particular to each weapon and that can be matched up exactly. In order to match a bullet from a shooting, then, another bullet fired from the same gun is needed. Therefore, the gun has to be recovered as well as the bullet. If the bullet passes through the body and is lost, or if the gun is never found, then the investigator is out of luck. Soft-nose bullets expand upon impact and hollow-point bullets explode; if they are too fragmented, the bullets cannot be matched.

One of the first cases in which ballistics figured importantly was the case of SACCO AND VANZETTI; another was the St. Valentine's Day Massacre (see BURNETT, W. R.).

BALLOU, KATE Ballou is the gorgeous redhead in Stanley Ellin's THE KEY TO NICHOLAS STREET (1952). A successful and glamorous commercial artist, she provokes envy and jealousy with her convertible Cadillac, her mink coat, and her body.

BALLOU, MICK The gangster friend and sometime sidekick of Matt SCUDDER in a series of novels by Lawrence BLOCK. The son of a butcher, he is nicknamed "The Butcher Boy," and is reputed to have killed a man and exhibited his head around New York's Hell's Kitchen, carried in a bowling ball case. His favorite weapon is a meat cleaver. Ballou runs a bar but technically has no possessions, a tax dodge. He does have a gang, however, which pulls off various jobs such as truck highjackings. His friendship with Scudder is interesting the more uneasy it is; in some cases, such as *Out on the Cutting Edge* (1989), he does things that Scudder wouldn't allow himself to do, and in others, such as A DANCE AT THE SLAUGHTERHOUSE (1991), Scudder drops his objections.

BALMER, EDWIN (1883–1959) Edwin Balmer is best known for *When Worlds Collide* (1933), a science fiction classic written with Philip WYLIE. But he was also a writer of mystery fiction. Balmer was born in Chicago and educated at Northwestern University and Harvard. He began writing as a reporter for the *Chicago Tribune,* and with his fellow reporter (and brother-in-law) William MACHARG, wrote *The Achievements of Luther Trant* (1916) and *The Blind Man's Eyes* (1916), the former notable for its use of psychology and the latter for its introduction of blindness into the plot (someone is trying to kill a famous blind lawyer, who must use his daughter and his secretary to see for him). Beginning in the twenties, Balmer was an editor of *Redbook* for many years.

BALZAC, HONORÉ DE (1799–1850) Like Charles DICKENS, Honoré de Balzac was a central figure in the development of the novel who also had an important effect on genre fiction. Born in Tours, Balzac went to Paris to attend the Sorbonne and became the equivalent of a PULP writer. He wrote a stream of sensational GOTHIC novels, imitating James Fenimore COOPER and Sir Walter Scott. But with *Les Chouans* (1829) he became a serious novelist and embarked on *La Comédie Humaine,* an enormous interconnected series of almost one hundred novels and stories, on which he spent twenty years of his life. Balzac revolutionized French literature and language by writing about every layer of society—including the poor and criminal classes. He is also credited with introducing more neologisms into the French language than any other writer. Balzac bridged literature and popular writing in a way that would have profound consequences, including for the crime and mystery genre. The encyclopedic social history of France between the revolutions of 1789 and 1848 embodied in *La Comédie* led Oscar Wilde to say that Balzac had invented the nineteenth century. His massive energies—he often wrote eighteen hours a day—and enormous ego (he even wrote reviews of his own books) were legendary. A spiritualist who examined him said, "What sort of a mind is that? It's a world! It scares me."

In *Le Père Goriot* (1834; tr *Old Goriot*), Balzac drew a vivid picture of a group of people living in a boarding house; among them was the criminal VAUTRIN, who was partly based on VIDOCQ. The kindly old Père Goriot sacrifices everything for his two well-married but selfish daughters, who do not even bother to go to his funeral. The opportunistic young provincial Rastignac is the lover of one of the daughters. Vautrin comes off as a sort of black knight, a man who adheres to a personal code; though he may be bad, he is at least not a hypocrite. In his experiment with the criminal-as-hero, Balzac anticipated DOSTOYEVSKY and the modern crime novel. Other works by Balzac that dealt with crime were the collection of interrelated stories about Vautrin, *Histoire des treize* (1833–35; tr *The Thirteen*), and *Une ténébreuse affaire* (tr *An Historical Mystery,* 1891; retr THE GONDREVILLE MYSTERY, 1958).

Graham Robb's *Balzac: A Biography* was published in 1994. *Le Père Goriot* has recently been translated into modern English by Burton Raffel.

BALZIC, MARIO Detective character created by K. C. CONSTANTINE. Balzic is half Italian and half Eastern European, and is the chief of police in Rocksburg, Pennsylvania. His hangout is Muscotti's Bar, where he sometimes drinks too much. He is married but has no children. Part of the appeal of Balzic is that, though he can be hard-drinking and foul-mouthed, he is far from the big-fisted tough-guy stereotype of the HARD-BOILED era; he is basically a recognizably average guy doing a job.

The author has taken realism about as far as it can go without becoming either dull or moronic. Balzic is a believably human person with flaws. His police work is realistic; it consists largely of talking to lots of people and squaring what they say with whatever physical evidence is on hand. Because his is neither a big town nor a big staff, the stories do not correspond to most PROCEDURAL writing. The feeling for nature and the changing of the seasons, the small town's passage from the dreariness of winter to the loveliness of summer, is also something rarely found in novels as gritty as these. Some of Balzic's best cases are THE MAN WHO LIKED TO LOOK AT HIMSELF (1973) and ALWAYS A BODY TO TRADE (1983).

The series has come to a kind of end, with Balzic retiring and being replaced by an acting police chief, Detective Sergeant Rugs Carlucci. The later books show Rocksburg in decline; the mills have closed and the municipal government is cutting back. In *Cranks and Shadows* (1995), his last appearance as chief, Balzic comes up against a paramilitary group. Balzic comes back in *Family Values* (1997) to investigate a murder almost two decades old, in the process of which he encounters a character who is like an evil version of himself. In *Brushback* (1998), Carlucci investigates the murder of "The Brushback Kid," a baseball player of the fifties who left the sport to become the owner of an illegal gambling club in Rocksburg.

BIBLIOGRAPHY Novels: *The Rocksburg Railroad Murders* (1972), *The Blank Page* (1974), *A Fix Like This* (1975), *The Man Who Liked Slow Tomatoes* (1982), *Upon Some Midnights Clear* (1985), *Joey's Case* (1988), *Sunshine Enemies* (1990), *Good Sons* (1996).

BANVILLE, JOHN (1945–) The Irish writer John Banville, known for lyrical, philosophical, modernist novels like *Doctor Copernicus* (1976) and *Kepler* (1981), has written two books on the fringes of the crime genre. Both are confessions of a sort: in *The Book of Evidence* (1989), Frederick Montgomery is being held for murder. A bizarre figure, a former scientist and expatriate with a past history of transgressions, he has become obsessed with a painting owned by an acquaintance, *Portrait of a Woman with Gloves;* the woman in the picture seems to live in a reality he would like to inhabit, and he impulsively (or perhaps insanely) decides to steal it. The book was nominated for the Booker Prize and was highly praised by Ruth RENDELL, among others. *The Untouchable* (1997) is a memoir by a seventy-two-year-old spy, Victor Maskell, who has been exposed as a double agent and publicly disgraced. Weeding through his own betrayals and lies, he tries to discover if there is a true self in him somewhere. The book is what a more literary, Irish George SMILEY might write.

BARDIN, JOHN FRANKLIN (1916–1981) Born in Cincinnati, Ohio, John Franklin Bardin had an unhappy childhood that haunted him for life and that had a deep effect on the books he would later write. Bardin's father was a coal merchant who died of a heart attack, leaving the family poorly provided for. Bardin was forced to drop out of the University of Cincinnati and get a job, first as a ticket-taker and bouncer in a roller-skating rink and later as a bookstore clerk. Meanwhile, Bardin watched his mother's mental condition—she was a paranoid schizophrenic—gradually deteriorate. He continued to educate himself, reading extensively, and developed a deep interest in psychology. Then, in the late forties, Bardin produced in a short space of time a series of three startling, original, and profoundly psychological novels. In a burst of creative activity between 1946 and 1948, he wrote three books that Julian SYMONS has described as "distinguished by an extraordinary intensity of feeling, and by an absorption in morbid psychology remarkable for the period." Symons also speculated that "the novels sprang out of nightmare experiences," and that they were "clearly a reworking of events in a stormy, painful childhood and adolescence."

In the first and most commercially successful of the books, THE DEADLY PERCHERON (1946), Bardin introduced Dr. George Matthews, a young but eminent psychiatrist, born in Indianapolis but educated abroad. Matthews suffers an episode of AMNESIA (a theme Bardin was obsessed with) during which he undergoes a catastrophic transformation. Bardin is primarily concerned with the loss of identity, brought about through a loss of memory that highlights the fragility or outright falsity of self-knowledge. Identity hinges on the question of evidence: how can we *prove* who we are? In addition, like Cornell WOOLRICH, Bardin was fascinated by dread and the reactions of people when the seemingly impossible happens (for example, in PHANTOM LADY, 1942). *The Deadly Percheron* begins as a preposterous tale of midgets and horses and then becomes deadly serious.

George Matthews reappears as a peripheral presence in *The Last of Philip Banter* (1947), an even more bizarre story. Banter is an alcoholic, a womanizer, and a narcissist; he also sometimes hears voices and suffers bouts of amnesia when drunk. He married his wife Dorothy partly because her father was the head of a major advertising agency where Philip has become an executive. Philip stumbles into work one morning and finds a manuscript on his desk entitled "Confession," written by himself. It purports to describe the events of the coming night: his old college friend Jeremy Foulkes and his new girlfriend, Brent Holliday, will come to dinner. Philip will be drawn inexorably to Brent, Jeremy will be called away by a phone call, and Philip will take Brent home and sleep with her—a flaunting of his infidelity in front of Dorothy. Horrifyingly, events tend toward the pattern of the confession, and a second installment follows. Banter desperately tries to do the opposite of what is predicted, but either way, he is allowing the confession to direct his life—a metaphor for neurotic obsession. Is he, Philip wonders, writing the confession himself? The ending is a mixture of tragedy and redemption, an equivocal answer to whether the neurotic can get outside the vortex of his thoughts.

The last book in the series was DEVIL TAKE THE BLUE-TAIL FLY (1948). Bardin later wrote novels under the pseudonym of Gregory Tree. He tried to create a series with *The Case against Myself* (1950) and *The Case against Butterfly* (1951), but it only lasted for two books. But as John Franklin Bardin, he had slipped back into obscurity. From 1968 to 1972, he was a senior editor with the New York publishing house Coronet. *Purloined Tiny* (1978), his last book, was also a crime novel.

Bardin lived to see his reputation revived, however, in 1976, with the publication of *The John Franklin Bardin Omnibus,* which included all three of the novels from the forties and for which Julian Symons wrote an introduction. Bardin himself was traced to Chicago, where he was editing a magazine for the American Bar Association. Among those writers who admired him was Kingsley AMIS.

BARING-GOULD, WILLIAM S[TUART] (1913–1967) Born in Minnesota and the son of a British consul general, Baring-Gould's criticism focused on the foremost GENIUS DETECTIVES on both sides of the Atlantic; he is known primarily for his extensive studies and annotated edition of the Sherlock HOLMES stories. He also wrote two "biographies" of his favorite fictional detectives: *Sherlock Holmes of Baker Street* (1962), and a similar book about Nero WOLFE entitled *Nero Wolfe of Thirty-Fifth Street* (1969).

BARNARD, ROBERT (1936–) Born in Essex, England, and educated at Oxford, Robert Barnard writes mysteries in the classic English vein, to which he adds bizarre twists. He has also used his extensive travels as backdrops from time to time. After leaving Balliol College, Barnard worked for the Fabian Society in London and later taught at a technical college. His acerbic social satire is a hallmark of his mystery writing. Barnard's next teaching job was in New South Wales, Australia, where he spent half a decade. Australia is the setting of his first mystery novel, DEATH OF AN OLD GOAT (1977).

After Australia, Barnard spent many years in Norway, first as a lecturer in English at the University of Bergen, and then as the head of the English department at the University of Tromso. *Death in a Cold Climate* (1984) was set in Norway; it is the soberest of Barnard's mysteries. During this period he was also writing mysteries that take place in England, some of them along traditional lines (*A Little Local Murder*, 1976, *Death of a Literary Widow*, 1979), and others more satirical, such as *Blood Brotherhood* (1977), which is set in a religious community.

In Barnard's series about Detective Superintendent Perry Trethowan, a self-loathing descendant of the country gentry, the author's humor went out of control. Previously, Barnard's work was reminiscent of Michael INNES; with Trethowan, Barnard went over the top in a way that exceeds Innes, in outlandishness and sometimes in poor taste. The first book, *Sheer Torture* (1981; U.S. title *Death By Sheer Torture*), is truly macabre: Trethowan has to solve the killing of his own father, who is found wearing tights and strapped into a medieval torture device. *Death and the Princess* (1982) mocks the royal family but is only shocking to those who can still respect them.

Barnard returned to England in the mid-eighties, and soon produced his best satirical book, *Political Suicide* (1986), about the death of a member of Parliament who jumps off a bridge (or is he pushed? one instantly asks). The humor and satire of politicians is broad enough to satisfy the non-anglophile. *The Skeleton in the Grass* (1987) is a HISTORICAL MYSTERY set in the GOLDEN AGE of the detective story.

Robert Barnard is also a critic, and in addition to works on DICKENS and the Bröntes he has written a book on Agatha CHRISTIE, *A Talent to Deceive* (1980).

BARNES, AL "MUSH HEART" The protagonist of DEATH AND THE GOOD LIFE (1980) by Richard Hugo, Al Barnes worked for seventeen years in Seattle, where his sympathy for those who find themselves on the wrong side of the law almost cost him his life. Forced to retire after a shooting, he has moved to Plains, Montana, where he works for Ray Yellow Bear, the chief of police. Barnes shares many characteristics with his creator, including the writing of poetry and an insight into people that is unfeigned and never ponderous; he would have made a more than usually successful series character.

BARNES, JULIAN [PATRICK] (1946–) Before he achieved fame under his own name with such novels as *Flaubert's Parrot* (1984) and *A History of the World in 10 1/2 Chapters* (1989), Julian Barnes wrote several detective novels under the name Dan Kavanagh. Beginning with *Duffy* (1980), he began exploring the seedy, economically depressed London of the late punk era. DUFFY is a bisexual security specialist and former cop who is frequently subjected to abuse for his sexual orientation. (In the first book, he gets a chance to get back at the cop who used his bisexuality to engineer his disgrace and to destroy his career.) Duffy worked in vice, and his work takes him into parts of London few English mysteries ever show (what other p.i. goes to a "wankpit"?). Duffy runs into an array of bizarre characters, including a man who has a dotted line tattooed around his neck and the legend, "Cut Here," as well as pathetic cheating husbands and sadistic thugs. The books are far more realistic than most mystery fiction, and very well written. They are gritty, full of frank and strong language, and sometimes graphically violent. In the opening scene of *Duffy*, a woman is terrorized and cut with a knife, and her cat is roasted. In the second book, *Fiddle City* (1981), Duffy gets a job at "Thiefrow" (Heathrow Airport) tracking down the crooks who are ripping off shipments from a freight company; he is physically tortured and psychologically tortures others. Duffy's methods are not always ethical, but practical. *Putting the Boot In* (1985) centers on soccer violence, hooliganism, and racism; Duffy also begins to worry about AIDS. The last book was *Going to the Dogs* (1987). All four were reissued as *The Duffy Omnibus* (1991).

BARON, THE A series character created by John CREASEY; the books were published under the pseudonym Anthony Morton. The Baron had a career almost as long as that of BLACKSHIRT. Creasey, with his usual efficiency, wrote the first book, *Meet the Baron* (1937; U.S. title *The Blue Mask*) in one week for a prize contest, which he won.

The Baron follows in a long line of hero thieves stretching back to RAFFLES and Arsène LUPIN, but with the difference that The Baron has gone legitimate and become an antique dealer. Now known as John Mannering ("The Baron" was his moniker as a criminal), he gives his assistance to Scotland Yard and Inspector Bristow, who grudgingly accepts it. Mannering is also married, to the beautiful Lorna Fauntley. Although they involve mysteries, the books are more in the THRILLER vein, with narrow escapes and numerous attempts on Mannering's life (even in a single book). Creasey wrote almost fifty Baron books, and in the process used almost every stock theme, from ART forgery to MURDER AFLOAT.

BIBLIOGRAPHY Novels: *The Baron Returns* (1937), *The Baron Again* (1938), *The Baron at Bay* (1938), *Alias the Baron* (1939), *The Baron at Large* (1939), *Versus the Baron* (1940), *Call for the Baron* (1940), *The Baron Comes Back* (1943), *A Case for the Baron* (1945), *Reward for the Baron* (1945), *Career for the Baron* (1946), *The Baron and the Beggar* (1947), *A Rope for the Baron* (1948), *Books for the Baron* (1949), *Cry for the Baron* (1950), *Trap the Baron* (1950), *Blame the Baron* (1951), *Attack the Baron* (1951), *Shadow the Baron* (1951), *Warn the Baron* (1952), *The Baron Goes East* (1953), *The Baron in France* (1953), *Danger for the Baron* (1953), *The Baron Goes Fast* (1954), *Nest Egg for the Baron* (1954), *Help from the Baron* (1955), *Hide the Baron* (1956), *Frame the Baron* (1957), *Red Eye for the Baron* (1958), *Black for the Baron* (1959), *Salute for the Baron* (1960), *A Branch for the Baron* (1960), *Bad for the Baron* (1962), *A Sword for the Baron* (1963), *The Baron on Board* (1964), *The Baron and the Chinese Puzzle* (1965), *Sport for the Baron* (1966), *Affair for the Baron* (1967), *The Baron and the Missing Old Masters* (1968), *The Baron and the Unfinished Portrait* (1969), *Last Laugh for the Baron* (1970), *The Baron Goes A-Buying* (1971), *The Baron and the Arrogant Artist* (1972), *Burgle the Baron* (1973), *The Baron, King Maker* (1975), *Love for the Baron* (1979).

BARR, ROBERT (1850–1912) Scottish-born Canadian writer Robert Barr created one of the best-known detectives of the Conan DOYLE era, Frenchman Eugène VALMONT. Barr was a co-founder with Jerome K. Jerome of the magazine *The Idler,* where Ernest BRAMAH worked as an assistant. Jerome eventually took over the magazine and left Barr high and dry.

Although born in Glasgow, Barr grew up in Canada, and his first writing job was with the *Detroit Free Press.* The newspaper sent him to London, where he became a familiar figure in English literary circles. Of all that he wrote, only the eight stories in *Triumphs of Eugène Valmont* (1906) are remembered. The title is ironic: Valmont has an ability to snatch defeat from the jaws of victory. Like POIROT, Valmont is a transplanted Continental working in London, and also has an elevated opinion of himself. Valmont fell out of favor after the era of the GENIUS DETECTIVE, of which type he was a parody. In addition, the fact that Valmont was a SHORT STORY character doomed him to obscurity. The Valmont stories are out of print, but one case, THE ABSENT-MINDED COTERIE, has been frequently anthologized. Barr also wrote a more direct PARODY of Sherlock HOLMES. His stories about Sherlaw Kombs were published under the name Luke Sharp.

BARTLETT, ADELAIDE Bartlett was the subject of one of the most famous British trials of the nineteenth century. A readable account of the trial and events leading up to it was written by Margaret COLE and included in one of the anthologies of the DETECTION CLUB. Cole points out that Victorian disapproval of any departure from sexual orthodoxy was at the heart of suspicion of Bartlett, who "was very nearly hanged because in the year 1885 she had in her possession a book which discussed birth-control, and, what was more, had actually lent it to a gentleman friend."

Adelaide Bartlett was an eccentric woman at the center of an eccentric household. In 1875, at the age of nineteen, Adelaide de la Tremouille (of Orléans, France) married Edwin Bartlett, a grocer. He sent his young wife off to be educated at a convent school, and they did not live together until two years later. Even then, their relationship remained non-sexual. Around 1878 or 1879, Adelaide ran away, but came back soon after. She later said that the only time during the decade of their marriage that they had had intercourse was in 1881 when Adelaide asked to have a child (the baby was stillborn). Edwin Bartlett, who was much older than his wife, also encouraged a friendship between her and a young Wesleyan minister, George Dyson. But no evidence was ever produced that Dyson and Adelaide Bartlett were lovers.

Edwin Bartlett became ill in December 1885; his symptoms included vomiting, diarrhea, and nervous exhaustion. The doctor thought Bartlett might be merely hysterical or suffering delusions. Edwin found relief by having his wife sit at the foot of his bed holding his toe, and said he drew strength from her through mesmerism. But on New Year's Eve he died, and an autopsy revealed that he had been poisoned with CHLOROFORM. Adelaide had bought chloroform because Edwin had suddenly decided that he wanted to be her lover, and she intended to stupefy him should he get into an amorous mood; she never used it, however, and threw the bottle into a pond. It was never found. Dyson admitted that he had bought the chloroform for her.

Whether she did or did not kill her husband, intentionally or by accident, Adelaide Bartlett would have hung if the prosecution could have conceived how she might have gotten a large amount of chloroform into Edwin Bartlett. But they could not, and she was acquitted. The mystery and its cast of strange characters continues to fascinate writers. *Sweet Adelaide* (1980) is a novel based on the case by Julian SYMONS.

BARZUN, JACQUES [MARTIN] (1907–) A noted scholar and critic, Jacques Barzun was born in France and emigrated to the United States as a teenager. He attended Columbia University, his studies being capped by a doctorate and a professorship. He became a full professor in 1947, and dean and provost in 1958. Barzun's training was in history and law, but his writing covers a range of subjects including language, art, pedagogy, and mystery and detective fiction. His books include *The Teacher in America* (1945), *The American University* (1968), and *Simple and Direct: A Rhetoric for Writers* (1975), co-authored with Georgia Dunbar. *A Word or Two Before You Go* (1986) is a collection of Barzun's essays. Barzun knew many of the great mystery writers of the mid-century, such as Rex STOUT, and was a student at Columbia at the same time as Cornell WOOLRICH.

Barzun's criticism rested on the distinction he drew between the "tale" and the novel. While perhaps valid for that branch of mystery story descended from POE, Julian SYMONS and others have shown that the mystery/detective novel had antecedents that went back before Poe to the rise of the novel, including outlaw biographies and PROTOMYSTERIES. Barzun also took the position that the mystery novel was basically a bloated version of the mystery short story with the addition of pointless RED HERRINGS whose only purpose is to make the book longer, an "artificial bustle and bulge which exists only to be deflated by a sentence or two near the end." His introduction to the anthology *The Delights of Detection* (1961) is the best expression of his views. He defended the story of pure detection as "the romance of reason" against the modern stories of suspense and psychology "which cater for the contemporary wish to feel vaguely disturbed."

Besides innumerable book reviews and articles on mystery fiction, Barzun co-authored with Wendell Hertig TAYLOR *A Catalogue of Crime* (1971; rev and exp 1989), which was recognized with a special EDGAR award. It is an enormous but uneven work, very extensive but also very opinionated. For example, there are no entries at all for Edgar WALLACE's books, and THE TIGER IN THE SMOKE (1952), considered by SYMONS and others to be its author's best book, is not even mentioned. The entries are often polemical, sprinkled with comments like "a book to be exiled from the premises" and "swallowed up in a surfeit of tripe," and therefore frequently more amusing than informative.

BASEBALL The American national pastime has often been combined with murder in fiction, for example in Ellery QUEEN's short story "Man Bites Dog" and Rex STOUT's novella "This Won't Kill You," both of which involve murder at the Polo Grounds, home of the old New York Giants. But a new group of writers have begun entire series of detective novels devoted to baseball, the most prominent of them being Troy Soos (see below).

In "This Won't Kill You," first published in *The American Magazine* and then in *Three Men Out* (1954), Nero WOLFE is persuaded to attend a baseball game because a visiting chef wants to. It is the last game of the World Series between the New York Giants and the Boston Red Sox, and it quickly becomes obvious that something is wrong when the Giants commit an incredible number of dumb errors. Then, a battered corpse is discovered in the Giant's clubhouse. Like most of the Stout novellas, there is less detection and more action than in the Nero Wolfe novels.

Of other baseball-oriented short fiction, Jon L. BREEN's stories about Ed Gorgan, a baseball umpire, should be mentioned. As yet they have not been collected.

Leonard HOLTON's Father BREDDER has such a reverence for baseball that he refuses to step on the pitcher's mound because it is "holy ground." In *The Devil to Play* (1974), he witnesses the shooting of a player on the field to prevent a winning run from scoring. The team hires him to investigate the shooting; he suspects the crime is related to illegal gambling on professional sports. The son of the author was a professional ball player.

The Troy Soos series revolves around Mickey Rawlings, the "oldest living baseball player." In *Murder at Fenway Park* (1994), he recalls a murder that he discovered in 1912 while playing for the Boston Red Sox. In *Murder at Ebbets Field* (1995), it is two years later and Rawlings has moved to the New York Giants, where his teammates include Casey Stengel and Christy Matthewson. In *Hunting a Detroit Tiger* (1997), he is in Detroit. Set during the post–World War I "red scare," it has Rawlings falsely accused of killing a player who was trying to unionize baseball—and getting lauded for it. One of his new teammates, of course, is Ty Cobb.

Donald Honig's baseball mysteries include *The Plot to Kill Jackie Robinson* (1992) and *Last Man Out* (1994). In the latter, set in 1946, Joe Tinker, a sportswriter, tries to clear a promising Dodgers rookie who is accused of killing his lover, a perverse New York heiress. Michael Geller's Slots Resnick, a former New York City chief of detectives and minor leaguer, sometimes gets baseball-related cases, such as *Major League Murder* (1988). L. L. Enger has also written a group of baseball mysteries, including *Comeback* (1990) and *Sacrifice* (1993). Crabbe Evers's *Bleeding Dodger Blue* (1991) is the first in another series, about an ex-sportswriter and sleuth named Duffy House, which also includes *Tigers Burning* (1994).

Many other writers have written single baseball-related mysteries. The Boston Red Sox figure in the early SPENSER novel *Mortal Stakes* (1975), which combines baseball, sex, blackmail, and corruption. Spenser is hired to find out if Marty Rabb, a Red Sox pitcher, has shady gambling connections. There is a rumor that he may be "shading a game" here or there. Harold Erskine, of the Boston Red Sox, hires Spenser, but no one else knows about it, not even the team's manager, giving a feeling that something is wrong from the start. Spenser does more digging than usual, and his investigation leads to a trip through the various levels of prostitution in New York City, and eventually to a meeting with the high-class madam Patricia Utley, who appears in other books.

Richard Rosen won an EDGAR award for *Strike Three, You're Dead* (1984), about a former Red Sox outfielder, Harvey Blissberg, who is sent to an expansion team ironically named the Providence Jewels. He is forced to investigate when his roommate, relief pitcher Rudy Furth, is killed.

William DEANDREA wrote a novel about a murder attempt against Mickey Mantle entitled *Five O'Clock Lightning* (1982).

Straight out of left field comes Ron FAUST's *Fugitive Moon* (1995), a bizarre, uproariously funny and sometimes offensive novel whose protagonist is Ted Moon, a pitcher with a bipolar mood disorder who makes $800,000 per year. To Moon, the television is "the black hole" (a portable t.v. is a "portable black hole"), and most of the consumers, fans, and drones who pass by are "the undead." Although he doesn't actively detect crime, a series of mysterious murders of transsexuals is the mainspring of the plot.

David Everson's *Suicide Squeeze* (1991) is a complicated plot involving Robert Miles, a former minor leaguer and ex-cop. He is invited to a "fantasy game," a re-enactment of the Chicago Cubs pennant loss to the New York Mets in 1969. It strays into political subplots and also has a sniper killing during a game.

Murder at the Baseball Hall of Fame (1996), written by David Daniel and Chris Carpenter, is about the murder of Herb Frowley, an ex-major league player, in Cooperstown, New York. An ex-New York City cop who happens to be visiting the Hall of Fame investigates his death. *Brushback* (1998), a K. C. CONSTANTINE novel, is about the killing of an ex-pitcher known for his aggressive style; Ted Williams makes an appearance (see Mario BALZIC). Under the name Paul Benjamin, the American writer Paul Auster wrote *Squeeze Play* (1982). In *Hand to Mouth: A Chronicle of Early Failure* (1997), Auster said that he wrote the book as "an exercise in pure imitation" in order to make money and pay off some bills (it didn't work out that way). The novel is about Max Klein, a private eye who is hired by George Chapman, a former baseball player who is entering politics and has received a menacing letter.

A true story that brings together baseball, mystery, and espionage is that of catcher Moe Berg, who played with several teams including the Boston Red Sox and the Washington Senators before World War II. A Princeton and Columbia graduate, a linguist, and a strange and secret man, Berg volunteered for the new OSS during the war. His espionage career involved spying on the German atomic bomb program (he was authorized to kill Werner Heisenberg if he thought the program was in danger of succeeding), and continued into the Cold War period. *The Catcher Was A Spy* (1994), by Nicholas Dawidoff, is a biography of Berg.

One former baseball player (and one of the best pitchers of all time) has written a mystery about the sport: Tom Seaver's *Beanball* appeared in 1989.

BATMAN Not the superhero, but the British term for an officer's servant. It sounds elegant and clubby, but comes from a Latin root meaning "pack saddle."

BAXT, GEORGE (1923–) Before he began his flashy series of CELEBRITY MYSTERIES, American author George Baxt created one of the earliest, if not *the* earliest, gay detective. His Pharoah LOVE trilogy was written between 1966 and 1968—thus before Stonewall—and provides a glimpse of the gay world in an earlier era, when harassment, violence, secrecy, and shame were more common.

Being black as well as gay, Pharoah Love has multiple reasons for fearing persecution. The books, frequently outrageous, have something of the feeling of underground comics and are still interesting as examples of avant-garde mystery fiction.

Any sixties time capsule would have to include one of George Baxt's works. In addition to the Love series, he wrote two books—the shortest possible "series"—during the same period about Detective Max Van Larson and Sylvia Plotkin. The first was A PARADE OF COCKEYED

CREATURES; OR, DID SOMEONE MURDER OUR WANDERING BOY? (1967). This duo reappeared in *"I!" Said the Demon* (1969). Like the Love series, these books are saturated with the hip attitudes of the decade, as well as Baxt's campy writing and joking.

The first of Baxt's celebrity mysteries was *The Dorothy Parker Murder Case* (1984). Others have involved Alfred HITCHCOCK (1986) and Bette Davis (1994). *The Tallulah Bankhead Murder Case* (1987) is set in 1952 against the background of the red scare and the House Un-American Activities Committee. Detective Jacob Singer investigates the murder of several HUAC informers from among the arts community. In addition to arrogant directors, alcoholic actresses, ingenues, a dancer whose name is Nance, and other extreme characters, there is George Baxt himself as talent agent—a role he played in reality from 1951 to 1957, before going to Britain to be a screenwriter. Tallulah searches for the killer while also stalking the attractive detective, then brings everyone together for a COUNTRY HOUSE finale. While Bankhead is an absurd detective, this dishy novel shows Baxt's inside knowledge of the period, and it has to be said that few mysteries deal so directly with politics.

See also AMNESIA.

BAY CITY The name by which Raymond CHANDLER referred to Santa Monica in his novels. MARLOWE has his most unpleasant dealings with Bay City politicians, cops, and residents (most of them crooked) in THE LITTLE SISTER (1949) and FAREWELL, MY LOVELY (1940).

BEAST IN VIEW (1955) One of the novels by Margaret MILLAR upon which her high reputation is based. Perhaps more than any other, it displays her interest in psychiatry. Helen Clarvoe is a cold, rational woman "shut off from the world by a wall of money and the iron bars of her egotism." When she receives a threatening call from the malicious Evelyn Merrick, she goes to her financial consultant, Paul Blackshear, in essence turning him into a private detective. His "investigation" probes the perverse relationships between Helen, her brainless and self-pitying mother Vera, and Douglas, her brother, a dilettante with no talent and no energy to make up for it.

Everywhere Blackshear turns, he finds self-deception. Vera prevents herself from seeing that Douglas is gay; Douglas hides from his own lack of character; Helen has shut herself up in the Monica Hotel in Hollywood and denies her own alienation; Evelyn deceives herself that her vicious phone calls, which play upon the fears of others, are really revelations of "truth." In each case, "the private I" is revealed as a retreat, a prison, and a fantasy. The ending of the novel now appears somewhat implausible and some of the psychology is leaden, but Millar created a deep sense of enmeshed relationships, jealousy, and spite raised to the level of evil.

BEAST MUST DIE, THE (1938) An early novel by Nicholas BLAKE, considered one of his best. It is fairly atypical, and ahead of its time, in using multiple narrators, the first of whom is Felix LANE. Lane is a mystery writer who announces in the first line that he plans to kill a man. Although this is a classic THRILLER opening, the story quickly develops into a double story of detection—first, Lane's clever identification of the hit-and-run driver who has killed his son, and then Nigel STRANGEWAYS's discovery of a murderer. Lane's diary is a complete artistic performance in itself; the second part of the book belongs to Strangeways, whose detection is understated (some of the clues are nearly invisible to the reader), but completely scoops Inspector Blount, the amateur's redoubtable but stolid official companion. The trail leads into a horrid family ruled over by a particularly repulsive matriarch—leading Georgia Strangeways (q.v.) to say of her husband, "The nose you have for skeletons in family cupboards is really too indecent." In George Rattery, Blake presents a perfect type, the bounder. The relationship between the Strangeways (married two years at the time of the story) is very effective, presenting a convincing intimacy into which the reader is invited.

Blake makes the motivations and emotions of the characters extremely vivid, no doubt partly due to the fact that the idea of the book came to him when his own son was almost killed in an accident, but primarily to his skill and interest in the genre as a vehicle for psychological and spiritual speculation. Blake has the right degree of ruthlessness to drive his characters into horrific predicaments, but the courage to empathize with them, which results in the only right conclusion.

BEAT NOT THE BONES (1953) A novel by Charlotte JAY that won the first EDGAR for best novel. Her second mystery, *Beat Not the Bones* is set in a small town on the coast of New Guinea a few years after World War II and before independence. It is one of those books that is a novel rather than simply a tale, in which the mystery is embedded in a larger narrative with wider interests.

As the story opens, the Australian administration in Marapai has begun a more liberal policy, but most colonials still look down upon the Papuans as inferior. Alfred Jobe, an adventurer, has found gold in the mountains near Eola, a town known for its *vada* men (sorcerers). Jobe cannot get help from the survey section chief,

Trevor Nyall, because the new policy forbids removing material of value to the local population. But they send an expedition to Eola, which includes David Warwick, the anthropologist chief of the cultural department. Warwick is later found shot in the head, an apparent suicide. His young wife Stella then enters the picture. She has led a very sheltered life; she has been taking care of her father, who dies with the word "murder" on his lips. She now comes to Marapai to investigate her husband's suicide. One of those who helps her is Hitolo, a native, and Philip Washington, an Australian who has a strong interest in and good relationship with the Papuans.

The mystery is really the backdrop for the story of Stella's education, and not the other way around—though the New Guinean background is a mystery itself, a world in which sorcery is a reality. The clash between Papuan and white culture is accurately described, the native characters are convincing and of some depth; a lot of ethnographic information is given along the way. Jay does leave behind clues, though the reader may be blinded to them by the other interest of the book.

BEAUMONT, J. P. See JANCE, J. A.

BEAUMONT, NED See GLASS KEY, THE.

BECAUSE OF THE CATS (1963) A novel by Nicholas FREELING, and one that bears out his reputation as a social commentator. In the opening chapter, Freeling writes about the pretentious, staid town of Bloemendaal aan Zee almost like a sociologist, but with a good deal of disgust at the inhabitants' hypocrisy and narrow-mindedness. Inspector VAN DER VALK is working for the "Zeden en kinder Politie," which deals with "Morals and Children." He is investigating a gang rape and burglary committed in Amsterdam; how he hits upon Bloemendaal as the likely source of the delinquents involved is unexplained, but he quickly focuses on a group that gathers at the Ange Gabriel cafe, and the owner, Hjalmar Jansen. The dialogue is cryptic, sometimes circular, but the book is curiously enthralling, as Van der Valk interrogates pompous industrialists and professionals who think they can buy the right future for their children, and whose morality is only about appearances.

BECAUSE THE NIGHT (1984) A novel by James ELLROY featuring detective Lloyd HOPKINS, who simultaneously investigates a gruesome triple murder in a liquor store and the disappearance of a legendary master detective. For much of the story, Hopkins's prey, a throwback to the "evil genius" figure (and, appropriately, a psychiatrist), outmatches him, leads him down blind alleys, and humiliates him. Realism gives way to surrealism as the Harvard-educated Dr. John Havilland (a.k.a. Dr. John the Night Tripper) brainwashes his covey of self-indulgent California narcissists into committing horrible crimes, and himself becomes involved in an Oedipal struggle with Hopkins. Hopkins is supposed to be a "genius," but he is rather easily duped by an appeal to his enormous libido. A final irony, in a book saturated with unmaskings of false knowledge and concocted truths and identities, is that Lloyd does not see the irony that he himself has become ruthless and pathological in his pursuit of an ambiguous culprit/victim.

Outlandish as the plot is, Ellroy starkly conveys how a culture founded on "psychobabble" masks a mass desire to be deceived. In light of Ellroy's later work, it is easy to see Havilland's disgust with the "feel good" society as the author's, which sometimes verges on an orgy of hatred of American society and its hypocrisy, from the sixties' "consciousness expansion" that was "fatuous and propagated by failures" to the "new reactionary fervor" that replaced it. Ironically, Hopkins's own hero is destroyed by unwanted but true self-revelation.

BECK, MARTIN The serious, sometimes self-lacerating homicide detective in the novels of Maj SJÖWALL and Per WAHLÖÖ. The avowed purpose of the Beck novels was to criticize Swedish democratic socialism from a political position further to the left. Beck is a brooding, idealistic man who does his job doggedly, but whose conscience reminds him of the bureaucratic structures that entrap him. His approach is mainly psychological, even though he works within a team of detectives and there is a PROCEDURAL gloss to the novels. More an antihero than a hero, Beck has plenty of faults, for example his continuing in a failed marriage with Inga, a woman he no longer loves.

Beck's best friend on the force is Lennart Kollberg, a savvy, middle-aged man who has a wife twenty years his junior. His sensual, uncomplicated marriage is contrasted with Beck's lonely and self-imposed isolation from his wife and children. Beck has less friendly relations with other members of the homicide unit, such as the enormous and handsome Gunvald Larsson, who has an active and indiscriminate sense of humor. Frederik Melander is grave and imperturbable; he is known for never forgetting a fact, a face, or a piece of information. Detective Ek is a white-haired, ghostly presence.

Beck is not always the central figure. For example, in *The Fire Engine That Disappeared* (*Brandbilen Som Försvann*, 1969; tr 1970), he functions like a Greek chorus, witnessing the actions of others in a series of calamities—a house under surveillance blows up in a terrible fire with multiple fatalities; two six-year-olds find a car in Malmö harbor, which holds a dead body; and a suicide victim leaves Beck's name on a note pad. THE LAUGHING POLICEMAN (1970) is the best-known book in the series; it won an EDGAR award. The Beck novel *Roseanna* (1967) is about the rape and murder of an American girl in Stockholm. *The Locked Room* (1973) is an interesting attempt to combine the socially conscious PROCEDURAL format the authors had developed with the archetypal situation of the classic mystery, the LOCKED ROOM. In addition, they added black comedy to the book by satirizing police procedure—the cops make the kind of mistakes that have lost cases in real life. THE MAN WHO WENT UP IN SMOKE (1969) takes Beck abroad.

Whether the authors succeeded in their political aim (to "use the crime novel as a scalpel cutting open the belly of the ideologically pauperized and morally debatable so-called welfare state") is a matter of opinion, but to deride the books for even trying to do so as some critics have done is witless—particularly as some of the same critics do not seem to object to writers whose books are imbued with sexism, racism, and troglodyte political views. Also, some of the Beck novels contain only a few passing remarks of a political nature, which are mildly "critical." If complaining about the commercialization of Christmas is socialist, then the United States must have more socialists than anyone expects. Whatever their political content, the novels' success as interesting mystery plots cannot be gainsaid.

BIBLIOGRAPHY Novels: *The Man on the Balcony* (1968), *Murder at the Savoy* (1971), *The Abominable Man* (1972), *Cop Killer* (1975), *The Terrorists* (1976).

BECK, PAUL See BODKIN, M. MCDONNELL.

BEEDING, FRANCIS (pseudonym of John Leslie Palmer, 1885–1944, and Hilary Aidan S. George Saunders, 1898–1951) The two Englishmen Palmer and Saunders, as Francis Beeding, wrote thirty-one mysteries, more than half of them about Colonel Alastair GRANBY. Both of the authors had attended Oxford University, and they met while working in Geneva for the League of Nations. Saunders had served in World War I, and wrote *The Battle of Britain* (1940) and *The Green Beret* (1949). Palmer was the drama critic of *The Saturday Review of Literature* and wrote books on the theater, as well as novels under the pseudonym of Christopher Haddon.

While the Granby novels are not greatly admired, another Beeding book, *The House of Dr. Edwardes* (1927), was the basis for Alfred HITCHCOCK's classic film *Spellbound* (1945). *Death Walks in Eastrepps* (1931) is a murder story set on the English coast. *The Norwich Victims* (1935) is another of their non-series collaborations.

BEEF, SERGEANT WILLIAM A character (at first a sergeant, then a private inquiry agent) created by Leo BRUCE. Beef is a no-nonsense Cockney who has quit the force on the strength of his successes and set up as a private detective. Beef's story could be called "The Case of the Hostile Watson": the narrator of his adventures is the snobbish Lionel Townsend, who looks down on Beef's lower-class behavior (he enjoys beer and darts) and doubts his intellectual abilities. Beef is large, with bad teeth and "a ginger moustache" (its tips "nourished in beer," Townsend sneers); his wife is a suitable complement, and decorates the Beef home in the out-of-date Victorian style.

Case with No Conclusion (1939) is Beef's first case after his "retirement," and his accent is at its thickest. Beef puts up signs advertising himself; Mrs. Beef complains over their cost. That Beef could be a successful private detective to Townsend exceeds "all human credulity." For his part, Beef complains about Townsend's written versions of his cases, which he thinks place him in a bad light and worse, are costing him business. Later in the series the conflict moderates, as do the personalities and accents. *Case for Three Detectives* (1936) is the most popular Beef novel because it humorously sends up Father BROWN, Hercule POIROT, and Lord Peter WIMSEY. Beef competes with them in solving a LOCKED ROOM mystery.

In *Case for Sergeant Beef* (1951), Townsend truly makes a fool of himself, first vowing to give up his chronicles, and then revealing his own pitiful deductive capacities. After a round of bickering, in which Townsend derides Beef as "bourgeois," they get down to the case itself, which imitates THE BEAST MUST DIE (1938) and does another turn on the INVERTED MYSTERY. Here, the would-be killer is Wellington Chickle, a retired watchmaker who plans an "art-for-art's-sake" murder—motiveless, and therefore undetectable.

Two of Beef's best are *Case Without a Corpse* (1937) and *Neck and Neck* (1951). Bruce ended the Sergeant Beef series with *Cold Blood* (1952).

BIBLIOGRAPHY Novels: *Case with Four Clowns* (1939), *Case with Ropes and Rings* (1940).

BEFORE THE FACT (1932) A novel by Anthony BERKELEY, published under the pseudonym Frances Iles. Howard HAYCRAFT's praise of the book was nothing short of astounding: "Not many 'serious' novelists have produced character studies to compare with Iles's internally terrifying portrait of the murderer in *Before the Fact*, his masterpiece and a work truly deserving the appellation of unique and beyond price." This novel followed MALICE AFORETHOUGHT (1931), in which Berkeley had developed the INVERTED MYSTERY and indicated the future direction of the modern crime novel. Despite Haycraft's judgement, Julian SYMONS thought *Before the Fact* inferior to *Malice Aforethought;* more pointedly, BARZUN and TAYLOR took Berkeley to task for inventing in *Before the Fact* a mysterious "alkali" that is supposed to be in "daily use everywhere" but is also an untraceable deadly poison. Whatever its faults, the novel remains a unique work in the genre.

As in his previous book, Berkeley announced the murderer in the first lines: "Lina Aysgarth had lived with her husband for nearly eight years before she realized that she was married to a murderer." But in this novel, one has to wait many pages before the sequel—the actual commission of murder. Instead, Berkeley gives us a kind of NOVEL OF MANNERS set in the same milieu as *Malice Aforethought:* a well-to-do community in the English countryside, with its tedious round of tennis parties and dinners, dominated by brainless conversation and gossip. Lina McLaidlaw is almost thirty and has given up on the idea of marriage when she meets Johnnie Aysgarth, a notorious and charming "rotter." Lina is not very attractive but she is intelligent; unfortunately, intelligence "was in her set the thing above all others which was not done"; in fact, "in a woman it amounted to the unforgivable crime." Johnnie seems willing to overlook it, perhaps because of the fifty thousand pounds she stands to inherit. They are married, and the majority of the novel is taken up with the development—deterioration, rather—of their marriage. Johnnie spends wildly, is addicted to betting on horses, and secretly sells off his wife's family heirlooms to cover his debts; and he commits other and worse crimes.

Completely aware of what her husband is, Lina still falls more and more wretchedly in love with Johnnie. The two are the only characters in the book who matter; one of the best sections is set in London during a brief separation, during which Lina meets a man who falls deeply in love with her, but whose love she is unable to return because of her moth-like attraction to Johnnie, whom she now sees as her "child." *Before the Fact* becomes not a masterpiece of mystery writing but a haunting portrait of a truly sick relationship. As in *Malice Aforethought,* the psychology is somewhat marred by the author's frequent statements of the things he thinks he knows about women ("women have not the class feeling of men"; "like all women, Lina was convinced she could arrange flowers just a little better than anyone else"; "Lina had not a very good imagination, except, like most women, as concerned herself"). Whether Lina's solution of her predicament is believable or not, the last scene is unlike any other in fiction of the GOLDEN AGE.

"BEFORE THE PARTY" A short story by W. Somerset MAUGHAM, first published in the collection *The Casuarina Tree* (1926). In this chilling and seemingly innocent tale set among the British upper class, the Skinner family is about to set out for Canon Haywood's garden party. Mr. Skinner is a successful solicitor in a proper, not to say stuffy old firm. His wife's main concern is whether she can wear her hat with egret feathers to the garden party. His two daughters are Kathleen and Millicent. Relations among the family are cordial, impersonal, and above reproach—except for the listlessness and bluntness of Millicent, who has returned from Borneo after the death of her husband, Harold.

The brilliance of the story lies in the way in which Maugham causes the carefully constructed world in which the Skinners have immured themselves to crumble slowly to pieces during a few moments while the family is waiting for the chauffeur to arrive with the car. It turns out that Harold was not quite what he appeared to be (a heavy-set, balding, successful civil servant). Millicent's appalling frankness is contrasted to the elder Skinners' shallowness and incapacity to react humanly. As for Kathleen—all she can say is that murder is "frightfully bad form."

BELLADONNA See NIGHTSHADE.

BELLAIRS, GEORGE (pen name of Harold Blundell, 1902–1982) Born in Lancashire, England, George Bellairs graduated from London University with a degree in economics and later received an honorary M.A. from Manchester University. Thereafter he worked in a bank, becoming chief of the Manchester office of Martins Bank, a post he retired from in 1962. Bellairs was also a freelance journalist, contributing regularly to the *Guardian.* He spent a good deal of time in France and wrote articles on France and its cuisine for various publications, including *Wine and Food.* After his retirement, Bellairs settled in the Isle of Man (his wife was a native). All of these experiences and settings provided material for his crime and mystery novels, most of which are about the affable and understated detective Inspector LITTLEJOHN.

Bellairs began writing while he was still working, and published his first novel, *Littlejohn on Leave,* in 1941. A stolid, efficient detective with many brothers in English detective fiction, Littlejohn is a better than average example of the type. Jacques BARZUN and Wendell TAYLOR remarked of *Death Before Breakfast* (1962) that the story was "more impressive than most of CREASEY's comparable turns with Inspector West." Some of Bellairs's best novels take place on the Isle of Man (*The Corpse at the Carnival,* 1958), or in France (*Death in High Provence,* 1957). *The Corpse at the Carnival* concerns the murder of a man known locally as "Uncle Fred," but who has also passed himself off as Fred Snook and Fred Snowball. Littlejohn, on leave, is completely entranced by the slow and dream-like Manx atmosphere, and pursues the investigation almost subconsciously. He becomes fond of the dead man, especially after the family Fred had abandoned in favor of a life of decrepit peace descends on the island to latch onto the spoils of Fred's estate. Bellairs expresses a feeling for place in this book almost like that of John Cowper Powys, though his style is far more restrained.

One of Bellairs's non-series novels was *Death Stops the Frolic* (1943; orig title *Turmoil in Zion*). It is about the murder of Alderman Harbuttle, a senior deacon of the church in Swarebridge. The murder method is strange if nothing else: while leading a group through the church, he falls through a trap door and is found below, stabbed to death. Superintendent Nankivell, however, is less interesting than Littlejohn. Bellairs also wrote *A Knife for Harry Dodd* (1953), *Death in Despair* (1960), *Intruder in the Dark* (1966), and *Fatal Alibi* (1968). See also MURDER AFLOAT.

BELLEM, ROBERT LESLIE (1902–1968) Robert Leslie Bellem was born in Philadelphia and became a prolific writer for PULP MAGAZINES, particularly *Spicy Detective.* Some of his stories about private eye Dan Turner have been collected in *Dan Turner, Hollywood Detective* (1983). The best introduction to Bellem's work is S. J. Perelman's essay SOMEWHERE A ROSCOE . . ." in which he analyzed with mock seriousness Bellem's ridiculous plots, Dan's absurd argot, and the posturing of the pulp detective. Bellem also collaborated with Willis Todhunter BALLARD, another pulp writer. Later in life, Bellem wrote for television, including the Perry MASON series.

BENCOLIN, HENRI The first detective character John Dickson CARR created, Henri Bencolin of the Paris police was probably inspired by such models as VIDOCQ and, more recently, Inspector HANAUD. He first appeared in stories that Carr wrote while still a student at Haverford College; some of these appear in *The Door to Doom and Other Detections* (1980).

In appearance, Bencolin seems more a villain than a hero. He is described as "Satanic," with a dark beard wound into two points "like horns." He has "cruel" lines in his face, drooping eyelids, and mysterious dark eyes. This figure from horror literature, however, attended college in the United States, where he met the father of Jeff Marle, a young American novelist who accompanies him on his travels and is the narrator of most of the novels. Bencolin wears a cloak and carries a silver-topped cane, prefiguring another Carr detective, Gideon FELL.

The first novel to include Bencolin was Carr's first novel as well. *It Walks By Night* (1930) is heavily influenced by GOTHIC literature (the original title was *Grand Guignol*). Psychoanalysis and plastic surgery are also brought into the plot. The case involves the insane Alexandre Laurent, who threatens the Duc de Saligny, who is planning to marry Laurent's ex-wife. The Duke is found beheaded in an empty room being watched by Bencolin himself, making this a LOCKED ROOM mystery. The other novels, including *Castle Skull* (1931) and *The Corpse in the Waxworks* (1932; British title *The Waxworks Murder*), have similar gothic overtones.

Marle undertakes an investigation in his own right without Bencolin's assistance in *Poison In Jest* (1932). Marle returns to his native Pennsylvania and finds things are much awry at the home of Judge Quayle, whose whole family has turned against him. Marle is pretty slow on the uptake as far as detection is concerned, and he also has some awfully strange ideas, including that murder is "inseparable from the weird minds of foreigners"—a conclusion drawn no doubt from his investigations on the Continent with Bencolin. The case is finally solved by Patrick Rossiter, an Englishman who at first appears as a buffoon.

BIBLIOGRAPHY Novels: *The Lost Gallows* (1931), *The Four False Weapons* (1937).

BENJAMIN, PAUL See BASEBALL.

BENSON MURDER CASE, THE (1926). S. S. VAN DINE wrote huge outlines for his first three books (25,000 words), but this, the first novel featuring Philo VANCE, was the first one to get into print. The story was also based on an actual New York murder case, the killing of Joseph Elwell in 1920. In the novel, the rich and dissipated stockbroker Alvin Benson is found shot to death in his home. Benson's house is scarcely less opulent than Vance's, though his taste runs to mounted trophy heads of big game and decorations suited to an opium den. But the motive is apparently not robbery; Benson is not wearing his toupé and false teeth; and some clues, as well as the man's reputation as a rake and a hedonist, point to a woman (CHERCHEZ LA FEMME). Vance's friend, District

Attorney John F.-X. Markham, calls in the amateur detective, who finds the prospect "most int'restin'."

Van Dine's writing is ornate to say the least, but more successful here than in other books. His facts and handling of details are hazy, or lazy: on one page a .45 bullet "grinds" through brain tissue, on the next it passes through the head "like it was cheese"; Van Dine thinks army ammunition is "steel capped," and that "nothing smaller than a .44 or .45 will stop a man" (the victim was sitting in a chair). Vance is flippant with everyone, and every precious little object is exactly described. The world of the book is a giant curio, and the murder is an amusing bauble for Vance to play with.

Perhaps more than the murder of Elwell, which is mostly forgotten, the reader may notice a similarity to the murder in THE LEAVENWORTH CASE (1878), a book still admired and read in Van Dine's time. Jonathan GOODMAN wrote a book about the Elwell case, *The Slaying of Joseph Bowne Elwell* (1987).

BENTLEY, E[DMUND] C[LERIHEW] (1875–1956) English writer, creator of Philip TRENT. Bentley and G. K. CHESTERTON were childhood friends; Bentley dedicated his classic TRENT'S LAST CASE (1913) to the author of the Father BROWN stories. After winning a scholarship to Oxford, where he became friends with John BUCHAN, Bentley went on to become a lawyer and a journalist. Partly under the influence of Chesterton, he turned from the political conservatism of his family toward liberalism and took an unpopular position against the Boer War. *Trent's Last Case,* however, betrays a strange mixture of criticism of the ruthless practices of the captains of industry and a fear of radical workers' movements (implicitly attributed to the machinations of "foreigners"). Bentley gave up the law shortly after he was called to the bar and instead devoted himself to journalism. He joined the *Daily Telegraph,* and remained there until his retirement.

Bentley was already thinking of writing a detective novel when the London publisher Duckworth announced a competition for a new novel with an offered prize of 50 pounds. Bentley wrote his book in between assignments and submitted it under the title *Philip Gasket's Last Case.* He later withdrew the manuscript when he learned (through another literary eminence, Edward Garnett) that it was not going to win. Happily, he met an American publisher who offered him a $500 advance for the book, but changed the detective's name to Trent and issued it as *The Woman in Black.* Bentley's old friend Buchan, who was working for an English publisher, brought out a British edition simultaneously, and the book was an instant hit on both sides of the Atlantic.

Trent's Last Case was extravagantly praised by Chesterton, Dorothy L. SAYERS, and others as a landmark work. It has been cited as the first modern detective story with characters who are like real human beings. Others, however (Raymond CHANDLER most notably), have found it flawed and its characters unbelievable.

Those who admire the book may turn to *Trent's Own Case* (1936), the sequel Bentley co-authored with Herbert Warner Allen, and the stories collected in *Trent Intervenes* (1938), but neither is likely to prove as satisfying. *Elephant's Work* (1950) is his only other mystery, but belongs more in the thriller genre, of which it is not a very distinguished example. (See AMNESIA.)

Bentley was also a charter member of the DETECTION CLUB and its second president; he had a hand in the group writing project THE FLOATING ADMIRAL (1931). He edited *The Second Century of Detective Stories* (1938), an anthology.

BERESFORD, TUPPENCE AND TOMMY A beloved pair of characters in books by Agatha CHRISTIE. Christie invented them in the thirties and then abandoned them for a long time, supposedly bringing them back owing to popular clamor for more of their adventures.

The wife and husband team began as young friends in *The Secret Adversary* (1922). Prudence Cowley (Tuppence), like Christie herself, had been a volunteer during World War I. Tommy is a wounded war veteran, and both are unemployed. Having not seen each other for five years, they meet, decide to set up an agency called Young Adventurers, Ltd., but are overheard talking about it and a man approaches them with a mission even before they can place the ad. In a startling bit of coincidence, the man, Whittington, is looking for a woman named Jane Finn. The mystery goes back to the sinking of the *Lusitania* in 1916. They learn from a Mr. Carter, a secret agent, that Jane was a survivor of the disaster and was carrying a secret document of profound importance. Tuppence and Tommy become entangled in the search for Jane. Among those also looking for Jane is an American millionaire who claims to be her cousin. At the center of the confusing web of intrigue is Mr. Brown, a NAPOLEON OF CRIME. One of the deaths is by chloral hydrate (a MICKEY FINN).

Tuppence and Tommy also appear in the delightful PARODY, *Partners in Crime* (1929), in which they temporarily run a detective agency, again at the behest of Mr. Carter. In *N or M?* (1941), they are again called out of retirement, this time to identify and fight NAZI agents in England. Christie last wrote about them in *Postern of Fate* (1974), in which the now elderly couple is living in quiet retirement in an English village—until Tuppence finds a children's book with underlined letters in it that add up to a message about the murder of Mary Jordan.

BERGER, THOMAS [LOUIS] (1924–) Thomas Berger is known for satirical, black humor that veils deeper explorations of contemporary society. Born in Cincinnati, Berger graduated from the University of Cincinnati in 1948, having served in an Army medical unit at the end of World War II. Berger arrived in Berlin only weeks after the city's fall. His five novels about the G. I. Carlo Reinhart began with *Crazy in Berlin* (1958). *Little Big Man* (1964) became well known through the 1970 film version with Dustin Hoffman. Through the narrative of 111-year-old Jack Crabb, the only white survivor of the Little Big Horn and Custer's "last stand," Berger told a picaresque tale that was also a commentary on genocide.

Berger is an extremely thorough writer who read sixty or seventy books in preparation for writing *Little Big Man*. KILLING TIME (1967) is a convincing crime story but is also funny. *Who Is Teddy Villanova?* (1977) parodies the HARD-BOILED subgenre. Two of Berger's most well-received books concern the eruption of crime in placid, conventional settings, and use premises that remind one of Donald WESTLAKE's humor. *The Feud* (1983) is set in the thirties. Dolf Beeler goes into a hardware store to buy paint remover and an argument ensues over his unlit cigar as a potential fire hazard. The owner's cousin forces him out of the store at gunpoint, unleashing a feud that leaves several dead (the store is also burned to the ground). In *The Houseguest* (1988), Chuck Burgoyne insinuates himself into the Graves household as a chef and handyman, but after he steals from them and takes liberties with their daughter, they decide to kill him.

There is nothing funny about *Suspects* (1996), however; a PROCEDURAL-style mystery, it begins with the discovery of the brutally slashed body of a beautiful woman, Donna Howland, and her small daughter. The gruesomeness is over quickly, however, and then the story becomes an engrossing drama, not so much for the search for the killer as the development of the relationships between the cops, as well as between an older detective and Donna Howland's suspicious brother-in-law, Lloyd. Lloyd, who worshipped Donna, is an unstable and shiftless young man, a complex and interesting character. Berger avoids the often parched style of procedurals but never loses the thread of the mystery while exploring complexities of personality.

BERK Contemporary English expression meaning "jerk." A peculiar etymology has been given for this word: it is a shortening of an earlier term of insult, "Berkeley Hunt." Berkeley Hunt was a rhyming euphemism for a much more offensive term.

BERKEY, BRIAN FAIR See THE KEYS TO TULSA.

BERKELEY, ANTHONY (pen name of Anthony Berkeley Cox, 1893–1970) The English author Anthony Berkeley Cox had a relatively brief career as a fiction writer—he stopped in 1939, though he continued to produce journalism—but what he wrote was consistently innovative. Berkeley had served in World War I, graduated from University College, London, and written humorous pieces for *Punch* when he created the infamously nasty detective Roger SHERINGHAM, who first appeared in *The Layton Court Mystery* (1925). The book was published anonymously, perhaps because Sheringham was based on a real person. Cox never disclosed who that person was, but said he had to tone down Sheringham's offensiveness when people failed to treat him as simply a joke. In fact, according to HAYCRAFT, Sheringham was "a breath of fresh outside air" among the too-eminent and factual detectives of the era—Sheringham was in both senses a character. He appeared in two short stories and some novels, including *The Poisoned Chocolates Case* (1929), based on THE AVENGING CHANCE.

Berkeley also wrote many books under the pseudonym of Frances Iles, including two classics, MALICE AFORETHOUGHT (1931) and BEFORE THE FACT (1932). He consciously steered the detective story away from pure puzzles toward a more psychological and character-oriented novel. Instead of railroad timetables, maps, and alibis, the reader would be held by the interest of the characterizations. These psychological novels are more "serious" novels, about the development of the murderer's personality, than they are mysteries, and any element of detection is in the background. Berkeley was one of the first to put the reader inside the murderer's head: in *Trial By Error* (1937), a man who is doomed to die from an aneurysm searches for someone—preferably the rottenest possible—whom he can take with him.

Berkeley also exercised his influence by founding the DETECTION CLUB and participating in their collaborative novels, and was a reviewer.

BERLIN NOIR (1993) A trilogy of novels, originally published separately, by Philip KERR. The stories are set in Germany and deal with the work of a private investigator named Bernhard Gunther. A World War I veteran and famous former member of Kripo, the criminal police section, Gunther first appears in *March Violets* (1989), set in Berlin in 1936. The "March Violets" are the Germans who hastened to convert to Nazism after Hitler's rise in 1933. Gunther and many others in the novel are sarcastic and disparaging about the NAZI regime, and Kerr vividly evokes the embarrassment of the civilized in the face of barbarity and their inability to meet it with anything more consequential than cynicism. In this, his first effort, Kerr's influences were not fully assimilated to a style; *March Violets* is clearly an effort to transplant the private eye novel of the thirties and forties to Nazi Berlin, and the Chandlerisms sometimes jar with the surroundings. With movie stars, millionaires, gangsters, Nazi top brass (one of whom—Herman Goering—hires the detective), and Gunther's incarceration at Dachau, the book is a bit overdone, a defect remedied in the best of the series, THE PALE CRIMINAL (1990). *A German Requiem* (1991), set in 1947, brilliantly depicts the cynicism of the victorious Allies—who sheltered war criminals who would be useful in the upcoming Cold War and executed others—as well as the guilt, bewilderment, and resentment of the conquered. In a well-constructed piece of deception and counterdeception, Gunther is hired by a Soviet colonel to defend a German war criminal who is also an unjustly accused man, on trial in Vienna for the murder of an American captain who was a Nazi hunter. Kerr's research is meticulous, even though he imagines unlikely situations for Gunther and involves him with historical figures whose very names preclude imagining them as human—perhaps the very feature that makes the stories absorbing.

BERTIE AND THE SEVEN BODIES (1990) A novel by Peter LOVESEY in which the detective is Albert Edward, Prince of Wales, the son of Queen Victoria, who later became King Edward VII of England. The atmosphere is therefore suitably Edwardian: the story takes place at Desborough Hall in Buckinghamshire, a COUNTRY HOUSE to end all country houses, with ninety-odd rooms. The Lady of manor, Amelia Drummond, gives a week-long shooting party and invites the Prince in order to lend the affair cachet. As the title indicates, a series of murders occurs, committed with firearms, knives, a poker, and poison. The first victim is "Queenie" Chimes, a minor actress. An essay in fun rather than a believable mystery, Lovesey shows considerable fluency with the material.

The ancestry of the novel is in Agatha Christie's AND THEN THERE WERE NONE (1940), though Lovesey mixes aristocratic philandering in with the murder plot, and the narration, by the Prince himself, is a piece of ventriloquism in Edwardian style. Cleverly, Lovesey also has each new murder shatter the theories that have been built up over the previous ones, until the apparent paradoxes are suddenly resolved by a final plot twist.

BERTILLON SYSTEM A system for the identification of criminals. Photographer Alphonse Bertillon's "anthropometrical" method relied on the measurement of an individual's physical features, such as the length of certain bones. First used in 1888 in Bertillon's native France, the system was adopted in England in 1894. The science of FINGERPRINTING later superceded Bertillon's methods.

BEYOND THE GRAVE (1986) A novel co-written by Bill PRONZINI and Marcia MULLER; it is a HISTORICAL MYSTERY set in California involving religious artifacts and treasure hunting stretched out over 200 years. Elena Oliverez is a Chicana amateur sleuth who is working for a museum of Mexican artifacts. At an auction, she finds a secret drawer in a chest. It contains part of a report by a detective named QUINCANNON, who worked for a San Francisco detective agency in 1894. (Like Matt SCUDDER, Quincannon quit his official job—the Secret Service—and started drinking after he accidentally killed a bystander in a pursuit.) The documents reveal that Quincannon wasn't having much luck with the case of some artifacts, including an El Greco, lost when the last owner of Rancho Grande was killed. Oliverez digs up some more records of the now-defunct agency.

Although a bit too complex, the plot and particularly Quincannon are engaging, and the old documents are well-done. The romantic subplot proves a little too convenient in the end. Quincannon had previously appeared in a book authored by Pronzini.

BEYOND THIS PLACE (1950) A novel by A. J. CRONIN, first serialized in *Collier's* magazine. It is a compelling tale of a son's efforts to clear the name of his father. Cronin avoids the potential sentimental pitfalls of the plot, providing a cast of characters, none of whom are quite what they seem. Paul Burgess is barely twenty-one years old when a teaching job in Belfast necessitates submission of his birth certificate. He learns that his real name is Paul Mathry and that his father, Rees Mathry, is serving a life sentence in an English prison for the brutal slaying of a woman fifteen years before in the Midland city of Wortley. On an impulse, Paul takes a tramp steamer across the water and begins a combination pilgrimage and investigation. He receives assistance from some odd quarters: the nervous little tobacconist Albert Prusty, who lived downstairs from the victim; Inspector James Swann, a man ruined by the case, reduced to an alcoholic wreck dying in a hospital; and Lena Anderson, a sad young woman with her own horrible secret.

Cronin is well known for his socially conscious novels. While Paul's descent into hell parallels his father's, questions arise about the strangely ignored clues in the case—a wallet made of human skin, a mysterious green bicycle—and why the police, egged on by a viciously ambitious prosecutor, are willing to thwart and even persecute Paul at every turn. Meanwhile Paul's pious mother, her clergyman and his witless daughter, slowly give up on Paul just as they once had turned their backs on his father. Most interesting of all is Rees Mathry himself, who, when he finally emerges into view, is a startlingly believable personality, a mutation of the affable charmer met in the early pages of the book. Questions are raised about the morality of CAPITAL PUNISHMENT, and more generally about the efficacy and hypocrisy of the penal system. Cronin portrays the law as being more an instrument of social control than of justice; but the ending slips into no easy formulas, neither narratively nor morally. It is a crime story that gets at the *matter* of crime, showing its effects on a group of people—both good and bad—who are worth caring about.

"B-FLAT TROMBONE, THE" (1911) Average JONES's first case. Having been prodded by a fellow club member, Mr. Waldemar, to go after the "advertising crooks," Jones gets on to a case involving a corrupt politician with designs on the mayoralty who has been blown out the window of his home in Brooklyn. The method employed is delightfully original and far-fetched. The author, Samuel Hopkins ADAMS, was himself a crusader against false advertising.

BIBLIOPHILE MYSTERIES See BOOKS.

BIG BOW MYSTERY, THE (1891) A short novel by Israel ZANGWILL, usually considered the first book-length treatment of the LOCKED ROOM puzzle. (The locked room had previously been used in a short story by POE, and before that by LE FANU.) Zangwill was a journalist, but far from a hack; he was educated and had earned a reputation as a committed Zionist. *The Big Bow Mystery,* however, was written in only a couple of weeks for serialization in the *London Star,* and combines elements of political journalism, sensational fiction, PARODY, and socially conscious tract writing. It begins with the discovery by Mrs. Drabdump (a rooming-house keeper) that her gentleman tenant, Mr. Arthur Constant, has overslept. Constant is a philanthropist and activist who has chosen to live among the poor in the squalid London community of Bow; as his name indicates, he is good and true, and has no enemies. It is surprising, then, that he should be found in his bed with his throat cut and the doors and windows locked and bolted. The first sleuth on the scene is the retired SCOTLAND YARD detective George Grodman; he later vies with his own successor, Edward Wimp, in trying to solve the mystery. Whereas Grodman is a practico-analytical sort of detective, Wimp is a genius who might have done great things, except that "an intellect which might have served to unveil the secret workings of nature was subverted to the protection of a capitalistic civilization."

Despite Zangwill's odd, quirky humor, his strange reversals of old clichés, and his jokes about the fads of the day (Madam Blavatsky's theosophical movement, vegetarianism, freethinking) the story only takes off when the foolish poet Denzil Cantercot comes on the scene. Long-haired, eccentric, and broke, Cantercot is a parody of the fin de siècle *decadent;* while he debates the Beautiful and the True with his friend, a skeptical cobbler, he gradually becomes a suspect. Tom Mortlake, a more professional labor organizer who resented Constant's amateur poaching on his area, becomes another. The solution revealed by Grodman is as beautifully simple as it is unlikely. Critics have seen *The Big Bow Mystery* variously as ridiculous, brilliant, or merely a parody, but all have recognized its significance for the genre.

BIG CLOCK, THE (1946) A novel by American poet Kenneth FEARING, well known through the successful 1948 film version starring Ray Milland and Charles Laughton. The mainspring of the plot is ingenious: a magazine publisher, Earl Janoth, kills his lover Pauline then sends his best reporter, George Stroud of *Crimeways* magazine, to hunt for a missing witness whom he has chosen to frame—Stroud himself. Part of the effect of the book comes from the fact that the author worked at *Time* and convincingly portrays the magazine milieu and the tyrannical editor. In Janoth Enterprises, Fearing tries to create the feeling of a giant corporation with a "Big Brother" personality; the novel is vaguely sociological and critical without ever taking a definite position.

The first five chapters, told in the first person by Stroud, describe the magazine world, his own life (he becomes involved with Pauline), and his interest in a particular female painter (a fact of later importance). After a weekend away with Pauline, Stroud sees Janoth's confrontation with his unfaithful lover. Janoth then describes his own view of the story. After arguing with Pauline about her unfaithfulness and her lesbianism, Janoth hits her with a decanter. The technique of alternating narrators continues throughout, while the noose tightens around George Stroud, who is trying to thwart the best efforts of the *Crimeways* staff to find the missing witness. *The Big Clock* is a suspense story rather than a mystery, though the ending is mystifying for several reasons.

BIGGERS, EARL DERR (1884–1933) American writer best known for his creation of Charlie CHAN, the Honolulu police detective. Biggers was born in Ohio, attended Harvard University and then became a newspaperman in Boston. His first big success was *Seven Keys to Baldpate* (1913), a mystery that was adapted for the stage by George M. Cohan (1878–1942), who later played in the first of several film versions (1917).

To his credit, at a time when evil Asian characters were *de rigeur* (see Sax ROHMER), Biggers wanted to create a Chinese-American policeman who was recognizably human as well as admirable. He gave Chan a taste for philosophy as well as good manners, intelligence, and a friendly appearance. Chan is fat and has a comical, delicate gate; his moon-like face is pale, a deliberate contrast to the "sallow"- and "yellow"-complexioned Chinese common in the era's popular fiction. Biggers's sensitivity did not seem to extend to other races, however, or at least not consistently; Japanese are regularly referred to as "Japs," and other non-whites are similarly dismissed. None of this was unusual for the day. But the scene in THE HOUSE WITHOUT A KEY (1925), in which a Japanese woman stares when a proper Bostonian begs her pardon—because "no one had ever begged her pardon before"—is a surprise. Biggers became interested in theater during his journalist years, and his novels are like conventional melodramas in their characterizations and conventional mysteries in their plots. While he veers between ethnocentrism and insight, the books are still readable because of Chan. The Chinese detective is treated as a figure of fun by the white characters, until they are shown up by his superior reasoning.

Charlie Chan's long film career made him more famous than the mere six books that Biggers wrote before his early death from heart disease. The first and most famous screen Chan was actually Swedish—Warner Oland. In order to keep the successful film series going, the device of a world cruise was adopted, during which Chan investigates murder in various exotic settings—from *Charlie Chan in London* (1931) to *Charlie Chan in Shanghai* (1935). Sidney Toler later replaced Oland. A total of almost fifty Charlie Chan movies were made in the thirties and forties.

BIG SLEEP, THE (1939) One must read this novel by Raymond CHANDLER to understand how confused the 1946 Howard Hawks film version—through which most people know the story—really is. The novel focuses on the corrupt family of the oil millionaire General Guy Sternwood. His two daughters, Carmen and Vivian, are wild, and the younger (Carmen) is a nymphomaniac and a drug abuser as well. Vivian is still married to her third husband, Rusty Reagan, a former bootlegger who has run off. His mysterious absence is the hole that paradoxically holds the plot together.

Bernie OHLS sends Philip MARLOWE to the general to help him get out from under a blackmail scheme; the dirty-book dealer Arthur Gwynn Geiger has some gambling IOUs signed by Carmen and has taken some compromising photographs of her. Geiger and several other people involved in his grift wind up dead. Geiger's house is owned by a gambler, Eddie MARS. Lash CANINO works for Mars, and Vivian Sternwood is at once threatened by and protective of Mars when questioned by Marlowe about her relationship with him.

The plot has been called "incomprehensible," but it isn't really; it has the structure of a shell game, with information and evidence passing from hand to hand, always one move ahead of Marlowe. Some of the shells get crushed. A grifter named Joe Brody takes over Geiger's game, but Marlowe makes him cough up the pictures. Brody also has some vital information, but before he can spill it he's killed. Then a tough guy named Harry Jones approaches Marlowe with a lead on the same information. Jones is killed, and the wheel turns again.

Chandler wrote *The Big Sleep* in three months. It was based on his earlier stories including "Fingerman" (the famous scene in which Vivian wins money at roulette from Eddie Mars is closely modeled on a similar scene in "Fingerman").

Chandler found it amusing that Eugene O'Neill used the phrase "the big sleep" throughout *The Iceman Cometh*, apparently thinking that it was an existing piece of underworld slang meaning "death." In fact, Chandler said, he made it up himself.

BILLION DOLLAR BRAIN, THE (1966) One of Len DEIGHTON's best books, this spy novel is full of sparkling, Chandleresque wit; the one-liners and metaphors ("His head looked like that of a statue that someone had found and rolled home so that all the delicate parts had broken off") are nearly always on target. Harry PALMER is sent to Helsinki to suppress the work of a Finnish journalist, then becomes involved in a plot to smuggle half a dozen eggs out of England. Even more than the other books in the series, *The Billion Dollar Brain* has a vivid cast of supporting characters. Palmer meets the charismatic Harvey Newbegin, an American agent who is so romantic that he is almost mad; Colonel Stock, a KGB boss, ruthless but respectable; and General Midwinter, an anti-communist fanatic from Texas with his own private intelligence network. The nursery rhymes that head each chapter emphasize that the games these characters play are at once childish and deadly. It is a sad, cruel business in which all are implicated. Palmer's "nobility" is that, while his boss equivocates ("responsibility is just a state of mind"), he prefers to say nothing.

BILLINGSGATE SHOAL (1982) This EDGAR-winning novel by Rick BOYER introduced the character Charles Adams, otherwise known as Doc ADAMS. Even as the good doctor is discussing with his wife on the porch of their Cape Cod home how dull he feels his life as a successful oral surgeon has become, mysterious events are unfolding before their eyes: they observe a dragger that has been stranded on Billingsgate Shoal at low tide. His curiosity about the vessel leads him to encourage a scuba-diving friend of his son's to check out the boat when it limps into Wellfleet, with disastrous results. The boy turns up dead, and the guilt-ridden doctor is driven to search for the *Patience* up and down the coast. As the story develops, it becomes more a case of suspense than mystery, since the central question is not who did it as much as why they did it (though at least one paperback edition gives the central motive away right on the back cover).

BIMBO The term "bimbo," now usually used to refer to a dumb woman, originally meant a dumb man. It was probably borrowed from Italian ("boy child"), in which *bimbo* is still in use, along with the feminine form *bimba*. Neither, however, has a connotation of stupidity in Italian. In English, the word was extended to include women but without the correct gender ending.

BISHOP, ROBIN See HOMES, GEOFFREY.

BITTERSOHN, MAX See KELLING, SARAH.

BLACK, FINNY The fascinatingly repulsive dwarf servant of the Seaton family in Nicholas Blake's HEAD OF A TRAVELER (1949).

BLACK, GAVIN (pseudonym of Oswald Morris Wynd, 1913–1988) A Scotsman born in Tokyo, Gavin Black has modeled his series character, Paul HARRIS, on himself. Harris is a Singapore businessman who gets into trouble all over Asia, and sometimes in Scotland. Wynd graduated from Edinburgh University and served in World War II, leaving the service a lieutenant. After the war, he became a freelance writer. Wynd has also published some books under his own name. All his works are thrillers and suspense stories rather than novels of detection.

BLACK, LIONEL (pseudonym of Dudley Barker, 1910–1980) Dudley Barker did not begin publishing mystery novels until he was fifty years old, but in the following three decades he produced more than a dozen. Many of them were about Kate Theobald, a reporter in London whose husband is a barrister. Black's first book was *Provincial Crime* (1960). Black was in a sense a throwback to the GOLDEN AGE, though he also wrote some thrillers on more contemporary themes, such as *Outbreak* (1968), in which the terror of smallpox afflicts England.

Black was born in London and attended Oxford. He was a journalist before World War II, in which he served in the Royal Air Force. Later in life, he worked for a literary agent. Perhaps his most enduring work is his biography of G. K. CHESTERTON.

BLACKBOARD JUNGLE, THE (1954) A novel by Ed MCBAIN concerning World War II navy veteran Rick Dadier's first year as a teacher. An idealistic but courageous greenhorn, Dadier teaches English to a multiracial collection of hoods at North Manual Trades High School. The book is driven by Dadier's struggle with gang leader Artie West, and his simultaneous forging of a relationship with a black student, Gregory Miller. The novel was made into a hit film with Sidney Poitier, Vic Morrow, and Glenn Ford.

BLACK CHERRY BLUES (1989) An EDGAR-winning novel by James Lee BURKE. Partly because it uses the mystery form to deal with loss and pain felt by middle-aged men haunted by Vietnam, alcoholism, violence, and past griefs, the novel is reminiscent of the work of James CRUMLEY. Also, half of the book is set in Montana, where Dave ROBICHAUX goes to track down the man who has framed him for murder. The plot is looser than in the earlier books in the series; the author seems to have let go of the reins in some way, having Robichaux soliloquize about God, memory, guilt, and his black depressions; discuss the meaning of his dreams with a psychiatrist; and receive visits from the ghosts of his wife and his father. As before in the series, minor characters play a central role. Dixie Lee Pugh is a childhood friend and white blues singer, a good-hearted alcoholic who always falls in with the wrong people, and to whom Robichaux brings the good news of Alcoholics Anonymous. In his briny speech, happy-go-lucky attitude and underlying weakness, Pugh is almost a reincarnation of Abraham Trahearne in Crumley's THE LAST GOOD KISS (1978). Cletus Purcel, Robichaux's former partner, plays the role of a black angel whose image wavers between that of a good man who does evil things and an evil man who does good.

BLACK CURTAIN, THE See AMNESIA.

BLACK DAHLIA, THE (1987), This classic work of HARD-BOILED fiction by James ELLROY is one of the most *noir* of NOIR novels. Set in 1940s Los Angeles, it presents a good cop/bad cop scenario of two men investigating the same, almost unbelievably grotesque crime. An aspiring actress is found dead in a vacant lot; that the victim was cut in half is only one indication of the horrible tortures she was subjected to. The book is strangely free of scenes of direct violence; Ellroy gives second-hand details and lets the reader's imagination do the rest. It is a book over which one could lose sleep.

The two detectives are Dwight Bucky Bleichert and Lee Blanchard, both former light heavyweight boxers. Bleichert is intelligent, naive, and fundamentally honest, while Blanchard is more experienced, ambitious, and willing to cut corners. Revolting and corrupt aspects of police work are revealed, from the planting of evidence and beating of suspects to remote spots used by the cops to get rid of unwanted bodies. Blanchard becomes obsessed with the case and is put under more and more pressure, partly because of politicking in the background. When Bleichert is left to follow the case alone, he picks up the same obsession, which imperils his job, his marriage, and his life. As over the course of two years he gradually unravels the threads and puts little pieces of the story together, he becomes more and more marginalized. When the case is finally solved, it reveals a far more horrible scenario than one could have imagined—where it was done, how it was done, and by whom. *The Black Dahlia* takes a modern realism into the heart of the romantic private-eye novel, Los Angeles in the forties, and produces something quite unforgettable.

BLACKHEATH POISONINGS, THE (1978) A HISTORICAL MYSTERY by Julian SYMONS set in London in the 1890s. A sad book, it shows Symons's interest in social history. After some difficult chapters explaining a nest of relationships by blood and marriage, the novel becomes enthralling. It begins like a Victorian family saga, except for the series of poisonings among the Collards, who own a prosperous toy company. Harriet is the matriarch, George her ineffectual son; he has made a rather inappropriate match with Isabel, the daughter of an important client of the firm. Whereas George is outwardly dull and too satisfied, his wife is a romantic, seductive woman with ideas of her own. The toy company is really run by Roger Vandervent, who is married to Harriet's daughter, Beatrice. Much of the action is seen through the eyes—and diary—of Paul, Roger's intelligent, poetic, and radical son. Although inspectors and constables appear, the only real sleuthing is done by Paul, who tracks down the blackmailer who has gotten a hold of Isabel's love letters. He also discovers the identity of the poisoner.

Symons strives to recreate the class feeling of the 1890s. The lower classes—including the police and to some extent even the doctors—are loath to confront their "betters" with their suspicions, thereby allowing the murderer to commit further crimes. Their hypocrisy is such that, when the truth finally forces itself on their attention, they are more severe in their judgements of sexual misbehavior than they were bothered by evidence of a murderer at work. Even the murderer is to an extent the victim of Victorian prudery; the family, when it veers beyond the narrow confines of licit behavior, tragically disintegrates. The house itself, a mansion designed by an illustrious architect, turns out to be a kind of prison, whose inmates practice lying and concealment. George's incompetence and frustrated dandyism, Beatrice's dimwittedness, Harriet's velvet fist in an iron glove, and the passions of those inmates who realize they are like moribund flies caught in a spider's web give the book its intensity. Symons, however, does not neglect to include the spying of servants, consulting of poison registers, and other features of classic detective fiction.

"BLACKMAILERS DON'T SHOOT" (1933) Raymond CHANDLER's first detective story, which appeared in BLACK MASK. It has been reported that Chandler was paid one cent per word for the story, or $180, which was a considerable sum for a story at the time. Chandler said that it took him five months to write and that it had "enough action for five stories." The prose is jerky and the descriptions are not up to Chandler's later vivid *bons mots* and memorable similes (except for "hair the color of the inside of a sardine can"). Although there are more stiffs than style, the subplot of the crooked cop who leans on a private detective for help is interesting.

Chandler had grave reservations about the worth of his early PULP stories. "Blackmailers" was republished in *Red Wind* (1946), but is not included in any of the story anthologies now readily available (*Trouble Is My Business,* THE SIMPLE ART OF MURDER, and *Killer in the Rain*).

BLACK MASK The magazine *Black Mask* (1920–1951) played a vital role in the development of the HARD-BOILED style of the indigenous American detective story. The stories in *Black Mask* depicted the violent and disillusioned spirit of the post–World War I United States. Raymond CHANDLER, Erle Stanley GARDNER, and Dashiell HAMMETT all achieved fame through its pages. It was said that Carroll John DALY, creator of Race WILLIAMS, boosted sales of the magazine by 20 percent when his name appeared on the cover.

Black Mask was co-founded by one of the most important literary figures of the time, H. L. MENCKEN, along with George Jean Nathan (1882–1958), a theater critic with whom he often collaborated. *Black Mask* was not originally the forum for hard-boiled writing that it became long after Mencken sold it. At first it was composed of rejects from *Smart Set,* another Mencken-Nathan publication, and included conventional romance and adventure fiction.

Apparently Mencken was more interested in making money from detective fiction than reading it (he called the magazine a "louse"), and wanted to use *Black Mask* to fund his other literary enterprises. He was never listed as an editor of *Black Mask,* and he sold the magazine for a profit after only six months (the oft-quoted figure of $100,000 is probably ten times what Mencken and Nathan received). *Black Mask* was not a bad return on the $500 Mencken had invested.

It was the ten-year editorship of Joseph T. SHAW (1926–1936) that really made *Black Mask* and saw the perfection of the hard-boiled style. He cultivated Hammett, Chandler, Gardner, and the other famous writers now associated with the magazine.

Black Mask was hugely successful: circulation estimates as high as 175,000 to 250,000 have been given but are probably inflated. Among those who liked to read it were Woodrow Wilson, Harry Truman, and Al CAPONE. Like all the PULP MAGAZINES, it eventually succumbed to the television era.

BLACK MASK, THE (1901) The second collection of stories by E. W. HORNUNG about A. J. RAFFLES, the genteel thief. Bunny Manders, Raffles's biographer, had left Raffles swimming for his life in the last story of *The Amateur Cracksman* (1899), THE GIFT OF THE EMPEROR. In his note prefacing *The Black Mask,* Bunny announces a change in the pair: they are no longer amateur cracksmen, but "professionals of the deadliest dye," signaling a more cynical turn. In one of his innumerable cricket metaphors, he says "it was a new match; and we played no more for love." Among the cases in the book is the often anthologized THE WRONG HOUSE.

BLACK MOUNTAIN, THE (1954) A novel by Rex STOUT. The absurd Cold War plot has Nero WOLFE tracking down the killer of his best friend among communist villains in Yugoslavia. Thin though it is, Wolfe's visit to the house he was born in, his overnight trekking through mountains, and his involvement in a knife fight endear the story to true fans. As an appropriate climax of this uncharacteristic violence, Nero Wolfe is shot.

BLACK MUSEUM, THE A collection, belonging to SCOTLAND YARD, of paraphernalia of crime, mystery, and murder. It includes macabre objects and relics of famous cases such as bloody clothes of the slain and myriad weapons. The Black Museum is not ordinarily open to the public. Some of its contents are described by Jonathan GOODMAN and Bill Waddell in *The Black Museum* (1987).

BLACK PATH OF FEAR, THE (1944) A novel by Cornell WOOLRICH of bad luck and gangsterism told in the HARD-BOILED style. It was also the last in his BLACK SERIES. The narrator, Bill Scott ("Scotty"), is down on his luck when he finds a wallet. Being honest, he returns it to its owner, gangster Eddie Roman. To show his gratitude, Roman hires Scotty as a chauffeur. This lucky break further leads to Scotty's meeting Mrs. Roman, with whom he falls in love. The two decide to flee to Havana, but on the way Scotty stops to buy a knife, a fatal decision that leads to a classic setup: the innocent man framed for murder who must turn sleuth to find the real killer and clear himself. By the end, Woolrich has taken a romantic story (boy finds wallet, boy gets job, boy meets girl) and ironically turned it into a tale of unmitigated disaster.

The movie version (*The Chase,* 1946), with a fine performance by Peter Lorre, unfortunately made a complete hash of the story.

BLACK SERAPHIM, THE (1984) Probably the second-best mystery novel by Michael GILBERT, after SMALLBONE DECEASED (1950). It shows the author's versatility in its handling of forensic details. A pathologist, Dr. Scotland, is required to go on a holiday for his health. He returns to Melchester—the town featured in Gilbert's first mystery novel, *Close Quarters* (1947)—and finds the town riven by a political feud involving villagers, the town council, and the Church of England. The core of the dispute is whether to develop cathedral-owned land into condominiums; one of the participants is murdered with nicotine. Gilbert's picture of an English village is entertaining. The crime is solved based on the forensic evidence, though there are classic touches, such as the importance of Chinese ceramics and music. A very British mystery, it also describes the local boys' school and the covert homosexuality within.

BLACK SERIES A group of novels by Cornell WOOLRICH, all of which have the word "black" in the title. They are all dark novels in the HARD-BOILED tradition, though detection does not always play as great a part as coincidence, the macabre, and bad luck. The books are: THE BRIDE WORE BLACK (1940), *The Black Curtain* (1941) (see AMNESIA), *Black Alibi* (1942), *The Black Angel* (1943), and THE BLACK PATH OF FEAR (1944).

BLACKSHIRT By an odd coincidence, it was the year after Mussolini (of the *camice nere*) came to power in Italy (1922) that Bruce GRAEME decided to call his thief-hero "Blackshirt." (Graeme said that he was inspired by his mother's wearing of a black dress.) A burglar, Blackshirt's real name is Richard Verrell. He is a successful author who steals only for fun. The short stories were first collected in *Blackshirt* (1925), soon followed by *The Return of Blackshirt* (1927), and eight further titles, the last in 1940. As his first Blackshirt wore out, Graeme got another one—a French ancestor of Blackshirt, a seventeenth-century Monsieur Blackshirt who was good for another four books beginning with *Monsieur Blackshirt* (1933). The stories were so popular that yet a third Blackshirt was required, this one Lord Blackshirt. His genealogy shows the romantic underpinnings of the Blackshirt series: Lord Blackshirt is actually an RAF pilot who discovers that his father was an earl separated at birth from his family and whose identity was forgotten. He appears in several short story collections (see series III).

Under the name Roderic Graeme, the author's son, Roderic JEFFRIES, wrote about the fourth (and final?) Blackshirt, who returns to the formula of Blackshirt No. 1: once again, he is a mystery author who likes to steal for thrills. He appeared in *Concerning Blackshirt* (1952) and nineteen other books, making a series total of thirty-seven books, all with "Blackshirt" in the title.

BIBLIOGRAPHY Short Stories (series I): *Blackshirt Again* (1927; U.S. title *Adventures of Blackshirt*), *Alias Blackshirt* (1932), *Blackshirt the Audacious* (1935), *Blackshirt the Adventurer* (1936), *Blackshirt Takes a Hand* (1937), *Blackshirt, Counter-Spy* (1938), *Blackshirt Interferes* (1939), *Blackshirt Strikes Back* (1940).

Novels (series II): *Monsieur Blackshirt* (1933), *The Vengeance of Monsieur Blackshirt* (1934), *The Sword of Monsieur Blackshirt* (1936), *The Inn of Thirteen Swords* (1938).

Short stories (series III): *Son of Blackshirt* (1941), *Lord Blackshirt: The Son of Blackshirt Carries On* (1942), *Calling Lord Blackshirt* (1943).

Novels (series IV): *Blackshirt Wins the Trick* (1953), *Blackshirt Passes By* (1953), *Salute to Blackshirt* (1954), *The Amazing Mr. Blackshirt* (1955), *Blackshirt Meets the Lady* (1956), *Paging Blackshirt* (1957), *Blackshirt Helps Himself* (1958), *Double for Blackshirt* (1958), *Blackshirt Sets the Pace* (1959), *Blackshirt Sees It Through* (1960), *Blackshirt Finds Trouble* (1961), *Blackshirt Takes the Trail* (1962), *Blackshirt on the Spot* (1963), *Call for Blackshirt* (1963), *Blackshirt Saves the Day* (1964), *Danger for Blackshirt* (1965), *Blackshirt at Large* (1966), *Blackshirt in Peril* (1967), *Blackshirt Stirs Things Up* (1969).

BLACKSTOCK, CHARITY (pseudonym of Ursula Torday, 1888–?) English writer of mystery and suspense novels, sometimes involving the OCCULT. Anthony BOUCHER said that she "writes with authority and power and subtlety." *The Foggy, Foggy Dew* (1958) takes place during a Soviet invasion of "Mittel-Europe," probably meant to mean the invasion of Hungary in 1956. In London, a man discovers the body of a murdered girl he had met at a party in the ladies' room after a theatrical performance, and realizes he will have a lot of explaining to do. The apparent motiveless crime is given far-ranging ramifications. *Monkey on a Chain* (1966) is about a sister who revenges herself on the man who killed her twin brother in a prison camp on the River Kwai twenty years before. Blackstock also wrote books as Lee Blackstock (*The Woman in the Woods*, 1958) and as Paula Allardyce.

BLACKWATER (1993; orig title *Händelser vid vatten*, tr 1995) This prize-winning novel by Kerstin EKMAN takes place in a remote town near the Norwegian border in northern Sweden. It has been called a THRILLER and includes three murders and a search for a killer, but no labels really apply. European fiction is less hampered by the invidious distinction between popular writing and "literature," and so Ekman's novel is richer, slower, and less plot-driven than American thrillers. Three very different characters are examined and developed in detail. Annie Raft is a teacher and a musician with stage fright whose mother was a famous actress. She quits her job and agrees to become the teacher at the Starhill commune outside the town of Blackwater; when her boyfriend fails to show up, she and her six-year-old daughter Mia try to find their way up to the commune themselves. They become lost and stumble upon a tent containing the savagely stabbed bodies of a tourist couple. The first part of the book is mainly about her experience in the commune and the strange silence about the killings. The main suspect seems to be Johann Brandberg, a sixteen-year-old who is half Sami (Lapp) and is persecuted by his brothers. He flees Blackwater on the day of the killings and has bizarre experiences with an older woman in a hunting lodge in Norway, where he is taken in by relatives.

Meanwhile, the crime is investigated by Birger Torbjörnson, a middle-aged doctor whose marriage has failed.

Twenty years later Annie, who has settled in Blackwater, sees someone whom she thinks is the killer. Johann has become Mia's lover, Birger has become Annie's. A number of issues are embedded in the story, including the environment versus development and the loss of the Sami traditional way of life, which appeals to romantics but entails horrible poverty. Ekman's descriptions of place go beyond landscape to evoke the whole physical and historical climate—beginning with the surreal timelessness of Midsummer (the day of the murder). Through Annie Raft, she describes an almost physical pain at the scouring of the shrinking wilderness. The murder is only one of several things the community would like to stay buried, but Annie, the troublemaker and outsider, refuses to discreetly let it go. Birger's love for her is beautifully shown, and Johann's equivocal nature acts as a fulcrum for the final surprising discoveries.

BLACK WIDOW The black widow spider has achieved a legendary reputation, even though most of its bites are not fatal. They do, however, give rise to such spectacular symptoms as vomiting, convulsions, sweating, muscle spasms, and delirium. The black widow has a distinctive red hourglass shape on its underside. The male of the species is smaller and not poisonous. Appropriately, in Patrick QUENTIN's *Black Widow* (1952), Peter DULUTH is hounded as a murder suspect and comes in contact with a *femme fatale.*

BLACKWOOD, ALGERNON (1869–1951) Born in Kent, England, Algernon Blackwood spent the first thirty years of his life traveling. He worked at a variety of jobs in New York, Canada, and Alaska, before returning to England in 1899. Blackwood became one the foremost authors of OCCULT and supernatural fiction. His first collection of stories was *The Empty House* (1906). *Tales of the Uncanny and Supernatural* (1949) is a selection of stories from his previous books. Blackwood's contribution to the mystery genre was *John Silence* (1908), whose main character used his extrasensory perception to investigate crimes.

BLAISE, MODESTY A comic strip, film, and novel figure (in that order) created by Peter O'DONNELL. The first novel, *Modesty Blaise* (1965), was actually developed from O'Donnell's screenplay for the movie, released in 1966. A criminal turned spy, Blaise works for British Intelligence, along with her sidekick, Willie Garvin. The pair had formerly operated "The Network," an international crime ring. Before that, Modesty was a street urchin in the Middle East after the war until she met her mentor, "The Professor." After his death, she became involved in organized crime. In her novel appearances, Modesty Blaise remains a comic strip kind of character, and is often compared to James BOND.

BIBLIOGRAPHY Novels: *Sabre-Tooth* (1966), *I, Lucifer* (1967), *A Taste for Death* (1969), *The Impossible Virgin* (1971), *The Silver Mistress* (1973), *Last Day in Limbo* (1976), *Dragon's Claw* (1978), *The Xanadu Talisman* (1981), *The Night of Morningstar* (1982), *Dead Man's Handle* (1985).

BLAKE, ANDY See POWELL, RICHARD.

BLAKENEY, SIR PERCY See ORCZY, BARONESS.

BLAKE, NICHOLAS (pseudonym of Cecil Day-Lewis, 1904–1972) The English poet C. Day-Lewis, who was named poet laureate in 1968, wrote sixteen books about the character Nigel STRANGEWAYS, one of the most appealing sleuths of detective fiction. Day-Lewis used the materials of his life perhaps more transparently in his fiction than have other mystery writers, and the books are among the most emotionally subtle of detective stories.

Cecil Day-Lewis (he removed the hyphen as an act of rebellion, then reinstated it late in life) was born in Ireland, the son of a curate in the Church of England. Day-Lewis studied at Oxford in the twenties (he received his M.A. in 1927), where he came to know Rex Warner and fellow poet W. H. AUDEN; he would later use Auden as the model for Strangeways. He became caught up in the postwar disillusionment and the Marxist politics then prevalent among his social group and was a member of the Communist party from 1935 to 1938. The rebellion against authority and the upper classes is evident throughout the Strangeways series, which exposes corruption, but more importantly hypocrisy and moral bankruptcy in high places. At the same time, all the books to one degree or another concern and show a respect for tradition. At the end of his career Day-Lewis had come full circle, and wrote an anti-communist thriller.

The Strangeways books show more character development than most detective novel series. Day-Lewis incorporated his experiences—his emotional life, not only his knowledge—into his books, and also fit the mystery story into a highly developed philosophical framework. He said that detective fiction had become a substitute for the religion in which people could no longer believe, and that it offered a similar kind of absolution of guilt; both religion and the mystery provide narratives that reach ultimate conclusions and a corresponding release of the tensions and emotions they strive to evoke. In this idea, Day-Lewis was borrowing from the theory of catharsis in Greek tragedy. Strangeways's strange philosophy, "We're not meant to be happy," whether it reflects the author's own personal life or not, bears out his taking seriously these ideas.

The first book in the series, however, *A Question of Proof* (1935), was written simply to pay for the repair of a leaky roof. It met with critical acclaim and was a selection of the Crime Club. It is set in a preparatory school similar to Cheltenham, where Day-Lewis was teaching at the time. The young poet almost lost his job because the story dealt with a teacher having an affair with the headmaster's wife. In his first mystery, Day-Lewis relied on the conventional trappings of the detective novel, and of the nineteenth century novel as well, including the narrator's habit of addressing the reader, heavy foreshadowing, and the detective's staging of a reenactment of the crime. He must have drawn on his own experience for the masters: the browbeaten milquetoast; the irreverent (but secretly conventional) young Turk; the vain, bullying headmaster; and the ex-military bore with a weakness for drink. There are also flashes of brilliant language, as well as social-critical excursus, as when a master thinks of a gathering of parents, "It was to maintain this portentous scum that millions sweated or starved beneath the surface." The book is also notable for its portrayal of the class system among the boys, who are neither too cute nor too vicious to be amusing.

Day-Lewis's own affairs and unconventional attitudes toward relationships had parallels in the series. Although a love story is built in the first novel, it is not given the usual "happily ever after" resolution; neither is the author's sympathetic portrayal of an adulterous relationship typical of the times. Strangeways meets Georgia Cavendish in *Thou Shell of Death* (1936); she appears in the books up to and including *Minute for Murder* (1947). At about this time, the author's relationship with the writer Rosamond Lehmann began, and Day-Lewis dedicated HEAD OF A TRAVELER (1949)—of all the books, the most concerned with poetry—to Lehmann's children.

Day-Lewis far exceeded his journeyman work in *Thou Shell of Death,* his second book but the first in which he tried to raise the genre to the level of literature—not, however, through devices of style (he never overloaded his books with "poetic" language). Instead, he tries to raise the story itself to the level of tragedy, which is shown in the first place by his choice of title—a quote from Tourneur's *The Revenger's Tragedy* (1607). The killing takes place at the COUNTRY HOUSE of Fergus O'BRIEN, one of Day-Lewis's most memorable characters, who transcends the good guy/bad guy dichotomy of genre writing in more ways than one.

In *The Corpse in the Snowman* (1941), the archaeology of complex family relationships is again important. Strangeways is called to a little village to investigate the strange behavior of a cat in the local manor, and becomes involved in the investigation of the life of a young woman who seems to have hanged herself. Lovely and corrupted, her personality is slowly unraveled by Nigel; she contrasts with her younger brother, a liberated spirit, and her older brother, who is stiff and traditional. The psychology of sexuality is treated seriously and well. THE BEAST MUST DIE (1938) is the most highly regarded Strangeways mystery.

Day-Lewis also wrote several non-series novels. A TANGLED WEB (1956) was based on a real case, that of the murderer John Williams. *A Penknife in My Heart* (1958) has a similar plot to Patricia Highsmith's STRANGERS ON A TRAIN (1950). Day-Lewis's last novel, THE PRIVATE WOUND (1966), is his most autobiographical.

Day-Lewis was the father of the respected actor Daniel Day Lewis. See also MURDER AFLOAT.

BLAKE, SEXTON A character similar to Nick CARTER, created only a few years later than Carter by Englishman Harry Blyth (1852–1898). Like Carter, Sexton Blake has been written about by many hands—eventually 200 of them. In his first appearance, *The Halfpenny Marvel* (1893), he is a Sherlock HOLMES for boys and lives in Baker Street. Blake would later grow up into an espionage/thriller hero.

BLEAK HOUSE See BUCKET, INSPECTOR.

BLEECK, OLIVER A pseudonym of Ross THOMAS. See ST. IVES, PHILIP.

BLEILER, E[VERETT] F. (1920–) English editor and scholar of mystery and detective fiction, particularly of the nineteenth century. Bleiler did not write fiction himself, but he compiled important information on obscure authors and publicized important work that had been forgotten. Bleiler's *A Treasury of Victorian Detective Stories* (1979) contains stories by the elusive WATERS and Andrew FORRESTER JR., as well as more familiar writers such as C. L. PIRKIS, Arthur MORRISON, and L. T. MEADE and Robert EUSTACE. Bleiler also wrote introductions to collections of stories by twentieth-century authors, including R. Austin FREEMAN.

"BLESSINGTON METHOD, THE" A story by Stanley ELLIN that can be seen as utterly fantastic or chillingly topical. A man named Treadwell is visited by a representative of a gerontology association that has developed the Blessington Method to cope with the "Frankenstein" of science, which has prolonged human life beyond its usefulness. Ironically, science itself is in the way of "progress"—defined by the desire of people like Treadwell to be freed from burdensome relatives. The story won an EDGAR in 1956.

BLIND MAN WITH A PISTOL (1969) A novel about "Coffin" Ed JOHNSON and "Grave Digger" Jones, the detectives created by Chester HIMES. Their hair is gray, they have put on weight, but they are still the HARD-BOILED cops of the earlier books. In this novel (their last), they are unable to pick up the pieces when Harlem is riven by political conflict. Himes said that he got the idea from a story of a blind black man who shot at a white man who had attacked him; he missed, and struck another black man instead. This kind of bitter irony permeates the novel. *Blind Man with a Pistol* takes place on a holiday commemorating Nat Turner's rebellion, the celebration of which gives rise to a conflict between the hippie March of Brotherhood, the Black Power group, and Black Jesus, a Christian organization. Himes looks with a critical eye at the struggles between various approaches to civil rights in the sixties. The satire is humorous but the outcome is not, and the two old detectives are powerless to stop a generational crisis. The character of "Michael X" is based on Malcolm X, who had visited Himes in Paris.

BLINNEY, OSCAR The main character of Henry Kane's THE PERFECT CRIME (1961). A bank teller, Blinney is a "chump," a real "goof-ball," and an honest man. His well-intentioned foolishness is the heart of the story.

BLOCK, LAWRENCE (1938–) Block has become one of the most popular and prolific of American mystery writers. Along the way he has created two of the most distinctive contemporary series characters, Bernie RHODENBARR and Matthew SCUDDER. The former is a burglar with a gift for lockpicking who steals as much for the thrill of being in other people's houses as for the loot. Scudder, on the other hand, is an alcoholic ex-cop—a subtle reinterpretation and updating of the classic tough guy. The first of the burglar books was *Burglars Can't Be Choosers* (1977); among the strongest are *The Burglar Who Liked to Quote Kipling* (1979), THE BURGLAR WHO STUDIED SPINOZA (1981), and *The Burglar Who Traded Ted Williams* (1994).

The immensely popular Scudder series is consistently readable but uneven. Set in New York City (also Rhoddenbarr's haunt), the books rely neither on local color nor wise guy humor, but on the insidious appeal of Scudder's somehow fascinating ordinariness. *The Sins of the Fathers* (1976), the first book, remains one of the best. Its violence is sordidly realistic and shocking rather than cinematic and "entertaining." *In the Midst of Death* appeared in the same year, and has Scudder trying to clear a cop who has been framed because he has reported corruption in the department, though he seems none too clean himself. EIGHT MILLION WAYS TO DIE (1983), the book in which Scudder decides to stop drinking and get into Alcoholics Anonymous, also has some of the best writing and one of the strongest plots in the series. In the following books, Scudder's descriptions of AA procedures and his feelings about the organization are often repeated, sometimes virtually word-for-word, and his earlier morbidness becomes a tendency to sermonize.

Although Scudder is presented and presents himself as a pragmatic moralist, he sometimes crosses the line into expedient justice in a disturbing way. In *A Ticket to the Boneyard* (1990), Scudder and his girlfriend are pursued by a monomaniacal killer from their past; A DANCE AT THE SLAUGHTERHOUSE (1991) dealt with "snuff" films and sexual perversion, and was an EDGAR award winner. In both cases, the horror of the crimes involved is used to justify what amounts to homicide. Some of the violence in the books is revolting, not apparently from manipulativeness but laziness in creating a meaning for it.

A Long Line of Dead Men (1994) is refreshingly strong on plot; verging on camp, it is an homage to the great age of the American detective story and bears a strong resemblance to Rex Stout's classic THE LEAGUE OF FRIGHTENED MEN (1935). It was followed by *Even the Wicked* (1997), in which a serial killer calling himself Will ("Will of the People") murders an acquitted child molester and targets his defense attorney, who is a friend of Scudder's. Scudder has mellowed over the course of the series, and the grim realities have been softened. Indeed, everyone seems to redeem themselves and open an art gallery. Scudder's girlfriend quits prostitution, and they are living together in the most recent book.

Block has written more than two dozen books, including yet a third series, about the spy Evan Tanner. In 1987 Block published INTO THE NIGHT (1987), his completion of an unfinished novel by Cornell WOOLRICH. He seems especially adept at the short story, and these have been collected in *Sometimes They Bite* (1983) and *Some Days You Get the Bear* (1993).

BLOFELD, ERNST STAVRO The arch villain in some of the James BOND novels. Blofeld is part of the criminal organization known as SPECTRE. He first appears in *Thunderball* (1961). In *On Her Majesty's Secret Service* (1963), he conducts biological warfare; in *You Only Live Twice* (1964), he seems completely mad.

BLOOD ON THE BOSOM DIVINE (1948) A novel by Thomas KYD (Alfred Harbage). Although not terribly complex in plot, it has strong characterizations representing a range of social types, beginning (at the bottom) with the down-on-their-luck vaudevillians at the center of the story. Lilith "The Bosom" Devine is performing in a strip show, "Frivolities Forty-Two," along with her husband, the comic "Loopy" Anderson, and the aging dancers, the "Curvacious Cuties." The place is not given, but Harbage's background and Lilith's real name (Stouffer) suggest Philadelphia. Trouble comes when the police decide to shut the strip show down; in the event, murder (by poisoned arrow) intervenes. One of the suspects is the Reverend John McKenna Tumpton, a virulent anti-pornography campaigner. Both the subplot involving detective Sam Phelan's romantic interest in stripper Mary Keeley and the murder mystery hinge on questions of modesty and men's expectations of women. Characteristically, Harbage treats pomposity with sarcasm, hypocrisy with irony, and failure with gentleness.

BLUE HAMMER, THE (1976) A novel by Ross MACDONALD featuring detective Lew ARCHER. One of the best books in the series, it begins with the theft of a painting by famous artist Richard Chantry. The painting, whose authenticity is brought into question, belonged to Ruth Biemeyer, wife of Jack Biemeyer, a mining magnate. The couple's daughter also goes missing during the story. The Biemeyers live in the posh California community of Santa Teresa, where Chantry also lived until he disappeared thirty years before, supposedly in pursuit of wider horizons and new inspirations. His wife jealously guards his memory, as does most of the town, milking his fame for tourist dollars.

Archer tries to begin tracing the painting from both ends, through the suspected thief (the daughter's boyfriend, an aspiring but apparently unbalanced art student) and the art dealer who sold the painting to Biemeyer. He quickly finds himself searching for several different people at once as well as for the painting itself. His search takes him back to Copper City, Arizona, where he begins to unravel complex relationships between the many characters, stretching back forty years. The plot twists are expertly handled and so woven into the story that they seem immediately logical more than surprising. Macdonald had almost outgrown the crime story; the novel makes one wonder what direction he would have taken next.

The Blue Hammer was Macdonald's last book. What makes it so strong is its many layers; the complicated bonds between the characters as well as between the present and the past give it the fullness of a nineteenth-century Russian novel. None of the characters are mere ciphers to fill in a blank in the plot. The fact that Macdonald seems to take an equal interest in all of them expands the book beyond the solution of a crime to an examination of human destiny. Macdonald meditates again on time, which flows in circles that connect the beginning and ending. He explores the complexities of maturity through characters who, having survived the vicissitudes of youth, are even more frightened than they were as children.

Finally, Archer's relationship with a much younger newspaper reporter adds an interesting emotional dimension. His attitude is protective and worried, almost rueful; his vulnerability allows Macdonald further reflections on aging.

Macdonald dedicated the book to William Campbell GAULT.

BLUNT INSTRUMENT, THE (1938) A novel by Georgette HEYER. It is a very original book, from the opening scene in which P. C. Glass finds Ernest Fletcher sitting quietly at his kneehole desk with his head bashed in and Simmons the butler comes in with the whisky and siphon Fletcher isn't going to need anymore. Glass, a quiet, Bible-quoting constable, is an effective foil for the meticulous Inspector Hannasyde. Even the romantic twit element is carried off lightly. The mystery of what the blunt instrument is is only the beginning of a plot with many turns and a solution staved off to the very end; its ingeniousness is such that little can be said about it without spoiling the story.

BLUNT INSTRUMENT One of the trio of basic murder weapons, along with the knife and gun. The classic blunt instrument has taken many forms; in addition to hammers, clubs, baseball bats, golf clubs, and oars, there have been more offbeat weapons, from a fireplace poker (in *The Emperor's Snuff-Box* by John Dickson CARR) to such ingenious choices as pieces of sculpture (a statue of Venus, in one Agatha CHRISTIE story), a doorknob (in Michael DELVING's *Smiling the Boy Fell Dead*), an ashtray (in THE TALENTED MR. RIPLEY), a geranium urn (in THE CASE OF THE LATE PIG), a paperweight (in Christie's *Hickory, Dickory, Death*), a frying pan (in *The Six Iron Spiders*, by Phoebe Atwood TAYLOR), and a quern (in Christie again, in *Murder in Mesopotamia*). The most famous blunt instrument of all is Roald DAHL's classic, a leg of lamb.

BLYTH, HARRY See BLAKE, SEXTON.

BOBBY Sir Robert Peel, the British prime minister (1841–1846), provided two nicknames for policemen, one fond and the other less so. As a Cabinet member, Peel was charged with the overhaul of the criminal code (1825–1830), part of which was the setting up of the Metropolitan Police of London (1829). From the name Robert was derived "Bobby's men" as a nickname for the police, and thence "bobbies." Peel was also Irish chief secretary (1812) and an opponent, in his early career, of liberal policy on the Irish question. "Peelers," another nickname for the police, had a pejorative edge when applied to the Irish constabulary.

BODKIN, M[ATTHIAS] MCDONNELL (1850–1933) Judge Bodkin—hence the publication of his work under the name M. McD. Bodkin, Q.C.—wrote an early series of stories about a female detective (Dora Myrl) and a series about an anti-HOLMES detective (Paul Beck), and then combined the two series by having the characters marry each other. *Dora Myrl, Lady Detective* was published in 1900, two years after *Paul Beck, the Rule of Thumb Detective* (1898). In *The Capture of Paul Beck* (1909), they are opponents, but later reconcile and marry.

Bodkin was born in Ireland and in his youth combined his career as a barrister with freelance journalism. In 1892, he was elected to Parliament from the Roscommon district and supported the Irish nationalist cause. His career was brief, however, and he became a judge, eventually being appointed County Court Judge in Clare. During the Irish war for independence, he wrote a famous report denouncing atrocities on both sides. He also wrote books on the law and on Irish history. In between all these activities, he managed to write six volumes of detective short stories between 1898 and 1929. *Recollections of an Irish Judge* (1914) is a collection of reminiscences.

In his taste in mysteries, Bodkin followed the pattern of an earlier era; he disliked the fact that the detective story was given over more and more to murder rather than to the cleverness of con men. Paul Beck, like Martin HEWITT, was a reaction against the GENIUS DETECTIVE and relied on common sense to "muddle and puzzle out" his cases. Dora Myrl, on the other hand, was a romantic heroine. The second volume of Paul Beck stories, *The Quests of Paul Beck,* appeared in 1908, before his encounter with Dora. The couple have a son who is also a detective and appears in *Young Beck, A Chip Off the Old Block* (1911), a collection of short stories.

BOGMAIL (1978) A "novel with murder" by Irish author Patrick McGinley (1937–). The subtitle is just: the story reads as much like a novel of rural Irish life as a murder story, with a tactile sense of environment and nature. Set in the small Donegal community of Glenkeel, a village of fishermen and farmers, the novel centers around the frequenters of the pub owned by Tim Roarty. Among them are the ancient Old Crubog, dispenser of wisdom and witticisms; the Marxist Cor Mogaill Maloney; and Kenneth Potter, an Englishman working in the area exploring for a mining company. After Eamon Eales, Roarty's debauched assistant, is found murdered, the murderer himself becomes the hunted, receiving blackmail notes from the "Bogmailer." McGinley's fine writing is not the gem-like purity of modernism but something older, the artfulness of the tale that does not wish to advertise its artiness. Whether discussing techniques of fishing, theology, or sex, the dialogue of the characters is relaxed, humorous, and engaging; rather than academic, it reflects a Catholic background and a lifetime's education in casuistry (that of the cynical Canon Loftus, for example).

BOHUN, HENRY A character in SMALLBONE DECEASED (1950) who assists Inspector HAZLERIGG with his investigations—and in fact upstages him. Bohun is a genius and mathematician who suffers from para-insomnia, the inability to sleep more than a couple of hours per night, though without ill effects. Out of boredom he moonlights as a night watchman, which leads to an important clue.

BONAPARTE, EMPEROR NAPOLEON See ARSENIC.

BONAPARTE, INSPECTOR NAPOLEON An Australian detective of mixed race created by Arthur W. UPFIELD, and one of the most interesting sleuths in detective fiction. "Bony," as he likes to be called (it was also the nickname of the original Napoleon), is the son of a black mother and a white father. Born "way up in Queensland," he is tall, elegantly dressed, and has disconcerting, penetrating blue eyes. Particularly in the earlier books, it is clear that Bonaparte was envisioned as a Sherlock HOLMES of the bush. Like Holmes, he is conceited and has utter confidence in his methods, though they are entirely original. Bonaparte's main weapon is his "inexhaustible" patience; though a dogged pursuer, he shows none of Holmes's sleepless frenzy when he is on the scent. He is as leisurely as a glacier and just as inexorable. His ability as a tracker is famous, as is his perfect record (no fugitive has ever escaped him).

Most interestingly, Bony attributes his patience to the aboriginal conception of time: "I am able to exclude from my mind the inherent sense of Time." Thus, his most difficult cases are the ones involving aboriginal people, because they share this traditional view of temporality and are as patient as he is (see, for example, THE BONE IS POINTED, 1938). The white detective lives with modern time pressures, races against them, and becomes discouraged; like a mystical philosopher, Bony sees the moment as the flowering of the seed of eternity, and has a capacity for total absorption, whether he is examining the momentary configuration of the sky, a broken branch, or events of the past. He will get his man, even if it takes forever. It is one of the conceits of the series that Bony's boss, the chief commissioner of the Queensland Police (Colonel Spendor), has fired him several times for failing to return to headquarters when his allotted time has expired.

Bonaparte's tracking occupies some of the most engaging passages in the books. Upfield, who himself traveled around Australia for years, not only has Bony pounce on the ignored bit of cloth clinging to a bush, much as Holmes collected cigarette butts; he also explains the physical aspects of tracking, describing how to look for an old hoofprint on a dried bed of clay, and the combinations of wind and light that allow Bonaparte to see what others cannot. *Winds of Evil* (1937) contains an interesting chase through the treetops along a country road, in which Bony plays cat-and-mouse with a serial strangler and almost becomes a victim.

Bony reveals that his mother was killed because of her alliance with a white man, and the child Bony was found under a sandalwood tree. Raised in a mission, he went on to attend the University of Brisbane and receive a B.A. He is married to Marie, who is also a "half-caste," and they have three children. In general, the farther into the outback the story is, the better the novel: the few cases with an urban setting, such as *An Author Bites the Dust* (1948), do not have the same energy and enthralling atmosphere. *The Sands of Windee* (1931) is Bonaparte's most famous case because it led to a real murder (LIFE IMITATES ART). THE TORN BRANCH (1959, rev 1965; orig title *Bony and the Black Virgin*) is one of the most interesting of the books from several perspectives, including its poetic language and the surprising treatment of race. In *The Will of the Tribe* (1962), the body of a white man is found in the middle of a meteor crater in the desert of the Kimberley Region, with no traces of how he got there. The police wonder how a white man penetrated unnoticed into a remote area where the appearance of a stranger is an event. Bony travels to the central homestead in the area, which has a mixture of white and aboriginal members and is very close to the local tribe. Many "walkabouts," lots of tracking, and Bony's knowledge of aboriginal culture precede and contribute to the well-conceived denouement.

Upfield left a manuscript of a Bony novel uncompleted at the time of his death. *The Lake Frome Monster* (1966) was finished using the author's notes by J. L. Price and Dorothy Strange.

BIBLIOGRAPHY Novels: *The Barakee Mystery* (1929; U.S. title *The Lure of the Bush*), *Wings Above the Diamantina* (1936; U.S. title *Wings Above the Clay Pan*), *Mr. Jelly's Business* (1937; U.S. title *Murder Down Under*), *The Mystery of Swordfish Reef* (1939), *Bushranger of the Skies* (1940; U.S. title *No Footprints in the Bush*), *Death of a Swagman* (1945), *The Devil's Steps* (1946), *The Mountains Have a Secret* (1948), *The Widows of Broome* (1950), *The Bachelors of Broken Hill* (1950), *The New Shoe* (1951), *Venom House* (1952), *Murder Must Wait* (1953), *Death of a Lake* (1954), *The Cake in the Hat Box* (1954; U.S. title *Sinister Stones*), *The Battling Prophet* (1956), *The Man of Two Tribes* (1956), *Bony Buys a Woman* (1957; U.S. title *The Bushman Who Came Back*), *Bony and the Mouse* (1959; U.S. title *Journey to the Hangman*), *Bony and the Kelly Gang* (1960; U.S. title *Valley of the Smugglers*), *Bony and the White Savage* (1961, U.S. title *The White Savage*), *Madman's Bend* (1963; U .S. title *The Body at Madman's Bend*).

BOND, JAMES The secret agent in a series of novels by Ian FLEMING. The Bond novels began to be published in the fifties, but it was the films of the sixties with Sean Connery as agent "007" that made Bond the most famous spy of all time. Actually, what Bond does has little to do with espionage in the sense of collecting information or operating networks. Instead, he is used like a hit man and is sent to destroy the leaders of diabolical conspiracies that threaten Great Britain—hence his famous "license to kill." Julian SYMONS called Bond "a more sophisticated version of Bulldog DRUMMOND," and it is true that the books are nothing like the novels LECARRÉ and DEIGHTON wrote at about the same time. England can do no wrong, and must defeat the devious foreigners by any means necessary. The popular appeal of the books was that they tried to put the "great" back in Great Britain at a moment when, as can be seen from realistic crime fiction (or literary fiction, for that matter), it was undergoing a decline into economic non-viability and overall drabness. Nothing but the best of everything is good enough for Bond, who wines, dines, and sleeps his way through Europe, Asia, the Caribbean, and other exotic settings.

The biggest difference between the Bond books and films is that the former did not rely on gadgetry and explosions to the extent that would eventually make the Bond films into ridiculous parodies of themselves. On the other hand, Bond's sexual exploits are far clumsier and embarrassing in print than when viewed on the screen. Another difference is that Fleming researched his books with care, and there are substantial passages during which he explicates international finance, smuggling, the gold standard, and whatever other background there is to the case at hand.

In *Casino Royale* (1953), the first book, Bond takes on SMERSH, the secret Russian organization that is one of his main opponents. *Live and Let Die* (1954) combines SMERSH with voodoo as Bond pursues the master criminal "Mr. Big" and a pirate treasure. No Cold War spy series would be complete without nuclear weapons, and these are the focus in *Moonraker* (1955) and *Dr. No* (1958); in both books, the Soviet Union uses criminal evil geniuses as surrogates to destroy the West. The Russians try to kill Bond in *From Russia, With Love* (1957). Bond gets married in *On Her Majesty's Secret Service* (1963) but the marriage does not last (neither does the bride).

The villains of the Bond series are only slightly less famous than Bond himself. The title character of *Goldfinger* (1959) tries to steal the gold from Fort Knox, aided by his agent, Pussy Galore. (At this point, the series seems to spoof itself.) The opening, in which Bond helps a Miami millionaire get back at Goldfinger for cheating at canasta, is a memorable scene. Goldfinger is the richest man in England and the "banker" of SMERSH; counter to type, he is short, with a moon-like face surrounded by red hair. Clownish as he appears, he is infinitely clever. Fleming's greatest criminal mastermind, however, was undoubtedly Ernst Stavro BLOFELD.

BIBLIOGRAPHY Novels: *Diamonds Are Forever* (1956), *Thunderball* (1961), *The Spy Who Loved Me* (1962), *You Only Live Twice* (1964), *The Man with the Golden Gun* (1965), *Octopussy and The Living Daylights* (1966).

Short Stories: *For Your Eyes Only* (1960).

BOND, MICHAEL (1926–) The English writer Michael Bond, famous for his children's books, might not have become a writer at all except for a chance purchase in 1957, when he bought a stuffed animal in a London store and took it home. He named the bear after nearby Paddington Station; later, he began to write a children's story about it. The bear from Peru, wearing a duffel coat and Wellington boots, has since appeared in many collections of stories, which have been translated into twenty languages. Through other spin-offs, Paddington Bear has become about as ubiquitous as Winnie-the-Pooh.

After a long career as a writer for children—he has written many other books besides the Paddingtons—Bond decided to write mysteries for adults. The Monsieur PAMPLEMOUSSE series was launched with the novel *Monsieur Pamplemousse* (1983). Although Pamplemousse's France is "real" and not magical, fantasy and the ridiculous are always present. The novels are about circumstances and Pamplemousse's humorous efforts to deal with them rather than about detection. Although not to everyone's taste, the Pamplemousse books have been praised by Reginald HILL and other writers.

BONE IS POINTED, THE (1938) One of the best-known cases of Arthur W. UPFIELD's Inspector Napoleon BONAPARTE. Five months after the disappearance of a cruel stockman, Jeffrey Anderson, known for his brutal raping, whipping, and beating of Aborigines, Bonaparte travels to the remote area of Meena Lake. The territory is dominated by the Lacy family's huge Karwir Station, and the much smaller Meena Station, home of the Gordons, a family who have fought to protect local Aborigines who still practice a traditional tribal culture. The tribe is naturally suspected in the Anderson disappearance, and they fear Inspector Bonaparte's knowledge of their ways. It is here that Bony remarks that "the bush is me: I am the bush: we are one," and his closeness to the land and the Aborigines almost causes his death.

Of all the Bonaparte books, *The Bone Is Pointed* focuses most directly on relations between blacks and whites. The destruction of the Aborigine way of life is discussed as an inevitable fate that the Gordons have tried to put off as long as possible by shielding them from misguided government attempts to "integrate," "civilize," and Christianize them. Bonaparte goes so far as to say "I stand midway between the black man, who makes fire with a stick, and the white man, who kills women and babes with bombs and machine guns." It is easy to see this in-betweenness as Upfield's own and as a sign of his ambivalence. He takes a bleak view of Western civilization, which massacred the Aborigines and then exculpated itself by depicting "the victims of its curse as half-wits in its comic papers." Yet Bonaparte sees some aspects of Aborigine culture as evil. In the end, he must turn inward and improvise his own justice.

BONFIGLIOLI, KYRIL (1928–1985) British author and creator of Charlie MORTDECAI, one of the more bizarre characters of crime fiction. Mortdecai appears in a trilogy of interrelated novels, which should be read in chronological order (though it is not the order in which they were written): *Don't Point That Thing At Me* (1972; also published as *Mortdecai's Endgame*), *After You With the Pistol* (1979), and *Something Nasty in the Woodshed* (1976). With the exception of one other novel, *All the Tea in China* (1978), the trilogy constitutes Bonfiglioli's entire literary output.

Bonfiglioli was, like his main character, an art dealer. He also owned a bookstore in Oxford, served in the Army, and was a lecturer as well as a writer. His life is more than a little reminiscent of Mortdecai's: the first editions of his books said he was "abstemious in all things except drink, food, tobacco and talking." Bonfiglioli also wrote in the science fiction genre, and was a friend of Brian Aldiss. Aldiss relates the story that Bonfiglioli found a painting by Giorgione, the Venetian master, for sale in a junk shop for sixty pounds (Bonfiglioli tried to beat the price down, though the painting was worth thousands).

Bonfiglioli's writing owes much to P. G. Wodehouse—he even uses some of Wodehouse's characters. Mortdecai talks like a corrupt and lower-class Bertie Wooster, and his sidekick, Jock, is a crude Jeeves with a LUGER. A pastiche at times, the books are by turns witty, amusing, and belabored.

BONNAMY, FRANCIS (pseudonym of Audrey Walz, 1907?–1983) Born in Mobile, Alabama, Audrey Walz wrote historical novels in collaboration with her husband, Jay Franklin Walz, as well as mysteries under the pseudonym Francis Bonnamy. Jay Walz was a journalist who started out with the *South Bend News-Times* in Indiana. He began working for the *Washington Post* in 1935, and in 1943 joined the Washington desk of the *New York Times*. The Walz's historical novels were *The Bizarre Sisters* (1950) and *The Undiscovered Country* (1958).

Not surprisingly, the Bonnamy mysteries were set in the capital; the main characters were Peter Utley Shane, a criminologist, and homicide detective Orson "Mac" McCullough. Shane had taught in the Criminology Department at the University of Chicago before World War II, and later worked for an intelligence agency. Shane's method depends less on evidence gathering than on piecing together the elements of a puzzle. The characterizations and the language are not elaborate, but the plots move right along. "Bonnamy" is not just a pseudonym, but also a character in the story (like S. S. VAN DINE in the novels about Philo VANCE); a former assistant professor in Shane's department at Chicago, Bonnamy works for the same intelligence agency in some nebulous capacity, but mainly follows Shane around during the investigations. McCullough is a typical bluff Irish cop.

In *Dead Reckoning* (1943), the first murder takes place in the map division of the Library of Congress; Hugh Mattson is pushed down the stairs after being hit on the head. He was about to set out on a sailing voyage with his best friend, Charlie Hogan. Hogan eventually goes out in the *Quest* with Joe Even, a reporter. They are hailed by a motorboat pretending to be in distress, but another murder happens when they go to aid the boat. A flighty young librarian named Miss Fly also appears. PORTRAIT OF THE ARTIST AS A DEAD MAN (1947), another Shane-McCullough mystery, deals with ART.

BONNER, DOLL A detective character created by Rex STOUT. She appeared as the protagonist in one mystery (*The Hand in the Glove*, 1937), which was not a very successful piece of work. Stout then integrated her into the Nero WOLFE stories as an independent operator sometimes consulted, grudgingly, by Wolfe.

BOOKS The book business and book collecting feature in an enormously large number of mysteries. Recently, John Dunning has written a successful series about a rare-book dealer, and Joan Hess has published several novels about the Arkansas bookseller Claire Malloy, but the subgenre has a long history. Henry GAMADGE, created by Elizabeth Daly, is a specialist in rare books. Another early bibliophile sleuth was Thomas B. DEWEY's Singer Batts, who runs a hotel in a small Ohio town and solves mysteries on the side. Marco PAGE wrote a series about Joel Glass, another bookseller who becomes a detective.

More recently, Michael DELVING's *Bored to Death* (1975) was the first of a series featuring the book dealer Dave Cannon. Other bookselling sleuths include Carolyn G. HART's Annie Darling, formerly Annie Laurance. In the first book of that series, *Death on Demand* (1987), Laurance is operating a mystery bookstore by that name. She teams up with, and marries, Max Darling, in a series similar to the COZY mysteries of Charlotte MACCLEOD. M. K. WREN has written a series featuring an Oregonian, half-Irish, half-Indian bookstore owner named Conan FLAGG, and Bruce GRAEME a series about Theodore Terhune. Frank GRUBER wrote books featuring bookseller Johnny Fletcher, and the adventures of bookman Matthew Coll have been chronicled by Roy Harley Lewis. Jon L. BREEN's *The Gathering Place* (1984) and *Touch of the Past* (1988) are about Rachel Hennings, a bookstore owner.

Bookselling turns up tangentially in many other individual mysteries. In L. A. G. STRONG's *All Fall Down* (1944), his series characters Ellis McKay and Inspector Bradstreet meet for the first time when a bibliophile is killed. The rare-book business is a feature in *Death Claims* (1973), a Dave BRANDSTETTER mystery. Bernie RHODENBARR buys a bookstore after his first two novels; collecting is an aspect of *The Burglar Who Traded Ted Williams* (1994), but in that case it is baseball cards. Other authors who have dealt with publishing and books in their mysteries include Amanda CROSS and Patricia MOYES. Ralph MCINERNY's *Frigor Mortis* (1989) is a comical crime novel set in Minnesota about the murder of George Arthur, pushed to his death by his wife's lover while ice fishing. Steve Nicodemus, owner of a used bookstore and a former marine, buys Arthur's large book collection. Later, it turns out that Arthur used the books as hiding places, and the widow wants the books back.

Not all book collecting mysteries are musty and genteel. In Bartholomew GILL's *The Death of an Ardent Bibliophile* (1995), Inspector McGarr investigates the poisoning of a rare-book expert and curator. The narrator has occasion to return repeatedly to the scene of the putrefying corpse, which has been in a warm humid room for a week. It appears the man had been replacing some of the library's collection with period forgeries based on contemporary pirate editions.

Missing manuscripts and forgeries are a frequent source of plots. Edmund CRISPIN's *Love Lies Bleeding* (1948) concerns a lost and rediscovered Shakespeare manuscript—which is a sub-subgenre in itself. In *Drury Lane's Last Case* (1933), a mystery by Ellery QUEEN, Inspector Thumm and his daughter, Patience, search for a thief who steals copies of "The Passionate Pilgrim" (1599), which contains many poems by Shakespeare; however, the thief returns the books by mail (See Drury LANE). Crispin's short story, "Merry-Go-Round" (1953), is about an interlocking series of forgeries used to humiliate an overbearing policeman. In the Gideon FELL novel *The Mad Hatter Mystery* (1933), by John Dickson CARR, part of the plot hinges on the theft of a manuscript of a previously unknown story by Edgar Allan POE.

In Ross Thomas's *No Questions Asked* (1976), a copy of Pliny's *Historia Naturalis* worth almost a million dollars is being ransomed by thieves who took it while it was on loan to the Library of Congress. Philip ST. IVES must recover it for the owner, Maude Goodwater, widow of "The Uranium King" Joiner Goodwater. Another p.i. is already missing on the case and presumed dead when the book opens.

The Godwulf Manuscript (1973), the first SPENSER novel, concerns a stolen medieval manuscript. Spenser is hired by the college to recover it, and becomes involved in radical politics, cults, and organized crime. The original theft is harebrained; the speeches by the radical professor are too absurd to credit. There is as yet no Hawk, and no Susan Silverman—a plus or minus depending on one's taste. Yet Spenser gets in a few good cracks (and shots), the writing is livelier than it would later be, and Boston is at its most charmingly seedy.

A. S. Byatt's POSSESSION (1990) is one of a number of books that probably owe their existence to Henry James's ASPERN PAPERS (1888).

Also of interest to bibliophiles are the vast number of mysteries dealing with publishing. One of the best books in this subgenre was co-authored by John Rhode and Carter Dickson (John Dickson Carr): in *Fatal Descent* (1939), the machinations in a publishing house lead to a murder committed using a booby-trapped elevator. In *Write Murder Down* (1972), a LOCKRIDGE mystery, a woman found with her wrists slashed in a Greenwich Village apartment turns out to be a well-known author. The Lockridges also wrote MURDER BY THE BOOK (1963), a Pam and Jerry NORTH mystery (Jerry is himself a publisher). Rex STOUT wrote a Nero WOLFE novel of the same name (1951). In the Nigel STRANGEWAYS mystery END OF CHAPTER (1957), controversial passages in a general's memoirs impugning the conduct of some of his colleagues during the war are tactfully deleted but then surreptitiously reinstated, with dire results. (The author, Nicholas BLAKE, worked in publishing for a number of years.) Julian SYMONS contributed two novels to the subgenre, *The Narrowing Circle* (1954), which deals with forgery, and *The Plain Man* (1962), in which an editor at a magazine conglomerate solves a murder. In a more recent novel, William DOUGAL, a series detective and failed graduate student created by Andrew TAYLOR, investigates a murder having to do with publishing in London.

BOOMERANG CLUE, THE See GOLF MYSTERIES.

BOOTHBY, GUY [NEWELL] (1867–1905) The Australian-born novelist and short story writer Guy Boothby was a shooting star of the Sherlock HOLMES era. He might not even have been an author at all, considering that he did not begin to publish until ten years before his death (from influenza) at thirty-seven; but when he did, he did so with incredible passion, publishing more than fifty novels in a decade.

Boothby was born in Adelaide but was educated in England. He returned to Australia after his schooling, and became an assistant to the mayor of Adelaide. In 1894, he decided to make a name for himself as a writer (he had written some plays, but they were failures), and returned to London. The following year, he published the appropriately titled *A Bid for Fortune*, which was an immediate success. It was not about his own bid, however; it is a suspense thriller about an evil genius known as Dr. Nikola, who would appear also in *Dr. Nikola* (1896), *The*

Lust of Hate (1898), *Dr. Nikola's Experiment* (1899), and *"Farewell, Nikola"* (1901). Much of Boothby's writing could be called slapdash, but like Rider HAGGARD, there is a relentless pressure to his narrative. He was interested in the OCCULT, elements of which colored many of his books. In *Pharos the Egyptian* (1899), a mummy come back to life—a favorite theme at the time—tries to launch a plague that will destroy Western civilization.

Boothby's most important contribution to the mystery genre was Simon CARNE, a gentleman thief who was the hero of several stories. He has been considered the original of the type; E. F. BLEILER wrote that Carne was "a criminal of much more imagination and ingenuity than the more famous RAFFLES."

BOOTLEGGER The term for a person who sells illegal liquor supposedly dates from American frontier days, when it applied to those who sold whisky to Native Americans and carried the bottles in the tops of their boots. The word "bootleg," however, was also used by convicts to refer to what passed for coffee in prison.

BOOTLEGGER'S DAUGHTER (1992) The EDGAR-winning novel by Margaret MARON that started the Deborah Knott series. Knott is a feminist North Carolina attorney who is running for judge. The book raises a lot of issues dealing with the "New" and "Old" Souths, but they are not just window dressing; the question of attitudes toward homosexuality, for example, is integral to the plot. In 1972, a woman named Janie Whitehead is found shot to death in a mill beside her three-month-old daughter. Almost twenty years later, the daughter, Gayle, approaches Knott, who reluctantly agrees to help search for the killer. Janie had disappeared after being seen talking to an unknown man in a car. The trail leads to a pair of gay men who are in a difficult position as an "out" couple in a traditional Southern family. Knott is assisted in her investigation by Dwight Bryant, an agent of the State Bureau of Investigation and an old high school friend. There is also a passel of Knotts in the book, including the bootlegger of the title.

BORDEN, LIZZIE Elizabeth Borden (1860–1927) became the subject of one of the most famous trials of all time when she was indicted for the double murder of her father and stepmother with an axe, memorialized in the anonymous rhyme beginning, "Lizzie Borden took an axe/And gave her father forty whacks." The murder occurred in the Borden home in Fall River, Massachusetts, on August 4, 1892. Borden was acquitted and the crime was never solved, though it has been the subject of much speculation. Those who agreed with the verdict include Edward Radin (*Lizzie Borden: The Untold Story,* 1961) and most recently Frank Spiering, who argues in *Lizzie* (1985) that Emma Borden, Lizzie's older sister, was the real murderer. Edmund PEARSON (*The Trial of Lizzie Borden,* repr 1937) felt that Lizzie was guilty. Julian SYMONS pointed out that Lizzie had not only opportunity but ample motive: her resentment of her stepmother and the $175,000 she and Emma inherited.

Fictional works based on the Fall River murder include the novels *The Long Arm* (1895), by Mary E. Wilkins Freeman; *Lizzie Borden: A Study in Conjecture* (1939) by Marie Belloc LOWNDES; a novel by Anthony ABBOT; and the plays *Nine Pine Street* (1933), by John Colton, and *Goodbye, Miss Lizzie Borden* (1947), by Lillian DE LA TORRE. Like Billy the Kid, Lizzie Borden even inspired a dance: Agnes de Mille's ballet *Fall River Legend* (1948). De Mille discussed the genesis of the work in *Lizzie Borden: A Dance of Death* (1968).

Geoffrey Homes wrote a Humphrey CAMPBELL mystery, *Forty Whacks* (1941), about a "new" Borden killing. A more recent novel based on the case is by Evan Hunter (Ed MCBAIN), and was exhaustively researched; *Lizzie* (1984) uses verbatim testimony from the trial, culled from the 1,930-page typescript. It begins with Lizzie's 1892 trip to Europe, and conjectures Lizzie's lesbianism. Hunter presents the trial first, then visualizes the murder in a brutal, graphic, and stunning conclusion. His solution would require some revision to the anonymous rhyme of the period.

It seems that appetite for the subject has still not been exhausted. *Lizzie Borden* (1991), by Elizabeth Engstrom, is the latest novel based on the crime. There is now even a *Lizzie Borden Quarterly,* catering to public fascination with the case.

BORGES, JORGE LUIS (1899–1986) The Argentine poet, short story writer, and essayist Jorge Luis Borges was one of the great modernist writers and a developer of the tradition that would become known as magic realism. He was a lifelong friend of his countryman Adolpho Bioy Casares (1914–1984), and they collaborated often. Under the pseudonym of Honorio Bustos Domecq, together they wrote *Seis problemas para Don Isidro Parodi* (1942; tr *Six Problems for Don Isidro Parodi,* 1980). Don Isidro is a barber who has been falsely imprisoned, but in his jail cell he is consulted by people in trouble. The stories are a satire on Argentinean society and political figures. Borges and Bioy Casares also edited *Los mejores cuentos policiales* (*The Greatest Detective Stories,* 1943), and an enthusiasm for crime and mystery fiction is also evident in Bioy Casares's best-known work, *La invención de Morel* (1940; tr *The Invention of Morel and Other Stories,* 1985). Borges's contribution to the mystery genre was recognized with a special EDGAR award in 1976.

BORUVKA, LIEUTENANT JOSEF Lieutenant Josef Boruvka is a heavy, sad-faced, tired "old criminologist" (even though he is only forty-eight) when he first appears in THE SUPERNATURAL POWERS OF LIEUTENANT BORUVKA. He has taught criminology and is a long-suffering veteran of the force. Twenty years before, he played alto saxophone in the military band, which comes in handy in the case of "That Sax Solo."

Boruvka also appears in two of the stories in a collection Josef Skvorecky wrote in defiance of the rules of Monseignor Ronald KNOX, in which all of the "rules" of FAIR PLAY were systematically violated.

BIBLIOGRAPHY Short Stories: *The Mournful Demeanor of Lieutenant Boruvka* (*Smutek porucika Boruvky,* 1966; tr 1973, repr 1987), *Sins for Father Knox* (*Hrichy pro patera Knoxe,* 1973; tr 1988), *The End of Lieutenant Boruvka* (*Konec porucika Boruvky,* 1975; tr 1989).

BOSCH, HARRY See CONNELLY, MICHAEL.

BOSTON BLACKIE (1919) Like Michael ARLEN's single story that led to the FALCON industry, Jack Boyle's one collection of stories about the thief Boston Blackie kept radio and film producers busy for decades. Blackie is a gentleman thief and one of many descendants of RAFFLES.

BOSTON STRANGLER The name of the person responsible for a reign of terror in Boston in the early sixties. Between June 1962 and January 1964, thirteen women between the ages of nineteen and eighty-five were sexually assaulted and strangled to death, not only in Boston, but in nearby Cambridge and as far away as Lawrence, Massachusetts. As hysteria in the city increased, law enforcement turned to computers, various specialists, and even clairvoyants to help find the Strangler. In the end, a man named Alberto DeSalvo, in custody on other charges, confessed to the crimes. DeSalvo turned out to be a character as bizarre as any in fiction. He came from what would now be called a dysfunctional family; his alcoholic father would bring prostitutes home and then beat his wife in front of them. DeSalvo had an enormous libido. As "The Green Man," he had attacked as many as three hundred women across New England (his sexual compulsion was so great that he assaulted four different women in one day alone). Earlier, he had been "The Measuring Man," who conned his way into women's apartments and got them to undress and be measured for their suitability as models. DeSalvo was diagnosed as a sociopath with schizophrenic symptoms. The flamboyant lawyer F. Lee Bailey was his defense attorney. *The Boston Strangler* (1966), by EDGAR-winning author Gerold Frank, is the primary book on the case. VÁZQUEZ MONTALBÁN recently wrote a novel from the perspective of the Strangler.

BOUCHER, ANTHONY (William Anthony Parker White, 1911–1968) One of the most important mystery critics and reviewers of the twentieth century, Anthony Boucher was also a mystery author himself. He was particularly a devotee of Sherlock HOLMES, and wrote two mysteries under the pseudonym H. H. Holmes (it was actually the name of a famous murderer). Boucher was influential for almost two decades as the mystery critic for *The New York Times Book Review, Ellery Queen's Mystery Magazine* and other publications, helping to win attention for mystery writing in the mainstream press. He also won several EDGARS for his criticism. Boucher translated from French, Spanish, and Portuguese, including works by Jorge Luis BORGES. Despite his distinctly un-hard-boiled style and preference for the outlandish and bizarre murder, Boucher corresponded and was friendly with Raymond CHANDLER, premiere exponent of the realistic private eye novel.

Boucher was born in California and attended school in Pasadena. He began by studying physics (several works had scientific or SCIENCE FICTION elements) and later changed to linguistics. He graduated with a B.A. from the University of Southern California in 1932 and received a master's degree from the University of California two years later. His first literary efforts were in drama, and he was an amateur actor and director. Boucher wrote seven mystery novels. *The Case of the Seven of Calvary* (1937) had a Sanskrit professor at the University of California for its sleuth. *The Case of the Crumpled Knave* (1939) introduced Fergus O'Breen, about whom he would write four novels. *The Case of the Solid Key* (1941) is a LOCKED-ROOM mystery, a form of which Boucher was especially fond. O'Breen is assisted by an Oklahoma playwright whose plans to make it with the Carruthers Little Theater in Hollywood are dashed when Rupert Carruthers himself is killed.

In this same period, Boucher was publishing science fiction stories and was reviewing science fiction for the *San Francisco Chronicle.* This subject turned up in one of his novels, ROCKET TO THE MORGUE (1942), set at a science fiction writers' convention. NINE TIMES NINE (1940), often singled out as Boucher's best work of fiction, concerns a Southern California cult. Both of these books were published under the pseudonym H. H. Holmes but have recently been reprinted under the name Boucher. His best-known Holmesian work is *The Case of the Baker Street Irregulars* (1940), which features a group of like-minded Holmesians writing a film and uncovering villainy in Hollywood.

The two-volume *Crimes and Misfortunes* (1970) is a collection of stories in honor of Boucher with brief remarks about him by such writers as Georges SIMENON, Rex STOUT, Margaret MILLAR, Bill PRONZINI, and Ellery QUEEN. It also lists some of Boucher's other interests as "football, basketball, rugby, Elizabethan drama, food, Gibsons, imported dark beer."

BOUCHERON The annual World Mystery Convention, named in honor of Anthony BOUCHER. The mystery awards given at the convention, similar to those of the Mystery Writers of America (the EDGARS), are also named for Boucher and are knows as the "Anthonys."

BOW STREET RUNNERS The forerunners of the London Metropolitan Police, the Bow Street runners were private agents of the courts. There was a court in Bow Street, and in 1748 Henry FIELDING was appointed magistrate. He organized the Bow Street Police to patrol the surrounding district. Even so, London remained an extremely dangerous place—after all, the Bow Street Police initially had only fifteen detectives, and they did not go outside their own district.

The Bow Street runners remained in existence for a decade after Robert PEEL established the first Metropolitan Police (see BOBBY). DICKENS offered the interesting information that, in his time, the Bow Street runners met in a pub across the street from the police station, where they could consort with crooks.

BOX, EDGAR The pseudonym of American writer Gore Vidal (1925–), under which he wrote three fluent, clever mysteries. All three feature public-relations man and amateur sleuth Peter Cutler Sargeant III. The first of the novels, *Death in the Fifth Position* (1952), takes place in a Russian ballet company; the most remarkable thing about it is how it mocks Red-baiting and conservative fears of communists, although it was published during the heyday of McCarthyism. It also treats homosexuality with a combination of humor and respect. Vidal said in his autobiography, *Palimpsest* (1995), that he got the idea for *Death in the Fifth Position* after watching Alicia Markova bickering with her partner in *Swan Lake* from backstage. In addition, he had taken ballet lessons to rehabilitate his knees, which had plagued him since his treatment for exposure in Alaska during his service in World War II.

Vidal has said that he wrote each of the books in eight days, composing seven chapters of ten thousand words each, and editing on the eighth day. He lived off the proceeds of the three Box books for several years. Vidal said that he was forced to write under a pseudonym because he had been blacklisted for the attitude toward sexuality expressed in his early fiction.

In *Death Likes It Hot* (1954), the best of the books, Vidal transplants the English COUNTRY HOUSE mystery to the Hamptons on the shores of Long Island. His handling of the plot shows his intimate knowledge of the snooty, rich, and artistic set who inhabit the summer enclave. It is almost a roman à clef, in that the painter Brexton could be a portrait of Jackson Pollock. This time, Sargeant is drawn into a mystery when Brexton's wife drowns. Vidal delights in using Sargeant to make fun of his own social set ("my interest in modern painting ranges somewhere between zero and minus ten"), and his highly original wit is neither half-baked nor hard-boiled. The Box novels are, as the author said, historical portraits of "the noon-like fifties, when the American empire was at its peak, and everything worked, and New York City glittered." *Death Before Bedtime* (1953) is set in Washington, D.C., however, and so lacks some of the energy of the other books. Sargeant is backing Hermione the singing poodle for a dog food company, and gets invited to a house party where a senator is blown up by a bomb rigged to go off when the fireplace is lit. Political wrangling, paranoia, and reactionary politics are in the background; everyone warns Sargeant not to investigate. Box reaches a surprise ending by means of an enormous RED HERRING, but the conclusion is unsatisfying.

Vidal was born Eugene Luther Vidal in West Point, New York, and graduated from Philips Exeter Academy. He served in World War II and then lived in Europe, South America, North Africa, and the United States. His novel *The City and the Pillar* (1948) dealt frankly with homosexuality. He later became known for a series of historical novels—*Burr* (1974), *1876* (1976), and *Lincoln* (1984)—and for his political writings and opinions.

BOYER, RICK [RICHARD] (1943–) The American author Rick Boyer has written eight novels about Doc ADAMS, the first of which, BILLINGSGATE SHOAL (1982), won an EDGAR award. Born in Illinois, Boyer received an M.F.A. degree from the University of Iowa in 1968. Thereafter he taught high school English in Illinois, then moved to Boston and switched to publishing, becoming a salesman and then an acquisitions editor. His first book was *The Giant Rat of Sumatra* (1976), a Sherlockian pastiche. Boyer now lives and teaches in North Carolina.

Boyer's work reflects the expansion of the regional mystery novel and the burgeoning of specialist detectives since the 1980s. In the first novel, however, Adams is just an oral surgeon who finds his life boring and safe, until his curiosity about a stranded boat leads to a young man's death. *Billingsgate Shoal* remains the most satisfying of the books, partly because of the series format itself; Boyer runs into the problem confronted by anyone who tries to write a series of mysteries about a character who is not a detective and not a cop. While it is plausible that through a series of circumstances Adams could be drawn into contact with murderers, violence, and death, to believe that such events impinge on his life again and again requires either the reader's willing suspension of disbelief or that the character become a "professional" sleuth (Boyer chooses the latter option, making Adams become a forensic consultant to the police).

Boyer's style combines elements of the standard suspense and mystery stories; although there are COZY aspects to the Adams novels, there are also some graphically violent scenes, such as when a man's head is "canned" by having a cast-iron pipe dropped on it from three stories. The cliffhanger approach—a series of climaxes, each of which might have been the final rather than penultimate one—is reminiscent of Donald WESTLAKE or Max BYRD. Boyer's writing also becomes looser and even careless as the series progresses: the boy whose death Adams accidentally caused was an eight-year-old in *Billingsgate Shoal,* but is a six-year-old in *Yellow Bird* (1991).

BOYLE, KAY (1903–1992) The American-born writer Kay Boyle, who lived much of her life in Europe and set many of her novels there, is known for her psychologically penetrating studies of character. Boyle married a Frenchman and lived in France, England, and Austria from 1922 until 1941; after the war she was a foreign correspondent for *The New Yorker.*

Romantic relationships (often unfulfilling) and political and social issues are recurrent themes of Boyle's work. In *Avalanche* (1944), she combines her usual preoccupations with a story of murder and espionage. The book also reflects her sympathy with the French Resistance movement. The plot is not terribly complex, but the setting forth of the characters' thoughts and emotions is excellent, as is the feeling of suspense. Fenton Ravel is returning to the village near Mont Blanc where she grew up for needed rest after her volunteer work in Lyon. She is also searching for the man she loves, Bastineau. On the train, she meets two somewhat mysterious men, De Vaudois and Jacqueminot; she also learns of a rumor that Bastineau has been killed in an avalanche. Her efforts to discover the truth have unexpected consequences.

BOZO Although this word for a stupid (and usually big) man reminds most people of Bozo the Clown, the term has been around since the beginning of the century. Several Spanish derivations have been proposed: *bozo,* meaning "the hair on the cheeks of boys" (i.e., "peach fuzz"), or *bozal,* "muzzle."

BRADBURY, RAY [DOUGLAS] (1920–) The American writer Ray Bradbury is one of the most important science fiction authors of all time; among his books are *The Martian Chronicles* (1950) and *Fahrenheit 451* (1953). Bradbury is known for the socially critical edge of his work; the last-named novel refers to the burning point of paper and concerns a "fireman" who is responsible for destroying rather than saving books.

In addition to his many science fiction stories, Bradbury has written two mysteries. *Death is a Lonely Business* (1985) is dedicated to the "big four" of the HARD-BOILED genre: CHANDLER, HAMMETT, Ross MACDONALD, and James M. CAIN. Dream-like, poetic, sometimes florid and overwritten, the novel takes place in Venice, California, in 1949, where the old carnival amusement park is falling into the sea. The narrator, a young writer who has published in BLACK MASK and *Dime Detective,* finds an old man's body floating in a sunken lion's cage. He begins an investigation, but his findings are at first ignored by a typical grouchy detective, Elmo Crumley. Despite the detection, the story has more the feeling of Bradbury's *The October Country* (1955), in which the tactile force of the present coexists with an almost surreal kind of reverie in which the past and future are physical presences. Bradbury can't maintain the down-to-earth hard-boiled style because of the slippage of time, centuries, and eras in the narrator/author's mind. Oil wells remind him of "great pterodactyls"; a frail old woman in her bed, of archaeopteryx. Although a detective novel, it betrays the obsession with the nature of time that marks the author's other work; this, in fact, is its greatest strength. *A Graveyard for Lunatics* (1990) is another novel in a similar vein, set in Hollywood in 1954, in which a scriptwriter makes a bizarre discovery.

BRADDON, MARY (1837–1915) Like C. L. PARKIS, Mary Braddon was a popular nineteenth-century English novelist, only more so. *Lady Audley's Secret* (1861-62), her first book, was also one of the most successful novels of the century, on both sides of the Atlantic, and was adapted for the stage. It is a crime story in which a woman does away with her husband by pushing him down a well. Braddon went on to write some eighty novels, some under the pseudonym of Babington White. William Rose Benét said that her novels were "of a high-flown, romantic character," which, "though ephemeral, were not devoid of quality."

Mary Braddon was born in London, the daughter of a solicitor who also was a writer on sporting subjects. She was educated at home but was highly literate. Her first story was written for a publisher who went out of business before her work could appear. Five years later, the publisher John Maxwell bought the rights to *Lady Audley's Secret* for the magazine *Robin Goodfellow*, which also failed, and so the novel was serialized in *Sixpenny Magazine*. It was published as a book in 1862. The success of the novel meant that Braddon was instantly rich, and she had no financial need to go on writing. Yet she wrote plays and poetry in addition to her heaps of novels. Some Victorian critics took Braddon to task for "immorality" and for making crime seem attractive, while others attacked her sensationalism. But she was well regarded by many, including STEVENSON and other important literary figures.

Braddon married John Maxwell in 1874 and had five children. Two of her sons also became writers. Like Mary Roberts RINEHART, she was able to keep a publishing company afloat single-handedly. She went on to write a total of eighty novels, among them *Dead Men's Shoes* (1876), *Phantom Fortune* (1883), and *Rough Justice* (1898). She also edited *Belgravia Magazine* and *Temple Bar*. Braddon's short stories ranged all over the map of popular literature, and included mystery and crime. "Levison's Victim" is a tragic story with a predictably happy ending. The theme is a daughter's sacrifice for a worthless father, and the revenge of her heartbroken suitor.

BRADLEY, BEATRICE ADELA LESTRANGE One of the most odd detectives in mystery fiction, Dame Bradley was created by Gladys MITCHELL. Dame Bradley is an old woman, but she is not cute and charming; neither is she a paragon of common sense. She is a noted psychiatrist, even though she looks like a witch, and her explanations of crimes involve analysis of the criminal's mind. Small and wizened, she is described by one character as looking like a "macaw," decked out in hideous garments of blue, orange, and sulfur. She tends to poke people in the side with her claw-like hands and to poke fun of them as well. Other people shrink from her as from a reptile.

The ageless Dame Bradley has been married three times and has a large extended family even as the series begins. Her fourth case, THE SALTMARSH MURDERS (1932), takes place in a small village. In *Laurels Are Poison* (1942), she meets Laurel Menzies, who helps her in other cases and becomes her secretary. THE RISING OF THE MOON (1945) is one of the best novels in the series. Another is *Spotted Hemlock* (1958), whose title refers to the murder method used to kill a young woman whose decayed body is found inside an old stage coach near an inn. A feud erupts between Highpepper Hall, a men's college, and the Calladale College of Agriculture for women, where Dame Bradley's nephew is teaching, being a "pig-fancier" himself. The appearance of a headless ghost on horseback and patches of asparagus planted over decomposing rats leads him to call in his aunt. The setting, the pranks, and the style are similar to Charlotte MACLEOD's work, though earlier.

The Crozier Pharaohs (1984) was the last book Mitchell completed, and was published after her death. It shows her powers sadly on the wane; the story is told in the third person and is very heavy on dialogue, which lacks the usual wit. Two sisters, Bryony and Morpeth Rant, set off the mystery when they decide to breed Egyptian Pharaoh hounds, the oldest breed in the world.

BIBLIOGRAPHY Novels: *Speedy Death* (1929), *The Mystery of a Butcher's Shop* (1929), *The Longer Bodies* (1930), *Death at the Opera* (1934), *The Devil at Saxon's Wall* (1935), *Dead Man's Morris* (1936), *Come Away Death* (1937), *St. Peter's Finger* (1938), *Printer's Error* (1939), *Brazen Tongue* (1940), *When Last I Died* (1941), *Hangman's Curfew* (1941), *Sunset Over Soho* (1943), *The Worsted Viper* (1943), *My Father Sleeps* (1944), *Here Comes a Chopper* (1946), *Death and the Maiden* (1947), *The Dancing Druids* (1948), *Tom Brown's Body* (1949), *Groaning Spinney* (1950), *The Devil's Elbow* (1951), *The Echoing Strangers* (1952), *Merlin's Furlong* (1953), *Faintley Speaking* (1954), *Twelve Horses and the Hangman's Noose* (1956), *The Twenty-Third Man* (1957), *The Man Who Grew Tomatoes* (1959), *Say It with Flowers* (1960), *The Nodding Canaries* (1961), *My Bones Will Keep* (1962), *Adders on the Heath* (1963), *Death of a Delft Blue* (1964), *Pageant of Murder* (1965), *The Croaking Raven* (1966), *Skeleton Island* (1967), *Three Quick and Five Dead* (1968), *Dance to Your Daddy* (1969), *Gory Dew* (1970), *Lament for Leto* (1971), *A Hearse on May Day* (1972), *The Murder of Busy Lizzie* (1973), *Winking at the Brim* (1974), *A Javelin for Jonah* (1974), *Convent on Styx* (1975), *Late, Late in the Evening* (1976), *Noonday and Night* (1977), *Fault in the Structure* (1977), *Wraiths and Changelings* (1978), *Mingled with Venom* (1978), *The Mudflats of the Dead* (1979), *Nest of Vipers* (1979), *The Whispering Knights* (1980), *Uncoffin'd Clay* (1980), *The Death Cap Dancers* (1981), *Here Lies Gloria Mundy* (1982), *Death of a Burrowing Mole* (1982), *Cold, Lone and Still* (1983), *The Green Stone Griffins* (1983), *No Winding Sheet* (1984).

BRAIN, MISTER A character in G. K CHESTERTON's story, "The Hole in the Wall." A judge and investigator who has returned from India, this "brown skeleton of a man" is known for his ruthlessness in the pursuit of criminals. As his name suggests, Mr. Brain represents the potential for abuse in a solely intellectual justice lacking in compassion.

BRAMAH, ERNEST (pen name of Ernest Bramah Smith, 1868–1942) The Englishman Ernest Bramah was one of the most admired mystery writers of the period after Sherlock HOLMES and before the GOLDEN AGE, when novelty and ingenuity were stressed and the idea of FAIR PLAY was not as emphasized. He created one of the most startling detectives, the blind Max CARRADOS, who appeared in no novels but several volumes of short stories. Bramah got the idea for a blind detective from seeing a mystery play that he thought a blind man could have figured out.

Very little is known about the author himself because he guarded his privacy—so much so that some people seriously doubted that "Ernest Bramah" existed at all, and thought it was a pen name. He wrote to Howard HAYCRAFT (who greatly admired his stories) that "my published books are about all that I care to pass on to the reader." His first book, however, is a nonfiction account of his abandoned attempt to become a farmer, *English Farming and Why I Turned It Up* (1894). Born in Manchester, Smith worked in London for Jerome K. Jerome, editor of *The Idler* and author of the very popular novel *Three Men in a Boat* (1889).

The first collection of Max Carrados stories, entitled simply *Max Carrados,* appeared in 1914. Carrados performs some incredible feats and often seems not to be hampered by his blindness at all, and was criticized by some for being unbelievable. In his introduction to *The Eyes of Max Carrados* (1923), Bramah documented incredible but true stories regarding real blind people and the development of the other senses when one is lost. *Max Carrados Mysteries* followed in 1927. *The Specimen Case* (1925) and *Short Stories of Today and Yesterday* (1929) contain a few other Carrados stories, but the first two books contain the best work. Bramah also wrote a series of Chinese stories narrated by Kai Lung, which have not stood up as well as the Max Carrados stories.

BRAND, CHRISTIANNA (pseudonym of Mary Christianna Lewis, 1907–1988) English mystery writer. Brand based her detective character Inspector COCKRILL on her father-in-law, who was a doctor. Cockrill is a policeman in Kent, though not all the books take place there. Brand's mysteries are in the line of Dorothy L. SAYERS. Brand said that murder was so improbable among the kind of people she wrote about that the mysteries amounted to "fantasy," but that she then tried "to make the unreality as real as possible." On the other hand, her first murder story was inspired by her own dislike of a co-worker; called *Death in High Heels* (1941), it is set in a dress shop.

Brand was born in Malaya. She lived with her family in Malaya and India until being sent to school in England. Owing to a family financial disaster, Brand worked at low-paying jobs for years to support herself, including sales girl, governess, and ballroom dancer. She later married a surgeon, and used medical knowledge to great effect in her fiction.

The first novel to feature Cockrill was *Heads You Lose* (1941), which not surprisingly involves decapitation. GREEN FOR DANGER (1944) is generally considered Brand's best mystery novel and is a classic in the genre. Cockrill investigates suspicious deaths at a military hospital during the Blitz. Brand wrote the novel during the attack, and the descriptions of the bombing are evocative. In addition, the book is a strong puzzle in the GOLDEN AGE tradition, with a multiplicity of viable suspects and a clever but fair obscuring of the killer's identity. *London Particular* (1953; U.S. title *Fog of Doubt*) was Brand's own favorite of her books, perhaps because of its personal associations (it takes place in a fictional version of her own house, and she based several characters on people she knew). Like Sayers, Brand tightly weaves the net of relationships, and the plot is made as perfect a puzzle as possible. The writing, though secondary—she made it deliberately accessible—is literate if not literary. ("London particular" is an expression meaning an especially thick fog.) *Tour de Force* (1955) has a more unusual atmosphere than *Fog of Doubt* but is not necessarily a better story. Some of the background necessary to create the suspense—and to satisfy the traditional mystery "rules"—are a little stretched, even for 1955 (an island-state in the Mediterranean ruled by a Grand Duc in a primitive style typical of the middle ages, embellished by "operetta" characteristics and situations). The author submerges the reader in a plethora of subplots and leads that lead away from the real clues (RED HERRINGS were popular with Brand). The inner story, which is well constructed and tight, could have done without this rind. Brand used the island as a setting again in *The Three Cornered Halo* (1957), which features not Cockrill, but Cockrill's sister, as the main character.

Brand wrote several other novels, including *Starrbelow* (1958), a historical novel published under the pseudonym China Thompson. *Cat and Mouse* (1950) is set in

Wales and shows GOTHIC inspiration. Brand eventually abandoned the novel form and wrote short stories instead, and published two collections, *What Dread Hand?* (1968) and *Brand X* (1974). *Buffet for Unwelcome Guests* (1983) contains a selection of mystery short stories by Brand, which are considered finely crafted examples in a now neglected medium. *Heaven Knows Who* (1960) is a nonfiction study of a historical murder case.

BRAND, DINAH See RED HARVEST.

BRANDSTETTER, DAVE The first major (mainstream) gay detective, in a series of novels by Joseph HANSEN. Brandstetter is an investigator for insurance companies specializing in suspicious deaths. At first he works for his father's company, Medallion Life, and then on his own. His father dies later in the series. Brandstetter takes and leaves various lovers along the way, but it is as irrelevant as the bimbos who throw themselves at innumerable HARD-BOILED detectives, and is done with considerably more class.

Some of Brandstetter's cases take him into the gay community, such as *Troublemaker* (1975), in which he investigates the murder of a co-owner of a gay bar. In an apparently open-and-shut case, the mother of the victim finds a naked man standing over her son's body, a pistol in his hand. *Early Graves* (1987) deals with the AIDS crisis. Other socially relevant topics are not far from the surface. In *Nightwork* (1984), Brandstetter goes into the poor neighborhood of Gifford Gardens in search of the murderer of two truckers, one white and one black. In the polarized community, he encounters hate-filled and resentful whites, a paralyzed rich man who lives like a lord in a high-security castle, brainless gang members, and resigned or suspicious members of a black congregation.

Because Hansen had Brandstetter age realistically, he is seventy years old in his last case, *A Country of Old Men* (1991), in which he investigates the shooting death of a rock guitarist named Cricket Shales.

BIBLIOGRAPHY Novels: *Fade Out* (1970), *Death Claims* (1973), *The Man Everybody Was Afraid Of* (1978), *Skinflick* (1979), *Gravedigger* (1982), *The Little Dog Laughed* (1986), *Obedience* (1988).

Short Stories: *Brandstetter and Others* (1984).

BRASHEAR DOUBLOON, THE The original title that Raymond CHANDLER wanted to give to *The High Window* (1942). His publisher, Alfred Knopf, forced him to change it. Chandler partly attributed the book's comparative lack of success to this change.

BRAUN, LILLIAN JACKSON See CATS.

BRAUNKOPF, HILDEBERT A supporting character in several novels by Michael INNES, beginning with ONE-MAN SHOW (1952), an Inspector APPLEBY mystery. Braunkopf is an art expert who runs the Da Vinci Gallery. He is a suspect in *A Family Affair* (1969). "Blond, spherical and boneless," the excitable Braunkopf speaks in a comical but wearying accent. His favorite word is "voonderble." Innes used him also in *Money from Holme* (1964), a novel without Appleby.

BRAZIL The enigmatic central character of Dashiell HAMMETT's "lost" novella, *Woman in the Dark* (1933; repub 1988). The story, first published in *Liberty* magazine, begins in a rural cottage north of San Francisco, and has the flavor of an Irish short story. Brazil, it emerges, is an ex-convict who is living quietly in the country until a woman excites his intense, noble, and almost grim passion. Robert B. PARKER wrote an introduction for the reprint.

BREAN, HERBERT (1907–1973) Herbert Brean is best known for his nonfiction works about mystery writing, particularly *The Mystery Writers' Handbook* (1958). Brean was born in Detroit and attended the University of Michigan. He entered journalism after his graduation in 1926 and went on to work for the *Detroit Times,* later moving to *Time* and *Life* magazines. After his move to New York City, Brean taught writing at Columbia University and New York University. He also wrote self-help books and works on jazz in addition to his mystery genre writings.

Brean's detective novels often have OCCULT or supernatural overtones. Several of them are set in New England and use journalist Reynold Frame as a series sleuth. *Hardly a Man Is Now Alive* (1950), which takes its title from the famous poem, "The Midnight Ride of Paul Revere," is set in Concord, Massachusetts, and features some ghosts from the Revolutionary War. The plot deals with a missing manuscript. *The Clock Strikes Thirteen* (1952) takes place on an island in Maine, where a scientist's experiments with bacteriological weapons lead to panic. *Wilders Walk Away* (1948) is set in Vermont. *A Matter of Fact* (1956; British title *Collar for the Killer*) was an early police PROCEDURAL.

BREDDER, FATHER Father Joseph Bredder, created by Leonard HOLTON, was the leading priest-sleuth between the periods of Father BROWN and Father DOWLING. Unlike the other two priests, however, Bredder is something of a tough guy, a former marine and Golden Gloves champion boxer. He also killed people during

World War II; it was seeing a Japanese marine incinerated with a flame-thrower that finally drove him to become a priest.

Bredder is a chaplain in a Los Angeles convent in a marginal neighborhood. A big, burly man, he continues to lead an active life; his hobbies are fishing, scuba diving, and cultivating roses. His cases range from the grim to the exotic. In his first case, *The Saint Maker* (1959), he finds a human head in his church. *Deliver Us from Wolves* (1963) has a GOTHIC theme: werewolves in a Portuguese castle. His aquatic interests play a part in some of his mysteries, for example *Out of the Depths* (1966), in which he hooks onto a corpse while fishing. *A Touch of Jonah* (1968) is an example of MURDER AFLOAT, set during a trans-Pacific yacht race. Holton himself sailed all his life, and participated unofficially in the Transpac, which he described as a horrible 17-day voyage and that undoubtedly gave him the idea for the novel.

Bredder is a psychological detective, and as with other religiously oriented sleuths, his interest is redemption, not punishment. One of his companions is Father Armstrong, a learned medievalist from a rich English family. Bredder's strongest virtue is humility; he gets a stipend of thirty dollars per month and feels bad about making extra money as a detective. The secular end of the mystery is held up by Lieutenant Minardi of the Los Angeles Police. Minardi grew up in Sicily and is a great admirer of Bredder for his enormous strength, which is more characterological than physical; Minardi's boss is Captain Ernest "Normal" Redwood, who is staid, competent, and unimaginative. In *The Mirror of Hell* (1972), Minardi's own daughter attends a cheerleading course, and her roommate is murdered. *The Problem in Angels* (1970) centers around a violist who drops dead during a performance.

Holton tried to work contemporary themes as well as theological and moral issues into the novels, though this often comes about in sudden outbursts over abortion, crime, the loss of manners and traditional values such as civility. *The Devil to Play* (1974) begins as a BASEBALL story. Bredder is hired by the L.A. Miners after a base runner is shot down between third base and home. The baseball mystery is quickly superseded by the murder of a fellow priest, a young man who got his calling during an LSD trip and who had done time in prison. Holton's commentary touches on church revisionism and youth masses, drugs, the professionalization of sports, and urban decay.

BIBLIOGRAPHY Novels: *A Pact with Satan* (1960), *Secret of the Doubting Saint* (1961), *Flowers by Request* (1964), *A Corner of Paradise* (1977).

BREDON, MILES This detective, created by Monseignor Ronald KNOX, is an early example of a popular subgenre: the insurance investigator. He appeared in only five mysteries, including THE FOOTSTEPS AT THE LOCK (1928). Bredon is one of several detectives of the GOLDEN AGE who were interesting in their time but, in hindsight, are cast completely in the shade by the more flamboyant POIROT, WIMSEY, and CAMPION. Bredon, however, is painted in a more playful spirit than any of these. He is described as "indolent," a man who prefers his cottage, his pipe, a game of solitaire and the company of his wife to pursuing investigations for the Indescribable Insurance Company. The Indescribable takes on risks that all others reject, and so supplies Bredon with some extraordinary scenarios.

Although the Bredon novels are lighthearted—Julian SYMONS said that Knox did not allow "the faintest breath of seriousness to disturb the desperate facetiousness of his style"—Knox stuck to his own commandments of FAIR PLAY. The formula Knox used was referred to as the "Lord, what fun!" school of detective fiction, in which the characters were impossible and the murder an excuse for an amusement. Thus, the appeal of the books depends entirely on plot, because there is nothing to fall back on in terms of character interest, except for the clever patter back and forth between Bredon and Angela, his wife. Knox's style, however, is that of the previous century, with the author addressing comments to the reader along the way ("Let me give you, then, the next stage of my story . . ."). One can almost see him drawing back the curtain from each successive scene. Some of his remarks are quite comical ("I am sorry that so many characters in this story should appear only to disappear").

Whatever may be said against Knox's old-fashionedness, his plots were in fact interesting. In *Still Dead* (1934), a drunk driver who had run over a child is murdered; Knox's use of the theme predates that of Nicholas Blake in THE BEAST MUST DIE (1938). The puzzle in *The Body in the Silo* (1933) is evident from the title (which may explain why it was issued in the United States as *Settled Out of Court*). In *The Three Taps* (1927), a man is gassed to death in a hotel room.

BIBLIOGRAPHY Novel: *Double Cross Purposes* (1937).

BREEN, JON L[INN] (1943–) A mystery parodist and critic, Jon L. Breen earned a degree in library science from the University of California. Breen was an undergraduate at Pepperdine University and also served in Vietnam. For many years, he reviewed mystery books for the *Wilson Library Bulletin*, a publication of the company that was once headed by Howard HAYCRAFT, and also for *Ellery*

Queen's Mystery Magazine. Breen won an EDGAR award for *What About Murder* (1981), a bibliography of studies of the mystery genre. In *Novel Verdicts* (1984), he discussed courtroom fiction; *The Girl in the Pictorial Wrapper* (1972) is a bibliography of PAPERBACK ORIGINALS.

Breen's most recognized fiction is his parodies of other mystery writers, from S. S. VAN DINE to John D. MACDONALD. Some of these stories were collected in *Hair of the Sleuthhound* (1982). Breen has also written mystery short stories about BASEBALL, BOOKS, and horse racing.

BRETT, MICHAEL (pseudonym of Miles Barton Tripp, 1923–) The English barrister Miles Barton Tripp is known for stories with bizarre characters, such as Hugo Baron, a combination barrister, journalist, and killer. In *Diecast* (1963), Baron becomes involved in the familiar case of an illegitimate child appearing and asking for money—blackmail—from a very rich father. To a conventional story, Brett adds his own peculiar and violent twist. *A Man Without Friends* (1970) is another book in the Hugo Baron series.

Brett served in the Royal Air Force in World War II and studied law after the war. His other series character is a private detective, John Samson, who appears in books written under the author's real name.

BRETT, MICHAEL (1928–) An American author with the same name as the English author listed above. He wrote a series of novels about a standard HARD-BOILED detective, Pete McGrath. His typical case has a predictable plot but some unusual additions; in *Lie a Little, Die a Little* (1968), about blackmail involving sex, the target is Jason Dominique, "The Fertilizer King," who has been photographed with three different women. Dominique, who is eighty years old, somewhat sheepishly hires McGrath to get him out of trouble. *The Flight of the Stiff* (1967) includes a bizarre scene in which McGrath shoots a corpse through a window using a circus canon. Other books by Brett include *Malice and the Maternal Instinct* (1969).

BRETT, SIMON (1945–) A British television and radio producer turned author, Simon Brett is known for his Charles PARIS novels and for A SHOCK TO THE SYSTEM (1984), the book on which a 1990 film with Michael Caine was based. Another of his sleuths, Mrs. Pargeter, is the widow of a criminal who finds that her late husband's friends are sometimes useful. Brett's work is COZY and usually intended to be humorous; the Paris series combines quirkiness, coziness, occasional sleaziness, and show-biz plots in a soufflé that often fails to rise. Charles Paris is a middle-aged, broken-down actor with a taste for whiskey. The author uses the theatrical and entertainment background, and plays the murder story more for laughs than anything else. In *The Dead Side of the Mike* (1980) he sets the crime at BBC radio, where Brett himself worked. *Murder Unprompted* (1982) uses an old device of mystery fiction, the murder on stage. The central improbability of this long series is that whenever Paris lands an acting job, people around him get killed; SCOTLAND YARD would probably start to suspect him as a serial murderer. But of course, realism is not a cozy virtue.

Tickled to Death (1985) is a collection of Brett's short fiction.

BRIDE WORE BLACK, THE (1940) A novel by Cornell WOOLRICH, the first in his BLACK SERIES. The book is at once traditional and experimental; Woolrich appends a list of characters at the front of the book in Ellery QUEEN style, but the complicated organization of the book marks it as not a traditional mystery. Each chapter is divided into three parts: "The Woman," a part named for a man, and a "postmortem" on the man. The book begins with a woman buying a train ticket to Chicago, only to get off at the first stop without ever leaving New York City. In the second chapter, a woman at a party lures a man to a ledge to retrieve her scarf, then pushes him off. Woolrich often used inexplicable events and behavior to create mystery. In this case, the setup is intriguing, though the writing is some of Woolrich's weakest: "An indistinctly outlined, pearly moon seemed to drip down the sky, like a clot of incandescent tapioca thrown up against the night by a cosmic comic." PHANTOM LADY (1942), only a few years later, would avoid such obvious blunders as putting "thrown up" and "tapioca" in the same phrase.

BRIGHTON ROCK See GREENE, GRAHAM.

BRINK'S JOB, THE See CAPER.

BRINVILLIERS, MARQUISE DE (Marguerite d'Aubrai, 1651–1676) The Marquise de Brinvilliers was one of the great poisoners of all time, and her capture and execution were an enormous scandal, reflecting badly on prominent figures. She was married to the Marquis at a young age and seems to have been happy until she met a young officer, Goden St. Croix, with whom she fell madly in love (her husband introduced them). When her father learned of it, he had St. Croix thrown in the Bastille for a year. The opposition of her family engendered an intense hatred: St. Croix apparently learned a lot about poisons in prison from another convict, and when he got out, he and the marquise began to experiment. The Marquise de

Brinvilliers used her charitable visits to hospitals to test the poisons on patients. In 1670, she poisoned her father, sister, and two brothers (but not her husband). She also apparently baked pigeon pies filled with poison, serving them to her guests to observe the effects. St. Croix may have been an indifferent chemist: the marquise poisoned her father ten times before she managed to kill him.

The crimes might never have been discovered except that St. Croix accidentally killed himself in the course of further chemical experiments. After her arrest, it emerged that the Marquise had instructed others and provided them with poisons. Some prominent people had died about the same time, and it has been suggested that she was swiftly executed in order that further scandalous murders be hushed up. She was beheaded and burnt on July 17, 1676. Madame de Sévigné recorded details of the scandal in her famous letters, and remarked that, because Brinvilliers's ashes were scattered to the wind, everyone might breathe them and become poisoners themselves. DUMAS discussed the case in his *Celebrated Crimes,* and John Dickson CARR resurrected her for *The Burning Court* (1937).

"BROKEN NECKS" The title story of Ben HECHT's collection *Broken Necks* (1924; expanded 1926) is a powerful and minutely observed description of a hanging. The narrator is among several witnesses who watch as two men, one who prays monotonously and the other a maniac who remains silent, are hanged inside a prison. Hecht uses a number of details drawn from ordinary life to throw into relief the horrible extraordinariness of the act. The observers sit at benches "such as picnickers use" and stare at the "furniture" of hanging—scaffold, nooses, hangman's shed—"as do children in a strange house." In this manner, Hecht brings home without histrionics or moralizing the methodical and cruel transformation of a young man who looked "as if he had been interrupted while washing dishes" into a corpse: "their masks had been moved, and their faces, colored like stained glass, watched us with mouths opened."

BROMFIELD, LOUIS See PRIME OF LIFE.

BROOKE, LOVEDAY Created by C. L. PIRKIS, Loveday Brooke was one of the earliest female sleuths and probably the best of her generation. Loveday Brooke appeared in a series of short stories in *The Ludgate Monthly* in 1893, which were collected in the volume *The Experiences of Loveday Brooke: Lady Detective* the following year. Brooke is described in a manner different from other female detectives of the time. She is in her early thirties, and is neither ravishingly beautiful nor matronly. The author goes to some length to dispel any impression that this is a romantic heroine: "She was not, tall, she was not short; she was not dark, she was not fair; she was neither handsome nor ugly." In fact, her appearance is "altogether non-descript." Another important feature of the stories is that emphasis is placed on her intelligence and rationality, not on "feminine intuition." Brooke is given undercover assignments on the theory that a woman is less likely to be noticed. She poses in a variety of roles, but usually as a servant.

Owing to some undisclosed tragic turn of "Fortune's wheel," Loveday became penniless and had to start working as a detective out of necessity. Having "defied convention" and stooped to sleuthing, she has lost what was presumably a higher position in society. Thus, she is an outcast. After five or six years of struggling at her trade, Loveday begins to work as a freelance operative for Ebenezer Dyer, the head of a big detective agency in Lynch Court, Fleet Street. He acts as her WATSON—he marvels at her intelligence, but is not bright enough himself to figure out how she arrives at her conclusions. In "The Black Bag Left on a Door-Step," Loveday simultaneously investigates a burglary at the Cathrow's country house, in which "To be let, unfurnished" was scrawled on the empty safe, and the appearance of a black bag containing a suicide note from a disgraced clergyman left in front of a house. Brooke is given a complacent opposite number in this as in other stories, who thinks he has the answer right away, and of course doesn't. In "The Redhill Sisterhood," Brooke investigates a group of Christian women suspected of running a front for a burglary ring. "The Murder at Troyte's Hill" is about the killing of a lodge keeper on the estate of a deranged philologist with a wastrel son.

BROOM, ANDREW Ralph MCINERNY's Andrew Broom, a lawyer in Wyler, Indiana, is living out the Middle-American dream—a big fish in a small pond, he has a beautiful wife, money, and plenty of time to play GOLF. The town has two tournament golf courses, one designed by Arnold Palmer. Broom has even lured his brilliant nephew Gerald away from a promising career in Chicago to share in this "paradise." While Gerald thinks the town has "a caste system that makes India's seem flexible," Andrew considers it the "real America" and wants to grab all he can of the good life while it lasts. The only blot on the picture is Frank McGough, Broom's rival for the big fish role.

The Broom series seems to have come along at just the right time to replace the long-in-tooth Father DOWLING series. In a mild sort of way, Andrew and Gerald's disagreements are a satire of conservative visions of family America. The only really common value is materialism. After twenty or so Dowling books, the author's writing is more deft. *Mom and Dead* (1994) is about the controversial sale of a riverfront property where a skull of indeterminate age is found. In *Law and Ardor* (1995), the body of Edgar Bissonet, a prominent businessman, is found on the seventh hole at the local country club.

BIBLIOGRAPHY Novels: *Cause and Effect* (1987), *Body and Soil* (1989), *Savings and Loam* (1990).

BROWN, CHARLES BROCKDEN (1771–1810) Considered the first professional U.S. author, Charles Brockden Brown was a fascinating and strange writer. At times melodramatic and verbose, he yet had a strong, even obsessive interest in psychology, abnormal experience, psychotic behavior, and the conflict of civilization and savagery. Thus, his writing anticipates many of POE's themes. He was also the first U.S. fiction writer to use Native American characters. Of his six novels, EDGAR HUNTLY (1799) has the most relevance to the later development of the mystery genre. His novels contain bizarre scenes, and he is famous for having a character die of spontaneous combustion in *Wieland* (1798).

Brown was born into a Philadelphia Quaker family. He was an early feminist, was a friend of noted physicians who shared his interest in understanding abnormal psychology, and became the "father" of the American novel. His influence was felt by Poe, COOPER, and other nineteenth-century writers. Although his dark view of human nature—"Disastrous and humiliating is the state of man!"—and the influence of English writers and his fascination with the DOPPELGÄNGER link him to the GOTHIC movement, his use of mystery and even detection is remarkable, and is one of the features that evinces the influence of William GODWIN on his work. Brown intentionally avoided "puerile superstition and exploded manners" and "Gothic castles and chimeras." As an American, he chose to examine psychology through and in the context of "the field of investigation opened to us by our own country." Edgar Huntly could be claimed as the first detective created by an American, almost half a century before Poe's C. Auguste DUPIN.

BROWN, FATHER Ellery QUEEN once called G. K. CHESTERTON's Father Brown the greatest detective of them all, and his adventures are some of the most well written, ingenious, entertaining, and above all thoughtful in the genre. A Catholic priest, the short, round-faced Father with the umbrella and the flat hat is neither dour nor sparkling; adjectives like "plucky" and "endearing" fail to do him justice, or to indicate Chesterton's purpose. Father Brown is simply a good man. In him Chesterton illustrates his own moral principles. The superior Brown is rarely sanctimonious or self-important, for as much as Chesterton was repelled by many aspects of "modern" society, he also had a profound horror of spiritual pride. Of the virtues, Father Brown most epitomizes humility and charity. His "large, grey, ox-like eyes" are those of a sufferer for humanity, his "stubbly brown hair" a sign of saintly contempt for vanity.

The first book of stories, *The Innocence of Father Brown* (1911), contains the cleric's most anthologized case, THE HAMMER OF GOD, and other famous detective puzzles such as THE INVISIBLE MAN, THE SECRET GARDEN, and THE QUEER FEET. In his first case, "The Blue Cross," Father Brown interferes with the plans of FLAMBEAU, a jewel thief whom he will eventually succeed in bringing over to the side of good (Flambeau becomes a private detective), and cleverly exposes a phony priest. Another character is Aristide Valentin, the most brilliant detective of the French police force—clearly inspired by VIDOCQ. In "The Secret Garden," he also turns out to be rabidly anti-Catholic.

The motivations and the morals drawn from the stories are often couched as Christian polemics, whether Father Brown is railing against "that great brutality of the intellect which belongs only to France," the French Revolution, or faith in science alone. Sometimes they are noble sentiments, as when he chastises the pride of the rich in "The Queer Feet," but it is not always so. In "The Wrong Shape," a version of the "inscrutable Asiatic" theme, Father Brown attacks Hinduism for its desire for "annihilation" and failure to admit sin, and Eastern art for its "evil" shapes. In "The Honor of Israel Gow," he criticizes the irrationality of paganism and compares demon worship to Puritan theology. Chesterton makes Father Brown appear humble, but meek he is not.

The titles of the collections have real meaning: the last of the five, *The Scandal of Father Brown* (1935), comes from the first story, which implies that in a corrupt world it is the priest's sense of right that has become scandalous. By helping a woman elope *back* to her husband, he combats license but ends up labeled a libertine. Father Brown doesn't care; he goes on, "accepting the world as his companion, but never as his judge."

The later stories tend more toward morality play than detective fiction. In "The Resurrection of Father Brown," he is in haste not to have himself canonized and foils a plot to calumniate his religion. Sometimes, his usually wry speeches become sermons. The first book and the second (*The Wisdom of Father Brown,* 1914) contain the best stories, though many in the later collections are well worth reading.

Father Brown is guided partly by intuition. He tries to imagine himself inside the mind and soul of the person he is pursuing. His work among "the criminal classes" gives him insight into the minds of the suspects. Sometimes, however, it seems he is led almost by divine light (not in the spirit of FAIR PLAY), but it really turns out to be the divine light of reason. He is also a careful observer and pays attention to material clues others ignore. When he traps Flambeau in the disguise of a priest, he points out that the imposter's remarks were "bad theology." Critics may cavil at this or that aspect, but it is undeniable that Father Brown's adventures are the most serious games in the genre. Chesterton's character was based on a real person, Father John O'Connor.

BIBLIOGRAPHY Short stories: *The Incredulity of Father Brown* (1926), *The Secret of Father Brown* (1927).

BROWN, FREDERIC (1906–1972) American mystery and science fiction writer. Born in Cincinnati, Frederic Brown lost his parents when he was still an adolescent. He attended college, then worked in the newspaper business in Milwaukee before becoming a fiction writer. He began by writing short stories for PULP MAGAZINES in the late thirties, eventually producing over 150 pulp pieces, some of them the "short shorts," stories of only a few hundred words, for which he is particularly known. One of them is "Mistake" (1961), a story of only 38 words. The story shows Brown's ability to frame a situation, a character, or an enigma in just a few words.

Brown himself is as enigmatic as some of his strange and quirky pieces. He was married twice and had a lifelong drinking problem, was a watercolorist and a flautist, a man who enjoyed conviviality but who also took lonely bus rides to think over ideas for stories.

Brown's stories are reminiscent of the work of Cornell WOOLRICH in their bizarre characters and plots. They were first collected in *Mostly Murder* (1953) and *The Shaggy Dog and Other Murders* (1963). Although Brown was hardly a household name during his lifetime, his work has recently been rediscovered and reissued in several editions. The title work of the short story reprint *The Freak Show Murders* (1985) shows Brown at his best. In a sense, he lets the setting tell the story—a series of murders among a collection of misfits, fire-eaters, snake-handlers, knife-throwers and dwarves—and avoids the straining after wild effects of some of his lesser efforts. *Carnival of Crime: The Best Mystery Stories of Frederic Brown* (1985), edited by Bill PRONZINI, contains such classics as "Don't Look Behind You," a clever story of counterfeiting in which the narrator/murderer's intended victim is the reader; "The Djinn Murder," which combines Brown's interest in mystery and the OCCULT; and THE CASE OF THE DANCING SANDWICHES (1951). In the same vein is the later novel *Night of the Jabberwock* (1950), which takes place during one night in a Midwestern town. The story owes much to Lewis Carroll, and the entire town becomes a kind of funhouse gone out of control.

Brown's first novel, THE FABULOUS CLIPJOINT (1947), introduced Ed Hunter, who along with his Uncle Ambrose would appear in seven mystery novels. Brown won an EDGAR award for best first novel for *The Fabulous Clipjoint;* the title refers to Chicago, which is the setting for many of Brown's works, and which he depicts with as much stark realism (and even more romanticism) as that other great Chicagoan, Nelson Algren.

Brown wrote many non-series mysteries, including one of his most famous novels, THE SCREAMING MIMI (1949)—which is not, however, one of his best. His writing is uneven, which partly accounts for his being less read than other writers of the time such as Woolrich. Brown had something in common with Algren, who also wrote about the "city of big shoulders" and its netherworld of hustlers, hoods, and criminals, but with considerably more realism and stress on poverty and political issues. However, some of Brown's books, such as *The Lenient Beast* (1956), are notable for their relatively early exposure of racism in American society: here the relationship between Frank Ramos and his boss, Walter Pettijohn, shows the subtle ways through which whites degrade blacks and other minorities. On the other hand, the book is overloaded by a romantic subplot that adds nothing to the story. Brown's prose in his short stories was terse and the narratives HARD-BOILED, but his novels sometimes meander needlessly. Such was not the case, however, with the intense and chillingly matter-of-fact HIS NAME WAS DEATH (1954).

Brown published his first story, "The Moon for a Nickel," in 1938, and moved to New York City in 1948 to pursue his career. In 1949 he went to New Mexico, moving on to California in 1952 and Tucson in 1954. He also made use of these settings, for example in *The Far Cry* (1951), a tale of obsessive, grim passion that has an extremely disturbing ending. *Knock Three-One-Two* (1959), about an insane rapist and murderer, also builds to a shocking ending. Although the criminal is a monster, the other people in the book, in their weak and scheming ways, are also monstrous. Both books show the turn away from the Woolrich, carnivalesque early style toward believable explorations of what might be called the psychologically misshapen.

Other collections of Brown's work include *Homicide Sanitarium* (1984) and *The Case of the Dancing Sandwiches* (1951; repr and exp 1985).

BROWN, RITA MAE See CATS.

BROWNE, HOWARD (1908–) Howard Browne was born in Omaha, Nebraska. His mother was a schoolteacher; his father died before Browne was born. He dropped out of high school and hitchhiked to Chicago, where he worked for many years in publishing. First, however, he worked at a series of jobs as various as waiter in a tuberculosis sanitarium and installer of Venetian blinds (more in line with his later work, he was also a skip-tracer for a department store).

Browne begun as a PULP writer, which was a stepping stone to an editorial job with the Ziff-Davis publishing company. Eventually, he became the editor of all the company's pulps. He published more than 200 stories of his own. Browne's first detective novel, *Halo in Blood* (1946), was published by Bobbs-Merrill under the pseudonym John Evans. It introduced his series detective, Paul Pine, a Chicago-based private eye in the HARD-BOILED tradition. Similar to Philip MARLOWE, Pine is a former employee of the State Attorney's office.

As Browne would later write in a preface to a reissue of *Halo in Brass* (1949), his first novel sold well, and he "developed delusions of grandeur, quit [his] job as a magazine editor" and went freelance—and almost starved to death as a result. Browne moved with his family to Burbank, California, and bought a new house, leaving him only five weeks to turn out his next contracted book, *Halo for Satan* (1948). The second Pine story has a plot more likely to be found in the pages of Ellery QUEEN than a pulp novel: his client is a bishop, and Pine is on the trail of a missing Aramaic manuscript worth millions of dollars. Among the others who want the manuscript are a Chicago mob boss, mysterious women, and Jafar Baijan, a NAPOLEON OF CRIME figure.

Browne's move to Burbank was fortuitous: he began working in the film and television industry, and over the next three decades wrote about 130 teleplays for various series. He also wrote four feature film scripts, including the one for the 1967 film *The Saint Valentine's Day Massacre,* with Jason Robards as Al CAPONE. He continued working into the eighties and wrote for the television detective show *Simon & Simon.* He also taught his craft at the University of California, San Diego.

The Paul Pine series continued with *Halo in Brass* (1949), in which the author used his Omaha background. He did not show the city to advantage, however; Pine is hired by a rather dense farm couple to search for a daughter who has gone missing in Chicago, and meets a number of repulsive individuals in a whorehouse—as well as finding the first battered body of the story. Pine picks up the trail of the girl, Laura Freemont, in Chicago, but quickly stumbles on the strangled corpse of another woman who may have some connection with her. Browne later wrote forthrightly about the attitude toward homosexuality expressed in the book, which was the prevailing view of the period in which it was written. At the end, however, Pine sets a police lieutenant straight after the cop talks about "perverts" and people who "don't matter."

The Taste of Ashes (1957), another Paul Pine novel, was the first that Browne published under his own name. Once again, Browne used a familiar hard-boiled plot (from THE BIG SLEEP, for example): Pine is hired by a wealthy man to find a "wild" daughter, who may be a victim of blackmail or involved in pornography. In *Thin Air* (1953), which does not have Pine, Browne used a more ingenious device, that of an advertising executive who uses his firm as a detective agency in order to track down his wife.

Although he was one of many hard-boiled practitioners who followed in the wake of CHANDLER, HAMMETT, and others, Browne was above average. His writing is clear, his jokes are funny more often than not, and if his work was not inspired, he did know what *not* to do; because he had more ability and more modesty than many other writers in the genre, his books are still readable today. Some of the Paul Pine novels were reprinted in the late eighties by Dennis McMillan Publications. Browne was also a member of the MYSTERY WRITERS OF AMERICA.

With his work back in print, Browne made a comeback in 1988 with *Pork City,* a fictionalized account of the murder of a *Chicago Tribune* reporter, Alfred J. Lingle, in 1930. Browne's style had changed dramatically from his early books, partly under the influence of his movie work; the opening line ("On the last morning of his life . . .") recalls the quasi-documentary format Browne had used for *The Saint Valentine's Day Massacre.* Al CAPONE, *Tribune* owner Colonel Robert Rutherford McCormick, and real reporters who Browne had known all make appearances in this cinematic, episodic novel, saturated with Chicago history and the atmosphere of lawlessness and corruption that prevailed in the PROHIBITION era. An interesting contrast is also provided by the language; the book is liberally sprinkled with the four-letter words banned by publishers when Browne wrote his earlier books, but the change adds little realism and actually sacrifices the crystal clarity he had earlier achieved.

BRUCE, LEO (pseudonym of Rupert Croft-Cooke, 1903–1979) English mystery writer, creator of Sergeant William BEEF (a John Bull of detectives), as well as Carolus DEENE, an altogether different type. Beef is almost the opposite of the classic GENIUS DETECTIVE: instead of suddenly springing his deductions to make himself seem brilliant, he calmly explains and makes them seem like common sense, thus placing himself in the tradition of Martin HEWITT. Beef is enough impressed with himself, however, to quit the force and strike out on his own as a p.i.

Croft-Cooke studied in Buenos Aires from 1923 to 1926, where he first became involved with a literary magazine. He served in British intelligence in World War II and also commanded a Ghurka regiment. At one time he was an antiquarian bookseller. All of these qualities are reflected in Carolus Deene, to whom he turned after he had stopped writing the Beef stories in the 1950s.

Bruce's ability as a mystery writer is disputed. One of the weaknesses that has been pointed out is the classism of the Beef stories. The impression is reinforced by the fact that Bruce abandoned the low-brow Beef in favor of Deene, a character much more like himself—thus, Bruce appeared to side with Lionel Townsend, Beef's chronicler, who always thought that the Cockney sergeant was beneath him intellectually and socially. Stereotypes and derivative plots are the other main objections. Leo Bruce seems to be particularly neglected, or disliked, by North American critics such as Otto PENZLER and Chris Steinbrunner, who left him out entirely when they compiled their *Encyclopedia of Mystery and Detection* (1976). H. R. F. KEATING, however, found Bruce's work "consistently excellent," and liked both of the author's sleuths.

Bruce wrote a long series of novels about Carolus Deene known as the "Death" series, all of which had death in the title. They include some of his best works, such as DEATH IN ALBERT PARK (1964), *Death of Cold* (1956), and *Death at Hallows End* (1965). Unlike many mystery authors, Bruce improved toward the end of his career. FURIOUS OLD WOMEN (1960) is perhaps the best of the later works; Bruce's conservatism manifests itself in a more than usually humorous vein, as various characters inveigle against modernity. Bruce's attempts at humor are often feeble, such as having all the tradesmen in a town named after famous writers (MAUGHAM, HEMINGWAY, Powys, etc.), and he had a penchant for "bit of fluff" references to sex that are typical of a certain kind of prudish British comedy that may once have been amusing. At other times, he shows a wry wit, particularly in the Deene novels. Bruce's strength is that he keeps extraneous detail to a minimum and constructs plots that actually work, both providing adequate clues and still arriving at surprise endings; there is no sleight-of-hand or hoodwinking of the reader. His books are satisfying as mysteries, if not as novels.

One Leo Bruce character says "I've been pretty annoyed for years with this silliness called modern life." Bruce was undoubtedly nostalgic for the world of the GOLDEN AGE for which he had fought, which he perhaps imagined to have been free of feckless youngsters and in which his values were not so much defended as presumed. But Bruce *knew* that he was nostalgic and, to rephrase one of his titles, a bit of a furious old man; to his credit, he did not go on writing quaint Golden Age mysteries as if World War II had never happened.

Croft-Cooke also published books under his own name, including nonfiction, poetry, and plays. Some of them are quite different from his mysteries: *Paper Albatross* (1965) is a first-person suspense story about Max Toner, a self-described "villain" who has gotten away with 120,000 pounds from a big robbery, only to find that it is an albatross around his neck. As he drifts from town to town while other members of his gang are picked up one by one, he finds he can't do any of the things for which he stole the money in the first place. The author depicts the forces of mediocrity and conventionality converging on the hero, who at least has some creativity and courage. Even so, Toner is a bigot who thinks all women are "tarts," except the fifteen-year-old with whom he falls in love.

"BRUCE-PARTINGTON PLANS, ADVENTURE OF THE" (1908) A case of Sherlock HOLMES in which the body of a young engineer is found on the London underground tracks, three leaves of plans for a new submarine in his pocket. Holmes, with the assistance of his brother MYCROFT, unravels an international plot.

A similar story was written by Clifford ASHDOWN, "The Submarine Boat," and is included in *The Rivals of Sherlock Holmes* (1971).

BUCHAN, JOHN (1875–1940) Born in Scotland, John Buchan's adventurous career led from the Boer War to intelligence work in World War I, to eight years as a Member of Parliament, and eventually to the Governor-Generalship of Canada. Not surprisingly, Buchan considered himself a politician first and a novelist second, and called his tales of spying and intrigue "shockers." Today the stories seem to be literate, civilized adventures; in the character of Richard HANNAY, Buchan chose as his hero the fundamentally decent man. Although Buchan was a staunch supporter of empire, his attitude does not take the jingoistic forms of SAPPER's. Buchan was a conservative rather than a fanatic.

Buchan was the son of a minister in the city of Perth. His family later moved to Fife, where he enjoyed outdoor life, as would his characters. Buchan attended Glasgow University and Oxford and was called to the bar in 1901. From 1901 to 1903, he worked for the high commissioner for South Africa. After his return to England he worked in publishing as a director of Thomas Nelson and Sons, a position from which he encouraged E. C. BENTLEY and Valentine WILLIAMS. He also published his first successful book, *Prester John* (1910), a romance novel set in South Africa. During World War I, Buchan was at first a war correspondent, then became Director of Information and later Director of Intelligence.

The book for which Buchan is best known, THE THIRTY-NINE STEPS (1915), also introduced his hero, Richard Hannay. He wrote the book while he was in the hospital recuperating from an operation for a duodenal ulcer. Buchan's fluidity of style and fondness for chases and tight scrapes make his books extremely readable. He was influenced by two other countrymen, Sir Walter Scott and Robert Louis STEVENSON. Hannay returned in other adventures, the best of which is *Greenmantle* (1916). The hero of *Huntingtower* (1922) is Dickson McCunn; the novel is about the struggle between Bolsheviks and Russian aristocrats, and also involves the Gorbals Die Hards, a gang of Glasgow slum boys.

Buchan was made first Baron Tweedsmuir in 1935, at the same time as his move to Canada. He also wrote the biographies *Montrose* (1928), *Sir Walter Scott* (1932), and *Cromwell* (1934). Buchan's autobiography, *Memory Hold-the-Door* (also pub as *Pilgrim's Way*), appeared in the year of his death.

Buchan's South African years are the basis of the recent pastiche, *The Buchan Papers* (1996) by J. D. F. Jones, about "Kruger's gold," the lost treasure of the Boers.

BUCKET, INSPECTOR A character in *Bleak House* (1852–53) by Charles DICKENS, Inspector Bucket is the first important police detective in English fiction. Bucket is also assisted by his wife, making them the first husband-and-wife detective team as well. The case involves the death of the lawyer, Mr. Tulkinghorn, who had uncovered the true past of one of his clients, Lady Dedlock, whose illegitimate daughter, Esther Summerson, lives with Mr. Jarndyce at Bleak House. Lady Dedlock thus has a reason to kill Tulkinghorn and is the prime suspect until she also is murdered.

Bucket, like Charley Wield, another Dickens detective, was based on the real-life Inspector Field. He is a master of stealth and of disguise, and punctuates his observations with a fat index finger.

BUILD MY GALLOWS HIGH (1946) A novel by Geoffrey HOMES, which was the basis for the classic of film noir, *Out of the Past* (1947). The story follows the now-classic pattern of a man with a dark past who settles down to a normal and conventional life, only to have it disrupted when his former associates make an unwelcome appearance. The man, Red Bailey, is living in a small town when Joe Stefanos, Guy, and the dangerous femme fatale, Mumsie McGonigle, dig up a past that won't stay buried.

Build My Gallows High was filmed again, though less successfully, as *Against All Odds* (1983).

BULLET PARK (1969) A novel by John Cheever (1912–1982), who was more known for his short stories about middle-class white suburbanites. But even the suburbs contain potential violence. The story concerns Eliot Nailles, whose son Tony is menaced by Paul Hammer, a dangerously unbalanced man. Cheever also wrote the widely respected prison novel *Falconer* (1977).

BUNKER, EDWARD (1933–) A highly regarded writer praised by William Styron and other prominent figures, Edward Bunker spent most of the first half of his life in jail. Bunker was born in Hollywood, California, on New Year's Eve. After his alcoholic family broke up and his parents divorced when he was four, his life rapidly went downhill. Living in a succession of boarding houses, he became involved in petty crimes. Bunker was sent to reform school at ten, violated parole at thirteen, and went to prison at seventeen. He was sentenced to a year in the county jail in Los Angeles on a drug charge but escaped; after he was caught, Bunker was sent for a longer stretch to San Quentin. Then began a long period spent mostly behind bars for crimes ranging from forgery to assault with a deadly weapon and safecracking. Released at twenty-three, Bunker found it impossible to find an honest job with his prison record; not long afterward he was back in San Quentin and served seven years.

In prison, Bunker began writing and submitting work; he sold his blood to get money for postage. His first article, "Behind the Walls," appeared in *Harper's* in 1972. His first novel, NO BEAST SO FIERCE (1973), came out while he was serving a sentence at a maximum-security prison in Illinois for a foiled Beverly Hills bank robbery. During this last incarceration, he wrote *The Animal Factory,* his second novel. Bunker was finally released in 1975, and today lives in Los Angeles with his wife and family. *No Beast So Fierce* introduced the archetypal (and autobiographical) Bunker character. The ex-con Max Dembo is drawn inevitably back into crime because his former associates are the only friends he has in a world that brands him a pariah. A film version with Dustin Hoffman was released in 1978 under the title *Straight Time;* Bunker also wrote the script. *Little Boy Blue* (1981) reflects the earlier period of Bunker's life and deals with juvenile criminals. The protagonist is thirteen-year-old Alex Hammond; the novel follows his path through a series of group homes, mental institutions, and reform schools. After he shoots a man during a grocery store robbery, he meets two older junkies who teach him the code of criminality. Bunker shows the vicious circle that delinquents without parents are trapped in, and how institutions cultivate a sense of worthlessness in their clients and patients. The film director Quentin Tarantino called it "the best first-person crime novel I've ever read" (a statement all the more remarkable given that the book is written in the third person). Bunker appeared as the character "Mr. Blue" in Tarantino's 1992 film *Reservoir Dogs.*

The central figure of *Dog Eat Dog* (1996) is Troy, who has spent twelve years in prison and plans a final score: to steal $360,000 worth of cocaine and then retire to the tropics. The other members of his gang are Mad Dog, a violent coke head, and Diesel, a trucker. The gang kidnaps the one-year-old son of a drug lord, but things start to go wrong. In a series of battles with police, most of the gang is killed. The ending is a depressing, bloody finale, a further statement of the impossibility of redemption.

BUNN, SMILER One of the thieves who followed in the footsteps of RAFFLES—the third book of short stories was called *Smiler Bunn—Gentleman Crook* (1923). But Smiler Bunn's creator, Bertram ATKEY, made him different from Raffles. Bunn is fat and middle-aged, and his adventures are primarily comic. He is already rich and steals for the love of it, with the assistance of Henry Black, who is actually Lord Fortworth. Bunn's clever idea of stealing from people who are themselves crooked or shady—and so don't complain—is like the premise of Ross Thomas's THE PROCANE CHRONICLE (1972).

BIBLIOGRAPHY Novels: *Smiler Bunn—Manhunter* (1920), *The Man with the Yellow Eyes* (1923), *The Mystery of the Glass Bullet* (1931), *Arsenic and Gold* (1939), *The House of Clystevill* (1940).

Short Stories: *The Amazing Mr. Bunn* (1911), *The Smiler Bunn Brigade* (1916), *Smiler Bunn—Byewayman* (1925), *Smiler Bunn—Gentleman Adventurer* (1926), *Smiler Bunn, Crook* (1929).

BUNTER, MERVYN The butler and former batman of Lord Peter WIMSEY in a series of novels by Dorothy L. SAYERS. It is in the figure of Bunter that the inspiration of the Wimsey series by P. G. Wodehouse's books about Bertie Wooster is most evident. Bunter is a perfect match—or copy—of Wooster's servant, the famous and unflappable Jeeves. The resemblance is so strong that even Wimsey notices it, remarking in STRONG POISON (1930), "Don't talk like Jeeves. It irritates me." Bunter not only cooks, makes coffee, and keeps house; he also performs scientific experiments for Wimsey and goes out sleuthing among the servants.

BUNTLINE, NED See DIME NOVEL.

BURDEN, INSPECTOR MIKE See WEXFORD, CHIEF INSPECTOR.

BURGLAR WHO STUDIED SPINOZA, THE (1980) One of Lawrence BLOCK's novels about Bernie RHODENBARR, interesting for the nature of the crime, the plot twists, and the ancillary characters. Told in the thief's usual breezy style, it recounts how Bernie takes his friend Carloyn Kaiser, a pet shop owner, on one of his burglaries, which she actually suggests—the victim is the husband of one of her customers. But someone breaks into the house after Rhodenbarr and his friend have left and kill the couple; a glove found at the scene points to Rhodenbarr. The haul from the theft includes an extremely rare nickel, almost impossible to resell. Bernie leaves it with his friend Abel Crowe, a concentration camp survivor and fence. A second murder shocks Rhodenbarr and makes *The Burglar Who Studied Spinoza* his most violent and most personal case.

BURIED FOR PLEASURE (1949) A novel by Edmund CRISPIN, one of the Gervase FEN series. Fen goes to the country town of Sanford Angelorum to campaign for Parliament, and puts up at the Fish Inn, whose owner is in the process of destroying his premises through his incompetent efforts to renovate the old building. A murder case immediately crops up: a woman married to a solicitor in the area has been murdered by way of poisoned chocolates sent to her through the mail; earlier, she had sought help from the police against a blackmailer. Fen then runs into an old schoolmate who is conducting an undercover investigation. He also meets several odd people, from a detective novelist (male) who goes by the name of Annette de la Tour to a naked madman escaped from a local asylum who believes himself to be Woodrow Wilson.

Although all the elements of a "mad" Gervase Fen adventure are there, it remains a novel with several backgrounds and without any foreground. No sense of urgency about the murders or the investigations is created; Fen is hardly phased at discovering a man stabbed in the throat and on the point of death. His interest in his own election wanes. Faced with such overwhelming diffidence, the reader is thrown back upon the one perfection of the book, the style of scrupulous satire. The appearances of the "non-doing" pig, a runt of sorts, are a welcome addition. The narrative is most energetic in Fen's speech insulting his future constituents, and one could almost believe Crispin wrote the book for the pleasure of inveighing against the corruption of British politics and the stupidity of the public, and to delight in Fen's perverse praise of apathy.

BURKE Another one-name tough guy, Andrew VACHSS's Burke is a former New York City cop who has an enormous moral chip on his shoulder. An unlicensed private investigator, Burke hangs out with low-lifes in his never-ending crusade against evil and corruption, but preserves his disdain for almost everyone who isn't Burke.

Burke has been to jail twice and has a reputation, possibly undeserved, as a hit man because of the child abusers he has killed. Burke has enough attitude to be the mayor of New York: he complains about everything from murderers to jaywalkers. He says of the city, "I hate it all so much—now more than ever." Humorless and petulant, Burke acts like he has seen the *Billy Jack* movies a few too many times; his persistent sourness and tough poses are ultimately comical.

Burke's sidekick is Max, a deaf mute and martial arts expert whom he treats like a trusted pet. Pansy is Burke's hundred-and-fifty pound mastiff, which he has trained to climb the fire escape to relieve herself on the roof (his civic consciousness does not extend to hygiene). "The Mole" is a pale and goggle-eyed genius who lives in a bunker in the Bronx. "The Prof" is a fight promoter who talks in embarrassingly wooden rhymes ("they looking for you to be a sheep for the creep. But that ain't the way it's gonna play, okay?"). In one case, Burke and his multicultural team of avengers break into a house being used for child porn and kill the nine occupants.

The Burke novels are socially conscious, bleak in outlook, and critical, but their main achievement is to prove the truth that crusaders, regardless of their political stripe, can be self-righteous bores.

The overemphasis on the message causes the neglect of the medium. *Blue Belle* (1988) begins with short chapters and meaningless scenes that bear little relation to the plot (the reader does not get a glimpse of Burke for some seventy pages). They introduce a young boy and a woman whom Burke has saved from a life of abuse and prostitution. He arranges for the woman to mother the boy. The case itself concerns the "Ghost Van," linked to a series of murders of teenage prostitutes. Burke is hired by a pimp to find out who is abducting and killing his workers; they even take up a collection of $50,000 as a reward to whoever can nail the Ghost Van. *Footsteps of the Hawk* (1995) is another meandering novel, in which Burke is pursued by two police officers, the loud and unpleasant Jorge Morales and the dangerous and sexy Belinda Roberts.

In *Safe House* (1998), Burke gets involved with a group that provides refuge for women who are the targets of stalking. Then the head of the safe house is herself stalked. Vachss also throws in some neo-Nazis and a bomb plot like the real-life Oklahoma City bombing.

BIBLIOGRAPHY Novels: *Flood* (1985), *Strega* (1987), *Hard Candy* (1989), *Blossom* (1990), *Sacrifice* (1992), *Choice of Evil* (1999).

BURKE, JAMES LEE (1936–) James Lee Burke has become known for a series of novels that take place on the Gulf Coast, where he grew up. Born in Texas, Burke sets his mysteries about Dave ROBICHAUX in New Orleans and the surrounding bayou. Burke wrote mainstream literary novels prior to taking up the mystery genre, a background reflected in his focus on the context of the action and efforts to develop subsidiary themes and minor characters. Cajun culture, the sordid but lively French Quarter, and the contrast between rural Louisiana and the face presented to tourists are matters Burke tries to treat in a serious manner. That his elegy to a vanishing culture—pressured by immigration, the oil business, and the tourist dollar—sometimes becomes maudlin and sentimental does not wholly detract from its power. On the other hand, Burke has no problem with the violent aspects of genre writing, and serves up some grisly scenes, including torture. At times, Robichaux could be a guilt-ridden version of Milo MILODRAGOVITCH; at others, he is a southern Matt SCUDDER.

In addition to using the Louisiana background for more than just local color, Burke has tried to inject serious political issues into his novels. In *Heaven's Prisoners* (1988), the blowing up of a private plane kills a priest active in the sanctuary movement, and the U.S.-sponsored terrorism in Central and South America is brought in as a side issue, though it is never more than that. It is the primary focus, however, in *The Neon Rain* (1987), in which the sleazy underworld of New Orleans and the devils in Robichaux's own mind erupt into a very violent story that leaves no one untouched. Burke's vision of

America is nightmarish, from the punks who sell drugs to children up to the spooks who sell hardware to death squads. But however gung-ho the action, the author's position is essentially liberal and anti-war. Sometimes, Burke's infusion of themes leads to an embarrassment of riches, introducing more ideas than can be dealt with adequately. Like a medieval crusader, Robichaux's questing violence is entangled with religion, morality, and honor, knots he never quite manages to untie.

Burke was nominated for a Pulitzer Prize for *The Lost Get-Back Boogie* (1978), a novel about a blues singer and ex-convict working on a ranch in Montana and a struggle over the local papermill. Burke has taught at Wichita State University in Kansas.

BURLEY, W[ILLIAM] J[OHN] (1914–) Born the week that the European powers were declaring war on each other and that saw the start of World War I, W. J. Burley did not publish his first mystery until more than fifty years later, after two careers and another world war. The first of the books for which he is best known, the WYCLIFFE series, appeared in the late sixties, but after 1980 he turned out a Wycliffe novel practically every year, with a series of titles beginning *Wycliffe and the. . . .* The writer whose work the Wycliffe books most resemble in style is Dorothy SIMPSON.

Beginning in his youth, Burley was employed in the gas industry, a job he held until the late forties. He attended Oxford, where he received his degree in zoology in 1953, and began his second career as a teacher of biology in the Newquay School in Cornwall. Twenty years later, he became a full-time writer. *A Taste of Power* (1966) and *Death in Willow Pattern* (1969) were Burley's early books, and they dealt with the amateur investigator Henry Pym. Like many writers, Burley used for his first novel an autobiographical setting (in this case, a school), and the atmosphere is true to life. He has used his Cornwall experience for background, for example in *Wycliffe and the Scapegoat* (1978).

Wycliffe and the Beales (1983) deals with the poor cottager, Bunny Newcombe, who dies after inquiring about his parentage. Although his cottage is squalid, it contains an unexpected hoard of cash. Once again, a local well-to-do family is involved. The Beales have all the ingredients for the classic skeleton-laden family chronicle: success, murder, a painter in the family, hidden homosexuality, obsessive gambling, and pregnancy out of wedlock. It is one of Wycliffe's more complex plots, though RED HERRINGS abound.

Burley has continued to write non-series mysteries, though with much of the flavor and hallmarks of the Wycliffe series, such as lust and repression in small rural towns. These books include *Charles and Elizabeth* (1979) and *The House of Care* (1981).

BURMA, NESTOR A HARD-BOILED private eye invented by the French writer Léo MALET. Burma's philosophy combines the author's anarchism with an American p.i.'s cynicism: "I don't work for society—society's big enough to look after itself—I work for myself and my own interests. But when I fight, I fight." Burma's cases are unusual for the genre, however, because of the French setting and the more than a little outlandish people and situations.

Burma works for the Fiat Lux detective agency, but he is a prisoner of war in his first adventure, 120, RUE DE LA GARE (1943), a story involving AMNESIA and a mysterious character named EIFFEL TOWER JOE. In *Dynamite versus QED* (1945; 1991 tr of *Nestor Burma contre QED*), he becomes involved in a byzantine plot set during the occupation of Paris. In 1938, four men had held up a train carrying gold bullion bound for the Bank of France; in 1942, four bars are still missing. One man, Alfred Thévenon, got away. The man who denounced Thévenon and got a reduced sentence is killed during an air raid, at the same moment as Burma encounters Lydia Verbois, the novel's *femme fatale,* in the immediate area. The plot hinges on who knew about the robbery and would be motivated to commit murder. The description of occupied Paris and of the bombing is vivid. *QED* is the name of the tabloid that hires Burma to investigate.

A few of the Burma books have recently been translated into English; the use of Britishisms ("blokes," etc.) is somewhat jarring, given the French setting and the American inspiration for the novels. Some of the Nestor Burma titles fit into his "nouveaux mystères de Paris" series, which was based on the work of Eugène SUE and had one novel set in each *arrondissment* (administrative district) of Paris.

BIBLIOGRAPHY Novels: *L'Homme au sang bleu* (1945), *Solution au cimetière* (1946), *Le Cinquième procédé* (1948), *Coliques de plomb* (1948), *Gros plan du macchabée* (1949), *Les Paletots sans manches* (1949), *Direction cimetière* (1951), *Pas de veine avec le pendu* (1952), *Le soleil naît derrière le Louvre: les nouveaux mystères de Paris (1er arrondissement)* (1954; tr *Sunrise behind the Louvre*), *Des kilomètres de linceuls: les nouveaux mystères de Paris (2ème arrondissement)* (1955), *Fièvre au Marais: les nouveaux mystères de Paris (3ème arrondissement)* (1955), *La nuit de Saint-Germain-des-Prés: les nouveaux mystères de Paris (6ème arrondissement)* (1955; also published as *Les Sapin pousse dans les caves*), *Faux frère* (1955), *Les Rats de Montsouris: les nouveaux mystères de Paris (14ème arrondissement)* (1955; tr *The Rats of*

Montsouris), *M'as-tu vu en cadavre?: les nouveaux mystères de Paris (10ème arrondissement)* (1956), *Corrida aux Champs Elysées: les nouveaux mystères de Paris (8ème arrondissement)* (1956), *Pas de bavards à la Muette: les nouveaux mystères de Paris (16ème arrondissement)* (1956), *Broulliard au pont de Tolbiac: les nouveaux mystères de Paris (13ème arrondissement)* (1956; tr *Fog on the Tolbiac Bridge*, 1991), *Les Eaux troubles de Javel: les nouveaux mystères de Paris (15ème arrondissement)* (1956 or '57), *Boulevard . . . ossements: les nouveaux mystères de Paris (9ème arrondissement)* (1957), *Casse-pipe à la Nation: les nouveaux mystères de Paris (12ème arrondissement)* (1957), *Micmac moche au Boul'Mich': les nouveaux mystères de Paris (5ème arrondissement)* (1957), *Du rébecca rue des Rosiers: les nouveaux mystères de Paris (4ème arrondissement)* (1958), *L'Envahissant cadavre de la plaine Monceau: les nouveaux mystères de Paris (17ème arrondissement)* (1959), *Nestor Burma en direct* (1962), *Nestor Burma revient au bercail* (1967), *Drôle d'epreuve pour Nestor Burma* (1968), *Un croque-mort nommé Nestor* (1969), *Nestor Burma dans l'Île* (1970), *Nestor Burma court la poupée* (1971), *Les Neiges de Montmartre* (1974), *La Femme sans enfants* (1981), *Le Deuil en rouge* (1981), *Une aventure inédite de Nestor Burma* (1982), *Poste restante* (1983).

BURNETT, W[ILLIAM] R[ILEY] (1899–1982) W. R. Burnett wrote two books that made a major contribution to crime literature, *Little Caesar* (1929) and *The Asphalt Jungle* (1949), both of which also happened to be made into important films. The film version of *Little Caesar*, with Edward G. Robinson, is credited with being the first gangster picture. In fact, Burnett's impact on the movies was more considerable than that of his writing, because his PULP style has not weathered the years. Burnett was not a hack, however; although his talent was for dialogue—he won an EDGAR award for best screenplay in 1951—he also won an O. Henry award (a literary rather than a genre prize) for *Dressing Up* (1930).

Burnett was born in Springfield, Ohio, and studied journalism. He worked as a statistician for the state of Ohio until 1928, when he moved to Chicago, just at the height of Al CAPONE's dominance over the city (the St. Valentine's Day massacre the following year solidified Capone's hold and also started the first public outcry against him). In the story of Cesare Bandello, the punk who rose to a mob chieftain, Burnett perfectly captured the typical crook of the PROHIBITION era. The book is slangy and heavily dependent on dialogue, and has become more dated than the film version. *The Asphalt Jungle*, two decades later, was also innovative: it is a CAPER story, in which the criminal genius or NAPOLEON OF CRIME is replaced by a consortium of crooks who work as a team to pull off a complicated scenario. Burnett's style had not changed substantially since his earlier book. The film version by Walter Huston is justly famous; it has a highly romantic finish but contains several masterful performances, particularly by the former Yiddish actor Sam Jaffe (as the safecracker) and former sea captain Sterling Hayden (as the blond hunk and hired muscle). Burnett also wrote a screenplay of his novel *High Sierra* (1940); Humphrey Bogart starred in it in 1941, and Burnett adapted it again in 1955 as a vehicle for Jack Palance. In all, Burnett wrote thirty-five books. His swan song was, appropriately, *Goodbye Chicago* (1981), written at the age of eighty-two. It is set in the thirties in the milieu of Burnett's greatest success, and concerns the investigation of the murder of the wife of a cop. The search produces an exposure of city corruption as well as an apocalyptic gang war. Burnett was named a Grand Master by the Mystery Writers of America in 1980.

BURN THIS (1980) The last novel by Helen MCCLOY featuring Dr. Basil WILLING. It is about a female writer named Harriet Sutton who goes to Boston to settle her husband's estate. She buys a house, and then lets the other rooms to a collection of oddball writers, among them a strange woman poet and a drunken historical novelist. One day a paper blows in at the window with "Burn This" written on it, and notes regarding a plan to kill "Nemesis," the pseudonym of a hated book reviewer. This find is communicated to the other writers, some of whom have themselves been burned by Nemesis. Willing makes his appearance halfway through the book, after a murder and a surprising revelation has occurred.

BURTON, MILES The pseudonym under which Major Cecil Street (also known as John RHODE) wrote his long series of mysteries about Desmond MERRION.

BURNT ORANGE HERESY, THE (1971) A crime novel by Charles WILLEFORD. The story is told by an ambitious and unscrupulous young art critic who has an opportunity to interview Jacques DEBIERUE, a great surrealist painter. Debierue has an immense reputation despite the fact that the public has never been allowed to see his paintings. His one public work, exhibited in the twenties, was an empty picture frame. The young man displays great ingenuity in gaining access to Debierue's secluded studio in Florida. The personality of the narrator is strikingly conveyed in the first-person account of his search, and is the most engaging aspect of the book, far more so than the plot. The novel is a story of ruthless, cynical ambition, but with a surprising undercurrent (well-buried) of morality.

BURY ME DEEP (1947) The first novel by Harold Q. MAZUR, *Bury Me Deep* introduced Scott JORDAN, a lawyer who acts like a HARD-BOILED detective. Despite the pulpy beginning—Jordan returns home from Miami and finds an almost nude blonde drinking brandy on his sofa—the story has distinct merits. After Jordan puts the drunken woman in a cab and sends her away, he receives several other mysterious guests, one of them an enraged seaman who is looking for the woman, whose name turns out to be Verna Ford. Verna next turns up at the morgue, and Jordan is the most likely suspect in her murder. He soon finds out that Verna was a key witness in an estate case, and also that his drunken playboy friend Bob Cambreau had been using Jordan's apartment for purposes of his own. Although the writing is uneven, Mazur writes some clever hard-boiled dialogue. As a lawyer, he was also able (like Erle Stanley GARDNER) to use obscure points of law to provide motives for murder and other crimes. The dour Lieutenant Nola is a laconic foil for the dashing Jordan, who seems to be irresistable to women. When Mazur is writing about the tough guys, the cops, and the hoods, his style is readable; as soon as a woman comes into the room he falls into hard-boiled clichés.

BUSH, CHRISTOPHER (1888?–1973) The English author Christopher Bush wrote mystery novels for more than forty years; almost all were about Ludovic TRAVERS and were typical GOLDEN AGE mysteries. Like Inspector FRENCH, Travers was a breaker of alibis.

Bush was the illegitimate child of a Quaker family, and was unsure of his own birth date. He was a schoolmaster before he became a mystery writer, and served in World War I and World War II. Some of the Travers books reflected Bush's own wartime experience. Under the pseudonym Michael Home, Bush wrote about the English countryside where his family had lived for generations.

BUSHWHACK In the mid-nineteenth century, this word acquired its present meaning of "to ambush." Earlier, it had meant to move a boat by grabbing at underbrush; the noun "bushwhacker" probably came from Dutch *bosch-wachter*, or "forest keeper."

BUTLER, GWENDOLINE [WILLIAMS] (1922–) The British novelist Gwendoline Butler has made a mark in several genres. Butler received an undergraduate degree from Oxford, where she studied history. Her first novel, *Receipt for Murder*, was published in 1956. Over the next few years, she introduced two series characters, Inspector John COFFIN and Constable Charmian DANIELS. The novels about Daniels are published under the pseudonym Jennie Melville. She has written many non-series novels under both her real name and her pseudonym; one of them, *Olivia* (1973; orig title *A Coffin for Pandora*), won a Silver Dagger award from the British CRIME WRITERS' ASSOCIATION.

Although Butler's principal works, the Coffin and Daniels series, are about cops, she does not fit easily into the PROCEDURAL category. Her interest in romantic suspense and the GOTHIC frequently colors her work. After a hiatus, she began publishing prolifically again in the late eighties and nineties. Her writing is often choppy and full of one-sentence paragraphs. The starkness of Butler's earlier work has been modified with the introduction of a COZY element.

BUTLERS The line "the butler did it" may go back to Sherlock HOLMES, who encountered sinister butlers in the GLORIA SCOTT (1893) case and "The Adventure of the Musgrave Ritual" (1893). Even earlier, the butler was one of the narrators in one of the most famous mystery novels of all time, THE MOONSTONE (1868). William LEQUEUX contributed *Bleke, the Butler* (1924) to the tradition.

But more often than they do it, butlers get done themselves. Georgette HEYER's *Why Shoot a Butler?* (1933) is almost a dissertation on the subject, having two butlers, one dead, the other alive and sinister. Hired help in general are often done in, and frequently used as expendable characters. Partly this has to do with the classism of the mystery novel, particularly the English novel of the GOLDEN AGE. The servant class is often viewed as shifty, dishonest, lazy, and criminal. As one Agatha CHRISTIE character (a titled one) disarmingly put it, "Nobody looks at a chauffeur in the way they look at a *person*." Christie is one of the writers who most exemplifies the upper class disdain for the people who work for them. Agatha killed the doorman in *At Bertram's Hotel* (1965); in Frances and Richard LOCKRIDGE's *Night of Shadows* (1962), a Detective LANE mystery, the doorman also gets it; and a servant girl is murdered in P. D. James's COVER HER FACE (1962). Butlers also continue to be murdered, for example in Antonia FRASER's *The Cavalier Case* (1990).

In the world of the mystery story, it is still hard to get good help, as evidenced by Ruth RENDELL's *A Judgement in Stone* (1977), in which a previously docile servant kills her employers. Damon RUNYON mocked the butler cliché in the story WHAT, NO BUTLER? (1934).

BUZZER In twentieth-century detective stories, a "buzzer" is a policeman's badge, and to "buzz" someone is to interrogate them. But, going back another century or two, a "buzz" was a pickpocket.

BYATT, A[NTONIA] S[USAN] See POSSESSION.

BYRD, MAX (1941–) Max Byrd earned his undergraduate degree from Harvard University and his Ph.D. from King's College, Cambridge. While teaching English at the University of California at Davis, Byrd created a version of the HARD-BOILED detective story that is at once updated (in terms of scene) and contemporary (in the male/female relationships and the ironic posture toward the genre itself), yet is also encumbered with literary baggage. Byrd's private eye is Michael HALLER (only a double consonant away from HAMMER), who works out of San Francisco and specializes in missing persons. Byrd's style is heavily indebted to Raymond CHANDLER; Haller is capable of delivering some witty cracks ("the oldest structures I ever see in California are Chevrolets with running boards"), but he shoulders the burden of cleverness too self-consciously, and the metaphors sometimes miss the mark entirely ("nipples like split infinitives"?). The literary references are many and range from Shakespeare to Randall Jarrell to Nero WOLFE.

Haller is given a weightily intellectual biography, including some unnecessary literary credentials—he is a Bostonian and Harvard dropout who went off to Europe, worked for UPI in London and then for INTERPOL in some capacity, and was also an aspiring poet. *California Thriller* (1981), the first Mike Haller novel, was named Best Paperback Novel by the PRIVATE EYE WRITERS OF AMERICA in 1981.

Although the Haller novels were critically successful, Byrd turned to writing THRILLERS, though he continued to use devices developed in the Haller series. *Target of Opportunity* (1988), like *Fly Away Jill* (1981), the second Haller novel, concerns a present-day case with roots that go back to World War II and the French Resistance. Gilman, a California cop, is in a Tahoe convenience store with his brother-in-law when the latter is fatally shot in the chest during a robbery. The murderer is let off on a technicality, and Gilman is forced by his sister-in-law into tracking him down. The chase leads to Boston and becomes entangled with an international intrigue surrounding a Polish dissident and a Harvard professor (and former French Resistance hero).

CADEE, DON A detective created by Spenser Dean (Stewart STERLING). Don Cadee works as chief of store protection for Amblett's department store in New York City, a novel setting for a detective series, though fraught with improbabilities. In *Murder on Delivery* (1957), he arranges for a fur buyer and an assistant to deliver a sable coat worth a hundred thousand dollars to a television star; men and coat all disappear.

Cadee is a former Marine commando and veteran of the South Pacific. Little is said of his appearance; his most distinctive feature is his prematurely white hair. He lives at the Hotel Vauclair and drives a Porsche. His girlfriend is also his employee, the young store detective Sybil Forde. In *Dishonor Among Thieves* (1958), Cadee deals with spoiled socialites who become shoplifters and thieves. He actually gets fired and replaced by Sibyl because of his loyalty to store detective Andrea Rheinholt, a reformed drug addict and thief. Puss Halloran, Cadee's contact with the Protex security firm, shows a nasty side. A gang led by a figure known as "The Coach" tries to blackmail Andrea into assisting them and she disappears. Then, an Amblett's truck full of valuable merchandise is hijacked and the driver killed. The plot brings together heroin, couture, and the Miami jazz scene.

The last and best novel in the series was CREDIT FOR A MURDER (1961), which begins with the discovery of an Amblett's employee frozen in a block of ice.

BIBLIOGRAPHY Novels: *The Frightened Fingers* (1954), *The Scent of Fear* (1954), *Marked Down for Murder* (1956), *The Merchant of Murder* (1959), *Price Tag for Murder* (1959), *Murder After a Fashion* (1960).

CADFAEL, BROTHER A twelfth-century Welsh monk and sometime investigator invented by Ellis PETERS. Cadfael is a kind of Renaissance man, born a few hundred years too soon. He was born in Trefriw. Before taking his vows, he went on the first Crusade, was a sailor as well as a soldier, and did not display a natural predilection for celibacy.

Peters did not invent Cadfael as a series character, she has said; he simply came into being to enable her to write about Shrewsbury Abbey in the twelfth century, and only later did she decide to take up his story again. His full name is Cadfael ap Meilyr ap Dafydd. In *A Rare Benedictine* (1989), Peters went back and described his return from the crusades and his conversion. Cadfael works in concert with his friend, Hugh Beringar, the sheriff, in solving crimes. The prior of Shrewsbury Abbey is the Benedictine abbot Radulfus, who is "magisterial" and strong, and also supports Cadfael's activities up to a point.

The novels contain interesting history, but the plots, with a romance novel underpinning, are more reminiscent of fairy tale than history. Damsels in distress and handsome young swains abound. In *The Virgin in the Ice* (1982), set during the winter of 1139, two noble children have disappeared following the sack of Worcester. The search for them is complicated by the fact that their father is on the wrong side in the civil war—he supports the Empress Maud, cousin of King Stephen. The struggle for the English crown that took place during Stephen's reign (1135–1154) forms the background for many books in the series. The virgin in question is a girl found frozen in a block of ice in a brook.

The Heretic's Apprentice (1990) shows the strengths and weaknesses of the series. The time is 1143, when Owain Gwynedd, across the border in Wales, is struggling against the English barons and the king. The English crown is still in dispute, between the house of Normandy and the house of Plantagenet. The rise of heresy is also beginning to create concern—and harsh repression—among the clergy. Elave, a young son of Shrewsbury, returns after seven years on pilgrimage, bringing the body of his master home, along with a mysterious carved box of great value—so great, that some are willing to kill for it.

Summer of the Danes (1991) does not take place in the usual setting. The civil war between Stephen and Maud has momentarily stopped, and Cadfael is sent on a church mission to Wales, where there *is* a civil war. Prince Owain Gwynedd has banished his rival, Cadwaladr, who returns to Wales with a Danish army (Cadfael is captured, and investigates murder in the Cadwaladr camp).

BIBLIOGRAPHY Novels: *One Corpse Too Many* (1979), *Monk's Hood* (1980), *St. Peter's Fair* (1981), *The Leper of Saint Giles* (1981), *The Sanctuary Sparrow* (1983), *The Devil's Novice* (1983), *Dead Man's Ransom* (1984), *The Pilgrim of Hate* (1984), *An Excellent Mystery* (1985), *The Raven in the Foregate* (1986), *The Rose Rent* (1986), *The Hermit of Eyton Forest* (1987), *The Confession of Brother Haluin* (1988), *The Potter's Field* (1989), *The Holy Thief* (1992), *Brother Cadfael's Penance* (1994).

CADIN, INSPECTOR See DAENINCKX, DIDIER.

CAIN, JAMES M[ALLAHAN] (1892–1977) James M. Cain was one of those writers who defined the

American HARD-BOILED style, but unlike CHANDLER and HAMMETT his position in the "canon" is still being assessed, partly because Cain wrote far more than either of the other two writers and produced much work of limited quality. Cain's first novel, THE POSTMAN ALWAYS RINGS TWICE (1934), caused a sensation; it was banned in Canada and gained the author a reputation for using sensational sex and violence. Considered rough in its time, Cain's style today might be called existential or minimalist. Camus's acknowledgement of *The Postman*'s influence on his novel *The Stranger* (L'Etranger, 1941) is often cited by those who see Cain as a moralist presenting an amoral world and not merely a writer of PULP. But Edmund Wilson called him the finest of the "poets of the tabloid murder," and the reputation has stuck.

Although he became famous for his stories about uneducated and often brutal people, Cain grew up in a well-off middle-class family, the son of a college professor and an opera singer. Cain himself earned a bachelor's degree from Washington College (where his father was president) and a master's in theater. He later rebelled against this background, taking jobs in a gas and electric utility, as a highway inspector, and in a meat packing plant, before finally settling into the career that suited him, journalist—a career not coincidentally located midway between the cultured upper classes and the netherworld of crooks and losers that fascinated him. The competing facets of Cain's personality point toward the primary quality of his fiction: psychological and social tension.

Cain's father seems to have been demanding: young James entered college at age fifteen because his father had him skip two grades in elementary school. As a result, Cain's college experience was unhappy. Later, inspired by his mother, a *coloratura* opera singer (like Varda in MILDRED PIERCE, 1941), Cain tried opera singing, but quit his musical studies after a year—another example of the pressure of parent-child rivalry.

Cain had an extremely long career, but only a brief part of it could be considered successful. In his book on Cain, Paul Skenazy says that Cain had "written himself out" by 1941, and his later books failed to achieve the acclaim of *The Postman Always Rings Twice* and DOUBLE INDEMNITY (1943). Given the importance of his conflict with his father as a driving force in his character, it is interesting that Cain wrote only one critically successful novel after his father's death in 1938.

Cain began working for the *Baltimore Sun* after serving in World War I. It was through this paper that he met H. L. MENCKEN, who published Cain's first story in *The American Mercury.* Mencken also convinced Cain to move to New York in 1924 and helped him get a job at the New York *World,* under Walter Lippmann, who became a major intellectual influence on Cain. It was also around this time that Cain contracted tuberculosis, and entered his second marriage. With the failure of the *World* in 1931, Cain briefly became managing editor of *The New Yorker.* Afterwards he began an unsuccessful career in Hollywood lasting more than a decade; Cain liked the money but disliked the medium, and only got a credit for three movies. Raymond Chandler loathed Cain's writing and called him "a Proust in greasy overalls" and "a dirty little boy with a piece of chalk and a board fence and nobody looking," but Chandler nonetheless worked on the screenplay of *Double Indemnity.*

Too much can be made of Cain's upbringing as a result of "reading backward" from his novels. The extremely dark view of human relationships in his books can be traced more easily to things Cain did himself. He was married four times, and in his fiction dwelt on the misery and boredom of failed relationships; the desperation his characters feel, however, drives them to the extremities of violence and murder. While Cain's treatment of sex and violence is no longer shocking (later purveyors have made his scenes seem tasteful by comparison), his exposure of emotional violence and despair still stuns the imagination. He was particularly adept at showing the rapid changes of mood of those who have lost all hope, and who rush from apathy to murderous rage in the blink of an eye.

Cain's shorter works have been collected in THE BABY IN THE ICEBOX (1981). His introduction to the omnibus *Three of a Kind* (1944) provides a response to his critics and gives his own evaluation of his work.

CAIN, PAUL (pseudonym of Peter Ruric, 1902–1966) American author of mystery and crime stories in the HARD-BOILED style. Born in Des Moines, Iowa, Cain emerged as a writer in the heyday of the PULP MAGAZINES, and also wrote for Hollywood. The stories collected in *Seven Slayers* (1994) are set against the background of PROHIBITION and concern BOOTLEGGERS, turf wars between rival gangs (the story "Black" is in the manner of RED HARVEST [1929]), and murderous jealousies among various crooks. One story, however, combines the gun play with an old-fashioned GENIUS DETECTIVE.

Told in a deadpan style, Cain's stories contain violence somewhat like SPILLANE's, with bloody shoot-outs and faces kicked into red mush. The characters are tough to the point of being monochromatic; in their netherworld, the alternative to toughness is not weakness but simply defeat, which is rapidly followed by violent death. The novel *Fast One* (repr 1994) is more drawn out but follows the format of the short stories: rapid progression from scene to scene, and rapid escalation to confrontation within scenes. Gerry Kells is a "playboy" who sometimes consorts with crooks, but when he is set up for a murder charge he decides to play the game for real. No fewer than four mob bosses struggle for control of the city of Los Angeles, with Kells playing them off against each other. The visits to the gambling ships anchored off the coast and Kells's various escapes keep the plot moving; his befriending of a newspaperman and a mild-mannered hoodlum provide more depth than the hard-boiled loners in Cain's stories usually display. Despite its bleakness, the ending is still a surprise, and the last lines are as close to poetry as the author came.

CALAMITY TOWN (1942) One of the best Ellery QUEEN mystery novels, *Calamity Town* finds Ellery settling in WRIGHTSVILLE under the cover of being a famous writer, Ellery Smith. (Inexplicably, all but one of the townspeople can't put one and one together—in the Queen world, perhaps there are many famous authors with the first name "Ellery"). He rents a house that turns out to have a dark past: three years before, John F. Wright built the house (next door to his own) for his daughter Nora and her fiancée, Jim Haight, but Haight ran away and left Nora at the altar. Queen moves in, and also moves in on Nora's sister Pat, much to the displeasure of her boyfriend, County Prosecutor Carter Bradford.

Next, Jim Haight turns up, all is forgiven, and he and Nora marry at last. Jim's sister Rosemary also returns to cause trouble, however, and then dies on New Year's Eve, with all the evidence pointing to Jim. The second half of the book becomes a courtroom mystery à la Perry MASON.

The book is considered one of the best in the series not least because it adheres strictly to the rules of FAIR PLAY; in fact, it is not very difficult to figure out, particularly as the reader has the "essential fact" and Queen doesn't (the book is, necessarily, written in the third person). What also makes it strong is that it embodies many of the concerns of the "serious" American novel, particularly at that time, such as small-town life, with its personal warmth and humanity on the one hand and stifling provincialism and lack of privacy on the other. The style ranges from naturalistic descriptions of the change of seasons to parody of small-town nosiness: "Didn't Jim look interesting with those purple welts under his eyes? Do you suppose he's been drinking these three years? How romantic!"

CALEB WILLIAMS (1794) A novel by William Godwin (1756–1836), the full title of which is *The Adventures of Caleb Williams, or Things as They Are.* The representation of "Things as They Are" means an anarchist critique of early industrial capitalist society. Godwin believed that human beings could reach a perfected state in which law and institutions would be unnecessary for the regulation of their behavior; however, a revolution in human consciousness would have to take place before any revolution in human affairs. The author of the first modern crime novel wrote it to illustrate his vision of a world without crime.

In the novel, Caleb Williams, a servant, becomes suspicious of his master, Falkland, who has been tried and acquitted of the murder of an evil man named Tyrrell. Two other men, a father and son, are hanged for the crime. Caleb tries to detect evidence that will condemn Falkland, while Falkland uses his superior power as a squire to persecute Caleb and have him thrown in jail. Thus the law, in Godwin's view, is like a bludgeon that men struggle over, hoping to crush each other with it. The novel contains many of the features of the modern crime story in addition to suspense, including the discovery of clues and the planting of false ones—the frame-up. Very atypical, however, is the fact that the "detective," once he discovers the criminal, interprets his successful conclusion of the case as a *failure.* Instead, he should have resolved the conflict as one human being to another unmediated by institutions (as an anarchist would). Only in the postwar period has a similar anti-institutionalism gained prominence in the crime novel, and then from cynicism about corruption rather than Goldwinian idealism.

Godwin was married to the feminist Mary Wollstonecraft, and his daughter married the Romantic poet Percy Bysshe Shelley. Among those who were influenced by Godwin was Charles Brockden BROWN.

CALIBER (CALIBRE) The means by which firearms are categorized, "caliber" refers literally to the measurement of the inside diameter of the barrel of a gun. In the manufacture of a gun barrel, a solid piece of stock is drilled down the center; this is called the bore. Grooves are then cut on the inside of the barrel (the rifling, which causes the bullet to spin). The parts of the bore that remain in relief or stand proud from the grooves are the "lands." The caliber refers to the lands, i.e. the original bore, though a few calibers are measured from the grooves.

Caliber is only a general measure of the power of a gun. Power is determined by such factors as the size of the casing, amount of powder in the casing, type of powder, the weight of the bullet, and velocity. In the thirties and forties, very small calibers with enormous muzzle velocities (such as the .22 Swift and the .218 Bee) were developed and were used to hunt animals as large as moose.

CALLAHAN, BROCK A private investigator and former football player in a series of novels by William Campbell GAULT. Brock "The Rock" Callahan narrates his own adventures, which often involve sports and corruption. He follows in the footsteps of his father, a policeman who was killed when Brock was nine years old.

Callahan's girlfriend, Jan Bonnet, is an interior decorator. An odd and not enjoyable aspect of the series is the bickering that goes on between the pair. Jan nags Brock for not working enough, and they argue about getting or not getting married because she does not like her job and he is too proud to have a wife who makes more money than he does. In *The Convertible Hearse* (1959), the argument is about Jan's trading in her old car for a Cadillac convertible advertised by the shady used-car dealer, Loony Leo Dunbar, who is later killed. It is one of the few times when the tedious quarreling has any connection with the plot.

The Callahan books are like boys' stories for grown-ups. His jock ethos is always apparent, not only in his solidarity with the other "old warriors" of the L.A. Rams but in his brooding about Jan, his checking out of other women (he actually talks about "massive mammaries"), and his lonely beer drinking at his favorite bar.

In *Come Die with Me* (1959), Brock is hired by Gloria Malone, a blonde bombshell and heiress, to find her husband, jockey Tip Malone. Tip is a nasty little man and soon gets his. *Dead Hero* (1962) takes place within the circle of his former teammates, and has Brock suspected of murder after he investigates the wife of "Horse" Malone and finds her having an affair with "Scooter" Calvin. The Rock gets confused and angry when his attitudes toward adultery by women are challenged by Jan; it is, however, one of his better performances. After this novel, there were no more Callahan books until *The Bad Samaritan* (1982), the beginning of a brief comeback.

BIBLIOGRAPHY Novels: *Ring Around Rosa* (1955), *Day of the Ram* (1956), *Vein of Violence* (1962), *County Kill* (1962), *Death in Donegal Bay* (1984), *The Dead Seed* (1985), *The Chicano War* (1986), *Cat and Mouse* (1988).

CAMPBELL, HUMPHREY A roguish, milk-drinking, accordion-playing detective created by Geoffrey HOMES (Daniel Mainwaring). Campbell is large and heavy, but has a cheery manner to balance his HARD-BOILED side. Publicity called him "the dick with a hard fist and a soft heart." He is also part Native American, though nothing he does really confirms it. Campbell is assisted by his putative boss, the hopeless and comical dipsomaniac Oscar Morgan, who holds (and presumably loses) a variety of jobs through the series. Campbell appeared with Robin Bishop, another Homes character, in the book *Then There Were Three* (1938), before being spun off into his own set of adventures.

There is something winning about Campbell, perhaps his equanimity, or his youthful exuberance. Mainwaring had some experience as a private investigator in California, where he also worked as a Hollywood screenwriter. In *Finders Keepers* (1940), Humphrey's dialogue is at its best, though the plot is weak (see ICE PICK), and his romantic interest is prominent. *Forty Whacks* (1941) plays on the Lizzie BORDEN case; here the setting is California and the supposed killer is Joe Borden, who is accused of dumping the hacked corpse into a rowboat.

Six Silver Handles (1944) is one of the best in the series. It was first published in *Bluebook* magazine in May, 1944; a later edition changed the title to *The Case of the Unhappy Angels* (1950). Oscar Morgan has somehow landed a job as assistant police chief in Joaquin, an agricultural California town. Campbell is about to enter the army but is hired by a Mr. Moise, a wealthy collector of paper money, to find a "fruit tramp"—a migrant worker. Meanwhile, in a plot similar to Henry KANE's *Edge of Panic* (1947), another recruit, Johnny Foster, drinks too much at a party and wakes up next to a corpse with its head bashed in. Campbell takes on this case as well. A jailbreak, a further murder, a missing collection, and the distracting (to Campbell) presence of Foster's sister provide further twists.

BIBLIOGRAPHY Novel: *No Hands on the Clock* (1939).

CAMPION, ALBERT The detective who is featured in all but a few of the books of Margery ALLINGHAM. Campion is at first almost a parody of the detective of the GOLDEN AGE, remarkable in every way: "Campion" is an assumed identity, for he comes from royalty and his real name is "Rudolph." In the early books he is rather affected, wearing glasses he doesn't need and talking in a high-pitched voice; he is such a genius that he pretends to be stupid in order to disguise himself. Campion's companion is the lag, Magersfontein LUGG.

Campion makes a gradual transition to normality. He has a long engagement to Amanda Fitton, who is something of a mechanical genius. Their relationship is not helped by the fact that he completely forgets who she is when he has AMNESIA. Campion's change from a buffoon in the early works to a more sober, mature detective is noticeable; even one of the other characters remarks in *Dancers in Mourning* (1937) that Campion is acting "less of an ass than he had ever seen him."

Other characters accompany Campion in his adventures, including the great-hearted Uncle William, who appears in three books, the last being *The Beckoning Lady* (1955). He overlaps with Charlie Luke, a brash young policeman who, in THE TIGER IN THE SMOKE (1952), handles the investigation while Campion looks on. Despite Campion's inactivity in this novel, it has been universally recognized as the author's greatest achievement. It is more of a crime story than a mystery, an all-out suspense adventure about the hunt for an exceptional criminal. DEATH OF A GHOST (1934) has a cast of very strange artistic characters and is also highly regarded; THE CASE OF THE LATE PIG (1937) is one of Campion's most bizarre puzzles. *More Work for the Undertaker* (1948) shares some qualities with *The Tiger in the Smoke,* most notably the relegation of Campion to a subsidiary role. Julian SYMONS remarked of these later novels that "they would have been better still without the presence of the detective who belonged to an earlier time and a different tradition."

Allingham's last book, *Cargo of Eagles* (1968) was unfinished at the time of her death and was completed by her husband, the artist Youngman Carter. He went on to write the final two books in the Campion saga by himself.

The Campion novels are famous and continue to be reprinted regularly; that Campion also appeared in a large number of short stories is perhaps less known. In addition to two collections (see below), *The Allingham Casebook* (1969) has eight stories about Campion, *The Allingham Minibus* (1973) three.

BIBLIOGRAPHY Novels: *The Crime at Black Dudley* (1929; U.S. title *The Black Dudley Murder*), *Mystery Mile* (1929), *Look to the Lady* (1931; U.S. title *The Gyrth Chalice Mystery*), *Police at the Funeral* (1931), *Sweet Danger* (1933; U.S. title *Kingdom of Death*), *Flowers for the Judge* (1936), *The Fashion in Shrouds* (1938), *Traitor's Purse* (1941), *Coroner's Pidgin* (1945; U.S. title *Pearls Before Swine*), *The Beckoning Lady* (1955; U.S. title *The Estate of the Beckoning Lady*), *Hide My Eyes* (1958; U.S. title *Tether's End*), *The China Governess* (1962), *The Mind Readers* (1965), *Mr. Campion's Farthing* (1969; by Youngman Carter), *Mr. Campion's Falcon* (1970; U.S. title *Mr. Campion's Quarry;* by Youngman Carter).

Short Stories: *Mr. Campion: Criminologist* (1937), *Mr. Campion and Others* (1939), *The Case Book of Mr. Campion* (1947).

CAN To be "in the can" means to be in prison. The word does not come from the object *can,* however; according to MENCKEN it is a gypsy word, from Romanian *caen,* meaning "to stink." Similarly, to be "in stir": from Romanian *staripen,* "prison."

CANINO, LASH A killer in Raymond Chandler's THE BIG SLEEP (1939). Canino (which in Italian means "little dog") is a small, tough, brown man: he has brown hair and brown eyes, always wears brown clothes and a brown hat, and even drives a brown car. He has a voice that purrs "like a small dynamo behind a brick wall." As the brown man he is in contrast to the "gray man" of the book, Eddie MARS, for whom he works.

CANNING, ELIZABETH A young servant girl whose disappearance became the subject of a famous case of the eighteenth century. It has been treated in fiction by Josephine Tey in THE FRANCHISE AFFAIR (1948) and by Lillian DE LA TORRE in *Elizabeth is Missing* (1945). A contemporary account is given by Henry FIELDING.

CANNING, VICTOR (1911–1986) Born in Plymouth, England, Victor Canning achieved the rare feat of becoming a full-time writer with his first book; such was the success of *Mr. Finchley Discovers His England* (1934). Published when Canning was only twenty-three, it was followed by several other humorous non-mystery novels. Canning's first attempt at the mystery and suspense genre, *The Chasm,* appeared in 1947. During his early career Canning also wrote feature articles for the *Daily Mail.* He served as an officer in the Royal Artillery during World War II.

Canning's varied experiences and his extensive travels provided the background for his THRILLERS and mysteries, which had ingenious though often unbelievable premises but were carried off with good humor. Canning's books lack the heavy-handedness of many thrillers. Several of his favorite themes come together in *The House of the Seven Flies* (1952), which combines a sea mystery with a war story. In the prologue, a German captain and his men rob a Dutch bank in 1944, but their launch is destroyed by partisans as they make their escape. Years later, an English sailor who was in the war and is trying to make a living with his pilot cutter—sometimes by smuggling—takes on a mysterious passenger, who promptly dies, leaving behind a trail of clues to a treasure. The story was filmed as *The House of the Seven Hawks* (1959).

Canning's only series character is Rex CARVER, a private detective who frequently is drawn back into his old profession, spying. A short-lived series, it ran to only four books. Among Canning's non-series novels are *A Forest of Eyes* (1950), in which an English engineer travels to Yugoslavia and stumbles into an intrigue; *The Scorpio Letters* (1964), about a mysterious blackmailer; and *Queen's Pawn* (1969), set aboard the ocean liner *Queen*

Elizabeth 2. While many of Canning's plots were intriguing, some were not. *The Doomsday Carrier* is about an escaped chimpanzee named Charlie who carries a deadly virus. *The Rainbird Pattern* (1972), about the kidnapping of an archbishop, was made into a film by Alfred HITCHCOCK under the title *Family Plot* (1976). Canning wrote over thirty novels, and won a Silver Dagger from the British CRIME WRITERS' ASSOCIATION.

CAPER To "caper" has for several hundred years meant to leap or jump about (from the Italian, *capriolare*). Its usage in criminal slang dates from the nineteenth century, when to "cut capers" could mean to dart through crowds pursuing thievery or otherwise hustling. "A caper" could also mean a drunken spree. The most common current meaning is a criminal plan, a job, especially if it involves complexity and several players.

The two most famous real-life capers of the century are probably the "Brinks job" and the "Great Train Robbery." The former occurred in Boston in 1950. Eleven criminals spent eighteen months casing the Brinks garage, even doing several rehearsals in which they got inside the building, copied keys, and covered every possibility. They got away with one and a quarter million dollars, and would never have been caught had not one of the gang informed. The London train robbery of 1963 involved several times as much money, most of which was never recovered. Thirty men were involved in this caper, and few of them ever went to jail. They stopped a mail train by means of a false signal, uncoupled it, and drove it to a spot where the two and a half million English pounds could be offloaded. The gang had stolen over a hundred thousand dollars from Heathrow Airport the previous year to use as operating money.

CAPITAL PUNISHMENT For most of the period during which modern mystery and crime fiction has been written, capital punishment has been legal in the major "mystery-producing" nations: Britain, France, and the United States. Ruth Ellis, an attractive blonde model, was the last woman executed in Britain (1955); her hanging aroused enormous public outcry. (Britain did not formally outlaw capital punishment, but discontinued it in practice.) *The Trial of Ruth Ellis* (1974) is a book about the case written by Jonathan GOODMAN and Patrick Pringle. Capital punishment was abolished in France only in 1981; West Germany had ended it in 1949, and other European countries such as Italy had given up capital punishment in the previous century. The first major philosophical attack on capital punishment (and the use of other cruel punishments, such as torture) was made by the Italian Cesare Beccaria (1734–1794) in *Dei delitti e delle pene* (1764; tr *Crime and Punishments,* 1963).

Capital punishment was never abolished in the United States; instead, the Supreme Court returned the question to the power of the states, some of which abolished it and some of which kept it. Recently, there has been a renaissance in legalized execution, spearheaded by conservative law-and-order groups and the growing public fear of violent crime. It has never been demonstrated that capital punishment is a deterrent, which is often given as an argument against it. Other obvious arguments are that an innocent person might be put to death for a crime he or she did not commit, and that long stretches spent on death row awaiting execution constitute cruel and unusual punishment and are in violation of the Constitution. Both of these arguments were involved in the case of Caryl Chessman. Chessman was found guilty in 1948 of several times forcing women into his car and making them perform oral sex at gunpoint; although the women were then released and not otherwise harmed, Chessman was found guilty of kidnapping and sentenced to death. He claimed that he did not commit the crimes. His execution was delayed for almost twelve years, during which time he wrote three books, including *Cell 2455 Death Row.* He was gassed at San Quentin in 1960.

While use of the death penalty is on the rise in the United States, in Europe it is headed for oblivion. The new constitution of the European Union includes the abolition of capital punishment as a principle; in some member states, such as Turkey and the Eastern European countries, it is still legal but is not in use. Russia and the Ukraine imposed a moratorium on capital punishment in 1997.

As in society, in fiction the attitude toward capital punishment varies widely. Some detectives take almost a pleasure in it. Nero WOLFE says that he tries to kill murderers or get them executed, and often lets them commit suicide. In one case, he lets one murderer kill another murderer and then himself. Other detectives, however, are not so sanguine. In the last novel to feature Lord Peter WIMSEY, he is reduced to tears because the murderer he has caught is put to death. The villains of the Nigel STRANGEWAYS books rarely make it to the gallows. See also GUILLOTINE.

CAPONE, ALPHONSE (1899–1947) The notorious gangster whose mob virtually ruled the city of Chicago during part of the PROHIBITION era. Capone was born in Brooklyn and began his rise to power in Chicago in 1920 shortly after the beginning of Prohibition. He based his criminal empire on bootlegging, but it came to include prostitution, gambling, and other rackets. He was thought to be behind the infamous Saint Valentine's Day Massacre of 1929, in which several members of the rival "Bugs" Moran gang were shot dead in a Chicago garage, along with some innocent bystanders. Capone's career came to an end in 1931, when the authorities successfully prosecuted him for tax evasion. He was sentenced to eleven years, of which he served nine. Capone retired to his estate on Palm Island, Florida, where in 1947, destroyed by syphilis, he died.

Capone has exerted a fascination for writers because of his reputation for ruthlessness and because of the nature of the times in which he lived and helped to create. He appears in various historical novels, including Howard BROWNE's *Pork City* (1988).

CAPOTE, TRUMAN (born Truman Streckfus Persons, 1924–1984) The American writer Truman Capote is known by many who never read his books merely as a flamboyant personality or celebrity of the sixties and seventies. Yet his contribution to American letters—as a proponent both of the "New Journalism" and the Southern "gothic" tradition—is impressive. Born in New Orleans, Capote moved to New York City and first made his mark as a short story writer. He won his first O. Henry award in 1946 for "Shut a Final Door." His first story collection was *A Tree of Night* (1949), his first novel *Other Voices, Other Rooms* (1948). Many of his short stories first appeared in *The New Yorker.*

Capote later ranged through several genres, writing travel sketches, screenplays, and essays. The novella *Breakfast at Tiffany's* (1958) was made into the classic 1961 film with George Peppard and Audrey Hepburn. Like Tom Wolfe, Capote experimented with a new type of journalism modeled on prose fiction; it was in this area that he made his single but very significant contribution to the crime genre, IN COLD BLOOD (1965/66). With the suspense, plotting, and pacing of a novel, Capote shaped his research into a 1959 multiple homicide into an engrossing narrative. The book has served as a benchmark and model for later true crime stories, but its meticulous journalism and gripping but unexploitive style have rarely been equaled.

CAPTAIN SWING See SWING, CAPTAIN.

"CARDBOARD BOX, ADVENTURE OF THE" (1893) A Sherlock HOLMES story, originally published in the *Strand* magazine but later suppressed and left out of Conan DOYLE's story collections because of its sexual undertones. A Croydon spinster receives a box in the mail from Belfast containing horrible tokens that suggest a double murder. Holmes finds it a "simple" case. The ending, with its vivid depiction of a confrontation of the murderer and his victims in two small boats in the haze, is rendered more powerful by Holmes's expression of a Conradian skepticism. Another interesting aspect of the case is that Holmes performs a feat of apparent mind reading similar to that of C. Auguste DUPIN in the story THE MURDERS IN THE RUE MORGUE (1841) (Holmes gives credit where credit is due, and mentions POE's work).

CARNACKI Thomas Carnacki is an OCCULT detective in a series of stories by William Hope HODGSON. Most of the Carnacki tales first appeared in *The Idler,* a magazine founded by Robert BARR and Jerome K. Jerome. They were collected in *Carnacki, the Ghost-Finder* (1913; exp 1947).

Carnacki uses scientific or pseudo-scientific methods to discover the causes of the phenomena he investigates, which may be natural, supernatural, or both. In "The Horse of the Invisible," a fraud is unmasked, only to disclose something more horrible behind it. Because of an ancient curse, a giant, invisible horse torments a family in a remote house. Like his creator, Carnacki is adept at photography, and uses it to make pictures of spirits. He also has an electric apparatus called "the pentangle" to protect himself from the evil agents.

CARNE, SIMON A gentleman thief written about by Guy BOOTHBY prior to the appearance of Colonel CLAY or RAFFLES, making Boothby almost the inventor of the type—almost, because there were plenty of precedents in ROGUE LITERATURE and other PROTOMYSTERIES. Boothby also made Carne a detective, through his second identity as KLIMO.

The Carne stories first appeared in *Pearson's Magazine* in 1897, and were collected in the book *A Prince of Swindlers* in the same year. Like Raffles, Carne is urbane and upper class, but has a trusted accomplice who is also a servant. His valet, Belton, assists in his daring burglaries, and also serves him at his house in Park Lane. His butler, the mysterious Ram Gafur, is one of several other Indian servants. When Carne returns from India in "The Dutchess of Wiltshire's Diamonds," he is hailed as a great expert in china and Indian art. With a wan face peering from between the collars of his fur coat, he appears frail and stooped, but this is only one of his disguises—he is wearing a papier maché hump on his back.

The top of Carne's house is a laboratory, where he constructs burglary tools and soporifics and also melts down the proceeds of his crimes. Some of the crimes, to a cynical reader, will seem to have been poorly thought out, and Carne's escape a little unbelievable, but Boothby did not work under the same stringent demands for realism as later writers. In "The Wedding Guest," Carne finds a way to rob the crass Greenthorpe of the seventy thousand pounds worth of wedding gifts his daughter has received upon her marriage to a worthless marquis. Part of the charm (and justification, no doubt) of these crime stories that made them palatable to a moralistic age is the way Carne uses crime to punish fools and ostentatious braggarts. Neither is his career purely criminal, since reference is made to secret services performed for the government. Carne is not above robbing his friends, however: "his conscience was sufficiently elastic to give him no trouble."

CARR, A. H. Z. (pen name of Albert Z. Carr, 1902–1971) An economist and advisor to presidents Franklin Delano Roosevelt and Harry S. Truman, A. H. Z. Carr is the only writer to receive an EDGAR award for best first novel after he was dead. His one and only novel, FINDING MAUBEE (1971), has attained the status of a modern classic.

Carr was born in Chicago and attended the University of Chicago. He also studied at Columbia University, where he earned his M.A., and at the London School of Economics. Carr became a governmental advisor during World War II. His writing career had begun in the thirties, when he began publishing short stories. He won three prizes from *Ellery Queen's Mystery Magazine* for his short stories during the fifties. Unfortunately, Carr's short fiction has never been collected in a book. He was also the author of a self-help book, *How to Attract Good Luck* (1952).

CARR, CALEB (1955–) Born in New York City, Caleb Carr attended Kenyon College and New York University. A military historian, he achieved instant fame in 1994 with his second novel, *The Alienist.* This HISTORICAL MYSTERY is set in New York in 1896 and uses both fictional and real characters. The story is about psychologist ("alienist") Laszlo Kreizler's search for a serial murderer who preys on male prostitutes. Carr's research is impeccable and the historical detail extensive, perhaps even excessive; the historical matter sometimes becomes turgid and the style is deliberate and academic more than expressive and novelistic. Into the New York of 1896, Carr imported the methods and concerns of a century later, having Kreizler use the technique of psychological profiling, which tells him that the killer was an abused child.

Carr brought Laszlo Kreizler back in *The Angel of Darkness* (1997). A Spanish consular official's baby is kidnapped, and Kreizler is recruited by Sara Howard to assist in the recovery amid growing political tensions between Spain and the United States. Although Carr uses many real personages of the time in the novel (including Clarence Darrow, who defends the villain of the piece), he also introduces some ridiculous characters and motifs. The real weakness is the narrator, Stevie Taggert, who thinks and sounds like a person of the nineties—the nineteen-nineties.

Among Carr's nonfiction works is *The Devil Soldier* (1992), about Frederick Townsend Ward (1831–62), an American soldier who offered his services to imperial China. As a mercenary, he introduced modern weapons and warfare, but his modernizations were brought to an end by his own death in combat.

CARR, JOHN DICKSON (1905–1977) Born in Pennsylvania and a graduate of Haverford College, John Dickson Carr lived in England for many years before World War II, and it was there that he achieved his reputation as a mystery writer—he was the first of only two Americans to be elected to the DETECTION CLUB. Under his own name and under the pseudonym of Carter Dickson, he became known as the master of the LOCKED ROOM mystery, in which it seems impossible that the crime could be committed or that some event (such as a disappearance) could have happened. In fact, Carr said that "the miracle problem," of which the locked room was only one variety, was the most difficult situation in crime fiction.

Carr's father was a U.S. Congressman, and so Carr spent several of his early years in Washington. After he finished college, he went to Paris in hopes of studying at the Sorbonne. Instead, he began writing. He later married an Englishwoman and settled in England, and his writing reflects the values of the GOLDEN AGE to such an extent that he has been called the most British of mystery authors. He would not return to the United States to live until 1965, when he settled in Greenville, North Carolina.

Those who admire mysteries of the puzzle variety have praised Carr's works for their carefully constructed plots. His solutions are usually simple but almost impossible to guess (not least because key information is withheld). Sometimes his efforts to conceal the solution from the reader exceed the bounds of FAIR PLAY, for example in reporting that someone said "something," but not what the thing was. Carr was not a very talented writer, and he is often criticized for the lack of believability and characterization in his novels. Julian SYMONS astutely observed of Carr's stories that "what one remembers about them is never the people, but only the puzzle." Carr included comments on the art of the locked room mystery in *The Three Coffins* (1935, repr 1979; British title *The Hollow Man*), in which he clearly lays out the method. Another text for understanding Carr's work is his essay,

"The Grandest Game in the World" (1963), in which he says that the three key elements of a detective story are fair play, a good plot, and ingenuity. Good writing, significantly, is not among them.

Carr also brought the GOTHIC back into the mystery after a period of disfavor, making use of creepy old houses, weird atmosphere, swamps, severed heads, suspicious dukes and duchesses, pale brides, bats and things that go bump in the night. This quality is particularly noticeable in such books as *It Walks By Night* (1930), which he later said was "pretty terrible," *Hag's Nook* (1933), and *The Burning Court* (1937). The "supernatural" element, however, was introduced to make the rational solution seem that much more impossible; of course, a realistic explanation was given at the end. Still, Carr was fascinated by the occult and the macabre. Carr's best-known detectives are Dr. Gideon FELL, an overweight, beer-drinking lexicographer, and Sir Henry MERRIVALE (who features in the Dickson books), a doctor and barrister. Henri BENCOLIN was the first detective he created, and Colonel March was another. His detectives, like the other people in Carr's fiction, are unrealistic and showy about it. March was probably the least eccentric; it is his cases, and not the detective himself, that are weird. Retired from the military, March is a SCOTLAND YARD detective who smokes a pipe and has sandy hair and a moustache. He only appeared in short stories, which were collected in *The Department of Queer Complaints* (1940) and *The Men Who Explained Miracles* (1963).

Carr's formulaic style and principles meant that the writing often lagged behind the plot. *The Emperor's Snuff-Box* (1942), considered one of his better books, is a case in point. It depends entirely on plot, elements of which are improbable, coincidental, or absurd. The characters are rather woodenly confined to type—the arrogant rake, the damsel in distress, and the French inspector with the volatile temper and the faux naif, ungrammatical English. Instead of a series detective, Carr uses Monsieur Goron and an eminent English doctor, Dermot Kinross (a psychological rather than scientific sleuth). Carr's writing is sometimes downright embarrassing, including such gaffes as when he says of zookeeper Mike Parsons in *He Wouldn't Kill Patience* (1944) that he was a "misogynist" because he "disliked the zoo, he disliked animals, he disliked everything else too."

An aspect of Carr's work not often remarked upon is his penchant for romantic subplots, a "fault" which is often imputed to authors when they happen to be women. The sentiments and sex roles in Carr's stories are often as mushy and predictable as anything involving Miss SILVER, and usually less sophisticated. BARZUN and TAYLOR said of one of Carr's books that the sex was "amateurish and repulsive at the same time."

The area in which Carr did much of his controversial late work was the HISTORICAL MYSTERY. Of these, SCANDAL AT HIGH CHIMNEYS (1959) is the best known. Another is *The Ghost's High Noon* (1969), set in New Orleans. Many have said that Carr's work began to fall off during this period. Unlike some other writers of historical mysteries, Carr included notes at the end of his books documenting his facts. THE MURDER OF SIR EDMUND GODFREY (1936) is an account of an actual murder of the seventeenth century, and is one of Carr's best and most readable works.

Carr's other contribution to the genre was his scholarly and critical works, including the authorized biography of Conan DOYLE, *The Life of Sir Arthur Conan Doyle* (1949), for which he won a special EDGAR award. He won another special Edgar in 1970 in recognition of his four decades of mystery writing. *The Door to Doom and Other Detections* (1980) includes Carr's essay, "The Grandest Game in the World," as well as short stories, some of them dating back to his college days. See also ARCHAEOLOGY, BOOKS.

CARRADOS, MAX The amazing blind detective in stories by Ernest BRAMAH. Carrados was blinded as an adult in a riding accident; undaunted, he keeps up his active life, and is a golfer and boxer as well as a music lover and coin collector. (Like his creator, he is also a chess player.) In "The Coin of Dionysus" he meets his WATSON, a private detective by the name of Louis Carlyle. It turns out that the pair knew each other under Max's real name, Wynn, which he was forced to drop by the terms of a will that left him a fortune.

Carrados is confident, and finds that his other senses have made up for his loss of sight—to such an extent that he can detect a fake moustache by the smell of the glue that was used to adhere it, and read newspaper headlines by feeling the print (a perhaps possible but certainly agonizingly slow method); for his coin work, he has an assistant, Parkinson. The earlier stories are accounted the best, and include TRAGEDY AT BROOKBEND COTTAGE. Another highly admired story, however ("The Ghost at Massingham Mansions"), came from the later collection *The Eyes of Max Carrados* (1923).

Carrados was not the only blind detective; Clinton Stagg's Thornley COLTON and Baynard H. KENDRICK's Captain Duncan Maclain are two others.

BIBLIOGRAPHY Novel: *The Bravo of London* (1934).

Short Stories: *Max Carrados* (1914), *The Specimen Case* (1924; 1 story), *Max Carrados Mysteries* (1927).

CARRAWAY, NICK See FITZGERALD, F. SCOTT.

CARRICK, WEBB A character created by Scottish author Bill KNOX. Of all branches of law enforcement, fish and game would seem to offer the fewest opportunities for fictionalized exploits of violent drama. Yet Knox has made Webster Carrick, a Chief Officer aboard the *Marlin,* a cutter of Her Majesty's Fishery Protection Service, the center of an engaging mystery series. A veteran of the merchant marine, Carrick has his own master's license, and very late in the series gets his own ship.

Carrick is stocky and powerful, a taciturn man of large experience, with lines of care already furrowing his young face. Dark haired, five-foot-ten, and "short of being handsome," he is a subdued hero. He steers clear of his captain, James Shannon, when he goes into one of his frequent rages; nearing retirement, Shannon has great respect for Carrick but doles it out grudgingly and hardly effusively (the same policy holds for his supply of single malt scotch). Other crewmen include bos'un William ("Clapper") Bell, a good-natured hulk who, like Carrick, is also a diver; the freckly second mate, Jumbo Wills; and the mysterious second officer, Pettigrew, a middle-aged man who returned to the sea to escape some undisclosed entanglements ashore.

Knox overcomes two problems, the first being that the Fisheries Service is supposed to supervise the fishing industry in territorial waters, not chase shore-going criminals. Knox makes use of local hotspots (Northern Ireland), industries (oil), and sea-borne crime (smuggling, primarily). The second problem, that the ship is an all-male environment, he manages less well, the romantic subplots being rather predictable and the women characters not very interesting.

In *The Scavengers* (1964), a marine biologist and diver is killed while on an expedition near Ayr; the plot has some similarities to *Hellspout* (1976), but it remains one of the best books in the series. The professor's innocent-seeming mission provides no motive for his murder, and Carrick must do some digging—and diving—to find out what the professor knew or inadvertently discovered. *Devilweed* (1966) ingeniously linked a bank robbery plot with the sea. *Blacklight* (1967) concerns the hijacking of an oil rig in the North Sea. A more believable plot is used in *Hellspout* (1976), in which the *Marlin* is taking two environmentalists to a remote island where two of their colleagues are studying seals. The two men have vanished, but a recent violent gale makes their departure from the island seem impossible. The obvious answer to their whereabouts is eventually found, but this raises even more questions, which are neatly tied up in the course of Carrick's investigations in the grungy town of Port Angus. Typically, the finale occurs at sea. *The Klondyker* (U.S. title *Figurehead,* 1968) and *Blood Tide* (1983) both concern smuggling, and are among the best (and most salty) of the Carrick mysteries.

In *Wavecrest* (1985), Carrick gets his own command, a small technological marvel called the *Tern,* designed for in-shore work. The mystery begins with the discovery of a small oil slick on a treacherous part of coast near Dunbrach, and the corpse of a woman trapped in the sludge. She turns out to be one of a couple living in an abandoned lighthouse on a desolate island, their only neighbor a wealthy Danish shipping and oil magnate. Atmospherically, the story is reminiscent of P. M. HUBBARD, until Knox introduces the usual series elements—Celtic lore, scuba diving, chases by sea, professional rivalries, etcetera. The Bagman, a misanthropic beachcomber, is a curious figure, but underdeveloped.

BIBLIOGRAPHY Novels: *Blueback* (1969), *Seafire* (1970), *Stormtide* (1973), *Whitewater* (1974), *Witchrock* (1977), *Bombship* (1980), *Dead Man's Mooring* (1988).

CARTER, NICK A character originally created by John R. Coryell (1848–1924). Carter, a private detective in New York City, was a staple of the DIME NOVEL and was featured in more than 1,000 stories. Thomas Chalmers Harbaugh (1849–1924) and Frederick van Rensselaer Dey (1861–1922) were among the many who wrote Nick Carter stories. Thomas W. HANSHEW was another. The first Nick Carter story was *The Old Detective's Pupil* (1886). Nick has learned the business from his father, and is tough but also as informed on obscure subjects as Sherlock HOLMES. The Nick Carter character was also used on radio and in film.

Carter is a combination superhero of incredible strength and GENIUS DETECTIVE with all sorts of knowledge at his command. Successive authors have updated Carter so that in later appearances he is a dashing modern spy. Sexton BLAKE is like an English version of him.

CARUSO, ENRICO See CELEBRITY MYSTERIES.

CARVALHO, INSPECTOR PEPE See VÁZQUEZ MONTALBÁN, MANUEL.

CARVER, FRED A Florida private detective created by John LUTZ. The first Carver novel was *Tropical Heat* (1986). Formerly of the Orlando police force, Carver was made to retire after he was shot in the kneecap. Carver is blue-eyed, curly haired, and muscular from swimming and using his cane; he looks like a "feral cat." His friend in the department is Alfonso DeSoto; his enemy is Lieutenant William McGreggor, a sadist who does not bathe regularly. Huge and blond-haired, McGreggor is an unpleasant presence in the series. He is mean and extremely vulgar, and expresses opinions so backward it is a little hard to believe—not that someone would *have* them, but would voice them. He hates both women and non-whites.

The Carver novels are set in sunny, seedy Florida but adhere to the old school of private eye writing, with brooding reflections on corruption and greed. In both *Kiss* (1988) and *Spark* (1993), Lutz used Florida retirement communities as settings. Another retiree (a Milwaukee cop) in *Hot* (1992) gets Carver involved in what appears to be a drug smuggling case—or just an old crank's harassment of his neighbor.

Some of the novels reflect Lutz's reputation for ingenuity and clever plots. In *Burn* (1995), a man thinks he is being falsely accused of stalking a woman he says he has never met; he believes she is trying to entrap him so that she can kill him and claim self-defense against a "stalker." He lives alone, and so when she reports his presence to the police, he cannot prove that he was sitting around at home. The man, however, looks disturbingly like the serial killer Ted Bundy, and the woman seems to be an ordinary freelance writer. Carver can't find anything wrong, but then is warned off the case in a violent manner by a giant with smelly feet. In *Torch* (1994), a married woman hires Carver to watch her and her lover for mysterious reasons; moments afterward, she is run down by a truck.

During the series, Carver undergoes dreadful experiences similar to Dave ROBICHAUX's. In *Scorcher* (1987), Carver has been living with Edwina, a real estate agent who is unpredictable and demanding. His former wife lives in St. Louis (scene of the Alo NUDGER novels) with their children, Ann, six, and Chipper, eight. When they come to visit Florida, a serial killer with a flamethrower made from a scuba tank incinerates Chipper. In *Bloodfire* (1991), a man named Ghostly hires Carver to find his missing wife. He pays with a thousand-dollar bill, and does not seem to be quite what he says he is. Like other books in the series, *Bloodfire* contains extremely violent scenes; Carver is in the same room with a woman when she is shot in the head with a .30-06 rifle. In this book, he meets Beth Jackson, a black woman who later becomes his girlfriend. He moves back to his beach cottage in Del Moray, twenty miles from Orlando. Beth becomes a reporter for an alternative newspaper, and also becomes Carver's de facto partner.

BIBLIOGRAPHY Novels: *Flame* (1990), *Lightning* (1996).

CARVER, REX A former spy and private detective in a brief series of novels by Victor CANNING. He first appeared in *The Whip Hand* (1965), in which Canning capitalized on the popularity of the horse racing mysteries of Dick FRANCIS and the spy novels of Ian FLEMING. Carter meets a beautiful girl in Brighton and follows her to the Continent, becoming involved with neo-NAZIS. *Doubled in Diamonds* (1966) involves drug smuggling and gems. *The Melting Man* (1968), the last book in the series, has a macabre setting in the waxworks of a mountain chateau. The other book in the series was *The Python Project* (1967).

"CASE OF OSCAR BRODSKI, THE" One of the cases of Dr. THORNDYKE, collected in R. Austin FREEMAN's *The Singing Bone* (1912). Often anthologized and cited as one of the most significant detective stories ever written, it is perhaps the most satisfying of Thorndyke's INVERTED MYSTERIES because of the sheer number of clues left by the killer, which are in the second part believably seized upon by the inexorable doctor. Silas Hickler, a burglar and jewel thief, is waiting outside his house to catch the boat train when by chance Oscar Brodski, a respectable jeweler, asks him the way to the station. Realizing why Brodski is going the same way, Hickler struggles with his conscience but finally invites Brodski into his home. Freeman's writing is particularly clear and vivid, especially in the realistic murder scene and Thorndyke's subsequent following up of the clues, which include not only the usual stray matches and unusual tobaccos, but such oddities as a pair of crushed eyeglasses that, when fully pieced together, leave a small pile of glass left over.

"CASE OF THE DANCING SANDWICHES, THE" (1951) A story by Frederic BROWN, one of his longest as well as best. It is about Carl Dixon, a nice guy who falls into the hands of con man Jerry Trenholm; Trenholm is running a double con, part blackmail and part revenge scheme. The result is that Dixon gets a life sentence, and the case against him is open and shut. Dixon's fiancée, Susan Bailey, is the only one who believes in him. She goes to New York City Police detective Peter Cole for help when all other avenues have been exhausted, and the results are surprising—to Cole and Susan, as much as to Carl himself. "The Case of the Dancing Sandwiches" was first published in *Mystery Book Magazine* in 1950, and later as a short novel.

CASE OF THE LATE PIG, THE (1937) This novel by Margery ALLINGHAM has nothing to do with pigs; "Pig" is the nickname of the victim. Naturally it features Albert CAMPION and his assistant companion LUGG, though Lugg seems to be more of a nuisance for his continuous nagging and criticism of Campion than a help. He does come up with one stroke of genius—he recognizes a typewriter's brand, model, and approximate use just by looking at a few typed lines. The story includes some inventive murder weapons, including a stone geranium urn.

The novel illustrates the author's main weaknesses, the prime one being that Campion as narrator is constantly characterizing the facts he is reporting with judgements on how he should have interpreted them differently, or how wrong it proved to be later, and how risky it was that he took such decisions in the light of further events, etc. There is a conscious effort to be funny, aping Wodehouse. Allingham goes overboard on romantic subplots: at the end of the novel wedding bells can be heard for *three* couples. Last, there is a violation of FAIR PLAY in that when Campion discovers something he does not say what it is.

The setup, however, is ingenious: having received an anonymous letter, Campion goes to the funeral of Peters ("Pig"), a grade school classmate hated by all the boys for his cruelty. Months later, Campion is called in by his good friend Leo Pursuivant—Chief Constable of the same village where Pig had been buried—in the case of a mysterious death. Campion is shocked when he recognizes the corpse. The book is also unusual in that Campion narrates his adventure in the first person. The book lies at the boundary between the early silly/detective Campion and the later wise/observer Campion, combining elements of both.

CASE OF THE TERRIFIED TYPIST, THE (1956) A novel by Erle Stanley GARDER, one of the Perry MASON series. The book is almost completely free of description, and, with the exception of the "French babe," of juvenile humor. It offers a distilled version of what Gardner did best: legal procedure. As the story opens, Mason has been cutting a brief to ribbons and needs a temporary typist to make a fresh copy. When she turns up half an hour later, she is exceedingly nervous, but very competent—she makes the typewriter sound "like a machine gun." Then, she disappears. After he learns that the office of the South African Gem Importing and Exploration Company down the hall has been burgled, Mason gets suspicious; when Della Street finds a wad of gum embedded with diamonds, he gets *very* suspicious; when he is hired to defend one of the company's employees, Duane Jefferson, on a charge of murdering a smuggler, he knows he has a very strange case indeed. Mason's (and Paul Drake's) investigation, particularly his ruse to find the terrified typist, take up a more considerable part of the book than usual. District Attorney Hamilton Burger is tickled to death, and Mason doesn't know why; the courtroom battle, Mason's questions, and the technical points are engaging. Mason's loss of the case—his first ever—calls for a surprising ending, and it may not be the expected one.

CASE OF THE TURNING TIDE, THE (1941) One of the non-series mysteries by Erle Stanley GARDNER, over which he seems to have labored more than with his other books. In his introduction, Gardner said that mysteries were "escape fiction" that had become "highly standardized through too much usage," and that in *The Case of the Turning Tide* "events are permitted to stream across the page in just about the way they would have in real life." The clues appear "naturally," and the story is told in a more lifelike manner; hence the "extra effort" that the book cost him.

The novel is a story of MURDER AFLOAT. The traveling salesman Ted Shale is walking along the beach at Santa Delbarra, hoping to catch the wealthy Addison Stearne leaving his yacht, the *Gypsy Queen,* so that he can sell him some paper products for Stearne's chain of hotels. Instead, he sees a young woman come up the yacht's companionway, lean over the rail and fall in, apparently unconscious. Shale and a woman on a nearby yacht, Joan Harpler, rescue the unconscious woman, the beautiful Nita Moline. When Shale goes aboard *Gypsy Queen,* he finds two corpses, one of them Addison's and the other his associate, C. Arthur Right. The ensuing investigation has several people trying to find out the truth at once. Prominent among the official investigators is district attorney Frank Duryea, assisted (at first unwillingly) by his wife's grandfather, Gramps Wiggins, a hard-drinking ne'er-do-well and mystery addict. What makes the book interesting is that, apart from major villains, Gardner presents most people as semi-honest, trying to do the right thing except when opportunities for feathering their own nests prove too good to pass up. Shale agrees to Anita Moline's proposal that he spy on the *Gypsy Queen* from Harpler's yacht, the *Albatross,* in exchange for a paper contract after she inherits Stearne's business; after Shale goes to his cabin for a nap, he finds himself shanghaied. Meanwhile, Stearne's lawyers and a pair of oil speculators play tug-of-war over some oil leases Stearne held an option on—which was due to expire on the night he died. The usual love triangle is expanded into a quadrangle involving Stearne, Right (referred to comically as Mr. Right), Right's wife, and Nita Moline. As in the Perry MASON series, Gardner inserts some legal snags, such as a will that depends on whether Right or Stearne died first. Another realistic element is that the private eye in this novel appears on the wrong side—he is employed to get at any cost (in other words, fabricate) evidence that shows that

Right died first. For once, Gardner gave almost equal weight to developing all the characters, and there is no star series character to hog the attention.

CASE OF WILLIAM SMITH, THE See AMNESIA.

CASEY, JACK "FLASHGUN" A character who was featured in BLACK MASK stories by George Harmon COXE. Casey fit the tough-guy mold of the PULP MAGAZINES, being big (an ex-sergeant) and hot tempered. He works for the *Globe* at first and then switches to the *Express.* Coxe abandoned Casey for a long time while he concentrated on his other main series character, Kent MURDOCK, but Casey returned in several novels written in the sixties.

BIBLIOGRAPHY Novels: *Silent Are the Dead* (1942), *Murder for Two* (1943), *Error of Judgment* (1961), *The Man Who Died Too Soon* (1962), *Deadly Images* (1964).

Short Stories: *Flash Casey, Detective* (1946).

CASK, THE (1920) The first mystery novel by Freeman Wills CROFTS, well written if long-winded. The book is written almost in real time, with every detail described without eliding the secondary or even trivial episodes. A strong feeling of suspense is built up by the initial discovery of a woman's hand in a barrel of gold sovereigns by a clerk in a London steamship company. Shortly thereafter, a man calls for the cask and absconds with it. The police (and Inspector Burnley) are called in, and the chase begins, leading back to France, from whence the *Bullfinch* had sailed with the mysterious cask. In Paris, Burnley calls upon the aid of the French detective LeFarge; from here on, the story shows its ancestry in the long and complex novels of GABORIAU. Yet a third detective (this one private), Georges La Touche, joins the hunt.

The Cask is far longer than later mystery novels, an outgrowth of its day-to-day, hour-by-hour pace (when the detectives wait for a lab report, the reader waits, too). Its slowness is not necessarily a fault. On the one hand, it is replete with clues, while on the other it is equally glutted with detail. Some of Crofts's favorite devices, such as unbreakable alibis and train and ship schedules, are central to the story.

CASPARY, VERA (1899? 1904?–1987) The American author Vera Caspary is best known for her mystery novel LAURA (1943), which became the basis for an enormously successful film directed by Otto Preminger. Like Caspary's other detective novels, the romantic element is at least as important to the plot as the crime story.

Caspary was born in Chicago and worked as a freelance writer before moving to New York, where she edited *Dance.* The experience of moving to New York was transmuted in her first novel, *The White Girl* (1929), into a story about a black woman who goes to New York and "passes" as white. Drawing on her own ethnic background (Portuguese/Jewish), Caspary then wrote *Thicker Than Water* (1932). She also wrote plays; *Blind Mice* (1931), a collaboration with Winifred Lenihan, was made into the film *Working Girls* (1931), which gave Caspary an introduction to Hollywood, where she would have a long career. Several films were based on novels she had published, and she also wrote or collaborated on many films over a period of decades, including *Such Women Are Dangerous* (1934), *Scandal Street* (1938), and *Lady from Louisiana* (1941), in which young heroines and the falsely accused are common plot elements. *I Can Get It for You Wholesale* (1951) and *Les Girls* (1957) were among her other scripts.

Caspary's books are sometimes said to be primarily "for women" because of their romantic focus, but it should be specified that they are for women *of the forties.* The notions behind the plots can be hopelessly outdated, as in Caspary's next novel after *Laura, Bedelia* (1945), also a commercially successful mystery but one that has not stood the test of time. Set in pre–World War I Connecticut (Caspary sometimes lived in Norwalk), the book makes an attempt to overcome prudishness that is more objectionable than prudishness itself, for example the effort to establish the central relationship between Bedelia and her husband, Charlie. For Charlie, "his wife's careless tresses had sluttish charm"; he had, "like every other respectable man, known a number of wantons," and his wife's "easy pleasure gave to the marriage bed a fillip of naughtiness without which no man of Puritan conscience could have been satisfied." Meanwhile, this stereotypical saucy wench "had a genuine talent for housekeeping," important because "a woman's most fundamental job . . . is to make a man comfortable."

With her husband, film producer I. G. Goldsmith, Caspary traveled to London to work on the screen version of *Bedelia* (1946). None of Caspary's other films had the success of *Laura,* perhaps with the exception of *The Blue Gardenia* (1953), directed by Fritz LANG. Her other romantic novels that feature an element of crime include *The Husband* (1957), about the nightmare of a homicidal spouse, and *Evvie* (1960), which is set in the twenties. One of Caspary's best later books was *The Man Who Loved His Wife* (1966), a tense story about an enraged and impotent tycoon, Fletcher Strode, who has cancer of the larynx and wants to commit suicide. He is worried, however, that when he dies his second wife, Elaine, will take up with another man. Elaine loves

Strode even though he abuses her mentally and physically. While Strode begins to write a diary that he hopes will ensure that Elaine is blamed for his death if he commits suicide, Strode's selfish daughter Cindy and her penniless husband Don also want to ensure that Elaine is charged with murder so that she cannot inherit.

CASTANG, HENRI The second series detective created by Nicholas FREELING, after the demise of Inspector VAN DER VALK. Castang is French, and thus brought Freeling even closer to his model, Georges SIMENON. The stories are set in France, but some critics have considered the Holland of Inspector Van der Valk to have been more interesting; however, the French setting is less lugubrious than that of the first series of Freeling novels. Castang has a Czechoslovakian-born wife, Vera, who assumes a prominent role in the stories. Castang is more in the background than Van der Valk, and more room is given to the author's free-ranging commentaries; actual police work is less evident.

Dressing of Diamond (1974) was the first Castang case, concerning the disappearance of a little girl. The crimes in the Castang novels tend to be more sensational than the sometimes all too believably sordid matters that engaged Van der Valk. Sometimes, crime is used as a pretext for comparative sociology and political commentary. *No Part in Your Death* (1984) contains three cases set in three countries, interrelated by their similar ambiguities. In Munich, after he advises a young woman whose enemies are trying to get her psychiatrically committed, Castang is sapped and taken in for questioning by German (*West* German) security police. In another story, the wife of an old friend disappears mysteriously.

After the European Union, Castang evolves from a cop to a bureaucrat. In *The Pretty How Town* (1992; U.S. title *Flanders Sky*), Castang is eased out of his job and sent to Brussels to be France's representative in a new European department of judicial services. His new boss is Mr. Claverhouse. An intrigue erupts right away when Claverhouse's wife is raped and murdered, and Claverhouse himself is one of the suspects. *You Who Know* (1994) takes Castang to Ireland after one of his Brussels colleagues, Eamonn Hickey, is murdered. Among the things that Castang learns about his former friend is that he was in reality an inveterate philanderer, and was also suspected of IRA involvement. The case becomes a travelogue and suspense story with Castang discovering the victim's former girlfriend in the Italian Alps—and, of course, a whole lot more. The possibility of extending the series through the change to Brussels seems not to have worked, since Castang spends little time there and because the series ended soon after. A DWARF KINGDOM (1996) was announced as the last Castang novel; it was nominated for an EDGAR award.

BIBLIOGRAPHY Novels: *What Are the Bugles Blowing For?* (1975; U.S. title *The Bugles Blowing*), *Lake Isle* (1976; U.S. title *Sabine*), *Gadget* (1977), *The Night Lords* (1978), *Castang's City* (1980), *Wolfnight* (1982), *Cold Iron* (1986), *Lady MacBeth* (1988), *Not as Far as Velma* (1989).

CATS The latest gambit in the chase after novelty in the mystery genre is the mystery for cat lovers. It was invented by Lillian Jackson Braun, who started her "The Cat Who" series in 1966 with *The Cat Who Could Read Backwards* (1966). After a hiatus of almost twenty years, she began again with *The Cat Who Saw Red* (1986), which was nominated for an EDGAR award. She has now written some twenty "Cat Who" books, all of which feature former police reporter Jim Qwilleran and his cats, the insipidly named Koko and Yum Yum.

By making the novel's "cattiness" its center, the cat phenomenon substitutes the principles of marketing for those of fiction. The writer Lydia Adamson is another author who has staked everything on the cat theme, closely modeling her series on Braun's—each title follows the "Cat [preposition][subject]" format: *A Cat in the Manger* (1990), *A Cat in the Wings* (1993), *A Cat on the Cutting Edge* (1994), etc. Adamson's human series character is Alice Nestleton, a struggling actress in New York who has two cats, Bushy and Pancho. Adamson and Braun are the leaders but are by no means alone. Among those who have followed in their paw prints is Rita Mae Brown, with the insufferable "Sneaky Pie." Brown was once considered a serious writer for such feminist novels as *Rubyfruit Jungle* (1973). Conan FLAGG, the Oregon bookstore owner, is also devoted to his pet. Several cat mystery-story anthologies have been published.

The cat series is a feeble concept indeed; there has always been a tension between realism and the demands of fiction in the mystery story, but with the cat novel realism flies out the window. Sentimentality replaces emotion, and striving to be cute replaces striving to be meaningful. Stephen King wrote that "the cat is a shortcut, a kind of emotional shorthand employed by writers who can't really write for readers who can't really read." Marion Babson's *Nine Lives to Murder* (1994) is perhaps the ultimate cat mystery because it completely abandons realism and puts into effect the fantasy of every real cat lover, that of *being* a cat. A Shakespearean actor is nearly killed in an "accidental" fall from a ladder, as a result of which he and a cat switch bodies (yes, his mind is transported into the feline, and the cat's "mind" into his body). As a cat, the actor investigates the attempt on his own life. Paul GALLICO wrote a book about a dead cat that seeks vengeance on its murderer.

To be fair, one has to admit that other detectives have been aided by their pets—Norbert DAVIS's Doan-and-Carstairs series is one example. Carstairs, however, was a dog, a tractable animal often used in law enforcement, and thus there was some grounding in reality.

CAUDWELL, SARAH (pseudonym of Sarah Cockburn, 1939–) The English barrister Sarah Cockburn was born into a family of writers: her father Claud was a writer, and she is the sister of the journalist Alexander Cockburn. Her first mystery was *Thus Was Adonis Murdered* (1981), which introduced the series character Hilary Tamar. This character, who may be a man or a woman, is an Oxford don and professor of medieval law. Hilary has several young former students who are now practicing at Lincoln's Inn and call on Tamar for advice when they stumble upon mysteries. In the first book, one of the young lawyers, Julia Larwood, sends back letters from Venice describing how she has become a murder suspect while on an art tour. (The plot is derivative of WYLDER'S HAND [1864]). Caudwell's characters are updated versions of the "Bright Young Things" of the mystery novels of the GOLDEN AGE. Moneyed, pretentious, and given to dropping bits of the education they have no real use for, they muddle their way through improbable plots while Hilary, the sexless and godlike figure, uses his or her knowledge of medieval law to solve the case. Railery, love triangles, and sex fill in the gaps. Caudwell's style, though a throwback, has been much admired.

CECIL, HENRY (pen name of Henry Cecil Leon, 1902–1976) During a long career as a lawyer and judge, Henry Cecil kept a sense of humor about the law, expressed in a series of novels combining PROCEDURAL accuracy with humorous and even farcical plots. Cecil was born in London and graduated from St. Paul's School and King's College, Cambridge. He served with distinction in both world wars. From 1949 to 1967, he was a county court judge. *Just within the Law* (1975) is his autobiography; Cecil was also the author of a practical nonfiction guide for the layman, *Know about English Law* (1965).

Cecil wrote some two dozen novels as well as two volumes of short stories, *Full Circle* (1948) and *Brief Tales from the Bench* (1968). His gift for humor, love of the perplexing and madcap, and the fast pace of his novels made his books easily adaptable for the stage. BARZUN and TAYLOR said that some of the conversations in *Natural Causes* (1953), a novel about the blackmailing of a judge, were "worthy of Shaw at his best." *Settled Out of Court* (1959) was made into a play by the author and William Saroyan. *Brothers In Law* (1955) was adapted by Cecil in collaboration with Ted WILLIS, was later filmed and also was turned into a television series. Cecil's work has been highly praised by critics, and several of his novels have recently been reprinted by Academy Chicago Publishers. Anthony BOUCHER said that "few men write so wittily and perceptively about The Law as Henry Cecil." *No Bail for the Judge* (1952) turns the legal mystery on its ear and has a judge, on trial for murder, being rescued by a clever criminal.

One of Cecil's most curious books is *Independent Witness* (1963), which was written as a radio play and then made into a novel by the author. It is not a murder story at all but a farcical courtroom drama that illustrates the unreliability of "eyewitness" testimony. A member of Parliament, Michael Barnes, is driving a car when a motorcyclist runs straight into him outside the Blue Goose pub. Barnes panics and leaves the scene of the accident; he is later prosecuted, and plenty of witnesses are on hand to give a totally different and in some cases totally false account of what happened. Cecil parodies such types as the dotty old military man (Colonel Brain) and the bibulous, lower-class rustic (Mr. Piper).

CELEBRITY MYSTERIES There are two types of celebrity mysteries: those involving celebrities and those written by them. Of the former, perhaps the best known are George BAXT's series of mysteries that variously feature Dorothy Parker, Tallulah Bankhead, Alfred HITCHCOCK, Greta Garbo, Noel Coward, and Marlene Dietrich, and Stuart KAMINSKY's novels about Toby PETERS, which also feature Hollywood personalities. Another series focusing on theatrical personalities is by Barbara PAUL: with *A Cadenza for Caruso* (1984), she began a group of novels featuring the famous Italian tenor as a detective. Many other famous historical figures have been recreated in mystery fiction, including Howard Hughes and Theodore ROOSEVELT. Many of these efforts fail to come off, usually not for lack of research but of imagination and writing ability. Eric Zencey's *Panama* (1995) casts historian Henry Adams as a sleuth looking for a missing woman against the background of the scandal surrounding the bankruptcy of the French Panama Canal Company in 1892. Hard on the heels of the Jane Austen "revival" comes a mystery that casts the English novelist as a sleuth; *Jane and the Unpleasantness at Scargrave Manor* (1996) is a book lacking in all of the great qualities of Austen's writing, for which it substitutes a ridiculous pastiche of eighteenth-century prose. Lillian DE LA TORRE's mysteries with Samuel Johnson as the detective are far better than most of the above; she has been praised for her understanding of Johnson and for her prose—a high compliment, given that Johnson is the second most quoted author in the English language after Shakespeare.

Baxt's *The Bette Davis Murder Case* (1994) includes not only the famous actress but Agatha CHRISTIE as characters, making it part of the sub-subgenre of the celebrity mystery involving a famous mystery writer. It is hard to write one of these without at least appearing to cash in on a name more famous than your own; William F. Nolan has initiated "The Black Mask Boys" series, featuring HAMMETT, CHANDLER, and GARDNER. The first two are *The Black Mask Murders* (1994) and *The Marble Orchard* (1996). First, one has to ignore the fact that, while Chandler and Gardner were friends, Chandler and Hammett met only once in real life. The first book, narrated by "Hammett," doesn't sound anything like Hammett. Instead, it is a tissue of hard-boiled cliches ("long-lashed bedroom eyes and a figure with more curves in it than Sunset Boulevard") and shop-worn lines ("She was like a rare hothouse flower"). Fistfuls of facts are given in a shotgun approach to authenticity—and the picky reader will notice inaccuracies. Joe GORES used Hammett as the main character in *Hammett* (1975), which was disastrously filmed by Wim Wenders in 1982. John Dickson CARR's *The Hungry Goblin* (1972) has Wilkie COLLINS as a character.

Many famous people have tried to write mysteries; a few have had the modesty or good sense to find a coauthor. Just as football has produced the actors Jim Brown and Joe Namath, celebrity fiction has its share of mediocre performances.

Among the best and most literate celebrity authors are two children of former U.S. Presidents, who have written mysteries about the White House, international politics, and diplomacy. Margaret Truman, daughter of Harry Truman, sets her many detective tales in Washington. *Murder on the Potomac* (1994) is a local color mystery about yuppies, drugs, gambling, and the re-enactment of famous murders. Elliot Roosevelt, the son of Franklin and Eleanor Roosevelt, went her one better by making his mother the detective. (Eleanor also appears in Stuart Kaminsky's *The Fala Factor,* 1984.) Roosevelt left many manuscripts at the time of his death, so his books continue to appear with regularity. In 1935, a book called *The President's Mystery Story* was published; its plot had been suggested by Franklin Delano Roosevelt himself, and was written collaboratively by seven writers who included S. S. VAN DINE, Anthony ABBOT, and Samuel Hopkins ADAMS.

Bill Shoemaker, one of the winningest jockeys of all time, has begun writing a series of detective novels, thus making himself an American competitor of England's Dick FRANCIS. Some critics have even said that he excels Francis in his accurate depictions of the horse racing world. Martina Navratilova has written mysteries centered on the international tennis circle (*Breaking Point,* 1996, is the second) with a co-writer (Liz Nickles), but not to advantage. Stephen Humphrey Bogart, son of the actor who made himself synonymous with Sam SPADE and Philip MARLOWE, made his debut with *Play It Again* (1995; the writing is choppy and the plot predictable). Other novels have followed. Political commentator William F. Buckley, who has endeavored to make himself into a celebrity, has written a number of mystery-suspense novels, as has his opposite (i.e., liberal) number, Robert MacNeil. MacNeil has further encroached on Buckley's turf by writing a novel (*The Voyage,* 1995) having to do with sailing; more a what-happened than a whodunit, it focuses on a diplomat whose career is threatened when a former mistress disappears from a sailboat in the Baltic.

There is another, highly exclusive writer's club, that of the celebrity ex-con. Patricia Hearst, who became famous when she was kidnapped by the Symbionese Liberation Army, arrested in 1974 for bank robbery and later convicted, has now authored *Murder at San Simeon* (1996) with Cordelia Biddle. The novel is based on an actual unsolved death at San Simeon in the twenties; although Charlie Chaplin and his son, John Barrymore, Eleanor Glyn, and other celebrities are on hand, Hearst/Biddle cannot get the plot moving, and the slow set-up feels like a tour of all of San Simeon's 250,000 acres. In a plot that jumps back and forth between present and past, the detective learns that her grandmother was the secretary to William Randolph Hearst's lover and was implicated in the death. (Another *Murder at San Simeon* predated Hearst's book; published in 1988 by Robert Lee Hall, it featured Chaplin, Jean Harlow, and Clark Gable as country house guests. But with the addition of a dwarf and a communist as suspects, it descended into spoof.)

E. Howard Hunt, the convicted Watergate conspirator, has written dozens of novels, both before and after his trip to the pen; his first book was *Maelstrom* (1948). Hunt's co-conspirator, John Ehrlichman, has also become a mystery and suspense author.

Other celebrity mystery and suspense authors include former New York City Mayor Ed Koch; comedian and television personality Steve Allen; actor Kirk Douglas; and director Oliver Stone. Even Willard Scott, the *Today* show host, has written a mystery, *Murder Under Blue Skies* (1998), with Bill CRIDER.

See also HISTORICAL MYSTERIES.

CELLINI, DR. EMMANUEL Yet another character created by John CREASEY, this time writing under the names Michael Halliday (in the U.K.) and Kyle Hunt (in the U.S.). Creasey came relatively late to the psychiatrist-sleuth subgenre, long after Basil WILLING and others had become popular. Creasey's handling of psychology suffers from the breakneck pace of his composition.

BIBLIOGRAPHY Novels: *Cunning as a Fox* (1965), *Wicked as the Devil* (1966), *Sly as a Serpent* (1967), *Cruel as a Cat* (1968), *Too Good to be True* (1969), *A Period of Evil* (1970), *As Lonely as the Damned* (1971), *As Empty as Hate* (1972), *As Merry as Hell* (1973), *This Man Did I Kill?* (1974), *The Man Who Was Not Himself* (1976).

CHAMBERS, PETER The New York–based "private richard" created by Henry KANE. Spanning four decades, the Chambers novels are a sociological mirror, capturing the changes in mores of the postwar period as well as literary styles. The first book in the series was *A Halo for Nobody* (1947). Chambers starts out as another HARD-BOILED private eye in the then-regnant manner, albeit with Kane's sense of humor already showing through. Eventually word play, parody, and language games would submerge the murder puzzles, even if they were fairly tight. Chambers develops into a Beat-generation hipster and a sixties libertine, fond of jazz, booze, and sex. Kane may have become bored with pun-engorged prose ridden with riddles, dropping this act somewhat in such books as *Better Wed Than Dead* (1967; orig title *Unholy Trio;* British title *The Devil to Pay*), which is written in a comparatively austere hard-boiled style. In that novel, Chambers is hired to marry Nora Bradley, sister of senatorial hopeful Hunt Bradley, so that she can meet the provisions of the will that will bring her millions of dollars. He then becomes involved in an intrigue involving the neo-Nazi group America Always, a cabal of dangerous bigots and right-wing fanatics. Chambers's gay hairdresser friend is one of the more interesting characters, and homosexuality is presented in a far more positive light than in many hard-boiled novels.

In the final novels, Kane takes the covert or offstage sex that had always been a part of the p.i. novel and makes it explicit, punctuating the stories with graphic and steamy scenes. Even here, the author's sense of humor proves irrepressible, epitomized in such titles as *The Glow Job* (1971) and *The Tail Job* (1971). The series is not always so daffy, however; *Too French and Too Deadly* (1955; British title *The Narrowing Lust*) is a LOCKED ROOM mystery. Chambers is courting a nightclub owner, Carlotta Cain, when her friend Gordon Clark comes into town. Clark is involved in a business shipping used cars to Europe and selling them at a profit (even ten years after World War II, automobiles were in short supply). Clark is found shot to death in the office inside the firm's garage; both the outer door and the office door are locked and barred from the inside, making it a locked room within a locked room. The solution is elegant and Kane plays no unfair tricks on the reader. The story itself is full of crooks and nightclub atmosphere, but the accents are terribly done.

Confusingly, Kane's Chambers novels appeared under different titles at different times.

BIBLIOGRAPHY Novels: *Armchair in Hell* (1948), *Hang by Your Neck* (1949), *A Corpse for Christmas* (1951), *Until You Are Dead* (1951), *The Case of the Murdered Madame* (1955), *Who Killed Sweet Sue?* (1956; British title *Sweet Charlie*), *Fistful of Death* (1958; British title *The Dangling Man*), *Death is the Last Lover* (1959; British title *Nirvana Can Also Mean Death*), *Death of a Flack* (1961), *Dead in Bed* (1961), *Death of a Hooker* (1961), *Kisses of Death* (1962; British title *Killer's Kiss*), *Death of a Dastard* (1962), *Never Give a Millionaire an Even Break* (1963; British title *Murder for the Millions*), *Nobody Loves a Loser* (1963), *Snatch an Eye* (1963), *Don't Call Me Madame* (1969), *The Schack Job* (1969), *The Bomb Job* (1970), *Don't Go Away Dead* (1970), *Come Kill with Me* (1972), *The Escort Job* (1972), *Kill for the Millions* (1972).

Short Stories/Novelettes: *Report for a Corpse* (1948), *My Business Is Murder* (1954), *Trinity in Violence* (1954), *Trilogy in Jeopardy* (1955), *The Name Is Chambers* (1957), *Death on the Double* (1957), *Kiss! Kiss! Kill! Kill!* (1970).

CHAMBRUN, PIERRE The suave hotel manager and sometime sleuth in a series of books by Judson PHILIPS, written under the name Hugh Pentecost. Chambrun manages the Hotel Beaumont, supposedly New York's best. Like other Philips heroes, Chambrun remains at the level of a sketch: he is stocky and has "the brightest black eyes you ever saw," and his employees "love him and respect him because they know he will always be fair and just." These employees include the narrator, public relations director Mark Haskell; his perfect secretary, Miss Betsy Ruysdale, who "reads his mind"; and the hotel dick, Jerry Dodd, an implacable terrier type. In addition to the SUPERLATIVE COMPLEX, the books are hampered by the limitations of the setting. To get around the problem, Philips was forced to create improbable and sensational plots. In *Time of Terror* (1975), a terrorist group of Vietnam veterans led by Colonel Coriander (an echo of Colonel Mustard from the board game *Clue*) seize a floor of the hotel, mine it with explosives, and threaten to blow the Beaumont up (or down) unless the army brass who prosecuted the war are put on trial. They also threaten to rape and mutilate young women and girls. Similar ploys are made in *The Fourteenth Dilemma* (1976), in which a twelve-year-old girl (a deaf mute) has her skull bashed in while she is staying in the hotel with her family—who, to make things interesting, have just won a quarter of a million dollars in a lottery. Philips managed to keep the hotel on the verge of disaster and full of maniacs for twenty-one episodes.

BIBLIOGRAPHY Novels: *The Cannibal Who Overate* (1962), *The Shape of Fear* (1964), *The Evil That Men Do* (1966), *The Golden Trap* (1967), *The Gilded Nightmare* (1968), *Girl Watcher's Funeral* (1969), *The Deadly Joke* (1971), *Birthday, Deathday* (1972), *Walking Dead Man* (1973), *Bargain with Death* (1974), *Death after Breakfast* (1978), *Random Killer* (1979), *Beware Young Lovers* (1980), *Murder in Luxury* (1981), *With Intent to Kill* (1982), *Murder in High Places* (1983), *Remember to Kill Me* (1984), *Nightmare Time* (1986), *Murder Goes Round and Round* (1989).

CHAN, CHARLIE Detective character created by Earl Derr BIGGERS. Chan is a Chinese American policeman working in Hawaii. When he first appears, in THE HOUSE WITHOUT A KEY (1925), he is a subordinate of the arrogant and impulsive Captain Hallet. Later he rises in rank and becomes such an eminence that he travels to other districts, such as California, to solve baffling cases.

Chan is a physical opposite of Dr. FU MANCHU, as well as being amiable and on the side of the law. Chan is rotund, almost cherubic, and a family man (he has eleven children), and is unlike the stereotypical lean, silent, and deadly Chinese of the period. His English is something else again; an attempt to get away from pidgin, but unrealistic and in some ways inept. Chan's dialogue is liberally sprinkled with long and specialized words, and he seems to have bypassed basic vocabulary altogether. Biggers's presentation of cultures and races is a far cry from what would be considered sensitive today, but then, it is also remote from the vicious caricatures of his own period. Biggers's appeal to his contemporaries was great; Rex STOUT said that he considered Chan one of the ten best fictional detectives.

As a detective, Chan describes his success as partly a result of "Oriental intuition," but he also subscribes to the "Scotland Yard" method of following the "one essential clue." One device used to maintain suspense is that a clue is made visible, but Chan does not discuss it until later.

Chan appears in only six books. The second novel is *The Chinese Parrot* (1926) and concerns the Phillimore pearls, a string worth $300,000. Through her friend Chan and the jeweler Alexander Eden, Evelyn Phillimore sells them to millionaire P. J. Madden. Trouble starts even before Chan gets off the boat in San Francisco; the participants feel that a crime has been committed, even though there is no trace of a victim. The first corpse to be found belongs to P. J. Madden's Chinese-speaking parrot. Bob Eden, the son of the jeweler, acts as Chan's WATSON in this case, and is much more puzzled by the case than is the reader.

Better in terms of its detection is *The Black Camel* (1929). Chan is back in Hawaii, investigating the murder of film star Shelah Fane, whose career is starting to fade. She is trying to decide whether to accept a millionaire's marriage proposal—with the help of her fortune teller—when she is murdered in her pavilion on Waikiki beach during a party. Among those present and under suspicion are her suitor, her ex-husband, her secretary and unofficially adopted daughter, and assorted actors. The cast of characters also includes a failed painter turned beachcomber. Assistance comes to Chan from an unlikely quarter—Tarneverro, the fortune teller. The solution is one of Chan's best.

Charlie Chan Carries On (1930) introduced an idea that was later used ad nauseam in the Charlie Chan films; the detective is on a cruise ship returning from an around-the-world voyage. *Behind That Curtain* (1928) uses the common mystery plot of two crimes widely separated in time and place (London and San Francisco). The clue, however, is unusual: pairs of Chinese slippers. *Keeper of the Keys* (1932), the last of the novels, is set in Lake Tahoe and deals with an opera singer. The novels were first serialized in the *Saturday Evening Post.*

CHANDLER, RAYMOND [THORNTON] (1888–1959) One of the acknowledged masters of the HARD-BOILED style, Chandler is perhaps the most famous American mystery writer. His work, however, is idiosyncratic, and stands apart from that of both Dashiell HAMMETT, who preceded him, and the many imitators who followed. Chandler was so widely and shamelessly copied that in once instance (the case of the author Raymond Marshall) his publisher brought a plagiarism suit and won.

Chandler was born in Chicago, but moved to England with his mother in 1895. He often remarked on the importance of the classical education he received in England to his development; he remained an Anglophile even though he did not return to England until the end of his life.

After studying in France and Germany, Chandler worked as a clerk in the Admiralty and embarked on a literary career in London, writing criticism, book reviews and poetry; he later spoke of these early efforts with deep sarcasm. Chandler returned to the United States and lived in California until 1917, when he joined the Canadian Army and served in France. Upon his return to California after the war he entered the oil business, rising to an executive position with the Dabney Oil Syndicate.

Chandler's career as a mystery author began after he was fired from his job for drinking. He had also fallen in love with a married woman much older than himself, and after she divorced they married. Living primarily on his savings, Chandler began to write, and sold his first story to BLACK MASK. Chandler later came to view these early stories as generally very poor; even THE BIG SLEEP (1939) he once said contained scenes that were "much too pulpy." It would be wrong, however, to say that Chandler aspired to be a serious novelist, since he felt contempt for most so-called serious fiction. What he wanted, instead, was to do something with the mystery story that had never been done before, to turn it into a vehicle for the kind of explorations found only in the most ambitious literature.

Chandler was an exacting critic, as is clear in his famous essay THE SIMPLE ART OF MURDER (1944). He thought that most mystery writing was bad, and referred to Rex STOUT, Ngaio MARSH, and Agatha CHRISTIE as "smooth and shallow operators." (His friend Erle Stanley GARDNER he considered hardly a writer at all, though he respected his work within the confines Gardner set for himself.) As a writer, Chandler had quite different goals, having little to do with the genre per se. Despising so-called significant literature that claimed to be important, and impatient of intellectual claptrap generally, he was interested instead in "the creation of emotion through dialogue and description" and the development of character. Chandler thought the writer should write from the "solar plexus," not from an intellectual agenda. He said that plot bored him, though he recognized that stories involving violence and murder held a central place in literature, probably because such extreme situations reveal character most nakedly. What Chandler had in mind was to say something about the human condition without *thinking* about saying something about the human condition.

Chandler was extremely interested in the American idiom, which because of his English upbringing he said he had to learn almost as a foreign language. His use of similes and lyrical phrasing is only the most obvious evidence of his preoccupation with style. He was a scriptwriter in Hollywood (Chandler worked on the screenplay for the film of James M. Cain's DOUBLE INDEMNITY (1943), though privately he despised Cain's writing), which helped him to think of the novel in terms of a series of scenes. Some works, however, use a more conventional narrative structure, such as *The Lady in the Lake* (1943), which is built around the familiar device of the two seemingly unrelated plot lines that turn out to be connected. This novel is more exactly plotted, and the relationships are much easier to spot, than in others of his works. Like many writers, Chandler was unable to take his own advice, and the later works especially contain more "philosophizing" than his critical strictures would allow. Although Chandler had no patience with the didactic novel in the proletarian mode, he has Philip MARLOWE say at the end of THE LONG GOODBYE (1953) that "We're a big rough rich wild people and crime is the price we pay for it, and organized crime is the price we pay for organization."

Selecting the best of the seven Chandler novels is a matter of opinion. *The High Window* (1942), however, is generally considered the weakest by authorities (including Chandler) but was selected as one of the hundred best mysteries of all time by H. R. F. KEATING. THE LITTLE SISTER (1949) has a similar lopsided reputation. *Playback* (1958) has been considered hardly a novel at all, because it reworks a story Chandler developed for a script (published only recently). Its very leanness, even emptiness, however, gives *Playback* a nihilistic feeling that shows Marlowe exiting the hard-boiled era and entering the rootless late fifties and early sixties.

After the death of his wife, Chandler became a wanderer, moving back and forth between England and the United States and feeling at home in neither. Frank MacShane's *The Life of Raymond Chandler* (1976) is almost documentary and shows each period of Chandler's life in detail. MacShane also edited *Selected Letters of Raymond Chandler* (1981). Chandler slaved over his letters and wrote several drafts; they are clever, intelligent, funny and often biting, but are deeply revealing of Chandler's personality. Tom Hiney's biography, *Raymond Chandler,* appeared in 1997.

CHANT DU MONDE, LE See THE SONG OF THE WORLD.

CHARABANC English expression for "motor coach," or bus. From French *char a bancs,* a coach with bench seats.

The Charabanc Mystery (1934) is a case of Desmond MERRION'S.

CHARLES, NICK AND NORA The most famous detecting married couple, the Charleses were created by Dashiell HAMMETT and appeared in only one book, THE THIN MAN (1933). The film version and its many sequels made the Charleses famous and boosted the careers of William Powell and Myrna Loy.

CHARTERIS, LESLIE (pen name of Leslie Charles Bowyer Yin, 1907–1993) While he was studying law, Charteris began reading books about burglary, and out of that study the idea of a RAFFLES-like "hero" evolved. The name of his hero was THE SAINT. Charteris said, "Sometimes when I hear fools complaining that life is dull, I want to advise them to knock their bank manager over the head and grab a handful of money and run." But the novels do not illustrate the real consequences of taking such advice.

Born in Singapore to an English mother and Chinese father, Charteris learned Chinese before he learned English. He became successful as a writer at an early age, which caused him to leave Cambridge University after only a year. Here was one author whose taste for adventure was not sated by fiction; Charteris at one time was a pearl diver, a bartender, and a policeman, as well as trying half a dozen other professions. The name Charteris, which he adopted in 1926, was that of a famous member of the HELL-FIRE CLUB. Charteris moved to the United States in 1932 and became a citizen in 1946; he worked in Hollywood during the time when the Saint movies were being made and enjoyed its glamour. By the time Roger Moore brought the Saint to television in 1962, the character had already appeared in almost a dozen films and been portrayed on radio by Vincent Price and others. Charteris was married four times, and returned to Europe at the end of his life.

Burl Barer won an EDGAR for his *The Saint: A Complete History* (1993).

CHARYN, JEROME (1937–) Born in New York City, the son of a furrier, Jerome Charyn now divides his time between New York and Paris. Charyn graduated from Columbia University and was for a number of years a professor of English at the City College of New York, and later taught in the creative writing program of Princeton University. He tries to make his crime novels more than just genre fiction; underlying his Isaac SIDEL stories is a pessimistic view of society and human nature, as well as a pervasive cynicism conceived as, or perhaps masquerading as, a philosophy. The realism of the contemporary novel is present in the use of sordid and gritty detail, but Charyn's work is on another artistic plane than simply showing the dirt of modern society. In Charyn, the HARD-BOILED school meets the *Professorenroman.*

In 1989, Charyn was made a Chevalier de l'Ordre des Artes et des Lettres. He has also won the Prix Alfred and the Rosenthal Award (American Academy and Institute of Arts and Letters).

CHASE, JAMES HADLEY (pseudonym of René Raymond, 1906—1985) Chase was a HARD-BOILED English mystery writer, a rare article in his time; unfortunately, he is also considered to have been an extremely bad writer. The only one of his books that today would evoke recognition, though not praise, is NO ORCHIDS FOR MISS BLANDISH (1939), which, appropriately, was made into one of the all-time worst films. As a book it was a bestseller, even though it was obviously modeled on William Faulkner's SANCTUARY (1931). It was also Chase's first book, and was followed by *Twelve Chinks and a Woman* (1940), the title of which indicates Chase's level of mind. He seems to have known little and cared less about the United States, beyond using it as an excuse for luridness, violence, and vulgarity. In the manner of Edgar WALLACE, he wrote the book in a matter of days, using an American slang dictionary.

Chase wrote dozens of other novels, and used other pseudonyms, including Raymond Marshall and Ambrose Grant. He jumped aboard various other bandwagons, including the CIA-agent THRILLER and the paramilitary subgenre. Under the name Marshall, he was sued for plagiarism by Raymond CHANDLER. Many of Chase's books continue to be reprinted in France.

CHEE, JIM Sergeant Jim Chee is one of the Navajo policemen who appears in novels by Tony HILLERMAN. Although Chee is studying to be a *yataalii* (a "singer," or what whites call a shaman), he also has an "intense" curiosity about all aspects of the white culture. Chee has attended the University of New Mexico and holds a degree in anthropology. All of these features allow Hillerman to work a great deal of discussion of Navajo and white culture into the stories, as in the novels about Joe LEAPHORN, with whom he is sometimes teamed (see below).

Chee first appears in *People of Darkness* (1980). The people referred to belong to what might be called an underground religion; arising in the late forties, they still use the drug peyote to achieve hallucinations. A court found that their peyote use was a legitimate rite, but mysterious events—for example, the theft of a box of "keepsakes" from the home of a wealthy white man—focus light on them once again. The murder method in this novel is extremely ingenious and subtly cruel. Chee's investigation of families in remote areas is vivid. In *The Dark Wind* (1982), Chee witnesses a plane crash while staking out a windmill that has been repeatedly vandalized. Another strange strand involves a corpse whose finger pads and foot soles have been cut off—pieces used in the preparation of "corpse powder." As well as witchcraft, the book deals with drug smuggling and intertribal politics between the Hopi and the Navajo (and the inept intercession of the Bureau of Indian Affairs).

THE GHOSTWAY (1984) is one of Chee's most complex cases, and also the one in which his conflict with his white girlfriend, Mary Landon, comes to a head when she forces him to chose between the two cultures. After this novel, Chee only appeared together with Leaphorn.

BIBLIOGRAPHY Novels (Chee and Leaphorn): *Skinwalkers* (1987), *A Thief of Time* (1988), *Talking God* (1989), *Coyote Waits* (1990), *Sacred Clowns* (1993), *The Fallen Man* (1997), *The First Eagle* (1998).

CHEEVER, JOHN See BULLET PARK.

"CHERCHEZ LA FEMME!" French phrase meaning "Look for the woman!" It was first used by Alexandre DUMAS in his novel *Les Mohicans de Paris* (1855).

CHESSMAN, CARYL See CAPITAL PUNISHMENT.

CHESTERTON, G[ILBERT] K[EITH] (1874–1936) A biographer, journalist, historian, and essayist known for his conservative Catholic philosophy, the English writer G. K. Chesterton may seem an unlikely giant of detective literature. Yet in Father BROWN he created one of the most lasting characters of the genre, and one who exemplified all of the Chestertonian qualities. Ellery QUEEN called Brown one of the three great detectives of all time (the others being HOLMES and DUPIN). If Rex STOUT was correct in saying that people who don't like mystery stories are anarchists, then in Chesterton's case love of the detective genre evinced a passion for order.

At the start of the new century, Chesterton began to make a name for himself as a polemicist with such books as *Heretics* (1905) and *Orthodoxy* (1908). Chesterton had always been politically conservative and a traditionalist, and these qualities would be accentuated after his 1922 conversion to Catholicism. He looked back fondly to the Victorian age and opposed some of the noted progressives and socialists of his era, including H. G. WELLS and George Bernard Shaw. His hostility to modernity was expressed in the title of *What's Wrong With the World?* (1910), and even permeates his detective stories. (At the beginning of his first mystery, he seems even to regret the invention of apartment buildings.) Among his friends he numbered Hilaire Belloc and E. C. BENTLEY; the former shared his conservative Catholicism while the latter did not. Bentley, of course, shared Chesterton's interest in the detective story, and succeeded Chesterton as the head of the DETECTION CLUB.

The detective priest Father Brown first appeared in 1911, and rapidly became famous. Father Brown was not, however, Chesterton's first sally as a mystery writer. THE MAN WHO WAS THURSDAY (1908) predates it, as do the stories concerning Rupert and Basil GRANT, Mr. TRAILL, and Horne Fisher. Chesterton published the collections THE CLUB OF QUEER TRADES (1905) and *The Man Who Knew Too Much* (1922); some of these mystery stories not about Father Brown are collected and reprinted in *Thirteen Detectives* (1987).

Chesterton's influential essay "A Defence of Detective Stories" dates from 1901, and reflects his interest in the medieval period: like AUDEN, he likens mystery fiction to quest literature and tales of chivalry. In his first story, however ("The Tremendous Adventure of Major Brown"), he seems most of all to be influenced by POE, even more than by Conan DOYLE. In quick succession, Major Brown has a series of bizarre and uncanny experiences: finding a plot of daisies, which he loves, spelling out "Death to Major Brown"; hearing a disembodied head renew the threat; and being grabbed by a giant pair of hands in a coal cellar. (The story could be said to look back to Poe, or, equally, ahead to the Kafka of "The Country Doctor.") Chesterton filled his detective stories with morals and maxims as he did his essays, such as that men with vague ideas become bullies when pressed, and that "a man will cheat in his trade but not in his hobby." Moral and political concerns are particularly obvious in the early stories. In "The Hole in the Wall," a murder story becomes an allegory of the dispossession of the Church during the Reformation; it also includes the symbolic Mr. BRAIN. In "The Bottomless Well," a story set in a colonial outpost in the desert with *Arabian Nights* overtones, the philosophical Horne Fisher is anti-jingoist but also is anti-Semitic. "The Garden of Smoke," with an opium-addicted artist, the exceptionally strange and memorable retired sea captain Fonblanque, the theosophist Miall, and the enigmatic Traill presents several philosophies of life at once.

CHEYNEY, [REGINALD EVELYN] PETER [SOUTHOUSE] (1896–1951) Peter Cheyney belongs with James Hadley CHASE and Sydney HORLER in that category of mystery writers who are more notorious than famous. Like Chase, Cheyney wrote HARD-BOILED mysteries in the style developed in the United States without knowing anything about that country, and wrote terrible pseudo-American dialogue, typified in the name of his first detective, Lemmy Caution ("let me caution"). He might have been better named Lemmy Atem; Cheyney gained a reputation for the cruelty and violence of his books. A supporter of the British fascist party before the war, he had ideas on a level with Horler's. Julian SYMONS said that Lemmy Caution was "the first 'good' man in crime fiction to torture for pleasure." Using the "kill the killers" formula, Cheyney justifies having the good guy perform horrible acts on an enemy because they are so evil they (supposedly) do not deserve any better. Cheyney's other detective of this period was Slim Callaghan, a London private eye. The author himself once ran a private eye agency, Cheyney Research Investigations, though the experience seems not to have made improvement in his books. During World War II, Cheyney wrote a series of novels with "black" in the title in which British agents battled the Axis forces.

Cheyney was born in London and was a lawyer. He was wounded at the Somme in World War I, and after the war became a hack journalist, short story writer, and songwriter. Perhaps the most remarkable thing about Cheyney was his success: he sold hundreds of thousands of books every year in England, France, and the United States. Like Chase, he was taken more seriously in France than in English-speaking countries (unfamiliarity or translation somehow screening his bathetic qualities); according to William DEANDREA, Jean-Luc Goddard used Lemmy Caution as the basis for *Alphaville* (1965). The original title of the film, *Tarzan versus IBM,* has a muddledness Cheyney would certainly have appreciated.

CHILDERS, ERSKINE (1870–1922) Anglo-Irish political activist, diplomat, and writer. THE RIDDLE OF THE SANDS (1903), his only novel, is considered the first modern spy novel (depending on one's definition of "modern"). It predates Joseph CONRAD's *The Secret Agent* (1907) and *Under Western Eyes* (1911). Despite its reputation as a spy novel, however, *The Riddle of the Sands* has more in common with the Victorian detective story, on which it is modeled, than later spy-genre "mysteries." It relies on deduction, characterization and wit rather than violence or the accoutrements of techno-suspense thrillers. Childers's writing is masterful, evocative, and technically accurate—not surprising, given that the author was an expert sailor who had sailed the waters of the Frisian coast and knew them intimately. Childers used his own boat to smuggle guns to the Irish during the failed Easter Rebellion of 1916.

Childers was born in London but grew up in Ireland. He fought on the British side in World War I, but then joined the Irish Republican Army. Along with Michael Collins, he was part of the group that negotiated the treaty that created the Irish Republic and resulted in the controversial partition of Ireland. Childers was executed by firing squad during the ensuing Irish Civil War.

CHILDREN A character in INTO THE NIGHT (1987) says, "there isn't anything on the face of this earth more hideous than child murder. Adult murder is a clean, upright thing by comparison." The most disturbing crime that can be treated in a mystery story, it is also the most dangerous from an authorial standpoint, in that it is difficult for the author to avoid seeming to exploit the reader's emotions. In many cases, unfortunately, the author *is* exploiting the reader in a sensational and offensive manner, for what is revolting is not necessarily moving. Many of the great mystery writers have avoided the subject, and some of the poorest have capitalized on it. It does not take much talent to write a story about a child being killed that grabs the reader by the throat. Some of the crudest pieces of writing dealing with crimes against children have been written by John GRISHAM, Jonathan KELLERMAN, and Dorothy UHNAK.

Some mysteries that involve child murders, however, are more disturbing than they are sensational, and explore the essential insanity of the act. Murder is usually committed for adult motives that children are supposed to be incapable of exciting. Among the books that deal seriously with this crime are Friedrich DÜRRENMATT's *The Pledge* (1959) and Gerald Kersh's PRELUDE TO A CERTAIN MIDNIGHT (1947). The death of a child occurs "offstage" and sets off a chain of events in Nicholas Blake's THE BEAST MUST DIE (1938). In Elizabeth DALY's *Deadly Nightshade* (1940), Henry GAMADGE is called in to investigate the poisoning of several children. In Tony HILLERMAN's *Dance Hall of the Dead* (1973), there is a twelve-year-old victim and a fourteen-year-old suspect. One of the most recent books to deal effectively with the theme is Peter Hoeg's SMILLA'S SENSE OF SNOW (1994). Theodore Weesner's THE TRUE DETECTIVE (1987) is a realistic novel about the abduction of a boy by a child molester. The haunting THE NIGHT OF THE HUNTER (1953), in which a nine-year-old boy and his younger sister are relentlessly pursued by a murderer, is also a meditation on the helplessness of children. Despite the title, James M. Cain's THE BABY IN THE ICEBOX is about a courageous rather than an abusive mother.

Many other mysteries feature children as prominent characters or, in juvenile literature, as detectives. Perhaps surprisingly, some of the major writers of children's stories have also written tales that are strictly not for bedtime. These mystery authors include A. A. MILNE (creator of Winnie the Pooh), Michael BOND (author of the Paddington Bear stories and Monsieur PAMPLEMOUSSE mysteries), Roald DAHL, Carolyn WELLS, and Michael DELVING (whose children's stories appear under his real name, Jay Williams). But most surprising of all is the fact that Mickey SPILLANE wrote two children's books.

CHILL, THE (1964) A novel by Ross MACDONALD, considered by many to be the best in the Lew ARCHER series. The author called it "that basilisk of a book," and it has one of the most twisted surprise endings of mystery fiction. It also has one of Macdonald's most memorable characters, Mrs. Bradshaw, the mother of Roy Bradshaw, a narcissistic, childish man who is dean of a college in Pacific Point, California. Archer is about to depart on a fishing trip when he is approached by a typical Macdonald character, a likeable, spoiled, and confused young man named Alex Kincaid, whose domineering father runs an oil company office in Long Beach. Kincaid's young wife, Dolly, has suddenly abandoned him during their honeymoon after being approached by an ex-con who thinks she might be his daughter. The scene in which Archer and Bradshaw meet is one of the best in the Archer series.

Dolly is soon found, enrolled under a false name at the local college where Bradshaw teaches; but that is only the beginning of an intergenerational tangle of murders and lies that stretches back to the killing of a police lieutenant twenty-two years before in Illinois. Macdonald said of *The Chill* that it was "perhaps one of the stronger single plot ideas that ever came to me." Its numerous pieces are easy to get hold of but hard to fit together, though in the end the fit is perfect, almost too much so. Although there is no central figure—other than Archer himself—who is as sympathetic and compelling as the protagonists of *The Doomsters* (1958) or *Black Money* (1966), *The Chill* stands out for its plot and perfection of the Macdonald style.

CHINESE BELL MURDERS, THE (1951) The first of the Judge DEE mysteries, written in Tokyo in 1950 by Robert VAN GULIK. It is one of the novels most closely tied to Chinese models, and also the longest. The prefatory story, told by a later narrator (also fictional), describes his discovery of Judge Dee's mirror and ceremonial cap; when he puts it on, he is overcome by visions of violence and death.

Judge Dee has just arrived in Poo-yang (magistrates were moved every three years) and takes up the pending case of the rape and murder of a young woman, Pure Jade, who had been having an illicit affair with a student. In accordance with Chinese practice, the student has been tortured but has refused to confess. At the same time, Judge Dee investigates two other cases. One concerns a temple of Buddhist monks who are reputed to be very rich and to spend their time drinking, eating meat, and entertaining themselves. The third case is of a family feud, and involves the motif of the Chinese bell. The realistic tribunal scenes include the execution of the grisly sentences meted out to the culprits.

CHINESE NAIL MURDERS, THE (1957) One of the later cases of Judge DEE. Robert VAN GULIK based the book on more than one documented Chinese case, including an example of the "nail murder," which was "one of the most famous motifs in Chinese crime literature."

Judge Dee has been sent to the frigid northern city of Pei-chow. It is twelve years since he made Hoong a sergeant, and nine since he took on Tao Gan, the former crook (in *The Chinese Lake Murders* [1953]); both men are now elderly and suffering in the cold. Into this straightened atmosphere erupts a bold series of murders, beginning with the discovery of the bloody headless corpse of the wife of a dealer in antiques. The dealer himself has left town. As more murders occur, the town gets in an uproar, and Dee is brought under pressure to find the culprit or be discharged. The minor characters, such as the ascetic boxing instructor, are especially interesting. Ingeniously, one of the clues is the "Seven Board," a series of seven paper triangles that can be combined to depict almost any scene. The nail murder was included in the first Chinese case that Van Gulik translated, *De Goong An* (1949), and this novel has a particular wealth of detail.

CHISELER "To chisel" is a verb of Scottish origin meaning to cheat, to gain by fraud or mooching. In English, the word dates from the beginning of the nineteenth century.

CHITTERWICK, AMBROSE See DETECTION CLUB.

CHLORAL HYDRATE See MICKEY FINN.

CHLOROFORM One of the most widely used anaesthetic agents in the nineteenth century, chloroform has been abandoned because of its dangers and side effects, including cirrhosis of the liver. Chloroform (trichloromethane) is a hydrocarbon and is used in industry as a chemical solvent. Its depressive effect on the central nervous system led to its introduction as a surgical anaethestic in 1847. Overdoses of chloroform can cause not only severe organ damage, but death—as in the most famous thriller of the nineteenth century, THE MYSTERY OF A HANSOM CAB (1886). The book was published, interestingly, at the time of the trial of Adelaide BARTLETT, who was accused of killing her husband using chloroform.

CHRISTIE, AGATHA (1890–1976) Probably the best-known mystery writer of all time (Conan DOYLE being less famous than his creation), Agatha Christie has been translated more than any other author in English. She wrote more than eighty novels, most of them featuring either Hercule POIROT or Miss Jane MARPLE.

Her most highly regarded books are THE MURDER OF ROGER ACKROYD (1926), MURDER ON THE ORIENT EXPRESS (1934), AND THEN THERE WERE NONE (1940), and "The Mousetrap," which became the longest-running play in history. She left behind two books to be published posthumously, in which she did away with her two famous detectives. Her vast output includes books on every popular mystery subject, from ART and ARCHAEOLOGY to GOLF and MURDER AFLOAT.

Born Agatha Mary Clarissa Miller in England, Christie was the daughter of an American father and an English mother. Her father died when she was still a child. Christie was raised by her mother, who encouraged her talents, even sending her to Paris for voice training. Christie married Colonel Archibald Christie in 1914. During World War I, she was a volunteer nurse, an experience that gave her a working knowledge of medicine and drugs (poisons were to be a favorite murder device in her fiction). It was also during the war that she began writing detective stories; earlier, she had written poetry. Her first novel featuring Poirot, THE MYSTERIOUS AFFAIR AT STYLES, was published in 1920, but her first great success was *The Murder of Roger Ackroyd* (1926), partly because of the debate over her "trick" ending.

Christie was herself the object of a mystery that same year; her car was found in Surrey abandoned by the roadside. She was missing for eleven days. Christie had checked into a hotel under the name of her husband's mistress, apparently following some kind of breakdown upon learning of her husband's infidelity (Christie was a religious woman). This episode in Christie's life is the subject of *The Lost Days of Agatha Christie* (1995), a novel by a licensed therapist, Carole Owens, in which Christie is referred to an American psychotherapist for treatment of her "amnesia" about her disappearance.

Two years after her disappearance, Christie was divorced from her unfaithful husband, and two years after that she married Sir Max Mallowan, an archaeologist whom she had met in Egypt. She visited the Middle East many times and assisted Mallowan at the archaeological digs, and used the Middle Eastern setting as a background for several mysteries, including the HISTORICAL MYSTERY *Death Comes as the End* (1944). Christie was a member of the DETECTION CLUB and became its president in 1954.

Despite the pre-eminence of Poirot and Marple, Christie experimented with other series characters and with other genres. She wrote six romantic novels under the name Mary Westmacott, a psychological THRILLER (*Endless Night*, 1967), detective short stories about Parker Pyne, and novels about Tuppence and Tommy BERESFORD that sometimes included espionage. One of her stranger creations features in THE MYSTERIOUS MISTER QUIN (1930).

Christie's protagonists tend to be members of the upper classes, and the supporting characters include the usual fawning or gruff tradesmen, grumpy or sniveling servants, and all the other stock figures of the COUNTRY HOUSE and GOLDEN AGE mystery. Her strength was not character but plot; hers are some of the most finely constructed puzzlers in the genre. Ingenuity and realism tend to be inversely proportional, and Christie has been criticized by such authors as Edmund WILSON and Raymond CHANDLER for the unreality of her characters, their actions, and the world they live in. But Christie was not trying to create a skillful whodunit *and* write a novel about the way people live, or to explore character and deep emotions. She once said "Murder has no emotional connotation for me," which may explain why she was so good at creating fictional murder puzzles, applying to the writing of the murder story the same purely "analytical" approach that detectives like Sherlock HOLMES were supposed to use in unraveling them.

Among the many books about Christie are her own *An Autobiography* (1977), *A Talent to Deceive* (1980), by Robert BARNARD, and *Agatha Christie: A Biography* (1984), by Janet Morgan. *The Agatha Christie Companion* (1984) and *The New Bedside, Bathtub & Armchair Companion to Agatha Christie* (1979; rev 1986) are two source books including biographical data, plot summaries, trivia, interpretations, and appreciations of Christie.

CHRISTOPHER, PAUL See MCCARRY, CHARLES.

CHUMP Now considered very *au courant,* this term for a stupid person or someone easily gulled may date from the seventeenth or eighteenth century, when it meant a block of wood, and was used to imply stupidity in the same manner as "blockhead."

CIRCULAR STAIRCASE, THE (1909) A novel by Mary Roberts RINEHART, in which she supposedly invented the HAD-I-BUT-KNOWN genre. The story has elements of the COUNTRY HOUSE type and of the classic form of the mystery, and involves such devices as disguises, hidden rooms, mantelpieces that slide aside and GOTHIC touches. Some of the characters are stock figures of nineteenth-century romance, such as the superstitious black servant and the faithful maid and companion to the heroine.

Rachel Innes, an aging spinster, rents a house on the New England coast, an imposing old pile owned by the Armstrong family. After she moves in, she finds out the "cottage" is haunted. Rachel wakes up at night hearing loud noises, but instead of a ghost she finds the body of the owner's son Arnold shot dead at the foot of the staircase. It turns out that he has been embezzling from the Armstrong family bank. The house continues to be the focus of the mystery; there are four more deaths and an exciting chase at the end. Rachel finds that her life is invigorated by the horrifying events, and she concludes that she never really lived before this experience.

In terms of her style, Rinehart is not yet out of the nineteenth century and has not reached the maturity exemplified by THE STATE VERSUS ELINOR NORTON (1934).

CLACK, MISS DRUSILLA The niece of Sir John Verinder in Wilkie Collins's THE MOONSTONE (1868). A prim, opinionated distributor of tracts, Miss Clack thinks the worst of everyone. She resents being asked to contribute her narrative to the "deplorable scandal" of the Moonstone, and also the offer of payment (which she accepts). Her narrative occupies the middle of the book and is a comic satire, though it contains important information as well.

CLANCY, LIEUTENANT A detective in a series by Robert L. FISH but published under the transparent pseudonym Robert L. Pike. The Clancy books are yet another example of the PROCEDURAL boom of the sixties. What is most notable about the series is that the first book, *Mute Witness* (1963), became the very successful film *Bullitt* (1968). By that time, the series was already over, Fish having written the last Clancy novel in 1965; however, after the success of the film, Clancy was reborn as the San Francisco detective Jim Reardon.

BIBLIOGRAPHY Novels: *The Quarry* (1964), *Police Blotter* (1965).

CLANCY, PETER A private detective in a long series of novels by Lee THAYER. Clancy is a typical GOLDEN AGE detective and even has an English valet named Wiggar, but the stories are set in New York City, where the author lived. One of the longest mystery series ever written, it is now all but unknown.

BIBLIOGRAPHY Novels: *The Mystery on the Thirteenth Floor* (1919), *The Unlatched Door* (1920), *The Affair at "The Cedars"* (1921), *Q.E.D.* (1922; British title *The Puzzle*), *The Sinister Mark* (1923), *The Key* (1924), *Poison* (1926), *Alias Dr. Ely* (1927), *The Darkest Spot* (1928), *Dead Man's Shoes* (1929), *They Tell No Tales* (1930), *The Last Shot* (1931), *Set a Thief* (1931; British title *To Catch a Thief*), *The Glass Knife* (1932), *The Scrimshaw Millions* (1932), *Counterfeit* (1933; British title *The Counterfeit Bill*), *Hell-Gate Tides* (1933), *The Second Bullet* (1934; British title *The Second Shot*), *Dead Storage* (1935; British title *The Death Weed*), *Sudden Death* (1935; British title *Red-Handed*), *Dark of the Moon* (1937; British title *Death in the Gorge*), *Dead End Street, No Outlet* (1936, British title *Murder in the Mirror*), *Last Trump* (1937), *A Man's Enemies* (1937; British title *This Man's Down*), *Ransom Racket* (1938), *That Strange Sylvester Affair* (1938), *Lightening Strikes Twice* (1939), *Stark Murder* (1939), *Guilty* (1940), *X Marks the Spot* (1940), *Hallowe'en Homicide* (1941), *Persons Unknown* (1941), *Murder Is Out* (1942), *Murder on Location* (1942), *Accessory After the Fact* (1943), *Hanging's Too Good* (1943), *A Plain Case of Murder* (1944), *Five Bullets* (1944), *Accident, Manslaughter, or Murder?* (1945), *A Hair's Breadth* (1946), *The Jaws of Death* (1946), *Murder Stalks the Circle* (1947), *Out, Brief Candle!* (1948), *Pig in a Poke* (1948; British title *A Clue for Clancy*), *Evil Root* (1949), *Within the Vault* (1950; British title *Death within the Vault*), *Too Long Endured* (1950), *Do Not Disturb* (1951; British title *Clancy's Secret Mission*), *Guilt Edged* (1951), *Blood on the Knight* (1952), *The Prisoner Pleads "Not Guilty"* (1953), *Dead Reckoning* (1954; British title *Murder on the Pacific*), *No Holiday for Death* (1954), *Who Benefits?* (1955; British title *Fatal Alibi*), *Guilt Is Where You Find It* (1957), *Still No Answer* (1958; British title *Web of Hate*), *Two Ways to Die* (1959), *Dead on Arrival* (1960), *And One Cried Murder* (1961), *Dusty Death* (1966; British title *Death Walks in Shadow*).

CLARK, DOUGLAS [MALCOLM JACKSON] (1919–1993) The English author Douglas Clark is best known for his stories of poisoning, running to more than two dozen novels. The reason behind his predilection for poisoning cases is that, after serving in World War II, Clark went to work for a pharmaceutical company. He introduced the series detectives George MASTERS and Bill Green in *Nobody's Perfect* (1969).

Clark's writing is awkward and even clumsy. The stories are old-fashioned, showing people interacting in the present in the roles of fifty years before (the sexism is also a problem). His expert knowledge and ability to create puzzles make some of his books worth reading. In *Premedicated Murder* (1975), Masters and Green work with two sergeants, Hill and Brant. It is an unhappy team, however, because Masters and Green are truly tired of each other. All four of the quartet would like to escape, but they are kept together because they are so successful. Clark favors unusual poisons, and in this case the murder is effected with RICIN. He also uses elements of the LOCKED ROOM mystery. In *Plain Sailing* (1987), Clark again constructs a plot in which someone seems to be poisoned in an impossible way. But in this case, it is a fast-acting poison (CYANIDE), and it seems the victim had no opportunity to take it before his death. At this point in the series Masters has become detective chief superintendent, outranking Green even though he is younger. The pair, however, have mended their fences and are friends. The victim is the son of another police officer in a northern town near where Masters and Green are vacationing.

The Clark series is the English mystery at its most orthodox; as in the novels of John RHODE, character and writing fall far behind the puzzle element. Interestingly, Masters and Green are contemporaneous with another English police pair, WEXFORD and Burden; in terms of mentality, however, they might be living in different countries. Clark and Ruth RENDELL are worlds apart in what they are trying to do with the mystery, Rendell responding to the postwar movement toward realism and psychology, Clark continuing on in the GOLDEN AGE tradition.

CLARK, MARY HIGGINS (1929–) The American mystery author Mary Higgins Clark did not begin publishing novels until middle age, but she has since become a leading, if not the leading, writer of suspense novels. Her first novel, *Where Are the Children?* (1975), set the pattern: plots often involving CHILDREN, in this case two children living on Cape Cod who are kidnapped. Their mother had previously been suspected of murdering two children, and the kidnapper is trying to frame her. Clark based the book on a real case. Her novels are carefully researched; one of her assistants was her daughter, Carol Higgins Clark, who later went on to write a series about a Los Angeles private detective named Regan Reilly, beginning with *Decked* (1992).

Clark has also published short stories, collected in *The Anastasia Syndrome and Other Stories* (1990).

CLAY, COLONEL The first—or almost first—"rogue" or "gentleman thief" character in mystery fiction, a type that became famous through the RAFFLES stories. Unlike Raffles, Colonel Clay appears in only one book, *An African Millionaire* (1897), the best-known work of British-Canadian author and doctor Grant ALLEN. Colonel Clay also only has one victim, Sir Charles Vandrift, whom the colonel is able to swindle and rob time and time again owing to his talent for disguise.

Slightly before the publication of Allen's novel about Clay, Guy BOOTHBY had introduced in a series of stories a similar character, Simon CARNE.

CLEEK, HAMILTON A thief and nobleman in a series of stories begun by Thomas W. HANSHEW and carried on by his wife and daughter. Hanshew's stories about the villain were collected in *The Man of the Forty Faces* (1910; rev 1913). Cleek's features are so mobile that he can alter his appearance just by assuming an expression, without using the usual trappings of disguise. Later in his career, he uses his talents in the service of justice. Subplots in the series involve his love affair with a woman named Ailsa and his rejection of the throne of the fictional kingdom of Maurevania. Hanshew also wrote several novels. After his death, his wife Mary and his daughter Hazel Phillips Hanshew continued the series under the name of T. W. Hanshew as well as their own. The last two books were written by H. P. Hanshew alone.

BIBLIOGRAPHY Novels: By Thomas Hanshew—*Cleek of Scotland Yard* (1914), *Cleek's Greatest Riddles* (1916; U.S. title *Cleek's Government Cases*). By Mary E. Hanshew and Hazel Phillips Hanshew—*The Riddle of the Night* (1915), *The Riddle of the Purple Emperor* (1918), *The Frozen Flame* (1920), *The Riddle of the Mysterious Light* (1921), *The House of Discord* (1922; U.S. title *The Riddle of the Spinning Wheel*), *The Amber Junk* (1924; U.S. title *The Riddle of the Amber Ship*), *The House of the Seven Keys* (1925), *Murder in the Hotel* (1931), *The Riddle of the Winged Death* (1932).

CLEMENS, SAMUEL LANGHORNE See TWAIN, MARK.

CLEMONS, FRANK A policeman in a series of novels by Thomas H. COOK. Clemons starts out as an Atlanta cop and later moves to New York City. The first book, *Sacrificial Ground* (1988), was nominated for an EDGAR award. *Streets of Fire* (1989), set in 1963, is about the murder of a black girl in Birmingham, Alabama, against the backdrop of Martin Luther King's movement. In *Flesh and Blood* (1989), Clemons has quit the Atlanta force and set up shop as a private investigator in New York. This case focuses on the murder of a clothing designer, and allows Cook to plunge into the corruption and competition of the garment industry. As often in his novels, the author develops sociological and historical themes, in this instance those of the Lower East Side of the thirties, with its sweatshops and labor battles, depicting the Jewish community and the subtext of racism. *Night Secrets* (1990) is about the Puri Dai, a kind of gypsy demi-goddess, and probes another New York subculture.

CLIMPSON, MISS A secondary series character in some of the mysteries by Dorothy L. SAYERS. Miss Katharine Climpson is an elderly spinster, but beneath her dowdy and comical exterior she is highly moral and extremely tough. She runs a typing bureau funded by Lord Peter WIMSEY; he calls it his "Cattery." The other employees are widows, spinsters, deserted wives and other women who appear helpless, but actually are not: the typing business is a cover for an investigation bureau. The women answer matrimonial advertisements and other ruses employed by men to trap unsuspecting women and rob them of their income. Miss Climpson has a "direct line" to SCOTLAND YARD, and the male customers of the bureau are often charged with fraud, blackmail and other crimes. Miss Climpson first appears in *Unnatural Death* (1927; orig title *The Dawson Pedigree*), and has her day in the sun in STRONG POISON (1930).

CLOACA-AND-DAGGER SCHOOL A term coined by Ross MACDONALD in a 1953 essay, "The Scene of the Crime." He used the term to describe the lowest form of popular literature—implicity, work that is sensational and dependent on gore and vulgarity for its effect.

CLOUDS OF WITNESS (1927) Dorothy L. SAYERS's second mystery novel about Lord Peter WIMSEY, in which he is called upon to defend his older brother Gerald, the Duke of Denver. Several of his other relatives, including his mother the Dowager and his sister Lady Mary, also enter into the story.

Wimsey is in France when BUNTER sees the headline that says the Duke of Denver has been arrested for murder. After going for a stroll, the duke found the body of Denis Cathcart, who had been betrothed to Lady Mary. The Duke refuses to put up a defense, which leads Wimsey to believe some matter of honor is at stake. The investigation is complicated by his brother's silence, and Wimsey himself is in peril. Clues, quicksand, and crotchety rustics are well done, and there is an unusual trial in the House of Lords. Sayers also takes advantage of Lindberg's famous solo trans-Atlantic flight and the first passenger flight, which took place three weeks later.

CLUBFOOT See WILLIAMS, VALENTINE.

CLUB OF QUEER TRADES, THE The title both of a book by G. K. CHESTERTON (1905; repr 1987) and of a strange organization in the story "The Tremendous Adventure of Major Brown." The stories in the book feature Rupert and Basil GRANT. Chesterton was writing under the long shadow of Conan DOYLE, and The Club of Queer Trades must have been inspired by the still more improbable Red Headed League (q.v). To be a member of the club, one must have invented a new kind of trade and be making a living at it. *The Club of Queer Trades* was reprinted in 1987 with the original illustrations, in the *Punch* style, by Chesterton himself.

CLUES Clues, in contradistinction to hunches, are the fictional detective's bread and butter. As the ratio of clues to hunches goes down, so does the believability of the mystery. A subset of course is the false clue, or RED HERRING, a preponderance of which is exasperating to the reader. Real police are naturally confronted with lots of useless information; but, because art is not life, what in reality would be the discovery of the irrelevant in fiction is construed as an attempt to mislead the reader.

Clues come in three main varieties: an object, a piece of information, or an act seen or described. In real detective work, the last category is the most common and useful—most crimes in which the perpetrator is not obvious are solved by tips from informants (known to their companions as STOOLIES). But because of the demands of fiction, it is not considered very entertaining—or sporting—for the detective to simply be told by someone who the culprit is—even in the PROCEDURAL. Anyone who knows who the killer is also gets killed, usually just after it becomes apparent that they have discovered the murderer's identity.

Because there is so little variation in the way clues are deployed in mystery fiction, great ingenuity has been used in the *choice* of clues. Clues change with the times; monogrammed cigarette cases left at the scene of the crime were once allowed, but would hardly be tolerated in a contemporary mystery. The current fad of the believable points up the fundamental contradiction at the heart of the mystery genre: the reader wants to be given an entertaining fiction, but also wants it to be rooted in the real world.

Some bizarre clues have been used in mysteries, including clues that weren't there, such as the famous "dog that didn't bark," encountered by Sherlock HOLMES in the story "Silver Blaze" (1892); a missing hat in THE ROMAN HAT MYSTERY (1929) as well as in THE GLASS KEY (1931); and a missing toupé and false teeth in THE BENSON MURDER CASE (1926). Sherlock Holmes stumbled on rather a lot of weird odds and ends, including the strange hieroglyphs in "The Adventure of the Dancing Men" (1903) DOYLE's contemporaries also excelled at the strange clue. In Rider HAGGARD's "Mr. Meeson's Will" (1904), for lack of the usual paper, the object in question is tattooed onto a woman's back. In THE CASK (1920), a barrel supposed to contain wine instead holds sawdust, gold, and a woman's hand. Major Brown, in an early story by CHESTERTON, is shocked to discover a bed of pansies spelling out a death threat. In "The Tea Leaf" (see Robert EUSTACE), a leaf is found deeply imbedded in a stab wound. Most bizarre were the papyrus scrolls smelling of honey and engraved with a picture of a man and woman sitting on a bench, found in the mouths of thousands of suicides in an adventure of Prince ZALESKY.

After Holmes, the GENIUS DETECTIVE survived as a figure for several decades, but there was a trend toward greater and greater realism, which has reached its height in the procedural. Strange pieces of evidence, however, continue to turn up. Gavin STEVENS makes much of a brass box filled with smoke in *Knight's Gambit* (1949). In Ross MACDONALD's story "The Bearded Lady," a moustache painted on a woman's portrait turns out to be a subtle psychological clue. The Ellery QUEEN stories often feature odd items; a red checker is found on the ground next to a headless corpse in THE EGYPTIAN CROSS MYSTERY (1932), and in *The Origin of Evil* (1951), the jeweler Leander Hill receives a dead dog in the mail. Severed body parts are common—for example, the finger sent in the mail in one of Margaret MILLAR's mysteries—and animals are useful not only dead, but alive. Birds, the only animals that can talk besides humans, may also "sing," for example in Erle Stanley GARDNER's *Crows Can't Count* (1946) and Nicholas Freeling's BECAUSE OF THE CATS (1963). One of Gardner's better clues is a wad of gum with diamonds embedded in it (in THE CASE OF THE TERRIFIED TYPIST, 1956). Leo Bruce's Inspector BEEF makes a subtle deduction from evidence in "The Clue in the Mustard" (the story is not, however, a throwback to THE TWO BOTTLES OF RELISH). Captain DA SILVA finds a radioactive shoe with a severed foot inside it. The oddest use of evidence, perhaps, is when Sergeant ZONDI identifies a killer from his prepuce cover in James MCCLURE's *The Blood of an Englishman* (1980). Anthony BOUCHER called the fly on a knife handle in Helen McCloy's CUE FOR MURDER (1942) "one of the cleverest and most imaginative clues in fiction."

The disclosure of clues in the whodunit sometimes seems to require that the criminal be unconscionably stupid; in a novel by Frank GRUBER, a bank robber who is buying Frankenstein masks to be used in a CAPER charges them to his hotel room rather than paying cash. Before we become exasperated with such lack of realism, however, we would do well to remember the bombing of the World Trade Center in New York City in 1994 and the fact that the bombers were caught because they tried to get back their deposit on the rental van they had exploded under the building.

CLUNK, JOSHUA An unpleasant character created by H. C. BAILEY in the tradition of Roger SHERINGHAM (though perhaps not so deliberately). The arrogant Clunk is described as "fond of himself as a cat with two tails." Clunk is a lawyer, and is also a consummate hypocrite; he sings hymns in his office and affects piety, but he can also definitely be bought, whether by criminals or by normal clients. His appearance is Dickensian: sallow, fat, short, and gray haired, he is a stereotypical slimy lawyer. Unlike Bailey's other series character, the amiable Mr. FORTUNE, Joshua Clunk appears only in novels (Clunk is like a Mr. Fortune who has gone sour). There are also two cases in which Clunk and Fortune work together, *The Great Game* (1939) and *The Wrong Man* (1944). Clunk is not evil enough to be really disturbing, and his predictability makes him tiresome.

BIBLIOGRAPHY Novels: *Garstons* (1930; U.S. title *The Garston Murder Case*), *The Red Castle* (1932; U.S. title *The Red Castle Mystery*), *The Sullen Sky Mystery* (1935), *Clunk's Claimant* (1937; U.S. title *The Twittering Bird Mystery*), *The Veron Mystery* (1939; U.S. title *Mr. Clunk's Text*), *The Little Captain* (1939; U.S. title *Orphan Ann*), *Dead Man's Shoes* (1942; U.S. title *Nobody's Vineyard*), *Slippery Ann* (1944; U.S. title *The Queen of Spades*), *Honour Among Thieves* (1947), *Shrouded Death* (1950).

COAT OF VARNISH, A (1979) The last novel by English novelist C. P. SNOW, the book was only his second mystery and was nominated for an EDGAR award. The murder is set in Belgravia, a London neighborhood whose upper-class, insular character Snow makes a forceful presence in the book. Humphrey Leigh is a retired spy who has cordial but fairly cold relations with his fashionable, well-to-do, and universally unhappy neighbors—until one of them is brutally murdered. Suddenly his rather dull circle of jaded, genteel acquaintances becomes more interesting, as each is a potential suspect.

As an amateur detective, Leigh is methodical if not desultory in his investigations; the book is structured less by his deduction than his relationships, particularly with Detective Chief Superintendent Frank Briers, a former protege, and with Kate Lefroy, an intelligent woman trapped in a marriage with a pathetic man who fancies himself a genius. Briers's investigation is like a PROCEDURAL novel interwoven with Snow's attentive and cumulatively compelling depictions of character—from weak and spoiled aristocrats to the powerful but socially insecure politicians who have replaced them. The world hidden by the coat of varnish turns out to be more repulsive than the crime.

COCKRILL, INSPECTOR A detective created by Christianna BRAND. Like his contemporary, Alan GRANT, Cockrill appeared in relatively few books and never achieved the brand recognition of the detectives of Agatha CHRISTIE, Margery ALLINGHAM, or Ngaio MARSH. In his shabby hat and battered overcoat, "Cockie" is an outwardly comical figure. Old and "brown," he chain smokes and grumbles through a series of novels. His suspects are sometimes personal friends, and he seems to be well known in Kent. Yet Cockrill can be nasty as well as nice, depending on how the mood strikes him. His second case, GREEN FOR DANGER (1944), is considered one of the best mysteries of all time, and is set in a hospital during World War II. *London Particular* (1953; U.S. title *Fog of Doubt*) also has a medical background. Cockrill is called to London to investigate the murder of one Raoul Vernet with a doctor's mastoid mallet. Vernet had been keeping an eye on young Rosie Evans in Switzerland; he turns up in London (and then turns up dead) while she is there on vacation. It emerges that he is the old flame of Rosie's sister-in-law, Matilda, and that the mallet belonged to Rosie's brother, Thomas, a doctor. Rosie is pregnant by a mysterious lover; two other men are in love with her, and one of them, a doctor who is in practice with Thomas, writes her a prescription for an abortifacient.

In *Tour de Force* (1955), Inspector Cockrill is a reluctant member of a guided trip to Italy. The rest of the group includes a middle-aged lady from Park Lane, very shy and gray, always tightly clasping her handbag under her chin; a famous London couturier who is gay, elegant, and effeminate; a once-famous pianist who lost his arm falling from a bicycle, and his wife; and the guide, a smiling, tanned, romantic, middle-aged man from Gibraltar. After one of the tourists is stabbed, Cockie is arrested as main suspect; the corrupt local police fail to find the real culprit, and then the Grand Duc of the island they are visiting intervenes, demanding a scapegoat in exchange for allowing the others to leave the island. The solution is dreadful since the law provides for hanging criminals or letting them die in the local prison, which dates back to the Middle Ages.

BIBLIOGRAPHY Novels: *Heads You Lose* (1941), *Suddenly at His Residence* (1946; U.S. title *The Crooked Wreath*), *Death of a Jezebel* (1948).

COFFIN, INSPECTOR JOHN The main figure in a series of books by Gwendoline BUTLER. Coffin has not received the praise that Butler's other series detective, Charmian DANIELS, has received. As far as PROCEDURALS go, the Coffin novels are rather staid, and Coffin himself is far from gripping. He is a policeman in London but is dispatched occasionally to other locations to enliven his investigations, for example in *Coffin in Malta* (1964) and DEATH LIVES NEXT DOOR (1960; U.S. title *Dine and Be Dead*). The latter takes place in Oxford, a setting the author knew well and revisited in other books. The Coffin series seemed almost to die out in the seventies, but there was a resurgence in the late eighties and nineties, introducing a "new" Coffin. *Coffin Underground* (1988) is set in the period when Coffin is still in charge of the Tactical Activity Squad. A house near his home in Church Row has historically been the scene of violence; in the latest incident, three students disappear without a trace, except for blood copiously splashed around the inside of the house. Another plot involves an ex-con who threatens Coffin.

Like the Daniels mysteries, the later Coffin novels sometimes read like COZY-procedurals. Coffin lives in St. Luke's Mansions in the tower of a converted church, and is preparing his "mad" mother's diaries for publication. He had been brought up by his aunt and grandmother and was told his parents were dead, but in fact his mother had many love affairs and he finds he has siblings in Scotland, New York, and god knows where else. He is tall, graying, and blue-eyed. His sister Laetitia, who runs a theater, was the developer who converted the church. Another recurrent character is the temperamental actress Stella Pinero, Coffin's sometime lover and, later, wife.

After hearing a speech by Lord David Owen, Butler got the idea of setting a series in a "Second City" of London made up of old boroughs. Coffin becomes Chief Commander of this New City Force. His beat includes the rough Docklands area. *Coffin on Murder Street* (1992) starts with the disappearance of a tourist bus on a "Terror Tour" of sites of crimes. There is also a child murderer in the area, and a grisly discovery of a severed hand is made. Butler is fond of such easy sensationalism. Jeremy Kay, one of Coffin's assistants, is the father of a boy murdered by other six-year-olds while playing. In *Cracking Open A Coffin* (1992), two students disappear, one of whom is the daughter of Coffin's former partner. A subplot involves a woman's shelter protected by a female gang leader. *The Coffin Tree* (1994) is about the mysterious death of two policemen who had been investigating money laundering in the City. Coffin comes in contact with one of his old lovers, now in charge of a new police unit.

BIBLIOGRAPHY Novels: *The Dull Dead* (1958), *The Murdering Kind* (1958), *Make Me a Murderer* (1961), *Coffin in Oxford* (1962), *Coffin for Baby* (1963), *Coffin Waiting* (1964), *A Nameless Coffin* (1966), *Coffin's Following* (1968), *Coffin's Dark Number* (1969), *A Coffin from the Past* (1970), *A Coffin for the Canary* (1974), *Coffin on the Water* (1986), *Coffin in Fashion* (1987), *Coffin in the Black Museum* (1989), *Coffin and the Paper Man* (1990), *A Dark Coffin* (1995).

COFFIN FOR DIMITRIOS, A (1939; orig title *The Mask of Dimitrios*) A novel by Eric AMBLER, considered one of the classics of spy fiction, but with a strong element of mystery. The "detective," Charles Latimer, is not a detective at all but a writer of mystery fiction who happens to be in Istanbul as the story opens. He stumbles into the matter of an apparent murder of a notorious international criminal, Dimitrios Makropoulos, known to the police of several Balkan countries and at various times involved in murder, white slavery, drug trafficking, espionage and political assassination. Latimer begins investigating the interesting life and murky past of the dead man, a trail beginning in Greece and Turkey fifteen years before. The trail gets warmer and warmer as Latimer encounters a series of people on both sides of the law who had been victims or accomplices of Dimitrios. When the major revelation comes, Latimer finds himself way over his head. Blackmail, shootouts, and changes of scene from the Balkans to Greece to Paris—the mystery proves to be far more exciting than anything Latimer himself could dream up.

COHEN, OCTAVUS ROY (1891–1959) Born in Charleston, South Carolinian Octavus Roy Cohen created one of the most popular "humorous detectives" of the early century, Florian Slappey. Cohen had a legal background, but the main inspiration for the Slappey stories seems to have been the Southern folkloric style (Cohen later wrote for the *Amos n' Andy* radio program).

Once considered very funny, the Slappey stories now seem very unfunny. Slappey is transparently based on the racist stereotypes of the minstrel shows, particularly the dandy figure who was supposed to illustrate the absurdities of black pretenses to education and culture. Florian is a private detective in Birmingham, Alabama. He is extremely elegant, but he writes "prices reasomble" on his door, and reassures his client "Ise the most deficient detective you ever met up with." His pathetic buffoonery is an offensive, grotesque parody. The stories are collected in *Florian Slappey Goes Abroad* (1928) and *Florian Slappey* (1938).

Cohen was born in the South and attended Clemsen College. He practiced law, but gave it up to write fiction in 1915. Later, he would publish in *The Saturday Evening Post* and other "slick" magazines. He settled in New York City.

In addition to Slappey, Cohen also wrote about the detective Jim Hanvey, a hulking, brutish detective who befriends some of those he puts behind bars. Later in his career, Cohen finally did change with the times somewhat, writing mysteries in a more contemporary style, such as *The Intruder* (1955; orig title *Love Can Be Dangerous*), about a police detective investigating the murder of a playboy. Cohen wrote non-series mysteries from the teens to the fifties; among them was *Romance in the First Degree* (1944), in which a war veteran investigates a real estate baron's son in the posh circles of New York City and encounters murder.

COLE, G. D. H. AND M. I. (pen name of Gordon Douglas Howard Cole, 1889–1959, and Margaret Isabel Postgate Cole, 1893–1980) Although it often evokes surprise that the detective stories of the noted English socialists G. D. H. and M. I. Cole are totally lacking in political relevance, there is nothing strange about it. G. D. H. Cole wrote the first of their mysteries, *The Brooklyn Murders* (1923), during an illness; his doctor said not to work, and Cole said writing detective stories wasn't work. The Coles never took the genre seriously—or rather, never acknowledged it as having the potential for seriousness—and were content to discharge their political energies in their many nonfiction books. Cole wrote the first book about Superintendent Wilson by himself, but he and his wife collaborated on another three dozen mystery books, with and without Wilson, including novels and short stories. The Coles' nonliterary interests may have revealed itself in Wilson's complete ordinariness. His most remarkable trait was that he grew six inches after *The Brooklyn Murders*.

M. I. Cole was the sister of Raymond POSTGATE. She wrote a biography of her husband, published in 1972. Both the Coles were influential in the Fabian Society, and G. D. H. was an adviser to politicians and sometime editor of *The New Statesman*.

If they wanted Wilson to appear to be an average Joe, they succeeded in spades. Wilson is gentlemanly in his manner, but he rose through the ranks at Scotland Yard and is not a high-born genius. He has a wife and children and is a family man; he is also passionately fond of beer. He is in his forties when he first appears. M. I. Cole said that many of his qualities were borrowed from her husband and co-author.

COLES, MANNING (pseudonym of Cyril Henry Coles, 1899–1965, and Adelaide Frances Oke Manning, 1891–1959) This team of writers, who were not husband and wife, combined experience in the two world wars in the espionage hero Tommy HAMBLEDON. Coles had begun working in British Intelligence in World War I, and Manning worked in armaments and the War Office. They did not meet until much later, shortly before their collaboration began. Coles had left England for a stint in Australia at various jobs, including journalist. He returned in 1928.

Coming out with the first book in 1940, Manning Coles capitalized on the national need at the time of the Battle of Britain for tales of triumph over the NAZIS. The

Nazis were portrayed as ruthless but stupid. The authors even lampooned the German language, having the characters use words like "soul-in-the-highest-degree-uplifting." Once the war was over, the formula gradually lost its appeal.

Pray Silence (1940; U.S. title *A Toast to Tomorrow*) is the best known of the books. It is also long, and covers the twenty-five-year period from when Hambledon is washed up on the beach, unconscious and with AMNESIA, at the end of World War I, to his final efforts to extricate himself from his position as Deputy Chief of the German Police. The propagandistic nature of the story dictates its terms, and the conventions of the genre are largely disregarded. From his chance meeting with Hermann Göering to his discovery of a likely double with a conveniently smashed face, Hambledon's adventure is a tissue of coincidences. Some of his double-agenting is clever though absurd. The Coles were clearly not fiction writers, though they were more literate than many who were. Their tracing of the rise of Nazism back to the punitive measures of the Versailles Treaty is surprising, given the date of the book, as well as their sympathy with the Germans. All in all, the novel is an amusing romp with a subsidiary historical interest.

Without the compelling war background, Hambledon lost much of his impetus. The later books are generally run-of-the-mill spy and adventure thrillers. Coles continued to work for British Intelligence until the late fifties. After Manning died, he wrote a few more books on his own. The pair also collaborated on a series of ghost stories: *A Family Matter* (1955; U.S. title *Happy Returns*), *The Far Traveller* (1956), and *Come and Go* (1958).

COLLINS, MAX ALLAN (1948–) Max Allan Collins is a prolific American writer who, as he tells it, keeps inventing new series characters in spite of himself. In an afterword appended to a 1985 reprint of one of his books about the hired killer named QUARRY, Collins said that only Nathan Heller was meant to be a series character from the first; the others were extended (some of them had to be resuscitated) at the request of publishers. The author's first novel, *Bait Money* (1973), was about Nolan, a one-name thief obviously modeled on PARKER, a series character created by Donald WESTLAKE in the early sixties. Collins killed off Nolan at the end of the first book but brought him back to life when "a series lured [sic] its seductive head." Collins has also written about Mallory, a mystery writer living in the Midwest; "had I intended a series, I'd have given him a better excuse to go tripping over corpses," Collins wrote; "I've been a mystery writer as long as I can remember and I hardly ever trip over a corpse."

In the Quarry series, Collins extended the Parker formula; Parker was a thief who killed when he had to, and Quarry simply leaves off the thievery and kills for a living. With Heller, Collins experimented with the HISTORICAL MYSTERY. Each of the books is based on a real case: *True Detective* (1983) on the Lindbergh kidnapping, *Damned in Paradise* (1996) on a Hawaiian rape-murder case in which the lawyer Clarence Darrow was involved. Each of the books has an afterword describing the facts of the case and the author's extensive research. In *Damned in Paradise,* Heller meets the real detective who inspired Charlie CHAN.

Among Collins's many other activities, he wrote the *Dick Tracy* comic strip for a number of years, and also the novelization of the 1990 film. He also wrote the *Batman* comic book, created the *Mrs. Tree* comic strip with artist Terry Beatty, and collaborated with Mickey SPILLANE on the comic *Mike Danger.* The Heller novels have routinely been nominated for the Shamus award, and two of them have won, *True Detective* (1983) and *Stolen Away* (1991) (See PRIVATE EYE WRITERS OF AMERICA).

COLLINS, WILKIE (1824–1889) Wilkie Collins was the leading English writer of sensational novels of the nineteenth century, owing mainly to his gift for plotting. A close friend of Charles DICKENS who was also interested in detection and its literary treatment, Collins surpassed Dickens in this field by producing two of the greatest mysteries ever written, THE MOONSTONE (1868) and THE WOMAN IN WHITE (1860). Critics alternately rate one or the other higher, but both are extremely satisfying stories to this day, whether evaluated on the basis of plot, writing, atmosphere, or characterization.

Collins and Dickens met in 1851. One of the things they had in common—besides an interest in writing and in the rakish life they pursued behind a front of Victorian respectability—was a background in law. Collins studied law at Lincoln's Inn, but even before he was admitted to the bar (1851) he was already aiming toward a writing rather than legal career. His first book was about his father, who was a painter: *Memoirs of the Life of William Collins, Esq., R. A.* (1848). Collins published his first novel, *Antonina; or, The Fall of Rome,* in 1850. The next year he met Dickens, and was soon contributing to the Dickens magazine *Household Words.* Collins's first detective character, Anne Rodway, appeared in the story "The Diary of Anne Rodway" in *Household Words* in 1856. This and other detective stories were collected in *The Queen of Hearts* (1859). *The Woman in White* and *The Moonstone* were serialized in another Dickens publication, *All the Year Round. The Moonstone* was the more complex novel, told from several points of view. In his second preface to the book (1871), Collins described struggling to finish the book in the throes of agonizing gout. Collins did not mention his increasing addiction to laudanum, his only relief from the pain. He later contracted an eye disease and sometimes wrote by dictation and had to sit in a darkened room. That he outlived his talent is a critical commonplace; his later works sold well but did not measure up to the great achievements of the sixties.

Collins had a similar (though lesser) ability to Dickens for creating memorable characters, such as Sergeant CUFF, whom he based on the real inspector Jonathan WHICHER. The three menacing Hindus of *The Moonstone* are also memorable, though they are almost more a part of the atmosphere than they are people. Where Collins really excelled was in the construction of plot. Just as Dickens is most often criticized for sentimentality, so Collins has his own Achilles' heel: melodrama. The criticism is somewhat unfair, if Collins is being judged in terms of a later tradition of crime fiction that upholds forms like the PROCEDURAL, from which melodrama—and often, drama, or even interest—is expunged. Compared with other nineteenth-century novels, what Collins was doing was not exceptional, and even Conan DOYLE was using melodramatic clichés twenty-five or more years later. When Collins was writing, the "tradition" of mystery and crime fiction hardly existed, and barely at all as a novel form. Instead, he took the NOVEL OF MANNERS, which was often preoccupied with marriage, and inserted sensational and even supernatural elements into it. Class issues and social problems are also more or less constant themes—indeed, these issues were Collins's chief interest, and it is not surprising that the culprit in the "mystery" is often barely concealed, and no premium is set upon detection simply for itself.

Collins wrote other mystery novels, among them *The Law and the Lady* (1875), which was partly based on the actual case of Madeleine Smith (see NOT PROVEN). Collins also wrote mystery short stories and tales of the supernatural. "MR. POLICEMAN AND THE COOK" (from *Little Novels,* 1887) was written in the manner of accounts of true crimes, which were much copied at the time by Victorian short story writers. By 1877, when he wrote MY LADY'S MONEY, Collins was a very sick man, gout having attacked his eyes and his drug habit reaching epic proportions (a servant who took half of one of his usual doses dropped dead). This novel concerns the theft of a £500 note from a table in the house of Lady Lydiard. As was common in the Victorian era, the identity of the criminal is hardly hidden at all from the reader; the entertainment comes rather from the suspense of the *characters'* not knowing. In this last significant mystery novel Collins created the memorable character OLD SHARON, who shines amid a cast of typical types from romantic melodrama.

COLT See PEACEMAKER; COLT FORTY-FIVE.

COLT, THATCHER Anthony ABBOT's Thatcher Colt was partly based on Theodore ROOSEVELT. Like Roosevelt, Colt is the police commissioner of New York City. Although he is burly, he is also very elegant as well as socially connected—as, of course, was Roosevelt. The first of the books, *About the Murder of Geraldine Foster* (1930), was based loosely on the case of Lizzie BORDEN.

The narrator of the cases is Anthony Abbot himself (a pseudonym); thus the format was similar to that of S. S. VAN DINE's mysteries about Philo VANCE. The similarity does not end there; Abbot seems clearly to have been influenced by Van Dine and the early Ellery QUEEN, in the creation of an Americanized GENIUS DETECTIVE who mimics the aristocratic detectives of the English tradition. But whereas Vance was overbearing and the early Queen pretentious, Thatcher Colt is a bit tougher (he was a policeman, after all). Colt is a World War I veteran as well; although he is wealthy and artistic in temperament, his fascination with criminology led him to the police force. Still only in his forties, Colt has already risen to the commissionership, had startling success, and retires during the series.

The plots used by Abbot in the Colt books are more interesting than those used by Van Dine, and his detective, though not believable, is less preposterous than Philo Vance; it is therefore puzzling that Vance lives on and Colt has drifted into obscurity. Abbot again used a real murder case as the basis of the second book, *About the Murder of the Clergyman's Mistress* (1931; British title *Crime of the Century*). He then branched out, using the circus as background in *About the Murder of the Circus Queen* (1932; British title *The Murder of the Circus Queen*), and psychic phenomena in *About the Murder of a Startled Lady* (1935; British title *The Murder of a Startled Lady*). *The Creeps* (1939; British title *Murder at Buzzard's Bay*) is a SNOWBOUND mystery. The last book to employ Thatcher Colt, *The Shudders* (1943; British title *Deadly Secret*), used the mad scientist theme. In addition to the novels, Colt was a character in *The President's Mystery Story* (1935), which was based on a plot suggested by Franklin Delano Roosevelt.

BIBLIOGRAPHY Novels: *About the Murder of the Night Club Lady* (1931; British title *The Murder of the Night Club Lady*), *About the Murder of a Man Afraid of Women* (1937; British title *The Murder of a Man Afraid of Women*).

COLTON, THORNLEY A sleuth who appeared in a series of stories before World War I, Thornley Colton was, like Max CARRADOS, a blind detective. Little is known about his creator, Clinton Stagg (1890–1916), other than the dates of his short life. On the other hand, much is known about Colton. He has the face of a GENIUS DETECTIVE: a thin, straight nose, pale skin, white hair, and elegant clothes. He carries a stick, and is able to navigate seemingly without effort because his assistant, Sydney Thames, has become expert at counting at a glance the number of steps required for any movement. Thames is named for the river that flows through London, where Colton rescued him while he was still in swaddling clothes. Colton is able to astound others by making observations that would normally require sight, but his other senses are so sharpened and his intelligence is so keen that he can tell that a fat woman is sitting at the next table by the squeak of her chair.

COMMUNISM Rex STOUT said famously that people who do not like detective stories are anarchists; however, the first detective novel, CALEB WILLIAMS (1794), was written by an anarchist. It is a platitude of mystery criticism that the genre is "conservative," and that it is strongly on the side of law and order, as Dorothy L. SAYERS implied. Nonetheless, many important crime and mystery writers have been communists rather than conservatives and have used the genre to criticize the hypocrisy or bankruptcy of social and economic institutions. Thus, a distinction can be made between stories that are on the side of law and order and those that are on the side of justice; for some writers, these are not the same things.

Of course, a writer's political beliefs do not have to be reflected in their work. G. D. H. and M. I. COLE were leading Fabian socialists, but never felt the need to inject a political message into their mystery stories. On the other side are writers like Dashiell HAMMETT and Jim THOMPSON. It is worth remembering that in Hammett's RED HARVEST (1929), often called a gangster novel for its innumerable shootouts, the trouble all stems from a labor dispute. Even before the book begins, Personville has been transformed into "Poisonville" because the industrial oligarchs have used gangsters to destroy the Wobblies, the Industrial Workers of the World. Thompson's earlier books were proletarian novels, dating from the period of his membership in the Communist party. Later, corrupt lawmen who use their power to commit murder for gain would reveal social hypocrisy at its hollowest. Like Hammett, Howard Fast (E. V. CUNNINGHAM) was jailed for his refusal to participate in the red scare, but the social criticism that filtered into his crime writing was far milder than in his "straight" novels. In England, Raymond POSTGATE used the mystery novel to illustrate Marxist principles and called into question the taken-for-granted notion of judicial "impartiality."

Outside the English-speaking world, the combination of the mystery with social criticism is more accepted. Maj SJÖWALL and Per WAHLÖÖ created the Martin BECK series in order to mount a Marxist critique of the socialist welfare state; they succeeded, though it has not made them popular outside their own country, and they are often said to have succeeded in writing good detective novels in spite of their message. Leonardo SCIASCIA used the genre to attack all illegal and unjust institutions, from the fascist regime to the Mafia. VÁZQUEZ MONTALBÁN's books also look back at a fascist past and its legacy in the present, from the perspective of police inspector and former communist Pepe Carvalho, who was imprisoned under Franco. The space between law and justice that Godwin identified is more at issue in crime fiction now than ever before, though a COZY tradition still continues to exist alongside it.

Robert B. PARKER expressed the opinion in "Marxism and the Mystery," an essay included in *Murder Ink* (1977), that the HARD-BOILED detective is "the last gentleman," interested in defending honor, not some political agenda. Parker felt that the discussion of the political or Marxist overtones of certain detective stories was a racket created by academics incessantly on the lookout for grist for the criticism mill.

CONFIDENCE-MAN, THE (1857) A novel by Herman Melville, author of *Moby Dick* (1851), which introduced an enigmatic figure into American literature: a combination devil-hero. The Confidence Man of Melville's novel could also be seen as the earliest example of the "rogue" figure typified by Colonel CLAY and RAFFLES. Melville's protagonist, however, is more frightening, anonymous, and morally chilling.

The novel takes place on a Mississippi riverboat on April 1, April Fool's Day. The Confidence Man appears in various disguises: as a crippled black beggar, a philanthropist, and salesman of such products as the Omni-Balsamic Reinvigorator. When he comes upon a skeptic, he alludes to some other avatars with whom the skeptic would get along. Thus having cleverly recommended himself, he reappears in this other disguise and successfully cages money from his dupe.

The Confidence-Man is a difficult book because the Confidence Man is constantly expounding bogus philosophies and wisdom to beguile his marks, revealing these people's "philosophies"—Christian, transcendental, pragmatic—as themselves no better than quackery. This revelation is for the reader only, however; these fools persist in their folly, and the Confidence Man's role is not to enlighten them but to egg them on to ruin and disaster while keeping his laughter to himself. The Confidence Man has been considered a Satanic figure and a tempter, but he is also a hero. The tricked are beneath the trickster because he at least *knows* that he is lying.

Like Jim THOMPSON's anti-heroes or Tom RIPLEY, the Confidence Man evokes unwilling admiration not for his crimes but because he lives at the bedrock, free of the socially approved hypocrisies of his victims. In the laying by the heels of the pompous, the arrogant, the miserly, the pietistic and the ungenerous, there is a kind of justice. His talk of "confidence" seems an incitement to doubt and distrust, but it really only exposes an emptiness that is already there.

CONFIDENTIALLY YOURS (orig title *The Long Saturday Night*, 1962) A novel by Charles WILLIAMS, one of the few of his books readily available, thanks to a reprint following the release of François TRUFFAUT's film version, *Vivement Dimanche!*, known in English as *Confidentially Yours* (1983).

Williams's novel follows the pattern of such works as THE CASE OF THE DANCING SANDWICHES (1951) and PHANTOM LADY (1942): an innocent man finds himself squeezed into an impossibly tight and perfect frame, and must turn to a courageous woman to extricate himself. John Warren, a real estate operator in Carthage, Alabama, is a big fish in a small pond, but a relatively complacent and unambitious man. One morning, a fellow hunter is found with part of his head blown off in a duck blind not far from Warren's own. Meanwhile, his extravagant and extravagantly beautiful wife, Frances, is on a mysterious trip to New Orleans, and calls demanding large amounts of money. Her sudden return sparks an explosive argument. When Warren finds himself on the run, pursued as a murderous psychotic, he adopts a resourceful plan to extricate himself. Part of the book's intensity is the compression of the story into a weekend.

CONIINE See HEMLOCK.

CONNELL, RICHARD [EDWARD] (1893–1949) Richard Connell is famous for just one story, THE MOST DANGEROUS GAME (1925), which is literally about a manhunt. It was first published in *Variety.* After attending Harvard University, Connell became a newspaperman in New York City. He served in World War I, and afterward was a freelance writer. Connell went to work in the film industry in Hollywood in the same year that his famous story was published. He wrote a detective novel, *Murder at Sea* (1929), and published hundreds of short stories, some of which were filmed. One of these was the basis for Frank Capra's *Meet John Doe* (1941), a much darker film than most of that director's work. Another story, "The Law Beaters," has a lawyer and a petty crook confessing to each other over a bottle of rye how they got away with murder; the punch line is that the setting is revealed only in the last lines.

CONNELLY, MICHAEL (1957–) The American mystery author Michael Connelly won an EDGAR award for his first novel about Los Angeles police detective Hieronymous "Harry" Bosch, *The Black Echo* (1992). Like Walter Mosley, Connelly received a boost when President Bill Clinton publicly claimed to be a fan of his HARD-BOILED hero. Although Bosch is a policeman, the series is more hard-boiled than PROCEDURAL and the focus is on Bosch, not on the "team." Like Inspector MORSE, Bosch is a loner who finds solace in drink and his favorite music. The influence of Raymond CHANDLER is most evident in *The Last Coyote* (1995), in which Bosch investigates the long unsolved murder of his mother (a theme dealt with in fiction and non-fiction by James ELLROY). *Trunk Music* (1997) takes Bosch to Las Vegas to investigate a mob-related killing. He also encounters his future wife, the former FBI agent Eleanor Wish.

Connelly attended the University of Florida, where he earned a degree in journalism. He covered crime for Florida newspapers before moving to the *Los Angeles Times.* He contributed to Pulitzer Prize–winning coverage of a 1985 Florida plane crash. Connelly's newspaper background was put to good use in his thriller, *The Poet* (1995), which won an Anthony award. In *The Poet,* Denver reporter Jack McEvoy investigates the apparent suicide of his brother, a homicide cop, and finds strange parallels in other cities. He uses the threat of publication to attach himself as an observer to an FBI team hunting for a possible serial killer. The murder of children and use of the Internet for trade in child pornography are central themes. While McEvoy narrates his story like a hard-boiled hero ("Death is my beat"), Connelly takes the THRILLER writer's easy way out by opening up a second plot line narrating scenes the protagonist could not have observed; the element of mystery is thus sacrificed to suspense. The tight detective-novel setup unravels into a typically implausible chase hither and yon, and the ending is even more incredible. *The Poet,* however, was vastly more successful than Connelly's stricter detective fiction. In the subsequent years the author has alternated between thrillers and further installments of Bosch, whose saga he fortunately does not intend to abandon.

CONNINGTON, J. J. (pseudonym of Alfred Walter Stewart, 1880–1947) One of the English writers of the GOLDEN AGE, Stewart was a chemistry professor who was known for the scientific elements of his detective stories. His father had been a professor at Glasgow University; Stewart studied there, at the University of Marburg, and at University College, London. He taught chemistry at the University of Glasgow and at the Queen's University in Belfast, retiring in 1944.

Most of Connington's mystery novels are about Sir Clinton DRIFFIELD, an aristocratic detective typical of the time, but, somewhat unusually, not an amateur. He is the chief constable of a fictitious English county, and his cases take him among the country gentry in and around Ambledown. Among the devices used by Stewart are nitrogen narcosis (known to divers as "the bends") in *Jack-in-the-Box* (1944), digitalis poisoning in *The Eye in the Museum* (1929), and cryptography in *Gold Brick Island* (1933). The latter two books are not Driffields; Stewart wrote a number of non-series novels, including two books about the lawyer Mark Brand (*The Counselor,* 1929; *Four Defences,* 1940). Stewart's first book, *Nordenholt's Million* (1923), was not a mystery at all, but a "doomsday" tale of the kind popular early in the century. While a plague threatens to wipe out humanity, a team of scientists backed by the millionaire Nordenholt work for a cure. Stewart also wrote the collection of essays *Alias J. J. Connington* (1947).

The Connington novels are out of print and likely to stay that way, unless the complicated puzzle comes back into fashion. Driffield is a somewhat chilly personality not likely to endear himself to the contemporary reader. As with John RHODE's books, there are occasional Conningtons interesting for their peculiarities and the odd character.

CONRAD, JOSEPH (adopted name of Teodor Joséf Korzeniowski, 1857–1924) The Polish-born writer Joseph Conrad is now recognized as one of the most important writers of the modern period. His lifetime bridged the nineteenth and twentieth centuries, and his literature helped bring about the transition to modernism. His best-known work is the novella *Heart of Darkness* (1902), told by Marlow, former captain of a Congo river steamer. He describes his search for the white trader Kurtz, who has gone over the edge and become an amoral, all-powerful tyrant among the natives of the Belgian Congo. The story's pessimism and vision of human evil prefigures much of twentieth-century literature. Conrad's stories are usually categorized as adventure, though the underlying themes are more weighty than those of, say, Rider HAGGARD. Much of his work is imbued with mystery, and suspense is a vital element; espionage and murder are also dealt with in *The Secret Agent* (1907), in which a group of anarchists plot to blow up the Greenwich Observatory, and *Under Western Eyes* (1911), about revolution and assassination in Czarist Russia. Conrad also wrote the short story "The Brute," in which a sailor overhears a discussion about a murderess—one of the most surprising in crime literature.

CONSPIRACY, THE (1972) This novel by John Hersey, the author of *Hiroshima,* can be read as a quasi-mystery, provided one does not know too much about Piso's Conspiracy, which took place in 65 C.E. during the reign of the Roman emperor Nero. Some of the central figures are the illustrious poet Lucan and the poet-philosopher Seneca, as well as Piso himself, a rich patron of the arts and influential Roman. Based on historical sources such as the *Annals* of Tacitus, Hersey has constructed what amounts to a PROCEDURAL novel in which the police are persecuting rather than investigating the suspects. The members of the Praetorian Guard track the movements of prominent Romans through stolen letters, police reports and memoranda, and the accounts of paid informants and spies—all of which Hersey has convincingly invented.

Although the end is an anticlimax (a complete one, if you are familiar with the history), the book is an interesting foray at the edges of the genre, as well as a historical novel that brings the sordid reign of Nero convincingly to life.

CONSTANTINE, K. C. (1935–?) The first mystery of K.C. Constantine is his—or her—identity. The Mario BALZIC novels are set in Pennsylvania and show expert knowledge of the territory, but that is not much to go on. Whoever he or she is, the author has no reason to be ashamed of the novels, which have won respect from critics and the public despite a harsh realism that some see as mere crudity.

Constantine has developed an updated HARD-BOILED style to describe Rocksburg, Pennsylvania, a depressed coal town where Balzic is the chief of police. The working-class characters are extremely well drawn, and the sociological aspects are a major focus, though not in an academic way. The dialogue is often praised as a highlight of the books, and it too is realistic—the vulgarity and profanity offends some readers. Balzic first appeared in *The Rocksburg Railroad Murders* (1972).

The insightful exploration of a rather unromantic setting elevates the books beyond mere genre writing. One could say that these are NOVELS OF MANNERS, and the manners are bad; it is a matter of opinion whether the level of swearing and cussing is justified in the interests of realism. An aspect of the novels that is particularly well done is the portrayal of small town politics—the infighting, gossiping, and backstabbing in a small place where everyone knows, or wants to know, everyone else's business. Balzic sometimes finds his office being used as a clearinghouse for dirt, and he must sometimes play one side against another while trying to keep his hands as clean as possible.

Among the best books in the series are THE MAN WHO LIKED TO LOOK AT HIMSELF (1973) and ALWAYS A BODY TO TRADE (1983). In 1996, Constantine retired Balzic in *Good Sons.* He is replaced by Detective Sergeant Rugs Carlucci, who investigates a grisly rape and murder; Balzic is definitely missed.

CONTINENTAL OP, THE Dashiell HAMMETT's Continental Op has no name, but that does not mean he has no personality; he is nameless, not faceless. The Op's name is unnecessary, because it is not who he is but what he is that is important. To lump him together with other PULP detectives is misleading, for the same reason that to place Hammett with the other pulp writers is like putting *Moby Dick* on the same shelf with *Field & Stream.* Hammett's prose is muscular without being muscle-bound in the way that HEMINGWAY's can be, and the Op is tough and sometimes thoughtful without being maudlin or artful. True, he enjoys working with his fists on a bad guy's belly; on the other hand, he doesn't force the reader to go through any elaborate justifications for his brutality à la SPENSER.

The Op works for the Continental Detective Agency, which was based on the PINKERTON Agency for which the author worked; the Op shares qualities with Hammett's former boss. (The Op's boss is "The Old Man"). The Op is middle-aged, short, and fat, but he is still tough, sometimes ruthlessly so. He combines occasional wry humor with an absolute lack of sentimentality. His absence of interest in women amounts almost to hostility; he rejects advances in THE GUTTING OF COUFFIGNAL (1926) not because he is immune, but because he will not do anything that interferes with the job he loves. Sometimes, however, he acts chivalrously, as in THE SCORCHED FACE (1925). He is well on his way to being like the man he esteems highest, The Old Man, the agency's San Francisco branch manager, and wants to get all the way there. The Op appeared in many stories in BLACK MASK. Among the collections of Op stories are *The Continental Op* (1945) and *The Return of the Continental Op* (1945). Op stories were later collected in *The Big Knockover* (1966), with an introduction by Lillian Hellman, Hammett's companion. The intervening story collections published during Hammett's lifetime contained a few Op stories each (see bibliography). The Op also appeared in the novels RED HARVEST (1929) and *The Dain Curse* (1929). The latter contains a violent but poorly constructed plot, and has been assailed as racist; it is Hammett's worst book.

The reason that the Op has stayed in print so long is that he is the most perfect hard-boiled character ever invented—or perhaps The Old Man is, with "his gentle eyes behind gold spectacles and his mild smile, hiding the fact that fifty years of sleuthing had left him without any feelings at all on any subject."

BIBLIOGRAPHY Short Stories: *Hammett Homicides* (1946), *Dead Yellow Women* (1947), *Nightmare Town* (1948), *The Creeping Siamese* (1950), *Woman in the Dark* (1952), *A Man Named Thin* (1962).

COOK, THOMAS H. (1947–) Thomas Cook is the author of over a dozen books, most of them thrillers. He had written several fine novels and had been nominated for the EDGAR award long before he finally won one. He remains one of the least recognized best writers in the genre; Cook himself, however, views his crime novels as a means of financing his more literary work.

Thomas Cook was born in Fort Payne, Alabama, and attended George State College. He later received advanced degrees from Hunter College and Columbia University in New York. The South and New York City provide the settings for his novels, the first of which was written while he was still a graduate student. That book, *Blood Innocents* (1980), is a police PROCEDURAL novel set in New York, and was nominated for an Edgar. Cook has written one mystery series, about detective Frank CLEMONS. The first of these books, *Sacrificial Ground* (1988), was also an Edgar nominee.

Cook's Edgar award, and with it, recognition, finally came with *The Chatham School Affair* (1996), a kind of HISTORICAL MYSTERY set on Cape Cod. It is less a mystery, however, than a psychological novel about a seventy-year-old murder. Cook has made historical mysteries a specialty. EVIDENCE OF BLOOD (1991) is one of his best: it concerns a true-crime writer who investigates a murder case in his home town. He only becomes interested in the case when he finds that an old friend whom he has come to town to bury was interested in it, too. Going through the papers of his friend (a former policeman), he finds references to the crime that tantalize his reporter's instinct, but in the end his meticulous investigation becomes suddenly personal.

One of Cook's trademark themes developed in *Evidence of Blood* is the pursuit of an activity whose results are totally different from those intended, though unconsciously the actor may be trying to expose some knowledge he or she has repressed. In *The City When It Rains* (1991), David Corman, a freelance photographer, listens one night to police radio calls about a suicide in his neighborhood (Hell's Kitchen, New York). A woman throws a doll from the roof of a tenement, then jumps herself. Himself a man in trouble, having lost his wife and about to lose his daughter and his home, Corman sees it as a great story. Once again, the idea of the "objectivity" of the investigator/researcher is questioned when the story of the suicide begins to intersect that of his own life.

Similarities to *The Chatham School Affair* are obvious, but in the later book, the mystery comes from the way in which veils shrouding the actual events are taken away one by one. The elderly narrator, who was a boy at the time of the mysterious death in question, slowly constructs the story through his reminiscences, which are all about his realization of human fallibility and the tragic consequences of miscommunication and stupidity. Like a spider spinning a web, with each strand he comes closer to completing the overall pattern in which the characters are trapped. Although the mystery is thus created through a narrative manipulation of the reader—since the old man presumably knows the whole truth from the outset—the tricks are generally well concealed.

Other novels by Cook also seem to demonstrate the opposite of the adage "time heals all wounds." In *Mortal Memory* (1993), a boy returns from a visit to some friends to find his entire family murdered and his father missing. As an adult, the now grown-up boy meets a woman who is writing a book about fathers who kill their families. Ben Wade is a small-town doctor in *Breakheart Hill* (1995) who is plagued by the memory of a girl he loved during high school who was murdered twenty-five years before the novel's "present."

Cook has also written nonfiction crime works: *Early Graves: The Shocking True-Crime Story of the Youngest Woman Ever Sentenced to Death Row* (1990) and *The True Story of an Infamous Mass Murder and Its Aftermath* (1992).

COOL, BERTHA A detective created by Erle Stanley GARDNER. Cool, partnered with Donald LAM, featured in a string of novels written between 1939 (*The Bigger They Come*) and 1970 (ALL GRASS ISN'T GREEN) and published by Gardner under the name A. A. FAIR. Cool is usually a sympathetic figure, with more believable humanity than most of Gardner's characters. Weighing more than 200 pounds, she isn't dashing; she has a keen eye for business (unlike Lam), and with her sharp mouth is far from a BIMBO. She describes herself as a "hard-boiled steamroller," and is one of the few HARD-BOILED women detectives of the period. Having run the agency on her own after the death of her husband, she takes on Lam as an operative. He proceeds to expand business into dangerous areas, but also makes the agency far more lucrative.

Not a very skilled writer, Gardner tends to make fun of his own character, but the laughs to be had from Bertha's weight and avariciousness aren't worth the weakening of the story and the alienating of the reader. Gardner also had little regard for consistency. In *Fools Die on Friday* (1947), Gardner portrays Bertha as cowardly, obsequious toward the police and anyone with money, and downright stupid. As one of the more interesting female characters of the time, Cool deserved better. Fortunately, in mysteries written during World War II (in which, like Archie GOODWIN, Lam decides to enlist), Cool gets to solve cases on her own. In *Cats Prowl at Night* (1943), Lam is "on vacation" and Cool narrates the story, in which most of the major characters and the corpse are women.

Despite cries of "Kipper me for a herring!" and other dotty expletives, Bertha is, like the title character of MILDRED PIERCE (1941), a woman running her own business, and Lam (at least at first) is only her employee. As a female detective created before the age of political correctness, Bertha both suffers from the patronizing ministrations of men (including her creator) and is refreshingly free from a superabundance of redeeming qualities.

In the first novel, *The Bigger They Come* (British title *Lam to the Slaughter*), Bertha hires the diminutive Lam to help her. A couple of years later, she makes him a partner in the business (*Double or Quits,* 1941). The early books are more hard-boiled and original. Gardner wrote quickly, and some of the plots are quite simple, even thin.

Owls Don't Blink (1942) takes the team to New Orleans, Shreveport, and back to Los Angeles, in a case that first involves a missing model named Roberta Fenn. Donald Lam takes her vacant apartment in New Orleans, despite the fact that there seems to be something fishy about the lawyer who hired them for the job (dishonest clients are recurrent in the Cool-Lam series). After the detectives track Fenn down the case seems to be over, but the appearance of a further corpse leads to typically wacky developments.

The Count of Nine (1958) is a much better story, with especially good dialogue between Lam, the police, and the two women—the wife and the mistress of the victim—

who come on to Lam. As in some other stories, Gardner shows a fondness for gadgetry, in this case an x-ray security device installed by soon-to-be-murdered adventurer Dean Crockett (he is killed by poisoned darts from his own blow gun). In *Bedrooms Have Windows* (1949), Cool and Lam are hired to tail Claire Bushnell. While on the job, Lam is lured by Lucille Hart, "a pocket-edition Venus," to the Kozy Dell Motor Camp, where Lucille's brother-in-law is found dead with his secretary, an apparent double suicide. Lam gets framed for the deaths, as well as a later sex murder. In both of these books, Bertha Cool is portrayed as less shrewish than in some of her other appearances.

Late in the series, in *Traps Need Fresh Bait* (1967), Bertha has become almost quiet compared with her earlier cantankerousness; she and Lam are hired to investigate an ad placed in a newspaper for persons willing to testify as accident witnesses—i.e., to commit perjury.

BIBLIOGRAPHY Novels: *Double or Quits* (1941), *Turn on the Heat* (1940), *Gold Comes in Bricks* (1940), *Spill the Jackpot* (1941), *Bats Fly at Dusk* (1942), *Give 'Em the Axe* (1944; British title *Axe to Grind*), *Crows Can't Count* (1946), *Top of the Heap* (1952), *Some Women Won't Wait* (1953), *Beware the Curves* (1956), *You Can Die Laughing* (1957), *Some Slips Don't Show* (1957), *Pass the Gravy* (1959), *Kept Women Can't Quit* (1960), *Bachelors Get Lonely* (1961), *Shills Can't Cash Chips* (1961; British title *Stop at the Red Light*), *Try Anything Once* (1962), *Fish or Cut Bait* (1963), *Up for Grabs* (1964), *Cut Thin to Win* (1965), *Widows Wear Weeds* (1966).

COOPER, JAMES FENIMORE (1789–1851). The American novelist James Fenimore Cooper would be an unlikely candidate as a "proto-mystery" writer, had not Dorothy L. SAYERS astutely pointed out that he enjoyed a great vogue in Europe and popularized Native American methods of "deduction"—that is, tracking and the reading of obscure signs. (From that perspective, the Leatherstocking and Chingachgook become ancestors of Jim CHEE and Inspector BONAPARTE.) Sayers saw an urbanized version of the Cooper methods in the works of Continental writers of the mid-nineteenth century such as Émile GABORIAU.

COP The single most common word for "policeman," cop is a shortening of "copper" and may come from Romanian *cappi,* meaning "gain, booty." Other etymologies have been suggested. It is certain that "copper" began to be applied to policemen in the mid-nineteenth century. Eric PARTRIDGE suggests the source was theatrical. "To cop" had long been an English verb meaning "to capture" or arrest. Hugh Rawson (see SLANG) suggests either the gypsy *cap,* "to steal," or Hebrew *cap,* meaning "hand," as the ancient root.

CORK, BARRY See GOLF MYSTERIES.

CORNWELL, DAVID JOHN MOORE See LE CARRÉ, JOHN.

CORNWELL, PATRICIA (1956–) In only a short time, Patricia Cornwell, whose first book was the biography of an evangelist, has become one of the best-selling mystery authors with her Kay SCARPETTA series. Scarpetta is a medical examiner in Richmond, Virginia. The first of the books, *Post Mortem* (1990), won an EDGAR for best first novel, the John Creasey award from the British CRIME WRITERS' ASSOCIATION, an Anthony, and other honors.

Cornwell worked as a crime reporter and as a technical writer and computer analyst in the Richmond, Virginia medical examiner's office for six years before she began writing her novels. This experience, plus her extensive research, provides the background for her books, which are extremely grisly. Cornwell won an award for her investigative reporting on prostitution while she was with the *Charlotte Observer.*

Cornwell was born in Florida and had a difficult childhood. Her father abandoned the family while she was still very young, and her parents divorced. She has spoken publicly about having been molested at the age of five by a security guard. During her mother's serious depression, Cornwell met Billy and Ruth Graham, the evangelists; Cornwell's first book was her 1983 biography of Ruth Graham. The first version of *Postmortem* was completed in 1984 and was rejected by several publishers. Cornwell rewrote the book with Scarpetta as the main character, and then revised the story in line with an actual series of rape-murders in Richmond. The man convicted of the crimes was executed in 1994. The structure provided by a real series of events seems to have provided Corwell's writing with its missing ingredient. Cornwell continues to base her books, such as *All That Remains* (1992), on real murders, and receives multi-million dollar advances. In 1991, a man in Sarasota, Florida, committed a murder following *Postmortem* in sickening detail.

CORPUS DELECTI A legal term derived from Latin, including but not restricted to corpses. In fact, it refers to everything of an evidentiary nature having to do with a crime, which would include a body, if there is one.

COSTA-GAVRAS, CONSTANTIN (1933–) The son of a World War II resistance fighter who was jailed after the war for his communist leanings, the Greek director Costa-Gavras became famous for a series of thrillers, most of them political. Banned from attending a Greek university and denied a visa to study in the United States, Costa-Gavras went to France. His first film, *The Sleeping Car Murders* (1965), was based on a mystery novel by Sébastien JAPRISOT and brought him commercial success. His second film had a far more profound impact. Z (1969), based on a novel (q.v.) by Vassilis VASSILIKOS, won the prize at Cannes as well as two Academy Awards, including the Oscar for best foreign film. Another thriller, *Missing* (1982), is about an innocent American searching for his missing son in Chile who comes face to face with American-sponsored terror. Like Vassilikos, Costa-Gavras was driven into exile for his political views and became a naturalized French citizen in 1956.

COUNTRY HOUSE A subgenre of the mystery story, particularly popular in England during the GOLDEN AGE, though this device continues to be used in endless permutations. The usefulness of the country house is that the number of suspects is limited to the guests, who can be picked over and interrogated by the sleuth at leisure (of course, everyone is loath to leave for fear of appearing to be guilty).

The country house murder is most often associated with Agatha CHRISTIE, though all of her contemporaries also used it. What the country house provides in terms of narrative shape and restricted setting is compensated, negatively, by the frequent unbelievability of the setup. Hugh GREENE blamed what he called the "monstrous regiment of women" writing between the wars (Christie, SAYERS, ALLINGHAM, MARSH) for taking the mystery out of the mean (or at least not nice) streets of Edwardian London and transplanting it to an unreal world. Ironically, the country house mystery was made popular at exactly the time when the social structure that supported it was going into irreversible decline; the end of World War I in 1918 was the beginning of the end for the *ancien regime* and the world of the stately English country mansion. After World War II, a new sub-subgenre would develop built on the ashes of the country house, and having to do with murder on the estate of an impoverished aristocrat who has to charge tourists admission to the country house in order to make ends meet. This satirical setup is used, for example, in Catherine AIRD's *The Stately Home Murder* (1970), Joyce PORTER's *It's Murder with Dover* (1973), and Christie's CURTAIN (1975).

In the United States, with its general lack of a landed gentry, the country house formula was modified. Mary Roberts RINEHART wrote about spooky deserted houses, while such writers as the LOCKRIDGES, Elizabeth DALY, and Edgar BOX used the country home outside New York City as a venue.

A popular variety of the country house murder is the SNOWBOUND mystery. MURDER AFLOAT achieves the same goal of isolating the cast of possible suspects.

COVE An English slang term dating from the sixteenth century, meaning "a guy," "a bloke."

COVER HER FACE (1962) The first novel of P. D. JAMES. If George Eliot had written a novel plotted by Agatha CHRISTIE, it might have turned out something like this. The center of the story is Martingale, the Elizabethan country home of the Maxie family. Simon Maxie is an invalid; his wife Eleanor entertains; his son Stephen is a doctor, and only comes home when he is not working at the hospital; and daughter Deborah is a young widow who lives at home and has a peculiarly possessive relationship with her brother. The Maxies have social position but little money—but Sally Jupp has no position at all. A young unwed mother, she comes to work as a maid at Martingale. From the moral height of their conventionality, the villagers view Sally as a "lucky girl," and like all lucky people, she is resented. Her relationship to Stephen particularly disturbs, and even enrages, other women in the story. The repressed spinster Miss Liddell says that the wages of sin are death; lo and behold, Sally is murdered.

Into the picture steps Adam DALGLIESH. The narrative, hitherto very subjective, becomes far more descriptive and detailed, which ingeniously reinforces the reader's sense of Dalgliesh's care with words and powers of observation. This manipulation of the novel's discourse is one of the author's hallmarks. When she writes that Mrs. Maxie "was either numbed by grief or thinking deeply," one forgets that an omniscient third-person narrator, who at other times renders people's inmost thoughts, could be presumed to "know" which state it was. Instead, this bit of coyness shows us how a policeman like Dalgliesh, unmoved by the scene, would view the woman's face. Only a few pages later, James plays an opposite sort of trick on the reader by using interior monologue. When Dalgliesh first appears, one character thinks he is "tall, dark and handsome," another sees "a supercilious-looking devil," and still another thinks he looks like a head by Dürer. She thus makes the policeman complex even while she communicates the suspects's apprehensions (in both senses). Few debut novels—or mature novels, for that matter—show such complete control of mood and character.

COVER HIS FACE (1949) A novel by Thomas KYD (Alfred Harbage) about a comical Ph.D., Gilbert Weldon, who teaches at the humble University of Allegheny.

Weldon has dreams of greatness (and marriage), and a lead on copies of Samuel Johnson's lost early works from *The Birmingham Journal* seems like just the opportunity to make a name for himself. He goes to the quaint English village of Fenny Dasset in search of further information, hoping to get some help from his distant relative, Lambert Weldon. His shocking first meeting with Lambert, however, leads to an entirely unexpected series of events. The story is told with Harbage's usual grace and satirizes intellectual pomposity, though it rates below BLOOD ON THE BOSOM DIVINE (1948).

COXE, GEORGE HARMON (1901–1984) George Harmon Coxe was working in advertising for a New England printer when he had his first big success with PULP MAGAZINES, particularly BLACK MASK. Born in Olean, New York, Coxe grew up there and in nearby Elmira. He attended Purdue and Cornell universities. Between 1922 and 1927, he worked for newspapers as a reporter—the Santa Monica *Outlook*, the Los Angeles *Express*, and the *Utica Observer Dispatch* and *Elmira Star-Gazette*. He used that background to create Jack CASEY, nicknamed "Flashgun" because he is a newspaper photographer. Casey was the subject of many pulp stories before he appeared in his first novel, *Silent Are the Dead* (1946). Casey was also adapted for film. Coxe himself had a career in Hollywood as a scriptwriter for Metro-Goldwyn-Mayer in the thirties and also wrote for radio. The photographer formula was successful and Coxe never strayed far from it, though he did write about the more conventional detectives Sam Crombie and Max Hale. Coxe's first novel, *Murder with Pictures*, appeared in 1935, and concerned another newspaper photographer, Kent MURDOCK, who is a less HARD-BOILED version of Casey. Murdock seems either more human or watered down, depending on one's taste for the pulp style. Unlike many pulpsmiths, Coxe did not often resort to violence to bolster a flagging narrative; instead, he wrote tight plots. Murdock is assisted by private detective Jack Fenner. Toward the end of his life, Coxe spun off a separate Fenner series, beginning with *Fenner* (1971), about a woman missing from a mental hospital.

Coxe also wrote non-series mysteries, such as *One Hour to Kill* (1951). Freed from the series format and sleuths who were tied to their desks in Boston, Coxe could use "exotic" locales and drop the photographic element completely. In *One Hour to Kill*, an illustrator and artist named Dave Wallace finds himself both a suspect and a sleuth when a woman is strangled with a pearl necklace in his picturesque hut in Trinidad. *Double Identity* (1971) is set in Guyana, ONE MINUTE PAST EIGHT (1957) in Caracas, Venezuela; *Murder in Havana* (1943) is another non-series mystery.

Coxe received the Grand Master award of the MYSTERY WRITERS OF AMERICA in 1964. He had been president of the organization in 1952.

COZY The term "cozy" is not very precise. Sometimes it has the same implications as the "Lord, what fun!" school of mystery writing, in which the story is basically a game and murder is not recognized for what it really is. In some ways, it is easier to identify a cozy by what it is not. A cozy mystery is one in which realism is not followed; the description of the crime is not graphic and bloody; and a strong feeling of evil is not evoked. In fact, a benign view of human nature and the world is generally the main criterion for labeling a work or writer "cozy." The murder is an exception, an aberration, an accident in a world that is basically good. The opposite of the cozy world view is represented by NOIR writers like James ELLROY, for whom injustice is the single strongest thread running through history and human nature. If the noir writer is a pessimist, the cozy writer is an optimist.

In another sense, the cozy is the GOLDEN AGE mystery that refuses to die. Writers like Martha GRIMES are clearly influenced by CHRISTIE and SAYERS, writers of the last generation for which the COUNTRY HOUSE, the dutifully subservient lower class, and the "all's right with the world" attitude could be taken for granted, and for which fiction displaying that attitude could be taken seriously. But many writers have maintained a cozy optimism without insulting the reader's intelligence or making the story grossly unreal. Elizabeth DALY's mysteries are set in an upper class milieu, but did not banish reality entirely. She presents vice—drug abuse, adultery, greed, cheating of various kinds—as a foible rather than an evil. During the period in which Daly was writing, HARD-BOILED writers presented the same vices as signs of social decay, corruption, and human perfidy. The cozy attitude is compatible with the police novel, or even the PROCEDURAL, as much as with the GENIUS DETECTIVE or gifted amateur. The calm with which Lieutenant HEIMRICH goes about his business indicates a basic social stability which the murder is in no danger of disturbing.

At its worst, the cozy mystery deteriorates into the cutesy mystery, presenting a world in which CATS show preternatural ability to solve crimes, romance submerges detection, and realism is ignored. An award for cozy mysteries, the Agatha, is named for Agatha Christie. See MALICE DOMESTIC.

CRAIG, ALISA See MACCLEOD, CHARLOTTE.

CRAMER, INSPECTOR A supporting character in the Nero WOLFE novels, Cramer is exasperated by Wolfe's methods but is often forced to rely on his assistance. Most frequently he is seen in the red leather chair Wolfe reserves for guests of honor, chewing on an unlit cigar. Cramer is a memorable but undeveloped character. He does, however, get to solve one case on his own, in *Red Threads* (1940).

CRANE, BILL A private detective created by Jonathan LATIMER, Bill Crane fits between the CONTINENTAL OP and Philip MARLOWE, both chronologically and developmentally. Crane is the typical hard-drinking shamus who became such a cliché in the HARD-BOILED era, but he was there first, or at least second or third. Crane is a bachelor in his thirties, and gets married late in the series. Crane works for the New York detective agency of Colonel Black; Tom O'Malley, Doc Williams, and Eddie Burns are other characters in the series. These are some of the most alcohol-soaked books in the genre—even a bulldog drinks whisky in one novel. Despite its hard-boiled flavor, the series did not stint on detection; Latimer inserted clues and followed up the deductive process as assiduously as a writer of classic mysteries. *Headed for a Hearse* (1935) contains a LOCKED ROOM problem. Crane has only six days to prove that Robert Westland did not kill his wife or Westland will go to the electric chair.

Latimer was also like Craig RICE in his ability to create strange and original situations. In the first Bill Crane novel, *Murder in the Madhouse* (1935), the private eye impersonates a mental patient in order to investigate a theft inside an asylum and to protect the rich Miss Van Camp. He meets a strange collection of patients, including one who thinks he is the reincarnation of Abraham Lincoln. The first patient to fall victim is strangled with a bathrobe belt. The police think Crane is not a detective at all but just another patient suffering from delusions. Latimer also had Rice's flair for nutty, frenetic energy, for example in *The Lady in the Morgue* (1936), which is full of outrageous scenes, chases, and inebriated folly. In this novel, set during a hot Chicago summer, Crane tries to find out who "Alice Ross" really was. Crane is sent to the morgue to see if anyone shows up to identify the body of a beautiful young woman, found hanged in a Chicago hotel. The body disappears, however, and is replaced with that of a murdered morgue employee. Crane is suspected of the killing, and while he searches for the missing body, the police search for him. He also has to avoid two gangsters who think *he* has the corpse. This good crook/bad crook team is made up of one man who thinks the woman is his beloved wife who ran off, and the other the jilted lover she is supposed to have run off with. In a bar, Crane and friends meet a guru who has them smoke hashish. They also find the bulldog, Champion, who puts away almost as much booze as the others and helps sniff around for the corpse in a cemetery. *The Dead Don't Care* (1938) takes place on an estate near Miami and involves murder and kidnapping. The residents include a gigolo, a washed-up fighter, and an exotic dancer.

BIBLIOGRAPHY Novels: *Red Gardenias* (1939).

CRANE, FRANCES (1896–) Born in Illinois, Frances Crane lived in Europe before World War II and achieved probably her greatest popularity in England. Her series of novels about Pat and Jean ABBOTT, a husband-and-wife detective team, reflected her own passion for travel and used settings on several continents. Most, however, took place in the United States, and of those a large proportion were set in San Francisco, the home base of private detective Pat Abbott. *The Golden Box* (1942) is set in a fictionalized version of Crane's home town of Lawrenceville.

Before turning to mystery novels, Crane was a prolific writer of short stories, and published an astounding 100 stories in *The New Yorker.* Her mysteries depended heavily on local color, which she sometimes brought off well; however, she was criticized for her adherence to the HAD-I-BUT-KNOWN formula. Jean Abbott is the typical female of this subgenre, who forges ahead into trouble and then has to be pulled out of harm's way by her male companion, in this case her husband Pat. Crane wrote twenty-six novels about the Abbotts.

CREASEY, JOHN (1908–1973) Probably one of the most prolific authors of all time, John Creasey is left out of most literature reference books, excepting those devoted to the crime and mystery genre—and with good reason: anyone who writes more than 600 books in something like 40 years can hardly afford to revise much. Creasey wrote under almost 30 pseudonyms; he did much of his best work as J. J. Marric (the GIDEON series) and as Michael Halliday (the Dr. CELLINI series). He also created two of the longest-running series characters, the BARON and the Toff (also known as Richard ROLLISON). Creasey's work was derivative, capitalizing on innovations in the genre made by other writers. Other Creasey characters include Patrick Dawlish (a Bulldog DRUMMOND type), Mark Kilby, and Roger WEST (a Roderick ALLEYN type). Creasey delved into every subgenre, including the scientific cloak-and-dagger school and espionage (including an anti-NAZI fantasy written during the war). In *The Touch of Death* (1954), he wrote about a Dr. Palfrey and the discovery of a mysterious deadly metal in a uranium mine.

The difficulty that Creasey had in getting published has become as notorious as the success he had once he managed to get into print. He received over 700 rejection slips before his first novel was accepted. Creasey is usually praised as an adept plotter. Unfortunately, he had not much of a gift for language, and the psychology of his characters is schematic at best. He did win several awards for his writing, including an EDGAR for *Gideon's Day* (1961) and the Grand Master Award. The Gideon books are considered his best, and the West novels are relatively clean copy; both are less outlandish than the campy BARON and Toff series, in which Creasey strained to go his models one better. Creasey's faults were in a way also his strengths, however; since the writing is never noticeably good, his more ridiculous and escapist stories may hold the attention longer. (Realism plus flat writing often equals boredom.) Creasey's imagination went into scenarios and details, not words.

Creasey helped to found the British CRIME WRITERS' ASSOCIATION (its best first novel award is called the Creasey Award), and was a president of the Mystery Writers of America while he was living in Arizona. He also ran several times for Parliament but was never elected.

CREDIT FOR A MURDER (1961) The last of the Doug CADEE novels by Spenser DEAN. The story is set in the few days before Christmas, and has Cadee chasing through illegal New York nightclubs and coming up against hardened criminals and rhyme-spouting beatniks. The story is told in the non-stop style of the Bertha COOL/Donald LAM novels, but is better written. John Maisler, a weak-willed employee at Amblett's department store, is found in the Hudson River frozen into a block of ice and presumed murdered. At the same time, Cadee collars a slick-looking character who tried to steal a sapphire cufflink, who turns out to be a yacht captain, gambler, and lover of a suspicious cabaret singer. Meanwhile, Sibyl Forde, Cadee's girlfriend, disappears while looking into the shoplifting incident—fear for her safety being used as the device that explains why Cadee never goes to the authorities but pursues all the leads himself. The clues are often funny (stickup men with their "crimetables" taped to their wrists for easy reference), there are plenty of them, and Cadee never stops moving; the campy dialogue and changing venues—Cadee is almost never in the store—keep the light material from getting stale.

CREEP A word now used as a synonym for "jerk," it has, like that word (which formerly meant masturbator), lost the sense of its original meaning. A *creep* was a particular kind of criminal, a sneak-thief; a *creep joint* was a whorehouse where, while the customers were engaged with the prostitutes, the creep would stealthily go through the pockets of their discarded clothes.

CRIBB, SERGEANT See LOVESEY, PETER.

CRIDER, BILL (1941–) A native of Texas, Bill Crider has written mysteries with a western and southern feel. His best-known book, *Too Late to Die* (1986), won an Anthony award. This novel introduced Sheriff Dan Rhodes, an indifferent politician but determined investigator. Rhodes is up for re-election in Blacklin County, and must contend with a bunch of small town types while trying to solve a murder. The sheriff is a widower with a grown-up daughter, and the series is less subplot-ridden than many. *Death by Accident* (1998) begins with the discovery of a corpse in a swimming pool.

Crider wrote another series closer to his own experience as a teacher, featuring professor Carl Burns, and still another series about Texas private eye Truman Smith. Smith first appeared in *Dead on the Island* (1991).

CRIME AND PUNISHMENT See DOSTOYEVSKY, FYODOR.

CRIME AT GUILDFORD (1935) A novel by Freeman Wills CROFTS, one of two novels set at Guildford, where he lived at one time. It is a COUNTRY HOUSE mystery in the sense that the murder occurs at Guildford Hall, but then everyone disperses and it becomes a hunt for the killer by Inspector FRENCH.

The victim, the accountant for Norne's London jewelry firm, had gone to Norne's country house in Guildford to consult with the directors of the company about the financial crisis caused by the Depression. On the same day as the murder, the safe is found burgled at the London offices of the company. French must sift a good many clues in order to discover the murderer and the method of the safe-cracking, and the plot and clues are tied up very tightly. An absorbing chase sequence caps the tale.

"CRIME WITHOUT PASSION" A story by Ben HECHT, depicting the author's sense of "the folly and poison of life" as macabre comedy. Its opening line announces it as a story of half-humorous, half-bitter satire: "Mr. Lou Hendrix looked at the lady he had been pretending to love for the past six months and, being a lawyer, said nothing." Hendrix's shallow romance with a Broadway showgirl rapidly and surprisingly turns into a *murder* of a Broadway showgirl. No one is as surprised as Mr. Lou Hendrix, and momentarily he is bereft of reason; quickly, however, his natural faculties (cleverness, shamelessness, craftiness, a "villainous detachment") take over and he begins to set up the murder as the crime of someone else. In fact, Hendrix begins to enjoy himself. Hecht documents each of Hendrix's false clues, masterfully laid, and his carefully thought-out evidence tampering, with a mixture of amusement and cynicism. Immensely satisfied with himself, Hendrix returns to the cabaret where his lover worked, and in that scene Hecht delivers the walloping double surprise that makes the story a tour de force.

CRIME WRITERS' ASSOCIATION A British organization of crime and mystery writers, formed in 1953 by an eminent group of writers in the field, primary among them John CREASEY. The Crime Writers' Association of Great Britain (sometimes called the British Crime Writers' Association) like the Mystery Writers of America, gives annual awards; the British equivalent of the EDGAR Award is the Gold Dagger (see below). Three other awards have been added since the founding of the association: a Silver Dagger award; a first novel award, named for Creasey himself; and a Diamond Dagger, similar in purpose to the Grand Master award of the Mystery Writers of America (see EDGAR). The Gold Dagger was originally called the crossed red herrings; prior to the creation of the Silver Dagger, there was a "runner-up" prize given to one or more candidates for the Gold Dagger. In some years when the winner of the Gold Dagger was an American, a category was added for "Best British" mystery.

Gold Dagger. 1955, Winston Graham, *The Little Walls;* 1956, Edward Grierson, *The Second Man;* 1957, Julian Symons, *The Colour of Murder;* 1958, Margot Bennett, *Someone from the Past;* 1959, Eric Ambler, *Passage of Arms;* 1960, Lionel Davidson, *The Night of Wenceslas;* 1961, Mary Kelly, *The Spoilt Kilt;* 1962, Joan Fleming, *When I Grow Rich;* 1963, John Le Carré, *The Spy Who Came in from the Cold;* 1964, H. R. F. Keating, *The Perfect Murder;* 1965, Ross MacDonald, *The Far Side of the Dollar;* 1966, Lionel Davidson, *A Long Way to Shiloh;* 1967, Emma Lathen, *Murder Against the Grain;* 1968, Peter Dickinson, *Skin Deep;* 1969, Peter Dickinson, *A Pride of Heroes;* 1970, Joan Fleming, *Young Man, I Think You're Dying;* 1971, James McClure, *The Steam Pig;* 1972, Eric Ambler, *The Levanter;* 1973, Robert Littell, *The Defection of A. J. Lewinter;* 1974, Anthony Price, *Other Paths to Glory;* 1975, Nicholas Meyer, *The Seven Per Cent Solution;* 1976, Ruth Rendell, *A Demon in My View;* 1977, John Le Carré, *The Honourable Schoolboy;* 1978, Lionel Davidson, *The Chelsea Murders;* 1979, Dick Francis, *Whip Hand;* 1980, H. R. F. Keating, *The Murder of the Maharajah;* 1981, Martin Cruz Smith, *Gorky Park;* 1982, Peter Lovesey, *The False Inspector Dew;* 1983, John Hutton, *Accidental Crimes;* 1984, B. M. Gill, *The Twelfth Juror;* 1985, Paula Gosling, *Monkey Puzzle;* 1986, Ruth Rendell, *Live Flesh;* 1987, Barbara Vine (pseudonym of Ruth Rendell), *A Fatal Inversion;* 1988, Michael Dibdin, *Ratking;* 1989, Colin Dexter, *The Wench Is Dead;* 1990, Reginald Hill, *Bones and Silence;* 1991, Barbara Vine (Ruth Rendell), *King Solomon's Carpet;* 1992, Colin Dexter, *The Way Through the Woods;* 1993, Patricia D. Corwell, *Cruel and Unusual;* 1994, Minette Walters, *The Scold's Bride;* 1995, Val McDermid, *The Mermaids Singing;* 1996, Ben Elton, *Popcorn;* 1997, Ian Rankin, *Black & Blue;* 1998, James Lee Burke, *Sunset Limited*; 1999, Robert Wilson, *A Small Death in Lisbon*; 2000, Jonathan Lethem, *Motherless Brooklyn*.

Silver Dagger. 1969, Francis Clifford, *Another Way of Dying;* 1970, Anthony Price, *The Labyrinth Makers;* 1971, P. D. James, *Shroud for a Nightingale;* 1972, Victor Canning, *The Rainbird Pattern;* 1973, Gwendoline Butler, *A Coffin for Pandora;* 1974, Francis Clifford, *The Grosvenor Square Goodbye;* 1975, P. D. James, *The Black Tower;* 1976, James McClure, *Rogue Eagle;* 1977, William McIlvanney, *Laidlaw;* 1978, Peter Lovesey, *Waxwork;* 1979, Colin Dexter, *Service of All the Dead;* 1980, Ellis Peters, *Monk's Hood;* 1981, Colin Dexter, *The Dead of Jericho;* 1982, S. T. Haymon, *Ritual Murder;* 1983, William McIlvanney, *The Papers of Tony Veitch;* 1984, Ruth Rendell, *The Tree of Hands;* 1985, Dorothy Simpson, *Last Seen Alive;* 1986, P. D. James, *A Taste for Death;* 1987, Scott Turow, *Presumed Innocent;* 1988, Sara Paretsky, *Toxic Shock;* 1989, Desmond Lowden, *The Shadow Run;* 1990, Mike Phillips, *The Late Candidate;* 1991, Frances Fyfield, *Deep Sleep;* 1992, Liza Cody, *Bucket Nut;* 1993, Sarah Dunant, *Fatlands;* 1994, Peter Hoeg, *Miss Smilla's Feeling for Snow* (U.S. title *Smilla's Sense of Snow*); 1995, Peter Lovesey, *The Summons;* 1996, Peter Lovesey, *Bloodhounds;* 1997, Janet Evanovitch, *Three To Get Deadly;* 1998, Nicholas Blincoe, *Manchester Slingback*; 1999, Adrian Matthews, *Vienna Blood*; 2000, Donna Leon, *Friends in High Places*.

CRIPPEN, DR. HAWLEY HARVEY One of the most notorious criminals of the twentieth century, Dr. Crippen also committed one of the most colorful and ridiculous crimes, a refutation of the idea that real murders are not anything like those portrayed in books. Crippen was a weak man with a domineering wife. Mrs. Crippen went by the name of Belle Elmore and wanted to be an opera singer. In 1910, after Crippen fell for a typist named Ethel le Neve, he decided to kill Belle. Crippen poisoned her with HYOSCINE and then chopped up her body and buried it.

That Crippen had not thought things out very well is shown by the way that he excused her sudden absence: he said she had gone off to Los Angeles, California, had died there, and that the body had been cremated. Not everyone believed this, however, and Crippen decided to flee. Traveling under an alias, and with Ethel le Neve disguised as a boy, Crippen tried to take a ship to Quebec. The captain of the ship sent a wireless message back to England (the first time telegraphy was used to stop an escaping criminal), and the police pursued Crippen in a faster boat and captured him.

The case continues to attract comment; one of those who has written about Crippen is Michael GILBERT (*Dr. Crippen,* 1953).

CRISPIN, EDMUND (pseudonym of Robert Bruce Montgomery, 1921–1978) Edmund Crispin has been called "one of the most literate mystery writers of the century." He has also been considered one of the funniest, for those who appreciate his type of English humor. Crispin was actually the respected English composer, Robert Bruce Montgomery. He was a friend of Kingsley AMIS and other British intellectuals.

Montgomery was born in Buckinghamshire. He studied modern languages at Oxford, where he wrote his first mystery, *The Case of the Gilded Fly* (1944; also pub as *Obsequies at Oxford*) while still an undergraduate. Crispin traveled in Europe, including Germany, before World War II (one of his novels would deal with NAZI spies). He taught briefly after graduation, and then became a successful composer and writer. In later years, he wrote scripts and also scores for films. He lived in Devon, far from the "rapidly decaying metropolis" of London, which he disliked, and used the country as the backdrop for his novels. At least some autobiography must be hidden in the hilarious story, "We Know You're Busy Writing, But We Thought You Wouldn't Mind If We Just Dropped In for a Minute" (1969). The narrator describes himself as "forty-seven, unmarried, living alone, a minor crime-fiction writer earning, on average, rather less than £1,000 a year"; the first three facts, at least, describe Crispin. At a cottage in Devon, the poor narrator is just trying to finish one sentence—*"His crushed hand, paining him less now, nevertheless gave him a sense of . . ."*—but is interrupted by myriad visitors and phone calls, which begin to merge with the frustrated story he is working on.

In his first book, Crispin introduced Gervase FEN, an Oxford don and sometime sleuth who would appear in a relatively small number of novels (eight) written over several decades, and the last of which was published in 1977 (*The Glimpses of the Moon*). Fen is refreshingly dotty throughout the series.

Despite the "donnish" nature of his books and his obvious debt to Michael INNES, Crispin made some original contributions to the genre that were not often imitated. He adopted the modernist device of self-reference: sometimes Fen comments on the writing of the book itself, offers suggestions, or quarrels with his creator. Breaking the frame of the narrative and puncturing the reader's suspension of disbelief is only the most obvious example of the author's cheerful disregard for convention. The best of the novels about Fen are THE MOVING TOYSHOP (1946) and BURIED FOR PLEASURE (1948).

The cultural refinement of the books is genuine and they are refreshingly free of snobbery. Crispin loved poetry, and dedicated *The Moving Toyshop* to Philip Larkin. *Frequent Hearses* (1950; U.S. title *Sudden Vengeance*) is about the making of a film about the life of the seventeenth-century poet Alexander Pope; murder, and the exuberant figure of Fen, intrude. *Love Lies Bleeding* (1948) focuses on a lost manuscript by Shakespeare. Other books involve the author's musical interests to a lesser or greater extent, including *Swan Song* (1947; U.S. title *Dead and Dumb*), which uses opera.

The Long Divorce appeared in 1951. It was the last Gervase Fen novel for twenty-five years. During the fifties, Crispin wrote a number of short stories about Fen. *Beware of the Trains* (1953) was the first collection. The short story form prevents the humor and nuttiness from going sour or becoming excessive, but Fen seems more urbane and sober than in the novels. *Fen Country* (1979) contains further short stories—some of them very short—most of which appeared in the London *Evening Standard* in the fifties. Not all concerned Fen; a number are about Inspector Humbleby of SCOTLAND YARD. Each story hinges on one major clue, for example the etymology of the word "dandelion," a dropped box of china, the homophones "rowed/rode," or the luminous properties of diamonds. These straight, honest puzzles adhere to FAIR PLAY, contain little description and no padding or romantic melodrama, and show that the author was a master of the "principles" of the genre and not just a humorist.

CROCODILE ON THE SANDBANK (1975) The first of Elizabeth PETERS's books about Victorian archaeologist Amelia PEABODY. The story is not primarily a mystery but an examination and criticism of nineteenth-century mores, evidenced by the fact that there is no murder. Instead, Amelia, who is on her way to Egypt to pursue her archaeological interests despite disapproval, meets the beautiful Evelyn Barton in Rome, an Englishwoman who is extricating herself from the grasp of a churlish Italian lover. Together they proceed to Cairo, where a mummy attacks them in their hotel. They continue on their way to the city of the heretic king, Khuenaten, the mysterious mummy dogging their trail. They find the encampment of the Egyptologist Radcliffe Emerson, who is dying of a fever and is nursed by Amelia. Although there is a mystery to the mummy's "curse," the story could most accurately be described as a revisionist romance. The mummy theme was fascinating to Victorian England, which had just rediscovered Egypt and was in the process of stealing as many of its treasures as possible. The writing of *Crocodile on the Sandbank,* however, is completely contemporary, as are the minds of the characters.

CROFT-COOKE, RUPERT See BRUCE, LEO.

CROFTS, FREEMAN WILLS (1879–1957) Born in Dublin, Freeman Wills Crofts was educated in Belfast and was a railroad engineer in Ulster for twenty years. That experience provided not only matter for many of his detective stories, but seems to have encouraged a general sense of punctiliousness, fascination with time, and a sensitivity to minute fractions of difference or disturbances of order. These qualities were reflected in his series detective, the stolid Inspector FRENCH, as inexorable as a locomotive and with an equal amount of inertia.

Crofts's father, a doctor with the British army, died while Crofts was still young. His mother's second husband was an archdeacon in the Church of Ireland; Crofts represents the conservative British virtues. One of his non-mystery works was *The Four Gospels in One Story* (1949). His many other activities as a writer included BBC radio plays and a stage play, *Sudden Death* (1932).

Inspector French was only a gleam in the creator's eye when he wrote THE CASK (1920), one of the classics of the GOLDEN AGE (of which it is considered to mark the beginning). The story was written while the author was recovering from an illness, and was his first. The book involves three detectives and is highly complex, showing a debt to Continental models, with perhaps a touch of HANAUD; it went on to sell 100,000 copies and put the author suddenly on the map. The following year, Crofts published *The Ponson Case,* with an Inspector Tanner; it was not until 1924 that he introduced Inspector French. *The Pitprop Syndicate* (1922), one of the more often reprinted books by Crofts, is also not an Inspector French mystery. The rather charming background is a bicycle tour of France by two Englishmen, who turn amateur sleuths after they see a strange truck—a seemingly innocent but ominous event.

Although the title of the first French mystery, *Inspector French's Greatest Case* (1924), would indicate that the series had reached its pinnacle even before having begun, the somewhat bland detective was a success and Crofts went on writing about him for another three decades. Crofts became famous for the machine-like quality of his plots and the dogged breaking of alibis. French's forte is using documented events and sightings to prove that people could not have been where they said they were at a particular time; Crofts is at his best when dealing with the boats and trains he loved. Two of his books were set in the town (Guildford) where he lived. These books followed the more familiar patterns of the English GOLDEN AGE and the COUNTRY HOUSE style.

One does not read Crofts for characterization, rich descriptions, subtext, romantic subplots, or interesting language—but then, one would not go to the HARD-BOILED experts for intricate puzzles or rigid adherence to the rules of FAIR PLAY. Crofts's mysteries are of the "no-nonsense," classic English type, a form in which he excelled. Crofts was also a member of the DETECTION CLUB, and participated in some of the SERIAL NOVELS that the group wrote.

CRONIN, A[RCHIBALD] J[OSEPH] (1896–1981) A. J. Cronin was a Scottish doctor and novelist of liberal views who often used his writing as a vehicle for social criticism. Writing about twentieth-century Britain, it was almost inevitable that he would deal with the subject of crime and society. The result, BEYOND THIS PLACE (1950), is a fine combination of detection, *Bildungsroman,* and consideration of crime as a social phenomenon and punishment as a social institution. The young man who discovers that he is the son of a murderer is a consistently engaging figure, whose investigations are credibly successful—and just as believably ignored by everyone else.

Born in Dumbartonshire, Cronin studied at the University of Glasgow and was a Royal Navy surgeon during World War I. He practiced medicine in the mining country of Wales, where he later became a mine inspector. After practicing medicine in London, poor health led Cronin into an early retirement, during which he turned to writing (like Conan DOYLE and R. Austin FREEMAN). He used his knowledge of coal-related disease in his most famous novel, *The Stars Look Down* (1935), which could be considered a work of proletarian fiction. It depicts the grim and oppressed condition of miners in the north of England. The novel was filmed in 1939. *The Citadel* (1937) showed the corrupting influence of money on the medical profession; it was filmed in 1938.

CROOK, ARTHUR In the tradition of DICKENS and the nineteenth-century sentimental novel, Anthony GILBERT gave her barrister-sleuth a name that hinted at his character: Arthur Crook is wily at best, a scoundrel at worst. He is another manifestation of a type of character pioneered by Melville Davisson Post with Randolph MASON, except that Crook has been given a crass veneer of loud clothes, a flashy car, red face and hair, and a Cockney accent to soften his callous impression. Crook appeared in dozens of novels from the thirties to the seventies.

In *And Death Came Too* (1956), Crook is sent to the Riviera and back in one of his more active appearances. *The Innocent Bottle* (1948; British title *Lift Up the Lid*) is a lengthy story about a woman married to an invalid forty years her senior. The wealthy and cantankerous James East hires a shrewish nurse, Miss Beake, who sows discord in the household. After East dies, she ensures that Mrs. East is arrested for murder. Crook enters the case at this point. Although Crook's banter is lively and often funny, here as in other novels the slow pace and the thinness of the other characters fail to sustain interest.

BIBLIOGRAPHY Novels: *Murder by Experts* (1936), *The Man Who Wasn't There* (1937), *Murder Has No Tongue* (1937), *Treason in My Breast* (1938), *The Bell of Death* (1939), *The Clock in the Hatbox* (1939), *Dear Dead Woman* (1940), *The Vanishing Corpse* (1941; U.S. title *She Vanished in the Dawn*), *The Woman in Red* (1941), *Something Nasty in the Woodshed* (1942; U.S. title *Mystery in the Woodshed*), *The Mystery of the Tea-Cosy Aunt* (1942; U.S. title *Death in the Blackout*), *The Mouse Who Wouldn't Play Ball* (1943; U.S. title *Thirty Days to Live*), *A Spy for Mr. Crook* (1944), *He Came by Night* (1944; U.S. title *Death at the Door*), *The Scarlet Button* (1944), *Don't Open the Door* (1945; U.S. title *Death Lifts the Latch*), *The Black Stage* (1945), *The Spinster's Secret* (1946; U.S. title *By Hook or by Crook*), *Death in the Wrong Room* (1947), *Die in the Dark* (1947; U.S. title *The Missing Widow*), *Death Knocks Three Times* (1949), *Murder Comes Home* (1950), *A Nice Cup of Tea* (1950; U.S. title *The Wrong Body*), *Lady Killer* (1951), *Miss Pinnegar Disappears* (1952; U.S. title *A Case for Mr. Crook*), *Footsteps Behind Me* (1953; U.S. title *Black Death*), *Snake in the Grass* (1954; U.S. title *Death Won't Wait*), *Is She Dead, Too?* (1955; U.S. title *A Question of Murder*), *Riddle of a Lady* (1956), *Give Death a Name* (1957), *Death Against the Clock* (1958), *Third Crime Lucky* (1959; U.S. title *Prelude to Murder*), *Death Takes a Wife* (1959; U.S. title *Death Casts a Long Shadow*), *Out for the Kill* (1960), *She Shall Die* (1961; U.S. title *After the Verdict*), *Uncertain Death* (1961), *No Dust in the Attic* (1962), *Ring for a Noose* (1963), *Knock, Knock, Who's There?* (1964; U.S. title *The Voice*), *The Fingerprint* (1964), *Passenger to Nowhere* (1965), *The Looking Glass Murder* (1966), *The Visitor* (1967), *Night Encounter* (1968; U.S. title *Murder Anonymous*), *Missing from Her Home* (1969), *Death Wears a Mask* (1970; U.S. title *Mr. Crook Lifts the Mask*), *Tenant for a Tomb* (1971), *Murder's a Waiting Game* (1972), *A Nice Little Killing* (1973).

CROSS, AMANDA (pseudonym of Carolyn Heilbrun, 1926–) The Columbia professor Carolyn Heilbrun had to wait until after she had received tenure before she could reveal that she was the author of the Kate FANSLER mystery novels as well as her academic works, which says something about the pretentious and pompous atmosphere of academia. The vivid recreation of this atmosphere is one of the attractions—or repulsions, depending on your point of view—of the adventures of Kate, who like her creator is a professor of literature at an elite university in Manhattan.

Heilbrun received her education at Columbia University and began teaching there in 1972. She has published a number of works of feminist theory and criticism, including *Towards a Recognition of Androgyny* (1973) and *Reinventing Womanhood* (1979). Her honors and awards are many, though they are exclusively for her academic work (except for a Nero Wolfe award in 1981). The critical reception of the Fansler novels has declined, with the later works being judged confusing and unreadable.

The problem with the series has always been Kate Fansler herself. When she was introduced, there was nothing new about an academic amateur sleuth; Gervase FEN, to name only one, had been around for twenty years when Fansler first appeared in *In the Last Analysis* (1964), and the "donnish" school was well developed. What Fansler had that the dons didn't have, however, was an up-to-date political agenda. Most donnish mysteries, like Michael INNES's, are absurd affairs, fantasies that are not to be taken seriously but are only meant to amuse (they usually do). Heilbrun's books are more realistic, but they are also less funny; the humor that passes between Fansler and her husband, Reed Amhearst, is often wooden and pretentious—the kind of thing that people whisper to each other at department meetings or remark at faculty teas, hoping to be overheard. The portrayal of the "low" characters—workmen, neighbors, ordinary mortals—is sometimes embarrassing. Fansler's character is not entirely to blame, however, because the books have a third-person narrator also given to such one-legged circumlocutions as, "Grace Knole was nearly seventy herself, like the miles per hour they were travelling."

The early books in the series are accounted the best, such as *The James Joyce Murder* (1967), *Poetic Justice* (1970), and *The Question of Max* (1976). In 1997, Heilbrun published *The Last Gift of Time: Life Beyond Sixty,* reflections on the satisfactions of later life that she once meant to deny herself, having vowed in her youth not to live into old age.

CRUMLEY, JAMES (1939–) Dismissed by some, adored by others, the American writer James Crumley has created two memorable detective characters, C. W. SUGHRUE and Milo MILODRAGOVITCH, a pair of loser-heroes who work out of Meriwether, Montana. There is more information available about Crumley in literary than in mystery sources. Crumley's language is no worse and his violence no more appalling than that of many of his contemporaries, and his writing is often better. Crumley's real offence is to have used the mystery for his own ends.

Born in Texas, Crumley attended the Georgia Institute of Technology and the Texas Arts and Industries University. He is also a graduate of the Iowa Writer's Workshop. Crumley served in Vietnam from 1958 to 1961. His first novel, *One to Count Cadence* (1969), was about the war. In 1975 he turned to detection with *The Wrong Case,* which introduced the alcoholic Milodragovitch, who also appears in DANCING BEAR (1983), which has an environmental theme. THE LAST GOOD KISS (1978) is about Sughrue's search for a missing man and his subsequent obsession with a budding actress who disappeared a decade before. Crumley seems to have been influenced by Jack Kerouac, in that most of his stories involve being "on the road," which is a metaphor for the rootlessness and alienation of his characters. The alcoholic and depressed Vietnam veteran, returned to an America that is a bizarre collage of political lies and media images, is an archetype Crumley is constantly exploring. He is more easily compared to non-mystery writers like Harry Crews and Stephen Wright (see GOING NATIVE, 1994). Crumley's anger and political message is more integrated than what one finds in self-consciously "empowering" mysteries. It is true that the violence can get wearing; it is less offensive than simply monotonous. *The Mexican Tree Duck* (1993) is an extremely violent novel (a Sughrue) about drug dealers.

Crumley has also worked as a journalist; some of his pieces, including "orphans" that were rejected, are collected in *The Muddy Fork and Other Things* (1991). In *Bordersnakes* (1996), Sughrue and Milodragovitch appear together for the first time. It is a revenge story, in which Sughrue has been shot and Milodragovitch cheated out of his long-withheld inheritance, and once more takes them on the road.

CUE FOR MURDER (1942) One of the wartime adventures of Basil WILLING, the psychiatrist detective created by Helen MCCLOY. Willing, who has not yet joined the Navy but is still assisting the district attorney of New York City, investigates a murder onstage during a revival of a mediocre play, *Fedora,* by Victorien Sardou (1831–1908). The play is itself a murder story, and at one point the body of the dying Russian count Vladimir is supposed to be discovered in an alcove. On the opening night, the man playing Vladimir turns out to be not acting, but really dead, with a scalpel through his heart. The man's identity is not immediately known, so it is impossible to assign motives to the only people who might have killed him, who were also onstage: Wanda Morley, a prima donna who stars in bad plays to cover her lack of talent, and is cast as the wife of "Vladimir"; Rodney Tait, a handsome but unskilled leading man who played the doctor (and carried a medical bag and instruments); and Leonard Martin, a talented actor who has returned to the stage after a year-long disappearance to play the Russian policeman. A related plot involves a series of burglaries of a nearby knife-sharpening business; nothing is stolen, but the proprietor's pet canary is let loose each time.

Cue for Murder is one of McCloy's least rich novels psychologically—the motive is weak—but it is one of her best puzzles; Anthony BOUCHER said that "the clue-structure is so careful and so fair" that the reader should arrive at the solution at the same time as Willing. The theatrical people are just that, but their very superficiality places the detection at center stage; this is also one novel in which Willing is present from the very first act.

CUFF, SERGEANT The investigator in Wilkie Collins's THE MOONSTONE (1868). Cuff was modeled on the real detective Jonathan WHICHER. Cuff has an appearance somewhat like an aged, withered Sherlock HOLMES: he is tall, with a "hatchet" face and penetrating gray eyes that seem to pierce the interlocutor. Surprisingly, Cuff is described as "elderly"; he is cadaverous, with yellow skin and claw-like hands. Cuff does not smile, but only curls up the corners of his mouth when he is amused. Some people find him repulsive, while others, like Betteredge, find him fascinating. In his manner, Cuff is of the cryptic school, making tantalizing remarks that seem to carry some important information (one of the ways in which Collins keeps the reader engaged with the story). On the other hand, he talks at length with the gardener about the cultivation of roses, which he would like to grow when he retires—an instance of another feature that would become a convention in the genre: the humanizing hobby.

CUNNINGHAM, E. V. (pen name of Howard Fast, 1914–) Howard Fast is best known for his historical novels written from a radical perspective and his association with and then repudiation of COMMUNISM. Born in New York City, Fast was a high school dropout but published a novel before he was twenty. He served in informational posts in the Army during World War II and then was a war correspondent in the Pacific during 1945. He joined the Communist party in 1943. *Citizen Tom Paine* (1943) was one of a series of novels about the revolutionary war; *The Last Frontier* (1941) was a groundbreaking work that viewed the conquest of the Americas from the viewpoint of native peoples.

In 1950, Fast refused to provide names to the House Un-American Activities Committee and went to prison for three months. After his release, still blacklisted under the McCarthyist red scare, he found it difficult to get a publisher and so started a publishing company himself. Fast published the highly successful *Spartacus,* about the Roman slave revolt, in 1951. Later, in *The Naked God* (1957), he announced his disenchantment with the communist cause. *The Passion of Sacco and Vanzetti* (1953) is another important work of this period.

As E. V. Cunningham, Fast wrote two series of mystery and detection stories. One features Masao MASUTO, a Japanese American detective with the Los Angeles police. The other is a collection of books dealing with women, each named for the protagonist. Some of these books are experimental and quite odd, including *Sally* (1967), in which a woman who thinks she is dying of a chronic illness hires a man to kill her, and *Helen* (1966), about the murder of a judge. This book dwells morbidly on the corruption of Las Vegas, and rather spectacularly violates one of the more important rules of FAIR PLAY at its end. It also shows the continuing concern with social issues that marked Fast's non-mystery fiction. *Samantha* (1967) is a hybrid novel that also includes Masuto's first appearance. Although his mystery novels are written with popularity in mind in a way that his other works are not, Cunningham injects some political content in a casual way.

CURARE A poison extracted from the bark and sap of a species of South American trees known as *Strychnos toxifera.* The poison has long been used by the Indians of the region for poison darts. Curare is an extremely powerful alkaloid, a muscle relaxant that rapidly causes death through respiratory failure. One of the most interesting things about the drug is that it is harmless when swallowed, and has to be injected or otherwise introduced into the blood to cause death. Curare is also used as an anaesthetic; the active part is tubocurarine, which inhibits the action of acetylcholine, a neurotransmitter. There is no antidote for this rapid-acting poison.

CURTAIN (1975) Hercule POIROT's last case. Unlike other writers who decided to let their detectives simply fade away, or didn't get time or get around to putting them away themselves, Agatha CHRISTIE brought Poirot's career to a conclusion in *Curtain,* shortly before her own death. She brought Poirot back to Styles, where he had begun (see THE MYSTERIOUS AFFAIR AT STYLES). She also brought back Captain Hastings, summoned by Poirot to help him trap a Mr. X, a criminal who has been in the vicinity of five murders, in each of which the blame was clearly thrown upon someone else. The case is a FINAL PROBLEM for Poirot.

Christie makes it difficult, however, for the reader to guess who the hidden murderer is by a series of covering subplots. For example, Poirot is old and ill and confined to a wheelchair. Hastings, never brilliant, is easily distracted by his concern for his daughter, who is menaced by the attentions of Major Allerton, a notorious woman-chaser. As his anger becomes murderous, it begins to seem that Hastings himself might be the killer. Several other charming candidates present themselves, however, including Dr. Franklin, who thinks that most of the human race should be exterminated, and Hastings's daughter, who agrees with him. People do begin to die, and it seems the mystery will never be solved. In the end, it is up to Hastings (with a little help from a postscript).

CYANIDE This poison exists in many forms and is one of the most fast-acting. Among the types of cyanide is hydrocyanic acid, which exists naturally in peach, apricot, and plum pits as well as other seeds. (Eating pits, however, is not fatal, since the hard substance of the pit prevents absorption.) Hydrogen cyanide has been used in numberless mysteries, but in reality, like many poisonous substances, it is difficult to obtain and has primarily commercial uses, insecticides and rodenticides among them. In its gaseous state, hydrogen cyanide has been used in gas chambers. Other forms of cyanide include potassium cyanide and sodium cyanide.

Cyanide is famous for the smell of almonds it gives off (though not, perhaps, as strongly as some fiction would indicate). Death from cyanide is rapid and unpleasant; the chemical prevents the absorption of oxygen in the blood and leads to convulsions.

"CYPRIAN BEES, THE" See HAILEY, DR. EUSTACE.

DAENINCKX, DIDIER (1949–) Probably the foremost contemporary French mystery writer, Didier Daeninckx remains little known in the United States. He wrote his first novel, *Mort au premier tour* (1977), while he was unemployed; it is the story of a murder at a nuclear research center, and introduced the series character, Inspector Cadin. Cadin appeared in a series of books, until Daeninckx had him commit suicide in *Le Facteur fatal* (1992)—putting himself in the small group of writers like Nicholas FREELING who have killed off their detectives. Daeninckx's novels, like Freeling's, are intensely focused on the nature of society, and embed a cultural critique in an otherwise orthodox mystery plot. *Meurtres pour mémoire* (1984; tr 1991, *Murder in Memoriam*) is a political novel as well as detective story, and won the Grand Prix de Littérature Policière. In 1981, Inspector Cadin investigates the murder of a man named Bernard Thiraud, which relates to the murder of his father, Roger Thiraud, twenty years before. Roger was a history teacher, killed on June 17, 1961, when 400 protesters were killed by the French police during the Algerian War. Daeninckx shows how the writing of history obscures as much as it reveals, and how it serves a national compulsion toward forgetfulness that only aids the abuse of power. Other books, such as *Le ders des ders* (1984) and *Un château en Bohême* (1994), are also interrogations of history, the former set in post–World War I France, the latter in Czechoslovakia. Both expose the hypocrisy of the powerful and the crimes that are committed behind the facade of respectability.

Daeninckx has also written for television, and Novacek, the journalist turned private investigator of *Un château en Bohême,* became the basis of a series.

DAHL, ROALD (1916–1990) Known for his stories for children, the Welsh-born Roald Dahl also wrote some strange and clever tales of the macabre. The stories poke rather nasty fun at human pretension and callousness, often showing people betrayed by their own deviousness (like the wife in "Nunc Dimittis," who loses the mink she got from her secret lover to a rival she didn't know she had). Jealousy and revenge are recurrent motives for actions that sometimes go very much awry. Although he did not write mystery stories per se, the frustrated people of his stories sometimes resort to murder. One of these stories, "Lamb to the Slaughter," contains one of the most famous murders in crime fiction and is a perfect example of Dahl's black humor. In "The Way Up to Heaven," a man who takes an almost sadistic pleasure in making his anxious wife late for appointments has his game backfire on him; the surprise at the end is worthy of Cornell WOOLRICH.

Dahl's volumes of stories include *Kiss, Kiss* (1960) and *Switch Bitch* (1974). *Tales of the Unexpected* (1990) collects Dahl's best-known work.

DALE, JIMMIE A gentleman thief in a series of novels by Frank L. PACKARD. Like RAFFLES, Jimmie Dale is an upper-class gent who likes to steal (though sometimes he is forced to it). But unlike Raffles, he is an American, highly placed in New York society; he also has a Robin Hood streak in him, and steals for good reasons. Because of the mark he leaves on the safes he cracks, Dale is known as "The Gray Seal." He has two other secret identities: Larry the Bat, an underworld crook, and Smarlinghue, an artist.

BIBLIOGRAPHY Novels: *Jimmie Dale and the Phantom Clue* (1922), *Jimmie Dale and the Blue Envelope Murder* (1930), *Jimmie Dale and the Missing Hour* (1935).

Short Stories: *The Adventures of Jimmie Dale* (1917), *The Further Adventures of Jimmie Dale* (1919).

DALGLIESH, ADAM A detective created by P. D. JAMES. When he first appears in COVER HER FACE (1962), Adam Dalgliesh is a Detective Chief Inspector with some seven years of experience. Tall and handsome, Dalgliesh has some of the characteristics of the GOLDEN AGE detective, but not all; there is nothing flamboyant or aristocratic about him, though he is cultured, a published poet who appreciates distinctions. Slightly introverted, Dalgliesh is closer in kind to Alan GRANT and Nigel STRANGEWAYS than he is to Roderick ALLEYN. His habit of focusing all his attention on the face of the deceased when he first sees the victim is not only a way of fixing those features in his mind, but a quasi-mystical act of empathy. It is, however, an empathy he is careful not to reveal to others.

P. D. James has written that she adheres "to the view enshrined in English law that what consenting adults do in private is their own concern," and so the details of Dalgliesh's personal life are kept discreetly in the background. We learn that his wife died during childbirth, along with their baby son. Dalgliesh's sorrow acts as a foil for his logical precision and relentlessness, as does the fact that he is a poet. (A MIND TO MURDER,

1963, takes place at a psychiatric clinic a stone's throw from where Dalgliesh is attending a publishing party for one of his books.) It may have been a brilliant stroke to make Dalgliesh emotional, but even more so to hold this quality in reserve. Over the course of several books, Dalgliesh has an affair with Deborah Riscoe and debates marrying her.

Police work is well documented in the books, but so are Dalgliesh's instinctive reactions (what used to be called hunches). Although James says that Dorothy L. SAYERS was "a potent early influence," her books also reflect the postwar trend toward greater realism, though she does not carry it to the sometimes boring extremes of the worst of the PROCEDURAL subgenre.

In *Unnatural Causes* (1967), Dalgliesh has come to the end of a love affair and is also coming off a difficult case, which accounts for his more subdued performance. He goes to Suffolk to visit an aunt, Jane Dalgliesh, who lives in a small village near where the encroaching sea has already swallowed one town. The somber atmosphere of Monksmere and the writers (a romance novelist, a drama critic, a mystery writer) who live in the area and their very different temperaments are well described. The corpse is found floating in a dinghy, the hands cut off. The medical report, however, finds that the victim died of natural causes before the mutilation.

Original Sin (1996) is set in a venerable old English publishing house, Peverell Press, which is experiencing some financial trouble. Gerard Etienne, the unpleasant new managing director, dies in peculiar circumstances and Dalgliesh is called in. This killing is only one of several in the story, which gets involved in subplots more than James's other mysteries.

The spelling of the detective's name varies from edition to edition, some having "Dalgliesh" and others "Dalgleish"—one edition of *Cover Her Face* spelled it one way on the cover and another inside.

BIBLIOGRAPHY Novels: *Shroud for a Nightingale* (1971), *The Black Tower* (1975), *Death of an Expert Witness* (1977), *A Taste for Death* (1986), *Devices and Desires* (1990), *A Certain Justice* (1997).

DALY, CARROLL JOHN (1889–1958) One of the early writers associated with BLACK MASK, Daly created the first HARD-BOILED detective, Race WILLIAMS. Now often dismissed out of hand for his melodramatic style, Williams's ludicrous toughness, and, simply, for bad writing, Daly could write well on occasion. THE FALSE BURTON COMBS (1922) was a pioneering hard-boiled story, which not only did not feature the trigger-happy Williams, but still showed vestiges of conventional romance underneath the crime story. (For these romantic touches, too, Daly has been criticized, particularly when it comes to THE FLAME.)

Daly was one of the first writers to make it big through *Black Mask*, and he seems to have helped the magazine as much as he was helped by it: the name of his detective on the cover of an issue supposedly boosted sales 20 percent. In a famous poll of its readers, Daly came out well ahead of Erle Stanley GARDNER and Dashiell HAMMETT, who ran second and third.

Some of Daly's books have recently been republished, including the novels *Snarl of the Beast* (1927; repr 1992) and *The Hidden Hand* (1928; repr 1992). Both were serialized in *Black Mask*. In the first, Williams battles a simian monster with green eyes; in the second, he takes ship for Miami on the track of a NAPOLEON OF CRIME, the unnamed "Hidden Hand." The nonstop action is punishing for the reader and rapidly induces fatigue. An occasional nice phrase is buried under verbosity and banality, and Daly has an addiction to the interrogative mode, particularly directed at the reader: "Stumped? Sure I was. What do you think? Did I want to see her? I didn't know. And why?" The language is repetitive, sometimes bizarrely inappropriate; a blonde's hair looks like "a huge sponge from the museum of Natural History." Daly's short stories, which are still readable today, are available only in anthologies.

DALY, CONOR See GOLF MYSTERIES.

DALY, ELIZABETH (1878–1967) A near contemporary of Mary Roberts RINEHART, Elizabeth Daly had much in common with the more famous writer. The settings of their novels tend to overlap, including New York City, New England, and the coast of Maine. Daly was a better writer than Rinehart, and her books are still entertaining today.

Daly's detective is the bibliophile Henry GAMADGE; book collecting often figures in his cases. Among his best adventures are *Any Shape or Form* (1945), *The Book of the Crime* (1951), and *Death and Letters* (1950). *An Elizabeth Daly Mystery Omnibus* contains three novels: *Murders in Volume 2* (1941), *Evidence of Things Seen* (1943), and *The Book of the Dead* (1960).

Agatha CHRISTIE said that Daly was her favorite American mystery author; Daly's work is similar to Christie's in reflecting upper-class society and obeying GOLDEN AGE conventions. Daly was the daughter of a New York judge and was educated at Bryn Mawr College and Columbia University. After teaching at Bryn Mawr for several years, she became involved with amateur theater groups in New York. Her cultivated background is reflected in Gamadge's gentility and erudition.

Daly only began writing mysteries when she was sixty years old, but she still made a significant mark on the genre. In 1960, she received an EDGAR award for her detective oeuvre.

DALZIEL, SUPERINTENDENT ANDREW Andrew Dalziel is the rougher of the detective pair created by Reginald HILL. Dalziel is an old-fashioned copper who has seen everything and become tough and realistic. Middle-aged and almost bald, he is known for bluntness and coarseness (he is referred to as "that fat bastard," or, more politely, "His Fatship"). Dalziel's wife has left him, and women in the books tend to react to him with mingled distrust and horror.

Dalziel's partner is Inspector Peter Pascoe (only a sergeant early in the series, he gets promoted in A RULING PASSION), a younger, more idealistic man. Pascoe is politically more liberal than the bigoted Dalziel, and has a degree in sociology. Beneath the antagonism and chiding, there is friendship and respect. Pascoe's girlfriend and later wife Ellie seems to detest Dalziel in the earlier books, but comes grudgingly to like him. It is easy to prefer the aesthete to the Neanderthal, and one of Hill's most clever tricks is to get the reader to fall naturally into Pascoe's way of thinking—his is, after all, a modern, sensitive, and wholly typical intelligence—and then to hit you with the truth that Dalziel has ferreted out with his copper's harsh and cynical logic, which the reader has tended to ignore because of Dalziel's coarse exterior.

Pascoe meets Eleanor Soper in *An Advancement of Learning* (1971) and marries her in *An April Shroud* (1975). After the wedding, Dalziel takes a two-week holiday in Lincolnshire that begins inauspiciously with a flood. He is picked up by a water-borne funeral cortège towing a coffin; the widow, Bonnie Fielding, takes an interest in Dalziel and invites him to wait out the flood in the Fielding home, where he finds a bizarre collection of people, a dead rat in the fridge, and indications of something strange going on below the surface. Then he discovers that Bonnie's first husband also died somewhat mysteriously. Partly an updated GOTHIC spoof, partly a laughable and slightly grotesque romance, the novel has Dalziel acting more like a classic sleuth trapped in a COUNTRY HOUSE (albeit a bizarre one) than a policeman.

Many of the Dalziel-Pascoe books, unlike true PROCEDURALS, involve these personal cases that begin unofficially or revolve around people known to the main characters (*A Ruling Passion* most shockingly). In *A Pinch of Snuff* (1978), Pascoe's dentist tips him off to sadomasochistic movies being shown by a local men's club. After the head of the club is himself caned and murdered, the trail leads into the world of "snuff" film production, but Dalziel removes Pascoe from the case.

Asking for the Moon (1994) contains four novellas, one of which recounts the first meeting of Dalziel and Pascoe. One story is futuristic, and two play off OCCULT themes. In a speculation on the development of the European Union set in the year 2012, Hill has Pascoe "Commissioner of Eurofed Justice" and Dalziel retired. In "Pascoe's Ghost," a brother's claim that he is being haunted by his missing sister's spirit leads Pascoe to investigate. In "Dalziel's Ghost," the gruff inspector spends a night in a haunted farmhouse.

BIBLIOGRAPHY Novels: *A Clubbable Woman* (1970), *A Killing Kindness* (1980), *Deadheads* (1983), *Exit Lines* (1984), *Child's Play* (1987), *Under World* (1988), *Bones and Silence* (1990), *Recalled to Life* (1992), *Pictures of Perfection* (1994),*The Wood Beyond* (1996), *On Beulah Height* (1998), *Arms and the Woman* (1999).

Short Stories: *Pascoe's Ghost* (1979).

DAM, THE (1968) This novel by Angus MACLEOD takes place almost entirely on a single, unseasonably hot summer day in Scotland. Camusinnes is a village, but it is not a COZY village; a hydroelectric plant has brought prosperity and ruin. After seven years working on the dam's construction for good wages, the crofters are resistant to returning to subsistence farming. Then developer Drummond Elliot offers to buy their land to build a holiday camp and a factory where they can have year-round jobs making "tartan novelties"—souvenirs for the tourist trade. The drunken schoolmaster and respected poet Duncan MacLaine exerts his influence over Sorby MacIver, his pub mate, who happens to own a plot smack in the middle of the site.

MacLeod's view of the conflict is balanced; if the commercial culture is "shoddy" and crass, the traditional can be backward, spiteful, and dirty-minded. He devotes a chapter to the principle characters, who emerge as people, not types. Judith, Elliot's wife, admires the poet's work and they fall in love; Elliot is having an affair with the Laird's wife; and the Laird chases village boys. MacLeod also knows it takes more than sending a character to Oxford or Cambridge to make one sound intelligent. The heat and stillness give a feeling of eternal day, but MacLeod does not hide the backwardness behind the beauty: "However did they reconcile dirt and love? They didn't of course, at least most of them didn't. Most of them thought of sex in terms of lust, enjoyable but dirty. All was dirty, secretions were excretions. Semen was excrement—men getting rid of their dirt." The story is invested with a tart humor and beautifully written. There is not, however, an investigation. The smoldering resentments do build to a violent confrontation—which is as nothing to the incredible surprise of the ending.

DANCE AT THE SLAUGHTERHOUSE, A (1991) An EDGAR award-winning novel by Lawrence BLOCK, and one of his most action-packed. It begins with Matthew SCUDDER's accidental discovery of a misfiled "snuff" film from a video store. The film reveals a man and a woman sexually abusing and finally murdering a captive victim. Scudder later recognizes the man in the film at a boxing match, and his pursuit, well- and intricately plotted, begins. It might have been better had Block not made the man a German, for he is too reminiscent of the countless sadistic NAZIS spouting crackpot versions of Nietzsche familiar from books and film. Scudder's friend, the genial murderer Mick BALLOU, is drawn into the plot, and together they bring about the most stupendous and ambiguous of Block endings.

DANCE HALL OF THE DEAD (1973) The first mystery to feature the Navajo detective Joe LEAPHORN, and an EDGAR-winning novel. The title refers to a lake where the spirits of the dead congregate. The novel illustrates the legal and jurisdictional tangle that plagues the Tribal Police. When a young boy is brutally murdered, the F.B.I. try to take over the investigation. Arrogant and officious, they have no respect for the native policemen. On their side, the Tribal Police do not have much respect for the F.B.I.'s methods or competence. While Leaphorn discovers the real truth, the white men concoct another "truth" that satisfies their preconceptions. The lack of trust in and respect for the independence of the Native Americans by the white authority is forcefully brought home.

DANCING BEAR (1983) A novel by James CRUMLEY. Milo MILODRAGOVITCH is living in a log house, surviving on a diet of cocaine and peppermint schnapps. He has been working as a night watchman when he gets a series of absurd jobs. One of his father's old lovers hires him to watch two people she does not even know who have been meeting furtively near her home. This elderly woman has become a radical and a pot smoker under the influence of her grandniece, whom Milo tries to pick up. He also gets a job tailing a mysterious woman named Cassandra Bogardus. Meanwhile, an environmentalist group wants him to donate his grandfather's parcel of land for the Dancing Bear wildlife refuge. Through a series of morose, meaningless adventures that become progressively more violent, the frayed threads of Milo's life gradually get twisted together.

DANE, TIMOTHY A private detective in a series of novels written by William ARD. Ard wrote in the HARD-BOILED tradition, but, like Ross MACDONALD in the same period, revised the formula toward greater psychological complexity. His novels are not, however, anywhere near as complicated or subtle as Macdonald's. Dane is young and debonair, but is a more sensitive version of the classic tough guy, as was the older Lew ARCHER. Dane is more similar to such handsome stud types as Travis MCGEE. He lives in a dump on Fifty-Third Street in New York City and is a hard drinker. After serving in the Marines in World War II, Dane got his start in the detective business with the Pioneer Agency in Chicago.

Hell Is a City (1955) is the best-known of the Dane novels. It is a very ugly but believable story: a policeman tries to rape a young girl, and her brother shoots him to prevent the crime. The novel is set in the Latin American community in Brooklyn and shows the corruption of the administration of "justice" by racism. Dane is called in by a newspaperman to find out the truth, but the police, the mayoral government, and the press are against him, wanting to portray the incident as a brutal killing by a delinquent and to make the would-be rapist a hero in blue.

The Root of His Evil (1957; also pub as *Deadly Beloved*), the last novel in the series, has Dane acting as a courier for the nightclub singer Buddy Lewis. The private eye has to deliver a hundred thousand dollars to the gambling boss Johnny Cashman in Miami; a group of sinister "Latins" linked to a South American revolution are also after the money. Along the way, Dane gets involved with the erotic dancer Lissa, who also "belongs" to Cashman. This plot of the young woman under the power of a criminal recurs in *The Perfect Frame* (1951), in which Dane is approached by an innocent beauty who had been drugged and photographed in the nude. The case also involves arson and a mysterious suicide by an insurance executive who takes a dive from his forty-third story office. Dane also runs into Jocko Robinson, an older operative from his Chicago days. Like the first novels of Ross Macdonald, *The Perfect Frame* is a mixture of pulpy clichés and original writing. Ard is at his best in his asides describing New York in the forties.

BIBLIOGRAPHY Novels: *The Diary* (1952), *A Private Party* (1953), *Don't Come Crying to Me* (1954), *Mr. Trouble* (1954), *Cry Scandal* (1956).

DANIELS, CHARMIAN A series character created by Gwendoline BUTLER, Constable Charmian Daniels is a relatively early entry into the now large subgenre of female cops. Daniels first appeared in *Come Home and Be Killed* (1962); it and the succeeding novels have been published under the pseudonym Jennie Melville. The books have appeared sporadically, with a new burst of titles in the last decade.

Although the Daniels novels could be classified as PROCEDURALS, Butler invests them with humor and GOTHIC elements, as well as overtones of romance, a genre in which the author has also been successful. She likes to use such elements as ghosts and the OCCULT, even if they are given realistic explanations. The novels are also sometimes billed as COZY, though the crimes are often brutal. In *Making Good Blood* (1989), a woman and a horse both have their throats slashed. (This is one of the books written in the first person.) *The Morbid Kitchen* (1995) is about a murder committed ten years before the time of the novel, and uses the "body in the basement" theme.

Charmian Daniels is a red-headed Scot who brims with self-confidence. Her usual beat is the suburban town of Deerham Hills. During the series, she becomes the head of a regional crime unit outside London; she lives in Windsor. In *Witching Murder* (1990), Daniels is Chief Superintendent with the Metropolitan Police, specializing in crimes against women. On sick leave, she gets involved with her neighbor, who is rumored to be the head of a coven of witches—one of whom is found stabbed to death, her body surrounded with occult objects and symbols. In *Footsteps in the Blood* (1990), Charmian's goddaughter Kate Cooper and Sergeant Dolly Barstow become suspects when a woman is killed who tried to sell them information about a stalker. In *Whoever Has the Heart* (1993), Daniels buys a dilapidated cottage in the village of Brideswell. She is planning to marry Humphrey Kent but has not decided whether to live with him. Then she finds parts of a dead woman on the property, chewed by rats; at the same time, one of the lovers of a London playboy has disappeared, and pieces of her are turning up all over the metropolitan area.

BIBLIOGRAPHY Novels: *Burning Is a Substitute for Loving* (1963), *Murderer's Houses* (1964), *There Lies Your Love* (1965), *Nell Alone* (1966), *A Different Kind of Summer* (1967), *A New Kind of Killer, An Old Kind of Death* (1971), *Murder Has a Pretty Face* (1981).

DARE, SUSAN See EBERHART, MIGNON G.

DARK FANTASTIC, THE (1983) A novel by Stanley ELLIN. Set in New York City, the novel has two converging plot lines. One involves John Milano, who works for Watrous Associates in a detective capacity. His job is to recover high-priced missing merchandise for insurance companies—in this case, two valuable paintings stolen from a private collection. Milano lives in a posh apartment overlooking Central Park. Charles Kirwan, on the other hand, is a Brooklynite who is terminally ill with cancer and plans to blow up one of his own apartment buildings (and the people inside it). Kirwan and Milano alternately narrate chapters of the book. It at first is not clear what Kirwan's motive is, but it emerges that he is a terrible racist, and sees his action as invested with symbolic meaning. Kirwan also has a perverse interest in CHILDREN, one of whom he has catalog his library in the nude. The book has been controversial, even though the views Kirwan expresses are clearly imputed to him alone and are obviously an element of his perversion.

DARLING, MAX See DEATH ON DEMAND.

DA SILVA, CAPTAIN JOSÉ A series character created by Robert L. FISH. At the time he was introduced, in *The Fugitive* (1962), Da Silva was a relatively rare phenomenon: a non-Anglo detective, not working in the northern hemisphere. But although he is a policeman, there is nothing PROCEDURAL in his stories; rather, they are criminous adventures with a smattering of detection. Captain "Zé" Da Silva is a liaison officer between INTERPOL and the Brazilian police, and is feared in the Rio de Janeiro underworld that he knows so well (his cousin, Nestor, is a notorious criminal). He is tall, "copper" skinned, and has a pockmarked face; with his curly black hair and moustache, he looks like a "slightly satanic brigand." He comes, however, from an important family, and is sharply dressed and formal in his manners, though he has a tendency toward sarcasm. Da Silva works with an American named Wilson, a "nondescript" man with sandy hair and light eyes, "of a type to be passed unnoticed on the street any day." Although he is only the security officer at the U.S. embassy, Wilson has an INTERPOL connection as well.

Da Silva is given a partly American background (through his mother's family), which accounts for his facility in English and for the fact that, through INTERPOL, most of his work has to do with rich, powerful foreigners and only tangentially with the Brazilian world. Rio de Janeiro provides local color, while the cases themselves are typical of "Western" suspense and spy fiction. It is hard to say whether Da Silva's *machismo* is supposed to convey further his being Brazilian, or is just the usual generic sexism of the sixties action thriller. All unmarried younger women are "girls"; Da Silva seems to think all women are dumb, and he looks down on Wilson for letting a woman get an emotional hold on him.

In the first book, Da Silva hunts for a NAZI who has fled to Brazil. *The Isle of Snakes* (1963) has Da Silva and Wilson trapped on an island surrounded by thousands of reptiles in a sensational plot similar to a James BOND film. In *The Diamond Bubble* (1965), Wilson introduces Da Silva to U.S. Senator Joseph Hastings, whose wife had purchased an exquisite diamond at far below market price—and from Da Silva's ne'er-do-well cousin. Da Silva finds that a number of tourists have bought genuine stones at bargain prices from underworld figures, and his attempts to find out why lead to a series of murders. *The Bridge That Went Nowhere* (1968) begins with the destruction of a bridge in a remote corner of the country. The plot, set against the background of Brazilian colonization of the interior, is more or less obvious from the start. A young American woman comes to Wilson with a story about her missing brother, a geology professor from Berkeley. Da Silva remains skeptical, until he finds a radioactive shoe with a foot still in it.

BIBLIOGRAPHY Novels: *The Shrunken Head* (1963), *Brazilian Sleigh Ride* (1965), *Always Kill a Stranger* (1967), *The Xavier Affair* (1969), *The Green Hell Treasure* (1971), *Trouble in Paradise* (1975).

DAUGHTER OF TIME, THE (1951) In this novel by Josephine TEY, Inspector Alan GRANT takes on a mystery four hundred years old, and solves it without leaving his hospital bed. Confined due to injuries following an accident in the line of duty, Grant is presented with a sheaf of interesting "faces" to ponder to help while away the hours. One of the portraits is of Richard III, King of England. The detective delves into the traditional account of Richard's evil career, which is familiar from Shakespeare's play: Richard murdered the famous Princes in the Tower, his brother Edward IV's two sons, because they stood between him and the throne. Grant finds the story full of holes. For example, there is no contemporary account of the deed, and the bill of attainder passed by Richard's successor, Henry VII, in which Richard is condemned, doesn't even mention the crime. Grant is assisted by a young American researcher, Brent Carradine, one of Tey's more hokey portrayals. While the book is not Tey's best it is one of her best known, and contains much interesting and arcane history of England during and after the Wars of the Roses.

DAVIDSON, LIONEL (1922–) Born in Yorkshire, England, Lionel Davidson has written a small number of highly respected mystery thrillers. His first novel, *The Night of Wenceslas* (1960), won the British CRIME WRITERS' ASSOCIATION prize for best thriller, and also an award from the Authors' Club for the most promising first novel of the year. The story concerns a man who is sent behind the Iron Curtain (to Czechoslovakia) as a messenger. Too late, he finds out that he has been deceived, and that his errand has involved him in crime. Davidson's second book, *The Rose of Tibet,* was published in 1962; Graham GREENE praised it as a "genuine adventure story." *The Menorah Men* (also pub as *A Long Way to Shiloh*) appeared in 1966. The latter was a selection of the Book-of-the-Month Club and of the Book Society in England. Davidson's books frequently deal with Jewish experience and related themes. *Making Good Again* (1968) is preoccupied with the NAZI horror. Davidson emigrated with his wife and children from England to Israel.

Davidson's books are difficult to categorize, which has earned him praise from literary critics and blame from purists. Whether one thinks Davidson has failed to play by the "rules" or has transcended the genre, it is undeniable that he is a talented writer. The political and ethnic issues in his books matter, both to the author and the story, in a way that is uncommon in the thriller. One of his books, *The Chelsea Murders* (1978; also pub as *Murder Games*), is a straight mystery story in its use of clues and detection—though the story itself is not "straight," but twisted. It concerns a bizarre killer of CHILDREN who wears fake curls, a smile mask, and rubber gloves. Despite the macabre element in his work, Davidson has also been praised for his humor, which he introduces into even the most serious or disturbing situations. Because he has not created a series character and does not repeat himself (and also because of his relatively few works), Davidson is a little-known innovator in the field.

DAVIES, ROBERTSON (1913–1995) Davies, one of the foremost Canadian authors of the century, is often included among mystery authors, though his output of fiction was large and varied, including ghost stories and fiction of a historical and philosophical turn. *Murther and Walking Spirits* (1991) combines all of these: the narrator is killed by his wife's paramour on page one, then is forced as a ghost to sit through a film festival in which the films reveal his ancestors' lives and how he came to be the man he is (or rather, was). Davies's masterpiece, the Deptford trilogy, most warrants his reputation as a mystery writer, or more accurately, a writer of mystery. This collection of novels, *Fifth Business* (1970), *The Manticore* (1972), and *World of Wonders* (1975), centers around two central mysteries: the identity of the killer of Percy Boyd Staunton, who was in line to become Lieutenant-Governor of his province when he was found in his car in Toronto harbor with a stone in his mouth, and the identity (in the narrowest and the broadest senses) of the magician and circus artiste Magnus Eisengrim. The first and third parts are told by Dunstan Ramsay, headmaster of a boys school and childhood friend of "Boy" Staunton; in the second novel, David Staunton, Boy's son, is driven to seek help at the Jung Institute by his questions about his father's death. It is also a brilliant account of the talking cure of psychotherapy.

DAVIS, DOROTHY SALISBURY (1916–) The American writer Dorothy Salisbury Davis was voted a Grand Master by the Mystery Writers of America in 1984 and has won many other awards; she would be better known, however, if she had created a more distinctive series character earlier in her career. One positive result was that it prevented Davis from repeating herself. Another reason for her relative lack of fame is that she did much of her best work in the short story form; she won several prizes from *Ellery Queen's Mystery Magazine.*

Davis was born in Chicago and lived in the Chicago area for many years. *A Town of Masks* (1952) and *Shock Wave* (1972) are mysteries set in Illinois. Davis later moved to New York, which is the setting for many of her other novels.

Davis's most famous novel is A GENTLE MURDERER (1951), in which a priest, Father DUFFY, works to find a killer. Duffy's compassion for the man he is hunting makes him reminiscent of a more famous detecting priest, Father BROWN. In this and in other books, Davis is sensitive to poverty and its effects on human growth. The interaction of environment and psychology is a prominent theme in *A Gentle Murderer* and elsewhere; *The Clay Hand* (1950) takes place in a poor coal-mining region of Appalachia. *Where the Dark Streets Go* (1969) is another book about a priest working in the bleak slums of New York City who must turn detective. *The Little Brothers* (1974) is set in Little Italy. Also illustrative of the author's sensibility is her anthology, *Crime without Murder* (1970); as the title suggests, it is a survey of fiction in which violence is downplayed. Davis's dislike for gore ran exactly contrary to the trend of the genre in the last three decades, and harkened back to the Victorian period, when crimes against property were more written about than murder.

Only in the seventies did Davis create a series character, Julie Hayes. She first appeared in *A Death in the Life* (1976), in which Hayes opens a fortune-telling business in New York City. Later she becomes a newspaper reporter. There are four books in the series, the most shocking of which is THE HABIT OF FEAR (1987). The other Hayes novels are *Scarlet Night* (1980) and *Lullaby of Murder* (1984). Unfortunately, Davis's short fiction has yet to be collected.

DAVIS, NORBERT (1909–1949) The American writer Norbert Davis was one of the best second-tier PULP MAGAZINE writers of the thirties and forties, along with Paul CAIN and others. Davis's relative obscurity is explained by two things: toward the end of his life he switched from writing crime fiction to writing stories for the slick popular magazines, and after personal and professional disappointments he committed suicide at the age of forty. Thus, Davis died without producing a novel that (as in the case of Raymond CHANDLER and others) would have allowed him to make the transition from the doomed pulps to the burgeoning HARD-BOILED private eye novel of the forties and fifties.

Davis published his first story in BLACK MASK in 1932 while he was a law student at Stanford University. He went on to publish dozens of stories in the major pulps, including *Dime Detective.* He was so successful that he gave up a career in law and wrote full time. One of his series was about Doan and Carstairs; Carstairs was a Great Dane, Doan a hard-drinking p.i. Bail Bond Dodd was another creation. Some of Davis's stories and novelettes about the shady private eye Max Latin have been reprinted as *The Adventures of Max Latin* (1988). Latin is a decent guy who poses as a crooked one, or vice versa; he occasionally winds up on the wrong side—or in jail. His headquarters is the restaurant of the brilliant, irascible chef Gutierrez, who tries to drive away his excess of customers by being rude. The Latin stories are drily humorous and, though they are "pulp," are clearly written. Had he not dropped such characters in favor of humorous non-genre pieces that appealed to *The Saturday Evening Post,* Davis might not have ended as, in John D. MACDONALD's words, "a writer who almost made it."

DAVIS, RICHARD HARDING (1864–1916) The American journalist Richard Harding Davis was the son of Rebecca Harding Davis (1831–1910), an early muckraking journalist and realist novelist who wrote *Life in the Iron Mills* (1861) and other pioneering studies of industrialization. Richard Harding Davis, born in Philadelphia, was the most famous reporter and war correspondent of his time and covered stories all over the globe. He attended Lehigh University and Johns Hopkins, and after writing for newspapers in Philadelphia and New York became the managing editor of *Harper's Weekly* in 1890. Handsome, debonair, and known for his elegant dress, he would have made a perfect GENIUS DETECTIVE character; he typified what TWAIN called the "mauve decade" of the nineties. His fiction was slick, sophisticated, and rather shallow; among the characters he created was Cortland Van Bibber, a Robin Hood of the upper crust who appeared in *Van Bibber and Others* (1892). Davis's position in the mystery canon rests on a single short novel, IN THE FOG (1901), which is considered a classic. It is set in the London of the Sherlock HOLMES era. Davis wrote many other works of fiction and twenty-five plays, among them *The Dictator* (1904).

DAWLISH, PATRICK Gordon Ashe, one of John CREASEY's many alternate identities, created Patrick Dawlish in the mold of Bulldog DRUMMOND. Creasey, however, had the advantage of writing many years after SAPPER created his imperialist thug, and Dawlish is more human. Dawlish is powerful and blond, a superman who hates crime. He is chastised and coddled by Chief Inspector Trivett, his police contact. Dawlish later becomes an operative for British Intelligence, and in the last dozen or so books, has joined up with an organization called "The Crime Haters," introduced in a novel of the same name (1960). *The Croaker* (1937) was the first book in the Dawlish series. In the post-BOND seventies, many of the books were reissued and in some cases revised.

BIBLIOGRAPHY Novels: *Death on Demand* (1939), *Terror by Day* (1940), *Secret Murder* (1940), *'Ware Danger* (1941), *Murder Most Foul* (1941), *There Goes Death* (1942), *Death in High Places* (1942), *Death in Flames* (1943), *Two Men Missing* (1943), *Rogues Rampant* (1944), *Death on the Move* (1945), *Invitation to Adventure* (1945), *Here Is Danger* (1946), *Give Me Murder* (1947), *Murder Too Late* (1947), *Engagement with Death* (1948; rev 1970), *Dark Mystery* (1948), *Kill or Be Killed* (1949), *A Puzzle in Pearls* (1949), *Murder with Mushrooms* (1950), *The Dark Circle* (1950), *Death in Diamonds* (1951), *Death in a Hurry* (1952), *Missing or Dead* (1952), *The Long Search* (1953; U.S. title *Drop Dead*), *Sleepy Death* (1953), *Death in the Trees* (1954), *Double for Death* (1954; U.S. edition 1969), *The Snatch* (1955; U.S. title *The Kidnapped Child*), *Day of Fear* (1956), *Wait for Death* (1957), *Come Home to Death* (1958; U.S. title *The Pack of Lies*, 1959), *Elope to Death* (1959), *Don't Let Him Kill* (1960; U.S. title *The Man Who Laughed at Murder*).

DEADLY PERCHERON, THE (1946) A novel by John Franklin BARDIN about Dr. George Matthews, a New York psychiatrist who becomes involved in the solution of bizarre crimes. The book begins in the madcap style: Matthews is approached by a young man, Jacob Blunt, who claims that "leprechauns" are paying him to do absurd things—wear flowers in his hair, whistle during Carnegie Hall concerts, and give away quarters. Matthews goes to meet one of the leprechauns, who turns out to be a dwarf dressed in "a bottle-green velvet jacket, a tattersall waistcoat and mauve broadcloth trousers." The dwarf has an enormous Percheron horse in a van, which he wants Blunt to deliver to Frances Raye, the star of *Nevada!* (obviously based on *Oklahoma!*, which had premiered in 1943).

At this point, the reader could be forgiven for not expecting anything but a conventional zany comedy. But after George leaves Blunt a murder occurs, and very quickly the psychiatrist wakes up in a mental hospital under the name of "John Brown," Bowery bum, and with a horribly mutilated face. Scenes of the institution, the maddening affect of having one's statements smilingly disbelieved, and the loss of identity are superbly done. Eight months have gone by, and George's total AMNESIA has left them blank; he is forced to start a second life as a counterman in a Coney Island cafeteria, where he meets a collection of amateur and professional misfits from the carnival. This, the most powerful segment of the book, advances the themes that would obsess Bardin. Disfigurement is a metaphor for splitting of the identity, alienation, and the failure to recognize oneself. Matthews as detective—with little help from his friend, Lieutenant Anderson—begins to follow his own backtrail, in search for both the killer and himself.

DEAF MAN, THE A character in a series of novels by Ed MCBAIN. The first four books, written between 1960 and 1985, pit the 87TH STREET PRECINCT against this NAPOLEON OF CRIME. The Deaf Man is a laughing evil genius who likes to torment and humiliate the police. His taunting phone calls make him reminiscent of Arnold ZECK. Despite his vaunted realism, McBain harkens back in the Deaf Man stories to an earlier tradition of the mystery less constrained by plausibility. By the time of the third Deaf Man book, *Let's Hear It for the Deaf Man* (1973), the Deaf Man has killed the Parks Commissioner and the Deputy Mayor in earlier appearances, and announced a bank robbery in advance just to taunt the police (McBain had already explored the idea of a criminal who reveals his plans in *Lady Killer*, published back in 1958). Now the Deaf Man jousts with them by sending clues in the mail—pictures of J. Edgar Hoover, George Washington, and Japanese Zeros. He tells Detective Steve CARELLA that he is going to make *him* help him steal half a million dollars, and even names the date. In another subplot, a cat burglar leaves a kitten in each apartment he hits.

After a long hiatus, McBain brought the dangerous prankster back in *Mischief* (1993).

BIBLIOGRAPHY Novels: *The Heckler* (1960), *Fuzz* (1968), *Eight Black Horses* (1985).

DEAN, SPENSER See STERLING, Stewart.

DEANDREA, WILLIAM L[OUIS] (1952–1996) The American mystery author William DeAndrea is known for his novels set in the television industry and featuring the series character Matt Cobb. DeAndrea attended Syracuse University and earned a degree in communications in 1974. Only four years later, he won an EDGAR award for *Killed in the Ratings* (1978), the first book in the Cobb series. Cobb is a network vice president who handles special projects. He is also a veteran and has an attack dog named Spot. DeAndrea said that he modeled Cobb's narration on the style of Archie GOODWIN, narrator of the Nero WOLFE novels.

DeAndrea also wrote spy novels and HISTORICAL MYSTERIES (one included Theodore ROOSEVELT as a character), and he was a columnist for *The Armchair Detective.* DeAndrea won two more Edgars, for the novel *The Hog Murders* (1979) and for *Encyclopedia Mysteriosa* (1994), a guide to mystery fiction, film, and television.

DEATH AND THE GOOD LIFE (1980) A novel by the American poet Richard HUGO. Set in Montana, the book focuses on "Mush Heart" BARNES, a semi-retired detective who again finds himself in charge of a murder investigation, this time because he is the only one on his small-town force with the necessary experience. The suspect is a six-and-a-half-foot-tall woman with gray hair who has killed a fisherman with dozens of blows from an AXE.

The narration of the book is superb; Hugo imbues Barnes with a poet's sense of "a world where life is always too hard, where we are asked to endure more than we can ever really bear," but he avoids poeticisms for their own sake, and gives Barnes's voice the firmness of a man who became a cop simply because he was "desperate." It has the flavor of the famous Flitcraft story, attesting to the influence of HAMMETT and CHANDLER and also Hugo's philosophical disposition. The intersection of the axe murderer's trail with another mystery going back to 1959 shows the effect of Ross MACDONALD on Hugo; however, his gift for capturing the enigmas of everyday life ("Why does a Ferris wheel seem more still when it's stopped than a car does?") is uniquely his own.

DEATH BY WATER (1968; orig title *Appleby at Allington*) An Inspector APPLEBY mystery by Michael INNES, and one of the best. Appleby is actually Chief Commissioner, retired, and is suddenly thrust into the middle of a murder mystery in a small English town where he has settled. Innes deals humorously with such subplots as the local constabulary's suspicion of Appleby and reluctance to work with him.

Lady Judith Appleby is away when Sir John Appleby is invited to dinner by the local lord of the manor, Owain Allington, whom he scarcely knows. After dinner, he invites Appleby to examine the control booth of the *son et lumière* apparatus, which he has temporarily installed for a charity benefit. Appleby experiments, illuminating the ruined castle across the lake. When he is about to leave, Appleby finds what looks like a pile of rags, and it turns out to be someone else who has played with the lights—and been electrocuted. He is a local dim-witted character with the improbable name of Leofranc Knockdown. The next day Lady Appleby returns, and plays a part in the detection in what turns out to be a string of murders. Innes as usual uses the story to satirize the upper classes, with their oafish spouses, lazy children, and all-consuming passion for golf and tennis to the exclusion of literate interests. There is more to the gibes than in some of Innes's more absurd comedies, however, and the book's subtleties render it both more and less than farcical.

DEATH COMES AS THE END See HISTORICAL MYSTERY.

DEATH IN ALBERT PARK (1964) A Leo BRUCE novel about Carolus DEENE, set in the conventional district of Albert Park, an area of gloomy Victorian houses and excessive respectability. A schoolteacher is stabbed on her way from the girls' school to the bus stop near the park. A second and third murder, also motiveless, convince the authorities that the crimes are the work of a madman. Carolus Deene interviews the associates of the victims, looking for a link. He compares the case with JACK THE RIPPER. The early treatment of a transvestite character is interesting and sympathetic. Deene impressively solves the case by observation and discussion, without physical evidence. Bruce shows what would happen to an amateur sleuth in reality—the police don't like him—but narratively paints himself into a corner, because later Deene has to go to elaborate lengths to get the police to listen to him after he has discovered the killer.

DEATH IN THE STOCKS (1935) A novel by Georgette HEYER that goes beyond the usual GOLDEN AGE English mystery. Heyer's writing is light and amusing, the dialogue is excellent, and the story is funny but also psychologically true. The characters' extreme "Englishness" is the result of an attentive observation of her society and is neither a PARODY nor a satire of English peculiarities.

The story itself, like many mysteries of its day, takes place in upper-class society in London and involves complex family relationships. The plot is well constructed, except for one overused device. The Verekers are a strange bunch. Geoffrey had two sons by his first wife Maud: the pretentious and much-hated Arnold and the wild, debt-ridden Roger, who was killed in South America on one of his escapades. With his second wife he had a son, Kenneth, and a daughter, Antonia ("Tony"). With the parents dead, Arnold Vereker is the heir and guardian of his two younger half-siblings—both of whom despise him. Kenneth, an artist, goes to live in Chelsea with their old governess, and his sister joins him, amusing herself by breeding bull terriers. But Arnold is found dead in the stocks with a knife in his back on Ashleigh Green, the village where he goes with his "fancies" on weekends, and both half-siblings are suspects. Antonia was at Arnold's cottage waiting for him on the night of the murder. Superintendent Hannasyde of SCOTLAND YARD tries to extract the truth from the two siblings, who delight in making hypotheses aloud and exchanging piercing and witty remarks. The investigation is made even harder by the complete lack of clues. Hannasyde is baffled until a sudden reversal of the situation occurs: an extra is added to the list of suspects, and just as quickly removed (by murder). The victim's cousin, the lawyer Giles Carrington, finally puts together the truth and the proofs. As usual with Heyer, the romantic side is not neglected, with two impending marriages at the end.

DEATH LIVES NEXT DOOR (1960) An early novel by Gwendoline BUTLER about her series detective John COFFIN. Coffin, as a young inspector, becomes involved in the case of Dr. Marion Manning, a brilliant Oxford don who is being stalked by a character known as "The Watcher." Manning was an anthropologist in Central America, but gave that up after a tragic expedition and became a philologist. She lives with Joyo, a strange housekeeper/companion with a colorful past in Australia. The atmosphere of Oxford, its strange inhabitants and the impressiveness of Dr. Manning are the focus of the first part of the book, which is full of literary allusions and lacks the PROCEDURAL trappings of Butler's later work. Inspector Coffin only makes his appearance about halfway through the novel; while looking for a missing photographer who has a sadistic hatred of cats, Coffin stumbles into the Manning case, and as usual the plot lines converge.

DEATH OF A FOOL See MARSH, NGAIO.

DEATH OF A GHOST (1934) One of the most admired early novels of Margery ALLINGHAM. It centers around the Bohemian community of Little Venice and the legacy of John Lafcadio, a fin de siècle painter. In order to best his rival, Lafcadio left a series of crated paintings to be unveiled at the rate of one a year, thus extending his productive life beyond his physical one. His widow, Belle, and the dealer Max FUSTIAN, supervise the Lafcadio legacy. Albert CAMPION attends one of the unveiling ceremonies and soon finds himself involved in a murder investigation. The cast of failed artists and eccentrics is a catalogue of familiar types, including an annoying spiritualist. The plot relies more on suspense than mystery; Belle and Fustian polarize Campion's attention, while Stanislaus OATES conducts an offstage investigation.

DEATH OF A JOYCE SCHOLAR, THE (1989) A novel about Chief Inspector MCGARR by Bartholomew GILL. The book demonstrates the strengths and weakness of the series: the characters are well set up and an interesting situation is established, but the resolution is hasty and the set of interrelations created between the characters ends up not being really germane to the solution. With his freckled face and oft-broken nose, McGarr looks like "a Dublin navvy from the building trades whose specialty was poured concrete." He is contacted by the wife of Kevin Coyle, a Trinity College literature professor found stabbed to death; she informs him that she has the body, which friends had brought home in a cart, in her apartment. The professor has a forthcoming book on James JOYCE and Samuel Beckett, and is killed on June 16, or "Bloomsday"—the day on which Joyce's *Ulysees* takes place (in 1904). Coyle's jealous colleagues and the husbands of his many mistresses are suspects in an interesting but somewhat wasted plot.

DEATH OF AN OLD GOAT (1977) The first mystery novel by Robert BARNARD is an academic mystery as well as a satire of Australian life. The ancient Professor Belville-Smith is on a lecture tour in Australia when he meets an untimely end in the remote town of Drummondale. A witty and unorthodox mystery, it takes a rather sharp view of Australia—the dusty landscape, the food, the trains, the accents, the standard of cleanliness, the manners. From the yokels who crowd the saloons to the police inspector who must finally investigate a case rather than take a bribe to do nothing, Barnard leaves no one unscathed. The mystery itself is fairly plotted, and fairly easy for the attentive reader to solve.

DEATH OF A PEER (1940; British title *A Surfeit of Lampreys*) A novel by Ngaio MARSH that has both exasperated and charmed readers. BARZUN and TAYLOR called it "intolerable," while H. R. F. KEATING named it one of the 100 best mysteries of all time. The book's oddly mixed reputation stems from the Lampreys themselves—an eccentric, theatrical family of aristocratic spendthrifts. The story begins when the Lampreys return from New Zealand, where they had undertaken their latest nutty attempt at industry. Lord Charles Lamprey is forced to appeal to his older brother Gabriel for money, and this results in a ghastly murder (a grisly stabbing through the eye).

The Lampreys are seen from the vantage point of a young New Zealander named Roberta Grey, who finds the clan delightfully mad. There is a surfeit of Lampreys indeed, including a set of identical twins (banned, of course, by Monsignor Knox in his rules of FAIR PLAY). One of the author's most theatrical works, *Death of a Peer* can almost be read as a play—Marsh more or less baldly instructs the reader to do so ("the scene now developed in accordance with the best traditions of polite drawing-room comedy"). The action is totally indoors, and the story stands or falls on the appeal of the constant patter of the Lampreys. With their arch remarks ("I must say I do think money's *awful*"), they seem more suited to a Noel Coward play than a murder story. Inspector ALLEYN does his duty, but the Lampreys overshadow him. What sticks in the mind is that, had she ever considered writing a mainstream novel, this would have been it, given Marsh's obvious fascination with the Lampreys; indeed, in the character of Roberta Grey she seems to have written herself into their lives.

DEATH ON DEMAND The name of both the first book and the location of a series by Carolyn G. HART. In *Death on Demand* (1987), she introduced Annie Laurance, who owns a South Carolina bookstore of this name. Accompanied by Max Darling (who is of course her darling, and later her husband), Laurance solves mysteries with the help of her knowledge of crime fiction and famous writers. Thus, the series combines the CELEBRITY MYSTERY with the mystery about BOOKS and the COZY formula. These elements add up to an incredible popular success, though also, for some, an unbearable amount of cuteness.

BIBLIOGRAPHY Novels: *Design for Murder* (1987), *Something Wicked* (1988), *Honeymoon with Murder* (1988), *A Little Class on Murder* (1989), *Deadly Valentine* (1990), *The Christie Caper* (1991), *Southern Ghost* (1992), *The Mint Julep Murder* (1995), Yankee Doodle Dead (1998), White Elephant Dead (1999).

DEATH UNDER SAIL (1932) A mystery by C. P. SNOW. Although the author was a research scientist at Cambridge University, the novel shows many of the conventions of the GOLDEN AGE. Snow was only twenty-six when he wrote it. The novel is told from the perspective of Ian Capel, a middle-aged man who has joined a group of young friends for a yachting party. Some of the members of the group describe classic types of the Jazz Age, such as the sexually liberated Tonia Gilmour and her lover, Philip Wade, who is rich, lazy and charming. Others reflect Snow's own scientific milieu and his interest in its culture. The host, Roger Mills, is a fat and self-satisfied doctor; William Garnett is his collaborator, a restless, brilliant younger colleague. The generational split becomes even more pronounced and interesting after the arrival of Capel's friend Mr. Finbow, a colonial civil servant and amateur sleuth, himself a model of scientific rationalism. Very little yachting gets done because a murder occurs, as though to chastise Capel for his belief that "being smug is one of the compensations of getting old" and for his defense of social inequality and the class of "gay and pleasant idlers." Only the low characters provided for comic relief and the factual errors ("revolver" and "automatic" are not interchangeable) mar the story.

DEBIERUE, JACQUES The surrealist painter in Charles Willeford's THE BURNT ORANGE HERESY (1971). The elderly Debierue is supposedly the "greatest living surrealist," though no one has ever seen one of his paintings, unless you count an empty frame he exhibited on the wall of his apartment. Debierue bears not a little resemblance to Marcel Duchamp (1887–1968).

"DECLINE AND FALL OF THE DETECTIVE STORY, THE" A famous essay by Somerset MAUGHAM, collected in *The Vagrant Mood* (1952). Maugham makes the oft-repeated remark that, when critics look back at the twentieth century, they may "pass somewhat lightly over the compositions of the 'serious' novelists and turn their attention to the immense and varied achievement of the detective writers." This viewpoint does not prevent him, however, from saying that most mystery writing is bad, that Sherlock HOLMES is two-dimensional, that the detective story is "dead," and that after Raymond CHANDLER (whom he admired) there was nothing left undone in the genre except the endless production of feeble copies. Many of Maugham's remarks are penetrating, and some are perplexing, such as his stipulation that the style of detective stories should be unadorned (not only unlike Chandler, but his own ASHENDEN) and even that "fine writing" is "out of place" in the detective story. He attacked improbability in both motive and method, as well as the romantic touch. His analyses of particular stories, from THE MALTESE FALCON (SPADE has no evidence on Brigid O'Shaunnessy at the end) to THE MURDERS IN THE RUE MORGUE (DUPIN's solution is wrong) are penetrating and provocative. Of particular note is his statement that "specious novelty" should be eschewed.

DEE, ED (***) The American PROCEDURAL crime novelist Ed Dee was a New York City police officer for twenty years before he turned to writing. Dee also attended the Arizona State University Creative Writing Program, receiving his M.F.A. in 1992. Born in Yonkers, Dee had served in the army and graduated from Fordham University before becoming a cop.

Dee's first novel, 14 PECK SLIP, was published to favorable reviews in 1994. It introduced detective Anthony Ryan, a forty-three-year-old half-Irish, half-Italian cop just short of his twenty years of service—and possible retirement. His partner is the hotshot Joe Gregory, an abrasive and wisecracking tough guy who lives to be a cop, and does not have much else left in his life that would compete with it. In the second book, *Bronx Angel* (1995), Ryan has been promoted and transferred to the Chief of Detectives office. He becomes involved in the investigation of the murder of a beat cop named Marc Ross, who is found with his throat slashed and his pants pulled down in a BMW he should not really have been able to afford, apparently the victim of a prostitute. In *Little Boy Blue* (1997), "Johnny Boy" Counihan, a cargo handler at John F. Kennedy airport, is murdered when he is mistaken for a cop (he wears a surplus policeman's jacket). The man's mother is the wife of one of Gregory's old partners; thus, Dee returns to the theme of his first book: the ties, both legal and illicit, among the police fraternity.

Dee writes plainly about police corruption and gives an unromantic and unflattering portrait of the "cop culture." Gregory appears to be an alcoholic, and Ryan is not far behind; both spend a lot of time looking for bad people in bad places in the middle of the night, or drinking with other cops in Brady's Bar. Cynicism, pessimism, and difficulty communicating with people on the outside—anyone who is not a cop—are occupational risks. The language is honest and dirty, exactly what one would expect to hear passed around among angry drunks or men used to distancing themselves from scenes of violence and blood. Dee balances the investigation of character and the investigation of crime so that the story is neither technically tedious nor coyly arty, and he keeps his tendency toward the maudlin generally in check.

DEE, JUDGE Based on a real figure of the seventh century, Judge Dee became in the hands of Robert VAN GULIK a masterful detective in the Western manner. Chinese authors had been using the judge (Ti Jen-chieh, A.D. 630–700) as a character in stories of detection for centuries, one of which Van Gulik translated—*Dee Goong An* (1949), which was also published as *Celebrated Cases of Judge Dee,* and was the first in the series. The original Ti Jen-chieh eventually rose to the position of Minister of State, and advised the Empress Wu over the imperial succession. Another famous magistrate was Pao Sheng (999–1062); one of his most famous cases forms part of the plot of THE CHINESE BELL MURDERS (1951). Especially at the beginning, Van Gulik used Chinese criminological and fictional works for material for his plots, and in the original editions of the Judge Dee books he appended commentaries to the stories about his sources (reprinted in the University of Chicago paperbacks).

Van Gulik's novels sound as if they have been translated, though he wrote them in English. The effect is sometimes dry and stilted, particularly in the dialogue, which is riddled with exclamation marks. On the other hand, Dee sometimes sounds oddly like a HARD-BOILED detective ("I will have no truck with the Buddhist crowd"). The Dee stories sometimes capture the feeling of daily life in old China, but other times we seem to be looking at it through a telescope. Van Gulik eschews some of the conventions of the original Chinese sources, such as having the magistrate assisted by ghosts and spirits. An exception, however, is the enigmatic story told by a later narrator (also fictional) that prefaces each novel.

Van Gulik had originally hoped that an already established Western author would be interested in writing mystery novels set in ancient China, but when none volunteered, he undertook the task himself. He also meant to translate his Judge Dee stories into Chinese and Japanese, because he felt the crime fiction of ancient China he used as a model was much better than contemporary popular literature.

Judge Dee is a powerful man; he combines the duties of a policeman with the authority of a judge. Behind him, at the top of the Confucian order, is the emperor. The duties of a magistrate were arduous, encompassing not only criminal hearings but the collection of taxes, registry of deeds and births, and all other civic matters. Dee is an accomplished swordsman, but the roughhousing is usually done by his companions and admirers, who are reformed criminals. In *The Chinese Gold Murders* (1959), he meets Chiao Tai, the stern soldier, and Ma Joong, who provides comic relief. Sergeant Hoong is his companion in the early tales and is later killed in the line of duty. The sorrowful Tao Gan, disappointed in love, is introduced in *The Chinese Lake Murders* (1961).

The Confucianist Dee is pragmatic and practical. He adheres to the law, is not shaken by Buddhist metaphysics, and as a bureaucrat is quick to resent any encroachment on his jurisdiction. In line with his philosophy, his relations to others are paternalistic. In the original Chinese sources, foreigners, such as Tartars and Mongols, and non-conformists, such as Taoists and Buddhists, were usually villains. Judge Dee has two wives, referred to as his First and Second Ladies, and later acquires a third, Miss Tsao, in the story "He Came With the Rain." He also has several children.

A chronology of the fictional Judge Dee's life appears at the back of *Judge Dee at Work* (1967), a collection of stories.

See also THE CHINESE NAIL MURDERS (1957).

BIBLIOGRAPHY Novels: *The Chinese Maze Murders* (1951), *The Red Pavilion* (1961), *The Haunted Monastery* (1961), *The Lacquer Screen* (1962), *The Emperor's Pearl* (1963), *The Willow Pattern* (1965), *The Monkey and the Tiger* (1965; novelettes), *Murder in Canton* (1966), *Poets and Murder* (1968).

DEENE, CAROLUS A sleuth in stories by Leo BRUCE, Deene is a more sophisticated character than Sergeant BEEF, though not necessarily better. Wealthy, dapper, and pale, Deene is reminiscent of the GOLDEN AGE detective, though he is also a scholar and a widower, not a dashing young aristocrat. In addition, the police do not enjoy his pursuit of his hobby of investigation. The only inspector who favors him with assistance is John Moore, who appears in a few of the novels.

In several respects, Deene is modeled on the author himself. Deene is a former paratrooper and senior history master of the Queen's School, Newminster; he also has an antiquarian book interest, an independent income, and a Bentley Continental. Bruce gave him a WATSON, the precocious student Rupert Priggley, who is like a younger version of Beef's somewhat unpleasant biographer, Lionel Townsend. Priggley is indeed priggish; he nags Deene and is Deene's "least favorite student." Deene also has a cranky housekeeper named Mrs. Stick, who has taken care of him since his wife was killed in an air raid. Deene is an intuitive sleuth and finds the killer's identity mostly by psychology. He supposedly has written a book, *Who Killed William Rufus?,* in which he solved historical mysteries with modern methods.

Our Jubilee Was Death (1959) is about the murder of a mystery writer, and *A Bone and A Hank of Hair* (1961) takes place against the backdrop of an artists' colony. *Dead Man's Shoes* (1958) combines a quaint depiction of rural England with exotic scenes. Deene is called in to investigate the shooting of Gregory Willick on the grounds of his country house; the main suspect has fled to Tangier, decided to return to England to clear his name, and then jumped from the ship *Saragossa,* leaving a typed suicide note. Deene visits all these locations, and springs his solution in an "I've-gathered-you-all-together-because . . ." scene aboard the ship.

One of Bruce's most sustained novels is FURIOUS OLD WOMEN (1960); the story is set in a nasty modern English village, dominated by old women who drink, complain, bicker, and take tranquilizers. *Nothing Like Blood* (1962) takes place in a boardinghouse and has a Dickensian flavor, and DEATH IN ALBERT PARK (1964) has some unusual features and devices. Deene's headmaster, Mr. Gorringer, appears in several books, fretting about the negative effect of Deene's "sordid hobby" on the reputation of the school. In *Jack on the Gallows Tree* (1960), Deene is recovering from jaundice and Gorringer persuades him to go to the spa town of Buddington to recuperate. Two women are strangled to death on the same night shortly after Deene's arrival. The two women are complete strangers to each other, but Deene refuses to accept the coincidence of the crimes.

The main appeal of the Deene series is to the purist. The process of detection takes place almost entirely through dialogue, so that the reader is as aware of everything that was said as the detective. Refreshingly, Bruce avoids ponderous references to meaningful glances and startled shivers when suspects lie or reveal significant facts; neither does he treat us to the sleuth's introspections (no peppering of "What could it mean that . . ."). The detection of inconsistencies and errors is generally left to the reader. Subplots about Deene's personal life, including his conflicts with Gorringer, are kept to a minimum. Not surprisingly, Bruce was praised by Jacques BARZUN, champion of the tale of pure detection.

BIBLIOGRAPHY Novels: *At Death's Door* (1955), *Death of Cold* (1956), *Dead for a Ducat* (1956), *A Louse for the Hangman* (1958), *Die All, Die Merrily* (1961), *Such Is Death* (1963; orig title *Crack of Doom*), *Death at Hallow's End* (1965), *Death on the Black Sands* (1966), *Death of a Commuter* (1967), *Death at St. Asprey's School* (1957), *Death on Romney Marsh* (1968), *Death with Blue Ribbon* (1969), *Death on Allhallowe'en* (1970), *Death by the Lake* (1971), *Death in the Middle Watch* (1974), *Death of a Bovver Boy* (1974).

DEEP BLUE GOODBYE, THE (1964) The first novel featuring John D. MacDonald's Travis MCGEE. It introduced a common villain of the series: a primitive but crafty man (Junior Allen) whose predatory sexuality and greed are both the expression of a Stone Age brutality and lust for domination. A very similar character appears in *Bright Orange for the Shroud* (1965).

DEFOE, DANIEL (born Daniel Foe, 1660–1731) The English novelist, journalist, and pamphleteer Daniel Defoe was also a biographer of criminals. Not only that, he was a "criminal" himself, sentenced to prison and the stocks for writing a satire against the High Churchmen.

He got a poem out of the experience ("Hymn to the Pillory") as well as a job: after being jailed for libel in 1703, the earl of Oxford had him released, in exchange for Defoe's services as an intelligence agent in Scotland.

Defoe's most famous work, *Robinson Crusoe* (1719), was based on the life and experiences of Alexander Selkirk. Using his journalistic skills, Defoe wrote other works depicting, embellishing, and fabricating events in the lives of famous people—most of them bad: he produced a series of lives of famous pirates, and he wrote a book about the most celebrated criminal of the age, Dick TURPIN. This type of criminal biography was very popular at the time; he also wrote *The Six Notorious Street Robbers* (1726) and *Street Robberies Considered* (1728).

Moll Flanders (1722), about a prostitute and her criminal life, was not a crime novel in the modern sense. The subtitle, however, was calculated to excite interest in the same way as the criminal biographies: "*The Fortunes and Misfortunes of the Famous Moll Flanders, who was Born at Newgate, and during a Life of continued Variety for Threescore Years, besides her Childhood, was Twelve Year a Whore, five times a Wife (whereof once to her own Brother), Twelve Year a Thief, Eight Year a Transported Felon in Virginia, at last grew rich, liv'd Honest, and died a Penitent.*" Although a great PICARESQUE story—and, unusually, about a woman—full of adventure and comedy, the purpose was to show vice reformed. Suspense is generated, of course, by Moll's escapades. See PROTOMYSTERIES.

DEIGHTON, LEN (pen name of Leonard Cyril Deighton, 1929–) Len Deighton's name is usually joined with those of Eric AMBLER and John LE CARRÉ, who preceded him as reinventors of the spy novel; together they changed it from the tale of adventure it had been for BUCHAN and PEMBERTON into a story of compromise, betrayal, and Faustian political bargains. Deighton, however, never lets himself get bogged down in this potentially lugubrious material, displaying a lighter touch and finer sense of humor than Le Carré. There is also more gadgetry in the Deighton books, though never is it taken to the idiotic excesses of other spy novels (not to mention films).

Deighton also made perhaps the most daring revision of the form in the area of class. He replaced the dashing upper-class hero with a working-class bloke, Harry, for whom the job of agent is just that, a job. He mocks his upper-crust superiors, with their delusions of nobility and talent for self-deception. And while others think a spy is just "the ink with which history is written," Deighton's modest hero tries to retain a minute area of personal responsibility.

Born in London, Deighton was a railway clerk and then served in the Royal Air Force, working as a photographer in the Special Investigation Branch. He later attended the St. Martin's School of Art and won a scholarship to the Royal College of Art. He worked at various occupations, including waiter, illustrator (in New York), and finally art director of a London advertising agency. In 1962 he published his first novel, THE IPCRESS FILE, which he wrote after moving to the Dordogne. This novel remains one of his best. It was made into a film (1965) and won attention for the young actor, Michael Caine. Caine played "Harry PALMER," the name given to the anonymous narrator who works for a secret British intelligence agency with the faintly ridiculous title, W.O.O.C.(P). Palmer keeps his own counsel, suspects everybody, and especially distrusts the Old Boy network at the top of the spying game. His assignments sometimes seem absurd on the surface, and his superiors usually withhold from him what is really going on. Thus, in *Horse Under Water* (1963), he is given diver's training and then sent to Portugal, ostensibly to head up a mission to salvage counterfeit currency from a sunken German U-boat and use it to finance Portuguese revolutionaries. Deighton is fond of attaching memos and document numbers to the stories, not so much to make them seem "real" as to satirize further the bureaucratic business of spying. Appendices provide information about real organizations and events. Other books in the series include *Funeral In Berlin* (1964), THE BILLION DOLLAR BRAIN (1966), *An Expensive Place to Die* (1967), and *Spy Story* (1974).

A decade after he finished with his anonymous hero in *Twinkle, Twinkle Little Spy* (1976), Deighton introduced a similar character, but with a name this time: Bernard SAMSON. He first appeared in *Berlin Game* (1983).

Deighton also wrote two books with a similar premise to Philip K. DICK's Hugo award-winning novel, *The Man in the High Castle* (1962). *SS-GB* (1978) is both a mystery and a fantasy about what would have happened if the NAZIS had successfully invaded Britain. Two English policemen, Sergeant Harry Woods and Detective Superintendent Douglas Archer, try to solve a murder in German-occupied England. The time is November 1941; a man is found dead in an apartment and is suspected of being a black marketeer. Interestingly, Woods is an older man who resisted the occupation, while the younger Archer was never a soldier and has the bureaucrat's apolitical desire to be left alone to "do his job." *XPD* (1981) focuses on a secret file relating to a fictitious meeting between Hitler and Churchill. *MAMistas* (1991) is another non-series novel, about a Latin American country called Spanish Guiana, which is being manipulated by the United States because oil has been discovered there. The characters include an idealistic doctor who has infiltrated the Marxist guerrillas opposed to the government and a ransomed CIA agent.

Deighton has also written military history, historical novels, cookbooks, and a comic strip. His reputation as a novelist has always been higher in Britain than in the United States, where he has been somewhat overshadowed by LeCarré, who captured the highbrow spy market. The *Sunday Times* of London, however, called Deighton "a poet of the spy story."

DEKOBRA, MAURICE See MADONNA OF THE SLEEPING CARS, THE.

DE LA TORRE, LILLIAN (Lillian de la Torre Bueno, 1902–1993) The American writer Lillian de la Torre had enormous gumption to write about a sleuth (Samuel Johnson) who was probably the finest prose stylist in the language, but most critics think she managed the trick fairly well. In her short stories, Johnson (1709–1784) has been turned into a eighteenth-century private investigator of sorts; the narrator is James Boswell (1740–1795), who was Johnson's frequent companion and biographer. The first collection of stories was *Dr. Sam Johnson, Detector* (1946).

De la Torre was born in New York City, and earned degrees from Columbia and Harvard universities. She became a teacher and a poet, and also acted. She often referred to herself as a "histo-detector," because she studied criminal cases of long ago, not only as entertainment but in order to solve them. She viewed crime as revelatory of human nature, quoting Alexander Pope's dictum that "the proper study of mankind is man." Her interest in crime was not restricted to the eighteenth century; she wrote a well-known work based on the trial of Lizzie BORDEN, and *Elizabeth Is Missing* (1945), about the Elizabeth CANNING case (which also inspired Josephine Tey's THE FRANCHISE AFFAIR [1949]).

Read with the perspective of fifty years, the Dr. Johnson stories hold up surprisingly well. She based the stories on real events into which she inserted Johnson, not too improbably—he did, after all, really investigate the case of the Cock Lane Ghost and show it was a fraud. In addition to Boswell, the Thrales, Fanny Burney, and others of Johnson's circle also appear in the stories. See TONTINE.

DELACOUR, STEPHANIE See KRISTEVA, JULIA.

DELAWARE, ALEX A psychologist and amateur sleuth in a series of novels by Jonathan KELLERMAN, Delaware specializes in therapy with children, though later in the series he branches out into other areas. Delaware's police contact is Milo Sturgis, a gay detective with the Los Angeles police, but it always seems to fall to Delaware to foil the villain. Sturgis has a lumpy face and wears loud clothing, and has black hair tinged with white. The first novel in the series was the EDGAR-winning *When the Bow Breaks* (1985).

Kellerman's biggest mistake in creating Delaware may have been to make him rich. A semi-retired consultant, he only takes a few cases (which coincidentally are those that bring him into contact with murderers). He sees himself as a white knight and protector of children, and his self-dramatizing and self-regard are rankling, despite displays of false modesty. The series has also not avoided the daytime drama format that has become so popular, with the relationship between the detective and his girlfriend always on the horizon. She is a builder of stringed instruments.

In *The Web* (1996), Delaware goes to the island of Aruk to help a Dr. Moreland prepare his papers for publication. He has been treating the island's medical problems and improving its infrastructure for decades. The islanders consider Moreland an Albert Schweitzer, but is he a Dr. Moreau instead? By this point, Delaware has acquired a French bulldog named Spike and is building his dream house, his previous home having been burned down by a psycho. *The Clinic* (1997) is the case of a psychology professor and self-help author on the subject of stalking who has been savagely stabbed to death.

BIBLIOGRAPHY Novels: *Blood Test* (1986), *Over the Edge* (1987), *The Butcher's Theater* (1988), *Silent Partner* (1989), *Time Bomb* (1990), *Private Eyes* (1992), *Devil's Waltz* (1993), *Bad Love* (1994), *Self-Defense* (1995), *Survival of the Fittest* (1997).

DELVECCHIO, NICK See RANDISI, ROBERT J.

DELVING, MICHAEL (pseudonym of Jay Williams, 1914–1978) Jay Williams was born in Buffalo, New York, the son of a vaudeville producer, and he himself had a career in show business before he wrote a novel. After attending the University of Pennsylvania and Columbia, he worked in the Catskills in the thirties in vaudeville shows and as a comic. He served in the army in World War II and was awarded a Purple Heart.

Williams's first books for children (written under his own name) appeared in the forties, and he eventually wrote more than two dozen of them. He also wrote juvenile fiction and co-authored SCIENCE FICTION stories with Raymond Abrashkin, starting with *Danny Dunn and the Anti-Gravity Paint* (1956). His mysteries were all written under the name of Michael Delving, and all had to do with ART or BOOKS.

Delving's sleuth is Dave Cannon, an American book and manuscript dealer from New Canaan, Connecticut, whose cases take place in England (where Delving himself died). Delving's dialogue is often clever and he sometimes played up the new-found sexual freedom of the sixties, albeit mildly. The first novel in the series was *Smiling, the Boy Fell Dead* (1966). Cannon goes to an English village to meet Mrs. Herne, the last in a long line of aristocrats, who wants to sell him "the Raimond." This manuscript is an account of the Third Crusade. Neville, an unpleasant local, is killed in the Herne house and Cannon is suspected. As he investigates, another murder committed seventy years earlier comes into play. *Die Like a Man* (1970) involves an even more valuable object, the Holy Grail. *A Shadow of Himself* (1972) is told by Cannon's partner, Bob Eddison, who is a Cherokee. In *Bored to Death* (1975), Cannon is married to an Englishwoman. The book plays on the habits of "the bore," a dangerous tidal surge. Cannon's adventures were seven in all; the last of the books was *No Sign of Life* (1978).

DEMARKIAN, GREGOR See HADDAM, JANE.

DENT, LESTER (1904? 05?–1959) One of the writers associated with BLACK MASK, Lester Dent's work sadly is out of print, except for some anthologized stories. Born in Missouri, Dent worked at a variety of jobs including teacher, journalist, dairy farmer, and telegraph operator. He created the character Doc Savage, a phenomenally popular PULP character whose adventures blend SCIENCE FICTION, suspense, and mystery. This aspect of Dent's work is similar to that of Manly Wade WELLMAN. The Savage stories appeared under the name Kenneth Robeson in *Doc Savage* magazine, though not all were authored by Dent.

Dent's output was prodigious: he wrote from breakfast time to early in the morning of the following day, and was so prolific that he made a substantial salary even in the lean Depression years. His success enabled him to travel extensively, including cruising from Florida to South America; he and his wife lived on a schooner until moving to Death Valley, where he became a prospector. Dent also became a licensed pilot, and at the end of his life returned to his hometown (La Plata) and became a dairy farmer.

Dent's sailing, prospecting, and love of adventure are reflected in such works as the pulp novel *Cry At Dusk* (1952), about a young man named Johnny Marks who is trying to escape the legacy of his father, a "buccaneer," and gets into trouble with his father's sinister associates (it even includes a treasure hunt). *Lady Afraid* (1948) and *Lady So Silent* (1951) are other novels. See also MURDER AFLOAT.

DEPTFORD TRILOGY, THE See DAVIES, ROBERTSON.

DE QUINCEY, THOMAS (1785–1859) English essayist and critic renowned for his memoir *Confessions of an English Opium Eater* (1822). Born in Manchester, De Quincey ran away at a young age and became a vagabond, travelling to Wales and London. After attending Oxford, De Quincey eventually settled in Grasmere, a village in the Lake District and the haunt of the Wordsworths (and of that other opium user, Samuel Taylor Coleridge). He became friendly with the Romantic poets, though he offended them with his later memoir of the period. De Quincey spent the rest of his life in Edinburgh, Scotland.

De Quincey was literally an opium *eater*, for the most popular form of opium at the time was laudanum. Chronically addicted and chronically in debt (he had a large family to provide for), De Quincey wrote voluminously. Among the fourteen volumes of his works was the essay "On Murder Considered as One of the Fine Arts," written in the form of a lecture to the "Society of Connoisseurs in Murder." He pretends "X.Y.Z" has gotten hold of it and written a pious and appalled preface.

The essay begins with a catalogue of the various "artists" who have tried their hands at murder, describing the "Augustan Age" of the art and criticizing modern "innovations" such as poisoning (as opposed to "the old honest way" of throat-cutting). De Quincey goes on to say that the purpose of murder as an art is the same as tragedy as defined by Aristotle: to purge the spirit through pity and fear. The satire, however, has a moral edge, in the manner of Swift's "Modest Proposal" (mentioned in the latter part of the essay). The public only wants a murder to be gory, and is not interested in murders of people who are themselves bad (thus evoking no pity); sick people should not be murdered, for it lessens the horror; and the victim should have a large number of dependent children, "by way of deepening the pathos." Whether one imputes it to an innate human curiosity or a historical barbarism that has only become possible with the anonymity of modern urban life, De Quincey indicts a phenomenon as grotesque and disturbing now as it was in his day.

The essay first appeared in *Blackwood's Edinburgh Magazine* in two parts (1827 and 1839); a third part, describing the Williams and M'Kean murders, was added later (1854) and is the most read today. It continues to provide fuel for writers, for example the novel THE TRIAL OF ELIZABETH CREE (1995). In 1812, John WILLIAMS, a former sailor, committed the killings known as the Ratcliffe Highway murders. De Quincey's satire ebbs, and then fades totally away, as he confronts the gruesome crimes. Williams was apprehended but killed himself before he could be executed.

DERLETH, AUGUST [WILLIAM] (1909–1971) Derleth was at one time a respected writer of "serious" fiction, notably his *Sac Prairie Saga.* Set in Wisconsin, this vast group of novels, stories, and poems was modeled on the European tradition exemplified most notably by BALZAC, chronicling a place and a people over a period of time. The series included several works featuring Judge PECK as sleuth. Derleth also created a detective modeled on Sherlock HOLMES, Solar PONS, with the permission of the estate of Holmes's creator.

Derleth was born in Sauk City, which was the model for the fictional Sac Prairie. He was the co-founder of Arkham House, a publisher of supernatural and science fiction. Mycroft and Moran, the imprint that published the Solar Pons stories, was named for Sherlock Holmes's brother and his implacable foe, Colonel Augustus Moran. Derleth's Wisconsin novels include *Still Is the Summer Night* (1937), *Wind Over Wisconsin* (1938), and *Restless Is the River* (1939).

Derleth's other crime work was *Consider Your Verdict* (1937), a collection of crime stories published under the name Tally Mason. It consisted of ten cases, each of which contained a flaw in the testimony that allowed coroner Dr. Everett Webster to spot the culprit. The District Attorney, Anthony Carden, is Webster's rather thick-headed companion. The reader was challenged to spot the flaw in the testimony, and a sealed section at the back of the book contained the answers. It was suggested as a party game to read the testimony out loud and for the participants to write separate answers to the problems.

DERRINGER A small, usually two-shot pistol with under-and-over barrels. The name comes from Henry Deringer (1786–1868), the Philadelphia gunsmith who invented it in the 1820s. The pistols were not more than six inches long (modern versions are smaller) and came in various calibers, including .36, .45, and .41, the latter being the most popular. The modern derringer is frequently of .22 caliber.

The unfortunate Deringer lived to see the gun that bore his name associated with one of the most infamous crimes of history, when John Wilkes Booth used one to assassinate President Abraham Lincoln in 1865. In coverage of the crime, a newspaper reporter spelled the gunsmith's name with two r's, and the misspelling "derringer" stuck.

Derringers appear in mystery fiction usually as women's guns; Milo MILODRAGOVITCH, however, uses a large-caliber derringer to gruesome effect in DANCING BEAR (1983).

DE SALVO, ALBERTO See BOSTON STRANGLER.

DETECTION CLUB An organization of British mystery and detective authors founded in 1928 by Anthony BERKELEY. The first and second "Rulers" to preside over the club were two friends, G. K. CHESTERTON and E. C. BENTLEY. Membership in the club is by invitation only. Berkeley used the club in his novels, under the pseudonym "the Crimes Circle": Ambrose Chitterwick and Roger SHERINGHAM are both members. They both appear in Berkeley's *The Poisoned Chocolates Case,* published the year after the author founded the club. The Detection Club Oath, in which members swore to adhere to the rules of FAIR PLAY, was reproduced in Howard HAYCRAFT's *The Art of the Mystery Story* (1946).

Detection Club members collaborated on a series of mysteries, including THE FLOATING ADMIRAL (1932). In *Ask a Policeman* (1933), a novel about the murder of a disliked newspaper baron, the members of the club took turns using and abusing each other's sleuths—Dorothy L. SAYERS writing about Roger Sheringham, Anthony Berkeley spoofing Lord Peter WIMSEY and so on. The problem is rather boringly introduced by John RHODE. In addition, the Detection Club published the true crime volume, *The Anatomy of Murder* (1936), in which different members each covered a famous murder case, discussing evidence and theories and sometimes coming to conclusions other than those reached at the time. Some of the essays were selected and reprinted in *The Anatomy of Murder* (ed 1989) and *More Anatomy of Murder* (ed 1990).

DEVIL TAKE THE BLUE-TAIL FLY (1948) This novel by John Franklin BARDIN often appears on "top 100" lists of crime fiction, though it is further toward the fringe of the genre than THE DEADLY PERCHERON (1946) and *The Last of Philip Banter* (1947), the other two books Bardin wrote during an intensive creative period. A psychological novel, a novel of terror, and a story of murder, *Devil Take the Blue-Tail Fly* also uses the DOPPELGÄNGER motif in a totally unexpected way. It perfectly develops the themes that obsessed Bardin in the earlier books and raises them to a new and even more disturbing level.

At the beginning of the story, Ellen Purcell, a concert harpsichordist, is preparing to leave a mental hospital after two years. Her attentive husband, Basil, is at the same time an egocentric conductor who does not share her tastes in music and who in fact simply uses music to enhance his own image and power. Trouble begins when they arrive home and Ellen finds her harpsichord locked and the key missing; then Basil miraculously finds the key and tells her it was there all the time. As suspicions about Basil's fidelity during her hospitalization grow, Ellen has more and more troubling flashbacks into a dark past. Bardin has an uncanny ability to represent seamlessly Ellen's drifting from reality into psychotic episodes, such as the moment when she slaps Basil's face: "she saw her hand outspread before her, saw, to her horror, that the blow she had struck had opened a great hole in his face, revealed a view, a distant, beguiling perspective, that peeped between the lattices of her fingers. Suddenly it was as if his face had ceased to exist, as if the slap of her hand had swept away a barrier that had stood between her and another scene, and she walked between her fingers, seeking what lay beyond." Ellen becomes increasingly unable to distinguish between dream and reality and describes the horror of an inward "pit" from which disturbing, rejected, and unassimilable memories flood upward, destroying her consciousness. The failure of her return debut and the reappearance of a seductive folk singer from her past hasten her collapse and the violent climax. *Devil Take the Blue-Tail Fly* is a psychopathographic novel—one which by its very style evokes confusion, fear, and dread in its reader similar to the experience of its characters. It is Bardin's most singular contribution to literature, as well as to the genre.

DEVINE, D[AVID] M[CDONALD] (1920–1981) This Scottish mystery author and lawyer wrote novels under two names, D. M. Devine and Dominic Devine. Encouraged by his publisher, he switched to the name Dominic after he had already written half a dozen novels. Devine earned an M.A. from Glasgow University in 1945 and an L. L. B. from the University of London in 1953. His first novel was published in 1961 (MY BROTHER'S KILLER); BARZUN and TAYLOR called it "a truly splendid piece of plotting and telling." Devine's second book was praised by Anthony BOUCHER. Critical praise has not saved Devine's work from that shared by many competent mystery writers of the past; although prolific, Devine died relatively early and has all too quickly slipped into obscurity and out of print.

Devine explored a limited range of settings and plots, but often did so skillfully. His strengths were his evocation of the Scottish environment, particularly Glasgow, and his knowledge of legal and medical detail; these were evident in his second book, *Doctors Also Die* (1962). *Three Green Bottles* (1972), in which a number of adolescent girls are strangled, also involves a medical practice. Devine's books often focused on such intimate professional or familial settings, and sometimes both: *The Royston Affair* (1964) is a prodigal-son story set in a family of lawyers. *This Is Your Death* (1982), published posthumously, is on the other hand reminiscent of a different archetype, the story of Cain and Abel.

Among Devine's "Scottish" tales is *His Own Appointed Day* (1965), which concerns what would today be called a dysfunctional family. Ian Pratt, aged sixteen, begins to undergo a personality change—for the worse—after he discovers that he is adopted. Then, he disappears. It is thought that he may be looking for his real father. His sister Eileen, a gym teacher in Silbridge, near Glasgow, is not completely satisfied, however. She searches for Ian with the help of Detective Inspector Nicholson, who develops a more than professional interest in her. He has his own problems, being an outsider who is mistrusted and mistreated by the rest of the force.

Silbridge's atmosphere is early sixties provincial, marked by heavy drinking and smoking, adultery, and professed puritanism about sex. The element of suspense, Devine's forte, is strong. Another complex family saga is the basis of *Sunk Without a Trace* (1979), also set in Silbridge, but with a stronger story and more developed characters. Ruth Kellaway, an illegitimate child, returns to the town after her mother dies; she begins to search for her father. Like Eileen Pratt, she is assisted by a police detective who takes a romantic interest in her. Missing files, tampered elections, and small-town corruption all swirl around her, until she disappears. At first she is presumed to have committed a murder, and then to have been a victim herself. Judy Hutchings, a colleague of Eileen's mother at the courthouse, then starts investigating in a story replete with sleuths, official and unofficial. A gauge of the plot's complexity is that the murder victim, Liz, is the lover of Ken (who was formerly the lover of Judy) and is divorced from a local politician, Peter Russell—who is now Judy's lover. Ken, Ruth, and Ruth's missing father are all suspects.

Devine held the posts of secretary and registrar at St. Andrews University, and the academic setting is used in several of his novels. In the first of these, *Devil at Your Elbow* (1966), Graham Loudon, the dean of the law school at an English university, must turn sleuth to solve a case of blackmail and murder. *Death Is My Bridegroom* (1969) is set in another university, this time rocked by late-sixties political unrest.

DEWEY, THOMAS B[LANCHARD] (1915–) A Midwesterner by birth (Elkhart, Indiana), Thomas B. Dewey had several different careers and lived in Hollywood and Arizona, but set his most famous mystery series in Chicago. These novels, about a private detective known as MAC, are respected but not widely known examples of the HARD-BOILED style. It is surprising, then, that Dewey's first novel, *Hue and Cry* (1944), was about a Shakespearean scholar named Singer Batts; if that were not enough to place him squarely among the eccentrics of detective fiction, Batts also owns a hotel in Preston, Ohio, and is a bibliophile.

Educated at Kansas State and the University of Iowa, Dewey worked for the State Department until moving to Hollywood after World War II. (Thus, he moved to California at the same time as Ross MACDONALD, with whom he has been compared.) Later, in the seventies, Dewey taught English at Arizona State University. In California, Dewey worked in advertising and continued writing, publishing in *Ellery Queen's Mystery Magazine* and other journals while also turning out three more stories about Batts: *As Good as Dead* (1946), *Mourning After* (1950), and *Handle With Fear* (1951). It was the "Mac" series that launched him into writing full time, with *Draw the Curtain Close* (1951). He went on to write sixteen novels about Mac.

In 1954, Dewey published two novels under the pseudonym Tom Brandt: *Kiss Me Hard* and *Run, Brother, Run*. He also wrote several other non-series mysteries in the fifties and sixties. In 1957, he started a second major series, about Pete SCHOFIELD, a Los Angeles private detective. Although Schofield is a swinger like Peter CHAMBERS (the books have titles like *The Girl in the Punchbowl* and *Nude in Nevada*), he is also married.

DEXTER, COLIN (1930–) Born the same year as Ruth RENDELL, Colin Dexter is one of the most respected English mystery authors of that generation. His work and his series character, Inspector MORSE, have achieved wide popularity through television adaptations. Dexter has been compared with Michael INNES, because of his academic background (he studied classics at Cambridge) and because he sets his stories in Oxford. There really is no similarity, however; the Inspector Morse stories are realistic, often dealing with sordid crimes and lower-class people. Morse himself is a rather unhappy man, a loner who would be bored to death or enraged by Innes's bubbling aristocrats. Dexter, however, appears to be a devotee of the classic mystery; despite the realistic settings and psycho-intuitive approach used by Morse, Dexter carefully inserts RED HERRINGS, builds false chains of assumptions, and fences with the reader in a manner to satisfy any fan of the GOLDEN AGE. It is this hybrid quality that is the author's greatest contribution to the genre, showing that a puzzle need not be silly or COZY, and a "modern" crime novel need not be just a weak plot cloaked heavily in atmospherics and violence.

Colin Dexter taught classics at a grammar school after earning his B.A. and M.A. from Cambridge and serving in the army signal corps. He later earned another M.A. from Oxford in 1966. Dexter is a crossword puzzle addict—he has won national championships—and an avid reader of poetry. Both activities probably help account for the allusiveness of some of the Morse books. Dexter combines the PROCEDURAL approach with the psychological, so that Morse always seems to be thinking along two lines at the same time. The stories are generally well written.

Morse's first case was *Last Bus to Woodstock* (1975). Dexter has made the most of the town-and-gown rivalry of Oxford, but this is more than just a convenient source of scandals; he explores the coexistence of two cultures that do not understand each other. Dexter has won two Gold Daggers (one for THE WENCH IS DEAD, 1989) and two Silver Daggers for the series.

DIABOLIQUES, LES See TUBS.

DIAMOND, LEGS See PROHIBITION.

DIBDIN, MICHAEL (1947–) Born in England, Michael Dibdin was educated at the University of Sussex and the University of Alberta in Edmonton, Canada. He has also lived in Perugia, Italy, and in Seattle. These experiences have all played a part in his fiction, but none so much as his knowledge of Italy, which forms the background to his series of novels about Aurelio ZEN. Among those who have praised Dibdin's work is Ruth RENDELL, another writer who adds a deeper level of social commentary to the basic whodunit plot. Dibdin's novels include *Ratking* (1988), which won a Gold Dagger Award from the British CRIME WRITERS' ASSOCIATION.

Dibdin's beginnings as a writer, however, were not so auspicious. His first book was the pastiche *The Last Sherlock Holmes Story* (1978), in which HOLMES is called in to catch JACK THE RIPPER. Reviewers criticized every aspect of the book, from its scholarship to its pseudo-Holmesian style. Dibdin tried writing a HISTORICAL MYSTERY with *A Rich Full Death* (1986), which involved the poet Robert Browning. But it was *Ratking*, the first of the Zen novels, that brought him the most attention.

Among Dibdin's non-series novels is *The Dying of the Light* (1993), which begins with a graphic and depressing depiction of life inside a mismanaged home for the elderly ruled by two sadistic alcoholics, and then develops into a clever and even funny whodunit disguised by the characters' own mockery of the whodunit form. Two elderly and lonely denizens of the home make up a mystery story about the wrecks around them, making one a retired colonel, another an American heiress, and one the "corned beef millionaire." Then suddenly, a real whodunit takes them in its anything but cozy grip, and not everyone escapes alive. A much more ambitious novel is *The Tryst* (1989), which combines several narratives, each of them full of psychological horror. The center of the novel is the relationship between a woman psychiatrist and a troubled boy.

Dibdin has also edited *The Picador Book of Crime Writing* (1993) and *The Vintage Book of Classic Crime* (1997).

DICK It has been said that this term for "detective" is simply an abbreviation of that word; but it has also been traced to the verb *to dick* (common in the nineteenth century) meaning "to watch," which comes from the Hindu *dekhna*.

Author-humorist Bruce Jay Friedman made a joke of the coincidence of the two English meanings of "dick" in *The Dick* (1968), about a hapless and sexually neurotic New York City homicide detective.

DICK, PHILIP K[INDRED] (1928–1982) One of the most prominent SCIENCE FICTION writers of the century, Philip K. Dick was dubbed "the poor man's Pynchon" for his multilayered narratives and preoccupation with the interpretation of reality, sometimes by highly disturbed minds. Interested in other states of consciousness (as opposed to other worlds), he wrote one novel of science fiction–detection, *A Scanner Darkly* (1977). The main character, an undercover cop named Fred, becomes addicted to a mind-altering drug in order to track down its producers. The drug, known as Substance D., splits the mind into two separate identities; Fred's other half, Bob Arctor, is the drug dealer he is pursuing, but he doesn't know it. (Fred, that is. Or Bob.) It is a gripping novel, and if there were any doubt about its seriousness, in an afterword Dick dedicated the book to those who were killed or mentally destroyed by drug abuse during "the bad decision," the decade of the sixties.

Dick studied briefly at the University of California at Berkeley before devoting himself to writing. He had been writing for ten years when he achieved prominence with *The Man in the High Castle* (1962), a Hugo award-winning novel imagining a world in which the NAZIS won World War II. This subject later fascinated Len DEIGHTON.

DICKENS, CHARLES (1812–1870) Perhaps the greatest and most popular novelist in English literature, Dickens created some of the best-known characters of English fiction—Oliver Twist, David Copperfield, Sydney Carton, Sairey Gamp, and many others. (Dickens also produced some of the most memorable crooks, including the Artful Dodger, FAGIN, and Abel Magwich.) It is less known that Dickens created the first private detective in English literature, and was writing crime and mystery stories ten years before POE.

Dickens grew up in poverty, the horrors of which became the central theme of his work. When his father, a clerk in the British Navy's pay office, was put in debtor's prison, the twelve-year-old Dickens was sent to work in a blacking factory making polish. These and other experiences are vividly reflected in such books as *Oliver Twist* (1839) and *Little Dorrit* (1857). The plot of the former is well known; Oliver, an orphan, falls in with a criminal gang headed by Fagin, a cruel old man who teaches young boys to steal for him. The book made the political point that the Poor Law of 1834, a utilitarian scheme for confining the poor to workhouses, was inhuman and only tightened the connection between poverty and crime.

Because of his family's poverty, Dickens never received much education. Instead, he became an office boy in a law firm, and later a reporter. Dickens entered into this career just at the time when Sir Robert Peel was organizing the first Metropolitan Police force (see BOBBY). Dickens was as fascinated by crime as he was by every other aspect of nineteenth-century London; his jobs brought him into contact with criminals, whose trials—and executions—he reported on (even renting a rooftop to see the double execution of Frederick and Maria Manning in 1849). He also accompanied the early police on their rounds and watched detectives in action.

Many of Dickens's books could be said to be germane to crime fiction because of his interest in the reasons for crime; however, he had a much more specific interest in mysteries and the activities of the police. Dickens was responsible both for the first official detective in English fiction (Inspector BUCKET) and the first private eye, Mr. NADGETT, who appears in *Martin Chuzzlewitt* (1844). Even before that, Dickens had brought the BOW STREET RUNNERS into *Oliver Twist*, and policemen had appeared in his very earliest works. Like his friend Wilkie COLLINS, Dickens also used real crimes and trials as material for his novels. The case of the Mannings helped provide the plot for *Bleak House* (1852). He also used the real policemen whom he met as models for his characters. Inspector Field, whose exploits he wrote about in his magazine *Household Words*, was the inspiration for Bucket as well as for Charley Wield, a large man with a "moist, knowing eye" who appears in other magazine pieces. Dickens did well what many mystery authors have done less well: used a few mannerisms, a peculiarity of speech, strange features or eccentricities to establish a character. Nadgett and Bucket are every bit as memorable as his other, more famous creations. One of Dickens's best-known detective short stories is HUNTED DOWN (1859). It is included in *Hunted Down: The Detective Stories of Charles Dickens* (1996), edited and ably introduced by Peter Haining; this volume makes many long-out-of-print stories available again.

When he died, Dickens was working on THE MYSTERY OF EDWIN DROOD (pub 1870); incomplete, it is a story that has become a fascinating mystery itself. He also left behind another, nonfictional secret that would take more than a century to unravel. In her award-winning book *The Invisible Woman* (1990), Claire Tomalin describes Dickens's decades-long relationship with Nelly Tiernan, an actress. The book contains a fascinating picture of Dickens's time and details of his relationship with Collins and the sometimes mysterious life of a Victorian gentleman.

DICKINSON, PETER (1927–) Born in Zambia, Peter Dickinson won a scholarship to Eton College. He later attended Cambridge and graduated in 1951. With a background in the classics and English literature, Dickinson began writing for *Punch* in 1951—about mystery fiction, among other subjects. His first novel did not appear until he was over forty, but when it did, he made an instantaneous impression. *The Glass-Sided Ants Nest* (1968; orig title *Skin Deep*) won a Gold Dagger from the British CRIME WRITER'S ASSOCIATION; Dickinson won another Gold Dagger the following year for *A Pride of Heroes* (1969; U.S. title THE OLD ENGLISH PEEP SHOW). Both novels feature the Dickinson series character, Inspector PIBBLE. Dickinson has been compared to the English writers of the GOLDEN AGE, though his writing is clear, modern, and without quaintness. More apparent is the influence of Graham GREENE and W. Somerset MAUGHAM, both in settings and the types of questions asked in Dickinson's work.

From his first book, Dickinson gained a reputation for an offbeat sense of humor and flare for the peculiar. *The Glass-Sided Ants Nest* concerns the murder of a New Guinean chief; his tribe, however, is living in the attics of some London townhouses. The tribe had been brought to London so that an anthropologist could study them further. In *The Poison Oracle* (1974), an Arabian sultan hires a bright but unsuccessful Englishman to try to teach a chimpanzee to read. A murder is committed, to which the chimp is the only witness. Despite the lack of realism and the apparent nuttiness of such plots, Dickinson uses them to make quite serious points. Two ongoing themes are the relationship of science to society and the politics of colonialism and postcolonialism. Dickinson's scientists are often likeable people with little imagination, who expertly manipulate the tools of science but accept its superiority and validity without question.

A typical example is Foxe in *Walking Dead* (1977), a young man who embraces the paternalism of the pharmaceutical company he works for until they start using him as a pawn in a dangerous game played against a dictatorial maniac. Foxe likes nothing better than working with rats, and accepts a posting to Hog's Cay, a Caribbean country somewhat like Haiti. He soon realizes that the experiment he is working on is worthless; the dictator, Dr. Onesiphorus Trotter, wants him to work on a drug that will make people "good" (i.e., submissive). Foxe finds himself under suspicion of murder, which Trotter uses to exact his cooperation. Trotter's contempt for his own people and his *realpolitik* allow Dickinson to make a point about the "do as I say, not as I do" hypocrisy of the European exploiters. At the same time, the characters' debates about social control veils (thinly) a meditation on the potential misuse of science for political reasons.

The Green Gene (1973) is an even clearer attempt to harness the crime story to political and social investigations. Technically SCIENCE FICTION, it is set in the near future and describes an England divided along racial lines. Humayan is a scientist who is kidnapped and stumbles into a murder case. Dickinson is obviously writing against the background of apartheid in South Africa, and uses science fiction and detection to question whether "it can't happen here." The novel is also a peculiar joining of his African and English interests. Another topical novel is *Play Dead* (1991), about the murder of a suspected child molester. The "hero" of the novel is a two-year-old.

Dickinson has said of his work, "I'm like a beachcomber walking along the shores of my imagination, picking up things and wondering what kinds of structures they could make." Dickinson has also won the prestigious Whitbread award.

The strangeness of some of his plots has sometimes led to a mistaken view of Dickinson as a satirical or perhaps even farcical writer. One of Dickinson's best books is THE YELLOW ROOM CONSPIRACY (1994), in which the apparatus of the crime or mystery story has been pared away, leaving a literary novel of sustained depth and character. The story looks back at the period of World War II from the perspective of today, using a murder as the thread tying the periods together. Dickinson has used this plot again and again, and the themes of memory and guilt have come to preoccupy the author more and more. In *Hindsight* (1983), a novelist's attempt to write about his childhood experience during the war dredges up repressed memories. *Perfect Gallows* (1988) is about Adrian Waring, a successful actor who discovered a black butler hanged in a dovecote on his uncle's estate in 1944. With American soldiers encamped in the area, it is possible that the murder was a lynching. Waring had turned down a family inheritance in order to make it on his own, and even changed his name; however, he returns to the house for an estate sale and is reminded of the events of August 1944 by certain objects.

DICKSON, CARTER A pseudonym of John Dickson CARR, under which he wrote his mysteries about Sir Henry MERRIVALE.

DIFFERENCE ENGINE, THE (1991) A novel co-authored by William GIBSON and Bruce Sterling. Both authors are known for their SCIENCE FICTION, elements of which are combined in *The Difference Engine* with crime, mystery, and the historical novel. Set in 1855, the book has as its premise that Charles Babbage's early protocomputers have been perfected into "Engines" that are mechanical (steam-driven) rather than electrical and that operate with punch cards. A further English revolution decades before the book opens has brought to power the Industrial Radicals, a progressive, pro-technology party at the head of which is Lord Byron (*not* killed in Greece, evidently) and his daughter, the "Queen of the Engines." A complicated plot weaves together the fates of Sybil Gerard, daughter of a Luddite executed by the "Rads"; Edward "Leviathan" Mallory, a paleontologist-adventurer who has earned fame by unearthing the first dinosaurs; a criminal-revolutionary named Captain SWING; secret agent Laurence Oliphant; and a mysterious set of punch cards that hold some wonderful or dreadful secret. The novel is a meditation on the use and misuse of information.

DILLON, ROY A character in THE GRIFTERS (1963), one of the best of Jim THOMPSON's novels. Roy is a clean-cut and ingenious crook who amasses a fortune not through a big score but from "the short con"—small swindles that fall to him through chance encounters in bars, coffee shops, and hotels as he travels around under the cover of being a salesman.

DIMARCO, JEFFERSON An insurance investigator in a series of novels by Doris Miles DISNEY, DiMarco works for Commonwealth Insurance in Boston. Disney also made him look the part, and instead of a dashing private eye type, DiMarco is short, gray, and heavy. Disney also made him fallible; in his first case he falls in love with a murderer. In *Straw Man* (1951; British title *The Case of the Straw Man*), the killer's identity is given away in the middle of the book. This novel was filmed in 1953. Another DiMarco novel, *Family Skeleton* (1949), was made into the film *Stella* in 1950.

BIBLIOGRAPHY Novels: *Dark Road* (1946), *Trick or Treat* (1957; British title *The Halloween Murder*), *Method in Madness* (1957; British title *Quiet Violence*), *Did She Fall or Was She Pushed?* (1959), *Find the Woman* (1962), *The Chandler Policy* (1971).

DIME DETECTIVE See PULP MAGAZINES.

DIME NOVEL Beginning during the American Civil War, the dime novel, like the RAILWAY NOVEL, catered to the burgeoning market for popular literature. The "penny dreadful" (in England, the "shilling shocker") was a shorter type of sensational story. The dime novel was usually of novella length and was printed at the lowest possible cost (like the PULP MAGAZINES that succeeded it). What made these forms of publication possible was the modern printing press and cheap paper. Dime novels might be mysteries, true crime, fantastic tales, adventure, horror—anything sensational. The Western as a genre began with the dime novel. One of the most successful dime novel publishers was Beadle and Adams, and one of their biggest sellers was the Westerns written by E. L. Wheeler about Deadwood Dick.

But another Beadle and Adams writer, E. Z. C. Judson (1823–1886), was the king of the dime novel. Judson wrote an incredible number of dime novels—over 400—many of them under the pseudonym of Ned Buntline. It is said that he wrote a six-hundred page novel in sixty-two hours. In addition to his writing, he fought a number of duels, led the Astor Place riots, and helped organize the xenophobic Know-Nothing Party.

The detective story was a later addition to the dime novel pool. Some of the Westerns included detection, but the detective story as a separate form had to wait until several years after the Civil War, and it only became dominant in the 1880s with the advent of Nick CARTER, the only dime novel sleuth who is still a household name. The dime novel declined just around the time that the pulp magazines were starting up, in the era of World War I.

DISNEY, DORIS MILES (1907–1976) Doris Miles Disney achieved a modest reputation as a mystery writer in the forties, earning the praise of Anthony BOUCHER, James

SANDOE, and others. Her strength was her portrayal of her native New England; her weakness was the technical flaws critics sometimes noted in her writing. Born in Connecticut, she spent most of her life in that state and worked in the insurance business in Hartford before her marriage. Her first novel, *Compound for Death* (1936), was about small-town cop Jim O'Neill, who appeared in several other books. David Madden, a postal inspector, was the sleuth in three books: *Unappointed Rounds* (1956; British title *The Post Office Case*), *Black Mail* (1958), and *Mrs. Meeker's Money* (1961). But it was the insurance investigator Jefferson DIMARCO who was to become her most recognized series character. After her husband's death, Disney supported herself with her writing. She wrote some two dozen non-series mysteries in addition to her three series. Among them was one of her last books, *Do Not Fold, Spindle, or Mutilate* (1970), which was filmed for television. *The Last Straw* (1954) is about a wealthy man pressured by his mistress and others who disappears, then turns up dead in a remote cabin. Disney wrote almost fifty novels, none of which are any longer in print.

DKA NOVELS See GORES, JOE.

DNA TESTING This method of identification, in use for approximately a dozen years, has been hailed as the greatest thing in forensic science since FINGERPRINTING. The complexity of the technique has hindered its acceptance, however, and some have suggested that the use of expert witnesses and attempts by defense counsels to discredit the technique have created a public sense that there is some scientific disagreement about the validity of DNA profiling that does not actually exist. Challenges regarding the security and handling of genetic material have some basis in reality, however; it was discovered that one technician involved in DNA profiling had been falsifying tests for years.

There are two types of DNA testing. The first involves *nuclear* human DNA. DNA can be recovered at a crime scene from spots of blood, semen, or other biological material. It has even been said that the saliva on the back of a postage stamp could be used. The genetic chain, made up of combinations of base pairs, is examined at various points or "loci"; the number of points can vary, and the width of the "point" can range from several hundred to several thousand base pairs, depending on which laboratory is doing the testing (imagine a license plate with millions of numbers, from which some sections will have to be compared to make an identification). What is agreed upon is that the odds that a sample from a crime that matches a sample from a particular person (the suspect) at four to eight loci are *not* from the same person are astronomical. But how astronomical the odds are has been the subject of debate, primarily because of the issue of "sub-populations." A specific genetic variation may be more frequent in a specific ethnic or racial population group; thus the odds are different when the sample is considered in relation to the population as a whole or the sub-population. In 1992, the National Research Council recommended a "ceiling principle" so that probabilities would be estimated as conservatively as possible.

A second DNA testing method involves *mitochondrial* DNA. Patterns are more difficult to establish with mitochondrial DNA, but on the other hand the technique requires a smaller sample of tissue. Mitochondrial DNA analysis has been favored by the military in identifying remains such as bone fragments, sometimes decades old. The technique has also been used to positively identify the remains of Tsar Nicholas II and the outlaw Jesse James.

DOBYNS, STEPHEN (1941–) An award-winning poet and essayist, Stephen Dobyns has written a series of mysteries set in Saratoga, New York, usually involving the horse racing crowd there. His series character is Charlie Bradshaw, a private detective and former cop. As a poet, Dobyns is known for his verbal displays and startling imagery in the surrealist vein. These characteristics carry over into his mystery stories, in which there is sometimes a GOTHIC undercurrent. *Saratoga Longshot* (1976) was the first book in the series, which has begun to show signs of age (not helped by a recent change of narrator). Charlie Bradshaw works out of an office over a used bookstore. His mother runs the Bentley, a Saratoga hotel. Bradshaw was a cop for twenty years before going private. He has aged realistically, and is now a middle-aged, gray-haired man with bifocals. Although Bradshaw is cool and mature, his hero is a murderer—Jesse James. Charlie is sometimes assisted by Victor "Vic" Plotz, a crude individual who speculates in various enterprises and always loses his shirt. In *Saratoga Backtalk* (1994), Vic began telling the stories, which was a disastrous change; his narration is choppy and his jokes are not funny enough. He also tells the story in *Saratoga Fleshpot* (1995), in which he gets a job guarding a horsey art exhibit because his investments have been wiped out. ("Fleshpot" is a horse.)

DOCTOROW, E[DGAR] L[AWRENCE] (1931–) A highly respected American novelist and author of such works as *Ragtime* (1975; film 1981) and *Billy Bathgate* (1989; film 1991), both of which have crime themes, Doctorow attempted to write a HISTORICAL mystery with

The Waterworks (1994). Set in the New York of the TAMMANY HALL era, it is a remarkable recreation of the squalid, bustling nineteenth-century city. Doctorow also captures the mood of fear that hung over the populace under the corrupt and lawless regime of William "Boss" Tweed.

The original "waterworks" was a magnificent neo-Egyptian reservoir that stood on the current site of the New York Public Library and Bryant Park, and took up the entire block bounded by 42nd and 40th streets and Fifth and Sixth avenues. A young newspaperman is walking by this structure when he sees a group of old men go by in a white carriage, one of whom is his father. This is not unusual, except that his father is supposed to be dead. His search for the answer to the mystery leads him to a NAPOLEON OF CRIME and bizarre goings-on in New York hospitals, all centered on the waterworks itself. Doctorow's research is meticulous and convincing, though the pace of the story is that of a historical novel of five times the length, and the detection element is outweighed by atmosphere. See also WHITE, STANFORD.

DOGGO, TO LIE The English expression "to lie doggo" means to conceal oneself, to lie motionless, to hide or wait and see.

DOLAN, BRAD See FULLER, WILLIAM.

DONNISH SCHOOL See INNES, MICHAEL.

DONOVAN, DICK (pseudonym of Joyce Emmerson Preston Muddock, 1842–1934) The English author J. E. Muddock wrote fifty detective stories and thrillers under the name Dick Donovan, as well as fifty historical novels and other books. Although his novels about the DONOVAN character brought him the most attention, he later disparaged his crime and mystery writing and, like Conan DOYLE, thought that his other work was better. He wrote a number of guide books, and also an autobiography, *Pages from an Adventurous Life* (1907). The adventure began early. Muddock was born in Southampton, he went to India in the employ of the East India Company, and survived the Indian Mutiny. Later he would travel in the Far East as a correspondent for the *London Daily News* and other journals. His spy novels gave rise to the rumor that he was working as an agent of the Russian government. One such work was *The Chronicles of Michael Danevitch of the Russian Secret Service* (1897). His Donovan stories appeared frequently in the *Strand* magazine. Many readers thought that "Dick Donovan" was a real person. Other works by Donovan, but relating tales about other characters, are *The Records of Vincent Trill of the Detective Service* (1899) and *The Adventures of Tyler Tatlock: Private Detective* (1900).

DONOVAN, DICK The character created by J. E. Muddock. Donovan-the-character is little more than a voice; he does not give many details about himself except his intelligence and his undaunted pursuit of problems others find impossible: "the seemingly impossible is frequently the most easy to accomplish, where a mind specially trained to deal with complex problems is brought to bear on it." The style of his accounts can be labored and overelaborate, with odd phrases and bits of alliteration: "a pathological conundrum was propounded which it was for the medical world to answer, and practically I was placed out of the running, to use a sporting phrase." The narrator's physical descriptions also lack the vividness of scene and character one finds in Conan DOYLE or Arthur MORRISON.

BIBLIOGRAPHY Short Stories: *The Man Hunter: Stories from the Notebook of a Detective* (1888), *Caught at Last!: Leaves from the Note-Book of a Detective* (1889), *Who Poisoned Hetty Duncan? And Other Detective Stories* (1890), *Tracked and Taken: Detective Sketches* (1890), *A Detective's Triumphs* (1891), *Wanted! A Detective's Strange Adventures* (1892), *In the Grip of the Law* (1892), *From Information Received* (1893), *Link by Link* (1893), *From Clue to Capture* (1893), *Suspicion Aroused* (1893), *Found and Fettered* (1894), *Dark Deeds* (1895), *Riddles Read* (1896), *Tales of Terror* (1899).

DON Q The character Don Quebranta Huesnos, created by Hesketh PRICHARD, is a dangerous and ambiguous type of hero who prefigures The Shadow and other similar characters—kind to their friends, but ruthless and even savage toward their enemies. Don Q is Spanish, and has a quasi-Catholic philosophy; he defends the poor and good against the powerful and evil. Don Q was a short story character and premiered in 1898. Several volumes of stories were collected.

BIBLIOGRAPHY Novels: *Don Q's Love Story* (1909).

Short stories: *The Chronicles of Don Q* (1904), *New Chronicles of Don Q* (1906; U.S. title: *Don Q in the Sierra*).

"DOOMDORF MYSTERY, THE" See ABNER, UNCLE.

DOOMSTERS, THE See ARCHER, Lew; MACDONALD, Ross.

DOORBELL RANG, THE (1965) A Nero WOLFE story containing an unflattering portrait of the Federal Bureau of Investigation. Rex STOUT wrote the novel after reading a book exposing the FBI's unappetizing methods and bloated power. In the end Wolfe symbolically shuts the J. Edgar Hoover figure out of his house.

DOPPELGÄNGER (German, meaning "double-goer") The figure of the double has roots in folklore, but it became popularized in literature in the romantic era. The GOTHIC movement used the figure of the double to the full; it often was connected to horror and imminent death. In *Armadale* (1866), Wilkie COLLINS wrote about two men who share the same name, Allan Armadale, and the fatal consequences of their encounter. The overuse of the *doppelgänger* partly accounts for Monsignor KNOX anathematizing its "secular" version, the identical twin. The *doppelgänger* is an irresistible figure, however, and the twin motif appears as recently as in the works of Walter MOSLEY. Another version of the *doppelgänger* is the split personality; a character is aware of another person who turns out to be a part of their own divided self.

The appeal of the *doppelgänger* is not simply the callow one of saving the author who has painted himself or herself into a corner. The psychic horror of being confronted with someone who is one's self, which so appealed to gothic writers, can be translated into the mystery or detective story as, for example, the shock of meeting the murder victim again, alive. Writers who have used the double figure include POE, DOSTOYEVSKY, and, more recently, Daphne DU MAURIER and Helen MCCLOY. John Franklin BARDIN used it most horrifyingly in DEVIL TAKE THE BLUE-TAIL FLY (1948).

DORRINGTON A character created by Arthur MORRISON who is part thief and part detective. Of the firm of Dorrington & Hicks, private inquiry agents, Dorrington describes himself as a "rascal," but he is a bit more than that. Dorrington uses lock-picks, disguises, and trickery to find out what he wants—and go to where he wants. He would as lief rob as detect. Once he solves the crime, he privately exposes the criminal, using his knowledge to line his own pockets ("Can I shut my eyes and allow a piece of iniquity like this to go on unchecked, without getting anything by way of damages for myself?"). In fine, he is a blackmailer.

Dorrington has slipped into obscurity, but he prefigures characters like Donald Westlake's PARKER—a much later generation of criminal heroes who are not gentlemen like RAFFLES, but rather nasty customers. Brazen and clever, "altogether an unscrupulous scoundrel," Dorrington is a good deal more realistic and unnerving than the debonair Edwardian hero-crooks. In the surprising end of "The Dorrington Deed-Box," he discovers two murderers whom he has been tracking throughout the story, but instead of turning them in, Dorrington takes them in his charge because he might have a use for them as professional killers. One of Dorrington's most amusing cases is "The Affair of the 'Avalanche Bicycle and Tyre Co., Ltd.'" Morrison was interested in sport, and in this case worked the bicycling craze into a tale involving speculators floating a stock issue for a bogus company.

BIBLIOGRAPHY Short stories: *The Dorrington Deed-Box* (1897).

DORTMUNDER, JOHN A thief in a series of novels by Donald WESTLAKE. Middle-aged and middle-class, Dortmunder is a working stiff who has bad luck; the "pessimistic" look in his eyes signals that something is always going to go very wrong. That he is Westlake's best series creation is a frequent but disputable claim. The humor is light, but the author strains after jokes and sometimes the books are quite childish. The first Dortmunder novel was *The Hot Rock* (1970); it was adapted very successfully to film (1972), with Robert Redford in the role of Dortmunder. Dortmunder's first tale began as a story about another Westlake character, PARKER, from whom he couldn't be more different. In *The Hot Rock,* Dortmunder is condemned to steal the same emerald again and again. An inability to hang onto his loot is a common feature of the novels. In *Nobody's Perfect* (1977), Dortmunder is hired by a blond New York playboy named Chauncey to steal a valuable Dutch painting so that the owner can collect the insurance money. To ensure that Dortmunder returns the painting after the claim is settled, Chauncey hires a hitman to threaten him. Dortmunder is accidentally caught in an elevator, so the gang goes on without him. The loss of the painting leads to a chase to Scotland, where Dortmunder and his childhood friend, Andy Kelp, battle in suits of armor under the moonlight. Among the other Dortmunder books is WHY ME? (1983), about another failed jewel robbery, and *Jimmy the Kid* (1974), in which Parker also appears. The Dortmunder novels are not supposed to be anything but preposterous, but the comedy of errors is a difficult act to repeat using the same characters; the best books in the series inevitably make the others seem lame.

BIBLIOGRAPHY Novels: *Bank Shot* (1972), *Good Behavior* (1986), *Drowned Hopes* (1990).

DOSTOYEVSKY, FYODOR [MIKHAYLOVICH] (1821–1881) Dostoyevsky is often classed as a "proto"-mystery or crime writer, primarily on the basis of the novel *Crime and Punishment* (1866). Julian SYMONS placed the novel among the hundred best works in the genre but later retracted his opinion. Symons recognized that Dostoyevsky's interest in crime was not sensational, nor was it even primarily sociological; it was theological. The question is moot, however, because Dostoyevsky had an enormous effect on later crime writers and practitioners of the "psychological" detective story or mystery, and also because *Crime and Punishment* is one of the most gripping novels ever written.

RASKOLNIKOV is a poor student who convinces himself that it is morally acceptable for him to murder a repulsive pawnbroker for the noble aim of rescuing himself, his mother, and his sister from grim poverty. His crime is one of the most piteous botched murders of fiction; he is discovered by the old woman's simple-minded sister, whom he must also kill. Dostoyevsky brilliantly portrays the unraveling of Raskolnikov's self-delusion under the pressure of his conscience. Once, he had grandiose dreams of achieving greatness through transgression, comparing himself to Napoleon; gradually his belief in himself as above morality crumbles, and he cannot even bring himself to spend the money his crime has earned. Meanwhile the detective Porfiry Petrovich watches him suspiciously, waiting for the confession that comes at the end of Raskolnikov's collapse, which also presages a rebirth.

Born in Moscow, Dostoyevsky was one of eight children. His father was a doctor; his mother died when he was sixteen. He studied at the Military Engineering School in St. Petersburg but was already bent on a literary career. His first book, *Poor Folk* (*Bednye lyudi,* 1846), dealt with poverty, which he had endured as a student. His second book, *The Double* (*Dvoinik,* 1846), is a story of mental derangement in which a failed man encounters his DOPPELGÄNGER. In 1849, Dostoyevsky experienced one of the most cataclysmic events in his life. He was arrested and actually taken out to be shot, but at the last minute his sentence was commuted to four years hard labor in Siberia. His prison experience both gave him an intimate knowledge of the underclass and developed his religious convictions.

The central act of *The Brothers Karamazov* (*Bratya Karamazovy,* 1879–1880), another masterpiece, is patricide. *Notes from the Underground* (*Zapiski iz podpolya,* 1864) attacks the kind of rationalist thinking by which Raskolnikov had deduced that he could commit murder for utilitarian purposes.

DOUBLE INDEMNITY (1943) This novel by James M. CAIN is yet another version of the "perfect" murder—this time involving TRAINS. Insurance salesman Walter Huff falls for Phyllis Nirdlinger, whose husband is an irascible and irritating older man. With his insider's knowledge, Huff helps Phyllis plan a murder no insurance company could detect—or so they think. As in other Cain novels, behind the pretense of love is cynicism and manipulation. The policy that the pair take out on the victim contains a "double indemnity" clause that doubles the payoff if the fatal accident occurs on a train. How they engineer such an "accident" is ingenious. In 1944, the novel was filmed with a screenplay partly written by Raymond CHANDLER.

DOUGAL, WILLIAM A series character in novels by Andrew TAYLOR, Dougal first appeared as a somewhat servile graduate student in the critically well-received novel *Caroline Miniscule* (1982). Dougal finds his tutor, Dr. Gumper, brutally murdered. He quickly becomes involved in a shady venture with the apparent murderer of Gumper, the suave and unscrupulous James Hanbury; not long after, events convince Dougal that Hanbury has been murdered himself. The crux of the story is a medieval manuscript written in Caroline Miniscule, the form of writing Dougal has been studying. Dougal becomes increasingly free of scruples as the story develops into a race to find the treasure of a canon of the Church of England who was also a master criminal. The final scenes aboard a small yacht and the ironic ending are well done.

Dougal reappeared in several later books. By the time of *Blood Relation* (1990), Dougal is working part-time for Custodemus, a security company, and also pursuing his literary career as a freelance editor. He is assigned to find Oswald "Oz" Finwood, the missing boyfriend of the daughter of Custodemus's chairman. The corpse is discovered impaled on an iron railing; Dougal's investigation leads into the nasty world of writers and publishing in London.

BIBLIOGRAPHY Novels: *Waiting for the End of the* World (1984), *Our Father's Lies* (1985), An *Old School Tie* (1986), *Freelance Death* (1987).

DOVER, CHIEF INSPECTOR WILFRED A grotesque detective created by Joyce PORTER and a complete parody of the GENIUS DETECTIVE. Dover is not only obese, but stupid; not only is he stupid, but he thinks he is intelligent. A "bird-brain," Dover typically makes all the wrong deductions; Detective Sergeant MacGregor thinks his boss is a "pig" but regularly saves his bacon. Dover is guilty of all of the seven deadly sins except lust. He is notoriously cheap, caging drinks and meals, and is inconsiderate of his wife and everyone else. The humor of the Dover books is related to bodily functions—Dover's either do not work or work too well.

While some critics have simply detested the Dover books completely, others have found that, beneath the detective's distracting crudity, these are well-written and plotted stories. The first Dover title was *Dover One* (1965). He is already middle-aged, repulsive, and the laughingstock of Scotland Yard. In the many novels that followed, the formula was not substantially changed. In *It's Murder with Dover* (1973), the chief of the Murder Squad sicks the "fat old layabout" on Lord Crouch, who has had to open his country house to tourists to raise money. The food prepared by his wife (a vegetarian), is a source of further Dover humor. *Dover Beats the Band* (1980), the last book in the series, has Dover following up on the murder of a man found on a garbage dump. To the last, Porter sticks to her formula, which is excess. The victim has been garroted, singed, mutilated, and stripped naked. Dover's pursuit of the killer (as the result of a bizarre clue found in the corpse's stomach) leads to a horrid holiday camp. The clumsy Chief Inspector then stumbles into a Special Branch investigation into a right-wing group called the Steel Band.

BIBLIOGRAPHY Novels: *Dover Two* (1965), *Dover Three* (1965), *Dover and the Unkindest Cut of All* (1967), *Dover and the Sense of Justice* (1968), *Dover Goes to Pott* (1968), *Dover Pulls a Rabbit* (1969), *Dover Fails to Make His Mark* (1970), *Dover Strikes Again* (1970), *A Terrible Drag for Dover* (1971), *Dover and the Dark Lady* (1972), *Dover Tangles with High Finance* (1975), *Dover and the Claret Tappers* (1976), *Dover Does Some Spadework* (1977), *When Dover Got Knotted* (1977), *Dover without Perks* (1978), *Dover Doesn't Dilly-Dally* (1978), *Dead Easy for Dover* (1978), *Dover Goes to School* (1978).

DOWLING, FATHER Father Roger Dowling is a Catholic priest and an unofficial detective in a series of novels by Ralph MCINERNY. A reformed alcoholic, Dowling used to work for the Archdiocesan Marriage Tribunal in Chicago making decisions about annulments, until suffering a sort of mental breakdown, bringing disgrace and transfer. In the novels, he has removed to Fox River, Illinois, where he helps local police detective Phil Keegan, his reactionary former classmate. Mary Murkin is Father Dowling's nosy housekeeper. Father Dowling is calm, intelligent, and unemotional; he pursues the truth, while Keegan pursues the criminal. The first Father Dowling novel was *Her Death of Cold* (1977). The series is not COZY, despite the potential of the setup; instead, some of the cases are sordid and realistic. They suffer not from the setup, but from the writing; execution often fails to measure up to conception. *Desert Sinner* (1992) concerns a woman who married at fifteen and had a child, then lost her husband; gave the child up for adoption and moved to Las Vegas, where she became a waitress and the lover of a mobster; and finally married a rich man, of whose murder she now stands accused. As a last insult, her long-lost son, now an ex-con, turns up and asks for money. It becomes apparent who did the murder, and the rest of the book hangs on the suspense of seeing if the killer will be caught and punished.

In *The Grass Widow* (1983), a disc jockey jokingly announces on the air that he is putting out a contract on his wife, who just left him. She goes to see Father Dowling in Fox River, and then is found dead at her motel, apparently a suicide, though the priest is not convinced. The motel is populated by a weird assortment of characters. As usual, the story is drawn out by adding analysis, details, and descriptions that are not always necessary. The story of double cuckolding, however, holds the attention.

Getting Away with Murder (1984) has an unusual twist. Howard Downs, with whom Father Dowling has held many conversations, is on trial for murdering his wife, and is surprisingly found not guilty. But after the trial, two odd things happen: Downs's attorney is found strangled, and Downs confesses to having killed him. Again, the overall idea attracts interest though the execution is less than inspiring.

As middling mysteries in a fairly unusual subgenre, the Father Dowling stories fall somewhere between well done and medium rare; in the class of priest detectives, Dowling can be rated above Father KOESLER but both are below the level of Father BROWN.

Father Dowling also appears in a GOLF mystery.

BIBLIOGRAPHY Novels: *The Seventh Station* (1977), *Bishop as Pawn* (1978), *Lying Three* (1979), *Second Vespers* (1980), *Thicker Than Water* (1981), *A Loss of Patients* (1982), *Rest in Pieces* (1985), *The Basket Case* (1987), *Four on the Floor* (1991), *Judas Priest* (1992).

DOXY This word has nothing to do with Greek *doxa,* or "praise, glory." *Doxy* dates as far back as the sixteenth century and was a term for "a beggar's wench" or a prostitute. It became an equivalent for a criminal's companion—a GUN MOLL. It has several possible roots: German *dukk,* or "bundle," or Dutch *docke,* meaning "doll." Another possible etymology is the English verb "to dock" (as with a dog's tail); thus, a doxy is a woman who has been deflowered.

Death of Doxy (1966) is one of the Nero WOLFE mysteries.

DOYLE, SIR ARTHUR CONAN (1859–1930) The most famous of mystery authors, Conan Doyle was also a rather unwilling one. He turned to the genre for economic reasons because of his failing medical practice. He tired of Sherlock HOLMES and thought to do away with him in THE FINAL PROBLEM (1893), only to be forced to bring him back by public acclamation. He preferred his other novels to his Holmes stories. Later in life he was dominated by his interest in spiritualism and the occult, seeming to forget Holmes altogether and writing books like *History of Spiritualism* (1926). But Doyle could not escape his own reputation, like Thomas Hardy, who thought of himself primarily as a poet but is most often remembered as an author of the novels he gave up writing more than thirty years before his death.

Conan Doyle made the genre vastly more sophisticated and respectable, but he did not invent it. Sherlock Holmes was modeled on an already extant literature and previous nineteenth-century detectives, particularly C. Auguste DUPIN and Monsieur LECOQ—who in turn were modeled on the real detective VIDOCQ.

Conan Doyle was born in Edinburgh but was of Irish descent. His father was an amateur painter, and his grandfather a cartoonist. The young Doyle was sent to Jesuit schools at home and abroad (Germany), and then settled down to study medicine at Edinburgh University (B.A. 1881, M.D. 1885). In the same year he received his doctorate, he married Louise Hawkins, with whom he had two children. Conan Doyle's medical studies had an important influence on his work. Not only is Holmes's amanuensis WATSON a doctor; one of the author's teachers, Dr. Joseph Bell, provided a model for Holmes in his careful forensic methods. A portrait of Bell (as well as of Doyle) may be contained in the story THE RECOLLECTIONS OF CAPTAIN WILKIE (1895), in which an Edinburgh doctor remembers his teacher's talent for deducing a man's profession from various outward signs, very much in the manner of Sherlock Holmes.

After graduation, Doyle made two voyages as a ship's surgeon, and his experience at sea would enter his work tangentially, for example in THE "GLORIA SCOTT." Conan Doyle had begun writing while still a student, and sold a story, "The Mystery of the Sassassa Valley," to the *Chambers Journal.* His first efforts at the novel were not auspicious: *The Narrative of John Smith* disappeared in the mail and was never found. His second book, *The Firm of Girdlestone,* would only be published in 1890 after Doyle's success with Holmes.

Conan Doyle set up as an eye specialist in Portsmouth, but the sluggish growth of his practice led him to devote himself to writing on the side. The first Holmes adventure, A STUDY IN SCARLET, was written in 1884 and serialized in 1887—not in the *Strand Magazine,* with which Holmes would become famously associated, but in *Beeton's Christmas Annual.* The second Holmes story, *The Sign of Four,* appeared in 1890. It was solicited by a Philadelphia editor from Lippincott Publishers at a famous luncheon (the other guest was Oscar Wilde, who also agreed to write a piece—what became *The Picture of Dorian Grey*). The stories that began to appear in the *Strand Magazine* in 1891 rapidly made Conan Doyle what we would call a celebrity, as well as inspiring myriad imitations, the best of which is THE MYSTERY OF A HANSOM CAB (1886). Hugh GREENE collected only a small number of the "Rivals of Sherlock Holmes" in his anthologies.

The style of the Holmes stories is typical of Victorian tastes. Particularly in his first adventure, which draws in not only murder but the wilds of the American West, a tragic love story, and religious fanaticism, Conan Doyle put in everything but the kitchen sink. The melodramatic element continues throughout the Holmes series; people have attacks of "brain fever" from stress, or are driven completely insane by their involvement in scandalous and mysterious events (as in the adventures of "The Crooked Man" and THE NAVAL TREATY). Conan Doyle made use of such sensational material as the Ku Klux Klan, in "The Five Orange Pips"; adventure on the high seas, mutiny, and murder, in "The 'Gloria Scott'"; and racism and interracial marriage, in "The Yellow Face." The rough-and-tumble of nineteenth-century America fascinated Doyle, and featured in "The Adventure of the Noble Bachelor" and most notably, *The Valley of Fear* (1915). Mark TWAIN took his revenge on Doyle for his Western absurdities in "A Double Barrelled Detective Story" by making Holmes the uncle of a dimwitted servant boy in a mining camp. The only really successful Holmes novel is THE HOUND OF THE BASKERVILLES (1902), which is also one of his greatest adventures.

As for the question of FAIR PLAY, Holmes himself observes of Watson's stories in "The Crooked Man" that Watson withholds "some factors in the problem which are never explained to the reader." Some stories, however, can easily be figured out, such as the well-known RED-HEADED LEAGUE.

So great was the hold of Holmes on the public imagination that people refused to believe that he did not exist, and actually wrote to him with their problems. They continue to do so to this day, and the Abbey Building Society, which now occupies the site of 221B Baker Street where Holmes supposedly lived, has a secretary who answers the letters addressed to Holmes. The letters include requests for help, criticisms of his cases, and endless questions about his personal life and tastes. Some of them have been collected in *Letters to Sherlock Holmes* (1985).

Conan Doyle twice did what few mystery writers (except those who were police officers themselves) have ever done: he tried to apply the methods used by his detective in fiction to real-life cases. The first of these, which occurred in 1906, was as bizarre and exotic as one of Holmes's own cases: Conan Doyle took up the cause of George EDALJI, a half-Indian student who had been sentenced to seven years for maiming horses. He later worked for the release of Oscar SLATER, a German Jew accused of robbery and homicide. Another case of LIFE IMITATES ART was Conan Doyle's volunteering in the Boer War, much as Doctor Watson had served in Afghanistan. His son by his first marriage (Louise Hawkins died in 1906, and Conan Doyle remarried the following year) was wounded in the war and later died of pneumonia. Conan Doyle wrote two books about the war, one a history and the other a piece of propaganda justifying British colonial policy. It was for *The Great Boer War* (1902), and not Sherlock Holmes, that Conan Doyle was knighted in 1903.

Conan Doyle was notoriously careless in his writing, confusing names, dates, and relationships of characters. Holmes fans and critics, most notably those belonging to the Baker Street Irregulars organization, have developed an ingenious method of dealing with these comic bloopers: much criticism has been written from the point of view that Holmes and his adventures really existed, and therefore the "inconsistencies" must be exegetically explained. These studies range from the charming to the insufferably boring. Enthusiasm for the Holmes stories is not universal: Somerset MAUGHAM said that upon rereading he was surprised by "how poor they were," and that "you know no more of Sherlock Holmes after you have read fifty stories than you did after reading one." Other mystery writers have not shared Maugham's view, including John Dickson CARR, who wrote a biography of Conan Doyle (1949) that won an EDGAR award, and Julian SYMONS, author of *Conan Doyle: Portrait of an Artist* (1979). BARING-GOULD wrote a well-known "biography" of Sherlock Holmes. See also A SCANDAL IN BOHEMIA; THE REIGATE PUZZLE; and the adventures of the ENGINEER'S THUMB, the GREEK INTERPRETER, and the EMPTY HOUSE.

DRAGOMILOFF, IVAN The founder of THE ASSASSINATION BUREAU LTD. (pub 1963) in the novel by Jack London. Even if the author had not written in his notes about Dragomiloff's "transvaluation of values," it is clear from the character's appearance that he is the embodiment of London's assimilation of Nietzsche's philosophy to his own stoical heroism. Dragomiloff is blond, leonine, and self-possessed, a man who has redefined all values for himself. Far from a "blond beast" or an irrational monster, it is Dragomiloff's absolute respect for reason that leads him, in the argot of a later age, to put out a contract on himself.

DRAKE, TEMPLE See SANCTUARY.

DRAM OF POISON, A (1956) A COZY novel by Charlotte ARMSTRONG. Although set in California, the people and the feeling are very English. The tragi-comic story hinges on an attempted suicide that could result in multiple killings; in spite of its anodyne subject matter—for a mystery—the novel is very suspenseful and won an EDGAR award.

The trouble begins when a poetry professor in his fifties—Mr. Gibson—goes to the funeral of an old colleague and takes pity on the deceased's daughter, Rosemary. Rosemary is devastated; in the days following the funeral, her depression worsens and she falls ill, so Gibson calls in his doctor and takes care of her rent. His do-gooding impulses still unsatisfied, he decides to marry her. In the meantime they move in together, and on the very day they have chosen to celebrate Rosemary's recovery they have a car accident and Gibson is gravely injured. He then calls upon his sister Ethel for help. Ethel is a paradox: an obviously good woman who believes that no one is good. She thinks her brother is naive and that his wife more or less tried to kill him in the accident in order to marry their young and handsome neighbor. She communicates the philosophy that human beings are slaves of their passions, often buried deep in their unconscious, and are therefore unable to help themselves. Gibson, convinced that he is doomed, resolves to kill himself, procures poison and goes home. But when he gets home, the poison has disappeared. Because of the way he had hidden it, there is a frantic search to find the poison before someone dies accidentally.

The story now develops in the manner of a silent movie, by foot, car, and bus. Along the trail, more and more people are picked up: the bus driver, a girl he loves, a rich matron, a famous elderly painter. They somehow cram into the car, where they discuss the events and their various philosophies of life while they hurtle toward disaster and the final resolution. The novel has a slack spot before Gibson's suicide decision, and the accumulation of people is a little forced, but otherwise the rhythm and pace are sustained throughout.

DREISER, THEODORE [HERMAN ALBERT] (1871–1945) One of the greatest American authors and certainly the leading Naturalist, Dreiser was raised in poverty, the twelfth of thirteen children, and was a lifelong critic of social injustice and hypocrisy. He revolted against his Catholic upbringing, and his books strenuously resist any Christian interpretation or acceptance of suffering and poverty, which the author sees as simply a waste of human life brought on by the bad values of society. Although poorly educated, Dreiser read extensively and was influenced by, among others, POE, Hawthorne, and BALZAC. His work often dealt with crime, or perceived crime; in *Sister Carrie* (1900), a supposedly "fallen" woman manages to escape the Chicago slums with a married man, and makes good while he deteriorates and finally commits suicide. Publication of the novel was delayed for years because of its "immorality."

Dreiser based his most famous work, AN AMERICAN TRAGEDY (1925), on a real murder case, which he used to attack American values, this time the fantasies of power and success that drive a man to seek the short-cut of murder to get what he wants. It addresses a central paradox that recurs in crime fiction: the loser who would not have been a loser if he hadn't tried so hard *not* to be a loser. Dreiser also wrote *The Hand of the Potter* (1919), a play about a sexually disturbed murderer that MENCKEN dismissed as pornography.

DREW, NANCY See STRATEMEYER, EDWARD L.

DRIFFIELD, SIR CLINTON Another of the also-rans of the GOLDEN AGE, J. J. CONNINGTON's Sir Clinton Driffield can be placed alongside Miles BREDON; once popular, these sleuths were rapidly eclipsed and have been out of print for decades. Driffield is the Chief Constable who often works in company with Squire Wendover, a justice of the peace and the local eminence in the county. Driffield and Wendover are also chess partners.

The series ought not to be entirely dismissed, however; the author had a background in science and introduced it plausibly, using details about BALLISTICS, medicine, and other matters. The Driffield case most singled out for praise by critics is *The Sweepstakes Murders* (1931), in which a group of people have shares in the winnings. They are bumped off, TONTINE fashion.

BIBLIOGRAPHY Novels: *Murder in the Maze* (1927), *Tragedy at Ravensthorpe* (1927), *The Case with Nine Solutions* (1928), *Mystery at Linden Sands* (1928), *Nemesis at Raynham Parva* (1929; U.S. title *Grim Vengeance*), *The Boathouse Riddle* (1931), *The Castleford Conundrum* (1932), *The Ha-Ha Case* (1934; U.S. title *The Brandon Case*), *In Whose Dim Shadow* (1935; U.S. title *The Tau Cross Mystery*), *A Minor Operation* (1937), *For Murder Will Speak* (1938; U.S. title *Murder Will Speak*), *Truth Comes Limping* (1938), *The Twenty-One Clues* (1941), *No Past Is Dead* (1942), *Jack-in-the-Box* (1944), *Common Sense Is All You Need* (1947).

DRUM, CHESTER A sleuth created by Stephen MARLOWE. A former FBI agent, Drum lives in Washington, D.C., and is a private investigator. His cases are more adventure and suspense than mystery, and often involve espionage. With Richard S. PRATHER, Marlowe wrote *Double in Trouble* (1959), in which Shell SCOTT also took part.

BIBLIOGRAPHY Novels: *The Second Longest Night* (1955), *Mecca for Murder* (1956), *Killers Are My Meat* (1957), *Murder Is My Dish* (1957), *Trouble Is My Name* (1957), *Violence Is My Business* (1958), *Terror Is My Trade* (1958), *Homicide Is My Game* (1959), *Danger Is My Line* (1960), *Death Is My Comrade* (1960), *Peril Is My Pay* (1960), *Manhunt Is My Mission* (1961), *Jeopardy Is My Job* (1962), *Francesca* (1963), *Drum Beat—Berlin* (1964), *Drum Beat—Dominique* (1965), *Drum Beat—Madrid* (1966), *Drum Beat—Erica* (1967), *Drum Beat—Marianne* (1968).

DRUMMOND, BULLDOG A retired colonel in a series of spy and adventure stories by SAPPER. Drummond places an advertisement in the paper to get himself work as an adventurer. The title of the first book, *Bulldog Drummond, The Adventures of a Demobilised Officer Who Found Peace Dull* (1920), says a lot about the values behind the book; that anyone could find peace "dull" after World War I shows Sapper's characteristic detachment from reality. Drummond literally wages battles in peacetime, wiping out scores of enemies and saving the damsel in distress, Phyllis, who becomes his wife. Carl Peterson is the name of his nemesis, a kind of international criminal who survives the first book but is later done in. Drummond is a man of action, an almost unbelievable stereotype of the imperialist boor to whom everyone not British is a "dago." Gerard FAIRLIE took over the series after Sapper died and toned down Drummond's racism, but the Bulldog couldn't really be house-trained (not surprising, since he found peace dull).

Drummond, like the Mounties, always gets his man, and what he does to him once he has him is usually disturbing. In *The Black Gang* (1922), he reviles two Jewish revolutionaries and then whips them with a cat o' nine tails. In *The Final Count* (1926), the book in which he defeats Peterson, he says Russia is ruled by a "clique of homicidal, alien Jews." Critics tend to allow that there is a fair amount of "excitement" in the Drummond books, but it is so saturated in hate, narrow-mindedness, preposterous plots (both narrative and political), and bad writing that one would have to say the ore is of too low a yield to be worth bothering over.

BIBLIOGRAPHY Novels: By MacNeile—*The Third Round* (1925; U.S. title *Bulldog Drummond's Third Round*), *The Female of the Species* (1928), *Temple Tower* (1929), *The Return of Bulldog Drummond* (1932; U.S. title *Bulldog Drummond Returns*), *Knock-*

out (1933; U.S. title *Bulldog Drummond Strikes Back*), *Bulldog Drummond at Bay* (1935), *Challenge* (1937). By Fairlie—*Bulldog Drummond on Dartmoor* (1938), *Bulldog Drummond Attacks* (1939), *Captain Bulldog Drummond* (1945), *Bulldog Drummond Stands Fast* (1947), *Hands Off Bulldog Drummond* (1949), *Calling Bulldog Drummond* (1951), *The Return of the Black Gang* (1954).

DUFFY The ex-cop and security specialist in the novels of Julian BARNES written under the name Dan Kavanagh. Nick Duffy is bisexual, but "a bit of a puritan." He has some odd traits, such as his dislike of ticking noises, which causes him to ask his overnight guests to leave their watches in a plastic container in the bathroom while they are sleeping together. The one person Duffy can't have a successful sexual experience with is Carol Lucas, his former girlfriend and coworker in the West Central police. He frequents the Alligator, a gay bar.

Duffy is stocky, powerful, hairy, and slightly bowlegged. His manners are curt to the point of being rude, his dialogue (and interior monologues) unrestrained.

BIBLIOGRAPHY Novels: *Duffy* (1980), *Fiddle City* (1981), *Putting the Boot In* (1985), *Going to the Dogs* (1987).

DUFFY, FATHER A priest and amateur sleuth in Dorothy Salisbury Davis's A GENTLE MURDERER (1951). The resourceful priest, who is knowledgeable about the world without being tainted by it, uses parish records, clerical contacts, and the tendency of others to confide in and trust a priest to discover the identity of a man who has confessed to a murder.

DULUTH, PETER A character created by Patrick QUENTIN. Duluth is an alcoholic theatrical producer who meets his wife, Iris Pattison, in his first adventure, *A Puzzle for Fools* (1936), while he is detoxifying in an institution where she is being treated for depression. Their courtship is cemented by a couple of murders in the hospital, which they solve together. The Duluths later break up and then get back together again. In *Black Widow* (1952), Peter Duluth is suspected of murder when a woman is found dead in their apartment. Some of the Duluth cases involve the detective's family and also have a theater background, though neither is an element in the bizarre *A Puzzle for Fiends* (1946); Iris—now a famous movie star—hardly appears in this novel, in which Duluth loses his memory and is drawn into a loony plot to save an inheritance (see AMNESIA). *My Son, the Murderer* (1954), has Duluth's nephew suspected of murder. The last two books use both Duluth and detective Timothy Trant, who appeared in another series by Quentin, published under the name Q. Patrick.

BIBLIOGRAPHY Novels: *A Puzzle for Players* (1938), *A Puzzle for Puppets* (1944), *A Puzzle for Wantons* (1945), *A Puzzle for Pilgrims* (1947), *Run to Death* (1948).

DUMAS, ALEXANDRE (1802–1870; known as Dumas *père*) The son of a general in Napoleon's army, Alexandre Dumas became one of the most prolific and successful French writers of the nineteenth century. He was highly praised as a dramatist in his time, though those works today are rarely read or performed; however, his lengthy romantic novels, including *The Count of Monte Cristo* (1844–45), *The Three Musketeers* (1844), and *Twenty Years After* (1845), are still popular. Although these are tales of adventure, Dumas was also interested in crime and mystery. He had a band of assistants who helped him sift through memoirs and journals for sensational reports that would make good plots. His multi-volume *Crimes Célèbres* (1839–40; tr *Celebrated Crimes,* 1869) dealt with the Borgia family, Ali Pasha, Mary, Queen of Scots (who is believed to have conspired to murder Lord Darnley, her husband and cousin), the Marquise de BRINVILLIERS, and other notable cases. For his *Mohicans de Paris* (1855), he may have borrowed the name of the celebrated MOHOCKS. This four-volume novel sets out to portray the lowest class of residents of Paris, "la moderne Babylone." Set in 1827, it revels in the lawlessness (there was no organized police force) of the time; always the dramatist, Dumas seized on the theatrical possibilities of bohemians, artists, and criminals mingling in a romantic milieu. Jacques BARZUN translated extracts from Dumas and included him in his anthology, *The Delights of Detection* (1961).

DU MAURIER, DAPHNE (1907–1989) The granddaughter of George DuMaurier, author of *Trilby* (1894), Daphne Du Maurier wrote with a similar feeling for romance and the uncanny. *Trilby* is the novel in which the original Svengali appeared; a Hungarian musician, Svengali's mesmeric powers turn the artist's model Trilby O'Farrall into a great singer. The magnetism of human relationships and the sometimes violent results are a major feature of Daphne Du Maurier's novels as well. Although she received the Grand Master award from the Mystery Writers of America, Du Maurier's work falls into the nebulous category of suspense.

Du Maurier was the daughter of the actor Sir Gerald Du Maurier, of whom she wrote in *Gerald, A Portrait* (1934). Born in London, Daphne spent most of her life in Cornwall, whose rugged coast and forbidding landscape were the perfect setting for her GOTHIC suspense and mystery stories. Her most famous book, *Rebecca* (1938), concerns the new Mrs. de Winter, whose husband Maxim lives up to his name by being a mysterious and chilly character. The mystery is the secret of Maxim de Winter's first marriage, to the beautiful and glamorous Rebecca, whose presence seems still to hang over the house.

A story involving mysterious deaths is *The Scapegoat* (1956). It uses the classic gothic device of the DOPPELGÄNGER. John, an English historian, meets his double in France, one Jean le Comte de Gué. Gué steals John's passport and car, leaving him to assume Jean's identity. Unfortunately, Jean is suspected in the death of the master of the family glassworks, which is bankrupt. John is introduced into a gothic dysfunctional family: Gué's mother is a morphine addict, his sister a religious fanatic, and his sister-in-law is his mistress.

One of du Maurier's admirers was Alfred HITCHCOCK, who filmed *Rebecca* in 1940. Edgar BOX co-wrote the script of the film version of *The Scapegoat* (1956; film 1959).

DUNNE, JOHN GREGORY (1932–) Born in Hartford, Connecticut, John Gregory Dunne is noted for his funny, critical, and penetrating insights into the American social scene, particularly his satire on Irish-American life. Dunne attended Princeton University and wrote for *Time* magazine before moving to the West Coast, where he wrote for the film industry and for magazines. His first book was *Delano: The Story of the California Grape Strike* (1967). TRUE CONFESSIONS (1977) is a crime novel based on the same sensational Los Angeles murder case as THE BLACK DAHLIA (1987), a novel by James ELLROY. Dunne's novel was filmed in 1981 with Robert Duvall and Robert DeNiro as two Irish-American brothers, one a cop and the other a priest. *True Confessions* was followed by *Dutch Shay, Jr.* (1982) and *The Red White and Blue* (1987). Dunne is married to the writer Joan Didion. *Harp* (1988) is an autobiographical work.

DUNSANY, LORD (1878–1957) Edward John Moreton Drax Plunkett, eighteenth Baron Dunsany, grew up in England until he succeeded to the ancestral Dunsany Castle, near Dublin, which had been the family seat since 1194. He was educated at Eton and then at Sandhurst, served in the British Army in the Boer War, and was permanently injured in the Easter Rebellion of 1916. Dunsany was a great sportsman, and there is a great sense of fun in many of his works, whether they are overlaid with the macabre or not.

Dunsany's early works were GOTHIC tales of horror and the supernatural. He was also a playwright, and one of his works, *The Glittering Gates* (1909), was staged at the Abbey Theater in Dublin (and produced by W. B. Yeats) and concerned two thieves who pick the locks to the pearly gates themselves.

Dunsany's contribution to the detective genre is *The Little Tales of Smethers and Other Stories* (1952). The detective is not Smethers, who is only a relish salesman, but the ingenious Mr. Linley. The Smethers stories abound with unlikely but clever murder methods, including a snake's fang hidden in a boot. Dunsany invented a neat method for sending a message, namely over the radio by a disguised Morse Code (coughing for a dot, blowing the nose for a dash). His most famous and widely anthologized story is THE TWO BOTTLES OF RELISH (1934). *The Curse of the Wise Woman* (1933) is a mystery set in Ireland; *Gods, Men, and Ghosts: The Best Supernatural Fiction of Lord Dunsany* (1972) collects shorter pieces.

DUPIN, C. AUGUSTE The detective created by Edgar Allan POE is often erroneously considered the first in English fiction (in fact, Charles DICKENS "beat" Poe by about a decade). Dupin is, however, a far more significant contribution to the genre, and could even be said to have *made* the genre, so many are the imitations of him, both conscious and unconscious.

Dupin is a young man of "illustrious family," but has been almost bankrupted and lives on a small income. He lives spartanly, his only luxury being books. At the beginning of the first of the three Dupin stories, THE MURDERS IN THE RUE MORGUE (1841), he and the narrator have taken up lodgings together in a deserted and "grotesque" mansion in the Faubourg St. Germain in Paris. The atmosphere is as GOTHIC as that of other Poe stories: the pair, owing to "the rather fantastic gloom" of their "common temper," live like vampires, shutting themselves up during the day (which they spend in reading, writing, and argument) and then making sorties into the night in search of "that infinity of mental excitement which quiet observation can afford." Thus, the detective and his sidekick are set up as two typical but somewhat weird *flaneûrs* of Baudelairean Paris.

The narrator's relationship with Dupin is the one that has most often been used in subsequent mystery fiction: he appreciates, even idolizes the sleuth, but is unable to make heads or tails of the same evidence upon which the detective bases his astounding deductions. Poe also created the idea of detection as a game, not only for the brilliant gentleman of independent means, but for the reader as well—in recognition of which, the first story is prefaced by a lengthy reflection on various games, including chess and card games, and the degree to which they engage the mental faculties in their "pure" form. Significantly, Poe is particularly interested in the role of intuition, which became more and more disparaged as science cast a greater and greater shadow over mystery fiction.

The other stories in which Dupin appeared were THE MYSTERY OF MARIE ROGET (1842) and THE PURLOINED LETTER (1844). In those stories, Dupin has been transformed into a Chevalier, and is now courted by the professional police who need his assistance. It has been revealed by the writer Michael Harrison that there was a real Chevalier Dupin (1784–1873), upon whom Poe's character was partially based.

DURELL, SAM A character in a series of novels by Edward S. AARONS, Sam Durell is a CIA agent, a Cajun, a Yale graduate, and a veteran of intelligence work in World War II. His adventures take him all over the world; like James BOND, he faces diabolical enemies and defeats them handily. Tall, dark, and strong, he also is irresistible and has sex with a prodigious number of women. These books are typical of the writing that was churned out for the PAPERBACK ORIGINALS market, with a lack of both believability and depth of character. Durell is a Cold Warrior and, were one to take them seriously as books, one might call the novels jingoistic. They are full of the it's-a-dirty-job-but-somebody's-got-to-do-it school of theatrics. *Assignment—Suicide* (1956), is the first book to have the hyphenated title formula. The hare-brained plot is that a renegade leader in the USSR plans to launch an ICBM at the United States on May Day, hoping to use the American counterattack as a pretext for massive retaliation. Durell parachutes into the USSR posing as a Soviet intelligence officer. Later books substituted sex for politics. In *Assignment—Sorento Siren* (1963), Durell is on the trail of Jack Talbott, a traitorous agent who tortures his own lover to death (she was unfortunate enough to take Durell's stern advice—"We have to go on. That's the job"). The plot also involves an international tin deal now imperiled by the theft of Prince Tuvanaphan's T'ang Dynasty Dwan Scrolls.

The last five novels in the series were written by other hands after the author's death and appeared under the name W. B. Aarons.

BIBLIOGRAPHY Novels: *Assignment to Disaster* (1955), *Assignment—Treason* (1956), *Assignment—Budapest* (1957), *Assignment—Stella Marni* (1957), *Assignment—Angelina* (1958), *Assignment—Madeleine* (1958), *Assignment—Carlotta Cortez* (1959), *Assignment—Lili Lemaris* (1959), *Assignment—Helene* (1960), *Assignment—Mara Tirana* (1960), *Assignment—Zoraya* (1960), *Assignment—Ankara* (1961), *Assignment—Lowlands* (1961), *Assignment—Burma Girl* (1961), *Assignment—Karachi* (1962), *Assignment—Manchurian Doll* (1963), *Assignment—Sulu Sea* (1964), *Assignment—The Girl in the Gondola* (1964), *Assignment—The Cairo Dancers* (1965), *Assignment—Palermo* (1966), *Assignment—Cong Hai Kill* (1966), *Assignment—School For Spies* (1966), *Assignment—Black Viking* (1967), *Assignment—Moon Girl* (1968), *Assignment—Nuclear Nude* (1968), *Assignment—Peking* (1969), *Assignment—Star Stealers* (1970), *Assignment—White Rajah* (1970), *Assignment—Tokyo* (1971), *Assignment—Bangkok* (1972), *Assignment—Golden Girl* (1972), *Assignment—Maltese Maiden* (1972), *Assignment—Ceylon* (1973), *Assignment—Silver Scorpion* (1973), *Assignment—Amazon Queen* (1974), *Assignment—Sumatra* (1974), *Assignment—Black Gold* (1975), *Assignment—Quayle Question* (1975), *Assignment—Afghan Dragon* (1976), *Assignment—Sheba* (1976), *Assignment—13th Princess* (1977), *Assignment—Tiger Devil* (1977), *Assignment—Mermaid* (1979), *Assignment—Tyrant's Bride* (1980).

DÜRRENMATT, FRIEDRICH (1921–1990) Although the Swiss writer Dürrenmatt is best known as one of the foremost playwrights of the twentieth century, he also wrote several detective novels. His detective stories share the concerns of his dramas: the breakdown of modern society, hypocrisy, alienation amid affluence, and the plight of the "hero," whose heroism must now be viewed ironically in the postwar world. One of his most famous plays, *Der Besuch der alten Dame* (1956; tr *The Visit*), is about a woman of unlimited means who returns to her home town and offers the townspeople a fortune if they will kill one of their number who betrayed her many years before. Murder for greed becomes a commentary on the thinness of human ideals. While these may seem to be heavy themes, they are actually tailor-made for the creation of a classic loner detective, who acts out of inner, "existential" impulses.

In *Das Versprechen: Requiem auf den Kriminalroman* (1959; tr *The Pledge,* 1959), a retiring detective who is about to take up a plum job in the Kingdom of Jordan becomes obsessed with a gruesome child murder that happens even as he is cleaning out his desk. A model of rationalism and rigorous analysis, Inspector Matthai, the perfect Swiss, is viewed by his colleagues as an "automaton." Now he must endure the incomprehension and ridicule of his associates when he inexplicably gives up his new job to pursue a hunch about a case they consider solved, solely because he has promised the murdered girl's parents that he will find the killer. Ironically, the closer he comes to the truth, the more aberrant his own behavior becomes. Dürrenmatt uses the story-within-a-story and other literary techniques, as well as his acute psychological insight, to create a mood as suspenseful as it is morally ambiguous.

Dürrenmatt's work shows how the mystery story need not be relegated to the basement of "genre" fiction;

his detective novels are read and taught alongside his other works because they are of a piece. THE JUDGE AND HIS HANGMAN (1955) most neatly combines his intellectual interests with the conventions of the genre.

DWARF KINGDOM, A (1996) A novel by Nicholas FREELING, the final one in the Henri CASTANG series. He is working at the headquarters of the European Community when two important events occur: one is a shocking act of violence, the other the death of his former boss in the Parisian police, who leaves Castang's wife, Vera, a house in Biarritz. The gift turns out to be something of a curse, however: a powerful criminal (a NAPOLEON OF CRIME type) who had been under investigation by Castang's late superior wants the house and its land overlooking the Bay of Biscay, and even resorts to kidnapping. Castang's pursuit of the "prince" of the dwarf kingdom leads him into the criminal underworld he has combated all his life; more, he is forced to ally himself with a group of terrorists and a killer known as "the Tigress." *A Dwarf Kingdom* is probably the most engaging and entertaining of the Castang novels, and contains less of the cynical brooding of the series.

DWYER, JACK See GORMAN, ED.

EASY THING, AN (*Cosa Fácil,* 1977; tr 1990) The most involved of the novels involving Hector Belascoarán SHAYNE, the detective created by Paco Ignacio TAIBO II. Taibo plays with the genre motif of converging plot lines, of which there are no fewer than three. First, the detective is asked to find Emiliano Zapata, hero of the Mexican Revolution, who would be ninety-seven years old at the time of the story (1976-77). Another case involves the daughter of an "actress" who made her career by taking off her clothes; the Catholic schoolgirl is pursued by seedy men driving a Rambler station wagon filled with soda pop. Lastly, Shayne agrees to investigate, for the management, the murder of an engineer on the eve of a violent strike at a metals plant. Other subplots involve the death of the detective's mother, his father's mysterious past, and the contents of a safety deposit box. Shayne, a former engineer, embodies the contradictions of Mexican society and wonders if he can erase his past as "Foreman-accomplice to The Bossman."

EBERHART, MIGNON G[OOD] (1899–1996) Mignon G. Eberhart followed in the wake of Mary Roberts RINEHART, both as a successful American professional female writer and as a stylist. Eberhart made a living as a writer at a comparatively early age, and eventually became president of the Mystery Writers of America, who named her a Grand Master in 1970. Born in Lincoln, Nebraska, Eberhart traveled widely, as indicated by the settings of *Message from Hong Kong* (1968), *El Rancho Rio* (1970), and *The Patient in Cabin C* (1982).

Eberhart's father ran an ice business. A voracious reader, she began writing stories as a child. She attended Nebraska Wesleyan University for three years just after World War I. After leaving college, she married Alanson Eberhart, a cousin of the poet Richard Eberhart. Her first published work appeared in a detective magazine in 1925.

Whereas Rinehart was the innovator, Eberhart was the consolidator. Like Rinehart, she created a nurse-sleuth, Sarah KEATE, who appeared in *The Patient in Room 18* (1929) and many other novels. Eberhart's stories also preserved the convention of the romantic heroine faced with thrilling, strange, and dangerous events—the conventions of the HAD-I-BUT KNOWN subgenre. The milieu was usually aristocratic (or its American equivalent, wealthy). Not known for its realism, this type of story seemed to be on its last legs toward the end of Eberhart's career; the publication of her last book, *Three Days for Emeralds* (1988), coincided with the rise of the HARD-BOILED female sleuth (exemplified by the works of Sara PARETSKY and Marcia MULLER), who acts out the same kinds of adventures as her male counterparts. Sue GRAFTON's novels about Kinsey Millhone and her minimalist, monastic existence seem to slay the dragon of romance once and for all. On the other hand, Eberhart exercises some lasting appeal—perhaps in reaction to the I-can-be-as-gory-as-you-can competition between all authors, female as well as male—and the Keate novels have recently been reprinted once again (by the University of Nebraska, 1995). Her other novels, however, have a certain sameness: *The Glass Slipper* (1938— "the clock struck midnight and she found herself in a murderer's arms"), *With This Ring* (1941—"a lovely bride—a perfect wedding—a flawless setting for murder"), *The Hangman's Whip* (1940—"suspicion and murder enmesh a girl with an ugly problem"), and *Fair Warning* (1936—"a beautiful girl runs terrified through a house of murder") .

At one time, Eberhart's short story character, Susan Dare, was as well known as Sarah Keate. Again, she was firmly in the WASP heroine tradition. (Virginia Dare, born in 1587, was the first child of English parents born in America, and disappeared with the ill-fated Roanoke colony.) Susan is a fair-haired young woman and crime author who wears glasses; she looks "not unlike a chill and aloof little owl." Her stories are collected in *The Cases of Susan Dare* (1934). "Introducing Susan Dare" shows her becoming involved in jealousy and murder among Southern aristocrats. In "The Calico Dog," she is in Chicago, helping the heiress of a $30 million patent medicine fortune who cannot decide which of two men is really the son who has been missing for twenty years and which is an impostor.

Eberhart was once hailed as "the American Agatha Christie." She wrote fifty-seven novels, but it is for her early work that she is most remembered. Her later novels usually involved wealthy characters in communities like Greenwich, Connecticut, where the author lived. Somewhat different is *Bayou Road* (1979), a HISTORICAL MYSTERY set in New Orleans during the Civil War. Eberhart received an award for lifetime achievement from the MALICE DOMESTIC organization in 1994.

EBERSOHN, WESSEL [SCHALK] (1940–) South African author of novels featuring prison psychologist

Yudel GORDON. Ebersohn has said that he set out to combine mystery with serious themes, and to prove that the thriller could also be art (would that more thriller writers felt that way); however, while readers of "serious" fiction will be grateful to Ebersohn for producing thrillers with real intellectual meat, thriller junkies will find Ebersohn's pace rather leisurely. The Gordon books were written at a time when Nelson Mandela had been in prison for decades, and they document the South African dilemma at the point when agitation against apartheid was at its height and hope was at its lowest.

Born in Cape Town, Ebersohn worked for the Department of Posts and Telecommunications before he began his career as a writer. *A Lonely Place to Die* (1979) introduced Gordon, and was followed by *Divide the Night* (1981). In the latter, an old store owner named Johnny Weizmann has killed eight people—the last a fourteen-year-old girl—in "self-defense," but is sent to Gordon for treatment. As he begins to probe the sources of Weizmann's murderous neurosis, Gordon immediately attracts the attention of the South African secret police. His pursuit of the truth about Weizmann involves him in the hunt for a fugitive black dissident, Munta Majola. Ebersohn has called South Africa "one of the most singular societies on earth," a view Gordon shares; he looks at the tremendous confusion of fragmented and opposed groups and "loved it all" because it made life interesting. But Gordon's aestheticism is challenged when he is forced to witness the torture (described in detail and at length) of a person who is trying to protect *him*, an act of resistance he cannot comprehend. Ebersohn seems to say that Africa has always been a dark continent for Europeans, but it is the darkness of the Europeans' own ignorance. In the end, Gordon is painfully confronted with what is really going on in his country and asks the ultimate question: how much pain would *he* be willing to suffer to get at the truth?

The didactic purpose of the novels is an inextricable part of the narrative, but Ebersohn does not come to any pat conclusions, which makes his books far more disturbing than the heap of "how we won the Cold War" thrillers. As South African society develops toward equality, Ebersohn's books will have historical as well as literary value.

ECO, UMBERTO (1932–) Critics have carped at the arcane philosophical background of Eco's THE NAME OF THE ROSE (1984), but its position as a best seller and probably the best medieval mystery ever written is unchanged. Eco said he wrote the book because he "felt like poisoning a monk." It took him two years, distilling a huge mass of medieval research and reading he had done over the previous two decades.

An Italian professor of semiotics, Eco included in *The Name of the Rose* a large dose of medieval theology and aesthetic theory because he wanted the book to be true to the time it was written about, not written in. The semiotic interest in signs and symbols dovetails neatly with the medieval intellectual tradition, which interpreted the world in terms of Christian dogma and iconography. Eco's major achievement, and what sets his novel apart from other HISTORICAL MYSTERIES, is that his investigator actually uses the form of reasoning (scholasticism, the method of the Schoolmen) that was current in the period, and not an anachronistic modern method transported backward in time. The Schoolmen tried to reconcile the classical learning then being rediscovered, particularly that of Aristotle (384–322 B.C.), with Christian dogma. Aristotle's dialectical method, his distinction between essence and existence, and his belief that knowledge comes from sensory experience (rather than divine light) all proved difficult to assimilate to medieval Christianity. The new learning—or the newly discovered old learning—constantly skirted the boundaries of heresy; in *The Name of the Rose,* the sinister figure of Bernard Gui, a historical inquisitor, plays an important part. The sleuth, William of Baskerville, is in the middle, using the emerging rationalism to analyze and penetrate the signs left by the murderer, who seems to be an ecstatic madman.

Eco's *Postscript to the Name of the Rose* (1983; tr 1984) is an account of the genesis of the book and its cultural-philosophical background. He has gone on to produce other novels such as *L'Isola del giorno prima* (1994; tr *The Island of the Day Before,* 1995).

EDALJI, GEORGE The first of the two celebrated criminal cases in which Sir Arthur Conan DOYLE lent a hand was that of the solicitor George Edalji. The Edalji family lived in Staffordshire in a mining area, and were the subject of racist harassment. For some reason, the police became convinced that George Edalji was responsible for threatening letters sent to his own family, but it was never proved. In 1903, some deranged person began maiming and mutilating horses and cattle in the area, ripping their bellies with a sharp instrument. This, too, was laid at George Edalji's door, and on very flimsy evidence—some of it probably planted by the police—he was sent to jail for three years. Upon his release, Conan Doyle took up the case. He deduced that because of Edalji's terrible eyesight, it was extremely unlikely that he had been sneaking around the English countryside at night attacking animals (he had trouble just reading the paper). Conan Doyle wrote letters to newspapers and found other inadequacies in the police case. In fact, there was no really good evidence at all; there was no obvious connection between his supposed earlier letter-writing and the assaults on animals. Although Edalji was pardoned, police wrongdoing in the case was never publicly exposed.

EDGAR The "Edgar" is the short name of the Edgar Allan Poe awards, given by the MYSTERY WRITERS OF AMERICA. The organization was founded in 1945 by a group of distinguished mystery authors, and it now has thousands of members. The Edgars have been given in a number of categories; new categories have been added from time to time and others have been abolished or replaced. (Year of publication is given below; award made in the following year.)

Best Novel:1953, *Beat Not the Bones,* Charlotte Jay; 1954, *The Long Goodbye,* Raymond Chandler; 1955, *Beast in View,* Margaret Millar; 1956, *A Dram of Poison,* Charlotte Armstrong; 1957, *Room to Swing,* Ed Lacey; 1958, *The Eighth Circle,* Stanley Ellin; 1959, *The Hours Before Dawn,* Celia Fremlin; 1960, *Progress of a Crime,* Julian Symons; 1961, *Gideon's Fire,* J. J. Marric; 1962, *Death and the Joyful Woman,* Ellis Peters; 1963, *The Light of Day,* Eric Ambler; 1964, *The Spy Who Came In From the Cold,* John Le Carré; 1965, *The Quiller Memorandum,* Adam Hall; 1966, *King of the Rainy Country,* Nicholas Freeling; 1967, *God Save the Mark,* Donald E. Westlake; 1968, *A Case of Need,* Jeffrey Hudson (Michael Crichton); 1969, *Forfeit,* Dick Francis; 1970, *The Laughing Policeman,* Maj Sjöwall and Per Wahlöö; 1971, *The Day of the Jackal,* Frederick Forsyth; 1972, *The Lingala Code,* Warren Kiefer; 1973, *Dance Hall of the Dead,* Tony Hillerman; 1974, *Peter's Pence,* John Cleary; 1975, *Hopscotch,* Brian Garfield; 1976, *Promised Land,* Robert B. Parker; 1977, *Catch Me: Kill Me,* William H. Hallahan; 1978, *The Eye of the Needle,* Ken Follett; 1979, *The Rhinegold Route,* Arthur Maling; 1980, *Whip Hand,* Dick Francis; 1981, *Peregrine,* William Bayer; 1982, *Billingsgate Shoal,* Rick Boyer; 1983, *La Brava,* Elmore Leonard; 1984, *Briar Patch,* Ross Thomas; 1985, *The Suspect,* L. R. Wright; 1986, *A Dark Adapted Eye,* Barbara Vine (Ruth Rendell); 1987, *Old Bones,* Aaron Elkins; 1988, *A Cold Red Sunrise,* Stuart M. Kaminsky; 1989, *Black Cherry Blues,* James Lee Burke; 1990, *New Orleans Mourning,* Julie Smith; 1991, *A Dance at the Slaughterhouse,* Lawrence Block; 1992, *Bootlegger's Daughter,* Margaret Maron; 1993, *The Sculptress,* Minette Walters; 1994, *The Red Scream,* Mary Willis Walker; 1995, *Come to Grief,* Dick Francis; 1996, *The Chatham School Affair,* Thomas H. Cook; 1997, *Cimarron Rose,* James Lee Burke; 1998, *Mr. White's Confession,* Robert Clark; 1999, *Bones,* Jan Burk; 2000, *The Bottoms,* Joe R. Lansdale.

Best First Novel: 1945, *Watchful at Night,* Julius Fast; 1946, *The Horizontal Man,* Helen Eustis; 1947, *The Fabulous Clipjoint,* Frederic Brown; 1948, *The Room Upstairs,* Mildred Davis; 1949, *What A Body,* Alan Green; 1950, *Nightmare in Manhattan,* Thomas Walsh; 1951, *Strangle Hold,* Mary McMullen; 1952, *Don't Cry for Me,* William Campbell Gault; 1953, *A Kiss Before Dying,* Ira Levin; 1954, *Go, Lovely Rose,* Jean Potts; 1955, *The Perfectionist,* Lane Potts; 1956, *Rebecca's Pride,* Donald McNutt Douglas; 1957, *Knock and Wait Awhile,* William Rowle Weeks; 1958, *The Bright Road to Fear,* Richard Martin Stern; 1959, *The Gray Flannel Shroud,* Harry Slesar; 1960, *The Man in the Cage,* John Holbrook Vance; 1961, *The Green Stone,* Suzanne Blanc; 1962, *The Fugitive,* Robert L. Fish; 1963, *The Florentine Finish,* Cornelius Hirschberg; 1964, *Friday the Rabbi Slept Late,* Harry Kemelman; 1965, *In the Heat of the Night,* John Ball; 1966, *The Cold War Swap,* Ross Thomas; 1967, *Act of Fear,* Michael Collins; 1968, *Silver Streak,* E. Richard Johnson, and *The Bait,* Dorothy Uhnak; 1969, *A Time for Predators,* Joe Gores; 1970, *The Anderson Tapes,* Lawrence Sanders; 1971, *Finding Maubee,* A. H. Z. Carr; 1972, *Squaw Point,* R. H. Shimer; 1973, *The Billion Dollar Sure Thing,* Paul E. Erdman; 1974, *Fletch,* Gregory Mcdonald; 1975, *The Alvarez Journal,* Rex Burns; 1976, *The Thomas Berryman Number,* James Patterson; 1977, *A French Finish,* Robert Ross; 1978, *Killed in the Ratings,* William L. DeAndrea; 1979, *The Lasko Tangent,* Richard North Patterson; 1980, *The Watcher,* Kay Nolte Smith; 1981, *Chiefs,* Stuart Woods; 1982, *The Butcher's Boy,* Thomas Perry; 1983, *The Bay Psalm Book Murder,* Will Harriss; 1984, *Strike Three, You're Dead,* D. D. Rosen; 1985, *When the Bough Breaks,* Jonathan Kellerman; 1986, *No One Rides for Free,* Larry Bienhart; 1987, *Death Amongst Strangers,* Deirdre S. Laiken; 1988, *Carolina Skeletons,* David Stout; 1989, *The Last Billable Hour,* Susan Wolfe; 1990, *Post Mortem,* Patricia Cornwell; 1991, *Slow Motion Riot,* Peter Blauner; 1992, *The Black Echo,* Michael Connelly; 1993, *A Grave Talent,* Laurie R. King; 1994, *The Caveman's Valentine,* George Dawes Green; 1995, *Penance,* David Housewright; 1996, *Simple Justice,* John Morgan Wilson; 1997, *Los Alamos,* Joseph Kanon; 1998, *A Cold Day in Paradise,* Steve Hamilton; 1999, *The Skull Mantra,* Eliot Pattison; 2000, *A Conspiracy of Paper,* David Liss.

Best Critical or Biographical Work: 1976, *Encyclopedia of Mystery and Detection,* Chris Steinbrunner, Otto Penzler, Marvin Lachman, and Charles Shibuk; 1977, *Rex Stout,* John McAleer; 1978, *The Mystery of Agatha Christie,* Gwen Robins; 1979, *Dorothy L. Sayers: A Literary Biography,* Ralph E. Home; 1980, *Twentieth Century Crime and Mystery Writers,* John Reilly; 1981, *What About Murder,* Jon L. Breen; 1982, *Cain,* Roy Hoopes; 1983, *The Dark Side of Genius: The Life of Alfred*

Hitchcock, Donald Spoto; 1984, *Novel Verdicts: A Guide to Courtroom Fiction,* John L. Breen; 1985, *John LeCarré,* Peter Lewis; 1986, *Here Lies: An Autobiography,* Eric Ambler; 1987, *Introduction to the Detective Story,* Leroy Lad Panek; 1988, *Cornell Woolrich: First You Dream, Then You Die,* Francis M. Nevins, Jr.; 1989, *The Life of Graham Greene, Volume I: 1904–1939,* Norman Sherry; 1990, *Trouble Is Their Business: Private Eyes in Fiction, Film, and Television, 1927–1988,* John Conquest; 1991, *Edgar A. Poe: Mournful and Never-Ending Remembrance,* Kenneth Silverman; 1992, *Alias S. S. Van Dine,* John Loughery; 1993, *The Saint: A Complete History,* Burl Barer; 1994, *Encyclopedia Mysteriosa,* William DeAndrea; 1995, *Savage Art: A Biography of Jim Thompson,* Robert Polito; 1996, *The Secret Marriage of Sherlock Holmes,* Michael Atkinson; 1997, *"G" Is for Grafton: The World Of Kinsey Millhone,* Natalie Hevener Kaufman and Carol McGinnis Kay; 1998, *Mystery and Suspense Writers,* Robin Winks and Maureen Corrigan; 1999, *Teller of Tales: The Life of Arthur Conan Doyle,* Daniel Stashower; 2000, *Conundrums for the Long Week-end: England, Dorothy L. Sayers, and Lord Peter Wimsey,* Robert Kuhn McGregor with Ethan Lewis.

Grand Master: 1955, Agatha Christie; 1958, Vincent Starrett; 1959, Rex Stout; 1961, Ellery Queen; 1962, Erle Stanley Gardner; 1963, John Dickson Carr; 1964, George Harmon Coxe; 1966, Georges Simenon; 1967, Baynard Kendrick; 1969, John Creasey; 1970, James M. Cain; 1971, Mignon G. Eberhart; 1972, John D. MacDonald; 1973, Judson Philips, Alfred Hitchcock; 1974, Ross Macdonald; 1975, Eric Ambler; 1976, Graham Greene; 1978, Daphne DuMaurier, Dorothy B. Hughes, Ngaio Marsh; 1979, Aaron Mark Stein; 1980, W. R. Burnett; 1981, Stanley Ellin; 1982, Julian Symons; 1983, Margaret Millar; 1984, John LeCarré; 1985, Dorothy Salisbury Davis; 1986, Ed McBain; 1987, Michael Gilbert; 1988, Phyllis A. Whitney; 1989, Hillary Waugh; 1990, Helen McCloy; 1991, Tony Hillerman; 1992, Elmore Leonard; 1993, Donald E. Westlake; 1994, Lawrence Block; 1995, Mickey Spillane; 1996, Dick Francis; 1997, Ruth Rendell; 1998, Barbara Mertz (Elizabeth Peters); 1999, P. D. James; 2000, Mary Higgins Clark; 2001, Edward D. Hoch.

EDGAR HUNTLY, OR, MEMOIRS OF A SLEEP-WALKER (1799) Although this novel by Charles Brockden BROWN is categorized as GOTHIC, it is not supernatural and contains none of the usual gothic elements. Instead, it is set in the American wilderness and evil is naturalized. The first part of the book deploys many features that would become standard in mystery stories.

The novel is set around the Huntly farm in western Pennsylvania in 1787. Huntly's friend Waldegrave is found fatally shot in the shadow of a great elm tree, with "no traces of the slayer visible, no tokens by which his place of refuge might be sought, the motives of his enmity or his instruments of mischief might be detected." Having thus established that there are no clues, Huntly examines the area immediately surrounding the crime scene, but finds nothing. Later, however, he finds a man (apparently sleepwalking) burying something near the tree. He does not recognize him, but quickly deduces a suspect: Clithero Edny, an Irish servant with an obscure past. Huntly takes up surveillance, and trails the sleepwalker into the wilderness. Later he confronts Clithero, hoping for a confession, but Clithero says his deductions are "a tissue of destructive errors." Clithero's lengthy confession involves several other deaths and mysteries instead. After making it, he disappears into the wilderness. The disastrous consequences of Edgar's actions illustrate a larger point about man: "By his own hands, is constructed the mass of misery and error in which his steps are forever involved." Finally, mental displacement merges with physical in Brown's linkage of the book's events with the dispossession of the Indians, demonstrating his claim to be "a moral painter."

EGAN, LESLEY The pseudonym under which Elizabeth LININGTON wrote her series of mysteries about Vic VARALLO.

EGERTON, SCOTT A sleuth created by Anthony GILBERT. The only unusual thing about Egerton was that he was a politician; otherwise, he was a second- or third-string genius of the GOLDEN AGE. Gilbert replaced him with the more interesting (and outlandish) Arthur CROOK.

BIBLIOGRAPHY Novels: *The Tragedy at Freyne* (1927), *The Murder of Mrs. Davenport* (1928), *The Mystery of the Open Window* (1929), *Death at Four Corners* (1929), *The Night of the Fog* (1930), *The Body on the Beam* (1932), *The Long Shadow* (1932), *The Musical Comedy Crime* (1933), *An Old Lady Dies* (1934), *The Man Who Was Too Clever* (1935).

EGG, MONTAGUE A character created by Dorothy L. SAYERS who features in a series of eleven stories but no novels, Montague Egg is a commercial traveler (traveling salesman) in wines who happens to stumble across a series of mysteries. These are collected in *Hangman's Holiday* (1933; repr 1995) and *In the Teeth of the Evidence* (1940; repr 1993). Egg offers an interesting contrast to that other Sayers creation, Lord Peter WIMSEY, in that he is middle class rather than aristocratic, and possessed of native good sense rather than otherworldly genius. In fact, he is a much nicer fellow. Unfortunately, it is a part of the snobbery of her age that Sayers felt she had to condescend to the artful Egg.

EGYPTIAN CROSS MYSTERY, THE (1932) A novel by Ellery QUEEN, which disproves the idea that mysteries have only recently become graphically violent. Ellery and his father visit the scene of the grisly murder of a schoolteacher named Andrew Van in Arroyo, West Virginia. Van has been murdered, decapitated with an axe, and crucified on a signpost near his house with four-inch iron spikes. There is also a religious lunatic in the neighborhood masquerading as a sun god. But this is only the first of a series of similar murders, each described by the fascinated Ellery. A millionaire importer is found crucified on a totem pole on Long Island, giving Ellery a whole new set of variables to fit into his psychological portrait of the killer. Inspector Queen bows out after the first murder. Ellery does some speculating as well as deducing, and becomes engrossed in the Egyptological significance of the letter "T," reflected in the shape of a decapitated body.

EIFFEL TOWER JOE The jewel thief and master of escape in Léo Malet's 120, RUE DE LA GARE (1943). Eiffel Tower Joe has gotten out of jails in London, Vienna, and New York. He is "a lover of puns, riddles, crosswords, and other childish amusements." A body thought to be his washes up on a beach in Cornwall, half-eaten by crabs.

EIGHT MILLION WAYS TO DIE (1983) A novel by Lawrence BLOCK, in which Matthew SCUDDER finally decides to stop drinking as a result of an extended and horrifying blackout. Paradoxically, though it is the novel in which Scudder is most on the skids, it is also the one in which he is most emotionally present, rather than self-abnegating or guilt-ridden. It is a realistic novel of addiction, in which other people try to set Scudder straight, to no avail. The actual crime is well set up except for the solution; the ever-present "Colombians" (a cliché of eighties crime fiction) are brought in to explain everything, à la *Miami Vice.*

87TH STREET PRECINCT The locus of a series of PROCEDURAL novels, probably the most successful procedural series yet written, by Ed MCBAIN. The author claims that they are set in a "fictional" city, but it resembles New York in many specifics (it even has Macy's). The district of "Isola," meaning "island" in Italian, is obviously Manhattan. "Stewart City," an enclave of "terraced luxury" apartments, is plainly Tudor City. The 87th Precinct is in a dangerous and run-down section of the city, full of old tenements, pool halls, bars, and small industries. "Riverhead" is like the Bronx.

The books are realistic in their depiction of teamwork; no one character is the star, though there are recurrent figures. The head of the precinct is Lieutenant Peter Byrnes, and Stephen Carella, the hero of the first book, is an important constant. His beautiful wife, Teddy, is both deaf and mute. Other characters include Meyer Meyer, who (like his father) is fond of jokes. Roger Havilland, a six-foot-four loudmouth built like a wrestler, is a brutal and a crooked cop. Cotton Hawes is a transfer from a precinct in a posh neighborhood.

McBain's insistence that the city of the books is "imaginary" emphasizes that it is a fictional mirror image, over which the author has artistic or poetic license. But it also points to an overlooked aspect of the series: it is not realistic. Events within books, the mutations that occur between books, and the treatment of time, are all dealt with "imaginatively." The early books are usually singled out as the best in the series. *Cop Hater* (1956) was the first book in the series and introduced Carella. In *Killer's Choice* (1957), Havilland is murdered, ironically because his better nature stages a brief rally and overcomes his usually nasty persona. In the same book Cotton Hawes appears, and, inexperienced with the violent crime of the 87th, makes a dumb play that almost gets Carella killed. The center of the story is a murdered woman who seems to have been several different women at once. *Lady Killer* (1958) is about a killer who announces his plans in advance, giving the cops only hours to pre-empt a murder.

Another famous book about the 87th Precinct, *Sadie When She Died* (1972), was chosen by H. R. F. KEATING as one of the hundred best mysteries of all time. The beautiful wife of lawyer Gerald Fletcher is stabbed to death, and the "killer" confesses. Carella, however, does not believe the confession, and is further disturbed by the husband's professed gladness at the decease of his wife.

Blood Relatives (1975) has one of the more gruesome plots in the series, involving the rape of two young girls, one of whom is also killed. A witness points the finger at one of Carella's colleagues. The title of *Long Time No See* (1977) is a "joke" of sorts; the story begins with the murder of a blind man.

Perhaps the oddest books are the series about a character known as THE DEAF MAN.

BIBLIOGRAPHY Novels: *The Pusher* (1956), *The Mugger* (1956), *The Con Man* (1957), *Killer's Wedge* (1958), *Killer's Payoff* (1958), *'Til Death* (1959), *King's Ransom* (1959), *See Them Die* (1960), *Give the Boys a Great Big Hand* (1960), *The Heckler* (1960), *Lady, Lady, I Did It* (1961), *Like Love* (1962), *Ten Plus One* (1963),

Ax (1964), *He Who Hesitates* (1965), *Doll* (1965), *Eighty Million Eyes* (1966), *Fuzz* (1968), *Shotgun* (1969), *Jigsaw* (1970), *Hail, Hail, The Gang's All Here!* (1971), *Hail to the Chief* (1973), *Let's Hear It for the Deaf Man* (1973), *Bread* (1974), *So Long as You Both Shall Live* (1976), *Calypso* (1979), *Ghosts* (1980), *Heat* (1981), *Ice* (1983), *Lightning* (1984), *Eight Black Horses* (1985), *Poison* (1987), *Tricks* (1987), *Lullaby* (1989), *Vespers* (1990), *Widows* (1991), *Kiss* (1992), *Mischief* (1993), *And All Through the House* (1994), *Romance* (1995), *The Big, Bad City* (1999).

Short Stories: *The Empty Hours* (1962).

EKMAN, KERSTIN (1933–) The Swedish writer Kerstin Ekman made her reputation in her native country with detective novels, as well as novels that explored issues of identity, particularly those affecting women. *Pukehornet* (1967) concerns the mysterious death of a woman, and is told from the alternate perspectives of her son and a writer who is a neighbor. Ekman is known to English speakers for *Händelser vid vatten* (1993; tr BLACKWATER, 1995), which won the Nordic Council's Literary Prize, the August Prize, and the Swedish Crime Academy award for best crime novel. *Blackwater* is a harrowing story about a murder that tears apart a community. A woman named Annie Raft travels to the far north of Sweden in 1974 with her six-year-old daughter to join her lover at a commune. When he appears to be missing, she begins a search through the woods and eventually finds two horribly stabbed corpses in a tent. Many years afterward she returns and the echoes of the killings erupt into the present.

Ekman was born in Risinge, a small village in central Sweden, and later moved to the north, where some of her works are set. She has published seventeen novels. In 1978, Ekman became the first woman in decades to be elected to the Swedish Academy. She resigned in 1989 over the issue of the statement to be made by the academy regarding the Iranian persecution of the writer Salman Rushdie.

It was inevitable that Ekman's novels would be compared with that of Peter HOEG, and her work was sometimes rated higher than SMILLA'S SENSE OF SNOW (1994). After the success of *Blackwater, Under the Snow* was published in 1996 in Britain and 1998 in the United States. It is actually the translation of *De tre smä mas mästerna* (1961), an extraordinary novel that evokes the incredible landscape of Lappland, where the Swedes are perceived as violent strangers and the native Somi people live in an almost mythic reality. After a mysterious killing occurs at a mah jong party, Constable Torsson skis out to the scene but finds only one clue (a bloodstained mah jong tile) and a mass of contradictory testimony, as well as a conspiracy of silence. The case is put down as an accident despite small unexplained facts. Later, a friend of the victim, an artist, arrives in town not knowing his friend is dead. He sees the town's beautiful English teacher with a bag containing a noose on which there are human hairs. The author just states the facts, repeats conversations, reports attitudes and changes in weather and light; each piece reinforces two truths, the accident and the mystery. The austerity of the land, the darkness of winter and the long day of summer, the feeling of the slowness of time, the closeness to nature, and the almost mystical atmosphere all make the story introspective, philosophical, and sad.

"ELEMENTARY, MY DEAR WATSON." Sherlock HOLMES never uttered these words, famous as they are. The closest he came was in "The Adventure of the Crooked Man," where he says simply "Elementary" in response to WATSON's amazement at a piece of deduction.

ELK, INSPECTOR A character created by Edgar WALLACE. Elk is a man of few words, but many of them are sarcastic. He is a friend of "The Twister" in the novel of that name. He has a passion for cigars, which he bums ("I left my case at home—some other fellow's home"), and once remarks that "I'd have let CRIPPEN go for a couple of boxes of good Odoras."

ELKINS, AARON (1935–) American author Aaron Elkins is known for his series of novels about Gideon OLIVER, a forensic anthropologist. Born in Brooklyn, Elkins attended Hunter College, the University of Wisconsin, and the University of California. He held various teaching posts and worked as a management consultant. For two years he taught in Europe, which has provided background for some of Gideon Oliver's exploits. Elkins did not try his hand at writing until he was forty-four.

Elkins has been a boxer as well as an anthropology professor, but Gideon Oliver is more versed in the latter than the former. Wherever he goes, his reputation has preceded him. His methods are non-violent; even though the crimes are sometimes gruesome, there is usually nothing left but skin and bones by the time they are discovered. Elkins also wrote the non-series mystery novel *A Deceptive Clarity* (1987).

In the nineties, Elkins began another quite different mystery series about a sleuth who is also an art expert, Chris Norgren. He first appeared in *Old Scores* (1993). Elkins has co-authored another series of mysteries with his wife, which are set on the professional GOLF tour and are about Lee Ofsted, a young pro.

ELLIN, STANLEY (1916–1986) The American writer Stanley Ellin gained the attention of the mystery reading public with his short stories, particularly his first, "The Specialty of the House," which won an award from *Ellery Queen's Mystery Magazine* and was instantly hailed as a classic; about all that can be said about it without spoiling the story is *bon appetit.* But, despite his legendary care and skill in constructing his stories, Ellin had a lot of difficulty getting into print. "The Speciality of the House" was rejected by many magazines before *EQMM* saw the value in it.

Ellin was born in Brooklyn, New York, and attended Brooklyn College. He worked as a dairy farmer, teacher, and steelworker. After serving in World War II, Ellin gave himself a year to write (with the support of his wife). His painstaking method of composition has been much remarked upon: Ellin would completely edit, polish, rewrite, and finish each page before he went on to the next. His short stories have been collected in *The Specialty of the House and Other Stories: The Complete Mystery Tales 1948–1978,* and they remain his greatest achievement. He won an EDGAR in 1956 for the short story THE BLESSINGTON METHOD, which shows his flair for the macabre. Although his methods of work might almost be called scientific, Ellin had no qualms about stepping outside the boundaries of the form. In "The House Party" (1954), also published in EQMM, he used horror and supernatural elements to depict a modern hell occupied by a temperamental actor, casting a psychoanalyst as the devil. Thus Ellin harkens back to the POE of "The Pit and the Pendulum" as much as the Poe who created C. Auguste DUPIN. THE NINE-TO-FIVE MAN (1964) shows another Ellin trait: revealing crime and the bizarre behind normal exteriors.

Ellin brought the same ingenuity to the novel as he employed in his successful nonfiction. His first novel was *Dreadful Summit* (1948), a revenge tale. He won a second Edgar for the novel *The Eighth Circle* (1958), about a private detective who doesn't want to clear his client (who is in jail) because he covets the client's wife. Another of his novels, THE KEY TO NICHOLAS STREET (1952), is interesting for its use of multiple points of view. Ellin was awarded the Grand Prix de Littérature Policière for the novel *Mirror, Mirror on the Wall* (1968).

The crime novel *Stronghold* (1974) further demonstrates Ellin's talent for creating surprising situations, and again he uses the technique of multiple narrators. The story rests on the question of how a Quaker, committed to non-violence, would react to a hostage situation. The wealthy, complacent, but not unsympathetic banker Marcus Hayworth is faced with just this problem when Jimmy Flood, a murderous delinquent whom he had tried to help, returns to his hometown after a prison stretch in upstate New York. Beginning like a conventional thriller, the novel quickly turns the tables on the reader with a series of surprises that are both ingenuous and psychologically believable.

With *Star Light, Star Bright* (1979), Ellin introduced a series character, John Milano, who also appears in THE DARK FANTASTIC (1983), his most controversial book. Ellin also wrote thrillers, such as *House of Cards* (1967). Set in Paris, Venice, and Rome, it focuses on former boxer Reno Davis and the young aristocrat from a strange family whom he is hired to protect.

Ellin was named a Grand Master by the Mystery Writers of America in 1981.

ELLIS, RUTH See GOODMAN, JONATHAN.

ELLROY, JAMES (1948–) James Ellroy's name is associated with Los Angeles, which he has portrayed in a series of crime novels. Ellroy spent a troubled youth in that city; it is where his mother was murdered in 1959. He has treated the murder in fiction (*Clandestine,* 1982), and in an even more startling work of nonfiction (*My Dark Places,* 1996). After years on the skids, Ellroy began working as a golf caddy and writing, a period that culminated in his first book, *Brown's Requiem* (1981), about Los Angeles p.i. Fritz Brown, who is hired by Freddy "Fat Dog" Baker, a sadistic caddy with mysterious sources of wealth.

The golf element continued but was entirely peripheral in *Clandestine,* a remarkable book about the meteoric rise and fall of Fred Underhill, a gifted golfer, pickup artist, and LAPD cop. His boundless ambition, his pursuit of a "wonder" that he finds in L.A. streets glowing with violence and the blown circuitry of lives, and his growing obsession with a brutal murderer of women lead him into a head-on confrontation with power—particularly in the form of Dudley SMITH—and a new knowledge he may not even want. The last quarter of the novel goes off into a multi-dimensional tangle of paternity, disloyalty, thievery, and decades-old secrets reminiscent of such books as THE GALTON CASE (1959). *Clandestine* was nominated for an EDGAR award.

THE BLACK DAHLIA (1987), a fictionalized account of a 1947 Hollywood murder, solidified Ellroy's already growing reputation. Several other novels set in Los Angeles during the same period and involving some of the same characters have followed: *The Big Nowhere* (1988); *L.A. Confidential* (1990), which was filmed in 1997; and *White Jazz* (1992). A theme throughout this series is that "the fifties weren't a more innocent time," and "the dark salients that govern life today were there then." The suaveties and witticisms that became a cliché of the lower echelon of HARD-BOILED writers are gone, and in their place is the brutality, racism, crudity, and callousness of people on the make, whichever side of the law they are making it on.

Ellroy's writing is often electric, nervously jumping from association to association, sometimes in a surreal manner, the prime example being *American Tabloid* (see below). Sometimes the torrent of words overrun the narrative they are meant to contain. Ellroy's experiments with various narrative forms include *Silent Terror* (1986; also pub as *Killer on the Road*), a serial killer book, but with the story told in the form of the murderer's autobiography. Ellroy also wrote a series of novels about Los Angeles Police detective Lloyd HOPKINS, probably the most innovative development in the California detective story since Ross Macdonald's. Instead of the moral firmament of Raymond CHANDLER (in which MARLOWE is a shooting star and Los Angeles a black hole), or the rueful elegies of Macdonald, what lies behind Ellroy's Los Angeles stories is barely suppressed rage and a vision of ghastly emptiness. In this world, "God was a malevolent jokester armed with a blunt instrument called irony."

With *American Tabloid* (1994), Ellroy struck out into bold—and bizarre—new territory. Set in the period leading up to the assassination of John F. Kennedy, the book is a ferocious jumble of covert operations, dirt, drugs, and organized crime, presided over by monstrous figures such as Howard Hughes and J. Edgar Hoover. The effect is the equivalent of photo montage, impelled by an enraged sense of betrayal and need to shatter phony nationalist images. The seams of the narrative open and a frenetic, almost psychedelic cultural critique bursts out. "America was never innocent," he says; "mass market nostalgia gets you hopped up for a past that never existed," and Kennedy was "the mythological front man for a particularly juicy slice of our history." It is Camelot viewed from the dungeon.

ELWELL, JOSEPH BOWNE See BENSON MURDER CASE, THE.

EMPEROR'S SNUFFBOX, THE See CARR, JOHN DICKSON.

"EMPTY HOUSE, ADVENTURE OF THE" (1903) The first of the adventures of Sherlock HOLMES after his supposed death in THE FINAL PROBLEM. The empty house is the building opposite Holmes's own lodgings at 221B Baker Street; from this vantage point, he surveys the attempts of his enemies (primarily Colonel MORAN) against his life, having first installed a wax dummy of himself in his rooms. The other part of the story is the mysterious murder of Ronald Adair, found shot to death by a revolver bullet in a locked room containing no revolver.

The story also contains Holmes's account of his miraculous escape from Professor MORIARTY at the Reichenbach Falls and his activities during the intervening three years since "The Final Problem," including two years in Tibet and a bit of exploring disguised as the Norwegian "Sigerson."

END OF CHAPTER (1957) A Nigel STRANGEWAYS mystery by Nicholas BLAKE (C. Day-Lewis). Set in a milieu the author knew well—a publishing house—*End of Chapter* would be interesting for its entertaining characters even without a murder. The dialogue among the intellectuals and pseudo-intellectuals is breezy and witty; when Strangeways asks Clare Massinger if she reads the "shiny magazines," she replies "they're written by career girls for veneer girls, aren't they?" The plot, however, is not one of the author's most complex; the two converging plot lines involve a general's memoirs and an unspeakably bad but very successful novelist. Strangeways is called in when some libelous passages in General Thoresby's memoirs that had been prudently cut somehow make it back into the published book. Millicent Miles, the queen of the bestsellers, is working in the office of the publisher (Wenham and Geraldine) on her steamy autobiography. When she is found with her throat slashed, Strangeways has to find the connection between her murder and the general's memoirs. BARZUN and TAYLOR called it "a happy return to Strangeways and straight detection."

ENGER, L. L. See BASEBALL.

"ENGINEER'S THUMB, THE ADVENTURE OF THE" (1892) One of the cases of Sherlock HOLMES that starts out as a case of Doctor WATSON's. The engineer, Victor Hatherley, appears at Watson's door one morning minus his thumb, which has been hacked off (Conan DOYLE's medical training helps him to present the scene with gruesome realism). Hatherley has been lured out into the country to examine an enormous machine for a group of suspicious characters, but he doesn't remember where in the country his disaster took place. His macabre experience in an isolated house and the pounding, room-sized machine recall Poe's "The Pit and the Pendulum."

ENGLISH MURDER, AN (1951) A version of the COUNTRY HOUSE murder (and also of the SNOWBOUND subgenre), this novel by Cyril HARE takes place over Christmas at Warbeck Hall. Hare uses the idea of a group of guests who are out of sympathy with each other, though in this case the conflict is intellectual and political. Sir Julius Warbeck is Chancellor of the Exchequer; his socialist government is raising taxes and forcing squires like the current lord, Thomas Warbeck, out of their ancestral homes. Lord Warbeck's son, the odious Robert, is the leader of an English neo-fascist organization, and is particularly offensive to the Hungarian Dr. Wenceslas Bottwink, a historian and concentration camp survivor who is studying the papers of Warbeck Hall. Mrs. Carstairs is the wife of a pushy, ambitious assistant to Sir Julius. Behind the obvious conflicts are more secretive ones that involve the servants. The characters of Bottwink and the Jeeves-like butler, Briggs, hold the story together. All the characters are stock types; the writing is enjoyable and literate, but the clues are few.

EPTON, ROSA Michael UNDERWOOD introduced Rosa Epton in *The Unprofessional Spy* (1964), at which point she is a lowly solicitor's clerk. He did not bring her back again until *Crime Upon Crime* (1980), by which time she has become a solicitor herself, the junior partner in a successful practice. This atypical novel concerns homosexuality and blackmail against a clubby London background. Arthur Kedly is thought by others at Noone's Club to be a secret agent; he's actually a blackmailer, and coincidentally sees a judge making use of the service of a male prostitute in Kedly's building. A petty crook, a lout, Kedly now finds himself out of his league. His neighbor the prostitute gets strangled with a belt; later, a grenade goes off in court. Underwood combines satire of hypocrisy with the legal and criminal aspects.

Epton is a defender, not a prosecutor; she is typically employed by clients whose status is ambiguous. At the least, Epton has to dig up some facts on her own. *Death in Camera* (1984) is about a judge who falls from the balcony of a new courthouse into the Thames. Rosa had seen the man touch his neck moments before during a photo session. It seems that he was shot with a RICIN pellet (see POISONED UMBRELLA). The judge's nephew hires Epton and tells her about being given a camera by a practical joker.

Underwood depicts the stresses of the legal profession in *Rosa's Dilemma* (1990). Epton has sworn up and down never to work again with old Malcolm Palfrey, but he convinces her to help him defend a couple charged with malicious damage after a drunken binge. Soon the girl starts shifting the blame onto her boyfriend, and the boy's father thinks Palfrey is putting her up to it. Palfrey does almost no work, and does not even show up for the trial. But he has a good excuse: he's dead.

Underwood has also written espionage novels, and some of Epton's cases are more than run-of-the-mill crime. In *A Dangerous Business* (1990), Epton is on vacation in Amsterdam with her lover, Peter Chen, when she sees a man she had defended unsuccessfully on a robbery charge and who is supposed to be in jail (the burglar, Eddie Ruding, had claimed that MI5 sent him to steal a code book). Then Epton is pushed in front of a tram and narrowly escapes. When she gets back to England, she discovers Ruding has been killed; in a strange twist, the robber's mother hires her to investigate his murder.

BIBLIOGRAPHY Novels: *Double Jeopardy* (1981), *Goddess of Death* (1982), *The Hidden Man* (1985), *Death at Deepwood Grange* (1986), *The Uninvited Corpse* (1987), *The Injudicious Judge* (1987), *Dual Enigma* (1988), *A Compelling Case* (1989).

EQMM See QUEEN, ELLERY.

ERRIDGE, MATT A character in a series of mysteries by Aaron Mark STEIN. Erridge is one of Stein's traveling heroes; a construction engineer, he takes jobs in foreign locales where he happens to get involved in murders. In *Deadly Delight* (1967), he is invited to visit a friend in Istanbul, and himself becomes a target for murder.

BIBLIOGRAPHY Novels: *Sitting Up Dead* (1958), *Never Need an Enemy* (1959), *Home and Murder* (1962), *Blood on the Stars* (1964), *I Fear the Greeks* (1966; British title *Executioner's Rest*), *Snare Andalucian* (1968; British title *Faces of Death*), *Kill Is a Four-Letter Word* (1968), *Alp Murder* (1970), *The Finger* (1973), *Coffin Country* (1976), *Lend Me Your Ears* (1977), *Body Search* (1978), *Nowhere?* (1978), *Chill Factor* (1978), *The Rolling Heads* (1979), *One Dip Dead* (1979), *The Cheating Butcher* (1980), *A Nose for It* (1980), *A Body for a Buddy* (1981), *Hangman's Row* (1982), *The Bombing Run* (1983), *The Garbage Collector* (1984).

ESCAMILLO Lily Rowan's nickname for Archie GOODWIN in the Nero WOLFE mysteries. This nickname is part of the case for the supposition that Lily and Archie are lovers throughout the series.

ESTLEMAN, LOREN D. (1952–) Loren Estleman has cut a wide swath through the crime genre, from Westerns to private eye novels to PARODY. Most noteworthy is his series about Amos WALKER, a p.i. based in Detroit. A divorced Vietnam vet living in a city that has become a byword for urban decay and the economic plight of the Rustbelt, Walker is a classic HARD-BOILED character living in a very tarnished world. The first Walker novel was *Motor City Blue* (1980). SUGARTOWN (1984) won a Shamus Award. Another series character created by Estleman is Pete Macklin, a professional killer.

Estleman was born in Ann Arbor, and still lives in Michigan. He graduated from the state university and worked for several Michigan newspapers. At one point he tried to become a painter. He has been writing fiction full-time since 1980. Estleman's first novel was *The Oklahoma Punk* (1976), which was based on a historical figure, a bank robber of the Dustbowl era. He wrote another book, *Aces and Eights* (1981), based on the life of the man who killed Wild Bill Hickock, which won a Golden Spur Award. *City of Widows* (1994), set in the New Mexico Territory in 1881, begins like a Western but has an element of detection (and a surprise, which is spoiled by the jacket copy).

In a preface to a reprint of his first book under its original title, *Red Highway* (repr 1994), Estleman said that he wrote it during his Elizabethan poetry class at Eastern Michigan University. The preface is more interesting than the book itself. Estleman says of this novel, published when he was only twenty-three years old, that it "says nothing new, lacks plot definition, and offers virtually nothing in the way of character, but there are some nice visuals," a comment that could be applied to much of PULP writing, which the book resembles. Estleman rejected the idea that the protagonist had to be in some way sympathetic ("he need merely be interesting"), and offered the dubious claim that "there is not a great deal of difference between the lawless and the law-abiding in our society, and that we are all killers who don't receive the same opportunities." The question is not one of opportunities, but whether one acts on them; in the book, even the other gangsters recognize in the killer Ballard a rare lack of conscience.

Such a view, though congenial to stories about gangsters and hit men, leads to contradictions when employed in the private eye novel. The Walker series could be compared to the Harry STONER novels of Jonathan VALIN, which are set in another Midwestern industrial center, Cincinnati. In other ways, Walker resembles the anti-heroes of James CRUMLEY: a Vietnam vet, a hard drinker, divorced, and plagued with money problems. Walker's love of films of the forties acts as a foil for the unromantic life of a p.i. in the economically distressed Midwest, the graveyard of the American dream. The background is good, even excellent, though some of the writing is bad, particularly in the romantic subplots ("she was wind in the pines, blue shadows on snow across a moonlit valley, the sudden scent of fresh flowers on a zephyr"). Estleman's writing has grown greatly, and his debts to his models are no longer as obvious.

Among Estleman's non-series novels is *Edsel* (1995), which takes place against the background of the Kefauver Commission investigation into organized crime under the Truman administration. It is a comic novel depicting the fifties in horrified and loving detail—including the much maligned Edsel, Ford's dream car that became the biggest bomb since the Chrysler Airflow. Connie Minor, a former newspaperman who hates the ad business and is mentally stuck in PROHIBITION, is hired by an executive—the "Devil in saddle shoes"—to protect the project. *Motown* (1991) is set in 1966, and is about an ex-cop and muscle-car nut who is hired by automakers to help sabotage efforts to improve automobile safety. Another historical crime novel set in Detroit is *Jitterbug* (1998), which takes place during World War II.

Estleman's nonfiction work includes "Plus Expenses: The Private Eye as American Hero" (1983).

EUSTACE, ROBERT [BARTON] (1854–1943) A British doctor and mystery writer, Eustace's mysteries are actually collaborations with others. He would provide the medical information behind the story and with the other writer would develop it into fiction. Not surprisingly, Eustace was strong on cases of poisoning, but he also invented many novel ways of killing people. "The Tea Leaf" is a locked hot room mystery—it takes place in a Turkish bath, where a man has been stabbed to the heart, but absolutely no pointed instrument capable of inflicting the wound can be found. The murder weapon is one of the most clever and far-fetched ever invented. Eustace provided his technical expertise to L. T. MEADE for other short stories, equally ingenious. They worked together on *The Brotherhood of the Seven Kings* (1899), which has a female villain leading a shifty group of Italians (a familiar stereotype of the period), and on a number of other books.

Eustace also collaborated with the English writer Edgar Jepson (1863–1938); their best-known story is "Mr. Belton's Immunity" (1926), which includes Bolshevism, cryptography, and snake venom. This was a less happy partnership because Jepson's writing is well below Meade's and is full of melodrama that today reads as comical and absurd ("A raging desire to balk the devils who had robbed him of Kitty and the bright world surged through him"). "The Tea Leaf," however, was a happy exception, carried through by its bold ingenuity rather than its writing.

If one assumes that Eustace thought up the mechanisms of all the stories, then he certainly had an ingenious mind. Eustace's most famous collaboration was with Dorothy L. SAYERS, which took place in 1930, three decades after he began his work with Meade. Thereafter, traces of Eustace vanished; Hugh GREENE claimed that

Eustace was alive and well and living in Cornwall in 1947, and would have been nearly a hundred.

EUSTIS, HELEN (1916–) The American writer Helen Eustis is one of a few writers who have earned a place in the mystery canon with only one book. THE HORIZONTAL MAN (1946) was critically acclaimed and won the EDGAR award for best first novel. The story is set at Hollymount College, which could be modeled after Smith College, which Eustis attended, or nearby Holyoke. Eustis wrote only one other mystery novel, *The Fool Killer* (1954), but it was not of the quality of her first; it was filmed in 1965.

EVANOVITCH, JANET (***) The American author Janet Evanovitch has won several awards, including the John Creasey award and the Silver Dagger of the British CRIME WRITERS' ASSOCIATION, for her series of comical novels about the bounty hunter Stephanie Plum. The series began with *One for the Money* (1994), in which Plum convinces her cousin Vinnie, a bail bondsman, to let her have a crack at a case despite having no previous experience. In this first case, she runs afoul of Joe Morelli, an unsavory vice cop who also happens to have been her first lover. Plum's turf is "the burg" of Trenton, New Jersey. The novels stress wacky characters and entertainment. In *Three to Get Deadly* (1997), Vinnie sends Plum to find Uncle Mo, a beloved candy store owner from the old neighborhood. Plum is in need of money (again) in *High Five* (1999) and so gets involved in a job with Ranger, a hard-core bounty hunter. In addition, her Uncle Fred is missing and a search of his desk yields pictures of a bag full of body parts.

EVANS, HOMER An eccentric detective created by Elliot PAUL. The author used his own experiences and interests as the basis for the Evans novels, combining such disparate elements as his life in Paris in the interwar period and his earlier time spent in the American West. Evans lives in Paris and is a talented painter in addition to being brilliant. He has a number of sidekicks who are parodies of mystery characters: instead of THE THINKING MACHINE, he has The Thinking Dog. Another assistant, Miriam Leonard, is an Annie Oakley who likes to play the harpsichord.

In the first three books, Evans investigates ART mysteries in Paris, aided by his entourage. The first novel was *The Mysterious Mickey Finn; or, Murder in the Café du Dôme* (1939). Paul later branched out, setting one book in Boston (*Waylaid in Boston,* 1953), and several out West. FRACAS IN THE FOOTHILLS (1940) takes place amid a Montana range war, but the same characters appear as in the Paris series. It is a monumental novel of almost seven hundred pages. *The Black and the Red* (1956), the last novel, takes Homer Evans to Las Vegas. The title is a parody of Stendhal and refers to gambling.

BIBLIOGRAPHY Novels: *Hugger-Mugger in the Louvre* (1940), *Mayhem in B-Flat* (1940), *Murder on the Left Bank* (1951), *The Black Gardenia* (1952).

Novellas: *I'll Hate Myself in the Morning and Summer in December* (1945).

EVERS, CRABBE See BASEBALL.

EVIDENCE OF BLOOD (1991) Like others of Thomas H. COOK's works, this novel is deeply concerned with examining how and why people act, and the divergence between their conscious motives and their unconscious ones. It also dwells upon evil acts, both public and private, committed for social expediency or inner compulsions. Cook shows how our inability to know ourselves is not a psychological cliché but an element of horror.

Jackson Kinley, an orphan, a genius, and a successful true crime writer, returns to his hometown of Sequoyah, Georgia, for the burial of a friend, former sheriff Ray Tindall. Kinley is an unemotional man, almost as cold as the sociopathic killers who fascinate him and who are the subjects of his books. He becomes interested in the case on which Tindall was working at the time of his death: a thirty-five-year-old murder for which a man was executed in 1954. Kinley's research—into trial transcripts, physical evidence, and accounts of surviving witnesses—is realistically done, so much so that the pace of the book is at times as slow as the real thing. But Cook wins the reader over with the intensity of the characters and the compelling nature of the central question: Was an innocent man burned in the electric chair? Along the way, Kinley meets a frightening sociopath who has undoubtedly committed crimes but remains free. At the end, however, having too effectively painted his investigator into a corner for suspense's sake, Cook asks the reader to believe totally in Kinley's phenomenal memory for details.

"EXCLUDE THE IMPOSSIBLE . . ." One of Sherlock HOLMES's most famous axioms exists in several different formulations. In "The Adventure of the Beryl Coronet" (1892), Holmes says, "when you have excluded the impossible, whatever remains, however improbable, must be the truth." In *The Sign of Four* (1892), Holmes said "Eliminate all other factors, and the one which remains must be the truth." In the late adventure of the BRUCE-PARTINGTON PLANS (1908), Holmes was still reminding Watson that "when all other contingencies fail, whatever remains, however improbable, must be the truth."

EXPENDABLE MAN, THE (1963) This novel by Dorothy B. HUGHES, like her earlier RIDE THE PINK HORSE (1946), is an odd combination of fairly weak writing but strong overall effect; the compelling situation and the suspense drive the reader on. Hugh Densmore, an intern at the UCLA Hospital, is young, tall, well-mannered, and black. He travels to Phoenix for his niece's wedding, and on the way he offers a girl a ride. He is concerned about leaving her alone in the desert at night, but is not happy about the possible consequences of being seen with a young white girl. Worse, the girl is suspicious and a liar; in front of some policemen, she makes up a story in order to oblige him to carry her all the way to Phoenix. Densmore hopes that will be the end, but his nightmare is only beginning: she comes to his hotel and demands assistance for an abortion. Outraged, he threatens to call the police. The next morning, the newspaper announces that a young girl answering to her description has been found, apparently killed by a botched abortion. Hugh knows he will be the main suspect. He needs to avoid not only being found guilty but being arrested at all, because his medical reputation would be ruined by the association with abortion (then illegal). With the help of friends and family, Densmore sets out to prove his innocence by finding the real killer. He gets the names of abortionists and starts tracing them himself. The marshall in town is open-minded, but his two helpers are ignorant bigots. In contrast, Hugh's family is strong, successful, and educated. The novel was daring for the time it was written. The mystery focuses not as much on who really did it—which becomes clear before too long—but on Densmore's identifying him and then convincing the police.

"EXTRADITION" (***) A humorous short story by Arthur C. TRAIN about a New York City assistant district attorney named Jack Dockbridge and McGinnis, his Irish cop sidekick. The pair are sent to California to bring back a bank swindler; because he is broke, Dockbridge decides to use the free trip as his honeymoon. The pair becomes a trio with the addition of Dockbridge's new wife, and then a quartet when they befriend the crook, who seems like a nice enough guy. The trouble occurs on the way back, when they defer to the villain's greater knowledge of train travel out West. Train uses a loophole in extradition law to create the disaster and then a "surprise" ending for a finale, but unfortunately telegraphs his punches.

FABULOUS CLIPJOINT, THE (1947) An EDGAR-winning novel by Frederic BROWN, *The Fabulous Clipjoint* introduced detectives Ed and Am Hunter. Wally Hunter, Ed's father, is shot to death in Chicago, and Ed gets his uncle Am to help him search for the killer. Ed, who is a boy and not a man, is the narrator of the novel; he tells the story of his coming of age as well as the whodunit. It is not only his virginity that he stands to lose; through the grimy world of Chicago, with its bums, petty criminals, and people who are just mean and small, he comes to understand what Nelson Algren called "the city on the make." Am Hunter used to work in the circus, and the novel shows Brown's characteristic fascination with the bizarre people of carnival life—itself a metaphor for the glitzy, loud, and sordid sham of urban "civilization."

FAHERTY, TERENCE (***) An American mystery author living in Indianapolis, Terence Faherty has introduced an original sleuth, Owen KEANE. Keane is an intelligent and educated former seminarian, but because of his philosophical disposition he works at low-paying jobs and investigates mysteries out of an overpowering inquisitiveness. Keane's curiosity is not about crime so much as the world itself. As is now the fashion, Faherty makes references to brand names, commercials, and other elements of popular culture, but his realism has more to do with attitudes of mind than the detritus of modern life.

Faherty has also written about Scott Elliot, a World War II veteran and former bit player in the movies who works for the Hollywood Security Agency. In this case Faherty is following a track whose grooves are well worn, for example by William DEANDREA. In *Kill Me Again* (1996), the year is 1947 and the House Un-American Activities Committee is investigating—witch-hunting—in Hollywood. Elliott's boss, the orotund and simply rotund Paddy McGuire, assigns him to keep an eye on a nasty writer from Brooklyn named Bert Kramer, accused of being a "Red."

FAIR, A. A. A pseudonym of Erle Stanley GARDNER, under which he wrote the novels featuring Bertha COOL and Donald LAM. The stories are less dramatic than Gardner's Perry MASON series, but the odd-couple detective duo and the humor—sometimes funny, sometimes flat—give them a distinct flavor. The identity of "A. A. Fair" was long a secret, and Gardner was not suspected, showing the degree to which he had developed a separate style for the series. The Cool-Lam books compare favorably with the Mason novels, and their lighter touch has given them staying power. The series began with *The Bigger They Come* (1939) and ended with ALL GRASS ISN'T GREEN (1970).

FAIRLIE, GERARD (1899–1983) The English writer and soldier Gerard Fairlie was the model for Bulldog DRUMMOND, the odious hero created by Fairlie's friend, SAPPER. Fairlie was educated at Sandhurst, served in World War I, and was decorated. After the death of Sapper, Fairlie took over the writing of the Drummond series, the bigotry of which he is said to have toned down.

Later in life, Fairlie wrote for film, and also created a postwar HARD-BOILED private eye named Johnny Macall, a former policemen. The series began with *Winner Take All* (1953) and ran to six books.

FAIR PLAY The idea that a mystery or detective story should in principle be solvable by the reader. Most importantly, this means that the clues the detective finds must not be withheld from the reader, and there must be no supernatural explanations. The "rules" of fair play were codified by Father KNOX in 1929; in addition to the two principles already mentioned, Knox specified that there be not more than one secret passage; no sudden appearances of twins or doubles; the detective cannot be the criminal; there can be no fortuitous accidents or intuitions to help the sleuth; the "WATSON" of the story cannot hide his thoughts from the reader, and he cannot be too much dumber than an average reader; and no unheard of poisons or complex gadgets can be introduced. Knox's famous "no Chinamen" rule was a reaction to the overuse of such characters at the time—and perhaps a dig at Sax ROHMER.

Knox made his list partly in a spirit of fun, and it is somewhat surprising that fair play is now practically written in stone. Also in a spirit of fun, Josef SKVORECKY wrote *Sins for Father Knox* (*Hrichy pro patera Knoxe*, 1973; tr 1988), a collection of ten stories, each of which deliberately violates one of the ten principles.

Dorothy L. SAYERS pointed out that fair play has not always been accepted as the standard of the genre; it was in fashion around the time of THE MOONSTONE (1868), which faithfully adheres to it, and then went into eclipse in the later nineteenth century. The form of the PROCEDURAL almost inherently includes fair play, but many good stories do not—including some of those of Sherlock HOLMES. Fair play is also in the eye of the beholder, to some extent, especially when there is a third-person or omniscient narrator. For example, in SMALLBONE DECEASED (1950), when Mrs. Chittering looks out over the transom just before she is killed and says to someone, "'Heavens, it's you? You did give me a fright,'" has the author unfairly concealed the person's identity? Fair play has often been sacrificed in order to save plots or revive suspense, but also in the interests of making stories readable.

FAIRY GUNMOTHER, THE (tr of *La Fée carabine,* 1987) The second of Daniel PENNAC's novels about the hapless Benjamin Malaussène. The fairy of the title is an elderly lady who shoots a policeman in the head with an explosive bullet; in the eyes of Piccolo Malaussène, she is a fairy who transforms the man into a flower. Elderly people are at the center of the story: the intricate plot features a murderer who kills them for their money and an organization of small drug dealers who take advantage of those who are depressed. Two policemen, Van Thian and Pastor, investigate the throat slashings of several old women. The crime is not funny, but their manner of investigation and the uproar it produces are. Meanwhile Julie, Benjamin's journalist fiancée, is delving into the problem of drugs and the elderly, which entails bringing the most intoxicated of the victims to Benjamin's house, where the whole Malaussène family takes care of them and helps them detoxify. Particularly important is Therèse, a girl with no charm but with the gift of foresight, who inspires them with a new faith in the future. The various crisscrossing stories—the murder of the policeman, the drug traffic, the killing of the elderly—are further complicated by a background story of building speculation, which also takes advantage of the elderly. Interwoven into this milieu are the personal stories of Pastor and Van Thian, who will eventually understand it all and save Benjamin, the scapegoat who is suspected of all the mentioned crimes.

FALCON, THE A character created by Michael ARLEN who in other hands became the vehicle for a long series of films in the forties. Gay Stanhope, the Falcon, looks like his nickname. Tall, dark, and somewhat sinister, he is a tough guy in the HARD-BOILED tradition. In his first and only case (in print), he steals back some jewelry that has been used for insurance fraud. George Sanders starred in the first batch of Falcon films (1941–1942).

FALKENSTEIN, JESSE See LININGTON, ELIZABETH.

FALL GUY The criminal who is set up to take the blame for a crime to allow the others to avoid being caught. The term comes, of course, from the phrase "take a fall," which had many colorful variants, such as "fall for the owl" (go to jail for burgling houses at night), "fall for the tools" (be convicted of possessing burglar's tools), and "fall for paper hanging" (counterfeiting or forgery).

"FALSE BURTON COMBS, THE" A story by Carroll John DALY, which appeared in BLACK MASK in 1922. The setting, Nantucket Island, is an unusual one for a HARD-BOILED detective story, nor is there a detective. The narrator, a man who describes himself as "an adventurer," is approached on a boat to Fall River, Massachusetts, by Burton Combs, the son of a rich family who has gotten involved in something illegal and subsequently has double-crossed his associates. He pays the narrator to impersonate him and travel to Nantucket in his place, because he fears the men he implicated (they have never seen him) are out of jail and are on their way to kill him. The job is complicated by the narrator's meeting a young woman, Marion St. James. Most critics consider the romantic angle a weakness of the story, but Marion's presence is vital to the functioning of the plot.

FAMILY AFFAIR, A (1975) The last novel by Rex STOUT, in which the killer comes very close to home. Stout uses the book as a vehicle for criticizing President Richard Nixon, whom he once described as "the greatest danger that ever occurred to American democracy."

FANSLER, KATE A literature professor and sometime sleuth in the books of Amanda CROSS. Fansler marries Reed Amhearst, who had previously assisted her, in *Poetic Justice* (1970). The books often involve literature, as in *The James Joyce Murder* (1967), in which Fansler is sorting through the papers of a great publisher who encouraged the major modernists. (Each of the chapters is named for a story in JOYCE'S *Dubliners.*) Kate and Reed talk to each other in a parody of nineteenth-century novelistic discourse: "I wait, ears eagerly attuned. . . . I have never fathomed the mystery of your familial connections." This from a boy who grew up in Baltimore. As the series continues, Kate and Reed mature without growing up. They continue to speak as if they had written down the dialogue while proctoring a final exam, and their cases become more bizarrely contrived. The political backwardness of Kate's colleagues and peers becomes more of a focus than the mystery. *Death in a Tenured Position* (1981; British title *A Death in the Faculty*) is about the poisoning of the first woman to receive tenure in the Harvard English department, where Fansler has a temporary position.

BIBLIOGRAPHY Novels: *In the Last Analysis* (1964), *The Theban Mysteries* (1972), *The Question of Max* (1976), *Sweet Death, Kind Death* (1984), *No Word from Winifred* (1986), *A Trap for Fools* (1989), *The Players Come Again* (1990), *An Imperfect Spy* (1995).

FANTODS An expression meaning worries, a case of the fidgets, or the heebie-jeebies.

FANTÔMAS A character created by Marcel ALLAIN and Pierre SOUVESTRE, introduced in the novel *Fantômas* (1911). The pair were hack writers at the time they were approached to write a series of five sensational novels by a Parisian publisher. Allain thought up the name "Fantômas" on the subway, and the first book was rapidly produced. Souvestre and Allain wrote so quickly—often by dictation—that ten more books were produced before the year 1911 was out. Eventually, a total of 32 Fantômas exploits were written.

It is at first hard to account for the furor that Fantômas aroused. The writing was mediocre and relied on the formulas of sensational nineteenth-century fiction. Fantômas is an anti-hero, an invisible thief and silent killer who stalks the dark streets of Paris. He was a fictional version of the kind of conscienceless monster who would fascinate Paris a few years later during the LANDRU case. But the romance of evil was hardly a new subject in 1911. Baudelaire's *Fleurs du Mal* and *Paris Spleen* and the decadent writers of the nineties had already explored it. The anonymity of the modern city, and its potential to breed violence and terror, had been a theme in literature for decades. The irony that the greater the number of people, the more the individual was alone and vulnerable, had not been lost on writers of sensational fiction.

The popular success of Fantômas was matched by a glowing reception among avant-garde artists and writers. At the time, European cultural circles had been swept by a wave of innovative "isms," including Cubism and Fauvism, and Dadaism and Surrealism were on the horizon. Each movement revolted against realistic representation and the safety of "bourgeois" art, even as anarchism and communism were attacking bourgeois social and political structures. The poet Guillaume Appollinaire called *Fantômas* "one of the richest works that exist," and founded a society of Friends of Fantômas. The character also appealed to the film director Louis Feuillade (1873–1925), considered the father of expressionist film and pioneer of the fantasy and suspense genre. His series of Fantômas films fanned the blaze even higher; in fact, this was one case in which the films were better than the novels.

Fantômas is less a NAPOLEON OF CRIME than a Prince Bernadotte, a madman and lover of crime-for-crime's-sake. Pursued by Inspector JUVE, his archenemy, Fantômas commits a non-stop series of crimes, including brutal murders. He has no redeeming qualities; he is not an avenger or a savior of the poor, nor an admirer of women—quite the contrary. The first novel begins with the discovery of the body of the Marquise de Langruen with her head almost cut off with a razor. Next, Lord Beltham, who had been missing for two weeks, is found (through Juve's cleverness) in an abandoned apartment inside a trunk, having been injected with a substance to prevent his decomposition. A handsome young man, Charles Rambert, who is in love with the granddaughter of the Marquise, is accused of the first crime, introducing a typical romantic subplot. As the mystery goes on and further crimes are attributed to the invisible hand of Fantômas, the reader begins to wonder if the anti-hero is going to appear at all, and if he is not just a name appropriated by various crooks, or a term applied to a nameless terror. Juve, however, continues to insist on his existence.

The main interest of the novels comes from this suspense, the non-appearance of the main character. Fantômas does become more corporeal—he has a mistress, Lady Beltham, and a daughter, Hélène—but is known mostly through his works. One thing Fantômas seems to lack is a motive, unless it is a perverse sense of sport or pleasure in the kill. In one case, he infects an ocean liner with the plague and kills everyone aboard.

The Fantômas novels are no longer readily available in English, tastes having changed. Mystery novels of their period tended to be long, and only the scenes of Parisian and provincial French life and the subsidiary characters continue to be of interest. The first novel (*Fantômas*), however, was reprinted on the seventy-fifth anniversary of its appearance (1986) in an updated translation with an introduction by the poet John Ashbery. Because the novels were sometimes serialized first, the publication history is confusing. In 1977, Léo MALET published an abridged version of one of the novels, *L'Arrestation de Fantômas* (1911). *Fantômas est-il ressucité* (1926) had first been published as a series of seven illustrated monthlies; it was adapted and translated as *The Lord of the Terror* (1925).

BIBLIOGRAPHY Novels: By Pierre Souvestre and Marcel Allain—*Juve contre Fantômas* (1911; tr *Exploits of Juve,* 1916), *Le Mort qui tue* (1911; tr *Messengers of Evil,* 1917), *L'Agent secret* (1911; tr *A Nest of Spies,* 1917), *Un roi prisonnier de Fantômas*

(1911; tr *A Royal Prisoner,* 1919), *Le Policier apache* (1911; tr *Slippery as Sin,* 1920), *Le Pendu de Londre* (1911), *La Fille de Fantômas* (1911), *Le Fiacre de nuit* (1911), *La Main coupée* (1911; tr *The Long Arm of Fantômas,* 1924; British title *The Limb of Satan*), *L'Arrestation de Fantômas* (1911), *Le Magistrat cambrioleur* (1912), *La Livrée du crime* (1912), *La Mort de Juve* (1912), *L'Évadée de Saint-Lazare* (1912), *La Disparition de Fandor* (1912), *Le Mariage de Fantômas* (1912), *L'Assassin de Lady Beltham* (1912), *La Guêpe rouge* (1912), *Les Souliers du mort* (1912), *Le train perdu* (1912), *Les Amours d'un prince* (1912), *Le Bouquet tragique* (1912), *Le Jockey masqué* (1913), *Le Cercueil vide* (1913), *Le Faiseur de reines* (1913), *Le Cadavre géant* (1913), *Le voleur d'or* (1913), *La Série rouge* (1913), *L'Hôtel du crime* (1913; repub as *Fantômas accuse,* 1934), *La cravate de chanvre* (1913; repub as *Le Domestique de Fantômas,* 1934), *La Fin de Fantômas* (1913). By Marcel Allain—*Fantômas of Berlin: The Yellow Document* (1919; not published in French), *Fantômas roi des receleurs* (1926; tr *Juve in the Dock,* 1925), *Fantômas en danger* (1926; tr *Fantômas Captured,* 1926), *Fantômas prend sa revanche* (1926; tr *The Revenge of Fantômas,* 1926), *Fantômas attaque Fandor* (1926; tr *Bulldog and Rats,* 1928), *Si c'était Fantômas* (1935), *Oui, c'est Fantômas* (1935), *Fantômas joue et gagne* (1947), *Fantômas contre les nains* (1941; serial only), *Fantômas contre l'amour* (1947), *Fantômas vole les blondes* (1948), *Fantômas mène le bal* (1963; serial only).

FAREWELL, MY LOVELY (1940) Raymond CHANDLER considered this his best novel, but it has perhaps worn less well than some of his others. Moose MALLOY, a prototype of the dumb giant character, is hard to take seriously; the portrayal of and attitudes toward blacks, who figure prominently in the early scenes, could charitably be called dated.

Chandler thought it his tightest and most complex plot. While looking for a Greek barber whose wife wants him back, MARLOWE runs into Moose Malloy, who has spent eight years in prison and is looking for his old girlfriend, Velma Valento. Moose discovers that the bar where she used to sing is now a black-only club, and is not too happy. Against his will, Marlowe is forced to trail along in the path of Moose's destruction.

Marlowe next digs up the widow of the club's previous owner, a broken-down alcoholic from whom he gets a picture of the missing woman. She also informs him that Velma is dead, which he wishes to communicate to Moose (who is now on the run) before he commits more mayhem. Before he can do that, another case comes up, involving the theft and return for ransom of a jade necklace. The deal goes sour, another murder is committed, and Marlowe himself is almost killed. The plot expands outward and, like a film script, is a structure of scenes rather than of a single, linear thread. It works through multiplication rather than deduction.

FAR SIDE OF THE DOLLAR, THE (1965) The title of this novel by Ross MACDONALD could be an echo of Philip MARLOWE's words at the end of THE LONG GOODBYE: "Organized crime is just the dirty side of the sharp dollar." It begins with Lew ARCHER's visit to a school for troubled boys, in search of a lead on Tommy Hillman, who has just escaped. The school is like most institutions visited by Archer, divided between petty tyrants and idealists who have given up, with the unfortunate inmates in between. It turns out that Hillman had borrowed and wrecked a neighbor's car, and was put in the school by his father to teach him a lesson. Next, Archer learns that a ransom of $25,000 has been demanded for the return of Tommy Hillman. The Hillmans are a typically horrifying wealthy couple whose life has become unmoored through too much lying. The investigation of their past at one point brings up a connection to Archer's, showing that he has more in common with these people than he at first supposed.

FAULKNER, WILLIAM (1897–1962) Recipient of the Nobel prize, William Faulkner is one of America's most respected writers. His novels about the families of imaginary Yoknapatawpha County, Mississippi, embody the ceaseless American search for personal and social identity, as well as the more particular and agonizing journey of the South. Faulkner deals with race relations, the brutal treatment of African Americans, the legacy of slavery, the southern aristocracy, and the painful transition from agrarian to twentieth-century industrial society and attendant shifts in morality and perspective.

The turmoil of transition creates an immense feeling of freedom that is often disappointed. The circumstances often lead to violence (most grotesquely, the castration and murder of Joe Christmas in *Light in August,* [1932]), and it is not a very great step from there to the crime and mystery genre; Faulkner took that step with SANCTUARY (1931), which was also his first great popular success. A deliberate attempt to write a money-making bestseller, Faulkner later famously disparaged *Sanctuary.* It is notable, however, that he wrote a sequel to it (*Requiem for a Nun,* 1951), and also produced other mysteries: INTRUDER IN THE DUST (1948) and the related stories of *Knight's Gambit* (1949). The figure of Gavin STEVENS connects the detective books to the other works in the Faulkner oeuvre.

FAUST, RON (***) Ron Faust is now praised for the lyricism of his writing and his plot construction, but recognition has come slowly and his work remains an acquired taste. Faust, a former minor leaguer, could not get his zany, baseball-oriented first novel, *Fugitive Moon*, published. He then turned to the subgenre of wilderness adventure mysteries. *Tombs of Blue Ice* (1974) is set in the Alps and concerns an American mountain climber, Robert Holmes. In a disastrous expedition, one of the other climbers is killed and a third is injured. Holmes goes for help for the injured man, Dieter Streicher, but when he returns, the body is gone. Across glaciers and an inhospitable landscape, Holmes searches for the reason behind Streicher's disappearance, which involves probing into the NAZI past. *The Wolf in the Clouds* (1977) also takes place against a rugged mountain background, the Rockies, and features the pursuit of a man. *The Burning Sky* (1978) is about the illegal killing of big game in New Mexico.

With *Lord of the Dark Lake* (1996), Faust made another change of pace. This novel concerns Jay Chandler, an archaeologist, who is the summer guest of Alexander Krisos on his Greek island. The Greek billionaire's entertainments include a week-long debauch, which culminates in a visit to the Minotaur (Krisos has installed a bull in the caves under the island). Even before the grisly myth can be re-enacted, one of the guests is murdered.

Since his other successes, Faust's first novel has finally gotten into print (see BASEBALL).

FEARING, KENNETH [FLEXNER] (1902–1961) The poet and freelance writer Kenneth Fearing was born in Oak Park, Illinois, but moved to New York in 1924, where he wrote for *Time* and other magazines. He was a graduate of the University of Wisconsin and had worked in various jobs, including as a mill employee and a salesman. He became known for his poems, some of which appeared in *Poetry* and *The New Yorker*, dealing with spiritual emptiness and the alienation of the individual in industrialized society. *Stranger at Coney Island* (1948) is one of his seven volumes of poems; his *Collected Poems* was published in 1940.

Although he wrote only a few novels in the mystery and crime genre, they are well-written and share the qualities of his poetry; one of them, THE BIG CLOCK (1946), is considered a classic of suspense, praised by Raymond CHANDLER at the time and afterwards by many others. His first thriller was *The Hospital* (1939). *Dagger of the Mind* (1941) was set in an artist's colony. In *The Loneliest Girl in the World* (1951), a daughter investigates when her father and brother fall to their death from a building.

FELICIA'S JOURNEY (1994) A novel by Irish author William Trevor (1924–). Long resident in Devon, England, Trevor often uses Irish characters and settings in his works, including *Felicia's Journey*, a suspense and crime story that concerns a young Irish woman's search through England for her boyfriend. Instead, she finds a serial killer.

Felicia runs away early one morning from her home and takes the boat to England to look for Johnny Lysaght, who has made her pregnant and whom she thinks is working in a lawnmower factory in the Midlands. Once there, she is unable to find any such factory, and runs into the heavy and bespectacled Mr. Hilditch, who seems pathetic, lonely, and helpful. He is in fact extremely cunning; with incredible patience, he has built up a "Memory Lane" of other girls he has "helped."

In a series of highly acclaimed novels and short stories, Trevor had previously dealt with violence and sometimes crime by people living on the margins of society. A powerful example comes from *Family Sins* (1990), the story "Events at Drimaghleen," about the disappearance of Maureen McDowd. She and her boyfriend, Lancy Butler, are found dead by the McDowds in the yard of the Butler's house, along with Lancy's mother. English newspeople trick the impoverished McDowds with an offer of money to give them information, which they then use to concoct a story that destroys the McDowds's memory of their daughter and their piece of mind.

FELL, DR. GIDEON A tall, fat (he weighs twenty stone, and a stone is fourteen pounds), gray-haired, and outlandish character who is also a sleuth. John Dickson CARR modeled him after G. K. CHESTERTON, who was his favorite writer. Carr wanted Fell to be likeable, but the pince-nez on a black ribbon, the pipe, his huge "bandit-like" moustache, *two* canes, and unmistakable hat make Fell seem like a walking closet of disguises, or simply a buffoon. Fell's character also contains echoes of Shakespeare's Falstaff and Dr. Samuel Johnson. Gideon Fell appeared in twenty-four novels, including *The Hollow Man* (1936), one of his best cases. *Fell and Foul Play* (1991) collects his short story appearances.

The Fell books are not ambitious in a literary sense, but the plots have been praised. These novels are generally better written than the Sir Henry MERRIVALE books by the same author. Even though Dickson Carr was most interested in plotting, the first book, *Hag's Nook* (1933), met with a cool reception by BARZUN and TAYLOR, who called it "unlifelike" and its detective "irritating and unsatisfactory." Set in Fell's hometown in Lincolnshire, it used the GOTHIC elements that Dickson Carr loved. It also introduced supporting characters, including Scotland Yard's Chief Inspector Hadley and young Rampole, Fell's acolyte. The second book in the series was *The Mad Hatter*

Mystery (1933), which concerns a "Mad Hatter," a thief who steals hats (and a barrister's wig) and places them on various monuments around London. The Hatter takes Sir William Bitton's top hat and places it on the head of his nephew, who is found murdered in the Tower of London and wearing a "golfing suit." There is nothing remotely believable about the Fell novels, and their appeal is to the fan of the puzzle; however, even critics of the old school have found the burlesque elements and the complete one-dimensionality of the characters annoying.

The Dead Man's Knock (1958) is set at Queen's College in Alexandria, Virginia, where a series of strange incidents occur in the gym, including the appearance of images of the founder's statue (a reference to Jefferson's statue at the University of Virginia) painted on the walls. The sexy and evil Rose Lestrange has been trying to seduce a Wilkie COLLINS expert, Mark Ruthven; Rose is found dead in her cottage (a LOCKED ROOM situation). The works of Collins and J. S. LE FANU are both worked into the story.

Besides the LOCKED ROOM problem, Dickson Carr faced Gideon Fell with the other usual mystery set-ups. *In Spite of Thunder* (1960) has Fell assisting rather than leading an investigation in a very strange COUNTRY HOUSE setting: actress Eve Eden brings together at the Villa Rosalind a group of people who were present at Adolph Hitler's Berchtesgaden in 1939, when her fiancé mysteriously fell to his death. There are two other investigators, Swiss policeman Gustave Aubertin and Brian Innes, a guest who is trying to protect a young woman.

BIBLIOGRAPHY Novels: *The Blind Barber* (1933), *The Eight of Swords* (1934), *Death Watch* (1935), *The Arabian Nights Murder* (1936), *To Wake the Dead* (1937), *The Crooked Hinge* (1938), *The Problem of the Green Capsule* (1939; British title *The Black Spectacles*), *The Problem of the Wire Cage* (1939), *The Man Who Could Not Shudder* (1940), *The Case of the Constant Suicides* (1941), *Death Turns the Tables* (1941; British title *Seat of the Scornful*), *Till Death Do Us Part* (1944), *He Who Whispers* (1946), *The Sleeping Sphinx* (1947), *Below Suspicion* (1949), *In Spite of Thunder* (1960), *The House at Satan's Elbow* (1965), *Panic in Box C* (1966), *Dark of the Moon* (1967).

Short Stories: *Dr. Fell, Detective* (1946), *The Third Bullet and Other Stories* (1954), *The Men Who Explained Miracles* (1963), *The Door to Doom and Other Detections* (1980).

FELLOWS, FRED A detective in a series of police PROCEDURAL novels by Hillary WAUGH. A few years before the Fellows series began with *Sleep Long, My Love* (1959), Waugh had published the ground-breaking procedural LAST SEEN WEARING . . . (1952), in which Bristol, Massachusetts, police chief Fred Ford tracks down the killer of a missing college student. Ford never became a series character, but Fellows is a police chief in Stockford, Connecticut, a small New England town not unlike Bristol. Whereas the fifty-eight-year-old Ford is intense, with closely cropped gray hair and a deeply lined face, Fellows is a more saturnine character, who does not ride his subordinates with grim persistence the way Ford does. Fellows is, however, also a skilled investigator, and the series is detailed. *Sleep Long, My Love* also dealt with the murder of a girl, a subject Waugh returns to again and again, for example in *The Missing Man* (1964).

BIBLIOGRAPHY Novels: *Road Block* (1960), *The Night It Rained* (1961), *The Late Mrs. D* (1962), *Born Victim* (1962), *Death and Circumstance* (1963), *Prisoner's Plea* (1963), *End of a Party* (1965), *Girl on the Run* (1965), *Pure Poison* (1966), *The Con Game* (1968).

FELO DE SE? (1929) A novel by R. Austin FREEMAN, issued in the United States as *Death at the Inn.* The inn in question is Clifford's Inn, London, the residence of John Gillum. The first part of the story is narrated by Robert Mortimer, a clerk in the bank patronized by Gillum. Mortimer has the misfortune to be involved in two ugly deaths; first, he discovers the body of a man in the porch of a church, dead from an injection of potassium CYANIDE. He is thought to have been murdered. Later Mortimer becomes friends with Gillum, hitherto known to him only as a customer of the bank. Mortimer had noticed that Gillum periodically received large checks, and also drew out sums of five hundred pounds or more on a quarterly basis, as well as smaller but still unusually large amounts of cash. After the men become friends, Mortimer learns that Gillum is an inveterate gambler—which, however, does not explain all his expenditures, and so Mortimer suspects blackmail. The relationship of the two men is developed through a series of conversations ranging over subjects such as the nature of gambling (to Mortimer merely an "insane hobby") and the justification of suicide. Mortimer has occasion to revert to these earlier conversations after Gillum's badly decomposed body is found in his rooms; bankrupt, he seems to have killed himself with morphine.

One man, Gillum's Australian cousin Arthur Benson, is not satisfied. He consults Dr. Thorndyke, who is convinced that Gillum did in fact commit suicide. Benson's aim is to get revenge on the blackmailers who drove Gillum to his death. Thorndyke advises him that this is almost impossible, but he proceeds anyway. Jervis, as usual, narrates this part of the story. Thorndyke's reconstruction of Gillum's predicament and identification of his associates calls for some of his best deductive efforts.

FELSE, GEORGE The policeman patriarch of a family of detectives created by Ellis PETERS, author of the Brother CADFAEL series. The first book in the series, *Fallen into the Pit* (1951), was not about George Felse but his thirteen-year-old son, Dominic, who grows up through the course of the series. The second book, *Death and the Joyful Woman* (1962), won an EDGAR award. George is a member of the Criminal Investigation Department (CID), but sometimes cases take him far afield. In *The Grass Widow's Tale* (1968), Peters gave George's wife Bunty a case to solve.

BIBLIOGRAPHY Novels: *Flight of a Witch* (1964), *A Nice Derangement of Epitaphs* (1965; U.S. title *Who Lies Here?*), *The Piper on the Mountain* (1966), *Black Is the Colour of My True Love's Heart* (1967), *The House of Green Turf* (1969), *Morning Raga* (1969), *The Knocker on Death's Door* (1970), *Death to the Landlords!* (1972), *City of Gold and Shadows* (1973), *Rainbow's End* (1978).

FEMALE DETECTIVES See WOMEN.

FEN, GERVASE The Oxford professor of English and Fellow of St. Christopher's who is the sleuth in novels and stories by Edmund CRISPIN. Although Fen is eccentric and donnish, the humor of the stories is sometimes reminiscent of Buster Keaton and Harold Lloyd. When Fen appears in THE MOVING TOYSHOP (1946), his large form is squeezed into "an extremely small, vociferous and battered sportscar" named *Lily Christine III*, with which he proceeds to tear up the college president's lawn.

Fen is tall, lanky, and fond of strange hats. His dark hair is a mess, and his disheveled appearance goes with his great energy and cheerfulness. He is vague when he wants to be, canny when it suits his investigations, and, like Mr. FORTUNE, is always hungry and makes strange exclamations such as "Oh, my paws!" The similarity in names between Gervase Fen and Gideon FELL is not accidental, as the author was influenced by John Dickson CARR. Fen even makes reference to Fell in the first book of the series, *The Case of the Gilded Fly* (1944). Another similarity between the two characters is their propensity for abstaining from discussing clues, while also professing to a full understanding of the affair, which is only made plain to the reader at the end. The big difference between the two detective series is that Crispin was a much better writer than Carr.

The Case of the Gilded Fly takes place against a theater background. The first murder victim is a person whom nobody likes, to the point that even Fen hesitates at unmasking the criminal. A second killing forces Fen to take action, which he does in the most theatrical way. Also written during the war, *Holy Disorders* (1945) involves spying. It has many bizarre touches, including Fen's preoccupation with butterflies, a plethora of curates, and, as usual, literary jokes (characters named Henry Fielding and Henry James). The author used his musical background more overtly here, making a composer, Geoffrey Vintner, the center of the story. Vintner is asked to fill in for a mad organist in the town of Tolnbridge, but is mysteriously attacked several times on the way there.

Love Lies Bleeding (1948) is a much bloodier story. On the eve of Speech Day at the public school of Castrevenford, where Fen is supposed to deliver the prizes, two masters are found shot, and a girl from a nearby school has gone missing. Mother Bly, a local witch who lives in an Elizabethan cottage, makes a startling discovery of a manuscript thought to be a play by Shakespeare; Fen throws a fit when he learns of her treatment of the find. In fact, he behaves quite pedantically throughout, and as usual knows what is going on but does not have time to inform the police (or the reader). The assumption and even reliance on the presumed ignorance of lower-class Britons is rather striking in this book, which BARZUN and TAYLOR called a "triumph." Crispin makes use of Shakespeare's most famous stage direction ("Exit, pursued by a bear") and even gives a sample of the Bard's "lost" work. BURIED FOR PLEASURE (1949) presents a much different Fen, this time campaigning for Parliament. He has no car; he wears no hat; he makes no outbursts—in fact, he seems diffident throughout, and the story is held up by the excellent writing, the country ambience, and the weird rural population.

The last novel, *The Glimpses of the Moon*, appeared in 1977, a year before the author's death. It is a late adventure, a slapstick romp in which Fen is on sabbatical and gets involved in a case involving dismembered bodies. The lunatic climax takes place during a foxhunt.

BIBLIOGRAPHY Novels: *Swan Song* (1947; U.S. title *Dead and Dumb*), *Frequent Hearses* (1950; U.S. title *Sudden Vengeance*), *The Long Divorce* (1951).

Short Stories: *Beware of the Trains* (1953), *Fen Country* (1979).

FENCE As a term for a receiver of stolen goods, this word has been in use at least since the eighteenth century.

FER-DE-LANCE (1934) The first of the Nero WOLFE/ Archie GOODWIN novels by Rex STOUT. The murder takes place on a golf course, and involves one of the most ridiculously contrived murder weapons of mystery fiction. It is also the longest of the books in the series, and is most indebted to the conventions of the GOLDEN AGE; it too is full of wit and charm. As the book opens, PROHIBITION is still in progress, and Wolfe is testing 49 kinds of the legal 3.2 beer. The case comes to him by way of Fred Durkin, a not very bright shadow who is often hired by Wolfe in the series, and whose wife has a friend with a problem.

Maria Maffei's brother Carlo is missing; an Italian metalworker, Carlo lived in a roominghouse on Sullivan Street. Stout's description of the immigrant ghetto is vivid and displays the author's love and complete knowledge of New York City. Even if the Italians are stereotypes, Stout at least doesn't stoop to the "whats-a-matta-wit-you" kind of dialogue that makes some "ethnic" mysteries impossible to read. Wolfe deduces a link between Maffei's disappearance and the death of a prominent man, Peter Oliver Barstow, on a Westchester County golf course. The investigation includes a stickup and an encounter with a fer-de-lance, a deadly pit viper of South America.

FERRARS, E. X. (U.S. pseudonym of Morna Doris Brown, 1907–1995) Morna Doris Brown's dozens of novels were published in her native England under the name Elizabeth Ferrars, and E. X. Ferrars in the United States. Brown was born in Burma and attended University College, London, where she studied journalism. Her first mystery novel was *Give a Corpse a Bad Name* (1940). The story concerned a woman author who runs over a drunk in the road; he later is identified as her husband. Women writers would appear often in Ferrars's novels as protagonists. She often wrote about strong female characters, but also specialized in COZY, domestic plots set in English villages. *Alibi for a Witch* (1952), however, was set in Italy. Ferrars did not create a widely recognized series character, which partly accounts for her lack of fame despite her large number of books. In many of her novels, there is no detective at all. Among her more unusual books is *With Murder in Mind* (1948), made up of conversations between a woman and her psychoanalyst.

Late in her career, Ferrars created Felix and Virginia Freer, one of the most oddball couples in mystery fiction. Felix is a liar and kleptomaniac who sponges on his wife, a physical therapist. Although they are married, they do not live together. In the first novel in the series, *Last Will and Testament* (1978), a rash of murders takes place near the town where Virginia Freer is living. Felix, though a small-time criminal himself, does most of the detecting in the series.

FIELDING, HENRY (1707–1754) Like DEFOE, Henry Fielding was one of the great developers of the novel in English. He also used the PICARESQUE model, for example in *Tom Jones* (1749), one of the masterpieces of English literature.

Fielding's early career was as a political satirist writing for the stage. His satire was so biting, in fact, that Robert Walpole passed a law (the Licensing Act of 1737) that essentially ended Fielding's career as a dramatist. Fielding got back at Walpole, however, in his fictionalized biography of the hated robber Jonathan WILD; Fielding's version of Wild was a thinly veiled portrait of Walpole himself.

Fielding studied law and became a magistrate after his playwriting days. He founded the BOW STREET RUNNERS, a private police force that was not replaced until the creation of the Metropolitan Police in the 1830s. His career was not without controversy; in 1749, a series of riots took place, in which sailors destroyed several houses of prostitution. One man who was hanged, Bosavern Penlez, was only accused of having stolen a few articles of linen. Fielding wrote *A True State of the Case of Bosavern Penlez* (1749), justifying his own harsh position as Chairman of the Westminster sessions at the time. Fielding also wrote *Enquiry into the Causes of the Late Increase in Robbers* (repr 1988), which describes several real (but in some cases somewhat fictionalized) crimes. See PROTOMYSTERIES.

FILM NOIR This French term ("black" or "dark film") for the moody, pessimistic style of film in the forties and fifties, many of them crime and mystery classics, actually stemmed from English literature. In the eighteenth and nineteenth centuries, the French referred to the English GOTHIC novel as the *roman noir. Film noir* was dark not only in its outlook, but in its look. Scenes of the criminal underworld, the night, and dingy haunts at the margins of the city were common. Unlike gangster films such as those of Edward G. Robinson and James Cagney, which took their style from melodrama, *film noir* had the look of German expressionist film, though technically it was far more advanced. The word "noir" is now broadly applied to crime fiction of a similar darkness of the fifties up to the present. (See NOIR.)

FINAL NOTICE (1981) A novel by Jonathan VALIN in which Harry STONER is asked to investigate a disturbing misdemeanor that threatens to turn into a very grisly felony: a vandal has been cutting out the genitals, breasts, eyes, and mouths in pictures of paintings in library books. Stoner connects the vandalism to a gruesome killing in the past that was never solved. Valin ambitiously tries to combine the search for "the Ripper" with explorations of Stoner's philosophy and past, as well as a romantic element. The detective's relationship with a young library worker, the development of which dominates the first half, is problematic because it invites cliché (the "brassy girl who was half denim and half lace"). Because the suspects are so few, the misdirection of the reader does not fool for long. Yet the book contains the elements Valin later more successfully combined and is an important transition work.

Final Notice (1973) is also the title of one of the DKA novels by Joe GORES.

"FINAL PROBLEM, THE" (1893) The case with which Conan DOYLE tried to do away with his creation, Sherlock HOLMES, in a battle with Professor MORIARTY. The story contains little detection, but is instead a tale of adventure. Holmes first seeks shelter with Doctor WATSON, having survived several assassination attempts earlier in the day, and tells him about the NAPOLEON OF CRIME whom he is stalking. Ominously, Holmes says that he would gladly sacrifice his own life in order to do away with Moriarty. First he and Watson must get out of the country, which involves the help of MYCROFT Holmes and a variety of clever devices, including a train chase. They go on to Brussels and then Strasbourg, where they learn that Moriarty has escaped the trap set for him by Holmes. The story culminates in Switzerland on a narrow path above the Reichenbach Falls, the "green water roaring forever down." Three years later, the author was driven by popular demand to revive Holmes, and did so in the adventure of the EMPTY HOUSE (1903).

FINCH, INSPECTOR See RUDD, INSPECTOR.

FINDERS WEEPERS (1983) Probably the most satisfying of the novels by Max BYRD about private eye Mike HALLER, because in it Haller loses his license and is placed in a more vulnerable and weaker role. Haller is set up by a vindictive cop while working on a case for Leo Matz, an elderly private detective who tracks down missing heirs. Someone does not want Haller to find Muriel Contreras, a prostitute and drug addict who has been left nearly a million dollars by an Armenian farmer and rug dealer for no apparent reason. Haller continues his search for Muriel, hoping also to get his license back. The story is tighter and more compelling than other books in the series: Haller has to depend upon the kindness of others, including friends among the criminal population.

FINDING MAUBEE (1971) The first and last mystery novel of A. H. Z. CARR; it won the author an EDGAR, which had to be awarded posthumously. The novel is PROCEDURAL and takes place on the Caribbean island of St. Caro. The tropical setting is more than just local color; Carr describes the culture and customs of the island, which have everything to do with the murder. A tourist named Carl Lattner is found hacked to death with a machete. At the scene of the crime a notebook is found. It belongs to legendary outlaw Dave Maubee and chronicles his sexual exploits. This practice is common to the island's men, who desire to distinguish between children fathered with their legal mates, illegitimate children they know they have fathered, and possible "bushbabies," an unfortunate class who, not knowing their fathers, are outcasts in society. Detective Xavier Brooke uses the notebook to track down Maubee's various women. Brooke happens to be an old friend of Maubee, and while the powerful of the island have decided on his guilt, the policeman is not convinced. As usual in the mystery novel, things are not exactly what they seem. In this case the complications are particularly interesting because they are political, racial, and cultural. A solitary, remarkable achievement, the book has a high reputation among mystery readers and critics.

FINDLEY, TIMOTHY (1930–) The respected Canadian novelist and playwright Timothy Findley won an EDGAR award for his novel THE TELLING OF LIES (1986). Findley began his career as an actor, and has gained respect as a novelist for such books as *The Last of the Crazy People* (1967) and *The Wars* (1977), a novel about World War II that won the prestigious Governor General's award. Findley's autobiography is *Inside Memory* (1990).

FINGERPRINTING The science of fingerprinting, known as dactylography, is over one hundred years old, but it was first used in a trial in 1905. Edward Henry (b. 1850) had pioneered the technique in India after he became inspector-general of police in Bengal in 1891. Fingerprinting was already in use, however, in Argentina, and the United States was also ahead of Britain in dactylography—in fiction as well as reality, for the first introduction of the technique in a story is credited to Mark TWAIN. The classic scientific work that put fingerprinting on the map as a crime-fighting technique was Sir Francis Galton's *Fingerprints* (1892; repr 1965).

Fingerprints were much abused as clues in fiction during the Edwardian period and the GOLDEN AGE, when they were produced in the most unlikely of circumstances from the most difficult of surfaces. For example, Arsène LUPIN gets a whole set from a much manhandled bloody cloth. Science, in the detective story, became a way of cheating, allowing the author to wriggle out of corners.

Today, owing to reader skepticism, an opposite kind of cheating takes place: the reader is told that fingerprints are rarely found, professional thieves are careful not to leave them, and textured pistol grips do not yield prints—thus opening the door for displays of miraculous deduction and more ingenious techniques. On the other hand, the potential for abuse of the *deus ex machina* is greater than ever: with the advent of computer modeling and databases, a print can now be sent off to the FBI or CIA in chapter III and, after days of off-stage number crunching, returned to the detective in chapter IX, just when the RED HERRINGS have begun to stink. For the true technophile, there are now far more gadgety and spooky scientific techniques, including DNA MATCHING.

FINISHERS Mystery authors, like other authors, often die with work left incomplete. Unlike other authors, they often have their works posthumously completed by other writers—whether for the venal reason that new works by dead authors can be lucrative (particularly in the case of a series character), or because everyone hates an unfinished mystery. In addition to the finishers who complete the works of others, there are continuers. Some of the characters who have been reprised by latecomers are RAFFLES, Nero WOLFE, and Philip MARLOWE. Rex STOUT said of writers who appropriate someone else's characters that he didn't know whether to call them "cannibals" or "vampires." This did not dissuade Robert Goldsborough (or the Stout estate, which gave him permission) from producing several Nero Wolfe novels in the 1980s.

Robert B. PARKER completed Raymond CHANDLER's unfinished novel, *Poodle Springs* (1989), for which he reportedly received one million dollars. Parker went on to write a "sequel" to THE BIG SLEEP (1939), entitled *Perchance to Dream* (1991).

Raymond Chandler's Philip Marlowe: A Centennial Celebration (1988) contains twenty-three "new" Marlowe stories by such authors as Loren ESTLEMAN, Sara PARETSKY, Stuart KAMINSKY, and Ed GORMAN. Most of the stories are dreadful, but Paco TAIBO's "The Deepest South" comes closest to pulling off this act of ventriloquism.

Lawrence BLOCK finished Cornell WOOLRICH's last novel, INTO THE NIGHT (1987).

The last Inspector Napoleon BONAPARTE mystery, *The Lake Frome Monster* (1966), was finished by J. L. Price and Dorothy Strange.

Margery ALLINGHAM's husband, who had helped her in writing her books, finished her last, *Cargo of Eagles* (1968), and then wrote two more featuring Albert CAMPION.

Henry Kitchell WEBSTER's *The Alleged Great-Aunt* (1935) was finished by two of his friends.

Robert L. FISH completed Jack London's novel THE ASSASSINATION BUREAU, LTD. (1963).

Ed MCBAIN finished Craig RICE's novel *The April Robin Murders* (1959).

Most recently, Jill Paton Walsh, using an outline left by Dorothy L. SAYERS, wrote a new Lord Peter WIMSEY mystery: *Thrones, Dominations* (1998). Set in 1936, the first hundred pages of the novel describe the changed conditions of the Wimsey household in detail. Harriet Vane, now Lady Wimsey, is adjusting to her new identity and wondering if she can continue to write murder novels. Lord Peter, meanwhile, is called away by the Foreign Office for political reasons (the abdication of Lord St. George and the rise of Hitler). Walsh also manages to marry off BUNTER. The author injects contemporary themes—the contrast of the wholesome and supportive marriage of the Wimseys and that of the victim, the vacuous and insipid redhead Rosamund Harwell—and is more explicit about sex than one would have expected Sayers to be.

The book that has attracted the most attempts at finishing is Charles DICKENS's last novel, THE MYSTERY OF EDWIN DROOD (1870). Dozens of writers have tried to resolve the mystery, which is left very open-ended because the book was only half completed at the time of the author's death.

FINNEY, MARY A doctor and amateur sleuth in a series of mysteries by Matthew HEAD. See also MURDER AT THE FLEA CLUB (1955).

FISCHER, BRUNO (1908–1992) One of the second- or third-tier writers who appeared in the PULP MAGAZINES of the thirties and forties, Bruno Fischer has yet to be rediscovered and reprinted, unlike some of his peers (Harold BROWNE, Norbert DAVIS, and others). Fischer was born in Berlin, Germany, and emigrated to the United States at the age of five, settling in New York City. After graduating from the Rand School of Social Sciences, he was a reporter in Long Island City and edited *Labour Voice* and the *Socialist Call.* His first published stories were not detective fiction but horror; he used the pseudonym Russell Gray. His first story was "The Cat Woman" (1936), for which he received sixty dollars. According to a *Writers' Digest* article of 1945, Fischer wrote two million words of horror stories between 1937 and 1941 and sold all of them. In this period he also began writing detective fiction. "Burn, Lovely Lady" was published in *Dime Mystery* in 1938. He created only one series detective, Ben HELM, who appeared in a few books in the forties and early fifties. Fischer also wrote many non-series novels, and a total of more than two dozen novels in all. He continued to write for pulp magazines for as long as they lasted.

Only a few of Fischer's short stories have been anthologized, but they show a degree of originality above standard pulp fare. "Five O'Clock Menace," which appeared in *Black Mask* in 1949, humorously makes use of two crime fiction archetypes: the romantic opportunities of the traveling salesman, and the murderous opportunity of the barber shaving a man in his chair with a straight razor. "The Wind Blows Death" is set in Florida. A group of people find themselves trapped in a roadhouse during a hurricane; one of them is Glenn Markham, a private detective from New York City. All of them are hoping to collect some stolen money, whether they have to kill the others or not.

In 1974, Fischer published his last novel, which he also considered his best: *The Evil Days.*

FISH, ROBERT L[LOYD] (1912–1981) Robert L. Fish was born in Cleveland and educated in the United States, though he lived in Brazil for many years, where he worked as an engineer. It was not until 1960, when he was forty-seven, that he published his first mystery, but he went on to make a mark in several subgenres. His first published story was a PARODY of Sherlock HOLMES and was published in *Ellery Queen's Mystery Magazine;* a long series of stories followed, which were collected in *The Incredible Schlock Homes* (1966) and *The Memoirs of Schlock Homes* (1974). Fish's sense of humor was also reflected in the piscatory pseudonyms he adopted for some of his mystery series: Robert L. Pike and A. C. Lamprey. One of Fish's early assignments was finishing the last novel by Jack London, THE ASSASSINATION BUREAU, LTD. (pub 1963).

In the early sixties, Fish began writing several different mystery and crime series at the same time. In 1962, he published *The Fugitive,* which introduced Captain José DA SILVA, a Rio de Janeiro police captain. This novel won Fish his first EDGAR award. Another series, about a New York City detective named CLANCY, was begun with *Mute Witness* (1963). This novel was filmed under the title *Bullitt* (1968), with Steve McQueen in the title role. The movie, which moved the setting of the novel from New York to San Francisco, was an enormous success. Although he started writing relatively late, it seemed that everything Fish did was destined to succeed. On the strength of *Bullitt,* he recycled Clancy in a series about a San Francisco cop named Jim Reardon who was essentially identical; he appeared in *Reardon* (1970), *The Gremlin's Grandpa* (1972), *Bank Job* (1974), and *Deadline 2 A.M.* (1976). Quite different from anything else he had done was Fish's series about the smuggler Kek HUUYGENS; the first book was *The Hochmann Miniatures* (1967). This novel employed a revenge theme about NAZIS living undercover, a subject Fish had also used in the first Da Silva novel. Fish's writing is on a similar level to that of John CREASEY, though Fish was not as productive. The Huuygens series was weaker than the books about Da Silva, which represent Fish's best work.

In 1971, Fish won a second Edgar award, this time for a short story, "Moonlight Gardener," published in *Argosy.* He was president of the MYSTERY WRITERS OF AMERICA in 1978; one of its awards is named for him.

FISHER, HORNE See CHESTERTON, G. K.

FISHER, STEVE (pen name of Stephen Gould Fisher, 1912–1980) The American writer Steve Fisher is best known for his work in and about Hollywood. Fisher published stories in PULP MAGAZINES and in *Ellery Queen's Mystery Magazine,* and wrote the screenplays for a number of films, including an adaptation of Raymond CHANDLER's *The Lady in the Lake* (1943; film 1947). *I Wake Up Screaming* (1941; rev 1960, repr 1991) is a Fisher novel that was made into a film in the same year as its publication. It is a grim story about an aspiring scriptwriter who becomes involved in a triangle involving a young would-be starlet and her sister, a singer. Fisher uses the names of real people in the book, giving his portrayal of Hollywood corruption an added feeling of reality.

Born in California, Fisher served in the Navy and later moved to New York City, where he became a friend of Frank GRUBER. As Stephen Gould, he published *Murder of the Admiral* (1936), *Murder of the Pigboat Skipper* (1937), and *Homicide Johnny* (1940).

FITZGERALD, F[RANCIS] SCOTT [KEY] (1896–1940) The author known for his portrayal of the glitter, cynicism, and decadence of the Jazz Age (a term he coined), was a young fan of Sherlock HOLMES; his very first story, written in 1908, was a Sherlock Holmes pastiche. The story has not survived, but Fitgerald's second effort, in the following year, was printed in his boys' school journal and is included in *The Fantasy and Mystery Stories of F. Scott Fitzgerald* (1991). Although this story had an original sleuth, the very Holmesian title, "The Mystery of the Raymond Mortgage," betrays its origins.

Born in St. Paul, Minnesota, Fitzgerald attended Princeton but did not graduate. He left school in 1917 to enlist and served as a first lieutenant. After World War I he worked as a copy writer in New York, but returned to St. Paul to finish his first book, *This Side of Paradise* (1920). Influenced by POE, Fitzgerald continued to write stories of mystery, suspense, and horror alongside his better-known work. Fitzgerald's fascination with crime and mystery fiction spilled over into his most famous novel. Fitzgerald was a friend of HEMINGWAY, who frequently depicted the lives of people several echelons below Fitzgerald's American aristocrats. Ultimately, Fitzgerald's view won out, in fiction if not in history; the Jazz Age is now remembered more for its flappers and wealthy decadents than for social misery. The two aspects, however, came together violently and memorably in THE GREAT GATSBY (1925).

FIVE RED HERRINGS, THE (1931) A novel by Dorothy L. SAYERS. During Lord Peter WIMSEY's stay in the Scottish Highlands among a community of artists, one of the painters, Mr. Campbell, is found dead at the base of a cliff, apparently having stepped back from his painting into oblivion. Wimsey is the only one who thinks that a murder has occurred; he announces that "something is missing" from the scene and asks the police to look for it—leaving the reader to guess what it is (which to some would be an offense against FAIR PLAY). Six people—all painters themselves—hated the rude artist Campbell and had a reason to kill him; one is the killer, and the other five, of course, are the RED HERRINGS. All six, however, are mysteriously not on the scene at the time of the murder. Lord Peter has to track them down, but their alibis seem ironclad. Wimsey is particularly witty and his mannerisms have been toned down. There is also real ratiocination involved in his investigation, including timetables and the matter of a stolen bicycle. The artistic element also figures importantly in the plot, and the painters are not mere caricatures.

FLAGG, CONAN A bookstore owner and private investigator in a series of mysteries by M. K. WREN. Flagg is half Nez Percé Indian and lives in the town of Holliday Beach, Oregon, where he runs the Holliday Beach Book Shop and Rental Library. Flagg is six feet tall with black hair and eyes; he is also a former operative of military intelligence, from which he has been retired for ten years at the start of the series. Flagg's attachment to Meg, his cat, adds a cutesy touch.

In this ethnic/regional/bibliophile/COZY series, one has the impression of a large shopping list of elements jumbled together. Variety cannot make up for the lack of subtlety, and the writing is not strong enough to make the combination work. In *Dead Matter* (1993), a famous author is murdered the day after he has an altercation with a jealous husband in Flagg's shop (the husband makes a mess of the shop with a chainsaw). The sensational autobiographical novel the author had been working on is missing. Written twenty years earlier, the first Flagg novel, *Curiosity Didn't Kill the Cat* (1973), was a less slapstick affair. The detective is called upon by an attractive older woman to discover who murdered her husband, a retired Navy captain who drowned on the beach near Flagg's shop during a gale. The widow reveals to Flagg that her husband, despite thirty years on ships, always remained afraid of the sea, and would not have walked on a storm-beaten shore for anything. Bookish interest is added by the appearance of a special edition of DOSTOEVSKY's *Crime and Punishment* (1866). Suspicious Russian trawlers, espionage, and former associates of Flagg's are also thrown in.

BIBLIOGRAPHY Novels: *A Multitude of Sins* (1975), *Oh Bury Me Not* (1977), *Nothing's Certain But Death* (1978), *Seasons of Death* (1981), *Wake Up Darlin' Corey* (1984), *King of the Mountain* (1995).

FLAMBEAU, HERCULE A thief who may have inspired the name of Hercule POIROT, Flambeau appears in the earliest tales of Father BROWN, including THE QUEER FEET and THE INVISIBLE MAN. A high-spirited Gascon who steals but rarely does physical harm, Flambeau is huge—he is able to run down the street with a policeman under each arm.

FLAME, THE "The Flame" is the girlfriend of Race WILLIAMS in the stories of Carroll John DALY. She has been dismissed as a ludicrous parody of a woman, typical of the smoldering sexpot of the HARD-BOILED era.

FLATFOOT This term came into use around the turn of the century, and was applied to the policeman who walked a beat—and, supposedly, got flat feet. But it has also been applied to soldiers and sailors.

FLEMING, IAN (1908–1964) The creator of James BOND, the most famous fictional spy in history, was born in London into a military family. Fleming's father was a conservative member of Parliament. The class values embodied in the Bond books reflect this background, and are closer to BUCHAN than to the "revisionist" spy writers who followed in the footsteps of MAUGHAM and AMBLER.

After his education at Eton and the military academy of Sandhurst, Fleming studied abroad, at Munich and Geneva. He became the Reuter's correspondent in Moscow, and then returned to England to be a stockbroker. Fleming's familiarity with espionage came from his involvement with British intelligence in World War II. He went to Moscow in 1939 as a reporter again but also was involved in intelligence gathering. During the war, he was an assistant to the Director of Naval Intelligence. Fleming himself typified the gentleman spy of pre–Cold War Britain, before the business got ugly—or rather before one was allowed to acknowledge the ugliness as DEIGHTON and LECARRÉ did. Fleming passed on to Bond his own sophistication and tall, dashing appearance. He made him an appreciator of the finer things at a time when few of the finer things were to be had in Britain during the rationing period after the war.

Fleming's idea of writing a spy thriller began to germinate during World War II, but he did not publish the first Bond book until 1953 (*Casino Royale*). The popularity of the Bond series built steadily until, with the films, it became a craze; Bond-wear, Bond-memorabilia, and other Bond spin-offs made the author a millionaire. Fleming wrote fourteen Bond books, and died before the film series had reached its peak of success. He had taken up writing to make money, and he succeeded. Fleming did not take the books very seriously, though leading intellectuals such as Kingsley AMIS did. They have been criticized as misogynistic and racist, though they are not in the same league with SAPPER or HORLER. The Bond books are pure entertainment and pure fantasy, pitting one man against evil (and always foreign) forces and coming out on top in death-defying, improbable encounters—but with enough time out to sample the most gorgeous women and the best booze. The biggest fiction of the Bond books, and the one that makes them so different from the "serious" novels of some of his contemporary spy writers, is that the Cold War was being fought from the East by people who were basically insane, like BLOFELD and Goldfinger, and not by good soldiers like James Bond, the comfortable organization man. This fact alone should demonstrate the spirit of unrealism in which the books were written; Fleming certainly knew enough about spying and politics to write a sobering LeCarré-type novel, had he the talent and inclination to do so. Instead, the plots that Bond is called upon to foil are usually suicidal, impossible, or moronic; the real politics of the era become invisible, replaced with the diabolism of OPPENHEIM.

Fleming wrote other books beside the Bond series, including *Chitty-Chitty-Bang-Bang* (1964), a delightful fantasy for children. *Thrilling Cities* (1963) is a personal memoir of his travels.

FLETCHER, JOHNNY See GRUBER, FRANK.

FLETCHER, J[OSEPH] S[MITH] (1863–1935) An English novelist whose fame derives primarily from an American President. Woodrow Wilson praised Fletcher's *The Middle Temple Murder* (1918), which insured its popularity. Fletcher was extremely prolific in the twenties but, sadly, wrote few books worth remembering.

Fletcher began his writing career with a series of romances and historical works; he became a fellow of the Royal Historical Society. In *The Middle Temple Murder*, Frank Spargo, a newspaperman, discovers a body of an elderly man beaten to death. The search for his identity leads to a variety of adventures. *The Charing Cross Mystery* (1923) of only a few years later uses a similar setup: a man (the barrister Hetherwick) stumbles upon a corpse, but here the coincidences are not redeemed as in the earlier book.

Fletcher's other notable work in the genre was *Paul Campenhaye, Specialist in Criminology* (1918). Campenhaye is a private investigator in the scientific mold. Julian SYMONS placed Fletcher among the "Humdrum" school.

FLIMFLAM The origin of this word is unknown, though Rawson (see SLANG) suggests Old Norse *film*, meaning "mockery or lampoon." The word refers to the particular con or trick that a crook uses to dupe his victims, or, in circus terminology, the "gaff."

FLITCRAFT See MALTESE FALCON, THE.

FLOATING ADMIRAL, THE (1931) A novel written collaboratively by members of the DETECTION CLUB. The authors include CHESTERTON, CHRISTIE, CROFTS, and SAYERS. In addition to her contribution, Sayers provides an introduction illuminating the procedure of the writing and offering general remarks about mysteries. The book was written sequentially, with each author taking up where the others left off, trying to tie up their loose ends while delivering a sockdologer at the close of the chapter. The author was bound to deal with the problems raised in the preceding chapters and to write with a definite solution in mind—in fact, they had to include a solution with their work. The solutions are printed as an appendix and can be read in correspondence with the chapters without ruining the mystery, since the reader knows no more than, say, John RHODE did when he created a solution after writing chapter V. Some of the solutions, Christie's particularly, are outlandish and weird. Cracks start to appear in the book's unity of style with Sayers's contribution, but the solutions become hysterically funny.

Inspector Rudge is called in to investigate the murder of retired Admiral Penistone, who is found floating on the river Whyn in the boat of his neighbor, the Vicar. Rudge is assisted by local constables and by the colorful Neddy

Ware, a retired seaman. The calculation of tides and times becomes very important, as does a murky story about earlier scandalous behavior in the opium dens of Hong Kong. Perhaps because he is a composite, Rudge is mostly free of mannerisms and quirks, a plain inspector of the ALLEYN style. He is exasperated that the victim's niece, her fiancé, and then the victim's best friend all run off after the investigation begins.

FLOYD, PRETTY BOY See PROHIBITION.

"FOOTPRINTS IN THE JUNGLE" (1933) A short story by W. Somerset MAUGHAM. Set in Malaya, it begins with the description of a bridge game that the narrator and the policeman, Gaze, play against an "almost elderly" couple named Cartwright (who beat them soundly). The Cartwrights are a striking pair, but the reader could be forgiven for thinking the account of a subdued entertainment in a colonial club a little pointless; only in the sequel is the force of this scene brought home. It is, in fact, a setup, for when the narrator and the policeman are alone, Gaze tells about the murder twenty years before of Mrs. Cartwright's first husband, Bronson, on a rubber plantation. Returning home with the payroll, Bronson takes a shortcut through the jungle and never arrives for another game of bridge, which is in progress; thus, Maugham inserts his characteristic balances and ironies. When the narrator remarks, "I have always thought the detective story a most diverting and ingenious variety of fiction, and have regretted that I never had the skill to write one," one detects the author having a bit of fun with the reader. The story even has a couple of well-planted clues, one of them having to do with footprints. The ending is obvious long before the end but is "somewhat of a shock," and Gaze's view on crime and human nature is provocative—"it's not what people do that really matters, it's what they are." This anti-existentialism opens up all kinds of disturbing possibilities and gives Maugham's tale an enigmatic twist.

FOOTSTEPS AT THE LOCK, THE (1928; repr 1983) A novel by Monsignor Ronald KNOX. Although not exactly farcical, Knox's stories had something of the madcap feel of the Gervase FEN novels, though Knox wrote in a less modern style—a sort of Victorian hand-me-down. The story is set in Oxford, and Knox made full use of the standard jokes about aesthetes, academics, and debt-ridden aristocrats. Miles BREDON is called in by the Indescribable Insurance Company when a young man mysteriously drowns during a canoe trip. The dour Derek Burtrell had stood to inherit £50,000 on his twenty-fifth birthday, but his excessive drinking made it unlikely—in addition, the money was already exceeded by his debts. If he died at twenty-four, the money would go to Derek's cousin Nigel, and Derek's creditors would get nothing, and so the creditors convinced him to take out an insurance policy (issued by the Indescribable). A doctor recommends a canoe trip on the upper Thames to improve Derek's health, and who should he take with him but cousin Nigel, a self-conscious aesthete, decadent, and snob who loathes Derek, the "hippopotamus." At Shipcote Lock, Nigel abandons the canoe and Derek to go take an exam; not long after, the canoe is found swamped with a splintered hole in the bottom and Derek is missing. Nigel has a perfect alibi.

Among the clues available to Bredon is a roll of film he finds in a tobacco pouch. One print shows wet footsteps on a bridge near the lock; another, what appears to be Derek's body floating in the canoe. Who took the pictures and why turns out to be a key question—never mind the unlikelihood that they should be taken at all, because in Knox's world, all details are worked into an intricate pattern, whether they be probable or not. Bredon and his wife Angela, with their constant repartee, are as earnest in their silliness as characters in a BBC comedy.

FORBES, [DELORIS] STANTON (1923–) A prolific novelist, both by herself and in collaboration, Stanton Forbes is best known for her series about Boston policeman Knute SEVERSON, published under the pseudonym Tobias Wells. Deloris Stanton was born in Kansas City, Missouri, and grew up in Wichita, Kansas. She studied at the University of Chicago and later went into journalism; she worked for newspapers in Oklahoma and Louisiana before moving to Wellesley, Massachusetts, where she was on the staff of the *Townsman*. Under the pseudonym Dee Forbes she published her first mystery short stories; with Helen Rydell, she wrote four mysteries as Forbes Rydell, beginning with *Annalisa* (1959). It was not until 1963 that she published her first mystery written entirely by herself, *Grieve for the Past*. It was an auspicious beginning, earning her a runner-up prize for the EDGAR.

Forbes wrote twenty non-series mysteries in the sixties and seventies. At the same time, she wrote her series about Severson. The first novel was *A Matter of Love and Death* (1966). Forbes retired from the newspaper business in the early seventies but continues to publish novels sporadically.

FORD, LESLIE (pseudonym of Zenith Jones Brown, 1898–1983) Now known as Leslie Ford, Zenith Jones Brown began her writing career during a stay in England; as David Frome, she published several novels beginning with *The Murder of an Old Man* (1929). She wrote two more mysteries under this name (one of them deals with GOLF) before starting her series about Evan Pinkerton. Pinkerton is a quirky character, a small Welshman who has inherited a fortune from a shrewish wife; the liberated widower now enjoys himself by going to the movies. He solves crimes with his friend, Inspector Bull, in such books as *The Hammersmith Murders* (1930) and the intriguingly titled *The Eel Pie Mystery* (1933; U.S. title *The Eel Pie Murders*). Pinkerton lives in London on his fortune of 50,000 pounds, which his wife had accumulated by taking in lodgers. He is so henpecked that even years after her death he is afraid to spend the money for fear of being chastised. Pinkerton's querulous personality is made fun of again and again, but he is not terribly funny or original.

Brown returned to the United States in 1931 and settled in Annapolis, Maryland, where her husband was an English professor. In the same year, she first used the Leslie Ford pseudonym. Her series of mysteries about Grace LATHAM and Colonel Primrose, begun in 1937, was published under this name.

Zenith Jones Brown got her unusual name from her father, who was an Episcopal minister. She was born in California but grew up in Tacoma, Washington, and graduated from the University of Washington. During World War II, she traveled extensively as a reporter, and also wrote novels dealing with nurses under the pseudonym of Brenda Conrad. She wrote many non-series mystery novels as well, including *Trial by Ambush* (1962), a more realistic work than many of her HAD-I-BUT-KNOWN efforts; it was also her last novel.

FORESTER, C[ECIL] S[COTT] (1899–1966) The British author C. S. Forester is remembered not as a crime novelist but as the author of the Hornblower saga, a dozen books that take Horatio Hornblower from his days as a midshipman and first prize command to his first "ship of the line" and finally to becoming an admiral and a peer of the realm. Set during the Napoleonic wars, the Hornblower series has pleased millions of readers. The development of the books was described in the autobiographical *Hornblower Companion* (1964).

Yet, Forester's first book was *Payment Deferred* (1926), an early example of the INVERTED MYSTERY. Set in London, it describes how a man murders his nephew for money and then, like Dostoyevsky's RASKOLNIKOV, begins to repent of what he has done. The novel was successful and later became a play and a film, both starring Charles Laughton. Forester wrote a second book, *Plain Murder* (1930), which resembled *Payment Deferred* and was also "inverted." These two books give Forester a significant place in the development of the crime novel.

Forester was born in Cairo and traveled extensively in Europe before the family returned to London, where (like Raymond CHANDLER) he attended the Dulwich school. He then trained at a hospital, but gave up medicine in order to write. Forester went to Hollywood after he became a successful writer and died in California. Many of his books were filmed, including the suspense and adventure novel *The African Queen* (1935; film 1951).

FORRESTER, ANDREW, JR. (***) Little is known about the British author who called himself Andrew Forrester, Jr. His name may have been a pseudonym, but his real identity has never been discovered; the place where he was born and where he died remain unknown. What is certain, however, is that he left a mark on the detective genre. He was the first writer to publish a collection of stories about a female police detective, MRS. G–. E. F. Bleiler wrote that Forrester "enlarged the scope of the British detective story with new themes, creating plotted stories as opposed to narrated reminiscences."

Forrester was strongly influenced by POE. In "Arrested on Suspicion" (1863) the narrator says that he intends to tell the story in the manner of Poe, as a "series of facts, inferences, and results"—thus, he helped define the classic form of the detective story, without psychology, melodrama, subplots, romance, or other distractions. Yet, Forrester's writing is very taking, and his characters convincingly human. The narrator of "Arrested on Suspicion" is a man whose sister has been taken in for shoplifting. Among the elements of later fiction that are included are the person cleverly framed for a crime and the re-enactment of a suspect's movements. Of particular interest is the discussion of ciphers and the description of the narrator's method of decoding. Ciphers also were involved in "The Forger's Escape," in which a police detective consults an amateur sleuth, a friend whose hobby is decoding messages in newspaper advertisements.

Forrester's stories were collected in three volumes: *Secret Service, or Recollections of a City Detective* (1863), *The Revelations of a Private Detective* (1863), and *The Female Detective* (1864). The latter contained the cases about Mrs. G–; one of them, "A Child Found Dead, Murder or No Murder," was modeled on a real-life mystery, the case of Constance KENT. Another, "The Unravelled Mystery," showed Forrester's debt to Poe and THE MYSTERY OF MARIE RÔGET (1842) in particular. Another work from *The Female Detective*, THE UNKNOWN WEAPON, was reprinted in the volume *Three Victorian Detective Novels* (1978).

FORSYTH, FREDERICK (1938–) The English journalist Frederick Forsyth turned to writing THRILLERS with *The Day of the Jackal* (1971) and won an EDGAR award on his first try. The novel, about a mysterious assassin who tries to kill French president Charles de Gaulle, was made into a successful film. Forsyth's novels are meticulously researched and cultivate a less sensational tone than many other thrillers. All have been commercially successful, though the only one that compares with *The Day of the Jackal* is *The Odessa File* (1972), about a secret organization of NAZIS in hiding. Forsyth won a second Edgar for a short story, THERE ARE NO SNAKES IN IRELAND (1982). His short fiction is collected in *No Comebacks* (1982).

Forsyth worked for the *Eastern Daily Press* in England, as well as Reuters and the BBC. His experience as a foreign correspondent has provided background for several novels, such as *The Dogs of War* (1974), about mercenaries in Africa.

FORTUNE, MR. REGGIE Pre-dating H. C. BAILEY's other series character, Joshua CLUNK, Mr. Fortune is a kinder, more sympathetic fat man, pink and cherubic rather than yellow and grub-like. Fortune is a doctor, though he is called "Mister." He acts as a consultant to Scotland Yard, dealing with the team of Stanley Lomas (head of CID) and Superintendent Bell. Lomas thinks Fortune is a very high flier, pursuing vague notions instead of facts. But that is his genius, of course; as one detective says of Reggie, "He feels life. We think about it." Some people find him tiresome, because Mr. Fortune is fond of absurd expostulations like "My only aunt!", and his accent and affected manner show a debt to other GOLDEN AGE detectives such as Albert CAMPION and Lord Peter WIMSEY. He sees himself as a champion of the defenseless, however, particularly children.

Mr. Fortune doesn't talk: he murmurs. He makes cryptic remarks (often dropping his articles and verbs) and occasional barbs at the police ("You're clumsy, but you move—sometimes—like the early cars"). Fortune has a wife, a Rolls Royce, and a love of fine food, and amuses himself in his spare time with his marionettes. Mr. Fortune first appeared in the short story collection *Call Mr. Fortune* (1920). There are a dozen volumes of short stories altogether, plus a few novels. The stories, particularly the early ones, are superior to the novels. See THE LONG DINNER.

Fortune's wife complains that it is hard living with "a small boy," but her husband's childlike qualities can be entertaining. It is not only his playing with toys that makes him seem boyish; Fortune has blond hair and a youthful, round, beardless face. In addition to the puppets, he enjoys his laboratory and his garden. Fortune believes in the "ultimate decency of people," though the atmosphere stops short of being COZY, and sometimes he must punish in his own way those beyond the reach of the law. His concept of decency includes a paternalistic attitude toward the lower classes and their stolid, plodding mentality, which he attributes to goodness rather than their being cemented into their roles and "knowing their place."

BIBLIOGRAPHY Novels: *The Shadow on the Wall* (1934), *Black Land, White Land* (1937), *The Great Game* (1939), *The Bishop's Crime* (1940), *No Murder* (1942; U.S. title *The Apprehensive Dog*), *Mr. Fortune Finds a Pig* (1943), *Dead Man's Effects* (1944; U.S. title *The Cat's Whisker*), *The Wrong Man* (1945), *The Life Sentence* (1946), *Saving a Rope* (1948; U.S. title *Save a Rope*).

Short Stories: *Mr. Fortune's Practice* (1923), *Mr. Fortune's Trials* (1925), *Mr. Fortune, Please* (1927), *Mr. Fortune Speaking* (1929), *Mr. Fortune Explains* (1930), *Case for Mr. Fortune* (1932), *Mr. Fortune Wonders* (1933), *Mr. Fortune Objects* (1935), *A Clue for Mr. Fortune* (1936), *Mr. Fortune Here* (1940).

FORTY-FIVE (.45) One of the best-known firearms ever invented, the Colt .45 semiautomatic pistol was the service pistol of the United States armed forces from 1911, the year of its patenting, until the late twentieth century, when it was replaced by an Italian Beretta 9mm pistol. Although once considered the premier combat handgun for its reliability and tremendous stopping power, it is relatively heavy (39 ounces) and difficult to conceal, and those characters in crime fiction who carry it are sometimes made fun of as shaky types who want to appear tough.

FOSCO, COUNT The villain of Wilkie Collins's THE WOMAN IN WHITE (1860), and one of the author's most famous characters, Fosco both followed and broke fictional conventions, and also established new ones. Like other bad men of English fiction (or bad women, for that matter; consider Madame de la ROUGIERRE), he is a devious foreigner. He is also charming, aristocratic, and cultured. But Collins also made Fosco grossly obese, in deliberate contrast with the "jolly fat man" then popular in fiction. Count Fosco created a new fashion for fat villains.

FOUR OF HEARTS, THE (1938) A novel by Ellery QUEEN, one of those written during the author's stay in Hollywood. Almost tongue-in-cheek, the story packs enough plot devices to satisfy any producer: a twenty-year-old feud, an eccentric millionaire living in a mansion in the mountains only reachable by air, gambling, two dead screen stars and two live ones, an agoraphobic gossip columnist who never leaves her house, pilots bailing out on their passengers (whether living or dead), and romantic trimmings. The focus is more on the writing than the plot, so the book is at once more entertaining and thinner than previous Queen stories. The novel revolves around two pairs of movie stars: Jack Royle and his son Tyler, and Blythe Stuart and her daughter Bonnie. The parents plan to marry (following a romance dating to before World War I), much to the disgust of the children, who appear to loathe each other.

FOUR SQUARE JANE A thief in a series of stories by Edgar WALLACE. Able to dress herself up as an innocent-looking girl, Jane gains access to the homes of the rich in order to rob them—but she has Robin Hood as much as robbery in mind. Jane donates the proceeds of her robberies to London hospitals and charitable organizations, or blackmails her victims into doing so. Her name comes from a peculiar little symbol with black corners that she leaves behind for the police as a signature on her crimes. Her adventures were collected in *Four Square Jane* (1928).

14 PECK SLIP (1994) The first novel by Ed DEE, a former New York City cop. The story is set in that city in the early eighties, when New York was at an ebb—economically depressed, corrupt, and divided. Dee's series detectives, Joe Gregory and Anthony Ryan, witness three men dumping a barrel in the East River near the Fulton Fish Market, which is under mob control. Believing that they have seen the aftermath of a mob hit, they investigate, thereby opening a much larger can of worms relating to the disappearance of the dirtiest of all corrupt cops, Jinx Mulgrew, ten years before. Mulgrew is thought to have fled to Ireland before he could be forced to "name names" to a grand jury. Gregory and Ryan come up against stiff resistance from the mob, and even greater resentment from their fellow officers; soon, everyone is treating Ryan and Gregory as if they were the bad guys. It turns out that no one liked Mulgrew, who was a "bastard," but no one wants to be brought down by his ghost, either. The book is particularly good in its evocation of nastiness—the surly attitudes of the older cops, the crude ostentation of mobsters, and the sordid atmosphere of a city suffocating under its own putrid lies and callousness. Although basically PROCEDURAL, Dee holds no brief for neatness or happy endings, giving the story a realistic edge.

FOX, TECUMSEH A detective created by Rex STOUT, and probably the first sleuth of Native American extraction to appear in fiction. Ellery QUEEN mistakenly gave that honor to Manly Wade WELLMAN's David RETURN, who appeared in the forties, but Fox premiered in 1939 in *Double for Death;* however, as nothing about Fox has anything to do with Native Americans except his name, his precedence is merely formal.

The main attraction of Fox is that he was apparently closely modeled on Stout himself. They are physically similar, live in the same town (Brewster, New York), and share interests and hobbies such as gardening. The three Fox books were written in quick succession, and then Stout never returned to Fox. The best of the books is *Bad for Business* (1940), though the author thought *Double for Death* was the best plot he ever invented, including those of the Nero WOLFE stories. The idea of *The Broken Vase* (1941) is clever (causing a violinist to commit suicide by sabotaging his New York premier), though the pace is turgid and the writing mechanical.

The character's full name, William Tecumseh Sherman Fox, is ironic: Sherman, the famous Civil War general, later fought in the Indian Wars. Tecumseh (1768?–1813) was a Shawnee chief who tried to prevent the westward expansion of colonial settlements, and fought on the side of the British in the War of 1812.

FOX, TOM (pseudonym of John Bennett, ***) Under this pseudonym, the British book publisher and writer John Bennett, about whom little is known, published *Tom Fox; or, The Revelations of a Detective* (1860). Bennett responded to the Victorian taste for fictional crime stories dressed up as actual accounts; POE had pioneered the technique, and DICKENS and WATERS also used it. The Fox stories were realistic, but it was a realism got up in the moral tones of "improving" literature; Fox's accounts of the lives of prostitutes and other street people of Victorian London may have been shocking at the time, but the moral of the story was heavily underscored, and the writing was a curious mixture of hard boiledness and Victorian morality play. One could say that Fox's writing had the outlines but lacked the spontaneity of life. Obviously influenced by naturalistic European fiction, his descriptions of characters, habits, and customs—like the pamphleteer in the shadow of the gallows selling "confessions" of the one about to be hanged—are forceful when looked at on their own.

Fox continued in this vein, developing into a writer of popular literature focused on lower-class life. He wrote a number of novels that, like RAILWAY NOVELS, were the PULP fiction of their day. These included *Revelations of a Sly Parrot* (1862), *My Wife's Earnings, A Tale of the Married Women's Property Act* (1873), and *Simon Peter and Pio Nino at the Gates of Heaven* (1880).

FRACAS IN THE FOOTHILLS (1940) One of the Homer EVANS mysteries by Elliot PAUL. Had it been written seriously, it would be a laughably bad mystery novel; what makes Paul's PARODY of the genre funny is how close he comes at times to the kind of writing indulged in by some of the hopeless practitioners who have attempted to write mysteries. In *Fracas in the Foothills,* Homer Evans goes "over the top" in terms of the absurdity of his adventures; in his introduction to the book, the author says that, in response to critics who felt his previous book was too long and rambling, he has doubled the length of the novel and thrown in "practically everything."

Having returned to Paris from the Moroccan desert, Homer Evans stops by the Café du Dôme, where he meets Rain-No-More, a Berkeley-educated Blackfoot Indian on a mission to deliver a message to Miriam Leonard, Homer's girlfriend. He tells of trouble in Circle, Montana, where Miriam's father is a cattleman; the sheep rancher Larkspur Gilligan is in league with the railroad, and a range war is heating up—in proof of which, Rain-No-More produces the scalp of Donniker Louey, a Chicago buttonman hired by Gilligan. The Indian's speech varies between Tonto-like mutterings and ordinary American speech (over and over he says, "I long for meat"). Miriam decides to rush back to her father's aid, and Homer decides to go with her—as does half of Paris, apparently. On the *Ile-de-France,* Homer's entourage also includes Chief of Detectives Frémont, who has taken credit for Homer's work in the past; Hjalmar Jansen, a Norweigan-American painter; and Hydrangea, Frémont's African-American lover. The gangsters, including Gilligan's son, are also on board, making for a journey as ridiculous as that of THE MADONNA OF THE SLEEPING CARS (1925)—and the voyage is just the beginning. In transporting the characters of the Parisian series to Montana, Paul reaches the pinnacle of his preposterousness.

FRAME, REYNOLD See BREAN, HERBERT.

FRANCHISE AFFAIR, THE (1949) A novel by Josephine TEY, perhaps her best; it is so good that it is not hurt by the absence of a murder. Instead, it deals with an alleged case of kidnapping and abuse. Tey based the story on the real case of an eighteenth-century Englishwoman who was hanged for abusing her servant, Elizabeth CANNING.

Robert Blair is a solicitor in the old firm of Blair, Hayward & Bennett in Milford, a highly respectable provincial English town. Robert is a bachelor of rapidly advancing age who lives with his devoted aunt in a comfortable but constricted world. His secretary, Miss Tuff, serves tea every day precisely at ten to four; his clients and callers are carefully screened by the aging Mr. Haseltine. Blair has always been satisfied with his quiet country life but has now begun to question whether this is enough—a question he finds very disturbing.

Into this world comes Marion Sharpe, an unmarried woman who, along with her mother, has recently moved into The Franchise, a forbidding old pile outside of town. The Sharpes are accused of kidnapping and beating a young schoolgirl, Betty Kane, in order to make a household slave out of her. Robert becomes convinced that there is some truth that Betty is withholding, though the evidence against the Sharpes is not inconsiderable. In addition to representing the Sharpes, he becomes an amateur sleuth, exceeding the police in the scope and thoroughness of his investigations (he even hires a private investigator to do some of his legwork).

Along with his rush to get at the truth before the case comes up for trial, Blair becomes increasingly preoccupied with his feelings for Marion. The question of whether there is more to life, which at the beginning he had considered with barely suppressed panic, becomes increasingly urgent. Along with the fine writing, it is the emotional dimension of the story that makes it absorbing, despite its "lack" of pyrotechnics and spilled blood.

FRANCIS, DICK (Richard Stanley Francis, 1920–) Born in Wales, Francis was the son of a jockey and became a champion steeplechase jockey himself. He first ventured into print with his autobiography, *The Sport of Queens* (1957). It was published in the same year that an accident ended his racing career. Francis's first mystery novel, *Dead Cert,* appeared five years later, and was set in the horse-racing milieu. Francis served in World War II as a bomber pilot, and after his retirement was a racing correspondent for the *Sunday Express.* He has used flying and turf journalism in some of his novels. Francis's own best and worst moment as a jockey was in 1956, when, moments away from winning the Grand National, his horse collapsed under him.

Not all of Francis's novels touch on the racing scene to the same degree, nor is the detective/hero always a jockey; one of his best books, *Blood Sport* (1967), features a government secret agent who is plagued by impulses toward suicide. Many of the author's protagonists have some kind of emotional or mental problem, usually related to their private lives—like the writer in *Forfeit* (1968) whose wife is paralyzed with polio, which supposedly drives him to risky behavior. In *Blood Sport,* the search for some lost horses and a killer ranges from London to Kentucky to the far West and contains some versatile writing. This novel is also less brutally violent than many of Francis's books, such as *Odds Against* (1965), about Sid Halley, an ex-jockey who also appears in *Whip Hand* (1979), which won a Gold Dagger from the British CRIME WRITERS' ASSOCIATION. Francis won EDGAR awards for *Forfeit* and *Whip Hand*.

Francis has set some of his books in other countries, including South Africa, but however the scene or circumstances are changed, the leading characters tend to all be versions of the same type. *For Kicks* (1965) is about an Australian horse breeder involved in probing a gambling ring in England. SLAY-RIDE (1973) is set in Norway. Francis's writing is straightforward, without a lot of inessential description or pseudo-artistic dithering. Unlike other thriller authors, Francis knows what he can do and does it; his prose is not beautiful, but neither has it to be slogged through. He also creates suspense through what happens, not through heavy-handed language (the equivalent of sinister background music). In recent years, his novels have become more concerned with feeling. TO THE HILT (1996) is about the theft of art objects.

A strong competitor in Francis's genre has emerged in Bill Shoemaker (see CELEBRITY MYSTERIES). Francis had several predecessors who were not jockeys but worked horse racing into their mysteries, including Edgar WALLACE, who bet extravagantly on horse races, and Arthur MORRISON.

FRASER, LADY ANTONIA (1932–) Better known as a biographer, English author Lady Antonia Fraser turned to mystery writing relatively late. She is the daughter of Lord Longford, who also was a writer. Fraser graduated from Oxford, taking an M.A. in history. She has written biographies of Mary Queen of Scots (1969), Oliver Cromwell (1973), James I (1974), and Charles II (1979). In 1977, she launched a series about Jemima Shore, a television investigative reporter, with *Quiet as a Nun*, in which Shore investigates a death in a convent. Fraser writes very much in the classic style of the GOLDEN AGE, but seems to have taken Dorothy L. SAYERS's advice about keeping romantic subplots under control. Fraser frequently deals with aristocratic and upper-class Britons. She has not strayed much from this territory, and her plots tend to be familiar ones, suitably updated with various outré and politically correct subject matter. In *Oxford Blood* (1985), she uses the ancient device of the babies "switched at birth." Shore is drawn into an investigation of a wild, degenerate, and aristocratic circle at Oxford, centered around Saffron Ivy, heir to Lord St. Ives. The Oxford scene is replete with eccentric characters, such as Professor ("Profy") Mossbacher and his mistress, Greek scholar Eugenia Jones. *A Splash of Red* (1981) features Lord Valentine Brighton, a sort of bisexual gadfly who is also Jemima's editor. Jemima borrows her friend (and romance novelist) Chloe's mod flat in Bloomsbury to get away from it all. Kevin John Athlone, a painter and Chloe's ex-husband, beats Jemima up to find out the whereabouts of the "vacationing" Chloe, who reappears soon enough—with her throat cut. Chloe was in love with the repulsive developer Richard Lionel, as (inexplicably) were other women. Radical politics, a troublesome squatter who is bothering Lionel, something about Chloes's recent book, and paternity are all thrown into the mess, but what really gets a lot of attention is Jemima's wardrobe. *Your Royal Hostage* (1987) tries to cash in on the various fads and causes of the day, including fascination with "the royals." A spying journalist is killed at a Royal Wedding press conference. Jemima is now working for American television. The Princess is kidnapped by an animal rights group, whose leader, funnily enough (or not) is named Lamb. Half the story is told in the omniscient third person, while the rest takes place in Lamb's head. The element of detection is minimal.

Jemima Shore at the Sunny Grave and Other Stories appeared in 1991, and rescues Jemima from her usual background, providing some relief from the sameness of the series. Some of the stories take place in the West Indies and Greece.

FREELING, NICHOLAS (1927–) Nicholas Freeling is one of those crime and mystery writers who tries to enlarge the boundaries of the genre and invest his novels with social significance. He started out with a belief that murder was not just a game, but an aspect of human life with many implications, which he tried to trace. Freeling has been criticized, however, for simply overloading his narrative with his opinions, whether put in the mouth of Inspector VAN DER VALK or simply grafted to the narrative. Of all his "social-critical" works, *The Dresden Green* (1966) has been most criticized, because of its importation into the narrative of a condemnation of the Allied destruction of that city during World War II. Yet this is a non-series work (no sign of Van der Valk), and is not a mystery but a spy story. It is an experiment, combining conventional elements (including a mysterious lost gem, a favorite item and theme since THE MOONSTONE) with techniques of the *nouveau roman* such as alternate endings. In this as in other books, Freeling also focuses on character, particularly the opportunist Louis Schweitzer, who fought both with the Resistance and the Waffen SS, and who has settled down to a life of quiet mediocrity.

Born in England but long resident on the Continent, it is not surprising that Freeling was influenced by French models, particularly the novels of Georges SIMENON. He has also said that Kipling has been an important influence since childhood. Despite the supposed problems with his books, which are mainly a matter of taste (the novels are certainly well written), Freeling has won the Gold Dagger award, the EDGAR, and the Grand Prix de Littérature Policière.

Freeling worked in hotels and restaurants before he became known as a novelist. He set his first mystery in Amsterdam, where he had been living. LOVE IN AMSTERDAM (1961) introduced Inspector Piet Van der Valk, a Dutch version of MAIGRET. Freeling based the case on his own experience: he was falsely arrested in Amsterdam and charged with stealing food; he served a sentence of three weeks in jail. In the book, however, he bumps up the charge to murder, and has a man accused of killing his ex-mistress.

The dialogue in the Van der Valk books, particularly the early ones, is a sometimes odd combination of Dutch accents and mod expressions. On the one hand, the Dutch characters sound as if they are speaking a second language, but they also use contemporary idioms ("just play it real cool"). One of the most introspectively Dutch books is BECAUSE OF THE CATS (1963). The most admired book in the Van der Valk series is KING OF THE RAINY COUNTRY (1966), which won an EDGAR award.

Van der Valk's wife, Arlette, is French, and Freeling uses her to give an outsider's view (hostile) of the Netherlands. After he eliminated Van der Valk in AUPRÈS DE MA BLONDE (1972), Freeling made Arlette herself into a detective for a couple of books (*The Widow,* 1979, and *One Damn Thing After Another,* 1980; U.S. title *Arlette*). Afterward, he created a second series detective, Henri CASTANG, who is not so very different as to justify getting rid of Van der Valk, though it enabled the author to change his setting to France. It is not so much the personality of the detective that changed between the two series as the personality of the author; his style becomes progressively more cryptic, giving freer play to his digressions, as though more concerned with pursuing his thoughts than conveying them. In *The Back of the North Wind* (1983), Castang deals with a grisly series of murders involving dismemberment and cannibalism—as well as subplots involving other sordid acts and activities.

In 1994, Freeling published *Criminal Convictions: Errant Essays on Perpetrators of Literary License,* which included reflections on CONRAD, SAYERS, Stendahl, Conan DOYLE, Kipling, and others. Freeling is unrepentant for his philosophical approach to the genre, through which he tries to make the crime novel *matter.* His style is sometimes epigrammatic, as though a Montaigne were trying to break into a MAIGRET novel at each point where the action sparks a reflection. In 1996, Freeling retired Castang in A DWARF KINGDOM. Freeling's first post-Castang novel was *One More River* (1998). The story is in the form of the last work by John Charles, an expatriate English writer living quietly in France who suddenly becomes the object of assassination and kidnapping attempts. His flight from danger eventually leads him to probe below the urbane superficiality of his life and discover shocking secrets—about himself.

FREEMAN, R[ICHARD] AUSTIN (1862–1943) Richard Austin Freeman was born to a poor family in lower-class London. He later tried to suppress facts about his humble origins, and asked members of his family not to reveal the details of the family's life. He responded to requests for interviews with the statement that he was not interested in publicity. The details have become common knowledge and, in a more lenient age, are no longer very embarrassing, only tragic. Freeman's father was a tailor and an alcoholic. Richard was the youngest son and grew up to be a rather stern parent, who was referred to by his own sons as "the emperor." The privacy of his study where he wrote his books was inviolate. One of his sons committed suicide, and the other seems to have never found his place in life.

Freeman studied pharmacology and then medicine at Middlesex Hospital Medical College, and would eventually become the head surgeon in the ear and throat section. He married in 1887, and the following year he shipped out for the Gold Coast (present-day Ghana). He spent the next seven years in the colonies in West Africa, which provided material for his later works. His first book, *Travels and Life in Ashanti and Jaman* (1898), was based on his participation in a British expedition to appropriate the African kingdom of Jaman. Another effect of Freeman's African period was the permanent ruination of his health. He contracted blackwater fever (the most deadly form of malaria) and was sent home. Freeman also seems to have picked up some unpalatable eugenic theories, which occasionally obtrude into his work and which he dealt with at length in the later *Social Decay and Regeneration* (1921). His work as a medical examiner of immigrants at the Port of London also apparently encouraged these ideas.

Having missed qualifying for a pension by only a few months of African service, upon his return to England Freeman tried to establish a medical practice, but his health would not allow it. He was informally employed at

Holloway Prison, which completed his preparation for writing medical-criminological puzzles by familiarizing him with criminals. He also met J. J. Pitcairn, the medical colleague with whom he would write his first works in the mystery genre. These stories were signed "Clifford Ashdown," and concern a flamboyant character named Romney PRINGLE, somewhat similar to RAFFLES. The stories were collected and issued as *The Adventures of Romney Pringle* (1902) and *The Further Adventures of Romney Pringle* (1907). They already display the scientific bent that Freeman's work was to take, foreshadowing his great detective, Dr. THORNDYKE. *From A Surgeon's Diary* (pub 1975) contains further medical detective cases co-authored by Freeman and Pitcairn. During World War I, Freeman was an induction physician.

Dr. Thorndyke first appeared in the classic THE RED THUMB MARK (1907). From the beginning Thorndyke was a scientific marvel, but his methods are well-documented (the author even conducted experiments to see if various techniques would work). Thorndyke employed technologies that were new at the time, including radiography, in such books as *The Vanishing Man* (1911) and *The Cat's Eye* (1927). Some of the forensic methods used in his works later became standard police practice, and some of the fictional cases were actually cited in British legal textbooks. Of the eleven novels, FELO DE SE? (1929), THE MYSTERY OF 31 NEW INN (story circa 1905; novel 1913), and THE STONEWARE MONKEY (1939) are among the best.

Freeman said he got the idea for *The Mystery of 31 New Inn* while working at the Westminster Ophthalmic Hospital, where it struck him that eyeglasses could be as much an identifying trait as an actual feature of the body. This book also contains the author's most famous "scientific" solution, in which the number of hoofbeats per minute made by a horse is used to calculate the location of a house.

Thorndyke's painstaking investigations are still entertaining, especially in that they involve real detection; the main flaw of the novels is that they tend to drag on too long, and too much of the sleuth's rehearsing of theories and rounding up of facts is shared with the reader.

Mistaken or altered identities were a favorite device of Freeman's. *Mr. Pottermack's Oversight* (1930) is a perfect example of its kind; Mr. Pottermack, an expert on snails, is also hiding from a previous criminal career as one Jeffrey Brandon. His past catches up with him in the person of a gambler who wants to blackmail him, and he deals with the threat—fatally, as it turns out. We then watch as Thorndyke inexorably uncovers him.

Freeman went on writing to the end of his life. *Mr. Polton Explains* (1939) was partly written in a London bomb shelter during World War II. Thorndyke's long-time assistant, the shadowy genius Polton, finally gives a full autobiography. *The Unconscious Witness* (1942) appeared when the author was nearly eighty years old, and deals with a surprising and unlikely impersonation.

Freeman is also known for his invention of the "INVERTED MYSTERY," in which the murderer is known from the beginning; these stories work, however, because the reader is held in suspense (particularly where Dr. Thorndyke is concerned) over the methods that will be used to entrap the criminal. *The Singing Bone* (1912) is a collection of stories featuring Thorndyke, all but one of which are inverted mysteries. Among the stories in this volume are THE CASE OF OSCAR BRODSKI and "The Old Lag." The degree to which the stories entertain is directly related to the number of clues dropped by the criminal, and the ease with which they can be picked out by the reader as the culprit commits them.

Thorndyke appeared in many other short stories, some of which are among his most famous cases, such as the title story of a 1925 volume, THE PUZZLE LOCK, which is not the best Thorndyke but certainly the most anthologized. *The Dr. Thorndyke Omnibus* (1932) gathers together many short stories, including inverted ones. One of the most accessible volumes of Dr. Thorndyke tales is the reprint *The Best Doctor Thorndyke Stories* (1973). *In Search of Doctor Thorndyke* (1971), by Norman Donaldson, is a major study of Freeman and his work.

FREEMANTLE, BRIAN (1936–) Born in Southampton, England, Brian Freemantle was a globe-trotting journalist before turning his hand to the spy thriller. Because he worked as a correspondent in literally dozens of countries before retiring from journalism in the mid-seventies, Freemantle's descriptions of settings bespeak an intimate knowledge of places and are among the strengths of his books. Among the London papers for which Freemantle worked were the *Evening News*, the *Daily Mail*, and the *Daily Express;* his assignments included covering the Vietnam War. Like Len DEIGHTON and John LE CARRÉ, who had both established themselves before Freemantle began writing, he dwells on the competition among the various intelligence agencies. The British agents' distrust of their American allies is almost as great as that which they feel toward the "bad guys," the Russians.

Freemantle has written series and non-series works. Charlie MUFFIN is his contribution to the anti-romantic subgenre of espionage writing, a sad sack agent who not only does not fit into, but gets kicked out of, the intelligence community. Although competent, Muffin has the lowest self-esteem of any spy in fiction; one's curiosity as to how he is going to extricate himself from hopeless situations, and hopelessness in general, overcomes the sometimes indifferent writing. His first adventure, *Charlie Muffin* (1976), involves the defection to the West of the highest ranking officer in Soviet intelligence. Only Charlie figures out what is really going on. In his second case, however, he manages to evoke the ire of British intelligence, the KGB, and the CIA; *Clap Hands, Hear Comes Charlie* (1978) is catastrophic for Muffin. The titles of the other books in the series indicate how the author has used his extensive travel experience to advantage: *Charlie Muffin's Uncle Sam* (1980; U.S. title *Charlie Muffin U.S.A.*), *Charlie Muffin and the Russian Rose* (1985), and *Charlie Muffin San* (1987).

Freemantle's first book, however, was not in the Muffin series at all. *Goodbye to an Old Friend* (1973) was written while the author was still working as a journalist. The book was a typical Cold War novel about the defection of two Soviet scientists. Freemantle's production rapidly increased: he published three books each in the years 1984 and 1986. Freemantle has also published under the pseudonyms Jack Winchester and Jonathan Evans.

FREMLIN, CELIA (pen name of Celia Fremlin Goller, 1914–) Celia Fremlin was born in London and studied classics and philosophy at Oxford. She won an EDGAR for her first novel, *The Hours Before Dawn* (1958). She published more than a dozen other novels over the following three decades. Fremlin's novels are noted for their portrayal of everyday life or "domesticity." They are novels more of menace and suspense than of crime, and some do not have murders at all.

In *The Jealous One* (1965), a smug suburban housewife sees her husband begin to change when a lively and attractive young woman moves in next door. In a high fever, the wife dreams of killing the new neighbor, then wakes to discover the woman has disappeared.

FRENCH, INSPECTOR JOSEPH Detective created by Freeman Wills CROFTS. Although writing in the GOLDEN AGE, Crofts was aiming for realism, so his detective is not an amateur, not a master of disguises, and has no royal connections or secret past. His enthusiasms are not for lofty things like music, but simple things like food. The convivial French, despite his name, is a version of the conventional Irish character of English fiction, with a twinkle in his blue eyes, a charming and friendly manner, and a taste for drink. French's wife, Emily, occasionally helps him with his detection. Like his creator, French likes to travel, which adds to the variety of setting in the novels.

French is most often described by critics as "plodding." He stops for meals rather than following up clues (which, as anyone who has sat in a coffee shop will know, could also be viewed as a realistic PROCEDURAL element). French's nickname is "Soapy Joe" because of his clean manners. His most outstanding quality is thoroughness; he does not simply fly to the solution on the wings of genius like Sherlock HOLMES, but works his way there, via railway timetables, ship sailings, and all. (French would be lost in a society in which nobody takes public transportation—perhaps a reason for his lukewarm appeal in the United States.)

Inspector French's Greatest Case (1925) was not really his greatest, but only his first. Involving a combined jewel theft and murder, it introduced a theme that Crofts returned to often (jewelry) and is one of his better books. The body of old Mr. Gething is found in the offices of the diamond merchants Duke & Peabody. The safe is open and the diamonds are gone; the chase leads French to Holland, Barcelona, the Alps, and through various European ports. CRIME AT GUILDFORD (1935) is one of two books set in the town in which Crofts lived toward the end of his life, and *The Purple Sickle Murders* (1929; orig title *The Box Office Murders*) is about a scam operating among a group of female ticket-takers at movie theaters. Crofts also used the classic COUNTRY HOUSE setup, sometimes with interesting changes. In *The Starvel Hollow Tragedy* (1927), the country house burns down. Ruth Averill is called away from her miserly old uncle's place by an invitation from friends, and so escapes death. Three bodies, however, are found in the ashes (Averill and the sinister butler and his wife), along with the remains of thirty thousand pounds. Some of the pound notes that were supposedly destroyed, however, are circulated after the fire.

Trains, of course, were Crofts's passion and his profession. French's best cases are those involving railroads, where the author's knowledge is given room to flourish, though the accounts can be tedious. *Death of a Train* (1946) is set during July 1942, and is about the shipment of England's entire supply of vacuum tubes to the army in North Africa facing Rommel. A special train is prepared, but is suspiciously destroyed in a horrendous accident. Crofts's description of signaling, loading, dispatching, switching, and other railroad matters is meticulous, but the political and historical background remains vaguely unreal (the prime minister is not Churchill, but Severus L. Heppenstall). Inspector French is called in to discover why the train crashed. For French, the next best thing to a train is a boat, and he has several cases of MURDER AFLOAT.

Crofts was also a prolific author of short stories, particularly at the end of his life; some of the stories concern Inspector French, and can be found in the collections *Many a Slip* (1955) and *The Mystery of the Sleeping Car Express* (1956). The former work also contains INVERTED MYSTERIES, a form that Crofts practiced successfully, though these pieces are now little known and hard to find. *The 12:30 from Croyden* (1934; U.S. title *Willful and Premeditated*) is a book-length inverted mystery in which a man plans a "perfect" murder involving the death of his wealthy uncle on a plane. Inspector French only appears late in the game.

BIBLIOGRAPHY Novels: *Inspector French and the Cheyne Mystery* (1926; U.S. title *The Cheyne Mystery*), *The Sea Mystery* (1928), *Sir John Magill's Last Journey* (1930), *Mystery in the Channel* (1931; U.S. title *Mystery in the English Channel*), *Death on the Way* (1932; U.S. title *Double Death*), *Sudden Death* (1932), *The Hog's Back Mystery* (1933; U.S. title *The Strange Case of Dr. Earle*), *Mystery on Southampton Water* (1934; U.S. title *Crime on the Solent*), *The Loss of the Jane Vosper* (1936), *Man Overboard!* (1936), *Found Floating* (1937), *Antidote to Venom* (1938), *The End of Andrew Harrison* (1938; U.S. title *The Futile Alibi*), *Fatal Venture* (1939; U.S. title *Tragedy in the Hollow*), *Golden Ashes* (1940), *James Tarrant, Adventurer* (1941; U.S. title *Circumstantial Evidence*), *The Losing Game* (1942; U.S. title *A Losing Game*), *Fear Comes to Chalfont* (1942), *The Affair at Little Wokeham* (1943; U.S. title *Double Tragedy*), *Enemy Unseen* (1945), *Young Robin Brand, Detective* (1947; juvenile), *Silence for the Murderer* (1948), *Dark Journey* (1951; British title *French Strikes Oil*), *Anything to Declare* (1957).

Short Stories: *Murderers Make Mistakes* (1948),

FRIDAY, THE RABBI SLEPT LATE (1964) This first novel in the Rabbi SMALL series by Harry KEMELMAN generated huge interest—it was a bestseller and won an EDGAR—and also a certain amount of confusion over who, or what, this innovative detective really was. The publishers received orders for *Friday, the Rabbit Slept Late, Freddy, the Rabbi Slept Late,* and, worst of all, *Freddy, the Rabbit Slept Late.* Once Rabbi Small became familiar, he would develop into one of the most successful "crossover" mystery characters, read by many people who did not have primary interest in the genre.

While the Congregation debates the first renewal of Rabbi Small's contract, the body of a young woman—a baby-sitter for an Italian family in Chilton (a section of Barnard's Crossing)—is found on the lawn of the temple. The rabbi, who was in his office studying until late at night, is a suspect; also, the girl's handbag has been found in the back seat of his car. But instead of trying to remove suspicion from himself, Small helps to clear and release from prison a member of the Jewish community who had been seen with the girl the evening she was killed. Because of increasing tension among the town's Yankee population and several unpleasant threats against himself and other members of the Congregation, Small is pushed into looking further into the murder. Rabbi Small is not a very inspiring figure, as far as his appearance goes: his hair is unkempt, his suit does not fit, and he does not notice his disheveled appearance. He is brutally honest and his ability to make distinctions is keen, however; he finds the culprit with only the help of his reasoning. He later presents his evidence to Police Chief Lanigan, who follows his deductions and is convinced. There is a twist at the end, though the ending is not spectacular. *Friday, the Rabbi Slept Late* is interesting because it avoids the pitfalls of "local color" and makes the cultural background and habits of thought an integral part of the mystery. Written before the explosion of regional and cultural subgenres and the vogue of the marginalized or special-interest detective, the novel makes its detection and its setting and characters a cohesive whole.

FRIEDMAN, KINKY (1944–) The American country/western singer Kinky Friedman has developed a following for his humorous private eye novels. Friedman is the leader of the group the Texas Jewboys, and has released some half-dozen CDs. He lives in Texas in a trailer, if his publicity is to be believed (it also says that millions of invisible ponies circle his home).

Kinky Friedman writes about a detective also known as Kinky Friedman, a private investigator who lives in a loft in New York City, smokes cigars, and wears a black cowboy hat. Friedman could be described as a jokester, who delights in verbal play, puns, and the more usual wisecracks of the HARD-BOILED genre. Not quite a send-up, the Friedman books do adhere to some of the genre's conventions and offer a real if rudimentary mystery, though they depend finally on their verbal games to sustain interest—sometimes becoming puerile and scatological. Friedman's language has more verve than many books in the humorous detective subgenre. The provocative titles of the novels hint, broadly, at their outrageous content, particularly *Elvis, Jesus & Coca-Cola.* In *The Love Song of J. Edgar Hoover* (1996), p.i. Kinky is hired by a femme fatale, Polly Price, to find her missing husband, Derrick. Another plot involves his drunken and paranoid journalist friend Michael McGovern, who is receiving threatening phone calls from Al CAPONE'S former chef. In deference to and parody of the contemporary CAT subgenre, Kinky frequently talks over the case with his cat, who is absolutely uninterested and useless as an assistant.

Friedman's political irreverence goes from a lampoon of the hypocrisy of J. Edgar Hoover that has an edge of outrage, to the truly outré: he uses "taking a Nixon" as a euphemism for a bodily function.

FROM LONDON FAR (1946) A donnish, tongue-in-cheek thriller by Michael INNES about an art theft ring discovered by scholar Richard Meredith when he mutters part of a poem by Alexander Pope. The timid don—"only a man chronically scared of life would have hidden behind that immense moustache"—decides to play out the role he has inadvertently stumbled upon. The first phase of the book ends with a shooting and an escape over the rooftops of London. Meredith finds himself in Scotland next, with his female accomplice (another scholar) and two bloodhounds. This second phase is dominated by a weird pair of Scotswomen living on an island whose major export is gull guano, exported by the mysterious Mr. Pepperjohn. The characters are eccentric stereotypes not meant to be taken seriously. In some respects the book is a PARODY of those by John BUCHAN. Although the book is overly long and the last sequence is more dull than droll, if one can enjoy its many unlikelihoods it is a good example of the humorous novel in which the author excels.

FROME, DAVID See FORD, LESLIE.

FULLER, WILLIAM (***) A Hemingway-esque figure in mystery and adventure literature, William Fuller was a sailor and fisherman in Florida and wrote novels about a character apparently much like himself, Brad Dolan. Dolan is an early example of a type later to achieve enormous popularity in the sixties, especially in the stories about Travis MCGEE by John D. MACDONALD. A veteran of the Second World War and Korea, Dolan worked as an ad man until he decided to drop out of the rat race. He is one of those characters who represent a revolt against the famous "organization man" of the fifties; tired of taking orders and not interested enough in consumerist prizes to play the game, he moves to Florida, buys an old boat, and sets up as a fairly legitimate charter operator. What is radical about Dolan is the truly heretical new goal (from an American point of view) he sets for himself: to work as little as possible. Getting ahead is replaced by getting along or getting by. Underneath his apathetic exterior, however, Dolan has the working-class American preference for the underdog and disgust at exploitation. Unfortunately, Fuller's writing rarely lives up to the potential to be explored in Dolan's character, and it would take John D. MACDONALD'S zest and fascination with counterculture to make the most of the knight errant of the marina. Fuller was also "an old Cuba hand," experience he put to use in TIGHT SQUEEZE (1959).

FUNERAL IN EDEN, A (1938) A novel by Paul MCGUIRE, set on the imaginary island of Kaitai. A Pacific paradise, Kaitai is ruled benevolently by George Buchanan, the "sultan" and a descendant of Buchanan the First, a Scottish tugboat captain who somehow made himself the king of the island. The white population of the island consists of various people who have made up new identities for themselves and "retired" to Kaitai, as well as a doctor, Alicia Murray, and Thompson, a former Scotland Yard inspector. Everything is peaceful in this ridiculous paradise until a man calling himself Goulburn shows up. No one is anxious for a stranger's presence—especially a former journalist given to prying—or to be forced to give up their secrets. Certain mineral deposits on the island, which Buchanan had hoped would not come to the attention of the outside world, have also aroused unwanted interest. When "Goulburn" is found dead, his dinghy foundered, everyone breathes a sigh of relief—until it becomes clear that he was murdered. The island has no criminal justice system, but the doctor, the sultan, and the retired inspector all have a hand in the detection.

FU MANCHU, DOCTOR A villainous master criminal created by Sax ROHMER, Fu Manchu had a long career, stretching from a short story appearance in 1912 (in "The Zayat Kiss," a year before the first Fu Manchu novel) to *Emperor Fu Manchu* in 1959. Fu arose at a time when the major colonial powers, including Britain, were fearful of the emergence of China into world affairs after several centuries of isolation, and alarmed by the increasing number of Chinese immigrants. The phrases "yellow peril" and "mongol hordes" were used to evoke xenophobic fear of this unknown people. The racism of the Fu Manchu stories makes them difficult reading today; Julian SYMONS called them "rubbish."

Fu Manchu has green eyes and a shaved head, making him appear somewhat reptilian. He is all villains rolled into one: a mad scientist, an organizational mastermind like MORIARTY, a leader of secret societies (like Sun Yat Sen, who launched his revolution in 1905). No mere gangster, Fu Manchu wants to control the world—prefiguring the villains of books such as the James BOND series. The doctor is opposed by the Englishmen Sir Denis Nayland Smith and another doctor, Dr. Petrie. At the end of the series, Fu becomes an anti-communist, a "good guy" at last.

BIBLIOGRAPHY Novels: *The Devil Doctor* (1916; U.S. title *The Return of Dr. Fu Manchu*), *The Si-Fan Mysteries* (1917; U.S. title *The Hand of Fu Manchu*), *The Golden Scorpion* (1919), *The Daughter of Fu Manchu* (1931), *The Mask of Fu Manchu* (1932), *Fu Manchu's Bride* (1933; British title *The Bride of Fu Manchu*), *The Trail of Fu Manchu* (1934), *President Fu Manchu* (1936), *The Drums of Fu Manchu* (1939), *The Island of Fu Manchu* (1941), *Shadow of Fu Manchu* (1948), *Re-enter Fu Manchu* (1957; British title *Re-enter Dr. Fu Manchu*).

Short Stories: *The Mystery of Dr. Fu Manchu* (1913; U.S. title *The Insidious Dr. Fu Manchu*), *The Secret of Holm Peel and Other Strange Stories* (1970; contains "The Eyes of Fu Manchu"), *The Wrath of Fu Manchu* (1970).

FURIOUS OLD WOMEN (1960) A novel by Leo BRUCE, one of his best about the scholar and amateur sleuth Carolus DEENE. The furious old women of the title are a group of ladies—three of them are the Griggs sisters—who dominate the town of Gladhurst. Were they generals, they would have destroyed it, for the women are constantly fighting over the town's morals and its primary institution, the church. The local vicar, Bonar Waddell, is torn between Millicent Griggs, who wants to keep the church as staid and Puritan as possible, and Grazia Vaillant, an eccentric woman with a Pre-Raphaelite air, a love of antiques and junk, and a penchant for the rituals of Catholicism. Waddell does not have to placate Millicent for long, because she is soon found dead.

Bruce populates the town with a collection of stock types—the town floozy, a retired military man, a poacher, unhappy lovers, and various bores—but Deene's conversations with them are well done. Well known for his conservative views, Bruce also puts in the mouths of his characters complaints about almost everything, from the Angry Young Men who dominated British fiction ("whining about their maladjustment or disillusionment or whatnot") to the decline of the English pub ("standardized swilling-houses for standardized products at standardized prices . . . in a few years their customers will be as standardized as they are") to taxes ("he had accommodatingly died before dying had been made too expensive") to nursing homes ("herded into homes to sleep in dormitories and obey the rules like children").

The structure of the mystery is admirable. An ingenious method of concealing the crime is used—lightly burying the body in the bottom of a grave already dug for someone else. Deene interviews everyone in the town, in the process uncovering a series of clues (missing galoshes, a loud motorcycle, a missing sheet) that lead to the solution. By suppressing any internal monologue or putting of two and two together by Deene, Bruce lightens the narrative and plays fair at the same time.

FUSIL, INSPECTOR ROBERT A second series character created by Roderic JEFFRIES, Inspector Fusil is less known than his Inspector ALVAREZ. In this PROCEDURAL series, Fusil is assisted by Constable Kerr and investigates crimes in a provincial English town. Jeffries's series lacks the power of some of the other English procedurals—the characterizations of Reginald HILL or Ruth RENDELL or the realism of Maurice PROCTER.

BIBLIOGRAPHY Novels: *The C.I.D. Room* (1967; U.S. title *All Leads Negative*), *Circle of Danger* (1968), *Murder Among Thieves* (1969), *Guilt Without Proof* (1970), *Despite the Evidence* (1971), *Call Back to Crime* (1972), *Field of Fire* (1973), *The Murder Line* (1974), *Six Days to Death* (1975), *Murder Is Suspected* (1977), *Ransom Town* (1979), *A Man Condemned* (1981), *Betrayed by Death* (1982), *One Man's Justice* (1983).

FUSTIAN, MAX A man of towering conceit but diminutive stature in Margery ALLINGHAM's DEATH OF A GHOST (1934). An art dealer and critic, Fustian's whole existence is based on riding the coattails of the dead painter John Lafcadio. In his absurd waistcoats and loud tweeds, Fustian is a figure of fun, but his unshakable faith in his own pompous self-presentation makes him a commanding presence in the community of "Little Venice."

FUTRELLE, JACQUES (1875–1912) There are two widely known facts about the American author Jacques Futrelle: that he created Professor S. F. X. Van Dusen, otherwise known as The THINKING MACHINE, and that he died on the night of April 14-15, 1912, on the ocean liner *Titanic.* Futrelle was born in Pike County, Georgia, of French Huguenot parents. His first newspaper job was in Richmond, Virginia; he also worked as a theatrical manager. Moving on to Boston (where the Thinking Machine stories are set), Futrelle joined the staff of the *Boston American.* He began his career as a fiction writer with humorous pieces. One of his early stories, very much in the style of Mark TWAIN, concerned a specially bred Kentucky racehorse with the legs of a kangaroo.

It was in the *American* that Futrelle's first and most famous story about Van Dusen appeared in October-November 1905, the often anthologized PROBLEM OF CELL 13. Futrelle had a gift for creating situations that seemed impossible but that the professor was able to reason himself out of. The Thinking Machine's problem in Cell 13 seemed so insurmountable, in fact, that it was published as a serial over the course of a week, and the *American* offered prizes for solutions sent in by readers.

The Thinking Machine's regular triumphs over the apparently insoluble was a quality at which some critics caviled. For example, in "The Phantom Motor," a car repeatedly enters a walled street from which there is only one outlet and in which there is no place to turn off, but the car never comes out the other end. Some of Futrelle's ideas were worthy of POE. In one of the most bizarre tales, "The Crystal Gazer," the victim sees his own murder in a crystal ball. The personality of Van Dusen, the dialogue, and the underlying humor give the stories more balance and weight than mere puzzles or attempts to baffle the reader. Futrelle also tried to make sure that the mechanics of the various "impossibilities" were sound.

Though he stands head and shoulders above most of his contemporaries for originality, some of Futrelle's work is pedestrian. "The Great Auto Mystery" is a conventional tale about a millionaire and a blonde actress, and lacks the quirkiness of the author's best work.

Futrelle wrote Westerns and romances in addition to his mysteries, and even touched upon SCIENCE FICTION. *The Diamond Master* (1909) is about a plot to produce artificial diamonds (a theme re-used twenty years later by Edgar WALLACE in *The Twister*). Futrelle's last novel was *My Lady's Garter* (1912), in which a burglary occurs. Another posthumously published book was *Blind Man's Buff* (1916), a crime story set in Paris that had been serialized earlier. After Futrelle's death on the *Titanic,* H. L. MENCKEN wrote that Futrelle "tempered the hot steel of derring-do in the oil of humor."

FUZZ This term for the police, now associated indelibly with the 1960s and 1970s, actually originated in the thirties.

FYFIELD, FRANCES (pseudonym of Frances Hegarty, 1948–) Frances Fyfield, the daughter of a doctor, graduated from the University of Newcastle-upon-Tyne and became a solicitor. Her fifteen years of experience in criminal law with the Crown Prosecution Service form a solid background for her work, which is technically exact but also has sociological and psychological aspects reminiscent of SIMENON, albeit explored in a very different style. Fyfield told *Contemporary Authors* that she lives alone and collects paintings, and she has written primarily about professional women who are often lonely and introverted.

Fyfield's first novel was *A Question of Guilt* (1988) and was nominated for an EDGAR award. Unlike the many imitators of GOLDEN AGE mystery fiction who continue to turn out COUNTRY HOUSE mysteries in a sixty-year-old literary style, Fyfield writes modern, even modernist English that sometimes proceeds by jerks, halts, and sudden torrents of words, nearly betraying grammar but stretching it to achieve effects. She is also modern in her exposure of the grim details of murder—without, however, rolling in the gore of the CLOACA-AND-DAGGER SCHOOL. There is still a sense of morality and the strong ethical core of the traditional mystery story, though at the same time a certain open-mindedness toward criminals and an insistence on social aspects of crime. She shares with Simenon a strong perception of the sadness of human weakness, and the sordidness of both human nature and modern urban society.

Crown Prosecutor Helen WEST and Detective Chief Inspector Geoffrey Bailey were Fyfield's first series characters. Two "pathologically reserved souls," they meet and warily overcome their professional distance and personal difficulties. Fyfield returns again and again to the disparities in the roles and mentalities of lawyers and policemen, who find themselves natural enemies rather than allies. Her writing has an almost obsessive quality that can be wearying. She brings third-person narration as close as possible to first, which requires substantial reporting of characters' thoughts. The characters are also vehicles for Fyfield's own often arresting perceptions, such as "the strange quality of fear, as varied as love in all its manifestations." The legal details are handled deftly and stressed more than the police investigation. In the manner that has now become almost *de rigeur,* West and Bailey start a relationship and thus become a male/female crime fighting "team," though their roles are complimentary rather than unified. An odd couple, they live in separate apartments until they decide to move to the country in *Not That Kind of Place* (1989).

In *Shadows on the Mirror* (1991), Fyfield created another series character, Sarah Fortune, who is also a lawyer. But hers is more a suspense story than a mystery; not a prosecutor, Sarah works for a stuffy law firm she finds rankling. Sarah's liaisons with men involve her in the case of a decayed body discovered off the coast of England. In *Perfectly Pure and Good* (1994), she becomes involved with a bizarre family through an estate case. Hegarty has also published several novels under her own name, including *Trial By Fire* (1990) and *The Playroom* (1991).

G–, MRS. Created by Andrew FORRESTER, JR., Mrs. G– was the first professional female detective in mystery fiction. A member of London's Metropolitan Police, her adventures were collected in *The Female Detective* (1864).

GABORIAU, ÉMILE (1832–1873) Gaboriau is not only the father of the French *roman policier;* his work had a strong influence on the development of the mystery and detective story in English as well. A keen follower of the methods of real policemen, Gaboriau was in a sense the first proceduralist. He based his hero, Monsieur LECOQ, on the first head of the Sûreté, VIDOCQ.

Gaboriau was born in Saujon, and was a young lawyer's clerk when Charles Baudelaire translated POE's tales into French in 1857. Gaboriau had quit the law and joined the cavalry by the time he published his first books, two collections of "humorous observations." Several novels followed. A writer of popular literature of no great distinction, Gaboriau first turned to the detective story with *L'Affaire Lerouge* (*The Widow Lerouge,* 1866), in which Lecoq makes a cameo appearance; thereafter, he would be the main character. Gaboriau was writing for *Le Pays,* a Parisian newspaper, in which the novel was printed in installments. Gaboriau's other detective novels also appeared first in serial form.

Gaboriau is often dismissed for having an even worse case of the melodramatic addiction of the nineteenth century than Wilkie COLLINS. Julian SYMONS, however, said Gaboriau was "an interesting and still underrated writer, whose crime stories are rooted in sound knowledge of police procedure." Gaboriau piled up a number of firsts, including being the first to use the taking of plaster casts of footprints in a detective story. It is not that Gaboriau was not skilled in the planting of clues or showing the methods of detection—he was; the problem is rather that the detective story is still wrapped up in the conventions of the sensational novel, the form in which the author had previously worked. The novels also contain an interesting picture of Paris around mid-century.

Of Gaboriau's other novels, *Monsieur Lecoq* (1869), built on the "manhunt" plot, and *Le Crime d'Orcival* (1867) are the most readable today. His other books, however, should not be neglected. *L'Affair Lerouge* is a proto-PROCEDURAL novel in that it has a plethora of detectives. In addition to Monsieur Daburon, the investigating magistrate, there is M. Gévrol, the Chief of the Sûreté, who is assisted by Lecoq, who in turn recommends that Gévrol call in the flamboyant amateur detective M. TABARET. Gévrol, pressured by Daburon, reluctantly agrees. Tabaret then embarrasses him further by solving the case, which concerns the Widow Lerouge, found beaten to death in her suburban home. Gaboriau uses the classic plot of the children switched at birth. The real vicomte is a driven, successful, but exhausted barrister; meanwhile, the bastard child lounges in velvet pants and enjoys the title that is not his. A cache of old letters in which the Comte revealed his plans to substitute his mistress's child for his hated wife's is part of the proof. The identities of the now cast-off mistress and of the nurse who witnessed the fraud are a shock to Tabaret.

After making Lecoq the focus of attention in later books, Gaboriau developed him into more and more of a hero, but there are still traces of the bare reality of Vidocq's world, in which criminals and police were almost indistinguishable. This kinship of the hunter and the hunted was something that would resurface again in the work of the greatest writer of *romans policiers,* Georges SIMENON.

Gaboriau also wrote short stories, the most familiar of which is THE LITTLE OLD MAN OF BATIGNOLLES (1876).

GAFFER An old man, a geezer. The word comes from "godfather." Godmother also had a contraction, *gammer.*

GALLICO, PAUL (1897–1976) Born in New York City of Italian and Austrian parents, Paul Gallico attended Columbia University and graduated in 1921, following his service in World War I. A larger-than-life figure, Gallico is more interesting to read about than to read. The six-foot-three Gallico worked his way through college as a longshoreman. He became one of the best-known sports reporters of his day through a series of sports stunts, the first of which was to go a round with Jack Dempsey (Dempsey knocked him out). Gallico also swam against Johnny Weismuller and got Dizzy Dean to pitch to him.

Gallico later worked for the *New York Daily News* (1922–1936). He then moved to South Devon in England, where he kept a Great Dane and twenty-three CATS. He was an avid fisherman and an expert fencer. His love of animals was expressed in his most famous book, *The Snow Goose* (1941), in which a bird adopts one of the boats evacuating soldiers from the beaches of Dunkirk. Among his many books about cats is *Thomasina* (1957), about the ghost of an injured cat who had to be destroyed and who takes vengeance on the veterinarian for her "murder." Gallico's books were popular in their time, but their sentimentality has palled. Gallico, who was married four times, later settled in Monaco.

During World War II Gallico was a foreign correspondent, which provided background for his thriller *Trial By Terror* (1952). This book used the Cold War theme of brainwashing by diabolical Communists years before Richard Condon's *The Manchurian Candidate* (1959), upon which the successful 1962 film was based. In Gallico's novel, an American businessman in Hungary has somehow been made to confess to acts of espionage he did not commit. Jimmy Race, a hot-headed young reporter in the Paris bureau of the *Chicago Sentinel,* is disgusted that everyone is sitting on their hands and gets himself sent behind the Iron Curtain to get the real story. He is promptly captured, and the Hungarians have announced that the next spy will be executed. The description of a newspaper office is well done, but the saccharine love story (a Plain Jane figure in love with the brash Jimmy Race, Jimmy Race in love with the boss's wife) and the story's heavy-handedness make it difficult to take seriously, except as an artifact of the fifties.

Late in life, Gallico wrote the thriller *The Poseidon Adventure* (1969), which was filmed in 1972 and spawned a disaster movie craze.

GALTON CASE, THE (1959) This novel is considered the pivotal mystery in the Lew ARCHER series by Ross MACDONALD for its development of his characteristic plot structure: the inevitable impact of past events on the present, and the search of a young man for his identity. The idea, however, that past actions (of which crimes are only the worst examples) are like seeds that bear fruit in the present had already been spelled out in *The Doomsters* (1958). The deeper source for Macdonald's "modern Oedipean legend" is of course Sophocles. Macdonald later wrote that "in the red spiral notebook where I made my original jottings for *The Galton Case,* I can still find this short note: 'Oedipus angry vs. parents for sending him away into a foreign country.'" The Oedipal figure—John Brown, alias John Galton, alias John Lindsay, alias Theo Fredericks—has a lot in common with Macdonald himself: "When this fictional John made his way to Ann Arbor and entered the University of Michigan, he was following in my footsteps. . . . We shared a sense of displacement, a feeling that, no matter where we were, we were on the alien side of some border. We felt like dubious claimants to some lost inheritance."

Archer is hired by lawyer Gordon Sable on a hopeless case: to search for the elderly Mrs. Galton's son and heir, Anthony Galton. What he quickly turns up is a decapitated corpse buried on the spot where Anthony had lived twenty years before, and a young man working in a gas station who looks exactly like Anthony and may be his son. The boy's name is John Brown, and like the young man in *Black Money* (1966) he has a yearning for respectability and success that is thwarted by his own dissimulation and the jealousies of others. Even before this discovery, however, another case enters the story at right angles: a thuggish servant of Sable's is stabbed to death on his front lawn. Archer, who "hates coincidences," investigates both cases at the same time. In addition to the overall shapeliness of the plot, the book has many individually memorable scenes. The Galton trail leads to a bleak provincial town in Canada, and Macdonald's wry and funny glance at the beatnik poetry scene in San Francisco enriches the early part of the novel, putting on display the strength and flexibility of Macdonald's mature style. With *The Galton Case,* Macdonald had "arrived," precisely by finding a mythical form for his own beginnings.

GAMADGE, HENRY Detective created by Elizabeth DALY. Gamadge is an amateur sleuth and a bibliophile who lives in New York, though his adventures take him to various, often picturesque locales. His home turf, however, is the Upper East Side of New York, where he lives with his wife, Clara, and their son. Neither poor nor rich, in between studying and acquiring rare books and advising clients Gamadge solves murders; unlike the NORTHS, Gamadge does not investigate crime with his wife's assistance.

Gamadge is born around 1907, and is mature and elegant upon introduction, as well as being erudite (his first commission, however, was at the age of thirteen, when he foiled his great aunt's plan to cheat her co-heirs). Gamadge is also one of the most well-spoken detectives, often correcting inarticulateness and prejudice in others with his more precise and measured use of words, which he respects as much as his books. Physically, Gamadge is somewhat colorless—medium height, a "figure in monochrome" whose most distinguishing traits are his gray-green eyes and lumpy gait. Befitting a scholar, he is somewhat stooped. Gamadge has two assistants. The first is Harold Bantz, a man whom Gamadge rescued from poverty. David Malcolm is a character more like himself, at least in his social class; however, he is more dilettante than detective, an enthusiastic neophyte to whom Gamadge is teaching both of his businesses—detecting and BOOK collecting.

Gamadge is wounded while involved in counter-intelligence during World War II. *The House Without the Door* (1942) maintains the prewar flavor; the sleuth is hired by Mrs. Curtis Gregson, who has been living in seclusion since 1938, when she was acquitted of murdering her husband with morphine. Now she thinks someone is trying to kill her. After packing her off to a sanitarium, Gamadge sets out to find the killer of her husband. In *Somewhere in the House* (1946), he is employed by what might be called a dysfunctional Social Register family on the eve of the settling of a trust with bizarre provisions. A room in the family mansion has been sealed for twenty years; inside is the wax figure of a young girl, a long dead relative memorialized by the ghoulish grandmother of the family. Again, Gamadge's encyclopedic knowledge of books is integral to his solution of the case, but he uncovers a far wider scandal going back a good number of years and involving a notorious murder case and other wrongdoing. The family habit of defacing old books proves important.

And Dangerous to Know (1949) has Gamadge drawn once again into a matter of family money, his bread and butter as a sleuth. An upper-class woman named Alice Dunbar disappears shortly after being seen buying cheap clothing and makeup, out of keeping with her usual behavior. She had expected to receive an inheritance from her Aunt Woodworth, who lived in a big house farther up the Hudson. The plot has both COUNTRY HOUSE and bohemian elements.

Night Walk (1947) takes Gamadge to the upstate New York town of Frazer's Mills, a resort town with a sanitarium, not unlike Saratoga Springs. He becomes embroiled in a rich network of relationships and resentments involving the wealthy sanitarium visitors and the locals. Garry Yates comes to town to be close to his sweetheart, Rose Jenner, but on the first night, a mysterious prowler leaves a fire axe outside his door. George Carrington (Rose is his ward) is found murdered; though this seems a classic case of a killing for profit, in fact the murder benefits no one, lending credence to the prowler theory. Gamadge investigates, though some might want the murderer to go free to protect the "flavor and bouquet" of Frazer's Mills (i.e., its reputation and income). Appropriately for Gamadge, he stages the denouement in the local library.

As can be seen in the summaries above, many of Gamadge's cases do not always have much, or anything to do with books. A volume of Byron, however, is central to MURDERS IN VOLUME TWO (1941). See also NIGHTSHADE.

BIBLIOGRAPHY Novels: *Unexpected Night* (1940), *Deadly Nightshade* (1940), *Evidence of Things Seen* (1943), *Nothing Can Rescue Me* (1943), *Arrow Pointing Nowhere* (1944), *The Book of the Dead* (1944), *Any Shape or Form* (1945), *The Wrong Way Down* (1946), *The Book of the Lion* (1948), *Death and Letters* (1950), *The Book of the Crime* (1951).

GARDNER, ERLE STANLEY (1889–1970) American lawyer and detective story writer, and one of the most prolific and successful mystery authors of all time. Gardner used his background as a lawyer to create one of the best-known mystery series characters, Perry MASON, as well as the District Attorney Doug SELBY. As A. A. FAIR, Gardner wrote a long series of novels about the private detective team of Bertha COOL and Donald LAM.

To say that Gardner wrote more than 100 novels (143, to be exact) is to give only a hint of his productivity; even before he created his most famous characters, he had had a successful career writing for PULP MAGAZINES. Gardner was born in Malden, Massachusetts, but his father was drawn west by his job as a mining engineer, traveling as far as California, Oregon, and even the Klondike. Gardner briefly attended college in Indiana, and after a short career in boxing (as both a fighter and promoter) he wound up working in a California law office. By dint of study, Gardner got his license to practice law without attending law school, passing the bar exam in 1911. His law practice was not lucrative (he defended poor immigrant clients), and he began writing. He made his first pulp magazine sale in 1923, and would become a big name with BLACK MASK.

Gardner wrote more than sixty novelettes about the character Lester Leith alone (five are collected in *The Amazing Adventures of Lester Leith,* 1980). Lester is a combination of RAFFLES and Travis MCGEE: he steals money back from criminals, pocketing 20 percent for himself as a fee and giving the rest to charity. Gardner's first series character was Speed Dash, a "human fly" with a photographic memory. Like many who wrote for the pulps, Gardner ranged from detective stories to fantasy to Westerns. His series characters from this period include Sidney Zoom and his police dog, Black Barr the gunslinger, Fong Dei, the slick Patent Leather Kid, Major Brane of the secret service, El Paisano (he could see in the dark), and Larkin, a juggler who fought with a pool cue. A few specimens of Gardner's pulp work have been collected: *Dead Men's Letters* (1989), featuring Ed Jenkins, the Phantom Crook; *Honest Money* (1989), about lawyer Ken Corning; and *The Adventures of Paul Pry* (1989). Gardner not only succeeded as a pulp writer, but became rich. He acquired a thousand-acre ranch (Ranch del Paisano), and virtually gave up pulp writing after the thirties and when his other series took off.

The pulp writings are very formulaic, and if he hadn't gone on to create his more famous characters Gardner might have sunk into oblivion. Even his friend Raymond CHANDLER said that Gardner was hardly a writer at all. The psychology and relationships of the characters are basic, though the dialogue can be sharp and HARD-BOILED. Gardner adopted the technique of dictating his books and stories, and eventually employed half a dozen secretaries, one of whom he married after the death of his first wife.

Despite their weaknesses, Gardner's books—the best ones, at any rate—are still entertaining, which was all that they were intended to be in the first place. Gardner stated frankly that he wrote for money and to provide "fun" for the reader. Later in life, he wrote books on such subjects as criminology and archaeology, and won an EDGAR award in 1952 for a book about an organization he helped to found, the Court of Last Resort, which reopened cases in which it was suspected that innocent people had been convicted.

One of Gardner's best books was the non-series mystery, THE CASE OF THE TURNING TIDE (1941).

GARDNER, TERRY A passenger on the *Goyaz* in Bruce Hamilton's TOO MUCH OF WATER (1958). One of the best characters the author invented, Gardner is a nervous, self-deprecating man who conceals his nervousness by making elaborate fun of himself. His antics entertain the increasingly apprehensive passengers as a series of murders occurs. Behind his facade, Gardner is quite intelligent and brave; insanely, he jumps into the sea to save a cat.

GARVE, ANDREW (pen name of Paul Winterton, 1908–) When he began writing fiction, Paul Winterton might have turned out to be another Eric AMBLER. Educated at the London School of Economics and London University, Winterton was a journalist for *The Economist* and other publications before World War II, and during the war was a correspondent in Moscow. These experiences provided material for such cloak-and-dagger suspense novels as *Murder in Moscow* (1951; U.S. title *Murder Through the Looking Glass*). Winterton also wrote nonfiction works about his experience in the Soviet Union: *Report on Russia* (1945) and *Inquest on an Ally* (1948). But although he had the credentials to be a serious spy novelist, he became an idiosyncratic genre writer who ranged widely and never allowed himself to become attached to a major series character. His one attempt at a series, three novels about the reporter Hugh Curtis (published under the pseudonym Paul Somers), are almost unknown. Winterton's early books were published under the pseudonym of Roger Bax; it was his series of adventurous tales written as Andrew Garve that would bring him recognition.

What Garve is most known for is original plots in exotic settings; he rarely repeats himself, except in his use of the Moscow scene and the newspaper business. The latter is dealt with, for example, in *The Press of Suspects* (1951; U.S. title *By-Line for Murder*), *The Megstone Plot* (1956), and *The Galloway Case* (1958). Although his strength is suspense, Garve has written some novels relying on detection, for example *A Grave Case of Murder* (1951), *Frame-Up* (1964), and *Murderer's Fen* (1966; U.S. title *Hide and Go Seek*). He has even written INVERTED MYSTERIES such as *Disposing of Henry* (1947). No respecter of convention (in this case the taboos of FAIR PLAY), Garve toyed with the identical twins theme in *The Far Sands* (1960).

The first novel published under the Garve pseudonym was *Fontego's Folly* (1950; also pub as *No Mask for Murder*). It is set in a British colony that could be British Honduras (now Belize) but also is reminiscent of Haiti. The hero is Martin West, an expert on leprosy who has come to rehabilitate the leper colony on the island of Tacri. The description of the abominable conditions and the political cynicism that prevents them from being changed is forceful, and West is a believable scientist–civil servant. Most of the rest of the colonials, such as Dr. Adrian Garland and his sluttish wife, are offensive racists. Essentially an inverted mystery, the story is engaging and shows much penetration in its analysis of the colonial mind. The second murder is incredibly cruel without being bloody—an example both of the author's writing skill and his capacity to surprise.

Another admired Garve book is THE ASHES OF LODA (1965), which combines his Soviet interest with journalism. Like *Fontego's Folly*, it shows his penchant for chases and harrowing escapes. *A Hero for Leanda* (1959) ingeniously blends Garve's usual political subject matter (the covert fomenting of revolution) and his love of sailing; like many of his books, it has a romantic subplot, which is more or less skillfully woven into the main action. MURDER AFLOAT figures in several other Garve novels. One of his most bizarre plots is *The Sea Monks* (1963), in which a lighthouse is taken over by some young punks and the keepers of the light are held hostage. THE LESTER AFFAIR (1974) is a very clever blending of disparate elements: a General Election, a yachting vacation in Scotland, and a newspaperman's view of British politics.

Garve was a founder of the British CRIME WRITERS' ASSOCIATION, and was its first secretary. Some of Garve's novels have been filmed, most notably *Came the Dawn* (1949), which as *Never Let Me Go* (1953) starred Clark Gable in the decline of his career.

GASH, JONATHAN (pseudonym of John Grant, 1933–) An English pathologist, John Grant has created a series of novels about an unscrupulous character named

LOVEJOY that could be called crime novels, burlesques, or fantasies. An antiques dealer, Lovejoy is also a criminal and on occasion a killer. The books have evoked a mixed critical response. H. R. F. KEATING thought Lovejoy's accounts of his adventures had "immense gusto," while the style was described in *A Catalogue of Crime* as "emetic."

Grant served in the British Army and later became a specialist in pathology. He has taught his subject all over the world, including at the University of London and in Hong Kong, and continues to practice in the field while pursuing his writing career, which began with *The Judas Pair* (1977). While still a medical student, Grant haunted London's markets and learned about antiques, storing up knowledge he would later use in the series. He has been awarded the British CRIME WRITERS' ASSOCIATION John Creasey award.

GAT A slang word for gun, "gat" derives from Gatling gun, the first machine gun, designed by Thomas Gatling. *Gat,* however, never applied to machine guns, but rather to all sorts of pistols, both automatic and revolver. It has been said that the name *Gatsby* in F. Scott FITZGERALD's most famous novel is a reference to "gat," meant to evoke Jay Gatsby's criminal past.

GAULT, WILLIAM CAMPBELL (1910–1995) American mystery writer who began writing for PULP MAGAZINES and first published in his twenties. Gault was born in Wisconsin, where he worked in the hotel business. He later became friends with Ross MACDONALD; like Macdonald, he had served in World War II and afterwards joined the postwar migration to California. It was against that background that he set his Brock CALLAHAN mysteries. Like Travis MCGEE, Brock Callahan is a hulking physical specimen, a former Los Angeles Ram who is now a private detective. Gault lived in Pacific Palisades, which he admired for its country club. His description of himself as a "low-pressure Republican," Big Ten football fan, and golfer makes him sound like the stereotypical "regular guy." His books were most frequently about sports, and scorned the corrupting influence of gambling and adulterous women.

Gault's initial success, however, was with non-series work, which was not always sports oriented. Gault won an EDGAR award for best first novel for *Don't Cry for Me* (1952). In *Blood on the Boards* (1953) Gault used a small theater group as a background for the murder of a Hollywood producer. One of the members of the group is Joe Burke, a former police sergeant who has inherited a fortune and retired. *Run, Killer, Run* (1954) is about a former bookie sent to jail for the murder of his wife. After his friend and defense lawyer is murdered, he escapes and tries to clear his name.

In addition to the Brock Callahan mysteries, Gault also wrote a series about Joe Puma, a private detective in the tradition of the PULP MAGAZINES. He appears in such books as *Sweet Wild Wench* (1959) and *The Wayward Widow* (1959). As the publication dates indicate, Gault could be a high-volume producer in the mold of GARDNER and COXE. The corruption of professional sports was used over and over in both series. In *Day of the Ram* (1956) a gifted young quarterback is pressured to cooperate with gamblers, then murdered. His father hires Callahan to investigate. In *The Hundred Dollar Girl* (1961) Puma investigates after the manager of a Mexican-Irish boxer is killed. The Puma stories are generally better, if only because they do not have Callahan's petulant and quarrelsome girlfriend, Jan.

Gault's mysteries were praised by critics but did not do well financially—just the opposite of what one would expect, for Gault's writing cannot be compared with other writers of the genre, lacking CHANDLER's surface brilliance, Macdonald's inwardness, or even DALY's brashness. At his best, Gault's style was like that of Thomas B. DEWEY, who at *his* best showed the value of restraint. *Come Die With Me* (1959), however, is typical: a horse racing story, it takes up many of the themes of earlier hard-boiled novels (with "a tall and busty bleached blonde," gamblers, and hoods), but with dull characterizations and writing.

In mid-career, Gault devoted himself to juvenile literature and football stories, but made a comeback as a mystery writer with a classic example of the "payback" theme. In *The Cana Diversion* (1982) Gault has one of his series detectives (Callahan) investigate the murder of another (Puma). The novel won a SHAMUS award. The later books were similar to what had gone before. *The Dead Seed* (1984) looks back to Chandler with its cast of Hollywood losers, stars, and everyone in between. It is an unhappy book, in which Callahan has retired but he and Jan wearily needle each other.

GAUNT, JONATHAN A character created by Bill KNOX. Knox was searching for a vehicle for a series that would take him beyond the bounds of his native Scotland, as can be seen from the titles of the books in this series, each of which uses the name of the "exotic" setting: *A Property in Cyprus* (1970), *A Killing in Malta* (1972), and *A Burial in Portugal* (1973) were the first three. The vehicle Knox found, however, was the little-known office of the Queen's "Remembrancer," an all-purpose attendant concerned with Scottish affairs. Knox takes considerable liberties with reality, however, and Gaunt is essentially a version of the espionage type.

BIBLIOGRAPHY Novels: *A Witchdance in Bavaria* (1975), *A Pay-Off in Switzerland* (1977), *An Incident in Iceland* (1979), *A Problem in Prague* (1981), *A Legacy from Tenerife* (1984), *The Money Mountain* (1987; U.S. title *A Flight from Paris*).

GAY MYSTERIES Mysteries in which the detective is explicitly identified as being gay are a relatively recent phenomenon (though many have idly speculated on whether earlier characters were gay, including Sherlock HOLMES). The Stonewall riots in New York City's Greenwich Village in 1969 marked the beginning of the movement for gay rights, and helped to make it "OK" to publish books with openly gay characters. Various claimants have been named for the honor of "first." Joseph HANSEN'S series featuring Dave BRANDSTETTER began with *Fadeout* (1970), a book that also includes a bisexual folk singer. The Pharoah LOVE series, however, had begun four years earlier.

Gay-centered mysteries have become progressively more political, and have also vastly increased in number (there is now a Stonewall Inn imprint that publishes many of them). Richard Stevenson's Donald Strachey mysteries, set in Albany, deal with gay issues and organizations, some of them real. In *Third Man Out* (1992), which has nothing to do with baseball, Strachey investigates the shooting of a Queer Nation activist. His other books include *On the Other Hand, Death* (1984), in which an elderly lesbian couple own eight acres of land that put them smack in the middle of a planned mall development. The developer cynically hires Strachey to investigate vandalism and threats against them. Jack Ricardo's first book, *Death With Dignity* (1991), is about a gay priest who has come out and is heading a group for gay Catholics when he is murdered. In *The Night G.A.A. Died* (1992), set in 1971, a gay cop inspired by Stonewall to come out loses his job; he gets involved with an activist group, one of whose leaders is killed. Molly Hite's *Breach of Immunity* (1992) is about a serial transvestite rapist. Other authors in the subgenre include Ronald Tierney, who writes a series about Deets Shanahan as well as non-series mysteries such as *Eclipse of the Heart* (1993). Others such as Steve Johnson have followed—as tends to happen with niche-marketing—with mechanical plots and immature writing. Another author of gay mysteries is Mark Richard Zubro, who writes about a gay Chicago cop.

The Dan Kavanagh (Julian BARNES) mysteries about DUFFY, however, are far more than subgenre novels. Another writer who transcends subgenre writing is Toby Olson. His novel *At Sea* (1993) is not even about a gay detective; however, it is set in Provincetown, Massachusetts, and issues of sexuality are prominent in the case (and in fact are the most interesting part of a sometimes improbable plot). Peter Blue is investigating the rape of a woman named Beth Charters, about whom he has romantic fantasies. Blue is married and has had several affairs, but remains detached from and is confused by his own sexuality. He is assisted in his investigations by Charters's father, a widower who has "come out" following the death of his wife.

Lesbian mystery novels are also becoming common. Laurie R. KING won an EDGAR for her first novel about a lesbian San Francisco detective. Sandra Scoppettone writes about a lesbian private eye named Lauren Laurano who lives in New York's Greenwich Village; her lover is a psychotherapist. Scoppettone first published her books under the pseudonym Jack Early. She won a Shamus award from the PRIVATE EYE WRITERS OF AMERICA for the first book, *Everything You Have Is Mine* (1991). She also won a Shamus for *A Creative Kind of Killer* (1984), a non-series novel.

Ellen Hart writes a series set in Minnesota's twin cities about a lesbian restaurateur named Jane Lawless and theater director Cordelia Thorn; the first book was *Hallowed Murder* (1989). Barbara Wilson writes two lesbian mystery series, one about a Spanish translator named Cassandra Reilly and the other about Pam Nielsen, who lives in Seattle and runs a printing business. *Gaudi Afternoon* (1990), the first of the Reilly books, won an award from the British CRIME WRITERS' ASSOCIATION.

GAY PHOENIX, THE (1976) A novel by Michael INNES. Imagine that two brothers are sailing the Pacific; the younger one, the sailor, is poor, and the older, a womanizing financier, is rich. When their boat is wrecked in a storm, the older brother is killed and the younger, who resembles him closely, is tempted to return to claim his brother's place in a glamorous world. The story is an INVERTED MYSTERY because we see the plan hatched aboard the wrecked yacht in the opening scene. A retired Sir John APPLEBY becomes interested in the case when the surviving brother takes over the ancestral mansion next door.

GAZEBO, THE (1955) A MISS SILVER mystery by Patricia WENTWORTH, which closely approaches the NOVEL OF MANNERS in its structure and tone. The plot could have been taken from a marriage novel of the previous century, for all its complexities of inheritances and obstructions to love. Althea Graham's father left the family home to her in his will, even though she was only ten years old at the time. Whatever his intention, this quixotic decision has made her a prisoner for life. As the novel opens, it is many years later and Althea is taking care of her invalid mother, Winifred, who is painfully aware that she is almost a guest in her own home. A hypochondriac, she has supposedly been on the point of death for years. She has extracted a promise form Althea not to leave her until she dies; she effectively blocked Althea's marriage to the journalist Nicholas Carey five years before. Carey went abroad, and Althea was left to a Cinderella-like existence, a virtual slave to her cloying and self-centered mother and both pitied (and humiliated) by the neighbors.

Carey has now returned, and courts Althea again. It is interesting that she first consults Miss Silver before any crime has been committed. Winifred shows no signs of dying, and Althea does not want to miss her second chance, so she asks Miss Silver for advice about marrying, not murder. Only after her mother is strangled in the gazebo do Miss Silver's deductive powers come into play.

GEE A slang word, meaning "a guy," the derivation of which is disputed. It may be a shortened form of GEEZER; derived from the first letter of the word "guy"; or a corruption of the French pronunciation of the name *Guy.* To complicate matters further, the word "gee" entered the language several centuries ago with the meaning of a docile mare. Supposedly, this came from the drover's phrase "gee up."

As an abbreviation from pronunciation of the letter "g," a *gee* could be a thousand dollars or, in hobo slang, a gallon of liquor.

GEEK A geek was a carnival performer who ate broken glass, bit the heads off chickens, and performed other outré or disgusting acts. Frederic BROWN said that geeks were often African Americans.

GEEZER An old man; a guy. The word comes from an alternate pronunciation of the Scottish/North of England word *guiser,* which meant a mummer (from French *guiser,* to disguise or masquerade).

GENIUS DETECTIVE. The dominant type of detective during the GOLDEN AGE, the genius detective was developed in the nineteenth century. POE established the pattern by making C. Auguste DUPIN a reclusive genius with mental powers far above those of the policemen he condescends to help. The genius is usually accompanied by a WATSON character who marvels at the genius' mental powers and often acts as his biographer. Sherlock HOLMES, of course, is the greatest genius detective ever created. The scope of his knowledge is indicated by his "publications," which range from treatises on bee keeping and the identification of tobaccos from their ash to *Upon the Polyphonic Motets of Lassus* and a linguistic study of the Chaldean roots of ancient Cornish. Conan DOYLE went so overboard in depicting Holmes' genius that the stories instantly invited PARODY.

The genius detective declined as a type in the twentieth century because of a greater interest in realism. The genius required a complex and brilliant crime to solve, and when writers (particularly Americans) began depicting street crime and murders without diabolical and ingenious planning, more realistic policemen and private eyes were wanted. The genius detective persisted, however, in characters like Nero WOLFE.

GENTLE MURDERER, A (1951) A novel by Dorothy Salisbury DAVIS, employing the classic situation of the priest to whom a murder has been confessed under the seal of the confessional. Father DUFFY and Sergeant Ben Goldsmith pursue parallel investigations, but the priest's methods are more factual and the cop's are intuitive. All the priest has to go on is that the killer had a gentle, sorrowful face like St. Francis, and a few hints about his personal life, but not his name. Much of Goldsmith's technique consists of following Duffy.

The story is set in Hell's Kitchen, on the west side of Manhattan. Davis uses slice-of-life techniques to portray Duffy's poor Irish and Italian parish. Ironically, Duffy elicits information from people by playing on the same impulse to confess that drove the killer to him. Thus he gets out of his own untenable position by gaining the confidences of others while concealing his own ulterior motives. The novel is almost an INVERTED MYSTERY.

GENTLY, INSPECTOR GEORGE This inspector with the English-sounding name is actually French in inspiration. Gently is gentlemanly, reserved, and competent. Created by Alan HUNTER, the series appeared when MAIGRET was at his height, and reviewers quickly drew comparisons between Gently and SIMENON's detective. Gently's cases take place in East Anglia, the author's home. Like Maigret, Gently smokes a pipe, but he also constantly chews on peppermints. Critics have also remarked on Gently's facility with interrogation, which is carried out at length. In the series, Hunter's native Norwich is transformed into the fictional town of Norchester. Despite the restricted setting, Hunter rings as many changes as possible on the traditional mystery motives and modi operandi. Gently is a thoughtful character, and his remarks on contemporary issues punctuate his investigations.

BIBLIOGRAPHY Novels: *Gently Does It* (1955), *Gently by the Shore* (1956), *Gently Down the Stream* (1957), *Landly Gently* (1957), *Gently Through the Mill* (1958), *Gently in the Sun* (1959), *Gently with the Painters* (1960), *Gently to the Summit* (1961), *Gently Go Man* (1961), *Gently Floating* (1963), *Gently Sahib* (1964), *Gently with the Ladies* (1965), *Gently North-West* (1967; U.S. title *Gently in the Highlands*), *Gently Continental* (1967), *Gently Coloured* (1969), *Gently with the Innocents* (1970), *Gently at a Gallop* (1971), *Vivienne: Gently Where She Lay* (1972), *Gently French* (1973), *Gently in Trees* (1974; U.S. title *Gently Through the Woods*), *Gently with Love* (1975), *Gently Where the Birds Fly* (1976), *Gently Instrumental* (1977), *Gently to Sleep* (1978), *The Honfleur Decision* (1980), *Gabrielle's Way* (1981; U.S. title *The Scottish Decision*), *Fields of Heather* (1982; U.S. title *Death on the Heath*), *Gently Between Tides* (1982), *Amorous Leander* (1983; U.S. title *Death on the Broadlands*), *The Unhung Man* (1984; U.S. title *The Unhanged Man*), *Once a Prostitute* (1984), *The Chelsea Ghost* (1985), *Goodnight, Sweet Prince* (1986), *Strangling Man* (1987), *Traitor's End* (1988), *Gently with the Millions* (1989).

GEORGE, [SUSAN] ELIZABETH (1949–) Born in Ohio, Elizabeth George received her undergraduate degree from the University of California and her masters from California State. She taught high school before becoming a writer. These do not exactly strike one as the credentials for a writer of British mysteries, but George's series about Inspector LYNLEY was a great success—the first book, *A Great Deliverance* (1988), won the Anthony Award of the BOUCHERON, the French Grand Prix de Littérature Policière, and other awards. The upper-class Lynley and his lower-class (and female) partner are another version of the odd couple theme.

George made the supporting characters the focus in *In the Presence of the Enemy* (1997). Apparently, George has gotten on the bandwagon of loading stories with "significant" social themes. Also set in England, the novel concerns the illegitimate child of tabloid editor Dennis Luxford; the mother is his political foe, Eve Bowen. The "ransom" is a simple request: to reveal the child's paternity, which would be disastrous for both of them. George makes her sleuths two of Lynley's helpers: Lady Helen Clyde and Simon St. James, a forensic expert. St. James's wife is infertile and loves children. One reviewer called the ending "hokey."

Like the works of Martha GRIMES, George appeals to those Americans who are fascinated with the royal family and things English. She also writes about England in a way that the English themselves never write.

GETHRYN, ANTHONY The amateur detective who appeared in a series of novels by Philip MACDONALD. THE RASP (1924) introduced Gethryn, who is clearly another version of Philip TRENT. Like Trent, Gethryn is wealthy and idle, has dabbled at painting, and specializes in investigative journalism, posting his astounding scoops from the scene of the crime. In their first case, both detectives are smitten by love at first sight and meet their future wives.

As if unwilling to leave a single chink in the detective's armor, MacDonald made Gethryn so polymathic that there is enough genius in him (to outward appearances) to make a dozen of Sherlock HOLMES. Gethryn is the son of a country gentleman (and brilliant mathematician) and an impoverished, artistic Spanish woman. He performed brilliantly at Oxford while appearing not to study at all, and excelled at rugby and "racquets"; he finished Oxford at the age of twenty-three, and "was called, but did not answer" to the bar. He enters World War I an infantry private, but, speaking perfect German, is transferred to the Secret Service and finishes up a colonel, while also winning the Distinguished Service Order and "a baker's dozen" of other awards. He has written two novels and a collection of poetry, and owns *The Owl*, the journal for which he writes his reports.

Gethryn has an upper-class disdain for what he calls "the unspeakable nasty work of the Private Inquiry Agent" which he laughingly shrugs off. As an "actor," he treats it all as a performance or game. With his "hawky" looks, flippancy, and obscure or supercilious remarks, he is similar to the early Albert CAMPION and Lord Peter WIMSEY. He is, however, supposed to have done "wonderful things" during the war, and one of his former subalterns, Superintendent Boyd, is now Colonel Gethryn's contact with Criminal Investigation Department (C.I.D.) at Scotland Yard.

Almost all the Gethryn novels were written within the space of ten years, at the heart of the GOLDEN AGE. They rely above all on clever plotting rather than character, realism, or polished writing. *The Polferry Riddle* (1931) is a LOCKED ROOM mystery that is so clever that the surprise ending makes the whole thing seem like a RED HERRING; one reader called it "318 pages of wool pulled over your eyes." Two men are driven ashore in their boat on the remote Wessex coast; the Hale-Storfords invite them up to the house they have been renting. Going to bed, the men discover a trail of blood under their host's door and open it to find Mrs. Hale-Storford with her throat cut with a razor. Nine months later, several other people who were in the house have died mysteriously. After a kidnapping and a chase across England, Gethryn uses that old trick, the re-enactment of the crime, to solve the mystery.

Warrant for X (1938; orig title *The Nursemaid Who Disappeared*) used the kidnapping theme. MacDonald did not mind coincidences: in this novel, someone happens to overhear the plot, and Gethryn is able to track down a NAPOLEON OF CRIME. Macdonald then wrote no Gethryn novels for twenty years, but in 1959 published the best of them, THE LIST OF ADRIAN MESSENGER.

BIBLIOGRAPHY Novels: *The White Crow* (1928), *The Link* (1930), *The Noose* (1930), *The Maze* (1931; U.S. title *Persons Unknown*), *The Wraith* (1931), *The Crime Conductor* (1931), *Rope to Spare* (1932), *Death on My Left* (1933).

Short Stories: *Fingers of Fear* (1952; U.S. title *Something to Hide;* 1 Gethryn story).

GHOSTWAY, THE (1984) A novel by Tony HILLERMAN about a Los Angeles Navajo who goes looking for his brother on the reservation and then kills a white man in a shootout. Jim CHEE discovers that the Navajo, badly hurt in the fight, sought refuge in the hogan of his uncle, the elder Hosteen Begay, and died there. (A "ghostway" is similar to an exorcism.) Certain aspects of the death ritual excite Chee's suspicions. For example, the body has been taken out through the door, instead of by cutting a hole in the side of the hogan, as is usually done when a person dies inside a dwelling (which must be permanently abandoned). A Navajo would usually make sure that a person did not die inside the house. About the same time, the granddaughter of Hosteen Begay disappears from school. Chee's investigation and search for the missing brother leads him into Los Angeles and into big crime. Chee also must deal with a white girlfriend who would like him to leave the reservation and live in the United States, culturally as well as geographically.

GHOTE, INSPECTOR A character created by H. R. F. KEATING, Inspector Ganesh Ghote (pronounced Ghoté, not "goat") is an Indian working for the Bombay Criminal Investigation Division, though the author has contrived to send him as far afield as London (*Inspector Ghote Hunts the Peacock,* 1968) and Los Angeles (*Go West, Inspector Ghote,* 1981). The first Inspector Ghote novel, *The Perfect Murder* (1964), won an EDGAR award. Keating went on to write a half-dozen of the books before he visited India for the first time.

To some, Ghote is a charming and quaint character. He is honest, committed, and honorable toward his wife, Protima, and his son. To others, Ghote is a Western stereotype of the polite and servile Westernized Indian, doing too much bowing and scraping, and being forever picked upon by others. His English, also, is considerably less "standard" than that of a typical educated Indian; when he travels abroad, his embarrassments and wonder at the great Western cities is what one would expect from a small boy, not an intelligent man who had seen a lot of crime. It is hard to say whether Ghote is made fun of more by his peers or by his creator. Capitalizing on "local color" and the comic possibilities thereof, the series is fundamentally unserious. As an "ethnic" detective, Ghote is not really more advanced as a characterization than Charlie CHAN.

Cultural questions aside, Jacques BARZUN made the insightful comment that Ghote was not believable simply because "the success of ineffectual people is rarely made plausible." *Under a Monsoon Cloud* (1986) is therefore doubly problematic, because the normally honest and timid Ghote commits a crime that is at once daring, indefensible, and incredibly stupid. It is not a mystery but a story of suspense. Ghote is sent to a remote village to put the police administration into shape. Very soon he is joined by Chief Inspector "Tiger" Kelkar, whom Ghote has idolized as his own opposite—forceful, irascible, and dashing. When Kelkar kills another policeman with a heavy inkwell, Ghote helps him conceal the murder.

The best of the Ghote books are the first, *Inspector Ghote Goes By Train* (1971), and *The Murder of the Maharajah* (1980), in which Ghote does not appear because the case involves his father and is set in the 1930s.

BIBLIOGRAPHY Novels: *The Perfect Murder* (1964), *Inspector Ghote's Good Crusade* (1966), *Inspector Ghote Caught in Meshes* (1967), *Inspector Ghote Plays a Joker* (1969), *Inspector Ghote Breaks an Egg* (1970), *Inspector Ghote Trusts the Heart* (1972), *Bats Fly Up for Inspector Ghote* (1976), *Inspector Ghote Draws a Line* (1979), *The Sheriff of Bombay* (1984), *Dead on Time* (1988), *The Iciest Sin* (1990).

GIBSON, JEREMIAH X. "Gibby" Gibson, a New York City district attorney, solves crimes in a series of novels by Hampton Stone (Aaron Mark STEIN). Gibson is a former policeman, and is assisted by another district attorney, "Mac," who also narrates some of the novels. The first book in the series was *The Corpse in the Corner Saloon* (1948). Stein's sleuths tend to be colorless, a possible fault that he made up for by creating outlandish secondary characters and strange situations. In the second book, *The Girl with the Hole in Her Head* (1949), the assistant D.A.s encounter Ellen Bennock, an eccentric woman who has a hole in her head covered by a steel plate. She has an equally bizarre family, but Gibson and Mac are skeptical of her story of threatening letters—until someone gets killed. Stein's search for novelty had some unexpected results; *The Murder That Wouldn't Stay Solved* (1951) has been praised because it introduced homosexuality into a story about a murder in a hotel. *The Real Serendipitous Kill* (1964) made use of the sixties counterculture, and has Gibson witnessing a murder on stage at a "happening."

Stein was known for his memorable titles. In the Gibson series, each title was like a nursery rhyme ("hickory dickory dock") and contained exactly eight syllables. As with some of Erle Stanley GARDNER's books, it seems that the title was thought up first and a plot dreamed up to fit it, however improbable.

BIBLIOGRAPHY Novels: *The Needle That Wouldn't Hold Still* (1950), *The Corpse That Refused to Stay Dead* (1952), *The Corpse Who Had Too Many Friends* (1953), *The Man Who Had Too Much to Lose* (1955), *The Strangler Who Couldn't Let Go* (1956; British title *The Strangler*), *The Girl Who Kept Knocking Them Dead* (1957), *The Man Who Was Three Jumps Ahead* (1959), *The Man Who Looked Death in the Eye* (1961), *The Babe with the Twistable Arm* (1962), *The Kid Was Last Seen Hanging Ten* (1966), *The Funniest Killer in Town* (1967), *The Corpse Was No Bargain at All* (1968), *The Swinger Who Swung by the Neck* (1970), *The Kid Who Came Home with a Corpse* (1972).

GIBSON, WILLIAM (1948–) The American author William Gibson is best known for his scientific and dystopic novels. He is responsible for the creation of the term "cyberspace."

Gibson's futuristic and science fiction work was influenced by Conan DOYLE's stories about Professor Challenger, and Gibson wrote an introduction to a recent edition of them. He also co-authored the novel THE DIFFERENCE ENGINE (1991).

GIDEON, GEORGE A character created by John CREASEY, Gideon appears in twenty-one novels, beginning with *Gideon's Day* (1955). Coming more than twenty years—and several hundred books—after the author's debut, the Gideon novels are by far the strongest of his works. *Gideon's Fire* (1961) won an EDGAR award. In that book, an arsonist burns down tenements to draw attention to conditions in the London slums.

The middle-aged Gideon is in charge of the Criminal Investigation Department at Scotland Yard. He is married and has six children; he says that London itself "had the comfortable familiarity of a good wife, and gave him just as must satisfaction," which about sums up Gideon's attitude to his world. In addition to ordinary crime, affairs of state intrude, as in *Gideon's March* (1962). Gideon has a cadre of loyal, even devoted subordinates, and their interaction gives the novels their PROCEDURAL feel.

BIBLIOGRAPHY Novels: *Gideon's Week* (1956), *Gideon's Night* (1957), *Gideon's Month* (1958), *Gideon's Staff* (1959), *Gideon's Risk* (1960), *Gideon's Ride* (1963), *Gideon's Vote* (1964), *Gideon's Lot* (1964), *Gideon's Badge* (1965), *Gideon's Wrath* (1967), *Gideon's River* (1968), *Gideon's Power* (1969), *Gideon's Sport* (1970), *Gideon's Art* (1971), *Gideon's Men* (1972), *Gideon's Press* (1973), *Gideon's Fog* (1974), *Gideon's Drive* (1976).

"GIFT OF THE EMPEROR, THE" An E. W. HORNUNG story, published in *The Amateur Cracksman* (1899). The last tale in the book, it shows RAFFLES and his partner Bunny Manders getting into trouble when they go after a pearl worth one hundred thousand pounds aboard the *Uhlan*, bound for Genoa. Actually, Raffles goes for the prize, luring Bunny—who had sworn off crime—into the CAPER and then typically leaving him holding the bag. Bunny's last view of Raffles is as a dot on the horizon; he himself is facing certain imprisonment.

GILBERT, ANTHONY (pseudonym of Lucy Beatrice Malleson, 1899–1973) One of the founders of the DETECTION CLUB, Beatrice Malleson wrote under the names of Anthony Gilbert, Anne Meredith, and J. Kilmeny Keith. Like Leo BRUCE, Gilbert created both an upper-class detective (Scott EGERTON) and a lower-class one (Arthur G. CROOK). Crook was a far more successful character than Egerton.

Malleson grew up in poor circumstances and supported herself from her late teens onward. Her first book was *The Man Who Was London* (1925). *The Tragedy of Freyne* (1927) was a thriller. Crook did not appear until more than a decade later, in *Murder by Experts* (1936). Malleson wrote mainstream novels as Anne Meredith; her autobiography, *Three-a-Penny* (1940), was also published under that name.

Gilbert was also a short story writer. Her one piece of short fiction about Crook, "You Can't Hang Twice" (1946), won a prize from *Ellery Queen's Mystery Magazine.* Under the name Malleson, the author also published "The Mills of God" (1969), a story that dealt with the subject of abortion.

GILBERT, MICHAEL [FRANCIS] (1912–) Michael Gilbert, a London solicitor, has carried on the English GOLDEN AGE tradition for five decades, updating it as he goes along with contemporary themes but preserving a style of superb clarity throughout. Gilbert has written all across the genre, including PROCEDURAL novels, spy tales such as *Game Without Rules* (1967), satirical legal mysteries in the manner of Cyril HARE, and even the currently popular forensic pathologist subgenre (see THE BLACK SERAPHIM, 1984). *Paint, Gold & Blood* (1989) is an INNES-like ART mystery into which Gilbert shoehorns a plot about terrorism by fanatical supporters of the Ayatollah Khomeini. Gilbert has also written for the theater, radio, and television. Gilbert's work has appealed to classicists as well as partisans of the psychological and literary crime novel; he is one of the few writers in the genre who could be said to have been almost universally praised.

Gilbert was born in Licolnshire and is the son of writers. He attended the University of London, earning his law degree before World War II. He served in the artillery during the war, in the African and Italian campaigns. Captured in Italy, he was interned near Parma but escaped. He used this experience as background for one of his most interesting books, *Death in Captivity* (1952; U.S. title *The Danger Within*), a murder mystery set in an Italian prisoner-of-war camp. Gilbert entered a law firm after the war and became a partner; he was also Raymond CHANDLER's London solicitor. Another legacy of his war experience was that his prison camp happened to have a copy of Hare's TRAGEDY AT LAW (1942). Gilbert's style has at times closely resembled Hare's, and Gilbert used his legal background to advantage, though his output has been far greater and more varied than Hare's. Gilbert began to write during his train journeys between his home and his office in Lincoln's Inn. He has written hundreds of mystery short stories and is one of the postwar masters of that form.

Close Quarters (1947) was Gilbert's first mystery novel and utilized the LOCKED ROOM situation. It introduced Inspector HAZELRIGG, who falls into the tradition of Inspector FRENCH. Critics have considered Hazelrigg to be bland and uninteresting, but this was the pattern of the classic prewar mystery as practiced by Freeman Wills CROFTS, John RHODE, and others. Hazelrigg is again the detective in Gilbert's fourth and best-known novel, SMALLBONE DECEASED (1950), in which a tiny corpse is found moldering like an old will inside a box. With this book, Gilbert had outgrown or perfected the prewar style, which he had enlivened with dry humor and deeper characterizations. In the fifties, Gilbert created a more interesting sleuth, the half-Spanish Scotland Yard detective named Patrick PETRELLA. Mainly a short story character, he is one of the least-known great detectives in the genre. Petrella's methods are PROCEDURAL; in addition to the stories collected in *Petrella at Q* (1977) and *Young Petrella* (1988), he also appears in some novels, including *Blood and Judgement* (1959) and *Roller Coaster* (1993).

Gilbert was a founder of the British CRIME WRITERS' ASSOCIATION, and was named a Grand Master by the Mystery Writers of America in 1988. His books have been critically acclaimed and added to many critics' "best" lists. Ellery QUEEN rated *Game Without Rules* second only to Maugham's ASHENDEN (1928) among spy stories. Other notable Gilbert books include *The Night of the Twelfth* (1976), a horrifying story about the torture and murder of three boys; books about the TICHBORNE CLAIMANT and Dr. CRIPPEN; and novels about art and the NAZI period. THE KILLING OF KATIE STEELSTOCK (1980) is an excellent mystery novel with an extensive trial scene.

The HISTORICAL MYSTERY is another area of interest; Gilbert combined it with espionage in the novel *Ring of Terror* (1995), about Russian revolutionaries in Edwardian London.

GILL, BARTHOLOMEW (pseudonym of Mark McGarrity, 1943–) The Irish-American Gill has created the character of Inspector MCGARR, a not very well disguised reference to the author's own real name. McGarr first appeared in *McGarr and the Politician's Wife* (1977). Gill is a graduate of Trinity College, Dublin.

Gill's novels often have a literary bent: other McGarr books deal with James JOYCE (DEATH OF A JOYCE SCHOLAR, 1989) and the antiquarian book business (*Death of an Ardent Bibliophile,* 1995). In the latter novel, a perverted book dealer acts out a Swiftean view of human nature by acting out the books themselves, with all of Swift's scatological humor intact. Gill's writing recreates the Irish atmosphere, usually without parody. BARZUN and TAYLOR unfairly accused him of "literary constipation"—which, given current tastes, is a charge likely to be aimed at anyone who cares about words. Gill's real faults have to do with plot and improbability. His taste for "theme" books has continued. *Death on a Cold, Wild River* (1993) has McGarr looking into the suspicious death of an old lover in a fly fishing accident.

"GIOCONDA SMILE, THE" A story by Aldous HUXLEY published in *Mortal Coils* (1922). Mr. Hutton is a callow, bored, and wealthy philanderer who spends most of his time ruminating on "the problem that was himself." He does not even derive much pleasure from his affairs, but they distract him from the tedium of living with an invalid wife; they make him feel independent while only demonstrating his fatal weakness. Hutton eventually turns his own lack of substance into a religion of "irresponsibility," which he imagines to be the source of all joy. One of the heavy ironies of the tale is that this "freedom" is also the seed of his own destruction.

GIONO, JEAN See THE SONG OF THE WORLD.

GIVE A MAN A GUN (1953; orig title *A Gun for Inspector West*) A mystery by John CREASEY, one of his Inspector WEST series. It seems to have been inspired by the case of Christopher Craig and Derek Bentley, which had gripped England the previous year. Craig was sixteen and Bentley nineteen when they tried to break into a warehouse but were caught when a constable saw them on the roof. Bentley, who was of low intelligence, told Craig to shoot Constable Miles, which he did, killing him. Since Craig was underage, he was sent to prison. Bentley had no gun, but he was hanged for inciting the murder.

The murder of PC Miles is echoed early in the book when a young bankrobber shoots a policeman between the eyes. Just as the real life case sparked public worry about growing violence among youth, so Creasey has West concerned about "dangerous misfits in society" and non-professional criminals who are "young, ruthless, [and] deadly." But Creasey's position is not of the simple law-and-order variety. As killings of policemen continue, West holds out against calls for the arming of British bobbies. He wants more police, not more guns. As the vendetta continues, West focuses on the daughter of a murdered fence whom he has some hope of redeeming.

GLASS KEY, THE (1931) A novel by Dashiell HAMMETT. Ned Beaumont is the right-hand man to Paul Madvig, a gangster who is running his own town as well as much of the state through politicians like Senator Henry. Beaumont is tall and lightly built, taciturn and fond of spotty green cigars. Madvig, who picked him "out of the gutter," is a big blond bruiser who relies on Beaumont's brains. An upcoming election provides the tension behind the plot, which heats up immediately when Beaumont finds Taylor Henry, the Senator's son, lying dead on the street only a couple of blocks from Madvig's club. The opposite side and some of Madvig's less reliable tools in the city bureaucracy think Madvig is the killer, and as he begins to lose his hold Beaumont turns detective in order to get to the bottom of the matter. The relationship between Beaumont and Madvig strains and breaks under the pressure (helped by the presence of Janet Henry, the Senator's daughter).

The novel is a subtler examination of political corruption than *Red Harvest,* published two years earlier, but has many of the same themes. Whereas *Red Harvest* was a true gangster story told by the wisecracking CONTINENTAL OP, *The Glass Key* is told rather coolly in the third person. The ending, however, reveals that an underlying emotional force has been built up. The relationship between Beaumont and Madvig is keenly felt, and rendered magnificently through offhand dialogue and body language. Beaumont himself is an enigma, a man who lives by his own code but doesn't bother to explain to anyone what it is.

GLASS VILLAGE, THE (1954) Written twenty-five years after Ellery QUEEN introduced a supercilious know-it-all detective of the same name in THE ROMAN HAT MYSTERY (1929), *The Glass Village* shows how much the Queen ideal had changed. In the late mysteries featuring Ellery Queen, such as *And on the Eighth Day* (1964), there is an increasingly serious undertone, mainly religious; with a similar seriousness, *The Glass Village* mirrored what was happening in the real world. In this novel, the author uses the mystery form to reflect obliquely on McCarthyism and the witch-hunting, hateful mood of American society. Shinn Corners is a typical New England town, an apparently serene old community with the usual village characters, one of whom is the ninety-one-year-old painter Aunt Fanny Adams. When she is beaten to death with a fireplace poker (a scenario exactly like that of *L'Affaire Lerouge*), the town goes mad, revealing an ugly, hateful side. Because a tramp had been seen leaving the house sometime before the murder, a lynch mob forms to see "justice" done. Instead, Superior Court Judge Lewis Shinn and his nephew, the former major in Intelligence Johnny Shinn, team up to find the truth and to uphold the honor of the name that their family and the town share. The novel is interesting not only in itself, but for the fact that it is a story that the authors had to go outside the boundaries of the Ellery Queen series in order to tell.

"'GLORIA SCOTT,' THE" (1893) A Sherlock HOLMES adventure that, he reports to WATSON, was his first case. It takes place while Holmes is still a student and concerns the father of his "only friend" at school, Victor Trevor. The elder Trevor is a Justice of the Peace, and drops dead when he receives a nonsensical message: "The supply of game for London is going steadily up. Head-keeper Hudson, we believe, has been now told to receive all orders for fly-paper and for preservation of your hen-pheasant's life." Hudson is a repulsive old sailor who seems to have Trevor in his power, and forces him to make him butler. Holmes solves the case using his analytic powers and cryptography.

GODEY, JOHN (pseudonym of Morton Freedgood; 1912–) John Godey had been writing for many years when he scored a major hit with the thriller novel *The Taking of Pelham One Two Three* (1973); along with the film version starring Walter Matthau, this book made Godey famous. The story concerns a gang who seize a New York City subway train and take the passengers hostage. This novel contained elements common to several other of Godey's books, in particular the New York setting and the use of the terrorist theme, but used them more successfully.

Born in Brooklyn, Godey attended City College and New York University and served in World War II. Later he worked in publicity and for the film industry. His novel *The Wall-to-Wall Trap* (1957) appeared under his real name. He also published articles and short stories in prestigious magazines such as *Esquire.* In the sixties, Godey turned to the mystery genre, but treated it with humor. *A Thrill A Minute with Jack Albany* (1967) introduced a comical, out-of-work actor who becomes involved in ridiculous escapades. Albany also appeared in *Never Put Off till Tomorrow What You Can Kill Today* (1970).

With *The Taking of Pelham One Two Three,* Godey began to publish non-series thrillers, some of them written earlier. *The Clay Assassin* (1959; pub 1973) is about Roy Hathaway, a heroin addict who murders a corrupt, powerful politician in exchange for a paltry sum—plus the promise of free heroin for the rest of his life. *Talisman* (1976) is a thriller with a political background reflecting the American identity crisis at the end of the Vietnam War. In the novel, the war is over but one anti-war protest leader—a priest—is still in prison. A group plans to "kidnap" an important piece of the national heritage (the "talisman") in order to draw attention to the priest's situation. The kidnapping is a metaphor for the placing in jeopardy of democratic political traditions by the undemocratic and lawless suppression of dissent, symbolized by the priest's incarceration.

Toward the end of the seventies, the end of the war and the ensuing somnolence of the American public made the political thriller less of a draw. Godey never regained the popularity he had had with *The Taking of Pelham One Two Three.* In *The Snake* (1978), Godey used a rather absurd device instead: a black mamba, the most poisonous of snakes, is released in New York's Central Park, unleashing a citywide terror. Godey has also published a book about growing up in New York City, *The Crime of the Century and Other Misdemeanors* (1973).

GODWIN, WILLIAM See CALEB WILLIAMS.

GODWULF MANUSCRIPT, THE (1973) The first novel about SPENSER, the Boston private investigator, by Robert B. PARKER. See BOOKS.

GOING NATIVE (1994) A novel by the American author Stephen Wright that combines the crime novel's preoccupation with character with the open-endedness of postmodern fiction. Characters appear and disappear throughout the novel, and sometimes seem to change identities. The discontinuous nature of the self is typified by Wylie Jones, who suddenly disappears from a drunken, boring cookout, leaving his wife and their plastic friends confronted with reality. Wylie says that "life is a haunting," and that close beneath the surface of convention is "the place where the black stuff hides," ready to erupt. Although told in the third person, the narrative is dazed, electric, and invasive—like the cop at a convenience store shooting, who catches the eye of an onlooker and "looks right inside easy as checking the contents of a boiling pot." Each person's viewpoint is radically subjective, and "the world" is not an outside realm, but a collection of projected mental interiors. The effect of the narrative is claustrophobia combined with weightlessness, and identity is no guide to behavior that is often disturbing and violent.

GOLD BULLETS (1929) A novel by Charles G. Booth (1896–1949) that shows the excesses of ingenuity practiced by third- and fourth-string writers of the GOLDEN AGE. A revolver is found that belonged to an old-time Californian who used gold bullets; lengthy messages written thirty years before are found rolled up inside unspent cartridges; and a butler, confronted with a man with a jeweled dagger protruding from his neck, says "He's not—he's not *dead?*"

GOLD DAGGER See CRIME WRITERS' ASSOCIATION.

GOLDEN AGE Criticism demands that every genre and form have its "golden age," and the mystery is no exception. Imprecise as ever, the term is usually taken to include the British mysteries written between the two world wars. The major figures are Agatha CHRISTIE, Margery ALLINGHAM, Ngaio MARSH, and Dorothy L. SAYERS. These mysteries all featured methodical detectives—private and public—in the HOLMES manner. *The Mysterious Affair at Styles* (1920) and THE CASK (1920) are often cited as the "official" beginning. The other major writers were John Dickson CARR (English in style, if not in nationality) and Freeman Wills CROFTS.

What was golden about the period was the number of good writers who devoted themselves to the genre. As usual, the top writers had many imitators, and much of the lesser work is unreadable today. This is partly because of the accepted "rules" of the period: character was de-emphasized in favor of the perfection of the puzzle; RED HERRINGS were used; and the plot was elevated above all other considerations (primarily believability). These rules are the subject of ongoing debate; as late as the 1980s,

BARZUN and TAYLOR said that "the detective story does not really permit true character study," while Julian SYMONS observed that "the best Golden Age writers . . . were unable to stick to those injunctions about subduing characters." Because of the focus on finding out who did it—the puzzle element—the term "whodunit" was coined to describe the classic mystery of this period. Popular interest in psychology and the gradual enervation of the puzzle (ever more tricky but less and less real) led later writers and readers to demand to know more than just "whodunit."

The English mystery of the Golden Age often fell into the COUNTRY HOUSE or LOCKED ROOM subgenre. In addition to the run-of-the-mill poisonings, shootings, and stabbings, ingenious murder methods were favored, such as Sayers's bell ringing murder, Christie's chess piece wired for electricity, and Robert EUSTACE's self-destructing dagger fashioned from frozen carbon dioxide. This aspect of the Golden Age connected it to the prewar period, when the detective story retained a strong connection to adventure literature, the GOTHIC, and tales of the fantastic, and could still be unapologetically "unfair." Thus, although the idea of FAIR PLAY was "codified" by Ronald KNOX in 1929, plenty of mysteries of the Golden Age continued to violate it. The most famous sleuths of the period were all amateurs: Hercule POIROT, Lord Peter WIMSEY, and Albert CAMPION. The influence of Sherlock Holmes was still strong. It is noteworthy that the best writers of the Golden Age in England were all women (leaving out CHESTERTON, who continued to write through the period but belonged to the one prior to it); Philip MACDONALD and John Dickson Carr come a long way below Sayers and Allingham in their control of language and feeling for style. Toward the end of this period, Josephine TEY began writing, and excelled all of them.

One could speak of a "golden age" of American mystery fiction at the same time, but much of it would be of an entirely different character from the English mystery of the period. Three of the greatest American detectives in the classic mold got their start in the golden age: Philo VANCE in 1926, Ellery QUEEN in 1929, and Nero WOLFE in 1934. But there was another renaissance of the detective story in the United States, beginning with the founding of BLACK MASK and taking a totally different direction. The writing of Dashiell HAMMETT, Carroll John DALY, Erle Stanley GARDNER, and Raymond CHANDLER (the HARD-BOILED style) had much different sources. In a sense, British writers wrote as if World War I had never happened, because they often wrote about upper-class people insulated from the disastrous postwar recession; the Edwardian mood of TRENT'S LAST CASE (1912) is not much different from that of many Golden Age books. The hard-boiled writers, however, were working in a new genre, one that reflected COMMUNISM, proletarian literature, the destruction of the ancien regime, the failed peace, and modernism. Through the hard-boiled school, the common man entered detective fiction not as the victim, the villain, or the hired help, but as the protagonist—the detective. See also GENIUS DETECTIVE.

GOLDEN ASHES (1940) A novel by Freeman Wills CROFTS featuring Inspector FRENCH. One of Crofts' later novels, it has more characterization and attention to mood and atmosphere than French's early alibi-busting, timetable-reading exploits. Geoffrey Buller is the grandson of a man who had broken with the family by marrying for love and emigrating to North America. Buller has just inherited the ancestral home and the title. Returning to England by ship, he meets Joan Stanton, a ship's nurse; Sir Geoffrey is looking for an expert hostess for his new home, and Joan's sister Betty needs a job. Betty's husband had abandoned her and she is almost penniless.

The story is told in two parts: First, Betty's story—the start of the job and her suspicions about Buller's secret meetings with a Mr. Davenport, which he later denies. The second half gives Inspector French's view of the case. Sir Geoffrey grows to dislike the manor house and does not fit in with local society. He has some of the best paintings in the manor's invaluable collection cleaned, and then decides to sell them. He is traveling in Italy when a fire destroys the manor. At the same time, Charles Barke, a friend of Betty's and an art expert who had visited the manor, disappears. The whole affair smells of arson and murder; French and the insurance man Shaw slowly unravel the quite skillful and cunning plan for burning down the house. As for the possible murder, French is quite baffled. The investigation takes him back and forth between London and Paris following various lines and suspects that lead nowhere until one day, while having lunch in an expensive Parisian restaurant (French loves food), a possible solution dawns on him.

GOLDFINGER See BOND, JAMES.

GOLDFISH See SYPE, WALLY.

GOLF MYSTERIES Golf, the game that evokes love and hate, has been the basis of or a prominent element in a number of mysteries. It figures importantly in the first Nero WOLFE novel, FER-DE-LANCE (1934), though even golf is too vigorous an activity for Wolfe to have any use for it, and the murder occurs before the book begins. With distaste, however, Wolfe is forced to learn something about the game, and actually handles clubs.

Agatha CHRISTIE's *Murder on the Links* (1923) is an early mystery featuring another unathletic detective, Hercule POIROT. He receives an urgent message from France from Paul Renauld, who fears for his life, but Poirot is too late to save him. He is found dead on a golf course. In *The Boomerang Clue* (1933), a flubbed drive leads Bobby Jones (not *the* Bobby Jones) to discover the body of a man at the base of a cliff. Just before dying, the man utters the enigmatic words, *"Why didn't they ask Evans?"* (also an alternate title of the book). From the same era is Leslie FORD's novel *The Strange Death of Martin Green* (1931; British title *The Murder on the Sixth Hole*), published under the name David Frome.

The English writer Herbert ADAMS was an avid golfer himself. In *The Body in the Bunker* (1935), Crosbie, a hated member of a golfing club, is found in a deep sand trap near "Hell," a particularly difficult and hated hole (the custom of naming holes is Scottish). Mashies and plus fours abound, and a romantic subplot concerns an attractive pair of girls who live in a windmill near "Hell." Adams also wrote *The Golf House Murder* (1933; orig title *John Brand's Will*) and several other golf mysteries, and is a sometimes charming writer who is now completely forgotten.

E. C. BENTLEY's classic story "The Sweet Shot" (1938) concerns a golfer who is apparently killed by lightning while golfing alone on a cloudless day. What's more, he is struck while standing in a hollow, not on high ground. TRENT finds another solution, and his approach to the murderer is interesting and surprising.

The finding of a dead man on a golf course seems to hold an enormous attraction for mystery writers; Monsignor Ronald KNOX used it in his first mystery novel, *The Viaduct Murder* (1925). More recently, John IRVING's lengthy novel *A Son of the Circus* (1994) starts with the discovery of the body of an elderly man who has been beaten to death with his own putter behind the ninth green. Robert UPTON used the suspicious death of a golfer in *Dead On Stick* (1986), a novel about his series character, private eye Amos McGuffin. Amos is called to the most exclusive country club in the world, the Palm Island Golf Club in the Bahamas, to investigate the possible murder of a millionaire. The club itself and its twisted members are the focus of the novel. A puzzling case, called facetiously the Crailo Golf Club Alleged Murder Case, is a subplot of *The Hollow-Eyed Angel* (1996) by Janwillem VAN DE WETERING.

Quintin Jardine's *Skinner's Round* (1995) is set in Scotland. A PGA tournament is about to be played at the new course, Witches' Hill, when a developer is found in his bath with his throat slashed to the bone. Part of a series, the book has PROCEDURAL and graphically realistic elements, and has none of the "plus-four" quaintness of some golf mysteries. Jardine lives in East Lothian and presents a believable Scotland and normal Scots, not the wee stereotypes of other mysteries set in golf's homeland (see this entry). Another Scot who wrote a golf mystery was Angus MacVicar (1908–), whose *Murder at the Open* (1965) is set at golf's holiest site, St. Andrews in Scotland.

Other golf mysteries set in Britain include *Lying Three* (1979), a Father DOWLING mystery; Brian Ball's *Death of a Low-Handicap Man* (1978); and *An Awkward Lie* (1971), a Sir John APPLEBY mystery.

Later writers have tried (perhaps unwisely) to build mystery careers on golf by creating series detectives. Most of these recent series are way above par—in the golfing sense. Conor Daly's golf-pro sleuth Kieran Lenahan first appeared in *Local Knowledge* (1995) and *Buried Lies* (1996). Another series began with *Murder on the Links* (1996) by John Logue, which boldly appropriated Christie's title. *The Feathery Touch of Death* (1997) is Logue's second, and takes place at St. Andrews. *Bullet Hole* (1986), by Keith Miles, likewise is set at the British Open. Bruce Zimmerman's *Crimson Green* (1994) is about a pro who loses his head on the last hole of the U.S. Open—literally.

The most successful of the new golf series is co-authored by Charlotte and Aaron ELKINS. The series is unusual because it focuses on the women's golf tour; it began with *A Wicked Slice* (1989). The series character is the golf pro Lee Ofsted, whose boyfriend is fortunately a cop. In *Rotten Lies* (1995), the second book in the series, Ofsted is set to win her first championship (Ofsted also plays a risky richochet shot used by Tom Watson in 1976). The murder of an obnoxious resort developer, however, interferes with her play. Ofsted goes to Block Island (off the coast of Rhode Island, where the authors live) in *Nasty Breaks* (1997) to give golf lessons to members of a salvage company. The head of the company is killed, and a plot develops having to do with sunken treasure. Although contrived, like any theme series, the books are well constructed and benefit from Charlotte Elkins's golf experience and the authors' research.

Barry Cork's *Dead Ball* (1988), the first in a series, illustrates in one book the traps and bunkers into which the golf mystery tends to fall. The Tamworth Classic is about to be played at the Royal West Wessex Golf Club when someone starts ploughing up the greens. In steps Inspector Angus Straun—a top amateur golfer, Straun is also a rich historical novelist who drives a Maserati. The book is competently written and uses good golf details, but goes utterly wild in matters of detail and plot. One suspect is an Asian golfer, who is actually described as "inscrutable" (shades of FU MANCHU), and we are told "they all look much alike to us." Another possibility is that feminist terrorists are using vandalism to protest the male domination of golf; but it is the use of *exploding golf balls* that leaves one speechless. Straun returns in *Unnatural Hazard* (1989), *Laid Dead* (1990), and *Winter Rules* (1991), which includes a political subplot about the building of a golf course in an African country.

GONDREVILLE MYSTERY, THE (1843; tr of *Une Tenebreuse Affaire*) This novel by BALZAC is his main claim to have been a pioneer of the detective story. In fact, an early editor commented that "it is certain as anything in history that Balzac begat Poe, and that Poe begat all our English crime-novelists." The novel also contains Michu, a figure nearly as great as Balzac's better-known VAUTRIN. Both are equivocal figures who combine disturbing amoral traits and a savage nobility. The story is set in 1803. Formerly a Jacobin during the Terror, Michu is a man of action whose red hair, pale skin streaked with broken blood vessels, and "fan-shaped beard" mark him as a wild and fanatic man. Gondreville is the ruin of a great aristocratic house where Michu lives. Everyone is terrified of him for miles around, not least because he is the bailiff for the area. The plot itself concerns Michu's revenge on the treacherous senator, Malin, and old scores that go back to the Jacobin period and the efforts of the greedy to take advantage of the revolution to dispossess the French noble families. Balzac also brings in the sinister figure of Jean Cottereau, who had been a character in *Les Chouans* (1829), Balzac's first novel to achieve literary acclaim.

GONIF (or ganoph, gonov, goniv) This word meaning a small-time thief comes from the Yiddish *gannabh*, and was introduced into English in the mid-nineteenth century.

GOODIS, DAVID (1917–1967) An American writer known for an outlook of unparalleled bleakness, David Goodis's books are often compared to those of Jim THOMPSON. The experience of the archetypal Goodis character—the man on the run—could be described as paranoia justified; although his heroes often turn out to be romantic and are basically good underneath, they are pursued by bad luck, bad people, and ill will.

Goodis was born in Philadelphia and graduated from Temple University with a degree in journalism in 1938. His first novel, *Retreat from Oblivion*, was published the same year, and in 1939 he moved to New York and began writing full time. During this early part of his career, he worked as a freelance writer and published in PULP MAGAZINES under various pseudonyms. He wrote not only crime and detective stories but horror, Westerns, and tales about pilots and other heroes. He later switched to screenwriting after his breakthrough novel *Dark Passage* (1946) was made into a film starring Humphrey Bogart and Lauren Bacall. The novel is about a man who is falsely convicted of murdering his wife and is sent to San Quentin for life but escapes, thanks to a woman. Goodis's years in Hollywood as a Warner Brothers screenwriter were not happy, and he went back to Philadelphia in 1950. He remained there for the rest of his life. He lived with his parents, and continued his odd and eccentric pattern of behavior. In Hollywood, he had gone out at night in a bathrobe; in Philadelphia he haunted the kinds of dives that appear in his books, and pursued his obsession with obese women (also familiar from his novels).

Goodis depicts a largely unheroic, violent world, in which criminals and their pursuers are often on the same moral level. In NIGHTSQUAD (1961), a crooked ex-cop goes to work for a mobster—in effect, tracking down one killer for another killer. But he was also obsessed with the idea of redemption and treated it like a bad habit. The protagonist of *Black Friday* (1954) embodies the dark ironic fate of the man who goes on hoping and struggling in spite of himself: "He wondered why he wasn't sick. He thought maybe he was beginning to get tough. He told himself it didn't really make any difference, because he didn't give a hang, but underneath he knew he did give a hang and it made a lot of difference and no matter what he kept telling himself he was really afraid of what was happening inside him." This character, Hart, is on the run for murdering his brother (for merciful reasons) and, having fallen in with a gang, has just helped cut up a body and burn it in a furnace. Unlike Thompson, Goodis usually wrote in the third person, and was able to describe scenes of incredible violence with a chilling objectivity; at the edge of horror, the real becomes surreal: "the sounds of the hack-saw and the knife were great big bunches of dreadful gooey stuff hitting him and going into him and he was getting sick and he tried to get his mind on something else, and he came to painting and started to concentrate on the landscapes of Corot . . ."

Goodis was a better writer than Thompson on the level of language, though in plotting he tended to use the same scenario (the fatal descent) over and over. His protagonists were often middle-class or wealthy men who had sunk to the level of the gutter, like Hart in *Black Friday* or Edward Lynn in *Down There* (1956). The last novel was filmed by François TRUFFAUT as SHOOT THE PIANO PLAYER

(1956); it was later reprinted under this title in the Black Lizard series, which has published new editions of many of Goodis's novels. In *Cassidy's Girl* (1951), an airline pilot whose career was destroyed when he was wrongly blamed for a crash is pursued by a similar evil fate in his new career as a bus driver. Goodis wrote during the high point of French existentialism, which may explain why his legendary "darkness" did not turn off European readers as it seems to have done in his own country. (The one biography of Goodis was written by a Frenchman, Philippe Garnier.) Whereas the fifties' private eye gets his man in the end and justice is somehow served (officially or privately), Goodis's people are beaten, often before they start. The truth that bad things happen to good people as well as bad is not a popular theme. Although Goodis's reputation in France never waned, thanks to the interest in his work by French intellectuals, Goodis had become almost unknown by the time his work was revived in the eighties. Geoffrey O'Brien wrote that "Nothing so downbeat, so wedded to reiterations of personal and social failure, would be likely to find a mass market publisher at present. The absolutely personal voice of David Goodis . . . emanated from the heart of an efficient entertainment industry, startlingly, like the wailing of an outcast."

GOODMAN, JONATHAN (1931–) English author of works on historical crimes, in the manner of PEARSON and others but with a more modern approach to scholarship. Goodman's works include *Murder in High Places* (1986), featuring notorious cases such as that of Lord LUCAN; *Murder in Low Places* (1988); and *The Slaying of Joseph Bowne Elwell* (1987), about the 1920 murder of a noted expert on the game of bridge, which was the basis for THE BENSON MURDER CASE (1926). Goodman's most notable feat was *The Killing of Julia Wallace* (1969), in which he actually "solved" the 1931 WALLACE murder. With Patrick Pringle he has written *The Trial of Ruth Ellis* (1974), about the last woman to be hanged in England. (Ellis's story was the basis for the film *Dance with a Stranger*). Goodman has also examined the case of Dr. CRIPPEN. *The Railway Murders* (1984) is a collection of accounts of killings on TRAINS beginning with the first in 1864. *The Oscar Wilde File* (1995) applied the same methods of his true crime works—going back to the original sources, news reports, and transcripts—to show the development of the Wilde affair.

GOODWIN, ARCHIE Without Archie Goodwin as a foil, Nero WOLFE might not be as deep (fat?) a character as he is. Wolfe's sedentariness—he rarely leaves his house, and then only under duress—would never work as a plot device were it not balanced by Goodwin's restless activity. Rex STOUT himself said that people think that they like reading about Wolfe, but what they really like is Archie.

Goodwin is a tough guy who rarely gets to shoot anyone or even hurt his knuckles, and lacks the machismo of a Mike HAMMER. In compensation, however, he is a rounded character who behaves like a human being, and is renowned for his wisecracking. Stout's biographer, John J. McAleer, observed that the relationship between Wolfe and Archie is essentially that of father and son.

When we meet Archie for the first time (in FER-DE-LANCE), he says he has already been working for Wolfe for five years. Goodwin is a transplant from Ohio and a college dropout. His duties include taking notes, keeping the germination records of Wolfe's orchids, chauffeuring, opening the mail, and filling Wolfe's fountain pen. He also knocks people down, occasionally shoots them, and interviews and tails suspects. Most importantly, he goads the lazy genius into activity, and his efforts to sting Wolfe where it hurts—in his pride—account for much of the humor. Goodwin never becomes too old for his work, because, like the other characters in the series, he doesn't age at all over the course of forty years. In *Some Buried Caesar* (1939), Archie meets Lily Rowan, his flame.

GOOF This now fairly innocuous word (witness the Disney dog character) has a complex history. While today a "goofy" person would be considered clumsy or silly, in the thirties a *goofer* was a simpleminded person, and a *goof* could mean a drug addict. To be *goofed up* was to be high—perhaps on a *goofball* or *goof-butt* (a marijuana cigarette; later, a cocaine-heroine mixture). On the other hand, to be *goofy* was to be suffering from withdrawal.

Some etymologists trace goof back to the now obsolete *goff*, a fool. In modern Italian, a person who is *goffo* is maladroit.

GOON The term goon, in the sense of hired thug or enforcer, may derive from the Hindu word *gunda*. (Hindu also gave us the word *thug*, from *thag*, meaning "thief." The Thugs were a notorious quasi-religious group who strangled and robbed travelers.) One authority, however, has given the uglier etymology of "goof + coon."

GORDON, MILDRED [NIXON] (1905–1979) **AND GORDON** (1906–) "The Gordons," as they were known, were a married couple who began their careers as journalists and later turned to writing thrillers. One of their characters, John Ripley, is an FBI agent; Gordon Gordon himself worked for the FBI during World War II in counterintelligence. The first Ripley book was *FBI Story* (1950). It was dedicated to J. Edgar Hoover, and reflected an admiring view of the agency; throughout the Gordons' work, operatives are shown to be tough, noble, and honest, ready to sacrifice themselves for others. The four other Ripley novels appeared sporadically between 1954 and 1973. The Gordons also wrote non-series novels, including *Power Play* (1966), in which the head of the FBI dies and there is a battle over the succession.

Mildred Gordon was born in Kansas and Gordon Gordon in Indiana. They met at the University of Arizona and married in 1932. While Mildred worked at the United Press agency and for the magazine *Arizona*, her husband was an editor of Tucson's *Daily Citizen*. He then worked as a publicist for a number of years during the Depression and in the early part of the war before joining the FBI. It was Mildred Gordon who was the first to become a novelist, with the mystery *The Little Man Who Wasn't There* (1946). The couple's first collaborative work was *Make Haste to Live* (1950). The Gordons may have been the first in the now popular subgenre of mysteries about CATS, of which they wrote three. The first, *Undercover Cat* (1963), was made into the Walt Disney movie *That Darn Cat!* (1965).

GORDON, YUDEL The Jewish South African psychologist in novels by Wessel EBERSOHN. Gordon is compassionate and unorthodox—he allows one troubled boy simply to sleep in his office to give him relief from his overbearing mother. Yudel also uses hypnosis, sometimes with unbelievable ease, to gain the information he needs to solve cases for the South African police. His long-suffering wife Rosa complains about his forgetfulness about bills and lack of solicitousness toward the patients she thinks "have nothing wrong with them" except being middle-class, boring, and spoiled.

Gordon is convincing as a psychologist because of his curiosity and constant observations of his surroundings (which reveal much about South Africa), and for his desire to preserve neutrality. This is not always possible. A decent man who believes in nothing, Gordon's adventures lead him to explore, partly unwillingly but also with a sense of moral duty, the horrors of the racist society of which he is a part.

BIBLIOGRAPHY Novels: *A Lonely Place to Die* (1979), *Divide the Night* (1981).

GORES, JOE (1931–) Joe Gores was working as a private investigator in San Francisco when he started publishing short stories in the late fifties. He won an EDGAR for his short fiction in 1970. In the same year, he also won an Edgar for his first novel, *Time of Predators* (1969). With his second novel, *Dead Skip* (1972), he created a series about a car repossession outfit known as Dan Kearny Associates (DKA). The action takes place in the same city where the author himself worked as an investigator—San Francisco.

Joe Gores was born in Minnesota and has led a wandering, adventurous life. He used to list on his dust jackets some of his prior occupations as schoolteacher (in Kenya), logger (Alaska), spear fisherman (Tahiti and the Seychelles), and carny (the Midwest). Gores also managed a hotel and a gym and wrote biographies of U.S. generals, as well as a marine salvage manual. He holds degrees from Stanford and Notre Dame.

Although the DKA series is about private investigators, its structure is PROCEDURAL. Like Ed MCBAIN's 87TH PRECINCT novels, it has a regular set of characters, including Larry Ballard, Patrick O'Bannon, and Bart Heslip. Ballard is a handsome, blond newcomer to the field in the early books. Heslip is African American, a former professional middleweight boxer. O'Bannon is an alcoholic but also the best operative in the office. There are two female characters, Kathy Onoda, the office manager, and Giselle Marc, a sexy young blonde who is also an ace investigator. The boss, Dan Kearny, is a classic hardass. The agency is housed in a former whorehouse.

Like McBain, Gores diverts attention from the characters' lack of complexity by keeping the players moving, with several stories taking place at once. The first book, *Dead Skip* (1972), begins with Heslip getting a beating from which he is lucky not to "wake up a carrot." Afterward, he is pushed off a mountain in a repossessed Jaguar. In *Final Notice* (1973), Ballard's lucky discovery of a wanted Cadillac convertible brings DKA into conflict with organized crime. Part of the excitement comes from the fact that repossessing cars sometimes amounts to stealing them, but for the bank. *32 Cadillacs* (1992) was based on an actual incident in which more than thirty Cadillacs were stolen in the Bay area on the same day. In the book, the death of the "King of the Gypsies" triggers the thefts, as everyone wants to drive to the funeral in a Caddy. Other books are *Gone, No Forwarding* (1978) and *Contract Null & Void* (1996).

Gores has also written non-series novels. *Dead Man* (1993) is about a man who seeks revenge on the hired killers who destroyed his family and maimed him. After being blasted with shotguns in a grisly scene, the hero emerges not quite all there mentally, and driven by his primitive, "reptile" brain to hunt down the murderers. Thus, the book takes on the popular "kill the killers" formula. *Menaced Assassin* (1994) is an improbable non-series story about a chain of killings by "Raptor," who calls up the detective Dante Stagnaro each time he strikes.

Among his other activities, Gores has been a very successful television writer. He has written episodes for some of the most popular cop and p.i. programs, including *Kojak, Columbo,* and *Magnum P.I.* He was not so fortunate with the screen version of his book *Hammett* (1975; film 1983), however; after being worked over by many hands, the screenplay was filmed by German director Wim Wenders and released in 1983 to a chorus of "boos" from critics.

GORMAN, ED[WARD] (1941–) A native Iowan, Ed Gorman is the premiere writer in the subgenre of the Western mystery. *Graves' Retreat* (1989) and *Night of Shadows* (1990) are two historical mysteries set in the West. Gorman is also a prolific writer of short stories, some of which are collected in *Prisoners* (1992) and *Moonchasers* (1996). Many of the stories in the latter collection are based on real events or the experiences of people known to the author. Gorman used his own experience of twenty years in the advertising business in his series of mysteries about private investigator Jack Dwyer; the first book in that series was *Rough Cut* (1985). Gorman is also an editor and co-founder (along with Robert J. RANDISI) of *Mystery Scene* magazine. Gorman has written non-series novels such as *Night Kills* (1991) and *The Night Remembers* (1991). In *Harlot's Man* (1997), Gorman wrote about Robert Payne, a former cop and FBI agent who specializes in "psychological profiling." He is called in when a priest is found dead in a cheap hotel room.

GORMLESS English expression meaning "foolish"; an approximate American equivalent would be "clueless." The word derives from the archaic *gaum,* or "understanding."

GOTHIC A literary movement that began in the eighteenth century and arose from renewed interest in the medieval period, which had been denigrated as barbarous ("the Dark Ages") during the heyday of neoclassicism. The gothic movement became one of the tributaries that led to the development of the mystery genre; the work of POE, considered the founder of the detective story, marked the highest development of the gothic. The gothic also heavily influenced such authors as Charles Brockden BROWN and Sheridan LE FANU, and, in a more moderated form, Wilkie COLLINS and more recent authors such as Mary Roberts RINEHART.

The gothic emphasized horror, medievalism, transgression and crime, perversion, and obsession. Matthew Lewis's *The Monk* (1795) takes these themes to an extreme that seems now almost ridiculous, but at the time was revolutionary and shocking. The gothic movement's treatment of criminality as an impulse and the interest in psychology played an important role in the development of writing about crime, particularly the concept of motive. The "psycho," as a character, is pre-gothic, going back to the Devil, the character who does evil things because he *is* evil, a complete tautology. Modern mystery writing—good mystery writing—demands more than that: the criminal must act from motives that the reader is capable of understanding and perhaps sharing. The thrill of the mystery story is identification, not revulsion.

The gothic movement also was seriously devoted to one theme that has been almost completely barred from the mystery/detective genre: the supernatural. Thus the gothic gave birth to two modern genres, horror writing (orthodox gothic) and mysteries (the secular form of the gothic). In writing about supernatural occurrences, however, nineteenth-century gothic writers often attempted to provide a plausible natural or scientific explanation, as in Ann Radcliffe's *The Mysteries of Udolpho* (1794).

GOULART, RON[ALD] [JOSEPH] (1933–) A former pupil of Anthony BOUCHER, Ron Goulart has carried on the tradition of blending mystery with SCIENCE FICTION. Like Boucher, in addition to his fiction writing he has written criticism about the genre. Among these works are *Cheap Thrills: An Informal History of the Pulp Magazines* (1972) and *The Adventurous Decade: Comic Strips in the Thirties* (1975). Goulart's own comic strip, *Star Hawks,* is a private eye series set in the future. Goulart has also worked with William Shatner (*Star Trek*'s Captain Kirk) and has turned his *Tek World* books into another comic series. Of Goulart's own novels, the series about private eye John Easy are best known. The books were all written in the early seventies and began with *If Dying Was All* (1971). Based in Hollywood, Easy usually investigates cases involving missing persons, women in particular.

Goulart himself worked in Hollywood for a number of years. He was born in Berkeley, California, and graduated from the University of California in 1965. He worked in advertising thereafter. He contributed pseudonymously to the Flash Gordon and Avenger series, and also wrote novelizations of film and television programs, including *Laverne and Shirley. Groucho Marx, Master Detective* (1998) is a CELEBRITY MYSTERY.

GRAEME, BRUCE (pseudonym of Graham Montague Jeffries, 1900–1982) Born in London, Bruce Graeme began his writing career after service in World War I. He wrote his first thriller in 1922, and by 1925 he was a best-selling author. He eventually wrote some sixty novels with several different series detectives. His son, Roderic JEFFRIES, carried on the family tradition and surpassed his father in the quality of his writing.

Graeme followed in the wake, as it were, of other writers; he created a RAFFLES-like character named BLACKSHIRT, and, perhaps inspired by A. E. W. Mason's Inspector HANAUD, a series with Inspector Pierre Alain, whom he teamed up with Scotland Yard Superintendent William Stevens. He wrote another series, in the COZY style, about Theodore Terhune, a bookseller, beginning with *Seven Clues in Search of Crime* (1941). Yet another detective was Sergeant Robert Mather, again in a French setting.

Ironically for someone who was so dedicated to series, Graeme's best books are non-series ones. In *The Undetective* (1962), he tells the story of a mystery writer who launches a new series under a pseudonym, only to see the "new" writer made the focus of a murder investigation. The appropriately titled *Through the Eyes of the Judge* (1930) used the interior monologue technique to give the thoughts of a judge during a trial.

GRAFTON, C[ORNELIUS] W[ARREN] (1909–1982) C. W. Grafton wrote only three mystery novels, but one of them is considered a classic. *Beyond a Reasonable Doubt* (1951) is a mystery of the INVERTED type, in which a lawyer commits an impulsive murder and then craftily tries to get away with it. Memorably, he conducts his own defense. Grafton's two other mysteries, *The Rat Began to Gnaw the Rope* (1943) and *The Rope Began to Hang the Butcher* (1944), were about a lawyer named Gilmore Henry; set in Kentucky, they were influenced by the HARD-BOILED style but were offbeat in setting and character.

Grafton was also the father of Sue GRAFTON.

GRAFTON, SUE (1940–) Sue Grafton launched her series of mysteries featuring detective Kinsey MILLHONE in 1982 with *"A" Is for Alibi*, which was the winner of an Anthony award. She has continued to work her way through the alphabet with enormous popular success; critical reaction has been mixed. One critic responded to *"A" Is for Alibi* that "no eagerness for volume 'B' is generated."

Sue Grafton was born in Kentucky and is the daughter of C. W. GRAFTON. She attended Louisville College and began publishing in the late sixties. After a couple of novels, she began to write for film and television.

Kinsey Millhone lives in Santa Teresa, California, and has an arrangement with California Fidelity, an insurance company. Here lies one of the hurdles that the author set for herself and then had to overcome, for most insurance investigations do not involve violent death, and murders and other stock-in-trade of the mystery story somehow have to be worked in. The missing person theme is therefore somewhat overworked. *"B" Is for Burglar* (1985) won a Shamus award, and deals with a wealthy widow gone missing. In *"C" Is for Corpse* (1986), Millhone meets a man with AMNESIA.

Grafton's books are reportedly meticulously researched, and the details are convincing. The same cannot be said for all of the plots, however. In *"H" is for Homicide* (1991), Kinsey passes herself off as a moll with a Hispanic gang for days on end, but her gum-in-cheek dialogue is rather square and out-of-date; they never seem to notice that she sounds like a character from *Happy Days*, and her survival (and especially rescue, a *deux ex machina*) is frankly unbelievable. Her regular gal-ism has attracted many readers, but Millhone's ordinariness acts as a drag on the narration: she often seems trapped within her own limited vocabulary. Her description of the "navy blue sea" leaves as little impression as her effort to convey her former boss's qualities in a flurry of boy-scout terms: "he's smart, meticulous, tireless, and very shrewd. . . . I've caught glimpses of the warmth and generosity that elicit much loyalty in his subordinates."

Grafton writes like many non-mystery novelists who gained notoriety in the 1980s and who portray the homogenized mall-world of consumer products, television, and condominium complexes that has come more and more to dominate the United States. Millhone's little speech about herself that is repeated with a few variations ("My name is Kinsey Millhone. I'm a private investigator . . . I'm thirty-two years old, twice divorced, no kids") is suitably bland. But remarks like "my life has always been ordinary, uneventful, and good," show a kind of willful neurotic repression, even if they make for banal reading. As if in an effort to find a psychological basis for Millhone's weirdly vapid narrative style, *"J" Is for Judgement* (1993) has her uncovering repressed memories that give the key to her neurosis. Millhone was orphaned at five when she was in an accident that left her trapped for hours in the car with her parents' corpses. She was raised by her aunt, and spent four or five months living in a "cardboard box filled with blankets," avoiding contact with others. (Her aunt must have been crazy herself, for she never "interfered.") Grafton seems, then, to have created the perfect detective for the era of victimhood: a former abused child whose ambivalence is revealed in her prudishness and choice of a violent profession. In a bow to the cutesy school of mystery fiction, the Millhone books are released every year close to the character's "birthday."

Grafton's short story "The Parker Shotgun" is one of the most anthologized recent pieces of short fiction.

GRAHAM, WINSTON (1910–) Born in Manchester, England, Winston Graham became famous for his series of historical novels set in Cornwall, beginning with *Ross Poldark* (1945) and collectively known as the Poldark saga. He also wrote a nonfiction book on the area, *Poldark's Cornwall* (1983). Parallel with his historical work, Graham wrote a series of thrillers, the best-known of which is *Marnie* (1961), the basis of the 1964 film by Alfred HITCHCOCK starring Sean Connery. It is a psychological thriller and mystery about the past of a female con artist; even she does not know what dark event she has repressed. Graham's other crime novels are *The Forgotten Story* (1945), *Fortune is a Woman* (1953), *The Little Walls* (1955), *After the Act* (1965), and *Stephanie* (1992).

GRANBY, COLONEL ALASTAIR An intelligence agent in a series of mysteries by Francis BEEDING. Written after BUCHAN and before AMBLER, the Granby novels left no lasting mark on the spy subgenre. Granby is a typical English spy, a recipient of the Distinguished Service Order and a hero. The spy novel of the day was still basically an adventure tale and not a vehicle for social or political commentary. The Granby novels are also considered to be inferior to the other books by Beeding.

Beeding did, however, respond to contemporary events, such as the Spanish Civil War. In *Hell Let Loose* (1937), Granby is dispatched to Spain to stop foreign agents from getting their hands on a secret weapon. In *The Twelve Disguises* (1942), one of his last adventures, Granby is the head of British Intelligence and sets out on a mission to save England.

BIBLIOGRAPHY Novels: *The Six Proud Walkers* (1928), *The Five Flamboys* (1929), *Pretty Sinister* (1929), *The Four Armourers* (1930), *The League of Discontent* (1930), *Take It Crooked* (1932), *The Two Undertakers* (1933), *The One Sane Man* (1934), *The Eight Crooked Trenches* (1936), *The Nine Waxed Faces* (1936), *The Black Arrows* (1938), *The Ten Holy Terrors* (1939), *Not a Bad Show* (1940), *Eleven Were Brave* (1941), *There Are Thirteen* (1946).

GRAND MASTER AWARD See EDGAR.

GRANT, ALAN Detective character created by Josephine TEY. Grant is an inspector with Scotland Yard. He talks little, except in THE DAUGHTER OF TIME (1951), in which he has nothing else to do; however, Tey conveys his thoughts, showing him to be a thoughtful and philosophical man. The contrast between what he says and what he thinks creates a strong dynamic in the novels.

The Grant novels were written at intervals over a period of almost twenty-five years, and each shows great care with setting, mood, and character. Tey wrote some of the most beautiful novels in the genre. Only *The Daughter of Time*, with its static hospital setting, is lacking in color—unless one enters with Grant into his enthusiastic imagining of the personality of Richard III. Grant is more three-dimensional than Roderick ALLEYN, whom he may have partially inspired. Although he has an artistic temperament, Grant is more believable as a policeman than the poet-sleuths Adam DALGLIESH and Nigel STRANGEWAYS, maybe because Tey seems to have more emotional distance from her detective than the writers responsible for these other two. Tey's spirit seems to be everywhere in Grant's world, but not in his head.

Grant has a gentle, self-deprecating sense of humor; he describes his fishing as "something between a sport and a religion." He attended public school with his friend, Tommy Rankin, who is married to Grant's cousin Laura, whom he once thought to marry. Grant always seems a trifle sad and lonely. In a late appearance, THE SINGING SANDS (1952), he is on sick leave following a nervous collapse accompanied by acute claustrophobia and panic attacks, which Tey vividly renders, along with the attendant embarrassment and bravery in trying to quell them that Grant displays. THE FRANCHISE AFFAIR (1948) was based on the case of Elizabeth CANNING. A SHILLING FOR CANDLES (1936) begins with a scrap of poetry written by a dead man.

BIBLIOGRAPHY Novels: *The Man in the Queue* (1929), *To Love and Be Wise* (1950).

GRANT, RUPERT AND BASIL A pair of brother detectives in short stories written by G. K. CHESTERTON. They first appeared in "The Tremendous Adventure of Major Brown." Rupert usually takes the lead, thinking that he is solving the mystery, when in reality he is just a slightly comical leg-man chasing down RED HERRINGS. His brother, a phlegmatic retired judge and poet, then comes to the rescue. Basil is the more interesting of the two. While on the bench, he developed such idiosyncrasies as charging defendants with egotism and ill-humor (he tells a Prime Minister to "get a new soul"), and has retired under a charge of insanity. Now he rarely leaves his garret (an inspiration for Nero WOLFE?) crammed with books, old swords and armor, and where he devotes himself to his art.

GRAY, CORDELIA See JAMES, P. D.

GREAT GATSBY, THE (1925) A novel by F. Scott FITZGERALD, one of the central works of American fiction. *The Great Gatsby* is not a mystery but is undeniably a crime story; like any great work of fiction, it can be read in a number of ways. Nick Carraway has graduated from Princeton and is now working, rather diffidently, on Wall Street. He has taken a house in West Egg on Long Island next to the grandiose dwelling of Jay Gatsby, where extravagant and uproarious parties are held, but which the mysterious Gatsby himself hardly attends. The book contains an accidental killing, and then a murder/suicide in which the murderer takes vengeance on the wrong person. The original cover, with its garish colors and haunting image of the eyes of T. J. Eckleburg, delighted the author, and was an unconscious tribute to PULP. One contemporary reviewer said, "one has the impression that the author entertained in his urbane and ever more polished imagination ideas for a melodrama, a detective story, and a fantastic satire." In the novel, the gangster Meyer Wolfsheim is modeled after the real-life gangster Arnold Rothstein. A friend of Rothstein's, Edward M. Fuller (a financier who eventually went to SING SING), was partly the model for Gatsby. Fuller's case was all over the New York papers at the time Fitzgerald was working on *Gatsby* in Long Island. In earlier drafts of the novel, Fitzgerald made Gatsby's involvement with crooked enterprises more clear.

GREAT TONTINE, THE (1881) A novel by Hawley SMART. The story combines mystery and suspense with some of the favorite Victorian themes: nasty, social-climbing petit bourgeois, hoping to join the squirearchy; impecunious noblemen hunting wives; and a widowed matriarch, a type that would be epitomized in later years by Victoria herself. Told in leisurely, readable prose, it describes how the "rabies of speculation" infects a group of people who subscribe to a TONTINE raised in 1860 to build an opera house. Each subscriber names a person sixty years old or more and pays a hundred pounds for a share, for which dividends are to be paid annually. As the old people die, those who nominated them lose their interest in the tontine; thus, they are betting on their nominees' lives as though they were so many thoroughbreds in the race of longevity. None of the nominees know that they have been chosen, which later on puts them at great peril.

Twenty years later, there are only a handful left in the game and the stakes are high, with the dividends mounting as each nominee dies off. Smart uses the tontine to give a cross section of Victorian society. Viscount Lakington, a spendthrift at the track, nominated his mother-in-law, wife of the magnate Anthony Lyme Wregis. When Lyme Wregis loses his money and blows his brains out, Lakington's interest in the tontine suddenly becomes more than a game. Paul Pegram, an ambitious and venal Welshman, sees the tontine as his only hope of establishing his son as a country gentleman, and thus he has to keep alive his nominee, a clerk who has gone senile. Most interesting of all is the nominee of old Miss Caterham. She chose a drunken Irish servant named Terence Finnigan who has gone to fight in the American Civil War and subsequently disappeared. While the race is on to find Finnigan (to preserve or do away with him), one of the last shareholders proposes a marriage to split the spoils between two families and end the tontine. But the various young people have other ideas. Smart thus weaves a typical Victorian NOVEL OF MANNERS into an amusing story of skullduggery and deceit.

GREAT TRAIN ROBBERY, THE See CAPER.

"GREEK INTERPRETER, THE ADVENTURE OF THE" (1893) Although the plot of this Sherlock HOLMES story has some holes and the ending is unsatisfying, it is noteworthy as the first in which Sherlock's brother MYCROFT takes part. His neighbor, Mr. Melas, has been virtually kidnapped, taken out into the country, and forced to interpret an interview with a Greek man who is being starved to death by his captors because he will not consent to his sister's marriage and give over an inheritance. Melas adopts an ingenious method of asking the man questions of his own, under the very noses of his abductors. The brothers Holmes also engage in an amusing bit of one-upsmanship using their deductive powers.

GREEN, ANNA KATHERINE (1846–1935) Although only one of her dozens of novels remains in print, Anna Katharine Green was a pioneer in the detective novel field. Her father was a lawyer, which provided her with material for the construction of her detective stories, the first and most famous of which was THE LEAVENWORTH CASE (1878), one of the most successful novels of the nineteenth century. The story has nothing to do with Kansas or the famous prison; instead, it is set in Old New York, the author's favorite milieu. It introduces the detective Ebenezer GRYCE, a New York policeman who investigates the shooting of the wealthy Mr. Leavenworth in his library with his own pistol—an apparent suicide.

Green was born in Brooklyn, New York, and attended Ripley Female College in Vermont. After her graduation in 1867 she returned to Brooklyn and began writing. Her father, James Wilson Green, was a well-known trial lawyer. She later married a furniture manufacturer and moved to Buffalo, New York. Her husband was also an amateur actor, and played in the stage version of *The Leavenworth Case,* which Green also wrote.

At the time, Green's novels were enormously successful, and the accuracy and detail of her legal and other details was praised. She was a thoroughly nineteenth-century writer, however, and added to her fiction high melodrama and romantic subplots, which are now rather hard to take. Green's books were often illustrated, and these dramatic old line drawings show the spirit of the novels to the fullest. Her works have been occasionally "rediscovered," though most of them are out of print. Gryce appeared with regularity over the years, most notably in *The Circular Study* (1900), a bizarre and complicated story that also takes place in a New York mansion; *The Filigree Ball* (1903), which features a strange and unbelievable murder weapon and has a long inquiry by the coroner appended to it; and *The Woman in the Alcove* (1906). Green also made the choice to age Gryce naturally, so that in the later books he is barely mobile.

Green wrote many other non-series mystery novels, which have shared the obscure fate of all but the first of the Gryce novels. These stories also used New York high society as a setting, and, in the absence of Gryce, are if anything more romantic. *The Millionaire Baby* (1905) is about the daughter of Mr. Philo Ocumpaugh. She is only six years old, and stands to inherit not one but three fortunes. The girl has disappeared and is presumed kidnapped. *Initials Only* (1911) is about a young woman who collapses in a New York hotel with no one standing near her. This fact becomes puzzling when it is found that she has not fainted, but has been stabbed. In *The Mayor's Wife* (1907), Mayor Henry Packard is running for governor, and wants to hire a companion for his wife, who has gone into a sudden decline (i.e., an embarrassing fit of madness). Her problems turn out to be related to the house itself, which may be haunted. Miss Saunders, the companion, tells the story and acts as the sleuth; both the narration and the setting mark the book as HAD-I-BUT-KNOWN *avant le lettre.* Green also wrote several other mysteries about female sleuths. Some of her stories featured sleuth Violet Strange, and one of Gryce's assistants was Amelia Butterworth.

Green was an ambitious writer, and hoped to become a poet. She published the collection *The Defense of the Bride and Other Poems* (1882), as well as a verse drama. Her talent as a writer, however, consisted in the construction of plot, and poetry has no plot; she also depicted people as types rather than creating convincing individuals. Thus, her works are more remembered than appreciated, and posterity has preserved only a single example, albeit the best one, of her ability as a technician of the murder story. Green will also always be recalled as the author of the first detective novel by a woman, even though the claim is untrue. Her position in the history of women's literature is slight but solid. Michele Slung anthologized one of the cases from *The Golden Slipper and Other Problems for Violet Strange* (1915) in *Crime on Her Mind* (1975). Slung points out that Green was three years old when POE died and lived to see Agatha CHRISTIE begin her own long publishing career; it has also often been noticed that *The Leavenworth Case* preceded Conan Doyle's A STUDY IN SCARLET by eight years. As a writer whose life spanned fully half of the entire history of the modern detective story, Anna Katherine Green is of historical rather than literary importance. Later critics have read her books more for their depiction of nineteenth-century society, especially its manners and relations between classes. It is perhaps ironic that the narration of detection, on which she had an important influence, is now less interesting than all that remains implicit in the books—from what the characters wore to how they spoke and how they thought.

GREEN ARCHER, THE (1923) One of the more often recommended novels of Edgar WALLACE, *The Green Archer* combines ghosts, gangsters, and murder. Although set in England, it is full of Americans, and like so many of Wallace's books, it also reflects his own journalistic experience (he said he was "first, last and all the time a newspaperman"). The young and ambitious reporter Spike Holland is charged with investigating the Green Archer of Garre Castle, a ghost of a man executed in 1487. He finds that the castle is currently owned by a former Chicago gangster named Abe Bellamy; as he is about to get a hot story, his source, Bellamy's associate Creager (a former prison guard) is found murdered with a green arrow. A mysterious green archer appears on the grounds of the castle, sometimes acting as a Robin Hood and saving damsels in distress—in this case Valerie Howett, daughter of a wealthy oil man.

In his preface to the 1965 Norton reprint of *The Green Archer,* Vincent STARRETT described Wallace's incredible working routine. He would get up at seven in the morning and smoke cigarettes and drink tea continuously throughout the day and often long into the night. His practice was to write out the first chapter of his books in longhand and then dictate the rest. The beginning of *The Green Archer,* like that of other Wallace novels, is slow; Wallace seems to have used the space to get his ideas straight but never went back and revised.

At the time that he wrote *The Green Archer,* Wallace had never visited the United States but was obviously fascinated by it. When he did make the trip in 1929, one of the places he went was Chicago, where he visited Al CAPONE's headquarters, the site of the St. Valentine's Day Massacre, and the flower shop where Dion O'Bannion was killed. (This research led to his famous play, *On the Spot.*) *The Green Archer* was filmed in 1925.

GREENE, GRAHAM (1904–1991) Graham Greene's novels are not, strictly speaking, mysteries (with the exception of THE THIRD MAN), although they often incorporate mystery and suspense. Sometimes the suspense is political, at other times it is theological—the suspense of the soul hanging in the balance of fateful moral decisions.

After studying at Oxford and pursuing a literary career, particularly as an editor and film critic, Greene served in British intelligence during World War II. After the war, Greene traveled the world as a reporter and correspondent, always seeming to be in the right place at the right time (he was in Cuba the year before the revolution). Hence he often dealt with political intrigue in his books, for example in the novels *The Comedians* (1966), about Haiti, and *The Quiet American* (1955), about Vietnam. Neither spy stories, conventional novels, nor mysteries, Greene termed such works "entertainments." One of the best known is OUR MAN IN HAVANA (1958), in which a sort of mystery develops when WORMOLD, an MI-6 recruit who has invented a string of informants and agents, finds that they have begun to exist in reality.

Greene's Catholicism and concern with philosophical questions pervades his work; the suspense of *The Heart of the Matter* (1948), about a colonial policeman in Africa during World War II, is really the suspense that Scobie feels as he hesitates between damnation and salvation. A smuggling operation, a shipwreck, and his loveless marriage all combine to entrap him in impossible choices. Although *The Power and the Glory* (1940) is a dystopic novel about religious persecution in a totalitarian society, the whisky priest's flight from his pursuers is less important than his gropings toward the truth and struggle with his own faltering and fallen self. Greene's stories are ambiguous because evil is more believable, and visible, than good: "one began to believe in heaven because one believed in hell, but for a long while it was only hell one could picture with a certain intimacy." *Brighton Rock* (1938) is the chilling story of PINKIE, a gang leader in England's most famous seaside resort. The story incorporates suspense and detective elements while exploring the possibility of redemption. The opening, in which a man tries to escape Pinkie's gang in the crowded Brighton waterfront, has a cinematic quality. Later Greene focuses on Pinkie's commission of mortal sin and the psychosexual sources of his delinquency.

Greene's postwar career as a journalist took him to many areas of upheaval, from Vietnam to the Congo. The morbid personalities and corrupt surroundings of his stories led critics to label his imaginative world "Greeneland." Other Greene entertainments include *Stamboul Train* (1932; also pub as *Orient Express*), about several people on the Orient Express, including a revolutionary named Czinner who is facing court martial and probable death; *The Confidential Agent* (1939), a suspense story about D., an agent from a civil war–torn country who is sent to procure a contract with the coal industry in England—a man who has lost his family and lost all hope; *Dr. Fischer of Geneva, or, The Bomb Party* (1980), about a perverse millionaire who stages dinners for his "friends" in which he humiliates them more and more grotesquely; and *Travels with My Aunt* (1969), about a charming elderly woman who is also a smuggler.

Greene wrote two volumes of autobiography, *A Sort of Life* (1971) and *Ways of Escape* (1980). Further volumes of writings have appeared posthumously, including the journal he kept of his dreams.

GREENE, HUGH (1904—) Brother of Graham GREENE, Hugh Greene had a similar career, though he did not become a writer of fiction. He worked as a foreign correspondent in the thirties, and then for the BBC as the head of the German Service throughout World War II. Greene continued with the BBC after the war, in Germany, Eastern Europe, and Malaya. He collaborated with his brother on *The Spy's Bedside Book* (1957), a compilation of short pieces, both fiction and reminiscences, having to do with espionage by a wide variety of figures, from the poet Edmund Blunden to the painter Paul Gaugin to T. E. Lawrence (Lawrence of Arabia). The book is dedicated to William LEQUEUX and John BUCHAN. The selections include Lord Baden-Powell's extraordinary description of butterfly hunting in the Dalmatians, during which he encrypted drawings of military fortifications (including number of guns and their calibers!) into his sketches of butterflies, and Colette's portrait of Mata Hari. Greene also edited *The Rivals of Sherlock Holmes* (1971), *Cosmopolitan Crimes: Foreign Rivals of Sherlock Holmes* (1971), and *Further Rivals of Sherlock Holmes* (1973), which collect many hard-to-find stories by contemporaries of Conan DOYLE.

GREENE MURDER CASE, THE (1928) One of the best-known novels of S. S. VAN DINE, *The Greene Murder Case* is something of a contradiction. Although it is better written than other books in the series, that almost makes it worse reading—the author is defeated by his own seriousness. Philo VANCE is supercilious, but he is not as studied in his pretentiousness and arrogance as in other appearances. Hence, *The Greene Murder Case* reads as a "straight" novel of the GOLDEN AGE, with all of the attendant flaws, and lacks the histrionics and unintentional humor that make some of the Van Dine books camp classics.

The story opens after the shooting of two sisters, Julia and Ada Greene, in the New York mansion they share with the rest of the members of this eccentric family. Van Dine deploys the stock device of a will with unusual provisions: Tobias Greene insisted that his family continue to live in the house for twenty-five years after his death or risk disinheritance. His widow is a self-centered hypochondriac; when her son is killed, her response is "Dear, dear! If people must do such things, why do they have to come to my house and annoy a poor helpless old woman like me?" All of the characters display a like unreality. For example, for a hundred pages the police and the district attorney are devoted to the theory that the first shootings were the work of a burglar, when it is plain to Vance—and even more so to the reader—that this is impossible. The Greenes are mildly amusing as a family of wealthy lunatics with skeletons to hide, even though they are completely unbelievable as people. Vance solves the case, famously, with the help of a German criminological treatise, Gross's "Handbuch für Untersuchungsrichter."

GREEN FOR DANGER (1944) A novel by Christianna BRAND set in a British military hospital in Kent during the Blitz. Considered a classic and listed on many "top 100" lists, it yet has a number of flaws. The motive of the murderer is hard to take without a dash of insanity thrown in; Brand employs the concept of the *idée fixe,* the mind normal but for one certain area. The novel also has one very unlikely clue, the difference between "astonishment" rather than "surprise" on a dead face. That it has as many romantic interconnections as a television hospital drama must be a fault to some, a virtue to others. The murder method, however, is brilliantly simple.

Amid daily and nightly German bombing raids, a group of doctors and nurses carry on almost normally—falling in love, becoming jealous, and committing murder. The hospital routine is described in detail, but then recedes into the middle ground. The persons assigned to the hospital have all more or less tragic—or at least dull—pasts from which they have momentarily escaped. Major Moon lost his son to a hit-and-run accident, and his wife died of grief; the anesthetist, Barnes, was accused of killing a girl on the operating table and is waiting for the affair to blow over; his love, V. A. D. (Voluntary Aid Detachment) Frederica Linley, is escaping from nothing more horrible than a dreary home life; and V. A. D. Esther Sanson is getting over the death of her mother, buried in an air raid under rubble for three days and nights.

One night, an air raid warden is brought in with a fractured femur; the next day, he mysteriously dies in the operating room. Only seven people knew that he was even in the hospital, one of whom soon learns the killer's secret and pays the price. Inspector COCKRILL also announces early on that he knows who did it, but has no proof. The denouement is drawn out as he tries to make the murderer crack. The story is clever, perhaps too clever by half. RED HERRINGS and diversions are almost too well laid out, but the clues are fairly dropped, and Brand expertly pulls off a surprise ending. *Green for Danger* reads very much like a book that could have been made into a typical forties film—which it was, in 1946.

GREEN ICE (1930) The first novel of Raoul WHITFIELD. A version of the book was first published in BLACK MASK, and it has very much the feeling of a series of episodes. Mal Ourney has been in SING SING prison for two years, having taken the rap on a vehicular homicide for a woman, Dot Ellis, who was driving his car. Ourney did the honorable thing because she was drunk on his liquor. He also expresses a noble desire to entrap and destroy some of the "breeders"—the big crooks who prey upon the small fry, setting them up and knocking them down. But before Ourney can even get to the train station at Ossining, someone has tried to set him up, and Dot is dead. Then, as he says, "a lot of guys quit breathing." Ourney follows the trail of corpses to the valuable stones—the green ice—for which all the crooks are ready to kill. He becomes a sleuth and enters into an uneasy alliance with a cop named Donnelly. Ourney also poses as a newspaperman in Pittsburgh (a job Whitfield once held).

Dashiell HAMMETT praised the nonstop action of *Green Ice,* though it falls well below the level of Hammett's own writing. Like a Paul CAIN story, Whitfield's work has the feeling of Carroll John DALY's with the extraneous words and expostulations combed out, leaving terse blow-by-blow descriptions: "Donnelly told his pal to take Red out. Red protested, and Donnelly told him to shut up. He shut up. Donnelly's pal took him away." There is less of a sense of artfulness than there is in Cain, who is more vigilant against romanticism. Ourney has seventy-five thousand dollars left from an inheritance, which makes his crusading almost on a par with WIMSEY's.

GREGSON, TOBIAS See STUDY IN SCARLET, A.

GRIERSON, EDWARD (1914–1975) Edward Grierson's output was small but his reputation as a mystery writer was large. Grierson was born in Bedford, England, and educated at St. Paul's and Oxford. He practiced law until World War II, in which he served in Egypt with the Sapper Territorials and rose to the rank of lieutenant colonel. After the war he was the senior legal adviser to an R.A.F.-Army organization. The latter part of his life was spent in writing and lecturing; he also spent a year as an announcer for the Australian Broadcasting Commission. Grierson also wrote books on history, including *The Fatal Inheritance* (1969), about Philip II of Spain.

Grierson began his writing career with historical works. His first mystery novel was *Reputation for a Song* (1952), which set the pattern for his other books, combining accurate trial scenes with an attention to character and psychological horror; Julian SYMONS called it "an outstandingly interesting account of crime as it is committed and endured." THE SECOND MAN (1956) is if anything even more highly regarded; BARZUN and TAYLOR said it was "altogether perfect." In this case, the lawyer protagonist is a woman, and the romantic subplot is ably handled and used neither as a diversion nor a space-filler. The novel is also somewhat reminiscent of the case of Oscar SLATER. Grierson's interest in history, criminal or otherwise, is most apparent in *The Massingham Affair* (1962), about an investigation into a robbery of the Victorian era in which two innocent men may have been sent to prison.

GRIERSON, FRANCIS D[URHAM] (1888–1972) English author, one of the lesser figures of the GOLDEN AGE. He belonged to the post-HOLMES reaction, and created a Bloomsbury doctor named Professor Wells. Like Doctor THORNDYKE, Wells was based on a real person, a scientist who was an acquaintance of Grierson's. Despite the supposedly realistic basis of the stories, there are unaccountable goofs, such as when the evil bookseller and criminal Gregory Marle poisons himself with STRYCHNINE at the end of *The Smiling Death*, and dies quietly in a few seconds without displaying any of the correct symptoms.

GRIFFITHS, MAJOR ARTHUR (1839?–1908) Major Griffiths served in the British Army for many years throughout the empire before he became a writer. Griffiths was a sixteen-year-old lieutenant at the siege of Sevastapol in the Crimean War; later he was stationed in India and Canada. After leaving the army with the rank of major, he worked in the British penal system, serving as deputy governor of several institutions. He then became a prison inspector, a position he held for twenty years. His first publications were military histories and books about crime. *Criminals I Have Known* (1895) is a collection of fictionalized short sketches based on his experiences. Of his thirty novels, about a third are mysteries. Other books by Griffiths include *Fast and Loose* (1885) and *Locked Up* (1887). *The Rome Express* (1896) is about a murder aboard a TRAIN, the *direttissimo* traveling between Rome and Paris, and shows the author's debt to Emile GABORIAU. After the bloody corpse is found in the sleeping car, suspicion falls immediately on an Anglo-Italian contessa. The crime is investigated by inspector Floçon, who blusters through a rather humdrum case with the bravado expected of a French inspector in a sensational Victorian novel. The British characters have dialogue that is equally, if unintentionally, funny ("If they stop us, I shall write to *The Times*").

GRIFTERS, THE (1963) A crime novel by Jim THOMPSON. The story is driven by the characters rather than the plot, which is a simple triangle. Roy DILLON is a grifter who lives in the Grosvenor-Carlton Hotel in Los Angeles, a run-down fleabag. His girlfriend is Moira Langtry, another hustler, who sometimes uses her body to get what she wants. Lastly there is Lillian, Roy's mother, who has an incestuous desire for her son (she gave birth to him when she was only fourteen) and for his money. Lillian hates Moira as much as she loves her son, though love is not really the word for her complex and perverse emotion. It is a fourth figure, the gangster Bobo Justus, whose actions bring out the latent violence in the triangle of Roy, Moira, and Lillian, producing a surprising and shocking outcome.

The tightness of the writing and the intensity of the small circle of manipulators who are themselves manipulated makes this novel one of Thompson's most effective. The familial aspect makes it almost primal; Dillon's efforts to distance himself from Lillian and her "love" for her son are a high-energy disturbance running through the story. Perhaps even more troubling than the violence is the mingling of love, hate, and naked self-interest, and the way in which the characters slip from one emotion to the next.

GRIJPSTRA, ADJUTANT HENK AND DE GIER, SERGEANT RINUS The two main characters in a series of novels by Janwillem VAN DE WETERING. The bluff

Adjutant Henk Grijpstra, middle-aged, fat, and with eyebrows "like steel wool," is a bit like Detective DALZIEL, and perhaps even cruder. For example, after his retirement from the force at the age of forty-eight and his move to private detecting, he does not take divorce or other romantic cases because "love is a fart in a brown paper bag." (Van de Wetering's scatological humor has long been a part of the series, but it has become more pronounced over time.) De Gier, on the other hand, has the practicality of Pascoe, Dalziel's assistant; his romantic streak, though, sometimes gets him into a tangle. (The title of the collection, *Sergeant's Cat and Other Stories* [1987], alludes to de Gier's other love, Oliver the Siamese cat). Grijpstra is stuck in an unhappy marriage for most of the series—hence the opening of *Just a Corpse at Twilight* (1994) is something of a shock.

The series has followed the pattern of the author's own life, beginning with a group of novels set in Amsterdam and then moving abroad. The first book in the series was OUTSIDER IN AMSTERDAM (1975), which is closer to the moodiness of Nicholas FREELING's Holland novels than to the jocular slapstick of the later Grijpstra and de Gier exploits. The contrast between the two men's viewpoints—Grijpstra's cynicism and de Gier's dreamy idealism—is brought out by the nature of the case: a man who has started a phony religious community is found hanged. Another Amsterdam case is *Death of a Hawker* (1977). Grijpstra and de Gier are dispatched to old Amsterdam to deal with violent riots against the tearing down of historic houses for the building of a subway. (The ruin of Rembrandt's Amsterdam by capitalists and politicians is a recurrent theme in the series.) Meanwhile a man, Abe Rogge, is found dead in his room by his sister; the murder weapon seems to have been a spiked object like a medieval mace. Grijpstra and de Gier are assisted by a retired transvestite policeman. Although Van de Wetering writes well, the case comes to a rather exaggerated finale involving a bulldozer; there is also a lack of explanation and analysis, and questions are left unresolved.

With *Just a Corpse at Twilight*, Van de Wetering revived the series after a hiatus of almost ten years. Grijpstra is now a private detective, but the next book, *The Hollow-Eyed Angel* (1996), flashes back to a time before his retirement from the force. A young gay reserve policeman asks the commissaris, who happens to be going to a conference in New York, to investigate the mysterious death of his uncle in Central Park. Rinus de Gier follows the commissaris, who is now very old and nods off during lectures. Meanwhile, Henk Grijpstra investigates the death of a baron on a golf course as a possible homicide. In *The Perfidious Parrot* (1997), Grijpstra and de Gier have retired and started a private detective agency. A sleazy character named Carl Ambagt twists their arms into investigating piracy on the high seas—the theft of a chartered oil tanker in the Caribbean. The case takes them to Key West and The Perfidious Parrot, a lap dancing bar, then on to St. Eustatius. Van de Wetering's ribald streak is getting stronger and stronger, his writing looser and looser; in *The Perfidious Parrot*, he writes like a Dutch Carl HIAASEN.

BIBLIOGRAPHY Novels: *Tumbleweed* (1976), *The Corpse on the Dike* (1976), *The Japanese Corpse* (1977), *The Blond Baboon* (1978), *The Maine Massacre* (1979), *The Mind Murders* (1981), *The Streetbird* (1983), *The Rattle Rat* (1985), *Hard Rain* (1986).

GRIMES, MARTHA (***) With a series of books all named for English pubs, Martha Grimes has become one of the leading Anglophile mystery writers. An American college professor, she helps to maintain the non-existent England of the GOLDEN AGE in a series of COZY mysteries and is almost a pastiche of CHRISTIE, SAYERS, and the other Golden Age masters.

Grimes was born in Pittsburgh and educated at the University of Maryland. She currently teaches at Montgomery College in Maryland. Her first mystery, *The Man With a Load of Mischief* (1981), introduced her series character, Richard JURY. Although Grimes researches her books in England and takes the names from real public houses, she has been criticized for the errors that crop up regularly in the novels. Among those most critical of her work were BARZUN and TAYLOR, who said of Grimes that "her work comes not from the imagination, but from other books, which take the real a little more seriously," and that she "allows her love for old English inns to blanket her attention to the mechanics of crime fiction." Grimes has written one non-series novel, *End of the Pier* (1992), which was set in the United States.

GRISHAM, JOHN (1955–) The U.S. author John Grisham could be described as the Steven Spielberg of mystery and suspense: hugely successful commercially, but often spurned by the critics. Grisham, however, has yet to create his *Schindler's List* and show that he is more than a producer of books that sell. But sell they do: a *Publisher's Weekly* article estimated the worldwide gross of his novels and their spinoffs at $1 billion. The "Grisham business" has a large effect on the book industry as a whole, dictating what other publishers print and when.

Born in Arkansas, Grisham initially wanted to play professional baseball. He later attended law school at the University of Mississippi, and practices criminal law. His first book was finished in 1987 and published in 1991. He has gone on to produce many other novels, several of which have been filmed. Grisham's novels are more dependent on suspense and melodrama than detection or mystery. The characters and descriptions tend to be wooden—with other suspense writers he shares the SUPERLATIVE COMPLEX: in *The Firm* (1989), the young protagonist is the best student from the best law school, the firm is the most selective and highest paying, etcetera. Unlike other attorneys, solicitors, and barristers turned fiction writers, like Cyril HARE and Frances FYFIELD, Grisham still writes like a lawyer, setting forth the argument and the parties rather than evolving the plot and the people. The books are readable precisely for this lack of style; moving along faster than the works of writers who attempt more and succeed less, they are primarily visual, like the films into which they are so easily made.

A Time to Kill (1989), his first novel, is based on an actual rape case. But the fact that a story is true does not therefore make it less obscene or liberate one from the demands of art. In the opening scene, the brutal rape of a ten-year-old black child, Grisham hangs the label "redneck" on the perpetrators; this technique of labeling rather than developing the characters (not particular to Grisham) establishes the invisible narrator's moral disapproval, thus providing permission for the depiction of a repugnant scene. But it also places the reader in the balcony with the omniscient narrator, not in the world of what is happening; a Jim THOMPSON or John LE CARRÉ would have made us stand in the rapist's shoes—horrible, but defensible for the same reason. Grisham's statement in a later introduction that he thought *A Time to Kill* was a "wonderful" story is amazing for its failure to grasp the irony or the subtleties of language. The Grisham book that most resembles a traditional mystery is *The Pelican Brief* (1992). It involves the assassination of two Supreme Court justices, and a female law student who thinks she has found the key to the crimes.

Grisham branched out in new directions with the ambitious novel *A Painted House* (2001), set in the rural Arkansas where he grew up. The story is narrated by a seven-year-old farm boy, Luke Chandler. Through the child's eyes, we see mysteries of the adult world—some of them shocking—gradually revealed.

GROFIELD, ALAN A thief, part-time actor and full-time lothario in several books by Donald WESTLAKE, written under the pseudonym of Richard Stark. Grofield first appeared in the PARKER series novel *The Score* (1964) as a bit of comic relief; Grofield quotes Shakespeare, acts out charades with the other bored thieves in their canyon hideout, and seduces one of the captives he is set to watch. Grofield was the first character to indicate the comic direction Westlake's work would later take. After appearing in two other Parker novels, Grofield had his first solo adventure in *The Damsel* (1967). The books in which Grofield is the protagonist differ in that he is also the narrator. Grofield disappeared at about the time Westlake's John DORTMUNDER came into being, giving wider play to the author's humor.

BIBLIOGRAPHY Novels: *The Dame* (1969), *The Blackbird* (1969), *Lemons Never Lie* (1971).

GRUB-AND-STAKERS See MACLEOD, CHARLOTTE.

GRUBB, DAVIS See NIGHT OF THE HUNTER, THE.

GRUBER, FRANK (1904–1969) One of the most prolific and successful of PULP authors, Frank Gruber was born in Elmer, Minnesota, but made his name in New York City as a freelancer. He wrote for trade journals and taught writing while trying to make it with the pulps; it was rough going at first, and Gruber's story, recounted in the autobiographical *The Pulp Jungle* (1967), is one of dogged determination rewarded. After breaking into magazines, he later branched out into novels, television, and film. Gruber eventually published more than three hundred short stories, over sixty novels, and over two hundred film and television scripts.

In his early years, Gruber worked on the family farm in Minnesota, then served in the army in the early twenties. During the rest of that decade, he held a variety of jobs ranging from ticket-taker in a movie theater to bellhop. The Depression found him, like most of the country, out of work. He had written for some agricultural trade magazines, and in 1934 he moved to New York. He published his stories in various pulp magazines, including the most prestigious—BLACK MASK. Like Erle Stanley GARDNER, Lester DENT, and others, he also branched out into other fields, including Westerns.

Of his novels, *The French Key* (1940) was probably Gruber's most successful. It introduced two series characters, Johnny Fletcher and Sam Cragg, who in addition to solving crimes are hawking a body-building manual. The book was a hit. Simultaneously, Gruber was making an impression on Hollywood, selling his first story (*Death of a Champion*, 1939), followed by a Western (*The Kansan*, 1943) and a film based on an Eric AMBLER novel (*The Mask of Dimitrios*, 1944). An adaptation of *The French Key* was filmed in 1946.

Oliver QUADE is another Gruber creation. Gruber had a flair for clever, intelligent characters rather than bruisers;

one of his best-known detectives was Simon Lash, a bibliophile like Gruber himself. The Lash adventures began with *Simon Lash, Private Detective* (1941). Simon and Eddie Slocum are down-and-out private eyes when they are approached by Joyce Bonniwell, a former girlfriend of Lash's. Her husband Jim, whom she believes suffers from AMNESIA, is missing; Lash believes Jim is faking amnesia in order to leave his wife. A detective hired to find Jim, however, has also disappeared. The story is told in an amusing style that is a cut above pulp writing and very readable.

Gruber's last book was *The Spanish Prisoner* (1969), about a former FBI agent vacationing in Spain who receives a letter dated 1520 from a man supposedly being tortured by the Spanish Inquisition. Attached to the letter is a genuine gold coin. He judges it to be a con game, but then the agent discovers the body of a tortured and crucified man. This story eventually becomes intertwined with the agent's previous failed investigation of a California bank robbery. Though unbelievable, the plot moves along with Gruber's usual brisk pacing.

In addition to his own name, Gruber wrote under twenty-five pseudonyms, including John K. Vedder and Charles K. Boston.

GRYCE, EBENEZER The detective introduced in Anna Katherine GREEN's best-selling novel THE LEAVENWORTH CASE (1878). Gryce is a policeman and suffers from an inferiority complex as a result. In his very class-bound view, he needs both a legman (Mr. Q) to do the dirty work and another helper, Everett Raymond, to pursue investigations in the high society to which Gryce feels unequal. Amelia Butterworth also helps him in the latter regard. A spinster and a busybody, Butterworth prefigured many later detectives such as Hildegarde WITHERS and Miss MARPLE, and to a lesser extent Miss SILVER. Amelia Butterworth first appears in *The Affair Next Door* (1897).

Like other GENIUS DETECTIVES, Gryce is incredibly well informed about a range of subjects. He is already middle-aged when the series begins; never an exciting personality, he becomes more and more subdued as he ages. The Gryce novels have not been reprinted, with the exception of *The Leavenworth Case.* Although Green used legal and medical detail to advantage, and Gryce is in some ways a preview of later offbeat detectives (his foibles and his fatness are not typical of the Victorian or Edwardian detective), her writing was stilted and artificial.

BIBLIOGRAPHY Novels: *A Strange Disappearance* (1880), *Hand and Ring* (1883), *Behind Closed Doors* (1888), *A Matter of Millions* (1890), *Lost Man's Lane* (1898), *The Circular Study* (1900), *One of My Sons* (1901), *Initials Only* (1911), *The Mystery of the Hasty Arrow* (1917).

Short Stories: *A Difficult Problem* (1900).

GUARNACCIA, MARSHALL SALVATORE The detective in a series of novels by Magdalen NABB. Guarnaccia is an Italianized version of MAIGRET: he pursues culprits through psychological clues rather than forensic evidence, using his empathy to understand how certain people would behave. A family man, Guarnaccia lacks Maigret's introversion; in his late thirties or early forties, he is married and has two sons, and his wife works in a school. Guarnaccia is Sicilian, from a little town near Syracuse, and experiences ongoing culture shock in Florence, where he lives above the Carabinieri barracks. His office is in the Palazzo Pitti.

Guarnaccia is overweight because he cannot resist food, a fact that his wife nags him about. He appears to be "asleep on his feet," an expression in Italian that also means mentally slow. Guarnaccia seems to think he is not very smart, though actually he is observant and canny. He is also old-fashioned, though in a good sense; in one novel, he encounters homosexuality, which he finds incomprehensible. Once he gets over his surprise, he accepts it—a realistically Italian reaction. Most of Guarnaccia's cases involve foreigners, but the Italians in the books are believable. *Death in Springtime* (1984) varies the scene of the series to include Sardinia. In *The Marshall and the Murderer* (1987), a pair of young Swiss women are visiting Italy to improve their Italian. One of them, Monica, becomes an apprentice potter in a small village, then disappears. Guarnaccia travels to the village to investigate and finds it to be a closed, inward sort of place that shuns outsiders. There he meets his alter ego, an exuberant Roman of the Carabinieri who has somehow made himself at home there. The roots of the crime go back to World War II and the German occupation. THE MARSHALL AT THE VILLA TORRINI (1993) is about the murder of a famous writer.

BIBLIOGRAPHY Novels: *Death of an Englishman* (1981), *Death of a Dutchman* (1982), *Death in Autumn* (1985), *Marshall and the Madwoman* (1988), *The Marshall's Own Case* (1990), *The Monster of Florence* (1996).

GUILLOTINE The guillotine is most famous for having been used during the French Revolution to cut off the heads of aristocrats and other opponents of the revolution. The word is derived from the name of a member of the Constitutional Assembly, Joseph Ignace Guillotin (1738–1814), who proposed that capital punishment be mechanized. The substitution of a machine for the traditional human executioner with his axe could be seen as symbolic of the birth of the modern state. The first version, designed by Dr. Antoine Louis of the French College of Surgeons, was known as the "louison" or "louisette." Contrary to legend, Guillotin did not die by the machine to which he gave his name.

The guillotine was only abolished in France in 1981. The last execution by guillotine took place in 1977. The guillotine was also the legal method of execution in Germany until 1947.

GUMSHOE This term for a detective came into use around the turn of the century, the idea being that gum-soled shoes allowed one to sneak around unheard.

GUN MOLL A gangster's woman; a woman who collaborates with gangsters or who is a criminal herself. Apparently a gun moll was said to carry a gun for the gangster. Hugh Rawson states, however, that the "gun" in *gun moll* comes not from the firearm but from the Yiddish GONIF.

"Moll" is a very old diminutive of the name Mary, and by the sixteenth century had taken on a pejorative meaning, which Defoe later helped to solidify with his *Moll Flanders,* who was a prostitute, thief, and convict all in one.

A *moll hook* or *mall tooler* was a female pickpocket.

GUNNER, AARON See HAYWOOD, GAR ANTHONY.

GUNSEL See GUNTZEL.

GUNTHER, BERNIE See KERR, PHILIP; BERLIN NOIR.

GUNTZEL This word has nothing to do with guns. From the Yiddish *gonzil,* it means a young man or boy, implicitly a homosexual who has yet to be "adopted" by an older man.

Anyone who has seen Humphrey Bogart's performance in *The Maltese Falcon* (1941) may recall his use of the word. According to Hugh Rawson, Dashiell HAMMETT, annoyed at the publisher's censoring of his books, snuck in the word guntzel (with its actual meaning); the editor, and later the director, both let the word slide because they thought it must have meant "gunman."

GUTMAN, CASPAR The Fat Man, the most vivid villain created by Dashiell HAMMETT. He is the large mass at the center of THE MALTESE FALCON (1929) around which the other scoundrels orbit. He is a jovial but dangerous mountain of flab with "a great soft egg of a belly" and "pendant cones for arms and legs." When he moves, the blobs shake in sympathetic motion. Full of well-formed maxims like "I'm a man who likes talking to a man that likes to talk," he is enormously entertaining.

"GUTTING OF COUFFIGNAL, THE" An idiosyncratic mystery featuring Dashiell HAMMETT's CONTINENTAL OP. It begins with the almost comical scene of the Op sitting in an armchair in an elegant house, guarding a pile of wedding presents. Meanwhile, the exclusive island community of Couffignal, joined to the mainland by a bridge, is about to be raided by a gang of crooks with machine guns and an armored car. The story first appeared in BLACK MASK in June 1926.

GYP This common word, meaning to cheat, is actually a racial slur based on the word Gypsy; thus, it is no more respectable than other race-based expressions, such as "welsh" (reneg, as on a bet) or "jew" (cheat someone out of something). There is another possible derivation, however: it has also been suggested that gyp could come from the obsolete word *gippo* (It.), meaning "scullion," which would make the term more palatable.

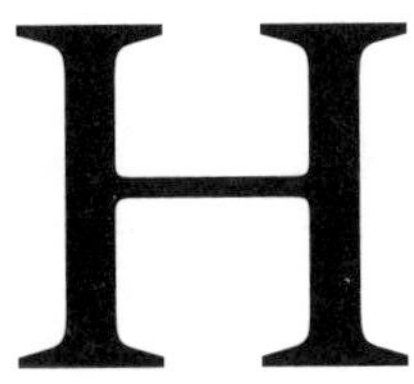

HABEAS CORPUS From the Latin, meaning "you must have the body," habeas corpus is the writ requiring that a person be produced in court in order to investigate the lawfulness of his or her detention. The Habeas Corpus Act was passed in England in May 1679.

HABIT OF FEAR, THE (1987) A novel by Dorothy Salisbury DAVIS, featuring her series character Julie Hayes. Hayes is writing a gossip column for the *New York Daily;* she is married to Geoffrey Hayes, a bigwig of journalism, but they have never been very close. Still, after he announces that he has fallen in love with another woman, Julie is shocked and humiliated. She leaves the house and goes for a walk, during which she is brutally assaulted.

All this is background, for the real mystery, which Julie decides to investigate after she gets out of the hospital, is her own past. She never knew her father, an Irish poet who had later disappeared. Hayes travels to Ireland in search of information about him, while the investigation into her attackers goes on, eventually revealing political and criminal complications. Although the story could be termed romantic suspense, the writing and characterizations are head and shoulders above the usual level. The psychology is interesting but not pushed too heavily; the characterizations are like quick dabs of color that bring people to life, even if they are not of much depth. The American characters are drawn better than the Irish, who tend toward cliché.

HABIT OF LOVING, THE (1979; orig title *Deadly Relations*) This novel by June THOMSON finds Inspector RUDD once again investigating heartbreak, frustration, and murder in the Essex countryside. Maggie Hearn is a middle-aged, unmarried woman who cared for her farmer father until he died. She has since let the land to other farmers, including the bitter Aston couple. Lonely, Maggie takes in a young man named Chris one rainy night. It turns out that he has a psychiatric history. Meanwhile, the philandering Ken Aston has been having an affair with his foreman's daughter, Jess, who is still a teenager but has already had a child out of wedlock. Then Chris begins dating Jess as well; after one of their meetings, Chris returns to Maggie's house in a rage, packs, strikes Maggie, and leaves. Soon he is hiding out in a quarry, suspected of murder. The plot is well constructed, with several suspects and no alibis.

This novel shows Thomson's ability to reveal strong emotions hidden under bucolic placidity. Her country people seem as complex, tortured, and sad as modern city dwellers. The psychology is penetrating but not presented in a heavy-handed way. Thomson has taken the English village mystery and shorn it of cuteness, substituting instead believable people and often harrowing situations.

HADDAM, JANE (pseudonym of Orania Papasoglou, 1951–) A former academic, Jane Haddam's first books were written under her real name, beginning with the thriller, *Sanctity* (1986). It is the Haddam books that have made her reputation, however; they feature detective Gregor Demarkian, a former FBI expert on serial killers who lives in an Armenian neighborhood in Philadelphia, where he grew up.

Haddam has gone rather overboard in the 1980s craze for gimmicks: each of the books occurs on a major secular or Judeo-Christian holiday, Demarkian has a smoldering-but-not-catching-yet romance with his sidekick (fantasy author Bennis Hannaford), and he reads about his own exploits in *People* magazine, where he is compared to Hercule POIROT. Luckily, Haddam leavens her concoctions with humor and local color, though the locales are sometimes unrecognizable.

The plots tend to capitalize on contemporary hot-button issues, and Haddam is fond of the religion-and-sex angle. Subplots are sometimes labyrinthine. *Dear Old Dead* (1994) concerns a Father's Day murder. At the center of the plot is a gay doctor with AIDS, Michael Pride, who runs a clinic in Harlem. He has recently been arrested at a gay porn shop; his priest is in love with him. His rich benefactor is killed in his clinic, and Demarkian is hired to investigate by the Archbishop, who wants to shut the clinic down. Subplots concern a Father's Day newspaper prize of $100,000, a teenage prostitute in need of rescue, and an anti-abortion clinic picketer. *Baptism in Blood* (1996) takes place at a camp in the South and teems with religious zealots and rednecks (and some lesbians). In this book, the widower Demarkian confronts his feelings for Hannaford. The first murder, of a baby, occurs during a hurricane, and the prime suspects are the mother or the lesbians. Satanic rituals and an atheist bookstore owner complete the mix. Demarkian is the most interesting character because he is the most neutral; by being ordinary in comparison with the various hyped-up characters he meets, he succeeds in seeming real. It is as if Inspector HEIMRICH suddenly appeared in an Almodovar movie.

Under her real name, Papazoglou has published novels about romance writer Patience McKenna. In *Wicked, Loving Murder* (1985), she takes a ghost editor job for a magazine and finds the body of Michael Brookfield, of the newsletter department, strangled with a typewriter ribbon. Felicity Aldershot, Ivy Tree, and the other romance writers and publishers are typically COSY and quite empty; the motives—drugs and money—do not bring their New York publishing world any closer to the real thing.

HAD-I-BUT-KNOWN A subgenre of the mystery story, usually involving a romantic heroine who retrospectively tells the story of her narrow escapes and brings the mystery to a conclusion. Thus, in a sense, a had-I-but-known novel is a shaggy dog story, the mystery created simply by the fact that the reader doesn't know the end of the tale, which is supposed to have already occurred when the book opens.

The invention of the genre is often credited to Mary Roberts RINEHART, whose THE CIRCULAR STAIRCASE (1909) begins with the line, "This is the story of how a middle-aged spinster lost her mind." The had-I-but-known novel, however, has its antecedents in the GOTHIC, borrowing many of its devices, including the retrospective element. In fact, as a label it sounds deceptively definite when in reality it is nebulous and imprecise. The term itself was coined for this subgenre by the poet Ogden Nash.

HAGGARD, SIR [HENRY] RIDER (1856–1925) English novelist of mystery and adventure, better known for the latter. His most famous works are usually included in surveys of the mystery genre because, in the broadest sense of the word, they deal with the mystery of the uncanny and unexplained. The roots of Haggard's work are in the ancient genre of quest literature, which may account for their incredible popularity.

Haggard was born in Norfolk but went to Natal in 1875, sent by his father to join the staff of Henry Bulwer, the lieutenant governor. He worked in the colonial administration in Africa for several years, met with Zulu leaders and learned about their culture. His African experience provided the background for a series of adventure tales, notably *King Solomon's Mines* (1885), which introduced the character Allan Quatermain. He is an elephant hunter who is recruited by Sir Henry Curtis and Captain John Good to search for Curtis's brother, who has disappeared while hunting for the legendary diamond mines of King Solomon. Haggard's stories caused some controversy because of their violence, which now seems unexceptional. The trap doors, stone slabs that open, and *Arabian Nights* flavor were liked by a vast readership that included such varied characters as Robert Louis STEVENSON and the poet Gerard Manley Hopkins.

Quatermain returned in *Allan Quatermain* (1887), which deals with the discovery of a white civilization in Africa. *She* (1887) is perhaps Haggard's most outlandish tale, about the immortal Ayesha, the queen of the "lost" city of Kor. She retains her youth (she is 2,000 years old) by bathing in a pillar of fire. Now considered Haggard's masterpiece, it was scandalous at the time—one reader wrote to Haggard that it was "sickening trash." Haggard's nearest contribution to the mystery story proper was MR. MEESON'S WILL. His stories were beloved by young boys. Ironically, Haggard's own son Jock died while still a child, a blow from which Haggard never fully recovered. Late in life he lost his ancestral home. Haggard's interests had always been social and political—reflected, for example, in his first book, *Cetywayo and His White Neighbors* (1882)—and he later wrote books on agricultural reform and sat on royal commissions dealing with environmental matters and surveying. Like Conan DOYLE, he was knighted for his public service rather than his writing.

One of those who read Haggard in their youth was Graham GREENE; he acknowledged the influence of Haggard in his review of Lilias Rider Haggard's biography of her father, *The Cloak That I Left* (1951). Greene pointed out the "adult" side of Haggard that children are apt to miss; mentioned his deep pessimism and obsession with death; and rated *Mr. Meeson's Will* as one of Haggard's "dull adult books."

HAGGARD, WILLIAM (pseudonym of Richard Henry Michael Clayton, 1907—1993) An English author of suspense and espionage fiction, William Haggard was a generation older than his compatriots LE CARRÉ and DEIGHTON but began publishing at about the same time. Although he wrote at the height of the Cold War, Haggard's work belongs to an earlier age. His hero is an aristocratic spy named Charles RUSSELL, who first appeared in *Slow Burner* (1958). Russell is much closer to Richard HANNAY than to Harry PALMER or George SMILEY, and though he is pragmatic he is still very much the "old boy," and more of an organization man than many other heroes. Julian SYMONS called Haggard a "right-wing romantic," a label that seems to have stuck. Haggard's books are less violent and more artful than many in the spy genre.

Haggard was educated at Oxford University and joined the Indian Civil Service in 1931 and eventually became a judge. He was in the Indian Army during World War II, returned to Oxford for his M.A. after the war (1947), and, at the time he began writing thrillers in the late fifties, worked for the Board of Trade.

Haggard has also written non-series thrillers, including *Closed Circuit* (1960) and *The Kinsman* (1974). Both these books are not so much about espionage as about money; in the first, an heir stands to lose his fortune because of an enemy who happens to be a Latin American dictator; in the second, a financial advisor to criminals is hired by a gambling boss to collect a £20,000 debt owed by a distant relative.

HAILEY, DR. EUSTACE The "Giant of Harley Street" is a character created by Anthony Wynne (pseudonym of Robert McNair Wilson, 1882–1963). Hailey treats crime as a disease, believing that "there are no great criminals," only people who have failed to adapt to circumstances and are driven to act criminally. Although a doctor, Hailey is not too impressed with science, only with the mind that applies it. His preference is for psychological detection, his method being to understand the character of the person who committed the crime. Hailey is tall and kindly, wears glasses (sometimes a monocle), and takes snuff. Hailey is also given to philosophizing and thinking out loud. He is remembered, if at all, for the unusual case "The Cyprian Bees." One of his best gestures is to produce the victim, alive, just as the "murderer" is being sentenced (in *Red Scar*).

HAILEY, J. P. See HALL, PARNELL.

HAIRLESS MEXICAN, THE A bizarre hired killer in ASHENDEN (1928), by W. Somerset MAUGHAM. He claims to be a general, and to have a vast hacienda in Mexico; he insists that he is irresistible to women; and he wears outrageous wigs and paints and sharpens his fingernails. Ashenden finds him to be a very dangerous clown, and their association is disastrous.

HALIFAX, DOCTOR CLIFFORD Dr. Clifford Halifax is both a pseudonym (of Dr. Edgard Beaumont) and a character in a series of stories written by Beaumont in collaboration with L. T. MEADE. They were collected in *Stories from the Diary of a Doctor* (1894, exp 1896), *Where the Shoe Pinches* (1900), and *A Race with the Sun* (1901). Halifax was a typical character of Edwardian fiction. The co-authors were pioneers of the medical detective, the finest example of which is Dr. THORNDYKE. The title story of *A Race with the Sun*, (which was reprinted by Hugh GREENE), however, is an outlandish tale more in keeping with the spirit of Max PEMBERTON. It involves the obsessive fear of a potential invasion of England, which was common at the time (and masterfully exploited in THE RIDDLE OF THE SANDS, 1903).

HALL, ADAM (pseudonym of Elleston Trevor, 1920–1995) Adam Hall's reputation rests mainly on the novel *The Quiller Memorandum* (1965), which was filmed in 1966 with an all-star cast that included Alec Guinness and Max von Sydow. This novel also won an EDGAR award and the Grand Prix de Littérature Policière. Hall went on to write a series of books about QUILLER, all in the spy-thriller-suspense vein.

Hall was born in England but later settled in the United States. He was a race car driver before World War II, and then joined the RAF. Hall has written many books under various other pseudonyms, including Caesar Smith and Mansell Black. A number of his books have been filmed. The flavor and attitudes of Hall's work are similar to those of William HAGGARD.

HALL, JAMES W. See MCGEE, TRAVIS.

HALL, PARNELL (1944–) Himself a former private detective, the American writer Parnell Hall has written a series about detective Stanley Hastings. This p.i. series is possibly more realistic than others precisely because of Hastings's ordinariness and the humdrum nature of much of his work. On the other hand, the detective is really a writer and actor who only works as a p.i. for the money. Hastings's main employer is the firm of Rosenberg & Stone, the kind of ambulance chasers who advertise on television and in the subway for personal injury cases. The first novel in the series was *Detective* (1987), and was nominated for an EDGAR award. In *Suspense* (1998), Hastings has opened his own agency; he is framed for murder in a case involving a successful but bad writer. All the Hastings books have one-word titles, and Hall has been turning out one a year; they include *Strangler* (1989), *Actor* (1993), *Movie* (1995), and *Scam* (1997). Dialogue is emphasized and the narration scrolls along, linear but without much shape.

Under the pseudonym J. P. Hailey, Hall began a series about a lawyer named Steve Winslow with *The Baxter Trust* (1988).

HALLER, MICHAEL Private detective created by Max BYRD. Haller is repeatedly called "the original missing person," an arty allusion to the fact that his business of seeking out missing persons is actually part of his search for self. Haller's partner is a retired cop known only as

"Fred"—cigar-smoking, fat, and looking like "a California sea lion." His girlfriend is a red-haired, "plump" psychiatrist named Dinah Farrell.

In his first case, *California Thriller* (1981), Haller looks for a missing journalist from the *San Francisco Constitution* who has supposedly run off with a woman not his wife. In *Fly Away Jill* (1981), Haller is hired to find the runaway daughter-in-law of a suspicious Italian whose business is oil tankers. The chase leads to London, where Haller finds that someone is following him, and finally to Bordeaux. As in a television thriller, the end is never the end, and explosions are piled on shootings in an attenuated denouement that brings in drugs, archaeology, and old scores going back to the French Resistance. In *Finders Weepers* (1983), the efforts to establish Haller's intellectualism are less obvious and the hair-raising, death-defying conclusion is less belabored. This book also shows Haller's typical feeling of displacement as a New Englander in California, and his delineation of San Francisco amounts almost to dislike.

HALLIDAY, BRETT (pseudonym of David Dresser, 1904–1977) Brett Halliday was one of the staple detective writers of the forties and fifties, during which time he published most of his novels about Mike SHAYNE. Halliday, who had started out writing for PULP MAGAZINES, had his greatest success with the Shayne character, and was one of the first writers to set a successful mystery series in Florida. Long before the creation of Travis MCGEE, Hoke MOSELEY, and a horde of other Floridian sleuths, Halliday had seen the potential of the regional setting. Unfortunately, however, the descriptions of Miami are not particularly vivid (Halliday did not live in Florida, but California), and the dialogue lacks the snap and cleverness associated with the HARD-BOILED school.

The Shayne series was written by other writers after Halliday gave it up, including Bill PRONZINI. Halliday was a founder of the Mystery Writers of America, and was at one time married to Helen MCCLOY.

HALLIDAY, MICHAEL A pseudonym of John CREASEY.

HAMBLEDON, TOMMY A fictional English spy created by Manning COLES. His full name is Thomas Elphinstone Hambledon, and he is represented as the wiliest and most daring of British spies (his assumed death after the first adventure allows his colleagues to give glowing eulogies of him). He is anything but impressive looking, however; "nondescript," short, thin-lipped, and square-jawed, with old wounds on his face that look like dueling scars.

Hambledon has a very long career, beginning in *Drink to Yesterday* (1940), set during the World War I. It is the second book, however, *Pray Silence* (1940; U.S. title *A Toast to Tomorrow*), in which, suffering from AMNESIA, he has his most outrageous adventure.

In *Green Hazard* (1945), Hambledon is shadowing an explosives chemist in Switzerland and happens to get blown up in the chemist's house; the unconscious Tommy is mistaken for the chemist and taken to Berlin. The humor comes from his efforts to appear to know something about his subject, and from the coincidence that the real professor winds up in Berlin impersonating *him*. Hambledon is suave but pulls some refreshingly dumb stunts, such as when, as the supposedly famous "chemist," he purchases elementary chemistry books right in front of his captors.

Always with a large element of fantasy, the Hambledon stories became progressively more strained in their plots. In *Now or Never* (1951), Tommy tracks down a resurgent Fascist movement known as the Silver Ghosts (that they named themselves after the most famous Rolls Royce is curious).

BIBLIOGRAPHY Novels: *They Tell No Tales* (1941), *Without Lawful Authority* (1943), *The Fifth Man* (1946), *A Brother for Hugh* (1947; U.S. title *With Intent to Deceive*), *Let the Tiger Die* (1947), *Among Those Absent* (1948), *Not Negotiable* (1949), *Diamonds to Amsterdam* (1949), *Dangerous by Nature* (1950), *Now or Never* (1951), *Night Train to Paris* (1952), *Alias Uncle Hugo* (1952), *A Knife for the Juggler* (1953), *Not for Export* (1954; U.S. title *All That Glitters*), *The Man in the Green Hat* (1955), *The Basle Express* (1956), *Birdwatcher's Quarry* (1956; British title *The Three Beans*), *Death of an Ambassador* (1957), *No Entry* (1958), *Crime in Concrete* (1960; U.S. title *Concrete Crime*), *Search for a Sultan* (1961), *The House at Pluck's Gutter* (1963).

Short Stories: *Nothing to Declare* (1960).

HAMILTON, [ARTHUR] [DOUGLAS] BRUCE (1900–) Bruce Hamilton wrote a handful of mystery novels in several different styles—the thriller, the courtroom novel, the INVERTED MYSTERY, and other subgenres. Hamilton was born in England and was a teacher in Barbados. He was the older brother of Patrick HAMILTON; *The Light Went Out* (1972) is his biography of Patrick. Hamilton's mystery novels include *Middle Class Murder* (1937; U.S. title *Dead Reckoning*), an inverted tale about a dentist who kills his wife. *Rex versus Rhodes, The Brighton Murder Trial* (1937) is a work of true crime. None of Hamilton's work is generally available, but TOO MUCH OF WATER (1958) is sometimes reprinted; it is a fine example of MURDER AFLOAT.

HAMILTON, DONALD [BENGTSSON] (1916–) Best known for his spy adventure series about Matt HELM, begun in 1960, Donald Hamilton had actually been publishing in the crime and Western genres of popular fiction since the forties. Hamilton was born in Uppsala, Sweden, and emigrated to the United States at the age of eight. After receiving his degree in chemistry from the University of Chicago in 1938, he entered the Naval Reserve. After World War II, he changed careers and became a freelance writer and photographer. In 1947, he published the spy novel *Date with Darkness* (1947). A lifelong outdoorsman, he also easily adapted to the Western mode; his novel *The Big Country* (1957) was filmed the following year and starred Charlton Heston and Gregory Peck. He later gave Matt Helm a similar biography to his own: at the outset of the series, Helm is living in the West and making his living at freelance writing. Hamilton has written articles about guns, hunting, yachting, and other outdoor subjects, and published *Donald Hamilton on Guns and Hunting* in 1970.

HAMILTON, [ANTHONY] [WALTER] PATRICK (1904–1962) Besides two plays that were made into famous films—Hitchcock's *Rope* (1948) and Cukor's *Gaslight* (1944)—the English writer Patrick Hamilton is remembered for one mystery novel: *Hangover Square* (1942), about the nightmarish existence of a schizophrenic criminal in a London slum. In the twenties, beginning with *Craven House* (1926), Hamilton produced a series of Dickensian works set in London. Of Hamilton's plays, *Angel Street* (1942), which was the basis for *Gaslight,* was the most successful, and ran for 1,295 performances.

HAMMER, MIKE The private detective created by Mickey SPILLANE, often called the toughest tough guy ever to appear in fiction. Hammer is more than tough; he is a sadist, particularly when it comes to women. Hammer is summed up by his most famous line in his first case, *I, the Jury* (1947): he shoots a woman in the stomach and as she dies she asks, "How could you?" He answers, "It was easy." Hammer is a far cry from Raymond CHANDLER's idea that down the "mean streets" must go a man "who is not himself mean"; Hammer is not only mean but cruel. Chandler himself said of Spillane, "pulp writing at its worst was never as bad as this stuff. It isn't so very long since no decent publisher would have touched it."

A common plot is Hammer meeting a hypnotically erotic woman, who offers herself to him; intensely aroused, he withholds his attentions, preoccupied by his desire to kill the murderer he is after. Thus, sexual lust is displaced by the lust to kill. Hammer's two desires are mixed up at a deep level; even when he likes a woman and embraces her, his "hands wanted to squeeze right through her waist until they met." That Hammer murders a psychiatrist in *I, the Jury* seems symbolic.

In the end, Hammer usually winds up burying the woman rather than sleeping with her, and thus he is oddly celibate during the series despite his violent sexual fantasies. In *Kiss Me, Deadly* (1952), Hammer burns a woman to death, and her agonizing end is depicted as an erotic parody of sex. *The Big Kill* (1951) is also about sexy, evil women—this time, a redhead, a term that is parodied in the end when her face is turned into "a ghastly wet red mask that was really no face at all." Again, punishment for such women is not so much death as torture and mutilation of their beauty. *My Gun Is Quick* (1950), however, shows Hammer in a more sympathetic light; he meets a red-headed prostitute in a hash house and feels sorry for her. He gives her money and beats up the thug who is after her, but she is the victim of a hit-and-run the next day. Hammer vows vengeance, but he does not even know her name. The plot is more complicated and involves more detection as Hammer investigates a prostitution ring.

William DEANDREA's idea that criticism of Hammer as pornographic resulted from some kind of forties prudishness is simply ridiculous. If such violence "wouldn't raise an eyebrow today" (which seems unlikely), it says more about the values of today than it does about Hammer. Hammer himself offers a muddle-headed justification of his violence: "I was the evil that opposed other evil," to the benefit of the good. This hardly seems to be the basis for a world in which "good and evil were sharply defined"—though Hammer's anti-Communist crusading in such books as *One Lonely Night* (1951) fit right into Cold War politics.

Hammer operates out of an office presided over by his secretary, Velda, who also has a private eye's license. His friend Pat Chambers works in the police department and gets him out of jams. In his first case, an old friend of his is killed, and Hammer vows to catch up with the murderer, shoot him in the belly with his .45, and watch him die. Hammer gets mixed up with a blonde bombshell who is also a psychiatrist; she is tired of neurotic men who have lost their masculinity, and finds Hammer to be a "real man."

Hammer becomes a drunk for seven years, thinking he has caused Velda's death. In *The Snake* (1964), it turns out that she has been behind the Iron Curtain, getting information that saves millions of lives. Reunited with Mike, she tells him that she is still a virgin. He refuses to take her, however, saying that they must get married. Still, the marriage is put off.

Hammer has mellowed somewhat over the years. In his latest adventure, he doesn't get to torture a mobster because Velda asks him not to.

BIBLIOGRAPHY Novels: *Vengeance Is Mine!* (1950), *The Girl Hunters* (1962), *The Twisted Thing* (1966), *The Body Lovers* (1967), *Survival . . . Zero!* (1970), *The Killing Man* (1989), *Black Alley* (1996).

"HAMMER OF GOD, THE" (1911) A Father BROWN story, which G. K. CHESTERTON based on the Cain-and-Abel story of good and evil brothers. One is the Honorable Wilfred Bohun, a pious clergyman; his brother is the dissipated Colonel Norman Bohun, a "tall, fine animal, elderly, but with hair startlingly yellow." Although Wilfred appears good, his "almost morbid thirst for beauty" and jealous love of his church is like his brother's lust and drunkenness. Wilfred predicts that Norman will be struck down by God when he tries to seduce the wife of the blacksmith—a huge and powerful man.

The crime is one of the most grisly in the Father Brown stories ("fragments of bone were driven into the body and the ground like bullets into a mud wall"), but the conundrum is how a small weapon could cause an enormous wound. Suspicion falls variously on the smith, his wife, and the village idiot. Father Brown's solution of the crime is well clued, and in a sense obvious. The solution also serves as the text for one of Brown's favorite themes, the sin of pride.

HAMMETT, DASHIELL (1894–1961) Born in Maryland, Dashiell Hammett did not go to school beyond the age of thirteen. He did not cultivate himself as a literary figure, and spent much of his time living in relative obscurity and isolation. His first works were published under a name (Peter Collinson) that came from underworld slang for "a nobody." During most of the second half of his life, he did not write at all. And yet, Raymond CHANDLER paid him the ultimate compliment, saying that Hammett "did over and over again what only the best writers can ever do at all. He wrote scenes that seemed never to have been written before." Only Conan DOYLE has had as profound an influence on the course of the development of mystery and detective fiction in the modern era.

Hammett worked for eight years as a Pinkerton detective out of Baltimore, a job that sent him all over the country (including to California, where he worked on the Fatty Arbuckle case) and provided the material for a series of ground-breaking novels and the stories featuring THE CONTINENTAL OP. He wrote advertising copy in the years after he left the Pinkerton agency. Hammett was one of the most popular writers who published in BLACK MASK, the magazine that defined the HARD-BOILED style. Hammett's first novel was RED HARVEST (1929), which featured the Op and was serialized in *Black Mask*. His next three novels would also appear serially in the magazine. What still impresses about the Op stories—sometimes dismissed as the "pulp" that led up to THE MALTESE FALCON in 1929—is their purity. They are not minimalist, because minimalism is a conscious reaction to some other literary convention perceived to be wordy or overwritten. Hammett was not so much naturalistic as simply natural. His Pinkerton experience gave Hammett's stories an authenticity many others lacked. But it was not because he knew the detective business that he wrote such powerful and unadorned stories—many ex-policeman have written mysteries, but none with Hammett's distinction—but because he knew how to write. Among the novels, all of which are distinctively different, only *The Dain Curse* (1928) is actually a bad book, dragged down by racial stereotypes and overloaded with exoticism.

Hammett had already created Sam SPADE, become famous, and started writing for Hollywood when he wrote THE THIN MAN (1934). In between, he published what he thought was his best work, THE GLASS KEY (1930). *The Thin Man* is a lighter, more comic work, and it led to a fantastically successful series of films. It was also the last novel Hammett published during his lifetime. The story collection *The Big Knockover* (1966) was edited by the playwright Lillian Hellman, Hammett's longtime companion, and contains a moving introduction by her. Hammett's earlier work continues to be reprinted. *Woman in the Dark,* a novella featuring the remarkable character BRAZIL, was published in book form in 1988 with an introduction by Robert B. PARKER.

Hammett wrote virtually nothing during the last twenty-five years of his life, during which he was constantly ill. He had served in both world wars, leaving the first with tuberculosis and the second with emphysema. In 1948, he gave up drinking after years of alcoholism. Although he did not write, he read with an insatiable curiosity about a vast array of subjects, from glassmaking to Hegelian philosophy to mathematics.

Hammett was imprisoned in 1951 in the same red scare that sent Howard Fast (E. V. CUNNINGHAM) to prison. Long a supporter of radical causes, he had been a trustee of the Civil Rights Congress and refused to name the contributors. He was also summoned to appear before Senator Joseph McCarthy's House Un-American Activities Committee. Hellman wrote that she did not know whether Hammett was a member of the Communist Party.

The various biographers of Hammett deal differently with his drinking, his abandonment of his family (he had been married in 1920 and had two children), and other controversial aspects. *Beams Falling: The Art of Dashiell Hammett* (1980) by Peter Wolfe and *Dashiell Hammett: A Life* (1983) by Diane Johnson are two books on Hammett's life and work.

HANAUD, INSPECTOR A French inspector of the Sûreté, invented by A. E. W. MASON. Hanaud is a large and affable man with great wit, though sometimes it fails—even Mason said that Hanaud's sense of humor at times was "too elephantine" and that he could be "quite, quite puerile." Hanaud is described as a "burly" man with thick dark hair and a round face and the "shaven chin of a comedian." His most distinguishing features are his light eyes and heavy lids. One character likens him to "a big Newfoundland dog." He has a taste for physical comedy, and sometimes seems like a giant inflated Charlie Chaplin.

Mason tried to make Hanaud as realistic as possible. The author knew personally Detective Beyle of the Parisian police, and also carefully studied the memoirs of chiefs of the Sûreté. Hanaud's WATSON is the bibulous Monsieur Ricardo. Ricardo thinks Hanaud a genius, a label the great detective resists, saying "Ascribe to me no gifts out of the ordinary run. I am trained, that is all." Mason further humanized Hanaud by having him commit errors.

The Parisian setting is well handled and Hanaud is charming, though sometimes he breaks the rules of FAIR PLAY (they were not "invented" until 1929); thus, Hanaud is a creature of the Edwardian era, even though, unlike Sherlock HOLMES, he is not a private detective but a policeman. Hanaud appeared in five novels but only one short story, "The Affair of the Semiramis Hotel," which was published in *The Four Corners of the World* (1917). Hanuad's dialogue is full of rhetorical flourishes, and his syntax is somewhat like Hercule POIROT's: "We are the servants of Chance . . . our skill is to seize quickly the hem of her skirt, when it flashes for the fraction of a second before our eyes." THE HOUSE OF THE ARROW (1924) is one of the most admired Hanaud tales.

BIBLIOGRAPHY Novels: *At the Villa Rose* (1910), *The Prisoner in the Opal* (1928), *They Wouldn't Be Chessmen* (1935), *The House in Lordship Lane* (1946).

HANNASYDE, SUPERINTENDENT See HEYER, GEORGETTE.

HANNAY, RICHARD The hero who ran away in THE THIRTY-NINE STEPS (1915) and other adventures by John BUCHAN. Hannay is a thirty-seven-year-old mining engineer from South Africa when he makes his first appearance. He meets an American, Scudder, who is killed in his apartment, leaving him with a puzzling, enigmatic message. Hannay is mistaken for a murderer and for a secret agent, from which his double dose of trouble stems. Hannay is clever and well educated (he speaks several languages), but he is also the most humble of fictional spies. He often finds himself being persecuted, and has to use both his wits and his mastery of disguises to escape while also trying to figure out what is really going on.

Hannay was based on a real person Buchan knew, "Tiny" Ironside, who became a field marshall (Hannay eventually rises to the rank of major-general). Among the other books in which Hannay appeared is *Greenmantle* (1916), in which he is sent on a secret mission based on a scrap of paper—again, a few meaningless words spark a mystery. It develops into an adventure to stop an Islamic holy war led by the prophet figure Greenmantle against the British Empire and Russia.

BIBLIOGRAPHY Novels: *Mr. Standfast* (1916), *The Three Hostages* (1924), *The Island of Sheep* (1936).

Short Stories: *The Runagates Club* (1928; 1 Hannay story).

HANSEN, JOSEPH (1923–) Joseph Hansen sent the manuscript of his first novel about Dave BRANDSTETTER, an insurance company investigator, to a number of publishers over the course of three years before anyone would take it. Insurance is hardly controversial, but Brandstetter's sexuality was: apart from Pharaoh LOVE, who was more of an underground phenomenon, Brandstetter was the first significant gay detective character (see GAY MYSTERIES).

Hansen was born in South Dakota but in his youth moved to California, where he has lived ever since. He moved to Hollywood during World War II, in which he was a conscientious objector. Hansen wrote for film, radio, and television, including the series *Lassie*. Although he published poems—which he had been writing since a young age—in prestigious magazines such as *The New Yorker*, it was with fiction that he had his major success. During the sixties, he became associated with the gay magazine *Tangents*. He wrote several gay novels, some under pseudonyms, including *Known Homosexual* (1968), a story about a gay man accused of murdering his lover. His first novel about Dave Brandsetter appeared in 1970. Hansen lives in Southern California with his wife and two sons.

Discussions of Hansen's work inevitably focus on Brandstetter's homosexuality, though not all of his cases involve the gay community, and sex is not a big part of the stories. Indeed, it is almost irrelevant, which is as it should be—part of Hansen's point seems to be that anyone can be a private detective just as anyone can be a cop. Hansen has said that he wanted to show that gays are just like other people, with the ironic result that Brandstetter is *not* "noticeably" gay, and that aspect of his personality does not set him apart from other people.

Twenty-five years after Stonewall, it should be easier to look at the Brandstetter books as books, and Hansen should get more credit for his writing than he usually does. Although he lacks the depth of Lew ARCHER, Dave Brandstetter covers the same territory—Southern California—with the same quiet efficiency and intelligent sympathy. Although less than dynamic, the books have a notably higher level of focus and observation than others among the horde of Californian p.i. books. Hansen's stories are good not because they are about gays but because he is a good writer; he has a no-frills style that, though it does not bristle with wisecracks or arty formulas, is perfectly suited to the kind of story he wants to tell.

In addition to the Brandstetter series, Hansen wrote several non-series novels. *Backtrack* (1982) is about a young man investigating the death of his father, who had abandoned him eighteen years before. The father was a small-time actor in Hollywood, and the son is forced to delve into the fairly sordid details of his life. Hansen adapted this novel for the stage. STEPS GOING DOWN (1985) is also a non-series novel, which engages gay issues even more forthrightly than the Brandstetter books.

Hansen has written two collections of short stories, *Bohannon's Book* (1988) and *Bohannon Country* (1993), about a former sheriff living in a rural area of California. Hansen has said that in his youth he was a great reader of Westerns and intended to write one but later lost interest. His periodic visits to some friends who live in an area like that of Bohannon's home led him to revive his early interest in the Western and to combine it with detection. In 1992, Hansen received the Lifetime Achievement Award from the PRIVATE EYE WRITERS OF AMERICA. Other awards include a fellowship from the National Endowment for the Arts.

HANSHEW, THOMAS W. (1857–1914) The English writer Thomas W. Hanshew could be said to have created the ultimate master of disguise with Hamilton CLEEK, a professional thief who can assume another identity simply by changing expressions. Hanshew produced several non-series mysteries and also wrote Nick CARTER books, but none of this work is as famous as Cleek—and even he is known mainly for his sheer preposterousness. Hanshew's family carried on his name, writing and publishing several Cleek books after Hanshew's death.

HARALD, SIGRID See MARON, MARGARET.

HARD-BOILED The hard-boiled style began with the tough guys of the PULP MAGAZINES after World War I. It has often been pointed out that the disillusionment and cynicism that followed the war embued the hard-boiled character. The first hard-boiled detective was Race WILLIAMS, created by Carroll John DALY—soon to be surpassed by other and better writers, primary among them Dashiell HAMMETT, whose hard-hitting CONTINENTAL OP remained forever nameless and was the most perfect hard-boiled character ever invented.

The hard-boiled novel was raised to the level of art by Hammett and Raymond CHANDLER; Chandler defined the knightly ethos of the hard-boiled character in his famous statement that began "Down these mean streets a man must go who is not himself mean." But a split had already occurred in the hard-boiled genre that would only get wider, between the knight-errant detective and the detective who was so tough that he was indistinguishable from the people he opposed. Ross MACDONALD defined the difference succinctly: "I think self-knowledge, and a matching knowledge of the world, are what the serious private detective may be after. . . . The fictional detectives who revel in killing don't belong to the real world. They inhabit a sadomasochistic dreamworld where no license is required, either for the detective or the wild dreamer at the typewriter." Race Williams and Mike HAMMER are the primary examples of the latter type of detective; Macdonald's own Lew ARCHER was the highest development of the serious, un-mean detective—who, it is important to note, Macdonald identified with *real* detectives he had met. "Sadists and psychopaths," he said, "don't last very long in this rather exacting work." This seems to indicate that the serious detective is also the more realistic detective.

The serious hard-boiled detective, however, often poses as a callous cynic. One of the conventions of hard-boiled fiction is a two-fold deception that conceals a moral battle between sincerity and insincerity. The detective is not a mean man (he is quite compassionate, in fact), but he hides his humanity behind a mask of cynicism—hence the wisecracks and ironic remarks that are the most notable stylistic feature of hard-boiled writing. On the other hand, the detective is usually confronted by a client who *is* insincere, who is a liar, or who at the very least is telling him only part of the story, but who hides his or her insincerity behind a mask of "sincere" emotion and concern. Brigid O'Shaughnessy in THE MALTESE FALCON (1929) is a perfect example of this type of deceiver, who may cry, make emotional pleas, and otherwise try to dupe the detective into taking the case. Another example is Chandler's Orfamay QUEST. Particularly in the earlier era of the hard-boiled story, this insincere character is often a woman—the *femme fatale*.

HARDIN, BART The sleuth Bart Hardin was obviously modeled on his creator, David ALEXANDER. Hardin works for a newspaper, the *Broadway Times*, which covers horse racing and the theater and is very similar to the paper Alexander once edited. Although a journalist, Hardin is still a tough guy in the HARD-BOILED tradition, a hard-drinking and scrappy former Marine. He lives in a Times Square tenement. In the first book, *Terror on Broadway* (1954), Hardin hunts down a serial killer who preys on women in the theater district. The book gives a nostalgic picture of the Great White Way. *Paint the Town Black* (1954), the next book, is about drug dealing.

BIBLIOGRAPHY Novels: *Shoot a Sitting Duck* (1955), *The Murder of Whistler's Brother* (1956), *Die, Little Goose* (1956), *The Death of Humpty Dumpty* (1957), *Dead, Man, Dead* (1959).

HARDY BOYS See STRATEMEYER, EDWARD L.

HARE, CYRIL (pen name of Arthur Alexander Gordon Clark, 1900–1958) An Oxford-educated barrister, Cyril Hare was extremely clever at using his legal background in his novels, a number of which were about barrister Francis PETTIGREW. Hare's pseudonym was made up anagrammatically from his addresses. An erudite and literate writer, Clark studied history at Oxford, but his first publications were humorous pieces for *Punch*. He was a friend of Michael GILBERT, whom he met at the DETECTION CLUB. Called to the bar in 1924, Hare later was a judge's marshall and during World War II worked in the British office of the Director of Public Prosecutions and for the Ministry of Economic Warfare. He became a county court circuit judge for Surrey in 1950.

Hare's first mystery was *Tenant for Death* (1937), and was a more conventional tale featuring Inspector Mallet of Scotland Yard. Supposedly, Mallet was not interesting enough to stand up on his own, but was later worked into the Pettigrew novels as a minor player. Mallet is an engaging character and a canny policeman; it sometimes seems odd that he does not arrive at the solution earlier, but it must be so for Pettigrew to have a role at all. Hare periodically renewed the series by adding new policemen who variously oppose, consult, and manipulate the barrister. Mallet reappeared in *Death Is No Sportsman* (1938), in which the sport is fishing. In *Suicide Excepted* (1939) Mallet begins to fade into the background, and a trio of amateurs do most of the sleuthing.

Hare shows the ins and outs of the legal world without sounding dry, and also with a good deal of humor. His style is similar to that of Edmund CRISPIN except that he is less self-conscious and circumlocutory and arch (some of Crispin's work seems to be written while daydreaming). Hare's experience as a judge's marshall forms the background of TRAGEDY AT LAW (1942), his own favorite among his works and a book singled out by many critics as a classic. It was the first book to feature Pettigrew. The circuit court judge, Justice Barber, meets with accidents as he is making his rounds, which leads his wife to think that someone is trying to kill him. Hare sometimes used obscure points of English law as the mechanism on which the plot turns. *When the Wind Blows* (1949; U.S. title THE WIND BLOWS DEATH), which is set in an amateur orchestra, is another of Hare's best mysteries.

Pettigrew was sent into rural retirement in *The Yew Tree's Shade* (1954; U.S. title *Death Walks the Woods*), in which he and his wife have settled in Yew Hill, Markshire, in the home of his wife's deceased uncle. A new cast of characters is brought on, including typical English village types. Chief Constable MacWilliam of Markhampton is the good cop who seeks out Pettigrew's advice; Superintendent Trimble, on the other hand, resents the semi-retired barrister's intrusions. With his typical understatement and reserve, Hare avoids the preciousness of the village subgenre.

AN ENGLISH MURDER (1951) is neither a Pettigrew nor a Mallet novel. Describing the conflicts among a group of people that includes some of the highest politicians in the land, Hare follows the usual whodunit structure only loosely. Hare also wrote detective short stories, collected in *Best Detective Stories of Cyril Hare* (1959). The volume was introduced by Michael Gilbert.

HARRIS, PAUL An amateur sleuth in a series by Gavin BLACK. Like Matt ERRIDGE, Harris has an unlikely profession: he is a wealthy manufacturer and shipowner living in Singapore whose business travels bring him into contact with mysteries. The novels are more about suspense and intrigue than they are detection. Harris is Scottish, and *A Big Wind for Summer* (1975) finds him in the Arran Islands working on a case involving a Renoir painting. Most of Harris's other cases take place in Asia and have been praised for their accuracy.

BIBLIOGRAPHY Novels: *Suddenly at Singapore* (1961), *Dead Man Calling* (1962), *A Dragon for Christmas* (1963), *The Eyes Around Me* (1964), *You Want to Die, Johnnie?* (1966), *The Wind *of Death* (1967), *The Cold Jungle* (1969), *A Time for Pirates* (1971), *The Bitter Tea* (1972), *The Golden Cockatrice* (1974), *A Book for Killers* (1976), *Night Run from Java* (1979).

HART, CAROLYN G[IMPEL] (1936–) Carolyn G. Hart is one of the large group of women writers who became popular during the eighties, but unlike Marcia MULLER, Sara PARETSKY, and Sue GRAFTON, Hart wrote COZY mysteries. Her novels about bookstore owner Annie Laurance and Max Darling have been dubbed the DEATH ON DEMAND series. These books have been nominated for awards a dozen times and won the Anthony and the Agatha, though never the EDGAR.

Hart was born in Oklahoma and studied journalism at the University of Oklahoma, where she later taught writing. Her first genre novel, *Flee from the Past,* was published in 1975; she wrote several other mystery and suspense novels before creating Laurance and Darling in *Death on Demand* (1987). A second series is about an Oklahoma journalist named Henrietta O'Dwyer Collins; Hart herself had worked as a reporter for the *Norman Transcript.* The first Collins mystery was *Dead Man's Island* (1993), which won an Agatha award. Hart also edited the fourth volume in the *Malice Domestic* series of traditional mysteries (i.e., cozies). Her introduction attempted to give the cozy mystery a literary and almost therapeutic status. She said that "Murder is *not* the focus of a mystery story. The focus of the mystery is fractured relationships. In trying to solve the crime, the detective searches out the reasons for murder by exploring the relationships between the victim and those around the victim. The detective is trying to find out what caused the turmoil in these lives." She then says that the reader relates this turmoil to fractured relationships in their own lives. She somewhat overreaches herself when she claims "No one ever captured the destructive power of greed any better than Christie did in *The Murder of Roger Ackroyd*" (What about DICKENS? Hardy? DOSTOEVSKY?). Her remark that "Malice Domestic reveals the intimate, destructive, frightening secrets hidden beneath what so often seems to be a placid surface" comes close to paraphrasing Julian SYMONS's remark about "violence behind respectable faces," which is interesting in that the cozy and the kind of crime story Symons was talking about are so much at odds.

HART, ELLEN See GAY MYSTERIES.

HARTE, BRET (pen name of Francis Brett Harte, 1836–1902) Born in Albany, New York, Bret Harte gained fame through his writings about the American West, later served as American consul in Germany and in Scotland, and retired to London, where he died. His was an illustrious career; he became one of the best-known Americans of his time. He employed Mark TWAIN to write articles for his *Californian,* and later collaborated with him on the play *Ah Sin* (1877).

Harte went to California in 1854, shortly after the Gold Rush. On the basis of his visit to the mining territory, he wrote his two most famous stories: "The Luck of Roaring Camp" (1868) and "The Outcasts of Poker Flat" (1869). In the 1860s, Harte also wrote his *Condensed Novels,* which were extremely clever parodies of other writers, ranging from James Fenimore COOPER to Charles DICKENS. Harte's single but noteworthy contribution to the crime and mystery genre was in the spirit of these: in "THE STOLEN CIGAR CASE" (1902), he wittily parodied the style of Conan DOYLE, making fun of the "genius" of Hemlock Jones.

HARVEY, JOHN [BARTON] (1938–) John Harvey was born in London, but he is most familiar through his Nottingham-based police PROCEDURAL series about Charlie RESNICK. Harvey attended Goldsmith's College, where he obtained his teaching certificate in 1963, and later received a master's degree from the University of Nottingham. Harvey has been extremely prolific, writing scripts for radio and television, novelizations from film and TV, poetry, and juvenile fiction. His novels include thrillers as well as a vast number of Westerns under his own name and several pseudonyms (William S. Brady, William M. James, John J. McLaglen, J. D. Sandon, L. J. Coburn, J. B. Dancer, and Jon Hart).

Harvey's Nottingham novels give a realistic picture of contemporary Britain, and Resnick is an interesting individual. Harvey's television work includes a series he told *Contemporary Authors* was closely modeled after *Hill Street Blues,* and so it is not surprising that his fiction follows the current vogue of imitating television. Harvey, like other contemporary writers, applies the procedural style not only to police work but to activities of daily living, generating a lot of extraneous detail that has to be waded through ("Resnick dropped a handful of Costa Rican beans into the grinder, sliced rye and caraway, set the kettle on to boil; he removed the outside layer from what remained of the Polish garlic sausage and cut thin slices from a stump of Emmenthal cheese. . . . He carried his breakfast through to the living room, switched the radio on low, and sat with yesterday's paper on the arm of his chair, while Miles assiduously cleaned himself on his lap, pink tongue licking deep between extended claws"). Whereas the HARD-BOILED p.i. was a man of mystery, the modern policeman is minutely described; but such details often show no more than that the detective, like several million other people, makes breakfast, has a cat, and follows the news. What the television imitators who have embraced "dialogue-driven" narration and minimized description fail to recognize is the non-transferability of the television show's aesthetic principles to the novel; once the "visuals" are taken away, the remaining "script" that is poured into the novel form is often banal. Bad dialogue may sound good when spoken against a dramatic background; in a book, it is merely bad dialogue.

The Resnick series has a number of good secondary characters whose activities are depicted in alternating narratives. At their best, Harvey's books are like a thickened Inspector MORSE novel and have the same dismal charm of that series—at least up until the point that the mass of material and the diversity of narratives dissipates the thrust of a central story.

HASTINGS, FRANK A police officer in a series of novels by Collin WILCOX. When he first appears in *The Lonely Hunter* (1970), he is a detective sergeant, but later becomes a lieutenant. The novels are PROCEDURAL and are set in San Francisco. In the pattern set after LAST SEEN WEARING . . . (1952), these procedurals have a large cast of characters, two if not several simultaneous investigations, and subplots about the main character's personal life. Hastings is a divorced alcoholic who has gone on the wagon; one constant theme in the series is the stress he endures coordinating the activities of various people who are not necessarily compatible, and how he manages to stay sober through it all. Wilcox preserves something of the flavor of the interior monologue of the classic private eye novel, though without the color and flair. Hastings is no Lew ARCHER, and his understanding of people is never amazing. These novels, however, are among the best contemporary procedurals. Hastings's cops include Inspector Canelli, a big, swarthy man who works stakeout, and Janet Collier, who is young, green, and sensitive. (In *Twospot* [1978], Hastings gets to work with the NAMELESS DETECTIVE).

Dead Center (1992) is the novel in which Hastings first meets Collier and begins to fall in love with her. The millionaire playboy Tony Frazer is shot to death by a street person, but Hastings cannot believe that a street person would use "the hit man's favorite weapon," a silenced .22 automatic. Other murders with the same M.O. (targeting rich and respected individuals) imply something more than a random killing. The romantic subplot seems to plunge the detective into a midlife crisis.

Switchback (1993) begins with the discovery of a wealthy young woman found shot to death at Baker Beach on San Francisco's Presidio. The crime seems senseless, but she may have been blackmailing one of her three middle-aged lovers. Then again, it could have been her drug-using roommates. There is no skimping on detail—neither the sights nor the smells of death. Hastings is a tough questioner, and much dialogue consists of his breaking down of people's façades. *Calculated Risk* (1995), in which the AIDS epidemic and California politics are yoked together in a murder story, has more the feeling of a cop show teleplay. The ending is concerned with Hastings's decision as to whether to leave Ann, the woman who had taken him in after he had been wounded in an arrest, in order to pursue a relationship with Janet Collier.

BIBLIOGRAPHY Novels: *The Disappearance* (1970), *Dead Aim* (1971), *Hiding Place* (1973), *Long Way Down* (1974), *Aftershock* (1975), *Doctor Lawyer* (1977), *The Watcher* (1978), *Night Games* (1979), *Mankiller* (1980), *Victims* (1985), *The Pariah* (1988), *A Death Before Dying* (1990), *Hire a Hangman* (1991).

HASTINGS, STANLEY See HALL, PARNELL.

HAVE HIS CARCASE (1932) A novel by Dorothy L. SAYERS. Harriet Vane, a mystery writer who had recently been tried for the murder of her lover and saved by Lord Peter WIMSEY's investigations (in STRONG POISON, published in 1930) discovers a dead body on the beach during a walking tour. With considerable sang froid, she takes pictures and observes as much as she can before the tide washes everything away, and then settles down to looking for help. Unfortunately it is market day, and nobody is around except some women and children. She finally gets to a village and calls the nearest police station.

Because the body has been washed away by the tide (and a helpful storm), it takes a long time for the police to locate the dead man. Meanwhile, Lord Peter (who has fallen in love with Vane) comes to her rescue once again because she is suspected of the murder. Eventually, Harriet and Lord Peter work together on what must be one of the most complicated plots ever invented. From every angle it looks like a suicide, yet there are many nagging facts that point toward murder. The detective duo faces unbreakable alibis, ciphers, mysterious Russian princesses, and itinerant barbers. Two-thirds of this lengthy book is interesting and suspenseful, but then the reader may start to fret, because it has become obvious who the murderer is, though there is no proof as yet. Introducing the corroborating facts presents Sayers with no small challenge: she has muddled things up so well that the detectives are completely baffled. It takes a couple of last-minute discoveries that, if they are plausible, are also a little too providential. It is not bad, only stretched a little too far. Would the dead man have burnt every trace of his identity? How disappointing that the ciphered letter he has in his wallet is not enough to bring much to light. An important paper is lost, and the recipient has forgotten all about it (until the end of the book). These technical problems are recognized in the book itself through Harriet Vane, who discusses the same kinds of problems (painting oneself into a corner) and enters into the details of some of the techniques of mystery writing. Sayers may just be showing off with this witty analysis of the genre in Vane's book-within-a-book, but it is bound to direct the attention of the reader to her own technique in *Have His Carcase.* It is inevitable that once one knows how the trick is done, the magician looses his aura.

HAVOC, JACK The ex-serviceman and ex-convict in Margery Allingham's THE TIGER IN THE SMOKE (1952), and one of her most compelling characters. Known as "the Gaffer" by his former comrades, Havoc's real name is Hackett. He is described as an animal, but not in the sense of being dumb. Like the tiger of the title, he is perfectly adapted to be what he is: a killer. His intense personal power makes him fascinating wherever he appears, like a figure of magic. But in foggy, depressed postwar London, he is frightening. Havoc's atavism is so frightening that the kindly Assistant Commissioner Oates says, "I should like to see him dead."

HAVOC, JOHNNY A private detective in a series of books by historical novelist John JAKES. Havoc is conceived counter to type, in that he is short (just over five feet), has comical red hair, and is involved in preposterous adventures. He appeared in a short-lived series of only four books; the author had hoped that the actor Mickey Rooney would be interested in starring in Havoc adaptations. The Havoc novels were all PAPERBACK ORIGINALS. The last book, *Johnny Havoc and the Siren in Red* (1991; repr of *Making It Big,* 1967), has Johnny working as a pitchman at an amusement park. He becomes involved in a mystery at a nearby army base, and at one point runs through a barracks full of naked female recruits. The puerile humor does little to enliven a farcical plot. Most of the Havoc novels have been reprinted by the Armchair Detective Library.

BIBLIOGRAPHY Novels: *Johnny Havoc* (1960), *Johnny Havoc Meets Zelda* (1962; repr as *Havoc for Sale,* 1990), *Johnny Havoc and the Doll Who Had "It"* (1963; repr as *Holiday for Havoc,* 1991).

HAWKSMOOR (1985) An award-winning novel by Peter ACKROYD. This disturbing story alternates between two narratives, one the first-person account of an early-eighteenth-century architect and protege of Sir Christopher Wren named Nicholas Dyer, and the other of a twentieth-century detective, Chief Superintendent Nicholas Hawksmoor, who is investigating a series of murders at the churches that Dyer built. While the historical sections are brilliant interpretations of eighteenth-century prose, the modern sections are forensic, and equally believable; both, however, are saturated with a peculiar mysticism, as time becomes a permeable membrane through which past and present influence each other. The conflict between eighteenth-century rationalism (the foundation of Hawksmoor's scientific method) and Dyer's worship of "dark Powers" blossoms into a metaphysical argument and philosophical investigation. Although inconclusive in comparison with a straight detective novel, it fully justifies the title of "mystery" and all that it entails in its original sense.

HAYCRAFT, HOWARD (1905–1991) The American mystery critic and publishing executive Howard Haycraft was the pioneer of scholarship related to the mystery and detective genre. Haycraft was born in Minnesota and worked for the H. W. Wilson Company (publishers of the *Reader's Guide to Periodical Literature* and a vast number of other reference books) for four decades, becoming president in 1953 and chairman of the board in 1967. He specialized in library services for the blind. In addition to a busy professional career, Haycraft produced two extremely influential and important works, *Murder for Pleasure: The Life and Times of the Detective Story* (1941), the first history of the mystery genre, and *The Art of the Mystery Story* (1946), an anthology of critical pieces that contains many important pieces now difficult to find. Haycraft compiled important bibliographical and biographical data on many mystery writers, and his *Murder for Pleasure* is still the authoritative source for information on many nineteenth- and early twentieth-century authors who are either obscure or famous but out of print.

Haycraft's contribution to the genre was recognized in 1975 with a special EDGAR award. He also received an Edgar in 1947 for his mystery reviews.

HAYWOOD, GAR ANTHONY (***) Gar Anthony Haywood is one of several writers of mysteries focused on the African American experience who have gained prominence in the wake of Walter MOSLEY's success. But in addition to producing another Los Angeles private eye saga (the Aaron Gunner novels), he has created the first series of black-oriented COZY novels.

Aaron Gunner is a middle-aged Vietnam vet who operates his private investigation bureau out of a barber shop in Los Angeles. We learn that Gunner made an attempt to become a cop but "flunked out" of the police academy after he smashed the jaw of a sadistic instructor. The first Gunner case, *Fear of the Dark* (1988), won a Shamus award. *You Can Die Trying* (1993) is an overt attempt to deal with the aftermath of the Rodney King case, interweaving the story with discussions of racism in the Los Angeles Police Department and American race politics. Gunner is hired, ironically, to prove that a vicious racist cop was set up for dismissal, even though he deserved it.

Haywood's other series is about the Loudermilk family and is less carefully written, though infused with some of the same themes. "Big Joe" Loudermilk is a retired California police officer; he and his wife Dottie (the narrator) travel around in an Airstream trailer named Lucille, hoping to avoid their five children but constantly being drawn into mysteries and disasters by them. In *Bad News Travels Fast* (1995) their political activist son is accused of murder.

HAZELL, THORPE The amateur detective in some of the stories in Victor WHITECHURCH's *Thrilling Stories of the Railway* (1912). Hazell is a photographer and book lover who has a fascination with TRAINS. He is also a vegetarian and physical culturist—in short, a health nut—and it is not uncommon for him to flail his arms like "a windmill" during an interrogation or confession. At one point, Hazell asks a shepherd's wife for two onions and a broomstick, and eats the former raw while vigorously twirling the latter around his head.

Thorpe solves a simple but perplexing case in "Sir Gilbert Murrell's Picture," in which the painting *Holy Family* by Velàzquez is stolen during its transportation to a gallery and replaced with a forgery. The conundrum is how a railway car was stolen from the middle section of a train while it was moving.

HAZLERIGG, INSPECTOR A detective character in a series of novels by Michael GILBERT. Although Hazlerigg could be considered bland, his flatness stems from the fact that the author did not follow the modern fashion of putting more energy into the sleuth's background—love affairs, personal quirks, distinctive vehicles, pets—than into the plot. Hazlerigg is a precise instrument for untangling the precisely tied knots in which Gilbert specializes. The inspector, however, sometimes behaves like Sherlock HOLMES or Nero WOLFE, sitting silent and inscrutable, so concentrated that "only the blinking of his eyes showed that he was alive."

We learn little about Hazlerigg's background, except that he is a Norfolk man, and at the time of SMALLBONE DECEASED (1950) has been thirty-two years in London, and has reached the rank of Chief Inspector. Hazlerigg appears in six other books, all written within a few years; *Close Quarters* (1947) and *Fear to Tread* (1953) are the first and last.

HEAD, MATTHEW (pseudonym of John Edwin Canaday, 1907–1985) Born in Kansas and educated at the University of Texas at Austin, John Edwin Canaday had a solidly American background; this is surprising, given that he wrote what might be called expatriate or Europhile mysteries about two women who have some kind of long-term relationship, and a casual WATSON who seems a curious and unattached *flaneûr.*

Canaday received his master's degree from Yale before World War II, and taught history at the University of Virginia. After serving in the Marine Corps during the war, he returned to his artistic and literary activities, including becoming an art critic for the *New York Times* and writing books about art history. His first mystery, *The Smell of Money* (1943), had appeared under the name of Matthew Head; *The Devil in the Bush* (1945) was the first to feature Mary Finney, the missionary doctor who is the sleuth in the remainder of the Head books, including MURDER AT THE FLEA CLUB (1955). The stories are told by a young man named Hooper ("Hoop") Taliaferro. *The Cabinda Affair* (1949), despite its "exotic" setting (the Congo), has the familiar retrospective plot structure (concluded events reported by Hoop to Mary Finney, who sees more in them than he does), but is rather plodding. This novel, however, gives more information about the intriguing Mary Finney and her younger assistant, Emily Collins, than *Murder at the Flea Club.* The devoted relationship of these two single women is probably due for critical re-evaluation. Hoop is working in the lumber business in Africa when he is called to Cabinda, becoming the guest of a beautiful Portuguese woman and her sadistic husband.

The other book in the series is *The Congo Venus* (1950). Like *The Cabinda Affair,* it is set in Africa, this time in Leopoldville, Belgian Congo, during the war. The story plays on the background of typical colonial life: dull parties, gossip, individuals marginalized by their study of native cultures, alcoholism, and other "peculiarities." Liliane Morelli is a beautiful young woman who has no sense of convention, and who allegedly dies of blackwater fever (to which R. Austin FREEMAN almost succumbed). It is more ambitious than Head's other African mystery; the narrative is therefore not as fast paced, but Head puts more into the scenic descriptions and studies of character.

HEAD OF A TRAVELER (1949) A novel by Nicholas BLAKE. Even without a murder, *Head of a Traveler* would be an absorbing book. Its fine writing and challenging vocabulary would make it stand up as a literary novel, as would its central figure, Robert Seaton, a poet admired by the amateur detective Nigel STRANGEWAYS—though the criminal events are dramatic as well. A headless body of an unknown man is found near the poet's property; the corpse bears a superficial resemblance to Oswald Seaton, the poet's brother who had committed suicide ten years before. While ostensibly gathering material for an article on Seaton, Strangeways investigates what happened on one fateful night, probing and questioning among the weird denizens of the Seaton household. He learns that Seaton is having difficulty in his work and feels entrapped by the gloomy house (called Plash Meadow) and his tragic past. Seaton is married to the daughter of the local squire, whose family once owned Plash Meadow. He has a son, Lionel, and a daughter, Vanessa. Lionel is involved with the psychologically troubled daughter of Rennell Torrance, a bad painter who lives in the barn of the Seaton house. The Seatons also have a simple-minded dwarf servant, Finny Black, whom they rescued from a gang of street toughs, a sign of their compassion that also emphasizes the GOTHIC element of the story.

This strange group of individuals lives in discordant concord at Plash Meadow, a stasis shattered by the discovery of the body. The nature of poetry and the poet's life are an important part of the book, as is the old mansion, which becomes almost a character itself, keeping further secrets. The finding of the head is a memorable scene—a restoring of the body's wholeness that ingeniously parallels psychological and narrative resolution.

HECHT, BEN (1893–1964) The American author Ben Hecht is best known for his contributions to film and theater, not for mysteries. His play *The Front Page* (1928), written with Charles MacArthur (1895–1956), was based on his experience as a newspaperman and was an enormous success; it remains his best-known work.

Hecht was born in New York City. His parents were Jewish immigrants from Russia, and the family later moved to Racine, Wisconsin, where Hecht grew up. A precocious boy, he displayed a talent for the violin at age ten, then became a circus acrobat, and finally, at seventeen, left home to become a newspaperman in Chicago with the *Chicago Journal* and the *Chicago Daily News*. He reported from Berlin on the political chaos that followed the German defeat in World War I, and used it as material for his first novel, *Erik Dorn* (1921). In 1926 he got an offer to write for Hollywood. The following year he earned an Academy Award at the first Oscar ceremony for best original story for *Underworld* (1927), Josef von Sternberg's pioneering film that inaugurated the gangster genre. He would later write screenplays for Alfred HITCHCOCK, including *Spellbound* (1945) and *Notorious* (1946). Among Hecht's seventy credited screenplays (he had a hand in many others, including *Gone with the Wind*) was a 1947 adaptation of RIDE THE PINK HORSE (1946).

Hecht became so successful that, according to his autobiography, he was able to write film scripts in two weeks and was paid between $50,000 and $125,000 for each one. Still, he managed to write thirty-five books, including several volumes of short stories, some of which deal with mystery and crime. Among them are *Broken Necks and Other Stories* (1924; exp 1926) and *Actor's Blood* (1936). Hecht also wrote two mystery novels, one of which was filmed: *The Florentine Dagger* (1923; film 1935) and *I Hate Actors!* (1944). Hecht's *Collected Stories* appeared in 1945. His autobiography is *A Child of the Century* (1954). *A Treasury of Ben Hecht* (1959) contains crime stories from *Broken Necks* and *Actor's Blood*, in edited or rewritten versions.

Hecht wrote of his work, "I have my periods of dullness, but they are not deliberate." He said that he did not write for "enigma fanciers," readers with "bobby-socks minds," and readers who like to read dull work "under the delusion that they, the readers, are coming to grips with Real Life." Although he injected humor into almost all his writing, he made it clear that it was a reaction against a natural sense of the evil in the world: "I know the world well and it fills me with an ugly mood. The stupidity of humans and their horrid incompetence toward life is a theme with which I have wrestled in many of my books." Nowhere is the horror more vivid than in the story BROKEN NECKS. "Actor's Blood," about the apparent murder of a Broadway star, harshly depicts the callousness of self-centered showpeople and the pathetic, grand gesture of the victim's father, a broken-down old hack. In "Café Sinister," a psychiatrist who frequents a certain club in order to observe neurosis and perversion stumbles on a revenge plot involving ART. Hecht's virtuosity is on display as he satirizes the bored fools of society who watch each other yawn, and the pursuit of fame, "a sort of mummy case in which the creative talents of yesterday lie in state and glitter with mania." His most viciously clever story is CRIME WITHOUT PASSION.

HEIMRICH, LIEUTENANT Detective created by Richard and Frances LOCKRIDGE, Heimrich has one of the most mercurial identities in mystery fiction. Lieutenant Heimrich's first name is probably Merton, but his initials have a disconcerting habit of changing from book to book. Heimrich works for the New York State Board of Criminal Identification, or Investigation (his employer changes, too), part of the state police. Although fully grown, he starts out small in the early books and gradually works up to being "a lumbering ox" or "a hippopotamus." His transformation from lieutenant to inspector, however, is a result of promotion. Heimrich is a circumspect, even taciturn man. His detection is methodical, and the stories that concern him are (sometimes) entertaining, but not gripping. For a policeman, he has few dealings with physical evidence, instead relying on his questioning of suspects, motive, and psychology. "The character has to fit the crime," he repeats. He has the habit of talking to people with his eyes closed, a mannerism of Nero WOLFE.

Heimrich began as a minor character in the Lockridges' series about Mr. and Mrs. NORTH, appearing in *Murder Out of Turn* (1941) and *Death of a Tall Man* (1946). He was spun off in *Think of Death* (1947). The Lockridges sometimes varied the setting of Heimrich's adventures from the detective's colorless surroundings in New York State: he investigates MURDER AFLOAT in *Inspector's Holiday* (1971); in *Death By Association* (1952), he becomes involved in the search for the killer of well-known anti-communist activist Bronson Wells while recovering in Key West from a gunshot wound received in a previous adventure. There are indications that Wells was connected to a senator resembling Joseph McCarthy. Another book with political underpinnings is *With Option to Die* (1967), which deals again with right-wing extremists, this time opponents of desegregation. Racism is also an issue in *A Risky Way to Kill* (1969). After a series of strange classified advertisements appear in the local paper of Heimrich's home town (Van Brunt, New York), offering an unused wedding dress, a rifle, and a horse for sale, Heimrich finds himself drawn into investigating the accidental death of a young girl a year before. The daughter of a Southern aristocratic family, she was inexplicably thrown from a horse into a stone wall during a hunt. Though the case is simple and the writing routine, Lockridge's portrait of the girl's alcoholic mother is one of his most poignant and believable.

Other Heimrich mysteries include *Not I, Said the Sparrow* (1973), in which Heimrich and his wife (Susan Faye, who first appeared in *Burnt Offering* [1955]) are invited to a party at the home of a wealthy neighbor who is shot through the neck with a hunting arrow the day after having announced his marriage to a woman fifty years his junior. One of Heimrich's best cases is LET DEAD ENOUGH ALONE (1955). After Frances Lockridge's death, Richard Lockridge continued the Heimrich series on his own, beginning with *Murder Can't Wait* (1964).

BIBLIOGRAPHY Novels: *I Want to Go Home* (1948), *Spin Your Web, Lady!* (1949), *Foggy, Foggy Death* (1950), *A Client is Cancelled* (1951; alt title *Trial by Terror*), *Stand Up and Die* (1953), *Death and the Gentle Bull* (1954; alt title *Killer in the Straw*), *Practice to Deceive* (1957), *Accent on Murder* (1958), *Show Red for Danger* (1960), *With One Stone* (1961; British title *No Dignity in Death*), *First Come, First Kill* (1962), *The Distant Clue* (1963), *Murder Roundabout* (1966), *Dead Run* (1976), *The Tenth Life* (1977).

HELLER, NATE See COLLINS, MAX ALLAN.

HELL-FIRE CLUB A club formed in 1745 by Sir Francis Dashwood that became notorious for its orgies and impious pursuits. The members, who also included John Wilkes and Bubb Dodington, met in Medmenham Abbey, a ruined Cistercian abbey on the Thames near Marlow. The club is mentioned by DE QUINCEY in his essay on the art of murder. In spirit, the Hell-fire club was like the MOHOCKS earlier in the century. See also CHARTERIS, LESLIE.

HELL HATH NO FURY See WILLIAMS, CHARLES.

HELLER, NATHAN See COLLINS, MAX ALLAN.

HELL IS A CITY (1953) The title of an early British police PROCEDURAL novel by Maurice PROCTER. It is also the title of a Timothy DANE novel by William ARD.

HELM, BEN A private detective in a series of novels by Bruno FISCHER. Although Fischer was a contributor to the PULP MAGAZINES at their height, Ben Helm is not really a HARD-BOILED type. Rather, Helm is an ARMCHAIR DETECTIVE who solves his conundrums without much blood. He was the author's only attempt at a series character.

BIBLIOGRAPHY Novels: *The Dead Men Grin* (1945), *More Deaths Than One* (1947), *The Restless Hands* (1949), *The Silent Dust* (1950), *The Paper Circle* (1951).

HELM, MATT Donald HAMILTON's Matt Helm was one of many sixties spies and fixers who followed in the steps of James BOND. Like Bond, Helm also made it to the big screen (as well as television), but the film Helm, played by Dean Martin, was something of a joke. In the books, Helm is a tough guy and a killer. *Death of a Citizen* (1960), the first novel, has him living a quiet life out West as a freelance writer and photographer on outdoor subjects. But Helm is a veteran of World War II and a secret espionage agency, and his old boss ("Mac" MacGilvray) calls him back into service after a fifteen year layoff. He has a wife, Beth, and three children, two boys and a girl. Later Beth becomes fully aware of his life of violence and brutality. Helm is a "remover," a man paid to get rid of other similar men who are the agents of the other side. He travels all over the world, foiling the communists and sometimes uncovering former NAZIS. The Helm novels were praised by Anthony BOUCHER and by John F. Kennedy, the latter endorsement doing much more for their popularity than the former.

Helm is six-foot-four and built like Travis McGEE; also like McGee, he thinks himself something of a philosopher, but more often he is a complainer like Brock CALLAGHAN. His wife is conveniently gotten out of the picture in the first book, opening up the possibility of sexual escapades with beautiful and dangerous women, a necessity of the Bond-style tale. There is little detection in the Helm books. Helm entertains, saves the West, and kills off the bad guys in the course of implausible plots. How Boucher could credit the series with "authentic hard realism" is puzzling; the killing of the opposition because they deserve it, the my-country-right-or-wrong attitude, the magical spiriting away of unwanted corpses by convenient local "contacts," and other features are far from realistic. Helm is really a descendant of the movie Bond, not the original character Ian FLEMING created. More off-putting than the unreality is the sadism and sexism of the novels; for example, Helm refers to rape as a method of breaking down a woman's composure. In *The Wrecking Crew* (1960), his wife has sued for divorce because she does not like being married to an assassin (she did not even like the way he brutally murdered the kidnapper of one of their children). Helm feels sorry for himself and expresses cynicism about women, though he is about to meet the girl of his dreams during a spying/killing operation in Sweden—a woman who can find her way through the woods without a compass. In *The Removers* (1961), Helm's ex-wife calls upon him for help; she has remarried, but her new husband is a former gangster's bodyguard and hitman. Helm gets his personal business mixed up with a job of tracking Martell, an oversexed killer who works for the Russians. In this book he talks more like McGee and shows signs of humanitarian scruples.

BIBLIOGRAPHY Novels: *The Silencers* (1962), *Murderer's Row* (1962), *The Ambushers* (1963), *The Shadowers* (1964), *The Ravagers* (1964), *The Devastators* (1965), *The Betrayers* (1966), *The Menacers* (1968), *The Interlopers* (1969), *The Poisoners* (1971), *The Intriguers* (1973), *The Intimidators* (1974), *The Terminators* (1975), *The Retaliators* (1976), *The Terrorizers* (1977), *The Revengers* (1982), *The Annihilators* (1983), *The Infiltrators* (1984), *The Detonators* (1985), *The Vanishers* (1986), *The Demolishers* (1987), *The Frighteners* (1989), *The Threateners* (1992).

HEMINGWAY, ERNEST (1899–1961) Probably the most imitated American writer of the twentieth century, Hemingway has been given credit for influencing the development of the mystery and crime story. His bold, clipped sentences and his lifelike dialogue—full of hesitations and things left unsaid—resemble to some degree the work of HAMMETT and other HARD-BOILED writers. But the relationship of Hemingway and hard-boiled fiction is basically a chicken-and-egg problem. Hemingway's first book, *Three Stories and Ten Poems* appeared in 1923, after BLACK MASK had become established; however, PULP MAGAZINES published all sorts of stories, and in the early days the terse, minimal style was not yet developed. Hemingway's *In Our Time* (1925) mostly contained stories about Nick Adams, a shell-shocked World War I veteran who looks back on the days in Idaho before the war. The masculine themes of independence, comradeship, and heroism, as well as postwar cynicism and alienation, are echoed in hard-boiled fiction. *Men Without Women,* which contains the story THE KILLERS, was published in 1927.

Hemingway was born in Oak Park, Illinois. After high school, he became a reporter for the *Kansas City Star.* Then he went to France in World War I and served as an ambulance driver, was wounded, and was decorated for heroism. After the war, he was part of the expatriate community in Paris (the Lost Generation), which included his friend F. Scott FITZGERALD. His first success as a novelist came with *The Sun Also Rises* (1926). *To Have and Have Not* (1937), about a cynical smuggler, became the first film in which Lauren Bacall and Humphrey Bogart appeared together. Hemingway's experience in Spain, where he covered the civil war as a correspondent, was embodied in his most successful novel, *For Whom the Bell Tolls* (1940). Later in life, Hemingway lived in Cuba until he was driven out by the communist revolution. He committed suicide shortly thereafter. Further writings appeared posthumously, including his memoir of Paris, *A Moveable Feast* (1964), and the novel *The Garden of Eden* (1986).

HEMINGWAY, INSPECTOR See HEYER, GEORGETTE.

HEMLOCK One of the most poisonous plants, known since ancient times. Its most famous victim was Socrates, who drank a decoction of spotted hemlock. The plant contains the alkaloid coniine, and death results from asphyxia through respiratory paralysis.

More horrible are the effects of water hemlock, a variety of the plant found in Europe and throughout North America. Also known as cowbane, water hemlock has a root resembling the parsnip and leaves like parsley; both parts are poisonous. One reason for accidental poisonings is this resemblance to edible plants (it is a member of the carrot family). In addition to respiratory impairment, the victim suffers nausea, vomiting, diarrhea, extremely violent convulsions, and finally, death.

HENBANE A poisonous plant, also known as "stinking" NIGHTSHADE. It is the most common member of that notorious family of plants known as the Solanaceae. It grows in North America, the British Isles, Europe, and parts of Asia, and its odor accounts for its nickname. It is also cultivated as a source of some drugs, including ATROPINE. Like tobacco, another nightshade plant, henbane, has been smoked for the "high" produced by its poisonous contents.

HERON, E. AND E. See PRICHARD, HESKETH.

HESS, JOAN See BOOKS.

HEWITT, MARTIN A detective created by Arthur MORRISON. Hewitt's main contribution to the genre is common sense: when he first appeared in 1894, the year HOLMES went (temporarily) to his grave in THE FINAL PROBLEM, Hewitt was comparatively staid. "Realistic" detectives would later have their vogue. Hewitt is not very eccentric and relies not on genius but native good sense. Very little is said about Hewitt's appearance, and his methods are illustrated rather than described. Hewitt's "Watson" is Brett, a journalist (like Morrison himself).

Hewitt's best-known case is "The Lenton Croft Robberies," in which a series of thefts occur in a country manor house, and each time a burnt match is left in the spot where an item of jewelry had been lying. A better story is "The Case of Laker, Absconded," which is about the "walk-clerk" Laker, whose job it is to travel from bank to bank exchanging bills for cash on behalf of his own firm. One day, Laker fails to return. The case hinges on that favorite clue of the Victorian and Edwardian detective story, the coded newspaper advertisement. In "The Loss of Sammy Throckett," Hewitt searches for a "professional pedestrian"—a track star—and reveals interesting details about sport in the late nineteenth century.

BIBLIOGRAPHY Short stories: *Martin Hewitt, Investigator* (1894), *The Chronicles of Martin Hewitt* (1895), *The Adventures of Martin Hewitt* (1896), *The Red Triangle* (1903).

HEXT, HARRINGTON Although it sounds like the name of a GOLDEN AGE detective, Harrington Hext is actually the pseudonym of a Golden Age writer, Eden PHILLPOTTS.

HEYER, GEORGETTE (1902–1974) As well as being a prolific romance novelist, the English writer Georgette Heyer was the author of a dozen detective novels, some of them very fine and all in the GOLDEN AGE manner. Like Margery ALLINGHAM, Heyer published her first novel when she was only nineteen and went on to become famous for her "Regency" romances, of which she wrote forty-five.

Heyer was born in England, but lived abroad from 1925 to 1929, first in East Africa and then for the last year in Yugoslavia. Her husband, George Ronald Rougier, was a mining engineer and later a barrister. Heyer was reclusive, and not much is known about her life beyond the barest details.

The best of Heyer's detective novels are DEATH IN THE STOCKS (1935), which introduced Superintendent Hannasyde, and A BLUNT INSTRUMENT (1938), the last of the four books to feature him. With *No Wind of Blame* (1939), she started a new series about Inspector Hemingway, who had been a supporting player in the previous series. This novel daringly appropriates Conan DOYLE's famous dog that didn't bark and uses an ingenious, far-fetched murder method. Heyer also put to good use the knowledge of mining she gained from her husband. Along COUNTRY HOUSE lines, *No Wind of Blame* uses a shooting party as its background. Prince Varasashvili visits Wally and Ermyntrude Carter at their home; Mrs. Carter hopes the houseguest will clinch her social standing in town, which suffers from the fact that Wally's business deals are all flops. After the Russian's departure, Wally is found shot. True to the formulas of the time, suspicion is divided among the shooting party, and blackmail, adultery, divorce, and money are the motives. Hemingway appears in three more cases: *Envious Casca* (1941), a LOCKED ROOM mystery; *Duplicate Death* (1951); and *Detection Unlimited* (1953), which continued an unfortunate downhill slide in quality.

The first Hemingway novel is the best, but none are as good as her humorous non-series work *Why Shoot A Butler?* (1933). The sleuth, a barrister named Amberley, comes upon a dead man sitting in a car on a country road with a bullet in his chest. He is Dawson, the personality-less butler of the local manor (hence, why shoot him?). A woman, Shirley Brown, is standing by the car. Amberley lets her go. The badinage between them throughout the book is entertaining. Insolent and conceited, Amberley refuses to help the bumbling local constabulary but conducts a secret investigation of his own.

Whereas Hannasyde was a bulbous detective presence like Inspector FRENCH, Hemingway is almost a Noel Coward character. Heyer liked to combine the conventional mystery with the romance and humor of her other non-mystery books, but at least she knew *how* to write romance, and used it in a way that is less gooey and bothersome than in the mysteries of many another writer—up to a point. Heyer also wrote some books that are, like Ngaio MARSH mysteries, encumbered with claptrap. *The Unfinished Clue* (1937), in the classic country house vein, is a highly romanticized story involving a Chinese dagger that winds up in the neck of the host of a house party. Inspector Harding investigates. The clue, the single word "There" written on a piece of paper, turns out to be a very ingenious one. The novel's dated attitudes ("when a woman powders her nose, Inspector, she loses count of time"), stereotypes (a Mexicanized version of Josephine Baker), and stock devices (a son disinherited for his choice of wife) make it all but unreadable.

Heyer wrote in a fashion that is now out of style, but her books continue to be reprinted while many of those by her contemporaries are not. At her best, she exemplified the cleverness of the Golden Age. Perhaps her most unusual turn on the mystery story was *Penhallow* (1942), in which the reader discovers the murderer but the participants in the action remain mystified.

HIAASEN, CARL (1953–) A native Floridian (one of the few, one would guess from his books), Carl Hiaasen began his writing career in journalism, and continues to write for the *Miami Herald.* He achieved notoriety, however, for a series of books that fall somewhere in the interstices of the crime novel, the CAPER, and social satire. His novels could be compared to those of Donald WESTLAKE, though they are more loosely plotted and with a humor closer to slapstick comedy. The style is journalistic, and at times even chatty.

Born in Fort Lauderdale, Hiaasen graduated from Emory University and worked for *Cocoa Today,* which is not a trade magazine but a paper in Cocoa, Florida. He moved on to the *Miami Herald* in 1976. He has won several awards for his reporting, and was a finalist for the Pulitzer Prize in 1980 and 1981 for his investigative reports on the medical profession and the illegal drug trade, respectively.

Hiaasen's serious crime reporting stands him in good stead in his fiction writing, which lampoons the many varieties of crooks: from machine-gun wielding gangs, to unscrupulous professionals, to corrupt evangelists, who pollute, in more ways than one, the Miami environment. The destruction of the Floridian habitat is at least as important, if not more important, to Hiaasen than the deterioration of society.

Hiaasen's first three novels were co-written with William D. Montalbano (who was a foreign correspondent for the *Miami Herald*): *Powder Burn* (1981), *Trap Line* (1982), and *A Death in China* (1984). The first novel written entirely on his own was *Tourist Season* (1986), which benefited from the boom in regional mystery and crime writing in the eighties. The story concerns a terrorist war on tourism; the assaults and indignities inflicted on visitors to Miami are comical, but in reality attacks against tourists, particularly Europeans, were becoming more and more common.

Double Whammy (1987) is about sleazy goings-on in the multimillion dollar bass-fishing industry. Although it has been said that Hiaasen is not really a mystery writer, *Double Whammy* is one of his works that follows closely the private eye novel format. The detective, R. J. Decker, is a former news photographer who is commissioned to get some incriminating pictures of a champion bass fisherman cheating in a tournament by "hooking" previously planted—or tethered—fish. *Skin Tight* (1989) also features a private eye. The detective, Mick Stranahan, is involved in the case of a slimy plastic surgeon and accused murderer, as well as a television host and other assorted villains. In this period, Hiaasen seems to have been influenced by the Hoke MOSELEY novels of Charles Willeford, which were written about the same time.

Hiaasen's books try to be comically violent, but in this attempt he often goes to extremes. One bad guy is crucified on a satellite television disk; another has his hand chewed off by a barracuda; and one body is found with a toy alligator crammed down its throat. The humor, though it tends to become crude and vulgar in its efforts to outdo itself, is nonetheless often funny. His technique is demonstrated in an extreme form in *Stormy Weather* (1995), an episodic narrative that intertwines the stories of numerous people in the wake of a hurricane. One is a thug, hunting down the builders and inspectors of his dead mother's mobile home; another is the owner of a wildlife park whose Cape buffalo, lions, and snakes have gotten loose. But the two poles of the story are the mad, prophetic Clinton TYREE and the shallow and villainous honeymooner Max Lamb, a New York advertising executive who amuses himself by taking movies of devastated hurricane victims with his camcorder. The ruination of the rapidly dwindling wilderness and "paving" of the state of Florida was the central theme of an earlier novel, *Native Tongue* (1991). Another of Hiaasen's novels, *Striptease* (1993), was made into a film in 1996.

He also participated in the comic SERIAL NOVEL *Naked Came the Manatee* (1996). *Lucky You* (1997) is a novel about an investigative journalist who helps a woman track down two insane men who have robbed her of her lottery winnings in order to set up a militia. *A Death in China* was reprinted in 1998.

HIGGINS, GEORGE V[INCENT] (1939–) George V. Higgins was an assistant to the U.S. attorney in Boston when he published his best-selling first novel, *The Friends of Eddie Coyle* (1972). Prior to that, Higgins had worked for the state attorney general following his graduation from Boston College law school in 1967. Higgins's novels are not romantic; his characters are cops (sometimes dirty), bureaucrats, hoods, and gangsters. Although he is respected for the way he employs his firsthand knowledge of the criminal world in his novels, it is really his style that has won Higgins a reputation. His books are heavy on dialogue, which he writes with great realism but also craft. The conversations sound like edited transcriptions of recordings, but unlike many tough-talk writers, Higgins punctuates his dialogue with banalities as well as vulgarity. Higgins's dialogue expresses how his characters think, which sometimes means badly or not at all. *The Friends of Eddie Coyle* and *Cogan's Trade* (1974) are his most admired works. Coyle and Cogan are both crooks, but Cogan is scarier, a professional killer.

HIGH HAT As a verb, a slang term for snub, condescend to, give the cold shoulder to, look down upon. As an adjective, the term means high-toned or classy.

HIGHSMITH, PATRICIA (pen name of Mary Patricia Plangman, 1921–1995) Born in Fort Worth, Texas, Patricia Highsmith created a body of work that has been described as more European than American. Highsmith lived in Europe after 1963, where her novels were not so much better received as better understood.

Highsmith graduated from Barnard College with a B.A. in 1942. Her first novel, STRANGERS ON A TRAIN, was published in 1950 and filmed the following year by Alfred HITCHCOCK (Raymond CHANDLER also worked on the film, in his one—uncomfortable—collaboration with Hitchcock). This book bore a resemblance to traditional suspense fiction, but with THE TALENTED MR. RIPLEY (1955) she tightened the screws, creating in the character Tom RIPLEY, a con man who kills with absolutely no feeling, neither remorse nor satisfaction. It has been said that Highsmith's work evokes horror, fear, and guilt, but the guilt is all in the mind of the reader; it is the *lack* of guilt that makes the stories horrifying.

What has shocked readers, and seems to have led to her greater acceptance in the existential philosophical atmosphere of Europe, is Highsmith's seeming contention that this is how people really are. Other writers explore the "fine line" between law and justice; Highsmith seems to say that there is no line, because there is no justice. Highsmith has been compared to Cornell WOOLRICH, but a better parallel would be Jim THOMPSON, in whose work regret, or even an understanding that they have done something wrong, is rarely a part of the characters' (the villains', anyway) makeup. Highsmith exceeds him, however, in having no heroes. The villains are only opposed by fools. Although Highsmith doesn't condone the success of the "villains"—she neither condones nor approves anything—her work bears some resemblance to the writings of Ayn Rand, whose "objectivism" held that selfish acts were not morally reprehensible but expressions of reason.

Highsmith had a talent for getting inside the minds of characters we perceive as deeply disturbed or sociopathic, revealing their thought processes in such a way that we understand them. Perhaps this is because, as she said in her *Plotting and Writing Suspense Fiction* (1966; rev 1981), she felt that "art has nothing to do with morality, convention or moralizing." In analyzing the development of detective fiction, Dorothy L. SAYERS said that it could only flourish once "public sympathy had veered round to the side of law and order." Perhaps, given Highsmith, it has veered again.

Ripley returned in four other books, and Highsmith continued to write non-series psychological novels as well as short stories, some of which are collected in *The Black House* (1981), *Mermaids on the Golf Course* (1985), and *Tales of Natural and Unnatural Catastrophes* (1987).

HIGH TIDE (1970) The masterpiece of novelist P. M. HUBBARD. It concerns a man named Curtis who has just been released from prison, having served a sentence for killing Evan Maxwell. One day Curtis had been walking in the fields with his Labrador retriever, and was crossing a road when Maxwell came barreling through in his Jaguar, killing the dog. Curtis, enraged, killed Maxwell. Now as he drives toward the coast, thinking to buy a yacht and go for an extended cruise, Curtis is followed by a man calling himself Matthews who wants to know the final words spoken by Maxwell. It emerges that Maxwell was on "urgent business," and people want to know what he told Curtis.

Hubbard's creation of Curtis is brilliant. A violent man, not because of brutishness but out of an absolute insistence upon autonomy, Curtis the killer feels violated:

"when I had set myself to defend the privacy of my mind, it had not occurred to me that there might be something in my mind which other people wanted." Hubbard shows also his gift for observation of small but important things: "It is always odd going back into a hotel after you have paid your bill and surrendered your key and left. The place is familiar, but you feel displaced." Displacements, large and small, and tremors of feeling that lead to large-scale and often tragic effects, are Hubbard's great strength.

Displaced, Curtis drives on in the ripple of his own shock, now searching his mind for the item of value, and already thinking of keeping it for himself.

HIGHWAYMAN English word for a robber of travelers. The most famous highwayman of history is Jonathan WILD. DE QUINCEY tells the story, in his celebrated essay on murder, of the highwayman who was suspected of killing one Mrs. Ruscombe and her servant in 1764 and who put socks over his horse's hooves so as not to attract his neighbors' attention. After his hanging, the highwayman's body was speeded away to the premises of a teaching surgeon in need of cadavers, where the moribund man was finished off by a student. Highwaymen like Wild became folk heroes (though their hangings were equally festive occasions), showing that it is not only in the twentieth century that the criminal has been glamorized in literature.

HILL, REGINALD (1936–) English author Reginald Hill has received less attention than P. D. JAMES, Ruth RENDELL, and Colin DEXTER, and he has taken a different course from any of them. Hill has departed more from the form of the classic English mystery, both in style and content. His detective duo, Superintendent DALZIEL and Inspector Pascoe, is not merely an odd couple, but a vehicle for Hill's commentary on class differences. Whereas WATSON simply agreed with HOLMES's opinions, with Dalziel and Pascoe there are always two perspectives on hand, which Hill exploits to the fullest—particularly because the subject matter is often volatile. But the polarity can sometimes lead to a kind of stasis, thereby stalling the story.

Hill served in the army and attended Oxford, and continued to pursue a career in education for some time after he had begun publishing mysteries. The Dalziel and Pascoe series is set in Yorkshire. The settings of the stories are well described, whether they are lonely rural spots or dismal suburbs. Sex and violence are generally treated more frankly in Hill's books than in those of his contemporaries.

RULING PASSION (1973) is an important book in the series, in which Pascoe gets promoted and has to deal with the murder of his friends. *A Pinch of Snuff* (1978) is about pornography and "snuff" films. While Pascoe is politically correct to a fault, Hill ingeniously reveals a clever intelligence behind Dalziel's apparently (and typically) boorish behavior. In *Bones and Silence* (1990), a murder occurs in the house just behind Dalziel's; he bursts in and finds the apparent killer holding a smoking gun. Meanwhile, Pascoe participates in amateur theatrics. *The Wood Beyond* (1996) is a long book with several strands, one of which is Pascoe's discovery of an ancestor who was shot for cowardice by his own side in World War I; the subplot recalls Sébastien JAPRISOT's *A Very Long Engagement* (1991). Subplots in general are becoming more obtrusive in Hill's novels.

Under the pseudonym Patrick Ruell, Hill has written a series of lighter mystery novels, including *Red Christmas* (1972), *Urn Burial* (1975), *Death of a Doormouse* (1987), and *Dream of Darkness* (1989). He has also written spy novels and THRILLERs under the names Dick Moreland and Charles Underhill. *The Spy's Wife* (1980) is a non-series novel published under the author's real name.

With *Blood Sympathy* (1993), and in the wake of Easy RAWLINS's success, Hill introduced a new series detective, Joe Sixsmith. A former lathe operator, Sixsmith is a middle-aged black man trying to make it as a private investigator. Despite his lack of experience and mild personality, he uses his severance pay to set up an agency in Luton. Hill has abandoned his usually intense manner, opting for a less literary, more comic style that is also more generic. Joe has a cat named "Whitey." The plots are clever and outrageous.

HILLERMAN, TONY (1925–) Tony Hillerman grew up in Oklahoma, far in distance but perhaps not in spirit from the Navajo lands that he would use as the basis for a series of extremely successful and well-respected novels about Native American detectives. In fact, Hillerman is at least as interested in communicating the Navajo way of life as in telling a whodunit. Therefore, his stories proceed at a modest pace while conveying a great deal of knowledge about the Navajo. While Hillerman does try to teach the reader about traditional societies and their anti-materialistic values, he treats the deep social significance imputed to his work with some humor. He said in an interview with Rosemary Frazer that the edifying material makes readers feel absolved for "wasting their time" enjoying a good yarn.

In Oklahoma, Hillerman lived on a small farm and attended a school for Indian children. It was the period of the Dust Bowl, and his family was poor, living without running water, a telephone, or electricity. Hillerman was decorated for his service in World War II, in which he was seriously wounded. After the war he embarked on a career in journalism, which eventually led to a move to Santa Fe and a professorship at the University of New Mexico. In 1954 he became executive editor of the *Santa Fe New Mexican.* It was almost twenty years later that he published DANCE HALL OF THE DEAD (1973), his EDGAR-winning novel featuring detective Joe LEAPHORN of the Navajo Tribal Police. Hillerman has also written about detective Jim CHEE, a much younger man than Leaphorn.

Hillerman's stories are believable and tight, with a characteristic twist at the end, though never too sensational to strain credulity. They display Hillerman's knowledge of Navajo rituals and beliefs, but are not pedantic or in any way cheap—the Navajo are not "local color." In fact, the stories have been much admired and praised by the Navajo community itself as well as the general reading public. The books almost enforce a grasp of feelings and questions that are the daily burden of today's Navajos, "an island" of 180,000 people in "a white ocean." The Navajo live on a reservation that occupies parts of Arizona, New Mexico, and Utah. It is larger than all of New England, and huge areas are uninhabited. Their lore says that this land was given by their gods for them to live in; therefore, to leave and go to dwell among the whites in cities is to cease to be a Navajo. The concept of *hosrah,* or living in beauty and harmony, is important to the culture and, of course, is violently shaken by the events in the novels.

Two of the writers who have influenced Hillerman are Arthur W. UPFIELD, whose aboriginal detective also tracks criminals across a desert landscape (Australia) using traditional knowledge, and Raymond CHANDLER, for his interest in depicting an entire society and the climate of crime (greed, particularly).

In reading Hillerman's exposition of the ways of the Navajo (Dine'ta), one is led to make a comparison and re-evaluation of one's own culture and beliefs, and to see even trivial aspects or "self-evident" values from a different perspective. For example, in *The Dark Wind* (1982), the detective has trouble understanding the motive of revenge because it is a concept foreign to Navajo thought. Different books focus on different aspects of the culture, for example witchcraft (*The Dark Wind* and *The Blessing Way,* 1970), and the Navajo taboos about death (*A Thief of Time,* 1988). A book that strongly foregrounds the interaction of the Navajo and white cultures is THE GHOSTWAY (1984).

In SKINWALKERS (1987), he first teamed Chee and Leaphorn in one adventure. Three apparently unmotivated murders occur on the reservation; then an attempt is made on Chee's life, leading Leaphorn to suspect that Chee himself is involved. They also collaborate in *Coyote Waits* (1990), in which the mysterious disappearance of the outlaw Butch Cassidy plays a part. In general, Chee's stories are slightly weaker than Leaphorn's. Where both are present, Chee gives a much better account of himself, probably because Leaphorn's intervention helps fill in the gaps and allows Chee to arrive at the solution without too many slips. And, as is clear in *Skinwalkers,* the relationship between the two men is complicated and not necessarily friendly at all times. In *A Thief of Time* (1988), there is no partner-and-sidekick or even "odd couple" feeling; Leaphorn sees Chee as a "romantic" and Chee's attempt to be a medicine man as a denial of modern reality. Meanwhile, Chee finds Leaphorn's uncommunicativeness annoying, but against his will he still wants to impress his hard-bitten superior. As a singer of religious rites, Chee's first customer proves to be Leaphorn.

After a three-year silence, Hillerman published *Sacred Clowns* (1993), which was greeted as his best book yet. In an unusual move, he disclaimed in a foreword that the Native American rituals depicted in the book corresponded to reality (in this case, the actual practices of the Hopi). But like his other books, the story is well researched and the author has consulted experts in the field. He continued to use Chee and Leaphorn in tandem, now in a task force of two, the Special Investigations Office.

Among the other awards Hillerman has received are the French Grand Prix de Littérature Policière and the Navajo Tribe's Special Friend Award.

HILTON, JAMES (1900–1954) The English writer James Hilton achieved enormous fame when he published *Goodbye, Mr. Chips* (1933), a novel set in an English boy's school, which has since been filmed and made into a play. Hilton's other great claim to fame is his invention of "Shangri-la" in the novel *Lost Horizon* (1933). A graduate of Cambridge University, Hilton had published his first novel as early as 1920. His one mystery, issued in the United States in 1933 as WAS IT MURDER?, was published under a pseudonym and is considered a significant work of the GOLDEN AGE. Two other Hilton works are of interest to the mystery reader. In *Rage in Heaven* (1932), Hilton uses the offbeat plot of a suicide made to look like murder. *We are Not Alone* (1937) is about a boy who poisons his mother; his father is arrested and tried for the crime.

HIMES, CHESTER [BOMAR] (1909–1984) The most important African American mystery novelist, Chester Himes's detective novels featuring "Coffin" Ed JOHNSON and "Grave Digger" Jones have become classics, discussed both as mysteries and protest novels. They were first published in French, however, by the Gallimard publishing house, which had suggested to Himes that he write a HARD-BOILED novel. Already a serious novelist with several books behind him, Himes moved to Europe in 1953 to escape the racism he felt in the United States and lived in Europe for the rest of his life.

Himes was born in Missouri and attended high school in Cleveland. He was a student at Ohio State University for two years but was arrested and convicted in 1928 for armed robbery, the last of several offenses. He had shown brilliance as a student, and intended to become a doctor but the other, self-destructive side of his personality drew him toward criminality and even led him to develop a separate criminal identity. In his two autobiographical works, *The Quality of Hurt* (1972) and *My Life of Absurdity* (1976), Himes reflects on the forces that shaped an almost "schizophrenic" dualism in his personality.

Himes was sentenced to twenty-five years for his armed robbery of a white home. It was during the six years he served that Himes began to write. From prison, he published work in *Esquire* and other magazines, and after his release he did manual labor for the Works Projects Administration (WPA) and was also employed by the Ohio Writer's Project. During World War II, Himes worked in the defense industry, which systematically passed over qualified blacks (like Himes) and relegated them to low-level jobs. This experience, and not his prison years, was the background of his first novel, *If He Hollers Let Him Go* (1945). The protagonist is Bo Jones, a black man who is working in a defense plant. Jones is the victim of racism and intimidation at work, particularly from a white female co-worker who abuses but also tries to seduce him, threatening to cry rape and using his race as a power over him. In his second novel, *Lonely Crusade* (1947), Himes dealt with similar themes but in the context of the labor movement. *Cast the First Stone* (1952), a novel about prison, was published shortly before Himes left the United States.

In 1957, Gallimard invited Himes to write a *roman policier,* sparking the Jones-Johnson series. *A Rage in Harlem* (1957; first pub as *For Love of Imabelle*) begins with a sucker who is done out of his money with the promise that ten-dollar bills can be chemically changed to a higher denomination. The other books include BLIND MAN WITH A PISTOL (1969), which ends with a race riot. The year before he began his detective series, Himes wrote *A Case of Rape* (1956), a novel in which four black Americans are put on trial in Paris for the rape and murder of a white woman. A black expatriate novelist tries to prove their innocence. Himes also wrote *Run Man, Run* (1966), a non-series crime novel.

Throughout his detective and crime writing, Himes revealed the disregard of black lives by the authorities, and the poor treatment dished out even to black detectives. He gave Jones and Johnson a sympathetic boss, Lieutenant Anderson, who sometimes acts as a buffer between them and uncaring higher-ups. Himes also brought the African American world into the crime novel as something other than a source of scenery. The world that the detectives deal with is very violent—in the first book, for instance, Jones has acid thrown in his face—and they are violent themselves. The political content of the stories is never far from the surface. In *Cotton Comes to Harlem* (1965), which revolves around a cotton bale filled with $87,000, he parodies Marcus Garvey's back to Africa movement. Himes treats the black community with humor and respect, but does not hesitate to show blacks victimizing each other; however, there are also powerful outside forces that thwart attempts to establish order (particularly by Jones and Johnson). The detectives try to even the score, in one case by failing to turn in the killer of a victim who was a brutal racist, in another by giving recovered money to a charity that helps inner-city kids. But the situation of the community at the end of the last book in the series seems depressingly hopeless.

Himes won the Grand Prix de Littérature Policière in 1957. Long appreciated in France, interest in Himes in his own country has steadily increased, especially since his death. Book-length critical works on Himes include *Two Guns from Harlem: The Detective Fiction of Chester Himes* by Robert Skinner, which appeared in 1989.

HIS NAME WAS DEATH (1951) A crime novel by Frederic BROWN illustrative of the snowball effect. Joyce Dugan, a widow, is about to go home for the day when an old high school friend turns up to collect ninety dollars which her boss owed him, having decided to trade cars with him the night before and pay the difference in cash. Joyce writes him a check on the boss's account, then decides to cash the check for him on the spot. Because of that, people lose their lives.

The other remarkable thing about the book is the personality of the murderer. A middle-aged loser whose wife cheats on him, he feels enlarged by committing the "perfect" crime, and begins to read true-crime stories and puff up his ego with reassurance of his daring, patience, and sang froid. The bland prose actually adds to the horrifying impression of this man who doesn't realize that he is still a loser, that his "brilliance" is the work of chance, and that his stupid errors are all his own.

HISTORICAL MYSTERY A mystery that is either entirely set in some particular period but was not written during it ("period" mystery), or that has a detective investigating an event more or less remote in time ("transhistorical" mystery). Of these two types, the former is the most difficult to handle. Examples of the latter include Josephine Tey's THE DAUGHTER OF TIME (1951), an acknowledged masterpiece in which Shakespeare's portrayal of Richard II as a vicious murderer is questioned. (Tey influenced Marvin Kaye's *Bullets for Macbeth,* 1976, which tells both the story of an onstage killing and the search for the identity of the third murderer in Shakespeare's *Macbeth*).

Some transhistorical mysteries actually shift back and forth in time and use separate narrators. Another method of accomplishing a time shift is through historical documents that the modern sleuth must interpret in the novel's present in order to unlock a mystery in the past. Examples of such "document novels" include A. S. Byatt's 1990 novel POSSESSION (the ancestor of which is Henry James's ASPERN PAPERS, 1888) and BEYOND THE GRAVE (1986), co-authored by Bill PRONZINI and Marcia MULLER.

Ruth RENDELL's *Anna's Book* (1994) charts the history of a Danish immigrant family in London in 1905. It begins with the diaries of Anna Westerby, an expectant mother alone in London with her two children while her neglectful husband Rasmus—a dreamer and motor car enthusiast—is preoccupied with his business and his own aims in Denmark. In the novel's "present," the diaries have become famous and been adapted to film. Anna's granddaughter, however, finds that a key page is missing from the diaries. Although a 1905 murder figures in the story, it is the identities of the several strong women in the book and the complexities of family that are the core of the novel.

The problem with the other type of historical mystery, the period mystery, is detail; authors often make the false assumption that masses of well-researched historical data bring the scene to life, when in actuality the characters seem to be living on a sound stage or a Hollywood backlot. Without believable characters, the historical detail achieves nothing. E. L. DOCTOROW is a master at creating characters who really seem to be comfortable in their period; they *believe* they live in it, rather than existing as the fantasies of some more modern mind (i.e., the author's). Doctorow's mystery and crime-related novels beg comparison with that of another writer whose historical mysteries are set in New York: Caleb CARR.

The husband-and-wife team "Maan Myers" has written a series of historical mysteries about New York, including *The Dutchman* (1992) and *The Kingsbridge Plot* (1993); the latter takes place at the time of the American Revolution and includes George Washington as a character. It also involves the famous *Turtle,* an egg-shaped wooden submarine that was used to try to drill holes in the hull of Admiral Howe's flagship (it failed).

Gillian Linscott has written revisionist history-as-mystery. Her heroine, Nell Bray, is an English suffragette; she experiences a level of freedom and empowerment that was extremely rare in the period (circa 1910) in which the novels are set. In *An Easy Day for a Lady* (1994), Nell goes to climb Mont Blanc on a "holiday" after committing a violent act of protest. She is hired to investigate the death of a mountain climber killed thirty years before and found in the ice. While this book sheds interesting light on family life and climbing, *Crown Witness* (1995) is an unbelievable story centered around the shooting of an anarchist.

Elizabeth PETERS uses her knowledge as a professional Egyptologist to supply background for her stories about a nineteenth-century Egyptologist, Amelia PEABODY. Michael Pearce, who grew up in the colonial Egyptian Sudan, has written a less-known series of mysteries. The stories take place just after the turn of the century, and concern the MAMUR ZAPT, the head of Cairo's Secret Police (a Mamur is a police inspector). Still further back, Agatha CHRISTIE set *Death Comes as the End* (1945) in 2,000 B.C. It has the classic scenario of the young vixen (Nofret) who comes between the older man (Imhotep) who dotes on her and his grown-up children from a previous marriage. Nofret is killed, but not before she has had Imhotep's three sons disinherited. That, however, is only the beginning of trouble, as Nofret's curse is blamed for a succession of suspicious deaths.

Robert VAN GULIK, an expert in Far Eastern languages, set his Judge DEE mysteries in medieval China. One of the best historical mysteries ever written was Umberto ECO'S best-selling THE NAME OF THE ROSE (1984), set in a medieval Italian monastery. Reaching even further back in history is the series by Lindsey Davis featuring an ancient Roman detective, Marcus Didius Falco. Furthest back in time is *The Stone Arrow* (1978), by the English writer Richard Herley; a thriller rather than a mystery, it is set in Sussex in the Paleolithic period (see ARCHAEOLOGY).

Many CELEBRITY MYSTERIES have been written using famous historical figures, most of which fail to convince. Several have featured Theodore ROOSEVELT. Historical mysteries have also been based on famous murder cases such as the trial of Lizzie BORDEN, the BOSTON STRANGLER, JACK THE RIPPER, and the Ratcliffe Highway murders, supposed to have been committed by John Williams.

Similarly, historical cases have been moved into the present: Josephine Tey also wrote THE FRANCHISE AFFAIR (1949), a modernized version of the Elizabeth CANNING case, and Nicholas Blake's A TANGLED WEB (1956) is an updated and fictionalized account of a 1912 murder case.

The two-volume anthology *The Mammoth Book of Historical Whodunits* (1993) contains a foreword by Ellis PETERS, one of the most popular of current practitioners in this subgenre and the creator of Brother CADFAEL.

Other writers who have written historical mysteries include Lillian DE LA TORRE, Thomas KENEALLY, John Dickson CARR, Peter LOVESEY, and Julian SYMONS. Even Cornell WOOLRICH wrote one mystery set in the nineteenth century.

HITCHCOCK, ALFRED (1899–1980) Born in humble circumstances in the East End of London, naturalized an American citizen in 1955, Alfred Hitchcock started his directorial career in silent films and ended as an idol of pop culture. One of the most successful directors of all time, he was known for his tremendous ego and he, not the actors, was the actual though (mostly) invisible star of his films. Dubbed the "Master of Suspense," he adapted works by some of the greatest writers in the crime and mystery genre, including John BUCHAN (*The Thirty-Nine Steps,* 1935), Patricia HIGHSMITH (*Strangers on a Train,* 1951), and Cornell WOOLRICH (*Rear Window,* 1954). Hitchcock's first major thriller, *The Lodger* (1926), was based on the novel by Marie Belloc LOWNDES, in turn based on the career of JACK THE RIPPER. Hitchcock's adaptation of Daphne DU MAURIER's *Rebecca* (1938) was filmed in 1940 and won an Academy Award for best picture. Confusingly, Hitchcock filmed some of Somerset Maughham's ASHENDEN stories as *The Secret Agent* (1936), and the same year filmed Joseph CONRAD's novel *The Secret Agent* (1907) under the title *Sabotage.* Among his most exciting thrillers are *The Lady Vanishes* (1938), *Suspicion* (1941), and *North by Northwest* (1959). Hitchcock reached his peak, of course, with *Psycho* (1960), whose "shower scene" is probably familiar to thousands who have never been able to bear to see the film.

Hitchcock, like Woolrich and others, often focused on the ordinary person suddenly caught up in incredible and nightmarish events. What Hitchcock had as a director was an ability to create edge-of-the-seat terror and horrifying scenes the viewer cannot stop watching. What he did not have was an ability to create believable female characters, and he overused the ingenue figure more than any other successful director. As a technician, he was a master, and he was also a brilliant psychologist—but it was the behavior and reactions of the audience member, and not the everyman who was depicted on the screen, that he understood most. While highbrow critics may dismiss him as a clever manipulator, French critics and directors (notably François TRUFFAUT) saw him as a genius who laid bare the fragility of calm social appearances and the horrors and anxiety of modern life. He received the American Film Institute's Lifetime Achievement Award the year before his death.

Hitchcock also had a career as a publisher by lending his name to the still extant *Alfred Hitchcock's Mystery Magazine,* as well as many books that anthologized stories of mystery and suspense. His television programs (1955–1965) did much to make his name a household word in his adopted country.

HODGSON, WILLIAM HOPE (1877–1918) The English author William Hope Hodgson is remembered as an important figure in the development of fantasy and horror literature. His place in the canon of mystery fiction was established by just one book, *Carnacki the Ghost-Finder* (1913), a collection of stories about an OCCULT detective. CARNACKI led the way toward SCIENCE FICTION by combining scientific methods with unnatural or fantastic situations. Hodgson's enormous novel *The Night Land* (1912), in which the sun has burned out and the remaining humans live in a metal pyramid eight miles high and one hundred deep, is considered a science fiction classic.

Born in Essex, Hodgson was the son of a nonconformist Anglican priest and the second of twelve children. Always an adventurous spirit, Hodgson joined the Merchant Marine at the age of thirteen. He spent eight years at sea, eventually earning his mate's certificate and becoming a skilled photographer. Later, after he gave up the sea as a brutal profession—"I dislike being a pawn with the sea for a board and the shipowners for players"—he traveled and lectured using his pictures of terrifying storms. He also was a "physical culturalist" (a bodybuilder) and ran a gym at one time.

Hodgson's first writings were tales of the sea that already showed his taste for the weird and dreadful. His first stories appeared soon after the turn of the century, and he became acquainted with writers such as H. G. WELLS, with whom he would be compared. His first novel, *The Boats of the 'Glen Carrig'* (1907), is in the tradition of POE's *The Narrative of A. Gordon Pym* (1838). After the *Glen Carrig* sinks, the crew sets off in lifeboats and is attacked by various monsters, including giant white slugs, the "Weed Men," and giant octopi. Some of Hodgson's other stories are collected in *Out of the Storm: Uncollected Fantasies* (1975). The collection's editor, Sam Moskowitz, gives a virtual biography of Hodgson running over a hundred pages.

At the outbreak of World War I, Hodgson returned to England from the south of France, where he had been living. He joined the Officer Training Corps at the University of London and was commissioned in the Royal Artillery, but after he was thrown from a horse and severely injured, he was discharged. Hodgson was an athlete, however, and got himself into shape and joined up again in 1917. He was killed in action on the Western Front, probably because of his lack of fear—it was reported that he was always volunteering for dangerous duty.

HOEG, PETER (1957–) The Danish author Peter Hoeg is known primarily for SMILLA'S SENSE OF SNOW (1994), a thriller that was an enormous bestseller in the United States and was later filmed. It would be a mistake to characterize Hoeg as a THRILLER writer, however; his work since *Smilla's Sense of Snow* has continued to show an unwillingness to be bound by genre. Hoeg's strength is his ability to combine suspense with psychology and a deep feeling for setting—Greenland, in *Smilla's Sense of Snow*—and to create narratives that instruct as well as entertain and that stand up on several levels.

Hoeg worked as an actor, dancer, drama teacher, and sailor before becoming an author. His persistent theme is the destruction of indigenous culture and of human spirituality by modern Western culture. *Borderliners* (1994) is about a prestigious school in Copenhagen covertly conducting an experiment on controlling children. Social engineering destroys the child's natural relationship to the world in the name of some kind of progress or enlightened thought. Hoeg's first novel, translated as *The History of Danish Dreams* (1995), follows several families through hundreds of years, focusing on the relationship between family and society that often leads to alienation of the individual and destruction of the spirit. *Tales of the Night* (1998) is a collection of stories, all of which take place on the night of March 19, 1929.

HOLMES, SHERLOCK Not only the most famous detective of all time, but one of the best-known characters in all of literature. Holmes is also a violinist and an expert in a wide range of fields; although he leaves the chronicling of his exploits to WATSON, he publishes such works as a "monograph upon the Polyphonic Motets of Lassus," and a frequently mentioned dissertation on the different varieties of tobacco ash.

Holmes's early life is notoriously unclear. He attended college for a couple of years, but it is not certain whether he finished or whether he went to Oxford or Cambridge. His place of birth is unknown, though the village of MYCROFT has been suggested. He meets Doctor Watson at the time of A STUDY IN SCARLET (1887) because both are looking for a roommate; Holmes is deeply involved in chemistry experiments, and has already worked on various cases in which he has been able to apply the "methods" he began developing as an undergraduate (see The GLORIA SCOTT case, Holmes's first). Particularly in the early stories, beginning with the "Science of Deduction" chapter of *A Study in Scarlet,* Holmes lays great stress on the scientific and objective nature of his methods, which, improbably, have more to do with finding faint "indications" than interviewing subjects as in real police work.

Watson's first impressions of Holmes are that he is eccentric (his odd habits, such as sticking his mail to the mantelpiece with a jackknife, are notorious). Extremely tall and thin with a hawklike nose, Holmes has penetrating eyes and a nervous manner; he immediately surprises Watson with his deduction that the doctor has just returned from Afghanistan. This episode introduces the Holmes trademark, which is to astound his clients upon their first meeting by displaying personal knowledge of them that he has deduced simply from their appearance. (Holmes is strong on tobacco ash, marks on cuffs, and the condition of shoes.) Perhaps his most astounding deduction is in "The Adventure of the Dancing Men," when he determines from a chalk mark between Watson's fingers that he has decided not to invest in South African securities.

After they move in to 221B Baker Street, Watson tries a little deduction of his own, and from Holmes's interests makes an effort to determine his profession, as yet a mystery. Watson rates Holmes's knowledge of literature as "nil," though he knows all about various arcane subjects related to detection and has a comprehensive grasp of "sensational" stories. (Conan Doyle rapidly amended Holmes's one-sidedness: already in the RED-HEADED LEAGUE he is quoting Flaubert, and by the time of the "Boscombe Valley Mystery" Holmes is carrying a "pocket Petrarch" and proposing to discuss George Meredith with Watson.) Holmes is, incredibly, ignorant of the theory of the solar system, because it has no bearing on his activities (a view he apparently thought better of, since in the GREEK INTERPRETER he discourses on "the causes of the change in the obliquity of the ecliptic").

As a doctor, it does not take long for Watson to discover that Holmes is addicted to cocaine, which he injects. It may help to explain why he (like Nero WOLFE) goes through periods of lassitude, moodiness, or the most abject laziness. The drug habit is dealt with rather lightly in the stories, and has led some later editors to excise mentions of Holmes's habit in juvenile editions of the adventures. Other facts about Holmes that eventually emerge are that he comes from an artistic family and has a brother named Mycroft. He owns a Stradivarius violin and plays it, badly. Surely the strangest thing that Holmes does is to die and come back to life. Conan Doyle had tired of him, seemed to have killed him pretty thoroughly in THE FINAL PROBLEM, and then had to go to some lengths in the EMPTY HOUSE mystery (including adding the Japanese art of "baritsu" wrestling to Holmes's many talents) to explain his reappearance. Holmes eventually retires to Sussex to keep bees, but comes out of retirement to save England in World War I.

In addition to the stories, Holmes appeared in four novels. The first was *A Study in Scarlet* (1887); it was in fact Holmes's debut, but the entire middle of the novel takes place in Utah and many people (including Loren D. ESTLEMAN, who wrote an introduction to Penguin's complete Holmes) believed that it could be skipped without hurting the story. THE HOUND OF THE BASKERVILLES (1902) is far and away the best of the novels and one of Holmes's greatest adventures. It was as a short story character that Holmes became famous, and it was as a short story writer that Conan Doyle excelled; perhaps it was this dependence that made Conan Doyle come to dislike Holmes. The publication of the stories in the *Strand* enriched both the magazine and the author.

Holmes has often been copied, both unconsciously and consciously. GENIUS DETECTIVES like Solar PONS and Nero Wolfe are descendants of Holmes (the former is actually a Holmes pastiche), as is Dr. THORNDYKE and the young Ellery QUEEN. *Son of Holmes* (1986) is a more literal attempt to copy Holmes; in this book by John T. Lescroart, Auguste Lupa is supposedly the son of Holmes and Irene Adler, whom Holmes so admired in A SCANDAL IN BOHEMIA. *Lupa* is also Latin for "wolf," and so Auguste Lupa could be Nero Wolfe—though how Holmes could have fathered a Montenegrin detective is a problem. Most Holmes parodies and pastiches have met with a lukewarm response from critics.

Encyclopedia Sherlockiana (repr 1997) is an exhaustive guide to Holmes, but no book could ever exhaust interest in him; writings about Holmes number in the thousands. BARING-GOULD's biography of Holmes is one of the better known.

BIBLIOGRAPHY Novels: *The Sign of Four* (1892), *The Valley of Fear* (1915).

Short Stories: *The Adventures of Sherlock Holmes* (1892), *The Memoirs of Sherlock Holmes* (1894), *The Return of Sherlock Holmes* (1905), *His Last Bow* (1915), *The Case Book of Sherlock Holmes* (1927).

HOLTON, LEONARD (pseudonym of Leonard Patrick O'Connor Wibberley, 1915–1983) Born in Ireland, Leonard Wibberly was a world-traveling journalist and a prolific author—almost one hundred books appeared under his own name and various pseudonyms. It is for one book alone, however, that he is most known: *The Mouse That Roared* (1955), which was made into a Peter Sellers film (1959). The story concerns a fictitious European country about the size of Andorra that decides to invade the United States.

Holton lived in England, Portugal, and other countries before moving to the United States. During World War II, he worked in a shipyard. He also worked for the *London Evening News* and the *Los Angeles Times.* Holton eventually settled in California, and he chose Los Angeles as the setting for his Father BREDDER novels. This was the first important mystery series with a priest as its sleuth since the Father BROWN stories; although Holton's writing is far below that of G. K. CHESTERTON, he did try to work in religious themes, albeit in a haphazard manner. Holton's numerous interests are reflected in his novels (see, for example, MURDER AFLOAT and BASEBALL). Holton was a violinist and also made musical instruments. In addition to mysteries he wrote plays and juvenile fiction.

HOMES, GEOFFREY (pseudonym of Daniel Mainwaring, 1901–1978) A former private detective and newspaperman, Daniel Mainwaring created two mystery series, one about Robin Bishop and the other about Humphrey CAMPBELL. Bishop is a reporter and detective in the subgenre at which George Harmon COXE excelled. Bishop, a married man and a less than flamboyant character, first appeared in *The Doctor Died at Dusk* (1936). Bishop's last book, *Then There Were Three* (1938), was also Campbell's first. The story concerns a woman who disappears on the evening of her wedding. Mainwaring produced four other novels about Bishop, including *The Man Who Didn't Exist* (1937), and four solo Campbell performances.

Born in California, Mainwaring attended the University of Fresno. He worked at a number of jobs, including migrant fruit picker; his rolling stone period would later provide material for his novels. Mainwaring's first writing job was for the *San Francisco Chronicle,* where he stayed for ten years. He later found his way into the film business through a job as a press agent.

All of Mainwaring's books except the first, *One Against the Earth* (1933), were written under the Homes pseudonym. He also worked for Hollywood as a screenwriter, and among his scripts was the one for *Out of the Past* (1947), which he based on his novel of the previous year, BUILD MY GALLOWS HIGH. It was to be Mainwaring's last book. With this fine example of FILM NOIR (it starred Robert Mitchum and Kirk Douglas), Mainwaring could be said to have quit at the top of his profession. He went on to write many more film scripts, over forty in all, the most famous of which would have to be *Invasion of the Body Snatchers* (1956). He also wrote a script about the gangster Baby Face Nelson (1957).

Mainwaring does not seem to have been able to take very seriously the HARD-BOILED style that was ascendant at the time he was writing, which is all to the good. Although not spoofs or parodies, his novels show a light touch, a healthy sense of humor, and a tendency to mock covertly the conventions of the genre. Mainwaring's non-series novels include *The Hill of the Terrified Monk* (1943), one of two novels based on his knowledge of the movie business. His late work was his most strange: in *The Street of the Crying Woman* (1942) he introduced José Manuel Madero, a Zapotecan Indian who helps a Spanish professor search for his missing son in Mexico.

"HOMESICK BUICK, THE" (1950) A story by John D. MACDONALD. It begins as the tale of a bank job in the one-horse town of Leeman, Texas. A nondescript little man named Stanley Woods turns up one day in 1949 apparently scouting for the site for a factory. But that isn't what he is really doing, as becomes obvious when the bank is robbed and two people are killed—one of them the driver of one getaway car, a Buick. MacDonald describes in detail the physical evidence gone over by the FBI, from dust in the corpse's pants cuffs to a crumb of bread under the seat. None of it results in anything until a homely fourteen-year-old named Pink, a misunderstood genius, comes up with a brilliant clue. The story, a model of clean, concise tale-telling, was originally published in *Ellery Queen's Mystery Magazine.*

HOODLUM This term for a tough guy or a thug arose in San Francisco, where it was first used in print in 1871. But its exact origin is unclear. The most imaginative theory is that a newspaper was looking for a name for the members of the Muldoon gang, and spelled the name backwards ("noodlum"), which was then was corrupted to "hoodlum" by the misreading of "h" for "n." Hugh Rawson gives as a more probable source the Bavarian word *hydelum,* meaning "disorderly."

HOOLIGAN A tough guy or street criminal, the word may have come from a proper name, such as Houlihan or Houlighan.

HOPE, MATTHEW A character created by Ed MCBAIN, after the success of his 87TH STREET PRECINCT series. Hope does what many New Yorkers have done: move to Florida. In the town of Calusa on Florida's west coast, he practices civil law in a small firm with one partner. Although he knows nothing about criminal law, he gets involved by chance in various criminal matters. The titles in the series refer to fairy tales and nursery rhymes, and the novels are as grisly as the stories they mirror (particularly *Three Blind Mice* [1990], in which it is not the victims' tails that are cut off). Hope's partner is Frank Summerville, a short and fat comic-relief character.

Hope first appeared in *Goldilocks* (1978), a bloody novel that also portrays Calusa as a sordid town full of middle-aged adulterers—including Hope. His client and friend, Dr. Jamie Purchase, returns home late at night to find his second wife and their two small girls horribly butchered. Hope believes Jamie is innocent, but has doubts about his alibi. Meanwhile, Hope is cheating on his own wife, and is at the point of asking for a divorce after many tiresome fights.

While in *Goldilocks* Hope had never had a criminal case, by the time of *Mary, Mary* (1992) he is one of the two best criminal lawyers in southwestern Florida. It is a sloppy book in which Hope has a preposterous love affair. The case involves an Englishwoman accused of killing three little girls and burying them in her garden. Realism, McBain's strength, seems to have left him, though there are lengthy courtroom and deposition transcripts. He uses one of the oldest of tricks to pull off the surprise ending.

BIBLIOGRAPHY Novels: *Rumpelstiltskin* (1981), *Beauty and the Beast* (1982), *Jack and the Beanstalk* (1984), *Snow White and Rose Red* (1985), *Cinderella* (1986), *Puss in Boots* (1987), *The House That Jack Built* (1988), *There Was a Little Girl* (1994), *Gladys the Cross-Eyed Bear* (1996), *The Last Best Hope* (1998).

HOPKINS, LLOYD A Los Angles police detective sergeant created by James ELLROY. Hopkins is a version of the "rogue cop" who breaks the rules in order to achieve justice, but also has elements of the classic p.i. Since his cooperation with his colleagues is almost nonexistent, he can operate like an enraged version of Lew ARCHER. Hopkins is physically large, powerful, and attractive to women. A womanizer, he is estranged from his wife and children. His hard-driving style and willingness to break the law in order to get his man has made him a departmental "legend" and oddball, earning him the nickname "Crazy Lloyd."

In *Blood on the Moon* (1984), Lloyd pursues a sex murderer, Teddy Verplanck. The Hopkins novels are more suspense than detection—INVERTED MYSTERIES with a twist: in BECAUSE THE NIGHT (1984), Ellroy uses the parallel narratives to show how Hopkins fails as a detective, chasing suspects who are already dead and being led around by the nose by a brilliant psychopath. In *Suicide Hill* (1986) Hopkins himself is being psychiatrically evaluated because of his violent and obsessive-compulsive behavior; the psychiatrist recommends early retirement. The story uses the device of converging plot lines, one involving the scary experiences of the prisoner Duane Rice, who is in charge of feeding, doping, and punishing a ward of mentally ill inmates. The other plot concerns the four Garcia brothers, who pose as priests and use psychological intimidation to deceive their gullible victims.

HOPLEY, GEORGE A pseudonym of Cornell WOOLRICH.

HORIZONTAL MAN, THE (1946) A novel by Helen EUSTIS that won the second EDGAR award for best first novel. The story reflects the interest in psychology and psychiatry at the time, and also uses the theme of AMNESIA. Irish poet, English teacher, and Lothario Kevin Boyle is murdered in the opening scene with a fireplace poker. The author lets the reader know that the killer is a woman, and so suspicion immediately falls upon Freda Cramm, a sexually liberated and wealthy professor in Boyle's department at Hollymount College in West Lyman, Connecticut. Then Molly Morrison, a girl who was madly in love with Boyle, becomes hysterical and signs a confession. Still, the book suffers from too many sleuths and too few suspects. Kate Innes, an unattractive but sharp student, and Jack Donnelly, a young reporter, team up to solve the crime. The cringing milquetoast professor Leonard Marks investigates, too—and so does the psychiatrist Julian Forstmann. Eustis uses themes that were beginning to interest writers of the era, and have been used countless times since; when she pulls off her surprise, the contemporary reader will have been onto it for some time. She also fails to make believable Molly's doubt of the evidence of her own senses and her conviction that she is insane. Eustis does better with the villain, but the shock is not as great now as it would have been originally. She did, however, know the small Berkshire women's college atmosphere from her own experience. The most convincing psychological aspects are her portrayals of Molly's difficult relationship with a stern and unloving mother, and professor George Hungerford's unresolved enmeshment with his mother.

The title is from a poem by a W. H. AUDEN.

HORLER, SYDNEY (1888–1954) The popular English novelist Sydney Horler was a sort of junior Edgar WALLACE in the twenties and thirties—in fact, he bought Wallace's desk and dictaphone after Wallace died. Those possessions did not, however, make him a writer of Wallace's quality. Although like Wallace he produced books at a furious rate (he eventually wrote about 150), and much of his writing was slapdash, he replaced Wallace's charm, essential good humor, and occasional vivid characterization with xenophobia, jingoism, and wretched stereotypes. All the same, Horler had an extremely high regard for his own work, and was positively bombastic on the subject. His autobiography is *Excitement: An Impudent Autobiography* (1933), which certainly justified its subtitle. The word "excitement" referred to the dust jacket slogan that made Horler's name famous during his lifetime—"Horler for Excitement!"

Such excitement as Horler provided was of a kind with SAPPER's; in his series about Tiger Standish, which began with *Tiger Standish* (1932), he has a dashing, devil-may-care English hero battling the supposedly subhuman peoples of the Mediterranean and the East. Standish is handsome, elegant, and brave, but does not have much in the area of brains. Another of Horler's heroes was Ian Heath, a spy. Perhaps his most bizarre character was "the Nighthawk," a perverted version of RAFFLES. George Frost, the Nighthawk, is a burglar who steals only from upper-class women whose morals he thinks are too loose; the Nighthawk takes their money and jewels and writes "wanton" on their pillows in lipstick. There were seven Nighthawk books, the first being *They Called Him Nighthawk* (1937).

Horler began his writing career as a reporter for the *Bristol Evening News* and other papers in the northern English industrial cities and London. In World War I he was a propaganda writer, an experience that no doubt carried over into his writings. His first novel was *Goal* (1920), and he wrote many sports-related stories. *The Mystery of No.1* (1925) was his first mystery novel.

Horler's books are out of print and likely to stay that way, given his racism, obsolete politics, and defense of a thankfully vanished code that was the essence of hypocrisy, meting out cruelty and death to its transgressors in violent fantasies. His views on writing were expressed in *Writing for Money* (1932), a thing he did well, though it did not produce anything of lasting cultural value.

HORN, FLETCHER A professional killer in Loren D. ESTLEMAN's *The Glass Highway* (1983), and a fine example of the type. Horn is neither a snide-talking sadist nor a cool customer with wing tips and a target pistol: he is just empty. Horn is one of the author's most effective creations.

HORNSWOGGLE A slang word meaning to trick, to deceive. Many dictionaries state that the word's etymology is unknown; however, the probable theory has been advanced that it is American cowboy slang, and referred to the slipping off of the lariat from the horn of a cow that a cowboy was trying to rope.

HORNUNG, E[RNEST] W[ILLIAM] (1866–1921) English writer and creator of RAFFLES, the famous thief and precursor of many modern scoundrel-heroes. Along with his partner Bunny Manders, Raffles burgles the homes of the rich. The stories do not have much detection, but are interesting for their humor, style, and portrait of England in the Edwardian era.

Hornung was born in Yorkshire but spent several years in Australia in his late teens and early twenties. This period of adventure was the incubator of his writing career. He taught at Mossgiel Station, Riverina. He returned to England in 1886, and in 1893 married Constance Doyle, the sister of the creator of Sherlock HOLMES. The Raffles stories were immensely popular and give an irreverent view of the period, whose charm and spirit was shortly to be destroyed by World War I. This era still exercises a fascination that has made writers as different as Conan DOYLE and Edith Wharton perennially popular, and for which the reader willingly suspends a horror of its politics. Raffles is one of the most intriguing characters of the period; on the one hand he upholds the public school values of a son of the British Empire, and on the other he shatters taboos. George Orwell wrote that Raffles had no social consciousness or morality but only his "reflexes"—"the nervous system, as it were, of a gentleman." In fact, Raffles steals in order to maintain the façade of a gentleman in society while being an amoralist in private; the keeping up of appearances is perhaps the only thing he takes seriously.

It is this moral ambiguity in the stories that makes them still readable today, gives them a more modern tone than Conan Doyle's stories, and makes Raffles more of a person of flesh-and-blood than Sherlock Holmes. Raffles views human nature as "a board of chequers," and thinks, "why not reconcile one's self to alternate black and white? Why desire to be all one thing or all the other, like our forefathers on the stage or in the old-fashioned fiction? For his part, he enjoyed himself on all squares of the board, and liked the light the better for the shade."

Hornung's early books such as *A Bridge from the Bush* (1890), *Tiny Lutrell* (1893), and *Irralie's Bushranger* (1896) were based on his Australian experience. Hornung had published some stories in the *Strand* before he created Raffles, but his amateur cracksman was his real success. Still, Hornung continued to write about Australia even after Raffles had become famous. Some of these books also dealt with crime, including *The Rogue's March* (1896) and *Dead Men Tell No Tales* (1899). Another genre work is *The Crime Doctor* (1914), about a psychological detective. Hornung also had a modest career as a dramatist. With Eugene W. Presbrey, he adapted his most famous character for the stage in *Raffles, The Amateur Cracksman* (1903), which played in London and New York; a sequel was entitled *A Visit from Raffles* (1909).

Hornung suffered from ill health all his life, but, like Raffles, was a good cricketer. He worked for the YMCA in World War I, operating a traveling library for the troops. *Notes of Camp-Follower on the Western Front* (1919) describes his experiences. Hornung lost his only son in the war.

The Raffles stories have recently been gathered together in *The Collected Raffles Stories* (1996).

HOUND OF THE BASKERVILLES, THE (1902) The best of the Sherlock HOLMES novels, and one of the very best mystery novels of all time. Conan DOYLE was able to combine his interest in the OCCULT with scientific detection most effectively. Jacques BARZUN complained of "those intolerable middle sections which potbelly three out of four of his longer tales"; this is the fourth, which preserves the flavor and techniques of the Holmes short stories while obeying a unity of time and action. It does not catapult the reader into the past or remote places to fill out its length with long historical digressions. However, *The Hound of the Baskervilles* does place Doctor WATSON at the center of the action.

Old Sir Charles Baskerville became rich in the South African gold speculation, but he had little peace at Baskerville Hall, situated on Dartmoor in Devonshire, because he believed his family lay under an ancient curse, explained in a document brought to Sherlock Holmes by Sir Charles's doctor, James Mortimer. On the evening of his death, Sir Charles walked out through the lane of yew trees at the hall and fell dead of heart failure. At the point where a gate opened from the lane onto the somber moor, the footprints changed, as if Sir Charles had been walking on his toes. Near the body, Mortimer found a frightening footprint.

While a "spectral" beast strikes terror into the neighborhood of Baskerville Hall, Sir Henry Baskerville, the heir, arrives from Canada. It is because Sir Charles's philanthropy had improved the district that a dilemma arises as to whether to allow the heir to take up residence at Baskerville Hall and continue the good works, thereby exposing himself to the curse and the risk of coming to a deplorably foul end. Even before he gets to Devonshire, strange things begin to happen to Sir Henry, so Holmes sends Watson down with him. The old, melancholy house depresses the spirits of both men, and on the first night Watson hears the sobbing of a woman—a suggestion of a ghost related to the horrible Baskerville legend. Conan Doyle takes evident delight in creating more gothic horrors. There is the Grimpen Mire, a bog that sucks creatures in like quicksand; the neolithic ruins and monoliths that cover the moor; the strange butler, Barrymore, and his troubled wife; and an escaped killer abroad on Dartmoor. The redoubtable Watson soon finds another mysterious figure hanging about the bleak tors and crags and ruined huts, and continues his investigations under an atmosphere of menace. The middle of the novel is told through Watson's reports to Holmes, who has stayed in London on a delicate blackmail case. The climax takes place in a dense fog and is one of Conan Doyle's most memorable.

HOUSEHOLD, GEOFFREY (1900–1988) The English suspense author Geoffrey Household wrote many books, but he is remembered almost exclusively for one: ROGUE MALE (1939), in which an English hunter goes after the biggest game of all (see NAZIS). H. R. F. KEATING felt that *Rogue Male* unjustly overshadowed Household's other books, to which he imputed strange and mysterious qualities.

Household graduated from Oxford University in 1922, and worked for four years in Romania as a banker. After that, he went to Spain, where he sold bananas. During the Depression he lived in the United States and wrote radio plays for children. He returned briefly to England and began selling printer's inks, traveling back and forth between Europe and South America. His first book was the novel *The Third Hour* (1937). He began publishing short stories and was encouraged by the *Atlantic Monthly,* which published "The Salvation of Pisco Gabar" in 1936; it was the title story of a collection of Household's short fiction (1938; exp 1940).

By the time that *Rogue Male* was published, World War II had already broken out and Household had joined the intelligence service. He was sent to Romania because of his previous experience there, and then to the Middle East, where he remained until 1945. Household was decorated for his war service.

Household's novels reflect his own peripatetic life. Just after the war he wrote two books set in the Middle East. He published *A Time to Kill* in 1951 (decades before the John GRISHAM novel of the same name), a story that, like *Rogue Male,* takes place in Dorset. Among his other thrillers and novels of intrigue is WATCHER IN THE SHADOWS (1960). Household's heroes tend to be upper-class Englishmen who reflect the prewar code of the gentleman. His books are usually not about detection, but rather the avoidance of detection; like Richard HANNAY, the Household hero scrambles to avoid malevolent agents whose purposes he may or may not understand, often trying selflessly to shield others from harm, whether they be friends or his nation itself. The code of ethics of the hero is such that a man who is at the mercy of Nazi captors chooses his words carefully so that he is not actually lying to them. Household's is an idiosyncratic elitism: anyone can belong to "class X," a kind of natural nobility, but whether proletarian or an aristocrat, they must have "the right stuff." In his democratic snobbism, "the only people who are class-conscious are those who would like to belong to Class X and don't."

Household's autobiography is *Against the Wind,* published in 1958.

HOUSE OF THE ARROW, THE (1924) A novel by A. E. W. MASON, the second in which Inspector HANAUD appears. It is a long and complicated novel, which begins with the receipt of a letter by the old London solicitor, Jeremy Hazlitt, from a half-mad Russian gambler named Boris Waberski. He asks for an advance on his expected inheritance from his sister-in-law, the widow Mrs. Harlowe, who lives in Dijon. As Hazlitt knows, Waberski stands to inherit exactly nothing. When Mrs. Harlowe dies three weeks later, Waberski is enraged and Hazlitt is thoughtful; he sends the young Jim Frobisher to look into the matter. Waberski makes accusations of murder against Betty Harlowe, who was the niece and adopted daughter of Mr. Harlowe.

Frobisher meets up with Hanaud in Paris on his way to Dijon and acts as his WATSON for the remainder of the story. Hanaud is actually more interested in investigating a rash of anonymous letters in Dijon that have caused a string of suicides.

HOUSE WITHOUT A KEY, THE (1925) The first Charlie CHAN book, by Earl Derr BIGGERS. As a mystery, it is a mixed bag; the plot is twisted enough, but the characters are so thin that one has difficulty caring who did it. The effort to make Chan's English seem ethnic is a failure, relying on the obvious device of having him confuse the singular and plural of the verb "to be," constantly saying "it are" and "they is." A genius at logic would no doubt be able to master such a fundamental aspect of grammar.

Set in Hawaii, the novel focuses on the death of Dan Winterslip, a black sheep of an old and proper Boston family. He lives next door to his brother, Amos, who has not spoken to him in thirty-one years because of his unsavory reputation. His cousin Minerva is visiting him (the most charming character in the book, who drops out after the first quarter); her nephew, John Quincy, arrives after Dan is already dead, and plays a large role in the investigation. Chan, in fact, is rather in the background, with John Quincy's overplayed Bostonian stuffiness and his romantic awakening taking up much of the book. The book dwells on the irresistible attraction of the Hawaiian islands and the pull they exert on outsiders, many of whom find they can never leave. Although written in 1925, it mourns the lost romance of Hawaii and the onslaught of modernity. The clues include a wristwatch with a dim numeral "2," a torn fragment of newspaper, and that staple of the period—a special brand of cigarette found at the scene of the crime. There is also an abundance of RED HERRINGS.

HUBBARD, P[HILIP] M[AITLAND] (1910–1980) An underappreciated writer, P. M. Hubbard is much better known in his native Britain than in the United States, where his books are scarce. Hubbard's work, particularly his late work, is admired for the depictions of nature and especially the sea. The understated but powerful effect of sexuality and violence in his novels has also been remarked. These two qualities are reminiscent of D. H. Lawrence, though Hubbard's style is spare and taut.

As a student at Oxford, Hubbard won the Newdigate Prize for Poetry (1933). He was employed in the civil service in India until Independence, and then returned to England. He eventually quit working in the fifties in order to devote himself to writing.

One of his best books is *The Causeway* (1978), which takes place on the coast of Scotland. A salesman and amateur sailor, Peter Grant, is forced ashore on an island when the rudder on his small sailboat breaks loose from its pintle. He doesn't know that the island is joined to the mainland at low tide by a causeway, and soon he is met by a stern and burly figure, Derek Barlow, who lives with his wife Letty in a house across from the island. Peter is attracted to Letty and senses something wrong in the house, but he can't help being shooed away by Barlow, who helps him fix his boat with the minimum of politeness and maximum of menace. The mystery builds with a suspense that is more like dread.

HIGH TIDE (1970) involves another coastal cruise, this one by an ex-convict who murdered a man for killing his dog (somewhat like a canine version of THE BEAST MUST DIE). Hubbard often wrote books with similar plots or characters; *A Rooted Sorrow* (1973) and *The Quiet River* (1978) both deal with writers with warped personalities. *A Thirsty Evil* (1974) is a suspense novel that also involves a writer, Ian Mackellar; he falls in love with a woman he sees on a train, and becomes caught in a dangerous triangle involving her seductive sister and emotionally disturbed brother. *The Whisper in the Glen* (1972) is a mystery set in the Scottish Highlands. The year before his death, Hubbard published *Kill Claudio*, in which Ben Selby, a secret agent of some kind, finds the corpse of his friend, who has been killed instead of him. The friend's wife asks Selby to find the murderer and, simply, kill him.

HUBIN, ALLEN J. See ARMCHAIR DETECTIVE.

HUCKLEBERRY FINN, THE ADVENTURES OF See TWAIN, MARK.

HUDSON, MARTHA Mrs. Hudson is the owner of 221B Baker Street, the address of Sherlock HOLMES. Her most active role in a Holmes case comes in "The Adventure of the Empty House," when she manipulates a wax dummy of Holmes in order to deceive Colonel MORAN.

HUGHES, DOROTHY B[ELLE FLANAGAN] (1904–1993) Named a Grand Master by the MYSTERY WRITERS OF AMERICA in 1978, Dorothy B. Hughes was active as a writer of mystery and suspense stories primarily in the forties, when she wrote eleven of her fourteen novels. She was born in Kansas City and settled in Santa Fe, New Mexico, after attending college at Columbia and the University of New Mexico. Many of her books are set in the Southwest. Hughes is known for depicting ordinary people who find themselves confronting unexpected situations. Many of her protagonists are WOMEN, and she also used the novel of mystery and suspense as a vehicle for social commentary, sometimes with religious overtones. Her first book, *Dark Certainty* (1931), was selected for the Yale Series of Younger Poets.

Her first novel, *The So Blue Marble* (1940), was set in New York and has a streak of the fantastic, making it somewhat reminiscent of Cornell WOOLRICH's novels. A wealthy fashion designer, socialite, and former movie star, Griselda Satterlee, is accosted by two TOFFS as she returns to her ex-husband's midtown apartment. The men, Danver and Davidant Montefierrow, are literally evil twins who happen to have taken up with Missy, Griselda's impish, monstrous little sister. The opening of the book is effective and chilling. From there, it spins a crazy plot involving a mysterious "blue marble," which is some kind of philosopher's stone, a secret "X" department in the U.S. government, and movie stars.

The drab Inspector Tobin is virtually a bystander. Hughes played on movie glamour again in *Dread Journey* (1945), which takes place on a TRAIN and again involves victimization of the heroine by malevolent forces.

RIDE THE PINK HORSE (1946), which was filmed in 1947 starring Robert Montgomery, is the best known of her novels, and broke with the pattern of romantic suspense. It is a Chicago gangster story, transplanted to the desert of the Southwest. A young man with a vendetta, a Chicago cop who tries to save him, and a crooked politician all come together in the heightened and volatile atmosphere of a fiesta.

Hughes reviewed mysteries for several newspapers across the country. Her critical works brought her attention as well as her only EDGAR award (1950). After *The Candy Kid* (1950) and *The Davidian Report* (1952), she stopped writing fiction for more than a decade. After this long hiatus, Hughes published THE EXPENDABLE MAN in 1963, in which the young black doctor, Hugh Densmore, has to clear himself of the murder of a white hitchhiker. It was her most highly regarded novel since *Ride the Pink Horse.* Hughes's prose is spare and without adornment, making little use of metaphor. Her talent was for suspense rather than detection, which she created through repetition and descriptions of mood. Her writing can be clumsy and odd, for example in her habit of turning nouns into unusual verbs.

In 1978, Hughes published a biography of a fellow mystery writer and personal friend entitled *Erle Stanley Gardner: The Case of the Real Perry Mason.*

HUGO, RICHARD (1923–1982) Few mystery writers have built a reputation on as small a foundation as the American poet Richard Hugo. He wrote exactly one detective novel, DEATH AND THE GOOD LIFE (1980), but it is of such quality that it leads to speculation as to what Hugo might have done in the genre had his life not been ended by leukemia.

Hugo was born in Seattle and spent much of his adult life in Montana, where *Death and the Good Life* is set. After serving in World War II as a bombardier, Hugo studied poetry and received his M.A. from the University of Washington. Thereafter he worked for more than a dozen years as a technical writer for Boeing, the aerospace company. His first collection of poetry appeared in 1961; he wrote ten books of poems, and was twice nominated for the Pulitzer Prize. Unlike many poets, however, Hugo developed a prose fiction that is not a heavily padded, stretched-out version of his poetic style, but a voice that is fully fledged.

HUGO, VICTOR See MISÉRABLES, LES.

HUME, FERGUS[SON WRIGHT] (1859–1932) The English author Fergus Hume was once a best-selling novelist, but is now often ignored or dismissed. He did, however, write *the* best-selling mystery of the nineteenth century, THE MYSTERY OF A HANSOM CAB (1886), which outsold the mysteries of Conan DOYLE and Wilkie COLLINS.

In reality, Hume's work is not any worse than that of many nineteenth-century authors who are still read. The genesis of the work is perhaps its most interesting quality. Hume was living in Melbourne, Australia, when he asked a bookseller what kind of book was selling the most copies. The bookseller told him GABORIAU's stories, and Hume, who had never heard of Gaboriau, decided to read him and to write a book along similar lines. Australian literature was not yet established and Hume had difficulty finding a publisher who would take him seriously. He decided to publish the book himself, and sold five thousand copies in three weeks. He then made one of the most famous bad decisions in publishing history: he sold the copyright to a London group of entrepreneurs for only fifty pounds. They published the book in edition after edition—complete with advertisements for corsets and other products—and sold hundreds of thousand of copies, for which the author received not a penny.

Hume was born in England of New Zealander parents. His father was a doctor and had been a founder of Dunedin College. Hume himself studied law at the University of Otago, and then worked in the New Zealand Attorney General's office. He was admitted to the bar in 1885 and moved to Australia, where he worked in Melbourne as a clerk in a solicitor's office. Hume said that he spent many nights in Melbourne's Little Bourke Street, the slum district that appears in *The Mystery of a Hansom Cab,* conducting research. His second book was *Professor Brankel's Secret* (1886), after which he decided to move to London and become a professional writer.

Hume went on to write many other novels (about 140) as well as eight plays, but only his first book is remembered, and then often as merely a footnote to the history of the detective story. After his return to England, he rarely used the Australian setting again in his books. One of the exceptions, however, is considered the second peak of Hume's achievement: MADAM MIDAS (1888). This novel is also set in Melbourne, and takes place against the background of the Australian gold rush. The title character is a self-made woman whose trouble starts when she returns to Melbourne with her gold. The novel was out of print for almost one hundred years when it was reprinted by Hogarth Press in the mid-eighties.

Late in life Hume became something of a recluse and lived a quiet, religious life in Essex, where he died. Hugh GREENE gives some interesting details about Hume's last forty years, living in a remote cottage with his companion, John Joseph Melville. Hume was a Theosophist, and believed that he was the reincarnation of a French aristocrat, and even remembered being GUILLOTINED during the French Revolution. Melville was supposedly a reincarnation of the philosopher Roger Bacon. Hume never achieved his greatest desire, to have a play produced in London; he attributed his bad luck to karma.

HUNT, E[VERETTE] HOWARD See CELEBRITY MYSTERIES.

"HUNTED DOWN" (1859) A story by Charles DICKENS. Often anthologized and recently republished, the story is based on the career of an actual poisoner, Thomas Griffiths WAINEWRIGHT. Ellery QUEEN called it a story of "pure detection," though it is hardly a model of FAIR PLAY; most of the detection goes on behind the scenes—i.e., nowhere—and is only alluded to in the solution.

A Mr. Sampson, who runs a life insurance company, is approached by a sinister figure, Mr. Julius SLINKTON. Sampson takes a dislike to the man on sight, but finds himself subtly manipulated and controlled. Sampson inquires about a life insurance policy for a friend, a Mr. Alfred Beckwith; despite his aversion, Sampson's firm makes out the policy. Through a series of encounters between Sampson, Slinkton, and Slinkton's ailing niece (sister of another niece, already dead), Dickens builds up an atmosphere of dread around Slinkton, whose favorite remark is "The world is a grave!" The ending comes as a surprise and shows Sampson to have been more perspicacious than he seemed.

HUNTER, ALAN [JAMES] [HERBERT] (1922–) The English author Alan Hunter was born in East Anglia and has lived there for most of his life. This part of the country forms the background for his long series of novels about Inspector George GENTLY. Hunter served in the Royal Air Force in World War II and published a volume of poems, *The Norwich Poems,* in 1945. He worked as a poultry farmer and sold books before becoming a full-time writer. His style depends heavily on dialogue, and his books have never had the appeal in the United States that they have had in England. Hunter has tried to renew the police story by making it more literary and by adopting narrative experiments.

HUNTER, ED AND AMBROSE See BROWN, FREDERIC.

HUNTER, EVAN See MCBAIN, ED.

HUUYGENS, KEK A notorious smuggler in works by Robert L. FISH. Fish invented Huuygens as a short story character, and then wrote a series of novel-length escapades. Huuygens lives in a luxurious apartment overlooking Paris's Bois de Boulogne; he has smuggled everything, even an elephant, but has always slipped past the customs agents. His real name is Mietek Janeczek. During World War II, he fled Poland and fought with the Resistance in France. In *The Hochmann Miniatures* (1967), Huuygens learns through his old Resistance comrades that his enemy, Wilhelm Gruber, is alive and living in Lisbon. As an SS officer, Gruber murdered Huuygens's parents and sister and married his girlfriend, a German Pole. The novel combines a revenge story with ART smuggling. Huuygens has a young admirer, the American reporter Jimmy Lewis, who assists the smuggler—whether he knows it or not.

BIBLIOGRAPHY Novels: *Whirligig* (1970), *The Tricks of the Trade* (1972), *The Wager* (1974).

Short stories: *Kek Huuygens—Smuggler* (1976).

HUXLEY, ALDOUS [LEONARD] (1894–1963) The English author Aldous Huxley is primarily known for his satires of the English intelligentsia, such as *Antic Hay* (1923) and *Point Counter Point* (1928), and for the dystopic novel *Brave New World* (1932). *The Doors of Perception* (1954), his other famous book, is about his experiment with natural hallucinogens and reflects his interest in Hinduism and mysticism.

Huxley's one contribution to the crime genre, the classic short story THE GIACONDA SMILE (1922), is an extension of his satirical work. It is both a murder story and a brilliant character study.

HUXLEY, ELSPETH [JOSCELINE][GRANT] (1907–1997) An English writer whose books are set in Africa, Huxley is best known for her nonfiction works about the continent, particularly the best-selling *The Flame Trees of Thikka* (1959), which discuss her early years in Africa. Huxley also wrote a string of entertaining colonial mysteries in the thirties, and then took thirty years off from the genre. Several of her books have recently been reprinted, including her best, THE AFRICAN POISON MURDERS, (1939) and *Murder at Government House* (1937), her first.

Huxley's father ran a coffee plantation in Kenya before World War I. During the war, Elspeth returned to England. In 1931, she married a distant cousin of Aldous HUXLEY. She began writing her mysteries during her long ocean voyages.

The protagonist of her mysteries is Superintendent VACHELL of the Chania police. He is sometimes assisted by his friend, anthropologist Olivia Brandeis, for example in *Murder at Government House.* In this novel the governor and commander-in-chief of Chania is found dead in his study during a party. The governor was strangled with cords cut from the Venetian blinds in the room, and the guests are all under suspicion (thus, for her first book, Huxley relied on COUNTRY HOUSE conventions). Vachell's investigation explores the consequences of drought in Africa, including tribal explanations for it and the sometimes brutal measures taken to exorcise whatever force is responsible for it. The detective's delving into the past opens up old wounds and exposes frictions between the British and the native Chanians. Despite some racial epithets that might offend some readers, it is actually an interesting reflection on the underlying similarities of the colonial subjects and the occupiers. Indeed, Huxley has been praised not only for her vivid portrayals of the landscape of Africa but her understanding of the traditions of both black and white cultures, which she depicts in an even-handed way. In MURDER ON SAFARI (1938), she looks critically at big game hunting when Vachell joins a safari traveling to an area where a murder has been committed.

Huxley returned to the African scene and the mystery genre with *The Merry Hippo* (1963); the title refers not to a friendly pachyderm but the name of a guest house. In a story about a dignitary murdered while visiting Africa on a diplomatic mission, Huxley at once lampoons colonialism, bureaucrats, and the natives. Once again, the satire has a serious edge, which is even sharper in *A Man From Nowhere* (1964). The crippled brother of Dick Heron has been murdered with a chainsaw. Heron decides to seek revenge on the person he feels is responsible—a British cabinet minister named Peter Buckle, whose African policy has led to chaos in an African state trying to achieve independence. Heron considers his loss of his ancestral home in Africa and his wife's suicide over this heartbreak to be the results of British policy as well. Heron gets a job on Buckle's farm, planning to kill him, but he has a change of heart; his final decision is something of a shock.

Huxley is as clear about her horror of African violence, disease, and death as she is about her love of the land and its people. Similarly, she presents the West as more advanced in some aspects but is highly critical of outside interference and the disastrous effect of the machinations and politicking of other powers, including the British.

HYOSCIN(E) An alkaloid associated with the NIGHTSHADE plant. In sufficient doses, it can cause paralysis of the central nervous system, delusions, and death. Like many similar substances, such as ATROPINE, hyoscine has medical uses. It occurs with surprising frequency in mystery stories; it was used by Agatha CHRISTIE in *Black Coffee* (1934), and by Margaret MILLAR in her first mystery about Paul PRYE. In real life it was used by the notorious murderer Dr. CRIPPEN.

I

ICE PICK Although no longer much in use, ice picks were of course quite common in the GOLDEN AGE, when ice was still delivered in large blocks that were deposited in an icebox, the forerunner of the refrigerator. Ice picks appeared as murder weapons rather more often in mysteries of that period than at present. Although still widely sold, as murder weapons they now have the savor of something almost exotic and certainly perverse—Matt SCUDDER puzzles over this impression in Lawrence Block's *A Stab in the Dark* (1981). *The Ice Pick Artist* (1997) is one of Harold Adams's Carl Wilcox mysteries set in the Midwest during the Depression.

The best of all mysteries in which ice picks figure is Raymond Chandler's THE LITTLE SISTER (1949). A silver ice pick turns up in Ross MACDONALD's story "The Bearded Lady," included in *The Name Is Archer* (1955). In *Finders Keepers* (1940), a Humphrey CAMPBELL mystery, the murder is committed with a similar weapon, a saddlemaker's awl—which is the most unusual thing about the book. In *Death on the Aisle* (1942), a Pam and Jerry NORTH mystery, the victim is found stabbed with an ice pick in a Broadway theater. Another ice pick murder occurs in *The Zebra-Striped Hearse* (1962), a Lew ARCHER novel.

IF EVER I RETURN, PRETTY PEGGY-O (1990) A critically praised novel by Sharyn MCCRUMB, set in the small Tennessee mountain town of Hamlin. The sheriff, Spenser Arrowood, investigates threats against a sixties folk singer, Peggy Muryan, who has moved to town to rest and revive her career. One of the author's more ambitious Southern mysteries, it relies on local history rather than local color; the older generation and the baby boomers share a tradition but not an understanding of it, like the old mountain songs whose words they interpret differently. The reactions of the various characters to the Vietnam War are central to the plot, especially after the grisly commando-style killing of Muryan's dog. Detection takes second place to exploring the memories of a town of 900 souls, many of them scarred—deputy and Vietnam vet Joe LeDonne ("a thin crust of snow over a pit of ice water") primary among them. The book ultimately evokes more issues than it can handle, and the big scene of redemption gives too large a burst of violins while leaving the central relationship between Arrowood and Muryan unresolved.

ILES, FRANCIS See BERKELEY, ANTHONY.

IMANISHI EITARO The Tokyo police detective created by Seicho MATSUMOTO.

I MARRIED A DEAD MAN (1948) A novel by Cornell WOOLRICH, originally published under the name William Irish. A murder is announced at the beginning of the book that both halves of a couple believe the other committed. In this highly deterministic story, chance is the opponent whose blows cannot be anticipated. People "break a rule" in the game of life, which sends them off in a direction from which there is no turning back. The unlikely but extremely clever premise is typically Woolrichean: Helen Georgesson, jilted by her lover and pregnant, takes a train back to San Francisco, on which she meets another pregnant woman, Patrice Hazzard. Patrice gives Helen her wedding ring for safekeeping for just a moment while they are getting ready to sleep, but fate only needs a moment: the train is wrecked, and Patrice and her husband are killed. Hazzard's rich parents then claim Helen as their daughter-in-law, based on the misleading ring. Helen cannot believe her miraculous rescue, and prays to fate, "Leave me in peace." But there is no such luck in this implacably dark novel, and a series of anonymous letters brings Helen's true past back into the equation (which equals murder).

IN ACCORDANCE WITH THE EVIDENCE (1915) A novel by Oliver ONIONS, almost as forgotten as its author. It was chosen by BARZUN and TAYLOR for their series of fifty great works of crime fiction and republished in the seventies, but remains an obscure classic. Written at a time when much of popular fiction continued to mimic the sensational and sentimental novels of the previous century, *In Accordance with the Evidence* is strikingly modern in its depiction, in the first person, of a narrator who is losing his mind even as he recounts the events leading up to a murder. James Jeffries is a poor business student who is jealous of his fellow student Archie Merridew. Merridew lives in a large apartment and is financially secure, in contrast to the narrator. Jeffries also confesses his love for Evie Soames, another student, but it becomes apparent that his "love" is obsessive. In fact, all of Jeffries's perceptions seem tainted with hate, jealousy, and frustration. The reader knows from the beginning that Archie Merridew is dead; the excitement of the narrative comes from Onions's skillful stoking of the reader's curiosity about how he met his end and the nature of Jeffries's relationship to Evie Soames. Like Camus' *The Stranger, In Accordance with the Evidence* is more a work of literature dealing with crime than a "crime novel."

IN COLD BLOOD (serialized 1965; book 1966) An account of a shocking 1959 murder case written by Truman CAPOTE, and termed by *The New York Review of Books* "the best documentary account of an American crime ever written." First serialized in *The New Yorker,* it is perhaps Capote's best-known work. In preparation, he traveled to the small Kansas town of Holcomb where the crime was committed and spoke with witnesses, investigators, and townspeople. The story is told with the suspense of a crime novel and the insight and depth of a sociological study.

Herbert William Clutter was a successful farmer whose sometimes innovative methods had been first laughed at and then appreciated by his neighbors. He neither smoke, drank, nor used coffee or tea. His wife suffered from mental problems and retired for extended periods to a psychiatric institution. Unfortunately, she, as well as two of the Clutter's four children, were at home on the night of November 14-15, 1959, when two parolees entered the Clutter home searching for a safe full of money they expected to find. The safe was not there, and the thieves gained only about forty dollars. They bound and gagged the adult Clutters and their teenaged son and daughter, then shot them point-blank in the heads with a shotgun. Capote describes how the crime stunned the community, and the process by which detectives of the state bureau of investigation tracked the killers all over the West and as far as Mexico. Their twisted and distorted lives, which led to their crime and their execution, are convincingly recreated through their own statements and Capote's imaginative reconstruction of their travels. The book is profoundly disturbing not so much for the violence of the subject as the emptiness it depicts—within the souls of the killers, within the damaged community, and even in the doing of justice, which seems an unsatisfying epilogue, a necessary mechanism that still does nothing to mitigate the horror and pathos of violent, meaningless death.

IN THE BEST FAMILIES (1950) A novel by Rex STOUT, in which Nero WOLFE must at last take on his enemy, Arnold ZECK. Wolfe had said earlier to Archie GOODWIN (in *And Be A Villian*) that, "If ever, in the course of my business, I find that I am committed against him and must destroy him, I shall leave this house, find a place where I can work—and sleep and eat if there is time for it—and stay there until I have finished." The book contains one of Wolfe's most surprising tricks: he must develop a reputation as a major criminal, which necessitates "a temporary abandonment of scruple" and the development of a swindling scheme.

IN THE FOG (1901) A novella by Richard Harding DAVIS, considered a classic and often reprinted (for example, in *Victorian Villainies,* 1984). The story is set in a London club, the very exclusive "Grill." A group of men are sitting around a table, and another is reading a detective novel; as he finishes, one of the men at the table points out that the man is a baronet, and is about to speak in the House of Commons in favor of a naval appropriations bill that will cost the people millions of pounds. The baronet is addicted to mystery stories, and his political opponent murmurs, "I would give a hundred pounds . . . if I could place in his hands at this moment a new story of Sherlock HOLMES." (The story was written and takes place during the eight-year period in which there were no Holmes stories because Conan DOYLE had "killed" the sleuth off in THE FINAL PROBLEM). The men around the table then begin a game of trying to detain the baronet by telling a series of mysterious anecdotes. The first, told by a man who represents himself as an American Naval attaché, makes use of the impenetrable fog outside the club, which is woven into a tale of murder involving two noble brothers and a Russian princess. The second story involves a diamond theft, and the third relates back to the first. Davis gave the novella a double surprise ending that is doubly satisfying in the way it neatly ties up all the loose threads of the narrative.

IN THE HEAT OF THE NIGHT (1965) With his EDGAR-winning first novel, John BALL did something that few writers have been able to manage: he used the mystery novel to address social issues without slighting the detective plot. He also created one of the most interesting personalities in the mystery genre, detective Virgil TIBBS, a black police officer from Pasadena, California, who happens to get stuck in a small southern town just as a sensational murder takes place. Wells is a town of only eleven thousand people situated somewhere in the Carolinas. It is suffering from economic decline, and the prospect of a new musical festival on the model of Tanglewood has filled some of the town council with hope of a renaissance and some badly needed revenue. Wells seems completely untouched by the civil rights movement: black males are referred to as "boy" or worse, and it is taken for granted that non-whites cannot think, perform jobs, or even feel pain on the same level with Caucasians.

The arrival of Virgil Tibbs becomes a test case for the members of the police department—as backward as most of the other people in town—and the town's leaders. Patrolman Sam Wood discovers the body of maestro Enrico Mantoli lying across the highway, his head bashed in. Tibbs is picked up at the railroad station where he is waiting for a train and immediately considered a suspect. Bill Gillespie is the chief of police; a huge but completely untrained Texan who dislikes blacks; he first kicks Tibbs out and then brings him back, planning to use him as a "fall guy." If Tibbs finds the killer, Gillespie can take the credit, and if Tibbs's can't, the chief can blame the failure of the investigation on the black man.

In a series of realistic and sometimes ugly scenes, Ball shows life in a backward, racist community. Tibbs, with his gentlemanly manners, education, social position, and investigative skill, becomes a magnet for all of the hate in Wells. The story demonstrates a truth that all victims of discrimination know: they have to be twice as competent and twice as circumspect to get even half the credit that others do. Tibbs's control of evidence and procedure (the plot is carefully constructed), his hunches and observations, and his grave manner begin to make some of the residents of Wells start to change their minds. But Ball does not give the reader a fairy story or politically correct fantasy in which everyone lives happily ever after; some of the doubts Tibbs creates are bleakly ironic ("Smartest black I ever saw . . . he oughta been a white man").

INDEMNITY ONLY (1982) The first novel by Sara PARETSKY about Chicago private eye V. I. WARSHAWSKI. *Indemnity Only* set the pattern for the series, which shows that crime is not only committed by mobsters and their goons but also by white-collar executives; however, here and elsewhere in the series, the latter sometimes associate with the former. In her seedy office, V. I. is consulted by a man calling himself John Thayer, an executive of the Ft. Dearborn Trust Company. His son, Peter Thayer, has gotten involved in radicalism at the University of Chicago, and wants to become a union organizer rather than a businessman like his "daddy." The father blames Peter's girlfriend, Anita Hill, who has disappeared, and Peter blames his father for her mysterious vanishing. Thayer Sr. wants her found.

The case sounds simple, but when Warshawski visits Peter's apartment she finds him with a hole in his head. She also finds the belongings of one Anita McGraw, and Peter's pay stubs from his job at Ajax Insurance Company. She visits the company and becomes suspicious of Peter's boss, Yardley Masters, but his assistant, Ralph Devereux, gives her important information about the indemnity claims business. She continues to look for the missing woman and is warned off the case by several people, including her father's old police partner. Paretsky strings the reader along and keeps the nature of the scam hidden as long as possible, partly through a romantic subplot between Warshawski and Devereux and run-ins with criminals in which the detective is beaten up. The pieces all come together in a violent confrontation between the various players. This book introduced most of the supporting characters of the Warshawski series and deployed with freshness what were to become its conventions.

INNES, HAMMOND (1913–1998) The English author Hammond Innes is known for stories of suspense rather than for crime or mystery, though his books often involve both.

Many of Innes's novels are about the sea. In *Dead and Alive* (1946), a group of men rescue a derelict landing craft and use it to start a smuggling operation. Smuggling and the ghost ship are two elements that Innes particularly liked. In *Gale Warning* (1947), British soldiers who are being repatriated find themselves on a ship that had been previously sunk, presided over by a deranged captain and carrying a suspicious cargo. *The Strange Land* (1954) begins with the wreck of a smuggler's ketch on the shores of North Africa. Latham, a former smuggler who has turned missionary, was waiting for a passenger on the boat (a doctor) who seems to have disappeared. In Tangier, Latham falls in with his former associates and with a mysterious young woman who was also waiting for someone supposed to be on the wrecked boat. Innes had traveled in Tangier and remote parts of Morocco in the early fifties, and the book is expressive of his romanticized vision of French colonial rule.

Probably Innes's best book is THE WRECK OF THE MARY DEARE (1956), a version of the ghost ship theme but without supernatural elements.

INNES, MICHAEL (pen name of John Innes Mackintosh Stewart, 1906–1994) Born in Scotland, mystery author and professor emeritus Michael Innes has created a detective in his own image: Sir John APPLEBY, a policeman whose knowledge of culture would be the envy of an Oxford don. Innes's father was a professor before him; the author himself attended Oxford, receiving his degree in 1929. While the Oxford strain is an obvious aspect in his work, his Scottish background is another; he uses it in such books as *Lament for a Maker* (1938), an

Appleby mystery whose title is an allusion to an early Scottish poet. Innes taught at the University of Leeds in the early thirties, and later at the University of Adelaide, Australia. He wrote his first mystery novel, *Death at the President's Lodging* (1936; U.S. title *Seven Suspects*), while en route by ship, à la Ngaio MARSH.

Following World War II, Innes returned to Oxford to teach. He became a fellow of Christ Church, Oxford, in 1949, and retired in 1973. As J. I. M. Stewart he has written critical studies of Shakespeare and modernist writers as well as biographies of Rudyard Kipling, Joseph CONRAD, and Thomas Hardy. His knowledge of literature and the academic (and sometimes the Australian) scene are woven into the Appleby stories, which are entertaining, humorous, and sometimes tongue-in-cheek. *Christmas at Candleshoe* (1953) is a pastiche of the COUNTRY HOUSE mystery and was later made into a film.

Innes's novels and his characters display no deep "subtext," unless it is a fascination with the queer goings-on among the English upper class. The author seems to reserve his more serious meditations for the non-mystery novels that he writes under the name Stewart. His detective stories stress mood, charm, and ingenuity over believability and tightness. Although Innes can construct neat puzzles, the amusements to be had along the way take precedence over the solution. His writing is fluid and polished, though sometimes a trifle too jaunty. Not surprisingly, given his background and the literary quips he puts into the mouth of Appleby, Innes has been called the founder of the "donnish" school, an especially useless label because of the number of English writers who have had, used, and not used the Oxbridge background. Nor was Innes the first to discover that Oxford was a potentially amusing setting for a murder. If a donnish school exists, however, Innes's books must be among the best of the lot, since he does not overload the formula—though sometimes even Innes's crooks quote Wordsworth and Latin maxims. Some of Innes's most donnish mysteries are his first, as well as *The Weight of the Evidence* (1943), in which a professor is killed by a very unlikely blunt instrument. Among the best known of the Appleby books are *Hamlet, Revenge!* (1937), in which a murder takes place during the performance of Shakespeare's play; ONE-MAN SHOW (1952), which has an ART theme; DEATH BY WATER (1968), set at a country house; and *The Open House* (1972), which has comically GOTHIC features. Innes also wrote short stories about Appleby; *Appleby Talking* (1946; U.S. title *Dead Man's Shoes*) and *Appleby Talks Again* (1956) are collections.

In addition to the Appleby series, Innes has written other mystery and spy novels. *The Man from the Sea* (1955) is a spy story with a Scottish setting. *Appleby and Honeybath* (1983), which also features Charles Honeybath of Scotland Yard who appeared in two other novels of his own: *The Mysterious Commission* (1975) and *Honeybath's Haven* (1978). Innes exercised his particular talent for the art-related mystery in *Money from Holme* (1964). Stewart has also written the memoir *Myself and Michael Innes* (1987). Among the books he published as Stewart was *The Man Who Wrote Detective Stories* (1959).

In all his genre writing, he has aimed at pure entertainment, and is unapologetic about the irrealism of his books. Some writers toy or juggle with the probable and the improbable, weighing how much the reader will be willing to swallow. Innes simply forges ahead with his tale (an Innes-like pun), making no effort to insert "markers" showing that we are dealing with a recognizable world. Hence his books have a stylistic unity that a temporizer with realism would not have achieved. On the other hand, some critics have seen Innes's style as a formula that does not bear dozens of repetitions.

Another author who writes donnish or academic mysteries is Robert BARNARD, who also taught in Australia, and who combined the Australian and English settings in his first novel, DEATH OF AN OLD GOAT (1977).

INNOCENT BLOOD (1980) A novel by P. D. JAMES. It is one of James's most famous works, which is strange (or maybe not) because *Innocent Blood* might better be described as a NOVEL OF MANNERS or a character study than as a mystery. It has a classic plot: an adopted child's search for her real parents. This theme had been masterfully treated by Ross MACDONALD in THE FAR SIDE OF THE DOLLAR (1965); in both cases, the quest has unintended and catastrophic results, and the past turns out to be a Pandora's box.

Philippa Palfrey seems assured and confident (even a bit arrogant) when she first requests information about her real parents, whom she believes were a servant girl and the aristocrat who fell for her. Philippa has won a scholarship to Cambridge, and with a famous sociologist as her adopted father, her future seems assured. The report on her parentage surprises and shocks her, however, and puts her on a collision course with the drab, middle-aged clerk Norman SCASE. Although the convergence of plot lines is a typical THRILLER setup, *Innocent Blood* is subtle and deeply unsettling. The case of child murder is sometimes difficult reading, not for grotesque scenes but for the painful emotions strongly evoked and deeply explored. In addition to a search for identity and a crime story, *Innocent Blood* is a sometimes damning novel of society. Beneath ordinary modern exteriors are personalities variously misshapen by grief, cynicism, or moral vacuity.

IN OUR TIME (1924) A collection of stories by Ernest HEMINGWAY. Hemingway's telegraphic prose influenced the development of the detective story, particularly the HARD-BOILED style (though it has also been suggested that HAMMETT's style influenced Hemingway). Although Hemingway never wrote a detective story, THE KILLERS is a crime story and indicates an awareness of the genre.

INSPECTOR IMANISHI INVESTIGATES (tr 1989) First published in 1961 as *Suna no Utsuwa (Vessel of Sand),* this novel by Seicho MATSUMOTO won the Akutagawa Literary Prize and the Japanese Mystery Writers' Prize. It concerns a baffling case that begins with a battered body of a man found in a Tokyo railway yard. Inspector Imanishi, a middle-aged detective with a high reputation, works on the case, but it is almost abandoned due to lack of progress. With the help of a young acolyte, detective Yoshimura Hiroshi, the tired but dogged inspector continues the hunt. The story begins as a procedural, but soon comes to focus on the individual effort of Imanishi, a classic loner detective. His approach, however, is not due to the Western concept of individualism but to Japanese customs: Imanishi is reluctant to bring forward leads until he is sure they will pan out, because otherwise he would lose face with his colleagues. Similarly, he disguises his travels around the country as vacation because he does not want to cost the department money if he does not turn up anything.

Part way through the book, another plot line is opened up, almost but not quite turning the story into an INVERTED MYSTERY. There are many complicated clues, which offer an interesting glimpse of Japanese society. Questions germane to the case include variations between Japanese dialects, the effects of World War II on the population, sexual mores, and the subordination of women. Fair play is occasionally circumvented, as in the case of letters with mysterious contents. Still, the investigation is absorbingly thorough and the light shed on Japanese culture is valuable.

INTERPOL "INTERPOL" was originally only the telex address of the International Criminal Police Organization (ICPO), now known as ICPO/INTERPOL. The origins of ICPO go back to 1914 and the First International Police Congress in Monaco. A second Congress was held in Vienna in 1923, which set up the International Criminal Police Commission. After World War II, the Commission was revived. It was renamed ICPO in 1956; in 1989, it moved from Paris to new headquarters in Vienna.

ICPO/INTERPOL is an organization for international cooperation, not a global police force. Its structure is similar to that of the United Nations, with a General Assembly and a Secretariat that ensure the exchange of information between the police forces of member states. INTERPOL currently has 176 members, but it has no powers of enforcement in member countries. Because INTERPOL's purpose is to compile data bases and provide technical expertise rather than to apprehend crooks, it has no agents roaming across borders pursuing criminals. This is not always the impression given in crime fiction, in which INTERPOL "agents" may pop up suddenly with vital information or blazing pistols.

INTO THE NIGHT (pub 1987) A novel begun by Cornell Woolrich and left unfinished at the time of his death. The book was finished by Lawrence BLOCK, who supplied the thirty-seven pages needed to complete the novel. The story begins with a classic Woolrich quirk: a young woman tries to kill herself with a pistol, which misfires. Taking it as a sign, she feels a surging appreciation for the value of life and tosses the gun down in joy—and it discharges, killing a woman passing on the street. At that point, the story slows down, and takes on an elegiac, dreamlike quality uncommon in Woolrich's other novels, exploring the thoughts of the woman, Madeleine Chalmers, who begins to merge her own identity into that of the woman she killed.

This structure is the more interesting because the opening was written by Block, and the story slows at the point where Woolrich's manuscript begins. It quickly becomes a detective story, however, with Madeleine's decision to turn detective and find out everything she can about her victim. The search leads to some surprising discoveries, a further murder, and a bizarre resolve on Madeleine's part. Among the other pieces of the novel written by Block is the crucial one—the ending.

INTRUDER IN THE DUST (1948) A novel by William FAULKNER, which Ross MACDONALD termed "our most ambitious American mystery novel." It centers on the fortunes of the elderly Lucas Beauchamp, a black man who is also a descendant of the white McCaslins, one of the central families in Faulkner's Yoknapatawpha County (they are the subject of *Go Down, Moses,* 1942, in which Lucas first appeared). Lucas is resented by certain members of the community because he will not kow-tow to whites; they try to railroad him for murder, and a mob tries to lynch him. Chick MALLISON, a boy whom Lucas has helped, decides to try to clear him. Lucas also is aided by his black friend, Aleck Sander, and the elderly Eunice

Habersham takes up Lucas's case. This socially diverse trio epitomizes the kind of tolerance and sense of justice that families like the McCaslins seem to lack because of their slave-holding past and moral corruption (including incest). Chick's friendship with Lucas, despite their differences in race and age, also illustrates a more hopeful vision of the possibility of understanding between blacks and whites.

INVERTED MYSTERY A mystery story in which the identity of the murderer or criminal is given away at the beginning. It was most associated with R. Austin FREEMAN, but many authors have subsequently tried it. The inverted mystery can be every bit as suspenseful as the more usual whodunit, sometimes even more so. For years films have used the device of the known murderer and the sleuth circling around each other in the same house or other location. This type of story may also exercise the reader's powers of deduction more than the whodunit by inviting a comparison of the detective's interpretation of the clues with the correct one.

The imprecise label "novel of suspense" is often applied to books that feature a detective and are similar to the inverted mystery. Often, they follow a chase from the perspective of both the hunter and the hunted.

"INVISIBLE MAN, THE" A short story by G. K. CHESTERTON, which begins as a romance, couched in a form resembling a parable. A young woman who serves at the Red Fish Inn is pestered by two suitors, the small and ridiculous Isidore Smythe and the tall, squinting James Welkin. Both are idlers; to taunt them, she says she will not marry anyone who has not carved a place in the world, and both go off to seek their fortunes. Smythe returns first, having made his fortune on robots that perform housework. Welkin threatens to return and prevent him from winning the girl. Father BROWN comes on the scene through the agency of his reformed criminal friend, FLAMBEAU. Once again, Father Brown reconstructs events in his head from a few simple clues, which he reveals in a modest and even bored manner to his friends, and identifies the "invisible man."

IPCRESS FILE, THE (1962) A novel by Len DEIGHTON, one of the most inventive in the spy subgenre. Most original, the story is written in the first person, and is told by "Harry Palmer," as the character came to be called after Michael Caine's brilliant portrayal of him in the 1965 movie. The unnamed narrator, a spy, goes to work for Dalby, the powerful head of W.O.O.C.(P), a tiny British intelligence unit operating in between the other more official units. There is a large element of satire in the depiction of intelligence activities, which the narrator views with ironic detachment and treats with wry humor. Because the story is told by a narrator who doesn't possess all the facts—sometimes he almost has none—the element of mystery is stronger than in most spy novels. The story begins with a mysterious man known only as "Jay" and the disappearance of top British biochemists who appear to have been kidnapped. Although Deighton gives a delightful portrayal of drab London and the even more drab routine of its civil servants (the narrator's overdue back pay is a constant preoccupation), he is equally good at evoking the surreal atmosphere of an atomic bomb test in the Pacific or a Hungarian torture chamber.

The "hero" who narrates the story escapes with his life partly because he distrusts the clubby upper-class and military types who run the intelligence establishment; taking his first job from Dalby, he remarks "If it doesn't demand a classical education, I might be able to grope around it." His origins and his humor show him to be more in the mold of the hero of the HARD-BOILED novel, a Philip MARLOWE type, than the suave and assured protagonist of most espionage stories. He is a cousin to Alec LEAMAS, but has not allowed bitterness to overwhelm him; instead, he maintains a cheerful cynicism.

IRISH, WILLIAM A pseudonym of Cornell WOOLRICH.

IRON GATES, THE (1945) A novel by Margaret MILLAR, a powerful story of psychic deterioration. The book opens with Lucille having a nightmare about the death of Mildred, her husband's first wife, fifteen years before. Mildred was married to Andrew Morrow, a doctor, and had two children, Polly and Martin. She was killed by a savage blow to the head from an axe in the park just outside the Morrows's house. Lucille subsequently married Andrew, but is not accepted by the children and is in competition with Edith, Andrew's possessive sister who also lives in the house.

After a strange, dirty-looking man brings a package to the house for Lucille, she disappears. Inspector Sands, who was never satisfied with the fact that Mildred's case was never solved, takes part in the search for Lucille, who ends up behind the iron gates—in a mental hospital. A combination of detection and chance helps Sands uncover several linked crimes and the events that have driven Lucille insane. It is an intensely morbid story of human destructiveness.

IRVING, JOHN (1942–) American author, famous *for The World According to Garp* (1978), a bestseller about the violent and outrageous life of T. S. Garp. Irving's novels have PICARESQUE foundations, though they are precisely plotted rather than episodic. His books have been noted, and criticized, for their extreme people and events; in the tradition of DREISER, they are self-consciously "big." *A Son of the Circus* (1994), a monumental novel (more than 600 pages) with all of the author's usual ribaldry, is a combination mystery and personal saga with obvious similarities to Robertson DAVIES's Deptford trilogy, including: the circus milieu; a retiring professional man and his relationship to a younger "star" of mysterious character for whom he creates a fictitious biography, but into which he writes his own dreams and fantasies; the Canadian background; and even a clue discovered in the corpse's mouth.

Dr. Farrokh Daruwalla is a renowned orthopedic surgeon who lives in Toronto but who returns periodically to Bombay, the city of his childhood; in neither place does he really feel he belongs. His hobby is collecting dwarf blood, in hopes of isolating the gene that causes achondroplastic dwarfism. He also writes screenplays for the vicious Inspector Dhar films. The actor who plays Dhar (and now essentially *is* Dhar) is hated by all Bombay, except its women. He and Daruwalla are lunching at the Duckworth Club when the elderly Mr. Lal is found in the bougainvillea beside the ninth green, clubbed to death. The murder sets off further events, including Daruwalla's ruminations on killings in the past, among them his father's death from a car bomb. A serial killer murders prostitutes and draws an elephant on their stomachs that looks vaguely like the Hindu god Ganesh. Irving's style is digressive, encompassing a vast number of characters, subplots, and anecdotes, which are often ribald.

JACKO A repulsive character in A TANGLED WEB.

JACKSON, SHIRLEY (1919–1965) Shirley Jackson was born in San Francisco and attended the University of Rochester and Syracuse University. Of her many books and stories, "The Lottery" (1948) is the most famous. Its appearance in *The New Yorker* and the author's dark view of human nature prompted a flood of letters, and the story was banned in South Africa. Like Patricia HIGHSMITH, Jackson shows people to be hypocrites when they try to be good, which is not often. Jackson's combination of subtle psychology with the GOTHIC and the OCCULT led some to dub her "Virginia Werewolf." Her brush with mystery fiction brought her an EDGAR award for LOUISA, PLEASE COME HOME (1960). In that story, too, she showed callousness, selfishness, and moral feebleness as the rule rather than the exception.

JACK THE RIPPER Perhaps the most famous unsolved murders of all time are those committed by "Jack the Ripper" in London in 1888 and 1889. The Ripper preyed upon prostitutes and mutilated their bodies in the most horrifying way, with a particularly pathological focus on their reproductive organs, which he sometimes removed. The subject of the Ripper murders has been done to death in books, film, and television. Many have claimed to have "discovered" the real killer; his identity, however, is still a mystery.

Of the many books based on the Ripper's killings, one of the most entertaining is certainly Ellery QUEEN's *A Study in Terror* (1966), in which Ellery receives a manuscript that purports to be Dr. WATSON's account of how Sherlock HOLMES was drawn into the hunt for the Ripper. The book skillfully recreates some aspects of the Conan DOYLE stories, into which Ellery's intrusions become more and more unnecessary.

The most prominent fictional treatment of the Ripper is Marie Belloc LOWNDES's *The Lodger* (repr 1964). *The Harlot Killer* (1953) is a collection of fiction and nonfiction writings about the Ripper, including newspaper articles of the period.

In *The Secret of Prisoner 1167* (1997), James Tully proposes that the real Jack the Ripper was one James Kelly, a convicted murderer and escapee from an insane asylum who was at large in London during the murderer's spree. Tully finds similarities between Kelly's obsessions and his murder of his wife and the Ripper killings; the fact that the Kelly files are officially sealed until the year 2030 adds the flavor of a conspiracy to Tully's evidence.

JACOBSEN, ROY (1954–) The Norwegian writer Roy Jacobsen is considered a rising star in his own country but has not achieved much notice in the English-speaking world, mostly because of a lack of translations of his work. His first book was *Fangeliv* (*Prison Life*, 1982), a collection of short stories. But it was his novel *Det nye vannet* (1987) that brought him notoriety (though virtually every one of his books has been an award winner). This novel has now been translated as *The New Water* (1997). The central character, Jon, lives on an island near a city in northern Norway. A hunter, Jon is less an outdoorsman than a part of the landscape. Considered strange or mentally ill, he does not fit into the society of the island, which is rapidly changing while he clings to a disappearing way of life. He witnesses what he thinks is the discovery of a corpse in a pond by two men working on a water project. This event inspires him to search for a missing woman, Lisa, another misfit and the companion and lost love of his childhood. The book is an intense psychological study, vivid in its depiction of scene and nature, and in the end is almost PROCEDURAL as Jon becomes involved in a murder investigation.

JACOBSON, DAN (1929–) Born in Johannesburg, South Africa, Dan Jacobson became known in the fifties for his novels displaying the racial inequalities of South African society. Jacobson's parents were Eastern European Jewish immigrants. He graduated from the University of Witwatersrand and then worked in public relations and in the family cattle-feed business. Jacobson then spent a period in Israel before moving to England in 1954.

One of Jacobson's early novels is *The Price of Diamonds* (1957), set in the rough, struggling mining town of Lyndhurst, South Africa. Manfred Gottlieb is the weaker partner in a respectable business. While Fink, his partner, is away, a down-and-out white man comes to the office and, after an incomprehensible speech (Gottlieb assumes he is crazy), places a small box on the desk. Later it turns out to be full of uncut diamonds. Gottlieb, a man "to whom things happened," keeps the illicit and illegal stones in order to impress Fink, a "big talker" who imagines himself a rebel. The seemingly inevitable train of ironic consequences that flow from Gottlieb's act shows the influence of MAUPASSANT.

JAKES, JOHN (1932–) Better known for a long series of historical novels set during the time of the American Revolution, John Jakes also wrote a group of novels about the detective Johnny HAVOC. Jakes wrote the books while employed in advertising in Rochester, New York, and Dayton, Ohio. Havoc's diminutive size, the ridiculous situations, and what Jakes calls the "Keystone Kops action" make the Havoc novels read like PARODY.

Jakes was born in Chicago and attended DePauw University and Ohio State. He began publishing while he was still in high school, and was a hack writer for many years, publishing Westerns, science fiction, and mysteries. He even wrote the novelization of the film *Conquest of the Planet of the Apes* (1972). He also combined the Western and sci-fi genres in *Six-Gun Planet* (1970). In 1974 he published *The Bastard,* the first of his American Bicentennial series; these books brought about his fame as a writer and sold millions of copies. Jakes has never enjoyed a very high reputation among critics (to which he responds, "sue me for not being Flaubert"). Under the name Alan Payne, Jakes also wrote *Murder, He Says* (1958) and *This Will Slay You* (1958).

JAMES, HENRY (1843–1916) Henry James was a contemporary of Mark TWAIN, but they represented opposite poles of nineteenth-century American culture. Whereas Twain captured the energies and wildness of the frontier and the youthfulness of the nation, James, a New Yorker and the grandson of one of the first American millionaires, represented such Establishment as then existed. As a writer, James looked—and went—to Europe for his models. James spent much of his life in Europe, and became a naturalized British citizen the year before his death. But both authors dealt with contrast between the New World and the Old, though they drew quite different conclusions from it. Growth and decay, the rise and decline of civilizations, and innocence and sophistication are constantly juxtaposed. Both Twain and James also had an influence on the mystery and detective genre. James's was the slighter, but in his ghost stories he showed himself to be a master of suspense and horror.

James attended Harvard Law School in 1862 but left to pursue his writing. He was the brother of the psychologist William James, who coined the term "stream of consciousness," in the development of which Henry James would be influential. In 1876 he settled in England, the same year that his novel *The American* was serialized in *The Atlantic Monthly,* whose editor (William Dean Howells) had done so much to encourage James. *The American* is a romantic story involving blackmail and murder. The American millionaire Christopher Newman courts Claire de Cintré, the daughter of a French aristocratic family, the Bellegardes, who reject his suit because of his mean origins. Claire's brother, about to die, tells Newman how he can blackmail the family by revealing a patricide. (Newman decides not to carry out his plan.) *The Other House* (1896), a much later novel, is about the murder of a child.

The Turn of the Screw (1898) is a ghost story in which a governess tries to protect two children from the evil influences of spirits; it shows James's handling of suspense and dread at their best. The nature of the spirits is ambiguous and has been much discussed. THE ASPERN PAPERS (1888) is a prototype of the CAPER story, in this case a literary one.

JAMES, P[HYLLIS] D[OROTHY] [WHITE] (1920–) Like several other notable mystery authors (including Raymond CHANDLER), English detective-story writer P. D. James came to the genre relatively late. James was born in Oxford. After the death of her husband, a surgeon, she became a hospital administrator. She worked for many years for the National Health Service and later was employed in the Home Office. Many of her books reflect this background and are set in hospitals. At the age of forty, James began writing the books for which she is now famous. She is best known for her stories featuring Adam DALGLIESH; though her female detective, Cordelia Gray, has also been praised, those books do not have the same reputation as the Dalgliesh series. Gray appears in *An Unsuitable Job for a Woman* (1972) and *The Skull Beneath the Skin* (1982).

Unlike many mystery writers, James did not begin working in the short story form, but always was and remains a novelist. (One of her few forays in the short story won a prize from *Ellery Queen's Mystery Magazine*). Dalgliesh made his debut in COVER HER FACE (1962), which was the author's first book, a well-constructed mystery along conventional lines but showing exceptional control and, already, a certain quality that transcended "genre" writing. Given James's background, it is not surprising that her work developed in the direction of psychology and sometimes unsettling realism (in, for example, A MIND TO MURDER, 1963), and that she did not shy away from volatile subject matter such as child murder. In style, as well, James has been daring. *A Mind to Murder* is for long stretches like a one-act play, with the setting unvarying and with little "action" to relieve its claustrophobia.

Among James's most accomplished works is INNOCENT BLOOD (1980), which is generally considered a work of literature first and a mystery second. In 1993 she published *The Children of Men*, an even greater departure. Set in the year 2021, it is a dystopic novel in which the human race is dying because all males have become infertile. Britain has become a dictatorship and there are prison camps and mass euthanasia. The protagonist, an Oxford professor, becomes involved in a revolutionary plot.

In the field of true crime, James co-authored *The Maul and the Pear Tree* (1971) with her colleague, T. A. Critchley. Based on exhaustive historical research, the book reconstructs the circumstances of the Ratcliffe Highway murders of 1811, usually attributed to John WILLIAMS.

JAMOKE Originally an army slang word for coffee ("java" + "mocha"), *jamoke* has come to mean a man, a guy.

JANCE, J[UDITH] A[NN] (1944–) Born in South Dakota, J. A. Jance earned her master's in education at the University of Arizona and worked in Arizona public schools as a teacher and librarian for several years. She later became an insurance salesperson; she published her first book, *Until Proven Guilty,* in 1985. This novel introduced the character J. P. Beaumont, a Seattle homicide detective. Two of the books in the series, *Without Due Process* (1992) and *Failure to Appear* (1993), won the American Mystery Award. After a dozen Beaumont novels, Jance created a new series character, Joanna Bradley, the widow of an Arizona sheriff, who first appeared in *Desert Heat* (1993).

Jance also writes children's books, such as *It's Not Your Fault* (1985), in which she tries to deal with current issues such as child abuse. Of her murder mysteries, Jance forthrightly told *Contemporary Authors* that they were "escapist fare with no redeeming social value."

JANES, J. ROBERT (1935–) The recent mystery series by Canadian author J. Robert Janes is either innovative or in very bad taste, depending on one's point of view. Set during the occupation of Paris during World War II, the books team a Gestapo detective with a Frenchman of the Sûreté Nationale. Janes's own modest opinion, expressed to *Contemporary Authors,* is that "the novels are great fun with a fantastic background, and truly wonderful characters." This view may be disputed: liking the books depends on whether one can bring oneself to believe that a middle-aged German who strongly disagrees with Nazi doctrine and refuses to do the "horrible things" the Gestapo did could still rise to a responsible position in the Nazi secret police (and, unlike Bernie GUNTHER, would even be sent abroad). Hermann Kohler is such an idealized Gestapo agent. A middle-aged Bavarian and former Munich cop, Kohler was an artilleryman in World War I; is a bomb-disposal expert; is beaten up by the SS because he hates them; and (like Hitler himself) loves children. His partner is Jean-Louis St. Cyr, a detective of the Sûreté who is the target of assassination attempts by the Resistance because they consider him a collaborator.

The first book in the series was *Mayhem* (1992; U.S. title *Mirage*). Janes has said that the idea of the books springs from the question of who solved the "everyday crimes of murder and arson" under the Occupation. The crimes in the novels, however, are not really everyday, and they are also sometimes grotesquely violent. In *Sandman* (1996), a young girl is found in a dovecote with a knitting needle protruding from under her chin; it had been stabbed upward into her brain. The crime appears to be the work of the "Sandman," a serial killer of girls who leaves one corpse in the belfry of Notre Dame. Another "ordinary" crime is the murder of a middle-aged postmistress in the Dordogne in *Stonekiller* (1994). She happens, however, to have been involved in the discovery of the cave paintings of Lascaux years before. A film crew happens to be making a movie about the historic find, and Joseph Goebbels happens to be one of the investors in the project. Hitler and Himmler are interested parties as well. Other books in the series are *Salamander* (1994) and *Mannequin* (1994). The dialogue and characters' thoughts are disjointed (presumably to indicate that the speakers are thinking in other languages).

Janes was born in Toronto and educated in Canada; he worked in the petroleum and minerals industries before becoming a teacher. He turned to writing full-time in 1970. His first book was about geology. Janes has written several other novels in addition to the St. Cyr-Kohler series.

JAPP, CHIEF INSPECTOR See POIROT, HERCULE.

JAPRISOT, SÉBASTIEN (pen name of Jean-Baptiste Rossi, 1931–) The French mystery author known as Sébastien Japrisot has written several sometimes macabre novels that have been translated into English. Each one of Japrisot's stories is unique, using different protagonists (no series detective) and striking, even alarming crimes that sometimes have philosophical or moral undertones. For example, he deals with questions of identity through a story about a woman who has had her face burned off and who is suffering from AMNESIA, in TRAP FOR CINDERELLA (1962). In *La Dame dans l'auto avec des lunettes et un fusil* (1966; tr *The Lady in the Car with Glasses and a Gun*), a beautiful blonde drives through France in a stolen Thunderbird, continuously encountering evidence of her own prior (and dangerous) presence. She begins to wonder whether she herself is a killer. It is a novel that reflects the uncanny and awful side of the mystery as much or more than the crime element, the POE of "Berenice" as much as the Poe of DUPIN.

In contrast, Japrisot's first mystery, *Compartiment tueurs* (1962; tr *The 10:30 from Marseille,* 1963; also tr *The Sleeping Car Murders*), was a more conventional mystery with an often-used setting. It was made into a successful film with Simone Signoret, Yves Montand, and Jean-Louis Trintignant. A woman is found dead in a sleeping car at the terminal in Paris, apparently having been killed just after the train arrived. Slowly the other passengers, who had meanwhile gone home, make themselves known and give their evidence. Then they start turning up dead, each shot with a silenced .45; the bullets had been cut across the ends to make them fragment on impact. The narrative is quite PROCEDURAL, with detailed reports of conversations and questionings. An incredible coincidence is used to achieve a surprise ending; only the motive is somewhat weak.

Japrisot, or Rossi, was born in Marseille. His first novel, *Les mals partis,* was published when he was seventeen. Japrisot worked in publicity and in the film industry (as a screenwriter and director). He also translated J. D. Salinger into French. He won the Grand Prix de la Littérature Policière for *Trap for Cinderella.*

Most recently, Japrisot's *Un long dimanche de fiançailles* (1991; tr *A Very Long Engagement,* 1993), won the Prix Interallié and was a bestseller. A HISTORICAL MYSTERY set during World War I, it concerns five soldiers who are court martialed for wounding themselves in an attempt to be sent away from the front. In a larger sense, it is about the bestiality of war. The men are condemned to be tied and sent "over the top," i.e., to be mowed down by the German guns. An outraged captain launches a counterattack to try to save the men, but he, and presumably they, are killed. The wife of one of the victims (a nineteen-year-old who was out of his mind at the time) tries to find out the truth about the five men.

Sébastien Japrisot is an anagram of Jean-Baptiste Rossi.

JARDINE, QUINTIN See GOLF MYSTERIES.

JAY, CHARLOTTE (pen name of Geraldine Mary Jay, 1919–) Born in Australia, Charlotte Jay traveled extensively and lived in England, Pakistan, Thailand, Lebanon, India, and Papua New Guinea. She also worked as a secretary in Australia and London. Jay was a stenographer in the Australian Court of Papua New Guinea in 1949; New Guinea was the setting of her EDGAR-winning novel BEAT NOT THE BONES (1953). She has written fifteen novels, nine of them mysteries. She now lives in her native city of Adelaide, Australia, where she works as an art dealer.

Jay strongly evokes the places she lived in; more than that, she communicates them. Her stories are pleasantly free of exoticism—the places and people are viewed locally, not from a remote Western perspective that renders them strange, barbaric, or primitive. Jay and her husband John Halls worked for UNESCO, and her understanding of other cultures is informed and sympathetic. Jay's weaknesses as a writer are matters of style; the dialogue tends to be stilted and her sentences are at times choppy. Jay's novels are mysteries rather than novels of detection and are, like the NOVEL OF MANNERS, concerned with character and human behavior under different conditions, cultural as well as circumstantial.

Among her other books is *The Feast of the Dead* (1956; U.S. title *The Brink of Silence*), which is about the strange childhood of Katherine Monroe, who was raised on a Pacific island before the war. Her brother Harry died under obscure circumstances. Katherine has no memory of the events; years later, a friend, Jim, reconstructs the truth from conflicting accounts. Although the reader is led to speculate about Harry's death, the story is primarily about complex relationships, intricately woven through the accounts of multiple narrators. *The Fugitive Eye* (1953), which was made into a film with Charlton Heston, and *A Hank of Hair* (1964) are also mysteries.

JEFFRIES, RODERIC (1926–) English mystery author Roderic Jeffries writes from a legal background, but with considerably more ingenuity than some of the others of that school. His series character, Inspector ALVAREZ, is mobile, dealing with cases in England as well as his home territory of Mallorca. One of the cases concerns a TONTINE and several involve peculiar and inventive MODI OPERANDI. Although his handling of legal matters is informed, his plots are often rather simple and sometimes thin. Particularly toward the end of the Alvarez series, which now runs to some twenty books, there seems to be a slackening of energy or effort, with the setting called upon to generate most of the interest. Jeffries is the son of Bruce GRAEME, and has continued his father's BLACKSHIRT series.

Before the Alvarez series was begun in 1974, Jeffries had published legal mysteries that benefited from his training and experience as a barrister. He published under the names Jeffrey Ashford, Graham Hastings, and Peter Alding. As Alding, he wrote about Inspector FUSIL and Constable Kerr. He has also written children's books and television and radio scripts.

JEPSON, EDGAR See EUSTACE, ROBERT.

JESSE, F[RYNIWID] TENNYSON (1889–1958) A grandniece of the English poet Alfred Lord Tennyson, F. Tennyson Jesse was a writer of true crime and some few detective stories. Jesse edited several volumes of the *Notable British Trials* series, including the Madeleine SMITH case, and was praised by William ROUGHEAD. *Murder and Its Motives* (1924) used case studies to examine the psychology of murder. Jesse wrote a number of books of fiction, though not all of them have to do with crime and mystery. *The Lacquer Lady* (1929) was one of her most admired non-crime novels. The best-known of her genre works is *A Pin to See the Peepshow* (1934), which was based on the 1922 Thompson-Bywaters case. H. R. F. KEATING called it "romantic, harrowing, an indictment of 1920s hypocrisy and the horror of capital punishment." Jesse and her husband, a playwright, dramatized the novel. Her other notable fictional work is a collection of short stories, *The Solange Stories* (1931), about a French private detective named Solange Fontaine who has clairvoyant powers.

Jesse studied art and then became a journalist before World War I, writing for various newspapers including the *London Times*. During the war, she was a correspondent and also worked for the Red Cross and the Ministry of Information.

JIVE *Jive* took over some of the original (probably nineteenth century) meanings of "jazz," such as idle or deceptive talk, lies, and sexual intercourse, when jazz became a respectable word applied mainly to a type of music.

JOE, NOVEMBER See PRICHARD, HESKETH.

JOHNSON, "COFFIN" ED One of two black detectives in a series of novels by Chester HIMES. Coffin Ed Johnson works with "Grave Digger" Jones in Harlem, though they live next door to each other in Queens. The reader rarely sees this comparatively calm atmosphere; instead, Himes plunges into the crime-scarred world of Harlem, where situations rapidly escalate into street war—which the two detectives meet with a drastic and violent response. In this friendly but sometimes volatile partnership, Johnson is the hothead of the two, often tempted to take shortcuts in the securing of information or the administration of justice.

The mood of the novels is something like that of the Wild West, because of the vacuum between two different and incompatible forms of order: the way in which the African American community regulates and defends itself, and the uncaring and racist white "justice" system. The two detectives are caught in the middle, picked upon or worse by their superiors (except for the uncomprehending but sympathetic Lieutenant Anderson) and treated with suspicion by the population. Supervision exists in the form of persecution rather than backup.

In their first case, *A Rage in Harlem* (1957; orig title *For Love of Imabelle*), Coffin Ed is disfigured with acid. The story starts with a con game and escalates into a series of bloody deaths. In *The Big Gold Dream* (1960), a woman is poisoned with holy water during a parade led by a phony revival preacher. A struggle ensues to find some money that may be hidden in her furniture. The book also contains an unpleasant depiction of a character referred to as "the Jew," a dealer in second-hand belongings. *All Shot Up* (1960) is about a multiple shooting that follows the appearance of a mysterious gold Cadillac in Harlem.

As in the novels of Walter MOSLEY, which also begin in the forties and stretch into the sixties, the situation of the African American community becomes worse, not better, ending in the chaos of BLIND MAN WITH A PISTOL (1969).

BIBLIOGRAPHY Novels: *The Crazy Kill* (1959), *The Real Cool Killers* (1959), *Cotton Comes to Harlem* (1965), *The Heat's On* (1966).

JONES, AVERAGE Created by Samuel Hopkins ADAMS, Adrian van Reypen Egerton Jones appeared in the short story collection *Average Jones* (1911). A.V.R.E.J., calling himself an "Ad-Visor," keeps a file of strange newspaper clippings as "grist for his mill" of detective cases. Jones is really average in appearance, except for the tell-tale deep-set eyes. He is twenty-seven and has an income of ten thousand dollars a year, with an expectation to inherit ten million. His first case is THE B-FLAT TROMBONE. Jones is assisted by the elegant and laconic Robert Bartram, with whom he engages in verbal sparring and jokes.

Adams used the device of the loony premise for all it was worth. In "The Million-Dollar Dog," Jones is intrigued by the advertisement, "Wanted: Ten thousand loathly beetles. . . ." In "The Man Who Spoke Latin," he finds an ad by a man calling himself Livius who claims to be an ancient Roman. Having been hit a strong blow on the head, Livius has forgotten his contemporary identity and regressed to a previous incarnation. He lives with the Latin scholar Colonel Graeme, and combs through the colonel's library looking for something. Detection is involved particularly in "The Merry Sign," about a missing laboratory assistant and the strange Mr. Smith, a creature with bloated face and hands.

JONES, "GRAVE DIGGER" See JOHNSON, "COFFIN" ED.

JORDAN, SCOTT A lawyer sleuth created by Harold Q. MASUR, Scott Jordan is, like John J. MALONE, a tough guy as well as a lawyer. But Masur substitutes for Craig RICE's drunken burlesque a more austere bachelor life. Jordan is sensitive and attentive to business, lacking the usual suave attributes of the HARD-BOILED detective. In fact, the author told *Twentieth Century Crime and Mystery Writers* that Jordan was partly modeled on Archie GOODWIN. Like Goodwin, he works in New York City, and injects a dose of humor into his stories. One of the comical things about the Jordan character is that he continually stumbles over dead bodies, even at his own door (*Suddenly a Corpse*, 1949). Jordan's first case is BURY ME DEEP (1947). Jordan was postal inspector before World War II and earned his law degree by going to school at night. After enlisting, he was assigned to intelligence work and served in Africa, India, and China. His first case involves divorce, mobsters, pornography, and a contested estate.

BIBLIOGRAPHY Novels: *You Can't Live Forever* (1950), *So Rich, So Lovely, So Dead* (1952), *The Big Money* (1954), *Tall, Dark and Deadly* (1956), *The Last Gamble* (1958; British title *The Last Breath*), *Send Another Hearse* (1960), *Make a Killing* (1964), *The Mourning After* (1983).

Short Stories: *The Name Is Jordan* (1962).

JOYCE, JAMES (1882–1941) The greatest Irish prose writer of the twentieth century has been "involved" in mysteries by Bartholomew GILL (see DEATH OF A JOYCE SCHOLAR, 1989) and Amanda CROSS. *Secret Isaac* (1992), one of the Isaac SIDEL mysteries, has a Joycean element (if a Joyce-scholar-turned-pimp could be called that) as well as being stylistically imitative.

JUDGE AND HIS HANGMAN, THE (*Der Richter und sein Henker*, 1955) A novel by Friedrich DÜRRENMATT. The focus of the story is the ailing Hans Barlach, police commissioner in Berne. Barlach is supposed to be investigating the murder of his most brilliant subordinate, Ulrich Schmied, but leaves the work to another young officer, Walter Tschanz. Barlach seems to be tired and apathetic, but he is an expert at fooling others (especially his officious and incompetent boss, Dr. Lucius Lutz) by showing them an appearance that fits their preconceptions. When the investigation turns toward a mysterious Herr Gastmann who has high-level political connections, Lutz tries to call it off. Although appearing in only a short novel, Barlach's character is wonderfully developed, culminating in a bizarre scene in which the dying detective with stomach trouble gorges himself in an almost unimaginable feast. Through Barlach's complete mastery, which is achieved precisely through his weakness rather than by force, Dürrematt comments ironically on conceptions of power and will. As the pieces fall into place, the question remains whether Barlach has fulfilled fate or invented it himself.

JUDSON, E. Z. C. See DIME NOVEL.

JURY, INSPECTOR RICHARD Martha GRIMES's Richard Jury is in a sense the least important thing in the author's series of novels set in Britain. Grimes is an American, and Jury's cases are more a vehicle for talking about England than the reverse. The plots are often tangled and farfetched and lack the neatness of their models—the English mysteries of the GOLDEN AGE. The influence of Dorothy L. SAYERS and others is visible in the choice of Jury's sidekick, Melrose Plant, an aristocratic amateur sleuth like Lord Peter WIMSEY.

BIBLIOGRAPHY Novels: *The Man with a Load of Mischief* (1981), *The Old Fox Deceiv'd* (1982), *The Anodyne Necklace* (1983), *The Dirty Duck* (1984), *Jerusalem Inn* (1984), *Help the Poor Struggler* (1985), *The Deer Leap* (1985), *I Am the Only Running Footman* (1986), *The Five Bells and Bladebone* (1987), *The Old Silent* (1989), *The Old Contemptibles* (1990), *Rainbow's End* (1995), *The Case Has Altered* (1997).

JUVE, INSPECTOR The opponent of FANTÔMAS in novels by Pierre SOUVESTRE and Marcel ALLAIN. Juve is the legendary agent of the Criminal Investigation Department who has sworn to bring the thief and killer Fantômas to justice. He is also a master of disguise.

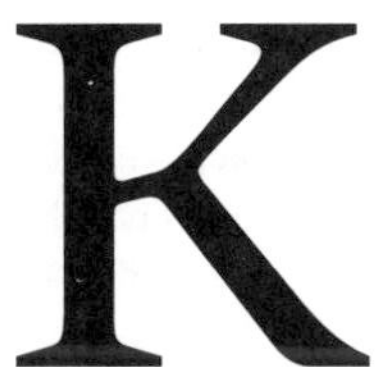

KAHAWA (1982) A novel by Donald WESTLAKE. The title refers to the central CAPER: an unlikely coalition of mercenaries, merchants, and idealists set out to steal a thirty-three-wagon train of coffee (*kahawa* in Swahili) belonging to Idi Amin, the former dictator of Uganda. Westlake was inspired to write the story by the tale of a real robbery. Although it contains the comical and farcical elements common to the author's work, because of the horrifying realities revealed by his research (Amin's security forces tortured and murdered half a million people), Westlake said, "I can't dance on all those graves." Thus, compared to Westlake's usual work, the novel is more realistic in its depiction of brutality and imbued with a variety of themes, touching on politics, race, and real-world evils—without, however, pursuing them to as bitter an end as does Wessel EBERSOHN. At the same time, *Kahawa* is a highly effective thriller, with a classic sleigh ride of an ending. The characters who assemble to mount the caper are varied and interesting: Lew Brady, a mercenary who has somehow remained idealistic and a little naive; his independent girlfriend, pilot Ellen Gillespie; Mazar Balim, the Indian wheeler-dealer who bankrolls the operation; and Isaac Otera, a Ugandan exile and mild clerk who discovers a streak of the patriot in himself.

KAMINSKY, STUART M[ELVIN] (1934–) Stuart Kaminsky could be called a professor of entertainment. He is, in fact, a professor of film, and his CELEBRITY MYSTERIES set in the Hollywood of the 1940s involve famous people as diverse as Errol Flynn and Albert Einstein. Kaminsky's first teaching post was in Chicago, where he was born. He also taught writing, and one of his students was Sara PARETSKY. Kaminsky graduated from the University of Illinois with a degree in journalism. He earned his Ph.D. in speech from Northwestern University.

Toby PETERS, a private detective, is the sleuth of the Hollywood series; his experience as a cop and as a guard at a studio give him an entree into the world of the stars. The stories are not realistic, nor are they meant to be; the emphasis is on mood and humor. Kaminsky has also written a series about Porfiry Petrovich Rostnikov, a one-legged Moscow policeman (his name is taken from DOSTOYEVSKY's *Crime and Punishment*). The second book in the series, *Cold Red Sunrise* (1988), won an EDGAR award. The Rostnikov books are set in the Soviet Union not many years before its collapse; the mood is somber, the people full of suspicion, fear, and hopelessness. Rostnikov himself is hindered rather than helped by the KGB, and the perversion of justice for political reasons is a constant theme. At the same time, Kaminsky manages to inject some humor into this depressing setting. *Rostnikov's Vacation* (1991) varies the setting and somewhat relieves the dark mood. But in *Tarnished Icons* (1997), the detective deals with some particularly ugly crimes—anti-Semitic violence in Moscow and a serial rapist who likes to use a knife. *The Dog Who Bit a Policeman* (1998) was the next book in the revived Rostnikov series and dealt with illegal dog fighting and battles between factions of the Russian mafia.

KANE, HENRY (1918–) The American author Henry Kane was one of those who benefited from the boom in PAPERBACK ORIGINALS in the fifties and sixties. Born in New York City, Kane had a successful career as a lawyer before he became a writer. Initially, he wrote short stories for magazines, including *The Saturday Evening Post* and *Esquire*. His first novel, about private detective Peter CHAMBERS, was *A Halo for Nobody* (1947). He stuck to Chambers through four decades, even while writing non-series and non-mystery novels. The novels about Chambers would eventually total thirty. *Kill for the Millions* (1972) was Chambers's last appearance, after which Kane focused on mass-audience THRILLERS.

From the moment he started writing, Kane was prolific, turning out several novels a year (not only about Chambers) and writing in several different styles at once. A typical apprentice work, *Edge of Panic* (1947) did not include Chambers; instead, it is a halting narrative in the style of Cornell WOOLRICH about a man who thinks he is a murderer. Harry Martin, an insurance salesman, has been sober for six years when he goes on a bender and finds that he still can't hold his liquor. Invited to a rich heiress's room to discuss annuities, he wakes up with a bloody hammer in his hand next to a faceless corpse. The detecting is done by his wife with the forbearance of a typical cranky, eccentric old homicide detective. *Sleep Without Dreams* (1958; orig title *Death for Sale*) is also about alcohol and the awakening of repressed impulses.

Chambers starts out as a typical HARD-BOILED dick early in the series. He becomes progressively more liberated, however; the late books are so sexually frank that they have been described as "x-rated." *Dead in Bed* (1961) finds Chambers right on schedule, a swinger of the sexually jaded, politically innocent post-Beat, pre-Vietnam period, as comfortable with marijuana as martinis. Leaving aside whether it is good or not, Kane's writing can be enjoyed as camp, or for the sheer excess of his word plays, puns, and fondness for alliteration reminiscent of Muhammad Ali. Chambers is awakened by a frantic phone call about a banker's disappearance ("the damned contrivance kept ringing like a toxic tocsin with a venomous clapper"), then finds a naked woman dead in his TUB. Police do not merely arrive; instead, "Coppers finally descended like pennies from heaven," and the detective "showed more interest than a gilt-edged bond." Everyone speaks in puns, as if collectively trying to find every permutation of a joke. Kane's self-parody reached a peak in *Kisses of Death* (1962), in which he teamed Chambers with a female sleuth, the blonde Marla Trent, who, with vital statistics of 96-67-95, is an impossible bombshell.

The best Kane book is not a Chambers novel, however; THE PERFECT CRIME (1961) is a perfect period piece set in Miami. Its cast of characters is sleazy, funny, and memorable. Kane's later work includes espionage and terrorism novels, such as *Operation Delta* (1966) and *The Tripoli Documents* (1976). He also wrote three "straight" or nearly straight detective novels about a retired New York cop, Inspector McGregor. In *The Midnight Man* (1965), he investigates loan-sharking. He gets caught up in Cold War politics in *Conceal and Disguise* (1966). *Laughter in the Alehouse* (1968) involves Israeli agents pursuing a suspected NAZI war criminal who ran a forced-labor camp. The man escaped with an acquittal at Nuremberg because he had killed his own father, an even bigger monster, in front of several Jewish witnesses who testified on his behalf. McGregor suffers slightly from the SUPERLATIVE COMPLEX: he was a legendary cop and turned down the commissionership, has become rich, is a gourmet cook, and has a photographic memory. The plot of the last book is particularly preposterous, with extravagant sexual subplots involving beautiful agents.

Kane's humorous work remains his most original and shows his real writing ability. Kane wrote the screenplays for two films based on Ed MCBAIN's 87TH PRECINCT novels, *Cop Hater* (1958) and *The Mugger* (1958).

KANTOR, [BENJAMIN] MCKINLAY (1904–1977) The Iowa-born author McKinlay Kantor began his career as a writer after high school when his hometown paper, *The Webster City Daily News,* gave him his first job as a reporter (his mother was the editor). He later moved to Chicago, where he continued to work as a journalist, and then eventually returned to Iowa. With *Long Remember* (1934), a novel about the battle of Gettysburg, he began the series of historical novels that would bring him notoriety and literary acclaim. *Andersonville* (1955), about the notorious Confederate prison, won the Pulitzer Prize. *Arouse and Beware* (1936) is another Civil War novel. Kantor also wrote the screenplay for the film *The Best Years of Our Lives* (1946), which was based on his own verse novel about World War II, *Glory for Me* (1945).

The less well-known part of Kantor's output is his contribution to the crime genre. Before he became successful as a historical novelist, Kantor had been writing for PULP MAGAZINES. In his stories, he drew on his Chicago experience during its colorful, gangster-ridden period. But Kantor's most important genre work was one of the earliest PROCEDURAL novels, SIGNAL THIRTY-TWO (1950); it appeared two years before LAST SEEN WEARING . . . (1952), and remains a unique work in the subgenre. Kantor brought to his description of the lower-class tenements of New York the same realism he would use in describing the horrors of Andersonville. Like other writers before and after, Kantor accompanied policemen on patrols in order to research the novel's background. *It's about Crime* (1960) is a collection of Kantor's short stories. *Midnight Lace* (1948) is a novel of suspense.

KARAPANOU, MARTA (1946–) Marta Karapanou moved from her homeland of Greece to Paris as a child, but writes in Greek. Her second novel, *O Ipnovatis* (*The Somnambulist,* 1985), is about a series of murders on a Greek island among a decadent group of expatriates. The book was translated into French and received the Gallimard Prize for foreign fiction.

KARMENSIN See KERSH, GERALD.

KAVANAGH, DAN A pseudonym of Julian BARNES, under which he wrote his detective novels. Barnes created a fictional biography for Kavanagh: born in County Sligo, pianist in Macao, pilot of drug planes in Colombia.

KAYE, MARVIN See HISTORICAL MYSTERIES.

KAYE, SIMON A detective created by Hillary WAUGH. Although Waugh is known first and foremost as a pioneer of the PROCEDURAL novel, Simon Kaye is a private detective of the HARD-BOILED school. The settings of the novels are contemporary however, and Waugh depicts the United States in the eighties in all its greed and sordidness.

Kaye is a former boxer and a former cop. One of his friends is district attorney Donald Maas, another is Father Jack McGuire, an ex-boxer. In *The Billy Cantrell Case* (1981), they witness the death of a promising young fighter in the ring. Kaye has the classic p.i.'s dingy office and a gorgeous, green-eyed secretary named Eileen. The writing and the treatment of sex (plenty of leering and "cleavage") make the story pulpier than the author's other work.

BIBLIOGRAPHY Novels: *The Glenna Powers Case* (1980), *The Doria Rafe Case* (1980), *The Billy Cantrell Case* (1981), *The Nerissa Claire Case* (1983), *The Veronica Dean Case* (1984), *The Priscilla Copperthwaite Case* (1986).

KEANE, OWEN An idiosyncratic sleuth created by Terence FAHERTY. Keane could be modeled on Demosthenes: he is a lost soul obsessed with finding the truth, wandering through the world with a certain passivity but questioning everything around him. A graduate in literature, Keane attended a seminary but left because of his doubt. He takes a series of jobs for which he is always overqualified—but Keane does not care about prestige or money. He dresses terribly, and endures the mockery of others at his trying to play "detective," a label he rejects, thinking of himself more as a searcher. Keane is fortyish and losing ground; his quest for enlightenment shows no signs of reaching an end. He is intelligent, cynical, and often funny. Keane knows he is doomed, like any philosopher, to be judged a failure in terms of the values of the modern world.

Keane first appeared in *Deadstick* (1991). *The Lost Keats* (1993) fills in the early part of the Keane story. It is set in 1973 when Keane was still in a seminary in Indiana. The murderer he helps put in jail in that book turns up again later in the series, out on parole. *Prove the Nameless* (1996) is the longest and most involved of the novels. Keane is working as a copyeditor with the *Post* in Atlantic City. He edits a story about the twentieth anniversary of a shocking murder: five members of a family were killed in their home, and only a baby of a few months was left alive. The case was abandoned after the two main suspects died. The "baby" is Barbara Lambert, now full-grown, who wants the police to reopen the case. Keane is assisted by Kate Amato, the young reporter who wrote the story. The characters are well drawn and the story suspenseful; only a purist would quibble at the way in which, having "stumped" Owen in his running down of all possible solutions, Faherty brings in events to help him break out of his deductive predicament.

BIBLIOGRAPHY Novels: *Live to Regret* (1992), *Die Dreaming* (1994), *The Ordained* (1998), *Orion Rising* (1999).

KEATE, SARAH A nurse sleuth created by Mignon G. EBERHART. The once-popular nurse-as-sleuth subgenre had already been firmly established by Mary Roberts RINEHART, with her mysteries about Hilda ADAMS, when Eberhart came on the scene. *The Patient in Room 18* (1929), the first Sarah Keate mystery, was an instant success. Sarah Keate is a red-haired, matter-of-fact character, not very young but still quite "presentable." The story takes place at St. Ann's Hospital, an old red-brick structure covered with ivy and perched on the side of Thatcher Hill, which we are told is a little east and south of the city of B—. In this GOTHIC setting, people are dying in Room 18 because of what seems to be a "curse." After this first success, Keate reappeared the following year in *While the Patient Slept*, even more reminiscent of Rinehart. Keate is working in the spooky mansion of the elderly Adolph Federie, who is bedridden by a stroke. There is a host of suspicious characters, including Genevieve, a black cat. This novel was also very successful, winning the $5,000 Scotland Yard Prize (not offered by SCOTLAND YARD, but a publishing company) for best mystery of the year. It was also adapted for the screen in 1935, one of half a dozen films about Sarah Keate. *From This Dark Stairway* (1931) was set in a lonely Nebraska hunting lodge.

At the beginning, Keate assisted, or was assisted by, the handsome detective Lance O'Leary. Perhaps significantly, Eberhart was later able to dispense with him—a sign that it was really the forceful Keate who attracted readers, or that the self-reliant fictional female sleuth had arrived.

BIBLIOGRAPHY Novels: *The Mystery of Hunting's End* (1930), *Murder by an Aristocrat* (1932), *Wolf in Man's Clothing* (1942), *Man Missing* (1954).

KEATING, H[ENRY] R[EYMOND] F[ITZWALTER] (1926–) H. R. F. Keating is best known for his works of criticism in the crime and mystery genre and for his series of novels featuring Inspector GHOTE. The first book in the series, *The Perfect Murder* (1964), won an EDGAR award and a Gold Dagger.

After serving in the army and then graduating from the University of Dublin, Keating worked as a journalist for the London *Telegraph* and the *Times*. He was the *Times'* reviewer in the genre for many years. Keating's critical works include *Crime and Mystery: The 100 Best Books* (1987), consisting of brief essays on 100 books Keating sees as the most important, encompassing the history of the genre from POE to P. D. JAMES; *Whodunit? A Guide to Suspense & Spy Fiction* (ed; 1982); and *The Bedside Companion to Crime* (1989).

In his mystery fiction, Keating falls somewhere in the same territory as Peter LOVESEY, being fond of exotic settings and periods. His early books, such as *Zen There Was Murder* (1960), were considered wacky interpretations of the mystery genre. Keating's is a particular kind of English humor, tending more toward Benny Hill rather than Monty Python. His work goes against the grain of the best postwar English mystery and crime fiction, represented by such authors as P. D. JAMES, Julian SYMONS, and Ruth RENDELL, and which stresses the psychological dimension. In addition to the Ghote books, Keating wrote *A Remarkable Case of Burglary* (1976), set in Victorian England. He has also written novels as Evelyn Hervey. Keating is a member and past president of the DETECTION CLUB.

KELLERMAN, JONATHAN (1949–) The American child psychologist Jonathan Kellerman has written a series of novels about a child psychologist, Alex DELAWARE. This began with *When the Bow Breaks* (1985), which won an EDGAR award. In a relatively short time, Kellerman became a bestseller, writing novels that rely on the shock value of crimes against CHILDREN. In one book, *Over the Edge* (1987), the child is the criminal, or is thought to be.

Kellerman received his B.A. in psychology from UCLA and his Ph.D. from the University of Southern California. He is married to the writer Faye KELLERMAN. The Delaware novels are set in the Los Angeles area. They have been praised for their informational quality, but though what Delaware says about his therapeutic practices is accurate enough, it is not always interesting. *Private Eyes* (1992) has an engaging plot; Delaware is called upon by an eighteen-year-old woman whom he had treated when she was seven for extreme anxiety and phobia. The girl's mother, an agoraphobic, was disfigured with acid by an assailant and never leaves her home. In Delaware's earlier successful therapy with the girl, he does hardly anything—he merely creates an atmosphere in which she can express her feelings, and she eventually is cured. The release of the attacker from prison and the disappearance of the mother provide drama, but Kellerman has difficulty knowing what to leave out of his story, which has only one pace.

Kellerman's books are often cluttered with extraneous and irrelevant detail: "Adding a pickle to Milo's sandwich, I put the plate back in the giant fridge, brewed some coffee, and reviewed the notes on my most recent custody consultation to Family Court." The writing is not so much bad as banal, a carelessness masquerading as style. Kellerman is fond of one-sentence paragraphs and sentence fragments, which tend to make the narration choppy. Sometimes the technique is used to represent Delaware's thoughts or notes on therapy sessions. Meanwhile, the story reads like a rough sketch for a second draft that was never made.

KELLERMAN, FAYE [MARDER] (1952–) Born in St. Louis, Faye Marder met her husband, Jonathan Kellerman, while both were studying at UCLA. Faye Kellerman studied mathematics and went on to become a dentist. Her first book, *The Ritual Bath* (1985), was published in the same year as her husband's EDGAR-winning first novel. Kellerman's series is set in Los Angeles and follows the fortunes of Peter Decker, a police detective, and Rina Lazarus, an Orthodox Jewish widow with two children, whom Decker meets on his first case and eventually marries. Much of the series is taken up with romantic subplot and with Peter's education in the Jewish faith (he was adopted by a Christian family as a child). Like her husband, Kellerman writes about abuse and crimes against CHILDREN. Pop psychology and doses of sensationalism are thrown in, often stalling the plot. *Prayers for the Dead* (1996) has Decker and other detectives investigating the murder of a doctor whose lab was testing a drug for the Food and Drug Administration and a drug company. The doctor's son is a priest. Subplots allow the author to inject into the story motorcycle gangs, the ethics of helmet laws and heart harvesting, the sexuality of priests, gay porn, sadism and masochism, and Decker's fears about infidelity. To pull this all together requires an improbable conspiracy and one character dropped into the story out of the blue.

Milk and Honey (1990), a book inexplicably praised by as good a writer as James ELLROY, is actually replete with not only flat writing but errors of grammar and spelling. ("Riding another mile, the trees disappeared and they came upon fields once more.") Kellerman is also prone to the same bathetic metaphors as Richard NEELY ("rows of tan-colored stucco homes had gelled into a lump of oatmeal") and problems with verbs ("his heart raced against his chest"). The plot is again top-heavy: a two-year old found wandering in blood-spattered clothes, a mass murder of a family, menacing beekeepers, hordes of angry insects, and an old army friend of Decker's accused of a rape-homicide. The writer of the jacket copy spoke more than he knew when he said "the motive behind [the] murder is lost in a sticky mess of blood, sex, and honey." For admirers of the CLOACA-AND-DAGGER school, there is plenty to savor: "yards of bloodless entrails, open shotgun blasts in the abdominal and thoracic regions, half a heart dangling out of one of the women's chests. The faces had become blackened with exposure, maggots crawling out of noses and eye sockets."

KELLERMAN, GENERAL FRITZ The NAZI overseer of police work in occupied Britain, introduced in Len DEIGHTON's *SS-GB* (1978). Kellerman uses British policemen as operatives to combat British resistance groups and persecute political refugees and Jews.

KELLING, SARAH Character created by Charlotte MacLeod. Kelling comes from patrician Boston stock, and the novels in which she has a part depict the upper crust as insular, vain, and back-stabbing. Orphaned in her youth, Kelling married a fifth cousin, and after he is killed in an accident she becomes an heiress. The scene of the novels shifts between her house in Boston, which she turns into a rooming house after she loses her money, and Ireson's Landing, a community on Cape Ann, where she meets Max Bittersohn, a Jewish investigator who works on art thefts. The two later marry.

This odd couple appears in many novels. After one of Sarah's tenants is murdered in *The Withdrawing Room* (1980), Max Bittersohn moves into the basement to protect her. A second victim is found dead in the Public Garden. Among the other characters is the butler Charles C. Charles, an actor who plays Jeeves and works for Sarah in his spare time. In *The Bilbao Looking Glass* (1983), the appearance of a mysterious mirror in the house in Ireson's Landing is linked to the murder of one older woman with an AXE and another with poison. Max is arrested for the crimes. *The Gladstone Bag* (1989) has one of Sarah's infinite list of relatives spending the summer at an artist's colony on an island off the coast of Maine. Emma Kelling, an active middle-aged woman, has to call on Sarah after a bag of stage jewelry she brought with her to repair gets stolen and the body of a mysterious man is found in the water. By the time of *The Resurrection Man* (1992), Sarah and Max are running a detective agency and the pretense of their just happening upon murders is made less obvious. The Countess Lydia Ouspenka is an artist and expert forger; she gets a job at the "guild" of Bartolo Arbalest ("the Resurrection Man"). Meanwhile, art burglaries have been multiplying in town, and one of Sarah's friends is killed in a robbery. Exoticism—including a mysterious Indian doing calisthenics in a red suit, spears, and icons—proliferates. Max is in Argentina looking for Watteaus in *The Odd Job* (1995). The couple try to get back pieces stolen from the Wilkins collection, a private museum in Boston.

BIBLIOGRAPHY Novels: *The Family Vault* (1979), *The Palace Guard* (1981), *The Convivial Codfish* (1984), *The Plain Old Man* (1985), *The Recycled Citizen* (1987), *The Silver Ghost* (1987), *The Balloon Man* (1998).

KEMELMAN, HARRY (1908–1996) Born in Boston, Harry Kemelman was a teacher and held administrative posts in the military before he began writing. His first mystery work, short stories about college professor Nicky Welt, was appreciated and published by Ellery Queen. Welt, solving cases with brains more than legwork, indicated the future scholarly direction of Kemelman's writing. The Nine-Mile Walk, the title story of a collection of Nicky Welt stories published in 1967, is a mystery classic.

Rabbi David Small, Kemelman's famous detective, is not only scholarly but talmudic; he follows the slow pace of exegesis, eliminating one by one all illogical possibilities and obscurities while Police Chief Lanigan and the *Rebbitzin* (rabbi's wife) Myriam help out with alternative theories and facts. It is an intellectual detection work in the armchair style, with reasoning predominating over facts and action. But unlike armchair geniuses like Nero Wolfe, Small is very matter-of-fact and seems like the neighbor next door. He is not eccentric, though his scholarly interests make him eccentric to some of the members of the board of directors of the synagogue in the town of Barnard's Crossing, all prominent New England commercial businessmen. Small's deduction is everything; the reader does not see much of Lanigan's wrapping up of the investigation. The pleasure is the intellectual one that comes from logical explanations. In the words of the rabbi, every piece of the picture falls into place simply, smoothly, and harmoniously. The first book in the Rabbi Small series was Friday, the Rabbi Slept Late (1964).

An independent thinker, the rabbi is in constant risk of having his contract not renewed and makes plenty of enemies. These conflicts in the Jewish community are often tied up with the resolution of the mystery and cleverly provide an opportunity to discuss doctrinal issues in a manner that is not irrelevant to the plot. Kemelman's recreation of New England society is extremely good, as are his descriptions of life in a small town, the typical characters, and the underlying tensions. But his best trait is the accurate depiction of Judaism, its spirit, and its differences with other religions. One discovers and is made to think about the alternative approaches to life that are produced by different religious beliefs, and is almost instructed in the history of religion. So prominent is this element that Rabbi Small's "teachings" have been collected as *Conversations with Rabbi Small* (1981).

The books in which the rabbi travels to Israel are the weakest. *Monday, the Rabbi Took Off* (1972) and *One Fine Day the Rabbi Bought a Cross* (1987) suffered from the removal of the Barnard's Crossing context, which was not made up for by the foreign surroundings and the rabbi's discoveries in the Holy Land—he already knew plenty anyway, and the find-a-killer-on-vacation gambit was hardly as original as the ordinary setting of the other books.

Kemelman lives in Marblehead, Massachusetts, not far from the fictional Barnard's Crossing.

KENDRICK, BAYNARD [HARDWICK] (1894–1977) American mystery writer and creator of a blind detective, Captain Duncan Maclain, along the lines of Max CARRADOS. In World War I, Kendrick met a blind soldier who astounded him with his ability to make deductions from things he could not see. Kendrick became interested in the blind, an expertise he used in his Maclain novels. Like Carrados, Maclain is active and refuses to be hampered by his handicap. Some critics have stated that Maclain is a more believable blind person than Carrados, and that his feats are at least possible. As pieces of writing, however, and as stories, the Carrados stories have won more praise. Even in the "outstanding" *The Odor of Violets* (1941), BARZUN and TAYLOR found Maclain "not so convincing" as Carrados.

Kendrick, born in Philadelphia, also lived in Florida and New York City. His first books, written before he invented Maclain, were set in Florida. Maclain first appeared in *The Last Express* (1937). The blind detective lives on Riverside Drive, has both a seeing-eye and an attack dog, and is assisted by Rena and Spud Savage. Kendrick was co-founder and the first president of the Mystery Writers of America.

KENEALLY, THOMAS (1935–) The Australian historical novelist Thomas Keneally is best known for *Schindler's Ark* (1982; repub as *Schindler's List,* 1993), a novel based on the historical figure Oskar Schindler, a German businessman who saved more than one thousand Jews from extermination during World War II. The novel won the prestigious Booker Prize and was made into a film by director Steven Spielberg. Keneally had dealt with crime in another well-known novel, *The Chant of Jimmie Blacksmith* (1972), which was also filmed. It was based on an actual crime that took place in 1900. Jimmy Blacksmith, half-black and half-white, has left his tribal life and wants to be assimilated into white society. He marries a white woman, Gilda, but their marriage is not accepted among whites, who try to pressure Gilda into abandoning him. This and other insults, including an attempt to starve him into submission, drive him to a murderous rampage (depicted with a shocking, matter-of-fact tone). *Victim of the Aurora* (1977) is a more conventional attempt to write a HISTORICAL mystery. Set in 1910, it concerns the murder of a journalist who is accompanying an expedition to Antarctica.

KENNEDY, CRAIG A detective character created by Arthur B. REEVE. Kennedy was the foremost American "scientific" detective of the period from before World War I to the rise of the HARD-BOILED school. A doctor at Columbia University, Kennedy was modeled on a real doctor, Otto H. Schultze, who advised the New York City district attorney's office at the time Reeve was writing.

The Kennedy stories are more dependent on then-novel scientific gadgets—the silencer, the dictaphone, x-rays—than on scientific method. Kennedy has his WATSON, Walter Jameson, a reporter with whom he shares rooms. Kennedy is as handsome as Dr. THORNDYKE but more of a tough guy underneath, carrying a gun and getting into scrapes. Whether because Reeve tried to be all things to all people or was an inferior writer to R. Austin FREEMAN, the Kennedy novels have not been reprinted.

BIBLIOGRAPHY Novels: *Gold of the Gods* (1915), *The Exploits of Elaine* (1915), *The Ear in the Wall* (1916), *The Romance of Elaine* (1916), *The Triumph of Elaine* (1916), *The Adventuress* (1917), *The Soul Scar* (1919), *The Film Mystery* (1921), *Atavar* (1924), *The Radio Detective* (1926), *Pandora* (1926), *The Kidnap Club* (1932), *The Clutching Hand* (1934), *The Stars Scream Murder* (1936).

Short Stories: *The Silent Bullet* (1912; British title *The Black Hand*), *The Poisoned Pen* (1913), *The Dream Doctor* (1914), *The War Terror* (1915; British title *Craig Kennedy, Detective*), *The Social Gangster* (1916; British title *The Diamond Queen*), *The Treasure Train* (1917), *The Panama Plot* (1918), *Craig Kennedy Listens In* (1923), *The Fourteen Points* (1925), *The Boy Scouts' Craig Kennedy* (1925), *Craig Kennedy on the Farm* (1925), *Enter Craig Kennedy* (1935; novelettes, finished by Ashley Locke Reeve).

KENT, CONSTANCE Constance Kent was still in her teens in 1860 when her four-year-old half-brother was taken from the family home at Road Hill, between Somerset and Wiltshire in England, during the night of June 29-30. After a brief search, the body was found in the morning in a disused "earth-closet" (an outhouse), the corpse's throat cut and the head almost detached. If ever there was a case of a crime being hushed up, it was the murder of Francis Saville Kent. The family was prominent (most of them were not even questioned at the inquest), and the crime was blamed, as in detective fiction, on a tramp or drifter. One of the clues was that a nightdress of Constance's was missing. Policemen actually found a bloody nightdress, but ignored it.

The most famous detective of the time, Jonathan WHICHER, thought differently. After examining the evidence he arrested Constance Kent, which evoked howls of protest from the community, sympathy for the "poor girl," and bad publicity for Whicher. He was vindicated in 1865 when Constance confessed. The crime fascinated the English public; the case had essentially been dropped and the culprit would have gotten away with murder had she not confessed. One of those who was influenced by the case was Wilkie COLLINS, who used Whicher as a model for the detective in his classic 1868 novel THE MOONSTONE. John RHODE later wrote an account of the Constance Kent case, and seems to have become fascinated with her as a precocious and adventurous girl, whose life (and mind?) was disturbed after her mother died and her father married the housekeeper, the oppressive Miss Pratt. Rhode speculated that Constance Kent killed the boy not from hatred of him or compulsion but in order to do something that would hurt her stepmother the most. After her confession, Constance was sentenced to death, which was commuted to life imprisonment. She served twenty years of her sentence and was a model prisoner, spending some of her time producing mosaics. After her release in 1885 she seems to have left the country and disappeared.

KERR, PHILIP (1956–) Scottish-born author of a series of mystery and suspense novels. Kerr's novels are divided between carefully researched historical mysteries on the one hand and imaginative, even futuristic, THRILLERS on the other. His work has been well received not only by the mystery press but mainstream reviewers as well, who have treated him as a "serious" novelist. *Granta* magazine chose him as one of the best young British novelists of the nineties, and he has been called "brilliantly innovative" by Salman Rushdie. Kerr worked as a freelance journalist for *The Times* and other periodicals before publishing *March Violets* (1989), the first of a series of novels to feature former policeman Bernie Gunther. Set in Berlin in 1936, it takes the private eye formula of the honest man in a corrupt world to an extreme; the detective's search for justice in NAZI Germany threatens to render the convention farcical, but it is just this tension that Kerr turns to his advantage. The Nazi characters are given personality, while Kerr tries to make Gunther a believable decent German. He is neither a hero—his independence is illusory—nor is he repugnant; like many, he dislikes what is happening but does not sacrifice himself to stop it. The other two books in the series are THE PALE CRIMINAL (1990) and *A German Requiem* (1991); all three were collected and published as BERLIN NOIR (1993).

Following his success with the Gunther series, Kerr has turned out a spate of mystery/thrillers. *Dead Meat* (1993) is most similar to his earlier work, and is set in St. Petersburg after the collapse of the Soviet Union. In another clever twist, Kerr grafts the PROCEDURAL mystery onto the shaky St. Petersburg Central Investigating Board, which tries to cope with a crime explosion with depleted resources. As the authorities try to redefine themselves in the new Russia, burgeoning mafias of Chechins, Georgians, and other *churki* ("people of the swamps") take advantage of the new openness. The chaos allows Kerr to indulge in one of his favorite devices, black humor. The book was nominated for a GOLD DAGGER award. In the same year he published *A Philosophical Investigation* (1993), his most sophisticated novel so far. After this ambitious work, however, he seems to have gone off the rails. Much of his later work has fallen into the silliness of the techno-thriller. *Gridiron* (1995, U.S. title *The Grid*) is about a "smart" building that starts killing people. *Esau* (1997) has a plot with a scientific background and a search for a new species, but could have been written by a dozen other thriller writers and uses the same clichés; it is a book that badly wants to be a movie and has skimped on its print version.

In *The Five-Year Plan* (1997), Kerr returned to the Russian theme. The central plot concerns the smuggling of "dirty" money in yachts, to be laundered in Russian banks. Kerr has also edited *The Penguin Book of Lies* (1991).

KERSH, GERALD (1911–1968) Born in England, Gerald Kersh achieved notice before World War II with NIGHT AND THE CITY (1938), an atmospheric crime novel set in London. Kersh had worked at a number of odd jobs—in both senses—before achieving success as a writer; he was a bouncer, a baker, and a professional wrestler. He served in World War II and produced films for the army. After the war he emigrated to the United States and lived in New York, but he continued to write fiction set in England, an example of which is PRELUDE TO A CERTAIN MIDNIGHT (1947). *Night and the City* was published in an American edition in 1946.

Kersh wrote several hundred short stories and was known for his macabre and bizarre flair and wild imagination. He was influenced by GOTHIC fiction, DICKENS, and other models of the previous century. The world his characters inhabit can be at the same time grimly realistic and nightmarish and fantastic. Karmensin, a thief and adventurer, was a series character in a number of stories. Some of Kersh's stories were collected in *Nightshade and Damnation* (1968).

KEYS TO TULSA, THE (1989) A crime novel by Brian Fair Berkey. The protagonist is a film professor at the University of Tulsa, Richter Boudreau, who has a weakness for young women and likes to get high on whatever is available. The entire story takes place during a week. Boudreau has a relationship with Vicky, a childhood sweetheart who is married to Ronnie, a Vietnam vet with a heroin problem. Ronnie is upset because, after he fronted Boudreau four ounces of dope, Boudreau spent all the money he made from it and owes the potentially violent Ronnie $500. The spark of the tale is that Ronnie suggests that Boudreau can do him a "favor" to make good on his debt: to use his media contacts to help Ronnie implement a blackmail scheme involving murder.

Brian Fair Berkey was a complete unknown when he published this highly acclaimed novel. He had been working as a carpenter while he wrote it. It could be compared to the work of James CRUMLEY and Charles WILLEFORD.

KEY TO NICHOLAS STREET, THE (1952) A novel by Stanley ELLIN in which five different narrators report on events on Nicholas Street in the town of "Sutton," not far from New York City. The first narrator, Junie, is a domestic worker in the home of the Ayres family, living at 161 Nicholas St. She also does work for the woman next door at 159, the beautiful red-headed commercial artist, Kate BALLOU. Mr. Ayres also paints, and Ballou gets him to "update" his style and paint geometric pictures of his garage. Mrs. Ayres is a straightlaced practical woman who does not approve of Ballou, and tries to make up for what she considers her husband's family's spinelessness. Trouble starts when the scruffy but irresistible ne'er-do-well Matthew Chaves, who has been dating Ballou, gets a job on a riverboat in town. He starts seeing the Ayres's daughter, Bettina, a twenty-one-year-old teacher—a sheltered schoolmarm type. Chaves virtually moves in, splitting his time between 159 and 161. With two "bad" (i.e., dangerously exciting) characters like Ballou and Chaves living next door to each other, murder becomes inevitable. Ellin shows sex and violence mixing turbulently under the somnolence of fifties suburbia.

KIENZLE, WILLIAM X[AVIER] (1928–) Born in Detroit, William Kienzle has based his series about Father KOESLER on his own twenty-year experience as a parish priest in Detroit —the major difference being that Kienzle later left the priesthood in order to get married. Since leaving the priesthood he has taught "contemplative studies" at the university level. Kienzle's writing career began with journalism; he edited a Catholic magazine for many years while he was still a priest. Although his novels use the church as a focus and plot source, the other aspects of the stories (the subplots, the romance, the sex, the lurid crimes) are straight out of the THRILLER genre.

KILLED BY SCANDAL (1962) A novel by Simon NASH involving the amateur detective and academic Adam Ludlow. The case begins innocently enough: another professor approaches Ludlow to ask him to give a lecture on Sheridan's *The School for Scandal* two weeks before the play is due to be presented. Ludlow reluctantly agrees. He is further talked into attending the dress rehearsal by the Haleham Green Thespians. An argument between the chairman of the group and his daughter's fiancé erupts in the middle of the play, and, not long after, a corpse is discovered. Ludlow is witty and amusing, with a characteristically dry sense of humor. *Killed By Scandal* is one of the best theatrical mysteries. At the same time, Nash executes his version of the "donnish" mystery with a light hand.

KILLER INSIDE ME, THE (1952) A novel by Jim THOMPSON. Although many "psycho killer" books have been written in the past few decades, *The Killer Inside Me* is an early, very believable treatment of that type of character. What is more, it is written from the first person point of view, and tells the story with a scary, absolute honesty. Deputy Sheriff Lou Ford of Central City, Texas, knows that he suffers from "the sickness," which causes him to kill repeatedly, but he cannot control his urges. The story is extremely violent, with Ford describing his murders in detail. But in the end this explicitness is justified.

Ford is ordered by his boss, Sheriff Bob Maples, to inquire into the activities of Joyce Lakland, a woman suspected of prostitution. He later develops a relationship with her. What makes the book the more disturbing is that, although Lou Ford is crazy, the mesmeric power of the narrative forces the reader to empathize with him at certain points.

"KILLERS, THE" A short story by Ernest HEMINGWAY, which appeared in the collection *Men Without Women* (1927), which also included such well-known Hemingway stories as "Hills Like White Elephants." "The Killers" is the closest Hemingway came to a mystery—a crime story about two gangsters who enter a diner where Nick Adams is eating. They take control and wait for the arrival of Ole Andreson, an ex-prize fighter whom they plan to murder. Adams manages to get to Andreson's rooming house to warn him, but finds him too sunken in apathy to even try to avoid his fate. This grim fatalism is the flip-side of the jadedness of enervated luxury that fascinated Hemingway's friend FITZGERALD.

KILLING OF KATIE STEELSTOCK, THE (1980) A novel by Michael GILBERT. In this and other works, Gilbert seems to be interested in the changes that have overtaken Britain in recent decades, particularly the alteration of the public perception of the policeman, from protector to potential enemy. Many social themes are treated, though not in depth—perhaps from their sheer number. The generation gap, the dissatisfaction of youth, the media, and homosexuality are among the issues touched upon.

The twenty-five-year-old victim is found dead at the end of the annual dance in Hannington, near Oxford. She is a television star, a country girl who had made good. Despite her success, she was keen on maintaining the family image and came back to Hannington whenever she could, living in a cottage adjacent to the family mansion. Yet, in London she appears to have been quite ruthless, a tough character who knew what she wanted and got it. One of the things she liked was to have power over others; another was sex. Chief Superintendent Charlie Knott has a choice of explanations for her death: it could have been her highly inflammable old boyfriend, or in her climb to the top she might have stepped on some unknown fingers a little too hard. At this point the equivocal image of the policeman comes into play. Knott is up for a promotion and wants to solve the case as quickly as possible, and chooses the easy way over the hard, despite the fact that an innocent man might be punished. The trial scene is vivid, and Gilbert's surprise ending is so well constructed as to all but guarantee satisfaction.

KILLING MISTER WATSON (1990) A historical novel by Peter Mathiessen (1927–). A naturalist and explorer, Mathiessen won the National Book Award for *The Snow Leopard* (1978), about Nepal, and *At Play in the Fields of the Lord* (1965), a surrealistic story set in the rain forest that shows the author's interest in traditional cultures untouched by industrialization. *Far Tortuga* (1975) is a novel about the death of turtle fishermen in the Caribbean.

With *Killing Mister Watson,* Mathiessen set out not to produce "docufiction" but to interpret and "reimagine" conflicting accounts of a legendary figure in southwestern Florida. Told in the voices of narrators who knew the man, it gives the illusion of historical fact. Edgar J. Watson was an outlaw wanted for murder when he came to the Thousand Islands, a remote part of Florida north of Cape Sable, in the early 1890s. He is an impressive man, and a dangerous one; with hair "the color of dried blood," blue eyes, and a sandy beard, he looks like a strange devil. Watson is an example of one of the most fascinating creatures of crime fiction, the man who rises above or simply ignores the rules that enchain those around him, for whom people are tools and for whom action, including violence, is untrammeled by conscience. How Watson gains power over the community, and how the people eventually turn against him, is a study of character as a volatile element in society. Mister Watson is that thing, an ambiguous personality, that promises both freedom and disaster to those who, lacking the man's ambition and dark passion, find it impossible to buck convention.

Mathiessen has gone on to make Watson the focus of an epic trilogy, but this first novel remains the most impressive and unified.

KILLING TIME (1967) A crime novel by Thomas BERGER. Publishers seem to enjoy giving away the plot details on the jacket of books they want to have read as "literature," as if to distance the books from "genre writing." In fact, there is more of the mystery in *Killing Time* than one is led to believe. The story begins with Betty and Arthur Bayson finding Betty's mother and sister, along with their male border, brutally murdered in their New York apartment on Christmas Eve. Betty's estranged (and deranged) father soon arrives. A Bowery bum, he is immediately suspected and taken into custody by detective James Shuster.

Berger uses the familiar device of the converging plot lines that bring about a resolution. The narration alternates between the fortunes of the family members and the story of a previous border, a young man of imagination and enthusiasm for life but with a very important screw loose somewhere in his mind. Berger's satire is apparent in the fact that the killing has the deepest meaning for the murderer, while for others it quickly becomes an opportunity, with Betty and her father selling their incoherent life stories to vulgar newspapermen. Betty lives in a selfish fantasy world and hardly notices that Arthur is mentally disintegrating.

KING, C[HARLES] DALY (1895–1963) C. Daly King was born in New York City and graduated from Yale University. He was an artillery lieutenant in World War I, and after the war worked in business before returning to school. With an M.A. in psychology from Columbia and a Ph.D. from Yale, King became a practicing psychologist and wrote several books on the subject, including *Beyond Behaviorism* (1923) and *The Psychology of Consciousness* (1932). He wrote very few mysteries, but those he did produce have been admired—and sometimes harshly criticized for not living up to their reputation. If nothing else, King was original. King's "obelist" series (an obelist is variously defined as an insignificant person or a person who is suspicious) combines weird settings with unusual plot twists and variations on the usual structure of the mystery. King's intellectual interests sometimes overwhelm his narratives. In *Obelists at Sea* (1932), four psychologists investigate a MURDER AFLOAT, and their interpretive differences receive more attention than the crafting of the story itself. OBELISTS FLY HIGH (1935) is a book about a surgeon who is threatened with death while on his way to save his brother's life (the brother is the secretary of state). King gave the book a list of clues and a prologue and epilogue; he also told the story in reverse, putting the prologue at the back. This novel has been universally rated King's best work. *Arrogant Alibi* (1938), one of his last books, was set in Hartford, Connecticut, during a flood. King's series detective in the novels is Inspector Lord, who is assisted by a psychologist. King wrote his last mystery novel, *Bermuda Burial,* in 1940, and then gave up fiction.

The most curious of King's books is *The Curious Mr. Tarrant* (1935), which was published only in England. A collection of short stories, it was included in QUEEN'S QUORUM. One of the stories was based on the mystery of the MARY CELESTE.

KING, LAURIE R. (1952–) American author of socially relevant mysteries about San Francisco homicide detective Kate Martinelli. King was educated at the University of California at Santa Cruz and the Graduate Theological Union in Berkeley. Her first novel about Martinelli, *A Grave Talent* (1993), won an EDGAR award. Martinelli is a lesbian; her partner, Lee, is critically injured in the first book. The sensational plot involves a woman, Vaun, who was imprisoned for strangling a six-year-old girl. She has served her time and now lives in an artistic enclave outside of San Francisco. Vaun is being hailed as the greatest living woman artist, but is also suspected in a new series of murders of girls in the area.

In *With Child* (1996), Martinelli and Lee have separated. Martinelli takes the precocious twelve-year-old daughter of a friend on a trip to the Northwest to visit Lee but loses her in an area where a series of child murders have taken place. Another book in the series is *To Play the Fool* (1995), a quite different novel based on the unlikely premise of a modern "fool" who can speak only through Shakespearean quotations. *A Letter of Mary* (1996) is the third in a series of Sherlock HOLMES pastiches. King pairs Holmes with a woman, Mary Russell, and the plot revolves around their relationship. The story is set in 1923 and involves ARCHAEOLOGY.

KING OF THE RAINY COUNTRY (1966) One of the most admired novels by Nicholas FREELING. Its title is taken from a Baudelaire poem. In the novel, Inspector VAN DER VALK operates like a private detective, "unofficially" investigating the disappearance of Jean-Claude Marschal, heir of enormous business interests. The most salient fact is that the man's wife, Anne-Marie, doesn't seem to want him to be found. Both husband and wife are former professional downhill skiers, as well as being handsome and rich. Van der Valk's investigation takes him to Cologne and Innsbruck, as Van der Valk's big hunch (making a link between two disappearances that have no apparent connection) turns the case into an international incident. Part of the book's popularity must stem from the fact that it is atypical of the brooding, gray atmosphere of the Van der Valk series, and that it launches him into a sphere of crime that seems glamorous in comparison with books like BECAUSE OF THE CATS (1963).

The structure of the book, too, is noteworthy. It begins with Van der Valk lying in a field in southern France not far from the Spanish border. The revelation of why he is there, when it is made, comes as a jolt. Then, retrospectively, the story is told from the point when Canisius, a high official of Marschal's company, arranges the highly irregular investigation even though no crime has as yet been committed. Freeling makes a conscious distinction between how the story would usually have been written and how things happen in the "real" world Van der Valk inhabits: "A private detective, the beautiful unspoiled darling of a detective story, would of course have leaped straight into bed with Anne-Marie, given Canisius the old right hook straight to the shiny false teeth, beaten Marschal by two seconds flat on the Olympic *piste* at Innsbruck, had the *tanzmariechen* fall in love with him instead, and been paid ten thousand pounds on the last page by grateful millionaires." That is not of course how it happens. The author's preoccupation with class shows up in the unreality of Marschal's flight—expensive cars bought and then abandoned, a helicopter stolen, people bribed—as seen from Van der Valk's practical middle-class perspective. The rainy country—which, to Freeling, stands for Baudelaire's idealistic self-torturing—has a fatalistic, oppressive boredom even for the rich, and it eventually reaches out to touch them all.

KING, RUFUS (1893–1966) Rufus King was born in New York City, which was the locale of his best known series of mysteries, about Lieutenant Valcour. Valcour is the son of a Parisian detective, and is unusual among fictional sleuths in that he starts out as a private detective and then joins the police force (of New York City). Valcour appeared in *Murder by the Clock* (1929), the first of eleven novels to feature him.

King's varied life included working in a silk mill, serving with distinction in the artillery in World War I, spending a period at sea, and tramping around Buenos

Aires. He was also a graduate of Yale University. His work combines some very effective writing with scenes that could have been written by anybody and the use of stock devices. King at one point lived on a farm in upstate New York, an area he also used as a setting. *A Variety of Weapons* (1943) is set at Black Tor, a spooky mansion in a remote part of the Adirondacks. The young photographer Ann Ledrick is sent there to photograph the pet ocelots of the wealthy Estelle Marlow. She meets the family patriarch, a dying old man whose life has been shattered by a murder twenty years before. King pulls a rabbit out of a hat when he has Estelle learn something startling about herself that explains her involvement in the case.

In *Murder in the Willett Family* (1931), featuring Lieutenant Valcour, King gave another picture of a family of eccentrics. In this case Valcour investigates the shooting of the young Arthur Willett, which is only the first in a series of murders. *Murder on the Yacht* (1932), another Valcour mystery, is an example of MURDER AFLOAT. Valcour joins a group of people on the luxurious *Crusader* because he believes a killer is on board.

Rufus King was also a short story writer of some note. In the twenties, he wrote about Reginald De Puyster, a millionaire playboy detective. Toward the end of his life, King wrote many stories about Stuff Driscoll, who works in southern Florida; they were collected in *Malice in Wonderland* (1958), *The Steps to Murder* (1960), and *The Faces of Danger* (1964). King also wrote murder dramas for the stage, and one of his books, *Museum Piece No. 13* (1946), was filmed by Fritz LANG. Lieutenant Valcour also appeared in screen adaptations.

KIRK, MICHAEL See KNOX, BILL.

KLAW, MORRIS See ROHMER, SAX.

KLIMO In a series of stories by Guy BOOTHBY, "Klimo" is the mysterious consulting detective who lives at No. 1 Belverton Terrace, Park Lane, next door to the master thief Simon CARNE. In fact, they are the same person, which enables Klimo to investigate the crimes he commits as Carne.

KNIGHT'S GAMBIT (1949) A collection of stories by William FAULKNER, focusing on the investigations conducted by Gavin STEVENS. They are stories of tragedy as much as crime, and include MONK, in which a meaningless sentence provides a clue to an injustice; "Hand Upon the Waters," about the drowning of a deaf-and-dumb man; and "Tomorrow," an intergenerational story about the strength of kinship that could have provided the plot for a novel. "An Error in Chemistry" is frequently anthologized.

KNOTT, DEBORAH See MARON, MARGARET.

KNOTT, FREDERICK M. P. (1918–) The English playwright Frederick M. P. Knott wrote the stage version of *Dial M for Murder* (1952), which was the basis for the 1954 film by Alfred HITCHCOCK. In the film, Grace Kelly played the wife who is being set up for murder by her husband. Knott's other mystery plays are *Write Me a Murder* (1961) and *Wait Until Dark* (1966). Knott was awarded special EDGARS for the first two plays; *Wait Until Dark* also became a successful film (1967). He emigrated to the United States at the time of the Hitchcock film and worked in Hollywood.

KNOX, BILL (WILLIAM) (1928–) The Scottish mystery author Bill Knox has made a mark in several mystery subgenres. He is a cross between a traditionalist and an experimenter, and writes better than many other authors who are similarly prolific. For many years, Knox alternated stories about Webb CARRICK, of the Fisheries Protection Service, with a more conventional series about Detective Chief Inspector Colin THANE. These are only the best known of his many series; he has written three others under pseudonyms.

Born in Glasgow, Knox worked as a newspaper journalist and later moved into television; later in his career, he hosted a well-known crime program. His first novel, *Deadline for a Dream* (1957), was a Colin Thane mystery and benefited from the author's experience as a crime reporter. Webb Carrick first appeared in *The Scavengers* (1964). While the Thane books are straightforward and PROCEDURAL, Knox took more of a risk in the Carrick series, simply because of the oddity of having a chief officer aboard a patrol ship as the detective. While the Thane series convincingly recreates the gritty Glasgow streets, the Carrick books are saturated with the mists of the highlands and evoke the harsh and beautiful Scottish coast and islands. Knox is not Sir Walter Scott, however, and his romanticism is tempered by realistic depictions of the routine of running a ship and the dreariness of some of the remote hamlets Carrick visits. Knox is praised for his plotting, as well as for his vivid use of "local color"—in his case a demeaning term, since Knox presents the Scots realistically, and the dialogue makes their language felt without descending into the "wee laddie" caricature. On the other hand, many authors do a better job than Knox at handling romance and sex. Knox also has a fondness for chases, whether by sea or land, and rousing conclusions.

Knox's boldest experiment was Talos Cord, a combination fixer and secret agent most improbably employed by the United Nations. The half-dozen Cord books, published under the pseudonym Robert MacLeod, were written in the sixties and seventies, the heyday of the Cold War and not coincidentally of the spy novel. Shortly after abandoning Cord with *Path of Ghosts* (1971), Knox began writing (as Michael Kirk) another maritime series, this one about a marine insurance investigator named Andrew Laird. Under the MacLeod pseudonym (and in the United States as Noah Webster), he produced a series about Jonathan GAUNT, who works for a little-known but real agency called the Queen's and Lord Treasurer's Remembrancer. Gaunt is based in Edinburgh, rival city of the author's native Glasgow, but his cases take him to various exotic locations. Knox has also written several non-series mystery thrillers.

KNOX, MONSIGNOR RONALD [ARBUTHNOTT] (1888–1957) Ronald Knox was a British mystery author, a Catholic priest, and the creator of the detective Miles BREDON of the Indescribable Life Assurance Co. But he is still most remembered for his promulgation (in the introduction to an anthology of detective stories) of ten rules of FAIR PLAY. Knox was also an early critic of and authority on Sherlock HOLMES, beginning with his "Studies in the Literature of Sherlock Holmes" (1912).

Knox's mysteries are today considered average at best; although a highly educated man and a gifted student—he graduated from Eton, and then took his B.A. at Oxford in 1910—he was not a master of the craft of fiction. Knox tended to imitate Conan DOYLE. Bredon smokes a pipe, like Holmes, but is married and lacks Holmes's restless energy. Knox is probably the only author to be ordered to stop writing mystery stories (by his bishop). After being ordained an Anglican priest in 1912, he was the chaplain of Trinity College at Oxford. In 1917, Knox converted to Roman Catholicism (he was later ordained in that church); he wrote about his conversion experience in *An Apologia* (1917). Given that his father and grandfather were Anglican bishops, his decision was momentous. He became Catholic chaplain at Oxford, a post he held for more than twenty years. His worldly pursuits included a stint in military intelligence during World War I as well as his mystery writing.

Like Dorothy L. SAYERS, Knox also wrote books on religious subjects. His attitude toward the mystery genre, however, was anything but pious; his work has a good deal of humor and even PARODY (for example, in his tongue-in-cheek Sherlockiana).

After his premature forced retirement from the mystery genre, Knox continued his work as a Catholic apologist. Accomplished in both Latin and Greek, he undertook English translations of the Old (1949–50) and New Testaments (1944).

The Viaduct Murder (1925) was Knox's first mystery. It begins with the discovery of a body on a golf course. Bredon was introduced two years later, in *The Three Taps*. Among the Bredon stories are THE FOOTSTEPS AT THE LOCK (1928), about two cousins (one of whom is about to become an heir) who go on an ill-fated canoe trip; *The Body in the Silo* (1934; U.S. title *Settled Out of Court*), possibly his best mystery; and *Double-Cross Purposes* (1937), involving a treasure hunt in Scotland. Evelyn Waugh's *The Life of the Right Reverend Ronald A. Knox* (1959) was the first biography of Knox. Knox was a member of the DETECTION CLUB and contributed to their SERIAL NOVELS. He was also elected to the Royal Society of Literature.

KOESLER, FATHER ROBERT William X. KIENZLE's Father Koesler seems to be modeled after the muscular, tough Father BREDDER rather than the more saintly cleric-sleuth Father BROWN. The Koesler series is set in Detroit, where the priest finds some rather HARD-BOILED mysteries to solve. The writing of the series is below the level of other practitioners of the subgenre; Kienzle tries to liven up his stories with sex, profanity, and other *noir* borrowings, and has a predilection for multiple murders and serial killers. In the first novel, *The Rosary Murders* (1979), a murderer is preying on priests and nuns. Kienzle tends to draw out his stories and sometimes abuses the reader's patience. This novel was filmed in 1987 with Donald Sutherland in the role of Koesler. Whereas some other priest sleuths get involved in cases that have nothing to do with religion, Koesler's usually have some doctrinal angle.

In the latter part of the series, Kienzle has added a secondary character, Father Tully, who is half African American and half white. His half-brother is Lieutenant Alonzo "Zoo" Tully, whose parents were both African American; his father abandoned the family. In *The Greatest Evil* (1998), Koesler is about to retire and Tully is his apparent successor.

BIBLIOGRAPHY Novels: *Death Wears a Red Hat* (1980), *Mind over Murder* (1981), *Assault with Intent* (1982), *Shadow of Death* (1983), *Kill and Tell* (1984), *Sudden Death* (1985), *Deathbed* (1986), *Deadline for a Critic* (1987), *Marked for Murder* (1988), *Eminence* (1989), *Masquerade* (1990), *Chameleon* (1991), *Body Count* (1992), *Dead Wrong* (1993), *Bishop as Pawn* (1994), *Call No Man Father* (1995), *Requiem for Moses* (1996), *The Man Who Loved God* (1997).

KOHLER, HERMANN See JANES, J. ROBERT.

KRAMER, LIEUTENANT TROMP Series character created by James MCCLURE. Kramer is a lieutenant of the Murder and Robbery Squad in Trekkersburg, South Africa. He is assisted by Bantu Detective Sergeant Mickey ZONDI. Kramer is realistically drawn: he has sympathy for blacks as individuals, but he doesn't question the racism of a social system that oppresses them. As a detective, he is clever but often obsessed by his hunches. Zondi is the more rational of the two, and his activities always seem to produce results. There are other series characters, primary among them Doc Strydom, the phlegmatic coroner with a disturbing sense of humor. Kramer has an affair with a widow, and his solicitous care for her and her son is an ongoing subplot.

From its inception, the series has been a critical success. *The Steam Pig* (1971) was awarded a Gold Dagger by the British CRIME WRITERS' ASSOCIATION. McClure won a Silver Dagger in 1976.

In *The Gooseberry Fool* (1974), a man is found brutally murdered in his kitchen. Zondi is dispatched to Natal to search for the victim's houseboy, where he witnesses an eviction, is attacked by a crowd of Zulu women, and is almost killed. Meanwhile, a superior bent on humiliating him sends Kramer to investigate a car accident. Once again it is Zondi's detection that wins the day. The author's taste for violence and morgue humor is less abated than refined as the series goes on. *Snake* (1975) begins with a highly original murder but is actually the most disjointed of McClure's narratives.

At his best, McClure satisfies both the reader's interest in seeing the reality of South Africa and the demands of the genre. *The Sunday Hangman* (1977) gives a plain description of everyday life in Trekkersburg, which is all the more scary for being matter-of-fact and not a political denunciation. A criminal whom Kramer had known is found hanged, but in all too professional a manner, leading the lieutenant to treat it as a faked suicide. Then a series of hangings stretching back over a period of years is uncovered, so that a question arises as to whether the recent crime is related. It is a very tight story in terms of clues and plot, more classic than PROCEDURAL. The motivations might not be believable were the book set in another developed country, but McClure shows how the South African setting makes people think and act as they do; this could be called critical psychology, and is one of the main appeals of McClure's work. *The Blood of an Englishman* (1980) is the most fully realized novel in the series. The hideous corpse of RAF veteran Bonzo Hookham is found in the trunk of his sister's car, shot and with hands so tightly bound that bones are broken; this turns out to be an important clue. Meanwhile, antique dealer Archie Bradshaw is shot in the collarbone and claims a giant with a silver gun attacked him. The weapon in both cases is the same gun. The novel is most procedural and most involved, with Strydom excellent and darkly acerbic, for example in the extensive description of his autopsy of Bonzo ("zealous rummaging had left his colorful contents in gay disorder").

BIBLIOGRAPHY Novels: *The Caterpillar Cop* (1972), *The Artful Egg* (1984), *The Song Dog* (1991).

KRISTEVA, JULIA (1941–) The French psychoanalyst and theorist Julia Kristeva has recently turned to the mystery genre. Kristeva was born in Bulgaria but emigrated to France in 1966, where she became a protégé of Roland Barthes. Kristeva's work is eclectic and combines several influences, including Jacques Lacan, Michel Foucault, semiotics, feminist theory, and structuralism. Among her works is *Desire in Language: A Semiotic Approach to Literature and Art* (1980).

Unfortunately, in her crime fiction this considerable sophistication goes for naught, for Kristeva does not know how to construct a mystery story. Her first book about her series character, Stephanie Delacour, was *Le vieil homme et les loups* (1994; tr *The Old Man and the Wolves*). The stories are set in a seaside town in the fictional nation of Santa Varvara. Delacour is a journalist and amateur sleuth. In the second book, *Possessions* (1996; tr 1998), she finds the decapitated body of her friend, translator and heiress Gloria Harrison. This scene is dramatic enough, but it becomes the pretext for one of Kristeva's endless digressions, this time on the theme of headless bodies in history and art: "Are we supposed to believe that women, eternal mourners over castrated corpses, can feel passion only for a guilty [*sic*] phallus? Maybe . . . the topped and gory remains of Gloria Harrison, lying at my feet exposed to the impotent curiosity of the police captain of Santa Varvara, shocked as much as it intrigued me. And try as I might to call painters and sculptors, the Terror and '93 to the rescue, such cultural digressions solved strictly nothing." The last statement, at least, can be agreed with. The mystery story does not so much unfold as get blurted out by the narrator in between postmodern homilies.

KUTTNER, HENRY (1914–1958) Born in Los Angeles, Henry Kuttner studied psychology and English literature at the University of Southern California. Kuttner began writing in the late thirties; he became acquainted with one of his fans and they later married. Kuttner moved to New York City, and he and his wife, a romance novelist, collaborated on several works. Kuttner also served in World War II. His books include *Man Drowning* (1952), *Murder of a Mistress* (1957), and *Murder of a Wife* (1958). The last was published posthumously. Kuttner's mysteries appeared under the names Will Garth and Lewis Padgett. He published science fiction under his true name. Kuttner's interest in psychology worked its way into his fiction, and he wrote a series about the psychoanalyst and sleuth Michael Gray.

Bill Blackyeard, writing in *The Armchair Detective* in 1983, claimed that *Man Drowning* was actually written by the African American science fiction writer Cleve Cartmill (1908–1964). Cartmill's own story is bizarre: after he published the novelette *Deadline* in 1944, a story that described the building of an atomic bomb a year before one was actually detonated on Japan by the United States, he was visited by agents who confiscated the correspondence between Cartmill and the publisher of *Astounding,* the sci-fi magazine in which the story appeared.

KYD, THOMAS (pseudonym of Alfred Bennett Harbage, 1901–1976) Alfred Harbage was a Shakespearean scholar at Harvard University, so it is not surprising that he chose the name of an Elizabethan dramatist as his pseudonym. His witty mysteries set in the university milieu are reminiscent of Michael INNES, though the flavor is distinctly American. Kyd's novels include *Blood is a Beggar* (1946), a professorial novel in which Biddle, who is showing his film about sound effects to his class, is shot in the projection room during the presentation. *Blood of Vintage* (1947), BLOOD ON THE BOSOM DIVINE (1948), and COVER HIS FACE (1949) are other novels.

Harbage was born in Philadelphia and received his B.A. (1924), M.A. (1926), and Ph.D. (1929) from the University of Pennsylvania. He taught there and at Columbia before joining the English faculty at Harvard University, where he spent most of his career. He wrote a number of books of Shakespearean criticism. He is known for the wit and deftness of his style, and his mysteries involving academics are without pretension.

L

LACY, ED (pseudonym of Len Zinberg, 1911–1968) Born in New York, Len Zinberg was a prolific author of mystery short stories and novels. Under the Lacy pseudonym he published what is considered the first series about a black private detective. Lacy himself was white, and gained some of his knowledge of African American culture through his interracial marriage.

Lacy was a correspondent for *Yank* magazine during World War II, and was also a boxing enthusiast. His first major success was the novel *Walk Hard, Talk Loud* (1940), which he published under his own name. It dealt with boxing (as did many of his works), and was made into a play in 1944. He went on to write a total of twenty-eight books, many of them PAPERBACK ORIGINALS.

Toussaint Moore was introduced in ROOM TO SWING (1957), which won the EDGAR award for best novel. Moore is a war veteran who hesitates between the security of taking a job as a postal worker (egged on by his socially ambitious girlfriend) and the excitement of detective work; the pay is better, even though the work is dirtier. In addition to the two Toussaint Moore books, many of Lacy's other novels also dealt with black characters. He wrote during the height of the civil rights movement, and the novels reflect Lacy's liberal ideas. Lee Hayes, another black detective, appeared in two novels, *Harlem Underground* (1965) and *In Black and Whitey* (1967).

Lacy also wrote mysteries in a more conventional vein; *Devil for the Witch* (1958) is about a policeman on vacation with his family on Long Island who discovers that a car accident was really a murder. Lacy's sensitivity to ethnic stereotypes runs all through his work; so also does his sense of humor. *The Hotel Dwellers* (1966) is a very funny novel set in the Hotel Times Terrace in New York City. Howie, who has suffered a heart attack, lets his wife run their concession stand inside the hotel—a perfect vantage point for observing the people who live and work in the Times Terrace. Lacy keeps introducing new and interesting characters while also dropping hints about a series of robberies plaguing the hotel.

LAG A British expression for an ex-convict. The term originally referred to the transportation of criminals to Australia, then came to mean an ex-convict returned from there (the "ticket of leave" man), and finally, to criminals generally.

LAIDLAW, JACK See MCILVANNEY, WILLIAM.

LAM, DONALD The partner of Bertha COOL in the series of novels by Erle Stanley GARDNER. Lam balances Cool's blustery, grasping ways with his suave and professional approach to cases and people. Slightly built and almost elegant, he is a tough guy in the forties manner, somewhat like an Archie GOODWIN without the quick wit and repartee. He also lacks the stature; Lam is described as short, a mere featherweight. Still, he is enormously successful with women and sometimes rumbles with his adversaries. Lam is a fairly rare type, an Americanized version of the elegant British detective of the WIMSEY style. He is "the class," as a contemporary saying would have it.

Lam was kicked out of law school for having devised a scheme for a "perfect" murder and then telling someone about it, who then put it into practice. He lands a job with Bertha Cool's agency and in a few books becomes a partner—a pretty quick rise for a little guy. Gardner never seems to have defined finally the relationship between Cool and Lam; sometimes he humiliates her, sometimes she humiliates him, sometimes she humiliates herself. Despite its sexism, in the series Donald always seems secretly to be shamming, Bertha to be exulting.

BIBLIOGRAPHY See COOL, BERTHA.

LANDRU, HENRI-DÉSIRÉ (1869–1922) The notorious serial murderer Landru was sent to the GUILLOTINE for killing eleven people, probably only a small fraction of his total victims. Landru's was the real-life version of a scenario often employed in fiction, that of a psychopath who entraps his victims through classified advertisements in the newspaper. His case was a sensation in Paris for three years, from his arrest in 1919 until his execution. But what was most remarkable about the Landru case was that no trace of any of his victims was ever found.

Landru's father was a factory worker who committed suicide in the Bois de Boulogne in 1912. A former choirboy, a lover of music and flowers, Landru was married and had a grown son when he started taking out matrimonial advertisements in Parisian newspapers. Estranged from his family, he met and charmed a number of lonely women, became engaged to each of them in succession, and, luring them to his villa in Gambais, killed them (probably by strangulation) and disposed completely of their bodies. The murderer chose women who had no family and therefore would not immediately be missed. Landru was a dealer in furniture and estates, and would sell off the belongings of his victims. Once, he made only four francs from one of his killings. Landru was trapped by his own acquisitiveness and meticulousness. His warehouse revealed such items as hair pieces, identity papers, and treasured belongings of women who had vanished. In his notebook were found accounts of trips to Gambais—two tickets outbound, one returning.

Only a few slivers of bone were ever found at Gambais, but police were able to prove that Landru was always the last to have seen the women; and, after seeing him, they had disappeared entirely from the earth. Carefully dressed and a punctilious observer of bourgeois manners, Landru entertained Paris at his trial with behavior that was bizarre given the circumstances, scolding the judge at one point for revealing that a female witness's age was greater than what she had claimed. The total number of women to whom Landru had been affianced was 283.

LANE, DRURY A character created by Ellery QUEEN. A retired Shakespearean actor, Drury Lane takes up detection and receives encouragement from Inspector Thumm of the New York City police department. The eccentric Lane has gone deaf and been forced to give up the stage. He lives on an estate called The Hamlet, surrounded by servants with Shakespearean names dressed in Elizabethan clothes. He amuses himself by solving mysteries. His first appearance was in THE TRAGEDY OF X (1932). The authors went on to write a "Y" and a "Z" in this series; having reached the end of the alphabet, they gave the last book the title *Drury Lane's Last Case* (1933).

Although overshadowed by the fantastic success of the mysteries about the character Ellery QUEEN, the Lane series is funny, better written than many of the Queen books (some of which are ponderous and heavy-handed), with ingenious and complex plots solved through real deduction—performed by Lane, not Thumm. *The Tragedy of X* contains a devious nicotine murder, and Drury Lane is every bit as clever in his thinking as Ellery Queen, and far more entertaining than the rather stuffy Ellery of that period. In *The Tragedy of Y* (1932), the main suspect seems to be a dead man; there is also a question involving syphilis.

In *Drury Lane's Last Case,* a bibliophile mystery and the best book of the series, a strange bearded figure appears in the office of Inspector Thumm and gives him an envelope, which he is told not to open unless the strange man fails to call him on an appointed day each month. Meanwhile, the Britannic Museum has been robbed and a valuable Shakespeare manuscript stolen—and Thumm's friend Donoghue, a museum guard, has disappeared. When the strange man fails to call, Thumm duly opens the envelope in the presence of Drury Lane. Among the suspects in the series of crimes are Hamnet Sedlar, a new curator, and Dr. Ales, a bibliophile.

BIBLIOGRAPHY Novels: *The Tragedy of Z* (1933).

LANE, FELIX The central focus in Nicholas Blake's THE BEAST MUST DIE (1938), Lane is an example of that familiar trope, the character who is himself a mystery writer. Blake, however, gives him two other important narrative roles, one of them being that of an amateur sleuth. Lane's diary comprises the first third of the book.

LANE, PAUL A character in a series of novels begun by Frances and Richard LOCKRIDGE with *Night of Shadows* (1962). Richard Lockridge continued to write about Lane after his wife's death in 1963. Paul Lane, however, never really got to stand on his own again.

Lane is a New York City police detective, and in the second book in the series he appears with Captain Bill Weigand, who was the friend of Pam and Jerry NORTH. Thereafter, Lane was a character in the series of books about Bernie SIMMONS, an assistant district attorney.

BIBLIOGRAPHY Novels: *Quest of the Bogeyman* (1962).

LANG, FRITZ (1890–1976) The son of a Viennese architect, Fritz Lang became one of the most important film directors in history, making vital contributions to the development of German expressionism and to FILM NOIR in the United States. After attending art school in Germany and France, Lang traveled for several years as an itinerant artist, visiting countries in Europe, Asia, and the Pacific. Lang's early film, *The Spiders (Der Spinnen,* 1919–1920), used a theme that would appear in his work again and again, the diabolical criminal out to conquer the world (which would also be one of the main plots of the James BOND series, four decades later). He returned to this idea in *Dr. Mabuse (Dr. Mabuse der Spieler,* 1922), introducing his famous NAPOLEON OF CRIME figure. Mabuse reappeared in *The Testament of Dr. Mabuse* (1933), which was banned by the NAZIS, who evidently saw versions of themselves in the evil criminals of the film—in spite of which Dr. Joseph Goebbels personally invited Lang to work on Nazi propaganda. (The story goes that Lang left the country the same day.) The other films from Lang's German period include *M* (1931), about a child murderer (played by Peter Lorre in his first screen role) who stalks Düsseldorf. Lang's films focused on the psychology of criminality and the corruption and violence of society; but while critics have often emphasized these sociological and political overtones, Lang was also a great artist of suspense, terror, and dread.

Lang eventually landed in Hollywood, where he found the studio system incalculably more restrictive than the situation in German cinema. He continued to make films with social themes, which were brutally cut and mutilated by the studio machine. Among his crime-related films of this period are *You Only Live Once* (1937), about a criminal accused of a crime of which he ironically is innocent; *Man Hunt* (1941), a version of Geoffrey Household's ROGUE MALE (1939); *Secret Beyond the Door* (1948), based on a novel by Rufus KING; and the classic *The Big Heat* (1953). Lang also made *Ministry of Fear* (1944), based on Graham GREENE's novel of the same name. *Beyond a Reasonable Doubt* (1956), another crime film, was Lang's last work in the United States before he left Hollywood in disgust. After his return to Europe, he made a final Mabuse episode, *The Thousand Eyes of Dr. Mabuse* (*Die tausend Augen des Dr. Mabuse,* 1960), which was also his last film. The atmospheric effects of Lang's movies and his ability to depict a climate of evil—as opposed to HITCHCOCK's situation tragedies—is unequalled.

LARCH, MARIAN A character created by Barbara PAUL. A New York City police detective, Larch has antecedents in the PROCEDURAL mystery (for example, Lillian O'Donnell's Norah MULCAHANEY), but resembles other feminist detectives introduced around the same time as Larch. The first Marian Larch mystery was *The Renewable Virgin* (1984). Larch is promoted to sergeant in *You Have the Right to Remain Silent* (1992) and reassigned to the Ninth Precinct on the Lower East Side. Although the author likes to involve Larch's romantic and personal relationships in the story, she can also be quite graphic and HARD-BOILED: the *You Have the Right to Remain Silent* case involves the grisly murder of a mother of four (stabbed forty-three times), and the subsequent execution-style killing of handcuffed victims. Despite the grimy setting, the victims turn out to be employees of an uptown laser technology firm. *Fare Play* (1995) takes place three weeks after Larch has been promoted to lieutenant. Seventy-year-old Oliver Knowles, a retired executive, is shot point-blank on a cross-town bus; no motive is apparent for this obviously professional hit. Paul throws in some curious details: no one on the packed bus saw the killer; the only picture in the victim's wallet is of a white Persian cat; a woman has been having Knowles tailed, but she has disappeared.

BIBLIOGRAPHY Novels: *He Huffed and He Puffed* (1989), *Good King Sauerkraut* (1989), *The Apostrophe Thief* (1993), *Full Frontal Murder* (1997).

LAST GOOD KISS, THE (1978) A novel by James CRUMLEY. C. W. SUGHRUE is hired to trace the missing and drunken writer Abraham Trahearne by the man's divorced first wife, Catherine. Catherine Trahearne is sexy, elegant, and ice-cold. She lives with Trahearne's ancient mother, Edna, across the creek from the house where Trahearne lives with Melinda, his second wife. The plot is episodic and keeps one bleary eye loosely focused on Trahearne's dysfunctional extended family.

Having chased Trahearne across several states, Sughrue finally runs him to earth in a Sonoma bar, drinking with an alcoholic bulldog named Fireball Roberts. Sughrue then gets drawn into another case, the search for Betty Sue Flowers, the daughter of the owner of the bar where Trahearne eventually turned up. The dog, the man, and his convertible Caddy all seem like elements from a comic Hollywood movie, but the underlying sordidness is as debilitating as it is real. The grown-up children trying to have fun, sticking out their tongues at their own disillusionment, seem almost noble compared to the self-pitying losers encountered along the way. There is a symbolic quality to the monotonous cycle of hope and disillusionment; like Sughrue's diet of "speed, codeine, beer, and Big Macs," there is something radically pointless about the simultaneous pursuit of stimulation and anesthesia. It is another of Crumley's comments on a culture that is dopey, in both senses of the word. Crumley dedicated the novel to Richard HUGO.

LAST SEEN WEARING . . . (1952) This novel by Hillary WAUGH is sometimes considered the first PROCEDURAL novel. Whether or not it is the first, it is still the best. In Waugh's hands, the "procedural" is not an exact reproduction of an investigation. Waugh walks a fine line between realism—reporting every move made by the police, dead ends, failed theories, and all—and making the narrative go. He succeeds brilliantly, eliding or glossing over some tricky maneuvers; for example, when the District Attorney is asked to call up a suspect's family in Virginia and, without identifying himself or arousing suspicions, find out when the person got home for Christmas break, how does he do it? We never know, beyond that the D. A. calls back half an hour later with the goods. If it is a great procedural, it is also a very atypical one. The taut and stripped-down story contains no romantic subplots, no weird characters (like the DEAF MAN, for example), no diabolical designs, no twisted motives, no melodramatic scenes, and little violence (only one person ever draws a gun)—only a sad, tragic, and completely believable crime.

The story is set in western Massachusetts at a women's college and could be modeled on one of several; which one doesn't matter. Lowell Mitchell, an eighteen-year-old freshman at Parker College in Bristol, disappears in the middle of the day on March 3. The search for her yields nothing. Waugh describes the hunt over several states, the agony of the family, and the complete competence of the impassive chief of police, Frank Ford. Ford is a marvelous character, a tough thirty-three-year veteran of the force who chides and instructs his right-hand man, Sergeant Cameron—a "college boy" with eighteen years on the force. But all the relationships in the novel are just there, not foregrounded or worked up; character, which is present in abundance, appears through action rather than being ladled on like a sauce after the basics are down. The story reads well as a mystery, and Waugh plants a big clue in plain sight. One can only wish that Ford and Cameron had become series characters (Fred FELLOWS, Waugh's series character, is a detective in rural Connecticut and is similar to Ford).

Last Seen Wearing (1976) is the second book in the Inspector MORSE series.

LATHAM, GRACE AND INSPECTOR PRIMROSE

A detective team created by Leslie FORD. Unlike the NORTHS and the CHARLESes, this pair of sleuths is unmarried. The series began in 1934 with *The Strangled Witness,* in which Primrose, a World War I veteran, operates alone. He first encounters Latham in *Ill-Met by Moonlight* (1937); she is an attractive widow and amateur sleuth, a perfect biography for a HAD-I-BUT-KNOWN (HIBK) heroine. While Ford's early work is definitely influenced by the HIBK school, and Grace Latham does get into situations from which she has to be rescued by her male partner, the series evolved over the years. The novels are set in Washington, D.C., with a few jaunts to other places, as in *Reno Rendezvous* (1939; British title *Mr. Cromwell Is Dead*) and *The Philadelphia Murder Story* (1945). The latter was perhaps a play on the title of the famous Cary Grant film of 1940. In Ford's novel, the murder takes place at the offices of *The Saturday Evening Post,* which had published many of her stories. In *Three Bright Pebbles* (1938), Latham appears by herself. Primrose is always accompanied by Sergeant Phineas Buck, his old friend from the war who tries to preserve their masculine camaraderie. He has little to fear from Latham, it seems: when Primrose proposes, the widow turns him down. Modern readers may find Primrose's attitude to his partner condescending; it embodies the usual feminine = intuition / masculine = rationality dichotomy of much of the fiction from its period.

Devil's Stronghold (1948), the next-to-last book, takes place mainly in California. Grace's son and a friend have gotten out of the service following World War II and are working in a glamorous hotel and trying to promote a new star. A girl dies in a fall down the stairs in the hotel; another guest, an aging silent film star, seems to be involved. The book hinges on the idea of concealed identities. The hotel seems to be based on the Garden of Allah, the former mansion of silent film star Alla Nazimova. Her career waning, she turned the mansion into a hotel in 1927 and it quickly became notorious. Various stars used it to conduct affairs or hide out during messy divorces.

BIBLIOGRAPHY Novels: *The Simple Way of Poison* (1937), *False to Any Man* (1939; British title *Snow-White Murder*), *Old Lover's Ghost* (1940), *The Murder of a Fifth Columnist* (1941; British title *A Capital Crime*), *Murder in the O.P.M.* (1942; British title *The Priority Murder*), *Siren in the Night* (1943), *All for the Love of a Lady* (1944; British title *Crack of Dawn*), *Honolulu Story* (1946; British title *Honolulu Murder Story*), *The Woman in Black* (1947), *Washington Whispers Murder* (1953; British title *The Lying Jade*).

LATHEN, EMMA

(pseudonym of Mary Jane Latsis, 1917?–, and Martha Henissart, 1927–1997) The two American writers who make up "Emma Lathen," an amalgam of their two names, chose as a hero a kind of character who more commonly turns up in mystery fiction as a villain: the Wall Street bigwig. John Putnam Thatcher's description makes him sound like a ringer for the actor John Forsyth; he is tall, silver-haired, and has obvious taste and class. Thatcher is a vice president with Sloan Guaranty Trust, the third-largest investment banking house in the country. His cases involve deals that go sour, bureaucratic back stabbing, and other shenanigans of high finance. The books could be called banking procedurals, because the two authors had long corporate careers themselves and depict the relationships within that select community with humor and authenticity.

Latsis and Henissart met while they were at Harvard. Latsis, an economist, worked for the UN Food and Agricultural Organization for a time, while Henissart worked in banking until the early seventies. They decided to keep their identities secret because of their fear of repercussions at their jobs. Surprisingly, the situation of women in the business world is not one of their major themes. Thatcher naturally has no trouble fitting in, with his patrician manners and appearance. The authors have, however, favored topical themes, as can be seen by comparing the titles and dates of such novels as *Death Shall Overcome* (1966) and *Double, Double, Oil and Trouble* (1978). Lathen has won two awards from the British CRIME WRITERS' ASSOCIATION: a Silver Dagger for *Accounting for Murder* (1964) and a Gold Dagger for

Murder Against the Grain (1967). The first of the novels was *Banking on Death* (1961).

LATIMER, JONATHAN (1906 – 1983) Born in Chicago, Jonathan Latimer was the son of a lawyer father and a violinist mother. Among his ancestors was Colonel Jonathan Latimer, an officer on the staff of General George Washington. He attended school in Arizona and later graduated from Knox College in Illinois. In school he was known for his athletic ability and unruly behavior. He spent two summers bicycling in Europe and also worked on a ranch. He joined the *Chicago Herald-Examiner* and the *Chicago Tribune* in the early to mid-thirties as a crime reporter and met Chicago gangland figures (including Al CAPONE). Around this time, he began writing his mysteries about Bill CRANE, which are scarcer today than works by other writers in the HARD-BOILED vein, but which did much to pave the way for them.

Like POE, Latimer was interested in the macabre, the uncanny, and the grotesque. In an essay on *The Lady in the Morgue* (1936), the Italian writer Alberto Moravia said that Latimer had "confronted frankly the necrophilia" that Moravia felt was a "poorly disguised but genuine" streak in American literature (and culture) going back to Poe, "the discoverer of American necrophilia." Moravia felt that an obsession with the dead human body was the source of the mystery genre. Certainly Latimer exploited the overlooked possibilities of the corpse as a *character;* this least likely person becomes in his books a bizarre and even humorous presence. Sometimes, it gets up and walks.

In the late thirties, Latimer went to California and began working as a screenwriter. He produced screenplays for THE BIG CLOCK (1948), THE GLASS KEY (1942), and other films. He also wrote for the Charlie CHAN series. During World War II, Latimer served in the Navy. After the war he continued as a screenwriter and also wrote more than fifty scripts for the Perry MASON television series. His written work never again attained the reputation of his Bill Crane novels. In 1955, he published *Sinners and Shrouds,* which returned to the Chicago setting with a story about a newspaperman who finds a nude female corpse in his room. Latimer's other non-series works include *Dark Memory* (1940), about hunting in the Congo; *Black Is the Fashion for Dying* (1959), in which he satirized Hollywood; *Solomon's Vineyard* (1941), a p.i. novel set in St. Louis; and *The Search for My Great Uncle's Head* (1937), which he published under the pseudonym Peter Coffin.

LAUGHING POLICEMAN, THE (1970) A novel by Maj SJÖWALL and Per WAHLÖÖ. Although it features Martin BECK, much of the detecting is done by other members of the staff, each of whom chips away at a very baffling case. A Stockholm city bus is found one rainy night with a cargo of bullet-riddled corpses. Nothing unites the passengers that could explain the mass murder, but one of the victims is a young colleague from the homicide division. Beck seems depressed throughout; he has taken to sleeping on the sofa to get away from his wife and stays up late smoking cigarettes and reading. The press attacks the police for their incompetence, but there are no clues to the identity of the murderer. The gloomy weather of the Swedish winter, the commercialization of Christmas, Vietnam War protests, and the low morale of the much-criticized police leave Beck and his harassed colleagues with not much to laugh about. The atmosphere and ingenious plotting of the novel make it one of the best in the series; the dead policeman turns out to be one of the most interesting and well-drawn characters. *The Laughing Policeman* is one of the few foreign language books to win an EDGAR award.

LAURA (1943) A novel by Vera CASPARY, which became famous as a result of the 1944 Otto Preminger film version featuring Gene Tierney and Dana Andrews—and the popular theme song. It is also far and away the author's best book, thanks to a clever plot. Highly atmospheric, it is an intoxicating portrait of New York City in the forties. The most memorable character is the columnist Waldo LYDECKER, a Walter Winchell type.

The story is broken up into five separate narrations, a device that allows Caspary to maintain suspense and interest and to selectively release details. In the first part, Lydecker describes how Detective Mark McPherson came to question him about the death of Laura Hunt, an advertising executive. Laura was engaged to Shelby Carpenter, a gallant Southern gentleman. Carpenter is also questioned by McPherson, along with Aunt Susan Treadwell. As the detective gets deeper into the case, it becomes clear to Lydecker that McPherson has fallen in love with the dead woman. In the second part, the detective himself takes up the narration. *Laura* has since been dramatized several times, including a television adaptation by Truman CAPOTE.

LAURANCE, ANNIE See DEATH ON DEMAND.

LAWLESS, JANE See GAY MYSTERIES.

LAWRENCE, HILDA (1906–) Hilda Lawrence had a brief career as a mystery writer in the 1940s. She wrote three mysteries about detective Mark East: *Blood upon the Snow* (1944), *A Time to Die* (1945), and *Death of a Doll*

(1947). Lawrence was born in Baltimore, the daughter of a U.S. congressman. She wrote about the South in the non-series novel *The Pavilion* (1946; also pub as *The Deadly Pavilion*), in which the innocent orphan Regan Carr answers an invitiation from her elderly cousin to come to live with him. Upon arrival she finds that he is already dead, the latest in a string of mysterious deaths in the family. Lawrence's writing reflects the formulas of the then-popular romantic suspense subgenre, but her books were critically well received.

LEACOCK, STEPHEN [BUTLER] (1869–1944) Born in England, Stephen Leacock emigrated with his family to Canada when he was only six and grew up to be one of that country's best-known writers. A humorist, economist, novelist, and parodist, he wrote several amusing spoofs on mystery and detective fiction.

Leacock attended the University of Toronto and the University of Chicago, and began teaching economics and political science at McGill University in Montreal in 1903. Leacock's *Elements of Political Science* (1906) was considered an important work, but it was his humor that proved most enduring. *Literary Lapses* (1910) was the first of a series of entertaining books that included *Arcadian Adventures with the Idle Rich* (1914) and *Frenzied Fiction* (1918). *Sunshine Sketches of a Little Town* (1912) is his best-known novel. The collection *Nonsense Novels* (1911) contained "Maddened by Mystery; or, The Defective Detective," a Sherlock HOLMES parody. Another Leacock humorous mystery story is "An Irreducible Detective Story" (1916). Leacock also wrote "Twenty Cents' Worth of Murder," a humorous essay in criticism advising writers what not to do in a detective story, which was collected in *Too Much College* (1940).

LEAGUE OF FRIGHTENED MEN, THE (1935) A mystery by Rex STOUT. It is not only the best of the Nero WOLFE mysteries, but is consistently chosen as one of the best mysteries of all time. Paul Chapin was crippled in a college prank at Harvard, and his guilt-ridden classmates have been paying him conscience money ever since. They approach Wolfe because they believe that Chapin has gone mad for revenge and is now killing them off one by one. The detection is superb, including Wolfe's devastating and humorous demolishing of the league's theory about the final murder ("[X] took the pistol from his desk and went to the foyer. Chapin, there waiting for him, took the pistol from him, shot him four times, turned out the light, threw the pistol on the floor and then got down on his hands and knees to look for it in the dark. What a picture!"). Wolfe's confronting of the league with Paul Chapin himself, Stout's insight into the often hypocritical behavior of those with a reputation to protect (and who do so through infamy) and his glance at Stephen Crane's "An Experiment in Misery" give the book a multi-dimensionality that some of the bread-and-butter Wolfe books lack.

LEAMAS, ALEC The central figure of John LE CARRÉ's novel THE SPY WHO CAME IN FROM THE COLD (1963), Alec Leamas is a study in contradictions. Although as a spy he cannot be honest with others, he takes pride in being brutally honest with himself. Leamas says he believes in nothing; he just tries to be a good (i.e., effective) player in what he knows is a rotten game. But the irony is that Leamas shows that it is impossible to be a consistently negative man, and he fails to achieve the true nihilism he cherishes. He disparages himself as one of the "crummy people," but keeps trying not to be one. At one point in the book an opponent accuses him of "selling loyalty"; Leamas's final, futile gesture is an attempt to give it away, but to someone whom it can no longer help.

LEAPHORN, JOE A Navajo detective created by Tony HILLERMAN. In the award-winning book DANCE HALL OF THE DEAD (1973), Leaphorn is a lieutenant. By the time of *The People of Darkness* (1980), the first Jim CHEE mystery, he is a captain. Both detectives combine their knowledge of Navajo culture with standard sleuthing techniques, but Leaphorn is more purely a cop than Chee. This is partly because he is a generation older than Chee and has a more pragmatic outlook, whereas Chee wants to become a medicine man, a goal Leaphorn finds nostalgic. Leaphorn holds a Master's degree in anthropology from Arizona State; he intended to become a professor but moved back to the reservation after he met his future wife, also a Navajo, on the campus.

Leaphorn is renowned for his toughness, his unorthodox playing of hunches, and his results. In the tough-guy tradition, Hillerman plays up to the reader less than in the Chee books, as though not caring whether one likes Leaphorn or not. Leaphorn's irreverence toward traditional Navajo culture is surprising, and is particularly effective when used as a foil for Chee's opposite attitude.

A Thief of Time (1988) involves parallel cases pursued by Leaphorn and Chee, but the book is really Leaphorn's. His wife Emma has died and he is planning to retire, but he becomes involved in the search for a missing anthropologist who specializes in ceramics. The story becomes deeply involved in the culture and fate of the Anasazi, the native people who preceded the Navajo and whose civilization mysteriously died out in the fourteenth century. Although protected, the thousands of

Anasazi sites are pillaged by thieves who sell the ceramics for high prices to unscrupulous collectors. Chee pursues the much more mundane (and humiliating) theft of a backhoe out from under his nose.

Leaphorn has several other cases with Chee, including SKINWALKERS (1988). In *Sacred Clowns* (1993), though Chee has made detective grade, he is still treated as a novice by Leaphorn, who sends him off on the mundane job of finding a truant schoolboy while Leaphorn investigates a teacher bludgeoned to death. But while Chee is attending a Hopi ritual, one of the participants, a clown, is murdered. *The First Eagle* (1998) concerns an outbreak of bubonic plague on the reservation.

BIBLIOGRAPHY Novels: *The Blessing Way* (1970), *Listening Woman* (1978), *Talking God* (1989; with Chee), *Coyote Waits* (1990; with Chee), *The Fallen Man* (1997).

LEASOR, [THOMAS] JAMES (1923–) James Leasor has modeled his series character, Dr. Jason LOVE, on himself. Leasor was interested in medicine as a young man; served in the British army during World War II; and is a collector of antique cars—all of which could also be said of Love. Leasor was born in Kent and rose to the rank of captain during the World War II, serving in the Far East. After the war he attended Oxford. He entered the field of journalism and worked for the *Express* in London for a number of years. The first book in the Jason Love series was published in 1964, when the revolution in the spy novel initiated by AMBLER, LE CARRÉ, and DEIGHTON was in full swing, and after the explosive success of the James BOND series. Leasor's work owes more to Ian FLEMING than to the other writers mentioned, and to an even greater extent is modeled on the much earlier John BUCHAN and the Edwardian generation of gentleman spies. Leasor did, however, borrow the new flexibility in subject matter (greater sex to go with the traditional violence) from the sixties spy novel.

LEAVENWORTH CASE, THE (1878) A novel by Anna Katherine GREEN. Subtitled *A Lawyer's Story,* the book benefited from Green's knowledge of the law (her father was a prominent lawyer). In fact, so accurate were its details that Yale University used the book in law classes to show the misleading nature of circumstantial evidence. The book was also a popular bestseller; in fifteen years, 750,000 copies were sold. *The Leavenworth Case* has been called the first detective novel written by a woman, but Seeley REGESTER had already published one in 1867.

The Leavenworth Case set the pattern for Green's other novels, introducing Ebenezer GRYCE and using the upper strata of New York City society as a setting. The wealthy Horatio Leavenworth lives with his two nieces, Mary and Eleanore, in his Fifth Avenue mansion. Mary is his favorite: she stands to inherit all when he dies—which he soon does. Leavenworth is found shot to death at a table in his library. Suspicion of course falls on the nieces. Gryce's detection is based on clues, rather than inspiration, and the novel has surprisingly solid underpinnings despite its romantic subplot. The writing, however, is a generic example of nineteenth-century popular fiction and is not distinctive.

LEBLANC, MAURICE (1864–1941) Born in Rouen, France, Maurice Leblanc studied law until his burgeoning writing career got in the way. Leblanc worked as a journalist and crime reporter, and in 1906 he was commissioned to write a crime short story for the journal *Je sais tout.* The story, "L'Arrestation d'Arsène Lupin," introduced the gentleman thief and detective Arsène LUPIN, about whom Leblanc would eventually write some sixty short stories and novels. The first collection of stories was entitled *Arsène Lupin: Gentleman-Cambrioleur* (1907). Leblanc continued writing about the character into the thirties, and received France's highest honor, the Lègion d'Honneur, for his work.

Early in the series, Lupin is a criminal like RAFFLES; later on he decides to use his abilities to help the police. There are many resemblances between the stories of Leblanc and his contemporary, Gaston LEROUX (see MYSTERY OF THE YELLOW ROOM, 1907), and the question of which are the better has been often debated. Julian SYMONS called Leblanc's writing "slapdash," but the verve of Lupin and his adventures redeems it. Not surprisingly, this kind of writing holds up better in short stories than in novels, the demands of which the style cannot sustain. Another problem is Lupin's invincibility, like that of the GENIUS DETECTIVES of the period; it reduces the suspense and, to maintain it, invites absurdities.

Leblanc lived a quiet and private life, so much so that it was thought at one point that he had died in 1926. He actually died during World War II, either in Paris or Perpignan. His other writings included plays.

LE CARRÉ, JOHN (pseudonym of David John Moore Cornwell, 1931–) Like his fellow Englishman Graham GREENE in the previous generation, John Le Carré has written espionage novels that have been accorded the status of literature. Also like Greene, Le Carré had first-hand experience on which to base his books. Beginning in 1959, he worked with the British foreign service in West Germany. He has also won every major award in the genre, and the book that made his reputation, THE SPY WHO

CAME IN FROM THE COLD (1963), has the status of a modern classic.

Le Carré attended Oxford and then taught French and Latin at Eton before entering the foreign service. Not long after, he published his first book, *Call for the Dead* (1961). This novel also featured George SMILEY, who plays a peripheral but important role in *The Spy Who Came in From the Cold* but later was made the center of the series of novels that is considered the core of Le Carré's work. The early books, however, are not to be dismissed; in particular, it should be noted that A MURDER OF QUALITY (1962) is a detective story (an excellent one), not a spy story, set in a boys' school.

Le Carré's work is an exploration of the spiritual emptiness and the lack of integrity of bureaucratic man (men in particular; women are rarely presented as villainous). The characters have the same disease as those in Greene's *A Burnt Out Case,* published the same year as *Call for the Dead:* an emotional leprosy, a preparedness for death not because they are brave but because they have already been eaten away from the inside (the best example is that of LEAMAS). But unlike Greene, whose heroes often find redemption (if not in faith, then in their faith that there could be faith), Le Carré has no ready antidote. Without belaboring the point, Le Carré has demonstrated the sociological implications of Cold War culture, which was inherently a spy culture; subterfuge, lying, and the sacrifice of people like chess pieces in the service of the "good cause" erodes whatever goodness the cause had. He implies that a democracy cannot survive with a cult of illegality and secrecy at the top. It is not only the members of the intelligence services who are seen as compromised, if not nullified; a couple watching television in their apartment are viewed as pathetic for "the crabbed delusion of their dreams."

The Little Drummer Girl (1983) is about an actress who is used as a pawn in the Arab-Israeli conflict. It and *The Russia House* (1989) were fast-paced books, and are more conventional thrillers; both were made into films. Since the Cold War has been declared over, LeCarré's work has changed, and he has suffered like other thriller writers from the need to invent new enemies or seek refuge in the implausible. *Our Game* (1995) finds new uses for a retired spy. *The Tailor of Panama* (1996) is about a tailor who dresses all manner of leaders and thugs, with the metaphor of clothing as a deception being heavily stressed.

LeCarre's *Single & Single* (1999) revolves around shady dealings between Western financial markets and the power groups, including criminals, in the chaotic states of the former Soviet Union. The novel begins with an extended and horrifying execution scene, viewed from the perspective of the victim. The plot focuses on the missing venture capitalist Oliver "Tiger" Single.

LECOQ, MONSIEUR A character created by Émile GABORIAU, based on the real detective François VIDOCQ. Lecoq has already some of the characteristics that Conan DOYLE would borrow for Sherlock HOLMES: he is egotistical, cocky, and able to make astounding deductions from very little physical evidence. He has a boss, the Chief of the Sûreté, Gévrol; their relationship could be the model for that between MAIGRET and his superior, Coméliau.

Gaboriau did make one vital change in concocting his hero, however; although early on he admitted that Lecoq, like Vidocq himself, had once been a criminal, he later explained this away as a mistake. Thus, the later Lecoq could become a prototype for the noble policeman of crime fiction, while his original, the ambiguous Vidocq, would inspire more roguish heroes.

Lecoq is one of several sleuths and not even the leading one in his first appearance, *L'Affaire Lerouge* (1866; tr *The Lerouge Affair*), a case in which he follows behind TABARET. In *Monsieur Lecoq* (1869), the balance has shifted: now Lecoq is the main sleuth and Tabaret is in the background (in both cases, Gévrol is disdained as a fool). THE LITTLE OLD MAN OF BATIGNOLLES (1876) is sometimes mistakenly listed as a Lecoq case.

BIBLIOGRAPHY Novels: *Le Dossier No. 113* (1967; tr *File No. 113*), *Les Esclaves de Paris* (1868; tr *The Slaves of Paris*), *Le Crime D'Orcival* (1871; tr *The Mystery of Orcival*).

LEE, GYPSY ROSE The first mystery to appear under the name of the famous stripper Gypsy Rose Lee was called, appropriately, *The G-String Murders* (1941). The book was looked upon favorably by BARZUN and TAYLOR. *Mother Finds a Body* (1942) was a second, less successful effort. Both books are thought to have been written by Craig RICE.

LE FANU, [JOSEPH] SHERIDAN (1814–1873) Born the son of a Protestant clergyman in Dublin, Ireland, J. S. Le Fanu is one of the least famous great figures of fiction. He did as much to develop the mystery, horror, and suspense genres as any nineteenth-century novelist, and won such later admirers as Anthony Trollope, M. R. James, Elizabeth Bowen, and Dorothy L. SAYERS. Yet while his work is reprinted from time to time, he is overshadowed by the great Victorian eminences Charles DICKENS and Wilkie COLLINS.

It has been said that Le Fanu wrote his mystery novels on the same desk on which his great uncle, Richard Brinsley Sheridan, wrote his brilliant comedies of manners. It has also been said that he wrote his books in bed on scraps of paper. Le Fanu's life was exceptional, tragic, and romantic—the kind to inspire myths. He has been compared to Edgar Allan POE, with whom he shared a consuming interest in the GOTHIC; other similarities may also have been assumed. Le Fanu was long thought (apparently incorrectly) to have had a secret drug dependency. His wife was afflicted with a neurotic disorder and was said to have died of a hysterical attack.

Le Fanu's early career was exceptional. He began writing poetry as a child and completed a long poem at fourteen. He entered Trinity College, Dublin, in 1833, and began contributing to the *Dublin University Magazine* as a student. By the time he became a barrister in 1839, Le Fanu had become so successful as a writer that he never actually practiced law. In the same year, he bought *The Warden* and the *Evening Packet*, and had an interest in the *Evening Mail*. He eventually combined the three newspapers under the latter name, and was the owner and primary contributor from then on. He used the *Evening Mail* as a vehicle for the Conservative party and it became a powerful paper. Yet despite his conservative allegiances, Le Fanu fell under suspicion during the 1848 rebellion in Ireland.

Despite his previous writing experience, what really made Le Fanu into a novelist was the death of his wife in 1858. The uxorious Le Fanu, who had enjoyed a gay social life and was accounted a brilliant conversationalist, never recovered from the loss and in fact became a recluse and "saw no one and went nowhere." Instead, his energies went into a dozen novels of tremendous imagination and darkness. As one critic wrote, "he is a master of the supernatural, as only a man obsessed by grief can be."

Le Fanu's fiction writing began in earnest when he became an editor of the *Dublin University Magazine* in 1861 (he later bought it, too), in which he would serialize eight of his novels, including UNCLE SILAS (1864), the work for which he is best known. Le Fanu is sometimes criticized as verbose, but it is more the pace of his novels than the writing that gives this impression—though pace is of course influenced by turgid passages, drawn-out scenes, and morbid theorizing that leads nowhere. His mysteries are well constructed and make use of the mood and props of gothic horror novels. He was adept at creating striking or innovative scenes; in *The House By the Churchyard* (1863), a drunken doctor opens the skull of a man beaten to unconsciousness, hoping to revive him so that he can identify his assailant. In *Checkmate* (1871), a criminal disguises himself through plastic surgery, one of the earliest examples of that theme in crime literature. Of all his novels, *Checkmate* most closely resembles a modern mystery novel, and shows a detective following the trail of a murderer and the use of dental and medical evidence for identification. Le Fanu's other principal works include WYLDER'S HAND (1864), in which a naval lieutenant disappears, is thought murdered, and then strangely seems to reappear; and *Uncle Silas*, which relates the slow, tense development of the relationship between a menacing guardian with a shameful past and his innocent but helpless niece. (It is impressive that he wrote these two novels in the same year.) His earlier story, "Passage in the Secret History of an Irish Countess" (1838), was the source for *Uncle Silas* and is the first instance of the employment of the LOCKED ROOM puzzle, predating Poe. *Guy Deverell* (1865), a tale of dueling and revenge, focused on the mysterious "Green Room" at Marlowe Hall, and contained one of Le Fanu's best characters, the sinister Monsieur Varbarriere, an old enemy of Sir Jekyl Marlowe, the owner of Marlowe Hall.

Le Fanu also wrote highly respected ghost stories, but mostly kept the supernatural out of his mystery novels (with one exception). His story "Green Tea" was included by Dorothy Sayers in her landmark anthology of detection and horror.

LEFT LEG, THE (1940) A novel by Phoebe Atwood TAYLOR, one of her Leonidas WITHERALL mysteries published under the name Alice Tilton. The story is set in Dalton, Massachusetts; Meredith Academy is a thinly veiled version of Philips Academy. Witherall, who deals in antique books, goes to examine a Shakespeare first Folio, and on the way home runs into a woman on the bus; after an argument, he is ejected and left by the side of the road. The woman turns out to be Myrna Riley, also known as the Scarlet Wimpernel because of the red wimple she wears. A blonde ingenue without much brains, she is funny for her many malapropisms. Witherall's troubles are only beginning; he is accused of a theft from Potter's store, and when the school headmaster is murdered, Witherall's galoshes are found by the body. Witherall and Link Potter have to rough up some cops in order to escape and find the "green man"—a green-clad figure with a harp who actually stole the money from Potter's store.

Like the other Witherall books, *The Left Leg* is pure farce. The plot piles one ridiculous incident on top of another. Myrna's purse is stolen; Witherall runs into Judy Brett at an auction, where the Wimpernel also shows up; the Reverend Evelyn falls in love with her; a photographer has pictures of the "green man"; and, of course, there is the mystery of the leg that was stolen. Maintaining the pace means everything in this kind of farrago, and *The Left Leg* is one of the more entertaining Witheralls.

LEHANE, DENNIS (1965–) Dennis Lehane acquired an instant reputation in the HARD-BOILED mystery field when he published his first novel, *A Drink Before the War* (1994), which won a Shamus Award. It launched a series set in the tough Boston community of Dorchester featuring two private detectives, Patrick Kenzie and Angie Gennaro.

Lehane was quickly compared to Raymond CHANDLER and Ross MACDONALD, which has become as routine for hard-boiled American detective novelists as "move over, Christie and James" on the covers of English mysteries. In fact, the series is a cross between a hard-boiled mystery and a soap opera; the "will-they-or-won't-they" sexual subtext is something that could have been learned from *Moonlighting* or *Hunter.* There are also a good number of those supposedly distinguishing props that have piled up in mystery fiction since the eighties. Thus, the detective has to have a cool (vintage Porsche Speedster) and a coolly uncool (Plymouth Volare) car, an office in the steeple of a church, and a .44 magnum, because he is a very bad shot and needs a big gun to hit things (though a sawed-off shotgun would be more effective). Kenzie's unattainable love is balanced on the other side by Bubba, his psychopath-with-a-heart-of-gold friend—a figure also becoming de rigeur after Walter MOSLEY's inimitable "Mouse" Alexander.

A Drink Before the War (1994) balances drunken cops, child abuse, racism, and war in the streets. In *Darkness, Take My Hand* (1996), the detectives become involved in a mob case. In *Sacred* (1997), they are hired by an ailing billionaire to find his missing daughter. *Gone, Baby Gone* (1998) deals with kidnapping. Despite the trimmings, Lehane knows what he is writing about, having grown up in Dorchester. He vividly recreates the feeling of Boston, particularly its hidden menace. He attended several colleges and graduated from Eckerd College in St. Petersburg. After a fellowship to the Graduate Writing Program at Florida International University in Miami, he moved back to Boston and did odd jobs while writing.

LEHMANN, KLAUS The "incorruptible" and deadly efficient head of the Nazi police who turns out to be British superspy Tommy HAMBLEDON with AMNESIA, and thus an unwitting early example of the MOLE in spy literature.

LEM, STANISLAW See SCIENCE FICTION MYSTERIES.

LEONARD, ELMORE (1925–) Elmore Leonard is one of the most widely admired and certainly most successful crime writers. He was born in New Orleans and served in the Naval Reserve before attending the University of Detroit, graduating in 1950. He settled in Detroit, which would later be the setting for many of his novels. Although he is known as a crime writer, his first fiction was in the Western genre. His first published story was "Trail of the Apache" (1951), published in *Argosy. The Bounty Hunters* (1953) was his first novel. Some of his Westerns from this period were made into films. Though he began writing in the early fifties, it was not until the late sixties that Leonard was able to start writing full-time and leave the advertising business, in which he had worked for more than a decade. Leonard had written scripts for educational films, and wrote a screenplay for Hollywood in the early seventies that he then novelized as *Mr. Majestyk* (1974). *The Moonshine War* (1969) bridged his early Western and his later crime work; set during PROHIBITION, it takes place in Kentucky and has to do with struggles between bootleggers.

It was really only in the mid-eighties that Leonard gained his wide reputation, based on several novels and their film adaptations. Reference works on crime and mystery fiction by Otto PENZLER (1976) and H. R. F. KEATING (1982) failed to mention him. *Stick* (1983) was made into a film starring Burt Reynolds; Leonard's fame skyrocketed after the movie version of *Get Shorty* (1990) was released. Like many writers who started out in television, Leonard's writing is facile and snappy; it exists mainly as dialogue, which has been praised for its "power" but is often pungently vulgar.

In a later series of novels, Leonard wrote about South Florida, frequently portraying the lives of street criminals, rich drug lords, corrupt businessmen, and policemen of varying degrees of honesty and brutality. Most of his characters have few redeeming qualities. Charles WILLEFORD wrote about the same setting and many of the same types of people, and most of what Leonard does Willeford did better.

Leonard has received several awards for his writing. *LaBrava* (1983) won an EDGAR. He received France's Grand Prix de Littérature policière for *City Primeval* (1980), in which a cop tracks down a savage killer. The International Association of Crime Writers gave him a Hammett Award in 1992.

LEONARDO'S BICYCLE (*La Bicicleta de Leonardo,* 1993; tr 1995) In this novel, which won the Latin American Dashiell Hammett Award, Paco Ignacio TAIBO II takes his conglomerated version of the detective novel to its conclusion. If "there is only one type of revenge, that which you take out on your own past," then the writer's revenge is upon history, which Taibo represents through alternating narratives. One concerns events in Barcelona in 1920, another the fall of Saigon in 1975, another the wanderings and lost works of Leonardo Da Vinci. Meanwhile, the crime writer José Daniel Fierro is laid up with a broken leg watching a Texan female basketball star on TV. She is later kidnapped and has her kidney stolen; Fierro simultaneously conducts an investigation and imagines a novel about it. Fierro is rather puerile and his quest is the least interesting part of the story, but as the novelist inside the novel he acts as an indispensable medium in whose mind the connections begin to be made and the mysteries to blend together. The well-researched account of the war between the unions and the bosses in Barcelona, when "the dead were calling out for the living to come and keep them company," is most gripping. In the middle of the story stands a diminutive tubercular journalist nicknamed "The Flea" and Fierro's grandfather, the anarchist Angel del Hierro. Taibo creates suspense by flashing images before the reader's eyes and whisking them away: Leonardo's mural disintegrating, melting, and dripping off the walls before his eyes; a CIA agent throwing a terrier from a helicopter, its "long growl fading away"; a corpse in a rowboat floating out in Barcelona Harbor at night. Ultimately, Taibo's style wears the reader down by its very saturation of images, and the narrative becomes clotted and the pace defeated by its over-richness.

"LEOPARD LADY, THE" (1939) This story by Dorothy L. SAYERS, which was included in the collection *In the Teeth of the Evidence* (1939), is neither about Lord Peter WIMSEY nor Montague EGG. The story prefigures Raymond Postgate's VERDICT OF TWELVE (1940) in its portrait of an unloved, imaginative young boy who is also heir to a fortune. Sayers also created an association, "Smith & Smith—Removals," which predates a very similar sinister group in Stanley ELLIN's more famous story THE BLESSINGTON METHOD (1955). When Arthur Tressider hears a mysterious message while standing in a bookstore, he thinks he is going mad. In a surreal encounter, the firm of Smith & Smith places a fortune within his grasp and bets that he is too weak to refuse. This simple short story presents a grimmer view of human nature than Sayers's more famous works and leaves the questions of justice and redemption more disturbingly open.

LEOPARD MAN, THE See WOOLRICH, CORNELL.

LEOPOLD AND LOEB In 1924, nineteen-year-old Nathan Leopold and eighteen-year-old Richard Loeb perpetrated a murder that gave a more than ordinary shock to the American public, because of the boys' backgrounds and the sheer pointlessness of the act. Leopold and Loeb were the sons of wealthy Chicago families and apparently without a care in the world when they decided to commit a crime for crime's sake. Loeb, who seems to have been the leader even though he was the younger, concocted a preposterous theory out of half-digested bits of Nietzschean philosophy that the two boys were superior beings, "supermen" who could commit a heinous crime with impunity. They lured a fourteen-year-old cousin of Loeb's named Bobby Franks into their car, where Loeb beat him to death. They dumped the body, poured acid on the face to hinder identification, and sent a ransom note to the boy's mother.

The crime was as dumb as it was motiveless, and the two were soon caught; Leopold's glasses were found near the crime scene, and the ransom note was traced to Leopold's typewriter. Well-heeled and well-educated (Leopold was at the time the youngest person ever to graduate from the University of Chicago), the pair of murderers were represented by the most famous lawyer of the era, Clarence Darrow. Their age and Darrow's passionate advocacy prevented them from being executed, but they drew life sentences plus ninety-nine years for the kidnapping. Loeb was stabbed to death in prison in 1936, and Leopold received parole in 1958.

Because of its crazy pseudo-philosophical justification, the Leopold and Loeb case was the kind of murder writers like to create but which hardly ever really happens. Not surprisingly, a number of authors have been fascinated by the murder. Patrick HAMILTON wrote a famous play based on the case, which Alfred HITCHCOCK in turn used as the basis for his film *Rope* (1948). James YAFFE's 1957 novel *Nothing But the Night* is still another fictional version of the case. Among the nonfiction treatments is Irving Stone's *Clarence Darrow for the Defense* (1941).

LEQUEUX, WILLIAM (1864–1927) English spy and mystery writer who probably based his spy stories on his own experiences. A journalist by trade, LeQueux was often said to be a spy, but was never exposed. (Perhaps, then, he was a remarkably *good* spy.) He was active during World War I but possibly was employed by the British Secret Service even before that. In any case, he played an indispensable role in the development of the subgenre and was one of the first modern spy novelists, producing his most famous books not long after Childers wrote THE RIDDLE OF THE SANDS (1903).

Born of a French father and an English mother, LeQueux traveled extensively in Europe in his youth. His first job was as a police reporter; he then moved into politics, again embarking on extended travel, which he loved. As a man committed to political principles—and involved in political intrigue—LeQueux's books, not surprisingly, have a didactic quality. Even in dealing with crime, he tends to moralize and pontificate against the criminal. These ideas may be admirable but they are also obvious. Some of his best work is contained in *Mysteries of a Great City* (1919); the titular subject is Paris, not London, and the tales concern the detective Monsieur Becq. *The Crimes Club* (1927) is a collection of short stories.

LeQueux's greatest successes were his spy thrillers. In *The Great War in England in 1897* (1894), LeQueux described a Franco-Russian invasion of Britain; Germany comes to England's defense. LeQueux seems to have been unable to make up his mind which Continental power was the real threat. In *England's Peril* (1899), it is France again. Hard on the heels of Childers, he predicted a German invasion in *The Invasion of 1910* (1906) (he drove thousands of miles, researching the island's weak points) and *Spies of the Kaiser* (1909). During the Balkan War in 1912–1913, LeQueux was a correspondent for the *London Daily Mail.* He also became an expert on wireless communication, and used it as the basis for several later books such as *Tracked by Wireless* (1922). He was also an automotive enthusiast, which spawned another group of novels including *The Lady in the Car* (1909). Some of his other espionage works are *Secrets of the Foreign Office* (1903) and *The Luck of the Secret Service* (1921).

Several of LeQueux's shorter pieces were collected and reprinted by Hugh GREENE, but LeQueux has long been mostly out of print. His output of novels was huge, totaling in the hundreds. They brought him wealth, which he used to procure villas in Florence and Signa. He also became chargé d'affaires for the Republic of San Marino. LeQueux's taste for espionage and luxury is reminiscent of E. Phillips OPPENHEIM. *Things I Know About Kings, Celebrities, and Crooks* (1923) is LeQueux's autobiography. *The Real LeQueux,* published in 1938, is a biography by N. St. Barbe Sladen. An older writer who encouraged LeQueux, whom LeQueux had met while he was a journalist in Paris, was the French master of naturalistic fiction Emile Zola.

LEROUX, GASTON (1868–1927) The French author Gaston Leroux is most remembered for *Le Phantome de l'Opera* (1911), which as a book was an indifferent success but years later became the basis for *The Phantom of the Opera* (1925), one of the most famous and startling films of all time, featuring Lon Chaney as a grotesque hermit who kidnaps the beautiful woman with whom he has fallen in love. Leroux wrote many mysteries and thrillers, the most important of which is *Le Mystere de la chambre jaune* (1907; tr THE MYSTERY OF THE YELLOW ROOM, 1908), which deployed many of the devices of the GOLDEN AGE mystery, such as the "least likely person" dodge and the LOCKED ROOM situation. This novel has a contested reputation: BARZUN and TAYLOR called it "unreadable" and Julian SYMONS thought it "preposterous," while John Dickson CARR praised it in his essay "The Grandest Game in the World" as one of the ten best mysteries of all time (at least up to 1946, when the essay was published—changes in postwar tastes might have led Carr to revise his opinion).

Leroux was born in Paris. He was a crime reporter and a war correspondent before he turned to mystery writing. Between 1894 and 1906 he sailed around the world reporting on his adventures as a correspondent. He witnessed the abortive revolution in Russia in 1905. Afterward, he began to write novels. The sleuth he introduced in *The Mystery of the Yellow Room,* Rouletabille, appeared in other novels, including *Le Parfum de la Dame en Noir* (1907; tr *The Perfume of the Lady in Black,* 1909), but none of these works were as successful as Leroux's first.

LESTER AFFAIR, THE (1974) A novel by Andrew GARVE. Part mystery and part political fable, it would make a fine cautionary tale for prospective presidents. It tells how in the space of eight days a progressive candidate for British prime minister goes from being a shoe-in to a man at whom people throw things during rallies, all over a sex scandal. The sex is not what brings down James Lester, but the public's belief that he has lied about it.

Lester and the progressives are twenty-five points ahead in the polls as the book opens. Then the candidate is handed a note by a woman, Shirley Holt, who says she had met Lester on Tobermory in Scotland the previous summer; more, she claims that Lester rowed in to the beach from his yacht, sunbathed in the nude with her, invited her back to his yacht, and had sex with her (consensually) that night. After Lester denies ever having met her at all, Holt is considerably put out, and offers corroborating details about the furnishings of the yacht. Lester claims that he tried to make a single-handed passage to Oban that night, experienced engine trouble, and turned back. Because there are no criminal charges, the investigation into who is lying and who is telling the truth falls to the newspapers—one of which, the *Post,* is run by Lester's old friend Oliver Tandy. The story is told largely through Tandy's daughter's diary and the bulletins sent in by reporters who are marshaled by Tandy to search Tobermory for witnesses, find the yacht (Lester had sold it after the summer), and delve into Holt's background. When a topaz that had fallen out of Holt's ring is found in the drain of the yacht's sink, it becomes a kind of locked-boat mystery; the yacht has been closed, padlocked, and under canvas since before Lester's candidacy was announced. The puzzle of motive is kept in suspense for most of the novel. Garve's handling of the nautical details (particularly the topaz problem) and the final surprises and ploys are excellent; the behavior of the politicians, the press, and the public, it almost goes without saying, are completely believable.

LESTRADE, INSPECTOR One of the SCOTLAND YARD detectives Sherlock HOLMES frequently encounters, and of whom he has a low opinion. Lestrade, however, often gets the credit for cases Holmes has actually solved. Lestrade is described as unattractive and rodent-like. In his first appearance, in A STUDY IN SCARLET (1887), he is "sallow," "rat-faced," and "ferret-like," with the dark eyes of an animal. Later, perhaps, the author felt more warmly about him, because he is then described as a "small, wiry, bulldog of a man."

Unlike other dutiful public servants throughout detective fiction who hinder GENIUS DETECTIVES or take the credit (for example, Inspectors Jiap and CRAMER), Lestrade never earns much respect. In "The Boscombe Valley Mystery" (1891), Holmes says that Lestrade is an "imbecile," and he does nothing to change this estimation. In "The Adventure of the Cardboard Box," (1893) he compliments Lestrade's tenacity but still finds him "absolutely devoid of reason."

LET DEAD ENOUGH ALONE (1955) A mystery by Frances and Richard LOCKRIDGE, one of the best featuring Captain HEIMRICH. The story is a variation on the COUNTRY HOUSE scenario. The host, psychiatrist Margaret Halley, invites a group of friends for New Year's Eve to her house in Upstate New York, where she lives with her rich husband, John. A snowstorm ensues, trapping the guests; the victim is found dead in the lake. The guests/suspects include a former patient of the doctor's, as well as a young woman who has been having an affair with the host's husband. Heimrich is his usual self, closing his eyes meditatively, asking questions, and giving the guests enough slack to slip up, and the psychology is better developed than in some of his other adventures.

LEWIS, ROY HARLEY See BOOKS.

LIFE IMITATES ART Unfortunately, it is inevitable that some deranged persons re-enact the events of murder mystery novels and stories. In Arthur W. Upfield's *The Sands of Windee* (1931), a body is burned and every trace of it destroyed, a seemingly perfect crime. One person who thought so was John Thomas Smith, alias Snowy Rowles. At a remote cabin in Australia's outback, he used Upfield's story as the template for the murder of one man and probably two, in order to get their vehicle. Smith was already a wanted man at the time; he was also less careful than Upfield's fictional killer. The victim, Louis Carron, was identified from a wedding ring and dental work found buried in the ashes. The wife of the other missing man begged Smith to tell what had happened to her husband, but he insisted on his innocence right up until the time he was hanged, in 1932.

Another writer unfortunate enough to have a work copied by an actual murderer is Patricia CORNWELL. And in a recent case, an adolescent's armed takeover of his school in a novel by the horror writer Stephen King was carried out in reality by a high school student.

LIFE'S WORK (1986) A novel by Jonathan VALIN in which private investigator Harry STONER is hired by the Cincinnati Cougars football team to find a missing player, Bill Parks, a noseguard who is a monster in both size and personality. What is interesting in this case—which involves an absolutely revolting murder—is not so much Stoner's commentary on the jock ethos of violence and buddyhood as the fact that he gives in to it, disastrously. Parks may be implicated in cocaine abuse, which has already cost the team three of its best players. In his search, Stoner quickly runs into a bunch of losers, some pathetic and others frightening, who are hangers-on trying to capitalize on Parks's success. One of them, Walt Kaplan, is a body-building guru whose gym is an outlet for crackpot machismo and possibly drugs. Another is a preacher and former used car salesman who has the team members' wives wrapped around his finger. And then there are the women, some of them prostitutes trying to make good, who think they can control overpaid and steroid-crazed animals like Parks. The most interesting relationship in the book is between Stoner and Otto Bluerock, a lineman who has just been given his waivers and somewhat unwillingly becomes Stoner's assistant. Initially as repellent as Parks, Valin gives him some bracing dialogue and a recklessness Stoner cannot help catching.

LINCOLN, ABRAHAM. See DERRINGER.

LININGTON, ELIZABETH (1921–1988) Early in the 1960s, Elizabeth Linington simultaneously launched several mystery series under various names and was immensely successful with one of them. Although born in Illinois, she grew up in California, and her detective PROCEDURAL novels were set in the Los Angeles area. She graduated from Glendale Junior College in 1942 (she used Glendale as the setting for one her series). Early in her writing career she wrote for radio and for the stage.

The best-known work by Linington is the series of novels she published as Dell Shannon: the Luis MENDOZA mysteries, which premiered with *Case Pending* (1960). As Lesley Egan, she developed the Vic Varallo series, a small town saga that began with *A Case for Appeal* (1961). In the same book, she introduced Jesse Falkenstein, a Los Angeles lawyer who has been brought in to defend a woman accused of performing illegal abortions that claimed the lives of two women. Falkenstein and Varallo later go their separate ways; the former features in a series with his brother-in-law, Sergeant Andrew Clock of the Los Angeles police. Other Falkenstein-Clock books are *Against the Evidence* (1962), *My Name Is Death* (1964), *A Serious Investigation* (1968), *The Blind Search* (1977), and *Look Back on Death* (1978). Like Mendoza, Falkenstein comes into some serious money and lives a luxurious life. As in the other series by Linington, the crimes are often grotesque and gruesome (rape of a child, for example), and meant to illustrate the depths of human depravity.

Although her most successful books, mysteries were not Linington's first. She had already written a number of historical novels, beginning with *The Proud Man* (1955), which reflected her preoccupation with Irish history. According to Otto PENZLER and Chris Steinbrunner, Linington abandoned the historical novel because, as she said, "leftist liberal publishers" would not accept one of her patriotic novels. Linington was for many years a member of the ultra–right wing John Birch Society.

Linington's books were written in a matter of weeks, and as can be seen from her bibliography, she regularly turned out several a year. She published some detective novels under her own name, a precinct-style series set in Hollywood. The first of this group of novels was *Greenmask!* (1964), which introduced Sergeant Ivor Maddox. He starts out as a bit of a rake, but later marries one of his colleagues, Sue Carstairs. Their domestic life looms large in the stories while they pursue separate cases. Rather holier-than-thou, they are shrill social critics on such subjects as feminism, abortion, and welfare. BARZUN and TAYLOR called *Date With Death* (1966) "a book to be exiled from the premises." Other books in the series include *Crime by Chance* (1973), *Perchance of Death* (1977), and *Skeletons in the Closet* (1982). In *Felony Report* (1984), Maddox investigates the killing of eleven people with Demerol through poisoned meat.

The violence and suspense of Linington's novels make them page-turners, unless one is interested in character. She tends to crowd the stage with people, rather than showing anyone in real depth; in particular, she produced few interesting villains, perhaps because of her black-and-white view of society, with the good (who are often also the well-off) menaced by the hordes of the shiftless, decadent, and evil. Anthony BOUCHER, one of her admirers, noticed that the criminals in her books commit crimes mostly for stupid reasons, as in real life. Life is not art, however, and Linington was not interested in embellishing it with NAPOLEONS OF CRIME or other such inventions. In an article written in 1970, she took to task "self-proclaimed" intellectuals who tried to make the mystery story into "an esoteric mystique" instead of entertainment.

A number of Linington's Mendoza novels have been reissued by the Mysterious Press, including *Knave of Hearts* (1962; repr 1984), which was nominated for an EDGAR, an award she never won. Others are: *Extra Kill* (1962; 1984), *Death of a Busybody* (1963; repr 1984), and *Double Bluff* (1963; repr 1985). Linington's last novels were *Blood Count* (1986), a Mendoza mystery, and *Strange Felony* (1986). Two books were published posthumously: *Alter Ego* (1988) and *Sorrow to the Grave* (1992), both under the pseudonym Dell Shannon.

LINSTOCK, GILLIAN See WOMEN.

LIST OF ADRIAN MESSENGER, THE (1959) An Anthony GETHRYN novel by Philip MACDONALD that combines features of the THRILLER with a mystery story. The first murder is spectacular: a plane with all its sixty-seven passengers is destroyed simply to eliminate one man—Adrian Messenger. The mortally wounded survivors manage to communicate Messenger's last words, which are so cryptic as to be nonsensical. Messenger had previously visited his old friend at Scotland Yard, George Frith, with a vague conspiracy theory; he presented Frith with a list of names and asked him to find out if the people on the list were still living at the same addresses. Nine of the ten people on the list are already dead.

Gethryn investigates the case with the help of a hero of the French Resistance with whom he had worked fifteen years before. Going through Messenger's papers, they begin to find links between the dead men that lead them to uncover a diabolical plot and a NAPOLEON OF CRIME. The locations range from the British Isles to California, and show MacDonald making the most of the newly revived spy thriller genre.

LITTLE CAESAR See BURNETT, W. R.

LITTLEJOHN, SUPERINTENDENT Tom Littlejohn is an invention of George BELLAIRS. Littlejohn is in the tradition of the bland English detective, although his mind is more romantic and his thoughts more explored (and more interesting) than those of Superintendent WYCLIFFE, for example. Littlejohn begins his career as an Inspector in *Littlejohn on Leave* (1941), but later he rises to the rank of Superintendent. He attends international police conferences, at which he confesses to having no method, and is considered a "venerable old buffer." One of his great friends is the Reverend Caesar Kinrade, Archdeacon of Man. He joins Littlejohn in the cases that take him to the Isle of Man and provides both local color and a sounding board for Littlejohn's speculations. Littlejohn's actual post is at Scotland Yard, though he manages to be sent far afield. *Death in High Provence* (1957) concerns the double murder of the brother and sister-in-law of a French cabinet minister. The story is set in the village of St. Marcellin, which is dominated by the Marquis de St. Marcellin, who rules the place like a medieval baron; this includes the imposition of silence through fear, a code that Littlejohn, again investigating unofficially, must break down. Bellairs was something of a Francophile (his journalism included writings about food and wine, among other things), and also set *Death in the Wasteland* (1963) and his last book, *Close All Roads to Sospel* (1977), in southern France. *The Corpse at the Carnival* (1958) is set on the Isle of Man, where the author often visited because it was his wife's birthplace. Other books with a Manx background include *Half-Mast for the Deemster* (1953), which deals with smuggling, and *The Night They Killed Joss Varran* (1970).

BIBLIOGRAPHY Novels: *The Four Unfaithful Servants* (1942), *Death of a Busybody* (1942), *The Dead Shall Be Raised* (1943; U.S. title *Murder Will Speak*), *Calamity at Harwood* (1943), *The Murder of a Quack* (1943), *He'd Rather Be Dead* (1945), *Death in the Night Watches* (1945), *The Case of the Scared Rabbits* (1946), *The Crime at Halfpenny Bridge* (1946), *Death on the Last Train* (1948), *The Case of the Famished Parson* (1949), *The Case of the Demented Spiv* (1949), *Outrage on Gallows Hill* (1949), *The Case of the Headless Jesuit* (1950; U.S. title *Death Brings the New Year* (1951), *Dead March for Penelope Blow* (1951), *Death in Dark Glasses* (1952), *Crime in Leper's Hollow* (1952), *Corpses in Enderby* (1954), *The Cursing Stones Murder* (1954), *Death in Room Five* (1955), *Death Treads Softly* (1956), *Death Drops the Pilot* (1956), *Death Sends for the Doctor* (1957), *Death in Desolation* (1957), *Murder Makes Mistakes* (1958), *Bones in the Wilderness* (1959), *Roll the Bell for Murder* (1959), *Death in the Fearful Night* (1960), *Death of a Tin God* (1961), *The Body in the Dumb River* (1961), *Death Before Breakfast* (1962), *The Tormentors* (1962), *Death in the Wasteland* (1963), *Surfeit of Suspects* (1964), *Death of a Shadow* (1964), *Death Spins the Wheel* (1965), *Strangers Among the Dead* (1966), *Single Ticket to Death* (1967), *Pomeroy, Deceased* (1971), *Tycoon's Death-Bed* (1971), *Murder Adrift* (1972), *Devious Murder* (1973), *Fear Round About* (1975).

"LITTLE OLD MAN OF BATIGNOLLES, THE" (*Le petit vieux des Batignolles*, 1876). A short story by Émile GABORIAU, interesting for its use of the problem of handedness and the narrator's ambivalent view of his neighbor, a police detective. One day the narrator, a medical student, accompanies the policeman to the Parisian neighborhood of Batignolles, where an old man has been stabbed to death in his apartment. The old man's nephew is arrested and subsequently confesses, but the detective is not convinced. Based on some evidence (including the behavior of a dog) he comes to another conclusion, but there is a surprise in the end about who drew the name of the nephew in blood next to the corpse.

LITTLE SISTER, THE (1949) A novel by Raymond CHANDLER, the merit of which has been contested by various critics. The book has been dismissed as confused in plot and overly violent, while other critics have placed it among Chandler's best. Chandler himself was aware of the weaknesses of the plot (he said it "creaks like a broken shutter"), but its combination of the HARD-BOILED style with Chandler's bantering, poetic dialogue and evocation of mood, which was to reach its most baroque in THE LONG GOODBYE (1953), is winning. Philip MARLOWE is approached by Orfamay QUEST to find her brother, Orrin, who had moved out West from Kansas to work in an aircraft factory and then disappeared. Marlowe takes the job for the ridiculous fee of twenty dollars. In a dirty rooming house in Bay City he does not find Quest, but he does come across the first of the ICE PICK murders in the book. The trail leads to rising movie star Mavis Weld and a shadowy gangster named Weepy Moyer. The book contains extended diatribes against Hollywood, with which Chandler was having trouble at the time ("the motion picture business is the only business in the world in which you can make all the mistakes there are and still make money"), and against the larger corruption, the "cold half-lit world where always the wrong thing happens and never the right." The fifth book in the Marlowe series, it shows the cynical and wisecracking detective becoming self-conscious and somewhat morose, but even Marlowe, tired of fending off cheap punks, cheap attitudes, and cheap sex, is a little surprised by the dirtiness of the sellout that climaxes the book. Perhaps *The Little Sister* has displeased readers because Chandler left off much of the gilding and romance that adorn the beautiful and damned in his others novels about Los Angeles, and allowed himself to come through (via Marlowe, of course) more as a moralist than a cynic.

LITVINOV, IVY (1889–1977) Born Ivy Low in England, Litvinov wrote only one mystery story, *His Master's Voice* (1930; U.S. title *Moscow Mystery,* 1943), but it exercises a continuing fascination because of the unusual background. The author's husband, Maxim Litvinov, was a Soviet official; after living in Moscow for twenty years, Ivy Litvinov accompanied her husband to Washington, D.C., where he was stationed as an ambassador during World War II. The U.S. edition of the novel dates from this period and includes a preface in which she reminisces about her life in Moscow. She also translated such authors as Pushkin, Tolstoy, and Chekov.

Litvinov's novel is a firsthand portrait of Moscow in the early days of the Soviet state. Supposedly, it was written after she consulted a German hypnotist who was examining the brain of Lenin, but nothing very outré seems to have rubbed off on the story. A high-ranking member of an American-owned firm is found murdered with a dagger in his neck. The victim, Arkady Petrovich Pavlov, was also a ballet enthusiast, and a young woman was seen entering his house not long before his murder. Detective Yanovitsky is called in; he is a rogue, and an expert in crimes because he has committed them himself. With his magisterial boss, "the Procurator," he begins to search for the woman. The book, when it can be found, is worth reading for its setting.

LIZZIE See BORDEN, LIZZIE.

LLEWELYN, SAM (***) The English mystery author Sam Llewelyn has written a mystery series devoted entirely to sailing. This theme, not a single series character, ties the books together. Llewelyn is a knowledgeable and experienced sailor, and has been compared to Dick FRANCIS in his recreation of a specialized milieu. Llewelyn favors the cliffhanger style of the THRILLER, which he does well, propelling the plot with action and danger rather than with detection; his books are also sometimes very violent.

Llewelyn's heroes are ordinary people caught in confusing and life-threatening events. In *Blood Orange* (1989), James Dixon is sailing through a storm off the Irish coast when a cable gives way; this "accident" turns out to be more than that. *Dead Reckoning* (1987) is about a yacht designer whose new rudder design makes him the target of a deadly sabotage campaign. In *Deadeye* (1991), a divorce lawyer's yacht is wrecked. This seemingly personal event is eventually tied to international conspiracy. Set in a Scottish fishing village, it has echoes of the Webb CARRICK mysteries.

More and more, Llewelyn has adopted the "big" plot of the contemporary thriller, sacrificing realism to keep up with the ever-growing pack. *Rip Tide* (1994) is filled with developers, yachts, racing, and very realistic scenes of the French nautical world and the French Riviera. The characters, however, are thoroughly romantic. The hero, Mick Savage, has circumnavigated the globe four times, met the woman of his dreams, had a daughter, played piano in cheap cabarets to survive, and worked for a floating circus (all before the book's events begin). In the vivid opening chapter, he is almost killed when a boat he is delivering nearly sinks. Toward the end, the hero starts to have too much of the luck of the *Indiana Jones* movies: he falls down an elevator shaft, but nothing can slow him down. Unusually, in this case the author makes a few errors in his descriptions of yacht construction. *Maelstrom* (1994) is about former eco-terrorist Fred Hope, a rammer of whaling ships and destroyer of fishing nets. He also is drawn into a web of intrigue that seems to spin out forever. *Death Roll* (1989) and *Clawhammer* (1993) are other Llewelyn novels.

LOCKED ROOM MYSTERY A mystery in which it seems physically impossible for the murderer to have entered or exited the room in which the killing has taken place. Edgar Allan POE is usually credited with having invented this subgenre of mystery with his short story THE MURDERS IN THE RUE MORGUE (1841). In fact, J. Sheridan Le Fanu used the locked room in an earlier story, "Passage in the Secret History of an Irish Countess" (1838), and adapted it again to UNCLE SILAS (1864), thus giving him a claim to the first employment of the locked room puzzle in both the short story and novel forms.

Many later writers used this motif, notably Israel Zangwill in the novel THE BIG BOW MYSTERY (1891) and Gaston Leroux in his classic THE MYSTERY OF THE YELLOW ROOM (1907). But no writer made the locked room his own like John Dickson CARR, who gave it endless permutations. Although it is associated with the GOLDEN AGE and has fallen into disfavor because of the manifold implausibilities and far-fetched mechanisms to which it has driven writers, the locked room scenario is occasionally revised. Maj SJÖWALL and Per WAHLÖO used it almost brazenly in one of their Martin BECK novels.

LOCKRIDGE, FRANCES (1896–1963) AND RICHARD (1899–1982) This husband-and-wife team wrote several series of mysteries, including one about the husband-and-wife team of Jerry and Pam NORTH. Less well known are the mysteries about Inspector HEIMRICH, who made his first appearance as a supporting character in two of the Norths' mysteries (*Murder Out of Turn*, 1941, and *Death of a Tall Man* 1946), and then became the subject of a series of his own.

Richard Lockridge was born in Missouri and attended the University of Missouri. He served in the Navy during World War I. He was a reporter for Kansas City newspapers and, after his 1922 marriage to Frances Louise Davis, who was also a reporter, moved to New York, where he was employed by the *New York Sun*. Richard Lockridge's first book was a biography of the nineteenth-century actor Edwin Booth. His first published fiction consisted of short stories printed in *The New Yorker*, to which he was an important contributor. The North mysteries grew out of Lockridge's association with the magazine, in which he had published non-mystery stories about publisher Jerry North and his wife, a cultured Manhattan couple. Both Lockridges were mystery readers, and after Frances' attempt to write a mystery novel stalled, Richard suggested that she use the Norths as characters in the mystery.

The Lockridges' method of composition was similar to that of Ellery QUEEN: one of them (Frances) contributed the plot, and the other (Richard) did the writing. The Lockridges used a variety of settings, but the majority of their stories take place in New York. Some of these are non-series mysteries. The fortunes of their characters followed their own, for after they left Manhattan they started the Heimrich series, which is set in the suburbs north of New York City where they lived. The interrelation of the several Lockridge series is somewhat involved. Heimrich began as a character in the North series. The Lockridges wrote another series about Nathan Shapiro, a New York City detective, and several books about detective Paul LANE; Lane, in turn, sometimes works for Captain Bill Weigand, who was a major figure in the North books (and who is also mentioned in the Shapiro series); Lane also makes some appearances in yet another series, about an assistant district attorney named Bernard SIMMONS, who was introduced in *Squire of Death* (1965).
The style of the books reflects Richard Lockridge's newspaper background and is more journalistic than literary. The Lockridges' books have been criticized for weak plotting, but the premise (as opposed to the plot) of the stories is often strong. In *And Left for Dead* (1961), a young man takes an apartment offered at below-market price because no one wants it; a certain Mary Smith has been murdered there. Some time later, a woman turns up claiming to be Mary, just recovered from a coma, and then mysteriously vanishes again. "Mary Smith" turns out to be the female equivalent of "John Doe" used in hospitals. The Lockridges were evidently fond of the "strange apartment" motif: in *Night of Shadows* (1962), a Detective Lane mystery, a man goes to meet a former girlfriend at her parents' apartment and finds a suspicious couple there instead, and his girlfriend vanished. In *Write Murder Down* (1973), a woman is found dead in a bathtub in a Greenwich Village apartment in which all personal affects and identifying objects have been removed. The woman's wrists are slashed but her body is full of barbiturates. Detective Shapiro traces the woman to a midtown hotel, where he discovers that she was a successful Southern novelist. The Lockridges also often used chase scenes in their books, and this became something of a trademark. Among the best Lockridge books are *Inspector's Holiday* (see MURDER AFLOAT), *Think of Death* (1947), and LET DEAD ENOUGH ALONE (1955).

After his wife's death, Richard Lockridge wrote no more North stories, but he did continue with the Heimrich mysteries and the other series. He remarried in 1965; his second wife was also a writer. Lockridge's two non-mystery novels are *The Empty Day* (1964) and *Encounter in Key West* (1966).

LOGUE, JOHN See GOLF MYSTERIES.

"LONG DINNER, THE" A short story by H. C. Bailey (from *Mr. Fortune Objects*, 1934) in which Mr. Reggie FORTUNE joins in a search for a missing Bohemian "degenerate" artist. Fortune finds a dinner menu in one of the man's jackets and leaps to the conclusion that the man is in Brittany. The case moves back and forth across the Channel, with Mr. Fortune mumbling to himself in his reverie while everyone is convinced he is totally off the track. (Unfortunately, his French companion out-Poirots POIROT in his bad syntax.) The scam he discovers is diabolical but could never hold up for long.

LONG GOODBYE, THE (1953) The next-to-last book featuring Philip MARLOWE that Raymond CHANDLER lived to complete. The book has a strong opening, with Marlowe assisting a helpless drunk (Terry Lennox) out of his car, which is then blithely driven away by the other passenger, a red-haired tramp who turns out to be his wife, Sylvia Lennox. Marlowe later lands in jail on suspicion of having helped Lennox flee to Mexico from a murder charge. When Lennox is found dead, a result of suicide, the case is quickly hushed up, and Marlowe finds himself the odd man out in still pursuing it. His method, however, is less a matter of detection than hanging around in the right places, waiting for something to happen.

The "Goodbye" has been criticized for being not only long but slow; however, it has the characteristic Chandler dialogue and some memorable one-liners: "I thought Southern California had a climate. . . . What are they doing, burning old truck tires?" At a deeper level, it is a mature novel with more serious undertones than, for example, a straight detective novel like *The Lady in the Lake* (1943). Not a few critics have ranked it as Chandler's best, the other candidate usually being FAREWELL, MY LOVELY (1940).

An interesting aspect of the book is that most of the characters, from the hundred-millionaire Harlan Potter to Detective Bernie OHLS, comment on the cynicism and corruption of the American culture and legal system. In addition, one of the main characters is a successful writer ashamed of his hack work but unsure whether he can do better; Chandler uses him to invest the story with meditations on the craft of writing and the nature of the writer. ("A writer needs stimulation—and not the kind they bottle.") This aspect sometimes gets out of hand (as in Marlowe's pointless exchange of quotes from T. S. Eliot with Potter's chauffeur), but shows Chandler's characteristic expanding of the boundaries of genre. The big "surprise" is not quite a surprise, but the many small touches, the elegant conversations over gimlets, and the ambiguous rescue all make it a memorable book.

LONG SATURDAY NIGHT, THE See CONFIDENTIALLY YOURS.

LOOKING FOR RACHEL WALLACE (1980) A novel by Robert B. PARKER. SPENSER undertakes a job for a publisher as a bodyguard for Rachel Wallace, a radical feminist and lesbian author whose revelations of discrimination against women in the workplace have provoked threats. Wallace disapproves of Spenser's violent way of earning a living and condemns him for his machismo; Spenser refuses to argue and treats her political views as irrelevant to his job. Eventually she fires him, but after she disappears Spenser is called in to find her. Suspects are few and the culprit, as well as the outcome, are not a surprise—though the treatment Spenser receives from the police (verging on sycophantic) is. Spenser's wise guy pose is carried off with a lighter touch than elsewhere in the series.

"LOUISA, PLEASE COME HOME" This 1960 story by Shirley JACKSON won an EDGAR award. The narrator, Louisa Tether, describes in detail her clever plans for running away from home on the eve of her sister's wedding. Louisa's clear and even cruel intelligence contrasts with the banality of the family circle; "I used to try and imagine Carol's face when she finally realized that my running away was going to leave her one bridesmaid short." Louisa escapes to a nearby town and sets up a new life for herself, anticipating the methods that will be used to find her and the thinking processes of the searchers. Years after her escape, chance finally throws a wrench into her plans. The ending is surprising in several ways—what are Louisa's real feelings?—and deeply ironic.

LOVE, DOCTOR JASON An espionage character in a series of novels by James LEASOR. Love is a British war veteran who practices medicine in the country. He is described as "Dr. Kildare with clandestine assignments." Although Love is a post-BOND creation and is sent on missions by British Intelligence, he harks back to the ordinary hero of an earlier period of British spy fiction exemplified by Richard HANNAY. The series is a hybrid, at once nostalgic and contemporary; Love's main passion, besides medicine and spying, is antique cars. He must be well compensated, because he drives a Cord convertible. In *Passport to Suspense* (1967; U.S. title *The Yang Meridian*), Leasor introduced another character, MacGillivray, an even more traditional older British military type. He reappears to help Love again in *Passport for a Pilgrim* (1968), which takes place in Damascus. First, Love encounters a woman who is supposed to be dead; the story also involves a FLEMING-esque plot to foment revolution by surreptitiously giving LSD to the masses.

BIBLIOGRAPHY Novels: *Passport to Oblivion* (1964), *Passport to Peril* (1966; U.S. title *Spylight*), *A Week of Love* (1969; short stories), *Love-All* (1971), *Host of Extras* (1973), *Love and the Land Beyond* (1979), *Frozen Assets* (1979).

LOVE, PHAROAH Detective character created by George BAXT. Pharoah Love is a gay, African American New York City cop. In his first three appearances, he deals with murders within the gay subculture of the city. The trilogy is made up of *A Queer Kind of Death* (1966), *Swing Low, Sweet Harriet* (1967), and *Topsy and Evil* (1968). There has been a recent resurgence of interest in these books, which have been reprinted.

Love returned more than twenty years later in *A Queer Kind of Love* (1994), which lacks some of the zest of the original books, which were the first GAY MYSTERIES to be published. Pharoah starts out by killing one of his childhood best friends, a drug dealer, and investigating the other, a mafioso.

LOVE IN AMSTERDAM (1962) The first novel in the Inspector VAN DER VALK series by Nicholas FREELING. In the first part, Van der Valk investigates the murder of a woman shot to death in her apartment. The story introduces the sketchy, pedantic, sometimes claustrophobic style of Van de Valk's method, as he investigates the case with the man who is the main suspect—Martin, a writer. The portrait of the victim, Elsa de Charmoy, emerges as that of a complicated, selfish, and masochistic woman; her relationships (particularly with men) are believable, fascinating, and perverse. An earlier phase of her life is described in flashback in the central section of the book. Taking up more than a third of the whole work, this second part reads as a free-standing novel (perhaps an effort to write a "serious" novel that was later turned into a mystery by Freeling) with similarities to MAUGHAM and GREENE, but even more reminiscent of the Dutch writer Jan de Hartog. It describes a romantic and impoverished literary and artistic circle in Holland just after World War II of which Else de Charmoy is the center. The style is quite different from that of the Van der Valk novels—more accessible, less talky, and more romantic in a not unpleasing way. The complete absence of Van der Valk from this section allows the other characters to be developed with a completeness otherwise impossible, even though the pursuit of the mystery as such is entirely suspended.

LOVEJOY A scoundrel and antiques dealer in a series of novels by Jonathan GASH, Lovejoy loves objects more than people; the latter he is only too ready to eliminate in his quest for the former. Lovejoy is a forger as well as an antiques "divvy" (from diviner, one who tells the value of or finds objects, like a water diviner). The stories are told in the first person in slangy English with plenty of Britishisms. Lovejoy is a bit of a misogynist and continually runs into (and of course sleeps with) beautiful women who are updated versions of the kind of women found in the James BOND series.

Lovejoy is frequently broke. In *The Vatican Rip* (1981), he agrees to a crazy plan concocted by a mysterious Italian to rob the Vatican of a Chippendale table. He takes on the nearly impossible task of robbing the Vatican museum because he has no money, and then finds he has been set up. This is not his most unbelievable adventure, however; *Spend Game* (1980) has him trying to unearth a solid silver model of a locomotive.

BIBLIOGRAPHY Novels: *The Judas Pair* (1977), *Gold from Gemini* (1978; U.S. title *Gold by Gemini*), *The Grail Tree* (1979), *Firefly Gadroon* (1982), *The Sleepers of Erin* (1983), *The Gondola Scam* (1983), *Pearlhanger* (1985), *The Tartan Ringers* (1985; U.S. title *The Tartan Sell*), *Moonspender* (1986), *Jade Woman* (1988), *The Very Last Gambado* (1989), *The Great California Game* (1990), *The Lies of Fair Ladies* (1992), *Paid and Loving Eyes* (1993), *The Sin Within Her Smile* (1994), *The Grace in Older Women* (1995), *The Possessions of a Lady* (1996).

LOVESEY, PETER (1936–) Originally a historian of sport, the English writer Peter Lovesey decided to enter a mystery contest sponsored by Macmillan Publishing. His entry, *Wobble to Death* (1970), not only won the prize but launched a series about a Victorian detective known as Sergeant Cribb. Lovesey has gone on to become one of the most respected writers of the HISTORICAL MYSTERY. He continued to run the education department of Hammersmith College until 1975, when he began writing full-time.

Sergeant Cribb works at Scotland Yard and looks like a character from *Punch:* short and muscular, he has prominent whiskers and an oftentimes comic manner. He is assisted by Constable Edward Thackeray. Cribb is a brilliant detective but has run into a glass ceiling at the Yard because of his lower-class origins. Lovesey has used his knowledge of sports in most of the novels. In the first, it was "wobbles," a six-day walking race; in *The Detective Wore Silk Drawers* (1971), boxing; in *Swing, Swing Together* (1976), punting. Lovesey has been praised for his research, but BARZUN and Taylor pointed out a number of inaccuracies.

More recently, Lovesey's historical work has branched out in all directions. He moved into the twentieth century with *The False Inspector Dew* (1982), set aboard the *Mauritania* in 1921. The book won a Gold Dagger from the British CRIME WRITER'S ASSOCIATION. *Keystone* (1983) is set in the early days of Hollywood and concerns an English stuntman and actor who unwillingly becomes one of Mack Sennett's "Keystone Cops" and then has to investigate a real crime. Most recently, returning to the nineteenth century, Lovesey began a slightly tongue-in-cheek series in which Albert Edward, the Prince of Wales, is the detective. A comparison with actual Edwardian prose—Conan DOYLE, or even Fergus HUME—will show that this series, stylistically at least, is somewhere between pastiche and historical mystery. BERTIE AND THE SEVEN BODIES (1990) involves the Prince in a COUNTRY HOUSE mystery, and *Bertie and The Crime of Passion* (1993) takes place in 1891 in Paris.

LOW, FLAXMAN See PRICHARD, HESKETH.

LOWNDES, MARIE [ADELAIDE] BELLOC (1868–1947) The English writer Marie Belloc Lowndes produced more than a score of novels, among which are scattered a couple of lasting achievements and not a few curiosities. She is best known for her fictionalized accounts of the most sensational murders of her time: JACK THE RIPPER and the Lizzie BORDEN case. Her first novel, *The Heart of Penelope* (1904), was a mystery; she also wrote an INVERTED MYSTERY, *The Chink in the Armour* (1912), almost two decades before Anthony BERKELEY is supposed to have invented that form. Lowndes also created a detective, Hercule Popeau, who is mostly remembered because he helped inspire Hercule POIROT.

Lowndes came from a distinguished and literary family. Her great-great-grandfather was the scientist Joseph Priestley, and her brother was Hilaire Belloc, who was a friend of G. K. CHESTERTON. Both Bellocs were born in France and emigrated to England. Marie Belloc Lowndes also wrote an autobiography, *I, Too, Have Lived in Arcadia* (1941).

LUCAN, LORD The Earl of Lucan was the subject of one of the strangest criminal cases in English history. On November 7, 1974, Lady Lucan was attacked by her husband in their home in London's West End. Bleeding from several head wounds, she fled to a nearby pub. When police entered the Lucan home, they found the dead body of Sandra Rivett, the nanny to the Lucans' three children, stuffed inside a mail bag in the basement. She had been bludgeoned to death, probably with a piece of lead pipe found at the scene. In Lady Lucan's bizarre version of events, Lord Lucan (from whom she was separated) tried to beat and strangle her to death, then desisted; both went upstairs to her bedroom, where she lay down and he examined her injuries, then went to get a cloth to wash her face (at that point, she bolted from the house).

Lord Lucan then disappeared. He spoke with his mother and with a friend before he vanished for good, saying that no one would believe his incredible story. A car he had borrowed was found two days later at Newhaven, a port city on the English Channel. One of the many odd things about the case was that another piece of lead pipe, similar to that found in the house, was discovered in the car, which was bloodstained. It was thought that the nanny had been mistaken for Lady Lucan and killed accidentally. A coroner's jury returned a verdict of "Murder by Lord Lucan," but the Earl was never seen again.

LUDLOW, ADAM See NASH, SIMON.

LUDLOW, JOHNNY See WOOD, MRS. HENRY.

LUGER The American name applied to the German Parabellum, originally an eight-shot, nine millimeter automatic pistol. The Luger is a powerful weapon and an ergonomic masterpiece, designed to point naturally as one points a finger. The gun has hateful associations from the NAZI period and from innumerable smirking film villains, but it was actually designed much earlier, in 1908. The Luger was the standard sidearm of the German armed forces in World War I, not World War II, when it was replaced by the 9mm Walther P-38 for almost all branches (the Gestapo used the WALTHER PPK).

The German manufacture of the Luger was forbidden by the treaty ending World War I, but a .30 caliber model was produced and was very popular in the United States—hence its appearance in books of the HARD-BOILED era. Detectives who carry a Luger include Philip MARLOWE; the grim and unbalanced narrator of Dick FRANCIS's *Blood Sport* (1967); and Charlie MORTDECAI's sidekick, Jock. Raymond Chandler seems to have been fond of them; he also put a Luger in the hand of the hero of his first story, BLACKMAILERS DON'T SHOOT (1933), and gave one to the villain Eddie MARS. Nero Wolfe is on the wrong end of a Luger in THE BLACK MOUNTAIN (1954).

LUGG, MAGERSFONTEIN A former criminal and servant of Albert CAMPION in the novels of Margery Allingham. Lugg is one of those characters people seem to either like or find insupportable (one critic called him "egregious" and "unspeakable"). Named after a battle in the Boer War, Lugg is a sad-looking, almost bald man who speaks with a Cockney accent. He "tsks" at Campion's adventures but assists, for example helping to drag a corpse up the stairs (*Pearls Before Swine,* 1945). He acts as butler in *Dancers in Mourning* (1937), and publishes a book of quotations in *The Fashion in Shrouds* (1938). The author compares him to a bull terrier, and he suits his tone and behavior to his appearance. As a servant, Lugg falls in the line of lower-class cantankerous assistants still popular today (like Pepe Carvalho's assistant/housekeeper).

LUPIN, ARSÈNE The sometime thief and sometime detective in a long series of stories by Maurice LEBLANC. Lupin has almost as many aliases as John CREASEY: Prince Serge Rènine, Paul Sernine, Luis Perenna, M. Lenormand, Jim Barnett, Paul Daubreuil, Captain Jeanniot, and more than half-a-dozen others. Lupin not only confounds the police but enjoys humiliating them, particularly his arch enemy Inspector Ganimard (whom he addresses as "friend of my youth"). He likes to discuss his capers in front of them, and says his criminal organization's budget is equal to that of a large town. The impotent Ganimard can only curse Lupin as "the scum of the earth." Lupin is a master of disguise, and for four years masquerades as the head of the Sûreté (a detail culled from VIDOCQ).

Leblanc parodied Conan DOYLE by opposing Lupin with a detective named Herlock Sholmes.

In "The Red Silk Scarf," Lupin is *both* thief and detective, solving a crime from a few bits of evidence—broken glass, an inkwell, a bloody scarf—and essentially sells the solution to Ganimard for a huge price. The arrogant Lupin describes his own deductions as "marvelous divination," and Ganimard is mute before "the master whom he could not choose but obey." Ganimard is not quite so idiotic, nor Lupin so irritating, in the much cleverer ARSÈNE LUPIN IN PRISON.

The translation of Leblanc's books into English has created a good deal of confusion. A single title sometimes appeared in translation under a variety of titles in Britain and the United States. The first book in the series was *Arsène Lupin: Gentleman-Cambrioleur* (1907; tr *The Exploits of Arsène Lupin* in U.S.; British title *The Seven of Hearts*).

BIBLIOGRAPHY Novels: *813* (1910), *The Hollow Needle* (1910), *The Frontier* (1912), *The Crystal Stopper* (1913), *The Teeth of the Tiger* (1914), *The Bomb Shell* (1916), *The Golden Triangle* (1917), *Coffin Island* (1920), *The Three Eyes* (1921), *The Tremendous Event* (1922), *Dorothy, The Rope Dancer* (1923), *The Memoirs of Arsène Lupin* (1925; British title *The Candlestick with Seven Branches*), *The Girl with the Green Eyes* (1927), *The Melamare Mystery* (1929), *Man of Miracles* (1931), *The Double Smile* (1933), *From Midnight to Morning* (1933), *Wanton Venus* (1935).

Short Stories: *Arsène Lupin contre Herlock Sholmes* (1908; tr *The Fair-Haired Lady*, 1909 (U.K.); also tr *Arsène Lupin versus Holmlock Shears* (1909) and *The Arrest of Arsène Lupin* (1911) in U.K., and as *The Blonde Lady* (1910) and *Arsène Lupin versus Herlock Sholmes* (1910) in U.S.), *The Confessions of Arsène Lupin* (1912), *The Eight Strokes of the Clock* (1922), *Arsène Lupin Intervenes* (1928; British title *Jim Barnett Intervenes*).

LUTZ, JOHN [THOMAS] (1939–) For a long time, John Lutz was a prolific and acclaimed writer in a neglected medium: the SHORT STORY. He began writing novels in the seventies and started series about two private detectives, Alo NUDGER and Fred CARVER. Nudger, who is based in St. Louis, was part of the Midwest revival that also included Amos WALKER and Harry STONER, though he preceded both by four years. Francis M. NEVINS, Jr. described Nudger as "Chaplinesque," and the Nudger series is closest in sensibility to Lutz's short story work. Carver also has bizarre adventures, but he is closer to the slick, made-for-TV p.i.'s.

Lutz was born in Dallas, Texas, but has spent much of his life in the St. Louis area. He worked at various jobs, including warehouse worker, switchboard operator for the St. Louis police, and forklift operator. He wrote dozens of stories before getting his first magazine acceptance in 1966—from no less a name than *Alfred Hitchcock's Mystery Magazine*. Lutz was laid off from his job in the early seventies and thereafter wrote full-time.

The strength of Lutz's work is his originality; particularly in the short form, he has the ability to find an ingenious "spring" that gives the story a simple but effective core. In "The Real Shape of the Coast" (1971), a murder occurs in a seaside mental asylum, and one of the patients is the sleuth. "The Shooting of Curly Dan" (1973) is a small HISTORICAL MYSTERY set among a group of gandy dancers straightening railroad track on a blistering hot day. In "Understanding Electricity" (1986), an enraged ratepayer takes bizarre revenge against a utility company. "The Second Shot" (1984) has a psychiatrist forcing a madman to choose between murdering someone he hates and escaping retribution through suicide. Lutz is more interested in surprising or stunning the reader and getting a laugh than he is in planting clues and presenting realistic methods. Lutz's fantastic situations sometimes border on the magical.

Lutz has written several non-series novels, including *The Eye* (1984), co-authored with Bill PRONZINI. Lutz's writing is somewhat like that of Pronzini or Loren D. ESTLEMAN, though it is less self-consciously clever than the latter. Alo Nudger is similar to Pronzini's medium-boiled NAMELESS DETECTIVE, though the fact that Nudger's stories are told in the third person makes him seem less neurotic. Viewing Nudger from the outside also prevents him from appearing to try to ingratiate himself with the reader—the Achilles' heel of many "sensitive" p.i. types. The Carver novels contain more sex, graphic violence, and the usual trappings of the cop novel (gushing blood, spattered gray matter, charred flesh, four-letter words). One might say that it is what Carver does that maintains the reader's interest, while what Nudger *is* provides a different and more unusual pleasure.

In *Shadowtown* (1988), Lutz brought back the two New York City cops who appeared in *The Eye*. The title of *Shadowtown* refers not to New York but to a soap opera; an ex-cop who is working security on the set is murdered. Lutz achieved wider recognition with another non-series novel, *SWF Seeks Same* (1992), which was filmed under the title *Single White Female*. In 1998, Lutz published *Final Seconds*, co-authored with David August (a pseudonym). The novel is about a former New York City bomb squad leader and a specialist in psychological profiling who try to catch a serial mail bomber.

Some of Lutz's short stories have been collected in *Better Mousetraps* (1988) and *Shadows Everywhere* (1994). He won the EDGAR award for best short story in 1986; he re-wrote the story as a novel the following year (RIDE THE LIGHTNING). Among his other honors is the lifetime achievement award of the Private Eye Writers of America, which he received in 1995.

LYALL, GAVIN (1932–) The English writer Gavin Lyall was a pilot in the Royal Air Force before he turned to writing, and this experience forms the background for several of his works. His first novel was *The Wrong Side of the Sky* (1961). Lyall was the son of an accountant and attended Cambridge University, where he edited *Varsity*, the university newspaper, and got his introduction to journalism. In the fifties, he worked for *Picture Post* and the *Sunday Graphic*, and then became a director for the BBC. He later returned to journalism and to aviation, becoming the aviation correspondent for the *Sunday Times*.

Lyall's second novel, *The Most Dangerous Game* (1963), was a new version of the Richard CONNELL classic; once again, Lyall used flying as a motif, and also added a treasure of the Tsars, counterfeiting, and scenes in Lappland. The chase, the manhunt, and the shootout became Lyall's stock-in-trade, with frequent additions of World War II agents, international intrigue, and pilots in trouble. *Shooting Script* (1966) takes place in the Caribbean. A former RAF pilot running a charter business in Jamaica gets mixed up in politics and the repressive Republica Libra. In one scene, he uses an unarmed plane to force a jet fighter to crash. Lyall knows about flying, but the Latins, Americans, and mercenaries are stock types, merely there to set up the action scenes. In *Midnight Plus One* (1965), Lewis Cane, a former British liaison agent with the French Resistance, is hired to drive a crooked businessman whose competitors are trying to kill him (and who is also wanted on a rape charge in France) to Liechtenstein. With the help of an American gunman and his former Resistance friends, Cane fights his way through a series of ambushes. Sometimes Lyall lets his love of romance, old cars, and vintage hardware run wild. *Judas Country* (1975) brings together veteran pilots and their aging aircraft with gun smuggling, Middle Eastern politics, and the sword of King Richard the Lion Heart.

With *The Secret Servant* (1980), Lyall belatedly got into the spy series market with Major Harry Maxim, who is an operative of the Special Services. *The Conduct of Major Maxim* (1982) and *The Crocus List* (1985) are other books in the series.

LYDECKER, WALDO The glittering wit, incorrigible cynic, and man-about-town who narrates the first part of Vera Caspary's LAURA (1943). A columnist, Lydecker describes how he first met Laura Hunt, an ad executive, when she tried to get him to endorse a fountain pen. Lydecker calls himself "the most mercenary man in America," and he loves to make people squirm. His repartee with Detective Mark McPherson is particularly clever.

LYNLEY, INSPECTOR THOMAS The main character in a series by Elizabeth GEORGE. Lynley is an updated, 1980s version of Lord Peter WIMSEY. He is an earl, and in a romantic subplot the books also explore his pursuit of Lady Helen Clyde. Lynley's assistant is the commoner Sergeant Barbara Havers; they overcome their class differences to become personal friends (not surprisingly, the books are written by an American). In *A Great Deliverance* Lynley and Havers investigate an AXE murder. Another regular figure in the series is forensic scientist Simon Allcourt-St. James. Lynley and St. James are childhood friends, though St. James was crippled in a drunk-driving accident (Lynley was the driver). Simon's wife Deborah is unable to have children, which causes friction between them. This subplot plays an important role in *Missing Joseph*, in which a vicar who had assuaged Deborah's grief is mysteriously poisoned. In *Deception on His Mind* (1997), Havers investigates alone in the case of a murder in a seaside town plagued by racial tensions.

BIBLIOGRAPHY Novels: *Payment in Blood* (1989), *Well Schooled in Murder* (1990), *A Suitable Vengeance* (1991), *For the Sake of Elena* (1992), *Playing for the Ashes* (1994), *In the Presence of the Enemy* (1996).

M

MAC A private detective created by Thomas B. DEWEY, "Mac" is a former Chicago police officer forced out of the department because he was too honest. Mac, we learn, solved a case that the corrupt powers-that-be wanted to quash. Like most ex-cop characters, Mac has a friend inside the department, Donovan, who can funnel him cases the cops will not or cannot work on, and also provides access to the resources of a big city police force.

The exposition of the Mac novels depends on dialogue. Mac's humor is of the dry rather than the wisecracking sort. *You've Got Him Cold* (1958) is a complicated case in the manner of Ross MACDONALD involving paternity, conspiracy, and rottenness among the rich. Mac is approached by a hunted man named Charles Traven, accused of murdering his wife; before Mac can help him, he is shot dead by a policeman in Mac's backyard. The case is officially closed but Mac continues to investigate, at first on behalf of Pete Bowman, a lawyer friend of Traven's. Bowman is married to the daughter of the wealthy and powerful Calvin Lloyd, founder of Green Acres, a rehabilitation facility for parolees.

In *The Chased and the Unchaste* (1958), published the same year, Mac is hired by abrasive film producer Julie Porter, who is married to a beautiful woman much too young for him. His daughter by a previous marriage, Linda, has been threatened, and a kidnapping attempt is feared. In this book, the vulnerability of the rich is not interesting; there is a lot of buildup and the story is rather slow. A large household of retainers and gophers fails to enliven the scene, also not improved by the wife's habit of swimming in the nude, a muted prurience that is nonetheless cheesy and juvenile.

In *Death and Taxes* (1967), Mac has a more interesting client, the retired mobster Marco Paul, who hires him to deliver ten thousand dollars to Paul's daughter. After Paul is killed, Mac has to look for the money while everyone else leans on, and beats on, him. Mac is dispatched to California again in *The Love-Death Thing* (1969), a case involving a young woman who has become mixed up in drugs. In his last appearance, *The Taurus Trip* (1970), he has decided to move to the coast (just as his creator did). He is hired by a silent film star in a book that also involves astrology.

Dewey tried to make the books topical, having Mac pursue runaways and neo-Nazis and descend into the counterculture, but underneath he is a tough, HARD-BOILED dick along prewar lines, which is all to the good. Mac is the fairly sensitive lonely guy of most good hard-boiled fiction, a sort of junior MARLOWE. He does not indulge in misogyny nor become caught up in saccharine romances, which makes many of the books still readable. Among the best Mac novels is *The King Killers* (1968; British title *Death Turns Right*). Published in the most tumultuous year of a strife-ridden decade, it both hits on Dewey's main political themes and hooks the reader with a hard-boiled plot. Mac is hired by his friend Nat Pines, who has not been paid for a shipment of dummy wooden guns sold to a group in California known as the League for Good Government, whose leaders, the brothers Edgar and Nick Royal, happen to be in Chicago. Mac grudgingly teams up with another p.i., Karl Schneider, who is looking for Nick Royal's wayward and apathetic daughter. They quickly stumble into a murder, for which Mac is framed. In the end, the size and power of the neo-Nazi group is less than believable, given their idiotic head, but the interaction of Schneider and Mac is entertaining.

BIBLIOGRAPHY Novels: *Draw the Curtain Close* (1951), *Prey for Me* (1954), *The Mean Streets* (1955), *The Brave, Bad Girls* (1956), *The Girl Who Wasn't There* (1960), *How Hard to Kill* (1962), *A Sad Song Singing* (1963), *Don't Cry for Long* (1964), *Portrait of a Dead Heiress* (1965), *Deadline* (1966).

MCBAIN, ED (pseudonym of Evan Hunter, 1926–) Born Salvatore A. Lombino in New York City, Evan Hunter—a.k.a. Ed McBain, Curt Cannon, Ezra Hannon, Hunt Collins, and Richard Marsten—has written scores of crime and detective novels. The best known are the 87TH PRECINCT novels written under the name McBain, which began with *Cop Hater* (1956); this series has made McBain the foremost PROCEDURAL author.

McBain grew up in New York and spent two years in the Navy before attending Hunter College. He graduated in 1950 and spent a "disastrous" few months teaching high school, which would prove to be a valuable investment. He published *The Evil Sleep* (1952), *The Big Fix* (1952), *Don't Crowd Me* (1954), and *Cut Me In* (1954), but had his first major success with THE BLACKBOARD JUNGLE in 1954. This novel was shocking at the time for its portrayal of violence and delinquency in an inner-city high school and was inspired by the author's own experience as a teacher. The famous film version, with Glenn Ford and Sidney Poitier, helped to advance the author's career.

The 87th Precinct series is set in a city that is obviously New York, despite disclaimers. The books are procedural, deadpan, and violent. McBain rode in squad cars, visited crime laboratories, and conducted other research to ensure that the details of the books were accurate. The precinct has the diversity of the city the novels are based on, and the volatility as well: as they say of one neighborhood, "somebody had set a pot to melting in Riverhead, and somebody else had forgotten to turn off the gas."

The multiplicity of players means that several plot lines can go on at the same time. Reading a McBain novel is rather like reading a *Hill Street Blues* script. The writing is variable, with grammatical errors not restricted to the colloquial dialogue. The realism of the books includes a lot of what might be called information-poor text—the kind of meaningless perfunctory remarks people make when they aren't thinking anything, repetitions, and facts one does not need to know. This aspect has been much commented upon and praised, even though it could also be seen as pointless, since in reading about an imaginary world one is suspending one's disbelief, *gratis.* Perhaps the most peculiar praise came from H. R. F. KEATING, who wrote of the mundane or dull conversations that "because you realize that these are absolutely insignificant, you hurry, hurry, hurry"—i.e., padding the novel with extraneous detail is good because it helps you to skim it, so that "you read a novel-length book with the speed of a short story." This would be a virtue, if it were one's goal to read as many novels as possible.

McBain's "realism" also does not square with other nonreal features, such as the fact that the process of aging gradually slows and finally stops, leaving the characters in permanent middle-age, or the unlikelihood of many events (in the DEAF MAN series, for example). In the tradition of Sherlock HOLMES, a character can die in one story and come back to life elsewhere. Among the best-known books in the series are *Cop Hater* (1956); *The Mugger* (1956), in which a charming mugger named Clifford punches his female victims in the face and then thanks them (both books were made into films scripted by Henry KANE); and the "Deaf Man" series.

The author continues to write novels under the name of Evan Hunter as well. *Privileged Conversation* (1997) is a recent example. It concerns David, a Freudian psychoanalyst who comes to the assistance of a young woman who has been mugged in Central Park; this chance event leads to an obsessive affair. The magnetic appeal of the woman and the mysteries about her true nature and identity—of obvious attraction to an analyst—create suspense, as does the threatened disintegration of David's marriage. The book is written in the present tense, and shows how the Hunter books are more psychological and experimental than the procedural novels about the 87th Precinct. Freed from the demands of the procedural, McBain has used less realistic and even romantic plots in the Hunter books. *Gang* (1978) is about a young Chicano gang member who falls in love with a rich girl. McBain also experimented in the series he started about Matthew HOPE, which he began in the late seventies, using different points of view (first and third person) and an entirely different setting (Florida). In a humorous interview, McBain and Hunter discussed their differences; the author expressed his dislike of labels, particularly "procedural."

McBain's other books include the short story collection *The Jungle Kids* (1956), which came shortly after and dealt with the same milieu as *The Blackboard Jungle.* His output of novels has been so great that his short stories have been left in the shade; but, as the collection *The McBain Brief* (1982) shows, his work in the short form is better. If, as Keating suggests, a McBain novel has a core the length of a short story surrounded by extraneous material, then the short stories are McBain's best writing, shorn of the "uh-huhs" and irrelevant mundanities.

Evan Hunter has also written an excellent HISTORICAL MYSTERY based on the Lizzie BORDEN case, and finished the last novel of Craig RICE. Among his screenplays are *The Birds* (1963), the famous film by Alfred HITCHCOCK. He wrote the teleplay of the Evan Hunter novel *The Chisolms* (1976). Hunter has also written several children's books.

MCCARRY, CHARLES (1930–) Only a year younger than Len DEIGHTON, his British counterpart, the American writer Charles McCarry is one of the heirs of the AMBLER-LECARRÉ spy story. Born in rural Massachusetts, McCarry worked for the U.S. Central Intelligence Agency for almost a decade. He was still a CIA employee when he published his first story in 1967, but he left the agency soon after.

The Miernik Dossier (1973), a novel about a group of agents trying to handle a Polish defector, introduced Paul Christopher, McCarry's series character. The book was stylistically adventurous—for the spy genre—in using multiple narrators and conflicting points of view, as well as the documentary technique (made-up reports, letters, and other material). It was praised by Eric Ambler and was a critical success. But as a series character, Christopher himself is less interesting than the events surrounding him. He is a poet as well as a spy, and an immature poet at that. The introduction of this "sensitive" side of his character does not square with the Cold War soldier aspect of his personality, and unlike the "heroes" or antiheroes of LeCarré and Deighton, Christopher's belief that he is deep is self-delusional. His love affairs also bulk large in the series. McCarry has ranged far and wide in search of plots. *The Tears of Autumn* (1975) has Christopher discovering a conspiracy behind the assassination of John F. Kennedy. *The Bride of the Wilderness* (1988) is a HISTORICAL MYSTERY.

MCCLOY, HELEN (1904–1994) The daughter of a New York newspaper editor and a well-traveled journalist herself, Helen McCloy created the first believable psychiatrist sleuth, Dr. Basil WILLING. He was introduced in *Dance of Death* (1938), McCloy's first, highly praised novel. Willing is a sleuth of the "tall and handsome" sort so popular in the GOLDEN AGE and dating back to Sherlock HOLMES, but in other ways he is highly original. Willing is a child of immigrants, a World War I veteran, and earned a degree from Johns Hopkins University; his cases are clearly described as victories of method rather than of intuition or genius. McCloy herself studied at the Sorbonne in the early twenties, was an art critic in Paris for ten years, and later was a London correspondent for the *New York Times.* Willing is also cosmopolitan, having rounded out his studies in Paris and, of course, Vienna.

McCloy was born in New York City, where her father managed the *New York Evening Sun.* She was educated both in New York and abroad. Her grasp of psychology is nuanced and its presentation in her books is more subtle than that of many other writers, even those with greater training (see for example Jonathan KELLERMAN). The mystery story became a vehicle for exploring McCloy's fascination with the mind. At one point, an assistant to Willing says that "Modern psychiatry is a form of detection; only, instead of detecting a criminal you detect a forgotten emotion that has festered in the dream layer of the patient's mind."

Like T. S. STRIBLING's Dr. Poggioli, Willing is an intellectual who advises law enforcement officers—in his case, the New York district attorney's office. His cases are mostly of the classic type, though there are sometimes bizarre or unusual touches. In *Through a Glass Darkly* (1950), McCloy employed the theme of the DOPPELGÄNGER. Willing also gets married in this book (to an Austrian noblewoman and refugee). Other important books in the series are *Mr. Splitfoot* (1968), which is set in the Catskills and alludes in its title to the Devil. McCloy was interested in the supernatural and it crops up as a minor theme in several books, though a scientific explanation eventually is given. In *The One That Got Away* (1945), which was much admired, McCloy displays an extensive knowledge of Scottish lore and customs, including superstitions. The title story of the collection *The Singing Diamonds* (1965) involves Willing and flying saucers; the story was actually written in the late forties when interest in extraterrestrials was high, and won a prize from *Ellery Queen's Mystery Magazine.* After Willing loses his wife, the psychiatrist moves from New York to Boston, where McCloy herself settled in later life. The last Basil Willing novel was BURN THIS (1980).

The forties, when McCloy wrote the bulk of the Willing novels, was a period of intense interest in psychology and psychoanalysis, which turn up in the mystery field in various ways, including a great flowering of books about AMNESIA. In the period after World War II, psychology came to dominate the mystery story, and some critics, notably Jacques BARZUN, deplored its displacement of ratiocination and the classically clued mystery based on evidence and deduction. Helen McCloy is almost alone in being praised both for her use of psychology and for her strict adherence to the classical model. Anthony BOUCHER called CUE FOR MURDER (1942) "one of the most detailed and intricately clued detective stories that I know." An indication of McCloy's adherence to FAIR PLAY is that the reader "should deduce (not guess) the answer at approximately the same time as Dr. Willing himself." McCloy was able to satisfy the stringent demands of the classical school while also creating characters who were not merely pasteboard masks but people one can actually care about.

McCloy wrote non-series novels, which were also preoccupied with psychology, including *Panic* (1944), *The Further Side of Fear* (1967), and *The Smoking Mirror* (1979). She used her experience as a speech writer in the novel *Minotaur Country* (1975). McCloy was the first woman to become president of the Mystery Writers of America, which she helped to found, and won an EDGAR for her criticism. She was married for some time to the author Brett HALLIDAY.

MCCLURE, JAMES [HOWE] (1939–) South African author of mysteries and nonfiction books on law enforcement. Born in English-speaking Johannesburg, McClure was educated in Afrikaner Pietermaritzburg, and this duality is exploited in his books, which deal with the separation between Afrikaners and English South Africans as well as between whites and blacks. McClure moved to England in the 1960s, where he pursued a career as a journalist.

In such books as *The Steam Pig* (1971), *The Artful Egg* (1984), *The Gooseberry Fool* (1974), and *The Blood of an Englishman* (1980), McClure has charted the investigations of Lieutenant Tromp KRAMER and Bantu Detective Sergeant Mickey ZONDI in the fictional town of Trekkersburg. It is remarkable that McClure has been able to create a successful series dealing with a group as hated as the

South African police; in fact, he has been highly praised for his depiction of South African society and the racial discrimination under *apartheid*, almost as if he were writing historical fiction rather than detective stories.

Although Kramer is white and Zondi is black, McClure mostly avoids any cheap comic possibilities in the interaction of this "odd couple." Psychologically, they are realistically drawn: implicitly, Kramer supports apartheid, and Zondi opposes it but must work within its restrictions. While the racist policies of the government of course extend to the police force, and Zondi must take a subservient role in public, McClure also explores the friendship between the two men. Most of the intuitive and logical leaps—the bread and butter of the GENIUS DETECTIVE—are made by Zondi rather than Kramer.

The writing in the earlier books is almost minimalist, and the PROCEDURAL element is clearer. The stories can be quite gory. There is a kind of sadistic delight in the first scene of *The Gooseberry Fool*, when the victim is said to have "his Adam's apple cored." Scatological and black humor are more pronounced in this book, as is Kramer's racism.

The Song Dog (1991) is a "prequel" that explains Kramer and Zondi's first meeting. It is set in 1962, not coincidentally the year of Nelson Mandela's imprisonment. Kramer is in Zululand following up the murder of a fellow policeman and his nymphomaniac pet, while Zondi is tracking a serial killer.

McClure's nonfiction *Spike Island* (1980) deals with police in tough inner-city Liverpool. *Cop World* (1985) examines policing in San Francisco. He has also written several non-series novels: *Four and Twenty Virgins* (1973), *Rogue Eagle* (1976), and *Imago* (1988).

Another author who writes about South Africa in the period before the end of apartheid, but with a more overtly political agenda, is Wessel EBERSOHN.

MCCONE, SHARON A private eye created by Marcia MULLER, Sharon McCone is a small woman with black hair and dark eyes, which reflects her part-Native American, part-Scots-Irish background. The series is set in San Francisco, where McCone works for All Souls Legal Cooperative. The approach is partly PROCEDURAL, partly HARD-BOILED, with a fairly unobtrusive romantic subplot involving McCone's disc jockey boyfriend. With her husband, Bill PRONZINI, Muller wrote a book in which McCone works with the NAMELESS DETECTIVE—*Double* (1984).

McCone's cases tend to be socially relevant; in *The Shape of Dread* (1989), she investigates the death of a stand-up comic, to which a crack addict has confessed. In *Till the Butchers Cut Him Down* (1994), McCone leaves her job with All Souls in order to set up her own agency, McCone Investigations. She loses her very first client, who disappears mysteriously. *Wolf in the Shadows* (1993) was nominated for an EDGAR award. *Duo* (1998) contains short stories by Muller and Pronzini, some involving McCone.

BIBLIOGRAPHY Novels: *Edwin of the Iron Shoes* (1976), *Ask the Cards a Question* (1982), *The Cheshire Cat's Eye* (1983), *Games to Keep the Dark Away* (1984), *Leave A Message for Willie* (1984), *There's Nothing to Be Afraid Of* (1985), *Eye of the Storm* (1988), *There Is Something in a Sunday* (1989), *Where Echoes Live* (1991), *Pennies on a Dead Woman's Eyes* (1992), *A Wild and Lonely Place* (1995), *The Broken Promise Land* (1996), *Both Ends of the Night* (1997), *While Other People Sleep* (1998).

Short Stories: *Deceptions* (1991).

MCCOY, HORACE (1897–1955) Horace McCoy began writing for PULP MAGAZINES in their heyday, but his biggest success came in 1935 with THEY SHOOT HORSES, DON'T THEY? The book was reissued at the time of the Sydney Pollack film (1969), but McCoy has since slipped into obscurity once again.

Horace McCoy was born in Tennessee and served in the Army Air Corps in World War I. He would later write pulp adventure stories featuring pilots, as well as his detective stories. After the war he settled in Dallas, where he became a sportswriter and also founded a theater. After publishing in pulp magazines, including BLACK MASK, in 1931 he went to Hollywood to become a screenwriter.

McCoy's other novels are *No Pockets in a Shroud* (1937), about a reporter, and *Kiss Tomorrow Goodbye* (1948), about a psychopath; the latter title hints at the bleak outcomes of McCoy's novels.

MCCRUMB, SHARYN (1948–) Sharyn McCrumb credits her great-grandfathers, who were both circuit preachers, with her storytelling ability. McCrumb has ranged over the genre from historical fiction to SCIENCE FICTION.

McCrumb's family settled in the Smoky Mountains in 1790, not far from the town in Virginia's Blue Ridge where the author now lives. Many of her works have an Appalachian setting, and folklore, legend, and superstition play a central part. These aspects are most evident in her series of mysteries set in Tennessee and featuring Sheriff Spenser Arrowood, the first of which was IF EVER I RETURN, PRETTY PEGGY-O (1990). This series includes McCrumb's most well-received work from a critical standpoint. *MacPherson's Lament* (1992) has to do with the mystery of the disappearance of the Confederate treasury at the end of the Civil War. *The Hangman's Beautiful Daughter* (1992) takes place in a Faulknerian familial setting. McCrumb's most complex book to date is *She*

Walks These Hills (1994), in which a historian's retracing of the journey of an eighteen-year-old girl who escaped from the Shawnee in the seventeenth century intertwines with an escaped convict's flight in the present. Typically, there are some peculiar twists: the convict, Harm Sorley, is a local hero because he killed the hated Claib Maggard, a pompous magistrate. Sorley also suffers from a memory loss syndrome and doesn't remember the crime.

Bimbos of the Death Sun (1988) is quite a different kettle of fish. McCrumb's science fiction mysteries are woolly parodies of the genre; *Bimbos of the Death Sun* won an EDGAR award. *Zombies of the Gene Pool* (1992) is a further adventure of Dr. James Owen Omega, who is also the science fiction writer Jay Omega.

Yet another series involves forensic anthropologist Elizabeth MacPherson, whose cousin is murdered in the first book, *Sick of Shadows* (1984). Even here, McCrumb avoids the run-of-the-mill. In *Paying the Piper* (1988), she uses multiple narrators and alternates from first to third person. MacPherson travels to Scotland to participate in a dig in order to be near her boyfriend Cameron Dawson, who is studying seals on a nearby island. While investigating some Celtic stone circles, the members of the expedition begin to die mysteriously; the improbable but ingenious cause is only revealed at the end. This series also includes *Missing Susan* (1991), set during a tour of England's most notorious murder scenes.

MCCULLOUGH, MAC See BONNAMY, FRANCIS.

MACDONALD, JOHN D[ANN] (1916–1986) Born in Pennsylvania, MacDonald moved to Florida after serving in World War II. MacDonald's son has written that, while on duty in the Far East, MacDonald was frustrated by the censoring of his letters and so wrote a short story and sent it to his wife. Seeing that the writing had merit, she submitted it to the prestigious *Story* magazine, where it appeared in 1946. After the war, MacDonald began writing for PULP MAGAZINES, and was almost inconceivably productive, writing hundreds of stories between 1947 and 1952. "I stayed with the pulp markets until the mid-fifties," he said, "when the last of them were shot out from under me." One of MacDonald's best short stories is THE HOMESICK BUICK (1950).

It was in his adopted state of Florida that MacDonald set the novels for which he is most famous, the Travis MCGEE series. He had already written forty books when the first McGee novel, THE DEEP BLUE GOODBYE, appeared in 1964. His earlier books foreshadow many of the themes of the McGee stories. For example, *A Flash of Green* (1962) concerns a ruthless group of real estate developers bent on filling in a shallow bay to make way for "progress"—an 800-unit housing development. Elmo Bliss typifies the corrupt, canny, and vicious local politician and investor of the McGee books, and Jimmy Wing is a weaker, corruptible, and in some ways more interesting prototype of Travis McGee. The third-person narration produces a more objective tone and generally better writing than in some of MacDonald's later books.

The McGee novels have an enormous following with readers and with other writers, though they are of variable quality. Among the best is *Bright Orange for the Shroud* (1965); despite the grisly rape scene, the portrayal of rural poverty and brutality gives the book a powerful foundation. At the opposite pole is *Dress Her In Indigo* (1969), a south-of-the-border adventure with very little plot, long monologues, and tedious Mexican stereotypes. Then there is the strange case of *The Green Ripper* (1979), which H. R. F. KEATING put on his list of the one hundred best mysteries and compared to DICKENS. A bestseller that won MacDonald new attention, the book is a sort of commando thriller in which McGee goes after terrorists who have killed his girlfriend with a variant of the POISONED UMBRELLA. The book is better, however, than many of the xenophobic and paranoid "terrorists-in-the-heartland" thrillers that have come along since. *Cinnamon Skin* (1982) also deals with the terrorism theme, this time Chilean. McGee's friend Meyer lends his boat, the *John Maynard Keynes,* to his niece and her husband; the boat is blown up and the terrorists claim responsibility.

Supposedly, MacDonald was unsure of his ability to carry on a one-character series and so wrote the first four McGee books simultaneously. The fact that the books published in 1964 were set in a variety of places supports the idea that he wrote several books at once, trying out the character in various situations. They are the best McGee books, because they don't depend so heavily on the Bahia Mar setup. *Nightmare in Pink* (1964), set in New York City, begins with some of the best MacDonald writing, includes some of the most extended sex scenes, and later veers into psychedelic fantasy. Its humor also makes it very entertaining.

One of the most interesting and perhaps disturbing aspects of the books is their sexuality. On the one hand, Travis McGee is a stud, but one who preaches against the emptiness of sex without love. On the other hand, the books are pervaded by a predatory sexuality. MacDonald dwells on the grotesque idea that a woman being raped could be made to experience orgasm against her will. Even when McGee says "it was a great season for girls," the hunting metaphor is slightly creepy, given the violence against women that is often the center of the stories. At its worst, McGee's tale-telling takes on a lubricous quality and the odor of dirty linen, such as when McGee sexually liberates yet another unmerry widow (*The Girl in the Plain Brown Wrapper,* 1968), their "secretions a bitter fragrance in the stillness of the bed."

The Good Stuff (1981) and *More Good Stuff* (1984) are collections of short fiction by MacDonald, including early stories from the pulps.

MACDONALD, PHILIP (1899–1981) The English writer Philip MacDonald was an ex-cavalryman, an equestrian, and a screenwriter (he wrote the screenplay for the film REBECCA, based on the novel by Daphne DU MAURIER). His grandfather, George MacDonald, was a Scottish poet and novelist. MacDonald's military and artistic background would have an important effect on his work, and his famous series detective, Anthony GETHRYN, bears some similarities to the author himself.

After service in World War I, MacDonald trained cavalry horses, but in 1920 took up writing. His first book, *Ambrotox and Limping Dick* (1920), was a collaborative effort with his father (whose name happened to be Ronald MacDonald) and was published under the pseudonym Oliver Fleming. A second novel, *The Spandau Quid,* followed in 1923. His first solo novel written under his own name was THE RASP (1924), a conventional COUNTRY HOUSE puzzle. MacDonald was also fond of the NAPOLEON OF CRIME figure, and though his work was imitative he often tried to go the classic authors one better by coming up with distinctive and even outlandish methods and conundrums—sometimes to the point of the ridiculous. THE LIST OF ADRIAN MESSENGER (1959) is the best-known novel to include Gethryn other than *The Rasp,* and is also the last. MacDonald takes the daring step of killing off the title character in the first few pages. MacDonald's style, unfortunately, is even in his best books rather stilted, and the stiff-upper-lip talk dated. MacDonald won two EDGAR awards (1953 and 1956), both of which were for short fiction rather than novels. In the novels one has the feeling that the writer is impatient to get the story down on paper, and never went back to iron out the flaws in the style; perhaps this explains why the writing in the short stories is better.

MacDonald wrote other mysteries under the pseudonym Martin Porlock. What may be his most successful book, *Patrol* (1927), was not a mystery at all, but a military adventure tale. MacDonald himself wrote the first of several screen adaptations of the book (1934). *The Rynox Murder Mystery* (1930; orig title *Rynox*) and *Mystery of the Dead Police* (1933; orig title *X v. Rex*) are two other non-series thrillers. MacDonald also wrote screenplays for Mr. MOTO and Charlie CHAN films, as well as adapting *The List of Adrian Messenger* (1963).

MACDONALD, ROSS (born Kenneth Millar; 1915–1983) Kenneth Millar was born in Los Gatos, California (near San Francisco) but grew up in Canada. His ability to look at the world and experience from multiple perspectives, an outsider and an insider at the same time, allowed him to write the greatest series of private detective novels in the genre. Millar's family moved to Vancouver not long after his birth. His father and grandfather had been journalists, and his interest in language began at an early age. He also came to know mystery fiction as a boy through PULP MAGAZINES: he later wrote that "when I was thirteen, the most important figure in my imaginative life was Falcon Swift the Monocled Manhunter."

The most important event of Macdonald's childhood was the breakup of his parents' marriage, which echoes throughout Macdonald's work. Because his mother was sometimes an invalid, he spent years being passed from one home or relative to another—a boarding school in Winnipeg, an aunt in Medicine Hat, Alberta, and a dozen other places. After graduating from the University of Western Ontario in 1938, he married Margaret Sturm, who later published her mysteries under her married name Margaret MILLAR.

Macdonald taught at the University of Michigan in the early forties and served in the Pacific in World War II. His first mystery was published in 1944 (*The Dark Tunnel*), and was based on his travels in Nazi Germany as a student before the war (see NAZIS). His Navy experience is echoed in many of his later books, in stories of men haunted by the war and what it showed them about themselves. One of the earliest, and a key book in terms of Macdonald's development, was *The Three Roads* (1948), a novel about a young Navy lieutenant with AMNESIA whose wife has been murdered.

Blue City (1947) tries to do what the later books do, but without any subtlety; a young man returns home to find his father has been murdered, and begins to mop up the corrupt town through violence à la RED HARVEST (1929), the gangster classic by Dashiell HAMMETT. The main character's extreme toughness (which begins to look like stupidity), a literary sensibility, and criticism of social conditions and hypocrisy exist as raw ingredients, which were patiently refined in the Lew ARCHER novels.

In the preface to the omnibus volume *Archer in Hollywood* (1967), Macdonald poignantly describes his and his wife's early years as writers before they became successful, and his own discovery of Lew Archer and of himself: "My wife and I used to sit and write in our overcoats. . . . I felt it was now my duty to write an autobiographical novel about my depressing childhood in Canada. I tried, and got badly bogged down in sloppy feelings and groping prose. . . . I was in trouble, and Lew Archer got me out of it. . . . I couldn't work directly with my own experiences and feelings. A narrator had to be interposed, like protective lead, between me and the radioactive material."

The first novel to feature Lew Archer was *The Moving Target* (1948), but he had already been developing in Macdonald's short fiction, though under another name. In the short stories, collected in *The Name Is Archer* (1955), Macdonald shows his debt to Raymond CHANDLER in the terse action, snappy dialogue, and HARD-BOILED flavor. Macdonald's books, however, seem more modern than Chandler's of the same era, particularly in their sensibility, which emphasizes heroism less than the moral courage required to remain an individual within society. Archer's work consists of what other fictional p.i.'s often loftily (but unrealistically) disdain—divorce work. "I'm a jackal," Archer says early in *The Moving Target,* but he doesn't mean it; divorce is just the family—and society, and culture—in decline. Archer, in a sense, is a physician.

Another interesting early book is *The Ivory Grin* (1952). It begins with the disappearance of a black servant and her white employer's ruthless attempts to find her. The racial aspects of the story are well handled (and with more compassion than Chandler usually showed), but toward the end the complexities unravel into frayed ends and implausibilities rather more than is usual for Macdonald.

The idea that Macdonald was simply the child of Chandler, however, does not bear scrutiny. Macdonald is a master of plot, which Chandler said he was not really very much interested in. Lew Archer also developed over the years more than Philip MARLOWE did. Marlowe does eventually get married, though not because of any softening of his cynicism. Archer, on the other hand, has been married (and divorced) before we ever meet him, and alludes to his past as the basis for the values he puts into play. Macdonald also made fewer mistakes than Chandler in terms of flashy displays, editorializing, or "good ones" he couldn't stand to leave out.

Macdonald was preoccupied by several themes, though to say that all of Macdonald's novels have the same plot is an oversimplification. (The story of Cain and Abel is an archetype of all murder stories, but that does not mean the variations are boring repetitions.) Sophocles was Macdonald's inspiration, which he said he realized in THE GALTON CASE (1959); however, the influence had already made itself felt. All his books operate on the principle that history is fate; typically, old lies, buried history, or undiscovered guilt resurface to disturb the present and its carefully constructed appearances. The idea is not simply that "murder will out." The time-frames involved are often not years but decades. There is also a strong Oedipal element in that people behave in certain ways because they do not know who they really are; often, this lack of self-knowledge has arisen because their parentage has been obscured. The disasters that occur are personal, familial and public—messy divorces and senseless murders, the southern Californian equivalent of Oedipus's crimes. The major difference is that Macdonald's characters are thoroughly modern, and only blind themselves metaphorically, through self-pity and rationalizations.

The Doomsters (1958) gives clear expression to Archer's (or Macdonald's) view when he says "an alternating current of guilt ran between her and all of us involved with her," and that it "flowed in a closed circuit if you traced it far enough." This outlook, however, extends even to a theory of time: "It isn't possible to brush people off, let alone yourself. They wait for you in time, which is also a closed circuit." Macdonald's conception of time was partly based on Nietzsche, and Archer alludes to Zarathustra's most famous dream of eternal recurrence: "The circuit of guilty time was too much like a snake with its tail in its mouth, consuming itself."

In such books as THE FAR SIDE OF THE DOLLAR (1964), *The Galton Case, Black Money* (1966), and *Sleeping Beauty* (1973), Macdonald dealt with a series of recurrent figures: the grown-up child searching for his past; the possibly willing kidnap victim; and the troubled person of some genius who reacts immaturely, and sometimes criminally (but with some justice) when his or her talents aren't recognized. In one novel, a mentally ill son is persecuted by his family because he wants to give back land his family stole from interned Japanese Americans during World War II; in another, an exceptionally bright Hispanic youth tries to pass himself off as a European to avoid prejudice.

One of Macdonald's most successful books was *The Drowning Pool* (1950), known particularly through the film version starring Paul Newman that was made a quarter century later. It is a more "straight" detective novel, however, with the skeletons in the family closet only beginning to rattle toward the end. Archer is hired by Maude Slocum in what seems a routine blackmail case. She is married to the pathetic rich boy Francis Slocum, who pretends to be an actor while waiting for his elderly mother to die. The family estate sits on millions of dollars worth of oil, but the older Mrs. Slocum refuses to sell out and keeps her family on a strict allowance—a perfect scenario for a murder. Although well written, in *The Drowning Pool* Macdonald tends to telegraph his punches, embellishes the story with few of his usually knotty complexities, and when the past finally does bounce up, the case is already closed. At the opposite end of the spectrum is THE CHILL (1964), a baffling and rewarding story that is Macdonald's most perfect plot. It was awarded the Silver Dagger by the CRIME WRITERS' ASSOCIATION of Great Britain. He won the award again the following year for *The Far Side of the Dollar.*

Macdonald's own life was full of tragedy. His only daughter died of a brain hemorrhage at an early age (Laurel Russo in *Sleeping Beauty* is thought to be a memorial to her). Alzheimer's disease prematurely ended Macdonald's writing career. THE BLUE HAMMER (1976), his last novel, shows him at the height of his powers and perhaps about to embark on new experiments that were never made.

MCGARR, INSPECTOR A character who appears in a series of novels by Bartholomew GILL, McGarr is a middle-aged Irishman who has returned to his native country after a brilliant career on the continent with INTERPOL and Criminal Justice in Paris. Now installed as the Chief Inspector of Detectives with the Garda Soichana, McGarr is something of a celebrity, though many resent his flamboyance and suspect his Continental connections and pretensions. McGarr (like Nigel STRANGEWAYS) is accompanied on his cases, somewhat improbably, by his wife Noreen. She is described as a small, sexy woman with copper-colored hair who is also an art historian.

McGarr and the Politician's Wife (1977) was the first book in the series. *McGarr and the Sienese Conspiracy* (1977) has a plot involving international intrigue, and the writing is weak. Throughout the series, McGarr's drinking and his sex life are rather boring. The best of the early books is *Inspector McGarr on the Cliffs of Moher* (1978), in which a female investigative journalist is found at the well-known tourist attraction in County Clare, stabbed to death with a pitchfork. She turns out to be the third of a trio of young Irish people who have recently returned from New York, having made their fortunes. The other two are a successful commercial novelist and a cold, idealistic doctor. Gill uses their intertwined fates to meditate on modern Ireland, including the IRA, for which McGarr has contempt.

The DEATH OF A JOYCE SCHOLAR (1989) is the most successful of Gill's books to date. It was nominated for an EDGAR award. In *The Death of Love* (1992), Chief Superintendent McGarr has a baby daughter and is starting to feel old. He investigates the mysterious death of Paddy Power, a millionaire who ought not to have had many enemies. But Power (is he named for the brand of whisky, or the brand of obsession?) had a diary containing dirty secrets about politicians, and his own life is hardly clean. As usual, Gill goes somewhat overboard on his bang-up ending.

BIBLIOGRAPHY Novels: *McGarr at the Dublin Horse Show* (1979), *McGarr and the P.M. Belgrave Square* (1983), *McGarr and the Method of Descartes* (1984), *Death on a Cold, Wild River* (1993), *Death of an Ardent Bibliophile* (1995), *Death of an Irish Sea Wolf* (1996), *Death of an Irish Tinker* (1997).

MCGEE, TRAVIS A character created by John D. MACDONALD. McGee is not properly speaking a private investigator, since he doesn't have a license. Nor is his ostensible object the pursuit of justice, though like every cynical tough guy he harbors a passion for doing good as though it were a vice. McGee often helps people who have been the victims of con artists—but the help is self-interested, since he takes half of whatever money he recovers. The first novel in the series was THE DEEP BLUE GOODBYE (1964).

McGee has many HARD-BOILED features: deep cynicism about human beings, enormous success with women, and a handsome, muscular physique. But he also lives on a houseboat in Bahia Mar, Florida (that he drives a Rolls Royce made over into a pickup truck is a typical bit of overkill) and is perhaps the first modern mystery hero to pursue a consciously "alternative lifestyle." He is, in the language of his times, a "swinger." Depending on the amount of sixties jargon, the books are more or less dated. Some of his sex-talk is frankly offensive or at least tacky, as when he laments the murder of a woman as a waste of "sweet flesh and heat and honeyed membrane."

McGee also delivers a large dose of pop psychology, which, thirty years later, seems often naive and embarrassing. In *Darker Than Amber* (1966), he describes how he frees a woman from self-delusion and frigidity through his talk and sexual therapy. McGee sees himself as something of a philosopher, and analyzes aspects of American society in his asides. This is one of the most often remarked upon aspects of the books, but it is also one of the weakest. Carried too far, McGee's self-absorption becomes absurdly melodramatic—especially when he speaks of himself in the third person—and the writing florid: "I had to be a roamer, a salvage expert, a gregarious loner, a seeker of a thousand tarnished grails, finding too many excuses for all the dragons along the way."

The battery of early books with which the series was launched are among the best. *A Purple Place for Dying*

(1964) takes place in the West, and deals with the common Western theme of the powerful rancher-speculator who has an entire community in his back pocket (one wonders, however, if any woman would refer to herself as "a big creamy bitch"). *The Quick Red Fox* (1964) is about a hunt for some dirty pictures and takes McGee to upstate New York (MacDonald grew up in Utica), California, and Phoenix. The best novel in the series, *Nightmare in Pink* (1964), is set in New York City. *Bright Orange for the Shroud* (1965) matches McGee against a sadist and has one of the neatest plots and some of the most repulsive sex of any book in the series. *Dress Her In Indigo* (1969) is a missing persons case that takes McGee to Mexico, where he meets an aristocratic English nymphomaniac, one of the author's silliest characters. *The Turquoise Lament* (1973) has a good plot but is spoiled by the poorer writing that plagues the later books. Two of McGee's friends who live on a boat break up because the woman thinks the man is plotting to kill her, and he thinks she is insane; it is up to McGee to discover the truth. Late in his career, *The Green Ripper* (1979) won MacDonald many new readers, though it was an atypical McGee novel.

McGee, oddly, bears comparison with Matt SCUDDER, who in a different time and place could be considered his smarter, post-sixties, post-sexual-revolution descendant. In fact, many contemporary novelists have turned out, wittingly or not, grown-up versions of McGee. Other writers who have set books on McGee's Florida turf are James W. Hall, who takes up MacDonald's attack on the corruption of real estate developers, and Carl HIASSEN. For the prehistory of McGee's Florida, see KILLING MISTER WATSON (1990) and the works of Lester DENT. The leading Florida mystery character before McGee was Mike SHAYNE.

BIBLIOGRAPHY Novels: *A Deadly Shade of Gold* (1965), *One Fearful Yellow Eye* (1966), *Pale Grey for Guilt* (1968), *The Girl in the Plain Brown Wrapper* (1968), *The Long Lavender Look* (1970), *A Tan and Sandy Silence* (1972), *The Scarlet Ruse* (1973), *The Dreadful Lemon Sky* (1975), *The Empty Copper Sea* (1978), *Free Fall in Crimson* (1981), *Cinnamon Skin* (1982), *The Lonely Silver Rain* (1984).

MCGIVERN, WILLIAM P[ETER] (1924–1982) The American author William P. McGivern is best known for his novel *The Big Heat* (1952), which was made into a FILM NOIR classic in 1953 by Fritz LANG. The novel tells the story of Dave Bannion, an offbeat version of the classic HARD-BOILED detective. Bannion is huge, a former football player turned Philadelphia cop. Though tough on the job, he also likes to read Kant and Benedetto Croce in his spare time. During the novel, he goes from being a highly respected, even-handed detective to a scary pursuer of revenge. McGivern liked the figure of the policeman gone wrong or pushed too far, and used this type again in *Rogue Cop* (1954) and *The Darkest Hour* (1955).

McGivern was born in Chicago and published his first detective novel, *But Death Runs Faster,* in 1948. He later worked as a screenwriter for television and film.

MCGUFFIN The term "McGuffin" is used to mean the thing—an object, money, knowledge, "the goods"—that drives the plot. In THE MALTESE FALCON (1929), the McGuffin is the falcon itself; in THE BIG SLEEP (1939), it is the knowledge of what happened to Sean Regan. The phrase has been attributed to Alfred HITCHCOCK.

Amos McGuffin is a private detective character in a series by Robert UPTON.

MCGUIRE, PAUL (1903–) Born in Australia, Paul McGuire was a historian, soldier, and diplomat. He served in the navy in World War II and later became his country's ambassador to Italy and was a delegate to the United Nations. All of his mystery writing was done before the war; his first mystery was *The Black Rose Murder* (1931; orig title *Murder in Borstall*). His most famous novels are A FUNERAL IN EDEN (1938; orig title *Burial Service*), which takes place on an island in the Pacific, and *Enter Three Witches* (1940; orig title *The Spanish Steps*), which was set in Italy.

MCHALE, TOM (1942–) The American writer Tom McHale achieved some notoriety in the early seventies, writing in a satirical style that reflected the social unrest caused by the Vietnam War. He was sometimes considered an epigone of Thomas BERGER. McHale grew up in Scranton, Pennsylvania, and later attended Temple University and the University of Pennsylvania. He also attended the Writers' Workshop at the University of Iowa. McHale was a caseworker with the Department of Public Assistance in Philadelphia before becoming a full-time writer. His first novel, *Principato* (1970), was published when he was only twenty-eight.

McHale's books depend heavily on their context. His satirizing of the traditional American values that had been discredited by the Vietnam fiasco and his instinct for ferreting out hypocrisy could hardly have failed to strike a chord at the time of publishing. In his second book, *Farragan's Retreat* (1971), he offered a perverse version of the middle-class family saga, set in his native Pennsylvania. The novel is about a middle-aged bus company executive who is being groomed as an assassin by his rabidly hawkish brother and sister, both of whom have had sons killed or maimed in Vietnam. Farragan's target is supposed to be his own son, who has fled to Canada after writing a "letter of condolence" to Ho Chi Minh. Another brother, a miserable Catholic priest who lives alone in an empty monastery and is tortured by unfulfilled sexual desires, is chosen to give Farragan an alibi for his murderous trip to Montreal.

If *Farragan's Retreat* was vaguely criminal, *School Spirit* (1976) was a straight mystery novel, or almost so; McHale still inserts large elements of social satire, this time taking aim at one of America's fattest and most ridiculous sacred cows: football. A coach investigates the death of a player during a hazing (the fat and ugly boy was locked in a freezer) twenty years before.

MACHARG, WILLIAM [BRIGGS] (1872–1951) William MacHarg was a familiar name in slick magazines of his day, such as *The Saturday Evening Post.* He is remembered now for two distinctive contributions to the mystery genre, both written collaboratively. MacHarg was born in New York but attended the University of Michigan and then became a reporter in Chicago with the *Tribune.* There he met native Chicagoan Edwin BALMER; together they collaborated on *The Achievements of Luther Trant* (1910), a collection of stories that was among the first to use modern psychology in fiction, little more than a decade after Sigmund Freud's epoch-making first publications. Trant scored another first when he used a lie-detector in one of his investigations. Balmer and MacHarg also wrote *The Blind Man's Eyes* (1916), one of the best uses of blindness in mystery fiction. MacHarg's solo work in the crime genre includes *The Affairs of O'Malley* (1940), a collection of stories about a clever Irish cop.

MACHEN, ARTHUR (pseudonym of Arthur Llewellyn Jones, 1863–1947) The Welshman Arthur Machen was one of the great writers of OCCULT fiction of the late Victorian and Edwardian periods. Many of his stories and novels are set in the medieval era in England and Wales. He published many works, including *The Great God Pan and the Inmost Light* (1894) and *The Terror* (1917), but he remained poor for most of his life and had to work at a variety of jobs, including teacher, actor, and translator. One of his translations was the memoirs of Casanova, which ran to a dozen volumes. *The Hill of Dreams* (1907), one of his best-known works, is about a Roman fort haunted by its own sinister history.

Machen's foray into mystery fiction was the collection *The Three Imposters* (1895), about two private detectives, into which he brought elements of horror.

MCILVANNEY, WILLIAM (1936–) A Scottish teacher and writer, William McIlvanney achieved sudden notoriety in the crime genre with *Laidlaw* (1977). Set in Glasgow, this dark, realistic novel was praised by Ross MACDONALD and also won a Silver Dagger from the British CRIME WRITERS' ASSOCIATION. McIlvanney had taught in France and Britain and had previously published literary novels, one of which won the prestigious Whitbread prize.

Jack Laidlaw is a Glasgow detective and tough guy of the old school; suspicious of authority, he acts more like a HARD-BOILED dick than a PROCEDURAL policeman. Like Philip MARLOWE, he has a inner moral compass that is belied by his public manner; thus he is always alone. The sequel to *Laidlaw* was long in coming: *The Papers of Tony Veitch* was published in 1983. In this book, Laidlaw's friend Eck Adamson, a vagrant alcoholic, summons him to his deathbed in the hospital and hands him a note containing the names of two people and a pub, "The Crib." Laidlaw thinks Adamson was murdered, and one of the people on the list is soon killed. Veitch is a student who seems to have the answers but has mysteriously disappeared.

The third book in the series, *Strange Loyalties,* did not appear until 1991. Laidlaw has to return to Ayrshire to investigate the death of his younger brother, who seems unmourned by his widow. It turns out that the marriage was on the rocks, and Laidlaw begins peering through the cracks in other people's façades, into souls in various stages of decomposition. A subplot involves the murder of a Glasgow drug dealer. McIlvaney handles the classic converging plot lines of the hard-boiled mystery with assurance; the design of the book is not new, but its intensity, setting, and earnestness are unusual.

MCINERNY, RALPH [MATTHEW] (1929–) Ralph McInerny was born in St. Paul, Minnesota, where he attended seminary and, later, the University of Minnesota. He received his Ph.D. from Laval University (Quebec) in 1954, and the following year began teaching at the University of Notre Dame, where he has established himself as a medieval scholar. He also co-founded the Catholic magazine *Crisis.* Beginning with *The Logic of Analogy: An Interpretation of Saint Thomas* (1961), McInerny published a dozen works on philosophy and religion. He has also written many novels, a number of which are humorous; this quality spills over into his genre writing. His first novel, written a full decade before he turned to mysteries, was *Jolly Rogerson* (1967). McInerny also directed the Jacques Maritain Center at Notre Dame and was co-editor of *The New Scholasticism.*

It is not surprising that the most familiar (to a general audience) of his many publications, his Father DOWLING mysteries, have a religious background. The first of these books was *Her Death of Cold* (1977). McInerny published another series, about the nun Mary Teresa Dempsey, under the pseudonym Monica Quill. "Attila the Nun" (Dempsey) is barely over five feet tall but weighs more than two hundred pounds. She is part of a dwindling religious order and lives with the two other surviving members in Chicago. Fortunately for the plots, one of the other sisters has a brother who is a cop.

McInerny's books can sometimes only be read with difficulty, and as mysteries, they do not serve up anything groundbreaking, though he does manage sometimes to bring Catholic theology into the plots. The writing style is not sharp; the sentences are often turgid, which is a shame, because the plots in outline are often interesting. McInerny's novels about lawyer Andrew BROOM have no religious connection and are written in a less heavy style.

One of McInerny's non-series books is *Romanesque* (1978), a comical novel with a protagonist who resembles the author himself. A specialist in medieval philosophy receives a fellowship to study at the Vatican (McInerny himself had been a Fulbright scholar), where he becomes involved in a mystery surrounding the theft of a manuscript of St. Thomas Aquinas. Another novel with a bibliophile interest is *Frigor Mortis,* published in 1989 (see BOOKS). In 1997, McInerny started a new series set at Notre Dame. *On this Rockne* (1997) is about gridiron fanaticism and the patron saint of Notre Dame football, Knut Rockne. A controversy between football-rabid alumni and trustees leads to murder.

MCKEE, INSPECTOR CHRISTOPHER Created by Helen REILLY, Inspector McKee is somewhat like a British detective trapped in an American milieu: pipe-smoking (or chewing), tweedy, tall, and dour, he is a Scottish version of the GENIUS DETECTIVE. McKee, however, is an inspector with the New York City Police Department, and later in the series becomes the head of the homicide department. The series has a reputation for its early use of PROCEDURAL elements, which was remarked upon by Howard HAYCRAFT in *Murder for Pleasure* (1941). McKee is assisted by Inspector Todhunter. Although neither man is married, BARZUN and TAYLOR said of one book that its romantic suspense elements were "meant for women readers who no longer exist." *Dead for a Ducat* (1939) is about the murder of a rich man's housekeeper. *Compartment K* (1955; British title *Murder Rides the Express*), a mystery involving TRAINS, is set in Canada.

BIBLIOGRAPHY Novels: *The Diamond Feather* (1930), *Murder in the Mews* (1931), *McKee of Centre Street* (1934), *The Line-Up* (1934), *Mr. Smith's Hat* (1936), *Dead Man's Control* (1936), *All Concerned Notified* (1939), *Murder in Shinbone Alley* (1940), *Death Demands an Audience* (1940), *The Dead Can Tell* (1940), *Mourned on Sunday* (1941), *Three Women in Black* (1941), *Name Your Poison* (1942), *The Opening Door* (1944), *Murder on Angler's Island* (1945), *The Silver Leopard* (1946), *The Farmhouse* (1947), *Staircase 4* (1949), *Murder at Arroways* (1950), *Lament for the Bride* (1951), *The Double Man* (1952), *The Velvet Hand* (1953), *Tell Her It's Murder* (1954), *The Canvas Dagger* (1956), *Ding-Dong Bell* (1958), *Not Me, Inspector* (1959), *Follow Me* (1960), *Certain Sleep* (1961), *The Day She Died* (1962).

MACLAIN, CAPTAIN DUNCAN See KENDRICK, BAYNARD.

MACLEOD, ANGUS (1906–1991) A generation before the current crop of Scottish crime writers—including Ian RANKIN, William MCILVANNEY, and Quintin Jardine—Angus MacLeod was writing suspense novels set in Scotland. Unlike the recent proceduralists who write about the grit of Glasgow and the evils of Edinburgh, MacLeod set his books in small Scottish villages and concerned himself with character, not plot. His outstandingly atmospheric THE DAM (1968) includes a shooting and a battle between developers and traditionalists, but does not involve detection. The characters are a real pleasure, however, and not the usual Scottish stereotypes. *The Tough and the Tender* (1960) is more of a crime novel, with a murder in a small Scottish community investigated by a police inspector. In *Blessed Above Women* (1965), Captain Ross, the owner of a fishing hotel, is secretly engaged to his mistress, with whom he had become involved even before his wife died in a mental hospital. His appeal to women creates plenty of jealousy, which seems to be the motive for his murder—until it is discovered that his will is missing. Complex relationships are again the focus. The inspector finds the will in a strange place, which, oddly, connects the murder to a series of thefts of women's panties by some prankster in the hotel.

MACLEOD, CHARLOTTE (1922–) Born in Canada and educated in Massachusetts, Charlotte MacLeod worked for thirty years for a Boston advertising agency. Her background provided the settings of her main detective series: upper-class Boston society for the team of Sarah KELLING and Max Bittersohn, the Massachusetts countryside for agronomy professor Peter SHANDY, and Canada for the two series she publishes under the name Alisa Craig—one about Inspector Madoc Rhys of the Royal Canadian Mounted Police and the other focusing on the Grub-and-Stakers Gardening and Roving Club of Lobelia

Falls, Ontario. The pseudonym pays tribute to the author's Scottish roots: Ailsa Craig is a rock in the Firth of Clyde.

MacLeod is considered to have revived the COZY mystery and probably hundreds of imitators have followed. In the cozy world of nice characters and homely settings, crime falls like thunder from a clear sky. MacLeod builds intriguing plots that tend to be overly intricate. Sometimes she may go to excess in pursuit of adventurous romanticism, and trades the tightness of the plot for the charm of a situation. To get out of impossibilities, she then has to perform sometimes less than elegant maneuvers. In *Trouble in the Brasses* (1989), an Inspector Rhys mystery, the detective comes to the rescue of his father—a well-known director—when murder breaks out in the orchestra during a tour. On their journey to an important stop, the hired plane gets lost and is forced down near an abandoned Canadian mining village, where Rhys encounters new murders and a nutty seventy-year-old boozer with a biplane. The atmosphere is wacky rather than cozy. *The Resurrection Man* (1992), a Kelling/Bittersohn novel, is a bizarre story that shows MacLeod's tendency to go off the rails in an everything-but-the-kitchen-sink manner. It concerns an expert antique restorer killed with a spear; a long-lost child; and a huge diamond taken from the head of an idol (the idol is cursed, of course).

MacLeod practices a form that is inherently unrealistic; it has no rules other than that developments be continuous. The characters need not be, and are not, believable. Whether one likes the form or not, it is clear that MacLeod has perfected it and is more skilled than her competitors.

MACLEOD, ROBERT See KNOX, BILL.

MCMURTRY, LARRY See PROHIBITION.

MACPHERSON, ELIZABETH See MCCRUMB, SHARYN.

MADAM MIDAS (1888; repr 1985) This long-forgotten novel by Fergus HUME is a partial sequel to his bestselling THE MYSTERY OF A HANSOM CAB (1886). The sleuth of the earlier novel, the lawyer Calton, reappears in another tale of greed, new-found wealth in Australia's gold fields, and Victorian class conflict. The title character is living in the former mansion of Mark Frettleby, who was at the center of *The Mystery of a Hansom Cab.* The MCGUFFIN of the story is "The Devil's Lead," a legendary gold mine some believe is just a myth. The sinister M. Vandeloup, accustomed "to carry[ing] on with guilty wives under the very noses of unsuspecting husbands," is one of the author's better villains. He also keeps the plot afloat with multiple crimes.

MADDOX, IVOR See LININGTON, ELIZABETH.

MADONNA OF THE SLEEPING CARS, THE (*Madone des sleepings,* 1925; tr 1927) A novel by Maurice Dekobra (1885–1973), known chiefly because it made use of the Orient Express years before Agatha CHRISTIE did. The book, which became a bestseller, was subtitled "un roman cosmopolite," and it certainly lived up to the sophisticated, hectic, and liberated spirit of the twenties. The plot is so outlandish as to be almost a PARODY; the book's patent ridiculousness can be read either as boring, historically curious, or delicious. Lady Diana Wynham is a nymphomaniac Scottish widow who is attended by her secretary, Prince Gerard Séliman. He left New York after his affair with his stepdaughter blasted his marriage, carrying with him only "a melancholy sketch of Lake Placid on an April afternoon." It emerges that the Lady is broke; however, she has 15,000 acres of oil fields in Georgian Russia that Prince Gerard is sent to recover. Along the way, he encounters Bolshevik agents, including the evil Irena Mouravieff, the "Marquise de Sade of Red Russia."

Although the translation is poor, some of the wit shows through: when Lady Diana asks the Prince if she is bad after yet another of her flings, he responds, "you are not a bad woman. You are a philanthropist." Besides the scenes satirizing the Revolution, there are many instances (for example, when the "Freudian" Dr. Traurig bombards Lady Diana with x-rays while she kisses Gerard in order to make a "spectral analysis" of her emotions) that show contemporary preoccupations and subjects of debate. The frank treatment of sex is certainly a far cry from the English writers of the GOLDEN AGE. Among Dekobra's many other books are *The Thirteenth Lover* (1928) and *Venus on Wheels* (1931).

MAGOOZLUM A word used in Raymond Chandler's THE LONG GOODBYE (1953) to describe bad writing. No source has been found for the word, which may be Chandler's own creation. It is probably related to "magoo" (a stupid or clownish man), the word that gave us Mr. Magoo.

MAIGRET, JULES A detective of the Parisian Sûreté, Inspector Jules Maigret appeared in a vast number of works by Georges SIMENON. Maigret is methodical and deeply psychological. He is, in a sense, the Sherlock HOLMES of non-English detectives, for his tenacity and not simply because of his pipe smoking. On the other hand, Maigret has more sympathy for his quarry than Holmes (though Holmes may also decide to let the culprit go, as in the case of "The Blue Carbuncle"). Maigret is also less scientific than intuitive, revealing the even deeper influence of POE on the Continent.

The outward facts of Maigret's life are that he, like many a Parisian, is actually a transplanted provincial. He and his wife Louise have an abiding relationship and live in an apartment in the Boulevard Richard-Lenoir. (It has been pointed out that Simenon was creating a fictional domestic tranquility that he himself did not enjoy.) Many of the novels do not take place in Paris, and some are set in the United States, where Simenon lived for a time. The inspector is irascible, sometimes harsh and often impatient; his nemesis is the magistrate Coméliau, who does not like Maigret very much. Maigret is a large man who likes to eat and drink—and, possibly showing his Belgian roots, prefers beer.

The "psychology" of the Maigret novels is often misdescribed; it has to do not with "psychos" and aberrations but with the psychology of everyday life—the way a woman takes a man's arm; the way one expects a person to be who has impressed you on first meeting, and the vague feeling of disappointment to discover on second meeting that they are just human; or, in one marvelous case, when Maigret is on his way to a murder scene, his stopping to pick up a puff ball left by some party goers in the back of a taxi.

The volume of Maigret's cases is astounding: if every Sherlock Holmes story were a novel, they would still fall far short of Simenon's productivity. Published in France as novels, the stories have recently begun to be printed in English-speaking countries in their original form (one title, one book), rather than as compilations. Many translations exist, including some by Anthony BOUCHER.

Simenon said that he deliberately used a limited vocabulary of only about 2,000 words in the stories, and, at least in the original, stock words and descriptions appear over and over. Yet the settings and the psychology of the stories are unique, for example the scene in *Le Pendu de St. Pholien* (1931; tr MAIGRET AND THE HUNDRED GIBBETS) in which Maigret accidentally causes a stranger to commit suicide. What is strongest in the novels is that one never knows what Maigret is going to do next. In *Le chien jaune* (1936; tr *Maigret and the Yellow Dog;* also tr *A Face for a Clue*), he appears to be doing nothing. Maigret is temporarily posted to Rennes and investigates killings in the town of Concarneau in which a yellow mutt seems to be an important clue. Maigret's assistant is a young man on his first case, Inspector Leroy, whose scientific approach is humorously contrasted with Maigret's cool and reserved psychologism.

François Mauriac's comment that Simenon depicted "nightmare" scenarios with "unendurable art" may seem lavish praise. Particularly in his books written during the economic depression of the thirties, however, Simenon sometimes evoked appalling squalidness, pathetic greed, and what he feared most of all, failure. *L'Ombre chinoise* (1932; tr *Maigret Mystified;* also tr *The Shadow in the Courtyard*) shows a set of interlocking relationships among the tenants of an apartment house, including a grasping shrew whose social climbing backfires: the no-good man she divorces becomes a millionaire, while her second husband, a spineless civil servant, fails to rise in his profession. They are all forced to live together in the same building—along with two insane sisters and a nosy landlady—without any privacy. Maigret, on the other hand, displays such sang froid (or contempt?) that, shut in a train compartment with the murderer, he falls asleep! In *Pietr-le-Letton* (1931; tr *The Strange Case of Peter the Lett*), a body believed to be that of a notorious criminal and master of disguises is found in the toilet of a train. But the elusive Lett has other identities, including a Norwegian sailor and a drunken Russian descended to the gutter. The murder of Maigret's friend, Inspector Torrence, provides him, unusually, with a motive of vengeance.

One reason there is a marked difference between the books of the thirties and the later Maigrets is that Simenon stopped writing about the Inspector for eight years; he returned in *Maigret Revient* (1942), which included three novelettes, one of which was *Les Caves du Majestic* (1942; tr *Maigret and the Hotel Majestic,* 1978).

In *Les Scrupules de Maigret* (1958; tr *Maigret Has Scruples,* 1959), Maigret faces the situation of a crime that has not yet happened, and may not—he has no legal obligation, but investigates anyway. Approached first by a possibly mad but likeable fellow who sells toys, then by his incongruously elegant and sophisticated wife, Maigret wonders who is a danger to whom. His interest leads to some consideration of psychiatry in search of a true diagnosis of the little "King of the Electric Train." Led astray by noble impulses or curiosity, Maigret finds a tragedy that expresses the Simenonian belief that "there exists, between responsibility and irresponsibility, an indefinite zone, a realm of shadows into which it is dangerous to venture." At this late date, Maigret and his wife are beginning to get old, each worrying that the other is concealing some serious illness—the most domestic subplot Simenon allowed himself.

The publishing history of the Maigret novels is tangled, to say the least. The first translations were omnibus volumes, which included more than one novella under a single title (see bibliography). Some Maigret novels were not translated at all, and some collections of novelettes were only translated in part; for example, *Signé Picpus* (1944) contained three pieces: *Signé Picpus* was translated as *To Any Lengths* in the omnibus collection *Maigret on Holiday* (1950), but the other two (*L'Inspecteur Cadavre* and *Félicie est Là*) were not. Translation titles in English and American editions sometimes differed; some English translations appeared in only one of the two countries. There are also several volumes of Maigret short stories that have never been translated (see bibliography); however, a selection of stories from a number of books was published as *The Short Cases of Inspector Maigret* (1959). Some of the Maigret short stories appeared in *Ellery Queen's Mystery Magazine,* and one of them was awarded the Ellery Queen international short story prize and reprinted in the anthology *Ellery Queen's Golden Thirteen* (1970).

BIBLIOGRAPHY Novels, by individual title: *M. Gallet Decédé* (1931; tr *The Death of Monsieur Gallet,* 1932), *Le Charretier de La "Providence"* (1931; tr *The Crime at Lock 14,* 1934), *La Nuit du Carrefour* (1931; tr *The Crossroad Murders*), *Un Crime en Hollande* (1931; tr *A Crime in Holland*), *Au Rendez-Vous des Terre-Neuves* (1931; tr *The Sailors' Rendezvous,* 1940), *La Tete d'un Homme* (1931; tr *A Battle of Nerves,* 1939), *La Danseuse du Gai-Moulin* (1931; tr *At the Gai-Moulin,* 1940), *La Guinguette à Deux Sous* (1932; tr *Guinguette by the Seine,* 1940), *L'Affaire Saint-Fiacre* (1932; tr *The Saint-Fiacre Affair,* 1940), *Chez les Flamands* (1932; tr *The Flemish Shop,* 1940), *Le Fou de Bergerac* (1932; tr *The Madman of Bergerac,* 1940), *Le Port des Brumes* (1932; tr *Death of a Harbour-Master,* 1941), *Liberty Bar* (1932; tr *Liberty Bar,* 1940), *L'Ecluse No. 1* (1933; tr *The Lock at Charenton,* 1941), *Maigret* (1934; tr *Maigret Returns,* 1941), *La Pipe de Maigret, et Maigret se Fâche* (1947), *Maigret à New-York* (1947; tr *Maigret in New York's Underworld,* 1955), *Maigret et L'Inspecteur Malchanceux* (1947; rev ed *Maigret et L'Inspecteur Malgracieux*), *Maigret et son Mort* (1948; tr *Maigret's Special Murder,* 1964; also tr *Maigret's Dead Man,* 1964), *Les Vacances de Maigret* (1948; tr *A Summer Holiday,* 1950; also tr *No Vacation for Maigret,* 1953), *La Premiere Enquete de Maigret* (1949; tr *Maigret's First Case,* 1958), *Maigret Chez le Coroner* (1949), *Mon Ami Maigret* (1949; tr *My Friend Maigret,* 1956; also tr *The Methods of Maigret,* 1957), *Maigret et la Vieille Dame* (1950; tr *Maigret and the Old Lady,* 1958), *L'Amie de Madame Maigret* (1950; tr *Madame Maigret's Own Case,* 1959; also tr *Madame Maigret's Friend,* 1960), *Les Mémoires de Maigret* (1950; tr *Maigret's Memoirs,* 1963), *Maigret au "Picratt's"* (1951; tr *Maigret in Montmartre,* 1954; also tr *Inspector Maigret and the Strangled Stripper,* 1954), *Maigret en Meublé* (1951; tr *Maigret Takes a Room,* 1960; also tr *Maigret Rents a Room,* 1961), *Maigret et la Grande Perche* (1951; tr *Maigret and the Burglar's Wife,* 1955; also tr *Inspector Maigret and the Burglar's Wife,* 1956), *Maigret, Lognon et les Gangsters* (1952; tr *Inspector Maigret and the Killers,* 1954; also tr *Maigret and the Gangsters,* 1974), *Le Revolver de Maigret* (1952; tr *Maigret's Revolver,* 1956), *Maigret a Peur* (1953; tr *Maigret Afraid,* 1961), *Maigret se Trompe* (1953; tr *Maigret's Mistake,* 1954), *Maigret et L'Homme du Banc* (1953), *Maigret à l'École* (1954; tr *Maigret Goes to School,* 1957), *Maigret et la Jeune Morte* (1954; tr *Maigret and the Young Girl,* 1955; also tr *Inspector Maigret and the Dead Girl,* 1955), *Maigret Chez le Ministre* (1954; tr *Maigret and the Minister,* 1969; also tr *Maigret and the Calame Report,* 1970), *Maigret et le Corps sans Tête* (1955; tr *Maigret and the Headless Corpse,* 1967; also tr *Maigret and the Headless Corpse,* 1968), *Maigret Tend un Piège* (1955; tr *Maigret Sets a Trap,* 1965), *Un Échec de Maigret* (1956; tr *Maigret's Failure,* 1962), *Maigret s'Amuse* (1957; tr *Maigret's Little Joke,* 1957; also tr *None of Maigret's Business,* 1958), *Maigret Voyage* (1958; tr *Maigret and the Millionaires,* 1974), *Les Scrupules de Maigret* (1958; tr *Maigret Has Scruples,* 1959), *Maigret et les Témoins Récalcitrants* (1959; tr *Maigret and the Reluctant Witnesses,* 1959), *Une Confidence de Maigret* (1959; tr *Maigret Has Doubts,* 1968), *Maigret aux Assises* (1960; tr *Maigret in Court,* 1961), *Maigret et Les Vieillards* (1960; tr *Maigret in Society,* 1962), *Maigret et le Voleur Paresseux* (1961; tr *Maigret and the Lazy Burglar,* 1963), *Maigret et les Braves Gens* (1962), *Maigret et le Client du Samedi* (1962; tr *Maigret and the Saturday Caller,* 1964), *Maigret et le Clochard* (1963; tr *Maigret and the Dosser,* 1973; also tr *Maigret and the Bum,* 1973), *La Colère de Maigret* (1963; tr *Maigret Loses His Temper,* 1965), *Maigret et le Fantôme* (1964), *Maigret se Défend* (1964; tr *Maigret on the Defensive,* 1966), *La Patience de Maigret* (1965; tr *The Patience of Maigret,* 1966), *Maigret et l'Affaire Nahour* (1967; tr *Maigret and the Nahour Case,* 1967), *Le Voleur de Maigret* (1967; tr *Maigret's Pickpocket,* 1968), *Maigret à Vichy* (1968; tr title: *Maigret Takes the Waters,* 1969; also tr *Maigret in Vichy,* 1969), *Maigret Hésite* (1968; tr *Maigret Hesitates,* 1970), *L'Ami d'Enfance de Maigret* (1968; tr *Maigret's Boyhood Friend,* 1970), *Maigret et le Tueur* (1969; tr *Maigret and the Killer,* 1971), *Maigret et le Marchand de Vin* (1970; tr *Maigret and the Wine Merchant,* 1971), *La Folle de Maigret* (1970; tr *Maigret and the Madwoman,* 1972), *Maigret et l'Homme tout Seul* (1971; tr *Maigret and the Loner,* 1975), *Maigret et l'Indicateur* (1971; tr *Maigret and the Flea,* 1972; also tr *Maigret and the Informer,* 1973), *Maigret et Monsieur Charles* (1972; tr *Maigret and Monsieur Charles,* 1973).

Omnibus Translations: *Introducing Inspector Maigret* (1933), *Inspector Maigret Investigates* (1933), *The Triumph of Inspector Maigret* (1934), *The Shadow in the Courtyard and The Crime at Lock 14* (1934), *The Patience of Maigret* (1939), *Maigret Abroad* (1940), *Maigret Keeps a Rendezvous* (1940) *Maigret to the Rescue* (1940), *Maigret Travels South* (1940), *Maigret and M. Labbé* (1941), *Maigret Sits It Out* (1941), *Maigret on Holiday*

(1950), *Maigret Right and Wrong* (1954), *Five Times Maigret* (1964), *Versus Inspector Maigret* (1960), *Maigret Cinq* (1965), *A Maigret Trio* (1973).

Short Stories: *Les Nouvelles Enquetes de Maigret* (1944), *Maigret et les Petits Cochons sans Queue* (1950), *Un Noël de Maigret* (1951).

MAIGRET AND THE HUNDRED GIBBETS (1931; orig title *Le Pendu de St. Pholien;* also tr as *The Crime of Inspector Maigret*) One of the earliest novels by Georges SIMENON about Inspector Maigret, containing startling psychological portraits and a fascinating, painful mystery. The suicide that leads to the unraveling of a cover-up is unwittingly instigated by Maigret himself. While on business in Brussels, he happens to see a disreputable man in a café stuffing thousands of francs into a brown paper package. Curious, he follows the man to the post office, where he mails the package, then to the train station, and eventually to Amsterdam and Bremen. At one point, Maigret substitutes an identical cheap suitcase for the one in which the man (Louis Jeunet) keeps his prized possession: a blood-soaked suit. Maigret's action leads to tragedy.

At the morgue, Maigret is approached by Joseph Van Damme, a French businessman. This highly effective character is loquacious, obsequious, sly, and dangerous. The trail leads to Liège (Simenon's birthplace) and to a group of middle-aged bourgeois men who once dreamed of being avant-gardists and have become cultivators and protectors of private property—except for the broken Jef Lombard, a photo-engraver whose obsession with the hanged hints at unfulfilled talent and great torment, as though he were dominated by the hanged character of the Tarot. A failed artist, his only work that shows real passion is a series of tormented drawings of hanged bodies. Maigret's investigation is satisfying, inexorable, and even a little cruel.

MAILER, NORMAN (1923–) One of the best-known contemporary American authors, Mailer has written an exceptional HARD-BOILED mystery novel, TOUGH GUYS DON'T DANCE (1984), and the espionage thriller *Harlot's Ghost* (1991), a thousand-page, unfinished tome about a CIA operative code-named Harlot. Earlier in his career Mailer published *An American Dream* (1965), a crime novel about a man who murders his wife.

Mailer attended Harvard University and served in World War II, which was the background for his first novel, *The Naked and the Dead* (1948), about a group of American soldiers on a Japanese-occupied island. It was immediately praised as one of the best works of fiction to come out of the war. It was also probably the first and last time that one of Mailer's works received an unequivocal response. Reputed for his ego and his courting of controversy, Mailer, in his second book, *Barbary Shore* (1951), began to show his radical political ideas. *Advertisements for Myself* (1959), a collection of short prose, fiction, and journalism, was a work of confessional literature. During the sixties, Mailer was one of the founders of the "new journalism," along with Truman CAPOTE and Tom Wolfe. He founded the *Village Voice* newspaper in New York, and won a Pulitzer Prize for *The Armies of the Night* (1968), which was about the peace demonstrations in Washington the previous year. Mailer won a second Pulitzer for *The Executioner's Song* (1979), an enormous book about the convicted killer Gary Gilmore.

MAINWARING, DANIEL See HOMES, GEOFFREY.

MAITLAND, ANTONY A barrister who acts as a sleuth in a series of novels by Sara WOODS. Maitland's relationship with his wife, Jenny, is a prominent feature of the novels. His uncle, Sir Nicholas Harding, is also important. Harding and the Maitlands share a building in Kempenfeldt Square, and he is also the head of Maitland's firm of solicitors. A wise old tortoise, he comes in on the cases toward the end. Maitland suffers from infirmities due to his capture and torture by the NAZIS in World War II.

The adventures are rather sedate, and the investigative method is usually heavily dependent on questioning. Some of the cases that go beyond the usual are *Error of the Moon* (1963), about top-secret missile research; *Past Praying For* (1968), a case of double jeopardy; and *The Law's Delay* (1977), in which Maitland gets his client acquitted and then worries whether he was right or not and has to investigate further in order to satisfy himself. A case that combines fact with fiction is YET SHE MUST DIE (1973). *A Thief or Two* (1977) has Maitland defending a man against a charge of having robbed and murdered a jeweler. As often happens, the evidence indicates that Maitland's client is guilty, forcing him into the role of investigator to see if he can dig up other facts.

The Third Encounter (1963; orig title *The Taste of Fears*) is of particular interest because it deals with Maitland's experience in World War II with the French Resistance and thus is more personal and less a matter of pure legal procedure and acumen. Still, Maitland is not the warmest of characters, and hardly flamboyant—high recommendations in the era of the kooky, cutesy, or chronically romantic detective.

BIBLIOGRAPHY Novels: *Bloody Instructions* (1962), *Malice Domestic* (1962), *Trusted Like the Fox* (1964), *The Little Measure* (1964), *The Windy Side of the Law* (1965), *Though I Know She Lies* (1965), *Enter Certain Murderers* (1966), *Let's Choose Executors*

(1966), *The Case Is Altered* (1967), *And Shame the Devil* (1967), *Knives Have Edges* (1968), *Past Praying For* (1968), *Tarry and Be Hanged* (1969), *An Improbable Fiction* (1970), *Serpent's Tooth* (1971), *The Knavish Crows* (1971), *They Love Not Poison* (1972), *Enter the Corpse* (1973), *Done to Death* (1974), *A Show of Violence* (1975), *My Life Is Done* (1976), *The Law's Delay* (1977), *Exit Murderer* (1978), *This Fatal Writ* (1979), *Proceed to Judgement* (1979), *They Stay for Death* (1980), *Weep for Her* (1980), *Cry Guilty* (1981), *Dearest Enemy* (1981), *Enter a Gentlewoman* (1982), *Villains by Necessity* (1982), *Most Grievous Murder* (1982), *Call Back Yesterday* (1983), *The Lie Direct* (1983), *Where Should He Die?* (1983), *The Bloody Book of Law* (1984), *Murder's Out of Tune* (1984), *Defy the Devil* (1984), *An Obscure Grave* (1985), *Away with Them to Prison* (1985), *Put Out the Light* (1985), *Most Deadly Hate* (1986), *Nor Live So Long* (1986), *Naked Villainy* (1987).

MAJOR, CLARENCE See SLANG.

MALET, LÉO (1909–) The French author Léo Malet was an important link between French mystery fiction and the American HARD-BOILED school represented by HAMMETT and CHANDLER. In 1943 he published the first of his mysteries about detective Nestor BURMA, 120, RUE DE LA GARE, which was a critical success. He went on to write sixty novels, many of them about Burma.

Mystery writing, however, was a second or third career for Malet. Born in Montpellier, he received no formal education. After moving to Paris, he became a cabaret singer at "La Vache Enragée" (The Enraged Cow) in Montmartre in 1925. Malet also wrote for various journals, including the *Journal de l'Homme aux Sandales* and *La Revue Anarchiste.* He worked in an office, as a ghost writer, as a movie extra, and as manager of a fashion shop. In the thirties, he was a member of the Surrealist group and a friend of the group's theorist, André Breton, as well as of the painters René Magritte and Yves Tanguy.

Malet's detective writing brought him France's most coveted prize in the genre, the Grand Prix de la Littérature Policière, in 1947. He also won the Grand Prix de l'Humour Noir in 1958 for a series of stories called "Les nouveaux mystères de Paris," each of which dealt with a different *arrondissement* of Paris.

MALICE AFORETHOUGHT (1931) This novel by Frances Iles (Anthony BERKELEY) was patterned on earlier INVERTED MYSTERIES (in which the killer's identity is disclosed at the beginning), but it was more than that; subtitled "the story of a commonplace crime," it prefigured the crime novel of the postwar period in which the puzzle is omitted and suspense comes from the plan, the execution, the chase, and the context. *Malice Aforethought* concerns itself not only with how little Doctor Bickleigh killed his wife, but why. The ambience of the English village where he lives and the pettiness, cattiness, and vindictiveness of the residents are constantly in the foreground. Character (its development and erosion) is paramount.

"It was not until several weeks after he had decided to murder his wife that Dr. Bickleigh took any active steps in the matter." The first sentence announces that the novel is not a whodunit, though written at the height of the GOLDEN AGE. Dr. Bickleigh is a much put upon man whose wife Julia delights in bossing him around, belittling him in public, and reminding him that she is a Crewstanton and thus ever so far above him in social class. The Bickleighs live in the Devonshire village of Wyvern's Cross, an incubator of small-mindedness and intrigue. Bickleigh is just trying to end his latest love affair when the wealthy Miss Madeleine Cranmere buys "The Hall." Bickleigh falls quickly in love with her and she, apparently, with him. He is afraid to ask Julia for a divorce, and in any case Madeleine says she could not marry a divorced man. Bickleigh's plan starts to form, and he subtly begins to change from a henpecked husband into a murderer—but already we have seen Bickleigh punch his previous lover in the face, a scene more shockingly realistic in its way than most of the murders done in Golden Age fiction. His MODUS OPERANDI, inspired by his medical knowledge, is ingenious; he carries it out over a period of weeks as carefully as if it were a scientific experiment. In fact, Bickleigh's crimes come to be nothing more heinous to him than "experiments" as his history progresses.

Berkeley's portrait of Bickleigh is the core of the novel and laid the foundation for many later fictional everymurderers like Julian SYMONS' Arthur Brownjohn in *The Man Who Killed Himself* (1967). What makes Dr. Bickleigh such a human villain is his capacity for self-deception; he can convince himself of anything, whether that "Madeleine's dislike of marrying a divorced man was not captious at all, but simply entrancing," or that the police are fools who could not possibly be onto him. The trial scenes are relatively brief but noted for their effectiveness and fine ironies. Perhaps the strongest proof of Berkeley's ability to bring life to a fictional world is that at the beginning of *Malice Aforethought* it is easy to detest everyone, and at the end hard not to pity them.

MALICE DOMESTIC The Malice Domestic annual convention honors writers in the COZY genre. Since 1989, Malice Domestic has given the "Agatha" award (named for Agatha CHRISTIE) for the best novel, best first mystery, and best short story in the subgenre. A nonfiction category was added in 1996; an award is also given for lifetime achievement. Although the winners of the award have almost exclusively been women, men have been nominated for Agathas. Dates listed below are publication dates; awards were made the following year.

Best Novel: 1988, *Something Wicked,* Carolyn Hart; 1989, *Naked Once More,* Elizabeth Peters; 1990, *Bum Steer,* Nancy Pickard; 1991, *I.O.U.,* Nancy Pickard; 1992, *Bootlegger's Daughter,* Margaret Maron; 1993, *Dead Man's Island,* Carolyn Hart; 1994, *She Walks These Hills,* Sharyn McCrumb; 1995, *Miracles in Maggoty,* Joan Hess; 1996, *Up Jumps the Devil,* Margaret Maron; 1997, *The Devil in Music,* Kate Ross; 1998, *Butcher's Hill,* Laura Lippman; 1999, *In Big Trouble,* Laura Lippman; 2000, *Storm Track,* Margaret Maron.

Best First Novel: 1988, *A Great Deliverance,* Elizabeth George; 1989, *Grime and Punishment,* Jill Churchill; 1990, *The Body in the Belfry,* Katherine Hall Page; 1991, *Zero at the Bone,* Mary Willis Walker; 1992, *Blanche on the Lam,* Barbara Neely; 1993, *Track of the Cat,* Nevada Barr; 1994, *Do Unto Others,* Jeff Abbott; 1995, *The Body in the Transept,* Jeane M. Dams; 1996, *Murder on a Girls' Night Out,* Anne George; 1997, *The Salaryman's Wife,* Sujata Massey; 1998, *The Doctor Digs a Grave,* Robin Hathaway; 1999, *Murder with Peacocks,* Donna Andrews; 2000, *Death on a Silver Tray,* Rosemary Stevens.

MALING, ARTHUR (1923–) An EDGAR-winning American novelist, Arthur Maling gained his reputation in the genre fairly late. After a career in business, he published his first novel, *Decoy,* in 1969. In this book, an anonymous narrator from Chicago has to deliver certain documents to Mexico. Maling has often used the Western states as settings, in for example *Lucky Devil* (1978), which takes place in Salt Lake City.

Born in Chicago, Maling attended Harvard University and then served in the Marines. He entered the newspaper business in Chicago but then moved to San Diego and worked for the *Journal.* He left the newspaper business in the late forties to open a chain of shoe stores. In 1972 he devoted himself to writing full-time.

One of Maling's trademarks is action. *The New Yorker* called *Shroeder's Game* (1977) "diverting and sufficiently blood-soaked entertainment." In this novel, Maling's series detective, New York private investigator Brock Potter, travels to Arizona to investigate a swindler. Many of Maling's books deal with crooked business dealings. Despite the presence of a private eye, Maling's books are based more on adventure and intrigue than detection.

Maling won his Edgar award for *The Rhinegold Route* (1979). His other novels include *Loophole* (1971) and *The Koberg Link* (1979).

MALLISON, CHARLES Chick Mallison, an important character in William Faulkner's INTRUDER IN THE DUST (1948), is one of the links between this mystery novel and the other "serious" books by Faulkner. Chick is the nephew of Gavin STEVENS. At the time of *Intruder* he is sixteen years old, but in filling in the interstices of his imaginative world Faulkner went back and used him as a child-narrator in *The Town* (1957) and then as a young adult in *The Mansion* (1959). Chick also appears in the mystery stories of *Knight's Gambit* (1939).

MALLORY See COLLINS, MAX ALLAN.

MALLOY, MOOSE An appropriately named character in Raymond Chandler's FAREWELL, MY LOVELY (1940). He is about six-and-a-half-feet tall and "not wider than a beer truck." Malloy has just gotten out of prison and is outlandishly dressed when MARLOWE meets him; he wears a gray sports coat "with white golf balls on it for buttons," alligator shoes with white tips, and matching yellow tie and handkerchief. Not very bright and seemingly unaware of his own strength, he has a habit of accidentally killing people. Chandler had toyed with a similar big moose character in PEARLS ARE A NUISANCE (1938).

MALONE, JOHN J. A hard-drinking lawyer and sleuth in a series of novels (as well as some short stories) by Craig RICE. Malone first appeared in *Eight Faces at Three* (1939), an unusual book that is still interesting for its concern with fantasy and dreams, as well as for its cast of vivid characters. Malone himself is a Chicago lawyer whose main interest is alcohol. He drinks whisky, gin, and beer—sometimes all three at the same time—and frequents Joe the Angel's City Hall Bar. He is short and unkempt, but this does not keep him from exercising the HARD-BOILED p.i.'s usual magnetic attraction for women. Among his friends are Jake Justus, a press agent, and Helene Brand, Jake's fiancé—both of whom help him solve his first case. Brand is a particularly enjoyable character, a well-known socialite who shares Malone's taste for booze and who injects an element of glamour that balances Malone's disreputable air. The red-faced and angry police detective, Daniel von Flanagan, is the typical exasperated cop-friend all p.i.'s seem to need. Maggie is Malone's devoted secretary.

In *Eight Faces at Three,* one of Justus's clients, band leader Dick Dayton, has just married Holly Inglehart. Holly, after having a nightmare with strong overtones of POE, wakes up to find her Aunt Alexandra stabbed three times. Later, an "oddly dapper little man" turns up (he sounds like J. G. REEDER), and he gets the same treatment. The dreams and images of clocks in the book suggest Rice's familiarity with surrealism and more particularly Salvador Dalí.

In *Having Wonderful Crime* (1943), Rice took all her Chicago characters on vacation to New York. There they meet the very drunk newlywed Dennis Morrison. The police come looking for him because his wife Bertha has been murdered; her corpse is found decapitated in the bed in a bridal suite—only, the head belongs to someone else. The father of this other head is a doctor from the country, and he shows up on Staten Island to investigate. What is unusual about the book is its use of lesbianism. One character uses her knowledge to blackmail the Greenwich Village poet Wildavane Williams into sleeping with her. The investigation is actually secondary to showing the three main characters racing around New York City, being glamorous (especially Helene), and drinking vast quantities of alcohol.

The Name Is Malone (1958) is a collection of short stories that show that the "little lawyer from Chicago" is not above bribing a judge or a jury. He brags that he has never lost a client, which is blatantly untrue. Imperturbable, when his client is killed Malone takes on the murderer's defense as his next case. The stories have far-fetched or farcical plots with motive given an easy ride. Rice is often entertaining without being very suspenseful.

Malone was adapted for both film and radio in the forties. In *The People vs. Withers and Malone* (1963), a collection of short stories, he teams up with Hildegarde WITHERS, the spinster detective created by Stuart PALMER. *But the Doctor Died* is a novel written by Rice in the mid-fifties but only discovered after her death and published in 1967. Helene is convinced by her friend Vivian Conover, a chemist, to take a secretarial job at a lab called Walden, and also to see psychiatrist Clifford Barnhall. Malone passes Helene in the street one day and sees she is clearly in a hypnotic trance; then, a man tailing him is shot to death. There is a Cold War plot involving "Operation Terminal," and Helene is charged with murder, but the story seems like a late work lacking the verve of the earlier novels.

BIBLIOGRAPHY Novels: *The Corpse Steps Out* (1940), *The Wrong Murder* (1940), *The Right Murder* (1941), *Trial By Fury* (1941), *The Big Midget Murders* (1942), *The Lucky Stiff* (1945), *The Fourth Postman* (1948), *My Kingdom for a Hearse* (1957), *Knocked for a Loop* (1957; British title *The Double Frame*).

MALTESE FALCON, THE (1929) If there is one novel in the mystery genre that needs no introduction, it is Dashiell HAMMETT'S *The Maltese Falcon.* First serialized in BLACK MASK, it was filmed more than once, the second version being the familiar one with Humphrey Bogart as Sam SPADE, Peter Lorre as Joel Cairo, and Sydney Greenstreet as Caspar GUTMAN. The Black Bird over which Cairo, Gutman, and Brigid O'Shaughnessy fight is a statuette supposedly given by an order of medieval knights to the king of Spain. The object and the myth are perfectly GOLDEN AGE, the plot and the characters perfectly HARD-BOILED. The dialogue in the book is so good that much of it went directly into the film. O'Shaughnessy hires Spade and his partner Miles Archer under false pretenses, and Archer ends up getting killed almost immediately. The fate of the Falcon and the mystery of the fate of Archer follow the classic converging plot lines.

One part of the book that was not filmed is an important story that Spade tells O'Shaughnessy about a man named Flitcraft. The story encapsulates the philosophy of Hammett's books in parable form. Flitcraft is walking to work one day when a beam falls from a building and nearly kills him; a steady and even complacent family man, the chip from the sidewalk that flies up and cuts his cheek is like the sharp jab of reality reminding him of his mortality and that his stable social world is an elaborate and delicate façade. Behind it lurks "blind chance." Shocked by this unveiling, Flitcraft abandons his life wholly and immediately. Spade meets him a few years later, living in Tacoma with a new wife and family. Flitcraft, with the most human and necessary self-deception, has forgotten again that life is chaos and accident; as Spade elegantly puts it, "He adjusted himself to beams falling, and then no more of them fell, and he adjusted himself to them not falling."

MAMUR ZAPT, THE A character in a series of HISTORICAL MYSTERIES set in colonial Egypt by Michael Pearce. The Mamur Zapt (chief inspector) is Cadwallader Gareth Owen, a middle-aged former soldier now in charge of political investigations. He has the usual virtues of a strong sense of justice and incorruptibility; he also knows Egyptian and Arab culture (Pearce grew up and taught in the region). His closest collaborators are the Greeks Georgiades and Nikos. Owen also works in cooperation with some members of the Parquet (a department of the Ministry of Justice) and some well-placed personal friends: Paul, the Consul-General's personal aide; Mahmoud el Zaki, a member of the Parquet; and Nuri Pasha, the father of his girlfriend, Zeinab. Owen meets a believable variety of people, from colonials who think that the natives are barbarians, to Egyptian patriots and corrupt officials who are in business only for themselves.

The Mamur Zapt and the Donkey-Vous (1990) has to do with a rash of kidnappings in Cairo. An elderly Frenchman disappears from Shepheards Hotel, a major tourist hotel, while on a business trip; Anglo-French conflict over construction contracts may be involved. Then an English tourist disappears from the same terrace of the hotel—while Owen is inside having a drink. The boys who run the donkey-vous—a kind of donkeys taxi stand—across the street from the terrace become important.

The Mamur Zapt and the Men Behind (1991) is set in 1908; people in the British administration are being followed, and a civil servant is shot. There is a link between the surveillance and the School of Law; law students are the target of a café bombing. Owen starts an investigation of the student world—the source of radical movements, secret political societies and support for the Nationalist movement. Investigation later leads Owen to Hamada, a village to the south, and to slavery and weapons traffic. The writing is not bad but neither is it masterful; the historical recreation of life in Cairo, plus some characterizations, is the strength of the book. Among the other Mamur Zapt books is *The Mamur Zapt and the Girl in the Nile* (1992).

MANCHURIAN CANDIDATE, THE See GALLICO, PAUL.

MANDERS, BUNNY See RAFFLES.

MANDERSON, SIGSBEE The tycoon in E. C. Bentley's TRENT'S LAST CASE (1912). Out of the stereotype of the American millionaire, Bentley makes Manderson into one of the most impossible people, from a psychological point of view, in mystery fiction.

MAN FROM THE SEA, THE (1955) This novel by Michael INNES, which has one of the most attention-grabbing opening scenes in espionage fiction, demonstrated that Innes could do more than write witty, donnish mysteries with farcical plots (see Sir John APPLEBY). In *The Man from the Sea,* two naked men meet on a Scottish beach at night. One is relaxing after a tryst with Lady Caryl Blair; the other is fleeing for his life. Without speaking, they enter into a bargain of mutual assistance as danger approaches. The book reaches an instant climax that shows the imposing character of the older man and reveals his own rash self to the younger. Each scene brings a new set of circumstances, and the disclosure of information is itself made an element of suspense (also making the plot difficult to summarize without spoiling it). The suspense continues without letup, and the story manages to roll uphill to further high points.

MAN IN LOWER TEN, THE (1909) A railroad mystery by Mary Roberts RINEHART and one of her best known works. Lawrence Blakely is a confirmed bachelor and a rising star among Washington lawyers. He and his partner MacKnight are involved in prosecuting a case against a forger named Bronson, and Blakely is entrusted with taking notes signed by the millionaire John Gilmore to Pittsburgh to verify that some are fakes. He boards the Washington Flyer for the return journey, and finds his Pullman car, the *Ontario,* filled with a strange assortment of characters, some of them suspicious. During the night, Blakely winds up in the wrong bunk, and the following morning a corpse is found in his own place. Incriminating evidence has been planted on him as well, and his clothes have been stolen. Just when things are looking black for him, the train crashes and most of the witnesses are killed. *The Man in Lower Ten* bears all the earmarks of a Rinehart story, including a prominent romantic subplot, questions of honor that bind the characters' hands, and a scene in a dark and spooky house. It is rather more dependent on coincidence than her other books, and is considered, probably wrongly, her masterpiece.

MANNINGOE, NANCY The black servant who cares for Temple Drake's children in William FAULKNER's *Requiem for a Nun* (1951). Temple takes Nancy into her confidence because she, like Temple in SANCTUARY (1931), has a past she would rather keep covered. Nancy had appeared earlier as a character in Faulkner's fictitious Yoknapatawpha County, and actually is said to have been murdered by her husband at the time of *The Sound and the Fury* (1929), but was later brought back to life by Faulkner.

MAN WHO LIKED TO LOOK AT HIMSELF, THE (1973) A short, grim novel in the Mario BALZIC series. It is even more dark than other books by K. C. CONSTANTINE because there are virtually no subplots to divert attention from the central murder, which occurs offstage but is certainly grisly. The book is a believable portrayal of primitive mentalities, expressed in strong (and bigoted) language.

Without much enthusiasm, Balzic agrees to go hunting with new state police chief of detectives Harry Minyon. The scene is the preserve of the Rocksburg Rod & Gun Club. A pretty poor bird hunter, their dog manages to find what seems to be a human thigh bone. Eventually, a skeleton that has been sawed up and scattered over acres of fields is pieced together. Balzic's investigations lead him to a local beef freezer plant and a group of former friends with their mouths clamped shut around some secret; the missing piece of the puzzle leaves the mystery open until the end of the book. There is little of the Rocksburg social background, and not enough character types to weave quite as rich a background as in the other books in the series. But as a wintry, outdoor, and even barbaric piece, it is powerful.

MAN WHO WAS THURSDAY, THE (1908) This novel of intrigue and political allegory by G. K. CHESTERTON would be more of a mystery if publishers would refrain from giving away certain facts on the cover. The first scene announces it as a philosophical adventure story. In the suburb of Saffron Park, a radical Bohemian enclave full of pseudo-artists, philosophers, and revolutionaries, a debate occurs between the "anarchist" poet Lucian Gregory and the "poet of order," Gabriel Syme. Syme thinks Gregory's anarchism pretentious and absurd; to prove he means what he says, Gregory takes Syme to an unprepossessing pub where, while they are eating, the floor suddenly drops like an elevator, propelling them into the subterranean chambers and armory of the New Anarchists. The group is about to elect a new representative to the European council, their previous representative having died "through his faith in a hygienic mixture of chalk and water as a substitute for milk, which beverage he regarded as barbaric, and as involving cruelty to the cow." If it is surprising that Gregory is really an anarchist, Syme's true identity is more so. The meeting develops hilariously, leading to a rollicking political adventure-farce.

Chesterton's political viewpoint is complex. He blames political extremism on the educated, who are out to destroy society because they have misguidedly blamed "civilization" itself for civilization's ills; but in defense of order he also makes the subversive point that "the poor have sometimes objected to being governed badly; the rich have always objected to being governed at all."

The idea of secret police who ferret out crimes from books of sonnets, trace the "dreadful thoughts" that lead to "intellectual crime," and believe "the scientific and artistic worlds are silently bound in a crusade against the Family and the State" sounds more horrifying at the end of the twentieth century than it must have at the beginning. But a decade after *The Man Who Was Thursday* was published, that world had been blown to pieces—but it had taken both anarchists and defenders of God and Country to do it.

MAN WHO WENT UP IN SMOKE, THE (1969) This novel by Maj SJÖWALL and Per Wahlöo, one of the Martin BECK series, takes place outside Sweden, and is for other reasons as well a kind of oddity. The beginning is somewhat sluggish, like the brief Swedish summer. Martin Beck's holiday is disrupted by the mysterious disappearance of a journalist in Hungary. Beck has only a week to find the man before the right-wing magazine for which he wrote creates a scandal and a diplomatic incident. While Beck is poking around, following up a few tips from his colleague Kollberg back home, he suddenly has to save his own life. Things then finally start to move; Beck and his Hungarian colleague come across drug trafficking and sex, but the journalist is still missing. Then suddenly Beck packs up and goes home, where he continues his investigation. The story arrives (perhaps unexpectedly) at a satisfying ending, and the second part of the book is real detection, thus delivering the PROCEDURAL element one expected from the beginning. In the middle, the investigation is drowned in an ocean of details about Budapest, the food, Beck's thoughts, etcetera—probably to render the idea of how hopeless the whole case looks, but certainly an excess of realism. On the other hand, the material sharpens the contrast between the two countries, the two investigations, and finally the two Becks: the sleepy one who has no clues, and the determined detective when the solution is in sight. Kollberg is helpful to Beck without even having being assigned to the case and provides the key links. Yet Beck mistreats Kollberg and hardly acknowledges his crucial help, which reveals their private way of relating to each other.

MARCH, COLONEL See CARR, JOHN DICKSON.

MARKHAM, ROBERT See AMIS, KINGSLEY.

"MARKHEIM" (1887) A short story by Robert Louis STEVENSON. "Markheim" is a tale of robbery and murder, in which the bright and dark sides of the killer's personality struggle over what he has done. Even though its Christian message is rather heavily laid on, it is one of the most vivid early stories that takes the murderer's point of view. The description of the panic that comes as soon as the crime is finished and the murderer's torture by his own imagination and fear of discovery are reminiscent of DOSTOYEVSKY.

MARKOV, GEORGI IVAN See POISONED UMBRELLA.

MARLE, JEFF See BENCOLIN, HENRI.

MARLOWE, PHILIP The series detective created by Raymond CHANDLER, and along with Sam SPADE a defining figure of the HARD-BOILED school. Marlowe is forever identified with Humphrey Bogart, who portrayed him in the film version of THE BIG SLEEP (1939), but in fact Chandler saw Cary Grant as the actor most like Marlowe. Marlowe is a large man with gray eyes, but what Marlowe looks like is less important than what he says and does, and Chandler never bothered to work up a full portrait of him. (He once answered a letter from a curious reader with a thumbnail biography of Marlowe, but this description lies wholly outside the works themselves. It does, however, include the interesting statement that Marlowe realizes he is a "loser" because he does not have money, the only thing his society respects.)

In the first novel, Marlowe says he is thirty-three years old, unmarried, and was formerly an investigator for the Los Angeles District Attorney; from this period dates his friendship with Bernie OHLS. In THE LONG GOODBYE (1953), Marlowe describes himself as being forty-two years old. In this novel, he has a one-night stand with Linda Loring, who is about to leave for Paris—though she asks Marlowe to marry her. He replies that he has been "spoiled by independence." She calls Marlowe from Europe at the end of *Playback* (1958) and renews her plea, with evident success, for Marlowe is married to her in the fragmentary *Poodle Springs* (pub 1989), which was finished by Robert B. PARKER. *Playback* is frequently dismissed as the weakest of the novels; it does, however, have interesting scenes in a hotel run by a suspicious character, and one great scene in which Marlowe discovers a corpse. His loyalty to Betty Mayfield, the *femme fatale*, is a little hard to understand. FAREWELL, MY LOVELY (1940), the second book in the series, is full of vivid characters; *The Lady in the Lake* (1943) is tightly plotted, and much of it takes place in the mountains.

"If I wasn't hard, I wouldn't be alive. If I couldn't ever be gentle, I wouldn't deserve to be alive." In these lines (from *Playback*, incidentally), CHANDLER gave the classic formulation of Marlowe's creed, which had spawned a whole subgenre. The tough guy with a conscience was a departure from earlier thuggish hard guys like Race WILLIAMS. MARLOWE and Lew ARCHER (and later Matt SCUDDER, Harry STONER, and others) have a tempered hardness that sets them apart. The last part of THE SIMPLE ART OF MURDER (1944) famously describes such a detective: "down these mean streets a man must go who is not himself mean, who is neither tarnished nor afraid." On the other hand, Marlowe does seem to have a nasty streak in THE LITTLE SISTER (1949).

In several of his novels, Chandler culled or adapted sections of his earlier short stories, which were later published under the title *Killer in the Rain* (1964). After he became famous, some of Chandler's early stories were "Marlowized"—republished with the name of the detective changed to Marlowe—including "Goldfish," which featured several memorable characters, among them Wally SYPE.

BIBLIOGRAPHY Novels: *The High Window* (1942).

Short Stories: *The Simple Art of Murder* (1950).

MARLOWE, STEPHEN (pseudonym of Milton Lesser, 1928–) Milton Lesser chose his pseudonym out of respect for Philip MARLOWE, and later legally changed his name. At the same time that he wrote SCIENCE FICTION as Milton Lesser, he produced a series of novels about a private detective named Chester DRUM (Lesser had been stationed at Camp Drum during his military service). Lesser wrote under several other pseudonyms; he used the name Jason Ridgway for a series about a former CIA agent named Brian Guy. Drum is a similar character, a retired FBI agent turned p.i.

Marlowe was born in New York City and graduated from the College of William and Mary in Virginia in 1949. He wrote for PULP MAGAZINES and published two science fiction novels, *Earthbound* (1952) and *The Star Seekers* (1953), before venturing into the field of the private eye novel. Despite his admiration for Raymond CHANDLER and the HARD-BOILED novel, he continued to pursue other interests. In 1987, he published *Memoirs of Christopher Columbus*.

MARON, MARGARET (***) Margaret Maron had already written an unremarkable series of novels about a Manhattan detective, Sigrid Harald, when she won an EDGAR for her novel BOOTLEGGER'S DAUGHTER (1992), the first of a series set in the South. It introduced Deborah Knott, a North Carolina attorney who is running for district judge and trying to solve an eighteen-year-old murder at the same time.

Margaret Maron was born in Greensboro, North Carolina, and grew up on a farm near Raleigh. She lived in Brooklyn, New York for many years before returning to the South. She was married in 1959. Maron has taught writing at Hunter College in New York and at Duke University. Her first mystery, *One Coffee With*, was published in 1981, and introduced Sigrid Harald. Maron continued the series for ten years, with such novels as

Death in Blue Folders (1985) and *Corpus Christmas* (1989); the latter book was nominated for several awards, but there is nothing exceptional about the Harald series. Many other women writers were coming out with series with female detective protagonists at the time and Harald is a not very compelling example of the type.

By leaving the fished-out pool of the New York detective story to better practitioners, Maron seems to have liberated herself and elevated the quality of her writing. The Knott novels are much more effective and relaxed, implementing the conventions of the genre less obtrusively. The author has a good ear for dialogue and Southern speech is rendered authentically. The Knott series should perhaps be subtitled "how the South deals with modern problems"; the first book deals with homosexuality, and *Southern Discomfort* (1993) with incest, relations between the sexes, foreign immigration, and other matters. In fact, the mystery itself is in some ways glossed over—for example, it is never adequately explained how a certain person was poisoned without killing others, and the murder only takes place on page 112. In this, the second book, Knott is sworn in as a judge and begins a progressive campaign, including building a home for a poor black family using only women as laborers. Knott discovers her niece Annie Sue, an unlicensed electrician, apparently raped. The suspected rapist, a man who beats his pregnant wife, is found killed with a hammer and with traces of ARSENIC in his body. Knott and some of her many family members are suspects. In *Up Jumps the Devil* (1996), an old neighbor of Knott's, a truck driver, is shot to death in front of his house, and because of the family connection she cannot resist investigating.

Maron's one non-series novel, *Bloody Kin* (1985), was reprinted in 1995. In a sense, it bridges her New York and North Carolina experience. In North Carolina, wealthy Hake Honeycott is killed with his own shotgun while out hunting. His wife, a New Yorker, is the amateur sleuth, and finds clues that indicate something more than an accident.

MARPLE, MISS JANE Agatha CHRISTIE's second-most-famous character, after Hercule POIROT. She appears in more than a dozen books and operates in a more COZY atmosphere than Poirot. A lifelong resident of the small village of St. Mary Meade, she is a vigorous (and nosy) old woman, very fond of knitting. Everything about her is Victorian. Christie first developed the character in short stories; the first Marple novel was *Murder at the Vicarage* (1930), a not unpredictable venue given the nature of the books. The second was *The Body in the Library* (1942), in which Christie tackled one of the most familiar settings for murder. An attractive young woman is found dead in the library of Colonel and Mrs. Bantry. Finally identified, she turns out to be Ruby Keene, a young girl missing from the Majestic Hotel in Danemouth. Miss Marple and Mrs. Bantry team up, going to the hotel to investigate undercover.

The premise of the Miss Marple stories requires a willing suspension of disbelief, because St. Mary Meade seems to have a crime rate to rival Raymond CHANDLER's Los Angeles. They are also oozing with charm and can be a bit treacly. They do, however, include some of the author's most ingenious plots and devices, for example the case directed from beyond the grave in NEMESIS (1971).

Miss Marple made her last appearance in *Sleeping Murder* (1976). Christie had written it some thirty years before and kept it in a safe. The book has to do with childhood memory and a murder far in the past. Gwenda Reed settles in a house in the small town of Dillmouth and begins renovating while she waits for her husband to arrive from New Zealand. Christie builds the suspense with a wonderful device: Gwenda discovers a house within the house, like a ghost. When she decides to have steps made, old, overgrown steps are found in the very spot. After walking into the wall several times she makes up her mind to cut a doorway between two rooms, only to find that a doorway once existed there. The coincidences unnerve her so much that she goes to London, where she accidentally meets Miss Marple. They attend a play, in which one line sends Gwenda over the edge (it is the same play from which P. D. James got the title for COVER HER FACE). The end, which hinges on logic and handwriting evidence, is brilliantly neat.

BIBLIOGRAPHY Novels: *The Moving Finger* (1942); *A Murder Is Announced* (1950), *They Do It with Mirrors* (1952; U.S. title *Murder with Mirrors*), *A Pocket Full of Rye* (1953), *4:50 from Paddington* (1957; U.S. title *What Mrs. McGillicuddy Saw!*), *The Mirror Crack'd From Side to Side* (1962; U.S. title *The Mirror Crack'd*), *A Caribbean Mystery* (1964), *At Bertram's Hotel* (1965), *Nemesis* (1971).

Short Stories: *The Thirteen Problems* (1932; U.S. title *The Tuesday Club Murders*), *The Regatta Mystery and Other Stories* (1939; one Miss Marple story), *Three Blind Mice and Other Stories* (1950; four stories with Miss Marple), *The Adventure of the Christmas Pudding and Other Stories* (1960; one Miss Marple story), *Double Sin and Other Stories* (1961; two Miss Marple stories), *Miss Marple's Last Cases and Two Other Stories* (1979).

MARQUAND, JOHN P[HILLIPS] (1893–1960) John P. Marquand's most famous statement about his detective,

Mr. MOTO, is that he only wrote the stories to provide shoes for his child. He called Moto his "literary disgrace." Ironically, the stories about the Japanese agent have proven more enduring than all but the best of his serious fiction.

Marquand was born in Delaware to what was then a well-off family. His father's financial failure, however, meant that he had to be sent away to live with other relatives, an event that marked him for life and led to the sensitivity to social distinctions that he documented in his novels. After graduating from Harvard University in 1915, Marquand served in World War I, becoming an artillery captain. In the twenties, he worked as a journalist and then concentrated on writing popular works of fiction. The first Mr. Moto novel, *No Hero,* appeared in 1935.

Marquand's most important works all deal with New England society, particularly with upper-class families who have fallen on hard times. *The Late George Apley* (1937) won a Pulitzer prize. It was followed by *Wickford Point* (1939) and *H.M. Pulham, Esquire* (1939). Throughout, Marquand satirizes genteel New England, but from a sympathetic point of view, no doubt developed out of his own experience. *Women and Thomas Harrow* (1958) was partly autobiographical.

MARRIC, J. J. The pseudonym under which John CREASEY wrote the GIDEON series.

MARS, EDDIE A shady character in Raymond Chandler's THE BIG SLEEP (1939). Appropriately, MARLOWE describes Mars as a gray man; he has gray hair, gray clothes, and a sinister mien.

MARSH, [DAME EDITH] NGAIO (1899–1982) In her autobiography, Ngaio Marsh described herself as having been "a morbid little creature" as a child. A melodramatic play her amateur-thespian parents performed gave her a terror of poison, an experience she would later put to good use in her writing. A native of New Zealand, Dame Ngaio (pronounced "Nye-o," a Maori word for a flowering tree) Marsh became one of the classic authors of the GOLDEN AGE.

Marsh grew up outside of Christchurch, New Zealand. Her father was English and her mother a New Zealander. Marsh's family was artistic and had come down in the world—they were "have-nots," in the sense that the family fortune had been lost a generation or two before, and they resembled the Lampreys in Marsh's most famous book, *A Surfeit of Lampreys* (1940; see DEATH OF A PEER). (The Lampreys, in fact, were based on a family the author met in New Zealand.) Marsh's mother, she felt, could have been a gifted professional actress had she had the inclination. Her father labored away as a clerk in a bank, employment totally unsuited to his humorous, absent-minded personality.

Marsh began her career as a playwright and actress while in New Zealand. She later produced university student productions, and continued her theatrical activities even after she became known as a mystery author (she was a producer in the British Theater Guild). This background is an integral part of her detective stories.

Marsh's sleuth is Roderick ALLEYN of Scotland Yard. An English gentleman, he is down-to-earth yet elegant, convivial and with a good sense of humor, a cosmopolitan who speaks French and Italian. At the time that she wrote the first Alleyn book (1934), Marsh was living in London, where she had set up a small gift shop with one of the "Lampreys." One rainy Sunday, she decided to start writing a detective story, and went out and bought some composition books. Because she had visited the Dulwich College Picture Gallery the day before, she named her detective Alleyn after the founder of the school (her father's alma mater).

Marsh's writing is pleasant and quite literate without being overly sophisticated. Strictly as a writer, she was closer to ALLINGHAM in spirit and better than CHRISTIE. Her stories are lively and can be realistic, and the characters are well-described and basically credible. One of Marsh's strengths, perhaps stemming from her training as a dramatist, is her psychological analysis of the characters' interrelationships.

The situations of the mysteries are interesting and reveal good background research and use of details; the plots are engaging without being far-fetched or uselessly intricate. Sometimes, however, obvious facts or events are treated as big mysteries. In *False Scent* (1959), one can tell from the first page who is going to be killed and how, though the murder takes place some sixty pages later; however, the discovery of why and by whom still comes as a surprise, and the end of the story provides an added twist. In *When in Rome* (1971), the victim and the MODUS OPERANDI are again fairly obvious—except to the characters in the book. The loss of a manuscript by an author researching a novel in Rome sets the mystery in motion. Though the discovery of the killer and his/her secret do not come as a complete surprise, Alleyn's covert investigation (he poses as a tourist) is suspenseful. The varied characters of *Colour Scheme* (1944), set in New Zealand, are especially distinctive (See NAZIS).

Marsh's books are suspenseful but the "dynamics" stay within a certain range—a steady pace with no crescendos. Alleyn himself is a bit too cold-bloodedly decent to excite intense compassion, but fortunately (or unfortunately), he is never confronted with believable, imminent peril. Many of the books deal with the activities of aristocratic socialites. *Death and the Dancing Footman* (1942) works some interesting changes on the COUNTRY HOUSE mystery: Jonathan Royal deliberately invites antagonistic guests for the weekend, including a disfigured woman and the plastic surgeon who maimed her twenty-five years earlier. On the other hand, it uses stock devices: the party is snowed in à la *Mousetrap* (1949). The much weaker *Death of a Fool* (1956) likewise uses a tantalizing, unlikely murder: the victim is beheaded behind a dolmen during a traditional winter-solstice sword dance. Yet the author combines her ingenuity of method with trite "Ye Olde" England language and mannerisms employed by lesser writers than Marsh, and the characters are once again stranded by snows.

Shortly after her first novel was published, Marsh's mother became fatally ill, and the author returned to New Zealand. She lived with her father for seventeen years after her mother died. She made frequent trips to England, and wrote her mysteries aboard ship during the long journeys. It was for her involvement in the theater that she was made Dame Commander of the Order of the British Empire in 1966, and she was designated a Grand Master by the Mystery Writers of America in 1977. Marsh's autobiography, *Black Beech and Honeydew* (1965; rev 1981), deals mainly with her early life, her family, the theater, and her development. *The Collected Short Fiction of Ngaio Marsh* (1989) contains not only Alleyn short stories but a previously unpublished script for a courtroom drama.

MARSH, RICHARD (1858–1915) The English writer Richard Marsh began writing stories for boys' magazines when he was still a boy himself (age twelve). Marsh attended Eton and Oxford, and by the time of his death at the age of fifty-seven he had published some seventy books of horror, mystery, and suspense. Marsh was an active man and an avid sportsman, but an impatient writer. Most of his works have been forgotten except for *The Beetle* (1897), in which a tramp is attacked by a huge, sickening insect. A down-and-out clerk, Robert Holt, takes shelter in a deserted house and is mesmerized first by the revolting beetle, and then by a strange man with hypnotic powers who turns him into a thrall. The story, one of horror, burglary, and intrigue, is told from several points of view.

Marsh's story "The Man Who Cut Off My Hair" was praised by BARZUN and TAYLOR and was included in one of Hugh GREENE's anthologies. Greene and his brother included *The Beetle* in their compilation *Victorian Villainies* (1984).

MARSHALL, WILLIAM [LEONARD] (1944–) An Australian by birth, William Marshall has lived in both Hong Kong and New York City. He used the former locale as the setting for his YELLOWTHREAD series, which combines the PROCEDURAL with outlandish and outrageous plots and murder techniques. After moving to New York in the eighties, he began a series of HISTORICAL MYSTERIES with *New York Detective* (1989), which he followed with *Faces in the Crowd* (1991). Marshall chose the post-TAMMANY period also favored by Caleb CARR. *New York Detective,* set in 1883, is as burlesque as its opening scene, set in a theater: an attempt is made to drown a man in a toilet stall. This is Marshall's humor at its most puerile; in the Yellowthread series he focuses more on violent crimes that are so strange that their gruesomeness is mitigated by the fact that they cannot be taken seriously.

In *Manila Bay* (1986), Marshall began a second series, about Lieutenant Felix Elizalde of the Manila police. The second novel was *Whisper* (1988). The Manila Bay series also focuses on bizarre crimes—such as the trade in skeletons—and depicts the poor and homeless of the Philippine city. This series seems to have lacked the energy or the appeal of the Yellowthread Street mysteries, to which the author returned with *Inches* (1994).

MARSHALL AT THE VILLA TORRINI, THE (1993) One of Magdalen NABB's novels about Marshall GUARNACCIA. This very civilized detective is sent to the Villa Torrini outside Florence one February day, where he discovers the body of a well-known writer in a bathtub, half submersed in bloody water. The immediate assumption is suicide, but when the water is drained, the body appears to have no marks on it. Then the police discover a broken wine glass under it—but that only accounts for the blood, not the cause of death. Guarnaccia's strict diet has him even more distracted and lost in his imaginary world of memories than usual. Scenes from another plot line—the trial related to an earlier homicide—punctuate the investigations of the Torrini case. The thin edge between "normality" and mental imbalance and the specter of "the sins of the fathers" play a role as Guarnaccia slowly tears away the veils of family and social history to reveal the truth.

This novel is one of the tightest in the series, with a satisfying intelligence and realism. Nabb has recreated a convincing Italian personality, based on her twenty years of residence in Florence. Guarnaccia is something like an Italian MAIGRET—though he takes himself less seriously and is not convinced of his own genius. He is also funny, and has a very humane way of approaching things: crime makes him sad. He slowly unravels his mysteries like a doctor unraveling the bandages of a rotten wound, with some repugnance for the foulness and a lot of empathy for the patient's pain.

MARTEL, CHARLES (probably the pseudonym of Thomas Delf, 1810–1865) Although there remains some doubt about his real identity, Charles Martel was one of the original generation of mystery writers after POE who set the genre on its feet. Like many of these writers, he is also almost entirely forgotten. He was much better known as a writer on art, his *Principles of Colouring in Ornamental Art* (1866) remaining continuously in print for decades. Delf was also a bookseller, and compiled *Appleton's Library Manual* (1847), a bibliographical work covering twelve thousand titles.

In the manner of DICKENS, WATERS, and other contemporaries, Delf published two books (under the Martel pseudonym) of purportedly true detective tales: *The Diary of an Ex-Detective* (1860) and *The Detective's Note-book* (1860). According to E. F. BLEILER, Martel anticipated later mystery fiction with his plots and was the first to write about the search for a stolen naval treaty (a subject treated by Conan Doyle in THE NAVAL TREATY).

Martel's work shows striking language, unique turns of phrase and expressions, and strong character development. "Hanged by the Neck: A Confession" is an early LOCKED ROOM problem but also an original case of bizarre abnormal psychology. It is about a man who craves what he considers one of the most rarefied and scarcely attained experiences—that of innocent men who are hanged, among whom he hopes to number himself! There may even be a Christian parallel in the story, though this narrator is interested, he says, in "the ecstatic sensations which I am convinced result from strangulation." Martel's startling evocation of mania shows real ability.

MARTINEAU, CHIEF INSPECTOR HARRY A series character in the long-running police PROCEDURAL saga by Maurice PROCTER. When he first appears in *Hell Is a City* (1953; U.S. title *Somewhere in this City*), Martineau is already gray and middle-aged. Since he has already put in twenty years, Martineau should be almost elderly by the time of the last book, *Hideaway* (1968). Martineau is a little bit like Inspector MORSE; he enjoys classical music and is visibly human (he even comes to wrong conclusions). On the other hand, he is happily married and not as morbidly romantic as Morse is. The novels take place in Granchester, a thinly veiled version of Manchester, England.

Two of Procter's recurrent themes are crimes against CHILDREN and the all-out manhunt. Both feature in *Killer at Large* (1959), in which Guy Rainer, already serving time in prison for the murder of his finacée's lover, escapes from prison. Meanwhile, a nine-year-old-girl named Dessie Kegan disappears. Martineau and Detective Sergeant Devery pursue the parallel cases while trying to determine the connection between them and also prevent a possible tragedy. Once again, Procter works in realistic and contemporary details in his depiction of the lugubrious atmosphere of lower-class Britain, particularly in the lives of the divorced parents of the girl, who are both living with other people but only a few blocks from each other. The various leads in the case cross and recross; the pace, however, lags. *Homicide Blonde* (1965; orig title *Death Has a Shadow*) deals with pedophilia.

Organized crime is another of Procter's repeated themes, with the Granchester mobster Dixie Costello at its center. Criminal gangs and robberies are involved in such books as *The Midnight Plumber* (1957) and *A Body to Spare* (1962). *Man In Ambush* (1959) is about the killing of a cop. In *Rogue Running* (1966), one of Martineau's subordinates, Detective Constable Brabant, has his warrant card stolen. This presents the possibility of the thief committing criminal acts under the guise of being a policeman—forestalling a feared crime wave being yet another variation on the manhunt theme. Procter as usual adds some other minor dramas. A businessman goes missing; he is suspected of having an illicit relationship with his secretary, who is herself married to a professional football player.

BIBLIOGRAPHY Novels: *Devil's Due* (1960), *The Devil Was Handsome* (1961), *The Graveyard Rolls* (1964), *His Weight in Gold* (1966), *Exercise Hoodwink* (1967).

MARY CELESTE A ship that became the subject of one of the most famous mysteries of all time. In 1872 the brigantine *Mary Celeste* set sail from New York City with a crew of ten. A month later, the ship was still sailing, but the entire crew had vanished without a trace. When it was found in the Atlantic, the *Mary Celeste* was under sail and nothing appeared to be wrong with the ship; food was on the table, tasks were half-done, but no one was aboard. The ship was towed to Gibraltar and sold.

The mystery of the *Mary Celeste* was the basis of a novel by Samuel Hopkins ADAMS and Stewart Edward White, *The Mystery* (1907). C. Daly KING is another writer who was influenced by the case of the *Mary Celeste.*

MASON, A[LFRED] E[DWARD] W[OODLEY] (1865–1948) The English playwright and novelist A. E. W. Mason had a successful career as an actor before he began writing the tales of the Parisian detective Inspector HANAUD, for which he is most remembered. Mason was educated at the Dulwich school (like Raymond CHANDLER) and then attended Oxford, graduating in 1888. Thereafter, he joined a theatrical touring company and was on the stage for six years. Not surprisingly, his first literary efforts were plays. In 1902 he published the novel *The Four Feathers,* about a man accused of cowardice and his struggle to vindicate his actions; it became a bestseller. He wrote a number of other novels of adventure, romance, and suspense. His first mystery (without Hanaud) was *The Watchers* (1907). *No Other Tiger* (1927) is another good mystery without Hanaud.

During the period from 1906 to 1910, Mason was a Liberal Member of Parliament. He also had an espionage career; during World War I, he was the civilian head of Naval Intelligence. Spying forms the backbone of *Fire Over England* (1936), but the book is set in the Elizabethan era.

Hanaud appeared in five novels, of which the best are the first two, *At the Villa Rose* (1910) and *The House of the Arrow* (1924). Critics have complained that Hanaud plays his cards too close to the chest—that he violates FAIR PLAY by not producing them immediately. Regardless, the stories have great strengths in terms of atmosphere, humor, wit, and skillful psychology. Writing at the height of the craze for the scientific detective, Mason produced something quite original and subtle. Mason said Hanaud was "a deliberate revolt from the superhuman passionless amateur who at that time . . . held the field." In a sense, Mason's books are closer to the nineteenth century and the mysteries of GABORIAU and COLLINS. Like theirs, his books are also quite long.

Mason's remarkable short story "The Clock" recalls POE. The murder seems impossible to solve; the solution involves a clever violation of fair play as well as of the laws of physics.

MASON, PERRY The best-known character created by Erle Stanley GARDNER, and probably the most famous mystery series character after Sherlock HOLMES, thanks to the television series that was based on the books. Mason first appeared in *The Case of the Velvet Claws* (1933), which seems surprisingly early; indeed, in the first few books Perry is more a rough-and-tumble investigator than the eloquent and masterful attorney he later became, able to break down culprits on the witness stand. Gardner used his own legal background in the creation of Mason, combined with his experience writing for the PULP MAGAZINES.

There are several constant characters in the Mason series, the most famous being his secretary, Della Street, who turns down repeated proposals of marriage from Perry, and relates to him with a respect tinged with amusement. Mason's most diehard opponent is District Attorney Hamilton Berger. Another associate of Mason's is the tall, "loose-jointed" Paul Drake, who runs the Drake Detective Agency; he does legwork for Mason, as well as providing comic relief with his desire to "keep his nose clean" and reluctance to be drawn into anything illegal, such as Perry's occasional breaking and entering in order to get evidence. Mason also has a clerk named Jackson. Lieutentant Arthur Tragg of Homicide and the coarse loudmouth Sergeant Holcomb also appear frequently. None of the characters, including Mason, is given much development.

Gardner wrote more than eighty books about Mason. The plots have a certain sameness; typically, a client comes in with a puzzle or problem, something they have been drawn into or events they do not quite understand. In *The Case of the Borrowed Brunette* (1946), Eva Martell is hired to impersonate a woman after she answers an advertisement. She is instructed to stand on a certain street corner in a dark dress and fur so the client can see her—there is another costumed girl on every corner for blocks. She later suspects the woman she's impersonating has been murdered. This could be called a "gimmick" case—one of those that starts with a conundrum. *The Case of the Buried Clock* (1943) is set during World War II and begins with a recovering soldier finding a ticking clock buried in a box by a mountain cabin. An engaging story that becomes more puzzling with each chapter, it ends in a train wreck of implausibilities and a RED HERRING the size of a whale. All in all, the early books make less use of gimmickry and shallow laughs. THE CASE OF THE TERRIFIED TYPIST (1956), perhaps the best of the series, is the only time that Mason actually loses a case; it is almost all dialogue, and the courtroom scenes are lively reading.

In *The Case of the Screaming Woman* (1957), Perry is approached by a woman who wants him to grill her husband and break down his alibi—but, supposedly, to save him. The legal details can be quite technical, but Gardner's explanations are clear enough. In *The Case of the Half-Wakened Wife* (1945), the crux is whether an oil lease to a certain island has expired or only lapsed (the leaseholder is murdered on a yacht while Mason is trying to help negotiate a settlement).

As the series went on, more novel ploys had to be invented, such as the ridiculous scene in *The Case of the Glamorous Ghost* (1955) of a young woman dancing naked in a public park under the full moon (by a torturous route, the "exhibitionist" finally gets charged with murder). Gardner only ever really had one joke, a kind of puerile sauciness about "babes" and scandalous women.

Gardner often dedicated the books to noted criminologists and law enforcement officers. He also prefaced the story with a cast of characters list (like the Ellery QUEEN novels) and catchy tag lines to describe them, for example, "Virginia Colfax—her figure was hard to believe, and so was her alibi." Perry sees her standing on his fire escape in the rather salacious opening of *The Case of the Dubious Bridegroom* (1949). When the wind blows her skirt up, she drops her gun and drops in on Mason.

Very few short stories were written about Mason. Those that were appeared in a series of volumes that also contained non-Mason short stories (see bibliography).

BIBLIOGRAPHY Novels: *The Case of the Sulky Girl* (1933), *The Case of the Lucky Legs* (1934), *The Case of the Howling Dog* (1934), *The Case of the Curious Bride* (1934), *The Case of the Counterfeit Eye* (1935), *The Case of the Caretaker's Cat* (1935), *The Case of the Sleepwalker's Niece* (1936), *The Case of the Stuttering Bishop* (1936), *The Case of the Dangerous Dowager* (1937), *The Case of the Lame Canary* (1937), *The Case of the Substitute Face* (1938), *The Case of the Shoplifter's Shoe* (1938), *The Case of the Perjured Parrot* (1939), *The Case of the Rolling Bones* (1939), *The Case of the Baited Hook* (1940), *The Case of the Silent Partner* (1940), *The Case of the Haunted Husband* (1941), *The Case of the Empty Tin* (1941), *The Case of the Drowning Duck* (1942), *The Case of the Careless Kitten* (1942), *The Case of the Drowsy Mosquito* (1943), *The Case of the Crooked Candle* (1944), *The Case of the Black-Eyed Blonde* (1944), *The Case of the Golddigger's Purse* (1945), *The Case of Fan-Dancer's Horse* (1947), *The Case of the Lazy Lover* (1947), *The Case of the Lonely Heiress* (1948), *The Case of the Vagabond Virgin* (1948), *The Case of the Cautious Coquette* (1949), *The Case of the Negligent Nymph* (1950), *The Case of the One-Eyed Witness* (1950), *The Case of the Fiery Fingers* (1951), *The Case of the Angry Mourner* (1951), *The Case of the Moth-Eaten Mink* (1952), *The Case of the Grinning Gorilla* (1952), *The Case of the Hesitant Hostess* (1953), *The Case of the Green-Eyed Sister* (1953), *The Case of the Fugitive Nurse* (1954), *The Case of the Runaway Corpse* (1954), *The Case of the Restless Redhead* (1954), *The Case of the Sunbather's Diary* (1955), *The Case of the Nervous Accomplice* (1955), *The Case of the Demure Defendant* (1956), *The Case of the Gilded Lily* (1956), *The Case of the Lucky Loser* (1957), *The Case of the Daring Decoy* (1957), *The Case of the Long-Legged Models* (1958), *The Case of the Footloose Doll* (1958), *The Case of the Calendar Girl* (1958), *The Case of the Deadly Toy* (1959), *The Case of the Mythical Monkeys* (1959), *The Case of the Singing Skirt* (1959), *The Case of the Waylaid Wolf* (1959), *The Case of the Duplicate Daughter* (1960), *The Case of the Shapely Shadow* (1960), *The Case of the Spurious Spinster* (1961), *The Case of the Bigamous Spouse* (1961), *The Case of the Reluctant Model* (1962), *The Case of the Blonde Bonanza* (1962), *The Case of the Icecold Hands* (1962), *The Case of the Mischievous Doll* (1963), *The Case of the Stepdaughter's Secret* (1963), *The Case of the Amorous Aunt* (1963), *The Case of the Daring Divorcee* (1964), *The Case of the Horrified Heirs* (1964), *The Case of the Troubled Trustee* (1965), *The Case of the Beautiful Beggar* (1965), *The Case of the Worried Waitress* (1966), *The Case of the Queenly Contestant* (1967), *The Case of the Careless Cupid* (1968), *The Case of the Fabulous Fake* (1969), *The Case of the Fenced-In Woman* (1972), *The Case of the Postponed Murder* (1973).

Short Stories: *The Case of the Crimson Case* (1970), *The Case of the Crying Swallow* (1971), *The Case of the Irate Witness* (1972).

MASON, RANDOLPH A popular but controversial series character created by Melville Davisson POST. Mason is a lawyer who uses his wiles to help criminals slip through loopholes in the law. Mason's easy conscience and ability to get the better of the legal system by adhering to the letter of the law rather than the moral ideas behind it was somewhat scandalous at the time, but he is a far more modern character than Uncle ABNER, whose prophetic religious outbursts and appeal to divine authority do not square with the direction that detective fiction, or modern society, has taken. Randolph Mason is all too current, however, in his insistence on a narrow and exact definition of crime, which to him is just a "technical word."

Mason takes the same approach to the law as the villain of the Uncle Abner story "The Tenth Commandment." He defines what is legal as what is right, and vice versa, and doesn't have any moral system of his own. His behavior is most shocking in the first two books, *The Strange Schemes of Randolph Mason* (1896) and *The Man of Last Resort, or, The Clients of Randolph Mason* (1897). Post defended Mason against charges that he was helping teach criminals new tricks, but he also seemed to have toned down Randolph's Machiavellian philosophy. In the last book, *The Corrector of Destinies* (1908), Mason has changed his spots and is working for good, not just for what is legal.

Born in Virginia, Mason practices law in New York City, where he helps people carry out legal but unscrupulous schemes. (It is surprising that the Mason stories have not been reprinted in the eighties or nineties, when they would have had a large and admiring audience.) Mason is an imposing man: he is tall and middle-aged, with brown hair streaked with gray and heavy eyebrows. The fact that he appears different from different angles—now stolid, now ugly, now monstrous—seems to emphasize his mercurial character. The other characters are in awe of him; Mason is "as grand, gloomy and peculiar as Napoleon."

In "The Error of William Van Broom" (1896), Mason helps a professional gambler down on his luck save his sister from poverty and prostitution. The gambler, Camden Gerard, writes a fake letter of introduction to the jeweler Van Broom to gain his confidence (and a valuable necklace). As with other stories, Post supplies references to actual cases to show that Gerard's "false making" of the letter "is no forgery, and that no crime has been committed." Post concludes that though the matter seems criminal to Van Broom, to Gerard's sister it is "kindness and sweet self-sacrifice," and muses "perhaps she saw it as it was." The story is one of Post's better flourishes of moral ambiguity.

MASTER OF THE DAY OF JUDGEMENT, THE (*Der Meister des Jungsten Tages,* 1921; tr 1994) A novel of mystery and dread by Austrian writer Leo PERUTZ. Set in Vienna in 1909, the story is told primarily by the Baron von Yosch; he is at an evening music party at the villa of the actor Eugen Bischoff when, after telling a mysterious story about a suicide, Bischoff goes into his pavilion across the garden and shoots himself. The Baron was previously a lover of Bischoff's wife, Dina, and falls under suspicion of having "driven" Bischoff to his death.

The novel is short but incredibly rich in texture, particularly because it reflects many of the themes of German romanticism as well as the contemporary movement of expressionism: the DOPPELGÄNGER or double; the nature of the unconscious, including the return of repressed guilt; erotic obsession; the uncanny and the unnatural; and the conflict between reason and irrationality. The last theme is symbolized by the confident, Sherlockian figure of Waldemar Solgrub, a coldly rational engineer who nevertheless sets out to find the killer and is overwhelmed by his own zeal and excitement.

The atmosphere of the book is somewhere between POE and the Edwardian world of Conan DOYLE. The novel also has one of the most unlikely and amazing murderers in mystery fiction.

MASTERS AND GREEN A detective team created by the English writer Douglas CLARK. They are an odd couple who needle each other through most of the series but eventually bury the hatchet. George Masters is a cultivated, conservative man, while Bill Green is an irascible, working-class character who tends to view events in terms of class conflict and who holds traditional moral views, to say the least. Their first case together is *Nobody's Perfect* (1969). *Premedicated Murder* (1975) takes place in a London suburb into which moves an obnoxious executive, Milton Rencory. He quickly makes himself hated, though his neighbor, the good-hearted war veteran Roger Harte, tries to help him. Then Harte is killed in Rencory's house by means of RICIN; because of the kind of poison, it seems impossible that Harte could have taken it, and yet he did. This is a typical problem created by Clark—the nature of the poison makes the time frame or some other aspect of the case fail to fit. In *Plain Sailing* (1987), a young man suddenly feels sick during a race at Wearbay, near Cullermouth, and dies before he can reach shore. Because death was rapid, the victim's crewmate seems to be the only suspect, though motive and opportunity are lacking.

Late in the series, Masters is promoted to Detective Chief Superintendent, his smoothness and middle-class manner no doubt lifting him over his mate, who actually has more seniority. In *The Big Grouse* (1986), Green is being kept on after retirement age by a special arrangement, but he refers to himself as a "has-been," and Masters treats him with an avuncular fondness that Green sometimes suspects is patronizing. When one of their subordinates is promoted, Masters and Green are sent a female constable. The case involves the disappearance of a sales representative who is a relation of their boss, the Assistant Commissioner.

BIBLIOGRAPHY Novels: *Death After Evensong* (1969), *Deadly Pattern* (1970), *Sweet Poison* (1970), *Sick to Death* (1971), *Dread and Water* (1976), *Table d'Hote* (1977), *The Gimmel Flask* (1977), *The Libertines* (1978), *Heberden's Seat* (1979), *Poacher's Bag* (1980), *Golden Rain* (1980), *Roast Eggs* (1981), *The Longest Pleasure* (1981), *Shelf Life* (1982), *Doone Walk* (1982), *Vicious Circle* (1983), *The Monday Theory* (1983), *Bouquet Gami* (1984), *Dead Letter* (1984), *Jewelled Eye* (1985), *Performance* (1985), *Storm Centre* (1986).

MASTERSON, WHIT See MILLER, WADE.

MASUR, HAROLD Q. (1909 or 1912–) Harold Q. Masur is known for one mystery series, about New York lawyer Scott JORDAN. Masur himself practiced law and wrote relatively few novels. He was president of the Mystery Writers of America and also served as counsel. Masur earned his Ll.D. from New York University Law School in 1934. He began writing mystery fiction in the early forties for the PULP MAGAZINES. In his Jordan mysteries Masur combined the action of the HARD-BOILED novel with courtroom drama and the legal procedure he knew well. Like most American sleuths of the time, Jordan was given an enemy (the District Attorney, just as in the Perry MASON novels of Erle Stanley GARDNER) and a friend in the police department. Masur's blending of various subgenres was on the whole successful and supported by competent writing. BURY ME DEEP (1947) was the first novel.

MASUTO, MASAO A Japanese American detective created by E. V. CUNNINGHAM (Howard Fast). Cunningham introduced Masuto in *Samantha* (1967), a book that belongs to another series, and did not write another book about Masuto for ten years. He returned to the detective series in *The Case of the One-Penny Orange* (1977).

Masuto is middle-aged and heads the Beverly Hills homicide squad, which consists of himself and one subordinate, detective Sy Beckman, a fat and well-meaning cop who fulfills the requirements of a sidekick. Masuto is married to a traditional, even submissive wife, Kati, also Japanese American, and they have two children. Masuto grew up in the San Fernando Valley, where his father farmed until he was interned in one of the infamous camps that were built to imprison Americans of Japanese descent during World War II. In *The Case of the Murdered Mackenzie* (1984), the last book, he visits Japan for the first time.

Known for his political non-mystery novels, Fast uses Masuto to make a variety of points about the society (modern Los Angeles) in which the detective operates. When he is condescended to because of his race, Masuto breaks into an impersonation of Charlie CHAN to put the offender in his place (though sometimes he sounds like Charlie Chan when he is *not* impersonating him). Masuto is a Zen Buddhist and also an expert in karate.

Masuto is given many Japanese-seeming characteristics, but he does not really come across as a personality, perhaps because the plots are often so slight. His detection is often "intuitive," for example in *The Case of the Russian Diplomat* (1978), where he searches the newspapers for any event of note that occurred at the same time as a faked suicide in a hotel swimming pool, and chooses the correct one because he has "a feeling." In *The Case of the Kidnapped Angel* (1982), about the murder of a movie star whose wife has a suspicious past, Masuto spends most of his time calling the principle characters together and trying to elicit a confession. The only real surprise comes with the autopsy of the second victim. In *The Case of the Poisoned Eclairs* (1979), Masuto tracks a killer who uses botulin to contaminate a box of eclairs. *The Case of the Murdered Mackenzie* is about the killing of an engineer involved in sensitive defense work. Since Masuto was in Japan at the time of the case, the victim's wife, a former movie star, is already on trial as the book opens. She insists that the man found in a bathtub in their home, apparently electrocuted by a radio that fell—or was dropped—into the TUB is not even her husband. The description of a trial does not seem to have been researched.

BIBLIOGRAPHY Novels: *The Case of the Sliding Pool* (1981).

MATHIESSEN, PETER See KILLING MISTER WATSON.

MATSUMOTO, SEICHO (1909–1992) The Japanese writer Seicho Matsumoto produced many crime and detective novels, most of which have not been translated into English. He began writing at the age of forty, and first published in the *Weekly Ashahi* in 1950. In 1952, *Aru kokura nikki den* received the prestigious Akutagawa Literary Prize, which since 1935 has been one of Japan's two top literary honors. He won the prize again for INSPECTOR IMANISHI INVESTIGATES (1961). *Ten to sen* (tr *Points and Lines*, 1970) was a million seller in Japan; it has a similar detective to Imanishi, an older, somewhat introverted man named Torigai. He investigates a case involving the apparent suicide of a man and a woman on a cold, deserted beach. The victim turns out to hold an important post in a government ministry under investigation for corruption, casting doubt on the "lover's suicide" hypothesis.

All of Matsumoto's works shed an interesting light on contemporary Japanese society, from the orthodoxy and narrowness of the professional classes to the disaffection and "nihilism" of youth born after World War II. *The Voice and Other Stories* (1989) is a collection of his short fiction in translation. The stories, all published in the fifties and sixties, show a mastery of style and a powerful sense of irony. In "The Accomplice," a man's fears about what his accomplice has been doing in the years since a successful crime drive him to bring about his own downfall. "The Face" is written in diary form. A young actor in a struggling theater company gets a series of opportunities to act in film because his looks are perfect for the role of the feckless young rebel. Hungry for fame, money, and status, he is strangely apprehensive, however, and his "lucky break" has the potential to bring disaster as he gets more and more important roles and is "rewarded" with more time on camera. His plan to suppress details of his past rests on an ironic misunderstanding.

MAUGHAM, ROBIN See TICHBORNE CLAIMANT, THE.

MAUGHAM, W[ILLIAM] SOMERSET (1874–1965) The English novelist, short story writer, essayist, and playwright Somerset Maugham is best known for the partly autobiographical novel *Of Human Bondage* (1915), and *The Moon and Sixpence* (1919), a novel based on the life of Paul Gaugin. During World War I, Maugham served as a secret agent; this experience became the basis for ASHENDEN; OR, THE BRITISH AGENT (1928), one of the classics of the spy genre.

Maugham was born in Paris, where he lived to the age of ten. Orphaned, Maugham was then brought up in the strictly religious household of his uncle, a clergyman. (Maugham would later call himself an atheist, and was renowned for his penetrating insight into human nature, which often cast its subject in a bad light.) He studied at Heidelberg and then at St. Thomas's medical school in London. His first novel, *Liza of Lambeth* (1897), was based on his experiences as an obstetrician. Genuine success as a writer would take him another decade, however, and eventually came from drama, not fiction. In 1908, he accomplished the feat of having four plays running in London at the same time.

During World War I, Maugham joined an ambulance unit. He was later transferred to the intelligence service and sent to Russia to "prevent the Bolshevik revolution" and to keep Russia from making a separate peace with Germany. As he said in a later preface to *Ashenden*, "the reader will know that my efforts did not meet with success." After the war, Maugham settled in France, living in a villa in Cap Ferrat from 1928 onward.

Maugham was also a respected author of short stories, which have now eclipsed his Edwardian dramas in popularity with critics and readers alike. His style appears to be modeled on that of MAUPASSANT, though the settings were often more reminiscent of CONRAD. One of his stories, BEFORE THE PARTY, is a particularly effective murder tale; it appeared in *The Casuarina Tree* (1926). The title story also concerned murder: set in Malaya, it is about a white colonial who shoots her lover after he confesses to having an affair with a Chinese woman. Maugham rewrote the story as a play under the title *The Letter* (1927). FOOTPRINTS IN THE JUNGLE (1933), possibly his most famous murder story, is also set in Malaya. As with his other work, Maugham's stories often reflected a cynical view of the barbarity of human behavior, concealed rather than ameliorated by convention and the appearances of civilization.

Maugham also wrote an influential essay, THE DECLINE AND FALL OF THE DETECTIVE STORY, which was printed in the collection *The Vagrant Mood* (1952). In it he provided a famous defense of *serious* detective fiction, but not the blanket praise of the genre with which he is sometimes credited.

MAUPASSANT, GUY DE (1850–1893) A protégé of Gustave Flaubert, Guy de Maupassant wrote some three hundred short stories and was a leading writer of the naturalist school. Maupassant was born in Miromensil and fought in the Franco-Prussian War. As a young man he contracted syphilis; later in life, he became a restless peripatetic. He tried to cut his own throat and, failing, died two years later in an asylum.

Although Maupassant did not write detective stories, some of his stories, particularly "The Horla," in which a man is deluded that an invisible parasite is attacking him through his lips, are sometimes considered tales of suspense or horror. Maupassant's stories are models of short fiction because they usually turn on a single action or element, the results of which are often deeply ironic. In the famous story "The Necklace," a couple borrow a diamond necklace and then lose it; terrified to admit the loss, they buy an exact duplicate and then work off the debt over a period of years. Later, they learn that the original necklace was paste. "The Hand" is a macabre tale set in Corsica about an Englishman who keeps a severed hand chained to his wall; one day, the man is found strangled.

MAURENSIG, PAOLO (1943–) An Italian businessman, Paolo Maurensig had never written a book when he published *La variante di Lüneburg* (1993; tr *The Lüneburg Variation*, 1997). The novel is a murder and suspense story with a political background, somewhat in the tradition of writers like Leonardo SCIASCIA, but with magical elements like the work of Leo PERUTZ. Most innovative is the story's use of chess: a particular gambit is cleverly used by a concentration camp victim to track down one of his former tormentors.

MAYERLING An Austrian village, Mayerling became internationally famous on January 30, 1889, when the bodies of the Austrian crown prince Rudolf and his mistress, Baroness Maria Vetsera, were found shot to death in a royal hunting lodge. The prince had been ordered to end the affair by his father; instead, he shot the baroness and then himself.

The Mayerling affair partly inspired Nicholas Freeling's KING OF THE RAINY COUNTRY (1966).

MAYO, ASEY An inhabitant of Wellfleet, Massachusetts, Phoebe Atwood TAYLOR's Asey Mayo is a former bos'n, first mate, and seaman who solves cases in his spare time. Although he is an ancient mariner, Mayo is a spry and still active retainer of the Porter family. He was the cook on Old Porter's yacht, *Roll an' Go*, and after Porter died, he became a helper to young Bill Porter. Bill's wife Betsey is also a significant character. Among the Porter family's interests is a line of luxury automobiles bearing their name. At one time Mayo was a daredevil race driver and the automotive equivalent of a test pilot.

Nobody can gauge Mayo's age accurately because he is so tanned, but he actually was born around 1875, and served against the Boxers in China in 1900. Lanky and tall, he goes around in corduroys, a Stetson hat, and a wool-lined canvas coat with innumerable pockets. Mayo is handy and can fix anything. Down to earth, he is not impressed by money or authority.

Mayo's mixture of Yankee homespun humor and philosophy is one of the charms of the series. The New England dialogue rings true, without forcing the reader to undergo a linguistics course. Although Asey's approach is to use hard sense, the puzzles he is presented with are humorous if not farcical. In *Out of Order* (1936), one of the members of Bill's club bets him $50,000—a huge sum during the Depression—that Asey can't even solve a grocery order. Mayo is compelled to return from Jamaica to a New England blizzard to sort out the mess, which soon comes to involve several murders.

Death Lights a Candle (1932), narrated by Betsey Porter's aunt Prudence Whitsby, also involves a SNOW-BOUND house. "Prue" is invited to a party at the Wellfleet home of Rowena Fible, a sculptress and daughter of an ex-governor of the state. It transpires that an old enemy of Rowena's—she threw a brick through his window and broke his teeth during her Suffragette days—has just built a house on the next hill and is throwing a housewarming party (men only). Rowena is roped into chaperoning the man's niece because she wants to sculpt another of the guests.

The events of OCTAGON HOUSE (1937) focus on a scandal caused by a public mural funded by the Works Projects Administration. Feuding relatives, a chunk of ambergris, and a cat named Emma Goldman make it a typically loony Taylor mystery. *The Six Iron Spiders* (1942) has Mayo returning to Cape Cod from the Porter tank factory during World War II. He finds his cousin Jennie and others doing a first aid demonstration in his house; later, in place of the dummy, he finds a corpse—Philemon Mundy, a businessman who was in trouble. The "spiders" are actually frying pans (one is thought to be the murder weapon). There are several suspects and a second death, but the book holds less interest than other Mayos.

Diplomatic Corpse (1951), the last novel in the series, is a comparatively dull affair in which the body of Muriel Babcock, one of the organizers of a historical pageant in Quanomet, is found stretched across a grave. Buff Orpington, a former college football star, is an important character; his boss, the ad executive George Pettingill, is Muriel's brother. Asey traps the killer with the help of Jennie Mayo.

BIBLIOGRAPHY Novels: *The Cape Cod Mystery* (1931), *The Mystery of the Cape Cod Tavern* (1934), *Sandbar Sinister* (1934), *The Tinkling Symbol* (1935), *Deathblow Hill* (1935), *The Crimson Patch* (1936), *Figure Away* (1937), *The Annulet of Guilt* (1938), *Banbury Bog* (1938), *Spring Harrowing* (1939), *The Deadly Sunshade* (1940), *The Criminal C.O.D.* (1940), *The Perennial Border* (1941), *Going, Going, Gone* (1943), *Proof of the Pudding* (1945), *Punch with Care* (1946).

Short Fiction: *Three Plots for Asey Mayo* (1942), *The Asey Mayo Trio* (1946).

MEADE, L[ILLIE] T[HOMAS] (pen name of Elizabeth Thomasina Meade, 1854–1914) L. T. Meade is most remembered for her short stories, many of which appeared in *The Strand* and other magazines of the day. She often wrote in collaboration with doctors, and the stories were physiologically and scientifically detailed. Meade's collaborations with Robert EUSTACE were among her most successful, and included *The Brotherhood of the Seven Kings* (1899), which is held to have introduced the first female criminal in the genre—leaving aside, of course, PROTOMYSTERIES, which present an impressive array of bad women.

L. T. Meade was born in County Cork, Ireland, and after moving to London began to work at the British Museum. She also edited a magazine, *Atalanta*. Although now remembered as a mystery writer, Meade also published 250 extremely successful novels for girls. They contained sensational, GOTHIC, and adventure elements, which also found their way into her collaborations with Eustace. Some of the Meade-Eustace books are *A Master of Mysteries* (1898), *The Gold Star Line* (1899), and *The Sanctuary* (1900). The collaborative short stories are rarely believable, but they are amusingly clever; "The Outside Ledge" (1900), published in *The Harmsworth Magazine*, makes the most ingenious (and what is more, purposeful) use of a CAT in detective fiction. No doubt it was Eustace, the doctor, who knew about the special properties of the herb valerian, often prescribed as a relaxant for persons of nervous disposition. Meade also wrote stories about Dr. Clifford HALIFAX with Dr. Edgar Beaumont.

The Sorceress of the Strand (1902) is Meade's best-known work; its subject is the female villain Madam SARA. The stories were published in *The Strand* as collaborations with Eustace but later collected under Meade's name. Madam Sara was innovative and evil enough to endure, but was only one of Meade's female protagonists. She wrote four stories (including "The Outside Ledge") about Florence Cusack, a young and beautiful detective with dark blue eyes and "raven-black" hair.

MEDMENHAM ABBEY See HELL-FIRE CLUB, THE.

MELODY SAM A character in Arthur W. UPFIELD's *Journey to the Hangman* (1959). Sam Loader is the patriarch of the remote Western Australia town of Daybreak—he even owns the church, and there is a statue of him in the main square. He is first encountered by Inspector BONAPARTE during one of his seasonal alcoholic binges, during which Melody Sam locks himself in the basement of his pub with a quantity of gelignite and refuses to be dislodged. He is a rustic autocrat like Old Lacy in THE BONE IS POINTED (1938).

MELVILLE, HERMAN See CONFIDENCE MAN, THE.

MELVILLE, JAMES (pseudonym of Roy Peter Martin, 1931–) There are certain similarities between the mystery novels of James Melville and his fellow British writer Magadalen NABB: both write about non-English settings in which a "native" detective deals with cases that often involve foreigners; both authors use these scenarios to present cultural contrast. Melville's Superintendent OTANI is a high-level policeman in the area of Kobe, Japan.

Melville was educated at the University of London, where he received his M.A. in political philosophy in 1956. His career as a diplomat, and more particularly his posting to Tokyo, provided background for the Otani series. Perhaps intentionally, Melville writes with awkward phrasings and peculiar word choices, making the novels seem almost to be translations from Japanese (though a good translation, of course, avoids awkwardness). The Japanese atmosphere is well done, though sometimes Melville digresses to the detriment of the narrative flow and the descriptions can be so detailed as to seem a little pedantic. (The average reader does not need to be extensively educated as to the Japanese custom of removing shoes before entering the home.) Regardless of how it is accomplished, the creation of a Japanese atmosphere has been praised by critics as authentic. The tempo of the books, the pacing of events and revelations, and the weaving of subplots into the main narrative are sometimes clumsy.

The greatest mystery and detective novels and stories set in Japan were written by the Japanese writer Seicho MATSUMOTO.

MELVILLE, JEAN-PIERRE (Jean-Pierre Grumbach, 1917–1973) This innovative and idiosyncratic French filmmaker took his screen name from his favorite novelist, Herman Melville. Born in Paris, he made his first films with a camera his father had given him as a present. After fighting in World War II, and disappointed in his efforts to crack the French film industry, he set up his own company and began making low-budget films with no-name actors. Melville later worked with stars like Jean-Paul Belmondo. In addition to films about war that reflected his own experiences, Melville made some classic crime movies that were influenced by Hollywood pictures of the thirties and postwar FILM NOIR. *Bob le Flambeur* (1955) is a suave, stylized black-and-white movie filmed with artful simplicity about a gang trying to rob the casino at Deauville. At the center is Bob, an ex-convict who has gone straight but cannot resist one more gamble. *Le Samouraï* (1967) is not a Samurai film but Melville's homage to *film noir* and the romantic-heroic figures of tough guys, crooks, and private eyes.

MELVILLE, JENNIE The pseudonym under which Gwendoline BUTLER has written her series of mysteries about the policewoman Charmian DANIELS.

MEMSAHIB In British English, an honorific term for the wife of a European. An Anglo-Indian word, it comes from "ma'am" and the Urdu word *sahib,* meaning "sir" (from the Arabic for "friend").

MENCKEN, H[ENRY] L[OUIS] (1880–1956) American critic, journalist, humorist, and instigator of controversies. In accounts of the literary life of the twenties and thirties, Mencken is a larger-than-life figure. Outrageous stories circulated about him, and he often delivered outrageous opinions. Yet Mencken played an important role in developing and legitimizing the canon of classic American literature. He and George Jean Nathan were editors and co-owners of *Smart Set* when they decided to found a new magazine, BLACK MASK. *Smart Set* was billed as "The Aristocrat Among Magazines," and it would not have survived without the subsidiary publications that bankrolled it—PULP MAGAZINES. The price that Mencken got when he sold *Black Mask* is often fantastically exaggerated. Mencken also had two other pulps, *Parisienne* and *Saucy Stories,* in which he sold his interest for about fifteen thousand dollars. He and Nathan went on to found *The American Mercury* in 1924, a journal of American literature and culture, which included articles by such figures as Lewis Mumford and Sinclair Lewis. Mencken also did much to build the reputations of Theodore DREISER and James T. Farrell, and shared their critical view of American society, religion, and morals.

For someone who professed no interest in the detective/mystery genre, Mencken had a strong effect on it, not only in founding *Black Mask*; Mencken also was a great fosterer of talent. He said that "Whenever a volunteer showed the slightest sign of talent, I wrote to him encouragingly, and kept on blowing his spark so long as the faintest hope remained of fanning it into flame."

Among those whom he encouraged were Theodore Dreiser and his fellow *Baltimore Sun* writer James M. CAIN, whose work he published in *The American Mercury,* including BABY IN THE ICEBOX. (Rex STOUT once said that he was planning to become a lawyer until he had a poem accepted by *Smart Set.*)

Mencken was also an authority on American speech, including SLANG, and his *The American Language* (first ed. 1919) was reissued and revised many times.

MENDOZA, EDUARDO (1943–) The Spanish novelist Eduardo Mendoza appeared on the literary scene at a time when experimentalism and magic realism were ascendant. Mendoza worked at the United Nations as a translator and then, in 1975, published the book that made his reputation, *La verdad sobre el caso Savolta* (tr. THE TRUTH ABOUT THE SAVOLTA CASE, tr 1992). The novel tells a story of revolution and intrigue in the period around the end of World War I. Set in Mendoza's native Barcelona, the book was praised as much for its portrayal of the city as its large cast of eccentric characters. Mendoza departed from the fashion of the time by his heterodox style, incorporating elements of the PICARESQUE, the HARD-BOILED, and romance; at times, the novel even reads like a PROCEDURAL. Two later books, *El misterio de la cripta* (1978) and *El labertino de las aceitunas* (1982), are hard-boiled parodies.

MENDOZA, LUIS Under the pseudonym Dell Shannon, Elizabeth LININGTON wrote almost forty novels about detective Luis Mendoza of the Los Angeles Police Department. Although a PROCEDURAL series, the Mendoza books are not terribly realistic, beginning with the detective himself. Mendoza is an heir and independently wealthy (despite the fact that he grew up in a slum), and pursues a career as a detective for the pleasure of it—qualities more commonly found in the GENIUS DETECTIVE of an earlier era than in a modern story of crime. Linington also used the series to illustrate her own conservative values; originally a card player, Mendoza narrowly escaped becoming a career criminal. He is a ladies' man and a natty dresser, but later settles down to an orthodox upper-class family life complete with pets and servants.

BIBLIOGRAPHY Novels: *Case Pending* (1960), *The Ace of Spades* (1961), *Extra Kill* (1962), *Knave of Hearts* (1962), *Double Bluff* (1963), *Death of a Busy-body* (1963), *Mark of Murder* (1964), *Root of All Evil* (1964), *The Death Bringers* (1965), *Death by Inches* (1965), *Coffin Comer* (1966), *With a Vengeance* (1966), *Chance to Kill* (1967), *Rain with Violence* (1967), *Kill with Kindness* (1968), *Crime on Their Hands* (1969), *Schooled to Kill* (1969), *Unexpected Death* (1970), *The Ringer* (1971), *Whim to Kill* (1971), *With Intent to Kill* (1972), *Murder with Love* (1972), *Spring of Violence* (1973), *No Holiday for Crime* (1973), *Crime File* (1974), *Deuces Wild* (1975), *Streets of Death* (1976), *Appearances of Death* (1977), *Cold Trail* (1978), *Felony at Random* (1979), *Felony File* (1980), *Murder Most Strange* (1981), *The Motive on Record* (1982), *Exploit of Death* (1983), *Destiny of Death* (1984), *Chaos of Crime* (1985), *Blood Count* (1986).

Short Stories: *Murder by the Tale* (1987).

MERLINI, THE GREAT Clayton RAWSON used his own experience as background for the four-book career of The Great Merlini, a magician who becomes a sleuth. He is first called in by the police in *Death from a Top Hat* (1940) to help solve a series of murders among magicians with the idea that it takes someone who knows the tricks of the trade to sort things out. Born into the circus, The Great Merlini has settled down to running a New York City magic shop after a world-traveling career. His shop assistant is Burt Fawkes, formerly known as "Twisto, the Man Who Turns Himself Inside Out." Merlini is tall and distinguished looking and seems younger than his sixty years. His contact is Inspector Homer Gavigan. Rawson was fond of the LOCKED ROOM situation, which so neatly fits in with the apparent impossibilities of the magic show. The title of *The Footprints on the Ceiling* (1939) indicates the clever, gravity-defying getaway of the murderer. *No Coffin for the Corpse* (1942) was the last novel in the series and focused on the millionaire munitions manufacturer Dudley Wolff, who is terrified of death. He funds research by a scientist and a psychic to find out what lies beyond the grave. His troubles start when he accidentally kills a blackmailer, who turns out to be an FBI agent. The Merlini books were typical of the novels by writers who had graduated from the PULP MAGAZINES in trying to find a hook that had not been used before, though Merlini used maps and other devices of the classic or GOLDEN AGE mystery. Some of his work seems to have been influenced by the early Ellery QUEEN.

BIBLIOGRAPHY Novels: *The Headless Lady* (1940).

MERRETT, JOHN DONALD See NOT PROVEN.

MERRION, DESMOND The second series character created by Major Cecil Street (John RHODE), writing under the name Miles Burton. Merrion is a former World War I intelligence officer who, after leaving the Admiralty, decides to become an amateur detective. He first appeared in THE SECRET OF HIGH ELDERSHAM (1930), which is somewhat unaccountably considered one of the author's best books. Merrion, whose ship was blown up off the Belgian coast during the war, now lives in luxury in

Mayfair (in the tradition of many Edwardian detectives, he is independently wealthy).

With the advent of World War II, the author sent Merrion back to the intelligence service, then demobilized him again in the late forties. Merrion's naval connection allows for plenty of cases of MURDER AFLOAT. Merrion is called upon by Inspector Henry Arnold of Scotland Yard's C.I.D., with whom he maintains a friendly but bantering relationship. Arnold is even allowed to solve some cases entirely on his own, such as *Death Leaves No Card* (1939). Merrion's wife, Mavis, hardly ever appears in the series.

BARZUN and TAYLOR summarized forty-seven Merrion stories in *Catalog of Crime* (1971; rev 1989), not one of which is in print in the United States. Although Merrion is active and the books are often inventive, Rhode's writing has palled with time; Merrion cannot compete with the great GOLDEN AGE detectives such as POIROT and WIMSEY, and even the adventures of Inspector FRENCH, who is hardly a flamboyant genius, are more often reprinted. Rhode devoted himself to the puzzle and to little else, and Merrion's hold on the imagination is too feeble to make his stories lasting.

Burton/Rhode regularly churned out two or three Merrion novels per year. He wrote one series with "death" in the title (*Death at the Club* [1937], *Death in a Duffle Coat* [1956], *Death Takes A Detour* [1958], etc.). Another group all began with "murder" (*Murder in Crown Passage* [1937], *Murder in the Coalhole* [1940], *Murder on Duty* [1952], etc.). The second of these, published in the United States as *Written in Dust* (1940), is one of the most diverting Merrion tales, if only for the coal mining background. THE PLATINUM CAT (1938) overcomes the usual weaknesses of stilted dialogue with a more than usually engaging plot. Other recognized high points in the Merrion series are *The Three Crimes* (1931), *Not A Leg to Stand On* (1945), and *Who Killed the Doctor?* (1944; orig title *Murder, M.D.*) As with the other series the author wrote, about Dr. PRIESTLEY, the earlier books are the better ones, but all are puzzle-oriented and in the style of the thirties.

BIBLIOGRAPHY Novels: *Menace on the Downs* (1931), *The Death of Mr. Gantley* (1932), *Death at the Crossroads* (1933), *Fate at the Fair* (1933), *Tragedy at the Thirteenth Hole* (1933), *The Charabanc Mystery* (1934), *To Catch a Thief* (1934), *The Milk-Churn Murder* (1935; U.S. title *The Clue of the Silver Brush*), *The Devereux Court Mystery* (1935), *Death in the Tunnel* (1936; U.S. title *Dark is the Tunnel*), *Murder of a Chemist* (1936), *Where Is Barbara Prentice?* (1936; U.S. title *The Clue of the Silver Cellar*), *Death at Low Tide* (1938), *Death Leaves No Card* (1939), *Mr. Babbacombe Dies* (1939), *Mr. Westerby Missing* (1940), *Death Takes a Flat* (1940; U.S. title *Vacancy with Corpse*), *Death of Two Brothers* (1941), *Up the Garden Path* (1941; U.S. title *Death Visits Downspring*), *This Undesirable Residence* (1942; U.S. title *Death at Ash House*), *Dead Stop* (1943), *The Four-ply Yarn* (1944; U.S. title *The Shadow on the Cliff*), *The Three-Corpse Trick* (1944), *Early Morning Murder* (1945; U.S. title *Accidents Do Happen*), *The Cat Jumps* (1946), *Situation Vacant* (1946), *Heir to Lucifer* (1947), *A Will in the Way* (1947), *Death in Shallow Water* (1948), *Devil's Reckoning* (1948), *Death Takes the Living* (1949; U.S. title *The Disappearing Parson*), *Look Alive* (1949), *Ground for Suspicion* (1950), *A Village Afraid* (1950), *Beware Your Neighbor* (1951), *Murder Out of School* (1951), *Heir to Murder* (1953), *Something to Hide* (1953), *Murder in Absence* (1954), *Unwanted Corpse* (1954), *A Crime in Time* (1955), *Murder Unrecognized* (1955), *Found Drowned* (1956), *The Chinese Puzzle* (1957), *The Moth-Watch Murder* (1957), *Bones in the Brickfield* (1958), *Return from the Dead* (1959), *The Smell of Smoke* (1959), *Legacy of Death* (1960), *Death Paints a Picture* (1960).

MERRIVALE, SIR HENRY Known as "the old man" and "H. M.," Sir Henry Merrivale is a sleuth who appears in the Carter Dixon mysteries of John Dickson CARR. A baronet, a doctor, and a barrister, Merrivale is large ("barrel-shaped"), ill-tempered, "pigeon-toed," and imposing; he wears an odd assortment of hats as well as horn-rimmed eyeglasses. He is noted for his forbidding aspect and his blustering manner. He says he has "pirate blood," and is fond of expletives like "Burn it!" and "Oh, Esau." Merrivale is also fond of jokes, sometimes descending to slapstick humor (squirting glue on a cabdriver's face and sticking a five-pound note to him). He is nominally employed by the War Office (head of military intelligence), but becomes embroiled in all manner of rather nutty adventures, exhibiting to the full the author's penchant for the impossible. Merrivale, of course, sails through with flying colors. In *He Wouldn't Kill Patience* (1944), a story involving snakes, growling Scotsmen and Cockneys, and a family feud between two dynasties of magicians, Sir Henry is chased around a reptile house by a lizard.

Merrivale's entourage is suitably eccentric as well: his wife Clementine, who was a dancer in a music hall; Inspector Humphrey Masters, who tags along in his footsteps but never quite gets to the solution, and who is also a magician; and his secretary, Miss Ffolliott. Merrivale is more of a caricature than a character, or a theatrical bit part raised to the level of a lead. His dropping of the letter *h* and use of "ain't" show a lineage going back to the affected early Peter WIMSEY.

As elsewhere, the author was interested in GOTHIC and ghostly themes. A mummy figures in *The Curse of the Bronze Lamp* (1945; British title *Lord of the Sorcerers*)—

(see ARCHAEOLOGY). During World War II, Merrivale gets involved in espionage. In *Murder in the Submarine Zone* (1940; U.S. title *Nine—And Death Makes Ten*), Merrivale is on a ship, the *Edwardic*. Against the background of the battle of the North Atlantic, a military secret leads to murder. In *The Skeleton in the Clock* (1948), Dickson Carr again uses the subject of ghosts. John Stannard, K. C., and his two young friends, Ruth Callice and Martin Drake, decide to spend the night in the "execution shed" of an abandoned prison, hoping to find evidence of troubled spirits. Meanwhile, through a bit of slapstick comedy, Merrivale buys at auction a tall case clock with a skeleton in it. In a complex romantic subplot, Drake is reunited with his lost love from the war, and involved in the investigation of her former fiancé's father's mysterious death. And then there is the skeleton. As often happens, Dickson Carr seems to be making up the plot as he goes along with little concern for pace or consistency.

Carr also wrote a few short stories about Merrivale, which are collected in several volumes along with other tales (see bibliography).

BIBLIOGRAPHY Novels: *The Plague Court Murders* (1934), *The White Priory Murders* (1934), *The Red Window Murders* (1935), *The Unicorn Murders* (1935), *The Magic Lantern Murders* (1936; U.S. title *The Punch and Judy Murders*), *The Ten Teacups* (1937; U.S. title *The Peacock Feather Murders*), *The Judas Window* (1938), *Death in Five Boxes* (1938), *The Reader is Warned* (1939), *And So to Murder* (1940), *Seeing Is Believing* (1941), *The Gilded Man* (1942), *She Died a Lady* (1943), *My Late Wives* (1946), *A Graveyard to Let* (1949), *Night at the Mocking Widow* (1950), *Behind the Crimson Blind* (1952), *The Cavalier's Cup* (1953).

Short Stories: *The Third Bullet and Other Stories* (1954), *The Men Who Explained Miracles* (1963), *March, Merrivale, and Murder* (1991).

MICKEY FINN A drink treated with "knockout drops," particularly but not exclusively associated with HARD-BOILED mysteries of the twenties and thirties. The drops were actually chloral hydrate, a treatment for insomnia; in heavy doses they could be lethal, as in Margery Allingham's THE CASE OF THE LATE PIG (1937). The Mickey Finn was especially popular with Raymond CHANDLER, who had his detective drink one in "Goldfish" and THE LITTLE SISTER (1949). Travis MCGEE is given a psychedelic Mickey (an LSD-like drug) in *Nightmare in Pink* (1964) in a restaurant and wakes up imprisoned in a mental hospital. A murder with chloral hydrate occurred in BURY ME DEEP (1947), the first case of Scott JORDAN.

Though the term did not yet exist, laudanum was used as a Mickey by the M'Kean brothers in a notorious murder discussed by DE QUINCEY.

MILDRED PIERCE (1941) This novel continues to be categorized and published as a mystery because it was written by James M. CAIN and because a murder was added to the powerful film version (1945) for which Joan Crawford won an Academy Award. To extend the term "mystery" to the suspense about what will happen to the hard-pressed protagonist of the book would also include most serious novels; it is, however, one of Cain's finest books. Mildred Pierce is a woman saddled with a philandering, not bright, and above all lazy husband. She finally manages to leave him and starts a pie business. A truly remarkable novel, it realistically portrays the struggles facing a divorced mother in the 1940s. The society that surrounds her is the same grim world of Cain's other novels, populated with heartless, unimaginative people whose only delight often is to crush the dreams of anyone less limited than they are. In Varda Pierce, the book also contains Cain's greatest portrayal of thoroughgoing amorality and evil. She is a prima donna as a little girl and then actually grows up to be an operatic singer. For her whole life, she "high hats" Mildred who keeps coming back for more. It is interesting that Varda's combination of cruelty and success was one of the things that had to be suppressed in the film, replaced with a more palatable theme—murder.

MILLAR, MARGARET (born Margaret Ellis Sturm, 1915–1994) The Canadian-born author Margaret Millar was married to Kenneth Millar (Ross MACDONALD); she has achieved a reputation equal to her husband among critics but less notoriety with the public. Millar actually began publishing before Macdonald did, with *The Invisible Worm* (1941), whose main character, the psychiatrist Paul PRYE, would appear in two more books. Psychology was to be the hallmark of her work; she often dealt with extreme states of feeling and mental derangement. Her grasp of child psychology—not in a clinical sense but as a mentality in which fantasy and reality merge—is unequalled in crime and suspense fiction. The invigorating but also dangerous persistence into adulthood of childlike ways of viewing the world is an important undercurrent in her stories.

Margaret Sturm was born in Kitchener, Ontario, and met Kenneth Millar when they were both teenagers. Although Millar at age fifteen had already decided he wanted to marry her, the first time they spoke was years later; he asked her to go on a trip to Ireland with him. She refused, she said, because "nice Canadian girls didn't go to Ireland on the first date." Sturm graduated from the University of Toronto in 1936 and married two years later. The couple moved to California after World War II. Ross

Macdonald described it as a tough, cold year—"My wife and I used to sit and write in our overcoats." THE IRON GATES (1945) is the first of her darkly psychological novels. It was related to the Prye series through the character of Inspector Sands, a Toronto policeman.

Like many of the works of Mary Roberts RINEHART, Millar's books display an interest in "mystery" in the broadest sense. But whereas Rinehart was drawn toward the occult and GOTHIC, Millar, writing under a Freudian influence, found all the horrors she needed in the human mind. The psychological thriller *The Cannibal Heart* (1949) is set in a remote spot on the California coast where a New York family, the Banners, have rented a house. The caretaker, Mr. Roma, and his Mexican wife and their daughter round out this isolated community, which Millar expertly develops through the eyes of the children. Strange tensions and relationships are already at work when the real mystery develops, upon the arrival of Mrs. Wakefield. She is the owner of the house, as well as the mother of a child who has died and the widow of a man who has disappeared and is presumed dead. Exploration of the minds of the various characters and elucidation of the past evokes a decidedly weird atmosphere.

Millar avoided the HARD-BOILED style prevalent in California in the forties and fifties, though she occasionally wrote novels in which a private detective appeared. In *The Listening Walls* (1959), p.i. Elmer Dodd investigates the murder of Wilma Wyatt, who had gone to Mexico City with her friend Amy Kellogg, a mousy rich woman from San Francisco married to the bland Rupert Kellogg, whose sole ambition is to run a pet shop. Consuelo Gonzales, the Mexican maid, overheard the women fighting and then found Amy knocked unconscious and Wilma dead. After Rupert imprudently checks Amy out of the hospital, she disappears. The complex network of relationships involves Gill Brandon, Amy's brother, and his wife Helene. Everyone tries either to shield or hurt everyone else. For example, Gill is obsessive about his baby sister, whom his wife so resents that she conspires with Rupert against Gill, her own husband. Once again Millar shows the fatal human inability to separate different motives and emotions.

Like POE, Margaret Millar had a talent for depicting what might be called primal scenes of horror touching on the most elemental of human fears. The best example is the scene in A STRANGER IN MY GRAVE (1960) in which the narrator dreams about her own grave and then comes upon the real thing. Millar won an EDGAR award for BEAST IN VIEW (1955), in which a mysterious telephone call leads to the disclosure of a horrifying human aberration or "monster." As a study of pure maliciousness, it is unexcelled. *Beyond this Point Are Monsters* (1970) is about the disappearance and presumed death of a California ranch owner.

The latter part of Millar's life was marked by two tragedies, the first being the death of her only daughter in 1970. Macdonald died in 1983 after a debilitating illness. Millar did not write any fiction for six years. With ASK FOR ME TOMORROW (1976), she introduced Tom ARAGON, a young Chicano lawyer who became her first series character since Paul Prye and Inspector Sands. Aragon appeared in two other books that contain mystery and crime elements but are most strikingly novels of character, place, and time.

In 1982 Millar was named a Grand Master by the MYSTERY WRITERS OF AMERICA, of which she had been president in 1957–1958. In addition to winning the Edgar for *Beast in View,* she was nominated for the award two other times, for *How Like an Angel* (1962) and *The Fiend* (1964). Unlike many writers who have started out average and stayed that way regardless of how many books they churned out, Millar began as a talented caricaturist (in the Paul Prye series) and developed into an acute humanist, an observer with the curiosity of a BALZAC and the wit to embody her wisdom in entertaining form.

MILLAY, EDNA ST. VINCENT See MURDER IN THE FISHING CAT, THE.

MILLER, WADE (pseudonym of Robert Wade, 1920–, and Bill Miller, 1920–1961) Robert Wade and Bill Miller met while they were in junior high school and began a collaboration that would eventually produce more than thirty novels and numerous short stories. Their best-known creation was the private detective Max Thursday. As Whit Masterson, they wrote the novel *Badge of Evil* (1956), which Orson Welles adapted for his classic film *A Touch of Evil* (1958).

Miller was born in Indiana, and met Wade after his family moved to San Diego. They worked together on their school newspaper, as well as on radio plays and movie scripts. Both attended San Diego State College; they co-edited the *East San Diego Press,* a weekly newspaper. Miller and Wade both served as sergeants in the Air Force during World War II, Miller in the Pacific and Wade in England and North Africa.

Miller and Wade both settled in San Diego again after the war and continued their collaboration. Their first mystery novel was *Deadly Weapon* (1946), which was praised by Anthony BOUCHER for its sharp writing and surprise ending. *Guilty Bystander* (1947) introduced Thursday, a former security man at an aircraft plant who has lost his wife and son and descended into the gutter. Wade and Miller did not simply want to write whodunits, but tried to put a deeper level of emotion into the HARD-BOILED mystery. They went on to write five more novels about the San Diego detective. The pair also won a short story award from *Ellery Queen's Mystery Magazine* in 1955, and published some memorable non-series novels. *The Devil May Care* (1950) is about Biggo Venn, an adventurer who is stranded in a sinister Mexican town. In *The Killer* (1951), a man tracks the murderer of his friend's son across the United States. Two novels, *Memo for Murder* (1951) and *Dead Fall* (1954), were published under the name Dale Wilmer (an anagram of Wade Miller).

Another of Miller and Wade's books as Whit Masterson was *All Through the Night* (1955), a kidnapping story (one of their favorite themes) which was also filmed. Wade continued to use this pseudonym after Miller's death, writing another twenty novels, some of them procedural. *A Hammer in His Hand* (1960) was an early mystery about a policewoman; in this case, a group of cops avenge their fellow officer's murder. Under his own name, Wade published *Knave of Eagles* (1969), a thriller about a BASEBALL player being held captive in Cuba.

MILLHONE, KINSEY A leading example of the new HARD-BOILED female detectives of recent decades, created by Sue GRAFTON—but with some strange eccentricities. The popular insurance investigator has exercised a somewhat inexplicable fascination for readers, and even for other characters; in Lawrence BLOCK's *The Burglar Who Traded Ted Williams* (1994), Bernie RHODENBARR and his pet-grooming friend Carolyn Kaiser speculate at length about Kinsey's sexual orientation and psychological profile. For something is definitely not as it seems beneath Millhone's chipper dialogue.

One might be tempted to ask what's eating Kinsey Millhone: like an *idiot savant,* by her guileless and casual remarks she reveals a character of which she is apparently unaware. A self-described "celibate," she is both repulsed and excited by other people's sexual behavior, particularly in *"H" is for Homicide* (1991), in which the plot hinges more on lust than criminality. Through a series of sexually charged episodes she repeatedly mentions that she can sense her companions' underwear "getting damp" (a peculiar remark to make once, but twice?). Is she simply fastidious, or a fetishist? In *"C" Is for Corpse* (1986), she says "I find myself keeping my guard up, along with my underpants."

A former police officer, Millhone lives in the California town of Santa Teresa (which was part of Lew ARCHER's beat). Her setup is this: she receives office space from California Fidelity, an insurance company, in exchange for which she renders investigative service. Her activities range far afield from the insurance business, however, and bring her into contact with murderers.

BIBLIOGRAPHY Novels: *"A" Is for Alibi* (1982), *"B" Is for Burglar* (1985), *"D" Is for Deadbeat* (1987), *"E" Is for Evidence* (1988), *"F" Is for Fugitive* (1989), *"G" Is for Gumshoe* (1990), *"I" Is for Innocent* (1992), *"J" Is for Judgment* (1993), *"K" Is for Killer* (1994), *"L" Is for Lawless* (1995), *"M" Is for Malice* (1996), *"N" Is for Noose* (1998).

MILLIGAN, RICHARD ("SMUT") The gas station owner in James Ross's THEY DON'T DANCE MUCH (1940). Greedy and coarse, it is Milligan's need for money to keep his illegal businesses going that leads him and an accomplice to commit brutal murder.

MILNE, A[LAN] A[LEXANDER] (1882–1956) The creator of Winnie the Pooh also wrote the classic, THE RED HOUSE MYSTERY (1922). Justly famous, it was not his only venture in the field. Milne's other mystery, *Four Days' Wonder* (1933), marked a decline from his first, but his mystery drama *The Fourth Wall* (1929; U.S. title *The Perfect Alibi*) is a classic INVERTED MYSTERY for the stage.

MILODRAGOVITCH, MILO An alcoholic, cocaine-addicted private detective in novels by James CRUMLEY. Milton Chester Milodragovitch III is the heir of a fortune based on land stolen from American Indians in Meriwether, Montana. DANCING BEAR (1983) involves environmentalists who want to get a hold of his ill-gotten property for a wilderness park. Because of a will designed to save him from himself, Milodragovitch has to wait until he is fifty-two to receive his inheritance. Milo is a Korean War vet with a large gun collection who sometimes works as a private eye, always seeming to land preposterous cases that turn out violently. He says "whiskey came in cases; the sort of work I did came in crocks." The bleakness of his life is underscored by the fact that both of his parents committed suicide.

BIBLIOGRAPHY Novels. *The Wrong Case* (1975), *Bordersnakes* (1996).

MIND OF MR. J. G. REEDER, THE See REEDER, J. G.

MIND TO MURDER, A (1963) A novel by P. D. JAMES. Superintendent Adam DALGLIESH is attending a party in his honor on the occasion of the publication of a volume of verse when he is called to the Steen Clinic on the opposite side of the square. Miss Bolam, the administrator, has been expertly stabbed to death with a chisel; a "fetish" carved by one of the patients is left with the body. At first the novel seems radically PROCEDURAL; some fifty pages are taken up with Dalgiesh's careful questioning of everyone in the clinic, from the porter to the psychiatrists, and all of this extended scene takes place in one drab little room. It seems as if we are reading of the investigation in real time. James flirts dangerously with the real tedium of any police investigation, but skillfully abridges some conversations and gives others in full. But all that emerges is that no one liked the straightlaced Miss Bolam, and that there were various jealousies within the clinic, where electroconvulsive therapy, LSD therapy, and classical psychotherapy are conducted for mostly privileged clients. Then a motive appears, and suddenly another; James's severe constriction of setting and action turns out to be a kind of delayed suspense.

MINUTE FOR MURDER (1947) A novel by Nicholas BLAKE. Set at the very end of World War II in the British Ministry of Morale, it reflects Blake's own war service. The device that opens the mystery is arresting: the secret mistress of the chief of the department is poisoned in front of several witnesses, including Nigel STRANGEWAYS.

MISÉRABLES, LES (1862) A novel by Victor Hugo (1802–1885). Influenced by Eugène SUE, Hugo created an epic novel of crime among the underclass of Paris. Jean Valjean, imprisoned for nineteen years for stealing a loaf of bread, returns to society and makes good, becoming the mayor of a town and a commercial leader. Hugo underscores the hypocrisy of industrial society by having Valjean pursued by Inspector Javert because of a previous crime; although Valjean has paid extravagantly for one crime, he is persecuted for another. He has reformed (the putative object of punishment), but reform is not good enough. Hugo, twenty years after POE, showed the social interest in crime that would not resurface in American literature for another eighty years.

MISOGYNY See WOMEN.

MISTER MEESON'S WILL (1888) A story by Rider HAGGARD, in which the publisher Mr. Meeson is shipwrecked along with his associates, including a young woman who is involved with the nephew he has disinherited. When it appears they are going to die, Mr. Meeson undergoes a change of heart and decides to change his will. Because there is no paper, he is forced to tatoo the will on the woman's back. The execution of the will in court calls for some risqué maneuvers, which made the book controversial at the time.

"MR. POLICEMAN AND THE COOK" (1887) A short story by Wilkie COLLINS. The story is told in the form of a confession by a former constable regarding the case that made him quit the force. It is a romantic tale, but one in which the hero is self-sacrificing and culpable at the same time. He is called upon to investigate a relatively simple crime, the stabbing death in a boardinghouse of a man who may have been killed by his wife during a moment of somnambulism (hers). Written in an era that had a nearly unshakable faith in the English social order and in the character of the policeman as a defender thereof—in contrast with GABORIAU and Continental fiction—the story is perhaps one of the earliest evocations of the "dirty cop," though the narrator (never named) does not commit his crime for money.

MITCHELL, GLADYS [MAUDE] [WINIFRED] (1901–1983) One of the lesser-known English writers of the GOLDEN AGE, Gladys Mitchell published scores of mystery novels. Described by the poet Philip Larkin as "the great Gladys," she was popular in England and was an early member of the DETECTION CLUB. Perhaps because of the quirkiness of her books and her brittle writing style, her work never caught on in the United States. She was, however, admired by James SANDOE.

Born in Oxfordshire, she attended University College, London, taking her degree in history. She then became an elementary school teacher, a position she held for decades, even though her first mystery novel appeared in 1929. That book, *Speedy Death*, introduced Beatrice Adela Lestrange BRADLEY. This eccentric character seemed to combine the author's two main interests, psychology and witchcraft. She is a psychiatrist but looks and behaves like a witch. Bradley appeared in sixty-six novels, including THE SALTMARSH MURDERS (1932), which was praised by Nicholas BLAKE. Edmund CRISPIN said that THE RISING OF THE MOON (1945) was "one of the dozen best crime novels that I know."

Mitchell's books, unlike those of some of her contemporaries, have grown in interest over the years. Her style is so over-the-top that it seems that she is satirizing conventions that were still being invented at the time she was writing. Dame Bradley is like a distillation of the Miss MARPLE type, but with dashes of nastiness and lunacy to sour the insipid sweetness that makes most old lady sleuths unbearable.

Mitchell's large output also included novels published under the pseudonyms Malcolm Torrie and Stephen Hockaby, as well as children's books and short stories. She retired from teaching in 1961 and lived in Dorset, but continued to write mysteries until her death, and in fact increased her production to two books per year. She was awarded the Silver Dagger by the British CRIME WRITERS' ASSOCIATION in 1976. Further books continued to be published after her death.

MODUS OPERANDI A Latin phrase meaning "mode" or manner of operating. (Pl. *modi operandi.*) The term is often abbreviated as m. o. and refers to a criminal's habitual methods.

MOHOCKS A group of aristocratic, upper-class hoodlums who preyed on Londoners by night during the early eighteenth century. The word was derived from Mohawk, the Native American tribe. Many references to the Mohocks turn up in literature, and apparently they inspired real terror. Jonathan Swift wrote to Stella, "Did I tell you of a race of rakes, called the Mohocks, that play the devil about this town every night, slit people's noses and beat them, etc.?", and the poet Matthew Prior wrote, "Who has not trembled at the Mohocks name?"

A hundred years later, Alexandre DUMAS borrowed the idea of the Mohocks for his novel *Les Mohicans de Paris* (1855).

MOJO A slang word for any narcotic drug. Mojo also means good luck, as in "to have your mojo working." Clarence Major, in his dictionary of black English, says that the word dates from the seventeenth century.

MOLE A double agent who has been inserted into an enemy organization many years before. The word was coined by John LECARRÉ, rather than by intelligence services, but it was not long before real spies began using it.

MOLL See GUN MOLL.

MOLL FLANDERS See DEFOE, DANIEL.

MOM See YAFFE, JAMES.

MONK The retarded young man in the story "Monk"(1949) by William FAULKNER. Abandoned more than once, Monk is raised virtually as an animal by mountain people who leave food for him but never see him. He apprentices himself to an old moonshiner, who dies. After Monk moves to town, he works at a gas station. By the time Gavin STEVENS comes to investigate the case of this strange and otherworldly young man, Monk has already been railroaded and executed for the murder of a prison warden.

MONKEY'S MASK, THE (1994) A free-verse novel by the Australian poet Dorothy PORTER. Made up of 185 short poems divided into a dozen "chapters," the novel tells the story of private investigator Jill Fitzpatrick's search for the killer of Mickey Norris, a teenage poetess, found strangled and buried in a shallow grave. Despite the unusual form, the story has most of the features of the HARD-BOILED novel: a p.i. who needs money badly; rich and corrupt people with plenty to hide; the cop friend who warns the p.i. off the case; the cover-up; and the shady witness/suspect who gets killed just before telling all. What makes the book different is that Jill is a lesbian, and her investigation takes her into the surprisingly slimy Sydney poetry world, with middle-aged poets trading their attention for sex with their young acolytes. Intertwined with the investigation is Jill's affair with Diana Maitland, Mickey's former poetry professor who is also married. Sexually explicit, the poetic form makes the language of *The Monkey's Mask* even more striking, while the simile-friendly hard-boiled subgenre is perfect for poetic interpretation. What emerges is a linguistically condensed tale of murder, sexual obsession, and opportunism.

MOONSTONE, THE (1868) First serialized in *All the Year Round*, the magazine of Charles DICKENS, *The Moonstone* is one of the greatest mystery novels ever written. T. S. Eliot said it was the very best, and there is certainly much in Wilkie COLLINS's most famous work to please a poet. At the same time, Collins was at pains to show that he had based his book on sound research, and thus Dorothy L. SAYERS said that *The Moonstone* was "probably the very finest detective story ever written." Although it is the complete development and control of suspense and mood that make the book haunting, Sayers noted that it adheres rigorously to the idea of FAIR PLAY.

The Moonstone, or the "Yellow Diamond," is a sacred Hindu stone taken by John Herncastle during the storming of Seringapatam in 1799. One of the priests he killed to get it lays a curse on him. The central action of the novel takes place in the spring of 1848. When Herncastle dies (six months before the novel's beginning), he leaves the gem to Rachel Verinder, daughter of his sister, Mrs. Julia Verinder, who had refused to see Herncastle for years because of his foul reputation. The question is whether he left the niece the stone out of some final turn toward benevolence or to pass on the curse to the relatives who had rejected him. Already, before the stone has even arrived at the Verinder's home on the Yorkshire coast, three Hindus have been seen in the neighborhood. In any case, Rachel has hardly had the Moonstone for a few hours when it mysteriously disappears. Sergeant CUFF is called in to investigate after the local police superintendent has proven incompetent.

The central conceit of the book is that Rachel's nephew, Franklin Blake, asks the principle parties in the story to write down what they know of the circumstances, and this allows Collins to use a series of narrators, beginning with the laconic house steward, the seventy-year-old Gabriel Betteredge. Another narrator is the comical Miss CLACK.

MOORE, BRIAN (1921–) The Belfast-born Canadian writer Brian Moore is best known for *The Lonely Passion of Judith Herne* (1955), a novel about a young Irish woman with dreams who suffers under the parochialism and bigotry of her surroundings, and *Black Robe* (1985), a historical novel about relations between whites and Native Americans that was the basis of a film by Bruce Beresford (1991). Moore has been called "one of the three or four practicing masters of the novel." Though not a "genre writer," Moore has written several books that involve intrigue, an element of mystery, or suspense.

Moore emigrated to Canada in 1948, where he lived for ten years before moving to California. He has won several awards for his fiction, including the Governor General of Canada's award (twice). Several of his works are suspenseful stories with mysterious elements, though they cannot be classed as genre novels. In *The Mangan Inheritance* (1979), Jamie Mangan, a failed poet whose movie-star wife is leaving him, undertakes a quest to discover whether he is related to the Romantic nineteenth-century Irish poet James Clarence Mangan (1803–1849). Moore has a superb gift for narrative and for the presentation of character, which, even when writing in the third person, emerges almost imperceptibly through dialogue and behavior. Jamie's search begins when he finds an old daguerreotype that looks exactly like himself; it leads him to Ireland and to the discovery of buried family secrets and horrifying crimes.

The Colour of Blood (1987), written on the eve of the collapse of the Soviet Bloc, is set in a thinly veiled version of Poland, and is reminiscent of Graham GREENE. Cardinal Stephen Bem, the highest figure in the Catholic church in his country, narrowly escapes an assassination attempt. Then he is arrested, or kidnapped, in the middle of the night by agents who say they are "protecting" him. Meanwhile, certain elements within his own church are planning to make an upcoming religious festival the pretext for an insurrection. The Cardinal escapes, and in a chase across the country must find out who is behind the plot and who kidnapped him and also prevent the futile uprising. *The Statement* (1996) is a novel about a NAZI war criminal in hiding whose identity is about to be uncovered.

MOORE, TOUSSAINT See LACY, ED.

MORAN, COLONEL SEBASTIAN The lieutenant of Professor MORIARTY, who tries to revenge himself on Sherlock HOLMES in the adventure of the EMPTY HOUSE.

MORIARTY, PROFESSOR JAMES The arch villain, the original NAPOLEON OF CRIME, whom Sherlock HOLMES vanquishes at the cost of his own life (or so it seemed) in THE FINAL PROBLEM (1893). For all his fame, Moriarity appeared, surprisingly, only in this one story. He is the classic evil genius, a man of good breeding and education, a mathematician, "a philosopher, an abstract thinker." Moriarty more than a little resembles Holmes himself: he is tall and thin, "pale," and "ascetic-looking."

James Moriarty is also the name of the professor's brother, Colonel Moriarty. The coincidence of two brothers being named James has puzzled Holmes scholars, and is one of Conan DOYLE's most celebrated gaffes.

MORLEY, CHRISTOPHER [DARLINGTON] (1890–1957) American essayist, novelist, and journalist, longtime editor at the *Saturday Review of Literature.* Morley was born in Haverford, Pennsylvania, and later became known for his column in the *New York Evening Post.* Some of his essays were collected in *Shandygaff* (1918). Morley was a Rhodes scholar in England, but even before that he had developed a love of the Sherlock HOLMES stories. He wrote the introduction to the *Complete Sherlock Holmes* (1930) and, with Vincent STARRETT, founded the BAKER STREET IRREGULARS in 1934. His other works on the genre include *Sherlock Holmes and Dr. Watson: A Textbook of Friendship* (1944), and the Sherlockian essay, "Was Sherlock Holmes an American?" Morley also wrote the classic mystery novel *The Haunted Bookshop* (1919), set in Brooklyn.

MORRISON, ARTHUR (1863–1945) The English novelist and mystery author Arthur Morrison was once considered almost alongside Conan DOYLE, the author whom he imitated in his stories about Martin HEWITT. Hewitt was also a fairly early imitation, first appearing in 1894. HAYCRAFT pointed out that, though Hewitt is less eccentric than HOLMES, he was the first in a reaction against eccentricity and in favor of more realistic, or at least conventional, investigators. Hewitt first appeared in *The Strand,* Holmes's magazine, and his stories were collected in *Martin Hewitt, Investigator* (1894), *The Chron-*

icles of Martin Hewitt (1895), and *The Adventures of Martin Hewitt* (1896).

After briefly working in the civil service, Morrison became a journalist with the *National Observer.* Morrison's first published novel was not a mystery at all, but a realistic work in the style of George Gissing; like Gissing, Morrison had risen to authorship from the slums, and documented this background in *A Child of the Jago* (1896). This book and his *Tales of Mean Streets* (1894) were serious works meant to excite public interest in the plight of the poor, and they succeeded. Most of the stories in *Tales of Mean Streets* first appeared in the *National Observer,* and helped to bring about new housing legislation. Although long out of print, these books were considered a lasting contribution; the *New York Times Book Review* said in 1925 that "the stories of Arthur Morrison fill the gap in the fiction dealing with the sinister streets of London between the days of Dickens and the writers of the present."

The Hole in the Wall (1902) was similar to these earlier works, though it also included murder—but not Hewitt, since it was set in the era of DICKENS. In *The Green Eye of Goona* (1904), he tried his hand at adventure à la Rider HAGGARD, telling the story of the pursuit of a unique jewel. One of Morrison's better efforts was *The Dorrington Deed Box* (1897), about a RAFFLES-type character—Morrison came first rather than second this time—named DORRINGTON, sometime detective and sometime crook. Morrison infused his stories with many details of lower- and middle-class life missing from the adventures of aristocratic detectives, including sport.

Morrison was also an art collector and wrote a study of Japanese art, *The Painters of Japan* (1911). In 1913 his collection of Asian art became part of the British Museum. He rated the importance of his mysteries below his socially critical work.

MORSE, INSPECTOR Colin DEXTER's Inspector Morse has a kind of intense, slow-burning appeal: although he has an "unorthodox, intuitive, and seemingly lazy approach" to solving crimes, the stories about him are very readable. Morse is a bachelor, an often lonely man, a drinker, and someone who has trouble getting close to other people. (The fact that he has everyone call him simply "Morse" is a typical example of his distancing.) Partly it is his shyness, but partly it is intellectual snobbery; in a town full of people with advanced degrees, Morse meets with stupidity at all levels. He is the head of CID for the city of Oxford, and is assisted by Sergeant Lewis, to whom he sometimes condescends but whom he could not do without. Above Morse is Superintendent Strange, a buffoon with a gratingly chipper manner. Morse loves classical music (particularly Mozart) and, like his creator, crossword puzzles.

If Morse were the narrator of the stories, he would probably be incomprehensible or unbearable, and certainly digressive. Part of the reason that the books work is that the omniscient narrator seems to be a person as well, who has a simultaneously critical and sympathetic attitude toward the main character. Dexter sometimes bends the rules of FAIR PLAY by having Morse discover clues and answers that are not shared with the reader.

Last Bus to Woodstock (1975), the first novel, set the tone for the series. Like the early books by Ruth RENDELL, it shows modern England to be uncomfortable rather than COZY. Amid the hallowed halls of Oxford, Morse finds poverty and sordidness, epitomized by sometimes shockingly brutal crimes like the rape and murder in *Last Bus to Woodstock.* Morse is in pursuit of a witness who refuses to come forward, which introduces another theme: human cowardice. Morse is constantly disappointed by the people he encounters, some of them his would-be lovers.

Some people are exasperated by Morse, while others admire him (aided no doubt by the excellent BBC television series, shown on *Mystery!*); the Morse novels have picked up several awards, beginning with a Silver Dagger for *Service of All the Dead* (1979). THE WENCH IS DEAD (1989) won a Gold Dagger award, as did *The Way Through the Woods* (1992). One of the best books in the series is THE RIDDLE OF THE THIRD MILE (1983). Morse's bad habits and diabetes catch up with him in the last book, *The Remorseful Day* (1999).

BIBLIOGRAPHY Novels: *Last Seen Wearing* (1976), *The Silent World of Nicholas Quinn* (1977), *The Dead of Jericho* (1981), *The Secret of Annex 3* (1986), *The Jewel That Was Ours* (1991), *The Daughters of Cain* (1994), *Death Is Now My Neighbor* (1996).

Short Stories: *Morse's Greatest Mystery* (1993).

MORTDECAI, CHARLIE A character created by Kyril BONFIGLIOLI. Charlie Mortdecai is part art dealer, part crook, and part detective. He is jocular, absurd, and sometimes annoyingly loquacious and juvenile. His speech is at times almost a parody of the simile-laden writing of CHANDLER, but with an English twist: "She paused, poised, for a second or two, drinking me in like Wordsworth devouring a field of daffodils." "Jock" is Mortdecai's simian, LUGG-like companion, whom he actually tries to euthanize in the first book of their adventures by kicking him in the head as Jock is about to be sucked into a pit of quicksand. His aide-de-camp's last name, not surprisingly, is Strapp.

Don't Point That Thing at Me (1972; also published as *Mortdecai's Endgame*) is Bonfiglioli at his freshest (and most ribald). The story begins with the theft of a Goya painting. As Mortdecai is drawn deeper into the plot, he is pursued by secret security forces as he makes a frantic journey across the United States in an antique Rolls Royce. The adventures become progressively more outlandish: in *After You With the Pistol* (1979), Mortdecai is coerced into an assassination attempt on the Queen of England, and just as improbably saved.

BIBLIOGRAPHY Novels: *Something Nasty in the Woodshed* (1976).

MOSELEY, HOKE Character created by crime and mystery novelist Charles WILLEFORD. Moseley has been called "the most clinically depressed of all heroes." His appearance is not very prepossessing: when he first appears, he has beautiful false teeth (later to be replaced by sickly gray ones), and lives in a tiny Miami Beach hotel room that reeks of dirty sheets and underwear, rum, and cigarette smoke. His father owns a big house near Palm Beach, where Hoke grew up. He has been divorced for ten years. He is, in short, a loser.

In *Sideswipe* (1987), Hoke is a Detective Sergeant and is forty-three years old. He is living in the Green Lakes development with Ellita Sanchez, his partner who is eight months pregnant, and his teenage daughters, Aileen and Sue Ellen. Hoke has been given charge of the "cold case" files—old unsolved murders, and some fairly warm ones that his colleagues dump on him because they have gotten stuck. Evidently it is too much for him, because he is suddenly struck with some form of post-traumatic stress disorder. He wakes up, decides to "simplify" his life, quits the force, and moves back to his hometown. The series comes to a memorable end in THE WAY WE DIE NOW (1988).

BIBLIOGRAPHY Novels: *New Hope for the Dead* (1985), *Miami Blues* (1988).

MOSLEY, WALTER (1952–) American mystery author Walter Mosley made a startling debut with *Devil in a Blue Dress* (1990), the first of his mysteries set in the Watts section of Los Angeles. Easy RAWLINS, an unlicensed investigator, does favors for both members of the black community and for the police. The first novel is set in the late forties, and has Rawlins duped into searching for a missing girl by men who want to kill her. Mosley's career received a boost when President Bill Clinton said publicly that he read the books; the film of *Devil in a Blue Dress* also won attention for the series. (Mosley, like John D. MACDONALD, uses a color in all his titles.)

Mosley grew up in Los Angeles. His African American father told him stories about Texas that would later provide the background for the Rawlins mysteries. He has said that his parents' experience of prejudice (his mother was Jewish) had a profound effect on his development. Mosley did not turn to writing until the mid-1980s, after he had worked as a potter, a caterer, and finally as a computer programmer.

Mosley is often praised for addressing a community that is not often dealt with in mystery fiction, and rarely treated with anything like fairness. His dialogue is convincing and uses black English without any of the hokiness that often attends the reproduction of dialects, and the development of the setting is rich. Mosley also confronts issues that are in the forefront of national debate: racism, discrimination, and violence. Although praise has been loud after the fact, the first Rawlins story, *Gone Fishin'*, was rejected by fifteen agents.

The weakness of the books is plot. The expositional phase, in which the mystery develops and the detective is faced with seemingly baffling events, takes up almost the whole of the book. The middle period in which the pieces fall together is too brief, with the solution coming hard upon its heels. Rawlins sometimes seems to endure rather than follow the mystery, though this is partly due to the fact that he is hampered, manipulated, and victimized by the primarily white police force. He is sometimes illogical, as in *A Red Death* (1991), when he finds out where "the goods" are halfway through the book but waits until the end to go get them. The clues that actually lead to the solution are sometimes too convenient to be believed—a list of illegal payments left in a drawer, a suspicious witness becoming suddenly gullible and being tricked into giving up information.

The least successful of the books is *A Red Death*, in which Rawlins becomes an unwilling pawn in the Red Scare of the 1950s. The most powerful is *White Butterfly* (1992), in which the mystery element (the search for a serial killer) is standard fare and perhaps secondary to the exploration of Rawlins' character and such issues as domestic violence and the relationships between men and women. Rawlins does some rather repulsive things, but whether he redeems himself or not is less a question than whether his redemption is simply assumed or, alternatively, is not even an issue at all. This novel and the following book, *Black Betty* (1994), dwell on the chilling fact that a white policeman can kill a black man and get away with it. But the division of good guys and bad guys does not follow racial lines; Rawlins's best friend, a black man named Mouse, is a pitiless killer who is incapable of understanding moral concepts. *A Little Yellow Dog* (1996) appears to be the conclusion of the series; to that end, the author seems to go through the motions, even using the tired device of identical twins.

Gone Fishin' was finally published in 1997 though written years earlier. It takes place in Texas when Rawlins is only nineteen, and regards an important incident that is often referred to in the later (or earlier) books: the killing of Daddy Reese by Mouse, in which Easy was implicated.

Mosley's best book to date is *Always Outnumbered, Always Outgunned* (1998), a connected series of stories about Socrates Fortlow, a convicted rapist and murderer. Although it contains crime, it is not a crime story; rather, in the manner of Richard Wright's *Black Boy,* Mosley examines the sociology of crime and the pathology of a racist society through an ambiguous victim/victimizer figure. The book was immediately turned into a film on the HBO television network. In 1998 he also published *Blue Light,* a weird science fiction story about a light from space that speeds up the evolutionary process when it strikes certain humans.

"MOST DANGEROUS GAME, THE" (1925) A story by Richard CONNELL, considered a classic of adventure and suspense. Sanger Rainsford, a rather callow big-game hunter, is traveling on a yacht with his friend and fellow hunter, Whitney, on a moonless night in the Caribbean. Rainsford makes light of his friend's sympathy for the fear felt by the animals they kill—"who cares how a jaguar feels?"—and also of the peculiar dread inspired by Ship-Trap Island, which they are passing. Rainsford's irreverence, of course, calls for divine punishment; when he hears shots from the direction of the island, he gets up on the boat's rail for a better look—a sign either that he is incredibly stupid or that Connell's technical skill was modest, since we have just been told that visibility is less than four yards. Rainsford falls overboard, and when he gets to the island he is taken prisoner (though he doesn't know that at first) by the evil General Zaroff. Bored with hunting animals, Zaroff kills men. Armed only with a hunting knife, Rainsford flees through the forest and gets a taste of how a jaguar feels, pursued by the general and the brutal giant, Ivan. The premise continues to be interesting, though the writing is that of a boys' magazine of the period.

MOTO, MR. I. A. The aristocratic, immaculate, gold-toothed Japanese agent and detective created by John P. MARQUAND. Mr. Moto appeared in six novels, displaying his psychological acumen and his mastery of skills ranging from navigation to being a butler, as well as knowledge of six Chinese dialects. Moto was popular, even though Japanese policies were not (ever since the 1933 invasion of Manchuria). After Pearl Harbor, one Moto book appeared (*Last Laugh, Mr. Moto,* 1942), but the series was then suspended until 1957 (*Stopover Tokyo*), at which point it was safe to revive Moto as an anti-communist Cold War agent. *Mr. Moto's Three Aces* (1956) contains short stories about Mr. Moto.

Moto is educated, short, elegant, and deadly with either a gun or his hands (he is a judo master). A putative servant of imperial Japan, Moto runs into Americans and other Westerners in his travels around the Pacific rim. He bears more than a passing resemblance to the earlier character of Charlie CHAN. Another thing he has in common with Chan is that he was very successfully adapted to the screen. Peter Lorre immortalized Moto in a series of eight films made in the short span of three years (1937–1939).

BIBLIOGRAPHY Novels: *No Hero* (1935; British title *Mr. Moto Takes a Hand*), *Thank You, Mr. Moto* (136), *Think Fast, Mr. Moto* (1937), *Mr. Moto Is So Sorry* (1938).

"MOUSETRAP, THE" See SNOWBOUND.

MOVING TOYSHOP, THE (1946) A novel by Edmund CRISPIN. Set in 1938, the story concerns the misfortunes of a young poet, Richard Cadogan, who is bored with life and seeks adventure. His choice of venue is somewhat strange (he goes up to Oxford), but when he gets more adventure than he bargained for he drops in on his former schoolmate, professor Gervase FEN, for help. The relationship between them is polite—even though the professor has panned Cadogan's poems and abandons him without scruple when they are caught breaking into a grocery store. Cadogan has lost some of his sense of humor since he was clubbed over the head after discovering a corpse (and a toyshop that disappears). The poet and the professor, interrupted by occasional attacks of pique and bickering, together pursue a trail of clues (including limericks) relating to a strange and unlikely conspiracy. It leads them through a chapel service and a university choir in full cry, through rooms where lazy undergraduates lounge in pajamas and feed their girlfriends chocolates, and into a great deal of trouble with a murderer and the police. The deftness and humor of the tale never falters, not even when Fen is suggesting titles to Crispin, or Cadogan is criticizing the story from inside ("If there's anything I hate, it's the sort of book in which characters don't go to the police when they've no earthly reason for not doing so"). For all its humor, the book is not a pastiche and is well if eccentrically clued.

MOYES, PATRICIA (1923–) Born in Ireland, Moyes has traveled the world and held various jobs, including secretary in Peter Ustinov's production company and editor for *Vogue*. She has created Inspector Henry TIBBETT of Scotland Yard, a character who falls into the tradition of Roderick ALLEYN and Alan GRANT, though he is less interesting than either of them. Tibbett is a somewhat bland character, not quite a wind-up policeman; he goes about his task with diligence but little flair. He is accompanied by his wife Emmy, who helps him to solve his cases.

Moyes was educated in England in the years before World War II. During the war she was a radar operator and then a flight officer in the Women's Auxiliary Air Force (WAAF). Her first husband was a photographer; her second, an international civil servant. The numerous countries where Moyes has lived or traveled provide the varied settings of the numerous Tibbett novels. She won an EDGAR for *Season of Snows and Sins* (1971), which takes place at an exclusive ski resort in the Swiss Alps. Moyes used her fashion industry experience in *Murder à la Mode* (1963), a tale of theft, smuggling, and murder in the fashion world. *The Coconut Killings* (1977) is set on the island of St. Matthew's in the Caribbean. Moyes's experience in the war is put to use in *Johnny Under Ground* (1965), in which it is revealed that Tibbett's wife Emmy was, like the author, in the WAAF. The story concerns a reunion twenty years after the war, and the murderous events of the present relate to Emmy's past love for a wounded pilot.

MUDDOCK, J. E. PRESTON See DONOVAN, DICK.

MUDROOROO (Colin Johnson, 1938–) See UPFIELD, ARTHUR W.

MUFFIN, CHARLIE Brian FREEMANTLE's Charlie Muffin is a dour, "nondescript" secret agent who appeared in several books, beginning with *Charlie M* (1976; British title *Charlie Muffin*). The second book was originally entitled *Clap Hands, Here Comes Charlie* (1978). But although the books are sometimes considered humorous spy spoofs, the cases themselves are not merely farcical. Charlie becomes a renegade spy because he goes against orders and exposes the failure and corruption of his superiors. This action leads to his wife Edith's death, and Charlie himself is forced to go underground. His one ally, his boss, commits suicide.

Muffin could be described as an anti-anti-hero. Like Len Deighton's Harry PALMER figure, Muffin is a working-class boy among Eton and Oxford men (Muffin's origins are even humbler than Palmer's: his mother was a prostitute, his father's identity is unknown). Muffin wears broken-down Hush Puppies, has hair like straw, and is poorly dressed. But unlike the usual competent and ruthless anti-hero of spy fiction since the fifties, Muffin is incapable of violence, not only for philosophical reasons but because "he just wasn't any good at it." This quality gets him into trouble in *The Inscrutable Charlie Muffin* (1979), a story inspired by the burning and sinking of the *Queen Elizabeth*. Charlie goes to Hong Kong on behalf of the insurer, who stands to lose twenty million pounds, and investigates the powerful owner of the *Pride of America*, a mysterious anti-communist named L. W. Lu.

In *Charlie's Apprentice* (1993), the mournful Muffin has been training a younger generation of spies. Muffin's bad luck continues: one of his students botches a mission in Beijing and Muffin is sent in to straighten things out.

BIBLIOGRAPHY Novels: *Charlie Muffin's Uncle Sam* (1980; U.S. title *Charlie Muffin U.S.A.*), *Madrigal for Charlie Muffin* (1981), *Charlie Muffin and the Russian Rose* (1985), *Charlie Muffin San* (1987), *See Charlie Run* (1987), *The Runaround* (1988), *Comrade Charlie* (1989).

MUG As a verb, of course, "mug" means to rob someone on the street. The meaning "to attack," especially by choking or strangling, comes from Erse *mugaim*, "to defeat," and Gaelic *much*, "to smother." It has been suggested, however, that muggers were so called because they picked out *mugs* ("foolish persons," or suckers) as their victims.

MULCAHANEY, NORA A New York City police officer in a series of PROCEDURAL novels written by Lillian O'DONNELL. The first book was *The Phone Calls* (1972). One of the themes of the series is Mulcahaney's struggle against the sexism of the police department; the development of her personal life is another. In a pattern that has now become common, much of the series is given over to her romance (with another cop), marriage, widowhood, and other personal matters. In *Lockout* (1994), she is investigated for shooting an unarmed mugger.

BIBLIOGRAPHY Novels: *Don't Wear Your Wedding Ring* (1973), *Dial 577 R-A-P-E* (1974), *The Baby Merchants* (1975), *Leisure Dying* (1976), *No Business Being a Cop* (1979), *The Children's Zoo* (1981), *Cop Without a Shield* (1983), *Ladykiller* (1984), *Casual Affairs* (1985), *The Other Side of the Door* (1987), *A Good Night to Kill* (1989), *A Wreath for the Bride* (1990), *A Private Crime* (1991), *Pushover* (1992).

MULLER, MARCIA (1944–) With her novels about Sharon MCCONE, Marcia Muller produced the first series in what was to be hailed as a "boom" in women's mystery writing about female detectives. *Edwin of the Iron Shoes* (1976) was the first novel in the McCone series. The novels are set in San Francisco, where Muller had moved in the sixties after taking a bachelor's and a degree in journalism from the University of Michigan.

Muller's first publisher went bankrupt, so the second novel in the series, *Ask the Cards a Question,* did not appear until 1982. A new McCone novel appeared yearly for the rest of the 1980s. At the same time, Muller was experimenting with other series detectives and other types of stories. One of the most interesting is Elena Oliverez, a Chicana art historian who first appears in *Tree of Death* (1983). In the Oliverez series, Muller gets away from the HARD-BOILED conventions of the McCone stories and writes with the social and historical context more in the foreground. The second Oliverez book, *The Legend of the Slain Soldiers* (1985), begins with a body discovered at Oliverez's mother's mobile home park. Like the novels of Ross MACDONALD, the story moves backward in time, locating the sources of the killing in the past. In the process, it shows the ugliness of a two-tiered society, with rich whites at the top living off the poor and immigrants. With her future husband, Bill PRONZINI, Muller co-authored the third in the Oliverez series, BEYOND THE GRAVE (1986). Yet another series also has an art theme: *The Cavalier in White* (1986) is the first book in a trilogy about a female security consultant for art museums unraveling a complex theft.

MURDER AFLOAT Murder and other crimes on the high seas have formed the basis of many mysteries, either because of the romance potential, the many opportunities for accidents, or the challenge to the author of handling such a cramped setting. In addition, like the COUNTRY HOUSE, murder afloat helps create the feeling of a limited number of suspects all kept in one place and in tension with one another. Although it does not follow this pattern, THE RIDDLE OF THE SANDS (1903) is one of the best nautical mysteries because of its author's expert seamanship and passion for his subject. C. P. Snow's first novel, DEATH UNDER SAIL (1932), is considered a classic, though of lesser quality.

R. Austin FREEMAN, a meticulous craftsman, showed particular care in the construction of the INVERTED MYSTERY "The Echo of a Mutiny" (1912), which takes place in and around a lighthouse. James Brown, an elderly sailor, has become a lighthouse keeper; he goes out to the light to relieve a wounded man and finds his new companion, Jeff Rorke, is the only other survivor of a mutiny committed many years before. Freeman's evocation of waterfront life, coastal navigation, and other nautical matters obviously reflects careful research and his experience as a port medical inspector.

The Gervase FEN story "Man Overboard" (1954) describes the classic murder gambit involving the sea: two people go out in a boat, a storm occurs, and one of them is lost overboard. When the survivor returns, who is to say that the death was not a bona fide accident?

The sea plays a role in many other mysteries that take place mostly ashore. THE FLOATING ADMIRAL (1931), a collaborative work of members of THE DETECTION CLUB, has strange doings by sailors on land. Lester DENT's story "Angelfish" (1936) begins with a faked murder on a beach and ends in a graphic and convincing depiction of a Florida hurricane from aboard a schooner. Conversely, *The Sea Mystery* (1928), by Freeman Wills CROFTS, begins with a man and his son out fishing and then moves ashore. In *Murder Adrift* (1972), by George BELLAIRS, Inspector LITTLEJOHN investigates when a man is found dead aboard his boat.

Agatha CHRISTIE's classic *Death on the Nile* (1937) is set on the steamship *Karnak.* Ngaio MARSH's *Singing in the Shrouds* (1958) is set on a freighter carrying nine passengers. Just before sailing from London to South Africa, there is a killing by "the flower murderer," who strangles young women, lays flowers on their bodies, and walks away singing. Inspector Alleyn joins the boat as a late passenger and investigates under that cover. Twenty years earlier, Alleyn met his future wife on a cruise in ARTISTS IN CRIME (1938).

Mary Roberts RINEHART's *The After House* (1914) was based on an incident aboard a real ship, the *Herbert Fuller,* which she changed from a cargo vessel to a schooner owned by a millionaire. The book includes some passing but gory descriptions of AXE murder and is marred by stereotypes and a pat ending. (For the details of the real case, see Edmund PEARSON's account.)

Valentine WILLIAMS's *Fog* (1933) is set during an Atlantic crossing by the liner *Barbaric.* In Richard LOCKRIDGE's *Inspector's Holiday* (1971), Inspector HEIMRICH travels to Spain by ship with his wife for relaxation and recuperation—but of course finds murder. Similarly, in Simon Nash's *Death Over Deep Water* (1963), an English professor who is on a holiday becomes involved in the search for a double murderer.

In *The Widow's Cruise* (1959), one of the later Nigel STRANGEWAYS novels by Nicholas Blake, the sleuth is on a cruise aboard the S. S. *Menelaos* in the Greek islands, along with his sculptor friend Clare Massinger. Also aboard are the classical scholars Jeremy Street (charismatic but shallow) and Ianthe Ambrose (serious but neurotic). Primrose Chalmers, a precocious child of two psychiatrists, goes around taping the other passengers' conversations, an activity that is not appreciated by someone (to say the least). Another mystery involving a Mediterranean cruise is *Murder in Absence* (1954), by Miles Burton (John RHODE). Many other of the Desmond MERRION mysteries also involve the sea.

Leonard Holton's *A Touch of Jonah* (1968) has Father BREDDER, the priest and amateur detective, pressed into service aboard Sir Harry Stockton's seventy-two-foot Transpac racer. Nasty, imperious, and autocratic, Sir Harry is known for his bad luck, and death visits the ship even before the race begins. Several people have already had fatal accidents around him—a gassed housekeeper, a gardener crushed by a felled tree—and others have reason to hate him. Holton's seamanship is impeccable, his writing, not. The ending is implausible but surprising. (The title refers to a famous sailors' superstition about passengers—including clergymen—who bring bad luck to their vessel).

TOO MUCH OF WATER (1958), a classic in the subgenre, was written by Michael Halliday. It involves the explosion of tensions, and resultant murders, among passengers thrown together in the cramped quarters of a ship. In one of John CREASEY's "Baron" novels, *The Baron on Board* (1964), his hero boards the *East Africa Star* in search of the Mask of Sumi, a jewel-encrusted Thai artifact. The Baron enters the case after his contact, Nikko Toji, is found poisoned, and the mask is missing.

Of earlier writers, Crofts was probably the highest producer of sea mysteries; he wrote half a dozen, some of them Inspector FRENCH novels. The better ones are: *Mystery in the English Channel* (1931), about a yacht discovered drifting, its crew murdered; *The Loss of the Jane Vesper* (1936), which involves the scuttling of a ship in an insurance fraud case, and one of the author's most liked books; *Cold-Blooded Murder* (1936), in which Crofts applied the same passion for detail to ships' sailings as he elsewhere did to railway schedules; and *Tragedy in the Hollow* (1939), which features the S.S. *Hellénique*, a casino ship. *Found Floating* (1937) is like a country house murder transplanted to a Mediterranean cruise ship.

Andrew GARVE has worked sailing into several of his suspense novels, including THE LESTER AFFAIR (1974). In this novel, a candidate for Prime Minister is accused of seducing a woman on his yacht and afterward lying about it. *The Narrow Search* (1957) and *A Hero for Leanda* (1959) both hinge on pilotage and navigation. In the latter, a sailor who has lost everything (including his boat) is roped into a scheme to rescue a political prisoner from an island. His first mate is a female militant.

Travis MCGEE lives on a houseboat, *The Busted Flush*, but it is not very seaworthy; however, THE DEEP BLUE GOODBYE (1964) and *Bright Orange for the Shroud* (1965) both have their climax and resolution at sea, and *Darker Than Amber* (1966) involves a scam aboard a cruise ship.

Other sea-oriented mysteries include THE GAY PHOENIX (1976); several powerful naturalistic works by P. M. HUBBARD; works by Victor CANNING; some novels of Douglas CLARK, better-known for his stories of poisoning; novels by Bill KNOX, particularly his series about Webb CARRICK; the works of Hammond INNES; and several books by Sam LLEWELYN, a writer and offshore sailor. Several books have been based on the actual mysterious case of the MARY CELESTE.

The ocean journeys during the age of the great liners were not only a good place for setting mysteries, but for writing them: Elspeth HUXLEY began writing her novels as a way of passing the time aboard ship, and Ngaio Marsh wrote hers during the long passages between New Zealand and England.

MURDER AT THE FLEA CLUB (1955) A peculiar though interesting mystery by Matthew HEAD. Its setting (Paris in the aftermath of World War II) probably accounts for what notoriety it has, though the City of Light is strangely vague and anonymous in the story. A collection of odd expatriates and refugees gather at the Flea Club, a private night spot. Head resorts to the "one-of-each" method of populating his novel: an aging heiress, an enigmatic piano player, a gigolo, a flamboyant homosexual. The story is told in a curiously detached manner by Hooper Taliaferro, the abnormally normal member of the club, in a series of shifts back and forth in time. Most interesting is that he does no investigating, but assists his friend, the brilliant Dr. Mary Finney, a missionary visiting from the Belgian Congo. The book has some of the feeling of the stories of Edgar BOX.

MURDER BY THE BOOK This title has been used at least twice, including by Rex STOUT (1951) and Frances and Richard LOCKRIDGE (1963). In Stout's novel, Archie GOODWIN narrowly misses being able to prevent the murder of a young typist, who is pushed out a window. Earlier, the body of a law clerk had been fished out of the East River, and in the man's pocket was found a list of names. One of the names turns up six weeks later in a letter sent by a prospective author to another typist, who was run over and killed in Van Cortland Park. Goodwin sets out on the trail of the manuscript and its author. It is one of the most action-oriented of the Nero WOLFE/Archie

Goodwin novels, and thus Archie is the focus because Wolfe never moves. Goodwin undertakes a cross-country journey in search of information and resorts to some clever ruses in unraveling the complex plot.

In the Lockridge's novel, Pam and Jerry NORTH are on vacation in Key West and Pam has taken to fishing from the hotel pier and feeding the pelicans. One day, a forensic specialist from New York is stabbed on the pier, and Pam is at first suspected. Appropriately, the story has many RED HERRINGS. *Murder by the Book* was the last Pam and Jerry North novel.

MURDER IN MESOPOTAMIA See ARCHAEOLOGY.

"MURDER IN THE FISHING CAT, THE" A comical story by the poet Edna St. Vincent Millay (1892–1950), set in Paris at the Restaurant du Chat qui Pêche. The owner, Jean-Pierre, is abandoned by his wife and daughter; as his business declines, he sinks into his own thoughts, his only confidant a large eel living in a tank in the restaurant whom he calls Phillipe. Eventually business picks up, and someone makes the mistake of ordering *anguille.*

The story was anthologized by Ellery QUEEN in *The Literature of Crime* (1952).

MURDER OF QUALITY, A (1962) A novel by John LE CARRÉ, the second involving his spy series character George SMILEY. The story, however, is a conventional English mystery rather than a tale of espionage. Smiley is in temporary retirement; his secretary from British Intelligence during the war gets in touch with him after she receives a letter from a woman who fears her husband is going to kill her. When Smiley arrives at Carne, a prestigious English public school, Stella Rode, wife of one of the masters, is already dead—brutally battered to death. Despite the setting in the Dorset countryside, and although Smiley helps out the local police (and of course comes up with the solution they are too dim to see), the tone of the book is unlike the English COZY. The atmosphere of snobbery is done with all of Le Carré's subtlety, and he uses the same unmasking of nastiness beneath polished, proper exteriors as in his other work.

MURDER OF ROGER ACKROYD, THE (1926) The novel that secured a readership for Agatha CHRISTIE, *The Murder of Roger Ackroyd* also provoked some disgruntlement on the part of critics because of its violation of one of the rules of FAIR PLAY. It has also been called a *tour de force* and a classic; Dorothy L. SAYERS and Julian SYMONS thought its deception of the reader fair.

The story is set in the village of King's Abbot. The widow Mrs. Ferrars is found dead, an apparent suicide from an overdose of veronal. The doctor who examines her, Dr. Sheppard, is the narrator. He discusses the case with Roger Ackroyd, who confides that he was planning to marry the wealthy widow, but that she broke off the engagement because she was a murderer herself, having killed her revolting husband a year before. Ackroyd also tells the doctor that another person knows about Mrs. Ferrars's crime and had been blackmailing her. Just then, Ackroyd gets a letter that Mrs. Ferrars presumably wrote before she died. He waits to open it in private. Before he can reveal its contents, however, Ackroyd is killed, and the letter disappears. There are a number of people in the house who are possible suspects, including his greedy relatives, a woman who wanted to marry him, and the butler. Poirot is called in by Ackroyd's niece, Flora.

Once one has swallowed the idea that Mrs. Ferrars would put the name of the murderer in a *letter,* the "shocking" conclusion shouldn't be much of a problem. As Julian Symons observed, "every successful detective story in this period involved a deceit practiced upon the reader."

Edmund Wilson wrote a famous essay, WHO CARES WHO KILLED ROGER ACKROYD?(1945), roundly dismissing the entire issue.

MURDER OF SIR EDMUND GODFREY, THE (1936) This HISTORICAL MYSTERY by John Dickson CARR combines scholarship and the techniques of the novel to examine and propose a solution to the crime that Thomas DE QUINCEY called "the finest work of the seventeenth century" in the art of murder: "in the grand feature of *mystery,* which in some shape or other ought to color every judicious attempt at murder, it is excellent." The mystery has remained unsolved for more than three hundred years, though Carr gives a plausible solution to it.

The murder in 1678 of Sir Edmund Godfrey, who was a prominent magistrate, was a part of the complex sociopolitical event known as the Popish Plot. This combination scandal and witch-hunt was fomented by the Anglican minister Titus Oates and another clergyman, Israel Tonge. The plot capitalized on anti-Catholic feeling in England, which had reached almost hysterical levels. The crux of the problem was that the king, Charles II, had no male heir, and so the next in line for the throne was Charles's brother James, Duke of York, who had converted to Catholicism around 1671.

Sir Edmund Godfrey lived in Hartshorn Lane, London. On Saturday, October 12 of 1678, he left home and was never seen alive again. Five days later his body was discovered; he had been stabbed and strangled. After Godfrey was killed, Oates was clever enough to invent evidence linking the murder to a plot to assassinate Charles and make James king. The queen herself and other prominent people were suspected; thirty-five were executed. The three people who were convicted and executed for the murder of Godfrey were innocent. Oates was rewarded with a pension, but under James II he was tried for perjury, flogged, and imprisoned.

MURDER ON SAFARI The title of two novels, the earlier by Elspeth HUXLEY (1938), one of her trilogy of novels set in Kenya and featuring Superintendent VACHELL. The first mystery of the book is why Lady Baradale brings a set of jewels worth a small fortune with her on safari; the second is whether her accidental shooting is really an accident.

Hillary WAUGH's *Murder on Safari* (1987) shows the changes that half a century can make. The safari is one for bird watchers, not big game hunters. James Addison is a newspaper reporter sent to cover the safari for a travel magazine. When the murders start happening, he collaborates with Colonel Dagger in investigating. The African background is generic, and less vivid than in Huxley's work; it does, however, have the novel method of death-by-hippo.

MURDER ON THE ORIENT EXPRESS (1934) Probably the best-known novel by Agatha CHRISTIE, thanks partly to an all-star film version (1974). Hercule POIROT starts out on the Taurus Express, in Syria. He is journeying toward Calais, and on the train he meets a cross-section of Europe: the Hungarian Count and Countess Andreyni, the English Colonel Arbuthnot, the obnoxious American, Mr. Ratchett, a Russian princess, and various other entertaining or annoying characters. Poirot hears a scream in the night, and the next morning one of the passengers is found stabbed a dozen times. Some of the wounds are deep, others minor; some were delivered after the victim was dead. Relying on the old stereotype of the Italian with the knife, Antonio Foscarelli—the only Italian on board—is suspected. One clue, a charred piece of paper, alludes to an American murder-kidnapping of the past, and other aspects lead Poirot to suspect a coldly rational murder instead of a crime of passion. The train is conveniently trapped in snow to retard the usual police procedures and to give "the gray cells" time to work.

Despite the proliferation of clues and RED HERRINGS, it is difficult not to know what the solution is partway through the book. It remains a Christie favorite—and is still better than the film.

"MURDERS IN THE RUE MORGUE, THE" (1841) A short story by Edgar Allan POE, the first in which the detective C. Auguste DUPIN appears. The tale concerns a grotesque murder of an old woman and her daughter in a poor district of Paris, the details of which Dupin and his friend, like HOLMES and WATSON, follow in the newspapers. A number of people passing in the street hear an argument going on in the apartment, and though a Frenchman, a Spaniard, a Dutchman, a German, and an Italian are present, everyone thinks that one of the speakers sounds "foreign." Upon investigation, the old woman is found with her throat cut almost to the point of decapitation and her hair pulled out by the roots. Her daughter is found stuffed head downwards up the chimney.

Dupin investigates the case purely as an amateur after an acquaintance is falsely accused. Visiting the crime scene, he amasses a series of clues. In addition to the detective's aiding of a suspected friend, the story contains many of the motifs of later mystery fiction, including: the inexplicably ferocious crime; the "motiveless" murder, with money and valuables left at the scene by the killer; the LOCKED ROOM problem; and the competition between the amateur and the police. Dupin even shows off his deductive brilliance in a small incident where he breaks in on the narrator's thoughts with an uncannily apt remark after many minutes of silence between them, thereby showing that he has correctly deduced the whole course of the narrator's mental associations from subtle non-verbal clues. Of the three Dupin stories, it is the most perfectly wrought and can bear comparison with any subsequent detective story. It is not, however, the *first* instance of the locked room puzzle, having been preceded by Sheridan LE FANU's "Passage in the Secret History of an Irish Countess" (1838), which was the basis of UNCLE SILAS (1864).

MURDERS IN VOLUME TWO (1941) A Henry GAMADGE mystery by Elizabeth DALY. Once again the bibliophile sleuth is drawn into a case involving family money among people he knows slightly. But this case has a decidedly weird element, as well as a more direct connection to Gamadge's bookish interests. He is consulted by the middle-aged Miss Robina Vauregard because Uncle Imbrie Vauregard believes that "somebody went into the fourth dimension and came out again." Robina tells Gamadge "you know queer things about books," and the mystery posed by Imbrie's assertion is very odd. It goes back to May 3, 1840, when Miss Wagoneur, an English governess, vanished from the Vauregard house arbor on Trader's Row (a cobblestoned Manhattan street) along with volume II of a set of Lord Byron's poems. Uncle

Imbrie believes that Miss Wagoneur has come back exactly one hundred years later, along with the book. It is feared that this woman, going by the name of "Miss Smith," is going to get her hands on the family fortune. This entertaining bibliophile puzzle becomes a murder case for Gamadge after one of the Vauregards is found dead (in the library, of course), murdered with poisoned coffee.

"MURDER WILL OUT" This oft-repeated phrase, used many times in novel titles, comes from Geoffrey Chaucer's "Prioress's Tale," one of the *Canterbury Tales.* The phrase means that murder cannot be concealed forever, and that the crime eventually becomes known.

MURDOCK, KENT A newspaperman-sleuth created by George Harmon COXE. Murdock was conceived as a character for the novel, and lacks some of the pulpiness of the very similar Flashgun CASEY. Coxe wrote a score of Murdock novels, beginning with *Murder with Pictures* (1935). Murdock's adventures—and problems—have to do with photographs, either ones he has taken that dangerously reveal the truth, or others that have been mischievously faked. In his first case, Murdock is covering a trial for his paper, the *Boston Courier-Herald.* A subplot involving Murdock's estrangement from his first wife, Hestor, turns out to be very important. The case turns into a gangster story within a romantic frame. Coxe made Murdock's second wife, Joyce, an attractive character (she solves a case in *Mrs. Murdock Takes a Case,* 1941), and also used private investigator Jack Fenner for some muscle. Other interesting Murdock cases include *The Charred Witness* (1942), whose title is self-explanatory, and *Eye Witness* (1949), in which Murdock has supposedly murdered himself. *The Jade Venus* (1945) is an ART mystery.

BIBLIOGRAPHY Novels: *The Barotique Mystery* (1936), *The Camera Clue* (1937), *Four Frightened Women* (1939), *The Glass Triangle* (1939), *The Fifth Key* (1947), *The Hollow Needle* (1948), *Lady Killer* (1949), *The Widow Had a Gun* (1951), *The Crimson Clue* (1953), *Focus on Murder* (1954), *Murder on Their Minds* (1957), *The Big Gamble* (1958), *The Last Commandment* (1960), *The Hidden Key* (1963), *The Reluctant Heiress* (1965), *An Easy Way to Go* (1969), *Fenner* (1971), *The Silent Witness* (1973).

MY BROTHER'S KILLER (1961) The first novel by D. M. DEVINE, and possibly his best. Agatha CHRISTIE called it "a most enjoyable crime story which I enjoyed reading down to the last moment." It is set in a fictitious city called Brickfield in the north of England or Scotland. The narrator, Simon Barnett, gets a call late at night from his brother Oliver, with whom he works in the family law firm. Simon shows up at the office and finds Oliver dead, a victim of a murder badly disguised as a suicide. The office safe is open and yields material that seems to indicate that Oliver—a brilliant, irascible, impatient man, and also a womanizer—may have led a secret life as a blackmailer. Simon, who had lived and worked quietly in his brother's shadow, is driven to find his brother's killer. Among the suspects are Simon's own estranged wife, daughter of one of the firm's other partners; Oliver's bitter wife Marion, who had been disfigured in a car accident and who was then ignored by Oliver; and a jealous husband. Devine's clues are presented in a manner that is fair but requires attention on the part of the reader. The whole performance is understated and subtle, from the dour provincial background, which the author develops without ever really having to focus directly on it, to the characters, who are like real people in being ordinary on the surface but revealing complexities after some acquaintance. The personal relationships are very convincing, not so much in the large emotions of love and hate but in the smaller pangs of pain and loss, envy, distrust, and, to a noticeable extent, wounded pride. A variety of themes are brought gradually into the story, including an illegal sex club, scandal and blackmail, and even plagiarism. Only in the ending is Devine forced to use an old trick—perhaps because of the fine net he had woven up until that point.

MYCROFT The name of Sherlock HOLMES's elder brother. He helps Holmes in several adventures, the first being that of the GREEK INTERPRETER (1893). His name comes from Mycroft, Yorkshire, which has sometimes been said to be the birthplace of Holmes, though there is no proof for the claim in the stories.

Mycroft works in the British government, though, like many facts in the Holmes stories, the nature of his post undergoes various mutations. In the adventure of the BRUCE-PARTINGTON PLANS(1908), he is not only *not* the holder of "some small office," as WATSON thought, but he is "the most indispensable man in the country." Holmes says that Mycroft's mental powers are even greater than his own, but because he is almost criminally lazy, Mycroft exerts no effort to verify his deductions, and would rather be thought wrong than go to the trouble of proving himself in the right. He is a huge man, with hands "like the flipper of a seal"; combined with his laziness, this makes him almost a proto–Nero WOLFE, a character he certainly influenced. He is antisocial and belongs to the Diogenes Club, in which the members are not allowed to speak to each other.

MYERS, ANNETTE AND MARTIN (MAAN MYERS) See HISTORICAL MYSTERIES.

MY LADY'S MONEY (1877) A late novel by Wilkie COLLINS that combines stock elements of Victorian melodrama with real detection. It was first serialized in the *Illustrated London News.* One of its stranger elements is that the key discovery is made by a Scottish terrier named Tommie, who belongs to the rich widow Lady Lydiard. Collins makes fun of her combination of wealth, aristocratic bearing, and low tastes (she asks a host for beer) assiduously cultivated to pique such pompous defenders of convention as Miss Pink, the aunt of Lady Lydiard's adopted daughter, Isabel Miller. Isabel encounters the brash young aristocrat Alfred Hardyman, who has thrown up his prospects and become a horse breeder, for which his father, Lord Rotherfield, considers him a "barely sane person." For Collins, the humor to be got from such reversals of class is endless, though for the modern reader perhaps less so. He also creates a typical triangle between Isabel and two suitors—Hardyman, and Lady Lydiard's dour steward, appropriately named Moody. When Isabel is suspected of stealing a £500 note left in an unsealed letter on Lady Lydiard's table, Moody employs the amateur detective OLD SHARON to sort out the mystery. The book would have no claim on the attention were it not for Old Sharon, perhaps the most interesting and original detective Collins ever created.

MYRL, DORA See BODKIN, M. MCD.

MYSTERIES OF PARIS (Les Mystères de Paris, 1842–1843) A romantic novel by Eugène SUE, showing in great detail the life of the Parisian underclass and the netherworld of prostitutes, *flaneûrs,* con men, rakes, and slumming aristocrats. The main character, Prince Gerolstein, lives among the proletarians of Paris and solves mysteries and crimes. Sue used the mystery and detective novel to express his socialist views.

MYSTERIES OF UDOLPHO, THE See GOTHIC.

MYSTERIOUS AFFAIR AT STYLES, THE (1920) The first mystery Agatha CHRISTIE published and the first to feature Hercule POIROT. It takes place during World War I at an English COUNTRY HOUSE owned—and ruled—by Emily Inglethorp, the classic country house dowager. Captain Hastings is present because he has been brought down to Styles by a friend, John Cavendish, who is the old woman's stepson. There are other interesting or eccentric characters in the area, including John's frustrated and unhappy wife Mary; Bauerstein, a bizarre doctor and a specialist in poisons, recovering from a nervous breakdown (*nota bene*)—and one Hercule Poirot. He is in the neighborhood because he has been sent there, a Belgian war refugee.

Mrs. Inglethorp is discovered in the morning, poisoned with STRYCHNINE. Her much younger husband, Alfred, is the immediate suspect, especially because of the way she has forced him to wait on her hand and foot (previously he was her secretary; now he does it for free). There is ample doubt and evidence for Poirot to work his brain over. Inspector Japp also makes his first appearance. In retrospect, it is strange that, despite the presence of all the elements of Christie's work, she had difficulty publishing this novel and was turned down a number of times.

MYSTERIOUS MR. QUIN, THE See QUIN, MR. HARLEY

MYSTERIOUS PRESS A press founded by Otto PENZLER, it later became part of WarnerBooks. The Mysterious Press publishes new work as well as reprints of out-of-print mysteries.

MYSTERY OF A HANSOM CAB, THE (1886) The best-selling mystery of the nineteenth century, written by barrister Fergus HUME, *The Mystery of a Hansom Cab* is one of the most famous and also notorious novels of the genre. More popular than the Sherlock HOLMES novels, the book was not an imitation of Holmes because it predated Holmes's appearance by a year. Instead, the author imitated Emile GABORIAU. Hume set out to write a best-selling mystery, and he did his homework: in addition to Gaboriau, he mentions DE QUINCEY's famous study of murder, Mary BRADDON, and THE LEAVENWORTH CASE (1878)—that other spectacular success of the nineteenth century.

It has become routine among critics to dismiss *The Mystery of a Hansom Cab* as unreadable—thus sparing one the trouble of reading it. In terms of style, there is nothing out of the ordinary about Hume's Victorian loquacity—a drunk is "addicted to the intemperate use of the flowing bowl"; a man is seen "screwing his eyeglass into his left organ of vision"—but on the other hand, the fact that a book is no worse than others does not equal a strong recommendation. A bowdlerized version of the novel, which suppressed some of its gritty scenes of Melbourne slums, may have contributed to its bad reputation. Yet Hume is capable of some memorable descriptions: "she was a small, dried-up little woman, with a wrinkled, yellow face, and looked so parched and brittle that strangers could not help thinking it would do her good if she were soaked in water for a year, in order to soften her a little." A more objectionable trait is Hume's "flair" for melodrama; his heroine is constantly swooning and falling to her knees. The detectives also have far too easy a time of it in collecting their clues.

The story begins with the discovery of a man murdered with CHLOROFORM in a hansom cab in Melbourne, Australia. Suspicion falls upon Brian Fitzgerald, a wealthy Irishman who is in love with Madge Frettlby, daughter of the even wealthier Mark Frettlby. The murdered man had been courting Madge, much to her and Brian's disgust. The detective, Gorby, builds up enough evidence against Brian to have him arrested. About a third of the way through the novel, Duncan Calton, the lawyer who must defend Fitzgerald, becomes the sleuth; even though Fitzgerald has an alibi, he refuses to divulge it because he is protecting someone, so Calton must discover the alibi through alternate means. Hume directs suspicion now here, now there, though rather obviously, and the killer is known to the reader long before the end. The finale includes as much melodrama as one can stand—awful secrets, swooning, somnambulism, brain-fever, and heart disease.

MYSTERY OF EDWIN DROOD, THE (pub 1870) The last, unfinished novel of Charles DICKENS. Left incomplete, it would have been Dickens's only mystery novel, though he had written detective short stories. The title character is an engineer and the young ward of Jack Jasper, a choirmaster in the town of Cloisterham. Although outwardly respectable, Jasper is in fact an opium addict. He is also in love with Rosa Bud, who happens to be Drood's fiancée. Drood and Rosa, however, fall out of love and their engagement is broken. Then Drood disappears. Rosa falls in love with another man, Neville Landless. He is arrested for the murder of Drood after Jasper produces certain evidence that incriminates him, though no body is found. Jasper tries to blackmail Rosa into marrying him by his threats against Landless. A new character, Datchery, then turns up on the scene, and shows himself to be a foe of Jasper. An admirable balance has been set up between these opposing characters, but unfortunately the novel fragment ends before it becomes clear what Dickens meant to do with these tensions and oppositions. It is not even clear whether Drood is actually dead.

More than any other unfinished manuscript, *The Mystery of Edwin Drood* has tempted FINISHERS—four appeared shortly after the author' death. R. Austin FREEMAN's *The Mystery of Angelina Frood* (1924) is more a rewriting than a finishing. In *Epilogue* (1934), Bruce GRAEME had two investigators go back in time to solve the mystery. Charles Forsyte's *The Decoding of Drood* (1980) includes a solution as well as a discussion of the mystery. *The Mystery of Edwin Drood*, by Leon Garfield, appeared in the same year.

"MYSTERY OF MARIE ROGET, THE" A story by Edgar Allan POE, his second about the detective C. Auguste DUPIN. It first appeared in the *Ladies' Companion* in 1842, and is the prototype of the mystery tale based on a real event. In 1841, the body of Mary Rogers, a young woman who had worked in a New York cigar shop, was found in the Hudson River, terribly battered. The case became a *cause célèbre* and inspired sensational news stories and the posting of reward money. Poe was in Philadelphia at the time; he decided to try out the deductive methods he had used in his first Dupin case, THE MURDERS IN THE RUE MORGUE (1841). Except for moving the story to Paris, Poe adhered closely to the facts of the case, and came up with what he thought was the correct solution. It was disturbing, then, that new evidence in the case of Mary Rogers was produced just as the final installment of his story was due to appear. The connection with a real case became a liability, and Poe's attempts to distance his fiction from its factual basis accounts for some of the story's stylistic defects.

An account of the Mary Rogers case and the genesis and development of Poe's story is given in *Poe: The Detective* (1968) by John Walsh, which won an EDGAR award for best fact crime book.

MYSTERY OF 31 NEW INN, THE (circa 1905; novel 1916) One of the most often discussed cases of Dr. THORNDYKE, *The Mystery of 31 New Inn* was R. Austin FREEMAN's very first work to include the doctor. Originally, it was written as a long short story in several chapters; this version was never published, however, and Freeman later worked it up into a novel, which saw print only after THE RED THUMB MARK (1907). The story version was finally published in *The Best Doctor Thorndyke Stories* (1973).

Dr. Christopher Jervis, Thorndyke's assistant, has not yet joined him as amanuensis when the story opens. Instead, he is covering another colleague's practice in order to gain money, of which he is in dire need so that he can get married. He consults Thorndyke after he is taken (in great secrecy) to see a man who is apparently dying of morphine poisoning. Because the carriage that took him to an unknown destination was blacked out, Thorndyke has constructed (by his servant, Polton) a device with a compass and notebook to enable Jervis to chart his course using such variables as direction, hoofbeats per minute, and external sounds. Next time the suspicious character summons him, Jervis is prepared—but finding the location of the house is only the beginning of the mystery. The case bears some resemblance to Conan Doyle's "The Adventure of the GREEK INTERPRETER" (1893).

MYSTERY OF THE YELLOW ROOM (1908; tr of *Le Mystère de la chambre jaune,* 1907) A novel by Gaston LEROUX, considered a classic for its early use of the LOCKED ROOM and its unlikely solution. The main detective in the case is the newspaperman ROULETABILLE; a mere teenager but already famous, he is obviously a GENIUS DETECTIVE. One of the things that has dated the book and makes it hard to take seriously is the almost absurd proofs of Rouletabille's amazing powers. When everyone except close relatives has been denied access to the crime scene, he utters the mysterious words, "the presbytery has lost nothing of its charm, nor the garden its brightness," and is instantly admitted. Leroux's melodramatic style is oftentimes unintentionally comic.

The story is set in 1892, and concerns an attack on Mademoiselle Mathilde Stangerson in the pavilion on the grounds of the Château du Glandier, where she had retreated with her father in order to conduct scientific experiments in solitude. Professor Glandier is a famous scientist whose new theory, the "dissociation of matter," is supposed to overturn all science based on the conservation of energy. Mathilde is beautiful, but for fifteen years has devoted herself to her father as an assistant; her many suitors have dwindled to one, Robert Darzac, and his persistence is about to pay off. Mathilde and Robert are soon to be married when she is shot in the Yellow Room of the pavilion. It is discovered that the attacker snuck into the room and hid under her bed, yet somehow escaped even though the doors and shutters were all locked after she entered. One of the clues is a bloody handprint on the wall.

In the investigation, Rouletabille vies with the famous detective Frédéric Larsan. Unlike Sherlock HOLMES, Rouletabille admires his police companion—at least when his conclusions coincide with his own—and they spar about their respective methods. Rouletabille rarely explains his discoveries to his fellow journalist, Sanclair, who acts as his WATSON, and thus the reader is left in the dark. What is the significance of the remark, "We shall have to eat red meat—now," or of the mysterious cries of a beast on the grounds of the château? Where exactly did Rouletabille find the woman's hair he takes out of the Yellow Room? The delay in divulging some of the secrets of the mystery is nearly interminable, put off over and over by the setting of traps, further attacks, and other melodramatic scenes, including the apparent dematerialization of the murderer and a victim's desperate measures to help the killer get into the château. The eighteen-year-old sleuth's sudden disappearance to gather evidence in the United States and return at the vital moment in the trial is the final imposition on the patience of the reader (if any have resisted skipping to the final chapters). *The Mystery of the Yellow Room* is probably more praised than it is read, and certainly merits reading less than some of the works of GABORIAU, Leroux's model.

MYSTERY WRITERS OF AMERICA See EDGAR.

NABB, MAGDALEN (1947–) Not long after she moved permanently from her native Lancashire, England, to Italy, Magdalen Nabb began a series of mysteries about a marshal of the Carabinieri, Salvatore GUARNACCIA. Nabb's reputation was established by the praise she received from her mentor, Georges SIMENON, and Guarnaccia's ancestry is clear in his psychological methods, which are similar to MAIGRET's. Nabb also may have drawn on the work of Leonardo SCIASCIA, whose detective novels highlight the differences between Sicilians and other Italians. Guarnaccia, a Sicilian living in Florence, has similar moments of misunderstanding, though they are treated as opportunities for "local color" and humor. Nabb does have an obviously great knowledge of Italy, however, and manages to work in a wealth of historical detail without seeming either pedantic or showy. She is interested in Italian politics and is knowledgeable about Tuscany's tradition as a bastion of COMMUNISM and the left wing. The first novel in which Guarnaccia appeared was *Death of An Englishman* (1981). He was assisted not only by his subordinates, but two Scotland Yard men as well. Many of the books deal with relationships between the Italians and various foreigners, and appear to be based more on the expatriate travelogue novel than the detective story. In THE MARSHALL AT THE VILLA TORRINI (1993), an Englishman is suspected of drowning his wife in a bathtub. Guarnaccia's self-doubts about his investigations among rich foreigners can be seen either as a human touch or as simply embarrassing.

"NABOTH'S VINEYARD" (1918) A story by Melville Davisson Post about Uncle ABNER. The irascible old Elihu March is shot dead in his house, and the hired hand, Taylor, has departed. He is overtaken, brought back, and cannot explain why his gun has obviously been discharged. There is a trial, and when it looks like Taylor will hang, March's housemaid confesses that she did it, because March had made remarks about her that drove Taylor away. Abner and Doctor Storm, who were the first to find the body, are able to solve the case using some very subtle clues. Most interestingly, Abner leads a virtual rebellion, which Post uses to show that the law rests on the will of the people, which in turn rests on a natural nobility that does not depend on birth but on "the sense of justice that certain men carried in their breasts."

NADGETT, MR. The sleuth in Charles Dickens's *Martin Chuzzlewit* (1844). Nadgett is a wizened, stealthy old man whose decrepit appearance belies his determination and persistence. Mr. Nadgett's mien is more in the tradition of fictional villains, but he is actually an employee of the Anglo-Bengalee Disinterested Loan and Life Insurance Company. He secretly investigates Jonas Chuzzlewit, the conniving nephew of Martin Chuzzlewit senior (whom Jonas tries to poison).

NAKED CAME THE MANATEE See SERIAL NOVEL.

NAMELESS DETECTIVE, THE A character in a series of books by Bill PRONZINI. He first appeared in the novel *The Snatch* (1971), and his name remained unknown for seven years. The Nameless Detective is a middle-aged private eye based in San Francisco, where he was a policeman for fifteen years. Prior to that, he was in Military Intelligence during World War II and served in the South Pacific. Despite his training, the Nameless Detective is unconventional. He does not carry a gun, has a paunch from drinking too much beer, and is a gray, haggard-looking man. He is also a voracious reader and collector of PULP MAGAZINES; in this he was modeled on Pronzini himself.

The Snatch, as the title indicates, is about a kidnapping; *The Vanished* (1973) is about a missing person. Pronzini later branched out from these stock plots, dealing with various scenes and milieu. One of the best scenarios occurs in *Blowback* (1977). On the eve of his fiftieth birthday, Nameless has found out that he has a lesion on his lung and is waiting to learn whether he has cancer. He accepts a request from an old war buddy who runs a fishing camp in the Sierra Nevada mountains, and steps into a volatile situation. One of the guests, Ray Jerrold, is insanely jealous, and his flirtatious wife Angela is the only woman in the camp. Then a van belonging to an Oriental carpet dealer mysteriously plunges into the lake, and Nameless finds a strange clue at the scene: a peacock feather.

The detective returns to the wilds of northern California in *Nightshades* (1984), which is about the case of *Northern Development vs. Ragged-Ass Gulch*. A group of three developers are trying to turn an old Gold Rush town into a theme park, but the sixteen residents—mostly artists and other oddballs—who have adopted the ghost town resist. Nameless is hired by the insurance company that held the policy on one of the developers, who was killed when his house mysteriously burned down. Kerry Wade, the detective's girlfriend, accompanies him on the case. By this time Nameless has also acquired a partner named Eberhardt, though he is occupied on another case.

The Nameless Detective did eventually get a name—but only from another author. In a work Pronzini co-authored with Collin WILCOX, *Twospot* (1978), the other major character, Lieutenant Frank HASTINGS, refers to the Nameless Detective as "Bill." The story is set in the Napa Valley wine-growing region. Another collaborative book was *Double* (1984), which Pronzini co-authored with his wife, Marcia MULLER. Nameless and Sharon MCCONE are both in San Diego (her hometown) for a private detective's convention. McCone calls Nameless "Wolf" because he is the last of the "lone-wolf" kind of private eye. In alternating chapters, the two p.i.'s describe their tandem investigation of two cases. First, Nameless sees McCone's old friend, who is the head of security at the hotel where the convention is held, fall to her death from a tower of the hotel. He suspects she was pushed. While McCone gets into trouble trying to find the murderer, Nameless investigates the disappearance of a strange woman and her son from the same hotel. This book is considerably weaker than Nameless's solo appearances.

Jackpot (1990) took Nameless into the gambling scene of Lake Tahoe, where a man who has won $200,000 mysteriously commits suicide. Labor relations provide the background for *Breakdown* (1991). In *Hardcase* (1995), the Nameless Detective is almost sixty, having aged only about thirteen years since his first appearance in 1971. In this book, he finally marries his longtime girlfriend, Kerry. In *Sentinels* (1996), Nameless travels to a small town in the wilds of northern California in search of a missing college student and her boyfriend who had disappeared while driving from Oregon to San Francisco.

In addition to the novels, Pronzini has published several volumes of Nameless Detective short stories. *Duo* (1998), a joint Pranzini-Muller collection, contains some Nameless stories.

BIBLIOGRAPHY Novels: *Undercurrent* (1973), *Hoodwink* (1981), *Scattershot* (1982), *Dragonfire* (1982), *Bindlestiff* (1983), *Quicksilver* (1984), *Bones* (1985), *Deadfall* (1986), *Shackles* (1988), *Quarry* (1992), *Labyrinth* (1992), *Demons* (1993), *Illusions* (1997), *Boobytrap* (1998).

Short Stories: *Casefile* (1983), *Graveyard Plots* (1985).

NAME OF THE ROSE, THE (*Il nome della rosa,* 1980; tr 1983) A novel by Umberto ECO, set in an Italian monastery in the fourteenth century. The "detective" is an old monk (fifty years, in 1327, was old) named William of Baskerville (Sherlockians take note), who has been sent to the Benedictine monastery to investigate a murder. His investigation itself provokes further violence, which takes on a pattern conforming to the Book of Revelation, including a drowning in a vat of blood. The story is told by Adso of Melk, who recalls the events seventy years later. Adso's simplicity, as well as the fact that he is recollecting a time that to him is distant and to us remote, helps to create the multiple frames that make the story "open-ended." This is one of the characteristics for which mainstream critics lauded the book and for which mystery critics have disparaged it. Eco has said that a novel is "a machine for generating interpretations," and that a historical novel should show "what happened then and how what happened then matters to us as well." *The Name of the Rose* meets both these criteria (not that it has many solutions—only many meanings), and its very length, complexity, and rhetorical style are truer to the medieval period than, say, the novels of Ellis PETERS, and convey a worldview in which the only great mystery was the mystery of God's will. The historical figure Bernard Gui, a persecutor of heretics, is particularly interesting as an evil version of the traditional sleuth represented by Baskerville.

NAPOLEON I. See ARSENIC.

NAPOLEON OF CRIME A phrase first used by Sherlock HOLMES to describe Professor MORIARTY. The genius master criminal, like the GENIUS DETECTIVE, has since become a stock figure, and the phrase "Napoleon of crime" recurs in many mysteries.

NARK This term, often used to indicate an officer of a narcotics squad, also has the much older meaning (from Dutch *narruken*) of "to spy or watch," which was current in the nineteenth century. To nark came to mean to inform, to SNITCH, to act as a STOOLIE. Another root could be French *narquois,* meaning "sly" or "cunning."

NASH, SIMON (1924–) The English mystery writer known by the name Simon Nash is of the second generation of "donnish" mystery writers, inheritors of the mode that Michael INNES fashioned. Nash writes about an amateur sleuth, Adam Ludlow, who is an Oxford-educated lecturer at the University of London (the author himself was a lecturer at the London School of Economics). Ludlow has "no expectation of further promotion" and so lives off a small private income and teaches. He doesn't mince words, particularly when it comes to criticizing other faculty members, and is fond of literary quotation. As an eccentric amateur, he advises Inspector Montero and Sergeant Springer of the CID. Nash is mainly interested in the puzzle, and no great effort is made to explain Ludlow's involvement. In *Dead Woman's Ditch* (1964), Montero investigates the killing of the mysterious Silas Taker at a country inn. Taker, it turns out, had lured the other guests (including a colleague of Ludlow's) to the inn with threatening letters. *Death Over Deep Water* (1963) is a case of MURDER AFLOAT. Ludlow is aboard the Mediterranean cruise ship *Inquirer* visiting ancient sites, which provides opportunities for his usual satirical remarks on modern education, the decline of civilization, and the naïve faith in science. Trouble visits the Acton family, whose relations have been strained by an unfair division of the family money. Ludlow is more similar to Francis PETTIGREW than Innes's wacky dons, though he is less entertaining. The best of the Ludlow cases is KILLED BY SCANDAL (1962), which has a theatrical setting.

"NAVAL TREATY, THE" (1893) Sherlock HOLMES's last case before he disappears in THE FINAL PROBLEM (1893). The story begins with a letter to Watson from his old school acquaintance, Percy Phelps, who is an example of Conan DOYLE's gently satirical treatment of the upper classes. Phelps is well connected, brilliant, but a bit silly, particularly in having left a naval treaty he was copying on his desk in the Foreign Office, whence it has disappeared. Percy has literally been driven mad by this career-ending disaster, having incurred the wrath of his uncle and patron, and is recovering under the care of his fiancée, Annie Harrison. The scene shifts to the country house where the invalid is convalescing. Several RED HERRINGS are introduced. Holmes is wounded during his unraveling of the case, and finally plays one of his typical practical jokes on Percy in the end.

NAZIS The Nazis, as the primary modern example of evil, have provided villains for numerous espionage THRILLERs, not to mention films and television. In a larger sense, the events of World War II have been credited with changing world fiction as a whole, producing a cynicism about human nature and the possibility of unalloyed good and making impossible the kind of cheerful naiveté about conflict and nationalism that infects such writers as BUCHAN and, in its most execrable form, SAPPER. This paradigm shift ushered in the era of the Cold War, during which writers such as LECARRÉ and DEIGHTON wrote about cynical warriors fighting over a ruined world.

Many if not most of the books with Nazi characters are not mysteries proper but stories of suspense. It is perhaps not surprising that Nazism could be exploited as thriller fodder, but it is startling that a phenomenon as complicated, horrifying, and important as the rise of National Socialism could also be made boring. Ira Levin's *The Boys from Brazil* (1976), about the cloning of Hitler, is only the most ridiculous of such books. Some of the major authors in the genre, however, were in their maturity during World War II and wrote stories and novels based on their own experiences with an authenticity later imitators rarely matched. Ross MACDONALD traveled in Nazi Germany before the war. Ngaio MARSH and Christianna BRAND lived in London during the Blitz, and C. Day-Lewis (Nicholas BLAKE) worked for the Ministry of Information; Frances Oke Manning and Cyril Henry Cole (Manning COLES) combined experience in the War Office and in British Intelligence in the series of novels about Tommy HAMBLEDON, which they began in 1940. Although the background was genuine, writers who were working at a time when the defeat of Nazi Germany was hardly a foregone conclusion often were writing what amounted to fantasies, in which the Nazis were dumber and more comical than they were in reality.

The Smiler with the Knife (1939), a Nigel STRANGEWAYS mystery, is set during the period of "the phony war." While on a retreat in the Devonshire countryside, the Strangeways stumble on a native fascist conspiracy, the "E.B." (English Banner). Georgia works undercover to infiltrate it, which necessitates her publicly separating from Nigel. She is discovered and must flee, which gives rise to an inventive chase. One may have to suspend disbelief in order to feel the threat of a pro-Nazi overthrow of the British government, but at the time of publication this was not inconceivable.

Ngaio Marsh's *True Colours* (1943) takes place in New Zealand at a run-down resort named Wai-ata-tapu and is one of her most interesting books. The story begins with the splenetic Dr. Ackrington suspecting one of the other guests, the vulgar bounder Mr. Questing, of signaling to enemy U-boats from a mountaintop. Marsh wittily recreates the ill-humor, fear, guilt, and controlled hysteria of those far from the front. The social background of the story is more developed than in most mysteries of the classic type, with two generations of Maori (the elders and the semi-Westernized youngsters), colonials of varying sensitivity, and "foreigners" such as a visiting English stage star and his entourage. The failure to take Maori customs seriously and the violation of *tapu* (taboo) sites is a minor theme. Inspector ALLEYN's name comes up only twice in the book. The murder is ingenious, if gruesome: a man is boiled to death in a volcanic mud spring.

ROGUE MALE (1939), by Geoffrey HOUSEHOLD, is considered his best novel. He indulges in some wishful thinking, telling the story of an attempt on a dictator's life by a vacationing British hunter. The hunter is trapped but escapes; there follows a suspenseful pursuit, which became Household's signature plot element. Intentional or not, the escape has similarities to the miraculous survival of Sherlock HOLMES.

Agatha Christie spent World War II as a volunteer nurse in London. *N or M?* (1941) is an espionage thriller featuring the BERESFORD couple, Tuppence and Tommy. They are hired to root out Nazi spies by going undercover at a seaside resort. Their clue is the last words of a murdered British spy ("N or M Song Suzie"). Christie deploys her usual cloak-and-dagger elements: sabotage, secret ink, kidnapping, Tommy about to be executed (again), etc.

Michael GILBERT served in the North African and Italian campaigns in a British artillery unit. *Death in Captivity* (1952; U.S. title *The Danger Within*) is a powerful murder story set in a prisoner-of-war camp in which the murder of a suspected informant imperils an escape plan. In the same year he published a novel about the French resistance, *Death Has Deep Roots.*

John CREASEY explained that his novel *Unknown Mission* (1940; repr 1972) was written at a time when "there did seem a very real chance that many of the neutral nations could be kept out of the Second World War," which would have led to the fall of Britain. Bruce Murdoch and Mary Dell pose as newlyweds in order to stake out a remote inn, reputedly a rendezvous for Nazi agents. The plot involves some valuable papers, supposedly containing secrets that will keep non-aligned countries out of the war. Murdoch and Dell are opposed by a host of other agents, including those of Scovia, a hybrid Scandinavian nation. Then Alloway, the author of the papers, is kidnapped. A non-stop chase across several countries ensues, with murders, parachutings into enemy territory, and other trappings of the wartime thriller.

If the fall of Hitler was a dream for this generation, then the possible resurgence of the Nazis was a nightmare. Household returned to the Nazi theme, but in a postwar setting, in WATCHER IN THE SHADOWS (1960). Gilbert's *After the Fine Weather* (1963) is about Nazis in Austria. Both Philip K. DICK and Len Deighton have written imaginative thrillers in which the Nazis are winning or have already won World War II. In Frederick FORSYTH's *The Odessa File* (1972), based on a real organization of former SS men, a German freelance journalist, Peter Miller, tries to track down a concentration camp commandant. SS Captain Eduard Roschmann really existed, and supervised the murders of thousands of Jews at Riga; around the story of Miller's efforts to uncover him Forsyth weaves a rather melodramatic personal saga as well as an international intrigue involving the beleaguered state of Israel. The author's research cannot be faulted, however, and he shores up the story with a considerable amount of history.

Philip KERR, a British author born in 1956, has written a series of mysteries set in the Nazi era (see BERLIN NOIR) remarkable for their depiction of the "banality of evil" and the chilling ordinariness of the monster. J. Robert JANES's mysteries have a Frenchman and a Gestapo agent working together on supposedly "ordinary" crimes.

NEBBISH A nebbish is a loser, a zero. The word comes from the Yiddish *nebekh.* Leo Rosten wrote that "when a *nebech* leaves the room, you feel as if someone came in." Alo NUDGER and Robert UPTON's Amos McGuffin appear to be nebbishes.

NEBEL, [LOUIS] FREDERICK (1903–1967) One of the better-known of the lesser-known veterans of the PULP MAGAZINES, Frederick Nebel, like Paul CAIN, has recently been brought back into print. Nebel was born in Staten Island, New York, and worked as a longshoreman and on a tramp steamer before he became a writer. A friend of Dashiell HAMMETT's, Nebel was already writing for BLACK MASK when he created Cardigan for *Dime Detective* in 1931. *The Adventures of Cardigan* (1988) collects stories from the thirties about Nebel's most successful HARD-BOILED detective. Jack Cardigan works for the Cosmos Agency out of St. Louis, but he also investigates in New York. He is described as a big, lumbering man with tousled hair. Nebel's other series characters include the team of MacBride, a hard-boiled cop, and Kennedy, an investigative news reporter. Donny Donahue was a private investigator for the Inter-State Detective Agency. These stories survive in old copies of the pulps but have not been collected in book form, except for some Donahue stories that were published as *Six Deadly Dames* (1950), the only story collection that appeared in Nebel's lifetime. Nebel also wrote two novels, *Sleepers East* (1933) and *Fifty Roads to Town* (1936).

NEELY, BARBARA (1942–) The African American writer Barbara Neely wrote her first mystery, *Blanche on the Lam* (1992), in order to call attention to the relations between domestic workers and employers in the United States. Neely had worked for the Women's Correction Center, a Pittsburgh alternative to incarceration program, and for other activist agencies. She chose as her sleuth a forty-year-old maid, Blanche White; Neely said that she tried to use humor to encapsulate the message of the book. The second book was *Blanche Among the Talented Tenth* (1994), in which Blanche accompanies her children to a black resort on the coast of Maine, where murder erupts among her children's rich private-school friends. *Blanche Cleans Up* appeared in 1998.

NEELY, RICHARD (1920–) Born in New York City, Richard Neely started out as a newspaper journalist and became an advertising executive, eventually rising to vice-president and director at major firms. He later moved to California, settled in the Bay Area, and devoted himself to writing full time. Neely's early novels focused on terror, sex, and suspense. *While Love Lay Sleeping* (1969) was his first novel.

Neely's books are disturbing, particularly in their scenes of violent crimes against women. They are as dark as anything written by David GOODIS or Jim THOMPSON, though Neely was not the equal of either; but like those writers, Neely achieved a reputation among French intellectuals, and the New Wave director Claude Chabrol would later film Neely's *The Damned Innocents* (1971) as *Dirty Hands* (*Les Innocents aux mains sales,* 1975). Another of Neely's early books, *The Plastic Nightmare* (1969), was republished in the Black Lizard series in 1991 as SHATTERED. Neely is so much associated with the other "noir" writers of the fifties that *Shattered* was billed as "a masterpiece of fifties high pulp," though the book was written at the end of the sixties.

For two reasons, Neely's resurgence has drawn less attention than that of other "rediscovered" writers. First, he wrote about the turbulent world of the sixties and seventies, after the sexual revolution and the advent of alternative culture. Neely's books remain uncomfortably contemporary, with nothing "retro" about them; they are scary rather than cool. The treatment of sex places the books midway between the puritanism of the fifties—partly that of the publishers—and the complete liberty available to writers since the eighties. Thus while Neely is graphic, some of his scenes are awkward, with the furtiveness of pre-liberation soft porn ("she enveloped the pulsating tumescence that now achingly demanded release . . ."). This is the second reason for his lesser popularity: some of Neely's writing was plainly awful. *The Ridgeway Women* (1975) is a wretched novel, full of bad puns, contrived and melodramatic scenes, atrocious similes and bad metaphors ("a lava spill of golden hair"), and clunky phrasing ("she banged the air in frustration"). The plot itself—a retired colonel's efforts to get his hands on his new wife's fortune—is preposterous, and only functions through the incredible obtuseness of the characters.

In THE WALTER SYNDROME (1970), Neely tried something more complicated and ambitious, a novel with multiple layers influenced by the late modernist or postmodernist fiction of Thomas Pynchon and Vladimir Nabokov. His move to California also seems to have brought Neely inevitably into the sphere of Raymond CHANDLER and Ross MACDONALD. *Lies* (1978) shows the Macdonald influence; the main character is a famous writer named Harper (also the screen name of Lew ARCHER, as played by Paul Newman), who is married to the former "Mrs. Archer." The story focuses on the battle over Harper's estate. *A Madness of the Heart* (1976) is about a series of rapes. A writer, Harry Falcon, steps out for a drink and on his way home rescues a woman who is being assaulted. At home, he finds his wife brutally raped, and he himself is the main suspect. He begins investigating other rapes as a way of clearing himself from suspicion but gets blamed for them, too. Neely likes to create puzzling or seemingly impossible situations in his books, but is prone to using psychosis or personality distortions as a device for wriggling out of them.

NEMESIS (1971) A Miss MARPLE mystery by Agatha CHRISTIE, in which the aging detective receives a windfall of twenty thousand pounds, left to her by an acquaintance, Mr. Rafiel. All she has to do is investigate a crime. Instructions left behind by Rafiel start arriving by mail, sending Miss Marple on a group tour to the countryside, then to a country house, where further clues reveal that Rafiel's son was convicted for the murder of his fiancée. Having given her the name "Nemesis," Rafiel has planned for Miss Marple to reopen the case. One of the results of her prying into the ten-year-old murder and the search for other suspects is a fresh crime, striking at one of her tour companions.

NERTS A euphemism for "nuts" (analogous to "darn" for "damn"), used as an expletive in the same way as *nuts!* to mean "No!" It came into use in the twenties.

NEVINS, FRANCIS M[ICHAEL, JR.] (1943–) A professor of law at St. Louis University, Francis M. Nevins is an important mystery scholar and critic. He has edited many anthologies, and has won EDGAR awards for his biographies of Ellery QUEEN and Cornell WOOLRICH. He has also written mystery novels and stories with a legal background.

NICOTINE See NIGHTSHADE.

NIGHT AND THE CITY (1938) The novel for which Gerald KERSH was best known in his own time. Set in the alleys, nightclubs, and rank spots of London's West End, it focuses on the slick and callow pimp, Harry Fabian, who passes himself off as an American songwriter. Harry concocts a scheme to promote "all-in" wrestling and lures the comical wheeler-dealer Figler into putting up half the money. Harry get his half—£100—from a nasty bit of blackmail. In the later part of the book, Harry's plans bring him into contact with the people of the club world: Vi, a pathetic tart; Helen, whose character is gradually being eroded by the life; and Adam, a penniless sculptor who hates his part in scamming the customers.

The plot gives Kersh plenty of opportunities to indulge his passion for description. Kersh can go into pages of ornate, metaphorical, and even purple prose when introducing a person: "Looking at him you had an impression of a large quantity of something soft poured into a smallish black suit with a pin stripe, overflowing at the wrists and collar; a long body supported by little crooked legs; a curved spine, round shoulders, a potbelly, and a face of the color and texture of a Welsh rarebit. In order to reproduce the way Figler spoke, put your tongue between your teeth, stop up your nose, half fill your mouth with saliva, and try to say 'This is the end of the matter.'" Kersh is as much in love with language as with the sound of his own voice, and sometimes dazzles with his inventiveness. A woman's smeared lipstick makes her look "like a newly fed ghoul that has forgotten to wipe its mouth," her hair "a dark fountain of accumulated wickedness squeezed out by the pressure of her corsets." The cleft in a man's chin and between his eyes is likened to "the remains of a central line about which his head had been mathematically constructed." Kersh's fascination with the disreputable and grotesque was like Hogarth's, though less moral; only his description of non-whites ("whose veins might have been slaughterhouse drainpipes carrying the watery overflow of a dozen different kinds of waste blood") is repulsive in its implications.

NIGHT OF THE HUNTER, THE (1953; repr 1988) A novel by Davis Grubb (1919–1982) in the manner of the best work of Jim THOMPSON. Set during the Depression, the story takes place near Moundsville, West Virginia, Grubb's native city. Ben Harper decides to rob the Moundsville bank, but the robbery goes sour. He kills two men, is wounded, and later apprehended. In prison awaiting hanging, Harper meets Harry Powell, known as "Preacher," a cold and opportunistic killer, a perverted man who despises sex and preys on women. Harper has a wife, Willa, a nine-year-old son, John, and a four-and-a-half-year-old daughter, Pearl.

Harper refuses to reveal where he stashed the ten thousand dollars he stole from the bank; after the execution, Preacher moves in on Willa, hoping to find out where the money is. It becomes evident that the children know. John is the only member of the small community who realizes the evil behind Preacher's pose as a "man of God." Grubb convincingly shows the children's thoughts and, particularly in the case of John, shows how children exposed to terror lose their trust in the benevolence of those around them, their belief in the solidity of the social world, and finally their childhood itself.

Moundsville lies on the Ohio River rather than the Mississippi, but the atmosphere is reminiscent of TWAIN and Melville's THE CONFIDENCE MAN (1857), overlaid with the twentieth-century nihilism of Thompson and others. The river scenes during the children's flight recall the adventures of Huck Finn. The freedom the river offers (both as a means of physical escape and the moral freedom implied by the shining glamour of the "sinful" riverboats) is a contrast to the grim trap of the town. Preacher's religion is grotesquely hypocritical, and the good townspeople who are taken in are less innocent than contemptible. Even their attempts to wipe out the guilt of their own gullibility are wrong-headed and immoral.

Grubb wrote many other novels, but none received the notoriety of *The Night of the Hunter,* which came as a result of Charles Laughton's stunning 1955 film version—the only film Laughton ever directed—starring Robert Mitchum and Shelley Winters.

NIGHTSHADE The name for a poison made from one of several nightshade plants, the most famous of which is "deadly" nightshade, or belladonna. Deadly nightshade is a shrub, even one of whose black berries can be fatal. It is common in many parts of the world, including North America and Europe. The Latin name of the plant (*Atropa belladonna*) combines the name of Atropos, one of the three Fates who cuts the thread of life, and the Italian words for "beautiful woman," a reference to the former cosmetic uses of the plant (in rouge, for example). The main chemical involved in nightshade poisoning is ATROPINE, an extremely toxic alkaloid that attacks the involuntary nervous system and can be fatal in very small doses. It also contains other alkaloids, including HYOSCINE. There is no antidote for deadly nightshade. Symptoms include nausea, vomiting, rapid heartbeat, disorientation, and convulsions. The name of this plant is also a popular title. *Deadly Nightshade* (1940) by Elizabeth DALY is superior to the *Deadly Nightshade* (1970) by James Fraser.

Despite its nasty reputation, deadly nightshade is cultivated for its beneficial medical properties (at low doses). It can be used as a sedative and as a pain reliever. Deadly nightshade is one of the Solanaceae family of plants, which also includes the potato. Another branch, including woody nightshade and black nightshade, is poisonous for a different reason: the presence of solanine, not atropine, makes them deadly. When ingested, solanine produces similar reactions to those induced by deadly nightshade, including a burning sensation, vomiting, abdominal pain, and possibly convulsions and death. Potatoes ordinarily contain only harmlessly small amounts of solanine. HENBANE is another member of this branch of the nightshade family.

Still another relative of nightshade is the tobacco plant, and it too contains a deadly poison—nicotine. Many mysteries have been written involving nicotine poisoning. They have also played on the fact that while smoking the plant does not lead to intake of sufficient nicotine to cause death, a single cigar does have enough poison to kill.

NIGHTSQUAD (1961) A novel by David GOODIS. The central character, Corey Bradford, is a former cop who was kicked off the force for shaking down hustlers. He engages in monologues with "the badge" in which he justifies his behavior. His father, an honest cop, died four months before Corey was born. He grew up in an area known as "The Swamp."

During a backroom poker game with several organized crime figures, two gunmen burst in and try to kill boss Walter Grogan. Bradford subdues one of the men, takes his gun, and uses it to shoot the other. Another of the card players kills the second man. Grogan is terrified, and hires Bradford to investigate the attack, offering a big reward if he can find out who was behind it. This group of murderers and criminals inhabits an even lower circle of hell than Goodis's other characters.

"NINE-MILE WALK, THE" A story by Harry Kemelman, which was collected in *The Nine-Mile Walk* (1967). It was one of the stories Kemelman wrote about Nicky Welt and first appeared in *Ellery Queen's Mystery Magazine.* Nicky is an urbane, brilliant man, the Snowdon Professor of English Language and Literature at a Connecticut college. Rather arch, he "could never drop his pedagogical manner," even with his friend the district attorney, who narrates "The Nine-Mile Walk." The case arises accidentally over breakfast at the Blue Moon; Nicky disparages the narrator's logical abilities and asserts that "an inference can be logical and still not be true." He dares the D.A. to give him a random sentence of ten or twelve words, from which he will construct "a logical chain of inferences that you never dreamed of when you framed the sentence." He fulfills the promise, in spades. The sentence picked out of the air by the D.A.—"A nine-mile walk is no joke, especially in the rain"—points to a real crime. The story is thus an exercise, literally, in pure deduction, but the consequences are totally surprising as well as logical.

NINE TIMES NINE (1940) Originally published under the name H. H. Holmes, this novel by Anthony BOUCHER is an intricate LOCKED ROOM mystery with a cast of outlandish characters. Many of them reappeared in ROCKET TO THE MORGUE (1942), but *Nine Times Nine* is considered Boucher's best novel. Sister Ursula of the Sisters of Martha and Bethany and Los Angeles police detective Terence Marshall are the oddball pair of sleuths. The plot focuses on a religious cult, the Children of Light, whose leader is Ahasva. He teaches his followers to hate everyone, especially his rival, the swami Virasenanda. Wolfe Harrigan, an exposer of cults, hires the unemployed writer Matt Duncan to assist him. When Harrigan is killed, Duncan gets drawn into the relationships among the murdered man's family and also begins to work with Detective Marshall. Duncan is a key witness, having seen a yellow-robed figure in Wolfe's locked study prior to the discovery of the body; the "yellow man" is believed to be Ahasva.

"NINE-TO-FIVE MAN, THE" (1964) One of the best known stories by Stanley ELLIN, "The Nine-to-Five Man" is about the methodical Mr. Keesler, proprietor of Keesler Novelties. Keesler lives with his wife in Flatbush, Brooklyn, and commutes to his office in the city every day with his sample case. But the sample case contains more than toys. The mystery of the story is the gradual discovery of Keesler's true business, and not a criminal investigation.

NIXON, RICHARD M[ILHOUS] See FAMILY AFFAIR, A.

NO BEAST SO FIERCE (1973) The first novel by Edward BUNKER, a first-person account by Max Dembo, a paroled burglar/bandit/forger whose life closely resembles that of the author. The story begins in prison the day before Dembo's release. During his final hours inside, he is terrified of being assaulted or killed just before regaining his freedom. Racial tensions are high in the prison and riots are frequent. Leroy, Dembo's black friend, gives him a couple of barbiturates to calm him down. The story is taut with suppressed violence and anxiety, and pulls no punches in the realism of its dialogue.

Max intends to stay straight once he is released, but in the event he finds it difficult. Bunker shows how the institutionalization of prisoners leads to recidivism—they are so accustomed to life in jail that they find it tough to make a go of it once released, and are further hampered by the fact that they are shunned by the rest of the population. Dembo contacts one of his former crime partners because he hasn't any other friends, and breaks one vow after another, the first being his resolution to stay off drugs. He and two other ex-cons end up planning a bank robbery (the crime for which Bunker received his last prison sentence). Bunker's realistic style creates an atmosphere similar to that of a Jim THOMPSON novel, though his dialogue is tightly written, clever, and often funny.

NOIR (Fr "black") A term now applied generally to crime writing of the forties and fifties, much of which wound up on the screen as FILM NOIR. The noir style is somewhat like the HARD-BOILED novel, minus the detective. The figures common in the fiction of Cornell WOOLRICH are like a tarot of noir: the sucker, the doomed man, the seductress, the insane killer, the frame-up, and bad luck. Drawing on the fiction of the hard-boiled era and even the symbolism of the GOTHIC novel and Romanticism, noir relies heavily on the contrast between dark and light, madness and reason, heaven and hell, sin and redemption.

These dualities and oppositions are further visible in noir sexual stereotypes. The central figure, usually male, is trapped between two women. The dark, sexy, and bad woman opposed by the blonde and good woman is a dynamic that goes back to the nineteenth century and beyond. In noir writing, the formula was sometimes varied by the trashy/dreamy duality; the seductress is a classic bombshell who oozes sexuality, while the "good" woman is younger, sexually unsure of herself, and inexperienced. One sends the hero into a rut, the other into a reverie. The sexually available woman excites an explosive but short-lived passion that proves to be a disaster for the hero, while the hopeful and adoring passion for the "good" woman is what drives the hero—who often as not feels completely sunk, set up, and gallows-bound—to make a final effort toward salvation.

Writers who have been associated with the heyday of noir include Charles WILLIAMS, David GOODIS, and Jim THOMPSON.

NOLAN See COLLINS, MAX ALLAN.

NO ORCHIDS FOR MISS BLANDISH (1939) The first novel by James Hadley CHASE and the only one still remembered. The novel is about a kidnapper and his victim (the daughter of a millionaire) who gradually fall for each other during the story. The book has more scenes of carnage and torture than RED HARVEST (1929), but cannot hold a candle to it in any other respect.

Chase, who worked in a library, wrote his first novel in his spare time over a few weekends, with the help of a dictionary of American slang. From his reading of pulp novels he extracted the most sensational elements and magnified them. His novels have a particular reputation for violent sex. Chase eventually produced some ninety novels, but none had the success of his first book. Tellingly, his reputation as a writer has always been lower in the United States, the culture he was supposed to be writing about; in France he has been extravagantly praised, though he was not a second POE.

NORTH, JERRY AND PAM Characters created by Richard and Frances LOCKRIDGE. The Norths inhabit the mildly swinging milieu of the forties and fifties bourgeoisie. The North novels gently poke fun at their society and the assortment of bores, crackpots, and villains that inhabit their "set." Stylistically, the Lockridges could have been imitating the Ellery QUEEN books of the Hollywood period, except that the Norths did not begin as mystery characters at all. They first appeared in a series of humorous sketches in *The New Yorker* depicting the life of young Manhattanites. These pieces were collected in *Mr. and Mrs. North* (1936).

Pamela and Gerald North are cultured and youthful. Pam is slightly built and has the curious and engaged expression of someone who is always enjoying life and new experiences, which causes people to confide in her. When excessive, her curiosity brings on crises (and the climax of the novel). Jerry, who runs North Books, Incorporated, is the picture of a publisher: he is tall, wears glasses, and has "ruffled" hair through which he is constantly running his hands. They live in an apartment with their cats—at first Toughy and Roughy, and later Sherry, Gin, and Martini. *Hanged for a Sheep* (1942) is mostly about Pam's relatives (and the behavior of the cats), who become murder suspects.

The North's cases and their detection are looser than the other Lockridge books. They work at detection in their whimsical way while their friend, police detective Bill Weigand, handles the mechanics. The Lockridges' writing is as usual uneven. *The Dishonest Murderer* (1949) is a sluggish book about the murder of a U.S. Senator on New Year's Eve. The language is repetitive, the phrases clumsily put together. *Dead as a Dinosaur* (1952) is a funny tale told in a different (and more lucid) style. Someone has been playing a joke on mammologist Orpheus Preson, taking out advertisements in his name asking for butlers, masseurs, and tree surgeons to apply in person to his apartment. Another ad says that he wants to buy a pony. It later becomes a murder case.

As in their Inspector HEIMRICH novels, the Lockridges made use of exotic locales, which are more believable—in that anything is believable—in the North series, given that they are amateurs. In *Voyage into Violence* (1956) the Norths are on a cruise to Havana and Nassau when a fellow passenger is killed. Members of an order of "Ancient and Respectable Riflemen" are on their way to a parade in Nassau; one of their ceremonial swords gets stuck through the murdered passenger, who turns out to be a private detective. The mystery is solved by Detective Bill Weigand with a little help from Pam North. The last novel in the series, MURDER BY THE BOOK (1963), is set in Key West, Florida.

BIBLIOGRAPHY Novels: *Murder Out of Turn* (1941), *A Pinch of Poison* (1941), *Death on the Aisle* (1942), *Death Takes A Bow* (1943), *Killing the Goose* (1944), *Payoff for the Banker* (1945), *Murder Within Murder* (1946), *Death of a Tall Man* (1946), *Untidy Murder* (1947), *Murder Is Served* (1948), *Murder in a Hurry* (1950), *Murder Comes First* (1951), *Death Has a Small Voice* (1953), *Curtain for a Jester* (1953), *A Key to Death* (1954), *Death of an Angel* (1955), *The Long Skeleton* (1958), *Murder Is Suggested* (1959), *The Judge Is Reversed* (1960), *Murder Has Its Points* (1961).

NOTHING MAN, THE (1954) A novel by Jim THOMPSON. It is quite unlike Thompson's other novels in that it is both disturbing and humorous; minus the murders, it could almost be a comic novel. What is disturbing is that one likes Clinton Brown—a washed up small-town newspaper columnist and an emasculated loser—and the way he spouts witticisms left and right, shows allegiance and loyalty to no one, and uses his nasty sense of humor to embarrass and humiliate others whom one suspects probably deserve it. The whole is seen through an alcoholic haze (probably more whisky is drunk in this novel than in any other). Brown evokes the same kind of ambivalent feelings as Tom RIPLEY.

NOTHING MORE THAN MURDER (1949) In this early crime novel by Jim THOMPSON, a frayed electrical cord is wired to the wet, sheet-metal walls of a rural movie showhouse, earning the book a place in the lists of ingenious if improbable murder techniques. Although Thompson was able to churn out pulp fiction on short notice, he spent eight years writing the novel, and it is one of his two best (along with THE KILLER INSIDE ME, 1952). The love triangle that turns into a murder plot is handled expertly (and with a twist: the unwanted spouse colludes in the deception) and the psychological states are developed rather than sketched.

NOT PROVEN A third verdict allowed for in Scottish law, midway between Guilty and Not Guilty. "Not Proven" indicates a strong suspicion that, were it not for the lack of evidence, the defendant would be convicted. A person released with a judgement of Not Proven, however, is acquitted and cannot be retried. Sir Walter Scott called it "that bastard verdict."

The Not Proven verdict has figured in a number of sensational cases, some of which are described in *Not Proven* (1960) by John Gray Wilson (1915–1968). Wilson makes the interesting point that only two verdicts are necessary—Not Proven and Not Guilty—because the defendant is not called upon to prove his *innocence:* rather, the prosecution is called upon to demonstrate his guilt. He ignores, however, that the defendant released with a verdict of Not Proven still has a cloud over his or her head, which only a verdict of Not Guilty could erase.

Among the cases described by Wilson is that of John Donald Merrett, also treated by William ROUGHEAD in *Trial of John Donald Merrett* (1929, Notable British Trials series). Merrett was only eighteen when he went on trial for shooting his mother in their Edinburgh home. Mrs. Merrett was writing letters at her table when a shot rang out; her son was the only other person in the room. He rushed out and told the maid that his mother had shot herself. Thus he was the only witness. Why Mrs. Merrett should have shot herself in the middle of a cheerful letter to a friend (which later vanished mysteriously—the police saw it on the table but did not take it away with them!) was a mystery. Young Merrett, it turned out, had been passing forged checks on her account and had robbed her of several hundred pounds. Mrs. Merrett took two weeks to die, and during completely lucid moments said that she knew nothing about a gun, and that she was sitting there writing when an explosion went off in her head. The police never bothered to take a statement from her of what happened, one of several lamentable errors. Merrett was convicted of the forgery but not of the murder. He served one year in prison.

Another notable case is that of Madeleine Smith, who in 1857 was tried for the poisoning of a former lover after having become affianced to a more desirable (and affluent) man. Despite strong disapproval, she was a charismatic woman who entered court "with the air of a belle entering a ballroom," according to one contemporary account. Smith was the daughter of a Glasgow architect and a noted beauty; her affair with the Frenchman Pierre Emile L'Angelier had almost reached the point of marriage when she threw him over for her wealthier neighbor, William Minnoch. It was demonstrated that Smith had purchased ARSENIC three times and had given L'Angelier cocoa, but not on the night in question, and L'Angelier's diary was not admitted as evidence. The verdict was Not

Guilty on one count, Not Proven on two others. During the trial Smith received several proposals of marriage.

NOVEL OF MANNERS That form of the novel toward which writers who are accused of trying to expand their mystery novels beyond the borders of the genre are often said to aspire. "Novel of manners" is a very imprecise term. It is supposed to apply to the type of novel that seeks to identify and explore the conventions and structures of society, constructing a sort of typology around the characters, who are often commented upon as fulfilling or transgressing certain norms. The novel of manners has been associated with such disparate writers as Jane Austen and Honoré de BALZAC, leaving a gap into which almost anything might fall. To let in Balzac is to let in DICKENS, and if Dickens, why not TWAIN? If Austen, why not Henry JAMES? The proletarian novel could be a political novel of manners; it meets the novel of manners coming the other way. The crime novel could be a novel of manners set among people whom society in one way or another anathematizes as not even part of society—the outlaw, the "underclass," or the *non compos mentis.*

NOVEMBER JOE See PRICHARD, HESKETH.

NUDGER, ALO A private detective created by John LUTZ. Nudger works in St. Louis, Missouri, and like Amos WALKER in Detroit is an idealist, a throwback to Philip MARLOWE and the "mean streets" code. But Nudger is a comic character because he is so hapless. The series began with *Buyer Beware* (1976), and Nudger seems to be the perfect private eye for the "malaise"-ridden seventies. His office is above Danny's Donuts, where he hangs out (instead of at the end of a bar). He drives a beat-up Volkswagen Beetle (later he trades down to a Granada), and business is always slow. Lieutenant Jack Hammersmith is "Nudge"'s former partner on the police force and is constantly amazed at the trouble Nudger can get himself into. Hammersmith smokes horrible green cigars and is a closed, watchful personality: "If the eyes were the windows of the soul, his shades were always down." The humor of the Nudger novels is understated and the texture more subtle than in Lutz's other series, about Fred CARVER.

Nudger is so nervous that he constantly chews antacid tablets. He tries to think tough, but his behavior is always giving him away. He is a sucker for innocence, a needy client, a hopeless case, or a sob story—particularly one delivered by a sympathetic woman. In *Dancer's Debt* (1988) the girlfriend of a troubled Vietnam veteran hires Nudger to find out what is causing his odd behavior. The wife of a man about to be executed brings him an even more dire case in RIDE THE LIGHTNING (1987).

Divorced from his wife Eileen (she constantly dogs him for dough), Nudger eventually gets a girlfriend, Claudia Bettencourt. In *Thicker than Blood* (1993), a serial killer is dumping women in the Mississippi, crimes that converge with Nudger's case. The humorous mystery is the most difficult to carry off, and sometimes it does not work. *Death by Jury* (1995) is about a man who stands a good chance of being executed for the murder of his wife (though her body has not been found) yet seems curiously confident that he will be acquitted. Nudger is hired by the defendant's lawyer to get new evidence. None of the characters is particularly engaging, and the lawyer is more annoying than he is funny.

BIBLIOGRAPHY Novels: *The Right to Sing the Blues* (1986), *Time Exposure* (1989), *Diamond Eyes* (1990), *Oops!* (1998).

OATES, STANISLAW The stolid official companion of Albert CAMPION in many of the mysteries of Margery ALLINGHAM. As Campion's SCOTLAND YARD contact, Oates was later replaced by the more dynamic Charlie Luke.

OATES, TITUS See MURDER OF SIR EDMUND GODFREY, THE.

OBELISTS FLY HIGH (1935) This much praised novel was C. Daly KING's most successful mystery. It is an offbeat version of a GOLDEN AGE detective novel in which King, a psychologist, uses long interrogations with the characters to present various competing philosophies and to debunk Christianity and "primitive beliefs." The story begins with an "epilogue" that describes a desperate situation aboard a Boeing airliner. Captain Michael Lord of the New York City police has been detailed to protect Dr. Amos Cutter, who has received a note saying that he will be killed precisely at noon on April 13—at which point Cutter is aboard the airplane, on his way to Reno to operate on his dying brother, the U.S. Secretary of State. In the epilogue, Lord has been shot, the plane is spiraling downward, and the situation is bleak.

The middle of the novel flashes back to the threat against Cutter and to Lord's elaborate plans to keep the bristly surgeon alive. The other passengers on the flight include an ingenue, an evangelical fanatic, a British novelist who believes thought can produce effects (including murder) at a distance, and Cutter's rabid assistant who thinks vivisection should be extended to include "idiots," "incurables," and other human beings. Coincidentally, Lord's friend Dr. L. Rees Pons (a WATSON figure) is also aboard. King concocts a LOCKED ROOM puzzle and throws in unpredictable plot twists. The prologue comes near the end of the book and is followed by a "clue finder," a list of forty clues that should have led the reader to the identity of the killer. The story is nothing if not ingenious, though pace, character, and style suffer from being made subservient to the puzzle element.

O'BREEN, FERGUS See BOUCHER, ANTHONY.

O'BRIEN, FERGUS The central character of Nicholas BLAKE's *Thou Shell of Death* (1936). A World War I flying ace so implacable toward the enemy that he scared even his comrades, O'Brien is rich, has a mysterious past, and is under a threat of death. O'Brien is one of the author's most lifelike characters because he is violent and kind, ruthless and perhaps sentimental—i.e., human and full of contradictions. He is also the lover of Georgia Cavendish, the future Georgia STRANGEWAYS.

OCCULT The detection of crimes that either apparently or in "actuality" involve supernatural causes or agents has long been a subgenre of mystery fiction. Mystery in the broadest sense could easily be traced back to the story of the supernatural—the fairy tale, the ghost story, the *Arabian Nights,* or any other of the forms of supernatural folktale that are found in every culture. But the ghost story as a modern form was first popular in the Victorian era and grew up alongside the mystery and detective story.

E. F. BLEILER credits Hesketh and Kate PRICHARD's Flaxman Low as the earliest important occult detective, a successful merging of the two genres. The Prichards based this series of stories on the folk motif of the haunted house—later to be exploited, in a secularized or de-supernaturalized version, by Mary Roberts RINEHART and others. The Prichards were part of a blossoming interest in the occult, horror, and the supernatural from the end of the Victorian period through World War I. Sometimes an incredible diversity of elements were mixed together. Richard MARSH's novel *The Beetle* (1897) was a wild combination of mystery, intrigue, murder, and grotesquerie. Archaeological discoveries in Egypt and the treasures brought back by expeditions led to the development of such favorite horror-mystery icons as the mummy and the ancient curse. Two main types of occult detective developed: the rationalist detective who investigates supernatural phenomena (such William Hope HODGSON's character, CARNACKI), and the detective who himself has unusual or fantastic powers (such as Algernon BLACKWOOD's "Psychic Physician," John Silence) and uses them to investigate ordinary crime, supernatural events, or both.

The tradition of the occult detective waned with the coming of the GOLDEN AGE, with its stress upon FAIR PLAY (one of Father KNOX's commandments was that supernatural causes had to be ruled out). The subgenre did not die out entirely, however, because writers like Manley Wade WELLMAN sometimes revived it. One surprising mingling of genres is the story "Handcuffs Don't Hold Ghosts," a Tommy HAMBLEDON adventure that won a prize from *Ellery Queen's Mystery Magazine* in 1946.

OCTAGON HOUSE (1937) A novel by Phoebe Atwood TAYLOR, one of her strangest and most humorous. Pam

Frye, the daughter of a somewhat daft retired professor, lives with her father in the Octagon House in Quanomet on Cape Cod. The town is in an uproar because of a mural recently painted at the town post office by Jack Lorne, who is married to Pam's slutty evil sister, Marina. The mural caricatures many of the townsfolk. National press coverage brings thousands of people to Quanomet.

Asey MAYO, just home from a trip, runs into Pam and learns about the mural; later, Pam drops by to tell him that she has found a 100-pound lump of ambergris on the beach (a valuable whale byproduct discussed in Melville's *Moby Dick*). Unfortunately, Marina has also seen it, and the sisters fight over it; even more unfortunately, one of them winds up stabbed to death. From that point, events become more and more outrageous. Pam and her father had been taking in borders, including Timothy Carr, who turns out to have a past connection to Marina. Then the ambergris disappears and the house's octagonal barn, where it is suspected the ambergris was hidden, burns down. Another suspect, Rodney Strutt, had recently bought a plane with his inheritance and then had his pilot deliberately crash it on the town square. Nettie Hobbs, the local busybody, and Peggy Boone, a cartoonist, also play a role. Mayo tries to figure out whether the killing has to do with the mural (later vandalized), the missing ambergris, or both. The novel gives a good impression of a sleepy seaside New England town in the thirties, not yet turned into a tourist mecca.

In a case of LIFE IMITATES ART, the town of Kennebunkport, Maine, received unwanted attention in 1941 when a WPA postoffice mural provoked the townspeople because it showed bathers (representing tourism) instead of scenes of the town's historic past. The resemblance to *Octagon House* was remarked upon at the time.

ODESSA FILE, THE See NAZIS.

O'DONNELL, LILLIAN [UDUARDY] (1926–) The Italian-born author Lillian O'Donnell wrote mystery and suspense fiction for years before she achieved notoriety with her series about Norah MULCAHANEY. Since then, O'Donnell has become one of the best-known PROCEDURAL authors. Begun in 1972 with *The Phone Calls*, the series now runs to more than a dozen books. One of them, *A Good Night to Kill* (1989), won an American Mystery Award.

O'Donnell was born in Trieste but her family is Hungarian. Before becoming an author she was an actress and director, having studied at the Academy of Dramatic Arts in New York City, where most of her mystery series are set. Her first mystery was *Death on the Grass* (1960). Although the Mulcahaney series is her most successful, O'Donnell has two others. She wrote three books about Mici Anholt, a Hungarian-American caseworker for the Crime Victims Compensation Board: *Aftershock* (1977), *Falling Star* (1979), and *Wicked Designs* (1980). In 1990, O'Donnell published *A Wreath for the Bride*, the first book in a new series about private investigator Gwen Ramadge. In *The Goddess Affair* (1996), Ramadge investigates the murder of a beautiful woman on a cruise ship. O'Donnell has also written many non-series mystery novels; the romantic suspense element of some of these works spills over into the Mulcahaney series.

OFSTED, LEE A character created by Charlotte and Aaron ELKINS. Ofsted is a professional golfer who solves crimes with the help of her policeman boyfriend. See GOLF MYSTERIES.

OHLS, BERNIE The District Attorney's chief investigator whom Philip MARLOWE encounters in several of his adventures. Ohls gets Marlowe his job with General Guy Sternwood in THE BIG SLEEP (1939). A former colleague of Marlowe's when he worked for D. A. Taggart Wilde, it isn't clear whether Ohls likes Marlowe, hates him, or respects him (perhaps a little of all three).

OKLAHOMA PUNK (1976) A novel by Loren D. ESTLEMAN. Set during the Depression, it is partly based on the exploits of a real bank robber, Wilbur Underhill. The story of Virgil Ballard (i.e., Underhill), a vicious criminal with no redeeming qualities, is told in the rapid-fire style of Raoul WHITFIELD, with numerous gory shootouts.

OLD BONES (1987) EDGAR-award winning novel by Aaron ELKINS, and the fourth book in the series about Professor Gideon OLIVER, the forensic archaeologist sleuth. The professor is forty years old at this stage and has been married for a year. He is invited to speak on his specialty at a police conference in France. The scene shifts between the conference and the story of an elderly man, Guillaume du Rocher, caught by the galloping tide while beachcombing at Mont St. Michel. His closest cousin is Claude Fougeray—a butcher, personally a pig, and a former collaborator. He is hated because another cousin of Guillaume was taken away by the German SS because Fougeray failed to warn him. Fougeray is nevertheless upset, however, when Guillaume, who had joined the resistance, leaves nothing to him in his will. Inspecteur Joly calls in Gideon Oliver when some bones are found in Guillaume's basement. The dismembered corpse is very incomplete, missing the key bones, but Gideon determines that it was a small person. Joly is not happy, because this conflicts with his theory that it is the body of an SS man killed by Guillaume. Further murders and attempts on Gideon's life ensue. The descriptions of Gideon's analysis, as well as the complexity of the relationships (only sketched here) make it the best of the Oliver books.

OLD ENGLISH PEEP SHOW, THE (1969; orig title *Pride of Heroes*) This novel by Peter DICKINSON won a Gold Dagger from the CRIME WRITERS' ASSOCIATION of Great Britain. Its outlandish plot centers around the Herryngs estate and a group of eccentric World War II heroes. Inspector PIBBLE is called down after one of the servants, Deakin ("a surly little gnome") hangs himself. The estate belongs to Sir Richard and Sir Ralph Clavering, who led a brave but costly raid during the darkest hours of the war and have been trading on their heroism ever since. Sir Richard is fascinated by lions and has a pride of them on the grounds of the estate. Ralph's daughter Anthea is married to Harvey Singleton, who has used the estate as the basis for "Old England," an English version of Disneyland with peasants and faked-up country charm. As usual, the aristocrats are only concerned about scandal, and try to impede Pibble's investigation at every turn. He survives lion attacks and makes some strange allies, including a Texan photographer in a purple suit. One of the clues Pibble has to collect is a pile of lion feces. Dickinson's combination of social satire, burlesque, and detection is less smooth than in some of his later works.

OLD MAN, THE See CONTINENTAL OP, THE.

OLD MAN IN THE CORNER, THE (1909; U.S. title *The Man in the Corner,* repr 1965) A collection of stories by Baroness ORCZY, featuring "the man in the corner," a bird-like man with bony fingers (named Bill Owen, though he remains "the old man"), prone to sniffling and lecturing on crime from his seat in the A. B. C. tea shop. The first group of Old Man stories appeared in the *Royal Magazine* in 1901–2, but were not published in book form until 1909. Further stories were collected in *The Case of Miss Elliot* (1905) and *The Unravelled Knots* (1925).

The Old Man's interlocutor is Polly Burton, who works for the *Evening Observer.* While he discusses crimes—often, in the style of the INVERTED MYSTERY, giving the solution first and then working backwards—he sits and plays at knotting pieces of string. One of his best stories is "The Fenchurch Mystery," an ingenious case of impersonation; the "Tremarn" mystery is one of his most violent.

OLD SHARON A detective in Wilkie Collins's novel MY LADY'S MONEY (1877), and an early example of the counter-type: he fulfills none of the usual requirements of the fictional detective. Old Sharon is a "rogue," apparently a lawyer who has been disbarred. He is dirty and disreputable, a drinker of gin with a sharp tongue for fools ("if I had lived to be your age, and knew no more of the world than you do, I'd go and hang myself"). He wears a frowzy gray overcoat, a tall white hat, and is accompanied by his pipe and his pug dog. He is rude and insolent, but also real; he precedes by half a century the many fat, coarse, or otherwise unpleasant detectives who would be created in reaction to the HOLMES model of unfailing genius and gentlemanliness.

OLD 'UN, THE The key character in Ngaio MARSH's *Scales of Justice* (1955). The Old 'Un is not an old man but a very large trout.

OLIVER, GIDEON A detective (technically, a "physical anthropologist") who is the protagonist in a series of mysteries by Aaron ELKINS. The fourth Gideon Oliver novel, OLD BONES (1987), received an EDGAR award. The premise of the series provides the author plenty of leeway in terms of plot construction: Oliver is a famous interpreter of human remains, and travels around the world giving his expertise to police and criminal justice systems in various regions. *The Dark Place* (1983) is set in the Pacific Northwest. In *Murder in the Queen's Armes* (1985), Oliver is visiting a friend at an early archaeological site in England when murders start happening. In *Icy Clutches* (1990), he attends a forest rangers' convention in Alaska (his wife Julie, whom he met in *The Dark Place,* is a ranger). Oliver learns of a case of thirty years before, when three people from a geological expedition were killed in an avalanche (it now turns out to be murder, of course). *Dead Men's Hearts* (1994) has Oliver taking part in the filming of a documentary in Egypt. *Twenty Blue Devils* (1997) is about the death of a Tahitian coffee plantation manager.

BIBLIOGRAPHY Novels: *The Fellowship of Fear* (1982), *Curses!* (1989), *Glancing Light* (1991).

OLSON, TOBY See GAY MYSTERIES.

OMERTÀ The "law of silence" of the Mafia.

"ON MURDER CONSIDERED AS ONE OF THE FINE ARTS" See DE QUINCEY, THOMAS.

ONE-MAN SHOW (1952; orig title *A Private View*) A novel by Michael INNES, one of his series with artistic backdrops. A memorial exhibition is being presented at the BRAUNKOPF gallery for the painter Gavin Lambert, who was shot to death. This provides Innes with an occasion for satire of the art world, one of his favorite themes. Inspector APPLEBY is in attendance and is depressed by the "oceans of twaddle and humbug" about art, particularly on the part of lecturer Mervyn Twist, who has the personality of a seagull. After the opening, it turns out that one painting was stolen just after Appleby looked at it. Lambert's model, Mary Arrow, also has disappeared. Meanwhile, the Duke of Horton has lost two valuable possessions he refers to as "Goldfish" and "Silverfish." The story becomes an artistic burlesque, with cracks at abstract expressionism (somewhat dated); a crude painter named Boxer; and Zhitkov, the Russian sculptor who feels put out because some of Lambert's blood dripped into his studio and fell on his statue of Venus.

ONE MINUTE PAST EIGHT (1957) A novel by George Harmon COXE. In this fast-paced, HARD-BOILED story, Jeff Lane of Boston must go to Caracas following his father's death in order to talk to his half brother, Arnold Grayson, about settling the inheritance. Arnold is not exactly a nice person, and has had trouble with the law in the States. On the way to meet him, Jeff is kidnapped and then just as mysteriously released. The pace picks up considerably once Jeff gets to Caracas, where he discovers that the detective he had hired to find his half brother is out of action. Jeff soon finds himself under suspicion of murder. Detectives then start to come out of the woodwork, including Karen Holmes (note the name), who is employed by a rival company that wants to control Jeff's firm. Coxe pays attention to psychology and provides a good climax and ending.

120, RUE DE LA GARE (1943; repr 1983) A novel by Léo MALET, the first to involve Nestor BURMA, who, instead of working for the Fiat Lux Detective Agency, finds himself in a German prisoner-of-war camp in World War II. In the camp he meets prisoner 60202, also known as "The Blob," and through him becomes involved in the mystery of EIFFEL TOWER JOE, a famous thief, and the gang headed by Georges Parris. The Blob is stricken with AMNESIA and is sent to the hospital, where he tells Burma with his dying breath, "Tell Hélène—120 rue de la Gare." Sent by train to Lyon with a group of other released P.O.Ws, Burma sees a mysterious woman on the platform; just as the train is pulling out, Burma's assistant from Fiat Lux rushes up to the train and gives the detective a message before being shot in the head. As Burma investigates the enigmatic message of the Blob and the identity of the woman on the platform, other forces try to stop him. The complicated plot has a riddle at the center of it, the solution of which could be lucrative. Malet combines French wartime atmosphere, the American HARD-BOILED idiom he had learned from his reading of HAMMETT and CHANDLER, and a surrealist edge reflecting his own artistic background to produce a unique Anglo-French mystery.

ONION FIELD, THE (1973) A chilling and frightening book by Joseph WAMBAUGH. Although it is based on a real case, and though Wambaugh read through the verbatim court report and did extensive research, the book reads like a novel. Both the cops and the killers are established as personalities, helping to explain the events of the night of March 9, 1963, when Los Angeles police officers Ian Campbell and Carl Hettinger were kidnapped by two parolees, Jimmy Smith and Gregory Powell. Wambaugh goes back into their childhoods to show Smith's experience of poverty and neglect and Powell's sexual confusion and years as a runaway. The relationship between the arrogant and irrational Powell, who is white, and the introverted Smith, who is black, is also complex, even though they had only known each other a matter of days when the crimes were committed. The terror-stricken flight of the surviving officer through the onion field at night, his disorientation, hysteria, and grief, is the most tormentingly powerful scene Wambaugh has written.

ONIONS, OLIVER (later known as George Oliver, 1873–1961) The English novelist Oliver Onions gained his literary reputation for his realistic novels and his ghost stories. He ventured into the crime genre in his trilogy *Whom God Hath Sundered* (1926), the first part of which was IN ACCORDANCE WITH THE EVIDENCE (1915). Onions was married to another English novelist, Berta Ruck.

Onions was born in Bradford, England, and studied at the Royal College of Art and later in Paris. Upon his return to London, he became an illustrator. He was also an amateur boxer and scientist. As a crime novel, *In Accordance with the Evidence* was years ahead of its time; its literary naturalism and first-person narrative give it the feeling of Camus's *The Stranger* (1942) or Ernesto Sabato's *The Tunnel* (1948). Onions's other books include *Widdershins* (1911), a collection of stories, *Mushroom Town* (1911), and *Poor Man's Tapestry* (1946). *The Story of Ragged Robyn* (1945) is a historical novel.

ON THE Q.T. See Q.T.

OPARA, CHRISTIE The first detective created by Dorothy UHNAK. When Opara first appears, in *The Bait*

(1968), she is described as a thin, freckled, flat-chested woman in her twenties, half-Greek and half-Swedish (though her name is Czech). A "tomboy," she has a young son and is the widow of another officer killed in the line of duty. Though slight of build, Opara is a determined and sometimes pugnacious woman; her difficulties in working in a (then) all-male environment are vividly depicted and no doubt depend on the author's own experience as an officer in the 1950s and 1960s. Opara appears in two other novels, *The Witness* (1969) and *The Ledger* (1970).

OPEN DOORS (*Porte operte,* 1987; tr 1991) A short novel by Leonardo SCIASCIA set at the height of the fascist period. It is also a meditation on law, and CAPITAL PUNISHMENT as inherently subversive of it. The year is 1937; Italy has seized Abyssinia and Mussolini is aiding the fascists in Spain. And in Palermo, a "little judge" is called upon to try a case involving the murderer of a prominent fascist. The Municipal Advocate Giuseppe Bruno had given away the murderer's job to another man, who was killed in revenge along with Bruno. The judge sees the defendant as desperately, almost nobly, mad, with a "fierce, twisted humanity." But since the fascists—who had reinstituted the death penalty—are clamoring for the man's execution, his friends are afraid to admit they know him, let alone act as character witnesses. It is up to the little judge to try to save the man from the gallows. In pursuing what he thinks of as justice, and in absolutely opposing capital punishment, he risks his career at the very least. That the trial goes on in a room used by the Inquisition (this is factually true; the real building, the Palazzo Chiaromonte in Palermo, was used by the Inquisition in the fifteenth century), with the centuries-old graffiti of its victims showing through the paint, further adds to the judge's feeling that he is trying to act a decent part in a very depraved play. Ruminative and philosophical, the novel's drama is an interior one: it shows the judge's effort to preserve "inner freedom, which is the prerogative of anyone called upon to judge."

OPPENHEIM, E[DWARD] PHILLIPS (1866–1946) Oppenheim was similar to his fellow Englishman, Edgar WALLACE, in his massive production, though he was a lesser writer than Wallace and concentrated primarily on the spy thriller. Oppenheim was a flamboyant man who was made rich by his 115 novels and dozens of other books.

Oppenheim's father ran a leather business, in which the author continued to work until the age of forty, though by then he had published many books. His parents helped to fund the publication of his first novel. Oppenheim worked in the Ministry of Information during World War I. Shortly after the war, he published his most famous book, *The Great Impersonation* (1920), an absurd story about a German, Baron von Ragastein, who impersonates his Eton schoolmate, an English aristocrat. The book is set in East Africa, but Oppenheim was known for placing his stories in the super-rich enclaves of the Riviera, where he acquired a home in 1922. Oppenheim lived the life of his aristocratic characters—and shared their views on the superiority of monarchism, disparaging socialism and democracy. Oppenheim's stories are proof that while wealth may be fascinating, many of those who have it are not.

The situations of Oppenheim's books are constructed sheerly for entertainment and are frequently fantastic. Some of them are even futuristic, accurately predicting political horrors in the near-term. Oppenheim also wrote an incredible 38 volumes of short stories, several of which were tales of detection in the classic line; these included *The Hon. Algernon Knox, Detective* (1920), *Nicholas Goade, Detective* (1927), and *Slane's Long Shots* (1930). Another collection was *The Ex-Detective* (1933). Oppenheim's two autobiographical works are *My Books and Myself* (1922) and *The Pool of Memory* (1941). The plot of his last book, *Mr. Mirakel* (1943), was indeed miraculous; the hero is a rich man who retreats from the monstrous inhumanity of World War II, setting up an ideal society for himself and his followers in a fantastic Shangri-La.

ORCZY, BARONESS [EMMUSKA MAGDALENA ROSALIA MARIA JOSEFA BARBARA] (1865–1947) Born in Tarna-Örs, Hungary, Baroness Orczy is most remembered for *The Scarlet Pimpernel* (1905), a story told against the background of the French Revolution. It deals with Sir Percy Blakeney, whose secret identity is The Scarlet Pimpernel, a notorious counterrevolutionary who rescues aristocrats and helps them flee the country. The story began as a play (1903) and was then novelized, and later filmed with Leslie Howard playing the publicly supercilious Blakeney. Orczy also wrote several sequels. It was the Baroness's favorite of her works; in her autobiography she claimed that it was inspired by God.

The Baroness's father, Felix Orczy, was a well-known composer, and as a child she socialized with his friends—Wagner, Liszt, Gounod, and Massenet. She herself was a musician and painter, and later married the painter Montagu Barstow. Baron Felix had innovative ideas about agriculture and was driven out of Hungary by his own peasants, who burned his crops and buildings in protest against the introduction of machinery in 1867. Educated in convent schools in Brussels and Paris, the Baroness did not learn English (the language in which she wrote her books) until she was fifteen. She had some success as a painter, attending the Heatherley School of Art and exhibiting at the Royal Academy.

In 1888 (according to Vincent STARRETT), one of the JACK THE RIPPER murders was committed near the Baroness's home in London. That, and the popularity of Sherlock HOLMES, started her thinking about detective stories. Orczy's aristocratic background (she was presented to the Empress of Austria, and her parents were the friends of royalty), reflected in the *Scarlet Pimpernel* and other romances, was suppressed in her mystery stories because she was striving for something different. Her most famous creation was THE OLD MAN IN THE CORNER, a consciously unromantic reaction against Holmes. The Old Man is an ARMCHAIR DETECTIVE who sits in a teashop and discusses crimes while nervously fidgeting.

Orczy created several other less popular detectives who are nonetheless interesting. They include Lady Molly Robertson-Kirk and the lawyer Patrick Mulligan; their adventures are collected in *Lady Molly of Scotland Yard* (1910) and *Skin o' My Tooth* (1928), respectively. In *Castles in the Air* (1921), she returned to the French scene of the Pimpernel stories in the deductions of M. Hector Ratichon. He and his valet Theodor are rather criminal themselves. *Links in the Chain of Life* (1947) is Orczy's autobiography.

OSS Office of Stratetic Services. The forerunner of the CIA, the OSS was formed at the beginning of World War II.

OTANI, SUPERINTENDENT TETSUO A Japanese detective created by James MELVILLE. Otani follows the example of Charlie CHAN—another Asian detective invented by a Westerner—in being round, smiling, and friendly, a type that is a reaction to another, more objectionable one: the inscrutable, cruel, and unsmiling "oriental" of an earlier period of popular fiction. The Superintendent is also intelligent, flexible, and open-minded. Otani is getting on in middle age; he and his wife Hanae have a grown daughter, a former political activist married to another political activist. They also have a son. Otani is the head of police in Kobe and has many subordinates, though Jiro Kimura and "Ninja" Noguchi are the ones who play a role in the novels. Melville includes a good deal of information about Japanese culture in the books, but without pedantry.

Hanae is an important part of the series—she takes a leading role, for example, in *The Ninth Netsuke* (1982). In that book she is involved, reluctantly, in her husband's investigation of the murder of a Filipino "hostess"—essentially an expensive prostitute—found dead in a hotel in Kobe that rents rooms by the hour. It is Hanae who finds the major clue, a small netsuke, or carved ivory figurine. A museum in Kyoto identifies it as one of a rare set depicting the Greek muses, and Otani causes a scandal when he refuses to turn it over because it is evidence. He is called on the carpet in Tokyo, during which time his wife is kidnapped. Otani's reaction is unusual for a detective story: he suffers a kind of breakdown, and is quite passive in the rest of the story and during its solution. *A Haiku for Hanae* (1989) is another case in which she has a major role.

The Chrysanthemum Chain (1982) is one of the many cases that involve Westerners. The English professor James Murrow is found dead in his home. Murrow was tall, blond, gay, and dressed in the Japanese style—in fact, he lived austerely, emulating medieval Japanese culture, even though he was extremely rich. His many connections in the Japanese world, including the government, reveal complexities of secrecy and corruption, which Otani unravels in tandem with the British consulate. Suspense is kept up through further murder and threats, but Otani seems old, and the pace lags a bit.

One of the best Otani books is *Death of a Daimyo* (1984). In alternating scenes, the novel describes Otani's visit to England—his first trip ever outside Japan—and the sometimes comical activities of his subordinates in his absence. Otani attends the dedication at Cambridge University of a new Japanese studies institute, at which a major Japanese businessman is killed. Meanwhile back home, the crime boss Yamomoto is dying; while a war of succession threatens, the old gang leader makes obscure and perhaps insane references to a "silent partner" and the renovation of the Empire. Cultural comparisons are more prominent in this book for obvious reasons, though Hanae's reactions to them make her come across as not very bright.

BIBLIOGRAPHY Novels: *The Wages of Zen* (1979), *A Sort of Samurai* (1981), *Sayonara, Sweet Amaryllis* (1983), *The Death Ceremony* (1985), *Go Gently, Gaijin* (1986), *Kimono for a Corpse* (1987), *The Reluctant Ronin* (1988), *The Bogus Buddha* (1990).

OUABAIN A toxic substance made from the leaves and bark of an African tree. Ouabain is a glucoside that paralyzes the muscles and causes death by heart failure. It was traditionally used by tribesmen to coat the tips of poisoned arrows for warfare and hunting. Like CURARE, it must be introduced directly into the bloodstream of the victim, and thus simple ingestion is not fatal. See THE AFRICAN POISON MURDERS (1939).

OUR MAN IN HAVANA (1958) One of the works Graham GREENE referred to as his "entertainments," this novel was based on Greene's visits to Cuba just prior to the communist revolution. It is a farcical spoof of espionage, but with a sting in the end. While WORMOLD does not take his ridiculous spy contacts seriously, it is precisely the contacts' loss of touch with reality that allows them to treat his fictional communiqués as if they were real, which leads to tragedy.

OUTSIDER IN AMSTERDAM (1975) In the first novel in the GRIJPSTRA and de Gier series by Jan Willem VAN DE WETERING, the two detectives are more intriguing and entertaining than in any other book. Grijpstra is an adjutant and de Gier a sergeant, and though neither is exactly young they are far from the old curmudgeons they would later become. Grijpstra is fat and badly dressed, while de Gier is handsome, curly-headed, and unmarried. The case begins with the apparent suicide of Piet Verboom, founder of the Hindist Society, a religious community based on Piet's smattering of Hindu and Buddhist philosophy—but whose real purpose seems to have been to make money for Piet through the restaurant, bar, and gift shop. Only a small bruise on his head indicates that Piet may have had help in hanging himself—or it may have been inflicted by a young member of the society whom he had got pregnant (she threw a book at him). It would be an ordinary, sordid little case were it not for the presence of two persons: Jan Karel van Meteren, a Papuan and former New Guinean policeman who has lived in the Verboom house, and Constanze, Verboom's attractive widow who had already separated from him and moved to Paris. There are few clues, but seventy-five thousand guilders are missing, and Verboom has inexplicably been importing huge quantities of miso soup paste.

Grijpstra and de Gier do not behave like typical policemen; Grijpstra keeps a drum set in his office and is sometimes accompanied by de Gier on the flute while they mull over clues. Grijpstra expounds a philosophy of society even more cynical than that encountered in the novels of Nicholas FREELING; he divides the population into the "bounders" or bosses, the "idiots," and the untrustworthy "idealists." The bounders run the government and economy and tell everyone what to think, and the idiots eat it up: "there is this type of idiot and that type of idiot but their skins are always gray, they have a variety of illnesses, they take a holiday once a year, they drive small secondhand cars that break down continuously and they buy the expensive rubbish the bounders sell to them." De Gier, on the other hand, is an ecstatic, living in a world of constantly changing, beautiful impressions: "De Gier believed in a miraculous surrealist world and he didn't want to give up his faith." Such detection as occurs is unobtrusive, even accidental, but van de Wetering delivers a few twists and surprises in the end.

PACKARD, FRANK L[UCIUS] (1877–1942) Born in Montreal of American parents, Frank Packard studied at McGill University and later returned to the United States and worked as a civil engineer. He wrote two dozen books, most of them mystery and crime stories; the ones for which he is famous feature Jimmie DALE, a RAFFLES-type of thief living in New York City. Among Packard's other non-series novels is *The Miracle Man* (1914), about a faith healer and con man.

PAGE, MARCO (pseudonym of Harry Kurnitz, 1909–1968) Harry Kurnitz was born in New York City and attended the University of Pennsylvania. He stayed on in Philadelphia and wrote for the *Philadelphia Record.* His first mystery was *Fast Company* (1937), in which an antiquarian bookseller and his wife act as sleuths in the case of a murdered bookstore owner. Kurnitz was a book collector himself. After the novel was published, Kurnitz went to Hollywood and wrote the screenplay for the movie version, which was filmed in 1938. He stayed in Hollywood and eventually wrote scripts for more than forty films. Among them was *Shadow of the Thin Man* (1941), one in the hit series of movies based on Dashiell Hammett's Nick and Nora CHARLES.

During his journalistic career, Kurnitz was a book reviewer and music critic, and he used artistic backgrounds to advantage in his mystery novels. *The Shadowy Third* (1946) is set in a concert hall; Kurnitz himself had studied violin. *Reclining Figure* (1952) concerns ART and forgery. Also a dramatist, Kurnitz wrote a stage version of *Reclining Figure* in 1954. *Invasion of Privacy* (1955) was set against the background of the movie business. A young woman who has written the story for a film gets into trouble when it turns out that the script mirrors a real killing. All of Kurnitz's books are deftly written and have comic and humorous elements. His dry sense of humor is perhaps best illustrated by his own biography of himself: "Harry Kurnitz, later Marco Page, later the fabulously rich Count Pierre Bezhukov, was born in New York City in 1909 on the site of what is now Knickerbocker Village, a housing project for low-income families which was then a slum for low-income families. A few years later, when Philadelphia was opened for settlement, his parents were in one of the first stampedes and settled on a tract of land approximately 28' X 97' in the northeastern district. After being educated fitfully in and around the public schools, including hitches at the U. of P. and Drexel Institute (whatever that is), he worked on papers in Philadelphia and New York and wrote fiction, most it for pulp magazines. He finally outwitted the depression in 1937 by selling a mystery novel, *Fast Company,* to MGM. He was given a four-week contract, later stretched to nine years for good behavior."

PALE CRIMINAL, THE (1990) A novel by Philip KERR, the second in his trilogy about Germany during the NAZI era. *The Pale Criminal* is set in 1938 against the background of the Sudeten crisis and the *Kristalnacht* pogrom against the Jews. In the first case, a rich woman pays private investigator Bernie Gunther to find a man who is blackmailing her son because of his homosexuality. Gunther is then compelled by SS General Heydrich to rejoin the police force in order to catch a killer who is murdering young Aryan maidens. Meanwhile, the anti-Semitic press tries to bring about large-scale violence against Jews. Gunther is aware of the irony that he is being made to investigate murders by "policemen" who are murderers themselves, and who only want to forestall an anti-Jewish riot because it will be expensive for the German companies that insure Jewish properties. The mood of the book is of impending disaster (though Kerr manages to suppress his own hindsight, so that Gunther really does not seem to know what is coming), and the sarcasm of the first book in the trilogy is no longer maintainable. Gunther knows that justice has become a joke, and even his own effort to strike a blow for it forces him into illegality. See BERLIN NOIR.

PALMER, HARRY The name given as a result of the film version of THE IPCRESS FILE (1962) to the anonymous narrator of several spy novels by Len DEIGHTON. Palmer is a "grammar school boy" (i.e., a product of public education), unlike his bosses and co-workers, who include the incompetent young Chilcott-Oates ("Chico"). An agent during World War II, Palmer also has a strong aversion to military types. He makes up for his lack of upper-class credentials by his cleverness, efficiency, and sometimes brutal honesty. As a character, his anonymity helps him to behave like a Demosthenes, reflecting the personalities and phonies around him, whose weaknesses he confronts with humor and sarcasm. Not surprisingly, he often gets on better with his enemies than with his friends (enemies don't betray you, but are honest opponents). Palmer's warmest relationship is with Jean, his secretary. They behave like two people parodying two people having an affair. A cynic who is ruthlessly honest with himself, he advises would-be spies, "Take a tip from the professionals; do it just for the money."

In *The Ipcress File,* Palmer temporarily becomes head of the organization W.O.O.C.(P.). One of his constant preoccupations is why his paychecks from his new job are so slow in coming. These touches of the mundane are a Deighton hallmark. In *Horse Under Water* (1963), the agent's last thought is to worry about being charged for diving equipment he used in a Navy course he took at the beginning of his mission. THE BILLION-DOLLAR BRAIN (1966) is one of his best exploits.

BIBLIOGRAPHY Novels: *Funeral in Berlin* (1964), *An Expensive Place to Die* (1967), *Spy Story* (1974), *Catch a Falling Star* (1976; British title *Twinkle, Twinkle, Little Spy*).

PALMER, STUART (1905–1968) The Wisconsin-born Stuart Palmer was an extremely lucky writer who achieved instant success. He attended the Art Institute of Chicago and the University of Wisconsin, and, after a series of jobs ranging from iceman to ad man, he wrote *The Penguin Pool Murder* (1931), the first of the Hildegarde WITHERS mysteries. The movie version, filmed the following year, ensured Palmer's success and gave him an entree to screenwriting. In recognition of his luck, Palmer made the penguin his personal charm and accumulated a collection of penguin statuettes.

Palmer's other series detective was Howie Rook, a reporter (as had been Palmer himself), but he only survived for two books, *Unhappy Hooligan* (1956) and *Rook Takes a Knight* (1958). Palmer's many screenplays included some for THE FALCON series, including one in collaboration with Craig RICE. Together they wrote a series of stories featuring the odd couple of Hildegarde Withers and Rice's John J. MALONE.

PAMPLEMOUSSE, MONSIEUR A character in a series of "gastronomic mysteries" by the children's book author Michael BOND. Pamplemousse (his name means "grapefruit") works undercover for *The Guide,* a French culinary guidebook. From this unlikely beginning, Bond creates absurd plots in which someone is always trying to kill Pamplemousse. In the first novel, *Monsieur Pamplemousse* (1983), while investigating the Hotel-Restaurant La Langostine, he tries the house specialty: a whole chicken sewed up and cooked inside a pig bladder. But instead of a chicken, the bladder contains a human head. The books are intended to be humorous, and so Pamplemousse strays here and there stirring up trouble in far-fetched situations. In *Monsieur Pamplemousse Aloft* (1989) he is invited to plan a gala meal for the first voyage of a new blimp, to carry both the British and French heads of state. A murder occurs at a gathering of famous mystery writers in *Monsieur Pamplemousse Rests His Case* (1991). *Monsieur Pamplemousse Investigates* (1990) involves an attack on the offices of *Le Guide* itself, combining piranhas and computer hacking. Pamplemousse's assistant is a dog named Pommes Frites ("french fries"), a real sleuth-hound who often has to rescue his master.

BIBLIOGRAPHY Novels: *Monsieur Pamplemousse and the Secret Mission* (1984), *Monsieur Pamplemousse on the Spot* (1986), *Monsieur Pamplemousse Takes the Cure* (1987), *Monsieur Pamplemousse Stands Firm* (1992), *Monsieur Pamplemousse On Location* (1992), *Monsieur Pamplemousse Takes the Train* (1993).

PAPERBACK ORIGINALS Books that appear for the first time in paperback without ever having been issued between hard covers. The practice of printing paperback originals began in the fifties and expanded the market for mystery and detective fiction. Authors such as John D. MACDONALD, Henry KANE, Stephen MARLOWE, and Richard S. PRATHER thrived on this market.

PARADE OF COCKEYED CREATURES, A; OR, DID SOMEONE MURDER OUR WANDERING BOY? (1967; repr 1986) A novel by George BAXT, one of those not concerning Pharaoh LOVE. It is memorable for its depiction of New York's East Village in the 1960s—cafés, bad poetry, and heroin—and for the construction of a mystery around the disappearance of a boy who has loyal, if weird, friends.

Detective Max Van Larson shows Baxt deliberately flaunting the conventions of big-city cop fiction of the previous decades: Van Larson is well-dressed, likes poetry and classical music, and keeps the pencils on his desk in a Toby jug. His partner is Sylvia Plotkin, who is not a cop but the high school teacher of the missing boy, Tippy Blaney, who disappeared after asking everyone he knew for $500. Seventeen-year-old Tippy was upset, having learned the truth about his parentage and that he was about to become a parent himself. Van Larson views Tippy's father, a nasty antiques dealer, as a "toad"; the mother, Wilma, comes on to Van Larson. Among the other characters in this milieu of young hippies and middle-aged losers is Madame Vilna, who reads poetry and speaks with a Yiddish accent, and Tippy's friend Ashley, who likes cemeteries and collects obituaries. Fittingly for the time of this period piece, all the characters are judged in terms of their ability to love.

PARAQUAT An herbicide used in weed killer; extremely toxic, it is usually very diluted. Paraquat became famous in the late seventies and early eighties when it was used by the U.S. government to discourage marijuana production. Head shops responded by selling test kits to enable end-users to determine whether the drugs they were taking were "safe." Paraquat causes violent internal pain and distress, though symptoms may take days to appear. Death results from damage to internal organs. See A SHOCK TO THE SYSTEM (1984).

PARETSKY, SARA (1947–) Sara Paretsky has written that on New Year's Eve, 1979, she vowed to write a mystery novel that year. Although she missed her deadline, and it took another year to find a publisher, the book, *Indemnity Only* (1982), successfully launched the V. I. WARSHAWSKI series. The novel was dedicated to Stuart KAMINSKY, with whom Paretsky studied and who helped her to get it into print.

Paretsky was born in Iowa and studied at the University of Chicago, where she earned a Ph.D. in history. She had been working in Chicago as a business writer and in direct mail for an insurance company when she decided to write the novel. These experiences have fueled the plots of her stories. Warshawski's cases all involve a business and finance background, but unlike that other insurance-oriented female investigator, Sue Grafton's Kinsey MILLHONE, Warshawski is firmly in the HARD-BOILED tradition. The business angle sometimes involves old-fashioned industry and the working class, not just paper-pushing service industry professionals. Of all the women who became well-known mystery writers in the 1980s, Paretsky is probably the most traditional in style. The subject matter, however, is often topical, as in *Bitter Medicine* (1987), written at a time of right-wing terrorist bombings of abortion clinics. Warshawski becomes involved in the case of a sixteen-year-old girl who is a patient of her friend, Lotty Herschel, a Viennese refugee from the Nazis, memories of whom are evoked by the destruction of her medical clinic. The book puts across a pro-choice message, but the pace is meandering (unlike, for example, the 1984 novel *Deadlock*). The main weakness is that the characters fail to evoke much sympathy: the villains are merely pathetic or stereotypical, and the only hero is Warshawski.

The effort to be timely is even more marked in *Tunnel Vision* (1994), which deals with abusive relationships, runaway children, and the broken family. In addition, Warshawski is having a relationship with an African American policeman and is helping a homeless family living in the basement of her building. The overload of subplots straining after significance and the corresponding lack of attention to the actual writing is a problem not unique to Paretsky. Her evocation of Chicago itself is well-done.

With *Ghost Country* (1998), Paretsky has branched out from if not necessarily given up on Warshawski. This novel is set in the world of the homeless of Chicago and concerns what appears to be a bizarre miracle and the appearance of a strange woman in the city. The consequences of these two odd events are examined through their effects on three women, but the ramifications extend, as usual, to the economic and political circles that control the city.

PARIS, CHARLES An actor-sleuth in a series of novels by Simon BRETT. At over a dozen books, the Paris novels, like other "concept" series, have reached the point of diminishing returns, but the author's knowledge of the British radio, television, and film business seems inexhaustible. The books are neither classic nor realistic and appeal mainly to people who cannot get enough of these subjects. Paris is a second-rate actor and hence almost always out of work; when he gets a paying job, somebody always ends up dying—in *Situation Tragedy* (1981), when Paris is cast in a sitcom, a lot of people die. Middle-aged, Paris has been married to his wife Frances for many years, though they continually fight and he keeps leaving her, so that they spend more time apart than together. Paris womanizes during his time off; he also drinks huge quantities of scotch. Brett's narrative style is brokenly chatty, with excess information about characters' artistic resumes, affairs, foibles, and entertainment histories swamping the occasional memorable phrase or line. *A Comedian Dies* (1979) begins with a scene as interminable as the string of variety acts Paris is forced to watch. After a performer is electrocuted through his guitar, Paris gets to exercise his "hobby" of sleuthing. *Murder Unprompted* (1982) gives him his biggest theatrical break yet, with the usual results. In *Sicken and So Die* (1995), Paris and Frances are back together once again and the has-been (or never-was) actor lands the role of Sir Toby Belch in Shakespeare's *Twelfth Night*.

BIBLIOGRAPHY Novels: *Cast, in Order of Disappearance* (1975), *So Much Blood* (1976), *Star Trap* (1977), *An Amateur Corpse* (1978), *The Dead Side of the Mike* (1980), *Murder in the Title* (1983), *Not Dead, Only Resting* (1984), *Dead Giveaway* (1986), *What Bloody Man Is That?* (1987), *A Series of Murders* (1989), *Corporate Bodies* (1991), *A Reconstructed Corpse* (1993), *Dead Room Farce* (1998).

Short Stories: *A Box of Tricks.*

PARIS GREEN Paris Green is a poison used as an insecticide and fungicide. Its green color comes from its copper content. The chemical is produced by combining copper acetate and arsenious oxide, thereby creating a copper-arsenic salt. Paris Green has also been used as a protective paint on ships.

PARKER In a series of novels written under the pseudonym Richard Stark, Donald WESTLAKE chronicled the adventures of a criminal anti-hero named Parker. Neither a NAPOLEON OF CRIME nor a gentleman thief like RAFFLES, Parker is an outgrowth of the NOIR hero of the forties and fifties. As we follow Parker's trail of robberies and collateral crimes (including homicide), we are enticed to hope that he gets away with it. A pure protagonist, we root for him not because he is good but because he is the center of attention.

The world depicted in the Parker novels is realistic, even if the CAPERS sometimes are not. His associates range from low-intelligence thugs to regular "mechanics" who have at least a sense of honor among thieves. Parker has only one name and virtually no personal life to speak of. He first appeared in *The Hunter* (1962), a revenge tale in which he has been double-crossed not only by his cohorts, but by his wife. The first novel was made into the film *Point Blank* (1967), and several other adaptations have been based on the series. In *The Man With the Getaway Face* (1963), Parker has plastic surgery in order to change his appearance and sever his connection to past crimes. For someone who says he kills only when necessary and without passion, Parker seems to spend a lot of time paying people back; *The Outfit* (1963) has him going up against a mob once again to settle a score. At the time of *The Mourner* (1963), one of his weirdest crimes, Parker is living in hotels as Charles Willis. He is blackmailed by a collector into stealing an alabaster statuette that comes from a fifteenth-century French tomb. The collector promises Parker fifty thousand dollars and the return of a gun Parker had used in a killing. Parker also appears less sympathetic than he would later in the series; in *The Mourner* he ties a woman up and tortures her with matches.

Like real criminals, Parker has a lot of trouble with unreliable confederates. In *The Seventh* (1964) someone takes off with Parker's share of the proceeds stolen at a football stadium. *The Score* (1964) involves a crazy caper similar to those of Westlake's DORTMUNDER books. Parker is approached by a man named Edgars, who convinces him that they can seal off and rob an entire city, the mining town of Copper Canyon, North Dakota. Parker assembles a team of a dozen crooks, including safecrackers, truck drivers, and lookout men. One of them, Alan GROFIELD, is a wise guy who acts in summer stock productions when he isn't pulling heists. Parker's apprehensions about Edgars, who seems to have obscure personal reasons for the robbery, are fully borne out when events inevitably depart from the script.

Parker's story is so realistic that he eventually finds another woman, Claire, and settles down in New Jersey. He disappeared after *Butcher's Moon* (1974). Almost twenty-five years later Westlake revived him in *Comeback* (1997). At this point, he is living by a lake in northern New Jersey with Claire. Although Parker does not seem to have aged at all, the world around him has been appropriately updated: he and his gang again hit a stadium, this time making off with the gate from a rally by a crooked televangelist. As usual, the people who are after Parker are far less sympathetic than he is, and include a sadistic police lieutenant as well as some pathetically inept young punks. His single combat with a turncoat in an abandoned house that seems to be modeled on Frank Lloyd Wright's "Falling Water" is epic. In *Backflash* (1998), the second of the new Parker novels, the target of his score is a gambling ship in the Hudson River.

BIBLIOGRAPHY Novels: *The Handle* (1966; British title *Run Lethal*), *The Jugger* (1965), *The Rare Coin Score* (1967), *The Green Eagle Score* (1967), *The Black Ice Score* (1968), *The Sour Lemon Score* (1969), *Deadly Edge* (1971), *Slayground* (1971), *Plunder Squad* (1972).

PARKER, ROBERT B[ROWN] (1932–) Robert B. Parker wrote his dissertation on Raymond CHANDLER and Dashiell HAMMETT, and these two writers are the model for his series of novels about a Boston private detective named SPENSER. Parker has identified himself so closely with Chandler that he was chosen by the Chandler estate to finish the last MARLOWE novel, *Poodle Springs* (1989).

Born in Springfield, Massachusetts, Parker has spent most of his life in the state and has been teaching at Boston's Northeastern University since 1968. After serving in the army he worked as a technical writer and in advertising before returning to school and earning a Ph.D. (1971). The first Spenser novel, *The Godwulf Manuscript*, appeared two years later (see BOOKS). Parker considered *Mortal Stakes* (1975) to be his best (see BASEBALL); this opinion appears to be confirmed by the critics, who have noted a general falling off as the series progresses. *Mortal Stakes* is satisfying because Spenser spends most of his time pounding the pavement rather than people's faces, though there is one stupendous pummeling. On another occasion Spenser's police friend, Marty Quirk, essentially accuses him of execution-style murder (but committed, fortunately, outside Quirk's territory). Spenser is a tough guy, certainly, and the books have a good deal of violence in them, especially the later ones. But despite the comparisons with Chandler and Hammett, Parker uses devices that neither of the earlier two writers would have touched. *The Godwulf Manuscript* uses a plot device that would have been perfect for a mystery of the GOLDEN AGE—the theft of a medieval manuscript (the crime, however, is totally pointless).

Spenser also has too many sterling qualities: a former boxer (he has had his nose broken eight times), policeman, and Korean War veteran, he is also sensitive, a "gourmet" chef, well-read (and given to quotation), and a pop philosopher along the lines of Travis MCGEE. The earlier books are the strongest; *Promised Land* (1976), which involves unscrupulous real estate speculators on Cape Cod, won an EDGAR. In *The Judas Goat* (1978), however, qualities of the THRILLER—primarily, unbelievability—crept in. Spenser is hired to avenge the murder of the Dixon family by powerful Hugh Dixon, who was paralyzed in the same terrorist attack. He offers Spenser $25,000 per head for the nine terrorists (plus expenses). Spenser goes to London, places an advertisement in the paper to lure the terrorists, and when two show up, he shoots them. And so it goes: he imports his friend Hawk to help him, meets a blonde female sadomasochist terrorist with redeeming qualities, and has to go to Montreal to save the Olympic games (and have the final showdown). LOOKING FOR RACHEL WALLACE (1980) and *Early Autumn* (1981), on the other hand, have very simple plots and little detection, relying instead on dialogue and exploration of character. In the former case, humor carries the day, while the latter book is a *Boys Own Paper* sort of story, in which the Ways of Spenser are solemnly inculcated to a shiftless teenager, Paul Giacomin, whom Spenser unofficially adopts. Through boxing, weight lifting, and Spenserian lessons in self-reliance, Paul's backbone is stiffened and he decides to become a ballet dancer, to the horror of his repulsive, selfish parents.

Taming a Seahorse (1986), in which Spenser tries to rescue a young prostitute, is one of the better later novels, though Parker's writing is becoming more and more offhand. It shows, however, that the author is at his best when he does not stray from the local scale that Hammett and Chandler used so effectively. It also brings back April Kyle, a prostitute who Spenser helped in *Ceremony* (1982). In that book, Spenser had been brought into the case of a runaway girl (April) by his girlfriend, Susan Silverman, who was the guidance counselor at her school. Like many of Spenser's cases, it becomes a personal crusade. Parker is not writing against the pressure of reality; Spenser acts out his knight errancy to a sweetheart audience that seems to include the Boston police and the criminal underworld. He makes grand gestures and waltzes into danger with the sangfroid of an actor who knows that death is scripted and he will come out all right. After committing a virtual double homicide, he is allowed to go home by the police with no questions asked. (In a strange counterpoint to his molding of Paul Giacomin, Spenser "accepts" in *Ceremony* that April's only possibility in life is to be a whore, and decides to make her a well-paid one.) Some of the recent books definitely taste canned rather than fresh: *Chance* (1996) is about the search for the missing wife of a mobster.

Parker has also written non-series novels, including *All Our Yesterdays* (1994), a historical crime novel focusing on an Irish-American family. He wrote a sequel to THE BIG SLEEP entitled *Perchance to Dream* (1990). More recently, Parker has announced a new series detective, Jesse Stone, though only the first book has been written (a sign of the times, perhaps). In *Night Passage* (1997), Stone is a washed-up ten-year veteran of the Los Angeles Police Department who has resigned after being found drunk while on duty. His wife, Jenn, had begun sleeping with a two-bit film producer. Stone is drunk again at his interview for the job of chief of police in the town of Paradise, Massachusetts, on Boston's North Shore, but oddly he is hired anyway. Soon after taking up his post, Stone's predecessor is blown up by a bomb, and Stone has an altercation with a thug named Jo Jo Genest and meets the gung-ho selectman and banker who runs the town. Except for an unbelievable white supremacist militiaman, the characters are realistic.

Abandoning Spenser is the best thing Parker could have done for his writing. Stone is tough, but does not advertise it; he drinks, but does not philosophize or agonize about it; he is intelligent, but does not try to be witty like Spenser. As a result, the novel is leaner and more ballasted than the later Spensers. It remains to be seen whether the plots can be tightened and whether the Stone series will fall into the PROCEDURAL or regional subgenre.

PARODY Any genre that adheres to conventions is open to parody, particularly of its greatest figures. Sherlock HOLMES parody and pastiche is an entire subgenre. Robert L. FISH's Yiddish pastiche of Sherlock Holmes, whom he renamed Schlock Homes, is one of the most famous (the character lived at 221B Bagel Street). Schlock Homes was not the only, or the funniest, parodic perversion of the master's name: there have also been stories about Sherlaw Kombs (by Robert BARR), Hemlock Jones (Bret HARTE), Holmlock Shears (Maurice LEBLANC), Shamrock Jolnes (O. Henry), and Picklock Holes (R. C. Lehmann). Mark TWAIN also made fun of Holmes.

Further jests at Holmes's expense and pastiches continue to be produced, including *A Three Pipe Problem* (1975) by Julian SYMONS; Nicholas Meyers's *The Seven Percent Solution* (1974), which made much of Holmes's drug use; and Loren ESTLEMAN's two books, *Sherlock Holmes versus Dracula* (1978) and *Dr. Jekyll and Mr. Holmes* (1979). Manly Wade WELLMAN united Sherlock Holmes with Orson Welles. *The Game Is Afoot: Parodies, Pastiches and Ponderings of Sherlock Holmes* (1994), edited by Marvin Kaye, offers an extensive selection of such writings.

Notable non-Holmes parodies include *Parody Party* (1936; repr. 1970) and "Greedy Night" by E. C. BENTLEY, parodies of Dorothy L. SAYERS; and S. J. Perelman's send-up of Raymond CHANDLER, "Farewell, My Lovely Appetizer." Bruce Jay Friedman's *The Dick* (1970), with its ludicrous protagonist, is a parody of all cop novels. John L. BREEN's parodies include one of Agatha CHRISTIE, "Hercule Poirot in the Year 2010" (1975). Another accomplished parodist was Stephen LEACOCK.

Christie parodied her own and other people's detectives in the short story collection *Partners in Crime* (1929). Tuppence and Tommy BERESFORD are hired to run the International Detective Agency as a cover for investigating Bolshevik activity. They do, however, have to take real cases and act like detectives, so Tommy comes up with the idea of laying in a library of mystery classics and using them as guides. The types of cases that come in include a Holmes, a Dr. THORNDYKE, and a Father BROWN.

Kingsley AMIS's *Colonel Sun* (1968), which he published under the pseudonym Robert Markham, is a pastiche of the most famous figure of spy fiction, James BOND.

PARTRIDGE, ERIC [HONEYWOOD] (1894–1979) Born in New Zealand, Eric Partridge became a philologist and lexicographer and an expert in American and British SLANG. Going back to original sources in newspapers, stories, criminological annals, and journals, he compiled exhaustive but very engrossing dictionaries, including *A Dictionary of Slang and Unconventional English* (1937; rev 1970; 8th ed. 1984), which was the first scholarly work on the subject. His *Dictionary of the Underworld* (1949; rev 1961) describes the etymology of criminal jargon stretching back for centuries, and has provided a source book for mystery writers as well as readers.

PATSY A sucker, an easy mark. According to PARTRIDGE, the word is an abbreviation of Patrick; as an affectionate diminutive, it gives the impression (false) that everything is OK.

PAUL, BARBARA (1931–) Barbara Paul (the name is a pseudonym) was an English and drama teacher before she became well known as an author. Paul's theater background was reflected in *The Fourth Wall* (1979), a mystery. Paul later started two mystery series in the same year (1984), one about New York police officer Marian LARCH and the other a group of CELEBRITY MYSTERIES featuring opera singers Enrico Caruso and Geraldine Farrar as detectives. She has also written several non-series mysteries, including *But He Was Already Dead When I Got There* (1986).

Paul was born in Kentucky and had a wide-ranging education: Bowling Green State, University of Redlands (California), studies abroad in Norway and Austria, and the University of Pittsburgh (Ph.D., 1969). Like Amanda CROSS, Paul was well established in her academic career before she turned to the mystery novel for diversion, and had a remarkable success. Paul also uses such literary techniques as multiple narrators, for example in *The Renewable Virgin* (1984), the first Marian Larch mystery.

Paul is fond of subplots. Often in the Larch series she adds romantic asides as well as copious material on her protagonist's psychological and emotional reactions to the crimes she investigates. She also brings in Larch's friend Kelly Ingram, a rising Broadway star, for diversion. Somewhat improbably, Larch also enlists her friend's help (and her acting talents) in catching killers. Larch is entangled in departmental sexism and politically corrects her colleagues.

Paul's celebrity mysteries are much weaker than the Larch novels. *A Cadenza for Caruso* (1984) might have been a better book without a murder—the impetus for Caruso's foolishly playing detective and appearing a bit child-like into the bargain. The background, however, is factual; the story takes place during the 1910 production of Puccini's *La Fanciulla del West*, based on David Belasco's hit play *The Girl of the Golden West* (1905). Both men are characters in the novel, and Puccini, who is being blackmailed, is also a murder suspect. *In-laws and Outlaws* (1990), another non-series novel, is Paul's worst work to date. Set in the wealthy Decker enclave on Martha's Vineyard, its five murders fail to redeem its heavy-handed plot and caricatures of people—two of whom are identical twins. Gillian Decker, the narrator, is a bumbling amateur who finally finds the killer (long after the reader has copped on) through a tortured process of questioning her family members. That the family wines, dines, sails, windsurfs, and has a good time after the brutal deaths of three of four children and the family patriarch is ridiculous, the events themselves extraneous and dull.

PAUL, ELLIOT [HAROLD] (1891–1958) Elliot Paul was an important figure in American letters before he became known as a mystery author. His early life follows the pattern of other members of the "lost generation," a term coined by Gertrude Stein for those who came of age during World War I. Paul was born in Malden, Massachusetts, and worked as a librarian and journalist in Boston, then spent a period "roughing it" in Idaho and Wyoming. When the war came, he served as a sergeant in the artillery, then stayed on in Europe as a journalist and writer among the expatriate community, which included Stein, HEMINGWAY, and FITZGERALD. Along with Eugene Jolas (1894–1952), Paul was one of the founders of the avant-garde journal *transition,* which published Stein, Hemingway, e. e. cummings, and portions of JOYCE's *Work in Progress*—later to be known as *Finnegans Wake.* Paul himself was writing literary novels that achieved a select audience and reputation; they included *Indelible* (1922) and *Imperturbe* (1924).

Paul spent a number of years on one of the Balearic islands, which led to his most famous book, *The Life and Death of a Spanish Town* (1937), about the destruction of a town by fascist forces during the Spanish Civil War. In *The Last Time I Saw Paris* (1942), Paul wrote nostalgically of Paris before the German occupation in a series of reminiscences. Between these two books, his most popular, he began to write mysteries. In *The Mysterious Mickey Finn; or, Murder at the Café du Dôme* (1939), Paul introduced the character Homer EVANS. These mysteries were comic, even burlesque; like his fellow New Englander, Phoebe Atwood TAYLOR, Paul combined bizarre and eccentric characters with outrageous situations. Evans is an expatriate in Paris, like the author himself. One has to wonder whether Paul's books inspired Matthew HEAD.

"PAVILION ON THE LINKS, THE" (1882) A long story by Robert Louis STEVENSON. The narrator, Frank Cassilis, returns to a desolate area of the Scottish coast and the estate of Northmour, a volatile and even brutish friend with whom he had quarreled. While camping near the house on the links—a Scottish word indicating not a golf course but sand hills overgrown with turf—Cassilis sees a schooner land a number of trunks and three mysterious passengers. His curiosity aroused, he braves the dangers of quicksand, revolutionaries, and his former friend. The love triangle is handled with all the melodrama of romantic suspense.

PEABODY, AMELIA A detective and archaeologist in books by Elizabeth PETERS, set in the late nineteenth century. In the first book, CROCODILE ON THE SANDBANK (1975), Amelia is traveling through Egypt and stumbles on a mystery. It is also the book in which she meets her future husband, Dr. Radcliffe Emerson, a fellow Egyptologist. *Crocodile* is the best of the books, partly because it predates the onset of the saccharine domestic scene, and more importantly because of the birth of the couple's son Ramses, an obnoxious little genius who blots the later books.

When she first appears, Peabody is thirty-one years old. She describes herself as "plain," but she intends to break out of the role of the stereotypical Victorian spinster. Her father, a scholarly man, left her a substantial legacy that enables her to gratify her intellectual interests.

BIBLIOGRAPHY Novels: *Curse of the Pharoaohs* (1981), *The Mummy Case* (1985), *Lion in the Valley* (1986), *The Deeds of the Disturber* (1988), *The Last Camel Died at Noon* (1991), *The Snake, the Crocodile, and the Dog* (1992), *The Hippopatamus Pool* (1996), *Seeing a Large Cat* (1997), *The Ape Who Guards the Balance* (1998), *The Falcon at the Portal* (1999).

PEACEMAKER COLT This revolver, particularly the 1873 model, is the famous one familiar from innumerable Westerns. It was manufactured in .44 caliber and its ammunition could also be fired from the Winchester repeating rifle Model 1873, the gun that "won the West." The Peacemaker Colt was manufactured into the 1940s.

PEARCE, MICHAEL See MAMUR ZAPT, THE.

"PEARLS ARE A NUISANCE" A short story by Raymond CHANDLER. Chandler said that he originally wrote it as a parody of the HARD-BOILED style he was then cultivating, but it was published in *Dime Detective* in 1938. Chandler also used the plot to make fun of the English style of detective story he later criticized in THE SIMPLE ART OF MURDER (1944). The wealthy Walter Gage is convinced by his prim fiancée to try to find old Mrs. Penruddock's pearls; the main suspect is the chauffeur, Henry Eichelberger, who is as huge and brawny as the more cultured Gage. After a knock-down fight, Henry becomes Walter's accomplice in the investigation. Walter narrates a hard-boiled story while apologizing for his anglophile language; Henry, on the other hand, talks like a hard-boiled mug. The contrast leads to some hilarious scenes, as when the two discover their mutual passion for alcohol and go on a bender ("I turned my head, which ached, and saw that Henry Eichelberger was lying beside me in his undershirt and trousers. I then perceived that I also was as lightly attired").

PEARSON, EDMUND (1880–1937) American writer known primarily for his writings on the Lizzie BORDEN case. Pearson first began to write nonfiction about true crime in magazines, notably *The New Yorker* and *Vanity Fair.* His *Studies in Murder* (1924; repr 1938) made his name well known; almost half the book deals with the Borden murders, the rest being given over to other cases, including the Lindbergh kidnapping and the case on which Mary Roberts RINEHART based her novel *The After House* (see MURDER AFLOAT). *More Studies in Murder* followed in 1936. Pearson later treated the Borden case in a book-length study. He also wrote about DR. CRIPPEN, JACK THE RIPPER, and other famous murderers; *Masterpieces of Murder* (1963) is a selection of his essays.

Pearson acknowledged his debt to DE QUINCEY when he said most murders were only worth "a paragraph in a newspaper," while "only two or three times a year, throughout the whole round world, may be discovered an almost flawless gem, meriting the attention of Thomas DE QUINCEY himself."

PECK, JUDGE Judge Ephraim Peabody Peck is one of the recurrent characters in August DERLETH's *Sac Prairie Saga,* a long series of novels and stories, most of which are not mysteries. Peck is a lawyer and former judge in the small town of Sac Prairie (based on the real Sauk City, Wisconsin). He is sixty years old and dresses in the style of an earlier age, with his ubiquitous bowler hat, old frock coat, and blue-black umbrella (the latter article a constant prop of Father BROWN). Peck's long face and "opaque" eyes conceal a sharp intelligence, but he is often described as tired and almost haggard. The novels are written in the third person, but the perception of Peck seems to be that of his friend, Doctor Considine, a heavy-set man with gray hair and a moustache. District Attorney Meyer is another series character.

Derleth's Sac Prairie, to which he devoted such an enormous amount of his creative energy, is a well-realized recreation of an American town in the early part of the twentieth century. The characters have connections to the town and to each other going back generations. But Sac Prairie is no ordinary village, at least where Judge Peck is concerned, because murder strikes often and sometimes in bizarre ways. *The Man on All Fours* (1934) is set in the Senessen mansion, a "gloomy pile locked in the marshes" south of town; in this and in other ways, it is like POE's House of Usher. The mansion was built by Everett Senessen, who went mad before he died. His widow, Gravisa, has lost two sons who also went insane. Dr. Considine is sent for by the matriarch of this menagerie (seventeen relatives and in-laws live in the house) when her son-in-law Roy Horrell becomes "sick." Actually, he has a huge, gaping chest wound, which Gravisa tries to conceal from the doctor—who immediately sends for Judge Peck. Once he is on the scene, Peck's tone and behavior are much like Dr. THORNDYKE's: serious but analytically detached, more thorough than zealous.

Most of the Peck novels were written during the Depression. One book, *Sentence Deferred* (1939), begins with a bank failure that leads to more than hard feelings. The murder element may retain for these novels more interest than other parts of the *Sac Prairie Saga.*

BIBLIOGRAPHY Novels: *Murder Stalks the Family* (1934; British title *Death Stalks the Wakely Family*), *Three Who Died* (1935), *Sign of Fear* (1936), *The Narracong Riddle* (1940), *The Seven Who Waited* (1943), *Mischief in the Lane* (1944), *No Future for Luana* (1945), *Fell Purpose* (1953).

PEDLEY, BEN Stewart STERLING's oddest specialist detective was his first, Chief Fire Marshal Ben Pedley. From his office in the Municipal Building near the Brooklyn Bridge, Pedley controls a network of investigators, tail men who act like forties p.i.'s, and fire officials who hunt down arsonists. The first Pedley novel was *Five Alarm Funeral* (1942) and presents the marshal as surprisingly HARD-BOILED. With "iron-gray" hair and a ruddy complexion, Pedley is a tough guy who sometimes engages in brutality. Here is how he deals with the little arsonist Harry Gooch: "Pedley got a grip in sandy hair, put a hundred and ninety-five pounds of beef behind the jerk which brought Gooch to his toes, flailing wildly with both fists. . . . He slammed Gooch's bony head against the concrete with a jolt that jarred tears into the other's eyes . . . hair came away in the Marshal's hand." Some of the hard-boiled dialogue is very good; on the other hand, Sterling has to come up with involved fire-related plots—like the arsonist mastermind in *Five Alarm Funeral* who insists that the fires be set with a ship's lantern. The accounts of arsonists' methods, burning buildings, and the crooked doings of fire inspectors and public officials all ring true.

BIBLIOGRAPHY Novels: *Where There's Smoke* (1946), *Alarm in the Night* (1949), *Nightmare at Noon* (1951), *The Hinges of Hell* (1955), *Candle for a Corpse* (1957), *Fire on Fear Street* (1958), *Dying Room Only* (1960), *Too Hot to Handle* (1961).

PEEL, SIR ROBERT See BOBBY.

PELECANOS, GEORGE P. (1957–) George Pelecanos was born in Washington, D.C. and has spent his whole life there. His crime and mystery novels show a side of the city not often seen in fiction. Instead of yuppie lawyers, high-powered lobbyists, and politicians of Capitol Hill, Pelecanos writes about "Chocolate City" and Washington's working-class poor and the African American community. In the HARD-BOILED tradition but with even more graphic violence and rough (but realistic) language, his books have received critical acclaim but only recently have attained commercial success. Pelecanos's series detective, Nick Stefanos, starts out as an appliance store PR manager in *A Firing Offense* (1997), in which he is called upon to find a missing boy. Pelecanos himself sold electronics and worked in a shoe store before becoming a writer. He attended the University of Maryland and worked in his father's coffee shop to put himself through school. Later he worked in film production. In other Nick Stefanos novels, such as *Nick's Trip* (1998), the character has become a bartender at The Spot and takes up the occasional case as an unlicensed p.i. Pelecanos's people are believable human beings, even when they are disturbing or repulsive; *King Suckerman* (1997) is about two friends, one Greek and the other black, who run afoul of a gang of sociopathic killers. Set in 1976, it has a cameo appearance by the young Stefanos and is saturated with the author's love of funk, muscle cars, basketball, and the D.C. streets.

PEMBERTON, MAX (1863–1950) English author of mystery and adventure stories, usually involving glamorous upper-class characters. Pemberton was far from a gifted writer, and is little read today. After graduating from university, he tried unsuccessfully to find a teaching job. Instead, he became a journalist on Fleet Street, and then took up the boys' paper *Chums.* Pemberton also wrote for *Cassell's Magazine,* which he edited from 1896 to 1906, and the *Daily Mail.* In *Cassell's,* which was a leading magazine in the mystery field, Pemberton published early work by R. Austin FREEMAN, Clifford ASHDOWN, and William LEQUEUX.

Pemberton's romanticism and love of the new—planes, automobiles, and steam ships—were boyish in themselves. His novels about Captain Black showed the influence of STEVENSON. In *The Iron Pirate* (1893), the technological marvel is a gas-powered ironclad capable of defeating all the navies of the world.

Pemberton's mystery stories include *The Man Who Drove the Car* (1910), written from the viewpoint of a chauffeur. His most strange character may have been Corinne de Montesson, who devotes her fortune to saving repentant criminals from a life of crime while wreaking vengeance on recidivists. *Jewel Mysteries I Have Known* (1894) is a collection of short stories.

Although his stories are sentimental and to many unbearably romantic, he had a gift for adventure and sometimes for powerful evocations of danger, as in *White Motley* (1911), in which he describes a flight over Mont Blanc, the highest peak in Europe. Pemberton was a member of Our Society, a club for the discussion of crime to which Conan DOYLE also belonged. He also belonged to the Savage Club, was knighted, and founded the London School of Journalism.

PENDU DE ST. PHOLIEN, LE See MAIGRET AND THE HUNDRED GIBBETS.

PENLEZ, BOSAVERN See FIELDING, HENRY.

PENNAC, DANIEL (pseudonym of Daniel Pennachioni, 1944–) Born in Casablanca where his father worked in the French colonial service, Daniel Pennac is one of a new generation of French crime and mystery writers. Pennac grew up in Africa and Southeast Asia, returned to France for his education, and became a literature professor. Along the way he worked as a woodcutter, a cab driver, an illustrator, and a teacher. He has written a series of novels about a character named Benjamin Malaussène, whose adventures and misadventures are reminiscent of those depicted in the novels of Donald WESTLAKE and Thomas BERGER.

Pennac writes an unusual kind of mystery novel, where the story is told with irony and cynicism and with no pretension to realism. The stories are set in Belleville, a suburb of Paris. Both the style and the characters are heavy with exaggerations; the characters go from incredibly unlucky people to supermen capable of impossible accomplishments. The protagonist—at times speaking in first person and telling his own story—is a professional scapegoat. First a department store and then a publisher hire him to receive the complaints and criticisms of their unsatisfied clients so as to arouse their pity with his looks and maladroit behavior. In *Au bonheur des ogres* (1985), Malaussène, working at the department store, becomes the prime suspect in a series of bombings. He has an extended and bizarre family, made up of the cast-off illegitimate children of his renegade mother (the number of sisters and brothers increases with each novel). There is no father, but there are a number of old and wise friends. Benjamin's fiancée is a sensual and aggressive journalist who often gets in trouble but is able to take care of herself.

The stories turn around themes that highlight sordid aspects of crime, vice, and social unrest. The crimes are interwoven with the characters' personal lives in a series of coincidences often unrealistic but enticing. While Pennac's imagination paints vividly the horrible and sanguinary crimes, he also provides a happy ending for those characters that are dear to the reader—and many laughs as well. The second book in the series, *La Fée carabine* (1987), was published in English as THE FAIRY GUNMOTHER (1997). Other novels are *La Petite Marchande de Prose* (1990) and *Monsieur Malaussène* (1995). Pennac's other work translated into English, *Comme un roman* (1992; tr *Better Than Life,* 1994), is an essay about reading and literature.

PENNY DREADFUL See DIME NOVEL.

PENZLER, OTTO (1942–) Otto Penzler was born in Germany and emigrated in 1947 to the United States, where he attended the University of Michigan. A journalist and a collector of mysteries, Penzler co-authored the *Encyclopedia of Mystery and Detection* (1975), which won the first EDGAR award for a critical work dealing with the subgenre. Penzler edited *The Great Detectives* (1978), a collection of "biographies" by writers of their famous creations—Roderick ALLEYN, Lew ARCHER, Virgil TIBBS, and others. Otto Penzler is also the publisher of *Armchair Detective* magazine.

PEREZ-REVERTE, ARTURO (1951–) Arturo Perez-Reverte was born in Cartagena, Spain. His career in television and as a war correspondent preceded his success as a mystery author. Several of his mysteries have been published in English, beginning with *La tabla de Flandes* (1990; tr *The Flanders Panel,* 1994). Perez-Reverte has been dubbed a "postmodern" writer because his novels frequently deal with the interpretation of signs, various kinds of games, and the way in which various texts interpenetrate. In *The Flanders Panel,* an ART restorer links a medieval painting of a chess game to a murder. Chess moves are likened to—and influence—the "moves" people make in everyday life. In *El club Dumas* (1993; tr *The Club Dumas,* 1997), the mystery has to do with rare BOOKS: *The Book of the Nine Doors to the Kingdom of Darkness* and a manuscript of *The Three Musketeers* by DUMAS. *La piel del tambor* (1995) was translated as *The Seville Communion* (1998). *El maestro de esgrima* (1988; tr *The Fencing Master,* 1999) is set in Madrid in 1868. Trouble starts when Doña Adela de Otero asks fencing master Don Jaime Astarloa to teach her his "unstoppable thrust," and he refuses because she is a woman.

PERFECT CRIME, THE (1961) A novel by Henry KANE, notable for its evocation of Miami in the early sixties and a string of curious characters. Evangeline Ashley is a floozy being kept by Señor Pedro Orgaz, but fooling around with his night-club manager, Bill Grant. When Orgaz finds out, he tries to rub them out. After a couple of well concealed murders occur, Oscar BLINNEY turns up on the scene, a hapless but honest bank teller from New York. After several twists and turns, Ashley winds up trying to convince Blinney to pay for her to go to Havana, ostensibly for an abortion. In reality, she and her old flame Grant hatch a plot for the "perfect crime," though there is some divergence over the details. Grant is a petty criminal, vain, and very imaginable in his silk slacks and elevator shoes. Blinney, an opposite type, is equally vivid in his bland and comical way. The writing is crisp, showing the best of what Kane could do; the plot takes a great unexpected twist at the end, leading one to wonder, "which is the perfect crime?"

PEROWNE, BARRY (pseudonym of Philip Atkey, 1908–1985) The nephew of Bertram ATKEY, Barry Perowne was once secretary to his uncle before he began writing mystery fiction himself. (He also married Atkey's daughter.) Perowne wrote about carnival people because he had gone to work for a maker of carnival equipment when he was only thirteen. He published stories in magazines and then went on to write a series of novels about highwayman Dick TURPIN. But Perowne's main claim to fame was that he was authorized to continue the stories of RAFFLES the gentleman thief, the precursor to his uncle's Smiler BUNN and other aristocratic robbers. *Raffles Revisited* (1974) is one collection of Perowne's stories, many of which appeared in *Ellery Queen's Mystery Magazine.* He also published several novels under his own name: *Blue Water Murder* (1935), *Heirs of Merlin* (1945), and *Juniper Rock* (1952).

PERRY, THOMAS (1947–) Thomas Perry was born in Tonawanda, New York, and received a bachelor's degree from Cornell University in 1967 and a Ph.D. in English from Rochester University in 1974. Perry's parents were both teachers. He worked at various jobs before becoming a professional writer, including teacher, commercial fisherman, and "weapons mechanic." He has also written and produced television programs.

Perry won an EDGAR award for *The Butcher's Boy* (1982), whose title character is an unnamed hitman who is supposed to kill a United States senator but winds up becoming a target himself. *Metzger's Dog* (1983), his next novel, is about a gang that tries to extort money from the CIA. Both these books are THRILLERS more than crime or mystery novels. Like Ross THOMAS, Perry intersperses tense scenes of action with sometimes long digressions and filling in of history. He favors rudimentary plots and the simplest of narrative devices, the "snowball" effect. Successive scenes are more and more outrageous or uncomfortable for the character, leading to a chase sequence and a bang-up ending. In *Metzger's Dog,* the gang finally shuts down the entire city of Los Angeles in order to coerce the CIA. In 1992 Perry brought back the "Butcher's Boy" in *Sleeping Dogs.* Having hidden out in England for ten years, the hitman is identified accidentally at a racetrack; he deals with the situation (dramatically) but draws wrong conclusions from it. He returns to the United States in further mistaken attempts to clear up the problem and be safe again, but his actions bring him closer and closer to the original players of *The Butcher's Boy.*

After his early thriller phase, Perry moved on to create a series about Jane Whitefield, a "guide" who helps people out of trouble. Whitefield is part Seneca and lives in upstate New York, but takes long trips during which she helps fugitives escape from murderers. Thus, chase sequences are again the mainspring of the plots. Her cases take her to Los Angeles, Las Vegas, and other haunts of organized crime, and the Native American culture and community thus do not figure largely in the stories. Whitefield has cat-like reflexes and an ability to slip about like a shadow. In *Dance for the Dead* (1996), she helps an eight-year-old boy, the heir to a hundred million dollars, escape from killers. A second plot line concerns a woman involved in savings-and-loan scams after the disastrous deregulation by the Reagan administration. In *Shadow Woman* (1997), she helps a casino executive who is being pursued by assassins.

Perry is known for his even-handedness in portraying good guys and bad guys. In *The Butcher's Boy,* he divided the narrative in two. Elizabeth Waring, a Justice Department investigator, tells of her pursuit of the killer, and in other chapters, the "butcher boy" himself describes his flight. The Butcher Boy is running not only from Waring, but from the Mafia, who believe that his scarred face will eventually lead to his capture and put them at risk as well. Perry told *Contemporary Authors* that "Criminals give a writer a chance to introduce confusion and disruption into the little world he's invented, and to test its limits." But in his books of the eighties Perry was dealing with a world that was already quite disturbed by greed, drugs, and the criminal behavior of governments. In *Metzger's Dog* both sides are equally villainous. A gang led by a Vietnam vet steals a million dollars worth of cocaine as well as a document showing the U.S. government's dirty dealings in Latin America. *Island* (1987) uses an idea familiar from the ending of Jim THOMPSON's *The Getaway* (1959) and other books: the private kingdom set up as a retirement community for major criminals. But this "paradise" is created by a married couple, and the clients are not the villains; the government agencies and banks who try to glom onto all that wealth appear to be greedier than the crooks.

PERUTZ, LEO (1882–1957) Born in Prague, Leo Perutz wrote in German and lived in Vienna until 1938, when he fled the Nazis and went to Palestine. Some years after the war, he returned to Austria, where he died. Perutz's work shows many of the obsessions of the Expressionist period, particularly the psychological, including the unconscious and the divided self. His characters are frequently unsure whether what they are experiencing is dream or reality. Perutz was admired by such writers as Jorge Luis BORGES, Graham GREENE, and Italo Calvino. Perutz's only true mystery story is THE MASTER OF THE DAY OF JUDGEMENT (1921), which incorporates his main themes. Others of his books, though not based in detection, incorporate elements of mystery, suspense, and especially that expressionist hallmark, dread. These works include *St. Petri-Schnee* (1933; tr *Saint Peter's Snow,* 1990), which explores questions of religious faith and political fanaticism under the guise of a mysterious tale that hinges on a baron, a young descendant of Frederick II, and a mildew that grows on wheat. The book was banned by the NAZIS.

PETERS, ELIZABETH (pseudonym of Barbara Louise Gross Mertz, 1927–) Born in Illinois, Barbara Mertz received her Ph.D. in Egyptology from the University of Chicago in 1952. Her subject has provided the background for a series of mysteries featuring Amelia PEABODY, a Victorian archaeologist who investigates crimes with her husband, Radcliffe Emerson (a cross between Ann Radcliffe and Ralph Waldo Emerson?), and sometimes their annoying son, Ramses. The first novel in the series was CROCODILE ON THE SANDBANK (1975).

Peters has also written a series about ART historian Victoria Bliss, who is beautiful, brilliant, and six feet tall. The first book in the series was *Borrower of the Night* (1973). The Bliss novels are set in Europe and make much of exotic settings and romantic conventions. More than the Peabody series, these books are like contemporary versions of the HAD-I-BUT-KNOWN (HIBK) school. *Silhouette in Scarlet* (1973) involves a search for Viking gold on a Danish island, and also brings in Victoria's friend, Sir John Smythe, a dealer in antiquities and an international playboy. Smythe is also an art thief. He and Bliss never become lovers because, though charming, he is dishonest and a criminal. *Trojan Gold* (1987) takes place in an Alpine ski resort. The stuff of romance is not the stuff of reality, and whatever entertainment the books provide depends on one's attraction to the heroine; BARZUN and TAYLOR found her "scatter-witted and a bore." Also very HIBK is yet a third series of novels, about college librarian Jacqueline Kirby, who later becomes a successful romance novelist (like the author). *The Murders of Richard III* (1974) is a COUNTRY HOUSE mystery in which everyone plays a role from Shakespeare's play. The book is also a tribute to THE DAUGHTER OF TIME (1951).

Under the name Barbara Michaels, the author has written a number of suspense bestsellers. Her nonfiction works on Egyptology appear under her real name.

PETERS, ELLIS (pseudonym of Edith Mary Pargeter, 1913–1995) English mystery author and creator of Brother CADFAEL. Born in Shropshire, Peters (like Agatha CHRISTIE) acquired firsthand knowledge of poisons from her several years as an assistant to a chemist (pharmacist). But as a writer, she first made a name for herself—under her real name—with her historical novels. Her first crime novel was *Murder in the Dispensary* (1938), which she published as Joylon Carr. It was followed by *Death Comes By Post* (1940). She then abandoned the genre for more than a decade, returning to mainstream novels.

After World War II, in which she served in the Royal Navy and was decorated, Peters began writing and translating full-time. In 1951 she published another mystery, *Fallen into the Pit,* under her own name. The book introduced the long-running FELSE family series. Dominic Felse, a thirteen-year-old, discovers a body in the first novel; he reappeared ten years later (but only three years older) in *Death and the Joyful Woman* (1961), in a murder case involving his girlfriend. The book received the EDGAR for best novel. Dominic's father, George, is a member of the CID and is the focus of later books, though Dominic continues to have a role, and his mother gets a case in *The Grass Widow's Tale* (1968). At the same time, Peters continued writing her historical novels, such as the four volumes on the Brothers of Gwynedd (1974–1977). She also won an award for her translations from Czech in 1968.

Peters was thus a successful and established author when her interest in local history sparked a series that would overshadow all her previous work. *A Morbid Taste for Bones* (1977) introduced the character of Brother Cadfael. The second book appeared two years later, and in the following decades well over a dozen further Cadfael stories have appeared. One of the books, *Monk's Hood* (1980), won a Silver Dagger from the British CRIME WRITERS' ORGANIZATION. Peters's other honors include the Diamond Dagger. The series has as much in common with the romance novel as the mystery. The local history is well-researched, though there are some peculiarities and anachronisms.

PETERS, TOBY A character in a series of CELEBRITY MYSTERIES by Stuart KAMINSKY. A former policeman and security guard at Warner Brothers, Peters's past gives him ample if implausible contacts with famous people. In his first case, *Bullet for a Star* (1977), his client is Errol Flynn. Kaminsky invented this kind of star-studded mystery, a formula copied by other writers (Kaminsky's major competitor in this field is George BAXT). Hollywood in its golden years is also the backdrop for a series by Terence FAHERTY.

Kaminsky switched to political figures with *The Fala Factor* (1984), named for Eleanor Roosevelt's dog, and *Buried Caesars* (1989), about the egomaniacal general Douglas MacArthur. Peters has two unlikely assistants, one a dentist, Sheldon Minck, the other a dwarf named Gunther. In *Think Fast, Mr. Peters* (1988), Minck thinks his wife has run off with the actor Peter Lorre. As with most celebrity mysteries, the introduction of "real" people actually makes the tale less real, because of the unlikely situations used to drag them in; the story must be taken with a large grain of salt and one must be a real fan to find them absorbing despite the siphoning off of reality.

BIBLIOGRAPHY Novels: *Murder on the Yellow Brick Road* (1978), *You Bet Your Life* (1979), *The Howard Hughes Affair* (1979), *Never Cross a Vampire* (1980), *High Midnight* (1981), *Catch a Falling Clown* (1982), *He Done Her Wrong* (1983), *Down for the Count* (1985), *The Man Who Shot Lewis Vance* (1986), *Smart Moves* (1987), *Melted Clocks* (1992), *The Devil Met a Lady* (1993), *Tomorrow is Another Day* (1995), *Dancing in the Dark* (1996), *A Fatal Glass of Beer* (1997).

PETRELLA, PATRICK A Scotland Yard detective created by Michael GILBERT, Patrick Petrella would be better known were he not primarily a short story character. *Young Petrella* (1988) contains early stories that first appeared in the *Edgar Wallace Mystery Magazine* and *Argosy* beginning in the mid-fifties. Petrella is a GENIUS DETECTIVE with a multicultural twist; his father worked for the Spanish government and the French police, and the family lived in Cairo, Casablanca, and France. "The Conspirators" describes Petrella's first murder case, when he was eleven years old and living in Perpignan. Petrella attended an English boarding school and the University of Beirut; he speaks four languages, and is as adept at wine-tasting as at lock-picking.

The Petrella stories are one of the bright spots in the general decline of the mystery SHORT STORY since the advent of television. Rather than gimmicky mystery "shorts" with cardboard people, Gilbert provides interesting background, believable people, and, as always, a highly literate style. Some of Petrella's puzzles are bizarre, and at times he is almost a superhero. The earlier stories evoke the comparatively innocent fifties, when the police were regarded as the "good guys" and drug smuggling was a relatively minor problem. Later, Petrella deals with corruption and all the evils chronicled in the contemporary crime novel. In *Roller Coaster* (1993), Petrella has become the Superintendent of the East London docklands and has to deal with such problems as race relations and allegations of police brutality.

BIBLIOGRAPHY Novels: *Blood and Judgement* (1959).

Short Stories: *Amateur in Violence* (1973), *Petrella at Q* (1977).

PETTIGREW, FRANCIS The barrister-cum-detective who features in a series of novels by Cyril HARE. Born in 1888, called to the bar in 1912, his practice is interrupted by his service in World War I and never recovers. Pettigrew is a rarity of the GOLDEN AGE—a modest sleuth (sometimes, he hardly does any sleuthing at all). In proposing to his wife in *With a Bare Bodkin* (1945), he says of himself, "I am old, I am unattractive, I am unsuccessful. I am crotchety and quirky and set in my ways. I am given to futile little jokes and I have been known to drink too much." His view of himself is borne out by his extreme reticence to get involved in other people's business, which is also a clever device on the author's part for delaying the solution of the case. Sometimes clues are not disclosed because Pettigrew does not ask an obvious question. Hare thereby observes the letter of FAIR PLAY, if not the spirit.

Pettigrew is a sophisticated, cynical upper-class lawyer, convinced of the virtues of hushing up scandal. He thus works against the law as well as with it. Covertly, he is an idealist, and one almost suspects him of murdering a judge in TRAGEDY AT LAW (1942) when his innocent client is hanged. His lost love, Hilda Matthewson, whom he pursued unsuccessfully, also appears in this, the first novel in the series. Pettigrew is more than a little embittered, having been up for but never receiving a judgeship. Struggling with an ailing law practice, he is reduced to editing legal textbooks for extra money. He honestly attributes his failure to something lacking in himself. These same qualities make Pettigrew a supremely human character, very unlike the dashing legal hotshots of contemporary thrillers. Pettigrew's wit and compassion, cleverly veiled by cynicism, also make him entertaining.

In *With a Bare Bodkin,* Pettigrew has been given a ridiculous wartime job in the Ministry of Pin Control. Based in Marsett Bay in the remote north, this governmental body supposedly oversees pin production and export to circumvent black market activities. Pettigrew acts as legal expert and cooperates with Inspector Mallet, who is in the area investigating a leakage of information. The murder, coming well along in the story, takes a surprising victim. The astute reader will have guessed the culprit, even though clues about the details are slow to be brought forth. In this book, Pettigrew also falls in love and marries. He and his wife Eleanor are living happily in Markshire in THE WIND BLOWS DEATH (1949). Having been cajoled into serving as treasurer to the Markshire Orchestral Society, Pettigrew is drawn into the investigation of the murder of an Anglo-Polish soloist.

Two Pettigrew short stories are included in *The Best Detective Stories of Cyril Hare* (1959).

BIBLIOGRAPHY Novels: *The Yew Tree's Shade* (1954; U.S. title *Death Walks the Woods*), *He Should Have Died Hereafter* (1958; U.S. title *Untimely Death*).

PHANTOM LADY (1942) Apart from his BLACK SERIES, *Phantom Lady* is the best-known novel of Cornell WOOLRICH; the story was made famous by the 1944 film that was based on the novel (with substantial and detrimental alterations). Scott Henderson has a fight with his wife just before they are supposed to go to dinner and a show; he goes to a bar, accosts the first woman he meets (who is wearing an outrageous pumpkin-like hat), and persuades her to accompany him instead. They decide not to exchange names or any personal information. Afterward, Henderson arrives home to find the police; his wife has been strangled with his own tie. When Henderson tries to establish his alibi, it is discovered that nobody can remember the woman or the hat, so he has no one to corroborate the time of the meeting, which would clear him. Henderson is sentenced to death.

The efforts of Henderson to wriggle out of the electric chair with the help of his friends are well done (for example, a pretty young woman menaces the bartender by staring at him for three days and nights). The story itself, as often with Woolrich, hinges on several improbabilities. A number of characters are inconceivably calm, hard-hearted, or forgetful.

PHILIPS, JUDSON P[ENTECOST] (1903–1989) In his early career, Judson Philips was as prolific as Erle Stanley GARDNER in producing a huge stable of private eyes and heroes for the PULP MAGAZINES, but in his later years as a novelist he never created a series character of major significance. Born in Massachusetts, Philips began publishing while he was still a student at Columbia

University in 1925. He wrote under several pseudonyms, including Hugh Pentecost. As Pentecost, he won a prize from the Dodd, Mead publishing house for his first mystery novel, *Cancelled in Red* (1939). Other Pentecost books include *I'll Sing at Your Funeral* (1942) and *Sniper* (1965). Philips often used a New England background for his novels, of which he eventually wrote almost one hundred. Under his real name he wrote a series of novels about a one-legged journalist-sleuth named Peter Styles, whom he introduced relatively late in his career in *The Laughter Trap* (1964). Pierre CHAMBRUN, a manager of a New York hotel that seems much like the Plaza, is another Pentecost character. Unlike others of his contemporaries, Philips never transcended his pulp background; his plots tend to be overwrought while the writing is underdeveloped. Philips's other series characters include an artist (John Jericho), a newspaperman (Grant Simon), and a public relations man (Julian Quist). Among his non-series novels is *Murder Clear, Track Fast* (1961), which has to do with horse racing and is set in Saratoga, New York.

Incredibly prolific as he was, Philips also produced and directed plays at the Sharon Playhouse in Connecticut (his father had been an opera singer and his mother was an actress), was a sportswriter for the *New York Times,* and wrote for Hollywood and for radio. He served a term as president of the MYSTERY WRITERS OF AMERICA, of which he was a founder. He was named a Grand Master by the organization in 1973.

PHILLPOTTS, EDEN (1862–1960) Born in India, Eden Phillpotts had settled in Devon when his neighbor, Agatha CHRISTIE, began writing mysteries. In the early twenties Phillpotts himself was writing mysteries, some of them under the name Harrington Hext. Phillpotts had published a mystery as early as 1888. He encouraged the young author next door, and she dedicated *Peril at End House* (1932) to him in recognition of his help.

Phillpotts had studied acting and worked in an insurance company before becoming an author. His strength was describing the scenery and manners of the countryside where he lived for the better part of his ninety-eight years, and in which he set his non-mystery novels. *The Thing at Their Heels* (1923) concerned the killings of members of a family who are in line for an inheritance. Believability was not his strong point, however; the motive for the killing is highly improbable and oddly humanitarian. Phillpotts's political views often were worked into his stories, for example in *Found Drowned* (1931). In *No. 87* (1922), which would have to be classed as a SCIENCE FICTION mystery because it involves the discovery of a new element, a high-tech weapon is used in the interests of world peace. In *The Red Redmaynes* (1922), written under his own name, Phillpotts used the idea of killing off several members of the same family. This novel is probably his best mystery. The detective is an American and the case also has something of the travelogue.

Julian SYMONS said Phillpotts's stories were "among the most ridiculous of the time," citing as an example a novel (*The Grey Room,* 1931) in which body heat applied to a mattress releases a deadly poison. *The Monster* (1925) has a Jekyll and Hyde theme, and *Lycanthrope: The Mystery of Sir William Wolf* (1938) plays up the GOTHIC elements and then explains them reasonably (a technique of John Dickson CARR).

Phillpotts also wrote an autobiography, *From the Angle of 88* (1951), plays, and several volumes of poetry.

P.I. In 1900, not many people would have bragged about being a p.i. (or "pee-eye"). Now taken to stand for "private investigator," in the earlier part of the century it still had the original meaning of *pimp.*

PIBBLE, INSPECTOR A detective created by Peter DICKINSON. James Pibble first appears in *The Glass-Sided Ants' Nest* (1968; orig title *Skin Deep*), the first of many peculiar cases. Pibble investigates a murder among a community of New Guineans established in London for anthropological study. Although Pibble is drab and ordinary in appearance, his career is decidedly strange. Born in 1915, Pibble is a policeman and nothing else; highly competent, but completely uncharismatic. After solving a number of baffling cases, he is actually fired from the force and thereafter sets himself up as a private investigator. Pibble's comrades find him "clever but quirky," and he himself is aware that he "never had the basic drive to make a topflight officer." The flashier, more socially adept members of the force sometimes steal the credit for Pibble's work. Pibble's wife is "overrefined" and thinks Jimmy doesn't assert himself or get enough credit for his genius. Pibble's favorite expletive is "CRIPPEN!"

The Sinful Stones (1970; orig title *The Seals*) incorporates several of Dickinson's signature elements, including science, obscure locales, and religious communities. The action takes place on an island in the Hebrides where a conflict has arisen between an elderly physicist and a group of monks. Pibble's own father was the physicist's lab assistant. Monasticism turns up again in *The Lizard in the Cup* (1972), another story set on an island, where Pibble is supposed to protect a Greek millionaire. An everything-but-the-kitchen-sink plot, it involves the Mafia, a stolen mosaic, drugs, and political subversion.

This series known for its oddity came to an end after only a half dozen books, partly because Pibble was so old to begin with. In his last case, *One Foot in the Grave* (1979), the elderly Pibble has retired to a nursing home, but becomes involved in the investigation of a murder when he discovers the body of a dead orderly in the home. Pibble struggles valiantly with criminals and lions in THE OLD ENGLISH PEEP SHOW (1969: British title *A Pride of Heroes*).

BIBLIOGRAPHY Novels: *Sleep and His Brother* (1971).

PICARESQUE A style of narrative originating in Spain having to do with the trials and fortunes of a roguish adventurer, or *picaro*. The first picaresque tale was the anonymous *Lázarillo de Tormes* (1554), about a young man named Lázaro. He is a servant to several masters, including a blind man, a miser (who is also a priest), and a mendicant. Lázaro believes mainly in himself; the next great picaresque hero, in *Guzmán de Alfarache, Vida del Picaro* (1599), believes in nothing. He supposedly composes his autobiography after being sentenced to a term in a galley for fraud. The picaresque first appeared in English with Thomas Nashe's *The Unfortunate Traveller; or, The Life of Jacke Wilton* (1594). The term "rogue literature" comes from an exact translation of *picaro*. Rogue literature, such as Nashe's work and the "con-catching" pamphlets of Robert Greene (1560?–1592), was about the doings of the London underworld and famous HIGHWAYMEN of the time (see PROTOMYSTERIES). The picaresque was a model for early novelists such as DEFOE and FIELDING, who were themselves progenitors of the modern crime story.

PICK-UP (1955) A novel by Charles WILLEFORD, a wrenching tale of alcoholism and suicide. It is more a tragedy than a story of crime, and has no detection, though there is a central mystery about the narrator's identity (no physical description of him is given until the last line). Extremely dark, it is a first-person narrative told by Harry, who works in a diner, where he meets Helen. They fall in love, but both are alcoholics, and being together makes it doubly hard for them to control their drinking. Helen prostitutes herself to get money for drink, which causes Harry deep distress; when they finally reach the lowest depths of despair, they make a failed suicide attempt. They enter a mental hospital together, are separated, and when reunited upon their release begin drinking again. The ending of the novel is a surprise, and reveals deeper reasons for the dooming of their love affair even as it shows Willeford to be ahead of his time.

PINAUD, INSPECTOR M. A character of Pierre AUDEMARS and an Inspector at the Sûreté in Paris. Pinaud is honest, strong, intelligent, religious, elegant, proud, incorruptible, dignified, and a loving husband and father. (Pinaud is elaborately over-described.) He is also an embittered, lustful, gluttonous moralizer, a heavy drinker and car lover who complains that he is too underpaid to afford to live according to his tastes. He loves food and fine wines and cannot turn his eyes from a beautiful woman, though he resists the impulse in the presence of his wife, Germaine. He has found a way of supplementing his meager salary and boosting his battered ego by getting a chronicler to write and publish the tales of his adventures.

BIBLIOGRAPHY Novels: *The Two Impostors* (1958), *The Fire and the Clay* (1959), *The Turns of Time* (1960), *The Crown of Night* (1961), *The Dream and the Dead* (1962), *Street of Grass* (1963; British title *The Wings of Darkness*), *Fair Maids Missing* (1964), *The Woven Web* (1965; British title *Dead with Sorrow*), *Time of Temptation* (1966), *A Thorn in the Dust* (1967), *The Veins of Compassion* (1967), *The White Leaves of Death* (1968), *The Flame in the Mist* (1969), *A Host for Dying* (1970), *Stolen Like Magic Away* (1971), *The Delicate Dust of Death* (1973), *No Tears for the Dead* (1974), *Nightmare in Rust* (1975), *One for the Dead* (1975), *The Healing Hands of Death* (1977), *Now Dead Is Any Man* (1978), *A Sad and Savage Dying* (1978), *Slay Me a Sinner* (1979), *Gone to Her Death* (1981), *The Bitter Path of Death* (1982), *The Red Rust of Death* (1983), *A Small Slain Body* (1985).

PINCH In the sense of "to steal" (from the motion of putting one's fingertips on something), the term dates from the seventeenth century. The other sense, to be arrested or nabbed by the police, is a nineteenth-century American usage. (*Nab*, incidentally, predates pinch as a term for "catch," going back to the sixteenth century).

PINE, PAUL See BROWNE, HOWARD.

PINKERTON, ALLAN (1819–1894) The founder of the most famous detective agency in the world. Pinkerton was also an author and wrote up his cases, with embellishments, and presented them as fact. These stories were first collected in *The Expressman and the Detective* (1874). Pinkerton was born in Glasgow, Scotland, and emigrated to the United States in 1842. His father had been a policeman, and he became a deputy sheriff in Chicago before founding his agency in 1850.

Pinkerton's method consisted of the amassing of huge dossiers on suspects, exhaustive surveillance by multiple operatives, and the use of undercover agents to win the confidence of the suspects and induce them unwittingly to confess. These techniques could be taken to ridiculous extremes, and some of Pinkerton's claims are unintentionally funny: he wrote in *The Expressman* that he had tailed a subject for *weeks* disguised as a German immigrant, with a yellow wig, a leather cap, a clay pipe and a carpet bag, even sitting next to the suspect on trains, and was never spotted. Pinkerton also wrote *The Somnambulist and the Detectives* (1875), so perhaps his suspect was asleep and didn't notice him. Mark TWAIN lampooned Pinkerton's methods in *Simon Wheeler, Detective* (1903).

Pinkerton's methods are also reflected in *The Valley of Fear* (1915) by Conan DOYLE, but in all seriousness. That story also contains hints of the most infamous reputation of Pinkerton agents: they were often used by industrialists and tycoons of the Gilded Age to suppress the American labor movement in the most brutal way, as in the Homestead strike of 1892, which devastated the metalworker's union.

Ironically, the most famous Pinkerton agent of all time was a suspected communist, Dashiell HAMMETT.

PINKERTON, EVAN See FORD, LESLIE.

PINKERTON, MISS The nickname of Nurse Hilda ADAMS, a sleuth created by Mary Roberts RINEHART.

PINKIE A character in Graham GREENE's *Brighton Rock* (1938). Pinkie is an early example of the sociopathic character in crime fiction. Pinkie Brown is a young and remorseless killer who marries a good but helpless girl, Rose, in order that she not be coerced into testifying against him. Even as he marries her, he plans to kill her if she shows signs of cracking. Although desperately callous, Pinkie is still only an adolescent.

PIRKIS, C[ATHERINE] L[OUISA] (?–1910) The British novelist C. L. Pirkis was known in her day for a dozen or so novels intended mainly for female readers. These included *A Dateless Bargain* (1877) and *Lady Lovelace* (1884). Popular in their time, these novels, like their subgenre, have faded from view along with their authors. Pirkis's major claim to fame other than her writing was that she founded an early British anti-vivisectionist organization, the National Canine Defense League.

Late in her career—with her last book, in fact—Pirkis made a contribution to the detective genre with the character Loveday BROOKE, a female private investigator. Her short stories about Brooke are comparatively well-written examples of the Victorian detective story during the post–Sherlock HOLMES boom. At a time when Holmes had inspired numberless imitators, Pirkis did something different; hers was not the first female sleuth, but has been sometimes called the best. One might, however, cavil at some of her methods. If the puzzle in the stories sometimes seems impossible to figure out, it may be because it is; writing in the days before FAIR PLAY was thought of, Pirkis had a habit of holding back information essential to the solution.

PITCAIRN, JOHN JAMES See PRINGLE, ROMNEY.

PLATINUM CAT, THE (1938) A novel by Miles Burton (John RHODE), one in his series about Desmond MERRION. Bordesley, the rector of Pascombe (near Dungeness), sees a fire in an empty cottage, but the building cannot be saved. Police find a human hand in the ashes, then a whole corpse. The cat of the title is a small figurine found with the body. The victim turns out to be an employee of the Defense Ministry, and of course was privy to a secret of "national importance" having to do with England's aerial defenses. All of these facts become known even before Merrion is called in by Sir Edric Conway, the assistant commissioner of the Metropolitan Police.

The Platinum Cat lies near the surface of the pool of obscurity into which the author's works have sunk. The plot and setting of the novel are more diverting than many of Rhode's products, and the writing is certainly clear; on the other hand, in good classical style the clues are heavily dropped, and some of them are old hat (a memo pad on which writing has left an impression on the sheet below the torn-off message). As for the dialogue, if ever people spoke this way, it was a long time ago, and their ideas embody the oldest clichés—"there's usually a woman at the bottom of these affairs" (i.e., CHERCHEZ LA FEMME). The author's rehearsing of the facts through the thoughts of the detectives is eminently fair, but plodding as a narrative technique. The book does illustrate some possible virtues of the classical form of the detective story. Since character is not an issue, there is nothing (romantic subplots, descriptions of the detective's home, furnishings, cuisine, etc.) to stand in the way of the laying out of the plot, and the body is found in the first chapter. Nothing except his datedness places Rhode below such modern writers as SIMPSON and BURLEY.

POE, EDGAR ALLAN (1809–1849) A poet, short story writer, novelist, and critic, Poe exercised a profound influence not only on the course of American literature, but, through his great reputation in Europe (particularly in France), on literature in general. The scandalous aspects of his life, however, including his notorious alcoholism and use of drugs, created a myth that at times almost overshadowed his achievement and prevented him from being taken seriously in his own country. One of the first great critics of American literature, Yvor Winters, said that Poe was the writer who most fitted his practice to his theory, "and was exceptionally bad in both." Poe considered himself more a poet than a fiction writer, but it is his prose that has proved most lasting, classics like "The Raven" and "Annabel Lee" notwithstanding. Poe's influence is still powerful; Jorge Luis BORGES wrote stories influenced by Poe's bizarre tale "Berenice."

Born in Boston of actor parents, Poe was orphaned at the age of two. Thereafter he lived with the family of John and Fanny Allan, with whom he spent five troubled years in England. Poe and his godfather never got along well. In 1826 Poe entered the University of Virginia, but had to leave after a year—he had resorted to gambling because of the stinginess of his allowance, and his godfather refused to cover his losses (Poe's room at the university is now a kind of shrine). Poe enlisted in the Army in 1827 and applied to West Point two years later. The peripatetic Poe returned to Virginia (Richmond), where he edited the *Southern Literary Messenger,* and moved to Philadelphia in 1839, where he edited *Burton's Gentleman's Magazine.* He published *Tamerlane and Other Poems* in 1827 and *Poems* in 1831. Five years later, Poe married Virginia Clemm, his thirteen-year-old cousin.

Poe's contribution to detective literature came relatively late in his career but was immense—most critics consider him to have created the form (see PROTOMYSTERIES). From poetry, Poe had gravitated to tales of horror and suspense (elements that had been present in his poetry already) such as "The Fall of the House of Usher" (1839). He introduced C. Auguste DUPIN in THE MURDERS IN THE RUE MORGUE (1841). Dupin, the first amateur GENIUS DETECTIVE in fiction, became the model for subsequent characters of this type, most importantly Sherlock HOLMES. Poe's detective is the subject of only three tales, the other two being THE MYSTERY OF MARIE ROGET (1842) and THE PURLOINED LETTER (1844), yet between them they established many if not most of the devices of later mystery fiction, including the LOCKED ROOM MYSTERY, the use of a slower-witted friend as chronicler and narrative foil for the detective, the story based on a true crime, the obvious but overlooked clue, and many other small details.

Although Poe's use of Dupin ended with "The Purloined Letter," it was not the end of his interest in the mystery story. "The Gold Bug" (1893) is also a problem of deduction, concerning treasure buried on Sullivan's Island, South Carolina, and THOU ART THE MAN (1844) is an entertaining mystery with a surprising ending.

Poe attained his greatest influence in his own century through Charles Baudelaire, who translated his tales into French (1857), and later was admired by Arthur Rimbaud and other symbolists. They were particularly drawn to his fascination with psychology (the abnormal especially), extreme experience, obsession, and hallucination. Poe himself was influenced by G. W. F. Hegel, and the Hegelian dialectic is reflected in the Dupin stories: the power of evil, madness, and passion represented by the murderer is countered by its antithesis, the rationality and order of Dupin's mind, leading to the synthesis—the solution of the mystery and triumph of understanding. Poe's tales, unlike much of the tradition he spawned, were above all concerned with evil and guilt. Ross MACDONALD wrote that "the scene of the crime for Poe is his own tell-tale heart. . . . Poe used and developed the Gothic tale to a new level, and invented the detective story in order to grasp and objectify the nature of the evil, and somehow place the guilt."

POGGIOLI, DR. HENRY See STRIBLING, T. S.

POIROT, HERCULE The famous Belgian detective created by Agatha CHRISTIE was introduced in THE MYSTERIOUS AFFAIR AT STYLES (1920) and became the most famous sleuth since Sherlock HOLMES. According to Poirot's fictitious biography, he retired from the Belgian police force in 1904. In his first appearance, he is staying in an English village as a refugee from World War I. Here he meets Captain Hastings, who is recovering from a wound (as is Poirot, who limps); Hastings is later his constant companion in his investigations (until Hastings is packed off to Argentina and a life of ranching). Like Holmes's Doctor WATSON, Hastings is a veteran and is slightly less intelligent than his genius friend; his grasp of his companion's mental operations is if anything thinner than Doctor Watson's. After Hastings bows out, other supporting characters become more important, particularly Poirot's secretary, Miss Lemon, and Mrs. Ariadne Oliver, who serves him as a freelance operative.

Poirot is like Nero WOLFE and other larger-than-life series characters in that he has a few dominant and often repeated signature traits: enormous conceit; sartorial elegance and immense fastidiousness ("a speck of dust would have caused him more pain than a bullet wound"); finicky habits where food is concerned; poor but often amusing English; and catch phrases, such as "the little gray cells," which he frequently uses. Poirot stands only five feet, four inches tall, and has a head like "an egg."

His perfect dress and his neat little moustache are striking. He regularly makes fools of the police, including Chief Inspector Japp.

Christie did not introduce Poirot with a long career in mind. Since he is already retired at the time of the first book, by the end of his adventures he would already have topped a century and a quarter. She did, however, kill the little detective off, in CURTAIN (1975). His death was announced in an obituary on the front page of *The New York Times,* an honor accorded to few people, even those who actually existed.

Poirot's most controversial case is THE MURDER OF ROGER ACKROYD (1926), and his most famous is MURDER ON THE ORIENT EXPRESS (1934). Although the novels are well known even to those who have never read them, Poirot also appeared in numerous short stories. There are several volumes in which some or all of the stories feature Poirot (see bibliography); there is one Poirot story in *Witness for the Prosecution* (1948), another in *Two New Crime Stories* (1929).

BIBLIOGRAPHY Novels: *Murder on the Links* (1923), *The Big Four* (1927), *The Mystery of the Blue Train* (1928), *Peril at End House* (1932), *Lord Edgware Dies* (1933; U.S. title *Thirteen at Dinner*), *Three-Act Tragedy* (1934; U.S. title *Murder in Three Acts*), *Death in the Clouds* (1935; U.S. title *Death in the Air*), *The A.B.C. Murders* (1936), *Murder in Mesopotamia* (1936), *Cards on the Table* (1936), *Dumb Witness* (1937; U.S. title *Poirot Loses a Client*), *Death on the Nile* (1937), *Appointment with Death* (1938), *Hercule Poirot's Christmas* (1938; U.S. title *Murder for Christmas*), *Sad Cypress* (1940), *One, Two, Buckle My Shoe* (1940; U.S. title *The Patriotic Murders*), *Evil Under the Sun* (1941), *Five Little Pigs* (1942; U.S. title *Murder in Retrospect*), *The Hollow* (1946), *Taken at the Flood* (1948; U.S. title *There Is a Tide*), *Mrs. McGinty's Dead* (1952), *After the Funeral* (1953; U.S. title *Funerals Are Fatal*), *Hickory, Dickory, Dock* (1955; U.S. title *Hickory, Dickory, Death*), *Dead Man's Folly* (1956), *Cat Among the Pigeons* (1959), *The Clocks* (1963), *Third Girl* (1966), *Hallowe'en Party* (1969), *Elephants Can Remember* (1972).

Short Stories: *Poirot Investigates* (1924), *Murder in the Mews* (1937; *Dead Man's Mirror* in U.S.), *The Regatta Mystery and Other Stories* (1939), *The Labours of Hercules* (1947), *Three Blind Mice and Other Stories* (1950), *The Under Dog and Other Stories* (1951), *The Adventure of the Christmas Pudding and Other Stories* (1961), *Double Sin and Other Stories* (1961).

POISONED CHOCOLATES CASE, THE See AVENGING CHANCE, THE.

POISONED UMBRELLA The poisoned umbrella affair was as incredible as anything in spy fiction, but it was, unfortunately, real. In September 1978, Georgi Ivan Markov, a Bulgarian defector who had fled to the West in 1969, was killed in London by secret agents who stabbed him in the thigh with a poison-tipped umbrella. A similar attack was made the month before in Paris on another dissident, Vladimir Kostov, but he survived. Markov, a novelist and playwright, had been making broadcasts for the BBC and for Radio Free Europe that were critical of the Bulgarian communist government. Doctors found in both Kostov's and Markov's bodies tiny spheres only 1.52 millimeters across, made of platinum and iridium. The inquest on Markov found that holes in the sphere contained RICIN, which caused Markov's death from septicemia and blood poisoning the next day.

This event partly inspired John D. MACDONALD's bestseller *The Green Ripper* (1979). In the 1990s, former KGB members confirmed that Markov was the victim of an assassination; Bulgarian journalists claimed that the killer was now a comfortable pensioner.

In what could perhaps be called a copycat case, agents of Mossad, Israel's secret police, in September 1997 attacked the head of the militant Islamic organization Hammas on the streets of Amman, Jordan, injecting him with a slow-acting poison. The agents were caught, however; King Hussein used the captives to compel Israel to supply an antidote (the victim recovered), and Israel was forced to release the founder of Hammas himself from prison.

POISONS See under individual names.

POLICE PROCEDURAL See PROCEDURAL.

PONCE "Ponce" started out in the nineteenth century as a word for a man kept by a woman. It then came to mean a man whose partner prostituted herself to support him—thus, a pimp. It is related to the French name *Alphonse,* which was slang for a man who lived off women.

PONS, SOLAR A detective—or rather "private inquiry agent"—created by August DERLETH. Conan DOYLE was still alive when Derleth created Pons as a direct copy of Sherlock HOLMES (with the author's permission). He is like Holmes in his speech ("I am always restless when I have no problem before me") and his methods ("Let me call your attention to the middle finger of the right hand"). Like Holmes, Pons gets away, figuratively speaking, with murder: the police let him take forensic evidence home to cogitate over. Pons even seems to be aware of Holmes, for in *Mr. Fairlie's Final Journey* (1968) he uses the adjective "elementary" over and over. Pons's WATSON is also a doctor, Dr. Lyndon Parker. Vincent STARRETT said that he found in the Pons stories a hint of "burlesque," though he admired some of Derleth's pastiches—particularly those in which he took up those tantalizing allusions made by Watson to cases of Holmes that were never chronicled afterward. One of these hints was expanded by Derleth into "The Adventure of the Late Mr. Faversham." The unevenness of the Pons stories becomes understandable when one considers that Derleth began them when he was nineteen years old.

Derleth wrote several volumes of Pons stories; many of them first appeared in *Ellery Queen's Mystery Magazine, Alfred Hitchcock's Mystery Magazine,* and other detective publications. He went a little overboard in giving Pons credentials: born in Prague, Oxford graduate, member of several prestigious clubs, intelligence agent in both world wars, widely traveled, and with residences in New York, Chicago, Paris, Vienna, and 7B Praed Street, London. In 1966, a Praed Street Irregulars was formed, similar to the organization of Sherlock Holmes fans.

BIBLIOGRAPHY Short Stories: *In Re: Sherlock Holmes: The Adventures of Solar Pons* (1945), *The Memoirs of Solar Pons* (1951), *Three Problems for Solar Pons* (1952), *The Return of Solar Pons* (1958), *The Reminiscences of Solar Pons* (1961), *The Adventure of the Orient Express* (1965), *The Casebook of Solar Pons* (1965), *The Adventure of the Unique Dickensians* (1968), *The Chronicles of Solar Pons* (1975).

PONSON DU TERRAIL, PIERRE ALEXIS (1829–1871) The Vicomte Ponson du Terrail, a French nobleman, wrote an extremely successful and lengthy series of adventures about the thief Rocambole. The first collection was *Les exploits de Rocambole,* published in three volumes in 1859. Written in a series of episodes to be serialized in newspapers (known as the *feuilleton* style), Rocamobole's stories caused a sensation. FANTÔMAS was one of those characters influenced by Rocambole.

POOLE, INSPECTOR John Poole is an inspector with Scotland Yard in a series of novels by Henry WADE. Poole is a fairly nondescript character, a competent policeman in the GOLDEN AGE tradition. He lacks the mannerisms and distinguishing traits of Inspector FRENCH, created by Freeman Wills CROFTS, the author with whom Wade is most often compared. Like Desmond MERRION, a similar type, Poole is not likely to excite the imaginations of postwar readers. Poole is middling in every way—size, class, imagination. He is a figure of a policeman more than of a man. On the other hand, Wade was attentive to detail, and clues are well-presented; some of the Wade books are proto-PROCEDURALS.

BIBLIOGRAPHY Novels: *The Duke of York's Steps* (1929), *No Friendly Drop* (1931), *Constable Guard Thyself* (1934), *Bury Him Darkly* (1936), *Lonely Magdalene* (1940), *Too Soon to Die* (1953), *Gold Was Our Grave* (1954).

Short Stories: *Policeman's Lot* (1933; half featuring Poole).

POPEYE An evil and sadistic figure in William Faulkner's novel SANCTUARY (1931). A gangster and rapist, Popeye is happy to see another man punished for Popeye's own crimes, and lives to suffer the same fate himself.

POPISH PLOT, THE See MURDER OF SIR EDMUND GODFREY, THE.

PORTER, DOROTHY (1954–) The Australian poet Dorothy Porter has made an intriguing contribution to the genre with a private eye novel written in verse. Born in Sydney, she graduated from the University of Sydney in 1975. *Little Hoodlum,* her first collection of poems, was published the same year. *Driving Too Fast* (1990) and several other books followed. Porter later began teaching poetry and writing in Sydney.

Essentially HARD-BOILED despite its lesbian detective and poetic background, THE MONKEY'S MASK (1994; repr 1997) has been critically acclaimed in Australia and abroad.

PORTER, JOYCE (1924–1990) Joyce Porter was born in the northern English town of Marple, which seems particularly appropriate for a mystery author, although she turned to writing rather late. She attended King's College, London, graduating with a degree in English. She was in the women's division of the army toward the end of World War II, and in 1949 joined the Women's Royal Air Force. Porter was sent to Paris to learn Russian, and in the following twelve years worked with the RAF in intelligence work. When she began writing after her retirement in 1963, Porter returned to her roots, writing stories set in small English villages. But her stories are hardly quaint; her main character, Inspector Wilfred DOVER, is gross in every sense. Crass, obese, and smelly, Dover is a bigot, a slob, and in Robert BARNARD's words, a man of "endemic malevolent sloth." Yet Porter was inspired by MAIGRET! *Dover One* (1964), a novel, was the unfortunate character's first appearance, and the ending has been praised for its grotesquerie. Dover's bowels also seem to be permanently out of order. Some people find this low comedy very funny, while to others it is just low. Dover is best taken as PARODY.

Eddie Brown, another Porter series character, is a parody of the kind of heroes found in the works of

LECARRÉ and DEIGHTON. The Honorable Constance Ethel Morrison-Blake (called the "Hon-Con"—perhaps a dirty joke, given Porter's knowledge of French), is a parody of detectives of the MARPLE/Miss SILVER type.

Porter considered writing a job, and finished everything she started. Her brother wrote that when she no longer needed to make more money, she stopped writing—a lack of egotism worth pondering. Her last novel was *Dover Beats the Band* (1980); *Dover: The Collected Stories* (1995) gathers eleven stories published in *Ellery Queen's Mystery Magazine* between 1968 and 1985.

PORTRAIT OF THE ARTIST AS A DEAD MAN (1947) Francis BONNAMY wrote a series of novels set in Washington, D.C., involving Captain "Mac" McCullough of the D.C. homicide squad and criminologist Peter Utley Shane. In *Portrait of the Artist as a Dead Man*, the body of painter Joe O'Donnell is found in his studio, dressed all in black. Beside his body lies "a portrait of the strangled man just as they saw him: heavy black eyebrows above distended eyes, glossy black hair covering a head that was twisted around and back, tongue thrust out and neck hideously drawn." The artist's real identity turns out to be Jose de Jiminez y O'Donnell, and he had important political connections through his patrons. O'Donnell had painted a number of old ladies, including Mamie Graeme, the "harridan hostess" of Virginia, and had imprudently had an affair with another. The investigation is aided by a German refugee and art expert named Franz Heiden. A clever ART mystery, *Portrait of the Artist as a Dead Man* is written in a witty style reminiscent of Thomas KYD, Bonnamy's contemporary.

POSSESSION (1990) A novel by the English author A. S. Byatt (1936–), part mystery and part romance. Highly acclaimed, it won the prestigious Booker Prize. The story revolves around two nineteenth-century poets and two twentieth-century literary critics. One of the latter, Roland Michel, steals two unknown letters by the poet R. H. Ash that suggest a passionate attachment to an unknown woman. He discovers the woman's identity (another nineteenth-century poet), and that the main archivist and scholar of her work, Maude Bailey, is also her descendant. They begin, through a process of detection, to try to find out the true relationship of the two poets. Their enemy is a rich—and, predictably, American—scholar who is trying to buy up all the materials on Ash. Byatt cleverly creates letters, poems, and documents purportedly of the nineteenth century, and pursues two plots in two different time periods, which in effect act as foils for each other and introduce the author's musings on late-twentieth-century love, sexuality, and society. A novel without murder, it is on the fringe of the HISTORICAL MYSTERY.

POST, MELVILLE DAVISSON (1871–1930) Howard HAYCRAFT called Melville Davisson Post's Uncle ABNER "the outstanding contribution of the United States between Auguste Dupin and Philo Vance." The setting of the stories—Post's native Virginia in the antebellum period—and the character of Uncle Abner himself are also purely American. Uncle Abner is a squire in the mountains who, like a superhero, takes it upon himself to protect those who cannot protect themselves and to punish those whom no on else can touch. His moral stance and allusions to the workings of God reinforce the sensation that Abner is an American Moses. His nephew reports that "Abner belonged to the church militant, and his God was a war lord."

Post was born in Clarksburg, West Virginia, received a law degree from the state university in 1892, and practiced law for several years before publishing his first book, *The Strange Schemes of Randolph Mason* (1896). He put his legal background to good use in the stories about MASON, but in an unusual way: Mason is a master of ruses for evading the law and has "no moral sense." These tricks of the trade were apparently so realistic that some readers protested that the author was aiding and abetting criminals. Two more Mason collections followed. Post's stories, like some of the writings of Arthur MORRISON, led to actual legislative reforms (in Post's case, the elimination of real legal loopholes Randolph Mason had exploited in fiction).

Post was an excellent plotter, and his writing is difficult to categorize. Its Biblical models and style are often remarked upon, but Post was also a natural storyteller, able to grip the reader at once with vivid settings and to maintain control of the pace of the narrative with the almost musical sense of phrasing of the spoken word. One can also hear echoes of the revival tent preacher (the first Abner story is about temperance). Post once said of himself, "I was born like the sons of Atreus in the pasture land of horses. I was reared by a black woman who remembered her grandmother boiling a warrior's head in a pot. I was given a degree by a college of unbeautiful nonsense. I have eaten dinner with a god." He certainly had a sense of theater and the magnetism of the human voice. Even when markedly old fashioned, his stories remain readable.

Post was tremendously successful at publishing in magazines, and never wrote an Uncle Abner novel. *Uncle Abner: Master of Mysteries* (1918) was the first collection of stories. More recently, *The Complete Uncle Abner*

(1977) brought all the stories together for the first time in a critical edition.

Despite the Jeffersonian setting of the stories, Uncle Abner is a figure from another age, perhaps from the Bible. His approach to justice is tribal rather than democratic. Not always does he turn evildoers over to the secular legal powers, and he is very far from a Sherlock HOLMES. Post did write some later stories with a more Holmesian air about *The Sleuth of St. James Square* (1920), Sir Henry Marquis, and even created a secret agent. *The Silent Witness* (1929) is a collection of stories set in West Virginia about crimes unraveled by Colonel Braxton. The key is that the lies with which the criminal must cover his tracks will have a hole in them somewhere, to be exposed by this "silent witness." *Melville Davisson Post: Man of Many Mysteries* (1973) is a biography by Charles A. Norton.

POSTGATE, RAYMOND [WILLIAM] (1896–1971) Although the English author, economist, and political theorist Raymond Postgate wrote only three novels in the mystery and crime genre, one of those books, VERDICT OF TWELVE (1940), is both an enduring classic as well as a most unusual one; his first novel, Postgate used it to elaborate his Marxist principles. Postgate was born in Cambridge and attended Oxford, studying classics and economics. After World War I he became a journalist, and was active in the socialist movement in Britain. His sister, Margaret Isabel Postgate, and his brother-in-law G. D. H. COLE, were also prominent socialists, in addition to being prolific mystery authors. Raymond Postgate's father-in-law, George Lansbury, was a leader of the Labour Party in the thirties, and Postgate became his biographer. Postgate was also a food and wine critic, and contributed to the *Encyclopedia Britannica. Verdict of Twelve* was followed by *Somebody at the Door* (1943) and *The Ledger Is Kept* (1953). In the second book, a desperate woman is trapped in a bad marriage to a bad man; keeping up-to-date, Postgate set his last novel in an atomic power plant.

POSTMAN ALWAYS RINGS TWICE, THE (1934) James M. CAIN was forty-two when he published his first novel, *The Postman Always Rings Twice,* and was instantly famous—which translated into infamous in Boston, where the book was banned as obscene. The violence of *Postman* was not new, but Cain's open treatment of sex caused a sensation. The story is set against the background of the Depression and has a bleak fatalism. At the opening of the story, Frank Chambers (the narrator) is kicked off the hay truck he is riding on and ends up at the Twin Oaks Tavern, a roadside lunchroom about twenty miles from Los Angeles. The owner, Nick Papadakis, offers him a job, which he is about to refuse when he sees Nick's wife, Cora. In his dialogue and his thoughts, Frank is a PULP character. His first reaction to Cora is: "her lips stuck out in a way that made me want to mash them in for her," which he does when they first kiss, biting her mouth until the blood flows down her neck.

Edmund WILSON called Cain the "poet of the tabloid murder," but Raymond CHANDLER thought the style struck a false note by trying to make the narrator of a novel be an average or perhaps sub-average Joe. Certainly, Frank and Cora are incredibly ignorant. Frank gets to Cora by making her think he believes her to be Mexican, and she complains about her Greek husband's greasiness. Their first attempt to kill Papadakis is a bad plan and they are nearly caught. A policeman shows up at exactly the wrong moment, and they are only saved by the accidental death of a cat. Yet they decide to try again. The second attempt is one of the best-known in crime fiction, only a bit less ingenious than the one in Cain's second novel, DOUBLE INDEMNITY (1935). The novel, however, gets better and better as one goes along; the double crosses, the rabid attorney Sackett, and the heavily ironic ending make *The Postman Always Rings Twice* a stunning debut novel.

The Postman Always Rings Twice has been filmed several times, including the famous 1946 movie with Lana Turner and John Garfield. An even earlier and more interesting version, however, was made by Luchino Visconti; under the title *Ossessione* (1942), he turned *Postman* into a gritty neo-realist drama and subtle critique of fascism.

POTTER, BROCK See MALING, ARTHUR.

POTTS, JEAN (1910–) Jean Potts won an EDGAR for best first novel in 1954 for a book (*Go, Lovely Rose*) based on an English murder case, but she changed the setting to a small town in the Midwest. Like Mabel SEELEY, Potts was to become known for books set in this milieu. Potts was born in Nebraska and attended Nebraska Wesleyan University. After moving to New York City, she began publishing short stories in various women's magazines as well as in *Ellery Queen's Mystery Magazine.* Her other novels include *Death of a Stray Cat* (1955), *The Man with the Cane* (1957), *Lightning Strikes Twice* (1958), and *The Only Good Secretary* (1965). In her later career she alternated between the Midwestern and New York settings. One book, *The Troublemaker* (1972), takes place partly on the coast of Maine. It concerns a *Lolita* situation in which a North Carolina professor, under the guise of bumming around on his own for a summer, actually runs off with one of his students, an irresistible nineteen-year-old.

Broke, they take menial jobs at the Seaview Inn. When word of their whereabouts leaks out, jealous wives and others converge on the spot, leading to panic and murder.

POWELL, HARRY The "Preacher" of THE NIGHT OF THE HUNTER (1953), Powell uses his hate-filled religion to mask misogynistic rage, greed, and murderousness.

POWELL, RICHARD (1908–) Richard Powell was born in Philadelphia and attended Princeton University. In 1930, he became a "cub police reporter" for the *Evening Ledger* in Philadelphia, and worked there for several years during the Depression, writing fiction in his spare time. With the outbreak of World War II, Powell enlisted and became a lieutenant colonel. After the war, he rose to vice president with N. W. Ayer & Son, a large advertising agency.

Powell wrote a dozen mystery novels, most of which were about Pentagon operative Andy Blake and his wife, "Arab." The first novel in the series was *Don't Catch Me* (1943). In *All Over But the Shooting* (1944), the trail of a spy leads to a mysterious house on Q Street in Washington, D.C., from which a number of workers from the War Department have disappeared. *Say It with Bullets* (1953) is a revenge story set in Philadelphia about a former American pilot abandoned by his friends during the war.

False Colors (1955; also pub as *Masterpiece in Murder*) is a non-series novel about Peter Meadows, a Philadelphia ART dealer with a small shop on Walnut Street. He gets involved in a case with two beautiful women and an art forgery and fraud plot.

PRATHER, RICHARD S[COTT] (1921–) Born in Santa Ana, California, Richard Prather wrote in the West Coast HARD-BOILED tradition, to which he added another Los Angeles p.i., Shell SCOTT. Prather made several embellishments of his own, however; with his cheerful outlook, colorful appearance, and easygoing manner, Scott is closer to Brett HALLIDAY than the CONTINENTAL OP. The plots of the Scott novels are propelled by rapid action and high body counts, showing the author's debt to Mickey SPILLANE, particularly in his early work. Prather wrote forty books, thirty-five of them about Scott.

During World War II Prather served in the merchant marine. After the war he was a civilian employee on a California air force base, and turned to writing in the late forties. His first novel, *The Case of the Vanishing Beauty* (1950), concerned narcotics abuse and also introduced Scott. Prather could be as prolific as any PULP writer: in 1952 he published *The Peddler, Dagger of Flesh,* and *Lie Down Killer,* all non-series novels. The first of these is about a nineteen-year-old punk who tries to get an old friend to help him worm his way into organized prostitution in San Francisco. In his enthusiasm, he starts killing people to get to the top (like W. R. BURNETT's Little Caesar). Perhaps sensational for its time, the story now seems hollow and sordid, the characters less shocking than merely unsympathetic.

In contrast with this grimly pulpy material, in the Scott series Prather relied heavily on comedy and unlikely situations; at one point, Scott uses balloons filled with natural gas to lift himself off the ground. Like Brett Halliday, he finds himself involved in embarrassing cases, such as *Strip for Murder* (1955), in which he investigates a killing in a nudist colony. While many critics have praised Prather, BARZUN and TAYLOR charged him with puerility, and PENZLER et. al. declined to mention him at all.

Other works by Prather include *Double in Trouble* (1959), which he wrote with Stephen MARLOWE, pairing Shell Scott with Marlowe's Chester DRUM.

PRELUDE TO A CERTAIN MIDNIGHT (1947) A novel by Gerald KERSH, better known for his short stories. The style of the book is episodic, Dickensian, and digressive; like DICKENS, Kersh writes of a lower-class London populated with strange characters, but in Kersh's work, it is a Jewish immigrant community. Among them are a retired boxer known as "The Tiger Fitzgerald," and Sir Storrington Thirst, who is described as "a wide flat man shaped like a bed-bug, who crept into the cracks of conversation and crawled out between rounds of drinks." When Sonia Sabbatini, the child of a poor tailor, is raped and murdered in the coal cellar of an abandoned house, two sleuths set out on the hunt: one is the close-mouthed Chief Inspector Turpin, the other his antagonist, Asta Thundersley. She pursues the murderer out of an obsession, based on a universal human response to the child murderer which she expresses simply: "I don't want him on earth." In her blustery manner, she is like an English Bertha COOL.

Kersh mimics Dickens's combination of gritty realism, stage comedy, sentimentality, and charm. His language can be flat-footed, often poetic, and sometimes arresting; he describes a toilet as "stuffed with used newsprint like the head of a plagiarist." Although there is little detection and the psychology is sometimes threadbare, the book is a peculiar, minor classic.

PRESIDENT'S MYSTERY STORY, THE See CELEBRITY MYSTERIES.

PRICHARD, [VERNON] HESKETH (1876–1922) Now sadly forgotten, Hesketh Prichard was a remarkable man and a prolific and interesting writer until his health was ruined and his life cut short by World War I. He is perhaps the only mystery writer who collaborated with his mother. Prichard was born in India, but after his father's death returned to England with his mother. He entered the civil service, eventually rising to the position of aide to the Lord Lieutenant of Ireland (1907). Prichard was also a big game hunter and cricket player of some repute. He served with heroism in World War I, winning the Distinguished Service Order (DSO), but was rebuked for suggesting sniper tactics as an alternative to the disastrous frontal assaults of trench warfare. Prichard's life was extremely vigorous, even though he had a heart defect.

In 1898, Prichard and his mother, Kate O'Brien Ryall Prichard, began to publish two series of detective stories. One was about Flaxman Low, a pioneering example of the OCCULT detective. In each of his cases, Low visits a haunted house and unravels a mystery. Sometimes, the monsters encountered were agglomerations of elements of several different horror genres popular at the time: in "The Story of Baelbrow," the "thing" that haunts the lonely Swaffam mansion is at first a dreadful shadow, then makes snuffling noises like a "bear," and yet appears to be bandaged. Unlike the story of pure dread, in the Low tales the supernatural agents actually kill people. The Flaxman Low stories were first published in *Pearson's Magazine* (1898–1899) under the pseudonym E. and E. Heron.

More famous than Flaxman Low was DON Q, a sinister character who also first appeared in magazines. Some of these stories were co-authored by the Prichards, and others were apparently written solely by Hesketh Prichard. Don Q was adapted for a film starring Douglas Fairbanks, *Don Q, Son of Zorro* (1925).

Another important pioneering effort—in more ways than one—was Prichard's series of stories about November Joe, who was termed "possibly the only backwoods detective in literature" by *The Encyclopedia of Mystery and Detection*. Prichard drew on his own experience as a hunter for these short stories, set in North America. November Joe is a Canadian woodsman who is employed by the authorities in Quebec as a consulting detective. His keen powers of observation, like those of Sherlock HOLMES, allow him to read clues that others miss, except that "the floor of the forest is his page" and not the streets of the metropolis. In stories like "The Murder at the Duck Club" (in which the killing is oddly like that in CONFIDENTIALLY YOURS, 1962), the tall and muscular outdoorsman shows himself to be "a courtier of the woods." The stories were collected in *November Joe: The Detective of the Woods* (1913).

Prichard was an inveterate traveler, and one of his strangest adventures was nonfictional. He joined an expedition to Patagonia to search for a giant prehistoric sloth, the Mylodon; he did not find it, but the journey led to the publication of *Through the Heart of Patagonia* (1902), written with his mother's assistance. Prichard also wrote a book about travels in Haiti.

PRIESTLEY, DR. LANCELOT A detective who appears in more than seventy novels by John RHODE. Priestley is not a medical doctor but a Ph.D., a retired professor of mathematics with a passion for logic. This sedentary detective mostly stays at home occupying himself with his writings on logic and the mystery puzzles brought to him by the police. A rather dry intellectual, Priestley wears strong glasses and is a cold personality. In his first case, *The Paddington Mystery* (1925), he meets and defends Harold Merefield, who becomes his personal secretary as well as his son-in-law. As an ARMCHAIR DETECTIVE, Priestley's habit is to hold a dinner every Saturday at his home in Westbourne Terrace. His friends, including Merefield, former Superintendent Hanslet, the retired Dr. Oldland, and Inspector Jimmy Waghorn join him and kick around theories about the latest case.

Priestley reflects the interest in scientific detectives at the time Rhode began writing. Dr. THORNDYKE was already well established; Priestley is similar to him in being aristocratic and blessed with superior intelligence, but eschewing intuition in favor of cold reason and analysis of facts. There the resemblance ceases. In contrast to Thorndyke, Priestley has few other characteristics—such as a sense of humor—to recommend him. Unlike Thorndyke's creator, R. Austin FREEMAN, Rhode was less careful of his science and was criticized for errors in his works.

Only a handful of the Priestley cases are worth looking for or likely to be found. BARZUN and TAYLOR called *The Corpse in the Car* (1935) a "near-perfect murder by poison." Of the generally better early stories, *Dr. Priestley's Quest* (1926) and *The Ellerby Case* (1927) are narrated by Merefield. *The Murders in Praed Street* (1928) and *Death in Harley Street* (1946) are among Rhode's best; the former was made into a film, probably because of its several killings and its atypical degree of action. *The Claverton Affair* (1933; orig title *The Claverton Mystery*) is notable for its use of the OCCULT. *Death at the Helm* (1941), obviously, is an example of MURDER AFLOAT. In *Murder at Derivale* (1958), Waghorn investigates a case of a country gentleman found dead in the back of a truck. Standard props include a ne'er-do-well brother and servants with criminal pasts. The "elderly" Priestley remains in the background in his "habitual attitude of apparent somnolence." The most interesting clue is a diary keyed to the shipping news.

BIBLIOGRAPHY Novels: *Dr. Priestley's Quest* (1926), *Tragedy at the Unicorn* (1928), *The House on Tollard Ridge* (1929), *The Davidson Case* (1929; U.S. title *Murder at Bratton Grange*), *Peril at Cranbury Hall* (1930), *Pinehurst* (1930; U.S. title *Dr. Priestley Investigates*), *Tragedy on the Line* (1931), *The Hanging Woman* (1931), *Mystery at Greycombe Farm* (1932; U.S. title *The Fire at Greycombe Farm*), *Dead Men at the Folly* (1932), *The Motor Rally Mystery* (1933; U.S. title *Dr. Priestley Lays a Trap*), *The Venner Crime* (1933), *The Robthorne Mystery* (1934), *Poison for One* (1934), *Shot at Dawn* (1934), *Hendon's First Case* (1935), *Mystery at Olympia* (1935; U.S. title *Murder at the Motor Show*), *Death at Breakfast* (1936), *In Face of the Verdict* (1936; U.S. title *In the Face of the Verdict*), *Death in the Hop Fields* (1937; U.S. title *The Harvest Murder*), *Death on the Board* (1937 U.S. title *Death Sits on the Board*), *Proceed with Caution* (1937; U.S. title *Body Unidentified*), *Invisible Weapons* (1938), *The Bloody Tower* (1938; U.S. title *Tower of Evil*), *Death Pays a Dividend* (1939), *Death on Sunday* (1939; U.S. title *The Elm Tree Murder*), *Death on the Boat Train* (1940), *Murder at Lilac Cottage* (1940), *They Watched by Night* (1941; U.S. title *Signal for Death*), *The Fourth Bomb* (1942), *Dead on the Track* (1943), *Men Die at Cyprus Lodge* (1943), *Death Invades the Meeting* (1944), *Vegetable Duck* (1944; U.S. title *Too Many Suspects*), *Bricklayer's Arms* (1945; U.S. title *Shadow of a Crime*), *The Lake House* (1946; U.S. title *The Secret of the Lake House*), *Nothing but the Truth* (1947; U.S. title *Experiment in Crime*), *Death of an Author* (1947), *The Paper Bag* (1948; U.S. title *The Links in the Chain*), *The Telephone Call* (1948; U.S. title *Shadow of an Alibi*), *Blackthorn House* (1949), *Up the Garden Path* (1949; U.S. title *The Fatal Garden*), *The Two Graphs* (1950; U.S. title *Double Identities*), *Family Affairs* (1950; U.S. title *The Last Suspect*), *Dr. Goodwood's Locum* (1951; U.S. title *The Affair of the Substitute Doctor*), *The Secret Meeting* (1951), *Death in Wellington Road* (1952), *Death at the Dance* (1952), *By Registered Post* (1953; U.S. title *The Mysterious Suspect*), *Death at the Inn* (1953; U.S. Title *The Case of the Forty Thieves*), *The Dovebury Murders* (1954), *Death on the Lawn* (1954), *Domestic Agency* (1955; U.S. title *Grave Matters*), *Death of a Godmother* (1955; U.S. title *Delayed Payment*), *An Artist Dies* (1956; U.S. title *Death of an Artist*), *Open Verdict* (1956), *Robbery with Violence* (1957), *Death of a Bridegroom* (1957), *Death Takes a Partner* (1958), *Licensed for Murder* (1959), *Three Cousins Die* (1959), *Twice Dead* (1960), *The Fatal Pool* (1960), *The Vanishing Diary* (1961).

PRIESTLEY, J[OHN] B[OYNTON] (1894–1984)

Rather late in a long career, the English novelist J. B. Priestley wrote a very good, very memorable mystery, SALT IS LEAVING (1966). But of his more than 120 books, few were mysteries.

Priestley was born in Yorkshire and studied at Cambridge University. He served in World War I and was wounded many times. After the war he became a journalist, and his first book publications were collections of essays. The book that made his reputation as a novelist was *The Good Companions* (1929). In the PICARESQUE tradition, it is about a Dickensian group of characters who tour English music halls. Priestley was also a playwright, and wrote for Hollywood in the late thirties. He was in London during World War II, and gave a weekly morale-boosting broadcast that made him famous.

Priestley's first thriller was *Benighted* (1927; U.S. title *Old Dark House*), a novel set in Wales about a group of five travelers who become stranded in a house owned by a suspicious family. They wind up telling their stories to each other, and there is a killing. The novel was made into a film. *Black-Out in Gretley* (1942) is a World War II espionage thriller. Among Priestley's many plays was *An Inspector Calls* (1946), in which the suicide of a girl sets off an investigation that exposes the sordidness beneath a family's conventional façade. It was successfully revived in the 1990s in London.

"PRIME OF LIFE"

A story by Louis Bromfield (1896–1956). Bromfield is best known for *The Green Bay Tree* (1924) and the other novels of his tetralogy, *Escape.* Like August DERLETH, he was noted for his presentation of agrarian life in the Midwest. Bromfield had a 1,000 acre farm and wrote several books about farming life.

"Prime of Life" springs from these same sources, but is less idyllic; instead, it presents the horrible frustration and emptiness of a man dying inside the shell of an unromantic and unrewarding conventional existence. A mystery in reverse, it tells how middle-aged hardware store owner Homer Dilworth came to be hanged. After an oppressive religious upbringing and marriage to a shrewish and repressed woman, Homer suddenly "turned young" again during a vacation. His abandonment of his family leads to his destruction, and is taken by the self-satisfied townspeople as proof that "the wages of sin is death." The narrator, however, draws a different conclusion. As a man who tries to break out of his enchainment into a somehow more authentic existence, Homer is an archetypal character similar to Dashiell Hammett's Flitcraft in THE MALTESE FALCON (1929).

PRIMROSE, INSPECTOR

See LATHEM, GRACE.

PRINGLE, ROMNEY A detective created by R. Austin FREEMAN in collaboration with his friend, the doctor John James Pitcairn (1860–1936). Pringle is a thief like J. J. RAFFLES, although he is more middle-class and his plans sometimes backfire. Some of Pringle's exploits were collected in *The Adventures of Romney Pringle* (1902), after appearing in *Cassell's Magazine.* Another collection of Pringle tales, *The Further Adventures of Romney Pringle,* did not appear until 1970. Freeman, who subsequently created the detective Dr. John THORNDYKE, went on to collaborate with Pitcairn on a series of medical detective stories, also published in *Cassell's* and collected much later (*From A Surgeon's Diary,* 1975).

Pringle is a handsome and educated scoundrel whose antique gem collecting is aided by his criminal schemes. Cheerful and polite, Pringle is a master of disguise; his main feature—a port wine mark on his face—is actually fake. In "The Assyrian Rejuvenator," he unmasks a quack medicine operation, drives off the proprietor, and then in disguise takes over the scam himself. An inveterate diner-out, Pringle picks up jobs by spying and eavesdropping on people in restaurants. In "The Submarine Boat," he overhears a deal being struck between a shipyard draughtsman and a French agent, and tries to horn in on the sale of secrets himself. When Pringle is not out drumming up scams, he pretends to be a literary agent, though he has no clients.

PRIVATE EYE WRITERS OF AMERICA (PWA) This organization was formed in 1982 and honors writers who write about private investigators, loosely defined. PWA's Shamus awards follow the model of the EDGAR awards and are given in the categories of best private eye novel, best paperback original, best first novel, best short story, etcetera. Dates below are for year of publication; award given in the following year.

Best Private Eye Novel: 1981, *Hoodwink,* Bill Pronzini; 1982, *Eight Million Ways to Die,* Lawrence Block; 1983, *True Detective,* Max Allan Collins; 1984, *Sugartown,* Loren D. Estleman; 1985, *"B" Is for Burglar,* Sue Grafton; 1986, *Staked Goat,* Jeremiah Healy; 1987, *A Tax in Blood,* Benjamin Schutz; 1988, *Kiss,* John Lutz; 1989, *Extenuating Circumstances,* Jonathan Valin; 1990, *"G Is for Gumshoe,* Sue Grafton; 1991, *Stolen Away,* Max Allan Collins; 1992, *The Man Who Was Taller Than God,* Harold Adams; 1993, *The Devil Knows You're Dead,* Lawrence Block; 1994, *"K" Is for Killer,* Sue Grafton; 1995, *Concourse,* S. J. Rozan; 1996, *Sunset Express,* Robert Crais; 1997, *Come Back Dead,* Terrence Faherty; 1998, *Boobytrap,* Bill Pronzini; 1999, *California Fire and Life,* Don Winslow.

Best First Novel: 1984, *A Creative Kind of Killer,* Jack Early; 1985, *Hardcover,* Wayne Warga; 1986, *Jersey Tomatoes,* J.W. Ryder; 1987, *Death on the Rocks,* Michael Allegretto; 1988, *Fear of the Dark,* Gar Anthony Haywood; 1989, *Katwalk,* Karen Kijewski; 1990, *Devil in a Blue Dress,* Walter Mosley; 1991, *Suffer Little Children,* Thomas D. Davis; 1992, *The Woman Who Married a Bear,* James Straley; 1993, *Satan's Lambs,* Lynne Hightower; 1994, *A Drink Before the War,* Dennis Lehane; 1995, *The Innocents,* Richard Barre; 1996, *This Dog for Hire,* Carol Lea Benjamin; 1997, *Big Red Tequila,* Rick Riordan; 1998, *A Cold Day in Paradise,* Steve Hamilton; 1999, *Every Dead Thing,* John Connolly.

PRIVATE WOUND, THE (1966) A novel by Nicholas BLAKE (C. Day-Lewis). Anthony BOUCHER called it "an intensely penetrating study of sexual passion, a powerful story of murder, constantly illumined by the author's lightning flashes of insight." The first part, about an Anglo-Irish writer's passion for a young woman in a small Irish town, would have stood alone as a novel even with an ending other than murder. It is refreshingly frank about sexuality without being cheap or sensational; Blake really is interested in the nature of sexual passion, which in this case survives even after the protagonist has recognized that no other bonds of sympathy or compatibility exist between himself and his lover. The author's own Anglo-Irish upbringing and his coming of age in the thirties (the time in which the novel is set) give the book an additional emotional force; Blake wrote about these aspects of his life in his partial autobiography, *The Buried Day* (1960).

Dominic Eyre is an Anglo-Irish novelist who was born in Tuam. During a driving tour of Ireland, he experiences car trouble and lands in the town of Charlottestown. He takes a small cottage where he intends to spend the summer writing. Some of the first people he meets in the town are Harriet ("Harry") Leeson and her husband, Flurry. A veteran of the Black and Tan war, Flurry was a ruthless and even savage fighter who seems to have settled into a clownish role in Charlottesville, a town practically owned lock, stock, and barrel by his younger brother Kevin. Ironically, while Flurry seems hardly to notice Dominic's intense affair with Harry, Kevin behaves extremely suspiciously. Inexplicably, Dominic's room is searched and attempts are made on his life (in one, he is left bound in a car on the sands, to be drowned by the rising tide). The murder, when it occurs, creates some strange alliances, and suddenly it becomes clear why the local priest and the populace wanted Dominic to leave: Charlottestown cannot bear much real passion, which risks to ignite its own repressed feelings and personalities. The various characters, especially Flurry's great ruined self, are powerfully drawn; it is a relatively simple story about complicated people.

"PROBLEM OF CELL 13, THE" (1905) The most famous and frequently anthologized case of Professor Augustus S. F. X. Van Dusen, the THINKING MACHINE. As the title suggests, it is a problem more than a case: the crotchety professor is having dinner with two esteemed friends when a discussion of prisons comes up. The Professor says that he could get out of a prison cell by using his wits. A bet is arranged, and he is promptly transferred to Cell 13, the "death cell" of Chisholm Prison. Bringing nothing with him but plain clothes and some tooth powder, Van Dusen is presented with The Problem—how to get out. Some of his procedures benefit from extreme luck, but the story is ingenious.

PROCANE CHRONICLE, THE (1972) A novel by Ross THOMAS, written under the pseudonym Oliver Bleeck. Professional go-between Philip ST. IVES enters a laundromat at three in the morning with a bag containing $90,000 in order to buy back some stolen property belonging to master thief Abner Procane. Instead, he finds a small-time con man murdered and stuffed into a crevice behind a dryer. Now it seems that the stolen property is in the hands of someone else, and *they* want the $90,000. So begins a trail of circumstances that leads the diffident St. Ives deeper and deeper into Procane's business—stealing. Procane has never been caught or even arrested because he only steals money and only robs people who are crooked themselves, taking money that they cannot possibly report stolen because then they would have to account for it. But if Procane does not get back his "chronicle" (an incriminating journal), he will lose his biggest caper of all, and his life. Thomas writes in the manner of Donald WESTLAKE, but without the comedian's need to draw attention to his own wit; the story is clever, the dialogue terse but very funny. Thomas never lets the humor take total control of the narrative, and so keeps a certain hard-boiledness and menace within sight, which finally erupts in the ending.

PROCEDURAL A type of novel in which the actual methods of police work are paramount. The police procedural, as it is often called, stresses realism of *action;* unrealistic characters still abound. It is interesting that Ed MCBAIN, the foremost of the police proceduralists, writes in the third person, as if in obedience to Raymond CHANDLER's dictum that the kind of person who would be a cop or private detective would probably not be the same as the introspective storyteller so common in the HARD-BOILED genre. Writing in the third person does away with this problem of suspension of disbelief. The tone of the procedural is not always objective, however. Many procedural writers are policemen (or policewomen, as in the case of Dorothy UHNAK) or ex-policemen, like Ed DEE and Joseph WAMBAUGH. English practitioners of the subgenre include John CREASEY, Maurice PROCTER, and John WAINWRIGHT. The first police procedural is often acknowledged to be Hillary Waugh's LAST SEEN WEARING . . . (1952). Ironically, this first bona fide procedural takes place in a rural rather than an urban setting.

The procedural novel rests on a contradiction: insofar as it tries to be truly objective—a bare statement of facts, like a policeman's notes—it is an inartistic formula. Dennis WHEATLEY produced some proto-procedurals that were actually dossiers of information rather than novels. In order to be readable, the procedural has to "borrow" the methods of art, which accounts for the unrealistic crimes and criminals that turn up, and the use of coincidences—the paramount one being the basic formula of the mystery, the "converging plot lines" device.

The popularity of procedurals has no doubt been encouraged by the television equivalent, the police show. Some procedural writers, like John HARVEY, have written television programs themselves and consciously use the cop show as model. On the other hand, everything for which the procedural book is praised is done better by television because the visual element enlivens the "text." In addition, mundane events that can be evoked with a second of film (getting up, eating, driving, etc.) often require many boring sentences to describe. Many procedurals read like teleplays, and as anyone who has read scripts knows, a great film may appear lifeless and dead on the page (see, for example, Graham Greene's comments on THE THIRD MAN, 1949). Hence, the best procedural books "cheat" by minimizing procedure and heightening suspense, character, and surprise—which is to say, their writers try to write like novelists. At its best, the procedural can say something about "the way we live now" (or in Charles Willeford's phrase, THE WAY WE DIE NOW) in a manner impossible in the COZY.

Jacques BARZUN summed up the procedural subgenre thus: "They should be taken in moderation unless one is a salesman and able to find a narcissistic pleasure in seeing other patient men ring doorbells."

PROCTER, MAURICE (1906–1973) The English writer Maurice Procter was a pioneer of the police PROCEDURAL style, based on his own experience as a policeman in

England. Procter ran away from home to join the army; extricated from that impulsive act, he later decided to become a policeman. He was on the force in Halifax, Yorkshire, for almost twenty years. His first books, written shortly after retirement, were novels about the police force: *No Proud Chivalry* (1946) and *Each Man's Destiny* (1947).

Procter's first mystery was *The Chief Inspector's Statement* (1949; U.S. title *The Pennycross Murders*), a disturbing novel about sex murder involving CHILDREN. *I Will Speak Daggers* (1956; U.S. title *The Ripper*) was also melodramatic, but it adhered closely to the pattern of the classic detective puzzle. In 1953, Procter published *Hell Is a City*, the novel that introduced his series detective, Inspector MARTINEAU. Martineau inhabits the dour, grim world of Granchester, a city in northern England (obviously based on Manchester). Although the series features teamwork, it is not as "decentralized" as other police procedurals—Ed MCBAIN's, for example—and Martineau remains the central hero. Procter also used the common mystery figure of the arch-enemy, or NAPOLEON OF CRIME. Martineau's particular nemesis is Dixie Costello, an underworld figure in Granchester. Procter wrote a handful of non-series novels. One of them, THE PUB CRAWLER (1956), is perhaps his best novel. In it he describes rather than shows police procedures with great care, in a manner almost documentary or nonfictional. Without the baggage of a series character, Procter is able to render the procedural in a purer form, free from the series props and gimmicks often used to make the procedural more "interesting."

Another Yorkshire policeman, who joined the force at the same time as Procter retired, was John WAINWRIGHT.

PROHIBITION The era during which alcohol was illegal in the United States came about through the passing of the Volstead Act (October 1919) and the Eighteenth Amendment to the U.S. Constitution. Beginning January 15, 1920, at the opening of the Roaring Twenties, the sale of wine, beer, and spirits was illegal.

The temperance movement had been lobbying for prohibition since the nineteenth century. It has been suggested that the effect of Prohibition was to make drinking more exciting by making it forbidden and clandestine, and that the rise of organized criminal mobs could also be attributed to it. "Speakeasies," the technically illegal clubs where alcohol was served, were quite unlike the traditional pubs and saloons of big cities, which had catered mostly to workingmen. Speakeasies made drinking glamorous, allowed women, fostered social mixing, and contributed to the freer atmosphere of the twenties.

Prohibition's contribution to literature was great, opening up a whole new range of criminal activity, whether one was taking a drink in a swanky bar or carrying a machine gun for a rumrunning racket. The background of HARD-BOILED stories is rooted in Prohibition. The Al CAPONE gang alone had an army of 1,000 men (the Commissioner of Internal Revenue only had 2,000 agents to enforce Prohibition in the whole country), and reportedly took in $60 million per year. In addition to the criminal gangs of Dion O'Bannion, Bugs Moran, and other bosses, Prohibition and the Depression saw the rise of outlaws like Bonnie and Clyde, John Dillinger, and Baby Face Nelson. Although all were murderers and some were insane, a few became folk heroes and continue to inspire novels to this day. Loren ESTLEMAN wrote *The Oklahoma Punk* (1976) about a comparatively minor gangster. William Kennedy's novel *Legs* (1976), the first in his Albany trilogy, is about Legs Diamond. Diamond was universally hated for double-crossing friends and enemies alike during his career as a bootlegger, drug pusher, and pitiless killer. He was finally killed by gangsters in 1931 after surviving previous attempts. A more romantic figure is Pretty Boy Floyd. Woody Guthrie wrote a folk ballad about Floyd, and ten thousand people came to view his body after he was trapped and shot by police and federal agents in 1934. Raised in Oklahoma, Charles Arthur Floyd began his criminal career as a teenager in the early twenties. He carried a gun for bootleggers, but really came into his own as a bank robber. His "Robin Hood" reputation stemmed from his habit of tearing up farmers' mortgages during hold-ups and giving away money and gifts. He killed at least ten people. A detailed portrait of Floyd is given in *Pretty Boy Floyd* (1994), a novel by Larry McMurtry and Diana Ossana.

Prohibition lasted a surprisingly long time; the Eighteenth Amendment was not repealed until 1933, when the Twenty-First Amendment was passed revoking Prohibition. During the battle over continuing or discontinuing it, those in favor of repeal were called "wets" and the opposition "drys." The Twenty-First Amendment, however, did not make drinking *legal;* it only returned the question to the power of the states, seven of which decided to remain dry. Mississippi was the last to repeal its dry laws, in 1966.

PRONZINI, WILLIAM [JOHN] (1943–) Born in California, Bill Pronzini turned to writing in the late sixties after various jobs, including one in the U.S. Marshall's office. He is one of the most prolific mystery and crime writers now working and has written many novels, literally hundreds of short stories, and critical articles, in addition to his best-known series about the NAMELESS DETECTIVE. Pronzini wrote some of his earlier books under the pseudonym Jack Foxx, and ghost-wrote some stories about Mike SHAYNE.

Pronzini is also a prolific collaborator. He has co-written several novels with Marcia MULLER, whom he married in 1992. The first was BEYOND THE GRAVE (1986), which included Pronzini's QUINCANNON. They also collaborated on *Double* (1984), a novel in which the Nameless Detective and Sharon MCCONE both appear. *Day of the Moon* (1983; repr 1993) is a novel co-written with Jeffrey Wallmann. It concerns a man named Flagg who is a "troubleshooter" for "the Organization," which is a criminal syndicate involved in trucking, smuggling, and other enterprises on the West Coast. Flagg is called in to retrieve some money when an armored car robbery financed by the Organization goes sour. His investigation, conducted in the manner of a HARD-BOILED p.i., comes to encompass other attacks on the Organization's operations. With John LUTZ, Pronzini wrote *The Eye* (1984). No doubt Pronzini's workmanlike writing style facilitates collaboration.

Pronzini's other non-series works include *Blue Lonesome* (1995), about a San Francisco accountant who becomes interested in a mysterious woman who then commits suicide. An unlikely hero, he travels to a small town in the Nevada desert to find out why the woman killed herself; his amateur investigations lead him into a murder case. This seems to be a new direction for Pronzini, for in 1997 he published *A Wasteland of Strangers,* another novel about pressures within a small rural community. Set in northern California, it concerns a stranger who comes to the town of Pomo for mysterious reasons, and soon becomes a murder suspect. Pronzini has carefully researched the culture of the Pomo Indian tribe.

Pronzini's non-series short stories have been collected in such volumes as *Small Felonies* (1988) and *Stacked Deck* (1991). A scholar of mystery fiction, particularly the PULP MAGAZINES, Pronzini has edited literally dozens of anthologies (including one about mysteries with TRAINS), and has published two humorous studies of the worst of mystery fiction, *Gun in Cheek* (1982) and *Son of Gun in Cheek* (1987). His anthology *The Arbor House Treasury of Detective and Mystery Stories from the Great Pulps* (1983) made available important stories otherwise difficult or impossible to find, including the first story about the CONTINENTAL OP. Pronzini was the first president of the Private Eye Writers of America, from whom he has received several awards.

PROTOMYSTERIES Broadly speaking, a term used to characterize works—written mostly before the industrial revolution—that are germane to modern crime and mystery fiction. The term is a catch-all meant to deal with two obvious facts: that crime has been an element of literature at least since Genesis, and that humans are fascinated with transgression. For her anthology *The Omnibus of Crime* (1929), Dorothy L. SAYERS chose examples from the Apocrypha, the *Aeneid,* and Herotodus, but other works or passages from Greek tragedy and the Bible have been produced as examples.

Two types of literature from the medieval and early modern period could also be said to have influenced the later development of the mystery. Quest literature, typified by the adventures of King Arthur and *Sir Gawain and the Green Knight,* was often highly suspenseful and violent; its purpose was to entertain and to illustrate the virtues of the Christian knight. One could see CHANDLER's HARD-BOILED credo ("down these mean streets a man must go . . .") as an echo of the code embodied in quest literature; the ancestry of the mystery story in earlier Christian models was noted by CHESTERTON, AUDEN, Nicholas BLAKE, and others. Rex STOUT said that people who did not enjoy mysteries were "anarchists," and every society has probably had protomysteries, in the sense of stories designed to epitomize the triumph of order over disorder.

Like quest literature, the PICARESQUE tale also involved adventurous journeys, but its hero was not a Christian knight; instead, he was a rascal of low birth. With its emphasis on realism, including the cynical attitude of the hero, the picaresque tale was well on the way to the modern novel. Daniel DEFOE wrote not only novels influenced by the picaresque, but criminal biographies and accounts of real crimes. FIELDING continued the development, writing both picaresque-inspired novels and criminal biography. (ZADIG [1747], by Voltaire, is often mentioned in this context, but there is only one chapter in which detection plays a part.)

William Godwin is usually credited with writing the first novel in which the detection was considered an object of interest in itself. In earlier novels, it was not the criminal's capture but his redemption that was of interest; up until the transition to the modern mystery, the criminal's ingenuity of escape rather than the subtleties of the pursuers was the focus. In CALEB WILLIAMS (1794), Godwin showed both the flight of the suspect *and* the deductions and pursuit by the "sleuth." Godwin was helped by the fact that he was an anarchist, since he was not caught up in any religious conception of redemption, but only a moral and social one. In the years between the turn of the nineteenth century and the work of POE, DICKENS is the pre-eminent figure, but the detective element was not "proto" any longer.

The background of the rise of criminal literature beginning in England has been amply described, for example in *Albion's Fatal Tree: Crime in Eighteenth Century England* (1975). This collection of essays makes the argument that, because rising commerce, the incipient industrial revolution, and the enclosure of public lands were rapidly making the rich richer while dispossessing the lower classes (see Captain SWING), more and more laws were passed, most of them protecting property—and a startling number with capital penalties. Simply put, more laws equaled more crime. People were actually hanged at TYBURN TREE for stealing a gentleman's wig, a watch, or in the famous case of Bosavern Penlez (see Henry FIELDING), a few handkerchiefs and caps. Hence, "the eighteenth century produced much genteel cant about justice, but it also produced a large popular literature marked by cynicism and disrespect for the law." It is interesting to compare this attitude with that of the HARD-BOILED mystery. The idea that the law was there to protect moneyed interests and maintain the status quo pervades the American hard-boiled novel, but not the COZY mystery or the later English mystery novel of the GOLDEN AGE. Writers like DEFOE began writing about crime and criminals, and street ballads and handbills purveyed the exploits of notorious wrongdoers such as Jonathan WILD and Dick TURPIN; some of these characters became folk heroes, while others were vilified and held up as models of all that was wrong with the age. The various branches of crime literature were already growing and would later lead to mysteries in which evil is exposed and punished and crime stories in which the malefactor is an interesting and sometimes heroic character. In the nineteenth century, BALZAC would do much to further this development.

While this whole growth process was taking place in the West, the detective story had already developed in China, as Robert VAN GULIK demonstrated.

PRUSSIC ACID Another name for hydrogen cyanide or hydrocyanic acid. Death from prussic acid can be as rapid as a few minutes. Hydrogen cyanide is used in many products, from metal polish to rat poison to insecticide. See CYANIDE.

PRYE, DOCTOR PAUL The first series character created by Margaret MILLAR. Prye appeared in her first book, *The Invisible Worm* (1941), and in two others. Prye is six-foot-five, slightly graying, and distinguished looking; however, he is only thirty-five years old, and clowns his way through Millar's humorous plots. He says he is interested in neurology, psychoneurology, psychiatry, abnormal psychiatry, and psychoanalysis, but prefers to be called a "quack" because it makes people feel more at ease. As his name suggests, Prye insinuates himself into people's affairs (including those of the police), satisfying his taste for sleuthing and insatiable curiosity about human peculiarities. In *The Invisible Worm*, he is staying at the home of George and Barbara Hays in Mertonville, Illinois. Barbara is a Merton, granddaughter of the founder of the town; she is also a mental case and a morphine addict. Their children are Eva, bewitching and sneaky, and Simon—"callow, sallow and shallow." Prye is actually a suspect when another resident, a suspicious Englishman named Thomas Philips, is found dead of HYOSCINE poisoning. The investigation is conducted by Inspector William Bailey, hindered by both his spinster sister and Prye himself. Meant to be lighthearted and comic, the book's humor seems rather dated and silly. The main interest of the novel today is to show from what beginnings Millar rose to become a master of mood and character. Prye's second appearance was in *The Weak-Eyed Bat* (1942), his last in *The Devil Loves Me* (1942).

PUB CRAWLER, THE (1956) A novel by Maurice PROCTER, and his most perfect PROCEDURAL novel. A team of detectives in the Midlands town of Airechester is sent into action after Sam Gilmour, the owner of The Starving Rascal Pub, is found with his skull bashed in with a coal hammer. The body is discovered by his daughter, Gay Gilmour; the head of the investigation is Detective Inspector Robert Fairbrother. These are the bare facts, and this is one procedural that basically sticks to them. The one convenient coincidence, that there is an undercover police agent in the area, is made to be convincing. The atmosphere of squalor and brutality in the run-down section of Champion Road and its population of victimizers and victimized is brought home to the reader particularly in the scenes of Ma Byles's guest house, where Polish and Irish laborers live in cramped quarters with other members of "non-respectable" society. Ma Byles herself is a disturbing example of callousness overlaid with pragmatism overlaid with vulgarity—and somewhere, a small and lukewarm heart. Her son is a petty thief, her older daughter a prostitute; the romantic triangle involving her youngest and unspoiled daughter and a man named Bill Knight is deftly handled and brought to a satisfying but surprising conclusion that, for once, also has a pertinent relationship to the solution of the crime.

Inspector Fairbrother and his associates never become much more than figures in uniforms or trench coats, but Procter so manages the handling of forensic evidence, the search for (and especially identification of) Gilmour's coin collection, and other procedures that the reader does not resent the tea-and-scones scenes to show how human the policemen really are. Procter's cops are not so much HARD-BOILED as well-trained. Only one implausible trick with firearms seems out of character.

PUBLISHING See BOOKS.

PULP MAGAZINES The pulp magazines were inexpensive, primarily weekly magazines that included but were not restricted to mystery and detective fiction. Their heyday was the decades between the end of World War I and the beginning or World War II, but the first of them appeared in 1889 (*The Argosy*), and the last finally disappeared in the fifties. Although the paper inside was cheap, the covers of the magazines were printed in garish, attention-getting colors. The pulp magazine was the inheritor of the DIME NOVEL, which had done so much to create the tastes of popular literature. Street & Smith, which dominated the dime novel business, got into pulps in the first years of the century and went on to produce many magazines, including *Detective Story,* which Bill PRONZINI has called "the first detective story pulp." It first appeared in 1915.

Many of the foremost American writers of the HARD-BOILED school started out in the pulps, most notably Dashiell HAMMETT, Raymond CHANDLER, and Erle Stanley GARDNER. Later, John D. MACDONALD would get his start writing short stories for pulps. Other writers identified with the pulps include Carroll John DALY, Horace MCCOY, Frederick NEBEL, Norbert DAVIS, Bruno FISCHER, Paul CAIN, Raoul WHITFIELD, and Lester DENT. Pulp writers often worked in various genres at the same time, writing everything from Westerns to science fiction in addition to detective stories. The best writers "graduated" from the pulps, while many others found that their style did not translate to the novel format.

The most famous pulp magazine was BLACK MASK. Under the editorship of Joseph T. SHAW, it sometimes raised pulp writing to the level of literature. Other pulp magazines included *Thrilling Detective* and *Dime Detective,* and many more specialized magazines that dealt with narrower themes such as courtroom cases or hero-thieves.

Television destroyed the pulp magazines, as part of its larger erosion of the habit of reading. The true heirs to the pulps are television-minded writers like John GRISHAM and Elmore LEONARD, whose work is more visual than verbal. The most familiar names from the pulp era are those of writers who went on to build reputations as novelists; even their pulp stories are often out of print. Anthologies such as Pronzini's *The Arbor House Treasury of Detective and Mystery Stories from the Great Pulps* (1983) and the *Black Mask* anthology, *The Hard-Boiled Detective* (1977), have rescued some of these stories from oblivion.

PUMA, JOE See GAULT, WILLIAM CAMPBELL.

"PURLOINED LETTER, THE" (1844) The last of the stories about C. Auguste DUPIN by Edgar Allan POE. Dupin is consulted by the Parisian prefect of police, Monsieur G—, about the case of a missing letter. The letter belongs to a female member of the royal household; the thief is even known (the ruthless Minister D—), but all searches of his apartments have failed. Everything has literally been gone over with a microscope. D—'s blackmailing in favor of his political stratagems is intolerable, but Dupin seems relatively uninterested in the problem. He recommends that the police search again. When G— returns months later, he reports no success, but tells Dupin that he will give him fifty thousand francs if he can assist him. Dupin thereupon produces the letter. The explanation of how Dupin found it is delayed by a long disquisition on his psychological/logical method, which involves replicating in the sleuth's mind the attitude of mind of the culprit. "The Purloined Letter" is the most purely ratiocinative of the Dupin stories and the most static in terms of action, all of which takes place offstage.

PUTZ From the Yiddish meaning penis, this word is now used metonymically (and derogatorily) for a man. It comes from the German *putz,* meaning ornament or decoration. It is thus very similar in derivation and usage to SHMUCK, though of much later date.

"PUZZLE LOCK, THE" (1925) A story by R. Austin FREEMAN, which appeared in a collection of the same name. One of the best known of the Doctor THORNDYKE stories, it is somewhat atypical in that it attempts to be humorous, and the story depends more on suspense than Dr. Thorndyke's ingenious methods. While dining at Giamborini's, Thorndyke and his assistant Jervis observe Inspector Badger, in disguise and making a fool of himself. The trail leads to a man named Luttrell, a cranky old character who deals in second-hand jewelry and antiques. The puzzle lock on his strong room is a sequence of fifteen letters, which no one except Dr.

Thorndyke is able to puzzle out because it has forty million combinations. The solution involves a seal ring with an apparently nonsensical message, partly in Latin. Thorndyke and Jervis are also inadvertently involved—or trapped—in a most interesting locked room problem.

Q, DON See DON Q.

Q, MR. An assistant to Ebenezer GRYCE, the series detective of Anna Katherine GREEN. Mr. Q is what a HARD-BOILED writer (Green's novels are anything but) would have called a legman. He gathers evidence for Gryce, going to places and meeting people, particularly the poor and criminals.

Q.T. An abbreviation for quiet; hence the expression "on the q.t." PARTRIDGE, however, says that q.t. was also used as an alternate, less obvious way of pronouncing *cutie,* meaning prostitute or whore.

QUADE, OLIVER A character created by Frank GRUBER. Although written in the HARD-BOILED era by a PULP writer, the stories of Quade have affinities with the styles popular during the Edwardian and post–World War I era. Quade has remarkable intellectual properties: a photographic memory and knowledge of arcane subjects have earned him the nickname the "Human Encyclopedia," making him a sort of hard-boiled THINKING MACHINE. His assistant is Charlie Boston. As a sideline, the duo go around selling a *Compendium of Human Knowledge.*

Most of Gruber's Quade stories first appeared in BLACK MASK, and were later collected in *Brass Knuckles* (1966).

QUARLES, FRANCIS A detective who appears in short stories by Julian SYMONS. There are two volumes of Quarles stories: *Murder Murder* (1961) and *Francis Quarles Investigates* (1965). The first book was never published in the United States. The stories are extremely brief examples of "instant detection," but are clued like classic mysteries.

QUARRY A killer for hire, Quarry appears in a series of four books by Max Allan COLLINS. The first two were published in 1976. Quarry is a vet who killed his wife's lover when he returned from Vietnam, was acquitted, and then became a professional murderer. In *Quarry's Deal* (1985; repr of *The Dealer,* 1976), he has acquired the "little black book" of his "broker"—a sort of murder-jobber—giving him access to the names of other killers. Quarry (or rather Collins) concocts the original idea of finding the intended victim of a hit and hiring out his services as a preventer, much as ex-burglars become security specialists. The first sentence of the novel describes a man who has sex as mechanically as he kills. Collins's basic prose achieves a necessary honesty in dealing with this murderer, and sometimes rises to another level (his view of farmer's faces "full of hard work and well-earned unhappiness," for example). Although his language is vulgar, it is when Quarry becomes "emotional" that he really seems crude.

Collins wrote the first Quarry book as a "one-off" with no plans for making him the center of a series—which is why he is about to die as the book closes. At the request of an editor, Collins wrote the other novels. "Ice man" characters usually melt quickly and are probably good for only one book. That is why the relentlessly hard character is rarely sustained; true to form, Quarry "retires," and then becomes a hero: in *Primary Target* (1987), a revenge tale, his pregnant wife is killed after he refuses the job of killing a third-party presidential candidate.

The early Quarry novels were later reprinted with their original titles restored.

BIBLIOGRAPHY Novels: *The Broker* (1976; repr as *Quarry*), *The Broker's Wife* (1976; repr as *Quarry's List,* 1985), *The Slasher* (1977).

QUARSHIE, DOCTOR SAMUEL An African doctor and sometime sleuth in a series of novels by John WYLLIE. Physically "immense," Quarshie is also impressive because of his medical knowledge, his impartiality, and his investigations, particularly his bringing to justice the killers of one of his country's presidents. Being incorruptible, he is viewed as a menace by the corrupt powers who are holding back African development to enrich themselves. One of Quarshie's parents came from the former English colony of Akhana, the other from the former French colony of Miwiland; he earned his medical degree in Canada. Thus, Quarshie is symbolic of a cosmopolitan, non-partisan African, staunchly anti-imperialist but wanting to take the best from both traditions. His solutions to problems often involve knowledge of both Western medicine and of African ritual and religion. His wife, Prudence, a beautiful woman who rejects Western customs, plays a central role, for example in *The Butterfly Flood* (1975).

Beginning with the first book, *Skull Still Bone* (1975), Quarshie's investigations have a political subtext; Wyllie provides slices of political theory and anthropology along with his depiction of contemporary African life. In *To Catch a Viper* (1977), the murder of two of Quarshie's relatives (using poisonous snakes) leads him into conflict with conspirators who want to bring back the tribal Goshi empire. Yet even behind this diabolical political thriller plot is a rumination on the "Balkanization" of West Africa and the dominance of its one giant, Nigeria. Political turmoil is again apparent in *A Pocket Full of Rye* (1978), in which Quarshie must do battle with corrupt officialdom.

QUEEN, ELLERY (pen name of Manfred B[ennington] Lee, 1905–1971, and Frederic Dannay, 1905–1982) Ellery Queen, created by two cousins from Brooklyn, is the most American of series detectives. Born Manford Lepofsky and Daniel Nathan, the pair invented one of the most recognizable mystery characters, and on the strength of his reputation went on to found a virtual publishing empire—books, anthologies, prizes, radio shows, and the ubiquitous *Ellery Queen's Mystery Magazine* (*EQMM*)—which had a sustaining influence on the genre for decades.

Lee and Dannay attended high school together in Brooklyn, and while still in their twenties decided to write a mystery story. This first novel, THE ROMAN HAT MYSTERY (1929), was written for a contest held by *McClure's Magazine* and the publisher Lippincott (the same house that commissioned *The Sign of Four*), and was heavily indebted to Conan DOYLE. Richard Queen with his snuff and Ellery with his pince-nez are very Edwardian, their house even more so with its pipe rack, sabers on the wall (a gift from "the old fencing master of Nuremburg with whom Richard had lived in his younger days"), and the hideous tapestry which was a gift from a duke. The story won the prize, but then the magazine was sold (to H. L. MENCKEN's *Smart Set*) and the new editors chose another winner. Having been done out of a $7,500 prize—a quite considerable sum in 1929—they still got the novel published, which was an immediate success.

In the opening of the series, Ellery is already a renowned amateur sleuth. His father, Inspector Richard Queen, works for the police of the City of New York. Thus, the HOLMES formula is reversed: the putative detective is the ordinary mortal, and the observer/assistant is the genius. Inspector Queen is irascible and feisty, a strong contrast to his son, who behaves throughout *The Roman Hat Mystery* like Oscar Wilde, though he is not half as clever. Father and son occupy a brownstone on New York's Upper East Side, where they are attended to by a male servant, Djuna, whom they have rescued from the street.

By the second novel, *The French Powder Mystery* (1930), one of the best of the early books, Lee and Dannay had already begun to modify their formula; their ability to adapt and change was to be one of the strengths of the series. Not only does Ellery have considerably more dash and muscle; the prose has been shorn of some of its decoration, and Ellery's speech has become laconic and enigmatic rather than artful and elaborate (though he still quotes Latin to strange cops). The case begins with the discovery of a corpse in the window a New York City department store. The third novel, *The Greek Coffin Mystery* (1932), was something of a relapse. Not only is it supposed to take place prior to the previous books (and just after Ellery has graduated from college), it also has the plodding pace and stagey flavor of a Philo VANCE novel. The case involves the death and the missing will of the blind gallery owner Georg Khalkis. The theft of a Leonardo da Vinci painting, the discovery of the corpse of a murdered forger, and a further killing punctuate a long novel full of interminable and stilted dialogue ("when I'm nervous, I become perverse, and I giggle like a callow baggage"). In the later novels, characters speak more naturally—possibly as a result of the authors' exposure to the medium of film.

Another shift was marked by THE EGYPTIAN CROSS MYSTERY (1932), when Lee and Dannay allowed more lurid entertainment to enter the series—in this case, murder by crucifixion. *The Spanish Cape Mystery* (1935) had a nude body found on a beach. Gradually the series moved away from the drawing room, though the books remained dialogue-heavy. The process continued during the thirties when the Queen team worked in Hollywood, which became the background for two of the best books in the series, *The Devil to Pay* (1938) and FOUR OF HEARTS (1938). Like Queen the writer, Queen the character is in Hollywood working as an "idea man." Ellery says that "anyone exposed to Hollywood more than six weeks goes suddenly and incurably mad," which must express the authors' own exasperation with the place. But Hollywood may have affected Lee and Dannay more than they affected it: the two novels written there are funnier and snappier, the dialogue has the pace of thirties' film, and the writing is leaner—a rare case of a writer's work being made *better* by Hollywood. Some of the scenes are straight out of film, such as the pilot of a plane bailing out on two passengers (both dead) in *Four of Hearts.*

Also during the thirties, Dannay and Lee wrote a short series of books about Drury LANE, a retired actor. The pair's theatrical interests extended to a lecture tour, during which Dannay played the role of author Barnaby Ross and Lee was Queen. Both wore masks and Ross served up crime mysteries for Queen to solve. They also wrote the radio plays for the popular *Ellery Queen* program, which further added to the character/author's fame.

CALAMITY TOWN (1942) was the first of the cases that took Ellery away to WRIGHTSVILLE, the setting of many novels, including *Ten Days' Wonder* (1948), an AMNESIA case, and *Double, Double* (1950; also titled *Seven Murders*), about a series of murders, including of the town hermit and the town drunk. The Wrightsville novels are less focused on pure detection and have a nostalgic, wistful quality, allowing Ellery to slow down and observe his natural and social surroundings (which may or may not have to do with the case at hand) and the tone is often rather somber. With recurrent characters and the town itself as a sort of protagonist, this series-within-a-series would seem to owe something to the sagas of DERLETH and FAULKNER.

Lee's and Dannay's method of working together was that Dannay provided the plot and the writing, and the embellishment fell to Lee. They said, however, that they varied the method of collaboration and tried different approaches—and argued a lot. Lee's style tends toward oratory, and sometimes his sonorities can't help but seem dated: "The living room was lined on three sides with a bristling and leathern-reeking series of bookcases." Toward the end of Lee's life, Dannay worked with other collaborators and then the product was revised by Lee. Dannay was nearly killed in 1940 in a car accident. The following year, *EQMM* first appeared; it was Dannay's personal project, as was the compilation of the Ellery Queen anthologies. Some of the anthologies, of which there were more than seventy, were pioneering, for example one collecting mystery stories having to do with sports and another with women (see SHORT STORY).

It has been said that the Queen novels are extremely fidelitous to the idea of FAIR PLAY. While it is true that clues are dutifully reported and the reader could in principle figure the mystery out, other "rules" are ignored, such as the outlawing of the fantastic and improbable, for example in *Ten Days' Wonder,* where a promising plot is ruined by the efflorescence of improbable motives and actions. But in the early books (up until their move to Hollywood) the authors focused on the puzzle aspect so much that the authorial presence intervened part-way through the novel and gave the famous "challenge to the reader"—a pause to consider and try to solve the mystery from the clues given. In their middle period, after they had glimpsed the possibilities of realism to add weight and color to the mystery story, the books are more satisfying as novels, while still retaining a solid and sober plot. They favored ingenious crimes and modi operandi. A tendency to insert religious mumbo jumbo or ancient secrets became a little too obtrusive at times, especially in *And On the Eighth Day* (1964). This novel, set in a California religious commune, is the most often debated and the most generally disliked of the Ellery Queen novels. Another late novel, *A Study in Terror* (1966), was based on the case of JACK THE RIPPER. Ellery Queen becomes involved in a reassessment of the evidence—supplied by Dr. WATSON.

Ellery Queen also appeared in many short stories. Several volumes of these were published, starting with *The Adventures of Ellery Queen* (1934). In *Calendar of Crime* (1946), the twelve stories each focus on a month; one involves a TONTINE, another valuable objects buried by George Washington on a Pennsylvania farm, another a pair of ruby dice said to have belonged to Caligula. The Ellery Queen short stories tend to have bizarre, outlandish plots. In "The Adventure of the Mad Tea Party," occurrences at a country house parallel those in Lewis Carroll's *Alice in Wonderland.* See also BASEBALL.

As scholar of mystery and detective literature and as editor, Ellery Queen was at pains to show that the mystery story had achieved not only literary respectability, but real literary excellence. In the introduction to the anthology *Ellery Queen's Book of Mystery Stories* (1952, repr 1957, 7th pr 1974; orig title *The Literature of Crime*), they even went so far as to claim that "nearly every world-famous author, throughout the entire history of literature, has tried his hand at writing the detective or crime story." As examples, they selected stories by Kipling, STEVENSON, MAUGHAM, H. G. WELLS, MAUPASSANT, and others.

Among the few non-series works by Ellery Queen are *Guess Who's Coming to Kill You* (1968), a novel of espionage during the Cold War, and *The Campus Murders* (1969), in which a detective named McCall has to solve the bludgeoning of a "coed" and the murder of a dean. (Some of the non-series works published under the Queen name were not actually written by Dannay and Lee.) THE GLASS VILLAGE (1954) was a parable of contemporary intolerance; after a murder is committed in a small town, the residents latch onto a newcomer as the prime suspect, showing how what is different is misunderstood and finally despised by the group mentality.

QUEEN, ELLERY The detective character created by Ellery QUEEN, one of the most successful sleuths of all time. At first he was a mere cipher, a boy imitating Sherlock HOLMES and Philo VANCE, but he grew to be a well-rounded man, a likeable character with a hint of sadness, loneliness, and romantic disappointment. In THE ROMAN HAT MYSTERY (1929), Ellery is bookish and learned but also conceited and silly, as well as somewhat condescending when he drops in on his father, Inspector Queen, at work. The killing takes place in a theater. One of the Inspector's regular assistants is the "black-browed giant," Sergeant Thomas Velie.

Large strides had already been taken in improving Queen in the second book, *The French Powder Mystery* (1930), a cool, intelligent, and sophisticated story surrounding the fortunes of Cyrus French, owner of the posh Fifth Avenue French's Department Store. Every day in the display window, a female model demonstrates a new kind of bed (a Murphy bed, essentially) that folds into the wall. On this occasion, it folds down to reveal the corpse of a woman.

Ellery is not only an amateur sleuth, he is also his own WATSON; one of the reasons for his interest in his father's activities is that Ellery writes mystery novels. To add further to the nesting of perspectives, an introduction by "J. J. McC." prefaces some of the early books. The introduction to *The French Powder Mystery* is lengthy; it informs us that the Queens have an Italian villa, provides details about Ellery's writing career, and says that he is a "pure logician" but uses "inspirational methods." To add further complexities, McC. tells us that Inspector Queen is a retired thirty-two-year veteran of the force and that this is "one of the older cases from the Queen's files," though the setting is clearly contemporary. It has been, supposedly, written up from Ellery's notes—the echo of Watson is still strong.

THE EGYPTIAN CROSS MYSTERY (1932), only two years later, presents a startlingly different Ellery: he first appears behind the wheel of a beat-up Duesenberg racing car, in which he and his father charge down to West Virginia to examine the scene of a combined beheading and crucifixion. With *Halfway House* (1936), the word "mystery" was dropped from the titles, a sign that Ellery was growing into a "real" character and not just a cutout of a detective or a thinking machine. In this novel, he investigates a case of a man who keeps up two separate identities and households (a plot device particularly attractive to mystery writers; used, for example, by Julian SYMONS in *The Man Who Killed Himself*, 1967). THE FOUR OF HEARTS (1938) sees Ellery in Hollywood, acting and sounding like a thirties leading man.

Beginning with CALAMITY TOWN (1942), Ellery is attracted to the town WRIGHTSVILLE. The New England setting gives the Wrightsville books a more intimate feeling, and the supporting characters shine more than they would against the background of the big city. Ellery himself is treated as an honored guest, and enters his maturity.

BIBLIOGRAPHY Novels: *The Dutch Shoe Mystery (1931), The Greek Coffin Mystery* (1932), *The American Gun Mystery* (1933), *The Siamese Twin Mystery* (1933), *The Chinese Orange Mystery* (1934), *The Spanish Cape Mystery* (1935), *The Door Between* (1937), *The Devil to Pay* (1938), *The Dragon's Teeth* (1939), *There Was an Old Woman* (1943), *The Murderer Is a Fox* (1945), *Ten Days' Wonder* (1948), *Cat of Many Tails* (1949), *Double, Double* (1950), *The Origin of Evil* (1951), *The King Is Dead* (1952), *The Scarlet Letters* (1953), *Inspector Queen's Own Case* (1956), *The Finishing Stroke* (1958), *The Player on the Other Side* (1963), *And On the Eighth Day* (1964), *The Fourth Side of the Triangle* (1965), *A Study in Terror* (1966; British title *Sherlock Holmes vs. Jack the Ripper*), *Face to Face* (1967), *The House of Brass* (1968), *The Last Woman in His Life* (1970), *A Fine and Private Place* (1971).

Short Stories: *The Adventures of Ellery Queen* (1934), *The New Adventures of Ellery Queen* (1940), *The Case Book of Ellery Queen* (1945), *Calendar of Crime* (1952), *Q.B.I.: Queen's Bureau of Investigation* (1955), *Queens Full* (1965), *Q.E.D.: Queen's Experiments in Detection* (1968).

QUEEN'S QUORUM A list compiled by Ellery QUEEN of the 125 most important books of detective and mystery short stories published since 1845. Queen's Quorum appeared in several forms at different times. The original source of the list was Howard HAYCRAFT's "Reader's List of Detective Story 'Cornerstones,'" which he included in *Murder for Pleasure* (1941). In 1948, "Queen's Quorum" was included as an addendum to the anthology *Twentieth Century Detective Stories;* at that point, the quorum contained only 100 titles. In 1951, *Ellery Queen's Mystery Magazine* published a hybrid version of the two lists, "The Haycraft Queen Definitive Library of Detective-Crime-Mystery Fiction," a collaborative work of Queen and Haycraft. This list covered the period 1748–1948 and had 167 entries. Queen's Quorum was first printed in book form in 1951; a revised edition (1969) carried the list up through 1967.

"QUEER FEET, THE" (1911) A Father BROWN story, which G. K. CHESTERTON selected as his best. It is one of the stories featuring the professional thief FLAMBEAU, whom Father Brown convinces to abandon his life of crime.

The story takes place in the Vernon Hotel, where an exclusive club, The Twelve True Fishermen, hold their exquisite dinners, which culminate in the consumption of a fish course using the club's solid silver fish service, each knife and fork being set with a large pearl. Father Brown is in the hotel for a less ostentatious purpose: to hear the confession of a dying Italian waiter. While he is sitting in an anteroom writing, Father Brown hears an odd procession of steps. First, there is a patter of rapid, light steps, which change to a slow and measured tread. The duple pattern repeats itself over and over, and from it, Father Brown deduces the crime. Besides the perfect simplicity of the clues, the story is the author's most perfect blending of his Catholic social criticism with a mystery; as a "fisher of men," he bests the shallow windbags of the club and wins a prize to him much greater than the taking of the thief, remarking on the oddity that "a thief and a vagabond should repent, when so many who are rich and secure remain hard and frivolous."

QUENTIN, PATRICK (pseudonym of several authors, including Hugh Callingham Wheeler, 1912–1987) Four English authors worked together and separately under the Patrick Quentin pseudonym. "Patrick Quentin" actually began as Q. Patrick, the pseudonym of Richard Wilson Webb (1901–) with Martha Mott Kelly. The first of their two Q. Patrick titles was *Cottage Sinister* (1931). *Murder at the Varsity Longmans* (1933; U.S. title *Murder at Cambridge*) was written by Webb alone. He then found another collaborator, Mary Louise Aswell, and wrote two more books. Not until Webb found Wheeler was "Patrick Quentin" born. Now the story becomes really confusing; Wheeler and Webb wrote several books about a Dr. Hugh WESTLAKE, which they published as Jonathan Stagge, and another series about Timothy Trant, an urbane police lieutenant who appeared in books sporadically from the thirties to the sixties.

Complicated as it was, all this activity did not amount to much beyond standard GOLDEN AGE fare with a touch of the bizarre. The Westlake books had OCCULT elements, and the Q. Patrick novel *S.S. Murder* (1933) was an admired example of MURDER AFLOAT. But when Webb and Wheeler launched the Peter DULUTH series, they struck upon something more original. Duluth is a theatrical producer and alcoholic whose first case, *A Puzzle for Fools* (1936), takes place inside a mental institution. In a series of bizarre cases, all of which have "puzzle" in the title, he meets murder with a theatrical (in both senses) background. Webb, who had been the core of the Patrick project, retired from the collaboration, and Wheeler continued on alone.

Wheeler was born in London and attended London University. Both he and Webb emigrated to the United States in 1934. Wheeler served with American forces in World War II (he became a U.S. citizen), and in later life was increasingly involved with theater and film. He wrote the screenplay for the film version of Graham GREENE's *Travels with My Aunt* (1972). He twice won the Tony and New York Drama Critics' Circle awards.

Patrick Quentin received a special EDGAR award in 1963 for the volume of short stories, *The Ordeal of Mrs. Snow,* which were written by Wheeler and Webb; it was also included in QUEEN'S QUORUM.

QUEST, ORFAMAY Philip MARLOWE's first client in THE LITTLE SISTER (1949). Orfamay is a prim, teatotalling, holier-than-thou girl from Manhattan, Kansas, who intrigues Marlowe in a perverse sort of way, at least enough for him to go to work for her. She later reveals that behind her proper exterior, she has one major vice: greed.

QUESTION OF PROOF, A (1935) The first novel to feature Nigel STRANGEWAYS. It is one of the best of that genre of mystery set in a British public school. See BLAKE, NICHOLAS.

QUICK DRAW Formulaic mystery writing lends itself to rapid production, if not to art. Some of the fastest authors are Edgar BOX, who wrote his 75,000-word novels in a week; Edgar WALLACE, who wrote the same amount in a weekend; and John CREASEY, who turned out almost 600 books under many names in only one lifetime. None of these, however, equaled BALZAC, who wrote a 15,000 word story in one of his long nights of coffee drinking.

QUILL, MONICA A pseudonym of Ralph MCINERNY.

QUILLER A spy in a series of novels by Adam HALL. Quiller is a stoic romantic who, like James BOND, always seems to have the right knowledge to get himself out of a jam, whether it is how to fly a plane or speak Chinese. He is a cartoon hero on the outside and neurotic intellectual on the inside, who for some reason remains loyal to the spy masters for whom he works. The first novel in the series was the award-winning *The Berlin Memorandum* (1965; U.S. title *The Quiller Memorandum*), about neo-NAZIS.

BIBLIOGRAPHY Novels: *The 9th Directive* (1966), *The Striker Portfolio* (1969), *The Warsaw Document* (1970), *The Tango Briefing* (1973), *The Mandarin Cypher* (1975), *The Kobra Manifesto* (1976), *The Sinkiang Executive* (1978), *The Scorpion Signal* (1979), *The Sibling* (1979), *Pekin Target* (1981; U.S. title *The Peking Target*), *Northlight* (1985), *Quiller* (1985), *Quiller's Run* (1988), *Quiller K.G.B.* (1989), *Quiller Barracuda* (1990), *Quiller Bamboo* (1991).

QUIN, MR. HARLEY An enigmatic character created by Agatha CHRISTIE. Quin is a kind of sprite who glides through *The Mysterious Mr. Quin* (1930), assisting Mr. Satterthwaite, an elderly man who has a talent for involving himself in the complex affairs of the young. The focus of the twelve stories in the book is love, though this love is too strange to be called romantic. "The Shadow on the Glass" has an uncanny quality: the title refers to a stain on the window at the spot where a previous owner stood and watched his wife run away with her lover. Hundreds of years have passed, but the stain remains. "The Face of Helen" concerns a woman whose beauty is like that of, and as tragic as, the original that launched a thousand ships.

Mr. Quin, in a sense, does nothing; Christie said he was "a catalyst," a Harlequin-like figure who represented both love and death. He is like an analyst as well as a catalyst, a changeable figure around whom the passions of others are projected, clarified, and resolved. Mr. Satterthwaite is the detective who actually picks up the pieces and solves the crimes (not all of which are murders). *The Mysterious Mr. Quin* shows the author at her most intuitive, perhaps allowing the unconscious to enter her work; it has a reputation for being one of Christie's best-written books.

QUINCANNON, JOHN A detective created by Bill PRONZINI, who features in the HISTORICAL MYSTERY *Quincannon* (1985), set in the year 1893. Quincannon is a big man with dark hair and a graying beard who wears a derby hat. He is the son of a cop and works for the Secret Service; he is tearing himself up inside, however, over an accident that happened in the line of duty. While in Virginia City, Nevada, he accidentally shot a pregnant woman in the stomach. Quincannon drinks gallons of whiskey in order to forget. He must be still on top of things because he is reading poems by Emily Dickinson, published only two years before, and he is also trusted with the investigation of a counterfeiting gang that takes him to Silver City, Idaho, a town both booming and corrupt. Quincannon is also an important character in the novel BEYOND THE GRAVE (1986).

RAFFLES A gentleman thief created by E. W. HORNUNG and, along with THE THINKING MACHINE and Doctor THORNDYKE, one of the great characters of the Conan DOYLE era. Being a thief, Raffles was on the opposite side from Sherlock HOLMES, but he is neither evil like MORIARTY nor as stupid or crude as some of the Holmes villains are (which made him no doubt all the more disturbing to Conan Doyle). But what really separates Raffles from Holmes is his sociability; he is a great cricketer (could Holmes ever play on a team?), wines and dines with the wealthy at country houses (which he robs), and is himself wellborn.

Raffles follows the line of Melville Davisson Post's Randolph MASON and Arthur Morrison's DORRINGTON: the rogue who is not a social outcast but a well-adapted member of society—an idea that in the late Victorian era many found objectionable. Conan Doyle disapproved of Raffles because he thought it was wrong to make the criminal into a hero. This type of subversive character went back to an earlier era (see PROTOMYSTERIES) and has continued to live on at the margins of literature and appears in many forms, from the ice-cold PARKER to the happy-go-lucky Bernie RHODENBARR. Hornung created Raffles in his own image, giving him an Australian background, a love of cricket, and a less conventional view of society than Conan Doyle's. Raffles was orthodox enough, however, to meet a patriotic end in the Boer War.

"The Ides of March" was the first Raffles story and appeared in *Cassell's Magazine* in 1898. Raffles is living in the Albany hotel in Piccadilly in the style to which he has become accustomed—through burglary. In the story he persuades his old school friend, Bunny Manders, to join him in a crime. Bunny, who narrates the stories, idolizes Raffles but is ambivalent about his criminal enterprises. Crime doesn't bother Raffles at all: "we can't all be moralists." Although he recognizes no law, Raffles is not violent because "violence is a confession of terrible incompetence."

Bunny pursues a desultory career as a freelance writer and versifier, but Raffles tempts him back into the life of crime that he plainly finds exciting. He would do anything for Raffles, and Raffles does not scruple to sacrifice him when necessary. The first collection, *The Amateur Cracksman* (1899), ends with THE GIFT OF THE EMPEROR. After serving a jail sentence, Bunny takes up the story again in THE BLACK MASK (1901). This collection contains one of their most anthologized adventures, THE WRONG HOUSE.

BIBLIOGRAPHY Novels: *Mr. Justice Raffles* (1909).
Short Stories: *A Thief in the Night* (1905).

RAILWAY NOVEL The equivalent of today's "airport novel," railway novels were sold in the nineteenth century in the waiting rooms of stations. They were manufactured cheaply and often contained sensational stories of crime; thus, they were forerunners of the DIME NOVEL and the PULP MAGAZINES, both of which flourished at times when there was a large literate but poor urban population.

RAMADGE, GWEN See O'DONNELL, LILLIAN.

RANDISI, ROBERT J[OSEPH] (1951–) Born in Brooklyn, Robert J. Randisi was at one time an administrator for the New York City Police Department. He is a prolific author of Westerns (more than 200 titles in one series alone), and has written mystery fiction. His first mystery was *The Disappearance of Penny* (1980), which featured private investigator Henry Po. Randisi's better-known series sleuth, Miles Jacoby, first appeared in 1982 in *Eye in the Ring* (Jacoby is a former boxer). Randisi founded the PRIVATE EYE WRITERS OF AMERICA (the organization that gives the Shamus awards) in 1981. He co-founded the magazine *Mystery Scene* with another American writer, Ed GORMAN. Randisi still lives in Brooklyn, where his series about private investigator Nick Delvecchio is set. In *The Dead of Brooklyn* (1991), Delvecchio's client is his brother, Father Vincent Delvecchio, who is accused of having had an affair with a woman and then murdering her. *Alone with the Dead* (1995) is another mystery set in New York but without Delvecchio. It shows how police work in response to a major crime involves other things besides detection. Detective Joe Keough forms a theory about the serial killer known as "The Lover," who leaves roses as a sign that he has struck. The brass is not interested in his theory because of their own political and public relations game.

Randisi has edited many anthologies, including two entitled *First Cases* (1996 and 1997), which collect the first appearances of famous private eyes in short stories.

RANKIN, IAN (1960–) Born in Scotland, Ian Rankin worked at jobs as various as swineherd and audiophile journalist before becoming a professional writer—which he did at a very young age. *The Flood*, his first novel, was published in 1986. With *Knots and Crosses* (1987), he introduced Detective John REBUS, an Edinburgh policeman. One critic called Rankin's work "tartan noir"; Scottish history, Scottish humor (a room outfitted with whips and chains has "more leather than in a bloody milking shed"), and the conflict of the high and low cultures of Edinburgh. The series is PROCEDURAL but with an interest in atmosphere, social setting, and character that bring it closer to VAN DE WETERING than MCBAIN. Rankin has also written novels under the pseudonym Jack Harvey: *Witch Hunt* (1993), *Bleeding Hearts* (1994), and *Blood Hunt* (1995). *A Good Hanging and Other Stories* (1992) is a sampling of Rankin's short fiction. Among Rankin's honors are a Chandler-Fulbright fellowship in detective fiction, a prize from the British CRIME WRITERS' ASSOCIATION for best short story in 1994, and the CWA Gold Dagger in 1998.

RANKIN, PAT The son of the cousin of Alan GRANT in THE SINGING SANDS (1953) and one of the few really enjoyable children of mystery fiction. The six-year-old Highlander has red hair and gray eyes, and fancies himself a revolutionary. When Grant says he hopes he won't have to arrest him, Pat answers, "Yu couldna."

RASKOLNIKOV, RODION One of the most famous characters in all of fiction, Raskolnikov is the self-deceived murderer whose spiritual redemption is the subject of DOSTOYEVSKY's *Crime and Punishment* (1866). He is probably the most sympathetic fictional murderer, whom through Dostoyevsky's intense art the reader gets to know to his very core.

RASP, THE (1924) A novel by Philip MACDONALD, and the first in which Anthony GETHRYN appears. It is also the novel in which Gethryn meets his future wife, who is for a short time a suspect. Whereas Macdonald shows an occasional flash of brilliance in Gethryn's sardonic humor, the detective's behavior is as moony and conventionally melodramatic as possible in the romantic subplot. There are, in fact, not one but two other romances going on at the same time.

Written at the beginning of the GOLDEN AGE, *The Rasp* (like Gethryn himself) is self-consciously aware of the shadow of Conan DOYLE, GABORIAU, and more recently, TRENT'S LAST CASE (1913). (The denouement, incidentally, gives away the central mechanism employed in R. Austin Freeman's THE RED THUMB MARK [1907].) The action takes place at a COUNTRY HOUSE, where a Cabinet minister, John Hoode, has been savagely beaten to death with the weapon mentioned in the title. But the story does not have the sense of confinement usual in the country house subgenre, Gethryn frequently leaves the scene to visit London and career around in his red Mercedes, and most of the denizens of Abbotshall are quickly ruled out as suspects. Gethryn goes down to cover the story for his newspaper, *The Owl*.

From the point of view of construction, the novel leaves much to be desired, even in so early a work of the Golden Age. While some clues are suppressed, most of those that are revealed are quite obvious, and the police appear especially dimwitted in their failure to put two and two together. All is revealed in a lengthy letter to the police of some forty-odd pages. The reader may be disconcerted to learn that, while a suspect's meticulous distinguishing of the Latin dative and ablative cases has been much remarked upon, more obvious clues, such as his ownership of the newspapers in which scurrilous articles about the deceased appeared, have been discovered behind the reader's back, so to speak. But were the "rules" of FAIR PLAY not skirted, the name of the murderer would have been blurted out at several points, destroying such suspense as there is.

RATCLIFFE HIGHWAY The site of a famous series of murders committed in 1812. See DE QUINCEY, THOMAS; WILLIAMS, JOHN; and JAMES, P. D.

RAWLINGS, MICKEY See BASEBALL.

RAWLINS, EASY A character created by Walter MOSLEY, and one of the most successful in recent fiction. Rawlins is an African American veteran of World War II and part of the postwar migration to California (in his case, from Houston). He finds that being a "war hero" doesn't last; the country quickly returns to its habitual racism when the euphoria wears off. In the first book, *Devil in a Blue Dress* (1990), Rawlins is working as a janitor and having a tough go of it, so he takes a job from a shady character that leads to his first experience with detection. Rawlins never gets a license or declares himself a private investigator. Instead, word gets around that he does favors for people. As the novels progress, he accumulates property and loses friends at the same time, and his integrity seems to crumble as he commits some rather questionable acts himself. Like many a character in American fiction, by the end of his chase after the American Dream he has found that he has lost at least as much as he has gained.

BIBLIOGRAPHY Novels: *A Red Death* (1991), *White Butterfly* (1992), *Black Betty* (1994), *A Little Yellow Dog* (1996), *Gone Fishin'* (1997).

RAWSON, CLAYTON (1906–1971) A famous magician of his day, Clayton Rawson put his knowledge of magic and sleight-of-hand to good use in a series of novels about The Great MERLINI. Rawson was born in Ohio and attended Ohio State University. He was an artist in addition to a writer, and studied at the Art Institute in Chicago. His long career as an editor included stints with *True Detective* and the Inner Sanctum series of Simon and Schuster. In Chicago, he worked for Ziff-Davis (publisher of many PULP MAGAZINES), as did Howard BROWNE. Rawson joined *Ellery Queen's Mystery Magazine* as an editor in 1963.

In addition to his Great Merlini novels, Rawson wrote a brief series of novellas about a character called Don Diavolo (also a magician); they were published under the name Stuart Towne. Rawson won two special EDGAR awards from the Mystery Writers of America, the first in 1949 for launching *Clue* magazine, and the second in 1967 for his service to the organization.

RAWSON, HUGH See SLANG.

"REAR WINDOW" See WOOLRICH, CORNELL.

REBUS, DETECTIVE INSPECTOR JOHN An Edinburgh cop in a series of novels by Ian RANKIN, Rebus is a stolid detective with a mild sense of humor and few memorable qualities. The quality of his intelligence, however, is what makes the books: Rebus's interest in other people makes him an attentive observer and describer as he prowls the winding streets of Edinburgh. The plots of the series are usually tight and involve important figures or weird criminals (Rankin follows the vogue for serial killers). In the first book, *Knots and Crosses* (1987), a serial killer preys on young girls. *Wolfman* (1992) is about a murderer who puts the bite on his victims, literally. *Strip Jack* (1993) has Rebus involved in a raid on a high-class whorehouse, where he views the whips and women in crotchless rubber suits ("Another looked like a cross between Heidi and Eva Braun") with a certain degree of amusement, while his staunchly Presbyterian boss fumes in righteous indignation. The case takes on a more serious coloring when they find a member of Parliament, Gregor Jack, among the customers. *Mortal Causes* (1995) is set during the annual Edinburgh festival, when Edinburgh's staid mask is dropped and its underside becomes momentarily dominant. On the last night of the festival, in an underground cavern, the grisly murder of Billy Cunningham takes place. He turns out to be the son of a notorious criminal whom Rebus had put away. The Northern Ireland problem is also brought into the story. Rankin won a Gold Dagger for *Black & Blue* (1997), a novel about a copycat serial killer who imitates the crimes of "Bible John," a murderer who terrorized the city decades before.

BIBLIOGRAPHY Novels: *Hide and Seek* (1991), *The Black Book* (1994), *Let It Bleed* (1996), *The Hanging Garden* (1998), *Death Is Not the End* (1998), *Dead Souls* (1999).

Short Stories: *A Good Hanging and Other Stories* (1992).

"RECOLLECTIONS OF CAPTAIN WILKIE, THE" (1895) A story by Arthur Conan DOYLE, one of the few mystery/crime stories he wrote that was not about Sherlock HOLMES. The story is told by a doctor on his way to Paris for a holiday. In the train compartment he meets a mysterious man, whose profession he tries to deduce solely from his appearance. The man eventually tells him a series of anecdotes about a reformed pickpocket, cracksman, and burglar. Conan Doyle's antipathy to the RAFFLES type, the criminal as hero, is well known; but in this story, he comes close to reveling in the adventure of stealing, just as Captain Wilkie's remorse and regret keep getting submerged in the thrill of the "old trade."

RED HARVEST (1929) The first novel by Dashiell HAMMETT, in which the short story character THE CONTINENTAL OP appears. The Op is called to Personville, nicknamed "Poisonville," by newspaperman Donald Willson, but before he can meet him Willson is shot four times in the stomach, back, and chest (people in Poisonville don't get shot only once). The Op goes to see Donald's father, old Elihu Willson, and there is a lot of witty byplay between them. Elihu's story is at the heart of the problem with Poisonville. He owned the town—"heart, soul, skin and guts"—because he owned the mine, the bank, and the press. When the I. W. W. (the Wobblies) began organizing Personville, union-busting Elihu imported a lot of thugs to crush them. The Wobblies lost, but the gangsters stayed. When the Op arrives, Poisonville is being fought over by Pete the Finn, Lew Yard, and "the kid," WHISPER. Thus, although the book is most remembered for its high body count (more than a couple of dozen), it has a political and sociological edge. The transition from "person" to "poison" is what happens when justice is ignored, and the poisoned atmosphere of the place affects even the Op, who fears in himself a growing blood lust (the first person he shoots is a deputy).

The action of the book is simple: one man can't slay a hundred, but he can have the hundred slay each other. To clean up the town, the Op sets one gang against another, a plot repeated ad infinitum in later books and films, from Kurosawa's *Yojimbo* to *A Fistful of Dollars.* The book also includes many memorable characters, among them the gold-digging Dinah Brand, the most lifelike woman Hammett ever created. With her broad shoulders, strong legs, and coarse brown hair, she is as tough as the Op and an inch or two taller. Hammett dedicated the book to Joseph T. SHAW.

"RED-HEADED LEAGUE, THE" (1891) One of the most familiar cases of Sherlock HOLMES, and one that sticks most closely to the rules of FAIR PLAY. Despite the seemingly absurd circumstances, the clues are all fairly laid out for the reader and the mystery is easy enough to discover. The case concerns a pawnbroker, Jabez Wilson, who is "obese, pompous, and slow." He also has an amazing head of red hair, and when he sees an advertisement for openings in The Red-headed League, he responds and is accepted. His only duties are to be present in the office of the league for a few hours each day and to copy out the pages of the Encyclopedia Britannica, for which he is well paid. This idiotic arrangement pleases him, and he understandably consults Sherlock Holmes when the league is suddenly and inexplicably dissolved. The story also contains a character, the corrupt genius John Clay, who is a precursor of Professor MORIARTY.

RED HERRING In mystery stories, a distracting detail, a dodge, or a diversion, often thrown in by the author to make the process of detection more mystifying. The overuse of red herrings is considered a sign of bad writing. Ross MACDONALD, for example, hardly used them at all.

The origin of the term, the story goes, is that a smoked herring (which is red) could be used by a person in flight to throw the dogs off the scent and so disguise the trail. This literal meaning dates to the seventeenth century; the contemporary figurative usage gained currency at the end of the nineteenth century.

RED HOUSE MYSTERY, THE (1922) An ingenious mystery by A. A. MILNE, better known as the author of the Winnie-the-Pooh books. Milne dedicated the book to his father, who was an enthusiast of the genre. Few writers who have attempted a first mystery have produced a classic, but Milne's interpretation of the COUNTRY HOUSE and LOCKED ROOM genres is accomplished as well as charming. The writer Alexander Woolcott called it one of the three best mysteries of all time.

Antony Gillingham, an unusually curious young man of independent means who likes to take up various professions until he masters (and tires of) them, is on vacation in the country. Learning that his friend Bill Beverley is staying at the nearby Red House, he strolls over one afternoon to say hello. He finds that Beverley is out playing golf, but, more importantly, the master of the house, Mark Ablett, has disappeared, and his ne'er-do-well brother Robert is lying on the floor of a locked room with a bullet in his head. Gillingham takes up the detection as his latest enthusiasm, assisted by the somewhat slow Bill. Mark had recently announced Robert's return from Australia to his friends and to the mother of his neighbor Angela Norbury, whom he had hoped to marry. The house has an interesting cast of visitors, including an actress, a Major, and Mark's adopted cousin. Milne almost mocks the rules of FAIR PLAY, cleverly incorporating many motifs that had become clichés when employed by less skillful hands. Raymond CHANDLER, however, had no use for the book, and cited it as a negative example in his essay THE SIMPLE ART OF MURDER (1944), the reading of which will spoil Milne's book for anyone who has not already read it.

RED THUMB MARK, THE (1907; repr 1967, 1986) *The Red Thumb Mark* stays in print because it is the first Dr. THORNDYKE mystery novel to be published (even though it was not the first to be written). It has other noteworthy features; R. Austin FREEMAN staked everything on a single clue, the bloody thumb print of the title, and took an idea that might have made a short story and expanded it into a novel. The amount of information and the level of detail about FINGERPRINTING and photography is almost staggering, but Freeman builds the mystery and suspense around the red thumb mark so well that one reads Dr. Thorndyke's courtroom exposition with interest.

As the story begins, Dr. Jervis (the narrator), an old school friend of Thorndyke's, has just met him again after a long period out of contact. He finds Thorndyke established in his premises at 5A King's Bench Walk with Polton, his devoted and gnome-like assistant. Jervis is somewhat embarrassed to admit that he is unemployed, but Thorndyke instantly offers him a job working on the case that has just presented itself. Reuben Hornby is accused of stealing a package of diamonds worth thirty thousand pounds from the safe of his uncle, Thomas Hornby, a dealer in valuable metals and occasionally diamonds. The thief had cut himself during the theft, and a bloody thumb mark left on a piece of paper inside the safe proves without a doubt to be Reuben's. The evidence seems incontrovertible to Scotland Yard, but Thorndyke is persuaded of Reuben's innocence. He proceeds with a series of experiments and deputizes Jervis to gather information on the Hornby household, which includes Juliet Gibson, an orphan taken in by the family.

Freeman finds several ways to string out the question of a single clue into a novel. Thorndyke keeps Jervis (and thus, the reader) almost completely in the dark; Jervis falls hopelessly in love with Juliet; and ingenious attempts are made on Thorndyke's life. The final courtroom scene, told in detail, prolongs the suspense and denouement. Thorndyke's exposition is so masterful that Jervis describes him in godlike terms.

REED, SIR CAROL See THIRD MAN, THE.

REEDER, J. G. A character created by Edgar WALLACE, Reeder appeared in some of his most popular books. Reeder is almost a composite of the great sleuths of the early century, or a detective designed by a committee: he carries an umbrella (unlike Father BROWN's, it has a knife concealed in it), and wears a pince nez and a bowler hat; he has big ears, a long face, sandy hair, and the mutton-chop side whiskers of an earlier age; and he also carries a pistol. All in all, Reeder is a homely article. He first appeared in *Room 13* (1923), which is about a criminal let out of prison who seeks revenge on those who put him there. Reeder's most famous exploit is *The Mind of Mr. J.G. Reeder* (1925; U.S. title *The Murder Book of J.G. Reeder*). The book is a collection of connected short stories in which Reeder, normally a private detective, is called in by the authorities and launches a one-man war against criminals in London. Despite the thinness of the premise, it is one of Wallace's best-written books.

BIBLIOGRAPHY Novels: *Terror Keep* (1927).

Short Stories: *Red Aces* (1929), *The Guv'nor and Other Stories* (1932).

REEVE, ARTHUR B[ENJAMIN] (1880–1936) The American mystery writer Arthur B. Reeve had the same kind of success in the heyday of the "scientific detective" as his British counterpart, R. Austin FREEMAN, but he lacked Freeman's scientific background. It was for this reason that his detective's science really boiled down to "pseudo-science" (Howard HAYCRAFT), and sleuth Craig KENNEDY does not have the enduring reputation that Freeman's Dr. THORNDYKE enjoys.

Reeve was born on Long Island and grew up in Brooklyn, later attending Princeton. He then studied law, but chose to become a journalist instead. Reeve started working as a freelance writer in 1906; four years later, he began a series of articles on scientific criminology that encouraged him to adapt the new techniques to fiction. The first Kennedy stories appeared in 1910 and were collected in *The Silent Bullet* (1912), and Reeve published one or more books a year through World War I. After that, his popularity began to decline. But during the height of his career, Reeve was fantastically successful, became rich, and saw his detective labeled "The American Sherlock Holmes." Reeve also wrote a book about a female sleuth: *Constance Dunlap: Woman Detective* (1916). Dunlap is a former criminal turned detective who uses scientific methods similar to Kennedy's.

The non-scientist Reeve must have had an incredible ability for absorbing information, because he was asked to set up a scientific crime lab during World War I. Like Erle Stanley GARDNER, he took a scholarly interest in criminology that increased as he got older. He wrote journalistic pieces and also directed radio programs on the subject, and was involved in movies. Some of his works were adapted for film.

REGESTER, SEELY (pseudonym of Metta Victoria Fuller Victor, 1831–1886) Under the name Seely Regester, Metta Victor published the first American detective novel by a woman, *The Dead Letter* (1867), a full decade before Anna Katherine Green's THE LEAVENWORTH CASE (1878), the book to which that honor is often attributed. Regester wrote several other books, beginning with a lost world novel, *The Last Days of Tul: A Romance of the Lost Cities of the Yucatan* (1846), published when she was fifteen years old. She went on to be a prolific dime novelist, but her one claim to fame was forgotten.

REGULATOR A fancy or respectable term for "vigilante," particularly but not exclusively used in Westerns. Regulators formed groups or committees when ordinary law enforcement was absent, ineffective, or insufficient. The word is also sometimes applied to private operatives (or hired guns) who were employed by railroads to maintain "order."

REICHENBACH FALLS The site of Sherlock HOLMES's apparent death in THE FINAL PROBLEM (1893).

"REIGATE PUZZLE, THE" (1893) One of the more inconsiderable of the adventures of Sherlock HOLMES, but notable for his seemingly bizarre behavior and clever ruses. He has a "nervous attack" and collapses on the floor, his eyes rolling about in his head. He deliberately knocks over a table with a dish of oranges and a carafe of water, then blames it on WATSON. The good doctor attributes his strange antics to his collapse after the strain of a previous investigation with international implications.

REILLY, CASSANDRA See GAY MYSTERIES.

REILLY, HELEN (1891–1962) Born in New York City, Helen Reilly was the daughter of the president of Columbia University. She began writing in the early thirties; with

The Diamond Feather (1930) she launched her long-running series about Inspector MCKEE. She also wrote under the pseudonym Kieran Abbey.

Opinions diverge about Reilly's writing. Some have considered her work an attempt to break out of the market for "women's mysteries," while others have seen it as an example of exactly that phenomenon (and what the reviewer Newgate Callendar rather insultingly called "ladyprose"). Her thirty-odd novels vary in quality and interest; some are historically important and have been called "proto-PROCEDURALS." With the novel *The File on Rufus Ray* (1937), a non-series novel, Reilly made an experiment similar to those of Dennis WHEATLEY with his "dossiers." Reilly's novel came equipped with objects and copies of documents related to the crime in the story. A fair assessment would be that Reilly's novels are interesting hybrids, sometimes involving romantic suspense but also making use of realistic elements that would become standard in the postwar period.

Two of Reilly's daughters, Mary McMullen and Ursula Curtiss, are also mystery writers.

RELIGIOUS BODY, THE (1966) Catherine AIRD's first novel. In the convent of St. Anselm, a nun gets up and begins the routine of waking the other sisters. One of them does not answer her knock, and her bed is made. After the morning service, the body of Sister Anne is discovered at the bottom of the basement stairs. There is no blood on the pavement and her glasses are missing.

Aird communicates both the strictness of the order and its rules, as well as the various personalities hidden under the conformity. Suspicion is fairly distributed among the nuns and other members of the community. Pranks by the boys of the local agricultural school on Guy Fawkes Day play a role, and the burning of an effigy yields puzzling clues. Inspector Sloan is tepid but likeable; he unearths plenty of clues and the whodunit is easily followed.

REMITTANCE MAN A black sheep of a family who is paid to stay away, or one who has committed a crime and so lives outside his native country. In mysteries, the remittance man is often an English gentleman who lives in America on his remittances—checks sent to him by his embarrassed family. One example is the main character in Stevenson's THE WRECKER (1892).

RENDELL, RUTH (1930–) Born in London of an English father and Danish mother, Ruth Rendell is one of the most popular English mystery authors writing today. After working as a journalist, she turned to mystery writing in 1964, and has since won three EDGAR awards and four Gold Daggers.

Rendell is a subtle writer, often employing a style of indirection which, however, does not resort to crude concealment. In *To Fear A Painted Devil* (1965), she suggests illicit relationships between the residents of a luxury housing development without having to state them; she shows their anger, fear, and jealousy, but also subtler emotions such as insolence, conceit, and shame. Some of the characters—like the victim, who appears to die of wasp stings—are bored, shallow-minded suburbanites, while others are appealing, including both the culprit and Max Greenleaf, a sympathetic but not saintly doctor who becomes an unwilling sleuth.

In *From Doon With Death* (1964), Rendell introduced her series detective, Chief Inspector WEXFORD, who is assisted by Inspector Mike Burden. The stories are set in Kingsmarkham, a typical postwar English town. One of the very best of the English writers working in the field, Rendell has learned from her GOLDEN AGE predecessors in terms of technique, but her values—literary and otherwise—are obviously different. Her depictions both of people and of the country are realistic, but without the satirical edge that creeps into the writing of Julian SYMONS (and sometimes Michael GILBERT) in the same period. Wexford's erudition never seems pedantic, and his shock at expressions of prejudice and bigotry seems normal rather than a superimposed political correctness. Because Rendell's interest in the human animal (literally) is strongly present in the Wexford-Burden series, it cannot be termed PROCEDURAL, even though care is taken to construct believable plots and to show a certain amount of routine.

A versatile writer, Rendell has also written non-series mysteries in which the procedural element is further suppressed and the psychological aspects are central. In *A Judgement in Stone* (1977), she eschewed the classic form in favor of an INVERTED MYSTERY, developing with great subtlety the mind of the person "whodunit," and why it was done.

In her more recent work, especially those books written under the name Barbara Vine, Rendell has gotten further away from the standard murder story and has focused more of her attention on portraying women's experience and dealing with social and cultural issues. The first of the Barbara Vine books, *A Dark Adapted Eye* (1986), won an Edgar award. Rendell continued to expand her scope in the following Vine books. *Anna's Book* (1994) is a more "literary" novel with a Danish background, and resembles a chronicle novel more than a crime story (see HISTORICAL MYSTERY). *No Night Is Too Long* (1994) is about a young man who commits a murder off the Alaskan coast and then is terrified of discovery; *The Brimstone Wedding* (1995) is an elegant tale of a dying woman and her secret past. *The Keys to the Street* (1996) illustrates the saying, "No good deed goes unpunished"; Mary Jago's donation of bone marrow is connected to a series of murders of homeless people, who are impaled on the spiked fence surrounding London's Regent's Park. A subplot involves Jago's efforts to extricate herself from an abusive relationship.

Rendell's other recent books include the novel *The Crocodile Bird* (1994), the story collection *Bloodlines* (1996), and *The Reason Why* (1995), an anthology of brief selections, both fictional and true, illustrating the psychology and sociology of murder. Although she is primarily known as a novelist, two of Rendell's Edgar awards were for short stories.

REQUIEM FOR A NUN See SANCTUARY.

RESNICK, DETECTIVE INSPECTOR CHARLIE John HARVEY's Charlie Resnick series is comparable in some ways to the John REBUS novels of Ian RANKIN. Resnick's Nottingham is as gray and crime-ridden as Rebus's Edinburgh. Both series have been called PROCEDURAL, but the Resnick novels come closer to the current fashion in procedurals and are less quirky and original than Rankin's work. Resnick lives alone in an apartment with an assortment of cats; like Inspector MORSE, he is a loner who does not like joining things—groups, clubs, fraternal orders—and also does not particularly care whether he is promoted or not. Resnick is divorced, and his ex-wife Elaine is in a mental institution. He is a fan of jazz and a bit of a slob, likely to turn up at work wearing part of his breakfast on his sleeve. The procedural has changed a great deal since LAST SEEN WEARING . . . (1952); like many of the current crop, the Resnick books often read like novelizations of a television cop show, padded out with domestic, romantic, and other scenes that are not germane to the investigation and are there either for mood enhancement or to fill in the background that the reader is presumed to want.

Resnick's boss is the graying and heavy-set superintendent, Jack Skelton. The other detectives include the thoughtful Graham Millington, the emotionally wounded Lynn Kellogg, and the loud-mouthed Mark Devine, who brags about his sexual exploits. The best thing about the series is its representation of life in modern Britain, with its lowered standard of living and lowered expectations: "Budgets were screwed down tighter than an Arctic winter. This was policing in the age of cost-effectiveness and consumer choice, when those at the top talked of minimal visual policing, counted the paper clips, put a ban on overtime, and sat up long into the night massaging the crime figures." In the procedural tradition, each novel weaves together multiple plot lines. In *Living Proof* (1995), Resnick searches for a woman who may be responsible for a series of attacks on men while also trying to protect an American mystery author (possibly meant to represent Patricia CORNWELL) who is receiving threats from someone who wants to do to her what she does to her characters. *Still Waters* (1997) is largely about spousal abuse, which is depicted in several scenes. *Last Rites* (1998) brings the series to an end.

BIBLIOGRAPHY Novels: *Lonely Hearts* (1989), *Rough Treatment* (1990), *Cutting Edge* (1991), *Off Minor* (1992), *Wasted Years* (1993), *Cold Light* (1994), *Easy Meat* (1995).

RESNICK, SLOTS See BASEBALL.

RETURN, DAVID A character created by Manly Wade WELLMAN. Return is a policeman on an American Indian reservation, where he works for his grandfather, Lieutenant Tough Feather. Return is like the detective used by Tony HILLERMAN, but appeared fully thirty years earlier. He uses Native American methods in his work and communicates much tribal lore and knowledge. Wellman based Return's imaginary tribe, the Tsichah, on the Cheyenne and Pawnee tribes. Wellman won the first international Ellery QUEEN prize for his David Return story "Star for a Warrior."

RHODE, JOHN (pseudonym of Cecil John Charles Street, 1884–1965) One of the most prominent of English mystery writers of the GOLDEN AGE, John Rhode is also one of the least read. Like Edgar WALLACE, his name is recalled, but most of his many books are forgotten. Rhode was a major in the British Army, and the virtues of his writing are in a sense martial; his plots were carefully constructed puzzles. He was fond of unlikely and clever murder methods. The characters, however, are mostly silhouettes. Rhode's people are like chess pieces, moved rather than motivated by the writer. In addition to his prodigious mystery output—140 novels—Rhode wrote nonfiction works on politics and history as well as biographies. He was a prominent member of the DETECTION CLUB and participated in its SERIAL NOVELS. Rhode also wrote about real crimes. He published a book on the Constance KENT case in 1928; remarkably, he received an anonymous letter following publication of the book from someone in Australia who obviously had intimate knowledge of Kent, who had disappeared in 1885.

Rhode's career spanned many decades, but his style remained that of the twenties and thirties. His first novel was *The White Menace* (1924), which dealt with cocaine trafficking. The next year Rhode introduced Dr. PRIESTLEY in *The Paddington Mystery* (1925). In this novel, Priestley, who is a logical rather than strictly scientific detective, clears Harold Merefield from a charge of murder. The early Priestley novels are considered the best; because Rhode made Priestley age more or less realistically, he becomes almost immobile as the series progresses, and in the later books most of the work is left to the supporting cast, including Inspector Hanslet. In *Hendon's First Case* (1935), Rhode added to the series the supporting character Jimmy Waghorn, an earnest young graduate of the Police College who becomes a detective. *Shadow of An Alibi* (1946; orig title *The Telephone Call*) is often mentioned because it is a fictionalized version of the Julia WALLACE case. *Invisible Weapons* (1938) is one of several Rhode books using the LOCKED ROOM scenario.

While the identity of the killer in the Dr. Priestley novels is often poorly concealed, the murder methods may be impossible for the reader to figure out since they may entail obscure scientific facts, rare poisons, or complicated mechanics. Poisoning was a Rhode favorite, but he also had victims done in by being struck with an automobile part (not the engine) and other unlikely techniques. Rhode was a competent writer on a mechanical level, but the very meticulousness and fairness of his blow-by-blow descriptions mean that his narratives rarely flow with ease. Each observation has to be introduced: "The next point of interest was the state of the doors and windows . . ." The clues are guaranteed to be apparent to the reader who can stand such tutelage.

Street adopted a second pseudonym with *The Hardway Diamonds Mystery* (1930), which was published under the name Miles Burton. As Burton, he wrote many mysteries about Desmond MERRION; incredibly, the fact that Rhode and Burton were the same person was not known until the sixties. Although his two sleuths belong to very different types—Merrion, like the author, is a former officer—the techniques and the style of the two series are essentially the same. Merrion is more mobile, however, giving a larger variety of scene. Like Freeman Wills CROFTS, Street was fond of murders on TRAINS and boats, and the greater freedom allowed to Merrion gave the author more room to indulge such interests. Among the Merrion novels are THE SECRET OF HIGH ELDERSHAM (1930) and THE PLATINUM CAT (1938).

Rhode wrote one novel in collaboration with John Dickson CARR, *Drop to His Death* (1939; U.S. title *Fatal Descent*), a murder story set in a publishing house. One of his Priestley books, *The Murders in Praed Street* (1928), was made into a film (*Twelve Good Men*, 1936), but with the sedate detective deleted from the story.

RHODENBARR, BERNIE A detective-cum-thief in a series by Lawrence BLOCK. Rhodenbarr first appeared in *Burglars Can't Be Choosers* (1977). Block himself has some skill in picking locks, which supposedly inspired the series. Bernie is a more comical, witty character than that other Block creation, Matt SCUDDER. His nemesis is a corrupt but genial policeman, Ray Kirshmann ("the best cop money could buy"), and he is sometimes assisted by his friend, Carolyn Kaiser, who runs a dog washing business. In THE BURGLAR WHO STUDIED SPINOZA (1981), he lets her come along on a job and she loses a glove, setting him up for a murder rap.

In the beginning, Rhodenbarr was a pure thief. But at the opening of the third book (*The Burglar Who Liked to Quote Kipling*, 1979), he has acquired a used bookstore. Most of his "cases" are not jobs; rather, he must solve the mystery before he is framed for the crime himself. In *The Burglar Who Traded Ted Williams* (1994), a case leads him to an ingenious way of buying his building from his landlord. The books' plots are becoming less tight as patter and ambiance become more of a focus, a weakness that detracts from *The Burglar Who Thought He Was Bogart* (1995).

BIBLIOGRAPHY Novels: *The Burglar in the Closet* (1978), *The Burglar Who Painted Like Mondrian* (1983), *The Burglar in the Library* (1997), *The Burglar in the Rye* (1999).

RHYS, MADOC See MACLEOD, CHARLOTTE.

RICE, CRAIG (pseudonym of Georgiana Ann Randolph Craig, 1908–1957) The American writer known as Craig Rice lived a short and tragic life and left behind a series of books that are widely revered, though not frequently reprinted. A measure of her fame at one time is that she was pictured on the cover of *Time* magazine on January 28, 1946—and very fortunately, because information about Rice is hard to come by. She was a native of Chicago, was married at least four times, and had three children. In Chicago, Rice wrote for newspapers and radio and also worked in public relations; one of her clients was Gypsy Rose Lee, for whom she ghost wrote two mysteries, *The G-String Murders* (1941) and *Mother Finds a Body* (1942). *Home Sweet Homicide* (1944) is a novel about a crime writer with three children and thus seems to have an autobiographical slant. In addition to writing novels, Rice also worked in the film industry. William DEANDREA wrote that she suffered from a drinking problem, which eventually killed her at the age of forty-nine.

Rice's best-known creation is John J. MALONE, a lawyer who solves crimes. The Malone novels are more playful and funny than those involving the reigning legal sleuth of the period, Perry MASON. Her other series characters have faded into obscurity. One was Melville Fairr, a psychological detective working in New York, and not a significant contribution to an already crowded field. The series appeared under the pseudonym Michael Venning. The characters Bingo Riggs and Handsome Kusak were more in the Rice line; a pair of photographers with grandiose ambitions for their fledgling film company, they get into all kinds of absurd adventures in three books with bird titles: *The Sunday Pigeon Murders* (1942), *The Thursday Turkey Murders* (1943), and *The April Robin Murders* (1959). The latter was finished by Ed MCBAIN.

During her career in Hollywood, Rice worked on the series about THE FALCON. One of her publicity clients, George Sanders, starred in the series, and it is thought that she ghost-wrote his mystery novel, *Crime on My Hands* (1944). Rice collaborated with Stuart PALMER, with whom she had worked on the Falcon series, on a number of short stories that paired Malone with Palmer's Hildegarde WITHERS. The stories were collected after her death in *The People versus Withers and Malone* (1963). Yet another facet of Rice's brief but diverse career was as a true crime writer. One of her books in this vein was *Los Angeles Murders* (1947), which dealt with actual cases.

RICHLER, MORDECAI See SOLOMON GURSKY WAS HERE.

RICHMOND; OR, SCENES IN THE LIFE OF A BOW STREET RUNNER (1827) One of the very earliest fictional accounts of the activities of a police agent, in this case a BOW STREET RUNNER named Thomas Richmond. The Bow Street Runners were not, properly speaking, policemen; the book was published two years before the establishment of the London Metropolitan Police (see BOBBY). *Richmond* stands at the beginning of an English tradition of stories purporting to document the activities of policemen and their procedures, a different branch of the detective story than that represented by POE. Among those who wrote fictionalized police chronicles was Charles DICKENS. *Richmond* was reprinted in 1976 by Dover Publications.

RICIN A poison made from the castor bean or castor oil plant. The familiar home remedy and laxative, castor oil, is made from the pressing of the bean, but the process leaves behind as a byproduct one of the most poisonous substances known to science—ricin.

Ricin has exerted a fascination for writers because the plant it is derived from grows wild in many areas and is readily available. The castor oil plant exists in many varieties and is even used as an ornamental shrub. In addition, ricin is a comparatively slow-acting poison, but a tiny amount is fatal. The mechanism by which the poison operates is still under study. Death is neither rapid nor pleasant, involving such symptoms as nausea, vomiting, and convulsions, which last up to a week or more. There is no antidote to ricin poisoning. Ricin has been used as the murder weapon in such mysteries as Douglas CLARK's *Premedicated Murder* (1975) and Charlotte MACLEOD's *Trouble in the Brasses* (1989).

The most bizarre RICIN murder was a real case: the strange and tragic affair of the POISONED UMBRELLA.

RIDDLE OF THE SANDS, THE (1903) This novel by Erskine CHILDERS is often considered the first modern spy novel, and is also a classic tale of the sea. Childers wrote *The Riddle of the Sands*—his only novel—with an avowedly propagandistic purpose: to warn Britain of the danger of a German invasion launched from the Frisian Islands.

In the novel, the narrator is invited by an old school acquaintance to accompany him for "a little yachting." Childers makes excellent use of the device of the naive narrator, who only gradually discovers that his host has an ulterior motive for cruising the treacherous islands. Among the shoals and barrier islands they encounter not only dangerous conditions but the mysterious Dollmann and his beautiful daughter. Childers' adventurous life and tragic fate have added to the book's enduring fame.

RIDDLE OF THE THIRD MILE (1984) An Inspector MORSE mystery, which begins at the battle of El Alamein in 1942, in which Lieutenant Browne-Smith orders a man to stop trying to rescue a comrade from a burning tank. Forty years later, Browne-Smith is an Oxford don; he vanishes at the end of term after grades are posted. Then Morse is faced with the discovery of a headless and handless corpse thrown into an Oxford canal. His search for Browne-Smith leads to a set-up in Soho where the don had been led to a certain flat with promises of sex. Morse's behavior is complicated physically by his agonizing toothache and emotionally by the fact that he failed in "Greats" at Oxford; had he passed (and not dropped out of school because of a love affair) one of his tutors would have been none other than Browne-Smith. An extremely complicated plot, it makes use of one of the proscribed devices compiled by Father KNOX in his definition of FAIR PLAY, and it also plays somewhat loosely with motive; traps, counter-traps, and ruses to divert suspicion are liberally sprinkled throughout the plot, whose twists and turns are a bit excessive.

RIDE THE LIGHTNING (1987) An Alo NUDGER novel by John LUTZ. The book is an expanded version of Lutz's EDGAR-winning short story of the same name. Nudger's client is the sweet, innocent, naive, or merely stupid Candy Ann Adams, who convinces him to take on his most hopeless case. Curtis Colt is about to become the first man to be electrocuted in the electric chair (to "ride the lightning") in Missouri in twenty-five years. In one sense, he is a victim of politics and the state's governor, who is out to fulfill his promise to get the chair operating again. On the other hand, Colt was convicted of shooting two old people in cold blood during a liquor store robbery. Candy Ann, his girlfriend, believes he is innocent, despite the word of four eyewitnesses. In her, Nudger encounters "foolish optimism that transcended even his own."

RIDE THE PINK HORSE (1946) A novel by Dorothy B. HUGHES, set in her adopted state of New Mexico. Sailor arrives from Chicago to an old Spanish town just in time for Fiesta, a three-day celebration. But Sailor is not there for a holiday; he is hunting for "The Sen," his old boss who owes him money. All the hotel rooms are full, which becomes the second source of his rage. He is forced to befriend one of the "spics," a man he calls Pancho who runs a merry-go-round during Fiesta. At first, Sailor appears to be nothing but a vicious little racist punk, but gradually his story unfolds. He meets up with MacIntyre, a Chicago detective who grew up in the same slum as Sailor but chose the path of good, while Sailor moved uptown and got involved with a political mob. While Sailor stalks the Sen, MacIntyre keeps an eye on both, amid the teeming masses of gringo tourists, Mexicans, and Indians. Sailor meets a young Indian girl named Pila. He is at first repelled by her expressionless dark eyes, which act as a disarming mirror, showing him that his vendetta is petty and he himself is less than nothing in terms of the ageless time of the Indian people and the emptiness of the desert. Sailor's other chance for enlightenment is MacIntyre's preaching to him about good and evil and offer of a break if he will tell what he knows about a murder back in Chicago. In a manner reminiscent of Graham GREENE—though the writing is not up to Greene's level—Hughes shows the contrasting mentalities of three cultures as they struggle for control of Sailor's soul.

RIFFRAFF This term for the lowest class of people dates from the Middle Ages; *rif and raf* meant "one and all," everyone.

RIGHT TO DIE, A (1964) A novel by Rex STOUT. The book was highly praised, particularly because it engages social issues more directly than other books in the Nero WOLFE series. It is also a sequel of sorts to *Too Many Cooks* (1938), which was praised for its delineation of race relations. Progressive in their time, both books now seem paternalistic as well as inconsistent in the way they deal with race, despite other strengths. Still, *Too Many Cooks* was hailed by *The New Yorker* as "by far the best of Mr. Stout's books," and the plot and dialogue are among the finest Stout constructed. The book was first serialized in *The American Magazine*, which sent the author on a promotional tour with a host of other artists as well as the great golfer Gene Sarazen.

In *Too Many Cooks*, Wolfe and Archie GOODWIN travel to West Virginia by train to attend a meeting of fifteen great chefs ("Les Quinze Maîtres") at Kanawha Spa, where Wolfe is supposed to address them with a speech ("Contributions Americaines à la Haute Cuisine"). Wolfe's ulterior motive is to acquire a sausage recipe from the chef Jerome Berin. During a taste test, one of the chefs is found stabbed to death, and Wolfe is drawn into the search for the killer. One of the young black employees of the spa (and a Howard University student), Paul Whipple, is instrumental in solving the murder. After Wolfe's speech about the rights of man and race relations, Whipple is persuaded to break his silence about what happened. The killer does not like this very much; this is the first book in which Wolfe is wounded.

Paul Whipple returns in *A Right to Die* as an adult, and with a problem: his son is engaged to marry a white woman with whom he works at a civil rights organization, and Whipple wants to stop it because of the social complications and disapproval. Wolfe first tries to talk him out of it, then agrees to look into the woman's background. As the plot develops, the point becomes moot.

RINEHART, MARY ROBERTS (1876–1958) Born in Pittsburgh, Rinehart became one of the most successful and well-known mystery authors and singlehandedly invented the HAD-I-BUT-KNOWN subgenre (now almost universally derided). Rinehart's eventful life was not without tragedy: her father was a failed inventor who committed suicide. Later, a financial crisis drove her to try writing to augment the family income. She succeeded in spades, eventually becoming the highest-paid U.S. author of her time. Rinehart invested some of her earnings in a publishing company, which eventually would bear her name (Farrar and Rinehart) and also publish her books (from 1930 onward).

Before her marriage, Rinehart trained as a nurse, background she would use in a series of mysteries featuring nurse Hilda ADAMS. The Adams stories, however, are today much less readable than her non-series work. Rinehart's stories are often laden with conventional and dated romance subplots. Her work matured as she got older, however; in THE STATE VS. ELINOR NORTON (1934), her highest achievement, she attempts to tell a story of murder with the sociological scope of DREISER set in the New York haute monde of Edith Wharton. (There are also some echoes of FITZGERALD's Nick Carraway in Carroll Warner's narration of Elinor's story from an intimate distance.) Rinehart's heroine lives morally in the nineteenth century, but the book manages to do much more than implant a murder into a novel that is essentially about a woman's need for marriage.

The Album (1933) is another late book, which, though long and almost somnolent at times, shows Rinehart re-evaluating Victorian conventions. There is even some incipient criticism of the roles imposed on women and the rankling confinement to domesticity—"the tyranny of the unimportant." The Crescent is a gated community of country mansions, now overtaken by the urban sprawl of an unnamed city. Widows and spinsters (at twenty-eight, the narrator is prepared to number herself among them) make up a large part of the neighborhood. In this community of the unhappy into which an AXE murderer strikes terror, everyone sees him or herself as having been more or less cheated out of life by someone else or by the repressive power of the group.

To her credit, Rinehart did not simply create a detective and then churn out a series, but varied her approach. Although she often focused on romantic heroines, one of her best-known books, *The After House* (1914; see MURDER AFLOAT) is written from the perspective of a man and is based on a real case. THE MAN IN LOWER TEN and THE CIRCULAR STAIRCASE (both 1909) are perennial favorites; the former is a classic case of murder on a TRAIN, while the latter is probably her most famous book and certainly the most remunerative, thanks to the stage version, *The Bat* (1920). A film was also made.

Old decrepit mansions are often symbolic in Rinehart's books of the decrepit families who live inside them, their jealousies and resentments eventually exploding into murder. Her own life probably gave Rinehart the ability to depict unhappy people living in painfully close proximity. Some of the defects of Rinehart's books are the intrusion of racist language and her heavy use of foreshadowing. In *The Door* (1930), suspense is maintained by having the murderer only unmasked in the penultimate line of the book. This novel is similar to *The Circular Staircase* in that a big house is central to the plot; it is owned by members of the American aristocracy, and the main character, Elizabeth Jane Bell, is a single, middle-aged woman. The mystery begins when a nurse who was out walking Miss Bell's dogs is found dead in the woods. Evidence points to her cousin, Jim Blake, but several other murders and questions about a will add complications, as does the panoply of servants.

The GOTHIC element of the "haunted" house appears again and again, for example in *The Confession* (1921), a novella that the narrator terms a "study in fear." One of Rinehart's better-written stories, it shows how the author could capitalize on the dread one experiences in a good ghost story, even when she had ruled out the supernatural. In a plot since endlessly repeated, a renter finds that a massive and silent old house has a menacing personality and horrifying secrets. The weakness, as in all but Rinehart's best works, is in the characterizations, which are often thin sketches of familiar types; the young heroine, the spinster, the superstitious servant. *Sight Unseen* (1931), a companion piece, involves the OCCULT. Several proper upper-class gentlemen are drawn into a mystery when their social club's innocent séance reveals a murder. The story is told sheepishly and rather charmingly by a timid lawyer who finds himself breaking into houses and getting into fights. The supernatural element seems not a plot device as much as an expression of the author's keen interest in mental phenomena.

Her weaknesses notwithstanding, Rinehart had versatility and an intuitive grasp of what would entertain her audience. Though she began writing out of necessity, her writing improved; she used the same formulas time after time, but polished them. In THE YELLOW ROOM (1945), she made her own house in Bar Harbor, Maine, the basis of one of her young heroine/sinister mansion plots. Rinehart's less melodramatic works often show a subtle wit. She created a humorous character in TISH, whose stories appeared in *The Saturday Evening Post.* Although they are only vaguely mysteries, these stories were immensely popular and she was paid the fantastic sum of $4,000 per story—a high price for a short story even today. Because the "had-I-but-known" style is now treated almost as a joke, it is hard to appreciate just how successful Rinehart was in her time. During the Depression, she regularly earned one hundred thousand dollars a year.

Rinehart's autobiography, *My Story,* was published in 1931 and revised in 1948. It reveals much about the person behind the famous author. She describes a lifelong conflict between her desire for and pleasure in success, and her persistent doubts, amounting almost to a guilt complex, about her departure from traditional women's roles. There is a seriousness behind her heroines that is not present in Rinehart's many inane imitators.

RIPLEY, CHARLES A character in novels by John WAINWRIGHT. The author said that this was his favorite of the characters he created. Ripley is a legendary "copper" among his peers. He is shot in *A Touch of Malice* (1973); paralyzed, he makes his last appearance in the melodramatic *Death of a Big Man* (1975). From his wheelchair, he squares off against Paul Gunther, a ruthless criminal who has beaten a woman with a hammer, murdered a policeman, and crashed a police gathering to drink a toast to the victim's widow.

RIPLEY, TOM A con man and murderer introduced in Patricia Highsmith's THE TALENTED MR. RIPLEY (1955). The title sounds ironic, once one knows who Ripley is, but it isn't; in the moral vacuum he inhabits, talent has no connotations of good and bad, and being good at killing people or good at impersonation is equally "good." Ripley, oddly (and disturbingly), is not a misfit; he can be charming and has friends, though he doesn't mind killing them if that suits his own needs. Not surprisingly, he is already on the run from the law when he first appears. He takes advantage of an offer from a friend in order to change his identity. Far from suffering for his behavior, Ripley prospers—marrying and adopting an outwardly conventional life.

The supporting characters in the Ripley novels are often not as developed as he is—his wife Heloïse, for example. The last book resembles a traditional mystery with the justice-in-the-end scenes shorn off. In *Ripley Under Water* (1991), Ripley is living in the French countryside and is involved in a plot to have an artist named Bernard Tufts forge some paintings. His co-conspirators are Jeff Constant and Ed Banbury, who never really become much more than ciphers. David and Janice Pritchard, however, are a well-drawn pair of flaky Britons who turn up and, through their nosiness, start to suspect Ripley. Another shadowy character named Murchison also gets on to the forgery, and Ripley deals with the situation with his usual murderous aplomb. *Ripley's Game* (1974) is vicious and viciously funny. In a chance meeting at a party, Ripley meets a picture framer who is seriously ill. Feeling snubbed by this character, Ripley plays a practical joke—a forged letter—in which he cruelly manipulates the man's fears for his health. He eventually manages to maneuver the picture framer into involvement in contract killings.

BIBLIOGRAPHY Novels: *Ripley Underground* (1970), *The Boy Who Followed Ripley* (1980).

RIPPER, JACK THE See JACK THE RIPPER.

RISING OF THE MOON, THE (1945) One might be forgiven for cringing before the idea of a novel that included the eccentric Dame Beatrice BRADLEY *and* a thirteen-year-old narrator, but Gladys Mitchell's *The Rising of the Moon* is one of the best books in the series and one of Dame Beatrice's most low-key performances. In fact, the cranky elderly psychiatrist only comes on the scene halfway through the story. The first part of the novel belongs wholly to the brothers, Keith and Simon Innes, two precocious boys whose Thames-side town is plagued by a series of "Ripper" murders. Simon, the elder, is the narrator; both boys speak very adult English (their thinking is equally advanced), and if this device is unrealistic, it also saves them from being cute, naive, or otherwise insufferable.

Keith and "Sim" are being brought up by their older brother Jack, his unsympathetic wife Jane, and their boarder, Christina. When the boys sneak out of the house to break into the circus visiting the town, they accidentally witness a sinister figure standing on a bridge, handling a knife in the moonlight. The first victim of the "Ripper" is one of the circus acrobats; the second is a barmaid; the third, a dairymaid. As the murders of young women pile up, the boys make some canny deductions and acquire some evidence. When circumstances begin to point toward their older brother, they try to lead suspicion away from Jack by stealing a knife similar to one he has "lost." Just as their scheme is unraveling, Dame Beatrice comes into the case, and deputizes Simon because of his local knowledge. After her appearance, the narrative becomes considerably less interesting, and the ending is drawn out long past the point when the murderer's identity is obvious. Edmund CRISPIN, however, praised the novel highly.

ROBICHAUX, DAVE A New Orleans homicide detective and later a private investigator, Dave Robichaux is the central character in a series of novels by James Lee BURKE. He first appeared in *The Neon Rain* (1987), probably the weakest book in the series, and the only one in which he is still on the police force. Robichaux was a lieutenant in Vietnam and spent fourteen years on the New Orleans police force. He is also an alcoholic; his meditations on his own dysfunctional mental processes (for example, in *Heaven's Prisoners,* 1988) are as lengthy as, and sometimes more informative than, those of Matt SCUDDER, though a bit florid. The detective's father was killed in an oil platform accident a couple of decades earlier than the setting of the novels, but he remains a haunting presence. In fact, history—from antebellum slavery to the trauma of the Civil War to Vietnam and the decay of American society in the 1980s—is a subject Burke puts in the foreground of the novels. A Catholic and a moralist, Robichaux says he dislikes the present and misses the past; hunting and fishing with his father and their closeness to nature represent a lost innocence. He is preoccupied by a personal sense of guilt and failure (his drinking, his inability to protect others), and by an almost physical feeling of the presence of evil in the world.

The books are violent, sometimes numbingly so. In the first book, he goes off the wagon and out of control, which is all the explanation given for some of his behavior. It also introduces the hallmark of the series, which is not detection but the pursuit of personal vendettas. Robichaux's violent streak and resorting to techniques the police are not supposed to use is subjected to some scrutiny—more than in the case of some other bruisers, like Mike HAMMER and SPENSER. But like these ultra-tough guys, a real Robichaux would be in jail for everything from arson to murder. Robichaux loses his wife in the second book. Because the series is almost like a saga, it makes more sense if read in sequence. The third book, BLACK CHERRY BLUES (1989), won an EDGAR for best novel—though it is more solemn, Dave Robichaux's meditations less integrated than in earlier books, and its plot looser. Robichaux's desire to hurt people reaches a new level, and in *Black Cherry Blues* he is at his scariest.

Some of Robichaux's most interesting exchanges are with Alafair, a Central American refugee who became his "daughter" in *Heaven's Prisoners* (1988), in which he rescues her from a plane crash. Despite the horrors she has seen, she remains guileless and innocent, and acts as a foil for Robichaux's own dark imaginings. Ironically, through the threats that the villains make against her, she releases him to indulge his most violent fantasies. *Heaven's Prisoners,* with its dramatic opening plane crash, grisly murder scene, and a plot involving multiple villains (some of them work for the government), is the best novel in the series. One of Robicheaux's oldest childhood friends is Bubba Rocque, a sadistic criminal to some, but to Robicheaux just a dumb redneck. In *Dixie City Jam* (1994), Robichaux gets involved in a case involving a Nazi submarine sunk in Louisiana waters.

BIBLIOGRAPHY Novels: *A Morning for Flamingos* (1990), *A Stained White Radiance* (1992), *In the Electric Mist with Confederate Dead* (1993), *Burning Angel* (1995), *Cadillac Jukebox* (1996).

ROCAMBOLE See PONSON DU TERRAIL.

ROCKET TO THE MORGUE (1942) A novel by Anthony BOUCHER, the second to involve the detective team of Lieutenant Marshall of the Los Angeles police and Sister Ursula of the Sisters of Martha of Bethany; other characters from NINE TIMES NINE (1940) also reappear. The plot centers on the Mañana Literary Society, a group of SCIENCE FICTION fans and authors. All have some reason to be frustrated with Hilary Foulkes, son and literary executor of the famous sci-fi writer Fowler Foulkes. Lieutenant Marshall is called in after the mysterious death of J. Tarbel, whose body turns up in the same building where Foulkes lives. Then an attempt is made on Hilary's life, which he barely escapes. After he gets out of the hospital, he throws a welcome home party for himself, at which the incident of the title occurs. A second attempt on Hilary's life is successful; like the first, it is a LOCKED ROOM problem. Suspicion falls on Matt Duncan, who wanted to reprint Fowler's stories but could not afford the exorbitant rates charged by the son. Fowler's death does not greatly disturb his unhappy wife, Veronica, who had wanted to become a nun, or Vance Wimpole, her brother, who wanted to be Foulkes' literary executor. Among the other members of Mañana is Anthony Boucher, who inserts himself into the story (just as George BAXT later would do in writing about Los Angeles in the fifties). The central conundrum hinges on a trick and the killer can be spotted fairly easily. The atmosphere of Los Angeles in the forties and the science fiction community is well done, though the book is rated below *Nine Times Nine.*

ROGUE LITERATURE A genre of the Elizabethan age, practiced by Thomas Nashe, Robert Greene, and others. The form was adapted from Continental models. The rogue is an important figure in later detective and mystery writing, and, it could be argued, the central one in crime fiction. See also PICARESQUE.

ROGUE MALE (1939) The narrator of Geoffrey HOUSEHOLD's *Rogue Male* never names himself, but we know that he is a famous English sportsman. His story is in the form of a diary, and everything flows from one hidden event that is not disclosed until the very end. The narrator travels to Poland and then crosses into a country ruled by a dictator—obviously Germany, though the NAZIS are never actually named. He is captured with a rifle and telescopic sight in range of the dictator, and tortured as an agent and assassin. He insists, however, that he was merely playing an academic and dangerous game: to see if it was possible to get close enough to the head of state to kill him, which he had no intention of doing.

A bungled attempt to kill the narrator leaves him severely wounded and embedded in mud at the bottom of a cliff; the mud saves his life by closing his wounds. His escape from Germany by boat and ship is told in great detail with plenty of local color. He is an engaging narrator who, in between the problems he encounters and their solutions, tells us about his personal code. He is a "rogue male," a man who thinks he owes no allegiance to anyone, and it takes the diabolical traitor Quive-Smith to reveal to him his true self and passions. As a dose of *bildung*, it is fairly mild, but there is an ingratiating quality about the narrator's chagrined self-revelation: "I, the civilized, scrupulous sportsman, was behaving like an ice-cream merchant with a knife." The non-stop chase through the London subways, into the countryside, and finally to Dorset, where the narrator literally goes to ground, is meticulously plotted; the rustic scenes reveal that behind the suspense yarn Household's true subject is his love of England.

ROHMER, SAX (pseudonym of Arthur Henry Sarsfield Ware, 1883–1959) There are details of Sax Rohmer's life as mysterious as the character for whom he is known, Dr. FU MANCHU. Some say Rohmer died in London, others that he died in a New York hotel; his real surname has been given as Ware, Ward, and Warde. But everyone agrees that despite his great success, Rohmer was always poor, a notoriously bad investor, and a spendthrift.

Ware was born in Birmingham and became interested in writing very early. He worked in the London financial world for a time before switching to journalism. Rohmer said that he papered an entire wall with rejection slips before he broke into print. He had been fascinated by the East and in the occult since childhood, and was particularly interested in Egypt, which he would later visit; his forays into the Limehouse district of London (the Chinese quarter) and his friendships there gave him material for the Fu Manchu stories. Rohmer said that one foggy night, he saw a Chinese man with a woman who appeared to be Arab leave a car and go into a cheap-looking house, and this inspired Fu Manchu. The first book in the series was *Dr. Fu Manchu* (1913).

Rohmer's writing is full of improbabilities, stereotypes, bathos, and pure absurdity. *The Exploits of Captain O'Hagan* (1916; repr 1968) is about a man who should have been born in the sixteenth century; an absolute monarchist with the personality of a musketeer, quick to take—or more accurately, give—offense, throwing down the gauntlet with such cries as "You are a puppy, sir!" Rohmer wrote better when he simply abandoned any pretense and admitted the supernatural into his stories, as in his "Tchériapin," from his *Tales of Chinatown*, about a scientist who has learned to turn organic matter into the hardest stone, and a violinist very like a devil.

Rohmer's *The Dream Detective* (1920) featured one of the most outlandish premises of detective fiction. Morris Klaw, the eponymous detective, is more than intuitive: he gets his insights into crime from sleeping on a special pillow and then interpreting the resultant dreams. Rohmer was capable of writing a fairly straight mystery, as in *Hangover House* (1949), featuring the dashing detective Storm Kennedy, whose client is the very "wot-ho" Lord Glengale. Late in life Rohmer created Sumuru, a female version of Fu Manchu.

ROLLISON, RICHARD A character created by John CREASEY and better known as "The Toff." Like most of the author's inventions, he is actually an imitation, clearly based on Leslie Charteris's THE SAINT. Outlandish plots, beautiful women, narrow escapes, and plenty of dashing around are staples of the series. Tall, tanned, and of course handsome, Rollison is the nephew of Lady Gloria Hurst, who runs the fashionable Marigold Club. He is assisted by a Jeeves-like valet named Jolly. Rollison has a "trophy wall" in his home in Gresham Terrace, London, covered with knives, pistols, a shrunken head, and women's nylons, all supposedly souvenirs of his adventures. He drives fast cars, plays fast and loose with the law, and is tolerated and sometimes abetted by Inspector (later Superintendent) Bill Grice of Scotland Yard.

Creasey wrote more than fifty books about The Toff. The writing is slapdash—he often wrote two Toff books a year, and it was only one of several ongoing Creasey series. The first book is *Introducing the Toff* (1938), the last *The Toff and the Crooked Copper* (1977). Each of the books has a stock setup. The Toff's aunt Mattie is nearly killed in *The Toff Goes to Market* (1942), which draws him into an investigation of smuggling and black marketeering. In *Model for the Toff* (1957), he is approached by a fashion designer whose models are being driven away by threats in order to destroy his business. In some of the books, Creasey uses the exotic-setting ploy—for example, *The Toff Down Under* (1953) and *The Toff in New York* (1956). The latter is about a criminal mastermind. In *A Rocket for the Toff* (1960), the Toff has to enlist the help of criminals in a desperate battle. Two of the books were filmed, both in 1952: *Salute the Toff* (1941) is about a kidnapping; *Hammer the Toff* (1947) is a thriller about scientific secrets.

BIBLIOGRAPHY Novels: *The Toff Goes On* (1939), *The Toff Steps Out* (1939), *Here Comes the Toff* (1940), *The Toff Breaks In* (1940), *The Toff Proceeds* (1941), *The Toff Is Back* (1942), *The Toff*

Among the Millions (1943), *Accuse the Toff* (1943), *The Toff and the Curate* (1944), *The Toff and the Great Illusion* (1944), *Feathers for the Toff* (1945), *The Toff and the Lady* (1946), *Poison for the Toff* (1946; orig title *The Toff on Ice*), *The Toff in Town* (1948), *The Toff Takes Shares* (1948), *The Toff and Old Harry* (1949), *The Toff on Board* (1973), *Fool the Toff* (1950), *Kill the Toff* (1950), *A Knife for the Toff* (1951), *Hunt the Toff* (1952), *Call the Toff* (1953), *The Toff at Butlin's* (1954), *The Toff at the Fair* (1954), *A Six for the Toff* (1955), *The Toff and the Deep Blue Sea* (1955), *Make-Up for the Toff* (1956), *The Toff on Fire* (1957), *The Toff and the Stolen Tresses* (1958), *The Toff on the Farm* (1958), *Double for the Toff* (1959), *The Toff and the Runaway Bride* (1960), *The Toff and the Kidnapped Child* (1960), *Follow the Toff* (1961), *The Toff and the Toughs* (1961; orig title *The Toff and the Teds*), *A Doll for the Toff* (1963), *Leave It to the Toff* (1963), *The Toff and the Spider* (1966), *The Toff in Wax* (1966), *A Bundle for the Toff* (1967), *Stars for the Toff* (1968), *The Toff and the Golden Boy* (1969), *The Toff and the Fallen Angels* (1970), *Vote for the Toff* (1971), *The Toff and the Trip-Trip-Triplets* (1972), *The Toff and the Terrified Taxman* (1973), *The Toff and the Sleepy Cowboy* (1973).

Short Stories: *The Toff on the Trail* (no date), *Murder Out of the Past* (1953).

ROMAN HAT MYSTERY, THE (1929) The first Ellery QUEEN mystery to appear in print, this one has been overrated. Inspector Richard Queen and Ellery Queen are an annoying pair, more caricatures than characters. It is interesting, however, to note how a few HARD-BOILED spices are thrown into the Holmesian pastiche; while Ellery is priggish, Richard is quite tough at times. The story begins with the discovery of a body in a theater. Inspector Queen is called in, and Ellery turns up soon after to watch the show. During the course of the evening's investigation, Richard takes snuff fifteen times and Ellery does an exceptional amount of pince-nez polishing and moping about a valuable book he has missed buying (he is an antiquarian book collector). This constitutes the substitution of mannerism for character; the most lifelike person in the book is ironically the dead man, a shady lawyer with many nefarious businesses and numerous enemies. His missing hat becomes the key to the problem. While the solution is ingenious, it strains credulity.

ROOM TO SWING (1957) In this EDGAR-winning novel, Ed LACY introduced a black New York City private detective, Toussaint Moore, who was to star in a short-lived series. The story opens in a similar setting to that of the more famous Edgar winner, IN THE HEAT OF THE NIGHT (1965). Moore, driving his Jaguar and looking very hip and well-to-do, is greeted by racist cops in the small town of Bingston, Ohio, near the Kentucky border. It turns out that Moore is on the run from a murder charge, having been set up by his client. In a long series of flashbacks, Lacy shows the detective being recruited by Kay Robbens, an advertising agent doing work for a new television true-crime program. Moore is hired to shadow Robert Thomas, a.k.a. Richard Tutt, a man wanted by the Ohio police for assault. The exorbitant fee encourages the p.i. to take the case despite the thinness of the story he is handed by Robbens. In a series of scenes, Moore is baited, exhibited, and exploited by "progressive" whites in Robbens's circle out to show how hip and liberal they are. This is only a foretaste of the treatment he receives once he is trapped into the role of murderer and has to punch a white cop to escape. Moore goes underground in order to clear himself of the crime, and once in Ohio has to shed his city ways and make himself acceptable to the white hierarchy. *Room to Swing* has a promising beginning and engaging characters, with interesting relationships, particularly between Moore and his girlfriend Sybil. The resolution of the mystery, however, is abrupt and surprisingly simple given the careful buildup.

ROOSEVELT, ELEANOR See CELEBRITY MYSTERIES.

ROOSEVELT, THEODORE (1858–1919) American politician, historian, and twenty-sixth president of the United States (1901–1909). Roosevelt had served as New York City Police Commissioner, and as such appears in the novel *The Alienist* (1994) by Caleb CARR. William DEANDREA had previously used Commissioner Roosevelt in *The Lunatic Fringe* (1980), a book set in 1896, and a younger Roosevelt appeared in H. Paul Jeffers's *The Adventure of the Stalwart Companions* (1978), a not very adept Holmesian mystery. Roosevelt also inspired the character Thatcher COLT.

President Roosevelt was friendly with one of the greatest mystery writers, though neither knew it at the time: the young Rex STOUT served on Roosevelt's yacht while in the Navy.

ROSENKRANTZ, PALLE [ADAM VILHELM VON] (1867–1941) The Danish baron Palle Rosencrantz (as a sign of his nobility, he is also called von Rosenkrantz) was a well-known literary figure in his time. Rosenkrantz was born in Helsingör, Denmark—the "Elsinore" of Shakespeare's *Hamlet*. In fact, it has been said that Rosenkrantz was a descendant of the man for whom one of the characters in *Hamlet* is named. That earlier Palle Rosenkrantz served as an envoy from the Danish crown to James I of England (he was accompanied by another Dane named Gyldenstierne; the pair were cast as killers by Shakespeare).

The modern Palle Rosenkrantz was a writer of mystery and adventure novels. He studied law at Copenhagen University and was called to the bar in 1909. He was an assistant to a judge and also worked for the telephone company before becoming a man of letters. His legal interests, concern for justice, and support of reform of the judicial system and the police can be seen in his work. In one of his stories about Lieutenant Holst, a Copenhagen policeman, the lieutenant tries to protect a beautiful Russian countess who says she is being unfairly persecuted by her brother-in-law, who believes she betrayed her husband to the Tsarist police. The brother-in-law, she thinks, is only after her money. Holst is chagrined to find in the end that everyone is innocent and guilty at the same time. One of Rosenkrantz's crime novels was *The Homburg Murder Case,* about the death of an English aristocrat killed in one of Europe's elegant spas. Rosenkrantz was prolific and also wrote dramas, autobiographies, historical novels, and radio plays.

ROSS, BARNABY See QUEEN, ELLERY.

ROSS, JAMES (1911–1990) Like Horace MCCOY, James Ross wrote one famous HARD-BOILED novel, THEY DON'T DANCE MUCH, which was published in 1940. Born in North Carolina, Ross attended Louisburg and Elon colleges and then served in World War II. He worked at various jobs, including farming, semi-professional baseball, and clerking for the Internal Revenue Service. He began writing with the *Greensboro Daily News,* and after 1954 supported himself as a journalist. His classic novel is a story of violence set during the Depression; Ross gave an unusual rural twist to the HARD-BOILED style.

ROSTNIKOV, PORFIRY PETROVICH See KAMINSKY, STUART.

ROUGHEAD, WILLIAM (1870–1952) Born in Scotland, Roughead became one of the most important criminologists of his or any time. He was an editor and writer of the *Notable British Trials* series, and wrote several volumes of essays on crime, including *Rascals Revived* (1940) and *Reprobates Reviewed* (1941). Roughead's attitude was like that of DE QUINCEY in his celebrated essay "On Murder Considered as One of the Fine Arts"; Roughead wrote that "to my mind, one cannot have too much of a good murder." His elegant essays are full of appreciation, though not admiration, for their subjects; his account of THE ARRAN MYSTERY reads like a suspenseful short story.

Roughead's writing impressed his contemporaries and even led to his involvement in real cases. Lillian Hellman, longtime friend of Dashiell HAMMETT, based her most celebrated play, *The Children's Hour* (1934), on a case dealt with in one of Roughead's essays, about teachers in a girls' school who are accused of lesbianism. Roughead wrote about the case in "Closed Doors, or The Great Drumsheugh Case," an essay from *Bad Companions* (1931). One of Roughead's volumes of *Notable British Trials* (1910) dealt with the case of Oscar SLATER, one of two men whose causes were championed by Conan DOYLE. Roughead published his book on the case the year after the trial, at which he was present. He and Conan Doyle worked tirelessly for Slater's release for two decades; Roughead was a witness at the final appeal in 1928. *Classic Crimes: A Selection from the Works of William Roughead* (1951; repr 1977) was published with an introduction by Julian SYMONS.

ROUGIERRE, MADAME DE LA The French governess in UNCLE SILAS (1864). An at once repulsive and comic villain, Madame de la Rougierre is a brandy-loving, craftily obsequious woman who becomes sadistic once out of sight of her employer. She is one of LE FANU's most memorable characters, and comes to an equally memorable end.

ROULETABILLE A sleuth invented by Gaston LEROUX and first introduced in the classic THE MYSTERY OF THE YELLOW ROOM (1908). Rouletabille's real name is Joseph Josephine, but because his head is as round as a marble, he is given the nickname Rouletabille ("roll your head"). At the age of sixteen, Rouletabille had disguised himself as a sewer worker and found the left foot of a murder victim, which he took to an editor. Much impressed ("'This foot,' he cried, 'will make a great headline'"), the editor hired him on the spot. Energetic, secret, opaque in his pronouncements, Rouletabille is a classic GENIUS DETECTIVE.

ROWCLIFF, LIEUTENANT GEORGE One of the recurrent characters in the Nero WOLFE series, Rowcliff is the adversary of Archie GOODWIN, and their tormenting of each other is used for comic relief. Rowcliff was based on a real Lieutenant Rowcliff, whom Rex STOUT met (and disliked) while serving on Teddy ROOSEVELT's yacht *Mayflower.*

RUBE A term meaning sucker or easily gullible person, *rube* is a diminutive of the name Reuben, which was used to denote a rustic, a hick, a farmer. Originating in the nineteenth century, it became a piece of carnival slang.

RUDD, INSPECTOR June THOMSON's Inspector Finch was imported to the United States under the name of

Inspector Rudd. Like the mysteries of Patricia MOYES, the Finch/Rudd novels have broken free of the classical COZY and have modern, very British characters, but Thomson is the better writer. Thomson also sets her novels in the English countryside (Essex), though the character of the books is largely PROCEDURAL, with a lot of attention to the gathering of evidence. Psychology, however, is almost more important. Jack Rudd is stocky and fresh-faced (is ruddiness the source of his American pseudonym?). He lives with his older sister Dorothy, who is in her mid-fifties, gray, and solicitous of Rudd's well-being. Rudd is assisted by the tall and broad Detective Sergeant Boyce. While Boyce is heavy, crisp, and official, Rudd hangs back, sizing people up. Thomson lets us see into his thoughts, intuitions, and estimates as he uses Boyce as a stalking horse.

Thomson is intensely interested in relationships, which are often dependent, unhealthy, or in some way aberrant. *Shadow of a Doubt* (1981) is set in an exclusive psychiatric clinic called Hawton Hall headed by Dr. Howard Jordan. Jordan is a typical arrogant doctor idolized by his female staff. While he becomes more and more of a big shot, his neurotic wife Claire seems to be fading away into his shadow; then she literally disappears. The novel is a painful portrait of a dead marriage and a woman driven into herself: "I'm not like my sister, Rose, she thought sadly. I haven't the courage to change the established order of things; Rose, who wore three rings on the same hand and had her hair tinted auburn and who had once called Father a bloody old bore to his face." Thomson's people are sometimes pathetic, but not unpitiable.

In *Case Closed* (1977), the inspector is followed for days by a man named Stoll, who seems to think that the shadowing will lead him to something valuable. Rudd receives a message from an ex-convict who overhead a fellow convict make the cryptic remark, "Melly Rudd Essex Transit." The inspector links this statement to the four-year-old case of Melly Thorpe, a sixteen-year-old strangled to death in the seaside town of Merestead. In *Rosemary for Remembrance* (1988), Finch investigates the murder of a womanizing teacher at a summer creative writing school.

No Flowers by Request (1987) is about the inexplicable shooting of David Hamilton, a successful lawyer in the village of Framden. The motives seem feeble—for example, his feud with his neighbor over the use of a path—but then, it is a constant of the series that the contraction of life in the country can lead to sudden explosions. In a way, Rudd is no different than the people he investigates. He lives a lonely existence in the suburbs and has painful epiphanies in which he sees his own life eluding his grasp: "As a child, he had longed to escape both from his mother and his boyhood home, irked by the restrictions they had placed on him, and yet here he was, reduplicating the relationship through his sister." Dorothy is also disappointed, her husband having been killed in a farm accident. Her desire for a family is channeled into mothering Rudd, who feels "stifled by so much unselfish devotion." Even his affair with Marion Greave fails: "there would be no escape for him through her, however much he might yearn for it, into a different, freer life." More than psychological procedurals, the Rudd novels are studies in unhappiness. THE HABIT OF LOVING (1979; orig title *Deadly Relations*) epitomizes this quality.

BIBLIOGRAPHY Novels: *Not One of Us* (1971), *Death Cap* (1973), *The Long Revenge* (1974), *A Question of Identity* (1977), *Alibi in Time* (1980), *To Make a Killing* (1982; U.S. title *Portrait of Lilith*), *Sound Evidence* (1984), *A Dying Fall* (1985), *The Dark Stream* (1986), *The Spoils of Time* (1989), *Past Reckoning* (1990), *Foul Play* (1991), *Burden of Innocence* (1996).

RUDGE, INSPECTOR See FLOATING ADMIRAL, THE.

RUFEE, REVEREND A character created by K. C. CONSTANTINE, the Reverend is actually a shady customer involved in various nefarious dealings. Rufee is black, and goes around in a white tuxedo with a white fur collar. When he entertains Mario BALZIC, there is a satin banner showing a coiled snake and the motto, "Don't Get Over On Me," a play on the most famous flag of the American Revolution.

RULING PASSION (1973) A novel by Reginald HILL. DALZIEL is mostly on the sidelines throughout the book, but shows rare vulnerability as he is forced to consult a doctor about his chest pains. The story begins with Pascoe traveling down from Yorkshire with his girlfriend, Eleanor Soper, for a reunion with some old friends from school. When they get to their friend's cottage in Thornton Lacey, they find a shocking scene: three of their friends—a gay couple and Rose Hopkins—all killed by shotgun blasts. The husband, Colin Hopkins, is missing. Although the story has a gritty, PROCEDURAL flavor, in classic English style Hill also provides plenty of suspects in addition to Colin: a flamboyant reporter who happens to be hanging around, a nasty publican, a local squire jealous of his land, and a neighboring couple with obscure problems of their own. There is perhaps one too many subplots (mining battle in Scotland, local environmental crisis, string of robberies back home in Yorkshire, and Pascoe's relationship with Eleanor), but the matter is not absurdly dragged out. Pascoe also does some clever detecting with urine in a tea kettle.

RUNYON, DAMON (1884–1946) The American journalist and short story writer Damon Runyon is most remembered for *Guys and Dolls* (1931), a collection of stories dealing with criminals, show people, and other denizens of Broadway that was made into a famous musical. (Runyon covered some of the same ground as Ben HECHT but was less biting.) A native of Kansas, Runyon made a career as a sports journalist and was a fan of horse racing (he even had a horse named after him). Track people, gamblers, and habitual losers often appeared in his humorous short stories. Many of Runyon's anecdotes take their departure from Mindy's restaurant on Broadway, where he runs into various tough, funny, or loony characters. Runyon did more than just insert SLANG into his stories; he recreated the New York City dialect with fidelity. The journalist Heywood Broun wrote that "To me the most impressive thing in *Guys and Dolls* is the sensitivity of the ear of Damon Runyon. He has caught with a high degree of insight the actual tone and phrase of the gangsters and racketeers of the town. Their talk is put down almost literally." Other writers also praised Runyon, including Walter Winchell ("the lethal sock he packs in his pillars of pithy patter for the paper . . . has driven mobsters out of New York faster than an extra girl in Hollywood says 'Yes'"). Winchell also said that Runyon was a "coffee fiend" (like BALZAC) and no doubt he soaked up stories along with his ten or fifteen cups at a sitting in places like Mindy's.

Guys and Dolls was included in QUEEN'S QUORUM and was reprinted in *The Damon Runyon Omnibus* (1944), along with *Money from Home* (1935) and *Blue Plate Special* (1934), which contained his PARODY of the classic mystery, WHAT, NO BUTLER? *Take It Easy* (1942) is another collection of short stories. In "Lonely Heart," Nicely Nicely Jones answers a matrimonial ad and winds up with a woman who always sets a mysterious empty place at the dinner table (there are several murders). In "Situation Wanted," Runyon conceals a dark political message in a hilarious story, in which the Depression finds even hired killers out of work. An unemployed torpedo who had worked for Al CAPONE finds new work in the Spanish Civil War. "A Job for the Macaroni" is a genuine mystery story about a murder and suicide. Runyon also wrote for Hollywood and co-authored a play, *A Slight Case of Murder* (1934).

RUSSELL, COLONEL CHARLES A character created by William HAGGARD. The Colonel, obviously a military man, upholds the aristocratic values of the English officer class, and is a contrast to other contemporary spy heroes. He seems more real than James BOND, but Harry PALMER would consider him a stuffed shirt, and George SMILEY might think him useful but a creature of the past. Russell fought in World War I and was later in India (like his creator), and works for the Security Executive in military intelligence. His cases, however, are not all military in nature, and some are quite wacky: in *The Unquiet Sleep* (1962), highly placed officials become addicted to a new drug. Haggard does not write about the foot soldiers of the Cold War, but the big wigs at the top, and for that reason his books seem more conservative than those of his peers. Add to that the old-boyishness of the mentality, and that the intelligence community is viewed with less irony and more respect, and one gets the feeling of a political descendant of BUCHAN without Buchan's style. Haggard peppers his novels with cranky remarks about the decline of Britain, the failure of American leadership, political cynicism, and feebleness of left intellectuals. In *Yesterday's Enemy* (1976), a garbled story about South American dictators, a plot to blame a theft of plutonium on West Germany and a Hiroshima survivor with a diabolical plan, all the political talk seems to exist in a vacuum; characters and settings never are more than a brief stroke of the pen. Haggard is never a very vivid writer, and the narrative tends to just plug along, alerting the reader to the plot's frictions rather than drawing one into them. He has been praised for his restraint in the area of violence, but Julian SYMONS observed in the later books "a distinctly thuggish mentality."

BIBLIOGRAPHY Novels: *Slow Burner* (1958), *Venetian Blind* (1959), *The Arena* (1961), *The High Wire* (1963), *The Antagonists* (1964), *The Powder Barrel* (1965), *The Hard Sell* (1965), *The Conspirators* (1966), *A Cool Day for Killing* (1968), *The Doubtful Discipline* (1969), *The Hardliners* (1970), *Bitter Harvest* (1971; U.S. title *Too Many Enemies*), *The Old Masters* (1973; U.S. title *The Notch on the Knife*), *The Scorpion's Tail* (1975), *The Poison People* (1978), *Visa to Limbo* (1979), *The Median Line* (1979), *The Meritocrats* (1985), *The Expatriates* (1989), *The Vendettists* (1990).

S

SACCO AND VANZETTI Nicola Sacco and Bartolomeo Vanzetti were two Italian immigrants who were put to death in Charlestown, Massachusetts, in 1927, while thousands protested and rioted not only outside the prison but as far away as Europe and South America. There are several reasons why a botched robbery six years earlier led to one of the most emotional and sensational criminal trials in history.

In 1920, Sacco was a factory worker and Vanzetti was a fish peddler. On April 15, a man carrying the payroll for a Braintree, Massachusetts shoe factory was held up for $15,000. The robbery went bad and two men, including the paymaster, were killed. For Sacco and Vanzetti, the timing of the crime could not have been worse: they were anarchists and immigrants, and the post–World War I red scare and xenophobia gave the trial a hysterical and racist cast. The entire American intellectual left took the side of Sacco and Vanzetti, believing them innocent. The trial was a mockery of justice, but later writers have felt that the evidence was against them, and particularly against Sacco, who possessed a pistol closely matching the one used in the killings. The governor of the state appointed a committee headed by the President of Harvard to review the case. They upheld the ruling, and after many reprieves the two men were electrocuted.

Among the literary works inspired by the case was Upton Sinclair's novel *Boston Massachusetts* (1927), and Maxwell Anderson's plays, *Gods of the Lightning* (1928) and *Winterset* (1935). The prison letters of Sacco and Vanzetti were published the year after the execution.

SAILING See MURDER AFLOAT.

SAINT, THE A character created by Leslie CHARTERIS, The Saint was one of the longest running series in the mystery and thriller genre. The name "The Saint" comes from the initials of his name, Simon Templar. The name alludes to the Knights Templars, an order founded in the early twelfth century to assist pilgrims traveling to Jerusalem. Despite their vow of poverty, the Templars became exceedingly rich and earned the jealousy of the royal houses of Europe. They were crushed and despoiled by the French king, Philip the Fair. The name Simon Templar is more appropriate than "the Saint" for Charteris's character, given his behavior.

Charteris said that his favorite proverb was the Moslem saying, "Paradise is under the shadow of a sword." The Saint's creed, like Bulldog DRUMMOND's, is not to die in your bed. He is a dashing two-dimensional hero who steals, flees, kills, and rescues ladies in a series of novels that began with *Meet the Tiger* (1928). The stories are pure escapism, a daydream for the tedium of modern civilization; their continuing appeal is evidenced by the many film and television adaptations, the most recent for the big screen (1997). The last Saint book that Charteris wrote himself was *The Saint in Pursuit* (1970). During the sixties, when Roger Moore starred as The Saint on television, many of the shows were "novelized" and published as books. Charteris did not write them himself, but gave them a final editing and put his imprimatur on them. The actual writing was usually done by Fleming Lee (sometimes with Norman Worker).

BIBLIOGRAPHY Novels: *The Last Hero* (1930), *Enter the Saint* (1930; three novelettes), *Knight Templar* (1930; U.S. title *The Avenging Saint*), *Featuring the Saint* (1931; three novelettes), *Alias the Saint* (1931; three novelettes), *She Was a Lady* (1931; U.S. title *Angels of Doom*), *Wanted for Murder* (1931; U.S. title of *Featuring the Saint* and *Alias the Saint*), *The Holy Terror* (1932; three novelettes; U.S. title *The Saint vs. Scotland Yard*), *Getaway* (1932), *Once More the Saint* (1933; three novelettes; U.S. title *The Saint and Mr. Teal*), *The Misfortunes of Mr. Teal* (1934; three novelettes), *The Saint Goes On* (1934; three novelettes), *The Saint in New York* (1935), *Saint Overboard* (1936), *The Ace of Knaves* (1937; three novelettes), *Thieves' Picnic* (1937), *Prelude for War* (1938), *Follow the Saint* (1938; three novelettes), *The Saint in Miami* (1940), *The Saint Goes West* (1942; three novelettes), *The Saint Steps In* (1943), *The Saint on Guard* (1944; two novelettes), *The Saint Sees It Through* (1946), *Call for the Saint* (1948; two novelettes), *Vendetta for the Saint* (1964),

Novelizations: *The Saint on TV* (1967; two novelettes), *The Saint Returns* (1968; two novelettes), *The Saint and the Fiction Makers* (1968), *The Saint Abroad* (1969; two novelettes), *The Saint and the People Importers* (1970), *Catch the Saint* (1974; two novelettes), *Catch the Saint* (1975; two novelettes), *Send for the Saint* (1977), *The Saint and the Templar Treasure* (1978).

Short Stories: *The Brighter Buccaneer* (1933), *Boodle* (1934; U.S. title *The Saint Intervenes*), *The Happy Highwayman* (1939), *Saint Errant* (1948), *The Saint in Europe* (1953), *The Saint on the Spanish Main* (1955), *The Saint around the World* (1956), *Thanks to the Saint* (1957), *Señor Saint* (1958), *The Saint to the Rescue* (1959), *Trust the Saint* (1962), *The Saint in the Sun* (1963).

ST. CYR, JEAN-LOUIS See JANES, J. ROBERT.

ST. IVES, PHILIP A former newspaperman and professional "go-between" created by Ross THOMAS, who wrote his series of novels about St. Ives under the pseudonym Oliver Bleeck. Somewhat like Travis MCGEE, St. Ives recovers stolen property and takes a cut. St. Ives, however, is a relaxed, unambitious man entering middle age. Having written a newspaper column dealing with New York City's criminal underworld, St. Ives has a lot of contacts among people who "hear things." His flamboyant and childish lawyer, Myron Greene, sets up his assignments. St. Ives is divorced, has a six-year-old son, lives alone in a tiny efficiency in the Adelphi Hotel on East Forty-sixth Street, and figures his few belongings are worth less than a thousand dollars. Though his pared-down lifestyle resembles Matt SCUDDER's, St. Ives has a self-deprecating attitude that is extremely funny. St. Ives is too lazy to be HARD-BOILED, and too intelligent to care. The first of the books was *The Brass Go-Between* (1969). St. Ives is hired by the Coulter Museum in Washington to get back a tenth-century brass shield, a venerated object to the Komporeen people of Africa, whose country is torn by civil war. Both sides want the shield as an edge in the conflict. The book has many of the Thomas hallmarks—everyone turns out to be greedy in one way or another—but the silliness of the central premise makes it less enjoyable than the later novels in the series. In *No Questions Asked* (1976), St. Ives is asked to look for a volume of Pliny worth one million dollars (see BOOKS). THE PROCANE CHRONICLE (1972) is one of Thomas's best novels. In it, St. Ives is lured into an apparently suicidal caper by Abner Procane, a man who seems to be (at first) St. Ives's ideal "good thief."

BIBLIOGRAPHY Novels: *Protocol for a Kidnapping* (1971), *The Highbinders* (1974).

ST. VALENTINE'S DAY MASSACRE See CAPONE, ALPHONSE.

SALT IS LEAVING (1966) The last mystery novel of J. B. PRIESTLEY. The story is set in the small, dreary English town of Hempton and the nearby city of Birkden. Dr. Salt has just disposed of his practice and is eager to bid good riddance to ugly Birkden. Before he leaves, however, he has one last detail to straighten out: a young patient, Noreen Wilks, is missing. She is a wayward girl who suffers from chronic nephritis; so many days have elapsed since her last treatment that Salt is afraid she must be dead. As he begins his inquiries, a young punk tries to hurry him out of town. Meanwhile in Hempton, Maggie Culworth is worried about her father, Edward, a bookseller and stationer. On a Monday in October, he got a call around lunchtime, left his shop, and has not been seen since. Culworth is so respectable and regular that even his son Alan does not react, because he cannot imagine that his father would be involved in anything untoward; Maggie is worried for exactly the same reason. Doctor Salt is commanding, even peremptory, from the moment he stalks into the police superintendent's office. A pipe smoker who loves classical music, his character is reminiscent of a more imposing (and perhaps a bit arrogant) Inspector MORSE, whom he pre-dates.

SALTMARSH MURDERS, THE (1932) A novel by Gladys MITCHELL, featuring the psychiatrist sleuth Beatrice BRADLEY. The story is narrated by the curate of the village of Saltmarsh, Noel Wells. He is both appalled by Bradley, who resembles a witch, and (WATSON-like) unable to follow the rapid and intuitive flow of her deductions. The story begins when a young boy tells Wells about the odd behavior of Mrs. Gatty, who seems to have lost her mind and is hinting that her husband has been murdered. Typical of the English village mystery, there is the matter of an illegitimate birth lurking in the background; but the conventional aspects of the gossipy and COZY situation are overshadowed by the weird personality of Mrs. Bradley. She has little patience for the villagers, and does not think they are charming—especially when incest and other crimes are concerned. Her very un-MARPLE investigation is meant to be uproarious, somewhat in the manner of the village mysteries of Phoebe Atwood TAYLOR in America.

SAMSON, BERNARD A character created by Len DEIGHTON, the successor to his Harry PALMER. Samson differs from Palmer in several respects. He is an old hand, a middle-aged man—a "wrinkled old fool"—when he first appears in *Berlin Game* (1983). Samson, whose father was the head of the Berlin unit of British intelligence years before, is disgusted with the younger generation of spies, full of theories and without much field experience. But the biggest difference between Samson and the earlier spy is the style. Samson's stories are colored by his tiredness, and are grayer and less humorous than those of Palmer, the smart young cynic. In *Berlin Game,* Samson is disturbed by the service's treatment of "Brahms Four," a highly placed East German official who had saved Samson's life almost twenty years before. The mutual suspicion of Samson and his beautiful wife Fiona, both of whom think the other might be unfaithful, forms a tense undercurrent, so that Samson does not feel safe either at work or at home. This feeling of advanced erosion—moral, personal, cultural—persists throughout the series. As the titles show, the

Samson books form trilogies. In *Charity* (1996), the conclusion, Samson's world (and family) are in the final stages of decay. Samson investigates his sister-in-law's murder against his bosses' wishes; Fiona is mentally disturbed after her experiences as a double agent; and Samson wants to flee with their children.

BIBLIOGRAPHY *Mexico Set* (1984), *London Match* (1985), *Winter: A Berlin Family 1899-1945* (1987), *Spy Hook* (1988), *Spy Line* (1989), *Spy Sinker* (1990), *Faith* (1992), *Hope* (1994).

SANCTUARY (1931) A novel by William FAULKNER, probably the mystery novel most "mistaken" as a serious novel, and, ironically, least read today as a mystery. Andre Malraux called *Sanctuary* "the detective story usurping tragedy" and Ross MACDONALD praised it highly, but Faulkner himself dismissed it as an effort to write a money-maker.

Horace Benbow, the narrator, relates the story of Temple Drake, a young woman who is raped by POPEYE, who also kills the simple-minded Tommy when he tries to protect her. Popeye then takes Temple to Memphis. Lee Goodwin is accused of the murder, and Benbow defends him. Temple, however, commits perjury in order to shield Popeye from justice; although it has sensational elements, such grotesque ironies as this give it a deeper—and darker—message. Its vision of violence, despair, and injustice is consistent with other stories set in Yoknapatawpha County. Faulkner set the tone for the reception of *Sanctuary* in a 1932 preface he wrote for the Modern Library edition. He deprecated the book, saying that his publisher had first refused to print it because he thought they would both end up in jail. He said he revised the book in order to bring it into line with (and up to the level of) his "serious" works. The *unrevised* version of the novel was published in 1981 as *Sanctuary: The Original Text.*

Temple Drake returned in the novelistic play *Requiem for a Nun* (1951), which takes place eight years after the action of *Sanctuary.* In a three-act combination of prose prologues and courtroom scenes, it tells how Temple is blackmailed by Popeye's brother Pete, with whom she plans to run away. Temple's only confidant is her black servant, Nancy MANINNGOE, who is charged with killing one of Temple's children. Temple's behavior is once again scandalously selfish, whereas Nancy behaves with dignity.

SANDOE, JAMES (1912–1980) During much of the postwar period, U.S. mystery critic and reviewer Sandoe was a pillar of mystery criticism, along with his friend Anthony BOUCHER. Sandoe was also a friend or correspondent of many mystery authors, from Raymond CHANDLER to Amanda CROSS. He was a personal friend of Lillian DE LA TORRE and others. Sandoe also seems to have been one of the most beloved figures in the mystery world; in a 1980 *Armchair Detective* article, Tom and Enid Schantz described him as "a friendly, inquisitive, and highly intelligent elf."

Born in Alameda, California, Sandoe received a Bachelor's degree from Stanford University (1934) and a Master's from Columbia University (1935). Afterward, he taught English at the University of Colorado, becoming a college librarian for a time when he was forced out of the English department for lack of a doctorate. He was the mystery and detective book reviewer for the *New York Herald Tribune,* among other journals. His "Reader's Guide to Crime" was included in Howard HAYCRAFT's anthology *The Art of the Mystery Story.* Sandoe also published *The Hard-Boiled Dick* (1952), a study of the HARD-BOILED genre, and edited *Murder Plain and Fanciful* (1948), an anthology by type of various mystery stories as well as true crime, which BARZUN and TAYLOR called "virtually perfect." Sandoe won two EDGAR awards for his criticism, in 1949 and 1956.

In addition to being a mystery critic, Sandoe directed theater, primarily Shakespearean drama, for many years. With impressive energy, he pursued several interests and careers at the same time; somehow, he still managed to review as many as six mysteries a week. Among the younger writers whom he encouraged was Joe GORES. Sandoe was particularly interested in the hard-boiled novel, but not to exclusion; he admired Cyril HARE, Christianna BRAND, and other English mystery writers. Sandoe also defended the hard-boiled short story—the finest examples of which he thought were Dashiell HAMMETT's writings and the early Chandler—by sharply criticizing some of its practitioners. He took Ross MACDONALD to task for his overuse of similes (learned from Chandler), and famously dismissed Mickey Spillane's first Mike HAMMER novel, *I, the Jury* (1947), in one sentence: "Boom-lay, boom-lay, boom-lay-boom." A devotee not of one writer or subgenre but rather of the well-written story wherever found, Sandoe's attitude toward the genre was similar to that of Julian SYMONS, whom he admired.

No collection of Sandoe's criticism has been published to date. Only his introduction to the recently reprinted collection of Dorothy L. SAYERS's stories, *Lord Peter* (1972), and perhaps his introduction to *Three By Tey* (1955), a collection of Josephine TEY novels, are readily available. He also contributed an essay to *The Mystery Story* (1976), edited by John BALL. Two of his important works were included by Howard Haycraft in *The Art of the Mystery Story* (1946); one was his famous "checklist" of the landmarks in the genre, and the other an essay on the psychological thriller entitled "The Dagger of the Mind," originally delivered as a lecture in a series sponsored by *Poetry* magazine.

SANDS OF WINDEE, THE See LIFE IMITATES ART.

SAPPER (pen name of H[erman] C[yril] McNeile, 1888–1937) The man who created Bulldog DRUMMOND chose as a pseudonym a name that recalled his own career as a professional soldier. McNeile was born into a military family (his father was a captain in the British Navy) and attended the Royal Military Academy. He served twelve years in the Royal Engineers (sappers), and rose to the rank of lieutenant colonel. Colonel was also the rank that he gave to Drummond, who is the exemplar of the English aristocratic military class. He displays the classic knightly virtues of loyalty, honesty, and bravery; he also shows all the faults of the colonialist era. What has made Sapper's spy stories age so badly, more so than those of BUCHAN and OPPENHEIM, is their open racism and xenophobia, in addition to sexism, upper-class snobbery, and the jingoism of empire that were a matter of course among most Englishmen of McNeile's class and profession.

In terms of the writing, McNeile wrote in generic Edwardian, the dialogue very haw-haw and the narration strong on derring-do and "once more into the breach" theatrics. On another level, McNeile knew how to inject excitement into an adventure story, though he did it less well than STEVENSON or Rider HAGGARD, and absolutely lacked the subtlety and sensitivity of CONRAD. The best comment on Sapper's style was perhaps given by George DuMaurier, Daphne DUMAURIER's grandfather: when Sapper showed him his first draft, DuMaurier read it through and singled out one line for praise—where the butler says, "Dinner is served."

McNeile called Sapper an example of "the Breed," a suitably eugenic term. They were the patriotic, public school Englishmen, loyal to certain values and contemptuous of those—intellectuals—who might ask what the values actually meant. The stories no longer work, if they ever did, for the reason that such a person can no longer be seen as a hero—"mine is not to reason why . . ." having been forever smashed as a basis for behavior by two world wars and numerous smaller ones. Drummond now seems not a "man of action," but simply irrational.

SARA, MADAME The best-known character created by L. T. MEADE. *The Sorceress of the Strand* (1903) chronicle's Sara's evil machinations and narrow escapes from justice. She operates a business as a "beautifier" in the Strand, where she is courted by high society. In addition to her depilatory and cosmetic operations—some employing secret potions learned from South American Indians—she also practices dentistry. In one case, she uses a poisoned filling containing HYOSCINE to do away with a victim.

Sara is described as having the appearance of a twenty-five-year-old because of her secrets of physical preservation, but she is probably double that age. She is small and fair-skinned (though she is half Indian and half Italian), with blue eyes and golden hair. But while she looks like a typical heroine of the day, she is in fact as ruthless and cold as MORIARTY, a subversion of type that probably accounts for her popularity. Madame Sara has an innocent and childlike manner that she is able to turn off and on at will, thereby charming everyone, from victims to judges.

SATTERTHWAITE, MR. See QUIN, MR. HARLEY

SAVAGE, DOC See DENT, LESTER.

SAYERS, DOROTHY L[EIGH] (1893–1957) Of all the masters of the GOLDEN AGE, the English writer Dorothy L. Sayers is the one who still most inspires critical debate. Some of her works have been dismissed as unreadable, and championed as subtle and complex. Her beloved creation, the aristocratic sleuth Lord Peter WIMSEY, is one of the most famous characters in detective fiction.

Sayers was born in Oxford, the daughter of the Reverend Henry Sayers, of Tipperary stock, and his wife Helen, whose side of the family (the Leighs) Dorothy preferred. Lord Peter certainly has more of the Leigh in him, who traced their ancestry back to the time of Henry the Third. At four, she moved with her family to Bluntisham, on the borders of the Fens (which would feature in the flood scenes of *The Nine Tailors* [1934]). There she lived in comparative isolation, immersing herself in books. Dorothy was intellectually encouraged by her parents from the start, and was even somewhat spoiled. She became one of the first women to receive a degree from Oxford itself, rather than from its women's college. She showed brilliance as a scholar (she had learned Latin at age seven) and earned first honors in medieval studies, eventually taking her M.A. in 1920. Her first job was as secretary to a shell-shocked veteran who was teaching in an English-style school in France, and with whom she was in love. Returning to London, in 1922 Sayers began working in an advertising agency, which would form the background for *Murder Must Advertise* (1933), one of her lesser productions. Two unpublished works deal with the early period of Sayers's life: *My Edwardian Childhood* and the unfinished autobiographical novel, *Cat o' Mary.* Both were used in the preparation of James Brabazon's biography of Sayers (see below).

The idea that Sayers went through a "wild period" (according to William DEANDREA) is far from the truth; her affair with John Cournos, and then the bearing of an illegitimate child to a man whose name has still not been divulged, were fraught with religious scruples and deep personal questions. Incredibly, she kept the birth of her son secret from her employers and her parents—forever. At the time of her death, very few people knew that she even had a son. In addition to the erudition and wit that grace her stories, Sayers had a less proper side: Wimsey's sexuality is handled with surprising openness, particularly in *Busman's Honeymoon* (1937), the last of her published mystery novels featuring Wimsey.

Sayers gave up mystery writing in the early 1940s and devoted herself to religious works—referred to by critics variously as "apologetics" or "propaganda"—including the essays in *Creed or Chaos* (1947). This aspect of Sayers's work is reminiscent of CHESTERTON, though she wrote from an Anglican rather than Catholic perspective. Sayers also worked on a translation of Dante's *Divina Commedia* (1949 and 1955), which was completed by Barbara Reynolds after Sayers's death. She wrote plays as well, including *The Man Born to be King* (1942), about the life of Christ. Sayers's abandonment of the mystery genre may be due to the fact that she said it could never reach the level of first-rate literature.

The first novel to feature Wimsey was *Whose Body?* (1923), in which the detective's mother ("the Dowager") asks him to investigate when her friend, the architect Mr. Thripp, discovers a corpse in his bathtub wearing gold pince-nez. The writing is rather dated and Wimsey's superciliousness a bit much. Sayers's second Wimsey adventure, CLOUDS OF WITNESS (1926), is more of a success. Now it is Lord Peter's brother Gerald who is in trouble; he has been having an affair and is on trial for murder. The writing of the book coincided with Sayers's affair and pregnancy. In *Murder Must Advertise,* the murders are many and various. The novel is set at Pym's Publicity, where Lord Peter must go undercover to investigate the death of a copywriter who died from a fall down a staircase. Particularly in the first half, the chatter of the many fatuous minor characters is hard to bear. *The Nine Tailors* (1934) is famous for its detailed and accurate rendering of the art of bell ringing, which is vital to the plot. Edmund WILSON attacked the book for what he thought was a ridiculously implausible murder method. H. R. F. KEATING put it on his "100 best" list, valuing its portrait of the fen country of the author's youth and its attention to serious matters such as religious faith.

Although she seems to have given her heart to Wimsey, Sayers also wrote a series of stories about the commercial traveler Montague EGG. Perhaps this was an acknowledgement of the Sayers rather than the Leigh side of her character—which would be borne out by the fact that she seems less comfortable with the lower-class setting of Egg, and that the stories fall into caricature. More likely, the stories reflect her experience with her son's father, who was not an intellectual but a mechanic, and with her husband, who was a Scottish war veteran and automotive journalist and probably not at all the kind of person her parents would have liked to see her marry. The Egg stories are interesting by their very contrast with Wimsey's cool and collected style. In fact, the stock view of Wimsey as Sayers's ideal bears re-examination, in which Egg should play an important role.

Sayers's most admired book is probably STRONG POISON (1930); her most controversial, THE FIVE RED HERRINGS (1931) and HAVE HIS CARCASE (1932); her worst, *The Unpleasantness at the Bellona Club* (1928). One of her most interesting books, *The Documents in the Case* (1930; repub 1949), co-written with Robert Eustace, is an epistolary novel dealing with a subtle case of poisoning and containing much technical information. The short stories in which Lord Peter made appearances—including his last, in "Talboys" (written 1942; pub 1972)—have been collected in *Lord Peter* (1972; repr 1987), with an introduction by James SANDOE.

Sayers also edited the wide-ranging anthology *The Omnibus of Crime* (1929). In a lengthy introduction, she laid out the history and principles of the detective, mystery, and mystery/horror stories. Some of the principles, such as the eschewing of romantic subplots, she later broke herself. Most surprisingly for a writer who would be criticized for her excessive intellectualism, she said that the mystery could never reach "the loftiest level of literary achievement." The mystery story in her description is a watch-like mechanism, in which any violent emotion "jars the movement" and disturbs the works. (One might ask what emotion could be more violent than the desire to murder; indeed, Raymond CHANDLER later questioned Sayers's theory on several points.)

Sayers wished that no biography of her be written until fifty years after her death, but such is the controversy surrounding her that her son and her literary executor authorized a biography of her to set the record straight. James Brabazon was given access to her private papers for his *Dorothy L. Sayers* (1981). *The Letters of Dorothy L. Sayers: 1899–1936* appeared in 1995. Sayers worked on but did not finish a further novel about Wimsey at the same time as she was co-writing a play based on *Busman's*

Honeymoon. The book was later finished by Jill Paton Walsh (see FINISHERS).

SCAM No convincing etymology has been offered for this word, which means swindle, fraud, or con game. It may have originated in the carnival.

SCANDAL AT HIGH CHIMNEYS (1959) A mystery by John Dickson CARR, set in the Victorian era. High Chimneys, in Reading, is the imposing home of Matthew Damon, a rich and respected barrister who is nonetheless pursued by rumors. (It seems, as a prosecutor, he enjoyed visiting female prisoners in their cells while they awaited execution.) Matthew's son Victor tries to convince Clive Strickland, a former barrister himself and now a mystery author, to arrange a marriage between Celia Damon and Lord Albert Tressider. When he gets to High Chimneys, Clive falls in love with the seductive sister of Celia, Kate. Meanwhile an intruder, thought by some to be a ghost, has been seen in the house the night before. Matthew Damon then tells Clive something of his secret past. At that point, Matthew is killed, and Clive is quite ingeniously made to look like the murderer.

"SCANDAL IN BOHEMIA, A" (1891) The first case in *The Adventures of Sherlock Holmes* and the one in which he encounters Irene Adler. The King of Bohemia is about to marry the daughter of the King of Scandinavia, and is anxious to get back a compromising photograph from the period of his dalliance with Adler. She enters into a battle of wits with Holmes, from which he emerges with a profound respect for her; she is "*the* woman." The King is impressed, too; when he regrets that he could not marry her because she was not of his level, Holmes archly replies that "she seems indeed to be on a very different level from your majesty."

SCARLET PIMPERNEL, THE See ORCZY, BARONESS.

SCARPETTA, DOCTOR KAY A sleuth in a series of mysteries by Patricia CORNWELL. Scarpetta is the chief medical examiner (M.E.) employed by the police department in Richmond, Virginia; she is also employed by the FBI. She is the foremost character in the forensic procedural sub-subgenre. The first book in the series was *Postmortem* (1990), whose instant success and shelf-full of awards established the author as a major crime novelist.

Scarpetta is an aging yuppie with ash-blonde hair, a doctor with a law degree and totally devoted to her work. Fortunately for her, the Richmond area seems to be a playground for serial killers. In *All that Remains* (1992), a psycho killer who likes to use a knife has murdered five couples. The remains are found deep in the woods by hunters. The detectives are Richmond homicide detective Pete Marino and FBI agent Benton Wesley, but of course Scarpetta is the one who pulls all the threads together after the daughter of the nation's "drug czar" and her husband are brutally slaughtered.

Cruel and Unusual (1993) won the Gold Dagger of the British CRIME WRITERS' ASSOCIATION. If possible, it is more grisly and gruesome than *All that Remains*—the whirring of saws, removal of organs, and other details are minutely described and almost outweigh the twists and turns of the plot. Scarpetta is completely unmoved by all of this, not even showing the morgue humor or any other sign of covert sympathy of other fictional M.E.'s. She is, however, devastated by the blowing up of an estranged lover, an F.B.I. agent. At the beginning of *Cruel and Unusual*, she is waiting at the morgue to receive the freshly killed body of Ronnie Joe Waddell, convicted of the gruesome murder of television newswoman Robin Naismith. But even after Waddell has been electrocuted by the state, a thirteen-year-old boy turns up dead, murdered in a similar fashion to Naismith. Then Waddell's prints start appearing, and a scandal erupts, linked to the highest levels in the state, that threatens to destroy Scarpetta's career.

The Scarpetta series continues to offer gore galore for fans of the CLOACA-AND-DAGGER school of mystery writing, and to re-run the same scenarios over and over. In *The Body Farm* (1994), a fresh killing reminds her of a murderer from the past. In *From Potter's Field* (1995), a fresh killing reminds her of a murderer from the past. The latter book is set in New York City.

BIBLIOGRAPHY Novels: *Body of Evidence* (1991), *Cause of Death* (1996), *Unnatural Exposure* (1997), *Point of Origin* (1998), *Black Notice* (1999).

SCASE, NORMAN A fifty-seven-year-old clerk in P. D. James's INNOCENT BLOOD (1980), Norman Scase quits his job in order to hunt down his daughter's killer. After eleven years waiting for the murderer to be paroled, Scase no longer even has a desire for revenge. Knowing himself to be a "non-entity," he has no hope for redemption or even cares. James paraphrases more than once T. S. Eliot's line that the human mind "cannot bear very much reality"; Scase is like J. Alfred Prufrock turned dutiful killer.

SCHMIDT, INSPECTOR A detective in a series by Aaron Mark STEIN, published under the pseudonym George Bagby. Schmidt has about as much personality as Merton HEIMRICH, perhaps less; a lot is made of his sore feet, his most notable feature. There is little physical description in the books, and the grim-faced Schmidt's technique relies mainly on interrogation of witnesses and suspects. Bagby is himself a character in the series, playing WATSON to the New York City police detective. This Bagby is a writer who has somehow convinced Schmidt to allow him to follow along during criminal investigations and write them up. The series began with *Murder at the Piano* (1935), the author's first mystery, and ended in 1984 with *The Most Wanted,* making it one of the longest-running series of all time.

As in Stein's other work, character receives little attention and plot is paramount. He tried to introduce novel themes and also made use of old ones. Ironically, while *The Murder That Wouldn't Stay Solved* (1951), a Gibby GIBSON novel, has been praised for its treatment of homosexuality, *The Corpse with Sticky Fingers,* a Schmidt novel written only the following year, mocks the character of a homosexual window designer in a manner both insufferable and jejune. The plot itself, which begins with the discovery of a corpse in a display window of a prestigious New York City department store, recalls the second Ellery QUEEN novel, *The French Powder Mystery* (1930). *Dead Drunk* (1953) has a more interesting premise. The alcoholic cop Al Malone has been dismissed from the force, but Inspector Schmidt keeps seeing him in strange places. He appears at a baseball game with a well-known gambler, then outside the Waldorf with a beautiful and apparently wealthy companion. Finally, he appears in the alley behind Schmidt's apartment with a bullet in his head, forcing the Inspector to investigate the drunken cop's decline and fall.

Like most mystery series, the Schmidt saga went on too long and whatever dramatic tension was originally there had dissipated. In *Innocent Bystander* (1976), "Schmitty" and "Baggy," who have become quite chummy over the years, investigate a series of suspicious muggings that may be premeditated murders.

BIBLIOGRAPHY Novels: *Ring Around a Murder* (1936), *Murder Half Baked* (1937), *Murder on the Nose* (1938), *Bird Walking Weather* (1939), *The Corpse with the Purple Thighs* (1939), *The Corpse Wore a Wig* (1940), *Here Comes the Corpse* (1941), *Red Is for Killing* (1941), *Murder Calling "50"* (1942), *Dead on Arrival* (1946), *The Original Carcase* (1946), *The Twin Killing* (1947), *The Starting Gun* (1948), *In Cold Blood* (1948), *Drop Dead* (1949), *Coffin Corner* (1949), *Blood Will Tell* (1950), *Death Ain't Commercial* (1951), *Scared to Death* (1952), *Give the Little Corpse a Great Big Hand* (1953), *A Dirty Way to Die* (1955), *Dead Storage* (1956), *Cop Killer* (1956), *Dead Wrong* (1957), *The Three-Time Losers* (1958), *The Real Gone Goose* (1959), *Evil Genius* (1961), *Murder's Little Helper* (1963), *Mysteriouser and Mysteriouser* (1965), *Dirty Pool* (1966), *Another Day, Another Death* (1968), *Honest Reliable Corpse* (1969), *Killer Boy Was Here* (1970), *Two in the Bush* (1976), *My Dead Body* (1976), *The Tough Get Going* (1977), *Guaranteed to Fade* (1978), *I Could Have Died* (1979), *Mugger's Day* (1979), *Country and Fatal* (1980), *A Question of Quarry* (1981), *The Sitting Duck* (1981), *The Golden Creep* (1982).

SCHOFIELD, PETE A private detective invented by Thomas B. DEWEY. Schofield offers a counterpoint to Dewey's MAC: instead of the mean streets of Chicago, Schofield walks the sunny streets of Los Angeles—not Raymond CHANDLER's Los Angeles, however. Schofield prefigures the swinging p.i. of the sixties, and in books like *Too Hot for Hawaii* (1960) and *Mexican Slayride* (1961), goes afield in life- and virtue-threatening adventures among blondes and bad guys. Schofield does, however, have a wife, a beautiful woman not surprisingly named Jeannie. Dewey wrote ten books about Schofield, but they have worn less well with time than his more HARD-BOILED work. The first novel in the series was *I.O.U. Murder* (1957), in which a millionaire diamond dealer and patron of young actresses is killed. Among the suspects are his wife, who is twenty years younger, and his son, a jaded playboy.

BIBLIOGRAPHY Novels: *Go to Sleep, Jeannie* (1959), *Go, Honeylou* 1962), *The Girl with the Sweet Plump Knees* (1963), *The Girl in the Punchbowl* (1964), *Only on Tuesdays* (1964), *Nude in Nevada* (1965).

SCIASCIA, LEONARDO (1921–1989) Born in Racalmuto, Sicily, the Italian novelist Leonardo Sciascia is best known to the English-speaking world as a writer of mystery stories that address serious social and political issues. Sciascia's work is deeply preoccupied with his native Sicily and the corrupting role of the Mafia in every aspect of life. But Sciascia's Mafia is not the romanticized, comic-book version of American novels and films; rather, it is the *real* and quite mundane (in the original sense of that word) Mafia, an organization embedded in Sicilian history and culture. A committed but independent writer with communist allegiances, Sciascia criticized both the Right and the Left. He also served on the Palermo city council and as a representative in the European Parliament.

Many of Sciascia's works have been translated and exist in numerous editions. Two novellas, *Il giorno della civetta* (1961) and *Il contesto* (1971), appeared together as *The Day of the Owl/Equal Danger* (1984) with a brief essay by the literary critic Frank Kermode. Sciascia's books brilliantly evoke the light and landscape of Sicily, and the oppressive pall of *omertà,* the rule of silence imposed by intimidation and fear. In *The Day of the Owl,*

Captain Bellodi investigates a Mafia killing, hampered not only by *omertà* but by the fact that he is from northern Italy, which causes the Sicilians (including his own subordinates) to view him as a "foreigner." Sciascia was also a playwright, and the interrogations are both lifelike and fascinating; Bellodi must pick his way through the unfamiliar Sicilian dialect and the prudent custom of nicknames to get at the truth. Meanwhile, the mafiosi try to stay ahead of Bellodi by manipulating the government to thwart his investigation. Corruption is so total that the cynical Don Mariano says to Bellodi at one point, "not even God will lead you to me."

Sciascia has been praised for expanding the bounds of the detective story. *Equal Danger* is a perfect example; Sciascia called it "a fable about power anywhere in the world." The story takes place in an unnamed country in which one Inspector Rogas investigates a series of murders of judges. As he begins to develop a theory with implications that do not please his superiors, the hunter becomes the hunted, as agents follow Rogas while he conducts his investigation. The supporting personalities include cynical communists who don't really want a revolution, ineffectual and pompous intellectuals, and an utterly cynical—or insane—judge who believes in his own infallibility. The figure of the detective (in the largest sense) who pursues the truth fatalistically, knowing that no one wants him to find it and that the search may in the end lead to his own destruction, is a recurrent figure in Sciascia's work (see, for example, OPEN DOORS, 1987).

Toward the end of his life Sciascia suddenly returned to the detective story after a lapse of a decade. One of these late works, *Una storia semplice,* (1989; tr *A Straightforward Tale,* 1991), is an almost classic detective puzzle with a strong humorous element. Set in Sicily, it concerns a man who is found shot to death in the long-shuttered house of a retired diplomat (shades of the LOCKED ROOM mystery). On the desk in front of him is the unfinished message "I have seen." Two detectives, one a brigadier and the other an inspector of police, develop divergent theories about the supposed "suicide." The brigadier is so irritated about the direction of the investigation that he gives his information to the rival law enforcement agency, the *Carabinieri* (technically part of the army). The story is well-clued and perfectly plotted; it also brings out the jealousies between and within the two agencies with a good deal of humor. This novella was published in English with three other pieces under the title *Open Doors and Three Novellas* (1992). Among the other pieces are *1912 + 1* (1986), an original type of true crime writing in which Sciascià examines an actual murder trial that took place during the hectic year of 1913. Futurism, incipient fascism, and conservative Roman Catholicism all play a part in the background of the story of a contessa who shot one of her husband's subalterns, a notorious womanizer. Sciascia compares the case to HUXLEY's famous story "The Gioconda Smile."

SCIENCE FICTION MYSTERIES Many writers best known for their science fiction have written mysteries, and many writers have combined science fiction with mystery and detection. The most famous of all science fiction writers, Isaac ASIMOV, wrote several mystery stories, as well as an article entitled "How Good a Scientist Was Sherlock Holmes?", published in 1980. William GIBSON co-authored the novel THE DIFFERENCE ENGINE (1991), which is both scientific and historical. Manley Wade WELLMAN, an author less known now but important in his time, wrote science fiction, mystery, and OCCULT works; one factored Sherlock HOLMES into Orson WELLES's "War of the Worlds" scenario. Ray BRADBURY, an author of the same eminence as Asimov, produced two "straight" mysteries toward the end of his career, but the plot of *The Martian Chronicles* (1950) was an early example of the "lost expedition" subgenre—what happened to group X on planet Y and why. Stanislaw Lem, another science fiction master, also used this plot, for example in *The Invincible* (1967). A spaceship travels to a planet where a previous expedition has disappeared after sending a final, meaningless message. The investigators find everything on the expedition's ship to be in order, except that the crew seems to have gone insane.

Frederic BROWN is one of those mystery authors who also doubled as a science fiction writer. Henry KUTTNER and Ron GOULART are others. William Hope HODGSON, whose CARNACKI stories are sometimes considered a relatively minor contribution to the mystery genre, was an extremely important progenitor of science fiction, and was of the same generation as H. G. WELLS, another writer who did work in both fields but made his greatest contribution through fantastic and apocalyptic speculations that sprang from science or pseudo-science. Within our own era, Philip K. DICK wrote the novel *A Scanner Darkly* (1977), which combines science fiction with detection in a seamless, hallucinatory, and totally captivating manner. Philip KERR's *A Philosophical Investigation* (1992) is a dystopian novel set in London in the twenty-first century.

Two works set at science fiction gatherings are Anthony Boucher's ROCKET TO THE MORGUE (1942) and the EDGAR-winning *Bimbos of the Death Sun* (1988), by Sharyn MCCRUMB.

"SCORCHED FACE, THE" (1925) A long story about the CONTINENTAL OP, with similarities to the Dashiell

HAMMETT novel *The Dain Curse* (1929). It begins as a missing persons case; the Op is hired to find two sisters, Myra and Ruth Banbrock. They were supposed to have gone on a visit to Monterey but never arrived. After well-conducted investigations by a lot of operatives, one of the girls is eventually found shot in the head. Then the case reaches a dead end, until the Op makes an intuitive leap that links the death to a string of other disappearances. Pat Reddy, a policeman married to a wealthy heiress, makes an interesting partner for the Op. The twist in the last line is worth waiting for.

SCOTLAND YARD Scotland Yard was originally a palace where Scottish royalty stayed when they were in London. Its site was occupied by the London commissioner of police; there, in 1842, the first Detective Branch was created. The first chief of the branch was Nicholas Pearce, a former BOW STREET RUNNER; under him he had two inspectors and six sergeants to cover all of London. The Criminal Investigations Department was established in 1876. The Metropolitan Police and the CID were later housed in new quarters, which were called New Scotland Yard.

Scotland Yard is not the equivalent of the United States's Federal Bureau of Investigation, because Scotland Yard is not a national entity but a local one. In order to investigate crimes outside of the London metropolitan area, Scotland Yard has to be invited into the case.

SCOTT, SHELL Sheldon Scott, a Los Angeles private detective created by Richard S. PRATHER, emerged during the postwar boom in California p.i. fiction. Perhaps that is why Prather gave Scott such odd and distinctive features. A bourbon-drinking ex-Marine, Scott is bizarrely un-HARD-BOILED. With a white crew cut, part of one ear blown off at Okinawa, a broken nose, and a physique like Brock CALLAHAN's, Scott is unlike the fedora-wearing and trench-coated private dick of the forties. In fact, Scott is a predecessor of the "alternative lifestyle" characters of the early sixties; like Travis MCGEE, he has a signature car (a Cadillac), and his wardrobe is casual and decidedly loud. He says his clothing combines "most of the visible spectrum." He also is a ladies' man, and the books are overflowing with beautiful and available women.

Scott first appeared in *The Case of the Vanishing Beauty* (1951). A patriotic anti-communist, he battles all sorts of vice and corruption while maintaining his *bon vivant* approach to life; this means that the books are heavy on jokes and wisecracks, while saving the reader from morbid philosophical speculations. In the earlier books, Scott is more a righter of wrongs (or a vigilante) in the manner of Mike HAMMER. *Bodies in Bedlam* (1951) deals with pornography, *Everybody Had a Gun* (1951) with illegal gambling. In *Ride a High Horse* (1953), Scott takes on greedy real estate developers. *Strip for Murder* (1955) uses a nudist colony as background. In *Slab Happy* (1958), Scott gets into trouble after he imprudently attends the funeral of a mobster he himself had killed. Another book in which Scott tangles with mobsters is *The Meandering Corpse* (1965). Prather's comic schemes with dead bodies show the influence of Jonathan LATIMER. *Double in Trouble* (1959) features both Scott and Chester DRUM. Scott also appeared in short stories, which have been collected in several volumes (see bibliography).

BIBLIOGRAPHY Novels: *Find This Woman* (1951), *Way of a Wanton* (1952), *Pattern for Murder* (1952; repub as *Scrambled Yeggs*, 1958), *Darling, It's Death* (1952), *Always Leave 'Em Dying* (1954), *Pattern for Panic* (1954), *The Wailing Frail* (1956), *Three's A Shroud* (novellas, 1957), *Take a Murder, Darling* (1958), *Over Her Dead Body* (1959), *Dance with the Dead* (1960), *Dig That Crazy Grave* (1961), *Kill the Clown* (1962), *Dead Heat* (1963), *Joker in the Deck* (1964), *The Cockeyed Corpse* (1964), *The Trojan Hearse* (1964), *Kill Him Twice* (1965), *Dead Man's Walk* (1965), *The Kubla Khan Caper* (1966), *Gat Heat* (1967), *The Cheim Manuscript* (1969), *Kill Me Tomorrow* (1969), *Dead Bang* (1971), *The Sweet Ride* (1972), *The Sure Thing* (1975), *The Amber Effect* (1976), *Shellshock* (1987).

Short Stories: *Have Gat, Will Travel* (1957), *Shell Scott's Seven Slaughters* (1962), *The Shell Scott Sampler* (1969).

SCRAM To run away; from *scramble.*

SCREAMING MIMI, THE (1949) One of the most famous works of Frederic BROWN, though not one of the best. The novel begins as a drunken newspaper reporter coming off a binge (Bill Sweeney) encounters a bizarre scene in the hallway of a Chicago apartment building: a beautiful woman (Yolanda Lang) who has been wounded by stabbing is undressed by her huge and apparently well-trained dog while a crowd watches through the door. Brown overworks the mildly titillating aspect of the story, while the mystery of what "Screaming Mimi" means is withheld as a rather obvious carrot. Sweeney's connection of the Screaming Mimi and the crimes of a Chicago "Ripper" is completely conjectural, a weak second leg for the plot to stand on (the other being his obsession with Yolanda Lang and desire to see her naked again, but not behind glass). The forties sensationalism no longer holds one's attention (nor the sneering "comedy" of a homosexual character), and the book lacks the true quirkiness of Cornell WOOLRICH, of whose work it seems derivative.

SCUDDER, FRANKLIN The American agent who Richard HANNAY meets and whose death sets off the chain of events in THE THIRTY-NINE STEPS (1915).

SCUDDER, MATTHEW A private detective character who appears in a series of novels by Lawrence BLOCK and who is one of the most well-known p.i.'s of contemporary fiction. The story of Scudder's life is dominated by his alcoholism, guilt, and redemption. In a sense, he atones for the things the dicks of the HARD-BOILED era didn't know they were supposed to feel bad about. On the one hand, he is the self-help detective, a dedicated AA member and proselytizer; on the other, he is a refreshingly real character who does not have it all "together," lives in a residential hotel, and has no flashy car or nifty gadgets; he does not even carry a gun. Scudder does not seem to read much, is not a gourmet chef, and does not claim to have discovered the meaning of life. Hence his broad appeal in a field increasingly dominated by self-actualized detectives convinced of their own wisdom and importance.

A former New York City policeman, Scudder was already a drinker before he quit the force. The primal scene (or original sin) of the series is years in the past: one night, Scudder is in a bar when a robbery occurs, and he shoots one of the escaping felons. Unfortunately, he also kills a young Hispanic girl with a stray bullet. This incident—for which, ironically, he receives a citation—proves to be the last straw for Scudder's career, his marriage, and almost his life. He nearly goes over the edge in EIGHT MILLION WAYS TO DIE (1983), in which he realizes that drinking is one of the eight million ways. Block's knowledge of New York is intimate, and the bars Scudder visits are often real places. During most of the series, Block's depiction of the city is extremely accurate, overdoing neither its romanticism or its grittiness. Later on it becomes imbued with fantasy, as when Scudder encounters a black pimp living in luxury in Greenpoint, or when the clichés of the late eighties become a substitute for novel situations. Block's New York encompasses five boroughs, however, not just Manhattan; as an author, he really owns the city in a way that is unique.

Early in the series, Scudder is still drinking. He is also tithing: though not religious, he gives ten percent of what he makes to various churches. With his friend Mick BALLOU, he often goes very early to mass in the city's meat district. Scudder is not very ambitious and doesn't bother to do the things necessary to get a private detective's license. He simply does "favors." His detective credo is "Knock on People's Doors." Block never romanticizes the boredom of detective procedure, but neither does he make the reader suffer through too much of it.

A Stab in the Dark (1981) is about an ICE PICK murder. *Out on the Cutting Edge* (1989) begins with a missing girl, and leads to a conflict between Ballou and Scudder before it reaches a bloody conclusion. A DANCE AT THE SLAUGHTERHOUSE (1991) won an EDGAR award, and is one of the most action-oriented Scudder novels. In *When the Sacred Ginmill Closes* (1986), Block described Scudder's life soon after leaving the police force. The story is set in 1975, and has Scudder involved in no less than three cases. One concerns a holdup of an after-hours club (which funnels money to the IRA) at which he is present; the second is about the murder of the wife of one of his barroom acquaintances, who hires Scudder to clear him; and the third concerns the theft of the "real books" of a bar-owning friend, which have to be ransomed if the barman's cooking of fake books for the government is not to be discovered.

Scudder's girlfriend, Elaine, is an expensive call-girl to whom he is usually faithful. (They marry, concurrently with her retirement.) In the more recent books, Scudder has put aside his crown of thorns, which will no doubt increase the appeal of a series whose realism made it appear a bit of a "downer," though Scudder seems somewhat lost without it. The books written in the eighties remain the best in the series, after the initial working out of the Scudderian personality and before his rococo period. In *Everybody Dies* (1998), Scudder finally gets his private detective's license; his first client as a legitimate p.i. is Mick Ballou.

BIBLIOGRAPHY *The Sins of the Fathers* (1976), *In the Midst of Death* (1976), *Time to Murder and Create* (1977), *A Ticket to the Boneyard* (1990), *A Walk Among the Tombstones* (1992), *A Long Line of Dead Men* (1994), *Even the Wicked* (1997).

SECOND MAN, THE (1956) This novel by Edward GRIERSON belongs among the very best legal mysteries ever written. It takes place in a provincial city in the north of England in the barrister's chambers of the old and imposing patriarch of the law, Mr. Hesketh. The narrator, Irvine, is a junior member, and an engaging personality and a modest man. When Marion Kerrison joins the firm—the first woman ever to do so—he recognizes her superior ability more readily and gracefully than some of the other men. The scenes of her early triumphs in court are convincing without ever really going into much legal detail; that is saved for the second part of the book.

Kerrison is at first a novelty, hardly taken seriously in the old boy society of the law courts (depicted by the author, who knew it well, with a mixture of affection and humor). Kerrison's personalities in and out of court are remarkably different, however, and she soon earns a reputation as a "firebreather." Her big prize is the defense in "The Maudsley Case," a murder of an elderly woman that is based in part on the case of Oscar SLATER. The detection, legal maneuvering, and trial scenes are handled skillfully without ever letting suspense lag; the narrator's mild tone but suppressed excitement is the perfect foil for Kerrison's grim determination and intuitive sense not of the right argument, but of the truth. She is convinced that John Maudsley, a rough, slightly shady, but courageous man lately come from Australia, did not kill his wealthy aunt. Irvine, on the other hand, is never able to trust the defendant's story, which adds yet another tension to his relationship with Kerrison. In a stunning courtroom scene, Kerrison promotes the theory of a "second man" (the killer), whom the chief witness, Jane Birman, deliberately misidentified as Maudsley. Doubt, distrust, and desperation continue to afflict the defense team's effort to get Maudsley off; rarely has the relationship between counsel and client been so subtly and tensely explored.

"SECRET GARDEN, THE" (1911) A Father BROWN story by G. K. CHESTERTON, one of the most frequently anthologized. Its popularity may be due to the lurid atmosphere and the seeming impossibility of the puzzle, although to modern tastes the motive is unconvincing. The story takes place at the sombre mansion of Aristide Valentin, the chief of the Parisian police, where he lives with his Russian servant, Ivan. The house is gaudily decorated with weapons, one of which is used to decapitate the victim. Father Brown is present, as is Julius K. Brayne, a multi-millionaire American philanthropist, and an assortment of other COUNTRY HOUSE types. RED HERRINGS are used to disguise the real nature of the crime, which is in any case unlikely to be guessed by a reader with a realistic frame of mind. The walled, impenetrable garden is a kind of LOCKED ROOM, and the killer exercises some ingenuity in getting around it, even if his purpose in doing so seems weak.

SECRET OF HIGH ELDERSHAM, THE (1930; repr 1976) BARZUN and TAYLOR defended their selection of *The Secret of High Eldersham* for their "50 classics of crime fiction" reprint series on aesthetic grounds, but the appeal of the book seems to extend little beyond the fact that it was the first of John RHODE's novels about Desmond MERRION, which Rhode published under the pseudonym Miles Burton. The book is also credited with using, for the first time, the topic of witchcraft as a device in a mystery story. The novel is set in High Eldersham, a remote English village of two or three hundred persons; the residents are suspicious, poor, and religious. Barzun and Taylor said that "murder and mysterious 'doings' in a remote East Anglian village must whet any reader's appetite"—exactly the claim of the "classic" mystery that later critics have disputed. The pure puzzle, without psychology, without the subtleties of character, appeals little to contemporary tastes. The attempts at humor are faint, and even some of the procedure is dubious (Constable Viney actually tests to see if one could stab oneself in the back). The setting is, however, of potential interest: the chronically unprosperous Rose and Crown pub has been taken over by Samuel Whitehead, a retired police sergeant from London, five years before the book begins. Miraculously, given the personality of the town, he has made a success of the place. Then he is found murdered in front of the fire in the pub with the door locked. Constable Viney, the first on the scene, is a very silly article, and Merrion's entry into the case is anti-climactic. Other Rhode/Burton mysteries better deserve to be resuscitated, for example THE PLATINUM CAT (1938).

SEDDON, FREDERICK Frederick Seddon was one of the most famous murderers of twentieth-century England. He was also a thoroughly unpleasant fellow; Edgar WALLACE described Frederick Seddon as "a mean, hectoring man, bombastic of speech, loud of voice." A greedy insurance agent who loved money, Seddon persuaded the middle-aged spinster Eliza Barrow to take lodgings in his home. Later, Seddon convinced her to take out an annuity and to sell her property and entrust the proceeds to him. Shortly thereafter, Barrow became ill and died. Seddon had had her make him her sole executor, and in that role he had her buried in a common grave. It was this act—and thus, his consistent miserliness—that drew the suspicion of Barrow's cousins. An exhumation was ordered, and the spinster's body was found to contain arsenic (one of those who examined the body was Sir Bernard Spilsbury, one of the most famous forensic pathologists of the century). It was never shown how Seddon had come by the arsenic, but his clandestine financial dealings with the victim were enough to hang him on April 18, 1912. At his sentencing, Seddon made a bizarre speech in which he signaled to the judge that he was a fellow Freemason, but he received no clemency. Seddon's wife was also put on trial, but was acquitted.

SEELEY, MABEL [HODNEFIELD] (1903–) Mabel Seeley was one of those American women writers who has been doomed to obscurity for her HAD-I-BUT-KNOWN (HIBK) practices. The blanket dismissal of her by some critics ignores the fact that she was an early practitioner of the regional mystery and that her stories were set among working-class people who were depicted with some amount of realism. Her first novel, *The Listening House* (1938), was based on her own experiences as a copywriter and was well received by critics.

Seeley was born in Minnesota and lived most of her life there, with the exception of a period in Chicago. She attended the University of Minnesota and after her graduation in 1926 worked as an advertising copywriter for department stores. *The Listening House* had a HIBK heroine, a young woman working in the same type of job as Seeley's, but in a fictitious Midwestern city. The action centers on the roominghouse of Mrs. Garr and the strange events there, in which dark secrets of the past cause violence in the present. James SANDOE thought that this book redeemed the HIBK formula. *The Chuckling Fingers* (1941) takes place in the Minnesota woods, and *Eleven Came Back* (1943) in Wyoming's Grand Tetons. After a promising start in the forties, Seeley's career waned. *The Beckoning Door* (1950) and *The Whistling Shadow* (1954) were later mysteries.

SELBY, DOUG Series character created by Erle Stanley GARDNER. Selby, like Perry MASON, is a lawyer, except that he is a district attorney—in some of the novels, at least. During World War II, Selby goes to work for military counterintelligence and rises to the rank of Major. His arch-enemy, the crooked lawyer A. B. Carr ("old A.B.C."), persists in calling him "Major Selby" in order to needle him. The wily Carr is constantly slipping through the hands of the law; at one point he cleverly marries the witness who could put him in jail.

The nine Doug Selby novels, beginning with *The D.A. Calls It Murder* (1937), all have the same small town setting of Madison County, California, an agricultural area. Selby is tall, wavy-haired, and young for his job. He is assisted by the canny old county sheriff, Rex Brandon, a former cattleman and expert tracker. On the other hand, Otto Larkin, the chief of police in Madison City (the county seat) is a blustering incompetent. Selby gets some help from Sylvia Martin, a reporter from *The Clarion* who idolizes him.

In the last Doug Selby novel, *The D.A. Breaks an Egg* (1949), it looks like Selby is finally going to hang a murder wrap on A. B. Carr. A woman who appears to be a Montanan named Daphne Arcola is found stabbed to death in a park shortly after checking into a hotel in Madison City. She turns out to be a friend of Mrs. Carr. Meanwhile, someone seems to be trying to frame Dorothy Clifton, whose fiancé is the son of a well-to-do family in town. The corpse is revealed to be a female private eye from Los Angeles, and when the misidentification is discovered, Selby's political enemies close in.

BIBLIOGRAPHY Novels: *The D.A. Holds a Candle* (1938), *The D.A. Draws a Circle* (1939), *The D.A. Goes on Trial* (1940), *The D.A. Cooks a Goose* (1942), *The D.A. Calls a Turn* (1944), *The D.A. Takes a Chance* (1948).

SERIAL NOVEL "Serial novel" here refers not to a novel printed in installments in a magazine but to a book produced serially by several different authors. The writers belonging to the DETECTION CLUB are best known for amusing themselves in this way; one example of their work is THE FLOATING ADMIRAL (1932). American mystery authors have also written serial novels. The hard-boiled serial *The Black Moon* (1989) was written by five American authors, including Loren ESTLEMAN and Ed GORMAN. The comic-book plot has five private eyes tracking down four paintings stolen in Italy after World War II and missing for decades. *Naked Came the Manatee* (1996), by a group of Floridian writers including Elmore Leonard and Carl Hiassen, was first serialized in the *Miami Herald Tropic* magazine. It begins with a riot in Coconut Grove, the loss of a mysterious package in the bay, and the rescue of a drowning man by a manatee named Booger.

SEVERSON, KNUTE A police detective created by Tobias Wells (Stanton FORBES). Handsome and blond, Severson also has a streak of bad temper and does not come across as particularly sympathetic. His wife is named Brenda; his son is Leif. Severson starts out as a Boston Police detective, but later he moves to Wellesley, Massachusetts. *Dead by the Light of the Moon* (1967) takes place during the famous blackout of 1965. In *Die Quickly, Dear Mother* (1969), Severson solves a case of digitalis poisoning.

Marital problems are a recurrent theme of the series, with Severson's grumpiness and his wife's snobbery—she is a little ashamed to be married to a policeman—creating tension. Their move to the suburbs is not an improvement. The world of women's clubs, "important" people in town, and social climbing is described neither with irony nor depth. In *Brenda's Murder* (1973), Mrs. Severson gets involved in a crime while Knute is away at a conference; she finds the body of a woman whom she was helping to organize a house tour stuffed in an appliance box.

Graves, Worms, and Epitaphs (1988) comes close to PARODY, and seems to blow the series to pieces. Severson, now chief of police, suffers a heart attack two-thirds of the way through the book. Brenda admits to having had an affair with the head of the library trustees, and she likewise exits the stage. The deaths occur among a group of elderly people who are under the spell of a ghoulish writing teacher. The interesting aspect of the story is that much of it is told through their submissions, which the detective reads for clues. The various victims are locked in a meat freezer; pushed into a swimming pool in a wheelchair; and shot.

BIBLIOGRAPHY Novels: *A Matter of Love and Death* (1966), *What Should You Know of Dying?* (1967), *Murder Most Fouled* (1968), *The Young Can Die Protesting* (1969), *Dinky Died* (1970), *The Foo Dog* (1971; U.K. title *The Lotus Affair*), *What to Do Until the Undertaker Comes* (1971), *How to Kill a Man* (1972), *A Die in the Country* (1972), *Have Mercy Upon Us* (1974), *Hark, Hark, The Watchdogs Bark* (1975), *A Creature Was Stirring* (1977).

SHAMUS (or shamos, sharmus) This term for a policeman or detective has been said to derive from the Irish name *Seamus,* because many early police forces (for example, in Boston and New York) were dominated by Irish immigrants.

SHAMUS AWARDS See PRIVATE EYE WRITERS OF AMERICA.

SHANDY, PETER A professor, avid birdwatcher, and horticulturist in the fictitious Balaclava County, Massachusetts, in a series of novels by Charlotte MACLEOD. Shandy is married to a younger woman, Helen, who works in the college library. It is a COZY series, and the couple is portrayed as open-minded, sensitive, kind, and down-to-earth. In *Something the Cat Dragged In* (1983), the cat finds a dirty item that turns out to be the hairpiece of an elderly man—found on the commons, killed with his cane. An interesting series of clues and deductions by Shandy follows; the story is less farfetched than others. *The Corpse In Ozark's Pond* (1987) was nominated for an EDGAR and takes place during the Spring celebration at Balaclava Agricultural College. Professor Shandy finds the half-frozen corpse of a man dressed in a 100-year-old suit who resembles Balaclava Buggins, the college's founder. Shandy investigates the Buggins family, who are now involved in a lawsuit. As she often does, MacLeod creates such complications that a triple somersault has to be performed to explain everything consistently. *Something in the Water* (1994) takes place in Maine, where Shandy is studying lupines. In *Exit the Milkman* (1997), another professor is stricken with AMNESIA after a car accident.

BIBLIOGRAPHY Novels: *Rest You Merry* (1978), *The Luck Runs Out* (1979), *Wrack and Rune* (1982), *The Curse of the Giant Hogweed* (1985), *Vane Pursuit* (1989), *An Owl Too Many* (1991).

SHANE, PETER UTLEY See BONNAMY, FRANCIS.

SHANNON, DEL A pseudonym of Elizabeth LININGTON, under which she wrote the Luis MENDOZA novels.

SHAPIRO, DETECTIVE NATHAN The evolution of Richard LOCKRIDGE's detectives seems to have been a literal descent of man. When Nathan Shapiro appears in an Inspector HEIMRICH novel, *Murder Can't Wait* (1964), he is even more subdued, or nondescript, than Heimrich is. Shapiro seems to be suffering from low self-esteem and is self-deprecating and moody. He gets promoted to lieutenant, which surprises him: "Lieutenant Shapiro has an abiding uncertainty that his rank is somebody's astonishing mistake and will one day prove a disaster to the New York Police department." A more humorous writer would have played up Shapiro's sad-sack personality, his "mournful" eyes, and his "dispirited" voice. Instead he remains a precursor of the dysfunctional detective type that became popular in the eighties. Shapiro may be no more lively or interesting than Heimrich is, but the settings of the stories are. Shapiro works in New York, and particularly Greenwich Village, where the author himself had lived for many years. In *Write Murder Down* (1974), a dead woman is found in a bathtub in the Village. *Preach No More* (1971) is about the murder of an evangelist.

Shapiro's earliest case is *The Drill Is Death* (1961), in which an English poet and teacher gets into a cab and finds a young woman stabbed to death. He is arrested by suspicious men calling themselves detectives, and soon finds himself on the run. The end is a chase, the Lockridge trademark.

BIBLIOGRAPHY Novels: *Murder for Art's Sake* (1968), *Die Laughing* (1969), *Or Was He Pushed?* (1975), *A Streak of Light* (1976), *The Old Die Young* (1980).

SHARK INFESTED CUSTARD, THE (1993, exp from *Kiss Your Ass Goodbye*) A bizarre, funny, and very disturbing crime novel by Charles WILLEFORD. This putative novel is actually a collection of four interrelated stories, set, like some of Willeford's other books, in Miami. Four friends share an apartment: Larry, an ex-cop; Eddie, an airline pilot; Hank, a drug company representative; and Don, a salesman. The first, second, and last parts are written in the first person, and the third quarter in the third person. The story begins when Hank bets that he can pick up any woman within an hour and a half. He succeeds, but the woman dies of an overdose in his car. This sets up a series of macabre events. In the second part, the hunter becomes the hunted as Hank is pursued by a jealous husband. Next, Don, who is mentally coming apart, tries to run away from his family. All of the characters are to some degree crazy; their story builds to a weird and surprising conclusion.

SHATTERED (1969, repr 1991; orig title *The Plastic Nightmare*) A novel by Richard NEELY. One of his first efforts, the book tries to ring new changes on the AMNESIA theme. The story concerns Dan Marriott, a San Francisco stockbroker who wakes up with no memory after his car plunges five hundred feet down a precipice as he is returning with his wife from a drunken party. Eight months have passed, and Marriott has been in a coma; in addition, his destroyed face has been repaired through plastic surgery. His wife Judith has devotedly nursed him through his reconstruction. They repair for a sex-filled vacation to San Clemente, during which she reveals insatiable passions of which he has not the slightest memory.

After they return to San Francisco, it rapidly becomes clear from clues discovered by Marriott that something is wrong. This part of the book is the most interesting, as Neely shows Marriott essentially investigating his own lost self. Everything that people report to him about what he did—and more importantly, felt—in the period before the accident has to be weighed. Marriott has to consider other people's subjective views, while having no subjectivity at all himself. His key discovery of evidence that he had hired a private detective leads to further revelations, and the past begins to repeat itself even as he reconstructs it. An ambitious novel let down by its writing and the author's attempt to put in one twist too many, it remains an interesting mixture of PULP, psychology, and suspense.

SHAW, JOSEPH T. (1874–1952) As editor of BLACK MASK from 1926 to 1936, Joseph T. ("Cap") Shaw did much to promote and shape the HARD-BOILED style and to advance the careers of writers such as Dashiell HAMMETT and Raymond CHANDLER. Shaw wrote some mystery stories himself, of which Chandler said "It's about the deadest writing I ever saw." Shaw's contribution as an editor, however, was vital to the mystery genre.

Shaw was a graduate of Bowdoin College, and had also served in World War I and with the Hoover Commission. At the time he was given the editor's job at *Black Mask,* he had never read a pulp magazine. After leaving *Black Mask,* Shaw went to work for the Sydney Sanders Literary Agency, representing such writers as John D. MACDONALD. He started his own literary agency at the age of seventy-eight. Shaw had won a fencing medal in the 1922 Olympics; MacDonald said he was the only man in New York City licensed to carry a sword cane.

SHAYNE, HÉCTOR BELASCOARÁN A private detective character in novels by Paco Ignacio TAIBO II. Shayne, whose mother is Irish and father Basque, could be called a postmodern HARD-BOILED detective. He carries a .45 or a .38 automatic, has a face scarred by earlier battles, and compares his own life to those of classic hard-boiled fictional dicks, but remains primarily a foil for Taibo's commentary on Mexican (and literary) history. Although influenced by Raymond Chandler's Philip MARLOWE, Shayne may also may owe something to Michael SHAYNE—who was also "born," the story goes, south of the border.

In his first appearance in *No Habrá Final Feliz* (1981; tr *No Happy Ending,* 1993), Héctor says "I got my license by mail for three hundred pesos, and I've never read a single British mystery novel. I don't know a fingerprint from a finger sandwich. I can only shoot something if it doesn't move very much." Thirty-three years old, divorced, and in business for three years, he shares his office with Gilberto Gómez Letras, a plumber; Carlos Vargas, an upholsterer; and El Gallo Villareal, a sewer engineer. Their seedy establishment and constant efforts to find work are a comic, realistic version of the hard-boiled p.i.

The inside of Shayne's head is like a Diego Rivera mural, across which dance images of his heroes (including John Reed and Robert Capablanca, the chess player), scenes from Mexican history, plus his own memories of "wasted passions, idiotic love affairs, old routines that had once seemed exciting." These elements merge most effectively in AN EASY THING (1990).

Shayne's first case comes about when he finds a Roman gladiator, complete with breastplate and helmet, sitting on the toilet in his bathroom, dead. The next day he receives a photograph in the mail of another man, killed the same way (his throat is slashed) and a one-way plane ticket to New York. Despite its absurd elements, the book is a reflection on the student movement of 1968 and the following crackdown and massacre. Shayne appears to die in the first book, but was brought back, as they say, by popular demand in *Return to the Same City* (*Regreso a la misma ciudad y bajo la lluvia,* 1983; tr 1989). He is recovering slowly and suffers from nightmares, from which he wakes in strange places: his closet; under his bed with his gun in his hands; on a plane to Tijuana; in a hotel registered under a false name. In *Some Clouds* (*Algunas Nubes,* 1985; tr 1992), Shayne has retreated from Mexico City to a village by the sea because he had crippled an eight-year-old boy with a stray bullet. Shayne is drawn back to Mexico City to investigate a case involving money-laundering, *judi-*

ciales who protect criminals, rape and murder, and the efforts of a writer to uncover the truth.

SHAYNE, MICHAEL A detective character created by Brett HALLIDAY. Shayne is a tall Irishman with a taste for cognac whose angular form conceals great strength. He has "violently red" hair, bushy eyebrows, and a freckled face. Shayne is one of many HARD-BOILED detectives who followed in the wake of HAMMETT, though his first appearance came relatively late. Halliday got the idea for the character from someone he met in a bar in Mexico. The cases are set in Miami. *Dividend on Death* (1939) was the first Shayne novel. The Freudianism—a novelty at the time—is brought out rather woodenly. A woman named Phyllis Brighton comes to Shayne because she is afraid she is going to kill her stepmother. It is not clear whether she believes that she "can't think straight anymore" and has "an Electra complex" or if she has been fed a line by the small, dark, "effeminate" Dr. Joel Pedique, who walks "mincingly" and purrs when he speaks.

Brighton became a series character (Shayne married her), but was later done away with and replaced by Lucy Hamilton. Shayne did not marry Lucy, which left more room for romantic escapades in the stories. In *One Night With Nora* (1953; British title *The Lady Came by Night*), a woman slips into Shayne's apartment, undresses, and gets into bed with him before she realizes she is in the wrong hotel room. She is looking for her husband, who is in the room directly above—dead.

Halliday gave up writing the series in 1958. For almost twenty years, ghost-written Mike Shayne novels continued to appear.

BIBLIOGRAPHY Novels: *The Private Practice of Michael Shayne* (1940), *The Uncomplaining Corpses* (1940), *Tickets for Death* (1941), *Bodies Are Where You Find Them* (1941), *Michael Shayne Takes Over* (1941), *The Corpse Came Calling* (1942; British title *The Case of the Walking Corpse*), *Murder Wears a Mummers Mask* (1943), *Blood on the Black Market* (1943), *Michael Shayne's Long Chance* (1944), *Murder and the Married Virgin* (1944), *Murder Is My Business* (1945), *Marked for Murder* (1945), *Blood on Biscayne Bay* (1946), *Counterfeit Wife* (1947), *Blood on the Stars* (1948, British title *Murder Is a Habit*), *Michael Shayne's Triple Mystery* (1948, 3 novelettes), *A Taste for Violence* (1949), *Call for Michael Shayne* (1949), *This Is It, Michael Shayne* (1950), *Framed in Blood* (1951), *Why Dorinda Dances* (1951), *What Really Happened* (1952), *She Woke to Darkness* (1954), *Death Has Three Lives* (1955), *Stranger in Town* (1955), *The Blonde Cried Murder* (1956), *Weep for a Blonde* (1957), *Shoot the Works* (1957), *Murder and the Wanton Bride* (1958).

SHERINGHAM, ROGER A detective created by Francis Iles, otherwise known as Anthony BERKELEY. Berkeley said that he deliberately made Sheringham obnoxious. Like Sherlock HOLMES, Sheringham has a high opinion of his ratiocinative powers and contempt for everyone else's, especially the police. An Oxford graduate, Sheringham is also a consummate philistine; he is a novelist who disparages his own works but enjoys their popularity, providing him with yet another opportunity to look down his nose at people. In the DETECTION CLUB novel *Ask a Policeman* (1933), he is appropriately referred to as "Snooty" Sheringham.

Sheringham may have been delightfully offensive when he first appeared, but now he can be annoying. The settings, plots, and people of the Sheringham novels follow the patterns of the GOLDEN AGE, but with several twists. Sheringham belongs to the Crimes Circle, a fictional version of the Detection Club. *Murder in the Basement* (1929) is a sort of proto-PROCEDURAL. One of Sheringham's most notable appearances is THE POISONED CHOCOLATES CASE (1929).

BIBLIOGRAPHY Novels: *The Layton Court Mystery* (1925), *The Wychford Poisoning Case* (1926), *Roger Sheringham and the Vane Mystery* (1927; U.S. title *The Mystery at Lover's Cave*), *The Silk Stocking Murders* (1928), *The Poisoned Chocolates Case* (1929), *The Second Shot* (1930), *Top Storey Murder* (1931; U.S. title *Top Story Murder*), *Murder in the Basement* (1932), *Jumping Jenny* (1933; U.S. title *Dead Mrs. Stratton*), *Panic Party* (1934; U.S. title *Mr. Pidgeon's Island*).

SHERLOCK HOLMES'S WAR OF THE WORLDS See WELLMAN, MANLEY WADE.

SHIEL, M[ATTHEW] P[HIPPS] (1865–1947) This English mystery author, born on the island of Montserrat in the Caribbean, is famous for bizarre characters (including himself). Shiel was the son of a shipowner and shop owner who was also a lay preacher, and in whom one sees a family talent for eccentricity: he had his son crowned "King of Redonda" by an Antiguan minister on his fifteenth birthday. The new king had no subjects, for Redonda was a small uninhabited island; Shiel took this coronation with all seriousness, however, and as an adult tried to hand on his title to a friend. Strangely, the mother of Shiel, a man who would sail dangerously close to racist supremacy theories, may have been partially descended from slaves—or perhaps the contradiction is in keeping with Shiel's bizarre nature.

In any case, Shiel was intelligent and wrote a novel when he was twelve. He was educated in London, which he called "the monster city in which all things lose themselves." He dropped out of school and began his writing career, producing reams of journalism and stories until he achieved fame with the very strange character of Prince ZALESKY. Shiel knew Edgar Jepson, Robert Louis STEVENSON, and other writers. He gained a reputation for wild imagination and even genius. Shiel's imagination was as explosive as a volcano, and just as indiscriminate.

In reality, Shiel was a borrower, and his verbose writings are full of half-digested occultism, political theory, war hysteria, eugenics, Bohemianism, and every other intellectual fad of the 1890s. In the Middle Ages, he could have been a visionary predicting the end of the world, or an alchemist. One of his best-known works is *The Purple Cloud* (1901), a novel about the last man on earth, who has triggered an apocalypse by a trip to the North Pole. It is not hard to guess the subject of *The Yellow Danger* (1898); this story of Asiatic "hordes" invading the West features the evil Dr. Yen How, who pre-dates Dr. FU MANCHU by more than a decade. It also includes genocidal germ warfare against the Chinese and Japanese and millions of deaths.

Critics have sought to find some sliver of redemptive value in Shiel's work. Some of it, like the title story of *Xélucha and Others* (repr 1975), is completely incomprehensible. The stories about Zalesky, a tiny fraction of his output, remain the most interesting and readable part of the Shiel oeuvre. *The Black Box* (1930) is one of his detective stories not about Zalesky. Shiel's stories are overwritten but unique in mystery literature. He was an intelligent man, and the way in which he refracted—or distorted—ideas and controversies of his time through his bizarre characters make the stories interesting if not easy reading.

SHILLING FOR CANDLES, A (1936) A novel by Josephine TEY. A woman is found by a local constable on the beach, a cloud of gulls wheeling around her, and "all over the world things happened because one woman had lost her life." Inspector Alan GRANT, from his first almost anonymous appearance, is an engaging person rather than a genius among fools; Tey doesn't need to slight her other characters or make idiots of them in order to puff up her sleuth. On the other hand, the dead woman becomes uncannily vivid and clear as the strange manner of her death is investigated. As a plot, the story is Tey's most perfect, and the atmosphere of coastal Britain is vividly rendered.

SHIV A knife; from the gypsy word *chiv,* meaning blade.

SHLEMIEL Yiddish word for a person who has bad luck or is clumsy. Leo Rosten quotes an old saying that the difference between a NEBBISH and a shlemiel is that a shlemiel is always knocking over what a nebbish has to pick up.

SHLOCK A Yiddish world meaning cheap, low-quality. Robert L. FISH wrote a famous PARODY using as his detective one Shlock Homes.

SHMUCK This word still means "jewelry" or "ornament" in German, but in Yiddish it means "penis," and is now in general use as a derogatory epithet. Considered very offensive, it gave rise to the euphemism *shmo.* According to Hugh Rawson, in this form it gave its name (and thus a secret, lewd past) to the Shmoo, the famous cartoon character.

SHOCK TO THE SYSTEM, A (1984) A novel by Simon BRETT, later filmed. It is a reverse or INVERTED MYSTERY about how Graham Marshal is caught after several murders. He electrocutes his wife by an elaborately rigged pipe in the attic, and blows up his boss in a similarly clever manner. This is perhaps the only mystery novel to use PARAQUAT as a murder weapon. Graham Marshall is a narcissist whose desires exceed his abilities, and who longs to live up to his parents' provincial, post–World War II idea of success. Faced with failure, he resorts to bizarre and criminal behavior.

SHOOT THE PIANO PLAYER (1956; orig title *Down There*) A novel by David GOODIS, later turned into a film by François TRUFFAUT. "Eddie" is the piano player at Harriet's Hut, a Philadelphia dive; he is the essence of cool, not only in his music but in his relations—or lack thereof—with others. Nobody knows where he came from or who he really is, and he takes no part in the brawls, passions, and conflicts that surround him—until, of course, the action of the book begins. Eddie's brother Turley, a criminal, comes to him in desperation, and in spite of himself Eddie helps Turley get away from a couple of killers. This action puts Eddie in jeopardy and begins the slow unraveling of his carefully crafted no-strings setup. His past identity as Edward Webster Lynn, a pianist of genius, is revealed, and he is also sucked down by the "bad" side of the Lynn family. Like other Goodis novels, *Shoot the Piano Player* is a story about redemption, in which a man is raised up by the almost chaste love of a woman (in this case, the waitress Lena). The writing of the book is more typical of fifties pulp than some of Goodis's extraordinary other efforts, but the suspenseful plot and the use of flashbacks and different time frames make it a rich narrative. The characteristic doom of Goodis's novels is lighter here than elsewhere.

SHORE, JEMIMA See FRASER, LADY ANTONIA.

SHORT STORY The mystery and detective story began as a short story form—one has only to think of the achievement of POE, DICKENS, and Conan DOYLE to remember that mysteries were first consumed by the public largely through serialization in newspapers. The mystery story was then still part of the "low" culture, a relationship that the PULP MAGAZINES cemented. With the death of the pulps, the mystery short story field is now dominated by two giants, *Ellery Queen's Mystery Magazine* and *Alfred Hitchcock's Mystery Magazine.* As Francis M. NEVINS, Jr. has written, no matter how good a writer is in the short form, "until and unless they also become known as the authors of mystery novels, the probability that any publishing house will be interested in a collection of their short stories is about as high as the probability that it will start handing out free copies of its best-sellers in Grand Central Station at rush hour."

The mystery did not become primarily a novel form simply because television killed the pulps, however; what really ended the heyday of the short story form was the conversion of the mystery into "serious" literature, which was already dominated by the novel. As early as 1941 Ellery QUEEN was writing that "in the 20th Century the publication of detective stories has proved commercially unprofitable." The function of the short story today may be, as Ross MACDONALD once wrote, "to sustain mystery writers between the novelist's widely separated paydays." But the short story still requires skills that producers of bloated novels laden with irrelevancies rarely have. (Jacques BARZUN was very critical of the heavily padded postwar mystery novels.) Some of the living mystery authors who are particularly known for their short stories are Ed GORMAN, John LUTZ, and Lawrence BLOCK.

SICKBED The prolonged immobility of the sickbed has led to a surprising number of mystery careers. Authors who began writing mysteries during convalescence from an illness or accident include some of the biggest names in the business: Catherine AIRD, John BUCHAN, G. D. H. COLE, Margaret MILLAR, Aaron Mark STEIN, S. S. VAN DINE, Freeman Wills CROFTS, and Valentine WILLIAMS.

SIDEL, ISAAC A series character created by Jerome CHARYN. Although Sidel is the Commissioner of Police in New York City, he is also a gangster, a romantic, a neurotic, and a slob. His adventures are the equivalent of postmodern PULP. Written in short, declarative sentences, they stumble through a Byzantine maze of corrupt policemen, FBI men, small-time hoods, bimbos, crime bosses, and mafiosi. The narrative space becomes chaotic and claustrophobic, like a stampede for the door in an illegal nightclub where the lights have gone out: "He'd forgotten to shave this morning. His shoes weren't tied. He had a Band-Aid on his finger. He was a detective who couldn't find his daughter or follow the clues of his own fucking life. Homicides were up in Manhattan. Handguns were everywhere. Hospitals were closing. There were crazies out on the street. The north woods of Central Park had become a private crib for crack babies. But he was the first Alexander Hamilton Fellow. He'd gone around the U.S. lecturing on crime. Justice and Frederic LeComte had sponsored Sidel, the Hebraic police commissioner who'd drawn Latinos and blacks into his Department, who had a Turkish chief judge, Chinese deputies, a Rastafarian lawyer. But he couldn't remember most of their names." (Neither can the reader.) Sometimes this unmodulated punchiness comes out like a graduate school version of Carroll John DALY.

A Sidel story does not so much proceed as accumulate. The books can be read as parodies of pulp, experiments with the novel, or semantic nonsense. Initially striking, betraying influences as diverse as James JOYCE and Raymond CHANDLER, their substitution of stuff for stuffing—a center, a heart, a point—eventually makes them implode under the burden of their own pretentiousness and attempts to be cool. And yet, they have amusing moments.

In *Montezuma's Man* (1993), Sidel teams up with Joe Barbarossa, a decorated cop, drug dealer, descendant of Chief Joseph of the Nez Piercé, Vietnam veteran, etcetera. Along with Sidel, they become the Black Stocking Twins, driving all over New York holding up Mafia social clubs in Sidel's ongoing war with the mob. *Secret Isaac* (1978; repr 1992) has Sidel battling the Guzman crime family as well as Dermott McBride, a former Joyce scholar and now the biggest pimp in New York—surprising, then, that after three months of undercover work dressed as a bum in Times Square, Isaac still has never heard of him. In his "investigation," Isaac always seems to be one or two steps behind.

BIBLIOGRAPHY Novels: *Marilyn the Wild* (1976), *Blue Eyes* (1975), *The Education of Patrick Silver* (1976), *The Good Policeman* (1990), *Maria's Girls* (1992), *Citizen Sidel* (1999).

SIGNAL THIRTY-TWO (1950) An early and ambitious PROCEDURAL novel by McKinlay KANTOR, unlike anything later written in that subgenre. Kantor's style is at first offputting and archaic, but the story builds to an almost surreal and violent climax that is incredibly sustained. Set in the 23rd Precinct in New York City, the novel revolves around the partnership of Joe Shetland and Dan Mallow. The former is a forty-two-year-old patrolman, a lonely and withdrawn man; Mallow is a rookie and "glamour-boy" type whose handsome youth conceals a serious mind. One of their first arguments is about police brutality after Shetland beats a suspect.

Like later procedurals, *Signal Thirty-Two* was carefully researched, and one can smell New York City, the "smutty wilderness," and feel the energy of the period, when many vets returned to become police officers. It is told much in the manner of a war novel, and the central event referred to in the title is preceded by myriad smaller episodes of action and repose. Through a jazzy train of incidents, people, tenement interiors, and cityscapes, Kantor builds a rich texture, using surprisingly realistic scenes of violence and harsh language that was unusual for the time (and some racial epithets that were all too common). He writes with a hankering after the sublime not yet undercut by cynicism and the minimalist pose: "He lay amid books and cigar butts and tumbled Coke bottles; he visited the past in its majesty and infamy. He peeked wonderingly into the discordant future, crowded up at a window which some bold preceptor of an earlier century had opened for him. He dulled his ears to the hopeless confusion of the present." There is also much more characterization than in later procedurals, and an extended romantic subplot. If we are embarrassed by naked sentiment, purple passages, and a sincerity we no longer believe, we are also impressed by the novel's vividness and cumulative force.

SILENCE OBSERVED (1961) A novel by Michael INNES. Sir John APPLEBY, aged but not yet retired, is at his club when he is approached by two members. One, Charles Gribble, collects forgeries of manuscripts, and is upset because he thinks he's been sold a *forgery* of a forgery of a Meredith manuscript. The other, the head of a national art institution, thinks he's been shown a mysterious but real Rembrandt by a strange, young, beautiful woman who has beguiled his assistant. The story gets off the ground slowly because of all the second-hand exposition, but once the crimes start (with the shooting in the head of an antiquarian book dealer), Appleby plays the serious detective.

SILVER, MISS An elderly spinster and detective created by Patricia WENTWORTH. Miss Silver is an antique, with her Victorian furniture, her respectable but well-worn clothes, and a cast of mind that goes back to HOLMES's era. Tennyson is her favorite poet and she thinks of Kipling as "modern." Miss Silver is connected to Scotland Yard through her former charge, Sergeant Frank Abbott. He is described as "high toned and classy"; dashing and elegant, he is a muted WIMSEY type, an aristocratic cop.

Mousy looking, wearing pince-nez and high collars, during her investigations Miss Silver knits small clothes for her niece's children and carries a flowered knitting bag. Hannah Meadows is her solid, matronly housekeeper. It has been suggested that Miss Silver is more believable than Miss MARPLE, another spinster detective, because she does not just happen to fall into all sorts of murder cases. On the other hand, it is hardly believable that Scotland Yard would consult this elderly amateur. Realism, of course, was not the fashion at the time the stories were written. *Grey Mask* (1927) was the first Maud Silver mystery. *The Case of William Smith* (1948) involves AMNESIA; THE GAZEBO (1955) is another interesting case.

BIBLIOGRAPHY Novels: *The Case Is Closed* (1937), *Lonesome Road* (1939), *In the Balance* (1941; orig title *Danger Point*), *The Chinese Shawl* (1943), *Miss Silver Deals with Death* (1943; orig title *Miss Silver Intervenes*), *The Clock Strikes Twelve* (1944), *The Key* (1944), *She Came Back* (1945; orig title *The Traveller Returns*), *Pilgrim's Rest* (1946), *The Latter End* (1947), *Wicked Uncle* (1947; orig title *The Spotlight*), *The Eternity Ring* (1948), *Miss Silver Comes to Stay* (1949), *The Catharine Wheel* (1949), *The Brading Collection* (1950), *Through the Wall* (1950), *The Ivory Dagger* (1951), *Anna, Where Are You?* (1951), *Watersplash* (1952), *Ladies' Bane* (1952), *Out of the Past* (1953), *The Vanishing Point* (1953), *The Silent Pool* (1954), *The Benevent Treasure* (1954), *Poison in the Pen* (1955), *The Listening Eye* (1955), *The Fingerprint* (1956), *The Alington Inheritance* (1958), *The Girl in the Cellar* (1961).

SILVERWIG Philip Marlowe's nickname for Mrs. Regan in THE BIG SLEEP (1939).

SIMENON, GEORGES [JOSEPH CHRISTIAN] (1903–1989) The Belgian-born French author Georges Simenon is one of the most important and most prolific of mystery novelists. Simenon wrote several hundred books, and his collected works run to literally dozens of volumes. Simenon was arguably the best-selling novelist of all time—an incredible half a billion books. André Gide called him "the greatest French novelist of our times." Yet his inner life is the subject of continued speculation, largely because of the myth he built around himself through volume after volume of autobiography, each piling on another layer of ambiguity, inconsistency, and even disinformation. His sexual conquests are notorious, yet he seems to have spent his life in pursuit of the loneliness his characters find all too readily. Simenon's early life was flamboyant; later he became almost a cult figure, and, finally, a recluse. The title of a recent biography, *The Man Who Wasn't Maigret,* shows how difficult it is to pry apart the Simenon of fact from the fiction.

Although he gained a reputation as one of the most literate and philosophical of mystery writers, Simenon's early biography is surprisingly similar to that of some of the American writers of the HARD-BOILED school who churned out books by the dozen in their early careers. Born in Liège, Simenon was the son of an unambitious but happy insurance salesman and his discontented and oppressive wife. Simenon loved the one and perhaps hated the other, and the desire to escape being trapped in the middle became the driving force of his existence. Simenon was writing for a newspaper at the age of fifteen and was already full of literary ambition. He moved to Paris in 1923, where he began producing PULP at a furious rate: in the next ten years, he wrote well over one hundred novels or novelettes. He was married by this time, and he and his first wife established a private bar in the Place des Voges where they threw extravagant parties. Simenon also began an affair with the dancer Josephine Baker, which he broke off when his work began to suffer (he was only able to write a dozen or so books that year). The pulp novels appeared under pseudonyms, and few people knew "George Sim's" real name.

Simenon became dissatisfied with his work, and, buying a tiny boat, went on a six-month voyage through the canals of France. It was less a vacation than an imaginative search. He then bought a fishing cutter, the *Ostrogoth,* on which he and his family would spend most of the next three years.

Worried by his publishers' lack of enthusiasm for his turn away from sensationalism and toward the *roman policier,* Simenon threw a ball in Paris to publicize the launch of his Inspector MAIGRET series and caused a sensation. Simenon referred to *Pietr-le-Letton* (1931; tr *The Case of Peter the Lett*) as the first in the series, but he had actually experimented with the character of Maigret in several earlier works. Simenon would eventually produce seventy-five novels featuring Maigret and more than half again as many stories. He also wrote over one hundred other "psychological" novels—though the Maigret books are themselves psychological.

Like the French existentialists who were his contemporaries, Simenon portrayed the lone individual alienated from society. He is interested in the psychological motivation of the person who is driven to neurotic or psychotic behavior and, sometimes, crime; of all mystery writers, Simenon is the one who most displays the view of crime as essentially a disease for which society itself is to blame, rather than a manifestation of the individual's "evil." Simenon once remarked that the policeman understands the criminal because he comes from the same strata of society and could as easily have become a criminal instead of a cop. Thus the criminal in Simenon's books is a far more sympathetic character.

Simenon also had great compassion for the poor among whom he had grown up, and again and again he depicts the failure and unhappiness that haunt society's nether regions. François Mauriac wrote of Simenon, "I am afraid I may not have the courage to descend right to the depths of this nightmare which Simenon describes with such unendurable art." The early Maigret novel *Le Pendu de St. Pholien* (1931; tr MAIGRET AND THE HUNDRED GIBBETS) exemplifies this descent, as Maigret's scalpel-like probing dissects the inner pain, disappointment, and guilt of a group of conspirators.

Some of Simenon's "psychological" novels are *Lettre à mon juge* (1947); *La Neige était sale* (1948; tr THE STAIN ON THE SNOW, 1953), considered by some his greatest work; *La Mort de belle* (1952); and *L'Ours en peluche* (1960; tr *Teddy Bear,* 1971), which concerns the gynecologist Chabot, who feels detached within the shell of his own reputation (like Simenon), and becomes more and more desperate to escape it and find his real self. In *The Man Who Watched Trains Go By* (1938), Simenon dealt with the theme of the psychotic killer. A clerk in a ship chandlery loses his job and turns an insane rage against what he considers to be an unfeeling world.

During World War II, the Simenons were caught in the German zone, then lived in unoccupied France and helped provide relief for refugees. In 1945, they left for North America, first living in Canada and then moving to Florida, Arizona, and California. Shortly after his arrival in the United States, Simenon met the woman who would become his second wife, an affair recounted in *Trois chambres à Manhattan* (1947; *Three Beds in Manhattan*). Simenon went to Reno, Nevada, in 1950 and was divorced from his wife Tigy one day and married to his lover the next; perhaps this was the quintessentially American experience that led him to contemplate changing his citizenship. He suddenly decided to return to Europe a few years later, however, and was greeted as a returning hero.

Simenon announced his retirement as a novelist in 1973. Apparently he meant it literally, for within days he had bought a tape recorder and began dictating memoirs that would eventually exceed twenty volumes. He died in Lausanne, Switzerland. The end of Simenon's life was grotesquely sad: his daughter Marie-Jo had long had psychological problems and committed suicide in 1978. Two years later, he published a work addressed to her; the year after that, his second wife sued to have passages in his memoirs stricken. In 1977, he made his famous claim to have slept with 10,000 women.

Simenon seems to have suffered from a lifelong ambivalence about his own worth and his achievement. The journals collected in *When I Was Old* (1970) show that he had been thinking about giving up his obsessive routine and stardom since the early sixties, and dreamed of a simpler life. He wanted to "just write," without thinking of plots or deadlines, and to find out whether, if he didn't have to write, he *would* write. For someone who seemed to seek fame intensely, Simenon was very disturbed by it; he said that by talking about himself "as if about a 'case'" and trying to fend off the myth, he ended up "not believing in myself." It was as if the one case the psychologist could not solve was his own. His distress over the question of identity led to what, for a writer, sounds like a kind of death wish: "I would like to be able to be silent."

Most of Simenon's autobiographical work is not translated. Patrick Marnham's *The Man Who Wasn't Maigret* (1992) takes account of the untranslated material and tries to separate the real man from the myth. Pierre Assouline's *Simenon: Biographie* (1992; tr *Simenon: A Biography,* 1997) takes a more narrative approach, but no one seems able to write about Simenon without entering into the psychology of this contradictory and mysterious man.

SIMMONS, BERNARD Assistant District Attorney Bernard Simmons is the last series character created by Richard LOCKRIDGE, and the only one he created completely on his own (i.e., without the collaboration of his first wife, Frances). Simmons is sometimes assisted by Detective Paul LANE, another Lockridge character. Nora Curran, who works as an editor, is Simmons's girlfriend. The Simmons series was a new departure in that Lockridge had not done any legal mysteries and had no background in the area. *Squire of Death* (1965) was the first novel and used the usual converging plot lines and tangled relationships. Simmons investigates the shooting of sixty-seven-year-old Jefferson Page, a much-hated millionaire about to marry a fourth wife. He may have been killed out of jealousy by Charles Halstead, but witnesses placed Halstead at the Café Bleu at the time of the killing. Lucy McClaren happens to sing at the Café, and she has gone missing; her husband James had been in law school with Simmons, and both McClarens knew Halstead. In *Something Up a Sleeve* (1972), Simmons has a good case against J. Stanley Martin, accused of killing his wife, but Martin's lawyer, Abe Levinsky, seems smug, as if he has a card up his sleeve. Then Levinsky is beaten to death in an apparent mugging. Part of Simmons's investigation is to go through the trial transcript for clues. The plotting of the Simmons series and the supporting characters are much like those of the other Lockridge mysteries. Simmons himself, however, fails really to come alive, and lacks even the minor eccentricities of Nathan SHAPIRO.

BIBLIOGRAPHY Novels: *A Plate of Red Herrings* (1968), *Twice Retired* (1970), *Death on the Hour* (1974).

SIMOLEONS This word for money may have been derived from the Italian *semola* or *semolina,* in the same way that "bread" or "chicken feed" also came to mean money in the industrial age, when the Biblical "daily bread" was earned in coin form.

SIMON, ROGER L[ICHTENBERG] (1943–) It was inevitable that the baby boom generation in the United States would produce a countercultural detective in its own image; Roger L. Simon was the writer who did it. Raised on the brainless commercialism and Cold War politics of the fifties, this generation reacted with the radical political critique of the sixties and the culture of openness, freedom, and permissiveness. When we first meet Moses WINE, the ex-campus radical turned private eye, he is smoking hash in his apartment and playing the board game *Clue*—a comic evocation and violation of GOLDEN AGE proprieties.

Simon studied at Dartmouth College and received a masters in fine arts from Yale University Drama School. He moved to California and had a career as a filmmaker; the first Moses Wine novel, *The Big Fix* (1973), was made into a movie starring Richard Dreyfuss (1978). Simon carried through the Wine-saga-as-baby-boom-parable by having the detective "sell out" in the eighties and go to work for a computer company. Approaching forty, Wine says "My political ideals, when I could remember them, felt like the rehash of a twenty-year-old Marcuse paperback."

Simon's other works include *Heir* (1968) and *The Mama Tass Manifesto* (1970). He also collaborated on the screenplay for *Bustin' Loose* (1981), a Richard Pryor film.

SIMON WHEELER, DETECTIVE See TWAIN, MARK.

"SIMPLE ART OF MURDER, THE" An essay by Raymond CHANDLER, which first appeared in *The Atlantic* magazine in 1944. Chandler's essay went a long way toward legitimizing the HARD-BOILED style of mystery writing that had grown out of the PULP MAGAZINES, and answered critics like Edmund WILSON, who had recently dismissed the entire mystery/detective genre with very few exceptions. Chandler had criticisms of his own, however; he attacked the English mystery of the GOLDEN AGE for its lack of realism and picked apart such classics as TRENT'S LAST CASE (1913) and THE RED HOUSE MYSTERY (1922). The essay was definitive in exposing a rift in the genre that still exists today. In the latter part of the essay, Chandler gave an extremely brief but brilliant analysis of Hammett's method and importance that has rarely been equaled, if at all.

What Chandler's argument boils down to is that the classic mystery is false in both action and character. By contrast, in the HARD-BOILED mystery, though it is still an entertainment (Chandler loathed didactic novels), there is something resembling real life. "Hammett gave murder back to the kind of people that commit it for reasons, not just to provide a corpse; and with the means at hand, not hand-wrought dueling pistols, curare and tropical fish." Chandler said, in essence, that to be relevant a novel had to be believable; a story that requires us to suspend our disbelief also suspends our involvement with reality. The classic mystery was second-rate literature because "if it started out to be about real people . . . they must very soon do unreal things in order to form the artificial pattern required by the plot." (Chandler admitted elsewhere, however, that the private eye of fiction is inherently unreal, because in real life such a person—thoughtful, often scrupulous, and morally refined, with a deep insight into human nature—would never become a private detective.)

The Simple Art of Murder is also the name of a collection that includes the essay and several of Chandler's early stories.

SIMPSON, DOROTHY (1933–) The English author Dorothy Simpson could be seen either as a reactionary, plodding along in the familiar English subgenre of the village mystery, or as a champion of the classic mystery. The reception of her Luke Thanet mysteries has ranged from cool to enthusiastic. H. R. F. KEATING called her work merely "pleasant" and "domestic"; BARZUN and TAYLOR, on the other hand, esteemed her highly, citing *Close Her Eyes* (1984) as the book in which she "perfected her craft" and achieved "complete mastery of the genre." They seem to have overlooked, however, the lack of psychological realism. (Is it believable that a parent, even a religious fanatic, would not want the police to look for a young daughter missing for three days because God would watch over her?).

Luke Thanet is an inspector working in Kent in southeastern England. His assistant is Sergeant Mike Lineham. Unlike the GOLDEN AGE mystery, these books are heavily padded with subplots about the domestic arrangements of the characters—including and especially the policemen. Here, domesticity is subject to the same pitfalls as romance in other writers; Thanet's wife, mother-in-law, and children do not help with the detection, and the amount of time spent on their troubles seems unwarranted. The writing is often stilted, the techniques wooden: in *Doomed to Die* (1991), the drab suburban households and their furnishings are contrasted with the tortured paintings of the artist-victim, Perdita Master, who is suffocated with a bag. The prevalence of clichés is also aggravating (lilac and orange blossoms "hung heavy in the gathering dusk").

Although the detection may be traditional, Simpson is up-to-date in her deployment of various hot topics, such as sexual abuse and family violence. Simpson aspires to some kind of realism and tends to present life in today's Britain as nasty, brutish, and long. Women are especially damaged, and are most frequently the murder victims in Simpson's novels: in *The Night She Died* (1981), an older woman who had witnessed a murder decades before; in *Close Her Eyes,* a fifteen-year-old girl whose family is made up of fundamentalist religious fanatics; in *Last Seen Alive* (1985), a widow who is only passing through town and is unaccountably strangled. Yet the atmosphere remains COZY and quaint. Thanet's beat is the town of Sturrenden, in the Kentish countryside. Simpson has tried to marry the cozy and the PROCEDURAL in a manner even more jarring than the novels of Gwedolyn BUTLER.

In *Dead on Arrival* (1986), Simpson took on the most risky and most often censured of Father KNOX's taboo subjects—identical twins. In *No Laughing Matter* (1993), the victim, Mr. Randish, is a wife-beater, philanderer, and rapist. His victim, his young niece, has become anorexic as a result of the rape and dies the same night that he is killed. Twins are again important. A subplot involves an Indian single-mother who is in love with her wheelchair-bound boss.

SINGING SANDS, THE (1953) The title of this novel by Josephine TEY comes from a scrap of adolescently romantic poetry written on a newspaper in the train compartment of a dead man. Alan GRANT is on his way to the Highlands to visit his cousin and recuperate from nervous exhaustion; the dead man seems to be a young poet who perhaps has drunk himself to death during the night. Grant goes on to Clune for his fishing holiday, but when the details about the man come out they seem all wrong, and he is steadily drawn into the case.

Despite the faltering ending, it is a fine novel as well as a baffling mystery (perhaps too much so). Even the minor characters, such as Pat RANKIN, are well realized, and the doubleness characteristic of a nervous state—appropriate social behavior and internal anguish—is strongly evoked. It is one of Tey's best attempts to combine the NOVEL OF MANNERS, the character study, and the mystery story; parts of it are worth reading out loud.

SING SING This famous prison in New York State was built between 1825 and 1828. The prison was named after the town where it was situated. After the prison became notorious, however, the town of Sing Sing disliked the association and changed its name to Ossining in 1901. Ossining is located on the Hudson north of New York City; Sing Sing is thought to be the source of the expression sent "up the river," meaning to be sent to jail.

SIX IRON SPIDERS, THE See MAYO, ASEY.

SIX SILVER HANDLES See CAMPBELL, HUMPHREY.

SJÖWALL, MAJ (1935–) **AND WAHLÖÖ, PE[TE]R** (1926–1975) This Swedish wife-and-husband team wrote a unique series of PROCEDURAL novels about Martin BECK and his colleagues in the Stockholm homicide division. Sjöwall and Wahlöö wrote with the point of view that crime represents a failure of society; this idea was much less controversial when the books were written—in the sixties and seventies—than it is now, with conservative retrenchment and the insistence that people commit crimes because they are "bad," not because they are encouraged or driven to it by the structure of society. Sjöwall and Wahlöö went further, however, in embedding the detective story in a Marxist critique of capitalism. Although they lived in one of the most liberal welfare states in the West, they saw modern Sweden as simply another bourgeois capitalist state, one that had cleverly accommodated itself to Marxism.

Despite these heavy intellectual underpinnings, the Beck books are also extremely funny at times. The authors' political views are often far less obtrusive than the protestations of critics would lead one to believe. (The commentary on the Greek situation in *The Fire Engine That Disappeared* [1969], is irrelevant, but it is also very brief.) Some of their criticisms are obvious or absurd, such as the comparison of the Christmas consumerist frenzy to the Black Death. The political critique is sometimes turned into a satire on the behavior of the policemen themselves and their bumbling of cases. The rich, who most benefit from the policing of the state, are not spared either. THE LAUGHING POLICEMAN (1970) is one of the best of the novels and won an EDGAR award. *The Locked Room* (1973) is a daring attempt to combine the Beck saga with a form that seems most inimical to it, the LOCKED ROOM.

Undoubtedly, the political message of the Beck series sinks the narrative under its weight in some of the novels. The first book, *Roseanna* (1967), is the closest to a classic detective story and has the least political content. A less often observed feature of the series is the Nordic frankness about sex, which appears as part of this Swedish "slice-of-life," and not, as is often the case with more prudish writers, as a naughty condiment, an approach as juvenile as it is sordid. The characters in the Beck series are built up slowly, and though not deep are believably human. The realism can be unnerving, as when summer vacation comes and the investigation—and the narrative—slow to a crawl. Painstakingly slow progress, while sometimes overdone, is more convincingly real. Aspects of the books are dated, while as a whole they are a lasting contribution.

Concurrently with the Beck series, Wahlöö was writing thrillers under his own name, which are generally conceded to be less interesting and even more focused on the political element. That view is not universal; Julian SYMONS thought *Murder on the Thirty-First Floor* (1966) and *The Steel Spring* (1970) were more ambitious than the Beck novels, though he said some of the latter were "among the most original modern crimes stories" and that they sometimes "succeeded in doing things that no other crime writers even attempted."

Prior to beginning the Beck books, Wahlöö was a newspaper reporter and writer for radio, television, and film. Sjöwall is also a poet.

SKINWALKERS (1988) A novel by Tony HILLERMAN. Navajo detective Jim CHEE wakes up in the night when an abandoned cat crawls into his trailer for shelter though the weather is turning mild. The circumstance of helping the cat leads Chee to meditate on nature (the Navajo don't like to interfere with its workings) and to suspect danger, which quickly materializes in the form of shotgun blasts fired into Chee's trailer.

Chee's report goes to Joe LEAPHORN, who has been investigating the stabbing of an elderly man, the bludgeoning of a sheep rancher, and the shooting of a woman. Chee finds a pellet of bone in his trailer; "skinwalkers" (witches) are said to use fragments of dead bones to give you the "corpse sickness," a lingering slow death. Leaphorn, through his grandfather, has inherited a strong belief against witchcraft. Meanwhile Chee discovers that "foreign matter" was found in the stabbing victim's wounds. The pattern of witchcraft develops slowly, though the dead woman, a social worker, doesn't fit into it. Leaphorn's and Chee's first collaboration becomes very vital indeed. The story is tight and the background, especially the Navajo concept and treatment of disease, is interesting and well-developed. As with the best of the author's works, suspense is built up but is ultimately less important than why and how acts are performed.

SKULLDUGGERY This word has nothing to do with skulls or digging. It comes from Scots *sculduddery,* which meant something considered obscene (eighteenth century). It became incorporated into English by the following century as "skull duggery," meaning suspicious behavior and underhanded or questionable actions.

SKVORECKÝ, JOSEF [VACLAV] (1924–) The Czech novelist and publisher Josef Skvorecký is well known in the West for his comic-satirical novels about Czechoslovakia in the period between the rise of communism and the "Velvet Revolution." These books include *Tankovy prapar* (1971; tr *The Tank Regiment*), *Bassaxofon* (1972; *The Bass Saxophone,* 1977), and *Miracl* (1972; tr *The Miracle Game,* 1991), which depict the depressing realities of Stalinism, but in a weird mixture of styles that might be called socialist magic realism. The scandal over Skvorecký's *Zbabelci* (1958; tr *The Cowards,* 1970), about the last days of World War II and the communist takeover, made him extremely unpopular with the ruling power.

Skvorecký has also had a very serious flirtation with the detective story. In a series of books about Lieutenant BORUVKA, he did not merely appropriate it for his own satirical assault on Soviet-style communism, but reflected on it, experimented with it, and twisted it into new shapes. If, as Dorothy L. SAYERS said, the detective story could not thrive until "public sympathy had veered round to the side of law and order," then Skvorecký's tales are inherently satirical, because they take place against a background of deep cynicism about whom "law and order" are supposed to protect in a totalitarian state. Boruvka is not, however, a dissident detective, nor does he hunt down political subversives. The stories in the first book, *The Mournful Demeanor of Lieutenant Boruvka* (*Smutek porucika Boruvky,* 1966; tr 1973, repub 1987), all take place among a sad collection of artists, dancers, and lackadaisical performers of an emasculated culture. No Holmesian idealism is possible if justice has already been misplaced and the whole society waylaid.

Like BORGES, Skvorecký performs twists on the detective story, and is less interested in working with its forms than commenting on them, or using them to comment on something else (namely, politics). This is clearest in Skvorecký's second collection of Boruvka stories, which are parodies and deliberate violations of the "rules" laid down by Father KNOX.

SLANG The word slang itself has a criminal past. Now taken to mean non-standard lingo in general, it originally (in the eighteenth century) specifically meant the language of criminals—the code phrases they used to communicate with each other over the heads of the authorities, the saps, and the suckers.

Slang is an important part of language that keeps it new and is a universal phenomenon: MENCKEN reported that Trappist monks who had taken a vow of silence had developed slang sign language. Mystery and detective fiction did much to legitimize the use of slang in fiction (PULP writers sometimes took slang to ridiculous extremes, as S. J. Perelman noticed in "SOMEWHERE A ROSCOE . . ." [1945]).

Some sourcebooks for slang are the works of Mencken and Eric PARTRIDGE, the two giants in the field; *Dictionary of American Slang* (3rd ed., 1995), by Robert L. Chapman with Barbara Ann Kipfer; *A Dictionary of the Old West* (1977), by Peter Watts; Clarence Major's *Juba to Jive: A Dictionary of African-American Slang* (1994); and Hugh Rawson's *Wicked Words* (1989).

SLAPPEY, FLORIAN See COHEN, OCTAVUS ROY.

SLATER, OSCAR If there is a "crime of the century," it may be the trial of Oscar Slater, a German living in Glasgow who was railroaded for murder in 1909. Slater spent nearly twenty years in prison while the battle to free him raged; one of Slater's champions was Sir Arthur Conan DOYLE. William ROUGHEAD, who was present at the first trial, wrote a book about it (1910) and was a witness during the appeal.

The crime took place just before Christmas, 1908. Marion Gilchrist, a Glasgow spinster in her eighties, was savagely beaten to death in her home. Gilchrist had a valuable collection of jewels and so kept many locks on her doors. On the evening of December 21, a neighbor heard a terrible struggle, and went upstairs to find Gilchrist lying dead. Both the neighbor and a servant saw the killer as he left; they described him as slim, dark-haired, and clean shaven. Gilchrist's jewels lay about, untouched, but her private papers had been rifled. All the evidence pointed to an attack by someone she knew (she would not have admitted a stranger), and in fact the servant thought she recognized the man.

Slater was arrested because he happened to try to sell a pawn ticket for a diamond brooch. Even though he had pawned the brooch *before* the murder happened and it was not Gilchrist's, once the police had him they never let go. Slater did not look anything like the man who had been seen; instead, he was heavily built and had a black moustache. But the servant's identification of the killer was suppressed, and later she changed her story. The numerous other irregularities included: the doctor who first saw the body was not allowed to testify; no fingerprints were taken at the scene (the technique was standard procedure at the time); and witnesses were given Slater's picture in advance to make sure they would pick him out. Most incredibly, the doctor who was first on the scene had found a chair leg dripping with blood, but it was never mentioned because police had decided that a little tack hammer Slater owned was the weapon (though it showed no trace of blood).

Slater was condemned to death but the sentence was commuted to life in prison. Some of the witnesses who told tales that helped put an innocent man away received monetary rewards. A detective in the Glasgow police named John Trench, who tried to blow the whistle on what had been done in the Slater case, was dismissed from the force and thereafter persecuted by the authorities. Slater was finally freed in 1927.

Many accounts of the case have been written; A. J. Cronin's novel, BEYOND THIS PLACE (1950), appears to use some aspects of the Slater case. Vincent STARRETT published a fictionalized version in his collection of stories, *The Blue Door* (1930).

SLAUGHTER ON TENTH AVENUE (1956; repr 1961) Originally entitled *The Man Who Rocked the Boat,* this book was both a work of true crime and a memoir by William J. Keating (1915–), a whistleblower who exposed waterfront gangs in New York City and illegal wiretapping by police. Keating came from a family of coal miners in Pennsylvania and joined the office of the District Attorney of New York County in 1942. In one of his first cases, one of the jurors was Octavus Roy COHEN. Another case involved the famous murder of Carlo Tresca, editor of the anarchist newspaper *Il Martello.* But it was Keating's prosecution for murder of John M. "Cockeye" Dunn, a boss in the corrupt longshoreman's union, that brought Keating national recognition. It was the first successful prosecution of a waterfront gangster, and Dunn went to the electric chair in 1949. At the time, half a dozen longshoremen were murdered every year to keep mob control of the hiring on the docks. The book offers a fascinating look into criminal investigation, political corruption, and particularly the rough world of the now-vanished West Side docks of New York City (portrayed, for example, in *On the Waterfront*), which once employed up to twelve thousand men a day unloading the ships. In massive "shape-ups," nearly twice that number of men would gather near the docks and wait to be hand-picked for the work, a procedure that was tailor-made for corruption, rivalries, and murder.

SLAY-RIDE (1973) A novel by Dick FRANCIS, one that involves a real mystery and a fair amount of detection by the protagonist, as well as the usual Francis action scenes and suspenseful finish. David Cleveland, an investigator for the British Jockey Club who is more used to ferreting out cheating, is sent to Norway to look for missing English jockey Bob Sherman. Sherman disappeared after a race—along with the day's take at the racetrack. Cleveland is assisted by a former pupil, Arne Kristiansen, responsible for security at the track. Before he gets to investigate anything, Cleveland is almost killed when a speedboat nearly crushes him and he is left floating in the icy waters near Oslo. Shuttling back and forth between England and Norway, Cleveland tries to find out about what happened to Sherman and what were the contents of a mysterious package Sherman had been given. The contents, when he discovers them, are surprising. The story culminates in a chase through the frigid Norwegian mountains.

SLEEPING MURDER See MARPLE, MISS.

SLINKTON, JULIUS A character in Charles Dickens's "HUNTED DOWN," his most famous detective short story. As was often the case, Dickens gave him a name befitting his character. About forty, dark, and well-dressed, Slinkton has oily hair parted in the middle. His appearance is that of a mortician, and he gives out the story that he is interested in becoming a clergyman. He is an engaging villain because, in addition to his repulsive qualities, he has a bewitching, mesmerizing manner that others find difficult to resist, as well as a facility for lying.

SLUNG, MICHELE B. See WOMEN.

SMALL, RABBI DAVID Harry KEMELMAN's Rabbi Small is not a politician, is not physically imposing, and is not a charming presence in his congregation. Instead, he is an intelligent and expert talmudist, able to solve problems with logic and finesse. He also refuses to do things just to be liked by his congregation, which provides the subplot of his life—his endless troubles with the community.

The pole-thin, gentle Rabbi Small lives in Barnard's Crossing (a fictitious small town between Lynn and Salem on Boston's North Shore), which consists of a harbor and an Old Town, mostly Yankee, and Chilton, the area where a large community of Catholics and another of Jews have come together. The Catholic police chief, Hugh Lanigan, is more Small's assistant than the reverse. The rabbi's logic helps clear away unwanted suspects and points toward the culprit, while the police provide clues and check the rabbi's hypotheses. Chief Lanigan is open-minded and interested in religion (a discussion comparing Judaism and Catholicism is what brought Chief Lanigan and Rabbi Small together; investigating homicides enhances their friendship).

The first novel was FRIDAY, THE RABBI SLEPT LATE (1964), and Small is still under thirty years old. In *That Day the Rabbi Left Town* (1996), Small finally leaves Barnard's Crossing and takes a job as a professor of Judaic studies at Windermere College in Boston, where he becomes involved in the case of the murder of an English professor.

BIBLIOGRAPHY Novels: *Friday the Rabbi Slept Late* (1964), *Saturday the Rabbi Went Hungry* (1966), *Sunday the Rabbi Stayed Home* (1969), *Monday the Rabbi Took Off* (1972), *Tuesday the Rabbi Saw Red* (1973), *Wednesday the Rabbi Got Wet* (1976), *Thursday the Rabbi Walked Out* (1978), *Someday the Rabbi Will Leave* (1985), *One Fine Day the Rabbi Bought a Cross* (1987), *The Day the Rabbi Resigned* (1992).

SMALLBONE DECEASED (1950) A mystery novel by Michael GILBERT, considered a classic. Set in the Lincoln's Inn solicitor's firm of Horniman, Birley and Craine, it is also a satire on the legal profession, which Gilbert knew first-hand. At the outset, Henry BOHUN has just joined the firm and Abel Horniman, the founder, has just died. Horniman was known for his efficiency, visible in the airtight strongboxes he designed for safeguarding documents after a mouse nibbled a signature off a deed. It is in one such box that Marcus Smallbone's decaying body is found one day, garroted with picture wire. Smallbone was co-trustee with Horniman of a trust worth half a million pounds, and was a nasty little fellow indeed, a man with a "small and uncomfortable mind." Inspector HAZLERIGG takes up the case, along with Bohun and some colorful assistants. Among the suspects are the surviving partners, the bullying Mr. Birley and the plump and proper Mr. Craine, as well as some office staff. With alibi-breaking, forensic data, and detailed auditing of the firm's books all playing a role, the book is basically PROCEDURAL and generally adheres to FAIR PLAY; however, it is really through its characterizations that it achieves staying power. Hazlerigg is the dullest of the lot, while a junior member of the firm, John Cove, is an acerbic wit whose dialogue associates him with the "angry young men" who dominated British fiction and drama in the fifties, a puncturer of pomposity and disrespecter of tradition and the Establishment. Despite some small errors ("Czechoslovakian" is not a language), the book is an impressive display of puzzle-building and solving, with a fine "novel of manners" thrown in for free.

SMART, HAWLEY (1833–1893) A prolific English novelist—he wrote two or three novels a year in the last couple decades of his life—Hawley Smart is mostly forgotten. He served as a captain in the army in the Crimean War and later in the Indian Mutiny. After he left the service and returned to England, Smart became a punter and gambled enormously and lost hugely on the horses. Short of money, he turned to writing, and produced many books dealing with the Crimea and with horse racing—leading Hugh GREENE to say, "he was near to being the Dick FRANCIS of his day." Stylistically, the comparison is not apt, owing to the customs of Victorian fiction and its preference for long, drawn-out plots. Of his novels with a mystery element, THE GREAT TONTINE (1881) continues to be reprinted and read.

SMERSH See BOND, JAMES.

SMILEY, GEORGE The so-called hero of a series of novels by John LE CARRÉ. Smiley first appeared in *Call for the Dead* (1961), and made a small (and not flattering) appearance in THE SPY WHO CAME IN FROM THE COLD (1963), but he is most associated with the Smiley "trilogy" of novels, *Tinker, Tailor, Soldier, Spy* (1974), *The Honourable Schoolboy* (1977), and *Smiley's People* (1980). It is in these novels that Smiley's own personal Cold War is settled. Smiley is also a character in the author's venture closest to the classic mystery, A MURDER OF QUALITY (1962). *Call for the Dead* is also more traditional.

In a couple of respects, Smiley is modeled on the author himself. Before he joins the British intelligence service, known as "the Circus," Smiley is a teacher with a specialty in languages. Smiley, however, is an ugly character—small, frog-like, middle-aged, slightly fat. But he is also a brilliant tactician, and the plotting in which he is involved equally so. The three books describe his battle against Karla, his opposite number among the Soviets; his enemy actually succeeds in cuckolding him. That is only a subsidiary battle, however; the main event is the finding of a "mole" within the Circus, a double agent who has been there for years. Whether Smiley is a hero depends on how much irony one sees in the account of his exploits, and how much of the ideal

"England" he adores is left after the compromises, infamy, and double dealing that go into defending it.

SMILLA'S SENSE OF SNOW (1992; also tr as *Smilla's Feeling for Snow*) A mystery by Peter HOEG that became a bestseller in English translation, and deservedly so. The story takes place in Copenhagen and Greenland, and concerns Smilla Qaavigaaq Jaspersen, who is a half-Inuit glaciologist. She discovers the body of her friend Isaiah, a young boy who is also part Inuit, in front of his building in Copenhagen. She begins to investigate whether his death was accidental or not, and in the process finds out more about her friend's real circumstances, such as having a junkie for a mother. The investigation also forces her to deal with the Danish Greenlanders whom she has avoided because she sees them as aggressive colonialists, even though her father is one. Isaiah, it turns out, was in possession of dangerous information that neither the police nor other heavy interests want to see leak out. They try to quash Smilla's unofficial investigation, and to get at the truth she must make a hazardous journey by boat to Greenland. A variety of themes—colonization, the survival of indigenous culture, globalization, business, and bureaucracy—are explored in a manner both serious and satisfying; they are integral to the plot, and make the reader care not only about the outcome but the issues themselves. Even Smilla's sharing of her knowledge of snow is an entertainment that instructs.

SMITH, DUDLEY A sadistic Irish-born, Los Angeles-bred cop created by James ELLROY. Tall, powerful, and imposing, Smith is a family man with five daughters. He can be charming, when he isn't behaving like a combination enraged psychopath and defender of decency against "degenerates"—drug users, homosexuals, minorities, and other marginalized Los Angelinos. Described as a gifted "actor" able to assume many roles, Smith often forgets that he is acting and goes insane. He is a dark center of energy in such novels as *Clandestine* (1982), *White Jazz* (1992), and, most famously, *L.A. Confidential* (1990).

SMITH, MADELEINE See NOT PROVEN.

SNITCH As a term for someone who informs or squeals to the police, "snitch" has been in use since the eighteenth century. It developed out of the older slang meaning of "nose."

SNOW, C[HARLES] P[ERCY] (1905–1980) C. P. Snow, who was Baron Snow of Leicester, is best known as a scientist and the author of semi-autobiographical novels about ethics and power. In *The Two Cultures* (1959), he postulated a split between upper-class/literary culture and lower-middle-class/scientific culture, seeing the former as conservative and the latter as progressive. His best-known novels were about postwar managerial and scientific elites. Snow's career as a writer, however, was bracketed by a pair of mystery novels: DEATH UNDER SAIL (1932), his first book, and A COAT OF VARNISH (1979), his last. The latter was nominated for an EDGAR. His sociological concerns are reflected in both books, but to a much greater degree in *A Coat of Varnish.*

SNOWBOUND In the famous story (and later, play) "The Mousetrap" (1949), Agatha CHRISTIE placed her characters in a classic COUNTRY HOUSE, and then produced a snowstorm to trap them there. The technique bears comparison with shipboard mysteries: in both cases, the suspects cannot leave the scene, and opportunities for spectacular death or narrow escape are increased. Suspense is almost automatic, even without a murder; when power fails, normal visits to the house are blocked, etc. Because of these strengths, the snowbound house theme has been explored by many other writers, including Ngaio MARSH, who used it in *Death and the Dancing Footman* (1942) and *Death of a Fool* (1956); Frances and Richard LOCKRIDGE (in *Let Dead Enough Alone,* 1955); and Helen MCCLOY (*Mr. Splitfoot,* 1968). Nicholas BLAKE used snowstorms as plot elements in several books, including *The Corpse in the Snowman* (1941). Cyril HARE introduced a snowstorm effectively in AN ENGLISH MURDER (1951). Phoebe Atwood TAYLOR's *Death Lights A Candle* (1932) takes place in March on Cape Cod. More recently, a snowbound house is the setting of *The Burglar in the Library* (1997), a Bernie RHODENBARR mystery.

An interesting version of the snowbound theme is *Fire Will Freeze* (1944) by Margaret MILLAR, in which a group of skiers are stranded when their bus breaks down during a blizzard. The climax of *The Blind Man's Eyes* (1916), by Edwin BALMER and William MACHARG, takes place on a train trapped by snows.

SNOW FALLING ON CEDARS (1995) A novel by David Guterson, set on an island in Puget Sound in 1954. San Piedro is an imaginary small island south of Lopez in the San Juan Islands. Carl Heine, a salmon fisherman of German descent, is found dead in his nets after a night at sea. A Japanese-American named Kabuo Miyamoto is charged with his murder, and a complicated case develops that has much to do with the shameful treatment of Japanese Americans by the United States government (and by their fellow Americans) during World War II.

Guterson, who has also written a collection of short stories and a book about home-schooling, achieved an amazing success with *Snow Falling on Cedars,* which won several awards, including the 1995 PEN/Faulkner Award.

Investigation reveals that Heine had just put down money on a strawberry farm that included seven acres that his mother had taken from the family of Kabuo when they were sent to an internment camp, and that Kabuo had approached Heine to buy them again. Heine's head injury resembles those inflicted by the Japanese during the war using kendo sticks. The story begins with the trial. The facts are presented to the jury by various witnesses, and we are treated to their reminiscences in full detail, including the story of the Japanese community, their arrival, their hardship, the culture they try to preserve, and clashes with the white culture, especially after Pearl Harbor. The war, and particularly the invasion of Tarawa, are depicted unsparingly through the eyes of the veteran Ishmael Chambers. A subplot involves his love (and later hate) for Hatsue Imada, a beautiful Japanese girl who married Kabuo. Ishmael's self-renewal plays a vital part in the resolution; when he finds that he holds a key to the mystery, he can barely bring himself to use it.

The most remarkable thing about the book (especially in a bestseller) is Guterson's style, which is encyclopedic, historical, and ponderous. He has a difficult time completing a sentence without a digression or several qualifiers: "Nels Gudmundsson turned toward the jury. 'No more questions,' he said. And with a slowness that embarrassed him—because as a young man he had been lithe and an athlete, had always moved fluidly across the floorboards of courtrooms, had always felt admired for his physical appearance—he made his way back to his seat at the defendant's table, where Kabuo Miyamoto sat watching him." The writing is affecting, but it becomes somewhat ridiculous when *every* paragraph is so constructed. The cascade of details and slightly different emotions that fall one after another is stimulating, however; Guterson's problem is quantity, not quality—and his mannerisms have a strange charm because he obliges one to accept a slowness in pace and in thoughts that is unusual in thrillers, and that is almost dreamlike.

SOLOMON GURSKY WAS HERE (1989) A novel by Mordecai Richler (1931–), the Canadian writer known for his often humorous novels that deal with questions of identity and values, particularly *The Apprenticeship of Duddy Kravitz* (1959). *Solomon Gursky* combines these elements with a mysterious disappearance. The story is complex and includes multiple flashbacks; it appears to be based on the Bronfman family of Montreal (and the Seagrams liquor empire). The Gurskys are Jewish-Canadian liquor barons, and their brand is "McTavish." Moses Berger, a brilliant writer and terrible alcoholic, is consumed by his investigation of the fate of Solomon Gursky, one of the three Gursky brothers who founded the family business early in the twentieth century. Berger had been a boyhood friend of the younger generation of Gursky children.

Solomon, the most enterprising of the brothers, was also closest to the almost mythical Ephraim Gursky, the first of the line to emigrate to Canada. He disappeared into the far north and is considered almost a god by the native peoples. Solomon has long been thought dead, too (in a plane crash), but peculiar events, including the appearances of a strange raven symbol, lead Berger to an involved research into Gursky's last whereabouts. The book has a freewheeling, historical feeling, not unlike Robertson DAVIES's writing, but one scene is a funny parody of the HARD-BOILED style.

SOME BURIED CAESAR (1939) A novel by Rex STOUT, who said that he considered it his favorite of his Nero WOLFE stories. Although the book's plot is neither Stout's best nor his tightest, it does, particularly in its opening scenes, convey a great deal of charm and an uncanny feeling that Archie GOODWIN and Nero Wolfe are real people.

Archie and Wolfe are on a car trip when they have a break down opposite a cow pasture, which happens to contain a very large prize-winning bull. The first scene includes the comical portrait of Wolfe standing on a tall rock in the middle of the field to escape the bull, and a winded Archie encountering Lily Rowan for the first time. The subsequent goring, pitchfork murder, and romance are well done, even though the setting is Upstate New York and not the West; one suspects that Stout has willfully shoehorned his Western adventures into a Brewster mold.

"SOMEWHERE A ROSCOE . . ." A famous essay by S. J. Perelman (1904–1979), reprinted in *Crazy Like a Fox* (1945), in which he recounts his discovery of Robert Leslie BELLEM's detective, Dan Turner, in the pages of *Spicy Detective,* a risqué PULP MAGAZINE. Perelman was a talented humorist who wrote for the Marx Brothers. His love of language and word-play made Bellem a natural target for his satire. With a number of hilarious quotes from various Dan Turner episodes, he shows how "the murders follow an exact, rigid pattern almost like the ritual of a bullfight or a classic Chinese play." Bellem rewrites the same scenes over and over: "From behind me a roscoe belched 'Chow-chow!' A pair of slugs buzzed past my left ear, almost nicked my cranium"; "The roscoe said 'Chow!'

and spat a streak of flame past my shoulder"; "From a bedroom a roscoe said: 'Whr-r-rang!' and a lead pill split the ozone past my noggin." Even funnier, however, are Dan Turner's relations with women: "The fragrant scent of her red hair tickled my smeller; the warmth of her slim young form set fire to my arterial system."

SONG OF THE WORLD, THE [*Le Chant du monde,* 1934, tr 1937] A novel by French writer Jean Giono (1895–1970). Giono said that he wanted "to make a story of adventure in which there should be absolutely nothing 'timely.'" The novel is set in a mythic version of Giono's Provence in which everything, including the stones, forests, and rivers, is invested with spirit and a poetic eroticism. The story concerns the disappearance of Sailor's red-haired son. A seventy-five-year-old man with a white beard and toughened body, Sailor sets out with Antonio, a golden-tongued man of the river, for the sinister Rebeillard country where the son has vanished. They quickly learn that the red-haired man and a woman are being sought all over the country by the servants of Maudru, a landowner and rancher who has made himself the tyrant of the Rebeillard. Giono's nature is cruel and violent as well as beautiful, qualities that erupt in people who are not separated from nature by even a hair's breadth.

SON OF THE CIRCUS, A See IRVING, JOHN.

SOUVESTRE, PIERRE (1874–1914) One of the French co-authors of the series of novels about FANTÔMAS. Souvestre was born to a wealthy family in Brittany and entered the field of law. Smitten by the newly invented automobile, he later gave up his career to become a writer for automotive journals and the magazine *Poids Lourds* ("Trucks"). He was also a drama critic. His meeting with Marcel ALLAIN led to their collaboration on the Fantômas books, which were an enormous success. Souvestre died in 1914 of influenza just at the height of the Fantômas craze, following the release of the first Fantômas films.

SPADE, SAM The tough and cynical detective in THE MALTESE FALCON (1929). Spade looms large in the history of detective fiction and in the minds of readers, despite the fact that he appeared in only one novel. Spade also does not look anything like Humphrey Bogart. The opening passage of the novel describes him as a "blond Satan," with a hooked nose and a V-shaped face. He is also not a very romantic character; cunning and cold, he is suspected in his partner's death because he does not even bother to look at the body before the police take it away. Somerset MAUGHAM called Spade "a nasty bit of goods," but what is really brilliant about Spade's portrayal is how it shows that a "code of honor"—the pride and joy of most HARD-BOILED dicks—is a two-edged sword, one side of which is always cutting. Spade's loyalty to the memory of a partner he didn't even like leads him to betray a woman he loved, much to the disgust of his secretary, Effie Perine. Spade is far more believable than other tough guys who never get any scratches on their escutcheons. Spade became a much more romantic figure on the screen. In the book he is tough and absolutely unsentimental.

The Adventures of Sam Spade and Other Stories (1944) includes three other appearances by Spade.

SPEAKEASIES See PROHIBITION.

"SPECIALTY OF THE HOUSE, THE" See ELLIN, STANLEY.

SPENSER The one-name hero of a series of books by Robert B. PARKER. Parker named his private investigator after the English poet Edmund Spenser and infused him with his own love of literature. A former policeman, Spenser operates in the Boston area. Supposedly, he lost his job with the District Attorney because of insubordination (shades of Philip MARLOWE). An avid cook and a weightlifter, Spenser is six feet, once inch tall and weighs two hundred pounds. Spenser's vaunted sensitivity and sophistication is sometimes perplexing; in his first case, *The Godwulf Manuscript* (1975), he doesn't know what an illuminated manuscript is, but is familiar with the philosopher Herbert Marcuse. Parker is an imitator of HAMMETT and CHANDLER, and some of Spenser's dialogue is very witty, particularly in LOOKING FOR RACHEL WALLACE (1980). At other times, he is childish and unfunny. Spenser's official contact is Lieutenant Marty Quirk who, in the tradition of Bernie OHLS, both likes and dislikes him.

Spenser is assisted by another one-name entity, Hawk, an African American distinguished by his lack of conscience. (Quirk calls him Spenser's "pet shark.") This type of character has since become very popular as a convenient source of shortcuts, whether to information or punishment. Hawk consorts with criminals as well as with Spenser; they met while both were pursuing boxing careers. Bald, dark-eyed, and snappily dressed, Hawk's presence sometimes has the effect of weakening Spenser's character: by having someone else do the things he would like to do but that violate his knightly code, Spenser essentially negates that code anyway, and worse, does it by proxy. But Spenser is often pretty lenient with himself. In *Early Autumn* (1981), Spenser refuses to kill a man whom he has just beaten senseless, so Hawk does; Hawk's amorality is consistent, at least, while Spenser's code comes out looking thin. In a book almost devoid of detection, Spenser uses burglary and blackmail to compel the neat solution he wants.

Unlike MARLOWE, one of his inspirations—he even has a torrid affair with a woman named after Linda Loring, Marlowe's love in THE LONG GOODBYE (1953)—Spenser kills a lot of people. If it weren't for his many other laboriously developed qualities, he would be more reminiscent of Mike HAMMER. As it is, demonstrations of Spenser's pugilistic vigor are frequent, particularly because of his lack of investigative finesse. Unlike his antecedents, Spenser primarily gets his information by threatening and quite often by beating up his informants. (A real Spenser would almost certainly be in jail.) On the other hand, Spenser has a long-term relationship (interrupted for a while in the series) with an independent woman, Susan Silverman, an educator and intellectual. His torrid affair with Brenda Loring in *Mortal Stakes* (1975) is uncomplicated, frankly physical, and without the usual mental gymnastics that Spenser and Susan force each other to perform. In some of the books, the consumption of bourbon, a time-honored tradition of the HARD-BOILED, is supplemented by long descriptions of the preparation of meals. The padding has come to take up a larger proportion of the stories as the series goes on.

BIBLIOGRAPHY Novels: *God Save the Child* (1974), *A Savage Place* (1981), *Ceremony* (1982), *The Widening Gyre* (1983), *Valediction* (1984), *Taming a Seahorse* (1986), *Pale Kings and Princes* (1987), *Crimson Joy* (1988), *Playmates* (1989), *Stardust* (1990), *Pastime* (1991), *Double Deuce* (1992), *Paper Doll* (1993), *Walking Shadow* (1994), *Thin Air* (1995), *Chance* (1996), *Small Vices* (1997), *Sudden Mischief* (1998), *Hush Money* (1999).

SPILLANE, MICKEY (Frank Morrison Spillane, 1918–) American HARD-BOILED detective story writer. With the character Mike HAMMER, Spillane created the toughest of private detectives. The stories have been criticized for excessive and even sadistic violence, as well as for sexism.

Spillane was born in Brooklyn. He served in the air force in World War II and now lives in North Carolina. He attended Kansas State College and worked as a lifeguard before becoming a writer. Initially, he wrote for PULP MAGAZINES and comic books. Although he has had several series characters (another is Cat Fallon, a pilot), they have not matched Hammer's enormous popularity. The first of the Hammer novels, *I, the Jury* (1947), sold six million copies.

Spillane has become the writer to cite when complaining about violence in the genre, but some other hard-boiled writers have done no better, or have done worse; however, they have disappeared and Spillane has not. Regardless, the Mike Hammer stories are really like comic books though some academics have treated them with comical seriousness. One essay, "Towards a Semiotic Reading of Mickey Spillane," makes such observations as, "The denomination [Hammer] has a definite semantic content which, at the lexamatic level, increases the disjunction murderer-avenger"—meaning that "Hammer" personifies a hammer. Hammer has mellowed overtime. Believability has not increased, however; in *Black Alley* (1996), Hammer has been shot in New York with a .357 magnum and nursed back to health by an alcoholic doctor in his own home and then is taken to Florida, without ever going to the hospital.

Just as the genius detective of the HOLMES era eventually could no longer be borne and gave rise to plain inspectors like FRENCH, the character who "lived to kill so that others could live," who justifies murder as "taking the blood of the bastards who make murder their business" is an anachronism. Hammer has been humanized somewhat, and, most recently, almost got married, but he has yet to join civilization. As far as the writing is concerned, Hammer's narration has the same staccato belligerence of Race WILLIAMS, while the romantic scenes are stagey and often inadvertently comical ("her breasts were laughing things that were firmly in place").

Spillane has written non-series work, and it is somewhat better. *Killer Mine* (1965), a novelette, is about a cop named Joe Scanlon who is sent back into the slum where he was born to find a serial killer who is murdering men who were all his boyhood friends. He is teamed up with Marta Borlig, whom he knew as a girl; their relationship, and Scanlon's feelings about his past, show degrees of intelligence and depth of which Hammer is incapable.

SPY WHO CAME IN FROM THE COLD, THE (1963) A novel by John LE CARRÉ, and one of the best spy stories ever written. Alec LEAMAS is a fiftyish spy who has come to the end of his career. He has been recalled from West Berlin after the last of his agents has been liquidated by the other side, led by the vicious head of the East German secret service, Hans-Dieter Mundt (who we learn almost killed George SMILEY, now in virtual retirement). Leamas is drawn into a plot to get rid of Mundt.

It is the essence of spying to say one thing and do another. Leamas is the one who most despises this falseness, yet is trapped into it just the same. Indeed, his efforts to escape it are factored into the game by his superiors as yet further tactical moves. Love and innocence can be turned into weapons—like beating ploughshares into swords—and make perfect covers for the subtlest manipulations. Leamas notes that the methods of both sides are Leninist—"the expediency of temporary alliances" reducing them to same level. But though they have become immoral and believe only in expediency, he defends the intelligence people for preventing even worse people who believe in something (the fanatics and ideologues of the Cold War) from blowing up the world. It is tempting to see the ending as redemptive along the lines of Graham GREENE's novels (Greene said it was the best spy story he had ever read), but LeCarré does not allow the idea of nobility of the soul (or the idea of a soul, for that matter) to come through untainted, as Greene does. In a sense, because Leamas's gesture is futile—it is already too late—it only satisfies his pride. Unlike the very similar situation of the whisky priest at the end of Greene's *The Power and the Glory* (1940), Leamas does not submit to fate, but creates it.

STAGG, CLINTON See COLTON, THORNLEY.

STAGGE, JONATHAN The pseudonym under which Patrick QUENTIN wrote about Dr. Hugh WESTLAKE.

STAIN ON THE SNOW, THE (*La Neige était sale*, 1948; tr 1953) One of the novels by Georges SIMENON not about MAIGRET, *The Stain on the Snow* has been more highly praised than any of his detective novels. It is a chilling story about a group of disturbed and disturbing people who frequent Timo's, a dive that attracts a macabre clientele from among the residents of an urban slum. "The Eunuch" is a gross beast who sits in Timo's with two thin brunettes (not always the same two), one on each knee. The braggart Kromer claims to have strangled a girl while he was having sex with her in a barn because she said she wanted to have a baby. Perhaps most disturbing of all is Frank Friedmaier, a young man who almost believes Kromer's tale and envies him his callousness about the supposed murder. Frank sets out to cold-bloodedly kill a man to make himself feel superior. He decides to borrow Kromer's knife and to murder The Eunuch with it. But as he waits in the shadows of a tannery for The Eunuch to come up the alley, he hears different footsteps, which turn out to be those of his stern neighbor, Gerhardt Holst. What Frank decides to do then is the heart of the novel.

Simenon uses these characters to meditate on the nature of evil. It seems less an actual quality than the complete absence of something else, perhaps a moral sense. Whether Frank is innately evil or whether it is something in his environment that leads him to commit acts without compunction is a problem of psychology Simenon wrestled with through much of his work, but never as shockingly as in *The Stain on the Snow*.

STANDISH, TIGER See HORLER, SYDNEY.

STARK, RICHARD The pseudonym under which Donald WESTLAKE wrote his series about the thief, PARKER.

STARRETT, [CHARLES] VINCENT [EMERSON] (1886–1974) Born in Toronto, Vincent Starrett moved permanently to Chicago, where he became a book reviewer for the *Tribune*. His greatest impact on the mystery genre was through his reviewing and his work on Sherlock HOLMES. His books include *The Private Life of Sherlock Holmes* (1933) and the Holmes pastiche, *The Unique Hamlet* (1920). He was one of the founders of the BAKER STREET IRREGULARS, and wrote some original detective stories himself, including those about Jimmie Lavender. *The Case Book of Jimmie Lavender* (1944) collects some of the stories. Another sleuth, Walter Ghost, appeared in such novels as *Murder on B Deck* (1929) and *The End of Mr. Garment* (1932). Starrett's correspondence with Anthony BOUCHER is contained in *Sincerely, Tony/Faithfully, Vincent* (1975). He also wrote an autobiography, *Born in a Bookshop* (1965).

STATE VERSUS ELINOR NORTON, THE (1934) A novel by Mary Roberts RINEHART, and her masterpiece. Set among the world of upper-class New Yorkers before and after World War I, the novel is about class morals and individual desires, particularly as it relates to a woman's need to conform socially in Rinehart's time and her contrasting need to be a person rather than the thing her society, and often her husband, considers her. Read in the context of Rinehart's autobiography and the questions with which she struggled, it is also a very personal book with no HAD-I-BUT-KNOWN camouflage.

The story begins with Elinor's trial for the murder of Blair Leighton. Carroll Warner, the narrator, then tells the entire saga in retrospect. He explains how Elinor, the most stunning young woman of her generation and class, came to marry the neurotic Lloyd Norton and not the massive, vibrant, and brutal Leighton, whom she really loved. The maturity of the book and the depth of its psychology are striking; it talks about estrangement, Elinor's womanizing father and his "final *faux pas*"—to sleep with his wife again after many years and thus to give her Elinor, before dying in the arms of a mistress. There is a frankness about sex, without ever directly revealing it. The complexity of Elinor's relations with her mother is related to the repression of her emotions and her feeling of an inability to love, which in turn leads her to marry Norton and to deny herself Leighton.

Warner met Elinor as a child and fell in love with her, though he was several levels below her in New York–Newport society; Rinehart describes a "social Rubicon" between the East Side and West Side, and Warner is on the wrong side. In 1913, she marries Norton, and Warner is crushed and does not see her for several years. The war changes everyone, Elinor perhaps most of all when she meets and falls in love with the blond and charming Englishman Blair Leighton. Warner returns from the war a different man; Norton returns a hero but hardly a man at all, with a "mental and physical impotence." Rinehart vividly suggests the hell of Elinor's life with Norton, who worships Leighton. The perversion of Norton's fascination with the man his wife loves is that of a neurasthenic for the "blond beast" he would like to be. It is easy to believe how Leighton lures Norton to Montana to start a ranch and live the rough, masculine life. After Leighton buys a half interest in the Norton ranch and moves in, a disastrous triangle is set up. From afar, Warner continues to play the best friend and is tortured by Elinor's confidences even as he seeks them. In the quadrangle of Elinor and the three men, Rinehart describes sex without love, love without sex, and nightmarish relationships with neither. She might not have added a killing to the book at all, but it gives the novel its sense of inevitability, as if it began at the top of a hill and accelerated downward.

STEIN, AARON MARK (1906–1985) A native New Yorker, Aaron Mark Stein used his extensive knowledge of the city to create several series characters, including a glum New York City police Inspector named SCHMIDT and Assistant District Attorney GIBSON. Of the hundred-odd novels Stein wrote, the Schmidt books are among the most readable. They were written under the name George Bagby, and the character Bagby is also the WATSON of the stories. Begun in 1935 (*Murder at the Piano*), the series gives colorful views of New York over a period of almost fifty years. One of the best books, however, takes place in Franco's Spain (*The Body in the Basket,* 1954), where Bagby has gotten into trouble and Inspector Schmidt must rescue him. The Gibson books were published under the name Hampton Stone.

Stein worked as a journalist for the *New York Post* and *Time* in the thirties before he started his career as a novelist. He graduated from Princeton in 1927 with a degree in classics and archaeology, and was also a Phi Beta Kappa member. He served in World War II, and because of his knowledge of languages was involved in cryptography.

Stein's first novels were experimental, literary, and unremunerative. With his scholarly background, it is not surprising that the details of atmosphere and setting in his mysteries are convincing. The style is generic, and as with any author who writes several books a year, there is a breeziness and lack of ballast. In his books, it is often where they are rather than who they are that makes people interesting. Stein liked to travel, and created a traveling pair of archaeologists, Tim Mulligan and Elsie Mae Hunt, who appeared in a series of eighteen mysteries concurrently with his Schmidt and Gibson books. He also wrote about an engineer named Matt ERRIDGE who works in exotic locales and investigates mysteries. Stein was named a Grand Master by the Mystery Writers of America in 1979.

STEPS GOING DOWN (1985) A novel by Joseph HANSEN, not part of the Dave BRANDSTETTER series. *Steps Going Down* is grimmer and more relentless than Hansen's p.i. novels, perhaps because of its lack of romanticism and stricter realism; it is a crime story rather than a mystery. Darryl Cutler is a hustler, a handsome gay man who lives off older, wealthier men. He is working and caring for Stewart Moody, an invalid who has a business typing movie scripts for authors, when he meets a younger, blonde version of himself, Chick Pelletier. Petulant, demanding, utterly selfish and cruel, Pelletier is like a gay version of Varda Pierce (daughter of MILDRED PIERCE). He "always tells the truth," and what he says cuts with a razor-like selfishness. What makes the book affecting is that Darryl is both victim and victimizer—a disappointed boy who craves love, and a manipulative man who craves power and comforts. Thus, he is no match for Chick's single-mindedness and peculiar, evil courage. The murders in the book are seemingly perfect, and Hansen pulls off a neat but believable tie-up at the end.

STERLING, STEWART (pseudonym of Prentice Winchell, 1895–?) Stewart Sterling wrote several mystery series, but it was the last of them, the books about Don CADEE, for which he is best known—or rather, for which Spenser Dean is known. Under this pseudonym-of-a-pseudonym, Winchell wrote nine novels about the head of store security for Amblett's, a swanky Fifth Avenue department store perhaps modeled on the now defunct Altman's. The first book in the series was *The Frightened Fingers* (1954).

Sterling was born in Illinois. He wrote for newspapers, PULP MAGAZINES, and for radio. Like many pulp authors, he used a variety of pseudonyms and wrote different lines of stories in various subgenres. Dexter St. Clair, Dexter St.

Clare, and Jay de Bekker were other avatars of Sterling. As a novelist, Sterling wrote about detectives in special professions, but he went far afield to avoid the more obvious subgenres, such as newspaperman detectives. He published in various magazines, including BLACK MASK, in which odd character types were common. Sterling must have invented the HARD-BOILED fireman in his first series, about a fire marshal named Ben PEDLEY who hunts down arsonists; the first Pedley novel was *Five Alarm Funeral* (1942). *Dead Wrong* (1947) introduced Gil VINE, a hotel detective at New York's Plaza Royale (fifteen years before the advent of Pierre CHAMBRUN).

Sterling's work bears comparison with that of Erle Stanley GARDNER. Gardner eventually turned to dictation to produce his hundreds of novels; Sterling's writing is similarly light, and sometimes sounds as rambling as a story told to a tape recorder without the subsequent developments previously thought out. Sterling, however, dutifully inserted clues, even if they were silly (a murder victim's monogrammed lighter pocketed by one of the conspirators). He also avoided scenes he could not or would not write, and thus his books are free of peek-a-boo sex or melodramatic romance. The Cadee novels are his latest and best work, leading to the tempting speculation that Sterling, at the end of his career, no longer had to write at the breakneck pace of a thirties pulpsmith.

STEVENS, GAVIN A lawyer in Jefferson, Mississippi, in several works by William FAULKNER, most notably *Knight's Gambit* (1939). He also appears in INTRUDER IN THE DUST (1948), though his role in defending Lucas Beauchamp is less important than Chick MALLISON's. Stevens also was a central character in *The Town* (1957), which deals humorously with his unrequited love, and *The Mansion* (1959). Neither is a mystery (though the latter deals partly with Mink Snopes's effort to murder his powerful cousin, Flem).

Stevens is presented as an educated and enlightened man, in high contrast to some of his neighbors, such as the Snopes clan. He has been educated at Harvard and Heidelberg (he is also a member of Phi Beta Kappa), and is now the county attorney in Jackson, Mississippi; thus, he is charged with investigating crimes like a D.A. He is "loose-jointed," with "a mop of untidy iron-gray hair," and is as comfortable discussing Einstein as he is jawing with the locals around the general store during one of his "vacations." This is how he picks up the information and local lore that he uses to help solve his cases. In fact, he says, what is needed for success in law and politics is not intelligence and eloquence but "an infallible memory for names."

Some of the stories in *Knight's Gambit* are told by Chick Mallison, including one of Steven's more deductive puzzles, "Hand Upon the Waters," a sad and beautifully written story having to do with the murder of one of two gentle and slow-witted orphans, found being eaten by fish on his own trot-line. (MONK is another retarded man, who is easily manipulated and railroaded.) "Tomorrow" is a retrospective story about the one case Stevens had before he became county attorney, and which he lost precisely because he didn't know some important local history about a couple—a hard-bitten grandfather and his dirt-poor but iron-willed son.

STEVENSON, ROBERT LOUIS (1850–1894) A writer known more for his adventure tales, such as *Treasure Island* (1883) and *Kidnapped* (1886), Robert Louis Stevenson skirted the mystery genre on many occasions. At the end of his life, Stevenson said with chagrin that he was read mostly by boys, thanks to his adventure stories and the huge success of *A Child's Garden of Verses* (1885). Yet many of Stevenson's best stories are adult tales of murder, suicide, and madness. Some are horrific, like *Dr. Jekyl and Mr. Hyde* (1886), or macabre, such as "Thrawn Janet" (1887), a story of demonic possession written mostly in Scottish dialect. However categorized, Stevenson was a master at creating the feeling of mystery and dread.

Stevenson was born in Edinburgh, Scotland. His father was an engineer, and Stevenson at first followed in his father's footsteps, studying engineering at the University of Edinburgh. He later abandoned that field and took up the law. He was called to the bar in 1875 but never practiced, instead becoming an essayist and travel writer. He went to California in 1879 in pursuit of the woman with whom he was in love, Fanny Vandegrift Osbourne, an American who was separated from her husband. The pair had met three years before while Stevenson was staying in an artist's colony in France. They married and returned to Scotland in 1880. Stevenson's restlessness continued, and the couple wandered about Europe until 1888. In that year, Stevenson, who was plagued by tuberculosis all his life, moved permanently to the South Seas. He died in Samoa. The book that Graham GREENE considered Stevenson's masterpiece, *Weir of Hermiston* (1896), was left incomplete at the time of his death.

Stevenson's most anthologized mysterious tales are THE WRECKER (1892) and THE SUICIDE CLUB (1882). *The Wrecker* was written in collaboration with his stepson, Lloyd Osbourne (1868–1947). In *The Wrecker*, smuggling was combined with murder and fraud. The same volume that contained "The Suicide Club" also included THE PAVILION ON THE LINKS (1882), a story set on the remote

Scottish coast that also brought nautical and crime themes together. In MARKHEIM (1887), Stevenson produced a prototypical study of the criminal mind that contains a shocking and all too believable piece of violence. "The Dynamiter" (1885) and "The Wrong Box" (1889) also involve mystery and crime; the latter hinges on a TONTINE.

There has been a great revival of interest in Stevenson in recent years (not only among boys). Graham GREENE established its terms in a now famous essay "From Feathers to Iron" (1948), in which he drew attention to what Stevenson was not (the "pale hollow stuffed figure in a velvet jacket"), dismissed his juvenilia, and praised his late work in which "the granite was coming painfully through." Recent biographies of Stevenson and also of Fanny Vandegrift Stevenson have been published: *Robert Louis Stevenson: A Biography* (1993) by Frank McLynn and *Fanny Stevenson: A Romance of Destiny* (1995) by Alexandra LaPierre. Lloyd Osbourne went on to write crime thrillers of his own, none of which were of Stevenson's caliber.

STIR, IN STIR See CAN.

"STOLEN CIGAR CASE, THE" (1902) A short story by Bret HARTE, parodying Conan DOYLE. The narrator, a doctor, visits the brilliant sleuth Hemlock Jones in Brook Street. This pseudo-WATSON, having sat himself at the feet of the great man and having "gently caressed his boot," is amazed when Jones demonstrates that it is raining merely by such indications as that the doctor's umbrella is wet. The cigar case, encrusted with diamonds, was presented to Jones by the Turkish Ambassador and is presumed stolen. In Jones's attempts to track down the thief, Harte parodies Sherlock HOLMES's famous techniques of disguise, his immodest speeches, and his condescension to Doctor Watson—only this Watson has the last laugh.

STONE, FLEMING A private detective in a long series of novels by Carolyn WELLS. Stone was the next major American detective character created by a woman after Anna Katherine Green's Ebenezer GRYCE. Stone differs from Gryce, however, in almost every respect, indicating changes in the genre in the generations that separated the two writers. Stone is a GENIUS DETECTIVE of the post-HOLMES era, attractive, tall, urbane, and possessed of encyclopedic knowledge. Others refer to him as "The Great Man." The books also have various bumbling policemen who are mystified by the cases Stone so brilliantly solves—another common element of the genius detective style. Wells realized that this kind of story absolutely ruled out realism; the books are only realistic in the sense of internal consistency.

Although Stone is a genius, Wells did not make him wildly eccentric in the manner of Philo VANCE or even mildly so, in the style of Lord Peter WIMSEY. He is not scientific, like his contemporary Doctor THORNDYKE; he is not vaguely comical, like HANAUD. His physical unmemorability and lack of bizarre attributes accounts for why Fleming Stone has been forgotten and left out of print, even though he appeared in more than sixty mysteries and had one of the longest careers of any fictional detective. His main feature is that he is a book lover—like his creator, who was a librarian.

It seems unfair, however, that while Vance is remembered as a literary excrescence, the more tolerable Stone is given short shrift by critics (none of the Stone books are discussed by BARZUN and TAYLOR, and he is not given an entry in PENZLER and Steinbrunner's work). Readers have not even the possibility of encountering his adventures except in antique book shops. *The Master Murderer* (1933) is about the death of an heiress and widow who has cancer. The question is immediately raised whether it was a "mercy death," or a venal one perpetrated by one of her three children and heirs. The book is not highly original, but it shows Wells working in the same milieu as Green, that of upper-class New York, but writing better. Titles like *The Importance of Being Murdered* (1939) also demonstrate that Wells had a sufficient degree of cleverness and wit. She also resisted the HAD-I-BUT-KNOWN formula so popular at the time, and her romantic subplots are less off-putting and silly than they might be. In such a long series, Wells found it necessary to vary her settings occasionally from the Fifth Avenue demi-monde. In *Triple Murder* (1929), Fleming Stone has gone to the Adirondacks to help a friend write a crime play. While staying at a hotel, he sees a woman murdered right in front of him. *The Beautiful Derelict* (1935) is not about a dissipated socialite, but a ship—a case of MURDER AFLOAT and a version of the by now ancient ghost ship or flying Dutchman theme.

BIBLIOGRAPHY Novels: *The Clue* (1909), *The Gold Bag* (1911), *A Chain of Evidence* (1912), *The Maxwell Mystery* (1913), *Anybody But Anne* (1914), *The Whit Alley* (1915), *The Curved Blades* (1916), *The Mark of Cain* (1917), *Vicky Van* (1918), *The Diamond Pin* (1919), *Raspberry Jam* (1920), *The Mystery of the Sycamore* (1921), *The Mystery Girl* (1922), *Feathers Left Around* (1923), *Spooky Hollow* (1923), *The Furthest Fury* (1924), *Prilligirl* (1924), *Anything But the Truth* (1925), *The Daughter of the House* (1925), *The Bronze Hand* (1926), *The Red-Haired Girl* (1926), *All at Sea* (1927), *Where's Emily* (1927), *The Crime in the Crypt* (1928), *The Tannahill Tangle* (1928), *The Tapestry Room Murder* (1929),

The Doomed Five (1930), *The Ghosts' High Noon* (1930), *Horror House* (1931), *The Umbrella Murder* (1931), *Fuller's Earth* (1932), *The Roll-Top Desk Mystery* (1932), *The Broken O* (1933), *The Clue of the Eyelash* (1933), *Eyes in the Wall* (1934), *In the Tiger's Cage* (1934), *The Visiting Villain* (1934), *For Goodness Sake* (1935), *The Wooden Indian* (1935), *The Huddle* (1936), *Money Musk* (1936), *Murder in the Bookshop* (1936), *The Mystery of the Tarn* (1937), *The Radio Studio Murder* (1937), *Gilt-Edged Guilt* (1938), *The Killer* (1938), *The Missing Link* (1938), *Calling All Suspects* (1939), *Crime Tears On* (1939), *Crime Incarnate* (1940), *Devil's Work* (1940), *Murder on Parade* (1940), *Murder Plus* (1940), *The Black Night Murders* (1941), *Murder at the Casino* (1941), *Who Killed Caldwell* (1942).

STONER, HARRY A private detective character created by Jonathan VALIN. Stoner is almost a composite of earlier detectives, yet remains distinct. Like Philip MARLOWE, he used to work for the district attorney's office; like Dashiell HAMMETT himself, he is also a former PINKERTON man; and like Brock CALLAHAN, he is a former football player. With a face like "a busted statue," Stoner is not quite as big as Travis MCGEE, but he has a similar "sensitive" side and a streak of the social critic. Stoner describes himself as "sixties to the bone," and he looks at America from the opposite end of that decade from McGee. He served in Vietnam, and says he has been drinking since he got back, because of "things you see, things you do . . ." Stoner misses the decade's lost idealism and freedom and feels contempt for the cynicism and greed of the Reagan-Bush era, which stands like a continental divide between the past and the current "era of bad feelings." His attitude is not purely nostalgic, however; he admits to being "square," and has no illusions about the havoc wreaked on those sixties casualties who could not move on and are permanently stuck in the past—or who did not survive at all.

Stoner's native turf, Cincinnati, looms large in the series. The economic decay of the Rust Belt and the subsequent social deterioration are foregrounded from the very first novel, *The Lime Pit* (1980), in which Stoner tries to find a teenage runaway who has disappeared into the sleazy world of crime and prostitution. In *Day of Wrath* (1981), he is again looking for a runaway, and in the process conducts another survey of corruption. *Natural Causes* (1983) has a murder investigation that takes Stoner inside the world of television. A writer for a soap opera has been killed, and behind the glamour and power of the medium Stoner finds the same base motives, exploitation, and greed that operate in the brothels and dives. FINAL NOTICE (1981) is about a crazed killer who begins by vandalizing library books. LIFE'S WORK (1986) is one of the most violent books and takes Stoner inside the world of professional football. *The Music Lovers* (1993) contains some of Valin's best characterizations and is set among a small group of mutually envious stereo geeks who obsessively collect albums but listen to their systems, not the music.

BIBLIOGRAPHY Novels: *Dead Letter* (1981), *Fire Lake* (1987), *Extenuating Circumstances* (1989), *Second Chance* (1991), *Missing* (1995).

STONEWALL See GAY MYSTERIES.

STONEWARE MONKEY, THE (1938) A novel by R. Austin FREEMAN. The first part of the story is told by Dr. James Oldfield, a young doctor who was a student of Dr. THORNDYKE. Oldfield has established a fledgling practice on the fringes of a rundown artistic neighborhood. There he meets an apparently famous ceramicist, Gannet, who comes to him with an unusual case of gastroenteritis—which turns out to be arsenic poisoning. Gannet's household consists only of himself, his wife, and a young maid; he shares his studio with his wife's cousin, a jeweler. He decides not to go to the police, and instead reveals to those close to him that he knows his illness was not an accident in order to deter further attempts. Oldfield becomes friendly with Gannet and learns a lot about his techniques (as does the reader). One day, Gannet disappears. His wife comes home to an empty house, and also finds that her cousin is missing. The case is taken over by Thorndyke and the police, and under the vigilant but mystified eyes of Dr. Jervis, the detective unravels the story.

Although the Thorndyke books are not known for their humor, in this case there is some humorous discussion of art from a period when modernism was still controversial. Freeman actually sculpted the object of the title in clay, a rather hideous humanoid figure.

STOOLIE A "stool pigeon" was literally a decoy. In the nineteenth century, it developed another meaning: someone who is used by the police to lure criminals into a trap. Hence the current meaning of *stoolie,* someone who betrays or informs on his fellows.

STOUT, REX (1886–1975) Born in Indiana from a long line of Quakers, Rex Stout lived an exciting, varied, and successful life before he created Nero WOLFE and Archie GOODWIN. Wolfe first appears in FER-DE-LANCE (1934), which Stout wrote when he was nearly fifty. Before that, Stout had published in PULP MAGAZINES and had produced several novels in that mode, most of which are now out of print, as well as several literary novels. He also wrote poetry and had spent periods in Paris exploring the Bohemian life and roughing it out West in the manner of Teddy ROOSEVELT (whom he would come to know). It is important to note, however, that though Stout wrote from a young age, writing was a pleasure rather than a vocation, and he continued to pursue a wide array of activities in other fields at the same time from his estate in Brewster, New York.

Wherever one turns in examining Rex Stout's life, one finds the exceptional and the strange. He was distantly related both to Mary Franklin, Benjamin Franklin's sister, and to the family of Daniel DEFOE, and was a sixth cousin twice removed of Hubert Humphrey. One of Stout's ancestors was shipwrecked at Sandy Hook, New Jersey, in 1642; after being scalped and partially disemboweled by Indians, she recovered and lived to more than one hundred. As a child, Stout showed exceptional intelligence. He had read the Bible through by the age of five, and at ten he toured Kansas, where the Stouts then lived, as a mathematical prodigy. Stout's parents did not have an easy relationship; they did not speak to each other during the last twenty-five years of their marriage except through a third party, though they lived in the same house.

In 1905, Stout joined the Navy, in which he learned accounting and was eventually assigned to President Theodore Roosevelt's yacht *Mayflower.* After serving for two years, he began a period of wanderings and started to write, at first for pulp magazines. In 1916, Stout's brother Bob and a partner came to him with an idea for a school banking system, later to be known as the Educational Thrift Service. This was not a bank for schools, but for their students. Stout designed the mechanisms of the ETS, which helped public school students save money while assisting the banks in keeping track of hundreds of thousands of tiny accounts. When implemented on a vast scale, the ETS proved highly profitable and made Stout financially secure. Stout traveled extensively during this period and met many of the famous writers of the time, including H. G. WELLS. *How Like A God* (1929), a serious psychological novel, was written while Stout was in Paris.

In the thirties Stout embarked on detective story writing. In addition to Nero Wolfe, he experimented with other characters, including the detectives Doll BONNER and Tecumseh FOX. Stout's contribution to the development of the genre was large: although Sherlock HOLMES had his WATSON, it has often been observed that by providing the GENIUS DETECTIVE (Wolfe) with a tough guy as an assistant (Goodwin), Stout effected a marriage of the English detective story tradition with the American HARD-BOILED school. This hybridization is most apparent in the early novels in the Wolfe series, which are noticeably more reliant on action. SOME BURIED CAESAR (1939), Stout's favorite among the Wolfe novels, concerns the projected barbecuing of a $45,000 prize Guernsey bull and contains one of the most stomach-churning murders in the series. It is also the novel in which Archie Goodwin first meets Lily Rowan, his friend and perhaps lover.

Stout had enormous energy, not all of which was expended on writing. (In fact, members of his family reported that he wrote only a couple of months a year.) A polymath, he designed and built his own furniture and the house he lived in. He cultivated food and flowers, and was active politically, particularly (and rather rabidly) as an anti-German propagandist during World War II. After the war, he was a promoter of world government and the United Nations, and a champion of author's rights. He was twice president of the Author's League, from which position he orchestrated a successful battle with publishing companies to try to get author's royalties improved.

Stout almost never revised and wrote his novels in a matter of weeks, which has been taken as a further testament to his genius. The books might, however, have had more depth and relied less on the redeployment of the stock situation had he reworked them. At the same time, Stout had a natural grace when he was "on" that makes the books perfect in their way. His stories might be called "entertainments" in the sense of the word given to it by Graham GREENE. Stout's novellas often appeared first in serialized versions in *The American Magazine.* An abridged version of *Fer-de-Lance* was published in the magazine in 1934, two days before the book came out.

The eighty-six novels and stories featuring Wolfe vary in quality. Among the most admired are THE LEAGUE OF FRIGHTENED MEN (1935), frequently listed as one of the best mysteries of all time; A RIGHT TO DIE (1964), the sequel to *Too Many Cooks* (1938); THE DOORBELL RANG (1965), Stout's attack on the extra-legal methods of the F.B.I.; AND BE A VILLAIN (1948), which begins with Wolfe volunteering to solve a case to pay his upcoming taxes; *The Rubber Band* (1936), which, like *The League of Frightened Men,* is based on an old pact between a group of men; MURDER BY THE BOOK (1951), in which an unpublished manuscript causes a woman to be pushed out a window and also leads to other murders; and *The Silent Speaker* (1946), involving union politics and in which a furious search is conducted by all hands for a cylinder from a dictaphone.

Another novel often mentioned in a list of Stout's best is *Prisoner's Base* (1952), in which, largely because of Nero Wolfe's notorious greed, a potential client is killed. Only Archie Goodwin feels guilty, however, and begins an investigation all on his own. He quickly gets himself arrested, and, for the first time, Goodwin becomes not Wolfe's assistant, but his client. *The Golden Spiders* (1953) has some similar features. Wolfe is approached by a twelve-year-old named Pete who washes car windows at stop lights. He has seen a woman passing in a Cadillac who mouths to him to get a policeman. A rapid series of deaths ensues before Wolfe has made up his mind what to do. As often happens in the series, he has no evidence, and fabricates ruses and temptations to trap the killer, such as offering information for sale (whether he has it or not) and seeing who wants to buy it.

Stout looked back fondly on his western experiences and tried to incorporate them into the Wolfe series, for example in the rescue from hanging in *The Rubber Band. The Mountain Cat* was set in the west, and concerned a rich woman rather than a puma. Stout was less successful with *Death of a Dude* (1969) in making something out of Wolfe's discomfort when leaving his house, his city, and his state. The ageless Wolfe seems rather tired on his trip to a Montana dude ranch, and is merely going through the motions. It might have been an interesting moment to let Archie handle a case himself, but the experiment was never made.

Often overlooked among the Wolfe output are the volumes of novellas, packaged in threes. Since Stout was best at developing plot through dialogue and Wolfe's disgruntled and laconic monologues, the compression of the short form was a problem. The short works do have some original touches, such as a murder by tetanus.

The authoritative biography of Stout is John J. McAleer's EDGAR-winning *Rex Stout: A Biography* (1977). The author knew Stout for years and provides a vast amount of information and anecdote, though it is not a very critical biography. See also BASEBALL.

STRANGER IN MY GRAVE, A (1960) Margaret MILLAR's *A Stranger in My Grave,* considered a classic by many, is a more orthodox mystery than most of her others. It focuses on a young woman in danger and a detective to whom she turns for help. The book begins by slowly evoking Millar's special brand of doom: a loving husband, a beautiful house, a lovely countryside, and a protective mother make a pleasant domestic scene, but a more disturbing element creeps in—a dream of death, and a feeling of imprisonment that slowly grows into a certainty of horror.

Daisy Harker and her mother were abandoned by Daisy's father when she was an adolescent; she only rarely heard from him—by letter, when he needed money. After moving to San Félice (half an hour from Los Angeles), Daisy married a promising young realtor, Jim Harker. Now very successful, he has built a house for them and a cottage nearby for his mother-in-law. The story begins eight years after their wedding.

Daisy has been getting over a depression that began when she learned that she could not have children. After deciding to adopt a child, she is now plagued by a recurrent, terrifying dream in which she walks up a hill to a cemetery and finds a grave marked by a cross in gray stone. Her own name is on the grave, with her deathday marked as December 2, 1955 (four years before). Daisy's formerly kind mother and husband ridicule her dream and her need to know what happened on that day. Daisy's crusade to rescue her lost day meets a wall of reticence, but through some odd circumstances she meets a private detective named Steve Pinata (a mystery himself) and decides to hire him. A mutual respect develops between the two while the scattered pieces of the puzzle are put together.

The novel is well balanced and suspenseful, though its romantic side could have been given a better foundation. Millar builds the eerie and menacing atmosphere by beginning each chapter with a line or two from a letter to Daisy from her father, which haltingly explain and simultaneously evoke the dark mystery—incomplete explanation as a form of suspense. The whole novel comes to be dominated by Daisy's father—his absence, his elusiveness, her desperate attachment to him and his continuous flight from it. Their relationship is the most powerful in the book. Some of Millar's other novels are stranger or more astounding—this, in the end, is a simple story—but in *A Stranger at My Grave* suspense and dread are expertly crafted and contained.

STRANGERS ON A TRAIN (1950) A novel by Patricia HIGHSMITH that presented an arresting premise: two people could "exchange" murders, each committing the killing the other had a motive for, and thus making the crimes seem motiveless while setting an alibi. On a train leaving New York, an architect, Guy, meets Bruno, a son of a rich family who chafes under his father's rule. Their discussion slowly turns to the subject of hatred. Bruno despises his father for not handing over some of his money; Guy's wife has been fooling around and may even be pregnant by another man. It is Bruno who suggests they do each other's murders, but Guy rejects the idea. When Guy's wife dies, it seems that Bruno has gone ahead with the plan; but if one of them "chickens out," the perfect arrangement becomes unbalanced. The book was filmed by Alfred HITCHCOCK in 1951. Raymond CHANDLER worked on the script but their two egos clashed; Chandler said that with Hitchcock there was no room for anyone else's personality. The same murder plot was used in a book by Nicholas BLAKE.

STRANGEWAYS, GEORGIA The wife of Nigel STRANGEWAYS in some of the detective novels of Nicholas BLAKE. Unlike spouses in many mystery series, Georgia is neither empty, cute, a saver of bad plots, or "just there" in the background. She is described as "the most famous woman traveller of her day." Strangeways meets Georgia Cavendish in *Thou Shell of Death* (1936) when they are both house guests of her friend, the aviator Fergus O'BRIEN, who saved her the previous year from a failed expedition to the African desert (during which she was forced to shoot her cousin because he had gone mad during a sandstorm). Georgia has an important role in THE BEAST MUST DIE (1938) and takes the lead in *The Smiler With the Knife* (see NAZISM). She does not appear in the later books because Blake has her die during the Blitz.

STRANGEWAYS, NIGEL Character created by Nicholas BLAKE (C. Day-Lewis), reportedly modeled after the poet W. H. AUDEN. (Strangeways does in fact have a literary turn of mind.) We learn that Strangeways left Oxford after two years, probably out of disgust (the opinion recurs that education "ruins" people for life), his last act of defiance being to answer his exams in limericks, for which he was expelled. His uncle, Sir John Strangeways, is the assistant commissioner of Scotland Yard. As a "private inquiry agent," Nigel has become rich, but his Philo VANCE-ish cases are all placed in the past, leaving scope in the present for interesting plots and unremunerative investigations.

As an amateur sleuth, Strangeways gets on unusually well with the police and gives them most of the facts and clues he uncovers. He has good relations with Inspector (later Superintendent) Blount and Inspector Wright, both of Scotland Yard. Strangeways has great sympathy with other people, does not think that murderers are inherently "monsters," and often finds the source of their crime in some psychological injury or damage done to them earlier in their lives. Murder may even be admissible under certain conditions; in these views, Strangeways resembles Jules MAIGRET.

In the first book in the series (*A Question of Proof,* 1935), Strangeways is clearly an eccentric of the GOLDEN AGE type. Tall, sandy-haired, short-sighted, and with a slightly rumpled elegance, he is not only the image of Auden, but of the young GENIUS DETECTIVE of the day. He drops snatches of quotations into his dialogue, talks loudly, walks like an ostrich, and bellows poetry at the top of his lungs during a car chase (Strangeways's habit of singing during a chase is probably based on the author's own experience as a boy, when he sang a patriotic Irish ballad from the top of an "ass cart"—and sent the animal galloping into town).

However much like the early CAMPION or WIMSEY, Strangeways is also a "human microscope" who shocks people because of his detached appreciation of a murder well done and thorough enjoyment of the solution. The second novel, *Thou Shell of Death* (1936), is notable for its ingenious plot, the appearance of Strangeways's future wife, and the central character of Fergus O'BRIEN.

There is not only a great variety of settings in the series, but of crimes, motives, and narrative techniques. *There's Trouble Brewing* (1937) is set in a brewery; THE BEAST MUST DIE (1938), a classic of mystery fiction, employs the INVERTED MYSTERY format in an original way; and HEAD OF A TRAVELER (1949) involves poetry and some of the most fascinating characters in the genre. *Malice in Wonderland* (1940), though unsatisfying as a mystery, is notable for its atmosphere of giddy hysteria and oppressive bonhomie. Strangeways is employed to find out who is behind a series of pranks at a holiday camp, which become progressively more and more sinister.

Strangeways is married once, to Georgia STRANGEWAYS, and widowed once (in MINUTE FOR MURDER, 1947). After he has gotten over Georgia's death, he begins a long affair with a sculptor, Clare Massinger, who appears in the later books. He accompanies her to Guest House in *The Sad Variety* (1964), a novel of the Cold War. Strangeways is keeping an eye on Alfred Wragby, a scientist who has made a discovery of military importance. Petrov, a Soviet agent, is planning to kidnap Wragby's daughter, assisted by Annie Stott, an ardent communist, and Paul Cunningham, a gay academic who is being blackmailed. Guest House is crowded with suspects: Admiral ffrench-Sullivan and his wife, private detective Justin Leake, and the obnoxious musician Lanie Atherson and his girlfriend. A SNOWBOUND mystery, *The Sad Variety* is also a return to the suspense style of *The Smiler with the Knife* (1939), in which Strangeways and his first wife battled the NAZIS.

END OF CHAPTER (1957) is set in the publishing world that Day-Lewis knew well (see also BOOKS); *The Widow's Cruise* (1959) deals with MURDER AFLOAT.

BIBLIOGRAPHY Novels: *The Corpse in the Snowman* (1941), *The Dreadful Hollow* (1953), *The Whisper in the Gloom* (1954), *The Worm of Death* (1961), *The Deadly Joker* (1963), *The Morning after Death* (1966).

STRATEMEYER, EDWARD L. (1862–1930) Although the name Edward Stratemeyer may not be widely recognized today, under twenty pseudonyms he wrote an incredible number of books—over four hundred—and invented such famous juvenile mystery characters as Nancy Drew and the Hardy Boys. As Arthur M. Winfield, he wrote about the Rover Boys, a long-running adventure series that began in 1899; he also invented Tom Swift, the boy-inventor. He founded the Stratemeyer Literary Syndicate in 1906, which employed ghost writers to turn out hundreds of titles in the various series.

Stratemeyer's writing career began in the days of the DIME NOVEL; he appropriated one of the great names of the Old West, Jim Bowie, as his pseudonym. Stratemeyer personally wrote only three Nancy Drew stories and nine Hardy Boys adventures. His daughter took over the company and continued the various series after Stratemeyer's death, winning millions of more young readers for the mystery genre.

STREET, DELLA See MASON, PERRY.

STRIBLING, T[HOMAS] S[IGISMUND] (1881–1965) American writer of mysteries and regional novels, Stribling lived in Europe and South America from 1908 to 1916. He used the latter as the setting for his most famous series of short stories, concerning Henry Poggioli. During his early career Stribling wrote for PULP MAGAZINES and produced one volume of short stories about Poggioli, *Clues of the Caribees* (1929), the concluding story of which ("A Passage to Benares") is an undisputed classic, and in which Poggioli himself is a suspect. The five tales, which are meant to be humorous, recount Poggioli's travels through the Americas, solving mysteries along the way. Poggioli is a psychology professor from Ohio State University. Among Stribling's non-mystery novels was the Pulitzer Prize–winning *The Store* (1932).

It is a shame that Dr. Poggioli has fallen into oblivion, because he still has the capacity to surprise. In "The Resurrection of Chin Lee," he demonstrates to a Florida mill owner that the ignorant belief that all Chinese people look the same has enabled a crime to occur.

More stories are collected in *Best Dr. Poggioli Detective Stories* (1975). *Laughing Stock: The Posthumous Autobiography of T. S. Stribling* appeared in 1982.

STRONG, L[EONARD] A[LFRED] G[EORGE] (1896–1958) The Anglo-Irish writer L. A. G. Strong did not make a definite mark on mystery fiction, but remains an interesting literary personage. He began as a poet, and collaborated with Day-Lewis (Nicholas BLAKE) on *A New Anthology of Modern Verse* (1941). His mysteries employed the series characters Ellis McKay, a Detective Inspector, and Inspector Bradstreet. In *Othello's Occupation* (1945; U.S. title *Murder Plays an Ugly Scene*), McKay is consulted by Claude Harrowby, a psychiatrist who believes one of his patients may kill someone. Strong wrote better fiction when he was not writing genre fiction. His collection of stories, *Sun on the Water* (1940), is a quiet book that deals primarily with the people and landscape of Ireland. There is often a crime element, as in "Shot in the Garden," in which a little boy finds a fattish woman stealing flowers from his grandfather's garden and, full of his Wild West fantasies, shoots her in the behind with his .22 rifle. In "Here's Something You Won't Put in a Book," an old woman takes her revenge on a writer who has put her and her family (libelously) into one of his works.

STRONG POISON (1930) A novel by Dorothy L. SAYERS, in which Lord Peter WIMSEY meets his wife-to-be, Harriet VANE, who is on trial for murder. It is one of the most entertaining books in the series, and has as a subtheme the lives of women who break with convention in one way or another. In the opening courtroom scenes, there is no doubt that the judge believes that Harriet Vane should hang for murdering her lover Philip Boyes with arsenic; perhaps, even, he thinks she should hang for her "immoral" conduct. Vane, a mystery novelist, had been living with Boyes, another writer who fancied himself to be avant-garde. The son of a parson, he did not believe in marriage, and convinced Harriet to live with him "in sin." When he changed his mind, threw over his radical ideas, and proposed to her, she became disgusted with the hollowness of his convictions and they separated. Much later, Boyes tried to patch things up, and arranged to meet Harriet after a dinner with his cousin, the solicitor Norman Urquart. Boyes fell ill, and three days later died. The case looks bleak, since Vane was the last person to see him alive, and all the food at Urquart's dinner was shared with other people who did not get sick—plus, she had bought arsenic and other poisons, ostensibly as part of her research for a mystery story.

Fortunately (but improbably) for Wimsey, his friend Miss CLIMPSON is on the jury, and gums up the verdict so that a new trial is declared. Having already fallen in love with Harriet Vane, Wimsey visits her cell in a number of embarrassing scenes and proposes. Then he begins to investigate what really happened to Philip Boyes.

Wimsey himself does relatively little detecting in the novel, and all the important work is done by women. Miss Climpson, whose "typing bureau" provides Wimsey with female operatives, is dispatched to try to find the will of Boyes's great aunt, a woman who led a famously debauched life in the Victorian era. Miss Murchison, a member of the bureau, is also a key detective (Wimsey takes her to the East End for lock-picking lessons), and she too runs up against moronic males who think that all she needs is to get married. While the policemen and the lawyers are clods, and Wimsey is in a flutter about Harriet, the women are intrepid and competent, and those who are scandalous are unrepentant. Sayers seems to have put more of herself into this novel (and, with Harriet Vane, literally inserted herself) than in any other.

STRYCHNINE This poison turns up frequently in crime fiction because of its violent effects (see, for example, the description in John D. MACDONALD's *A Purple Place for Dying* [1964]). Strychnine was once used as rat poison, and was thought to have beneficial medicinal properties, but no longer. The poison comes from the seeds of various kinds of plants, particularly the tropical *nux-vomica.* It can be swallowed, inhaled, or absorbed through the skin or eyes.

Strychnine acts on the nervous system. After poisoning, the facial muscles begin to contract, followed by the limbs and the rest of the body until the victim is asphyxiated. Light, sounds, or even movement can induce spasms. Despite its notoriously dramatic and gruesome results, strychnine poisoning is sometimes misdescribed in mysteries (see, for example, Francis GRIERSON).

STUDY IN SCARLET, A (1887) Sherlock HOLMES's first published case, in which he meets and takes rooms with Doctor WATSON, and ends by authorizing Watson to make accounts of his cases. This first, book-length adventure shows the strong influence of nineteenth-century Romantic and sensational literature on Conan DOYLE. He manages to fit a damsel in distress into a story, the middle of which takes place among the fanatical Mormons of Utah; Brigham Young makes a very unflattering appearance. The writing is much worse than in the later cases (it has been suggested that the North American section can be skipped entirely), and plenty of melodrama is thrown in. Still, Dorothy L. SAYERS called it a "bombshell" that forever changed mystery literature.

The case begins with the discovery of the corpse of Enoch J. Drebber in an empty house. The room is covered with blood but there is no wound on the body. Drebber hails from Cleveland, and is a drunk and a lecher. A woman's wedding ring is found under the body. The word "Rache" is written in blood upon the wall; the German word for "revenge," it suggests Continental entanglements and is the original RED HERRING.

In his first appearance, Holmes is surprisingly arrogant and condescending, including to Watson. Both Inspector LESTRADE and Tobias Gregson enter into the case for Scotland Yard, and are extremely jealous of each other. Gregson, who is tall, "white-faced," and "flaxen-haired," is the opposite of the ratty Lestrade. Holmes regards both with unconcealed disdain. His contempt for the investigative acumen of others is much broader, however: Holmes describes LECOQ as "a miserable bungler" and terms DUPIN "a very inferior fellow."

SUE, EUGÈNE (pen name of Marie Joseph Marie Sophie, 1804–1857) French novelist best known for the MYSTERIES OF PARIS (1842-43). This work has been described as a "kaleidoscope" of Paris at mid-century. Sue was one of the first to address the effects of industrialization and was influenced by socialist theory, just as he influenced Victor Hugo's LES MISERABLES (1862).

Prior to the *Mysteries,* Sue was a ship's doctor, the source of his adventure stories *Plik et Plok* (1831) and *La Vigie de Koatven* (1833). His other works include *Le juif errant* (tr *The Wandering Jew,* 1844-45).

SUGARTOWN (1984) A novel by Loren D. ESTLEMAN, and a winner of the EDGAR award. An Amos WALKER mystery, it uses the classic device of the converging plot lines. The opening overturns the HARD-BOILED cliché of the ingenue who slinks into the detective's office with a problem on her mind. In *Sugartown,* the woman in the black pillbox hat with the veil comes in a walker. Her name is Martha Evancek, and she is looking for her missing grandson, Michael, whom she has not seen in almost two decades. The Hamtramck police cannot help her because the trail is too old and they have little time for an elderly Polish woman who has only been in the country two years. The eleven-year-old Michael Evancek was not home when his father, Joseph (Martha's son), an unemployed auto worker, killed the rest of the family and himself with a shotgun. The boy was adopted by his aunt and disappeared. As Walker investigates, a mystery develops immediately when some details about the murder-suicide seem anomalous. Walker uses some clever moves to find Michael, and also becomes involved in a romantic subplot with the old woman's nurse. Just when the case seems wrapped up, another comes in, involving a Russian author who has defected but who believes Soviet agents have been sent to assassinate him. Given that his first client is a Polish immigrant, some connection seems likely between the two cases. The second case seems more exotic, but the best part of the book is made up of Walker's tramping around the decrepit city, chronicling the ongoing saga of destruction of old neighborhoods by "progress" ("We need another Cadillac plant like the world needs another moon"). Walker follows the trail over the battleground of the haves and have-nots, the last hold-outs against City Hall, and people with money. The old Polish neighborhood is being rolled up, taken by eminent domain with the help of city assessors who under-assess property and impoverish the working-class owners. Estleman's evocation of place and sense of injustice are as solid as ever, and Walker keeps his Hamlet-like (or Hammett-like) posing to a minimum.

SUGHRUE, C. W. One of two series characters invented by James CRUMLEY, Sughrue is the less likeable of the two. A Vietnam vet who was sent home after a Canadian film crew caught him committing atrocities, Sughrue then became a domestic spy, infiltrating the peace movement for the Federal government. Sughrue is like an imploded Philip MARLOWE, a moralist who knows he does not have a leg to stand on; hypocrisy is hell, because confessing does nothing to diminish it. Some may find Sughrue disagreeable, but one is not forced to take his inebriated adventures seriously, though their cumulative effect is to compel the reader to share his underlying depression about the way things are. See THE LAST GOOD KISS (1978).

BIBLIOGRAPHY Novels: *The Mexican Tree Duck* (1993), *Bordersnakes* (1996).

SUICIDE CLUB, THE (1882) A series of interlocking stories by Robert Louis STEVENSON, in which Prince Florizel and his trusted retainer, Colonel Geraldine, are involved with a sinister club run by a criminal genius. (People are not dying to get in, but getting in to die.) Although psychologically unbelievable as to motive and action, the stories are compulsively engaging. Florizel is a decadent at heart, jaded with privilege and searching for new forms of stimulation. A man appears in an oyster bar in London, giving away dozens of cream tarts; he also throws his money into the street because he is planning to die. Intrigued, Florizel allows himself to be drawn into a card game at the club where the stakes are one's life. The stories are not clued, but mystery develops—for example, how does a dead body planted on a gullible New Englander relate to the "doctor" who tells him to put it in a trunk and take it to London? How does the address he is given relate to Florizel and Geraldine? Stevenson handles the device of the seemingly unrelated plotlines like a master.

SUPERLATIVE COMPLEX The tendency to make characters superlative in everything to establish their "credentials," whether for good or ill. Thus, an evil scientist may have attended Harvard Medical School and graduated at the age of 17, discovered a new medicine that netted millions of dollars, found out the deadliest weapon of all time, and won the most beautiful woman. GENIUS DETECTIVES also attend the best schools, are the most talented, the most revered in their fields, excel even professionals when they take up hobbies, etcetera. Bad writers afflicted by the complex use superlatives to paste up characters as types instead of creating believable and more modulated portraits. THRILLER writers of all eras have been particularly prone to it.

"SUPERNATURAL POWERS OF LIEUTENANT BORUVKA, THE" (1966) The first adventure of Lieutenant BORUVKA, a satire of the PROCEDURAL story. Boruvka is called to a house where an old woman has hanged herself. He discovers a gung-ho former student of his, Sergeant Malek, who quickly inundates him with time schedules and diagrams in an attempt to show that the husband of the woman is the culprit. Boruvka can't get a word in edgewise while Malek tells him that he has begun "dactyloscopic examination" (fingerprinting); had the wall of the toilet in the tavern where the husband relieved himself removed to the laboratory; ordered a helicopter; taken plaster casts of *all* footprints and bicycle tracks between the house and the tavern; and set the principal, teachers, and students of the grammar school combing the woods.

Boruvka then makes one observation in the room itself that solves the case.

SURFEIT OF LAMPREYS, A See DEATH OF A PEER.

SWAG This word, meaning booty or ill-gotten gains, came from the Scottish word *swack*. For a time, it acquired a respectable meaning in English, i.e., goods of any type, not necessarily stolen. It must have been current but not very polite in 1839 when DICKENS footnoted it in *Oliver Twist* as meaning "booty."

SWING, CAPTAIN A fictitious revolutionary figure whose name was signed to threatening letters and proclamations during the English rural uprising of 1830. By the early nineteenth century, the English peasantry had virtually disappeared, replaced by relatively large farms worked by rural laborers who were paid casually—by the month, the week, or even by the hour. The inadequacy of wages and the Poor Law resulted in the total impoverishment of farm workers, who finally revolted against low pay and the introduction of machines that were both labor-saving and worker-starving. The mobs of 1830 destroyed farm machinery and burned the property of the rich, preferring to retain their anonymity behind the figure of "Captain Swing."

In THE DIFFERENCE ENGINE (1991), William Gibson and Bruce Sterling give Swing a face, making him into an actual person, and move the uprising ahead fifteen years to 1855. The authoritative account of the 1830 riots is *Captain Swing* (1968), by Eric Hobsbawm and George Rudé.

SYMONS, JULIAN (1912–1994) English mystery author and critic. Symons's approach to the genre, whether as a writer or critic, has been consistently literary, interested not only in good stories but good books. Some of Symons's work has the darkness of the crime genre proper: both victims and villains inhabit a grim social world, which they often confront with cowardice, dishonesty, and desperate violence. Others could be called satires of circumstance, about hapless or silly people entrapped by complexities that are only partially self-created. The types of failure he depicts range from the humorous to the ugly. In one of his earliest novels, *The Thirty-First of February* (1950), a policeman's suspicions, and the fact that his office gives him the power to indulge them, lead him to do a great injustice to an innocent man. *The Narrowing Circle* (1954) explores the theme of the individual pursued by circumstances, if not by enemies, and the persecution of the innocent. Gross Enterprises is bringing out a new crime magazine, and Dave Nelson is assured of being named editor, but at the last minute another man lands the plum job. After the man is killed, Nelson looks to be the most likely suspect and has to prove his innocence.

Perhaps the strangest of Symons's early novels is the award-winning *The Colour of Murder* (1957), a sordid picture of postwar England and the lives of people whose world is so small as to resemble a doll's house. Implicitly, Symons questions the meaning of punishing a disadvantaged and mentally impaired man. The murder is committed against the garish backdrop of a seaside town, and the macabre laughter that figures importantly in the book is a GOTHIC detail reminiscent of POE.

Like Poe, about whom he wrote, Symons began his career as a poet, and had achieved a literary reputation in that field before World War II. Prior to the war, Symons edited the poetry journal *Twentieth Century Verse* (1937-39), which showed an unusual interest in American poetry. Symons had many interests, including the history of the Victorian era, which he used as the background for THE BLACKHEATH POISONINGS (1978). *Sweet Adelaide* (1980) is based on the case of Adelaide BARTLETT. *The Detling Secret* (1982; orig title *The Detling Murders*) is similar in flavor, though more humorous. Sir Arthur Detling is an affluent member of the Conservative Club and is scandalized when his daughter, Dolly, decides to marry Bernard Ross, a Liberal member of Parliament. His other daughter, Nelly, is attending the Slade School of Art, having an affair with an impecunious artist named Charlie Bangs, and succumbing to fin-de-siècle Bohemianism. Symons's explication and use of the "Irish Question" as background and as plot device is masterful, and in many other spheres he reveals the impending conflict of orthodoxy and xenophobia with justice and emancipation that shattered the Victorian ideal.

Some of Symon's best mysteries concern the BOOK business (he began reviewing for the London *Times* in 1958, and was the editor of the Penguin Mystery Series from 1974 to 1977). Symons often gave his novels and stories a sociological edge, and said famously that he was preoccupied by the "violence behind respectable faces."

This sense of concealment and deception opens up the area of double identities, explored in *The Man Who Killed Himself* (1967), in which a man's crime annihilates not only his victim, but himself. Arthur Brownjohn is a failed inventor married to a woman of higher social status, which she never lets him forget; she keeps her inherited wealth out of his hands. She would be scandalized to know that his real income comes from a marriage bureau he runs. To compensate for his repression within the marriage, Brownjohn develops an alter ego, the boorish and promiscuous Major Mellon. When Arthur decides to kill his wife, he ingeniously frames the Major (i.e., himself) for the murder—a plot outline worthy of Donald WESTLAKE.

Another of Symons's "The Man Who . . . ," novels is *The Man Who Lost His Wife* (1970). Although only tangentially a mystery, this novel has a compelling central figure in Gilbert Welton, a confused middle-aged man like Saul Bellow's Herzog, who fails to understand the upheavals going on around him. It is a NOVEL OF MANNERS about the social chaos and comedy of the early seventies. Welton's publishing company, left to him by his much stronger father, is failing; his wife announces she is leaving him to "find herself," and runs off to Yugoslavia; Gilbert follows her, fails to find her but falls in love himself. Both passionate and comic, the story shows how a man deeply resistant to change constantly creates it by the pursuit of his desires. The mystery of a welt glimpsed on his wife's arm is enough to set off a bizarre quest. Most curiously, Symons shows how jealousy is a strange variety of the desire to know, and is a kind of self-torturing sleuthing. The deaths are incidental and tragi-comic. It is not clear how much the author endorses Welton's Panglossian solution to his doubts.

Symons's satire could be funny and, at the same time, ugly: in the title story of *The Tigers of Subtopia* (1982), a suburban businessman becomes a leader of a lynch mob. Sexual jealousy, infidelity, and plain selfishness are often motives for crimes by "respectable" persons. In *The Plot Against Roger Rider* (1973), a triangle develops between Roger, his wife, and his childhood friend Geoffrey Paradine. While they are all uncomfortably on vacation together, Roger disappears. *Death's Darkest Face* (1990) is an unusual work, and his last; Symons himself appears as a character, and is involved in the solution of the 1936 murder of a glamorous poet.

Symons's influence as a critic was as great, or greater, than his influence as a novelist. He won an EDGAR award for *Bloody Murder* (1972; rev 1985), a study of the development of the detective story and crime novel from their inception with PROTOMYSTERIES up to the present. Symons examined many individual authors in detail, and also left many out; he took the position that the best crime stories were written by artists, not artisans, and repeatedly said that the crime or mystery story could entertain *and* do something more. His high standards did not make him popular; one famous critic and publisher said unkindly that Symons "would find something to carp about at the second coming of Christ." Symons held the mystery story to a higher literary standard than any critic of the genre since Raymond CHANDLER. His nonfiction works include *A Reasonable Doubt, Crime and Detection from 1840* (1960), which deals with actual crimes, and *Crime: A Pictorial History* (1966). He wrote biographies of Conan DOYLE (1979) and Dashiell HAMMETT (1985), as well as *The Tell-Tale Heart: The Life and Works of Edgar Allan Poe* (1978). He also introduced a later edition of selections from the works of William ROUGHEAD.

Symons received many honors for his work. He was a member of the DETECTION CLUB, succeeding Agatha CHRISTIE as president in 1976. He was named a Grand Master by the Mystery Writers of America in 1982, only the fourth English writer to receive that honor.

SYPE, WALLY The train robber who stole the mysterious Leander pearls in Raymond CHANDLER's 1936 story "Goldfish," published in BLACK MASK. The detective, Carmady, goes to Idaho to find Sype, "a heavy loser" who is living quietly and raising fish, having done his time in Leavenworth. Also on the trail of the still-missing pearls are a cowardly lawyer and a hard girl named Carol Donovan, one of the most vicious characters Chandler created. The story was reprinted in *The Simple Art of Murder* (1950) and in *Trouble Is My Business* (1950), but with Carmady's name changed to MARLOWE.

There is an echo of Sype in the figure of Otto Sipe, a broken-down former house detective whom Lew Archer finds holed up in the Barcelona Hotel in THE FAR SIDE OF THE DOLLAR (1965).

TABARET, MONSIEUR An amateur detective created by Emile GABORIAU. Also known as Tirauclair, Tabaret is a proto-HOLMES: from a heel print, he deduces the rank and wealth of a suspect; he lies with his face in the mud examining tracks, with no thought to fine garments. But unlike the handsome Holmesian detective who later became the rule in English-language fiction, Tabaret is ugly. He has an upturned nose "like the broad end of one of Sax's horns"; receding hair; small red eyes; and long ears. In his sixties, he is short, thin, and bent.

As a romantic novelist, Gaboriau was bound to give Tabaret a full and tragic history. He is rich, and works for the "secret police" of the rue de Jerusalem. A collector of criminological books, his life was ruined by his father, who came to live with him when Tabaret was twenty-five, ostensibly helpless. Having slaved twenty years to support his father rather than marry, Tabaret learned on his parent's death that the man was wealthy, and had blasted all the son's romantic hopes simply to teach him economy.

TAIBO II, PACO IGNACIO (1949–) Born in Spain, Paco Taibo has lived in Mexico since 1958. He was one of the founders of the International Association of Crime Writers, and has received several awards for his writing, including the prestigious Planeta prize and three Latin American Dashiell Hammett awards. Taibo, in the European tradition, and even more than Manuel VAZQUEZ MONTALBÁN, combines the detective story with the novel of social commentary, and particularly satire. His stories also reflect the Latin American tradition and often involve outlandish humor, the absurd, and PICARESQUE elements. The main thrust of the earlier work is to uncover the sordid world of Mexican politics. Probably for this reason, and because the plots are rather sketchy, Taibo has been praised more in the mainstream press than by mystery critics. In the modern Mexico depicted by Taibo, the rhetoric of the revolution masks corruption at every level and massive poverty at the bottom; "justice" is a word that can only be mentioned with a sneer, and criticism should be accompanied by a look over your shoulder.

Taibo has created two series characters: one, Héctor Belascoarán SHAYNE, is a private detective. The other, José Daniel Fierro, is more an image of Taibo himself. Fierro is a crime writer who gets drawn into various adventures and finds himself much less prepared than would be the characters he writes about. In his first appearance, *Vita misma* (1990; tr *Life Itself,* 1994), he is invited to become chief of police in the corrupt mining town of Santa Ana, which is being fought over by a revolutionary city government and the powerful rich who want to steal it back. Fierro is chosen because they think a detective writer must know about policing (he doesn't) and none of the local hoodlums would dare shoot a man known nationwide (another false assumption).

Taibo's attitude is best summed up by the note that prefaced one of his novels: "Obviously, the plot and the characters in this novel belong to the realm of fiction. The country, however, although it may be hard to believe, is absolutely real." The oppressiveness of the ruling party and stifling of democracy are a constant theme, but Taibo's Mexico is also a churning, creative culture, and the books are ribald, frequently violent, and full of humor. Taibo translated several of his works himself. His most ambitious work thus far is LEONARDO'S BICYCLE (1993). He has also written the testamentary novel *Four Hands* (*Cuatro manos,* 1990; tr 1994), which does not involve any of his series characters but is a story of intrigue.

TALENTED MR. RIPLEY, THE (1955) The novel in which Patricia HIGHSMITH introduced Tom RIPLEY. Set in Italy and New York City, it vividly depicts both locales, is richly complex in plot and language, and deals masterfully with the problems of a narrative in which the main character assumes two separate identities (a technique William GIBSON used in a quite different context).

Tom Ripley is hired by the wealthy Herbert Greenleaf to help him find his son, Dickie. Ripley travels to Europe and catches up to Dickie in Italy, meanwhile corresponding with Greenleaf through the mail. Later, after he has assumed Dickie's identity himself, he keeps up the imposture by writing to Dickie's friends and avoiding personal contact. He continues, however, to be "Tom Ripley" when the occasion demands. Highsmith takes us into the mind of a repellent character but, through the sheer force of her communication of his personality, compels a sympathetic fascination on the part of the reader. Aspects of the plot seem to be taken from WYLDER'S HAND (1864).

TAMAR, HILARY See CAUDWELL, SARAH.

TAMMANY HALL The name for the corrupt administration of the notorious William Marcy "Boss" Tweed (1823–1878). Tammany Hall, located on Union Square, was the seat of the Democratic Party in New York City.

Tweed and his cronies cheated the city out of millions of dollars, and Tammany Hall became a synonym for corruption. The name of the hall itself comes from a seventeenth-century Delaware chief, Tammany, whose name was adopted by anti-British organizations in the following century. These political clubs died out after the American Revolution—except for Tammany Society No. 1, located in New York. Aaron Burr turned it into a vehicle for his political battles, and it helped to secure Thomas Jefferson's election in 1800.

The Tammany period has exercised a fascination for novelists. In E. L. DOCTOROW's *The Waterworks* (1994), he depicts the city as suffering from a post-Tammany hangover: impoverished, distrustful, cynical.

TANGLED WEB, A (1956; first pub as *Crime and Daisy Bland*) A crime novel by Nicholas BLAKE, based on the murder trial of JOHN WILLIAMS. Blake has moved the story ahead several decades, setting it in somber postwar London. He creates suspense by telling the story in retrospect: Daisy Bland, the lover of Hugo Chesterton, is waiting in a lawyer's office to hear what the verdict will be. Hugo has shot a policeman, but because of his "RAFFLES-like" character, the public has been swayed in his favor. There follows the story of how Hugo and Daisy literally bumped into each other, and how that encounter altered their lives and set him on the road to the gallows (hints are given that Daisy's testimony was the most damning). Blake handles love at first sight not as a romantic wonder but a queer, even disturbing process. Daisy's feelings are particularly stressed, because Hugo conceals as much about his burglarious career as possible. She is beautiful, with a kind of unearthly innocence—due, perhaps, to mental simplicity—that allows her to descend into the criminal underworld without being stained by it. Hugo's best friend is the impotent abortionist Jacko, a ghoulish parasite upon the passions of others. Blake develops both of the main characters fully and uses Hugo's desire to reform to heighten the tragedy.

TARANTELLA See TARANTULA.

TARANTULA The hairy tarantula spider has long inspired fear; legend had it that the tarantula bite was deadly. Although this is a myth, it is not true that the tarantula is harmless. This large, frightening-looking spider actually does have a weak venom, but it usually does not affect humans unless there is an allergy.

The *tarantella* is a dance that originated in Taranto, Italy, in the Middle Ages. People who were bitten by the European tarantula began to dance frenetically in the belief that violent excercise would lead them to sweat the venom out of their systems.

Because it is non-poisonous, the tarantula does not make a very good murder device. In Elliot PAUL's *Mayhem in B-Flat* (1940), however, Homer EVANS investigates a series of "tarantula murders" in Paris.

TAYLOR, ANDREW [JOHN ROBERT] (1951–) English mystery author Andrew Taylor was schooled as a librarian and has written that one day over lunch he began writing a mystery story, which became *Caroline Miniscule* (1982). This novel won the John Creasey Memorial Award and was nominated for an EDGAR. It is the comical story of William DOUGAL, a graduate student in medieval paleography who finds his tutor, Doctor Gumper, garroted to death in his office. It is typical of Dougal's outlook that his first thought is "how bloody inconvenient." A refreshingly anti-"donnish" mystery, the story deals with the jealousy-ridden and embittered lot of graduate students rather than the suaveties of the profs. This well-written story is a mystery and a crime novel at once, and the academic background is convincing while yet being unobtrusive.

Taylor's father was a teacher and minister. His mother was a physiotherapist. He attended Cambridge University, receiving a B.A. with honors, and then got his degree in library and information studies at the University of London. He told *Contemporary Authors* that the prospect of "a lifetime of undemanding and unsatisfying jobs" drove him to write, and he has not looked back since: Taylor has poured out a stream of books, many of them series novels. They include *Waiting for the End of the World* (1984), *Our Fathers' Lies* (1985), *An Old School Tie* (1986), *Freelance Death* (1987), and *Blacklist* (1988). The characters (thankfully) do not seem to have been conceived as series figures from the start, but they reappear (sometimes miraculously) in the later works. Taylor was nominated for a Gold Dagger by the British CRIME WRITERS' ASSOCIATION in 1985. *The Four Last Things* appeared in 1997.

TAYLOR, MITCH See TREAT, LAWRENCE.

TAYLOR, PHOEBE ATWOOD (1909–1976) Phoebe Atwood Taylor was born in Boston and educated at Barnard College. In 1931, she published her first mystery about Asey MAYO, *The Cape Cod Mystery,* which was a great success. She went on to write a total of two dozen mysteries about the Yankee amateur detective; the last, *Diplomatic Corpse,* was published in 1951.

Taylor is best known for her Yankee humor, her ear for dialogue, and her genuine and recognizable New

England characters. She certainly had ample bluestocking credentials herself, being a descendant of one of the passengers on the *Mayflower.* Asey Mayo, appropriately, is an old salt himself. The Cape Cod dialect in which Mayo and other characters speak includes much dropping of g's, t's, and r's, as well as a peppering of Yankee expressions.

The strength of Taylor's writing is in the characterizations and caricatures. The denizens of her New England towns and villages are interesting, even charming; their way of communicating with each other—they are given to a fair amount of chiding—is entertaining. Judged as books, therefore, the novels are "good reads"; as mysteries, however, they lack that obsession with tightness that marks many of the masters of the genre, and the motive behind the crime is often weak. For these reasons, Taylor's mysteries have been treated as spoofs or examples of a "wacky" mystery subgenre.

Although the Mayo books are often referred to as the "Cape Cod Mysteries," they do not always take place on Cape Cod. *Out of Order* (1936), for example, is set in western Massachusetts. Taylor also alternated between third- and first-person narration; *Death Lights a Candle* (1932) is told by Prudence Whitsby, the aunt of Betsey Porter, who is the wife of Bill Porter, Mayo's friend and the son of his former employer and protector. It is a SNOWBOUND mystery that also involves ART. Art is also a concern in OCTAGON HOUSE (1937), where it is treated in a humorous vein.

Under the name of Alice Tilton, Taylor also produced a series of eight novels about another New England sleuth, Leonidas WITHERALL. Witherall is a typical nutty professor. He has been a teacher at a New England prep school, and has at least three sidelines: he is a part-time antiquarian book dealer, a successful writer of thrillers, and, when he is drawn into bizarre events, an investigator. Typical of the lunacies to be encountered in his adventures is *The Cut Direct* (1938), which opens as the hero has just been hit by a car. Witherall's greatest fame is for his resemblance to William Shakespeare, which accounts for his nickname, "Bill." Taylor's Asey Mayo books are perennially popular, and were reprinted by Foul Play Books in a paperback edition of the late 1980s. Among those who had a high opinion of Taylor's books was Nicolas BLAKE.

TAYLOR, WENDELL HERTIG (1905–1985) A scientist by profession, Wendell Hertig Taylor also co-authored with Jacques BARZUN the massive *Catalogue of Crime* (1971, exp ed 1989), a landmark work of mystery criticism. Taylor graduated from Princeton University, where he would later teach; he also worked for the Du Pont company as a researcher.

TEDDY BOY During the 1950s, "Teddy boys" were young men who followed the fashion for Edwardian dress (hence Teddy, from Edward, Prince of Wales). Like their namesake, they had a raffish reputation.

TELLING OF LIES, THE (1986) An EDGAR-winning novel by Timothy FINDLEY. It takes place during the last summer of Vanessa Van Horne at the Aurora Sands Hotel, which is to be torn down to make way for a condominium development. The setting is a thinly veiled version of Prout's Neck, Maine. Fast approaching sixty, Van Horne is a photographer and landscape architect—forthright, unmarried, but far from a spinster in spirit. Her friend Lily Porter is having an affair with Calder Maddox, a world-famous pharmaceuticalist and a very nasty man. Van Horne is taking pictures on the beach when the ancient Maddox dies in his beach chair, apparently naturally. Anomalies about his death begin to turn up, however, and mysterious doings at the rival hotel down at the end of the Neck cause further alarm. Van Horne investigates with the help of a doctor who turns out to be a weak reed, and her childhood friend Mercedes Mannheim, a powerful socialite who is both charming and fearless. The characterizations—a broken Canadian civil servant; a shattered war veteran who is alcoholic, handicapped, and homosexual; a smarmy young politico—are superbly done and eschew caricature.

The story is told in the form of Van Horne's diary; cleverly, this prohibits any HAD-I-BUT-KNOWN overtones, since at every point Vanessa is totally ignorant of the final outcome. It also gives full play to her introverted, thoughtful nature; although the horrors of Reaganism are a clear inspiration for the novel, Findley keeps the politics wry and ironic. Vanessa is forced to ask what it really means to belong to the "ruling class," and indeed to admit that it really exists. Her coming to terms leads to a surprising change in her character.

TEMPLAR, SIMON The "real" name of THE SAINT.

TEN DAYS' WONDER See AMNESIA.

"TENTH COMMANDMENT, THE" (1918) A story by Melville Davisson POST. Before the story begins, a landowner named Dillworth legally swindles a man who has bought a faulty deed; the man hangs himself. Uncle ABNER enters the picture when he passes through the area with his cattle and finds a primed shotgun in a hollow tree. He goes to visit Dillworth, who is hoping to execute claims against his other neighbors, and they have a debate over the relationship between the law and justice. It is the clearest expression of Abner's philosophy in the stories: "The law is not always justice." Dillworth counters that the law says what is right and what is wrong, absolving people of deciding for themselves. Thus, he collapses the idea of what is legal and the idea of what is right. Uncle Abner, however, believes that every man knows justice, though not every man knows the law (witness Dillworth's hapless victim). The story, besides containing ingenious maneuvers on Abner's part, shows how he gets at others by reaching into their souls or the emptiness where their souls should be.

TERHUNE, THEODORE See GRAEME, BRUCE.

TEY, JOSEPHINE (pen name of Elizabeth Mckintosh, also known as Gordon Daviot, 1896?–1952) Josephine Tey is one of the more under-appreciated authors in mystery fiction. Although her historical mystery, THE DAUGHTER OF TIME (1951), usually appears on "all-time great" lists, it is an atypical book; the "action" is completely indoors, and the deduction all takes place from a hospital bed. THE FRANCHISE AFFAIR (1948) is probably Tey's second-most familiar work, and was also based on a historical case.

The details of Tey's life are sketchy, beginning with her birthdate, which is not known exactly. Born in Inverness, Tey taught physical education before she became a successful author. Her outdoor scenes in the highlands are vivid and full of energy. Tey also wrote plays. The young Sir John Gielgud starred in her historical drama *Richard of Bordeaux* (1933). Her historical interests emerged early, even though her famous historical mysteries were late works (*The Daughter of Time* appeared posthumously).

The Man in the Queue (1929) was her first mystery and appeared under the name Gordon Daviot. It also introduced Inspector Alan GRANT, a quiet Scot, remarkable in that he emerged at the time of Lord Peter WIMSEY and the outlandish early CAMPION. Although he has wealth, Grant is understated, lacking the aristocratic pretensions of Wimsey (royal pretensions in Campion's case) and the foreignness of POIROT.

Grant's next case, A SHILLING FOR CANDLES, appeared in 1936. It concerns the death of a woman found on a beach, and the setting—the Channel coast—is exquisitely rendered. It was used as the basis for Alfred HITCHCOCK's film *Young and Innocent* (1937). *Brat Farrar* (1950; also pub as *Come and Kill Me*) has the familiar plot (used both before and since) of a prodigal son returning to his family, but under a cloud of doubt as to whether he is not an imposter. THE SINGING SANDS (1952) is perhaps Tey's best book about Alan Grant, and the one in which he emerges as most human; it is also her most brilliant depiction of the "wide, unchanging, undemanding Highland world" of her childhood. Tey romanticized Scotland but also brought it physically to life on the page. (The pseudonym "Tey" comes from a river in Scotland.)

Miss Pym Disposes (1946) is a novel not about Grant but a former physical education teacher who investigates a killing at a girls' school. *To Love and Be Wise* (1950) has Grant, but no murder.

THANE, COLIN A detective created by Bill KNOX, and the least adventurous of all his characters. He was also the first, and Knox stuck to tried-and-true patterns and to the city he knew best, his native Glasgow, Scotland. Thane made his debut in *Deadline for a Dream* (1957). As far as Scottish detectives go, Thane is less interesting than Alan GRANT. A former boxer, Thane has a stable home life with his wife Mary and their children. He is tall, gray-eyed, and has unruly dark hair. Nondescript in appearance, in personality Thane is a stereotypical dour Scot. To give these investigations color, Knox adds a sidekick—but one who is older rather than younger than the hero. Phil Moss is efficient and takes care of the details while Thane speculates; Moss also takes care of his ulcer, which is the major component of his personality.

Thane rises from Detective Chief Inspector to the rank of Superintendent during the series, getting his promotion in *Live Bait* (1979). Although the Thane novels are considered PROCEDURAL, Knox uses a variety of plots and stratagems, some of them far-fetched, to get Thane away from old Glasgow or to introduce an exotic element. In *The Ghost Car* (1966), Knox even brings in the Russians, who are engaged in industrial espionage. After he becomes Superintendent, Thane joins the special Scottish Crime Squad, which further liberates him from the realities of the procedural format. In *The Taste of Proof* (1965) and *Rally to Kill* (1975), the crimes concern Scotland's liquor industry. The title character of *The Tallyman* (1969) is what in American terms would be called a loan shark. Other notable Thane books are *Who Shot the Bull?* (1970), which begins with the killing of a Highland bull but also involves Scottish separatism, and *A Killing in Antiques* (1981).

After almost thirty years writing Thane books, Knox gave the series a "facelift," adding younger characters and pushing Moss into the background. A later book is *The Interface Man* (1989); oddly, though Moss grows older and fades, Thane is still only in his early forties. Although he never had much of a sense of humor, Thane's promotion seems to have made him petulant and blunt with his inferiors. The jocose banter between the young detectives Sandra Craig and Joe Felix does not help. The story, about an international computer crime guru, now seems rudimentary given the development—sometimes outlandish—of the computer CAPER novel in the following decade.

BIBLIOGRAPHY Novels: *Death Department* (1959), *Leave It to the Hangman* (1960), *Little Drops of Blood* (1962), *The Grey Sentinels* (1962; orig title *Sanctuary Isle*), *The Killing Game* (1963; orig title *The Man in the Bottle*), *Justice on the Rocks* (1967), *Children of the Mist* (1970), *To Kill a Witch* (1971), *Draw Batons!* (1973), *Pilot Error* (1976), *The Hanging Tree* (1984), *The Crossfire Killings* (1986).

THANET, LUKE See SIMPSON, DOROTHY.

THATCHER, JOHN PUTNAM A banker-sleuth in a series of novels by Emma LATHEN. An executive vice president at the Sloan Guarantee Trust, Thatcher deals with financial crimes that often lead to broader implications—global ones in *Murder against the Grain* (1967), about a Russian wheat deal. Gray-haired and urbane, Thatcher never ages in the series, which began in 1961 with *Banking on Death.* The books have tried to deal with contemporary issues, fashions, and even consumer fads. In the recent *Brewing Up a Storm* (1996), a battle erupts between a consumer group opposed to the selling of nonalcoholic beer to minors and the makers of one such beverage, Quax. Over the decades Thatcher has dealt with the oil crisis (*Double, Double, Oil and Trouble* [1978]) and relations with Japan (*East Is East* [1991]).

BIBLIOGRAPHY Novels: *A Place for Murder* (1963), *Accounting for Murder* (1964), *Murder Makes the Wheels Go Round* (1966), *Death Shall Overcome* (1966), *A Stitch in Time* (1968), *Come to Dust* (1968), *When in Greece* (1969), *Murder to Go* (1970), *Pick Up Sticks* (1970), *The Longer the Thread* (1971), *Ashes to Ashes* (1971), *Murder without Icing* (1972), *Sweet and Low* (1974), *By Hook or By Crook* (1975), *Going for the Gold* (1981), *Green Grow the Dollars* (1982), *Something in the Air* (1988), *Right on the Money* (1993).

THAW, HARRY K. See WHITE, STANFORD.

THAYER, [EMMA REDINGTON] LEE (1874–1973) Lee Thayer was one of the most prolific of American mystery novelists, publishing them into her ninety-second year. All but one of her sixty novels are about Peter CLANCY, a private investigator similar to many other GOLDEN AGE p.i.s. Thayer was born in Troy, Pennsylvania, and lived in New York City for most of her life. She was a professional artist, having studied at Cooper Union and the Pratt Institute. Her work was exhibited at the Chicago World's Fair in 1893.

THEOBALD, KATE See BLACK, LIONEL.

"THERE ARE NO SNAKES IN IRELAND" (1982) An EDGAR-winning short story by Frederick FORSYTH. The story is set in Northern Ireland and concerns a poor Indian medical student named Harkishan Ram Lal who gets a job with a demolition crew headed by the bigoted Big Billie Cameron. While the men are taking down an old whiskey distillery, Cameron insults Lal; the rest of the story describes the Indian's intricate plans for revenge, which go awry more than once and come to a chilling conclusion.

THEY DON'T DANCE MUCH (1940) A crime novel by James ROSS, set in an unspecified North Carolina town in the Piedmont area between Charlotte and the South Carolina border. It is written in the Carolina vernacular. The story moves quickly, and its dark psychological profiles, though sometimes falling into cliché, have a resemblance to the work of Jim THOMPSON. The book is also extremely realistic, providing a wealth of detail about how devastating the Depression was to the rural working poor. Ross has an understanding of race relations during the period; nevertheless, racial epithets are used throughout, and at times it is difficult to determine whether or not the opinions about blacks belong to Ross or are used solely to convey the attitudes of the characters.

The narrator, Jack McDonald, is a smart man with a lot of common sense but not much education. Out of work, he accepts a job at a local gas station owned by Smut MILLIGAN. Milligan is greedy, and expands the place into a roadhouse where locals can buy liquor, gamble, and rent rooms by the hour. He is soon successful, but needs more money to keep his business going. He hears a rumor that Bert Ford has buried a large sum of money on his property, and decides to get it, which leads to the violent events of the novel, including shootings, poisoning with PARIS GREEN, and the drowning of a victim in a vat of beer.

THEY SHOOT HORSES, DON'T THEY? (1935) A novel by Horace MCCOY. Set in Hollywood, it concerns two extras who are on their uppers, Robert Syverton and Gloria Beatty. Neither of them is registered with the Central Casting Bureau or has much chance of getting into film. They meet accidentally at a bus stop, spend the day together, and wind up at a dance marathon held in a dance hall on an amusement pier. They decide to participate even though they hardly know each other because free food and a bed are provided for as long as each couple can keep going. Other couples, however, are professional dance marathoners, and have perfected techniques for sleeping on their partner's shoulders and taking care of all necessaries during the ten-minute break allowed every two hours.

The story is told in flashbacks. At the beginning, Robert has already admitted to killing Gloria and is on trial. A doubt is quickly opened up, however; he says that the one person who could have helped him is also dead.

The first week of the marathon is hardest. As the weeks go by, Gloria and Robert's clothing deteriorates; they acquire two sponsors, who supply them with new shoes and other articles; and Gloria's feeling of despair increases. The marathon becomes a metaphor for life. After 800 hours comes the climax that leads back to Robert's predicament. The narrative circularity reinforces the sense of meaninglessness created by the dance marathon itself, from which there is seemingly no exit except collapse.

The book was critically well received, but it was even more admired abroad, particularly by the French existentialists (much like the work of Jim THOMPSON, who was hailed by the great film directors Jean-Luc Goddard and François TRUFFAUT).

THINKING MACHINE, THE Professor S. F. X. Van Dusen, created by Jacques FUTRELLE, is "The Thinking Machine," one of the quirkiest, crankiest, most headstrong (in both senses) detectives in fiction. His best case is THE PROBLEM OF CELL THIRTEEN (1905), one of the most anthologized and admired mystery stories of all time. With thick glasses and eyes that are "mere slits of watery blue," and above them a tall, wide forehead and bushy yellow hair, Van Dusen is the very type of the nerd. He is scholarly and "remotely German," a descendant of noted scientists. Fifty years old, he spends most of his time in his laboratory, from which he emerges with startling discoveries. Van Dusen's appearance—weak, thin, pale—masks an improbable intelligence. The invincible professor is able to beat the world chess champion though he has never played the game himself; his logic is more miraculous than demonstrable. He is childlike not only in his appearance but in his egotism, which is quick to detect any slight toward his powers. Van Dusen refuses to accept any fee for his services. Futrelle does not overdo his quirks, and the professor is one of the most endearing fictional sleuths after Sherlock HOLMES.

The professor's WATSON is a Boston newspaper reporter named Hutchinson Hatch, who also brings him some of his cases. In "The Crystal Gazer," Hatch takes his life in his hands when he agrees to replace a man who has been told by a spiritualist that he will be murdered (the professor's comment: "A sense of humor ought to convince him that disembodied spirits do not come back and rap on tables in answer to asinine questions"). Another recurrent figure is the cigar-chewing, practical Lieutenant Mallory. In "The Problem of the Stolen Rubens," Hatch brings to Van Dusen's attention a loss suffered by a rather comical millionaire: "Matthew Kale made fifty million dollars out of axle grease, after which he began to patronize the high arts." Futrelle often began his stories with such arresting and amusing flourishes: "Douglas Blake, millionaire, sat flat on the floor and gazed with delighted eyes at the unutterable beauties of a highly colored picture book. He was only fourteen months old, and the picture book was quite the most beautiful thing he had ever beheld" ("Kidnapped Baby Blake, Millionaire").

No less arresting are the situations faced by the sleuth, for example the car that seems to vanish in "The Phantom Motor"—a story which is probably the earliest description of a police speed trap in fiction. In "The Superfluous Finger," Dr. Prescott is approached by a lovely young woman who wants him to amputate one of her fingers, though there is nothing the matter with it. When he refuses on ethical grounds, she conceives the idea of shooting the finger off with a pistol and then having him dress the (now legitimate) wound.

The Thinking Machine stories were first serialized in Boston newspapers beginning in 1905, but the two collections that were published in the author's lifetime only account for about half of them. A few of the uncollected stories have appeared in anthologies, and in *Best "Thinking Machine" Stories* (1973), edited by E. F. BLEILER. The one novel in which the Thinking Machine appeared was actually the first story to be written.

BIBLIOGRAPHY Novels: *The Chase of the Golden Plate* (1906).

Short Stories: *The Thinking Machine* (1906), *The Thinking Machine on the Case* (1907).

THIN MAN, THE (1933) A best-selling novel by Dashiell HAMMETT, later the basis for a very successful series of films. *The Thin Man* is not much liked by those who cleave to the morbid aspects of HARD-BOILED fiction, to whom it seems almost a betrayal of Hammett's usual style. It was to be Hammett's most popular book with the public, however, and although Nick and Nora CHARLES appeared in this novel only, they became household names.

At the opening of the novel, Nick Charles says he hasn't done any private detecting since 1927, when his wife inherited a lumber mill and a narrow-gauge railroad.

Nick is the original likeable lush, who has had at least two drinks by page two and a hangover by page four. Nora is charming, and the dog, Asta, is mischievous and endearing. All of these aspects, especially the husband-and-wife detecting team, have been much imitated.

The Charleses, of San Francisco, are on vacation in New York. The plot concerns the disappearance of a "batty as hell" inventor, Clyde Miller Wynant. His secretary is found shot to death in her apartment by Wynant's ex-wife. Nick Charles had worked for Wynant—who, standing more than six feet tall, with almost white hair and a moustache, is himself The Thin Man—when he was accused by a man named Rosewater of stealing an invention. Although the story is played for wit and laughs, there is also some detection, once Wynant's daughter Dorothy convinces Nick to look into the case. Her teenage brother Gilbert is an amusing nerd whose criminological and forensic theorizing provides further comic relief.

The Thin Man was filmed in 1934, starring William Powell and Myrna Loy, and was so successful that it spawned no less than five sequels. Hammett contributed to only the first of these, *After the Thin Man* (1936). Earlier, Powell had made a career of portraying Philo VANCE on the screen.

THIRD MAN, THE (1949) Graham GREENE wrote the screenplay for Sir Carol Reed's thriller set in Vienna and starring Orson Welles; but because plot, character, and atmosphere are "almost impossible to capture for the first time in the dull shorthand of a script," Greene wrote the story down as a work of fiction first. This version was included in *The Portable Graham Greene* (1973). The tone of the story, told by a British colonel and Scotland Yard agent named Calloway, is reminiscent of Joseph CONRAD (and one of the villains is named Kurtz). Once again, Greene takes an ordinary man and plunges him way over his head in intrigue. The Englishman Rollo Martins is an author of pulp Westerns under the name Buck Dexter. Martins doesn't take his literary efforts very seriously, though soon after he arrives in Vienna he is mistaken for another Dexter who is thought to be the next Henry JAMES. Martins is drawn to Vienna, despite the fact that it is still under occupation and technically off-limits, by a call from his old school chum Harry Lime. He gets to Vienna just in time to attend Lime's funeral, and then is thunderstruck to find out that Lime was a racketeer involved with murder. He vows to Calloway that he will probe the "accidental" death of his friend and clear his name. Greene's depiction of frozen, bombed-out Vienna, the terror of the Russian Zone, and the callousness of the various intelligence services is vivid. Calloway coolly watches Rollo Martins's private investigations with a mixture of admiration and dismay; Martins begins to find cracks in "the smooth wall of deception," though his "unhealthy curiosity" holds serious dangers. Against the background of a Cold War just starting to heat up, Greene has Martins make a shocking discovery.

THIRTY-NINE STEPS, THE (1915) The best-known novel of John BUCHAN. It is a brief, fast-moving tale about Richard HANNAY, a mining engineer who has returned from Rhodesia and is getting bored in England. Set before the Great War, the volatile Balkan situation is all important; the murder of the Greek premier is involved, as well as British naval secrets. Through chance circumstances, Hannay finds himself accused of murdering an American adventurer and spy interested in the Balkan matter. Even though he is innocent, Hannay already knows too much, and the people who really did kill the American want him dead as well. The chase through Scotland, the mystery of "the thirty-nine steps," the elaborate disguises used by Hannay, and his HOLMES-like powers of analysis make the book a tour-de-force. There is little extraneous material, and the language, though studded with Briticisms, is tight and literate. The novel was made into a famous film by Alfred HITCHCOCK.

THOMAS, ROSS [ELMORE] (1926–1995) A former public relations man who worked for the administration of President Lyndon Johnson, Ross Thomas won an EDGAR award for his first novel, *The Cold War Swap* (1966). More a THRILLER writer than a writer of mystery, Thomas often takes a cynical or satirical view of bureaucracies, from small-town governments to trade unions to superpowers. His main subject, however, is Washington, D.C., and the various corrupt characters who riddle the power nexus inside the Beltway like termites.

Thomas was born in Oklahoma City and served in the Army in World War II. After graduating from the University of Oklahoma in 1949, he wrote for newspapers, later switching to the public relations business. His work took him all over the world; *The Seersucker Whipsaw* (1967) was based on his p.r. work for a Nigerian chieftain. His African and Washington experiences come together in *The Brass Go-Between* (1969). *The Money Harvest* (1975) shows his Washington insider's knowledge to best advantage. "Crawdad" Gilmour is ninety-three years old and has been an advisor to six presidents. He is killed by mistake during an inept mugging. When the same gun used to murder Gilmour turns up in the death of a twenty-three-year-old ballet dancer, a Washington conspiracy for money and power is uncovered.

One of Thomas's best-known books is *The Fools in Town Are on Our Side* (1971), the story of the corruption of a Southern town, greatly lengthened by being sandwiched within a spy's recollection of his fall from grace. Lucifer Dye, formerly of the mysterious Section Two intelligence agency (fired after a deadly snafu in Hong Kong), is hired by an unlikely prodigy, Victor Orcutt, who wants to clean up crime and corruption by first making it "much worse." Yet a third story, about Dye's upbringing in a Shanghai bordello following the death of his missionary father, makes the book a top-heavy burlesque. *The Porkchoppers* (1972) is about unions, with which Thomas also once worked. His books are credited for their humor, but they are not always humorous enough to make up for sometimes turgid writing and lack of a center. The format is somewhat formulaic, consisting of swift, reader-catching scenes of action followed by sections where the author pulls back and fills in previous history, including biographies of the characters.

Thomas did not create a truly successful series character, though Philip ST. IVES appeared in several books. Two agents, McCorkle and Padillo, were introduced in his first novel. They also feature in *Cast a Yellow Shadow* (1967) and *The Backup Men* (1971). Thomas won a second Edgar for *Briarpatch* (1985). In this novel, set in the Sunbelt, the brother of a murdered police officer searches for her killer and uncovers political corruption.

THOMPSON, JIM (pen name of James Myers Thompson, 1906–1977) An out-of-print author of PAPERBACK ORIGINALS and ailing alcoholic at the end of his life, Jim Thompson predicted that he would be famous a decade after his death, and he was right. All of Thompson's work has been republished, including two early non-crime genre books, *Now and on Earth* (1942) and *Heed the Thunder* (1946). Critical studies and biographies of Thompson have proliferated, including *Jim Thompson: The Killers Inside Him* (1983), co-authored by Ed GORMAN and Max Allan COLLINS, *Jim Thompson: Sleep with the Devil* (1990), by Michael J. McCauley, and Robert Polito's EDGAR-winning biography *Savage Art* (1995).

Jim Thompson was born in Oklahoma when it was still a territory. His father, James Sherman "Big Jim" Thompson, was a sheriff. Big Jim Thompson was a huge, handsome man who became a significant political figure in Anadarko, Oklahoma, and once ran in the Republican primary for Congress. In 1907, he was brought down by criminal charges relating to misuse of public funds and had to flee to Mexico on horseback like the desperadoes of Western fiction, leaving his family to fend for themselves. Jim Thompson recycled the materials of his life in his fiction in sometimes bizarre ways: the narrators of THE KILLER INSIDE ME (1952) and *Pop. 1280* (1964) are both sheriffs who are also remorseless murderers. Elsewhere he championed his father, who was an important, ambiguous presence in his imaginative universe.

Big Jim was eventually reunited with the family, and became associated with crooked oil man Jake Hamon. In Texas, Jim Thompson stored up the material for his most powerful later work. He attended the University of Nebraska College of Agriculture, where he published his first work, but dropped out in 1931. Thereafter he was a hobo and did a series of odd jobs while trying to make it as a writer. He wrote guidebooks for the WPA Writer's Project, and his family helped him write stories for the true crime PULPS by collecting information on lurid murders. In 1936, he joined the Communist Party. Thompson's early novels were in the proletarian tradition. His first crime novel was NOTHING MORE THAN MURDER, which appeared in 1949, relatively late in his career. Most of his crime genre work appeared in the fifties, including THE NOTHING MAN (1954), the closest thing to a traditional mystery in Thompson's oeuvre.

Thompson's characters are sometimes described as psychotic killers, but they are sociopaths rather than "psychos." They have no delusions, no hallucinations, no clinical paranoia; instead, they are completely callous pragmatists who remove people who are in their way with the same level of feeling as for an insect. They do not live in a fantasy world, but rather a familiar world that they have grotesquely simplified by removing all the moral and legal limits placed on the realization of self-interest. The murderer in Thompson's books (often also the narrator) is like a man walking onto the set of a Western with a loaded gun; armed and dangerous in a way no one else knows, he makes others seem hopelessly hopeful and trusting. The victims only grasp the nature of the hidden power that confronts them just before the *coup de grace.* That power is nihilism; Thompson's sociopathic killers, as one of Charles WILLEFORD's characters says, understand the difference between right and wrong but "just don't give a shit." Thompson's most autobiographical books are *Bad Boy* (1953) and *Roughneck* (1954). THE GRIFTERS (1963), which has one of the most horrifying endings of any crime novel, was made into a film with a screenplay by Donald WESTLAKE. THE GETAWAY (1959) was also filmed (1972, 1994). Thompson, like other NOIR writers such as David GOODIS, was admired by French film directors (Bertrand Tavernier turned *Pop. 1280* into a film set in French Africa [*Coup de Torchon,* 1981]).

THOMSON, JUNE (1930–) June Thomson taught English for twenty years before she began her writing career. Born in Kent, she attended Bedford College, University of London, and graduated in 1952. Most of her work is about Inspector Finch, known in the United States as Inspector RUDD. A quiet policeman in rural Essex, Finch combines procedure with psychology, and hence the nature of character looms larger in this than in other PROCEDURAL series. The novels are somewhat reminiscent of the books of Ruth RENDELL, though even more focused on mood. Thomson's depiction of the English countryside has little to do with the COUNTRY HOUSE mystery; instead, it evokes spiritual, economic, and social decay, to which even the detective himself is not immune. Thomson has also written *The Secret Files of Sherlock Holmes* (1990) and *The Secret Chronicles of Sherlock Holmes* (1992), two volumes of pastiche.

THORNDYKE, DR. JOHN EVELYN The first fully fledged "scientific detective," R. Austin FREEMAN's Dr. Thorndyke made his debut in THE RED THUMB MARK (1907). Freeman himself was a medical man, and Thorndyke was partly based on one of the author's teachers in medical school. Thorndyke's knowledge, however, extends far beyond medicine, into a plethora of obscure subjects.

Thorndyke lives in King's Bench Walk, London, and has two assistants, Nathaniel Polton and Christopher Jervis. The latter is his WATSON, a fellow doctor who chronicles his cases—although Jervis was often supplemented with other narrators to bring out different perspectives. Polton, a genius as a practical mechanic and a highly educated man rescued from the gutter by Thorndyke, is able to make any device the doctor desires; he is described as "elderly" and "dry" even in his first appearance, dressed as a laborer but with a "refined and intellectual face." Thorndyke is tall and handsome, is both a doctor and a barrister, and like many contemporary detectives of his day, is invincible. In fact, Thorndyke is almost godlike, a reflection of an absolute faith in science that was largely unquestioned in Freeman's day. The author said he made Thorndyke handsome as "a protest against the monsters of ugliness" some authors had used as detectives. Thorndyke is muscular as well as classically good-looking, and ages little over his career. His genius is emphasized by Jervis's thick-headedness (he is "an expert misunderstander"). Polton was based on two people, a lab assistant and a watchmaker Freeman had known. Late in life, Freeman wrote *Mr. Polton Explains* (1940), putting the secondary character in the limelight for a change; the butler-cum-lab assistant turns out to be interesting in his own right.

Thorndyke is above all a professional, perhaps the first in crime fiction. He lacks any of Sherlock HOLMES's air of the *artiste*. In his methods Thorndyke is also a virtual opposite of Chesterton's Father BROWN. He uses physical evidence, not his knowledge of human nature, to track down the criminal. The dumpy, unassuming priest with a clumsy umbrella and a unique sympathy contrasts sharply with the handsome scientist with the green research case containing a miniature microscope, test tubes, and instruments. Dorothy L. SAYERS found Thorndyke "outwardly bonhomous, but spiritually detached." He is part of the reaction against the eccentric detective that began with Martin HEWITT. Thorndyke's only vice is the smoking of terribly pungent "Trichinopoly" cheroots ("I'd sooner smoke my own wig" jokes Anstey, the jovial but canny barrister who is an old friend of Thorndyke's). Like Sherlock Holmes, Thorndyke is an expert at identifying different varieties of pipe tobacco, makes of typewriters, etcetera. Also like Holmes, he occasionally does not mind if the criminal escapes. In the story "A Case of Premeditation," an INVERTED MYSTERY, a former crook who has become a respected gentleman goes to bizarre but explicable lengths to kill a man (his method necessitates the purchase of a dead rat) and keep his identity hidden; Thorndyke remarks that "To kill a blackmailer—when you have no other defence against him—is hardly murder."

Of all the scientific detectives who crowded the mystery field in the early part of the twentieth century, Thorndyke is far and away the best. The first Thorndyke novel and THE STONEWARE MONKEY (1938) are two of the most admired, and are also the most readily accessible thanks to fairly recent reprints by Dover. Although his characters are often weak, the plots of Freeman's stories are usually ingenious, and predate by decades their many descendants. In *The Silent Witness* (1914), a corpse is discovered but inexplicably disappears by the time the authorities arrive. In *The Eye of Osiris* (1911; U.S. title *The Vanishing Man*), an archaeologist is the victim of a clever faked disappearance. Disappearances, in fact, are a staple of the Thorndyke series. Archaeology again turns up in *The Penrose Mystery* (1936).

Freeman was interested in a large number of subjects, which he worked into Thorndyke's cases with his customary care and exactitude, for example the nautical details of the story "The Echo of a Mutiny" (see MURDER AFLOAT). While Freeman is famous for having actually tested out the methods incorporated into his books for their viability, Dr. Thorndyke himself has an even more startling practice: he keeps under lock and key six volumes of hypothetical murders of prominent people that he has worked out in detail, and just as carefully worked out the detective method of unmasking them. Thus, Thorndyke plays a private game of inverted mystery against himself.

A particularly good example of Thorndyke's art is FELO DE SE? (1929). THE MYSTERY OF 31 NEW INN was the first Dr. Thorndyke story; written around 1905, it was not published as a novel until 1916. The original short story was reprinted in *The Best Dr. Thorndyke Detective Stories* (1973).

BIBLIOGRAPHY Novels: *Helen Vardon's Confession* (1922), *The Cat's Eye* (1923), *The Mystery of Angelina Frood* (1924), *The Shadow of the Wolf* (1925), *The D'Arblay Mystery* (1926), *A Certain Dr. Thorndyke* (1927), *As a Thief in the Night* (1928), *Mr. Pottermack's Oversight* (1930), *Pontifex, Son and Thorndyke* (1931), *When Rogues Fall Out* (1932; U.S. title *Dr. Thorndyke's Discovery*), *For the Defense: Dr. Thorndyke* (1934), *The Jacob Street Mystery* (1942; U.S. title *The Unconscious Witness*).

Short Stories: *John Thorndyke's Cases* (1909; U.S. title *Dr. Thorndyke's Cases*), *The Singing Bone* (1912), *The Great Portrait Mystery* (1918; two Thorndyke stories), *Dr. Thorndyke's Case Book* (1923; U.S. title *The Blue Scarab*), *The Puzzle Lock* (1925), *The Magic Casket* (1927),

"THOU ART THE MAN" (1844) An at once comical and masterful detective story by Edgar Allan POE, but not involving C. Auguste DUPIN. Set in the country town of Rattleborough, it concerns two old cronies, Mr. Goodfellow and Mr. Shuttleworthy. One day, Shuttleworthy's horse returns to town bespattered with mud and wounded by a pistol bullet. The grief-stricken Mr. Goodfellow leads a search through the wilds of the neighborhood, but Shuttleworthy is not found. Instead, a chain of evidence (including an early use of BALLISTIC evidence) points to Mr. Pennifeather, Shuttleworthy's dissolute nephew. The narrator, who plays the role of detective very unobtrusively, produces a startling ending with a piece of whalebone and a box of Chateaux Margaux; the corpse itself has the last laugh.

"THRAWN JANET" See STEVENSON, ROBERT LOUIS.

THREE ROADS, THE See AMNESIA.

THRILLER A piece of literary terminology nearly as useless as "suspense," and liable to the same criticisms Jacques BARZUN made against the suspense label. If a thriller is supposed to be thrilling, then the term could as well describe *Moby Dick, Wuthering Heights,* and *Macbeth.* As a result of its imprecision, "thriller" is often used in conjunction with some other term; there is the spy thriller, the mystery thriller, the detective thriller, and the technothriller. Publishers often refer to books as "thrillers" when they do not want to admit that they are spy novels or mysteries. This fatuous attempt to make the "thriller" more respectable than genre fiction is all the more ludicrous because the thriller category includes as much if not more junk than the detective genre; the thriller is more prone to humorlessness and heavy-handed writing.

THUMM, INSPECTOR A character in four mysteries by Ellery QUEEN, published under the pseudonym Barnaby Ross. Thumm is a New York City police detective but is usually accompanied by his daughter, Patience. See Drury LANE.

THURSDAY, MAX See MILLER, WADE.

TIBBETT, INSPECTOR HENRY A policeman in a series of books by the English author Patricia MOYES. The first novel in the series was *Dead Men Don't Ski* (1959). Tibbett is a typical postwar English detective: mild-mannered, bland, and ruminative. More diligent than brilliant, Tibbett's hunches are acceptable and believable; the string of choice cases in exotic places is a piece of outrageous luck, not typical of the real SCOTLAND YARD. Tibbett's wife Emmy accompanies him frequently, and the cases often involve friends or family in trouble. During the series, Tibbett rises to the position of Chief Superintendent.

Season of Snows and Sins (1971), which takes place at an exclusive ski resort in the Swiss Alps, was awarded an EDGAR. The story is told in the first person by Jane Weston, an Englishwoman and sculptress. Ann-Marie Durey is found guilty of fatally stabbing her husband, a handsome ski instructor who had become infatuated with a famous actress, Giselle Anay. Inspector Tibbett, an old friend of Ann-Marie, arrives on vacation and takes up the case. The story appears straightforward initially, but complex subplots develop and take Tibbett to Paris for some research on the "beautiful people," such as Giselle, who have ruined his friend's life.

Falling Star (1964) has the typical strengths and weaknesses of the series. Although a Tibbett story, it is told from the perspective of Anthony (Pudge) Croombe Peters, an aristocrat who has backed an independent film. The device of having the first murder occur on camera is good; the characters, however—from the aristocratic types to the temperamental Italian actress—are run-of-the-mill. Tibbett enters rather late, and his stratagem for catching the murderer is a bit weak and heavy-handed. *Many Deadly Returns* (1970) has a more PROCEDURAL style and is better constructed, though it concerns a typical COUNTRY HOUSE setup: Lady Balaclava invites friends to her country home (where she lives with her longtime female companion, Dorothy Underwood-Threap) for her birthday, which of course winds up being her last. The murder occurs right under the nose of Inspector Tibbett, who must redeem himself by finding the killer.

In *Murder à la Mode* (1963), a top executive of a fashion magazine is found sprawled over her desk, poisoned with CYANIDE; one of the prime suspects is Inspector Tibbett's niece Veronica, a successful but young model whom the Tibbetts are supposed to be keeping an eye on as she gets her start in London.

The Tibbetts are themselves victimized in *Night Ferry to Death* (1985) when thieves break into their home looking for diamonds. The couple had previously traveled on the Amsterdam ferry when a suspected jewel thief was found dead, but with no diamonds on his person. All the major suspects are women. Despite the nautical flavor, the book is redolent of tweed and cardigan sweaters and is very English.

BIBLIOGRAPHY Novels: *Down Among the Dead Men* (1961), *Death on the Agenda* (1962), *Johnny Underground* (1965), *Murder Fantastical* (1967), *Death and the Dutch Uncle* (1968), *The Curious Affair of the Third Dog* (1973), *Black Widower* (1975), *The Coconut Killings* (1977), *Who Is Simon Warwick?* (1979), *Angel Death* (1980), *A Six-Letter Word for Death* (1983), *Black Girl, White Girl* (1989).

TIBBS, VIRGIL A detective in a series of novels by John BALL. An African American from Pasadena, California, Virgil Tibbs is visiting his mother in the deep south when he passes through the town of Wells in IN THE HEAT OF THE NIGHT (1965). After a concert conductor is murdered, Tibbs is grabbed from the railroad station as a likely suspect. When his identity is revealed, the Wells police—completely incompetent to solve a murder—obtain the loan of his services from his hometown force.

Tibbs has been a policeman for ten years at the opening of the series, and specializes in the investigation of murder and other serious crimes. He is slightly built and weighs only a hundred and fifty pounds, but he is trained in judo and other martial arts. Tibbs is quiet and turns the other cheek at many indignities he is forced to suffer for the color of his skin, but Ball reveals in subtle ways the detective's contained anger. When he is given the floor at the end of *In the Heat of the Night,* he delivers not an impassioned plea for equal rights but a cool reconstruction of the crime that could have come out of a classic mystery—except that Tibbs's racist listeners have already humiliated themselves and been forced to admit their ignorance by Tibbs's quiet dignity and efficiency.

In *Five Pieces of Jade* (1972), Ball dealt with racism within, as well as between, ethnic communities. A jade importer is stabbed with a Chou Dynasty dagger and is found by an Amerasian girl, half-black, half-Japanese, who is rejected by both communities. *The Cool Cottontail* (1966) was more offbeat: it is set in a nudist camp in California. *The Eyes of Buddha* (1976) begins with the disappearance of an heiress and the discovery of the decomposed corpse of a woman in Pasadena, California, but ends in Katmandu, Nepal.

BIBLIOGRAPHY Novels: *Johnny Get Your Gun* (1969).

TICHBORNE CLAIMANT, THE The Tichborne Claimant was one of the great fraud cases of all time, though whether the Claimant really was or was not who he claimed to be is still unresolved. It was a real instance of a plot that has fascinated many mystery writers: someone turns up and claims to be a person who has vanished years before.

Sir Roger Tichborne was an Englishman who disappeared in South America in 1853. Twelve years later, a man claiming to be Roger arrived in England. One person who was convinced of his identity was Tichborne's mother, as were other associates of the missing man, including the family lawyer. The would-be heirs of Tichborne, not surprisingly, said "the Claimant" was an imposter. Some of the reasons for rejecting him were that he could not recall his mother's maiden name and did not seem to have the education that the original Roger had had. A legal battle ensued, and the case dragged on in the courts for years. In the end, the Claimant was sentenced to fourteen years in prison.

Once the Claimant was in prison, bizarre things began to happen. His extreme loss of weight—in the neighborhood of 200 pounds, from Gideon FELL-size down to a mere Donald LAM—may have caused psychological aberrations, or perhaps corrections. The Claimant had previously appeared ignorant, and suddenly he was able to quote Latin literature in the original. FINGERPRINTING was not yet in use, and the BERTILLON system of measurements was inconclusive.

Among the writers who have used the plot of the suspicious return of a missing person are Josephine TEY (in *Brat Farrar* [1950]). In one of the cases of Susan Dare by Mignon G. EBERHART, there is not one claimant but two. Michael GILBERT examined the case in *The Tichborne Claimant* (1957) with both legal acumen and imagination. Robin Maugham (1916–1981), the nephew of Somerset MAUGHAM, wrote a novel based on the case, *The Link* (1969).

TIGER IN THE SMOKE, THE (1952) A novel by Margery ALLINGHAM, often considered her finest. The "Tiger" is Jack HAVOC, a prison escapee on the run. He is pursued by Charlie Luke, an ambitious detective who is himself described as "ferocious," while CAMPION assists. Havoc's presence is balanced by that of Canon Avril (Campion's uncle), the symbol of good, but whose goodness is anything but weak.

The story begins with a conundrum: Campion's cousin Meg, a war widow who is about to be married, receives pictures in the mail purporting to show her first husband, Major Elginbrodde, still alive and somewhere in London. The novel also includes a cast of Dickensian characters who speak in Cockney. The power of this most headlong of narratives comes also from "the Smoke"—London itself, blanketed by a fog so dense that early in the book it creeps in like "a third person." This London is a bad dream in which memories of the horrible glory of the war mingle with the tattered present: "Mr. Campion reflected that the evil smell of fog is a smell of ashes grown cold under hoses, and he heard afresh the distinctive noise of the irritable, half-blinded city, the scream of brakes, the abuse of drivers, the fierce hiss of tyres on the wet road." It is a book DICKENS would have appreciated, and has been justly called one of the best mysteries of any period.

TIGHT SQUEEZE (1959) A novel by William FULLER, one in his series about Brad Dolan. Fuller lived in Havana and its environs for several months at the height of the Cuban revolution while researching the novel. The six-foot-three, two hundred pound former Marine Dolan lives a boom-and-bust existence on his boat in Florida, making money from fishing parties and occasional black market activities. He enjoys his carefree lifestyle until the money is gone and he has to go back to work. The plot of *Tight Squeeze* expands the usual frame by incorporating historical events, the larger world, and more serious philosophical choices for Dolan. He is hired by the sexy Sheila Gaynor to smuggle a cargo of guns from the Florida Keys with his boat, but Dolan has hardly begun when he is boarded and hijacked. After a dramatic escape, he puts the cargo in a safe place and sets off for Havana to find a buyer but has a run-in with a powerful offshore American gangster instead. Dolan's debate with himself over the revolution is solved when he decides that Castro is the lesser of two evils and becomes, partly for reasons of his own, an irregular in Che Guevara's army and takes part in the attack on Santa Clara. Inklings come through of the terrible excitement of Havana at the time, but Fuller obviously was unable to put some of his experience into words.

TISH A character created by Mary Roberts RINEHART, Tish had a phenomenally successful run in *The Saturday Evening Post.* In a series of humorous adventures, she did little detection but got into all kinds of scrapes, along with her friends Aggie and Lizzie. Many of the tales are not criminal at all, but Ellery QUEEN singled out "Tish and the Treasure Hunt" for their landmark anthology of a hundred years of mystery stories (1945). Other Tish stories include "Hijack and the Game," in which she gets involved in smuggling liquor during PROHIBITION. The Tish stories are being rediscovered because they show a more "feminist" side of Rinehart, who has long been in disfavor for her HAD-I-BUT-KNOWN tendencies. Unlike the heroines of many of Rinehart's novels, Tish and her friends try such "masculine" activities as hunting, auto racing, and flying a blimp. *The Best of Tish* (1925) is a selection of her exploits.

TOBACCO The ubiquitous vice of the HARD-BOILED detective is also a poison. See NIGHTSHADE.

TO CATCH A THIEF A popular title that has been recycled more than once. Craig RICE wrote a novel of this name in 1943, under the pseudonym Daphne Sanders. David Dodge's book of that name would be unknown but for the fact that Alfred HITCHCOCK made it into a film in 1955.

TOFF A well-dressed, apparently well-to-do person. This English expression is derived from an old meaning of "tuft." A tuft was Oxford University slang for a student who had a title of nobility or was a gentleman; they wore gold tassels, or tufts, on their caps.

"The Toff" was a series character created by John CREASEY. The Toff's real name is Richard ROLLISON.

TOM SAWYER, THE ADVENTURES OF See TWAIN, MARK.

TONTINE A financial scheme, named for the Italian Lorenzo Tonti. Originally from Naples, Tonti set up the first tontine in Paris in 1653, whereby a group of individuals went in on an investment, with the understanding that each would be paid an income from it. As investors died, the proceeds of the investment would be split among a smaller and smaller group, and therefore individual income would increase.

It is not hard to see why the tontine would invite corruption by the impatient. By murdering other members of the group, an investor would increase his cut. In "The Tontine Curse" (1946), by Lillian DE LA TORRE, Sam Johnson says that the tontine is "inherently vicious." The story is set in 1779; in the tontine, twenty children have 5,000 pounds staked on them—which amounts to a price on their heads, because after only four years have passed only four of the children are left.

Hawley Smart's THE GREAT TONTINE (1881) adds further complexities to the tontine scheme. Sixteen-hundred shares are sold at the cost of one hundred pounds each, with the purchasers "nominating" a person sixty years old or older as the "life" by which their share should be measured. A dividend is paid, which mounts as the number of lives dwindles; the last speculator stands to gain £160,000. The "lives" have no idea that they have been nominated—nor of how much danger they are in.

"The Adventure of the Inner Circle," the first story in *Calendar of Crime* (1946), has Ellery QUEEN investigating a tontine subscribed to by the surviving members of the first class of the fictitious Eastern University. The members of this "inner circle" of the class of 1913 are getting old, but their suddenly escalating mortality rate cannot be easily explained.

More recently, the tontine features in Roderic JEFFRIES's *Troubled Deaths* (1978) and Charlotte MACLEOD's *Trouble in the Brasses* (1989).

TOO MANY COOKS See RIGHT TO DIE, A.

TOO MUCH OF WATER (1958) An example of MURDER AFLOAT, this novel by Bruce HAMILTON takes place on the *Goyaz*, a small steamer making its way from Europe to South America through several ports of call. It contains some excellent writing and vividly drawn characters, including Edgar Cantrell, a distinguished middle-aged conductor; Maurice Marcus, a counter-tenor; Terry GARDNER, a highly emotional buffoon; Major Major, an officer and a lush; two crashing bores, the know-it-all Mr. Rottentosser and the preachy Mr. Swete; and a dozen other passengers, including a retarded Paraguayan boy and a cold beauty who sets the men at each other's throats. Hamilton recreates the feeling of being on a small vessel for a long while and the effort to contain dislike and preserve social appearances. Things go wrong right away when the captain, recently widowed, proves incapable of performing his duties; then a passenger disappears during a storm in the Bay of Biscay. Though written in the third person, events are seen mainly through the eyes of Cantrell, who by force of circumstances is pressed into acting as the sleuth. But while his heart leads one way, the facts that pile up as a result of further crimes lead to the imprisonment of his friend Marcus in a temporary brig. Hamilton makes the most of the claustrophobic setting, but also employs the maps, alibis, and timetables of the traditional English detective story, all cleverly transplanted to what amounts to a sea-going country house.

TOPER An English term for a drinker, from the verb *tope*, "to drink excessively" (perhaps derived from a French source).

TORN BRANCH, THE (1959; rev 1965; orig title *Bony and the Black Virgin*) A novel by Arthur W. UPFIELD and one of the best books in the Inspector Napoleon BONAPARTE series, for its depiction of the desolation and beauty of the remote Australian bush. John Downer and his son Eric return to their sheep station on Lake Jane from their "annual bender" to find a murdered man in their house and their hired hand, Carl Brandt, mysteriously gone. They are losing their stock because of a prolonged drought; "there were children of two and three years who had never seen a raindrop."

Weeks pass. While Eric is nearly unmanned by the suffering of the animals that die in agony or which he is forced to shoot, the dead stranger is nearly forgotten; then the body of Brandt is uncovered by the wind. Bonaparte arrives to take the case in hand. His discovery of clues under a landscape turned to dust is convincing, and his timeless perspective contrasts with and throws into relief the attitudes of those around him, including the impatient Eric, the tough and unflappable John, and the other settlers, who are considerable figures and not just extras in the drama. The descriptions of tracking are vivid. The murders are not very important to the "pastoralists": everyone is focused too intently on the wait for rain. Upfield's depiction of the anxiety, fatalism, and heartbreak of the drought would make the book an intense and satisfying story even if the murder element were removed. Attitudes toward race play an interesting part.

TO THE HILT (1996) A novel by Dick FRANCIS about Alexander Kinmouth, a painter and nice guy in a squeeze. Despite some odd habits—living miles from everyone in a bothy on a huge Scottish estate, not divorcing his wife after five years of separation—he is the basic Francis hero. When his stepfather suddenly becomes ill and the family brewery gets into trouble, Alexander steps in to find the firms's stolen assets, including a medieval chalice (and, of course, a horse). A subplot concerns the possession and ownership of a hilt from the sword of Bonnie Prince Charlie, and seems to betray some anti–National Trust feelings. The ancillary characters include several nasty relatives and fossils with titles, like Alexander's uncle ("Himself") the Earl.

TOUGH GUYS DON'T DANCE (1984) A novel by Norman MAILER. Set on Cape Cod, it is told from the perspective of writer Timothy Madden, who tries to solve the mystery of whether he killed two women during a period of AMNESIA. A literary novel that is also suspenseful, it uses an engaging plot, the grisly nature of the murders, and the main character's apprehension that he may be involved in a series of killings to maintain the reader's interest. The pacing is excellent, and character is artfully developed through dialogue. On the other hand, Mailer abuses coincidence: the story's radically different people—street hoods, sex junkies, a DEA agent, two writers, a bisexual African American drug dealer, townspeople, socialites—all seem to have met, slept with, married, or fought with each other at some point in their lives.

One morning, twenty-four days after his wife Patty disappeared, Tim wakes up with a hangover, a tattoo on his shoulder bearing a woman's name, and no recollection of the night before. He also finds the front passenger seat of his Porsche covered with blood. After the acting chief of police—a sleazy and suspicious figure—suggests he look at his marijuana stash in the Truro woods, Madden finds a blonde head there. Mailer depicts Provincetown in the off-season as a beautiful but twisted place. The descriptions of the Cape are vivid and bring in history, social stratification, and relations among New Englanders, Portuguese, artists, and the gay community. Madden's horrifying predicament is reminiscent of the plots favored by Cornell WOOLRICH. The weapons used include a sword, a DERRINGER, and a knife.

"TRAGEDY AT BROOKBEND COTTAGE, THE"

(1914) A story hailed as the best of the Max CARRADOS tales by Ernest BRAMAH. It begins in the classic Holmesian manner with a visit by a client, Lieutenant Hollyer, and his exposition of a mystery. He is concerned that his sister Millicent is about to be killed by her husband, Creake. The writing is better than Conan DOYLE's, at least in the dialogue, which has more of the sound of real speech, though the solution is easy to guess at the penultimate moment. Carrados's uncovering of the clues and his use of his blindness to get the advantage over others are extraordinarily subtle. It is also the story in which Carrados says that one of the few things he misses since his blindness is the sight of lightning, adding poetically that he still "can hear a good deal of colour in it."

TRAGEDY AT LAW (1942) A novel by Cyril HARE. Set in 1939–1940, it focuses on Judge William Hereward Barber, a pompous old eminence whose legal wit depends upon the advice of his brilliant (but not practicing) lawyer wife, Lady Hilda. The first part of the story takes place mostly during the judge's transit along the southern circuit; as he goes from town to town, a number of mishaps occur that lead to the conclusion that someone is trying to kill Barber. A case involving an expired license, a concert pianist, and an amputated finger leaves the judge fighting for his professional life.

Also on the scene is the lawyer Francis PETTIGREW, who follows the circuit as a defense counsel and is treated shabbily by Barber throughout. Based on Hare's own experience, the recreation of circuit court life is vivid and detailed. Among the characters is the judge's Marshal, Derek Marshall, a young idealist to whom Pettigrew tries to teach the essential art of "hushing things up." Lady Hilda, who is much younger than her obnoxious husband, is engaging and charming, but Pettigrew is absent from the stage for a good part, and without him the interest of the story flags. The surprise ending, however, is not to be missed; the solution of the small crimes (and one major one) is made to hinge on an arcane point of tort law. The Falstaffian figure of Inspector Mallett is present intermittently, but the story relies more on suspense and curiosity than detection, of which there is little.

TRAGEDY OF PUDD'NHEAD WILSON, THE

(1894) This novel by Mark TWAIN is famous in the mystery genre for its early use of FINGERPRINTING in the resolution of a criminal case. In a larger sense, it is a bitterly ironic novel attacking the institution of slavery, which brings disaster to all who come in contact with it. The title character, David Wilson, is derisively called "pudd'nhead" by the townspeople because of his eccentricity. Wilson is a lawyer, and gets involved in a case that hinges on children switched at birth. The slave Roxana, who is light-skinned, exchanges her natural son for the son of her owner. Her real son, Tom Driscoll, grows up to be a criminal despite his advantages. In the book's cruelest irony, Tom sells his own mother to pay his gambling debts; he also commits a murder. The actual son of the Driscoll household goes under the name Valet de Chambre. While the guilty are punished and the good rewarded in the resolution, Twain shows how Valet de Chambre is made totally unfit for his role as a member of the landed gentry by the abominable treatment and irremediable ignorance of his upbringing as a slave.

TRAGEDY OF X, THE (1932) A mystery by Ellery QUEEN, but not an Ellery Queen mystery, *The Tragedy of X* was the first book to use Drury LANE as a sleuth. Before the story begins, the retired actor has already helped the police solve one case and has sent the solution to Inspector Thumm. The police then ask him to assist in the investigation of the murder of Hadley Longstreet, a Wall Street broker who had announced his engagement to Cherry Browne, an actress/floozie. The ingenious murder method is to drop a cork stuck with needles (coated with concentrated nicotine) into Longstreet's pocket while he is riding on a streetcar. The first suspect is Longstreet's colleague John DeWitt, who has professional and personal motives for wanting to get rid of Longstreet. Drury Lane examines the case and pays careful attention to facts overlooked by everybody else. Still, another two murders occur before the case is wrapped up.

The book, the authors later wrote, "stems from the deductive school—that special branch which makes a fetish of fairness to the reader." Despite this fetishism, Queen also pays attention to character, giving Drury Lane a curious all-male entourage: Quacey, aka "the hunchback," a "lump of evil"; Falstaff, his major-domo; Kropotkin, his director; and Hof, his scene designer. In the Lane series, the authors found a sense of humor that was lacking in the early Ellery Queen books, which were dependent on Philo VANCE as a model. With Lane, they brought their writing up to the level of their plotting.

TRAILL, MR. A semi-retired Scotland Yard detective who appears in G. K. CHESTERTON's "The Garden of Smoke," and one of the author's most memorable characters. Traill has large droopy eyelids and a cadaverous face, but also a mesmerizing power of sympathy. He appears at first as only an enigmatic top hat moving above a hedge.

TRAIN, ARTHUR C[HEYNEY] (1875–1945) Born in Boston, Arthur C. Train was a prolific author who wrote not only mystery stories but true crime and science fiction. Train followed in the footsteps of his father, who had been the attorney general of Massachusetts for almost twenty years. Arthur Train attended Harvard University and Harvard Law School, and afterward practiced law. He later became an assistant district attorney.

Of his hundreds of works, Train's most notable was the series about Ephraim TUTT, almost a lawyer version of Uncle ABNER, the crime solver and punisher of wickedness created by Melville Davisson POST. The numerous Tutt stories were collected in a dozen volumes. Artemus Quibble, who appeared in *The Confessions of Artemus Quibble* (1911), was a shifty lawyer similar to Randolph MASON.

Train wrote a long short story about a TRAIN, entitled EXTRADITION. *My Day in Court* (1939) is Train's autobiography.

TRAINS MURDER ON THE ORIENT EXPRESS (1934) is not the only mystery to take place on a train. It isn't even the first to involve the Orient Express (see THE MADONNA OF THE SLEEPING CARS, 1925). There are dozens of mysteries set on trains, including Mary Roberts Rinehart's THE MAN IN LOWER TEN (1909), in which the wreck of a train is used to help cover up a murder. Christie said that she "hated" her 1928 novel, *The Mystery of the Blue Train* (the blue train is the train to Nice, France).

Key events take place on trains in many other mysteries, such as Josephine Tey's THE SINGING SANDS (1952), in which a few cryptic lines of verse are found in the possession of a man who has been murdered on the London Mail on its way to Scotland; Jim Thompson's *The Getaway* (1959); Patricia Highsmith's STRANGERS ON A TRAIN (1950), later a famous HITCHCOCK film; and the Sherlock HOLMES stories "The Adventure of the BRUCE PARTINGTON PLANS" (1908) and THE FINAL PROBLEM (1893). Most famously, a train is the venue for murder in James M. Cain's DOUBLE INDEMNITY (1944). Tommy Hambledon discovers a body in his compartment in *The Basle Express* (1956), a scene repeated in various other mysteries. In Cornell Woolrich's I MARRIED A DEAD MAN (1948), a train disaster offers a pregnant woman bizarre opportunities.

As Hugh GREENE pointed out, the railway fascinated Victorian writers and was used in many mysteries—particularly as it was then possible to order a special train in an emergency. Arthur C. TRAIN wrote a short story, EXTRADITION, which depended on the route of an eastbound train through the United States and Canada.

"Famous last rides" include the Solar PONS novel *Mr. Fairlie's Final Journey* (1968), a Sherlock HOLMES pastiche. A much better final journey is *Sir John Magill's Last Journey* (1930) by Freeman Wills CROFTS. Crofts was himself employed by the railroad and wrote several books with trains and train journeys as a major feature. *Death of a Train* (1946) is almost a "train procedural," giving a detailed account of a wreck. *The Groote Park Murder* (1925) and *Double Death* (1932) also involved railways. John CREASEY's *Murder on the Line* (1960) did not benefit from Croft's kind of personal knowledge. Other ill-fated trains are *The 10:30 from Marseilles* (1963, by Sébastien JAPRISOT; tr *The Sleeping Car Murders*) and *The 4:50 from Paddington* (1957; a Miss MARPLE mystery, printed in the United States as *What Mrs. McGillicuddy Saw*).

A nonfiction collection about famous murders that occurred on trains is Jonathan GOODMAN's *The Railway Murders* (1984). Bill PRONZINI's *Midnight Specials* (1977) is an anthology of train-related mystery stories.

TRAITOR'S PURSE See AMNESIA.

TRANT, LUTHER See MACHARG, WILLIAM.

TRANT, TIMOTHY See QUENTIN, PATRICK.

TRAP FOR CINDERELLA (1963; orig title *Piège pour Cendrillon*) A novel by Sébastien JAPRISOT. The title is a dark joke: "Cinderella" is a woman who has survived the burning of a house on the French Riviera, but her hands are horribly scarred and her face has been restored with plastic surgery. When she wakes up in the hospital, she does not know who she is. The woman is believed to be Michele Isola, a flighty, promiscuous, and gaily cruel young heiress. Her friend, a former bank employee named Domenica Loi, is thought to have burned to death in the fire. Michele's former governess, Jeanne Murneau, checks her out of the hospital and takes her to a house in the Bois de Boulogne outside Paris. Gradually, Michele gets the impression that Jeanne is hiding her from her former friends, and not simply because she has AMNESIA. She even comes to doubt whether Domenica died in the fire and if "Michele" survived. Japrisot never pushes the psychology in a heavy-handed way, but interestingly, a third personality emerges, the present-tense "Michele/ Domenica" who does not feel that she is either woman. For her, her personal history began when she opened her eyes. She is repelled by the behavior of Michele, and equally unhappy to be identified with Domenica—and either may have been a murderer. Japrisot's unravelling of what really happened on that night in the burning house on the Côte d'Azur is ingenious and the ending packs several surprises and ironies.

TRAVERS, LUDOVIC A detective in a long series of novels by Christopher BUSH. The first book in the series was *The Plumley Inheritance* (1926); the last novel appeared forty-two years later. The series was begun in the era of John RHODE, and Travers, like Desmond MERRION, is a World War I veteran and amateur detective who assists the English police. The Travers novels never transcended their GOLDEN AGE inspiration. Superintendent George Wharton is Travers's police contact. Together they go about breaking down alibis (also the specialty of Inspector FRENCH). Travers lasted longer than most of his contemporaries, but faded sooner because detective competence was not supplemented with any great degree of originality or imagination.

Travers is six-foot-three and wears "monstrous horn-rims," which he polishes while he is thinking. He is an author and an expert on economics; he is reserved and diffident, almost shy; and he is imaginative and generous. His values are a thirties mixture of radicalism and tradition: "unconventional and even communistic in the things that really matter but holding tight as a limpet to those canons of living whose outward and cheaper expressions are an Oxford accent and the old-school tie." Travers *sounds* interesting when he is described, but Bush's writing could not translate this potential into what he does. The same is true of Wharton, with his comical "weeping-willow of a moustache," his brusqueness, and his decisiveness. At rest, they are curious personalities, but their activities are ordinary.

BIBLIOGRAPHY Novels: *The Perfect Murder Case* (1929), *Murder at Fenwold* (1930, U.S. title *The Death of Cosmo Revere*), *Dead Man Twice* (1930), *Dancing Death* (1931), *Dead Man's Music* (1931), *Cut Throat* (1932), *The Case of the Unfortunate Village* (1932), *The Case of the Three Strange Faces* (1933; U.S. title *The Crank in the Corner*), *The Case of the April Fools* (1933), *The Case of the Dead Shepherd* (1934; U.S. title *The Tea Tray Murders*), *The Case of the 100% Alibi* (1934; U.S. title *The Kitchen Cake Murder*), *The Case of the Chinese Gong* (1935), *The Case of the Bonfire Body* (1936; U.S. title *The Body in the Bonfire*), *The Case of the Monday Murders* (1936; U.S. title *Murder on Mondays*), *The Case of the Hanging Rope* (1937; U.S. title *The Wedding Night Murder*), *The Case of the Missing Minutes* (1937; U.S. title *Eight O'Clock Alibi*), *The Case of the Tudor Queen* (1938), *The Case of the Leaning Man* (1938; U.S. title *The Leaning Man*), *The Case of the Green Felt Hat* (1939), *The Case of the Flying Ass* (1939), *The Case of the Climbing Rat* (1940), *The Case of the Murdered Major* (1941), *The Case of the Fighting Soldier* (1942), *The Case of the Red Colonel* (1942), *The Case of the Magic Mirror* (1943), *The Case of the Running Mouse* (1944), *The Case of the Platinum Blonde* (1944), *The Case of the Corporal's Leave* (1945), *The Case of the Second Chance* (1946), *The Case of the Missing Men* (1946), *The Case of the Curious Client* (1947), *The Case of the Haven Hotel* (1948), *The Case of the Housekeeper's Hair* (1948), *The Case of the Seven Bells* (1949), *The Case of the Purloined Picture* (1949), *The Case of the Happy Warrior* (1951; U.S. title *The Case of the Frightened Mannequin*), *The Case of the Fourth Detective* (1951), *The Case of the Comer Cottage* (1951), *The Case of the Happy Medium* (1952), *The Case of the Counterfeit Colonel* (1952), *The Case of the Burnt Bohemian* (1953), *The Case of the Silken Petticoat* (1953), *The Case of the Three Lost Letters* (1953), *The Case of the Red Brunette* (1954), *The Case of the Amateur Actor* (1955), *The Case of the Extra Man* (1956), *The Case of the Flowery Corpse* (1956), *The Case of the Russian Cross* (1957), *The Case of the Treble Twist* (1958; U.S. title *The Case of the Triple Twist*), *The Case of the Running Man* (1958), *The Case of the Careless Thief* (1959), *The Case of the Sapphire Brooch* (1960), *The Case of the Extra Grave* (1961), *The Case of the Dead Man Gone* (1962), *The Case of the Three-Ring Puzzle* (1962), *The Case of the Heavenly Twin* (1963), *The Case of the Grand Alliance* (1964), *The Case of the Good Employer* (1966), *The Case of the Deadly Diamonds* (1967), *The Case of the Prodigal Daughter* (1968).

TREADGOLD, HORACE B. Probably the only tailor-sleuth in mystery fiction, Horace B. Treadgold was created by Valentine WILLIAMS. From his little shop in the West End of London, he solves mysteries in *Dead Man Manor* (1936) and *Mr. Treadgold Cuts In* (1937; U.S. title *The Curiosity of Mr. Treadgold*).

TREAT, LAWRENCE (born Lawrence Arthur Goldstone, 1903–1988) Several years before the publication of LAST SEEN WEARING . . . (1952), Hillary WAUGH's famous PROCEDURAL novel, Lawrence Treat wrote a series of novels about a New York City detective with a procedural flavor. In his "alphabet" books—a title gimmick later used by Sue GRAFTON—detective Mitch Taylor and lieutenant Bill Decker solve crimes in a realistically presented New York, using real techniques including forensic assistance. The first novel in the series was *V as in Victim* (1945). He kept up the pattern for four more books: *H as in Hunted* (1946), *Q as in Quicksand* (1947), *T as in Trapped* (1947), and *F as in Flight* (1948). Several other novels appeared with more conventional titles. Treat was born in New York City and graduated from Dartmouth College in 1924. He received his law degree from Columbia University in 1927. He became a mystery writer in the 1930s, and was particularly well known for his short stories, which are currently unavailable. Treat won two EDGAR awards for his work in the short form. Treat taught mystery writing for years and won a special Edgar for his *Mystery Writer's Handbook* (1977).

TRENT, PHILIP A character created by E. C. BENTLEY, Philip Trent is the classic English detective of the GOLDEN AGE. His first appearance, TRENT'S LAST CASE (1913), was not actually his last, but was by far the most significant; this book was considered by Agatha CHRISTIE to be "one of the three best detective stories ever written." Time has eroded that reputation, because Trent seems in retrospect to be almost a PARODY, and the book has some important technical flaws (see separate entry).

Blond, tall, and elegant, Trent has a "high-boned, quixotic face," is a painter like his father, and though he has an independent income he is well known as an artist and sells his paintings. We are told that he solved his first case in one day by reading newspaper accounts of a murder on a TRAIN. Although he is only thirty-two and began detecting after his artistic success, his name is "one of the best known in England." He certainly sounds like a genius detective and not a down-to-earth GUMSHOE.

Bentley brought Trent back in another novel and several short stories. One of the stories is a famous mystery about GOLF. In the novel *Trent's Own Case* (1936), the detective investigates the death of a philanthropist; Dorothy L. SAYERS said Trent had "all his old humor and charm" (he was one of the inspirations for her sleuth, Lord Peter WIMSEY). The reason that it is Trent's *own* case is that he is a suspect. The novel was written by Bentley in collaboration with Herbert Warner Allen.

BIBLIOGRAPHY Short Stories: *Trent Intervenes* (1938).

TRENT'S LAST CASE (1913) A classic though problematic mystery by E. C. BENTLEY. The book is typically Edwardian—quirky servants, an interest in the new "motor cars," useful old-school acquaintances, and country houses. The story falls into two halves. In the first, the amateur detective Philip TRENT goes down to Marlstone to investigate the murder of American financier Sigsbee Manderson, found shot in the head next to the tool shed in his own yard. Trent is dispatched by the *Record,* the London paper to which he contributes his investigative reports.

Trent is often cited as the first modern, recognizably human detective, but there have been dissenters from that view (including Raymond Chandler, who criticized the book in THE SIMPLE ART OF MURDER [1944]). Trent's approach to detection is certainly as "quixotic" as his appearance. Mabel Manderson, it emerges, was a beautiful woman trapped in an unhappy marriage to an older man seemingly as cold in his private life as he was in his business dealings. Trent falls madly in love with the widow of the murdered man. After cracking the case (thanks to some clues he doesn't share with the reader), he leaves his final dispatch to the newspaper in the hands of his prime suspect. Trent next turns up in Munich, where he is trying to forget his hopeless love. The book has a romantic ending, based on a vow Trent has made during the story.

TRETHOWAN, PERRY See BARNARD, ROBERT.

TREVOR, VICTOR The man who, in "THE 'GLORIA SCOTT'" (1893), tells the young Sherlock HOLMES that he should become a detective, and who sets him on the course of his adventures by supplying, with his own death, the first of them.

TRIAL OF ELIZABETH CREE, THE (1995) A much-touted novel by English writer Peter ACKROYD. Ackroyd is one of those writers whose every work is greeted with loud praise, though this title was merely interesting while Ackroyd's HAWKSMOOR (1985) was a work of real genius. *The Trial of Elizabeth Cree* is based on the Limehouse murders, which took place in London in 1880. The killer's choice of victims and grisly methods are reminiscent of JACK THE RIPPER. Because of certain of his acts, and because the murderer was never seen and seemed to vanish into the polluted fog of the Limehouse district, a popular belief sprang up that the killings were the work of a "golem"—a monstrous creature of Jewish myth. As a result, a wave of xenophobia and anti-Semitism was unleashed. Among the writers who were influenced by the killings were George Gissing and Oscar Wilde.

No one was ever tried for the murders, making the story ripe for Ackroyd's technique of mixing facts with fiction. For instance, he makes the scene of some of the killings the same house where John WILLIAMS committed the Ratcliffe Highway murders in 1812, and the suspects include the novelist George Gissing, Karl Marx, and Dan Leno, a precursor of Charlie Chaplin. The main detective lives in domestic homosexual bliss amid Victorian London. Ackroyd's method is ingenious and literary, if a little uneven—the book is a strange combination of extremely grisly scenes, compelling descriptions of nineteenth century London, believable but invented journal entries, and excursuses on literary history in which Ackroyd falls into the dead jargon of "lit crit." The writing is excellent, despite the lack of unity of style and the disjointedness.

TRUE CONFESSIONS (1977) A novel by John Gregory DUNNE, set in Lost Angeles in 1946. With strong language and sharp and sometimes bitter humor, Dunne paints a picture of a corrupt, racist city and the fates of two brothers, each entwined with the fortunes of the Irish American fraternity (one could almost say mob) that dominates two institutions: the police department and the Catholic Church. Tom Spellacy is a detective whose wife spends most of her time in a mental institution; his son is in the armed forces and his obese daughter ("a walking Hersey bar") is a nun. Desmond has become the elderly Cardinal's chancellor, a combination administrator and hatchet man. There is a huge network of relations between the two institutions and the two men, from the prostitute from whom Tom took payoffs (not only in coin) to the crook she worked for, Jack Armstrong, who also happened to be the main builder of the archdiocese's new churches, centers, and schools. The grotesque murder of a young woman, her body cut in half and dumped in a vacant lot, plays upon the relationships as though they were nerves. No one really cares about the "Virgin Tramp," only about how her murder might get their name in the papers.

Police work is only important in the first and last quarters of the book. Much of the novel concerns the friction between the brothers, their mutual lack of understanding, and their vague resentment. While Desmond finesses his way through contracting the archdiocese's building projects, easing out figures who are no longer useful and arranging "donations" to the church (he's bucking for bishop), Tom worries about his pregnant girlfriend, his incompetent boss (who is bucking for chief), and the imminent return of his wife from the mental hospital. By the end of the book, however, Dunne has woven such a net of favors requiring reciprocation and old wrongs requiring a different sort of payback that the mixture is explosive.

James ELLROY used the same historical murder case as the basis for THE BLACK DAHLIA (1987), though except for the dismembered woman the books are entirely different. Robert De Niro and Robert Duvall shared the best actor prize at the Venice film festival for their portrayals of Des and Tom Spellacy in the film version of *True Confessions* (1981).

TRUE DETECTIVE, THE (1987) A novel by Theodore WEESNER. Set in the small coastal city of Portsmouth, New Hampshire, it concerns the disappearance of twelve-year-old Eric Wells. He and his brother Matt live with their mother Claire in a poor, fatherless household. Weesner establishes the tension in the household caused by their neediness—emotional and financial—even before Eric is abducted by a pedophilic college student only ten years older than he is. Repulsive as Vernon Fischer is, Weesner shows how he is little more than a child himself. Physically an adult and, as his crimes show, fully capable of adult brutalities, Vernon nonetheless sees himself as a hurt and starved child searching for love. Detective Gil Dulac, a transplanted French Canadian, is just as attentively drawn. A huge man driven by his own strength and sense of right, he races against an internal clock that tells him Eric is still alive. But this is a story that hurts more than it terrifies, nakedly revealing its characters' emotions without destroying their dignity. Weesner takes on the most flammable of issues, sex crime against children, but not merely to shock. The novel shows crime to be a wound from which pain radiates in every direction. Gil's sense of inadequacy, of his own childlessness, of a life of "small successes adding up to overall failure," becomes entwined with the detailed and competent investigation that unfortunately lags painfully behind events. And after the climax, there is only emptiness. For those who were touched by it, Weesner seems to say, the aftermath of a crime is permanent; even the signs through which we read what happened—the images, the *story*—are now changed utterly. The loss and the feeble hope of recovery is summed up in the image of personal belongings and papers left in a dumpster: "They lie there as a mass of words and pictures, within the deflected light of the mall, within the faintest currents of summer air, as if in waiting, in some secret plan, to be found again."

TRUFFAUT, FRANÇOIS (1932–1984) The French filmmaker François Truffaut had a troubled childhood, which may have led to his becoming one of the masters of the crime thriller. His first major film, *The 400 Blows* (1959), was based on his own experience in a reformatory and his becoming a factory worker at the age of fifteen. At a young age he became a film critic for the influential magazine *Cahiers du Cinéma,* but trouble found him again: called up for military service, he later deserted, went to prison, and received a dishonorable discharge.

The autobiographical character of *The 400 Blows* (1959) is named Antoine Doinel, whose story was continued in *Stolen Kisses* (1968), *Love on the Run* (1979), and other films. At the same time, Truffaut pursued a quite different career as a director of films imitative of HITCHCOCK, whom he greatly admired (he almost married one of Hitchcock's daughters). This other interest in Hollywood-style thrillers was evident even from his second major film, SHOOT THE PIANO PLAYER (1960), which was based on a novel by David GOODIS. Truffaut was in fact an aficionado of the American NOIR style. He also brought the Charles WILLIAMS novel *Hell Hath No Fury* (1953) to the screen as CONFIDENTIALLY YOURS (1982), and filmed Cornell WOOLRICH's *The Bride Wore Black* (1940) in 1968. Other films, such as *The Woman Next Door* (1981), deal with explosive, violent passions that sometimes lead to crime. The two faces of Truffaut's artistic work are different facets of the same romanticism, one branch of which leads to alienation, sensitive introversion, and love, and the other to obsession, transgression, and often death. He seems to have been attracted to those American writers who explored the dark side of fate and the hellish irony that the same passion that leads to the happy romantic ending can also lead to absolute damnation. He wrote a book that deals with the "noir" side of his artistic personality and its inspirations, *Hitchcock/Truffaut,* published in 1983. Truffault's life was cut short by a brain tumor.

TRUTH ABOUT THE SAVOLTA CASE, THE (orig title *La Verdad Sobre El Caso Savolta,* tr 1992) This novel by Eduardo MENDOZA was voted the most important book to be published in Spain since the end of the Franco regime. A virtuoso performance encompassing several styles, it requires a process of adaptation by the English reader. The narrative method, in which a chronicle is built up through multiple narrators, invented newspaper pieces, letters, court statements, and fragments adapted from real sources, is a very common one in Spanish literature, but requires a special receptiveness and attention. But with familiarity the novel becomes engrossing, particularly its evocation of the hectic atmosphere of Barcelona in the years following World War I. The story combines crime (political, financial, and *passionnel*), love, espionage, politics, and social themes.

Javier Miranda Lugarte, a young man from Valladolid who has studied law, gets a job with a Barcelona lawyer named Cortabanyes. The lawyer is a strange man: not very strict, sloppy in dress, but very well connected. He assigns Miranda to assist a distinguished young Frenchman, Lepprince—a shady character who, though only newly arrived in Barcelona, is already an executive in the Savolta Company, which dominates the financial scene. Its officers are Mr. Savolta (the majority shareholder), Mr. Claudedeu (chief of personnel, nicknamed "the man with the iron hand" because he lost a hand in a terrorist attack), and Mr. Parells (an older executive). A fourth executive whose functions are unclear is Lepprince himself. The company plays a major role in the social unrest of the time (1917–1919) and in the confrontations between proletariat and capital.

Lepprince uses Miranda as a courier in his transactions with two strongmen of the underworld, circus performers accompanied by a young and mysterious gypsy woman of incredible beauty. Miranda also meets Pajarito de Soto, an anarchist journalist with whom he develops a friendship. He gets involved with Pajarito's wife, first as friends and then suddenly one evening as lovers—on the night before Pajarito is killed. While Miranda tries to find out who killed Pajarito, a whole series of murders take place that center on the Savolta company; the police "investigation" includes reprisals for the assassinations and terrible raids against anarchists and activists in which many are executed. The truth is finally revealed to an astonished Miranda by a policeman who is himself ideologically suspect and in danger. It is a mystery that ends with a mystery and the terrible pathos of *la comédie humaine.*

TUBS On July 13, 1793, Charlotte Corday entered history by stabbing the French revolutionary Jean Paul Marat to death in his tub. Corday supported the more moderate Girondists and was striking a blow against the excesses of the Reign of Terror conducted by Marat and Robespierre.

The corpse in the tub has since become a familiar trope of crime fiction, evoking helplessness, embarrassment, and even humor. (It is also, of course, a convenient place to drown someone, as well as a notorious site for household accidents.) A body, naked or clothed, is found in the tub in such mysteries as *Whose Body?* (1923) by Dorothy L. SAYERS, the first Lord Peter WIMSEY novel; *Write Murder Down* (1972) by Richard LOCKRIDGE, as well as in the Lockridge's first novel about the NORTHS, *The Norths Meet Murder* (1940); *The Case of the Murdered Mackenzie* (1984) by E. V. CUNNINGHAM; Stewart Sterling's *Dead of Night* (1950); Skinner's *Round* (1995) by Quintin Jardine; and INTO THE NIGHT (pub 1987), the last unfinished work of Cornell WOOLRICH. Drowning the victim in the tub is always popular; such drownings occur in *Dishonor Among Thieves* (1958), a Don CADEE novel, and George BAXT's *The Tallulah Bankhead Murder Case* (1987). A tub drowning is the central scene of Henri-George Clouzot's *Les Diaboliques* (1955), one of the greatest mystery-thriller films of all time; it was based on a novel by Pierre Boileau and Thomas Narcejac.

Corday went to the GUILLOTINE on July 17, 1793, almost exactly a year before Robespierre suffered the same fate. Agatha CHRISTIE, incidentally, wrote many of her mysteries in the tub.

TUPPENCE AND TOMMY See BERESFORD, TUPPENCE AND TOMMY.

TURN OF THE SCREW, THE See JAMES, HENRY.

TURNER, DAN See BELLEM, ROBERT LESLIE.

TURPIN, DICK [RICHARD] (1706–1739) Famous English criminal and the subject of numerous literary works, including Harrison Ainsworth's *Rookwood* (1834). Turpin's parents ran an alehouse, and as a young man he was apprenticed to a butcher, but this legitimate training failed to take. Turpin first became a smuggler, a widely practiced profession at the time, and then joined a gang that specialized in robbing houses. From there, Turpin graduated to highwayman. He became the partner of the notorious Tom King, whom he shot to death accidentally while aiming at a pursuer during a getaway.

Legend has it that Turpin once rode his horse, Black Bess, from London to York (a distance of some 200 miles) in a single night to establish an alibi. It was for horse stealing that Turpin was ultimately convicted and hanged. Among the places where Turpin's story is described are *The Book of Remarkable Trials and Notorious Characters* (1845), with illustrations by Phiz, the illustrator of DICKENS. See also PEROWNE, BARRY.

TUTT, EPHRAIM This lawyer, created by Arthur C. TRAIN, was once a famous character. His cases were serialized in the *Saturday Evening Post* and collected in many volumes, among them the highly regarded *Mr. Tutt's Case Book* (1937), which was assigned as required reading in law schools. The Tutt stories present cases in which the innocent party has been set up, and it requires great legal ingenuity—reflecting the author's own background as an attorney—to exculpate them. Tutt practices in New York and has never lost a case. Train also published a fictitious biography, *The Autobiography of Ephraim Tutt* (1943).

BIBLIOGRAPHY Novels: *The Hermit of Turkey Hollow* (1921).

Short Stories: *Tutt and Mr. Tutt* (1920), *By Advice of Counsel* (1921), *Tut, Tut, Mr. Tutt!* (1923), *Page Mr. Tutt* (1926), *When Tutt Meets Tutt* (1927), *The Adventures of Ephraim Tutt* (1930), *Tutt for Tutt* (1934), *Mr. Tutt Takes the Stand* (1936), *Old Man Tutt* (1938), *Mr. Tutt Comes Home* (1941), *Mr. Tutt Finds a Way* (1945).

TWAIN, MARK (1835–1910) Born Samuel Langhorne Clemens in Florida, Missouri, Twain is one of the greatest American writers, whose novels *The Adventures of Tom Sawyer* (1876) and *The Adventures of Huckleberry Finn* (1884) are classics of world literature. Twain had already learned the printing trade and become a newspaperman by the age of twenty. He then spent several years in St. Louis, Philadelphia, and New York before becoming a Mississippi steamboat pilot in 1857. He drew upon this period and the colorful, humorous, and dangerous river characters he met for the stories in his novels, and took his pen name from the riverboatman's call that meant "two fathoms" depth.

Twain is usually discussed among mystery and detective authors with reference to THE TRAGEDY OF PUDD'NHEAD WILSON (1894), in which David Wilson, a lawyer, defends a twin accused of murder. The defense makes use of FINGERPRINTING, a detail that Twain had already been the first to introduce into fiction with "A Thumb-Print and What Came of It," a story in *Life on the Mississippi* (1883). But crime and detection are prevalent in Twain's most famous works as well. Twain's books have their roots in the PICARESQUE, a form he transports to the banks of the Mississippi in the antebellum period and interprets with great humor and wit. In their first adventure, *Tom Sawyer,* Tom and Huck witness a murder (comically, Twain places the scene in a graveyard; the two boys are trying to cure warts with a dead cat at the time). There follows the classic flight of the witness afraid of the murderer and the hesitant but courageous return, a story repeated countless times in later mystery and detective books. The boys come back to town just as Muff Potter is being tried for the crime. In the first sequel, *Huckleberry Finn,* Huck tells the story of his escape from his drunken and violent father and his trip down the river in the company of Jim, a runaway slave. More than the first book, *Huckleberry Finn* is an exposure of social ills and the diseased slave-owning society from which the two principal characters are in flight. But Twain also captures the adventurous, romantic side of the life he knew first-hand; in the manner of Melville's CONFIDENCE MAN (1857), he portrays the seedy world of the river and its array of ne'er-do-well characters.

One of Twain's most important contributions to American literature was the use of the vernacular, to be emulated by many later writers, including detective novelists. MENCKEN credited Twain with having legitimized the use of the American form of the language in literature, but deplored that it was only late in Twain's life that he received the respect he deserved as "the first American author of world rank to write a genuinely colloquial and native American." Ross MACDONALD was conscious of the influence of the style of Twain, whom he said was "just about the last great American novelist who wrote to a whole civilization."

Twain's late, little-known works focused even more directly on detective elements, and responded to the astounding success of Conan Doyle's Sherlock HOLMES stories. These include *Tom Sawyer, Detective* (1896) and *Simon Wheeler, Detective* (1903). Twain worked on the latter off and on for decades but never finished it. The story begins with a murderous feud between two families, the Burnsides and the Dexters. Young Hale Dexter arrives in Guilford in order to kill Hugh Burnside, whom he unwittingly meets on the road, befriending him and also falling in love with his sister, Clara. Meanwhile, Hugh falls in love with Milly Griswold, whose father, Judge Griswold, is enthusiastic about the feud and offers to help Hale Dexter commit the murder. Into this romantic comedy steps Simon Wheeler, a parody of the PINKERTON detective. While tracking a fugitive, Wheeler learns from Dexter that he has seen no footprints but only cow and wolf tracks; from this they deduce that their man has disguised himself as a cow and a wolf, and they think they have brought him to bay in a tree.

In "A Double-Barreled Detective Story" (1902), Twain makes fun of the methods of Sherlock Holmes. The story begins with a young man, Archie Stillman, who is born with the olfactory abilities of a bloodhound because his evil father had set his dogs on his mother. The father abandons them, and when Archie grows up the mother charges him with hunting the father to the ends of the earth, which he does, literally following his nose. A grave error in the pursuit is revealed, however. Archie finally winds up in a mining camp, where he pits his skills against those of Sherlock Holmes in the investigation of the blowing-up of a widely disliked miner. In a parody of Conan DOYLE's scientific method, Twain has Holmes take the barometric pressure, the precise position of the cabin allowing for magnetic variation, and other irrelevant but scientific measurements. The solution he comes to is completely wrong, and a lynch mob pursues Holmes to burn him at the stake.

Another famous Twain parody is the story "The Stolen White Elephant" (1882), about the appropriately named Detective Blunt.

"TWO BOTTLES OF RELISH, THE" A well-known story by a little-known author, Lord DUNSANY, collected in *The Little Tales of Smethers and Other Stories* (1934) and at one time often anthologized, including by Ellery QUEEN. Smethers is a traveling salesman who sells relish. In the story, he takes an apartment with a man considerably above his station, Mr. Linley, who has recently "come down" from Oxford. In between selling Num-numo, Smethers follows the case of a man, Steeger, suspected of murdering his girlfriend in a country cottage. They went to the cottage together; she completely disappeared, but Steeger stayed on, spending his time furiously chopping wood. Scotland Yard can find no evidence in the house or on the property. Smethers tries to get the brilliant Mr. Linley to think about the problem, and goes down himself to poke around and gather information. He learns from a merchant that Steeger bought two bottles of Num-numo, and this, combined with other facts, leads Linley to the solution. The reason for the wood chopping is brilliantly deduced.

TYBURN TREE Tyburn, located on the outskirts of London approximately three miles west of Newgate, was the traditional site of public hangings. "Tyburn tree" was the particular hanging tree that had been used from time immemorial for this purpose; so, to be hanged was "to ride a horse foaled by an acorn." Hanging, up until the end of the eighteenth century, was almost a sport: accounts of the victim's misdeeds or confessions were sold, and vast crowds assembled—including relatives and friends of the soon to be deceased who hoped to free the prisoner, or at least rescue the corpse from being turned over to one or another scientific or surgical association for dissection. The Tyburn site was abandoned in 1783 because the riots associated with the hangings had become so violent and opposition so strong. Thereafter, executions were carried out inside prisons and out of public sight. However, the public continued to have a morbid interest in such proceedings (see Charles DICKENS). See also PROTOMYSTERIES.

TYREE, CLINTON A recurrent character created by Carl HIAASEN who first appeared in *Double Whammy* (1987). He is also at the center of *Stormy Weather* (1995). Known as "Skink," Tyree is a cross between Iago, the wild man, and a Shakespearean fool. A former Florida governor who has gone mad—though there is method in his madness—he lives off the land (including roadkills) or what is left of it. Tyree is anti-development and anti-tourism, his favorite theme being the greedy pillaging of Florida.

UHNAK, DOROTHY (1933–) A fourteen-year decorated veteran of the New York City Transit Police, Dorothy Uhnak published her first novel while she was still a cop. But it was *The Bait* (1968), published the year after she left the force, that attracted attention. Anthony BOUCHER praised the book lavishly, calling it the first true police-*woman* PROCEDURAL.

The story begins with the young detective Christie OPARA, who works for a special squad of the District Attorney, riding the train on her way to a very important drug bust that has taken months to set up. She spots an extremely bizarre man about to expose himself to two young girls, arrests him, and misses her appointment. The man, Murray Rogoff, is a hairless giant who wears special goggles to keep his eyes moist and a cap crammed down to cover his bald head. Pathetic at first, his mental incapacity increases to monstrousness. Although the procedural element is overdone ("Carefully, she placed scraps of paper against the carbon and scrubbed away a letter, then lining the paper up, hit the proper key sharply . . . she had placed the letter in the wrong spot, causing a strikeover. . . ."), the story is compelling, an unromanticized view of policing in the big city. Written in the pre-Stonewall era, it shows the hatreds, ignorance, and the clash of various groups.

Uhnak gave up the Opara series rather quickly. Her later books have not been so well received. *The Investigation* (1977) is a truly disgusting story of the murder of two boys; the excessive way in which this atrocious killing is made even more vile is sickening.

UNCLE ABNER See ABNER, UNCLE.

UNCLE SILAS (1864) A novel of mystery and suspense by Sheridan LE FANU. Young Maud Ruthyn lives happily with her father, a well-meaning man besotted with Swedenborgianism. Knowing that he is dying, he decides that he has been too harsh with his brother Silas, an aging rake who was a family scandal but now affects austere piety. As a gesture of his trust, he appoints Silas to be his daughter's guardian upon his death. By the terms of the will, if Maud dies before she reaches majority, her estate devolves upon Uncle Silas.

Maud is sent to live with Silas after her father succumbs to his illness. Her cousin Monica is alarmed, because she knows of the scandal in Silas's past: he is suspected in the death of a man who was staying in his house (he owed the man money). Silas has grown ill, bad-tempered, and seedy. He lives in his dilapidated gothic mansion, Bartram Haugh, with his brute of a son. The household is rounded out by the governess Madame de la ROUGIERRE, whose slithering manner, bad accent, and combination of fawning servility and cruelty (she tortures Maud when no one is looking) are vividly portrayed.

The plot involves several mysteries, including: What really happened to Uncle Silas's unfortunate guest? Why is part of the mansion closed up and off limits? and What is to be Maud's fate at Bartram Haugh? It being a novel in the GOTHIC mode, there are also narcotics, an attempted escape, a grisly murder, a romantic subplot, sympathetic servants, and ambiguous local characters. Le Fanu also used the LOCKED ROOM situation in the plot, a device he had experimented with even before POE. Like other works by Le Fanu, the novel has first to overcome its own inertia, and then mounts from terror to terror; he was a master of atmosphere and the conception of treacherous double characters whose words and actions strike alarmingly discordant notes for the reader.

UNDERWOOD, MICHAEL (1916–) Based on thirty years' experience with the Department of Public Prosecutions, the English barrister Michael Underwood has written several series of novels that could be called legal procedurals. Although his most interesting series protagonist, Rosa EPTON, is a lawyer, he has also written about two policemen, Sergeant Nick Atwell and Inspector Simon Manton.

Underwood was born in Sussex and graduated from Oxford in 1938. He was called to the bar the following year. His career with the Department of Public Prosecutions began in 1946, and continued long after he had made a name for himself as a writer. *Murder on Trial* (1954) was Underwood's first book, and introduced Inspector Simon Manton. Underwood wrote thirteen books about Manton over the next ten years, including *Death on Remand* (1956), one of his best novels. During the sixties and early seventies, Underwood focused on non-series novels, some of them involving espionage, and downplayed the courtroom element. Among these were *The Shadow Game* (1969), about a well-meaning barrister recruited by intelligence agents who gets into trouble behind the Iron Curtain, and *The Unprofessional Spy* (1964), a novel that is also about a barrister (this time in East Berlin) and that introduced Rosa Epton in a minor role. *A Trout in the Milk*

(1971) is unusual among the non-series mysteries in that it is a courtroom novel. Many scenes in Underwood's novels take place at the Old Bailey in London.

In 1977, Underwood wrote his first book about Nick Atwell, *Murder with Malice.* Atwell is assisted by his wife, a former constable. In *The Fatal Trip* (1977), a burglar is found guilty but Atwell still has his doubts. Risking official disapprobation, he puts his wife on the case, and much of the investigation is done by her more or less as a p.i. The least interesting of Underwood's series characters, Atwell was abandoned after three novels. Underwood brought Epton back in *Crime Upon Crime* (1980). Underwood's books could best be described as solid (generally), like the British legal procedurals of Sara WOODS, except that Underwood has experimented more over the course of his thirty-odd novels.

UNKINDNESS OF RAVENS, AN (1985) An Inspector WEXFORD novel by Ruth RENDELL, the title of which comes from an obscure linguistic oddity. Dora, Wexford's wife, tells him that her friend Joy's husband Rod has disappeared. Wexford calls on Joy and finds her to be a listless, lifeless woman living in an unbearable lower-middle-class milieu. Her teenage daughter Sara is equally unhappy and secretive. Wexford finds out that Rod had taken a leave from his job as a marketing manager, leading the inspector to suspect the classic "other woman" scenario. But when the missing man's suitcase turns up in a pond, the case takes on a different tone. Then two men are mysteriously stabbed by a young girl along the Pomfret Road, and finally Sara's cousin is killed. Wexford uses an ingenious plan to force the murderer into the open, but the motive that is finally revealed is questionable, depending on one's acceptance of the atmosphere created in the novel. As usual, Rendell's writing is literate and suspenseful; she injects into the novel the kind of issues she dealt with more explicitly in her books written under the pseudonym Barbara Vine.

"UNKNOWN WEAPON, THE" (1864) One of Andrew FORRESTER, JR.'s tales about the detective Mrs. G—. Collected in *The Female Detective* (1864), they could be seen either as long short stories or short novels; "The Unknown Weapon" was reprinted in *Three Victorian Detective Novels* (1976). In the story, Mrs. G— is not named, the narrator simply referring to herself as a female detective. She is amused but not surprised when the residents of the town of Tram "could not grasp the idea of a police officer in petticoats." She goes about undercover, investigating the case of a young man found dead outside his father's country house, murdered with a strange, barbed piece of iron found stuck in the body. There was no love lost between the elder Squire Petleigh, an avaricious collector of gold and silver plate, and his son, an inveterate poacher driven to crime by his father's stinginess and his own romantic disposition.

The narrator gives a lengthy description of the inquest in the style of the time, simulating as much as possible the matter-of-fact chronicles of real crimes. Yet those chronicles were usually short stories with little character or plot development, whereas "The Unknown Weapon" has a complex chain of evidence and a narrator whose tone of professionalism and amusement at her ability to deceive her interlocutors conveys a real sense of person. It is a sustained performance, in the course of which she remarks on the contradictoriness of human nature, apologizes for the detective's necessity of lying, and notes that the profession breeds the suspicion that everyone is guilty until proven otherwise—"a very dismal way of looking upon society." Forrester has her say that "our system is a necessary one (under the present condition of society)," at a time when that system—of criminal justice and policing—was still in its infancy. Writing four years before the publication of THE MOONSTONE (1868), Forrester had already grasped the possibilities of combining the new world of the policeman with the tradition of sensational literature in an extended format. At so early a date, it is also surprising to find Forrester already using such scientific techniques as the examination of fibers through a microscope.

UPFIELD, ARTHUR W[ILLIAM] (1888–1964) Australian mystery novelist Arthur W. Upfield is one of those novelists who, like Rex STOUT, led a life at least as exciting as his fictions. As a young man, Upfield was sent away to Australia by his father, who was convinced that his son was destined to be a failure. Instead, Upfield took immediately to the land and thrived. He wandered across the continent working at various jobs including cook, fence-rider on a sheep station, and miner. In 1914, he enlisted and fought in World War I, seeing action in France, Egypt, and at Gallipoli in Turkey, the fruitless nine-month campaign in which 300,000 men on both sides died.

After the war, Upfield married and returned to England, but the marriage was unhappy. He became estranged from his wife and son, and went back to Australia and a life of gold prospecting and fur trapping. His early books were derivative thrillers. Not until he met up with Tracker Leon, a half-aborigine who worked for the police, did he hit upon the idea of Inspector Napoleon BONAPARTE, who made his first appearance in *The Barrakee Mystery* (1929; U.S. title *The Lure of the Bush*). Bony is somewhat conceited in the HOLMES manner, a quality toned down in the later books, but the story and especially the descriptions of the Australian bush were distinctive enough to get the series off the ground. Upfield's most famous book, written two years later, was a case of LIFE IMITATES ART. While working as a fence-rider in the Australian bush, Upfield said out loud one evening that he would give "a pound" for the plot of a perfect murder. His friend George Ritchie obliged him, describing how a man could be killed, his body burned and then completely eradicated using only the resources available on a bush station. That idea became *The Sands of Windee* (1931). Before the book was even printed, another local man had taken the idea to the next step—reality.

Bony is an engaging character, and the author was sufficiently conversant with Aboriginal culture to make him more than just a native Holmes. But the star of the books is really Australia itself. Upfield's ability to evoke its sometimes cruel beauty and desolation alone makes the novels worth reading. Sometimes he poignantly portrays characters who are less complex than the land that surrounds them; their hopes are often dashed by floods, droughts, and other catastrophes. The Aboriginal characters are neither romanticized nor patronized; some are good and others bad. Upfield does betray white prejudices (such as the idea that all Aborigines are ugly), and calling the indigenous people "abos" would be considered offensive today. It is, however, an accurate depiction of the time in which the books are set. Upfield died before the first Aboriginal novel was even published—which was, incidentally, a sort of crime novel. Mudrooroo's *Wild Cat Falling* (1965) is about a young part-Aborigine man who has just been released from prison.

Upfield describes Bonaparte as a "romantic," and romantic subplots are pursued in several of the books (including THE BONE IS POINTED, 1938), though the outcome is sometimes a tragedy rather than a ride off into the sunset. Bonaparte sometimes goes undercover, in which case he is treated merely as a "half-caste" by white settlers. *Winds of Evil* (1937) has Bony investigating the activities of a strangler while posing as a "swagman"—a hobo and wandering laborer. In *Journey to the Hangman* (1959), he is Nat Bonner, an itinerant horse breaker who goes to the remote town of Daybreak (presided over by the comical MELODY SAM) in order to solve three brutal killings in which a former delinquent is suspected. This novel is similar to *The Bone Is Pointed* in that the rural community is treated as a closed system, in which a symbiotic relationship exists between tribal blacks who still maintain traditional practices (including telepathy and ritual murder by "the pointing of the bone") and the white ranchers.

Upfield's writing developed over the course of the series, and the books became shorter, though plot and the "rules" of the game were not always respected; the motive in *Journey to the Hangman* is impossible for the reader to deduce. Upfield's sometimes stilted language in the early works gave way to more fluid writing. THE TORN BRANCH (1959) most displays Upfield's love of the land and contains his best nature writing. He is less successful when Bony is removed to the city setting, as in *An Author Bites the Dust* (1948), but *The Devil's Steps* (1946), about Bony's efforts on behalf of national security, is one of the best books in terms of detection.

Follow My Dust! (1957) is a biographical work about Upfield by his companion, Jessica Hawke. *The Spirit of Australia* (1988), by Ray B. Browne, is a critical work.

UP THE RIVER See SING SING.

UPTON, ROBERT (1934–) Robert Upton was born in Illinois and studied law. He practiced in San Francisco while trying to write for the theater. Later he moved to New York City and had some success writing for film and the stage. His first novel, *Who'd Want to Kill Old George?* (1976), introduced Amos McGuffin, an amiable, hard-drinking private eye who lives on a houseboat in San Francisco and is somewhat similar to the hapless Alo NUDGER. In the first book, McGuffin is hired by a millionaire to find out if his estranged wife is cheating on him. When the detective reports back in the affirmative, he finds his client shot to death. Although the police think it was a case of burglary, McGuffin is intrigued by the presence of a movie projector in the room—without any film. The case leads McGuffin to a typical California consciousness-raising group—a cult—that supposedly had driven his client insane. In *Fade Out* (1984) McGuffin is dispatched by Nat Volpersky to look into the supposed suicide of his son, a Hollywood producer. Sinister Arabs and a suspicious cop add to his woes, but McGuffin has miraculous luck. One of McGuffin's cases involves GOLF. Other McGuffin novels include *The Fabergé Egg* (1988) and *A Killing in Real Estate* (1990).

URSULA, SISTER A sleuth created by Anthony BOUCHER who appeared in the novels considered to be his finest, NINE TIMES NINE (1940) and ROCKET TO THE MORGUE (1942).

VACHELL, SUPERINTENDENT A detective created by Elspeth HUXLEY who appears in her mystery novels set in Africa. Vachell is a Canadian, and studied with the F.B.I. and worked in Canada and India before becoming the head of the Chania police in British East Africa. With long legs and deep-set eyes, Vachell clearly has something Holmesian in his makeup. His curiosity and compassion and tendency to observe those around him while maintaining a neutral reserve are vaguely reminiscent of Lew ARCHER. Vachell is also, however, capable of making a complete ass of himself. His best case is the THE AFRICAN POISON MURDERS (1939). He also appears in *Murder on Safari* (1938).

One of the main problems he faces is that in rural Africa, people who are involved in or connected to a crime can simply vanish, drifting off into the bush (as in the Inspector Napoleon BONAPARTE mysteries). The author vividly recreates the vast and engulfing background that is Vachell's real adversary.

BIBLIOGRAPHY Novels: *Murder at Government House* (1937).

VACHSS, ANDREW (1942–) The American lawyer and writer Andrew Vachss has written both straight crime novels as well as detective stories about a private eye with the single name BURKE. Of these two halves of his output, the former is by far the best.

Vachss was born in New York City and attended Case Western Reserve University as an undergraduate. He received his law degree from New England Law School in 1975. He has specialized in public interest law, particularly cases involving the abuse of CHILDREN, a subject that is treated explicitly in his novels.

VALCOUR, LIEUTENANT See KING, RUFUS.

VALIN, JONATHAN [LOUIS] (1948–) A native of Cincinnati, Jonathan Valin has written a series of novels set in that city and concerning private investigator Harry STONER. Valin received his bachelor's degree from the University of Chicago in 1974, went on to study at Washington University in St. Louis, and briefly had a teaching career before he quit and devoted himself completely to writing. His first Stoner novel was published in 1980 (*The Lime Pit*), and they have appeared with regularity since then.

Valin is greatly concerned with history, and Stoner reflects on the changes in Cincinnati since the "good old days" of the sixties. The neighborhoods have become more integrated, but crime, hate, and racism have increased. Developers change the face of the city while its insides rot. Many of Valin's characters (including Stoner) are middle-aged people trying to find some meaning in a world unlike that of their youth. Valin is not peddling more sixties nostalgia, however. In *Fire Lake* (1987), Lonnie Jackowski, a former friend, uses Stoner's name to check into a hotel room, where he tries to kill himself. Stoner and Jackowski's wife try to find him after he disappears, somewhat unwillingly; both had rejected Lonnie because of his self-destructive drug use. In *The Music Lovers* (1993), Stoner's client is an audiophile with a collection of 23,000 records who thinks valuable disks have been stolen by another member of his stereo clique. The mystery deepens and involves a group of burnouts, "leftovers in the refrigerator of life" trying to cope in an era without values; the characterizations of the minor figures are among Valin's most subtle. Stoner is most Matt SCUDDER–like in *Missing* (1995), at the heart of which are issues of homosexuality and the AIDS crisis. It is a problematic work, not so much for a number of small mistakes as for its ultimate failure to render something intelligible from its own ambivalence. Stoner says that he does not like gays, and the cops are shown to hate them, as do the self-loathing gays the story depicts. A kind of homosexual original sin is conjured up, which settles like a rank fog in the empty spaces of the narrative. FINAL NOTICE (1981) was made into a film (1989). Valin won a Shamus award for *Extenuating Circumstances* (1989). LIFE'S WORK (1986) is thoughtful, funny, and violent.

The writer who seems closest to Valin in spirit is Loren D. ESTLEMAN, whose mysteries about Amos WALKER are set in another Midwestern city, Detroit. Valin's books, however, remain more individual and less dependent on the formulas of the HARD-BOILED school. In addition, Valin is one of a few writers in the genre whose writing has improved over time, becoming more involved with personality and the concerns of "straight" novels.

VALJEAN, JEAN See MISÉRABLES, LES.

VALLEY OF FEAR, THE See DOYLE, SIR ARTHUR CONAN.

VALMONT, EUGÈNE Created by Robert BARR, Eugène Valmont was a precursor of Hercule POIROT. Valmont is an amateur whose services are called for by Scotland Yard. At a time when invincible sleuths with remarkable powers were in vogue, Valmont was a talented but pompous ratiocinator who is brought down by his own hubris. He and his Scotland Yard contact, Spenser Hale, trade snide remarks about each other's intellectual abilities. Valmont, like Poirot, embodies the English comic stereotype of the French: he is elegant to a fault, excessively vain, and short-tempered. Agatha Christie, however, did not go all out for comedy in the way that Barr did, and so Poirot is a "serious" detective. Valmont's most famous case is "THE ABSENT-MINDED COTERIE" (1906). Only one book of Valmont stories was published, *The Triumphs of Eugène Valmont* (1906).

VANCE, PHILO Once an enormously popular character, S. S. VAN DINE's Philo Vance was the GENIUS DETECTIVE to a fault; today he seems like a caricature, an unbearable anglophile who would like to be Sherlock HOLMES, though he is so arrogant he would probably feel he was lowering himself. Philo Vance is Bernard Berenson with a sleuthing bug. Vance knows everything, permits himself everything (for example, killing the murderer himself), and understands everyone by virtue of his flawless intuition. He smokes his Régie cigarettes in a holder, has "chiselled features," and drops his final g's (a trait of Lord Peter WIMSEY's). He is one of the great snobs of fiction. At the beginning of *The Dragon Murder Case* (1933), the narrator remarks of Vance that "since the influx of post-war, *nouveau riche* Americans along the French and Italian Rivieras, he had forgone his custom of spending his summers on the Mediterranean." If the books are enjoyable, they are enjoyable as camp; Van Dine was funny unintentionally, as Elliot PAUL was by design.

Philo Vance is a very overdone example of the handsome detective type. He is tall, has a cleft chin, and "a slightly derisive hauteur in the lift of his eyebrows," which is appropriate given that he is an aristocrat. Vance has been to Oxford (like Holmes, he doesn't seem to have deigned to graduate), wears a monocle, drives a Hispano-Suiza, and has a house outside Florence, Italy. However, he does his detecting in New York from a Thirty-eighth Street townhouse crammed with *objets d'art,* including works of the Italian Renaissance and one of the best collections of Chinese prints. Ogden Nash immortally summed up exasperation with the character in two lines: "Philo Vance/needs a kick in the pance."

Seen in comparison with later tastes, Vance seems ridiculous. But in the GOLDEN AGE, he was not that much more eccentric, nor that much more brilliant, than many other detectives. He simply flaunted it, and that may account for his great success (the stories are said to have kept Scribner's afloat during hard times). Vance is a creature of the Jazz Age and can be admired for his nerviness. Whatever his defects, he is certainly a "personality." In fact, Philo Vance may have been wasted as a detective; he would have made one of the greatest villains of crime and mystery fiction for those very same qualities that make him so easy to hate as a detective.

Vance is assisted by "Van Dine," an old classmate and friend (from Harvard, of course). This narrator can be tedious, for example in his pages of description of his idol's great art collection, and the many pedantic footnotes, loaded with the author's cultural pronouncements (disguised as Vance's), and such minutiae as Vance's "interpuliary width" and angle of face, derived from x-rays.

The first Philo Vance book was THE BENSON MURDER CASE (1926), in which Van Dine as narrator describes how he came to be Vance's personal assistant and lawyer after Vance returned from his years in Europe. The book shows that, though Philo Vance may be a genius, his creator was not, for details seem to get away from him. He appears most interested in describing the luxurious atmosphere with an almost fetishistic relish. Yet, for their "grand imaginative folly," Julian SYMONS termed THE GREENE MURDER CASE (1928) and *The Bishop Murder Case* (1929) "among the finest fruits of the Golden Age." In the latter, the series of killings are based on nursery rhymes. In his most famous scene, Vance does in the killer at the end by switching drinks with him (his was poisoned). Even *The Dragon Murder Case,* which seems to be nobody's favorite, has some amusing details. It takes place at the Stamm mansion in upper Manhattan; the Stamms themselves are an "intensely inbred line." Sanford Montague, an actor with designs on the Stamm fortune, dives into the Dragon Pool during a party and fails to come up again. The other drunken guests don't much care, because they are also interested in the Stamm money. It would not be a Philo Vance mystery without some arcane subject matter—here, Native American lore about the "monster" believed to inhabit the pool. Manhattan's Inwood neighborhood (still a rural retreat and "hidden fastness" at the time!) becomes a sort of Sleepy Hollow.

The "Canary" Murder Case (1927) is about the killing of a Broadway star. *The Kennel Murder Case* (1933) is a LOCKED ROOM MYSTERY. The last Philo Vance story, *The Winter Murder Case* (1939), was only in outline form at the time of the author's death, but Van Dine's "outlines" were novel-length in themselves.

BIBLIOGRAPHY Novels: *The Scarab Murder Case* (1930), *The Casino Murder Case* (1934), *The Kidnap Murder Case* (1936), *The Garden Murder Case* (1937), *The Gracie Allen Murder Case* (1938).

VAN DER VALK, INSPECTOR PIET Nicholas FREELING's Piet Van der Valk is one of the most human of fictional detectives: when he gets shot, he dies. The author made the inspector convincingly imperfect, and just as convincingly got rid of him after ten books. Strangely, for an author so concerned with verisimilitude, he had the inspector's wife Arlette take up the case and solve it after his death (see AUPRÈS DE MA BLONDE [1972]). Arlette Van der Valk then became a series character herself.

Van der Valk is a veteran detective who works for the gruff, pipe-smoking Mr. Boersma, who is far more politic than Van der Valk, whom he thinks will never advance any further because he is "distrusted, higher up." Van der Valk is too sensitive; he wants to understand as well as detect. He respects the law but is willing to bend or break it in order to make his case. This shows a pragmatism—or cynicism, perhaps—that runs through his character. He is like MAIGRET in having a sympathetic understanding of criminals and an intuitive ability to feel his way toward the roots of their actions. In BECAUSE OF THE CATS (1963), he tries to understand what goes on in the minds of wealthy, bored adolescents who break into homes to defile and wreck them, and in one case rape the owner in front of her husband.

Freeling's outlook is bleaker than that of SIMENON, with whom he is compared. Whereas Maigret is a character of the thirties who survived into the seventies, Van der Valk is definitely a product of a postwar world in which any idealism is a drug that wears off quickly. Van der Valk calls himself a "poor sod of a policeman" because he needs other people before whom he can think out loud and thus arrive at his conclusions. He distrusts the system he works for and disparages his own job: "A Dutch policeman was really good for only one thing, and that was filling in a form explaining how some other very wicked asocial individual had filled in another form incorrectly." Van der Valk's consciousness as constructed in the novels illustrates the principle of mediation: he is part of the system, "a tool of government control," and he never can really see his own actions apart from the distorting lens of his own role. Thus a *leitmotif* of the series is that for Van der Valk, knowledge always seems to come too late. The detective's view of himself dovetails with the author's efforts at social criticism and his economic interpretation of police work: "in our days the government, in order to make headway against the pressures and distortions, the tides of economic change and the winds of upheaval, must possess a machine so complex and so detailed that its tentacles can grip and manipulate every soul within its frontiers." Van der Valk is a liberal man in a reactionary profession.

Although Van der Valk is sometimes assisted and even rescued by his wife, he tries not to use her as a sounding board; she punishes him with bad food when he gets too preoccupied with a case, so he prefers not to bring work home. Some of the best Van der Valk stories are LOVE IN AMSTERDAM (1962), the first case; *Gun Before Butter* (1963; U.S. title *A Question of Loyalty*), one of the most homely and believable cases of smuggling; *Criminal Conversation* (1965), about a neurologist accused of murder; and THE KING OF THE RAINY COUNTRY (1966), which won an EDGAR award.

BIBLIOGRAPHY Novels: *Double Barrel* (1964), *Strike Out Where Not Applicable* (1967), *Tsing-Boom* (1969), *Over the High Side* (1971; U.S. title *The Lovely Ladies*).

VAN DE WETERING, JANWILLEM (1931–) The Dutch police PROCEDURAL author Janwillem van de Wetering has used the genre to satirize and reflect on his native country, but his wide travels and philosophical interests transcend the procedural subgenre. As an alternative to military service, van de Wetering became a police officer with the Amsterdam Reserve Constabulary for ten years. He was a very unusual policeman: born in Rotterdam, he had studied Zen in the Daitoku-ji Monastery in Kyoto, Japan, and philosophy at the University of London. He had written two books about Zen, *The Empty Mirror* (1971; tr 1975) and *A Glimpse of Nothingness* (1975), before he produced the first of his Amsterdam police novels, OUTSIDER IN AMSTERDAM (1975).

The Amsterdam series focuses on Adjutant GRIJPSTRA and Sergeant de Gier, his junior partner. Their boss is the "commissaris" named Jan; an older man, he is a delegator rather than an investigator, though his wistful dialogue is an important counterpoint to the bluster of Grijpstra and the dreamy thinking of de Gier. Another important character is the "CC," the chief constable, a "decorative" man with an aquiline nose and silver hair who lost his wife when she crashed her plane into a peat bog, after which he engaged in a mechanical series of affairs. As may have become apparent, the Amsterdam series is very much focused on men, most of them reflective and to some degree alienated from the society that they serve.

Van de Wetering moved to the coast of Maine in 1975, and thereafter set several of the mysteries in the United States, including *The Maine Massacre* (1979). After *Hard Rain* (1986) there was a hiatus in the series, but the characters later returned in a reconfigured setting. In *Just a Corpse at Twilight* (1994), Grijpstra has become a private detective and de Grier is retired and living on an island off the coast of Maine. In *The Hollow-Eyed Angel* (1996), we flash back to a time when Grijpstra and the Sergeant are still on the force, and the commissaris seems to be on his last legs.

Van de Wetering has also written non-series crime novels, as well as a collection of short stories, *Inspector Saito's Small Satori* (1985), his clearest attempt to combine Eastern philosophy with the detective story. Inspector Saito Masonobu is an inspector third class in Kyoto. He comes from a wealthy family; both his parents were doctors, and were killed in a car accident. No inscrutable genius, Saito is an ambitious man who wants to publish an article about the criminal mind to annoy his boss and make himself famous. The philosophy, whether it is the Zen teaching of a monk (and suspect) that leads to Saito's small glimpse of enlightenment (*satori*), or the homespun Buddhism of his uncle, is well presented, and is clearly the main focus of the book; the mysteries cannot help but seem secondary.

Van de Wetering also wrote the biography *Robert van Gulik: His Life, His Work* (1988), about the author of the Judge DEE stories. Van de Wetering usually writes his procedural novels in English, though in some cases there have been Dutch versions.

VAN DINE, S. S. (pseudonym of Willard Huntington Wright, 1888–1939) An erudite critic of art and literature as well as a journalist, Willard Huntington Wright chose one of the most original methods of getting into crime fiction. He decided to write a mystery story while he was convalescing from an illness, and supposedly took the scholarly approach of first studying some 2,000 mysteries of the past century to get a grounding in the genre (Wright's claims have been disputed). He then wrote enormous outlines of the first three of what would be the Philo VANCE series of detective novels, some of the most popular of the century, even though they fell into disfavor relatively quickly.

Wright was born in Charlottesville, Virginia. He attended Pomona College in California as an undergraduate, and went on to study at Harvard University and in Europe. His first newspaper job was as the literary editor and art critic of the *Los Angeles Times*. He moved to New York in 1912, where he became associated with H. L. MENCKEN and George Jean Nathan. Wright was an editor of *Smart Set* and collaborated with Mencken and Nathan on *Europe After 8:15* (1914), a collection of travel essays. He was a frequent traveler to the Continent, and chose the initials "S. S." for his pseudonym in recognition of his shipboard travels. Wright also published poetry, a novel (*The Man of Promise*, 1916), a nonfiction book, *Modern Painting* (1915), and a book on Friedrich Nietzsche (1915).

Thus established as a literary figure, Wright saw himself as taking a serious step down when he decided to write a mystery (unlike C. Day-Lewis [Nicholas BLAKE], a poet laureate of England who never concealed his detective writing, despite the pseudonym). He was bound to create a detective somewhat in his own image, but Philo Vance is also clearly an Americanized version of Lord Peter WIMSEY. Many critics now complain about Vance's pretentiousness, extreme erudition, and loquaciousness. On the other hand, Wright himself was highly cultured, and Vance, though pedantic, actually does know what he's talking about. But Wright no doubt shared his friend Mencken's low opinion of the detective genre, some of which rubbed off on the books in the form of near-parody; one is never quite sure whether Wright is not actually laughing behind the mask of "S.S. Van Dine," who relates Philo Vance's adventures with a straight face. Footnotes are even included to increase the theatrically brainy and academic feeling.

The first book, also considered one of the best, was based on a real murder that took place in 1920 (for the killing of Joseph Elwell, see Jonathan GOODMAN). THE BENSON MURDER CASE (1926) makes better reading than the later books because Van Dine has not yet worked up Vance to be truly annoying. The author originally planned to write only six books and then stop; however, the first three were so successful that he went on to write a total of twelve Philo Vance novels. Wright regretted that he was no longer taken seriously as a literary figure after he devoted himself to the Vance series, as indicated by his essay "I Used to Be a Highbrow But Look at Me Now" (1929). But, while outdated books on Nietzsche and aesthetics are many and their authors forgotten, classic mysteries like the Philo Vance novels are perennially discussed (if little read). Sadly, Wright never seems to have recognized this, and clung to his "highbrow" image of himself.

The second Vance mystery, *The Canary Murder Case* (1927), concerned not a bird but a singer, and on its wings Wright soared to unheard-of popular (and financial) success. In the same year he published THE GREENE MURDER CASE (1928), which contained one of the author's most famous stunts: the murders are committed in imitation of a German criminological treatise. *The Bishop Murder Case* (1929) focused on a scientist accused of a series of murders; here the murders are inspired by nursery rhymes. Afterward, the books became progressively more ridiculous. Van Dine's novels were serialized in magazines including the *Pictorial Review* and *The American Magazine*.

Philo Vance is among the most despised creatures of the detective genre, dismissed out of hand by many who have never read him (a fate like that of THE MYSTERY OF A HANSOM CAB [1886] and its author). Yet there is a degree of pleasure in reading the novels, similar to that of watching old movies of the twenties and thirties: the acting is terrible, the dialogue absurd, but the very fact that the plot is acted out with high seriousness may be amusing, more so than later products (for example, the Inspector SCHMIDT novels) that are modest to a fault.

In 1992, John Loughery published *Alias S.S. Van Dine,* a biography that won an EDGAR award and also tore down the last shreds of the Van Dine myth, stating, for example, that the legendary reading of the 2,000 books was a fiction, that the author's "illness" was the product of substance abuse, and that Wright abandoned his wife and child. There is still something remarkable about his decision to turn himself into a popular novelist—and succeeding. He wrote about detective novel-writing in his introduction to *The Great Detective Stories* (1927) and in a 1928 essay, "Twenty Rules for Writing Detective Stories." He used his prodigious income from the Philo Vance novels and several film spin-offs in order to live like Philo Vance, enjoying Epicurean luxury during the Depression. In a sense, the most interesting Vance story is "the Van Dine case," or how a preposterous illusion became reality.

VANE, HARRIET D. The wife of Lord Peter WIMSEY, Dorothy L. SAYERS's great detective. Harriet's physical appearance is very similar to that of Sayers herself, which has led commentators to postulate that Sayers was so impressed with her own creation that she fell in love with him, and created a character (Vane) so that she could marry him herself. Harriet Vane is a mystery novelist, and also has an unconventional love life (like the author herself) which lands her in the dock on a murder charge in STRONG POISON (1930).

VAN GULIK, ROBERT (1910–1967) Robert van Gulik came to the mystery story rather late in a relatively short life, but still created one of the best-known characters in the genre. A man of broad experience and erudition, van Gulik was a Dutchman who grew up in Java and wrote about a Chinese detective, Judge DEE. The first Judge Dee book was not an invention but a translation of a seventeenth-century Chinese work about an eighth-century district magistrate, *Dee Goong An: Celebrated Cases of Judge Dee* (tr 1949). Van Gulik's first Judge Dee book of his own was THE CHINESE BELL MURDERS (1951). Van Gulik was a brilliant linguist and knew many languages, including Chinese dialects, Japanese, and languages of the Indian subcontinent as well as those of the countries where he served in the diplomatic corps.

Van Gulik was born in the Netherlands, but his father was a doctor in the Dutch colonial army, so Van Gulik spent the years from age three to twelve in Indonesia. Van Gulik returned to the Netherlands to attend school. Already his gift for languages had begun to show, and, under the guidance of a mentor, he studied Sanskrit, Chinese, and the Blackfoot Indian language (his first published work was about the Blackfoot language). His studies continued at the University of Leyden, where he earned his Ph.D. with a dissertation on the horse cult of the East.

Van Gulik then returned to Asia, serving in the diplomatic service in Japan from 1935 until World War II, when he was evacuated to China. He returned to the Netherlands two years after the end of the war. Van Gulik was an antiquarian book collector, and it was in 1940 that he first came across an old book about Judge Dee. In addition to *De Goong An,* he also translated *T'ang-yin pi-shih* (1956), a thirteenth-century casebook that provided much of the material for his Judge Dee stories. Van Gulik continued his diplomatic career after the war, serving in the Far and Middle East as well as in the United States. The pinnacle of his career came a couple of years before the end of his life, when he was appointed ambassador to Japan.

Van Gulik's books have been praised for their atmosphere and their plots, which he adapted from his Chinese sources. He was a significant figure in the opening of Chinese popular literature to serious scholarly attention. His focus as a Sinologist was on what would now be called popular culture; as well as being a student of literature, he collected art objects and was an accomplished player of the ancient Chinese lute. He thought that contemporary literature could be reinvigorated by the revival of the ancient detective genre, which, unlike the GOLDEN AGE detective story in the West, dealt with middle- and lower-class characters rather than aristocrats. The main criticism has been that the stories had to be thoroughly Westernized because the detective novel in ancient China was not a whodunit but a moral fable in which supernatural events often played a part. (THE CHINESE NAIL MURDERS [1957], however, begins with a wonderful ghost story.) Still, the Judge Dee mysteries were very popular and have recently been reissued. The earlier ones are generally considered the better, though *The Willow Pattern* (1965) is one of the best. The chronology at the end of the story collection *Judge Dee at Work* (1967) includes summaries of the plots of many Judge Dee novels (but not, of course, the solutions).

Van Gulik's scholarly works in Sinology dealt with such subjects as Chinese art and sexuality in ancient

China. One interesting aspect of the novels is that Van Gulik depicted the "Victorianism" of the Confucian gentleman, who often maintained a scandalous sex life behind an orthodox facade. The Dutch novelist Janwillem VAN DE WETERING wrote a biography of Van Gulik.

VARALLO, VIC See LININGTON, ELIZABETH.

VARGAS LLOSA, MARIO (1936–) Peruvian novelist Mario Vargas Llosa is best known for his penetrating and unsettling novels exposing the political violence and corrupt social structure of his native country. His novels are known for their complexity, including experiments with multiple points of view and layers of meaning, as well as shifts in time. Vargas Llosa, however, produced a mystery, *Quien mato a Palomino Molero?* (1986; tr *Who Killed Palomino Molero?*, 1987), that tightly adheres to the detective story genre while addressing the serious political and social matters dealt with in his other fiction. Palomino Molero is a young man who is found brutally murdered and mutilated near the town of Talara. Officer Lituma and Lieutenant Silva learn that he was a gifted *bolero* singer who for some reason enlisted in the Air Force and was stationed at the base outside of town. The two policemen get no help from Colonel Mindreau, the base commander, whose daughter Molero was in love with. While picking their way cleverly through military/civilian, white/Indian relations, the pair of policemen—a brilliant version of the classic detective duo—oppose corruption even though they have to swim in it. The plot is tight, the language vivid, the dialogue spicy. Some of the books of Paco Ignacio TAIBO have a similar flavor.

Lituma and Silva appear in other books by Vargas Llosa, including *Death in the Andes* (1995).

VASSILIKOS, VASSILIS (1933–) The Greek author Vassilis Vassilikos has been a leading writer of his generation from a very early age: his first novel was published when he was twenty, and in 1961 he became the youngest author ever to win Greece's most prestigious literary prize (the Award of the Group of Twelve). In 1959–1960, he traveled in the United States on a Ford Foundation grant. A highly political writer, Vassilikos has said that modern literature "should reflect modern life, and the essence of modern life is conflict." Vassilikos's novel *Z* was published in 1966; a thriller about a political assassination, it was based on an actual murder of a Greek pacifist and was banned in the author's own country. The novel was enormously successful in Europe, however, particularly after the film version by Greek director COSTA-GAVRAS won the Jury prize at Cannes in 1969. Vassilikos lived in exile from 1967 to 1974 in protest against military rule in Greece. In his preface to the twenty-fifth anniversary edition of the novel, Vassilikos said that he had been influenced by Truman CAPOTE, particularly his book IN COLD BLOOD (1966).

VAUTRIN One of the great villains of literature, Vautrin appeared in several novels by Honoré de BALZAC. It has been said that Vautrin was based on VIDOCQ, but Vautrin is a criminal through and through. In *Père Goriot* (1834), Vautrin lives in a boardinghouse with Eugène de Rastignac, the "hero" who compares unfavorably with Vautrin because of his weakness and willingness to abandon his principles to satisfy his ambitions. *Vautrin* was published in 1840.

VÁZQUEZ MONTALBÁN, MANUEL (1939–) This Spanish writer, who is also a poet and journalist, has become known to English-speaking readers as the creator of Detective Pepe Carvalho, a policeman with links to both the CIA and the Communist party. Carvalho, once driven into exile for his anti-Franco activities, has returned to prowl the streets of Barcelona as a private detective. He is like Nero WOLFE in only one respect: his gourmet tastes. The books have become renowned for their fine writing, which is marked by rich descriptions, poetic language, and political and psychological sophistication. There are now more than twenty novels in the Carvalho series, which began with *Yo Maté a Kennedy* (1972; "I killed Kennedy"). A number of them have been translated into English, including *Southern Seas* (*Los mares del sur*, 1979), in which the detective investigates an idealistic businessman's death before important elections. This was the first mystery to win the prestigious Planeta Prize for Spanish literature, and is an example of how Vázquez Montalbán weaves political intrigue and reflections on contemporary Spain into his mysteries. Other Carvalho novels include *Asesinato en el Comite Central* (1981; tr *Murder in the Central Committee*, 1985). In this novel, Carvalho is hired by the Spanish Communist party to investigate the murder of the head of their central committee during a meeting. The killing is a parody of the LOCKED ROOM problem: no one could come in or go out of the meeting room, but the other committee members are all suspects—all 139 of them. Carvalho has to leave his beloved Barcelona and travel to Madrid; a great deal of time is spent talking about food and the specialties he will miss. *The Angst-Ridden Executive* (*La soledad del manager*, 1977) is another humorous Carvalho adventure, satirizing the business class.

Vázquez Montalbán has also written non-series books within the crime genre. In 1994, he published *El*

Estrangulador, a novel told from the point of view of the BOSTON STRANGLER. It is written in the voice of Albert DeSalvo, the man thought to be the strangler, but it is also a postmodern novel, and DeSalvo reflects on such thinkers as R. D. Laing and Michel Foucault.

VERDICT OF TWELVE (1940) A novel by Raymond POSTGATE, a mystery with an avowedly political message. Postgate prefaced the book with Marx's statement of the theory of reification: "It is not the consciousness of men that determines their existence, but on the contrary their social existence determines their consciousness." The first third of the book introduces the jurors through biographies that are short stories in themselves. One juror is a murderer who has never been caught; another a Jewish woman whose husband was killed by a racist gang of thugs who were never punished; another a fat, revolting, and smug Oxford don. The second third of the book describes the murder. The last part is devoted to the trial and the decision of the jury. As Postgate intended, the jurors' class prejudices, life experiences, and above all the fears—of being found out, or thought stupid, or shown up—determine their votes, and not their examination of the evidence. In fact, their examination of the evidence is itself filtered through the unreliable sieve of their natures. No one is objective; even the foreman, the only one who tries to remain impartial, is betrayed by that very effort into downplaying his own reactions.

The murder story itself is as compelling as the lives of the jurors. Rosalie van Beer is a former shop girl whose war marriage and widowhood, as well as a couple of fortunate (for her) accidents, have left her one life away from a large fortune. She is made the guardian of her nephew, Philip Arkwright, simply because there is no one else left in the family. Philip is a sickly and troubled boy of eleven who stands to inherit the family fortune at twenty-one, if he lives that long. Van Beer is a stupid, weak, and bad-tempered woman, seen by Philip as a monster—particularly after a shocking scene in which she gasses his pet rabbit in the oven. Soon after, Philip dies of poisoning, and she is arrested.

Although one might expect that an author with Postgate's intentions would present mere effigies or cardboard cutouts, the characters are well formed and believable (the most two-dimensional happens to be a young Marxist intellectual). His portrait of the poor and failing old doctor who might have saved Philip illustrates Postgate's economics of character: "Lack of any other resources forced him to go on practicing when he should have retired. He had to live, and for that reason someone else was to have to die." The performance of the vain barrister Sir Isambard Burns is brilliant, including his use of a story by Saki as the center of the defense. The trial scenes are both entertaining and serve to confuse the reader—as Burns intends them to confuse the jury—about what really happened. The ending of the novel is one of the most stunning and clever in the genre, not likely to be forgotten quickly.

VIDAL, GORE See BOX, EDGAR.

VIDOCQ, FRANÇOIS EUGÈNE (1775–1857) The French policeman who inspired numerous fictional detectives, including C. Auguste DUPIN, and who could be considered the ancestor of all sleuths. Vidocq, who became the first head of the Parisian Sûreté in 1811, was the most famous detective of the nineteenth century. He inspired Emile Gaboriau's Monsieur LECOQ and Balzac's VAUTRIN, and also influenced SUE, DICKENS, and other writers. Vidocq was a master of disguise, and was the prototype of all those detectives who are on close personal terms with members of the underworld, by whom they are both feared and respected.

How Vidocq got his knowledge is legendary: he started out his career as a criminal. In his *Memoires* (1828-29) he says that he was a thief, and while serving an eight-year prison sentence became a police informer. His escape was arranged, and then the thief turned thieftaker. Vidocq's original force consisted of just four agents, and they, like Vidocq, were former criminals who had "reformed": it was charged that they would instigate crimes and then investigate them, because they were paid by the arrest, not on salary. It was even said that Vidocq once investigated a crime he had committed himself. Such rumors eventually forced his retirement, after which Vidocq started the first private investigation agency.

VIG (or viggorish) The profits from an illegal activity, particularly the interest, as in loan-sharking. Derived (through Yiddish) from the Russian *vyigrysh,* meaning winnings or profit.

VINE, BARBARA A pseudonym used by Ruth RENDELL.

VINE, GIL A sleuth created by Stewart STERLING. Like Sterling's other detectives, Vine is defined by his profession: he is the head of security at the Plaza Royale, a twelve-hundred-room New York hotel. Vine is helped by Reidy Dunn, the cool and quiet assistant manager, and other hotel personnel. The books are more slangy than those Sterling wrote pseudonymously about Don CADEE, and also have looser plots and more posturing and mugging around by the detective than actual detection. Sometimes, however, they reveal interesting aspects of culture. For example, Vine is only drawn into a murder story in *Dead of Night* (1950) because of a house policy against allowing single women to have men in their rooms. He investigates a report of a man seen in the room of Tildy Millett, an ice-skating star. He finds the playboy advertising executive Dow Lanerd; Millett is missing, and her bodyguard's bloody corpse is found in the closet—the first of several murders, including one in a TUB.

BIBLIOGRAPHY Novels: *Dead Wrong* (1947), *Dead Sure* (1949), *Alibi Baby* (1950), *Dead Right* (1956), *Dead to the World* (1958), *The Body in the Bed* (1959).

Novelettes: *Dead Certain* (1960).

VISCONTI, LUCHINO See POSTMAN ALWAYS RINGS TWICE, THE.

VON ROSENKRANTZ, PALLE See ROSENKRANTZ, PALLE.

WADE, HENRY (pseudonym of Major Sir Henry Lancelot Aubrey-Fletcher, 1887–1969) At one time the high sheriff of Buckinghamshire, the English writer Henry Wade had ample military and civic experience with which to write his detective novels. Yet his reputation is mixed. Some critics consider him a major figure in the prewar classical genre as well as in the postwar realistic police novel, while others dismiss him as dull. Had Wade "done more to explicate the psychology and mores of the English people than any other writer in the genre" (*The Encyclopedia of Mystery and Detection*), or was he just another "humdrum" (Julian SYMONS)? The reader will have to decide, but first the reader will have to find Wade's work, which is out of print.

Educated at Eton and Oxford, Aubrey-Fletcher served in World War I and received the Distinguished Service Order and the Croix de Guerre. After the war, he held a number of offices in Buckinghamshire, including alderman and justice of the peace. He published his first mystery in 1926, *The Verdict of You All.* Three years later, he introduced Inspector POOLE in *The Duke of York's Steps.* Wade wrote INVERTED mysteries as well as the usual GOLDEN AGE police story. He was also a short story writer, and one of his collections, *Policeman's Lot* (1933), was included in QUEEN'S QUORUM. In 1937 Wade succeeded to his baronetcy. After the outbreak of war a few years later, he rejoined the Grenadier Guards and served in World War II, though he was in his fifties. In the postwar period, he continued to write mysteries that reflected the English milieu.

WAHLÖO, PETER See SJÖWALL, MAJ.

WAINEWRIGHT, THOMAS GRIFFITHS (1794–1852) Thomas Griffiths Wainewright was an art critic for *London Magazine* under the pseudonyms Egomet Bonmot and Janus Weathercock; he published *Some Passages in the Life of Egomet Bonmot* in 1827. Wainewright also painted, and exhibited some of his work at the Royal Academy. None of this activity would make him deserving of attention; Wainewright's real achievement was as a poisoner. He is believed to have poisoned his mother-in-law and his uncle. Not content with having inherited his uncle's property, he insured his sister-in-law's life and then poisoned her, too. In 1831, Wainewright prudently left England for France, but he returned in 1837. At that point he was arrested, but Wainewright was only convicted of forgery. He was transported to Tasmania for the rest of his life, and so went down in history not as an obscure aesthete but one of those few known to have gotten away with murder.

WAINWRIGHT, JOHN (1921–) A former policeman in Yorkshire, John Wainwright is known for PROCEDURAL novels that are set in his old stomping grounds. Wainwright was born in Leeds and served in the Royal Air Force during World War II. After the war he began working in the West Riding Constabulary, which he continued to do even after his first books were published. He left the force in 1969, a twenty-two-year veteran and already a novelist (his doctor told him to stop burning the candle at both ends and staying up nights to do his writing).

Wainwright's first crime story was *Ten Steps to the Gallows* (1965). Like Ed MCBAIN, Wainwright uses a large number of series characters and depicts police work as a team effort, though different characters are emphasized in particular stories. He departs from reality (or probability) at times; for example, he has his force get caught up in international problems in *The Crystallized Carbon Pig* (1966). At the opposite pole, he has written a mystery in the classic English tradition (*High-Class Kill,* 1973). He also writes about hit men (*The Hard Hit,* 1974; *Portrait in Shadows,* 1986).

Among the characters in his Yorkshire series are Chief Superintendent Robert Blayde (see *Landscape With Violence,* 1975, and *Blayde R.I.P.,* 1982) and Charles RIPLEY. Although Wainwright's work often lacks depth and finish, it has plenty of realism. He writes about "bobbying" from experience, and his major characters get killed, have breakdowns, and quit. *All on a Summer's Day* (1981) and *All Through the Night* (1985) are most concerned with day-to-day procedure. *Cul-de-Sac* (1984) is more psychological, and was praised by SIMENON. Part of it is the diary of a man whose wife has fallen from a seaside cliff and been killed.

Tail-End Charlie (1978) is Waiwright's memoir of his service with the RAF.

WALKER, AMOS A private detective in a series of books by Loren D. ESTLEMAN, Walker is a romantic white knight who gets into trouble because of his lonely code of conduct. A Vietnam vet living in Detroit, Walker dropped out of the police academy and became a security guard for General Motors. He then worked for an older detective named Dale Leopold, who was subsequently killed before his eyes. Like the character in the Mike HAMMER television adaptation, Walker seems like a man plucked out of another era and dropped into 1980s America. He uses forties expressions ("Dangle, darling") and is so self-consciously HARD-BOILED and Bogart-ish (he has an original *Casablanca* poster on his wall) that even the other characters notice it. The writing of the series is reminiscent of Lawrence BLOCK, with the similes of CHANDLER and a straining after humor like Robert B. PARKER. Like Parker's SPENSER, Walker sometimes uses violence to get his clues (he chokes one informant with a telephone cord). He also has the cartoon indestructibility of Spenser (jumping out of a car at fifty miles an hour, getting up with only scratches and a sore knee).

On the other hand, Estleman writes novels such as *The Glass Highway* (1983), in which the similes crackle ("the soft leather seat wrapped itself around me like an amorous stingray"), the seams don't show, and the characters are memorable (including Fletcher HORN). Walker is hired to find the son of an air-headed television newsman. On the way, he must deal with the boy's cat-like half-sister, Fern, and his mysterious girlfriend, Paula, whose life story only seems to go back eighteen months. Estleman loses his license and does jail time before proving his honor once again.

In *Every Brilliant Eye* (1986), Walker's friend and war buddy, the syndicated columnist Barry Stackpole, disappears. Stackpole, who had appeared earlier in the Walker series, is wanted by a grand jury. The clues to his disappearance consist of the file of clippings of things he was working on: the recently murdered partner in a chop shop, a deceased organizer of a Jewish industrial union, and a cop who killed himself. The story owes something to Chandler's THE LONG GOODBYE (1953), particularly in the nutty, rambling paragraph written by a drunken writer that turns out to be a clue. Walker is in an exceptionally pugnacious mood, going out of his way to insult people. Hypocritically, he sleeps with a woman and then calls her a whore (something Mike Hammer would have done). In *The Hours of the Virgin* (1999), Walker gets involved in an ART mystery surrounding a fifteenth-century illuminated manuscript.

SUGARTOWN (1984) won an EDGAR award.

BIBLIOGRAPHY Novels: *Motor City Blue* (1980), *Angel Eyes* (1981), *The Midnight Man* (1982), *Lady Yesterday* (1987), *Downriver* (1988), *Silent Thunder* (1989), *Sweet Women Lie* (1990), *Never Street* (1997), *The Witchfinder* (1998).

Short Stories: *General Murders* (1988).

WALLACE, EDGAR (1875–1932) Incredibly prolific English author of mystery and suspense stories, as well as plays and journalism. While CHRISTIE and STOUT each wrote over eighty books (and lived into their eighties to do it), Wallace wrote 173 books in a life that was cut tragically short. He published eighteen books in 1926 alone, and it is often said that in the twenties and early thirties, one out of four books sold in Britain was by Wallace. Obviously such speed precludes consistency (Wallace once wrote a 75,000 word novel—*The Coat of Arms*—in a weekend). Wallace often dictated his books, like Erle Stanley GARDNER, but he did write them himself and even offered a reward of several thousand pounds to anyone who could prove otherwise. (It was never collected.)

Wallace was born in Greenwich of an unmarried theatrical couple and was adopted nine days later by a Billingsgate fish porter. He left school and worked as a plasterer, a printer, and at other trades until joining the army at eighteen. He was sent to South Africa, and published his first book, a collection of poems, in 1898. His first literary effort was actually some song lyrics; he was sentenced to a short period of hard labor when he went AWOL from his regiment to hear them performed.

Political journalism turned out to be Wallace's forte. According to his daughter, he bought his way out of the army and became a correspondent for Reuters and covered the Boer War. In fact, his "scoop" of the treaty-signing led to his being blackballed by Lord Kitchener, a ban that lasted until World War I. His outspoken political books continued to get him into hot water.

After his return to England, Wallace became a crime reporter and also developed his lifelong love of the turf, reporting (and betting) on horse races. Wallace's first novel, *The Four Just Men* (1905), is his most famous because he published it himself and because of a promotional gimmick that backfired. When it was serialized, a prize of five hundred pounds was offered for the reader who wrote back with the correct solution, but the promoters forgot to specify the *first* reader and so had to honor many claims to the money.

Among those books that reflect Wallace's interest in horse racing are the Educated Evans series. Horse racing also features in *The Twister* (1928), about Mr. Braid, an incredibly shrewd horse owner and financier, but also a man of honor. Typical of Wallace, there is a romantic subplot that underlies the murder story: when he offers to bail out the bankrupt father of the young woman he loves, only to hear that the man has inexplicably committed suicide, Braid uses his natural craftiness (he is "the Twister") to trap the killer. For characters who were literally dashed off, some of Wallace's creations hold up surprisingly well. *The Twister* includes the knowing and tart Inspector ELK, an example of how Wallace would use a single trait or nervous tic to establish a personality, albeit a shallow one. Wallace's women tend to be silly, however; wide-eyed and innocent, they are especially ridiculous when they open their mouths ("We are awfully well off, aren't we, Daddy?"). In some books, it is very evident that the author is feeling his way toward a plot, and the narrative is rambling and repetitive. *The Clever One* (1927), about a mysterious and brilliant forger, creates doubt early on about not only who the Clever One is, but who the sleuth will be. One of Wallace's best books is THE GREEN ARCHER (1923), a murder mystery with a haunted castle. Wallace also wrote a series based on his African experiences, about the colonial Commissioner Sanders.

Why did Wallace write so much? Not because he was crazed; in fact, his publisher is the one who seems to have come up with the idea of flooding the market with Wallace books, and demanded a very high rate of production. As a journalist, Wallace had developed the ability to write to deadline, and dutifully banged out his copy, smoking and drinking tea constantly. Another reason for his high output of books might be his high outflow of money; Wallace loved to bet large sums on horse races and often lost. Although he was making a huge income from his books, he also lived a life of luxury. Wallace was divorced in 1918 and married his secretary a few years later.

Wallace also wrote plays, eventually producing twenty-four. The novel *On the Spot* (1931), a treatment of the Al CAPONE story, was based on one of them. In fact, Wallace often transformed his plays into prose fiction. In 1931 he went to Hollywood to write screenplays. He is generally said to have written *King Kong* (1933), but the claim is disputed by William DEANDREA. Before he could do much film work, Wallace died of a combination of undiagnosed diabetes and complications resulting from pneumonia. The diabetes was said to have been caused by his consumption of tea, very sweetened.

Wallace's stories featuring J. G. REEDER are often considered his best work; *The Mind of Mr. J. G. Reeder* (1925) is routinely cited as one of the indispensable books of the mystery genre. Wallace created other notable sleuths, however, such as Chief Inspector O. Rater, who appears in *The Orator* (1928), and a female competitor of RAFFLES named FOUR SQUARE JANE.

WALLACE, JULIA Julia Wallace was the victim in a famous murder case of 1931 that has been much written about and much copied in fiction. The bone of contention was that her husband, William Wallace, claimed that he received a mysterious phone call that drew him away from the Wallace house in Liverpool; when he returned, Julia Wallace was found savagely beaten to death with a fireplace poker or metal bar (both objects were missing from the house).

Wallace's story was that a man calling himself Qualtrough lured him away from the house by suggesting that he was a possible client (Wallace was an insurance broker). "Qualtrough" called the Liverpool chess club where Wallace was to play a match the night before the murder. The prosecution asserted that the call was made by Wallace himself, trying to set an alibi by establishing that Qualtrough really existed. The following night, Julia Wallace was murdered, according to her husband, while he was vainly searching for Menlove Gardens East, the address to which Qualtrough had decoyed him.

The actual case against Wallace was weak, the only motive being that he may not have liked his wife after eighteen years of marriage, though whether that was sufficient reason to spatter their parlor with blood and brains was an obvious question. Besides motive, the timetable was weak: in one version it gave Wallace only twenty minutes to commit the murder and remove all traces of blood (none were found on his clothes or anywhere outside the parlor). A milk boy may have changed his testimony about the time under police pressure—in the original version, Wallace would only have had five minutes, an obvious impossibility. Wallace was convicted anyway, but a court of appeals held that the evidence was insufficient for a guilty verdict, which Dorothy SAYERS wrote was "the first time in English legal history that a conviction for murder had been set aside on those grounds."

Wallace was set free but died of cancer two years later; he left notes pointing to the identity of the probable murderer. Jonathan GOODMAN made a convincing case for his innocence. Several writers have based novels on the case, including Winnifred Duke, C. E. Bechhofer Roberts, and Sara WOODS.

WALSH, JILL PATON See FINISHERS.

WALTER SYNDROME, THE (1970) A novel by Richard NEELY, divided into three separate first-person narrations. The first narrator is Lambert Post, who describes how he met Charles Walter at work, selling advertisement space for a local newspaper. Post has extremely low self-esteem and latches on to Charles Walter because their association makes him feel "confidence" and "manliness." The two men have similar personal histories and become brotherly.

Walter narrates the second part. When Lambert is insulted by Sol Pincus, the star telephone solicitor in the office, he immediately tells Walter about it. Walter takes bizarre revenge on Pincus, calling a laundry where he knows Pincus has left a white cashmere jacket and, impersonating Pincus, asking them to dye the jacket black and replace the buttons with heavy, less attractive ones. Walter becomes an "avenger," committing crimes in order to avenge the humiliations inflicted on his friend, Post.

The third narrator, Mary Ryan, is a reporter investigating a series of brutal slayings. The way in which Neely weaves together the three strands of the story is skillful, and the method of resolution was more innovative than it would seem nearly thirty years later.

WALTHER PPK The 7.62 millimeter Walther PPK was the sidearm of the hated Gestapo in World War II, but it has escaped this association because of its later fictional connection with James BOND. (A quite different detective, Mickey ZONDI, is one of those fictional characters who also carries a PPK.) The Walther was originally manufactured in 7.62 mm (the equivalent of the U.S. .32 automatic), but in the United States PPKs were made in .380 auto and even some in .22 LR.

WALZ, AUDREY See BONNAMY, FRANCIS.

WAMBAUGH, JOSEPH (1937–) After a career with the Los Angeles police department, Joseph Wambaugh became one of the foremost writers of police PROCEDURAL novels. It is therefore strange that he has been ignored by prominent critics including Jacques BARZUN, William DEANDREA, and Julian SYMONS. Wambaugh's bestsellers include *The New Centurions* (1970), *The Blue Knight* (1979), and *The Glitter Dome* (1981), which are familiar from their popular film versions. Wambaugh's writing is in line with that of other writers in the procedural field. He does, however, make more use of sex and black humor, which sometimes spills over into bad taste. Wambaugh's most important book is not a novel at all but a novelization or work of "docufiction"; THE ONION FIELD (1973) is a deeply researched and chillingly imagined account of the murder of a Los Angeles policeman. It was given a special EDGAR award in 1974. Wambaugh's own favorite of his novels is *The Secrets of Harry Bright* (1985), in which detective Sidney Blackpool investigates the murder of a millionaire's son who has been shot and then incinerated in a burning Rolls Royce near Palm Springs. *Lines and Shadows* (1984) is about policemen patrolling the desert border with Mexico.

WARFARIN When a victim is said to have died from "rat poison," usually ARSENIC is the culprit; however, warfarin, an anticoagulant with medical uses, has largely replaced more dangerous substances like arsenic in commercially available rodenticides. Thus, one of the most common ways of doing in the victim during the GOLDEN AGE is now foreclosed. Warfarin is used to control blood clotting in postoperative patients. Despite its reputation as a "safe" household poison, warfarin is still dangerous and potentially fatal.

WARSHAWSKI, V[ICTORIA] I[PHIGENIA] A private detective character in a series of novels by Sara PARETSKY. "Vic" is the best of the HARD-BOILED female private eyes of the eighties (others are Sharon MCCONE and Kinsey MILLHONE). It may have been her hard-boiled reputation that led to Warshawski's conversion into an action hero in the 1992 screen adaptation, *V. I. Warshawski* (not based on any one book), which made her name well known. William DEANDREA, absurdly, compared Warshawski to Mike HAMMER (at one point, Vic says of Hammer, "Maybe Mike's secret is he doesn't try to think"). Actually, Warshawski is tough without being stupid, intelligent and sensitive without having a grating soapbox personality, and the action is not gratuitously violent. She is also able to have sex with someone without finding it necessary to kill them later, and she has a number of matter-of-fact affairs that are neither torrid nor tepid.

Warshawski is a divorced private detective working in Chicago, and the books are very much novels of place. Her mixed heritage (part Polish, part Jewish, part Italian) figures in the books not only as background but as an integral part of some stories. In *Deadlock* (1984), her cousin, the retired hockey player Boom Boom Warshawski, is working on the docks when he is shredded by the propellers of a Great Lakes freighter. Warshawski's cases usually begin with a person in trouble but lead into a larger web of corruption at higher levels. In *Deadlock,* her investigation takes her through the intricacies of the shipping business, onto the deck of a thousand-foot freighter, and to the mansions of Oak Bluffs. Paretsky researches her books thoroughly (though at one point Warshawski calls the stern "the frontmost tip of the vessel"). Warshawski also makes a very boneheaded play when she fails to see the obvious significance of the appearance of a scuba diver; but then, if she did, the book would end a hundred pages too soon.

Vic's mother was an Italian opera singer whose career was cut short when she had to flee Italy in 1938. Her father was a police sergeant. The Polish side of the family still lives on the South Side, and is treated less romantically. Warshawski herself worked for the public defender's office; combined with her background, this places her on the side of the underdog and the working class, and in her cases she attacks the head of the monster—the managers and big shots—and not the pawns, who are usually ignorant tools of the powerful. Paretsky's Chicago is teeming with life, but she suppresses none of its drabness. Among Warshawski's regular contacts are newspaperman Murray Ryerson, her sometime lover, and Lieutenant Bobby Mallory, a colleague of her father's who thinks she should go home, get married, and have babies. The central figure of *Bitter Medicine* (1987) is her friend, the doctor Lotty Herschel; a young patient of hers dies in premature labor while Warshawski is taking the girl's worthless boyfriend for a job interview. Although the problems of doctors afraid of malpractice suits are not inherently less interesting than those of longshoremen, Paretsky's writing seems to generate more heat when she is dealing with labor history and Chicago's colorful past.

Warshawski's first case was INDEMNITY ONLY (1982). There is one volume of Warshawski short stories, *Windy City Blues* (1995).

BIBLIOGRAPHY Novels: *Killing Orders* (1985), *Blood Shot* (1988; British title *Toxic Shock*), *Burn Marks* (1990), *Guardian Angel* (1992), *Tunnel Vision* (1994), *Hard Time* (1999).

WAS IT MURDER? (1931; orig title *Murder at School*) A novel by James HILTON (creator of Mr. Chips) published under the name Glen Trevor. Hilton used the same kind of setting as in his more famous book. Set at the Oakington School, it concerns the mysterious deaths of some of the boys. The sleuth, Revell, is twenty-eight and somewhat blasé. Revell won the famous Newdigate Prize and is writing an epic poem. Not a private detective, he has however won notoriety for solving a mystery of a missing manuscript while at college. The first mysterious death at Oakington occurs when a sleeping boy, Robert Marshall, is killed by a falling gas pipe. Strangely, the boy had written a sort of will shortly before his death. His brother, who is his heir, is also a pupil at the school. The death has been declared an accident by the police, but Revell is called in by the headmaster—a relation of the dead boy—to make certain. Revell can find nothing wrong, and goes away. Not long afterward, a second death occurs—the victim dives into an empty swimming pool. Revell returns and acts as a detective on behalf of the police. He is no genius, but gathers information through conversing with people and probing the secrets of the insular school community. In the end, Revell feels foolish when the real nature of his role is brought to light.

WATCHER IN THE SHADOWS (1960) A novel by Geoffrey HOUSEHOLD, almost a reprise of his best novel, ROGUE MALE (1939). The earlier story was about a big-game hunter who had tried to kill Hitler and was hounded through the English countryside by foreign agents. In *Watcher in the Shadows*, this plot returns in an ironic form. Dennim, an aristocratic Viennese who had spied for British Intelligence but had at one point worn a Gestapo uniform, is mistakenly hounded through the English countryside by a victim of the NAZIS who is bent on revenge. Dennim is a gentle zoologist who studies red squirrels, and would like to get close enough to his assailant to explain what his real role in the war was and whose side he was on; the only problem is that if he gets that close, his enemy will probably kill him. In the opening scene, Dennim's mailman is blown to pieces when he tries to stuff a package (a bomb) through his mail slot. Dennim goes to see Ian Parrow, his old British Intelligence contact, and tries to lure his antagonist into open country where he can be trapped. From this point on, Household uses the kind of up-hill and down-dale battle of wits as in *Rogue Male*, though he cannot equal that stunning performance. The Household code of honor and gallant understatement are still in place, however; when Parrow asks, "'Don't you care whether you are alive or not?'", Dennim makes the sublime response, "'Very much. I have a lot of work still to do on the red squirrel.'"

WATERS (***) Although he was "the originator of the British detective short story" (according to E. F. BLEILER), the writer known as "Waters" remains a mystery himself. In 1849 (the year of POE's death), Waters published "Recollections of a Police-Officer" in *Chambers's Edinburgh Review*, the first story of its kind to appear in Britain. Waters was an imitator of Poe, and his first collection of stories, *The Recollections of a Policeman*, was published in the United States (1852) before its British publication (in 1859, as *Recollections of a Detective Police-Officer*). Among Waters's other works are *The Experiences of a French Detective Officer* (1861) and *Experiences of a Real Detective* (1862).

Waters's work also followed the Victorian vogue, established by DICKENS, for fictional "reminiscences" of policemen and detectives. A hundred years before the PROCEDURAL was thought of, these authors were researching their subject, becoming friendly with policemen, and acquainting themselves with their methods. In an 1862 story, "Murder Under the Microscope," Waters used both the microscopic differences between human and animal blood and the comparison of hairs. The case is that of the murder of a hated absentee landlord who had swindled more than one tenant by selling them the same worthless farm.

The Waters stories were frequently reprinted, under a variety of titles, during the nineteenth century.

WATERWORKS, THE See DOCTOROW, E. L.

WATSON, DOCTOR JOHN The famous doctor who acts as Sherlock HOLMES's Boswell, writing his cases down and publishing them. The conceit of Watson's authorhood is bolstered by frequent references to "other" cases that are not yet written down, and Holmes's sometimes wry comments on Watson's publications, for example in "The Crooked Man." Watson is a bachelor when he is first introduced to Holmes in A STUDY IN SCARLET (1887), but meets his future wife in *The Sign of Four* (1890). Thereafter, Watson's wife makes many convenient trips in order for Watson to be caught alone by Holmes and drafted for further adventures. Watson narrates all but two of the Holmes stories.

Watson is like Archie GOODWIN in this respect: it is he and not the GENIUS DETECTIVE who makes the stories so entertaining. Not only is Watson the narrator; his is the viewpoint of an ordinary man suddenly involved in extraordinary events, and the excitement he communicates makes the stories so readable, for Holmes himself tends to be rather blasé on the one hand or insufferably arrogant on the other. When he is first introduced, Watson is recovering from a bullet wound received in Afghanistan. Courage and loyalty are Watson's main virtues. His mind is more cautious than Holmes'. It has been said that a great detective's chronicler should be slightly less intelligent than the reader, but Watson makes a truly dumb move in THE FINAL PROBLEM (1893) when he sees a man striding rapidly toward the Reichenbach Falls, where he has just left Holmes, and fails to grasp that he has been tricked. But Watson's descriptions of his own activities in the adventures—the visit of the engineer in the ENGINEER'S THUMB (1892), his anxious escape in "The Final Problem"—are vivid, and lack the woodenness of Holmes's pronouncements. Conan Doyle also put more of himself into Watson, who sometimes seems to have a failing medical practice, marries, and is then widowed. Holmes may be the greater character, but Watson is the better characterization.

It has been said that Watson had two or even three wives. In a famous speech to the Baker Street Irregulars, Rex STOUT beat the Sherlockians at their own game by using the evidence of the books to "demonstrate" that Watson was in fact a woman. Conan Doyle himself provided the loopholes for such speculations by his sometimes careless writing (Watson's wife's slip in calling him "James" at one point has provided further grist for Sherlockian scholars).

WATSON'S APOLOGY (1984) A novel by Beryl BAINBRIDGE, based on documents relating to an actual Victorian murder case. J. S. Watson is the headmaster of a boys' school, a classicist, and a frustrated poet and the author of *Geology—A Poem in Seven Books.* The story begins with his remarkable letters and offer of marriage to an impoverished Irish gentlewoman whom he had met briefly years before. Supplying the psychology to fit the skeletal historical account, Bainbridge turns the murder story into a character study. The Watsons' desperate entanglement and disappointment is as interesting as their own very different and peculiar personalities, which emerge in vignettes of marriage stretching over several decades.

The real Reverend J. S. Watson was a minor literary figure. The English clergyman savagely beat his wife to death in their house in 1869; afterward, he attempted to commit suicide and then confessed. His wife was mentally disturbed and was an intemperate drinker.

WATTS, PETER See SLANG.

WAUGH, HILLARY (1920–) A prolific American crime and mystery novelist, Waugh is often credited with having written the first police PROCEDURAL, LAST SEEN WEARING . . . (1952). Although there were other antecedents, Waugh was the first to perfect the form. He has said that a true crime book inspired him to try for the same level tone in a novel. Waugh has also rightly pointed out that complete realism is impossible, because that would involve the inclusion of masses of useless information. Like a vacuum cleaner, a real police investigation picks up any and all material that might be relevant. Waugh never loses sight of the fact that he is writing a *narrative,* and realizes that making a novel more like reality is also making art more like non-art. When he wrote *Last Seen Wearing . . . ,* Waugh had already published three novels: *Madam Will Not Dine Tonight* (1947), *Hope to Die* (1948), and *The Odds Run Out* (1949).

Waugh was born in New Haven, and Connecticut and New York City are his main settings. He graduated from Yale University in 1942, and later taught mystery writing there. After his success with *Last Seen Wearing . . . ,* Waugh began his series of novels about ebullient police chief Fred FELLOWS a generation before the "rural procedural" caught on. Fellows is chief in an imaginary Connecticut town, Stockford; he is also a pillar of the community and exactly what a "town father" should be (unlike a later and more famous rural police chief, Mario BALZIC). The first book in the series was *Sleep Long, My Love* (1959). Waugh switched to the Manhattan scene about the time he dropped Fellows, writing a series of 87TH PRECINCT-type novels about "Manhattan Homicide North," beginning with *"30" Manhattan East* (1968).

Since he stopped writing about Fred Fellows, Waugh seems to have been overtaken by other practitioners of the type of novel he helped to create. His ideas about the craft are put forth in *Hillary Waugh on Mysteries and Mystery Writing* (1991). Waugh has served as president of the Mystery Writers of America, and was named a Grand Master by the organization in 1989. One of Waugh's best recent books is the non-series novel *A Death in Town* (1989). About the rape and murder of a high school student, it is told through statements made by various townspeople. Waugh's other books include *Madman at My Door* (1978) and the comical MURDER ON SAFARI (1987). He has written suspense novels under the pseudonym of Elissa Grandower, and a series about private detective Simon KAYE, a throwback to the HARD-BOILED detective of the forties. The first of the six Kaye books was *The Glenna Powers Case* (1980).

WAXNOSE AND FRISKY A comical pair of killers in Raymond CHANDLER's story "Trouble is My Business." Waxnose is tall and deadly; the clownish and crazy Frisky is the kid brother he lets tag along. Waxnose has removed the firing pin from Frisky's gun so he won't hurt anyone; Frisky gets it back, with disastrous consequences.

A similar pair of hoods was used in the film version of THE BIG SLEEP (1939) for comic relief.

WAY WE DIE NOW, THE (1988) The last of the novels by Charles Willeford featuring Hoke MOSELEY. The title alludes to Anthony Trollope's *The Way We Live Now* (1875). Willeford was not the first to play on the title; Michael Lewin wrote an Albert Samson novel also called *The Way We Die Now* (1973).

In *The Way We Die Now,* Willeford ties together several plots, all focusing on Hoke. One involves a mysterious mission for Hoke among primitive and dangerous people in the Everglades. At the same time, he is preoccupied with the threat posed by a killer he had put in jail and who has been suddenly released. He also has time to cleverly trap a murderer in a "cold" case several years old. Among the targets of satire in the book are affirmative action, the psychologist Melanie Klein, and the 1980 Mariel boatlift. Moseley's visit to a brutal, poor, and depressing agricultural town in the middle of nowhere is one of the most powerful parts of the whole series; his showdown with the bad guys is one of the most violent and shocking.

WEBSTER, HENRY KITCHELL (1875–1932) Writing during the heyday of Anna Katherine GREEN, Henry Kitchell Webster produced mysteries that he referred to as "romances," and in which there was hardly ever explicit violence. His first book was actually about railroads—*The Short Line War,* published in 1899. His first mystery novel appeared in 1908 (*The Whispering Man*). It was about a lawyer and a painter who use detection to find out how a New York "alienist" was poisoned.

Most of Webster's books were set in the Chicago area, where he lived. Webster was born in Evanston, Illinois, and attended Hamilton College. His varied writing activities included opera, editing a boys' paper, poetry, and articles for magazines like *The Saturday Evening Post.* He wrote most of his mysteries later in life. Among the most highly regarded are *The Corbin Necklace* (1926), in which a young boy helps the bedridden narrator find some missing jewelry, and *Who Is Next?* (1931), which contains a double murder and also a love story. *The Clock Strikes Two* (1928) had a female heroine; *The Man with the Scarred Hand* (1931) was set in the mountains. *The Alleged Great-Aunt* (1935) was completed after Webster's death by Janet Ayer Fairband and Margaret Ayer Barnes.

WEESNER, THEODORE (1935–) Not primarily a crime writer, Theodore Weesner has written some highly praised novels that happen to fall within the bounds of the crime genre. Born in Flint, Michigan, he left school at the age of sixteen and was in the army for three years. He later attended Michigan State University and the University of Iowa. He has taught at the University of New Hampshire and Carnegie Mellon University.

Weesner is best known for his studies of character, particularly his "coming of age" novels about young men. His first novel was *The Car Thief* (1972). Set in 1959, it is about a sixteen-year-old named Alex Housman who is growing up in Detroit, where he lives with his father, an alcoholic. Alex's motives for stealing cars and his psychology are subtly explored. Joyce Carol Oates praised the novel for revealing "a kind of life, and a kind of human personality, that are totally foreign to most of us"—something that the best crime fiction aims at. The book was considered a vivid portrait of juvenile delinquency and was compared to TRUFFAUT's autobiographical film *The 400 Blows* (1959). *A German Affair* (1976) is set in Germany in 1952, and is about a kid from Detroit who discovers himself through his affair with a seamstress. Weesner's one real "genre" novel,

THE TRUE DETECTIVE (1987), is also one of the most sensitive books about crime against CHILDREN.

WELCOME, JOHN (pseudonym of John Needham Huggard Brennan, 1914–) John Welcome was born in Wexford, Ireland, but was sent to school in Yorkshire. He later attended Oxford, taking his degree in law in 1936. Welcome served in the artillery in World War II and attained the rank of captain. After the war he began his long career as a solicitor in the firm of Huggard and Brennan, writing his crime novels under a pseudonym.

Welcome started writing non-mystery novels shortly after the war. An avid fox hunter and follower of the turf, he wrote a number of fictional and nonfictional books on sporting themes. His first novel was *Red Coats Galloping* (1949). Later, he would edit many volumes of stories on various themes including gambling, smuggling, spying, motoring, and hunting. *Great Racing Stories* (1989) is one of the volumes he edited with Dick FRANCIS.

Welcome's first genre novel was *Run for Cover* (1958), which introduced his series character, Richard Graham, a sometime spy for British intelligence as well as a rogue. Welcome made a hero of a stock British character: the gentleman who is fond of horses, gambling, and women, and therefore often finds himself broke and in hot water. The author is a world traveler, and the books are set on several continents. Welcome's other main series character is a former racing driver named Simon Herald. He and Graham are two of kind, and even appear in some books together. *Stop at Nothing* (1960), a Herald novel, is about a substance that makes horses run faster. Welcome's books are remarkably like those of Dick Francis, but with a dose of Gavin LYALL thrown in; he loves chases, *femmes fatales,* and sadistic villains. On the other hand, Welcome's work is more conservative and lacks Francis's occasional introspectiveness and originality. His reputation in the United States has never compared with that of Francis. Surprisingly, for a lawyer, Welcome has never written a courtroom novel or legal thriller of consequence.

WELLMAN, MANLY WADE (1903–1986) U.S. author, known primarily for works of SCIENCE FICTION and fantasy. Wellman was born in Kamundongo, Angola, but returned to the United States with his family at the age of six. Wellman was a newspaperman in Wichita, worked for the WPA Writers Project, and later became a teacher of creative writing at the University of North Carolina. He had a strong interest in folklore, particularly of the South, which he used in his stories about "occult detectives" tracking down witches and other supernatural beings. One of his weirdest combinations of science fiction with the mystery and detective story is *Sherlock Holmes's War of the Worlds* (1975), in which Conan DOYLE's sleuth battles the Martians of H. G. WELLS.

Wellman also wrote some straight detective tales, and pioneered the Native American detective with David RETURN. His novels include *Find My Killer* (1948), *Fort Sun Dance: Candle of the Wicked* (1960), and *Not At These Hands* (1961). His vast output (he said that in the Depression he wrote eight to ten thousand words per day) includes many fantasy and horror novels (his last, *Cahena,* is set in Africa in the eighth century) as well as books on the Civil War, including one that was nominated for a Pulitzer Prize. He also won an EDGAR award in 1955 for his nonfiction crime study *Dead and Gone: Classic Crimes of North Carolina,* and a short story prize from *Ellery Queen's Mystery Magazine.*

WELLS, CAROLYN (1862–1942) Popular at one time, Carolyn Wells has followed Anna Katherine GREEN, whom she emulated, into a similar obscurity. BARZUN and TAYLOR called her *The Mystery of the Sycamore* (1921) "the worst cock-and-bull story ever put together by a rational being," which indicates in an extreme form the contemporary reaction to Wells's implausibility and weakness of style. In fairness, it should be pointed out that "realism" in the sense in which it now dominates the genre was something she did not even aim at, instead proposing in her critical writings an internal consistency like that of the fairy tale. Ironically, Wells is famous for having written the first critical work on how to write mysteries, *The Technique of the Mystery Story* (1913). It is also probably the only one of her works that will stand the test of time.

Carolyn Wells was born in Rahway, New Jersey, and became a librarian. Wells married Hadwin Houghton, son of the founder of the famous Boston publishing house. Her writing career began with poetry and humorous works; she first became known for a series of anthologies, which included the *Nonsense Anthology* (1902) and the *Parody Anthology* (1904). She wrote books for girls and a series for children known as *The Patty Books.* Her creation of the series detective Fleming STONE also dates from this early period, though she did not write a full-length novel about him until *The Clue* (1909); the 1906 story "The Maxwell Case" was published in *All-Story Magazine.* Wells got the idea to write a mystery after hearing an Anna Katherine Green story read aloud.

Fleming Stone appeared in some sixty novels, which represented not even half of Wells's total of 170 published books. She created numerous other series detectives. With Pennington "Penny" Wise, about whom she wrote eight novels, Wells contributed to the subgenre of the psychic detective. Another sleuth, Kenneth Carlisle, is a former actor of the silent screen. As in the Stone series, Wells often wrote about the upper crust of New York City, where she settled. This was also the territory of Green's mysteries. *In the Onyx Lobby* (1920) is about a feud between two society ladies living in The Campanile, a building situated between Columbus Circle and Times Square. *The Disappearance of Kimball Webb,* written the same year, was published under the pseudonym Rowland Wright. Also in that year appeared another Fleming Stone novel, *Raspberry Jam.* Her breakneck pace—later in the series she wrote three Fleming Stone novels a year—naturally affected the quality of her writing, though many who wrote less wrote worse. Barzun and Taylor said that she had "ingenious" ideas but that they were "swamped by a bad convention she did not resist or outgrow." Whatever that convention was, it was not the HAD-I-BUT-KNOWN style. Carolyn Wells was, like Agatha CHRISTIE, Ngaio MARSH, and Dorothy L. SAYERS in England, a woman writing about a brilliant man (Fleming Stone), but in the United States there was not such a firm tradition of women's writing that was not "for women," but for a general mystery reading public. The fact that so many reference and critical works still describe most of the women who wrote mysteries before World War II as appealing to "a feminine audience" shows what a lock this conventional thinking has had and still has on the industry. The reputations accorded to Elizabeth PETERS and other writers of romantic mysteries is also remarkable. Had Wells written silly romances, her reputation might be greater today.

The Rest of My Life (1937) gives details of a sometimes tragic biography: Wells lost her hearing to scarlet fever at the age of six, and lost her husband only a year after their marriage in 1918.

WELLS, H[ERBERT] G[EORGE] (1866–1946) The English SCIENCE FICTION writer, historian, journalist, and socialist H. G. Wells made a small but significant contribution to mystery fiction. Wells was a student of Thomas Huxley, the famous Victorian Darwinist, and his books and stories illustrated concepts of evolution. Underneath the veneer of civilization, the animalistic core of humanity is exposed, for example in the apocalyptic *The Time Machine* (1895). He advocated progressive social policy as the only way to avoid human self-destruction; among those who criticized Wells's radicalism was G. K. CHESTERTON. Wells was influenced by POE, and his early stories sometimes crossed over from suspense and horror into the crime genre proper. "The Thumbmark" (1894) involves FINGERPRINTING used to identify an anarchist. In "Pollock and the Porroh Man" (1895), an English colonial is terrorized by what he thinks is the ghost of a witch doctor of whose murder he is guilty. "The Thing in Number 7" involves a mysterious mutilated corpse. In 1895, Wells published *The Stolen Bacillus and Other Incidents,* which combined science, crime, and humor. In "The Hammerpond Park Burglary," a burglar disguised as a painter sets out to steal jewels from a country house, only to run into some real painters who ask him some difficult questions about his technique ("either that man is a genius or he is a dangerous lunatic"). *The Invisible Man* (1897) combined science fiction and crime in the story of an "evil genius" figure who discovers a chemical causing invisibility and plans to use it to control the world. The actor Claude Rains starred in the 1933 film version. *The Island of Dr. Moreau* (1896) is another mad scientist-criminal story.

WELLS, PROFESSOR See GRIERSON, FRANCIS D.

WELLS, TOBIAS The pseudonym under which Stanton FORBES wrote the mystery series about Knute SEVERSON.

WENCH IS DEAD, THE (1989) An award-winning novel by Colin DEXTER. The story seems to be modeled on Josephine Tey's THE DAUGHTER OF TIME (1951): Inspector MORSE is taken to the hospital because of a duodenal ulcer, and from his bed he investigates a murder that took place in 1859. The story is based on the author's research into an actual case.

While Morse is convalescing, he is put in a room with an old soldier, Mr. Denniston, who promptly dies. Denniston's widow gives Morse her husband's book on the drowning of a woman named Joanna Franks, *Murder on the Oxford Canal.* Dexter includes the invented text in its entirety. A system of canals, built long before the coming of the railroads, connected Oxford with the city of Coventry to the north. There is a lot of interesting information on little known facets of English history, and Morse's curiosity about the canal boat "culture"—how the boats were worked and who worked them—is contagious. Joanna herself is a sympathetic, pathetic victim. Though one could have done without a scene of the toileting of Morse, the contrasting contemporary and historical "texts" are well handled and it is a good example of this subgenre.

WENTWORTH, PATRICIA (pseudonym of Dora Amy Elles Turnbull, 1878–1961) Patricia Wentworth's mysteries about Miss SILVER are still in print, testifying to the continuing appeal of the dowdy former governess turned private investigator. Maud Silver first appeared in *Grey Mask* (1927), and more than thirty other novels followed. Miss Silver is often compared to Agatha Christie's spinster sleuth, Miss MARPLE. Some have felt that Miss Silver does not measure up to that standard, mostly because of the saccharine factor—the romantic subplots in which Miss Silver often plays matchmaker. This criticism is largely unjust. First of all, Wentworth was a better handler of language than Christie; second, as BARZUN and TAYLOR pointed out, in the Silver tales "the old clichés of women's magazine fiction are avoided" in the main.

Wentworth was born in India and, as was the colonial custom, sent off to England for her education. The daughter of a British general, she married an officer herself after her return to India. Widowed in 1906, she returned to England; her development as a writer was accelerated out of necessity. In 1911 she published her first novel, *A Marriage Under the Terror,* set during the French Revolution. In 1920, she married again (to another military man).

Wentworth's books are like NOVELS OF MANNERS with murder thrown in—the concerns are more those of Jane Austen than Agatha Christie. THE GAZEBO (1955) is a good example: the murder only occurs after a hundred pages describing a woman whose romance is blighted by the demands of her invalid mother. Romance is not the subtext of the Miss Silver mysteries, but the main event and motivating factor. *The Chinese Shawl* (1943) involves a wounded RAF pilot and the women who want him; Wentworth dwells on the pain and jealousy evoked by broken engagements. Similarly, in *Miss Silver Comes to Stay* (1948), James Lessiter's return to the town of Lenten opens up old wounds. Lessiter is a seducer who had abandoned a Lenten woman twenty years before, destroying her life. An outrage to the morals of respectable society, this act still evokes anger. It needs only for Lessiter to show his face again to provoke violence. *The Case of William Smith* (1948) is a romantic tale involving AMNESIA and is one of the author's strongest works.

Wentworth wrote a string of non-series mystery and suspense stories before bringing Miss Silver back in her second appearance, *The Case Is Closed* (1937). The non-series novels, in the style of Georgette HEYER, often featured innocent heroines getting their first taste of the world's rottenness, and after many trials emerging triumphant. Money, marriage, and relations are the substances from which these romances are made up. Many of these books have been recently reprinted. *Nothing Venture* (1932) is one of those mysteries that hinges upon a will with ridiculous conditions. Jervis Weare stands to inherit a great deal of money as well as property from his uncle Ambrose—unless he fails to marry his fiancée, Rosamund, within six months after Ambrose's demise. If he does not marry, all the money goes to his fiancée. Rosamund inconveniently backs out of the nuptials two days before the deadline. *Run!* (1938), like many of Mary Roberts RINEHART's stories, involves someone who stumbles on strange mysteries in a spooky old house—though in this case, the someone is a man. James Elliot is lost in heavy fog, then discovers himself on the driveway of a country mansion. As soon as he enters, he finds a breathless young woman who urges him to run away; at once, the pair are shot at from the gloom. Eventually, Elliot is embroiled in the case of Miss Aspidistra Aspinall and her aunt's diamonds. *Dead or Alive* (1936) is about Meg O'Hara, widow of a dashing, handsome, and cruel Irish spy—only Meg does not believe that Robin O'Hara is dead, because of some suspicious messages she receives. Bill Coverdale is the devoted admirer who helps her unravel the mystery.

The assumptions of the GOLDEN AGE in some cases have worn very thin, and at times Wentworth works them very hard indeed. In the non-series mystery *Mr. Zero* (1938), the titular blackmailer demands that Lady Sylvia Colesborough steal government papers from her husband's associates or else he will reveal her gambling debts. It is hard today to imagine oneself in such a state that one would not simply tell Mr. Zero to go to hell. Wentworth attempts humor and romance, but not with the lightness or wit of Heyer; Lady Sylvia is *so* silly that she cannot remember how old she is, and does not know what the world "sabotage" means (she must know French, though—she thinks it has something to do with shoes).

Wentworth's most lasting contribution is undoubtedly the Miss Silver mysteries. Compared with other spinster sleuths like Hildegarde WITHERS, Miss Silver is more readable today; though at times comical, she is not a caricature. Wentworth's writing is solid and understated, with a natural modesty that allows her to reach the target she aims at without a lot of extraneous demonstrations of cleverness. Critics have rightly considered her an assured craftsman of the genre.

WEST, HELEN A series character in novels by Frances FYFIELD. West is a modern female crime fighter in the manner of the *Prime Suspect* television series, though she is a Crown Prosecutor and not a policewoman. Slim, dark, and naturally graceful, she hates cooking and domestic chores. Her lover is Geoffrey Bailey, a Detective Chief Inspector. Bailey is not an unusual type—big, strong, handsome, sensitive, intelligent—but he is unusually inarticulate and has trouble putting his thoughts into words. It is a more interesting explanation of a policeman's businesslike and even insensitive treatment of fellow human beings. In Bailey's case, what he says (little) does not indicate what he feels. This trait renders him less weak than vulnerable, and also makes others uncomfortable. His bosses promote him in order to get away from him ("too good to push down, so he has to go up"). Over forty, he is somewhat older than West. Both are divorced.

In *A Question of Guilt* (1988), the first book, West and Bailey meet when both become involved in the case of the brutal murder of a London solicitor. The killer, a pathetic amateur private detective and Polish immigrant, confesses, but doubt remains about the role of Eileen Cartwright, an insanely embittered client of the victim's husband. Cartwright's unattractive exterior conceals an even more ugly soul, full of a longing for love that has curdled into something else—a desire to do evil. Bailey and West are complex and highly developed characters—in fact, their reactions to things are far more prominent than the things themselves. Fyfield takes a risk in making her protagonists two highly intelligent introverts, and the development of their relationship takes up at least as much space as the solution of the crime.

West and Bailey move to the village of Branston in *Not That Kind of Place* (1989). The village, situated on a triangle of land between three highways, is a new commuter village full of social climbers and "achievers," with pretensions overlaying the usual suburbanite mentality. West and Bailey find that they hate it. A woman's body is discovered by a scavenging fox in a small wood. The body bears no identifying marks, but is found near The Crown, a hated pub with very rude landlords with a somewhat retarded son. Fyfield lets the reader into the thoughts of the characters, including the retarded Henry and a young girl, and these passages are well done and create suspense. There are, however, long passages of description and irrelevant reflections in which the author's efforts to be "literary" go astray. Although the mystery plot is submerged beneath the "novelistic," it is nonetheless well constructed.

In *Deep Sleep* (1991), West and Bailey have returned to London, where West is recovering from a gynecological operation. In part an INVERTED MYSTERY, the story begins when the wife of a pharmacist dies, apparently of natural causes, though she has no real health problems. The special properties of CHLOROFORM play a part in the mystery, as does an unexploded World War II bomb. *A Clear Conscience* (1994) is generally interesting though the characters are almost all unlikable, apparently by intention. The author tells the reader about all of their faults: the lower-class ones are crude or drunks or both, while the upper-class types are callous yuppies or neurotic loners. Before the scene opens, Damien Flood, an ex-boxer, is stabbed to death with a bayonet by a gang of youths. He is survived by his sister Cath, who is beaten by her bartender husband. Before West and Bailey can solve Flood's murder, another similar killing occurs.

BIBLIOGRAPHY Novels: *Without Consent* (1997).

WEST, INSPECTOR One of the many sleuths created by John CREASEY, the Roger West series ran for more than thirty years, during which the character evolved from a Roderick ALLEYN-ish, quiet sleuth into a more PROCEDURAL policeman similar to Creasey's George GIDEON. The first novel in the series was *Inspector West Takes Charge* (1942), which introduces him as the youngest inspector at Scotland Yard. He is troubled by the case of the Prendergast family, heirs to a tobacco fortune, three of whom have died in quick succession—one by drowning, one from a fall from a cliff, and one in a hit-and-run accident. In *Inspector West at Home* (1944), West's enemies set him up to be arrested as part of a smuggling ring, and he faces jail time.

West's nickname is "Handsome," and he follows the pattern of the detectives of the thirties in being dashing, clever, and suave. He has a wife, Janet, and two boys, who make cameo appearances in the books. Later in the series, more attention is given to his helpers. West has a cozy relationship with the press through a private investigator and journalist named Brammer. The other policemen remain little more than names. West's assistants, Detective Sergeant Peel and Detective Inspector Sloan, are both described as "big" and "boyish." GIVE A MAN A GUN (1953) is one of the more interesting West novels.

BIBLIOGRAPHY Novels: *Inspector West Leaves Town* (1943; U.S. title *Go Away to Murder*), *Inspector West Regrets* (1945), *Holiday for Inspector West* (1946), *Triumph for Inspector West* (1948; U.S. title *The Case Against Paul Raeburn*), *Battle for Inspector West* (1948), *Inspector West Kicks Off* (1949; U.S. title *Sport for Inspector West*), *Inspector West Cries Wolf* (1950; U.S. title *The Creepers*), *Inspector West Alone* (1950), *Puzzle for Inspector West* (1951; U.S. title *The Dissemblers*), *A Case for Inspector West* (1951; U.S. title *The Figure in the Dusk*), *Inspector West at Bay* (1952; U.S. title *The Blind Spot*), *Send Inspector West* (1953; U.S. title *Send Superintendent West*), *A Beauty for Inspector West* (1954; U.S. title *The Beauty Queen Killer*), *Inspector West Makes Haste* (1955; U.S. title *The Gelignite Gang*), *Two for Inspector West* (1955; U.S. title *One, Two, Three*), *A Prince for Inspector West* (1956; U.S. title *Death of an Assassin*), *Parcels for Inspector West* (1956; U.S. title *Death of a Postman*), *Accident for Inspector West* (1957; U.S. title *Hit and Run*), *Find Inspector West* (1957; U.S. title *The Trouble at Saxby's*), *Strike for Death* (1958; U.S. title *The Killing Strike*), *Murder, London–New York* (1958),

Death of a Racehorse (1959), *The Case of the Innocent Victims* (1959), *Murder on the Line* (1960), *Scene of the Crime* (1961), *Death in Cold Print* (1961), *Policeman's Dread* (1962), *Hang the Little Man* (1963), *Look Three Ways at Murder* (1964), *Murder, London-Australia* (1965), *Murder, London–South Africa* (1966), *The Executioners* (1967), *So Young to Burn* (1968), *Murder, London-Miami* (1969), *A Part for a Policeman* (1970), *Alibi* (1971), *A Splinter of Glass* (1972), *The Theft of Magna Carta* (1973), *The Extortioners* (1974), *A Sharp Rise in Crime* (1978).

WESTLAKE, DR. HUGH A character in a series of novels written by the authors known as Patrick QUENTIN, but published under the name Jonathan Stagge. Westlake is a country doctor who manages to get involved in bizarre situations. In *Light from a Lantern* (1943; U.S. title *The Scarlet Circle*), Westlake is in New England. At Cape Talisman, he finds a half-finished grave with a Chinese lantern set over it. His investigation leads him to a twisted killer. *Call for a Hearse* (1942; U.S. title *The Yellow Taxi*) is about a sinister cab driver with a scarred face who terrifies a girl; she believes the car was responsible for her friend's death. *Funeral for Five* (1940; U.S. title *Turn of the Table*) involves vampirism. The authors' interest in the macabre and horrifying continued in the series about Peter DULUTH.

BIBLIOGRAPHY Novels: *Murder Gone to Earth* (1936; U.S. title *The Dogs Do Bark*), *Murder or Mercy* (1937; U.S. title *Murder by Prescription*), *Murder in the Stars* (1939; U.S. title *The Stars Spell Death*), *Death My Dear Girls* (1945; U.S. title *Death My Darling Daughters*), *Death's Old Sweet Song* (1946), *The Three Fears* (1949).

WESTLAKE, DONALD (1933–) The U.S. mystery author Donald Westlake has become the reigning king of the humorous mystery story. Although he began writing in the HARD-BOILED tradition, the tough-guy element was later submerged by humor. Westlake served in the U.S. Air Force before becoming a writer. His first books were salacious potboilers written in the fifties. Next he wrote a series about PARKER, a thief but no gentleman. Unlike the earlier charming cat burglars of fiction, Parker is humorless and vicious when necessary. Appropriately, the novels were written under the pseudonym Richard Stark. Westlake turned out books with the rapidity of a PULP writer, producing three Parker novels in 1963 alone.

The Fugitive Pigeon (1965) was the first Westlake novel in which comedy predominated. *The Spy in the Ointment* (1966) followed, and the next year *God Save the Mark* won an EDGAR. Westlake was off and running, and his novels became progressively looser, and then even absurd. *Bank Shot* (1972) is about a bank job that involves stealing the bank itself. It also brings in John DORTMUNDER, a recurrent series character whose attitude to life resembles Rodney Dangerfield's—the novel WHY ME? (1983) typifies his lucklessness. Dortmunder is sympathetic, but the humor in the novels is heavier than in the Bernie RHODENBARR books, to which they bear a resemblance. In a novel like *Two Much* (1975), in which a man tries to pass himself off as two identical twin brothers in order to get hold of the inheritances of a pair of female twins, Westlake leaves reality far behind.

The Parker novels, with their austere tone, are less dated than some of Westlake's sixties efforts, such as *The Spy in the Ointment*. Every age has its humorists, and what seems funny to one generation is simply dumb to another; one problem with PARODY is that cultural memory of the thing parodied fades, so that one no longer appreciates, or cares about, the thing being made fun of. In the case of *The Spy*, the object of the humor, the James BOND-type spy escapade that flourished in the sixties, is itself a joke when viewed decades later.

Using his humor, Westlake has evolved a type of story that might be called an anti-thriller. *Help I Am Being Held Prisoner* (1974) is about a practical joker with the unfortunate name of Harry Künt, one of whose gags accidentally lands him in prison. He meets a gang of crooks who have a tunnel to the outside, but rather than escape, they are planning bank robberies, thinking that they will have the ultimate alibi: being in prison. Humorous scenes rather than events carry the book along, and the only mystery to speak of is who is sending out the messages referred to in the title. The combination of the RAFFLES tradition of thievery with slapstick comedy has the potential to be entertaining (but only that) when the formula works. KAHAWA (1982) is a more effective book, perhaps because it is based on reality (the theft of a train full of coffee), and the setting—Uganda under the regime of Idi Amin—is largely not funny but quite bizarre. Another mating of humor with gruesome subjects is *Baby, Would I Lie?* (1994), about a broken-down country and western singer who is on trial for an ugly sex murder.

Westlake's humorous mysteries now overshadow his other work, but should not obscure his versatility. With *Anarchaos* (1967), he ventured into the SCIENCE FICTION crime subgenre. In the Mitch Tobin series, written by Westlake during the sixties and seventies under the pseudonym of Tucker Coe, crime stories were combined with explorations of subcultures and those disaffected with or outcast by society.

Never has Westlake written a novel as deadly serious as THE AX (1997), nor one that better shows his ability to remake himself as a writer.

WEXFORD, CHIEF INSPECTOR A character created by Ruth RENDELL who has appeared in a series running for more than a quarter century, since *From Doon with Death* (1964). Wexford in an everyday chap—heavy, with an unremarkable and even ugly face—but he is also special. Like Inspector MORSE, Wexford is educated and able to identify or use quotations from literature, even to the extent of noting similarities between the real situations that confront him and scenes from books. Yet he is too realistic to be a GENIUS DETECTIVE, and his education does not encompass fifty varieties of cigarette papers and rare pipe tobaccos or other GOLDEN AGE wonders. Wexford's wife is named Dora, and they have two children; his usual assistant is Inspector Mike Burden, a gruffer sort of character toward whom Wexford sometimes adopts a superior attitude.

A striking debut, *From Doon with Death* begins *in media res,* with Burden's efforts to calm the fears of a milquetoast husband whose wife is an hour late getting home. Refreshingly, Rendell dispenses with any "once upon a time" introduction of characters, setting, and narrative landmarks. The Parsons home is a sad and shabby house in provincial Kingsmarkham. Mr. Parsons, an avid reader of crime stories, terrifies himself with fears for his wife Margaret, which later turn out to be all too justified. The detectives' procedure is described with exactitude, but not pedantically. *No More Dying Then* (1971) focuses more on Burden than is usual because he has been left a widower. His grief is balanced by, but in conflict with, his love for one of the other characters. The investigation of a murder/kidnapping is carried on by Wexford, but he must also cope with his partner's incapacitating emotional trauma.

Other books in the Wexford series are *Shake Hands Forever* (1975), in which a man is suspected of killing his wife—even though it was his mother, previous wife, and daughter who hated her; *A Sleeping Life* (1978), in which a woman who has been missing for twenty years is found stabbed to death; AN UNKINDNESS OF RAVENS (1985), in which feminist themes emerged; and *Simisola* (1995), about a serial killer who preys on Nigerian women.

In *Speaker of Mandarin* (1983), Rendell experimented with the form by removing Wexford from his usual context. The first half of the book concerns his vacation in China at the invitation of his nephew, who is attending conferences. The story is well researched and shows a typical guided tour in communist China, with visits to schools, plants, and factories, some of which Wexford skips. A series of strange events occurs, including the death of a Chinese guide during a scenic tour down a river, as well as Wexford's experience of visions or hallucinations. The second half of the book is a typical investigation of a murder that reflects back upon the events overseas.

The recent Wexford novel, *Road Rage* (1997), deals with ecoterrorism, giving the Inspector a chance to sort through all manner of New Age enthusiasts and fools. Dora is among the abductees. The case turns more serious when the terrorists carry out their threat to kill hostages.

BIBLIOGRAPHY Novels: *A New Lease on Death* (1967), *Wolf to the Slaughter* (1967), *Best Man to Die* (1969), *A Guilty Thing Surprised* (1970), *Murder Being Once Done* (1972), *Some Lie and Some Die* (1973), *Death Notes* (1981; orig title *Put On by Cunning*), *The Veiled One* (1988), *Kissing the Gunner's Daughter* (1991), *Harm Done* (1999).

Short Stories: *Means of Evil* (1980).

"WHAT, NO BUTLER?" This story by Damon RUNYON was collected in *Blue Plate Special* (1934). It parodies the GOLDEN AGE mysteries (see BUTLERS) and that staple of the period, the LOCKED ROOM problem. The narrator goes along with a detective and the acerbic drama critic Ambrose Hammer to view the body of Mr. Justin Veezee, found dead in his own house one morning. Veezee was "an old stinker" who was always "on the grab for young dolls" around Broadway. His neck is broken, and the narrator thinks it a perfect setup for a butler, because that's how it is done "in all the murder-mystery books I ever read."

WHEATLEY, DENNIS (1897–1977) By all accounts a bad writer, Dennis Wheatley yet did something important that opened the eyes of mystery writers to new possibilities—or so the history of the PROCEDURAL has it. Wheatley wrote mysteries, spy stories, tales of the OCCULT, and romances; he sold literally millions of books. His books about Gregory Sallust, a secret agent who battles the NAZIS in seven books written during World War II, are stiff-upper-lip stuff. He wrote another stack of books about Roger Brook, a spy for the Younger Pitt, who became prime minister of Great Britain in 1783.

Wheatley was born in London to a family of wine merchants. He fought in some of the major battles of World War I, including Ypres. An artilleryman, he was injured in a gas attack in 1918. He entered the family business after the war and did not publish his first book until 1933. *The Forbidden Territory* was an immediate success. Only three years later he hit on the idea (with the help of J. G. Links) of the "murder dossier." As the name suggests, these were not books but collections of material and clues such as one would encounter in a real murder. The reader, or buyer, would get a folder containing envelopes that held hair, "poison," a shred of cloth, and other clues, as well as photographs of the suspects and the notes and reports of the police. The reader was supposed to deduce the solution like a real detective (the answer was in a sealed envelope). The first dossier in the series was *Murder Off Miami* (1936; U.S. title *File on Bolitho Blane*). Three others followed: *Who Killed Robert Prentice?* (1937; U.S. title *File on Robert Prentice*), *The Malinsay Massacre* (1938), and *Herewith the Clues* (1939).

The dossier was a step toward the procedural because it contained a classic puzzle but used real pieces. Instead of a little old lady finding the vicar with a dagger in him and then neatly unraveling whodunit, the reader is faced with a mess of the stuff that crimes are made of. One cannot say if Wheatley considered the question of whether people who read mystery stories wanted to hear a tale or turn over family trees and pictures of crime scenes; to enjoy reading about a crime does not entail that one would like actually to solve one. Few of the dossiers are left and they are much sought after as collectibles. Ironically, the best work that Wheatley did was not a book, but an artifact or an object. Because of their originality, they were remembered when his other work was forgotten.

WHICHER, JONATHAN One of the first detectives in nineteenth-century London (see SCOTLAND YARD), Jonathan Whicher became known as the "Prince of Detectives." His fame attracted the attention of and was promoted by Charles DICKENS and Wilkie COLLINS. Under the name of "Whichem," Dickens wrote about the detective in his magazine *Household Words.* Collins used him as the model for Sergeant CUFF in his novel THE MOONSTONE (1868). Features of Whicher's solution of the case of Constance KENT, who had murdered her younger brother, were also brought into the story by Collins.

WHISPER Max "Whisper" Thaler is one of the key characters in Dashiell Hammett's RED HARVEST (1929). First described as "a little slick dark guy with something wrong with his throat," the gambler Thaler is the most enduring—literally—and likeable of the host of gangsters who murder each other in the book.

WHITE, STANFORD At the time of his murder in 1906, Stanford White was a principal of the firm of McKim, Mead & White, one of the leading architectural firms in the United States. They popularized the neoclassical style, and created such monuments to it as the Boston Public Library, the old Pennsylvania Station in New York, the arch in Washington Square, and a number of buildings at Columbia University. White was having an affair with the actress Evelyn Nesbit Thaw, whose husband, Harry K. Thaw, was not only insanely jealous but insane, period. Thirty-four years old, Thaw was the heir to a $40 million fortune and a drug addict, and was judged so unbalanced by his father that he had left instructions in his will that an allowance be doled out to young Harry by his mother.

In June 1906, the love triangle exploded. Thaw encountered White at an opera, and afterwards shot him on the roof of the old Madison Square Garden (incidentally, a McKim, Mead & White building).

There was never any question of Harry K. Thaw's guilt. Nesbit and White, however, were demonized in the press, the one as a wanton woman and the other as a womanizer. (One of those who wrote about the trial was Samuel Hopkins ADAMS.) The only issue was Thaw's insanity. The first trial ended in a hung jury. The second, in 1908, resulted in Thaw's being confined in an insane asylum—where, in consequence of his wealth, he lived in extreme luxury. He escaped to Canada once, was brought back, and was finally found sane in 1915 and released.

The case has been rehashed in several books, including *The Murder of Stanford White* (1963), by Gerald Langford, and more recently *Stanny: The Gilded Life of Stanford White* (1989), by Paul R. Baker. The murder forms a subplot of E. L. DOCTOROW's *Ragtime* (1975).

WHITECHURCH, VICTOR [LORENZO] (1868–1933) The mystery writing career of Canon Whitechurch, an Anglican clergyman, fell into two distinct phases. His early stories were collected in *Thrilling Stories of the Railway* (1912), which was included in QUEEN'S QUORUM; more than half of them were about the unusual Edwardian sleuth Thorpe HAZELL. Later in life, he turned out a series of detective novels that have been widely praised.

Whitechurch was a country clergyman, and his stories often showed a bucolic England—unlike the work of many of his contemporaries, who wrote about the romance and grime of London. He was made honorary canon of Christ Church, Oxford, toward the end of his life. He wrote several novels about clerics, including *A Canon in Residence* (1904), *Concerning Himself* (1909), and *A Downland Corner* (1913).

Whitechurch introduced *The Crime at Diana's Pool* (1927) with his thoughts on detective writing; he went on to violate the rules of FAIR PLAY in the story itself, which is about a murder at a garden party. His novels of the twenties and thirties obey the rules of an earlier age. *The Robbery at Rudwick House* (1929) echoes the Victorian preference for crimes against property rather than the person. Whitechurch also used his background as a clergyman in these books, both in the choice of settings and in the use of clerics as characters and even sleuths.

The first novel of his late period was *The Templeton Case* (1924); others are *Shot on the Downs* (1927) and *Murder at the Pageant* (1930).

WHITEFIELD, JANE See PERRY, THOMAS.

WHITFIELD, RAOUL (1898–1945) Raoul Whitfield is one of those crime writers whose own life reads like an adventure—in his case, tragically cut short by illness. Whitfield was born in New York City but grew up in the Philippines, where his father was employed in the American territorial administration. Returning to the United States in 1916, he began to act in the early silent films. With the entry of the United States into World War I in 1917, Whitfield enlisted in the Air Force and became a flying ace.

After the war, Whitfield was a reporter for a Pittsburgh newspaper and also began writing for the PULP MAGAZINES, selling his first contribution to BLACK MASK in 1926. He published his first novel, GREEN ICE, in 1930. Whitfield used his Philippines experience in some short stories about Jo Gar, an early "ethnic" detective (they appeared under the pseudonym Ramon Decolta). Whitfield's writing is classically HARD-BOILED, much cleaner than DALY's; he emulated Dashiell HAMMETT and hit nearer the mark than many other pulpsmiths. His other novels are *Death in a Bowl* (1931), about a shooting at the Hollywood Bowl, and *The Virgin Kills* (1932). These novels were reissued in the 1980s in paperback editions. Whitfield wrote two other books under the pseudonym Temple Field, but they remain out of print. In *Death in a Bowl,* conductor Hans Reiner is directing the orchestra when he is shot in the back. *The Virgin Kills* is a case of MURDER AFLOAT. Eric Vennel is a millionaire, a gambler, and a yachtsman. He sails up to Poughkeepsie, New York for a regatta with his guests, a group of writers, thugs, and Hollywood types. An attack on the yacht and a murder occur during the voyage.

WHITTINGTON, HARRY (1915–1990) The Floridian writer Harry Whittington produced some one hundred and forty books under a variety of pseudonyms and in several genres, including mystery and crime. He turned out Westerns as Harry White and Hondo Wells, and novels about the South as Clay Stuart and Hallam Whitney. He even published a series of novels about a young nurse under the name Harriet Kathryn Meyers. Whittington sold his first short story in 1943 for fifteen dollars. He held a number of jobs in St. Petersburg, as a theater manager, a postal worker, and an editor before publishing his first novel, *Vengeance Valley* (1945).

With titles like *Murders My Mistress* (1951), *Swamp Kill* (1951), *So Dead My Love* (1953), and *You'll Die Next* (1954), Whittington contributed to the massive outflow of NOIR novels in the forties and fifties. He deployed such stock plots as the small town ruled by a corrupt "boss" figure, but also used ingenious murder weapons (such as an alligator). *Web of Murder* (1958; repr 1993) is the only Whittington book readily available. It is a classic double-cross story: Charley Brower, a successful lawyer, is trapped in a dull marriage with a rich wife who keeps him on a short leash as far as money is concerned. When Charley falls for his secretary, he decides that getting rid of his wife would be the best home improvement "since solid oak flooring." The complexity of the "perfect murder" is unlikely but entertaining, especially as it unravels.

Whittington also wrote for the television series *The Man from U.N.C.L.E.* Although not of the first rank, he remains an interesting writer, particularly as a regionalist.

"WHO CARES WHO KILLED ROGER ACKROYD?" One of a series of three essays by Edmund WILSON, first published in *The New Yorker* in 1944–45, in which the author lambasted mystery writers for bad writing and a dearth of imagination. In the first essay, Wilson attacked THE MALTESE FALCON (1929) but singled out Raymond CHANDLER for praise. (A great admirer of HAMMETT, Chandler wrote privately that Wilson's head was full of "mucilage.")

"Who Cares Who Killed Roger Ackroyd?" was the second essay in the series, written after an outpouring of negative letters from readers and critics, some of whom protested that Wilson had read the wrong mysteries. Taking their suggestions in mind, he re-examined the genre. Wilson dismissed Ngaio MARSH's writing as "unappetizing sawdust," and Margery ALLINGHAM as "completely unreadable." Wilson's most interesting point is that mysteries only appear good when the normal rules of critical reading are suspended; in short, the mystery reader makes the fish seem bigger by making the pond smaller. The true mystery "addict" engages in a form of cheating: he or she holds imagination and intellect in abeyance, focuses on the story purely as a problem (but usually does not pay close enough attention to solve it), and instead of going back and re-examining the book to see how the plot works, simply starts another.

The essay is reprinted in Howard HAYCRAFT's *The Art of the Mystery Story* (1946).

WHODUNIT See GOLDEN AGE.

WHO KILLED PALOMINO MOLERO? See VARGAS LLOSA, MARIO.

WHY ME? (1983) A novel by Donald WESTLAKE, a comedy of errors developing out of a jewel theft. John DORTMUNDER, the sad-sack thief, steals a 90-carat ruby, the Byzantine Fire, from a jewelry store in South Ozone Park, Queens. It is a Turkish national treasure, and was about to be returned to Turkey when it was stolen by Greek Cypriots, who placed it in the safe of the jeweler just as the unlucky Dortmunder was robbing the place. Soon he is being pursued by various law enforcement agencies as well as terrorists.

WIBBERLEY, LEONARD See HOLTON, LEONARD.

WICK, CARTER See WILCOX, COLLIN.

WILCOX, COLLIN (1924–1996) A leading American writer of police PROCEDURALS, Colin Wilcox began his career by publishing an offbeat series about a sleuth with psychic powers. Stephen Drake, a reporter in New York City, appeared in *The Black Door* (1968) and *The Third Figure* (1969). In his first case, Drake's murder investigation involves him with right-wing extremists. Wilcox later turned to a more conventional hero, Frank HASTINGS, a San Francisco cop with the brooding personality of a private eye.

Wilcox was born in Detroit and attended Antioch College. He was in the Air Force and then taught in San Francisco, later switching to the furniture business. Wilcox eventually founded his own lighting company. He has written non-series mysteries and has also entered the theatrical mystery sub-genre (Parnell HALL coincidentally writes about an actor/p.i. named Hastings) with his novels about Alan Bernhardt, an actor, director, and private eye who first appeared in *Bernhardt's Edge* (1988). *Find Her a Grave* (1993) is one of the later Bernhardt books, in which the illegitimate offspring of a Mafia boss recruit him in an underworld battle over their legacy—a million dollars in gold and diamonds buried behind a tombstone. The same old mob tough talk and the weak plot make this not one of Wilcox's best efforts. His Hastings novels remain his most successful work, though they get looser and looser, in line with current procedural fashion. Under the pseudonym Carter Wick, Wilcox published *The Faceless Man* (1975).

WILD, JONATHAN (1682–1725) An English highwayman and robber who was said to have six wives and who was hanged for burgling a house. Wild was immortalized in literature by DEFOE (*Jonathan Wild*, 1725) and FIELDING (*Jonathan Wild the Great*, 1743). In both books, Wild is portrayed unsympathetically—indeed, as a monster without feelings—and they offer an interesting contrast to romantic crime fiction, in which the criminal-as-outcast becomes a hero or anti-hero.

WILLEFORD, CHARLES [RAY] (1919–1988) Charles Willeford was one of the most versatile of crime and mystery writers, producing some of the funniest (THE SHARK INFESTED CUSTARD [1993]) and some of the grimmest (PICK-UP [1954]) books in the genre. Willeford was born in Little Rock, Arkansas, and was orphaned at the age of eight. He lived with relatives until he left home to become a hobo during the Depression. Willeford was sixteen when he lied about his age in order to get into the Army. His military career would last twenty years. Willeford served in World War II as a tank commander in the Third Army, fought at the Battle of the Bulge, and earned a Silver Star, a Purple Heart, and other decorations. A man of wide-ranging interests and abilities, Willeford's postwar career encompassed jobs as horse trainer, boxer, and radio announcer. He was also a painter and art critic, which provides the background for the novel THE BURNT ORANGE HERESY (1971).

Willeford's first book, however, was a volume of poems, *Proletarian Laughter* (1948). His first paperback novel was *High Priest of California* (1953). Willeford did not repeat himself, and the novels that followed were each different in kind, including *Cockfighter* (1962, rev 1972), the story of a cruel and depressing subculture.

Willeford portrayed a dark vision of American society and the madness it allowed; he often showed the cult of success rendered down in the mind of the "madman" (who carries the rules to their logical extension) to its essential element, a completely amoral desire for power. The difference is that Willeford still left enough oxygen inside the story for the reader to breathe. Thus, the narrator of *The Burnt Orange Heresy* adheres in the end to an almost Greek sense of the need for retribution for the circle to be closed and the tragedy ended. The ironies Willeford was so fond of also offer a comic release. The ex-con in *Sideswipe* (1987) who has stolen a look at his medical records and seen that he is "sociopathic" and "psychopathic" feels relief, considering his pathology an explanation of his behavior and even a license for it. If he can't help himself, why not help himself to whatever he needs or desires?

Recognition came late in Willeford's career. His best-known character is the toothless and somewhat grotesque Hoke MOSELEY, one of the most unlikely detectives in crime fiction. Willeford wrote all of the Hoke Moseley novels in a short period at the end of his life, and there are only four. The first was *Miami Blues* (1984), in which Moseley suffers the ignominy of having his teeth stolen, and tracks down a sociopathic recidivist. Hoke does some detecting, but not much; rather, he is shown on a collision course with trouble, and most often the reader knows who the trouble is before the detective does. The plot of *Sideswipe* mirrors that of the first book, but the pace is much slower because Moseley is in an almost catatonic funk.

Willeford also wrote two volumes of autobiography, *I Was Looking for a Street* (1988) and *Something About A Soldier* (1989).

WILLIAMS, CHARLES (1909–1975) Originally from Texas, Charles Williams led a richly adventurous and interesting life. Born in San Angelo, which was then a cow town, Williams spent his twenties at sea. His training in radio while in the merchant marine laid the groundwork for his later shoreside career in marine electronics and radar. His experiences as a sailor also provided material for his mystery and suspense novels with nautical themes, making him a master of MURDER AFLOAT.

In 1939, Williams married and left the sea, but he did not publish his first book until 1950. He wrote prolifically for a quarter century until his death. During this period Williams lived in Arizona, California, Florida, Peru, and Switzerland. His first books drew on his boyhood in rural Texas, but then he turned to novels of the sea. Among his works in the mystery genre are *Dead Calm* (1963), in which a mysterious shipwreck survivor is picked up by a couple on a pleasure cruise. It was made into a minor example of the FILM NOIR style (1989). A book that made it to the screen more spectacularly was *The Long Saturday Night* (1962), which was filmed by François TRUFFAUT twenty years later as CONFIDENTIALLY YOURS (1983). So adaptable to film presentation were Williams's taut, suspenseful plots and sympathetic characters that in all, fourteen of his twenty-one novels were sold to the movie industry.

Williams was an expert at evoking the pressures inside a small town: boredom, complacency, frustration, suppressed passion, hypocrisy, and incipient violence. He exploited the common NOIR sexual paradigm of the hero—or anti-hero—caught between two types of beautiful women, one sexy and dangerous, the other more restrained and virtuous and with an appropriately more subtle beauty. This dichotomy of course goes back to romantic and GOTHIC fiction, with its blonde heroines and dark villainesses. In the early novel *Hill Girl* (1954), however, a finely written story about a man who returns to the South to farm, Williams created Angelina, an overturning of the sexpot cliché and one of the best female characters in *noir* fiction.

Other books by Williams include *Scorpion Reef* (1955), *Aground* (1960), and *The Sailcloth Shroud* (1960). Another reflection of his maritime background is *And the Deep Blue Sea* (1960), in which a boatload of people are held hostage on a burning ship. *Aground*, about arms smuggling aboard a yacht, was praised by Anthony BOUCHER. Other novels were more in the mainstream of fifties *noir*. *A Touch of Death* (1954) is about a fight over some embezzled money between a man and a vicious killer—a woman. This was one of a number of books about dangerous females; *The Wrong Venus* (1966) had three. Lawrence Colby, a former paratrooper, newspaperman, and dealer in art forgeries, gets involved with an "Amazon," an author of sex novels, and an amoral member of the jet set.

Most of Wiliams's works are out of print. The only one that is readily available is *The Hot Spot* (orig title *Hell Hath No Fury*, 1953; repr 1990), which was reprinted at the time of the release of a film adaptation. In this novel, hot-headed Harry Madox gets a job selling cars in a small southern town and becomes involved with the boss's alcoholic sexpot wife. Then he falls in love with a quiet young woman who has a mysterious and painful secret. The rankling narrowness of small-town life and its festering, petty jealousies is aptly portrayed. Madox is a classic type, the loser who thinks of himself as a winner and who goes around with a chip on his shoulder, which fate eventually knocks off most spectacularly. The plot develops through chain reactions, the steps of which Madox is always too late to foresee. The ending is one of Williams's most hellish scenarios.

WILLIAMS, JAY See DELVING, MICHAEL.

WILLIAMS, JOHN A man who was arrested for the 1811 Ratcliffe Highway murders. He is discussed in DE QUINCEY's famous essay on murder that dealt with that incident. It was believed that Williams entered the household and shop of Timothy Marr at 29 Ratcliffe Highway and cut the throats of the father (possibly a former shipmate of Williams's) and mother, infant, and boy servant after first crushing their skulls with a shipwright's mallet. De Quincey, in Edinburgh at the time, reported national panic and outrage; there was no police force in England at the time. Thirty thousand people attended the Marr's funeral. Then, twelve days later, a tavern keeper named Williamson, his wife, and a female servant were all murdered, but a witness escaped. Williams was arrested for the crime but hanged himself in prison with his suspenders before he could be brought to trial. De Quincey reports that in accordance with tradition, Williams was buried at a crossroads with a stake driven through his heart. Although De Quincey says that a bloody knife in a cloak caked with blood was found in Williams's lodgings, other examiners of the case have doubted his guilt. The definitive account of the Ratcliffe Highway murders is by P. D. JAMES and T. A. Critchley, who termed De Quincey's essay "fanciful." One of the results of the Ratcliffe Highway murders was a public outcry for the reform of methods of protecting the public and keeping the peace.

Another John Williams was the subject of a celebrated case a hundred years later. This 1912 murder was used by Nicholas BLAKE as the basis for A TANGLED WEB (1956).

WILLIAMS, RACE Acknowledged as the first HARD-BOILED detective, Williams was created by Carroll John DALY and appeared in stories in BLACK MASK as well as in novels. Today the Race Williams stories are treated more or less with derision by critics for their melodrama, bad writing, and Race's ridiculous machismo (he carries not one, but two .44s). Large and muscular, with dark eyes and hair, Williams was the prototype for many later detectives. Race is not an introvert by any means; he kills often and broods little, thinking that his victims always "deserved it." Race says "with me the thought is the act," but unfortunately the converse is not true. Mike HAMMER is similar to Williams. Williams has a nemesis of sorts in "The Flame," a dangerous redhead, and his resisting of her attractions is again similar to Hammer's relations (if they can be dignified by that name) with women. Interest in the PULP MAGAZINES and the genesis of the hard-boiled style have led to the reprinting of several volumes in the Race Williams series in recent years, but contemporary readers are more sophisticated—not least because of having read the many authors who improved and updated the type pioneered by Daly—and unlikely to find Race Williams readable. *The Snarl of the Beast* (1926), for example, is a quagmire of bluster, not improved by senseless shootouts and Williams's incoherent commentary on the events.

BIBLIOGRAPHY Novels: *The Hidden Hand* (1929), *The Tag Murders* (1930), *Tainted Power* (1931), *The Third Murderer* (1933), *The Amateur Murderer* (1933), *Murder from the East* (1935), *Better Corpses* (1940).

Short Stories: *The Adventures of Race Williams* (1987).

WILLIAMS, VALENTINE (1883–1946) English mystery and spy writer and world-traveling journalist, creator of the memorable "Clubfoot." Williams was born a writer: his father was the chief editor at Reuter's News Agency, and his grandfather had also worked for Reuter's. Valentine joined the agency when he was only nineteen, and because he had been educated in Germany and was fluent in the language, was sent to Berlin as a correspondent in 1904, remaining there until 1909. He broke with tradition (and with his father's wishes) when he quit Reuter's to become the Paris correspondent of the *Daily Mail.*

Probably no spy novelist has come to writing in the same way as Valentine Williams. Seriously wounded at the battle of the Somme in 1916, Williams had a series of dreams while in the hospital that he was a British spy in Berlin and was being pursued by the Germans. With the encouragement of John BUCHAN, Williams turned those nightmares into fiction in *The Man with the Clubfoot* (1918). "Clubfoot" is the enormous, monstrous Dr. Adolph Grundt, the head of the German secret service. Williams eventually produced seven Clubfoot novels.

Williams's work took him to the United States, France, Egypt, and other countries, which he used as background for his fiction. Although World War I remained a deep source of material, he also wrote detective novels that had nothing to do with Clubfoot. Among them are *The Yellow Streak* (1922) and *The Three of Clubs* (1924), which includes scenes set on the Orient Express. As Clubfoot faded, Williams created the detectives Trevor Dene, a Scotland Yard man on loan in the United States, and Horace B. Treadgold, an English tailor working in the United States. Treadgold is also a stamp collector and an amateur sleuth, and appears in such books as *Dead Man Manor* (1936), a collection of short stories entitled *Mr. Treadgold Cuts In* (1937), and *Skeletons Out of the Cupboard* (1946).

Other works by Williams include *The Gold Comfit Box* (1932) and *Death Answers the Bell* (1932).

WILLING, BASIL The psychiatrist Basil Willing is the sleuth in a series of novels by Helen MCCLOY. Willing was introduced in *Dance of Death* (1938; British title *Design for Dying*), making his one of the first serious attempts to present a psychiatrist in mystery fiction. Prior to McCloy, the psychiatrist was more often the butt of humor, but Willing's psychological commentary is neither academic, ponderous, nor dogmatic. Instead, he is a quite convincing observer of words and gestures. His training is evidently Freudian, and he lays stress on dreams and the detection of repressed emotions.

Anthony BOUCHER said that *Dance of Death* would have deserved an EDGAR, had that award existed at the time; "few first mysteries have received such generous critical praise." Like many detectives of the time, Willing is elegant and urbane, but more emphasis is put on his intellect than on his other attributes. Born in the United States of a Russian mother and American father, the well-traveled sleuth studied psychiatry in Vienna, its birthplace. Returning to the United States, he assists the District Attorney's office in New York City. A World War I veteran, Willing also serves in World War II in Naval Intelligence; in *The One That Got Away* (1945), the war has just ended and he is searching for an escaped prisoner. The novel is narrated by Lieutenant Peter Dunbar, a subordinate of Willing's and himself a specialist in juvenile delinquency. Sent to the Scottish Highlands, Dunbar becomes involved in the case of Johnny Stockton, the adopted son of two writers, one a hack and the other a serious novelist. Dunbar's efforts to find out why Johnny keeps running away lead him into an intrigue that also involves a reclusive neo-Nazi philosopher—an American one. As in other novels in the series, Willing only appears later in the book after the plot has developed into a tangle that the other characters cannot untie. *The Goblin Market* (1943) is also set during the war.

McCloy was a relatively slow producer of mysteries—only fourteen Willing novels over a period of more than forty years—which shows in the quality and distinct merits of the books. *Through the Glass Darkly* (1950) is the most experimental novel in the series and is famous for its use of the DOPPELGÄNGER theme. The story is set at Brereton, a girls' school in New Jersey. An art teacher, Faustina Crayle, is fired without explanation. Her friend, Gisela von Hohenems, writes to Willing for help. (Gisela, an Austrian noblewoman, is Willing's future wife.) In the course of his investigation he discovers that Faustina's behavior had bizarre and even paranoid features. CUE FOR MURDER (1942) takes place during a theatrical performance and has been praised for the tightness of its plotting and the perfect arrangement of the clues. BURN THIS (1980) was the last novel to feature Willing. At this late date, he is living with his daughter and is a widower. Willing does not age realistically, because in *Burn This* he would be nearly eighty years old. The novel is extremely polished and noteworthy for the delicate sadness of its tone, established through the main character, a female writer.

BIBLIOGRAPHY Novels: *The Man in the Moonlight* (1940), *The Deadly Truth* (1941), *Who's Calling* (1942), *Alias Basil Willing* (1951), *The Long Body* (1945), *Two-Thirds of a Ghost* (1956), *Mr. Splitfoot* (1968).

WILLIS, TED (Baron Edward Henry Willis, 1918–1992) The English writer Ted Willis first became known for his work in the theater, radio, and television, and as the creator of Dixon of Dock Green, a policeman who first appeared in a 1949 film but was to have an incredibly long run as a TV character in the early decades of television. Willis was made a life peer in 1963. His books about George Dixon were spin-offs from the television and film productions. The best known is *The Blue Lamp* (1950). Willis went on to write other mysteries and thrillers, such as *Death May Surprise Us* (1974), in which a Labour Party prime minister, while visiting a country fair in Okefield, enters a fortune-teller's van and then mysteriously disappears, presumably kidnapped. His books often reflected political issues and his experience in the House of Lords. *The Churchill Commando* (1977) is about a paramilitary vigilante group that kills off undesirable elements in British society, from rowdies at soccer matches to kidnappers and leftists. Hiding behind the image of Winston Churchill and nationalism, the murderous gang become heroes. In *The Left-Handed Sleeper* (1975), a British agent looks for a member of Parliament who has disappeared and may have defected, and also falls in love with the man's wife.

WILSON, BARBARA See GAY MYSTERIES.

WILSON, EDMUND (1895–1972) The American critic Edmund Wilson, known for his work on the Symbolists and writers of the modernist period (*Axel's Castle*, 1931), took a brief interest in the mystery genre that has become famous. Known for his curmudgeony opinions, Wilson wrote three essays during World War II in which he almost completely dismissed the genre of mystery and detective fiction. The best known of the essays is WHO CARES WHO KILLED ROGER ACKROYD? (1944), the title of which sums up Wilson's point of view.

WILSON, SUPERINTENDENT See COLE, G. D. H. and M. I.

WIMSEY, LORD PETER Lord Peter Wimsey is probably the most imitated detective of the GOLDEN AGE. Although he is not hard-boiled, death is his middle name (Lord Peter Death Bredon Wimsey). Dorothy L. SAYERS made Wimsey handsome, aristocratic, and tall (like Superintendent Wilson, Wimsey grew several inches after his first appearance, topping the six-foot mark). He has "straw-colored" hair, which he wears slicked back, and is elegantly tailored. Sayers gave him a multitude of natural graces: like RAFFLES, he is a great cricketer; he has soldiered heroically in World War I, rising to the rank of captain, and his batman, BUNTER, is his loyal companion;

he plays the piano; he collects books and incunabula; and he has an encyclopedic mind. In fact, Sayers's books are overflowing with information about Wimsey and his clan. The progenitor of the Wimsey line, Gerald de Wimsey, was a crusading knight who fought at the Battle of Acre.

Viewed as a series, the Wimsey books are a family saga as well as a romance in four volumes. Wimsey's older brother Gerald is the Duke of Denver. The sleuth rescues him from trouble in CLOUDS OF WITNESS (1927), the second book in the series. His mother, the Dowager, is a comical, lovable presence, and brings Lord Peter his first case (*Whose Body?,* 1923) when a body is discovered in her TUB. Wimsey's sister Mary marries Inspector Charles Parker, who is a friend of Wimsey's within Scotland Yard. Parker assists Wimsey in his investigations, as does his team of women, headed by Miss CLIMPSON. In STRONG POISON (1930), Wimsey meets the mystery writer Harriet Vane under unusual circumstances, and their courtship runs through the rest of the series. THE FIVE RED HERRINGS (1931) is a case set in Scotland involving ART.

As time went on, the romantic aspect came to take up more and more of the series. The lengthy *Gaudy Night* (1936) does not even have a murder, and is more a NOVEL OF MANNERS set in Oxford. Action is displaced by Harriet's final acceptance of Wimsey's suit. HAVE HIS CARCASE (1932) is the intervening book, in which Wimsey continued his proposals to her while they solved a mystery together. The last book, *Busman's Honeymoon* (1937), had the provocative subtitle "A Love Story with Detective Interruptions," and given the direction in which the series was headed, it seems unlikely that it could have continued, even though Sayers left an incomplete manuscript of a further novel.

When he first appears, Wimsey affects an accent (dropping his g's), wears pince-nez, and is something of a twit. His volubility (he often inserts scraps of poetry into his jumbled thoughts) and Bunter's gift for understatement show the obvious influence of P. G. Wodehouse, who had published his first story about Bertie Wooster and his valet, Reginald Jeeves, in 1915. The first volume of collected stories, *My Man Jeeves,* appeared in 1919, and the second in 1923—the same year in which the first Lord Peter Wimsey novel was published.

Wimsey matured, however, when it became necessary for him to fulfill the conventional role of romantic hero. Some readers adore him as much as Sayers evidently did, while others find him as annoying as Philo VANCE. Lord Peter is "slight" and "fantastical in manner." If one hates the aristocratic English detective, he is an artificial, unnatural buffoon. If one can see him as a real person, he is a nervous, possibly bored man in flight from himself, playing the clown at parties, running after criminals instead of women, and thoroughly avoiding himself. No wonder Sayers wanted to rescue him from himself—by creating Harriet Vane. (The similarity between Harriet Vane and Dorothy Sayers herself has often been remarked upon). Howard HAYCRAFT felt that, because of her turn toward romance and the Wimsey-Vane domestic scene, Sayers's last two books were failures, "neither good detection nor good legitimate fiction."

Lord Peter Wimsey also appeared in quite a large number of short stories. *Hangman's Holiday* (1933) and *In the Teeth of the Evidence* (1939) contained a few stories about Lord Peter and several about Montague EGG. The last story to feature Wimsey, "Talboys," was not published until after the author's death. It is included in the anthology *Lord Peter* (1972; repr 1987), which collects all of the Wimsey short stories. In the end, Wimsey is a thriving father with three sons, and one of them is rambunctious enough to steal the neighbor's peaches.

BIBLIOGRAPHY Novels: *Unnatural Death* (1927; orig title *The Dawson Pedigree*), *The Unpleasantness at the Bellona Club* (1928), *Murder Must Advertise* (1933), *The Nine Tailors* (1934).

Short Stories: *Lord Peter Views the Body* (1929).

WIND BLOWS DEATH, THE (1949) A novel by Cyril HARE, which along with TRAGEDY AT LAW (1942) represents the height of his achievement. Introduced in the earlier book, Francis PETTIGREW has now married and settled down in Markshire with his wife, Eleanor, who plays violin with the Markshire Orchestral Society. Pettigrew is the amateur orchestra's treasurer, and so he is present at a concert when the guest soloist, violinist Lucy Carless, fails to appear on stage. She is found strangled with a stocking in the artist's room. Also missing is Bill Ventry, a passable organist and accomplished womanizer who had made overtures, so to speak, to the second wife of Carless's first husband, Robert Dixon, an aristocrat who serves as the orchestra's secretary. If these complications were not enough, Carless (née Carlessoff) had had a violent argument with the Polish clarinetist hired by the orchestra to fill out its ranks, necessitating the hiring of another woodwind player at the last minute—and there is some doubt about who that player really was.

Hare lays out the complex relationships focused on Lucy Carless with great simplicity. Pettigrew is an unwilling participant in the investigation, which he is drawn into by Chief Constable MacWilliam, a convivial Scotsman. His role is concealed from the ambitious yet insecure Inspector Trimble. The important clues are arcane but fit together nicely—a piece by Mozart, a point of English law dating back to Henry VIII, and Lucy Carless's positive hatred of DICKENS. Hare is as lucid and affable as ever. He combined a talent for puzzles—the preoccupation of the GOLDEN AGE—with an agreeable style and subtle humor. Pettigrew is also brilliant while remaining mortal and believable.

"The Wind Blows Death" (1942) is a short story by Bruno FISCHER.

WINE, MOSES A divorced Jewish sixties radical with two kids based in Southern California, Moses Wine is an atypical private eye, or was at the time Roger L. SIMON introduced him in *The Big Fix* (1973). There followed a host of post-sixties detectives, most of them Vietnam veterans of approximately the same age as Wine, but they were closer to the HARD-BOILED model and its values. (Wine, on the other hand, gets his picture on the cover of *Rolling Stone* as the "hippie" detective.)

The Wine adventures are laid-back and almost tongue-in-cheek, with fairly simple plots. In *The Big Fix,* Wine smokes a lot of hashish, though he figures he "hadn't yet passed Sherlock Holmes, who, in *The Sign of Four,* took three cocaine injections a day." The detective gets into trouble after an old girlfriend hires him to work for the campaign of a liberal senator running in the presidential primaries. His problem is that he has been endorsed by a far-left crank who sends out leaflets depicting the senator alongside Marx and Lenin. After a gruesome murder takes place, Wine also finds his case mixed up with a California-style religious cult. The story is neither long nor very complex, and the narration by Wine is completely straightforward, even artless—though he gets into trouble when he tries to throw in the traditional hard-boiled p.i.'s descriptive turns of phrase ("the sky was beginning to look like steamed piss"). Some of the time Wine sounds as if he belongs in a Hunter S. Thompson novel.

In the other Wine books, the private eye usually takes on some group of reactionaries and defeats them. *Wild Turkey* (1975), the second novel, is about the death of a famous writer—the standard murder-or-suicide puzzle, but with radical politics thrown in. The books in which Wine takes his crusade to the far corners of the globe are less than believable and descend to the thriller level. The author's penchant for adding irrelevant sex has been objected to, but all in all it is rather tame. As the series goes on, there tends to be more commentary and diversion and less and less substance to the novels. In *Raising the Dead* (1988), an Arab group hires Wine to investigate the killing of one of their leaders, and the case takes him to Israel, where he re-examines Jewish culture.

At the beginning of *California Roll* (1985), Wine announces "I never sold out because nobody ever asked me." Seeing that "all around me my sixties buddies were getting rich," Wine takes a job for a corporation at a big salary and moves to Silicon Valley. As the security chief for a firm that makes personal computers, he starts out by tracking down knock-offs being produced in the Far East. Then one of the company's whiz kids gets murdered, and shadowy figures who may be foreign agents start menacing Wine.

BIBLIOGRAPHY Novels: *Peking Duck* (1979), *Dead Meet* (1988).

WINSLOW, STEVE See HALL, PARNELL.

WITHERALL, LEONIDAS A comical amateur sleuth in a series of novels by Phoebe Atwood TAYLOR. Witherall looks like William Shakespeare, and people call him Bill. Under a pseudonym, he writes mystery novels about a Lieutenant Haseltine. Witherall is a retired teacher who lives in the Boston area and gets into a variety of crazy adventures, which always involve finding a corpse and (except in the first book) getting blamed for the murder. He spends a lot of time twirling his pince-nez, saying "M'yes," and dashing around town. Another hallmark of the Witherall series is the startling opening scene. In the first book, *Beginning with a Bash* (1938), he encounters a former student carrying a golf bag in Boston—not so odd, except that it is winter, and the student is being chased by the police. The man enters the bookstore where Witherall is working as a janitor (his pension from his private school is not enough). At the opening of *The Cut Direct* (1938), he has just been hit by a car. In THE LEFT LEG (1940), Witherall has a fight with a woman on a bus and gets kicked off. In *Dead Ernest* (1944), a freezer is unexpectedly delivered to him, but the contents are even more of a surprise (the pun in the title gives more than a hint).

By the time of *Cold Steal* (1939), Witherall is living in Dalton, Massachusetts, and teaching at a boys' school. Returning from a trip, he sees a mousy middle-aged woman hiding a bag that contains a gun and a pair of handcuffs, which are whisked away before he can secure them. A corpse is found on the train when it pulls in. Witherall gets a couple more nasty surprises when he arrives home to his new house, which the builder has made imposing and modernist rather than traditional. There is also a dead body in it.

Taylor used the same New England humor as in her Asey MAYO series, but Witherall's adventures tend to be set among a more sophisticated group. The main character is also fond of literary references and verbal jokes. In *File for Record* (1943), Witherall has become the owner of Meredith's Academy and is on the board of directors of a department store. All is not well, however; when he goes to get an umbrella because the weather has turned bad, he winds up unconscious in a bread basket on the back of a wagon. At home, he finds a corpse stabbed with a samurai sword, and, of course, he is the first suspect.

The Witherall books, like the Asey Mayo novels, have been republished by Foul Play Press. Both series are initially amusing but a steady diet of them becomes like one too many Yankee boiled dinners.

BIBLIOGRAPHY Novels: *The Hollow Chest* (1941), *The Iron Clew* (1947; British title *The Iron Hand*).

WITHERS, HILDEGARDE A sleuth created by Stuart PALMER, the frumpish, funny Withers is a homely and proper schoolmarm. Her first case, *The Penguin Pool Murders* (1931), involves the discovery of a corpse during a field trip. A busybody and a know-it-all, Withers has endeared herself to fans of the homespun or cute detective, and has been dismissed by BARZUN and TAYLOR as not even a good caricature. She is, in fact, an Americanized version of the familiar spinster detective of English mystery fiction. She wears ugly hats, smells of chalk, and of course is "horse-faced." Her surname, however, refers to another part of the horse's anatomy.

Withers is a thorn in the side of Inspector Oscar Piper of the New York City Police Department. He is the typical policeman who warns the amateur that he is going to do something about her meddling, but somehow never does. Later in the Withers series, the sleuth retires to Los Angeles (coincidentally, Piper often winds up there, too), where the author had gone to work in the film industry. Withers was a natural for movie adaptation, and starting in 1932 was the subject of half a dozen films. The last novel in the series, *Hildegarde Withers Makes the Scene* (1969), was finished by Fletcher Flora.

In a collaborative series of stories with Craig RICE, Withers was paired with her polar opposite, John J. MALONE. *The Riddles of Hildegarde Withers* (1947) is a collection of short stories featuring the schoolmarm alone.

BIBLIOGRAPHY Novels: *Murder on the Wheels* (1932), *Murder on the Blackboard* (1932), *The Puzzle of the Pepper Tree* (1933), *The Puzzle of the Silver Persian* (1934), *The Puzzle of the Red Stallion* (1936; British title *The Puzzle of the Briar Pipe*), *The Puzzle of the Blue Banderilla* (1937), *The Puzzle of the Happy Hooligan* (1941), *Miss Withers Regrets* (1947), *Four Lost Ladies* (1949), *The Green Ace* (1950), *Nipped in the Bud* (1951), *Cold Poison* (1954; British title *Exit Laughing*),

Short Stories: *People versus Withers and Malone* (1963).

WOLFE, NERO A GENIUS DETECTIVE created by Rex STOUT. Wolfe first appeared in FER-DE-LANCE (1934) and went on to have one of the longest and most successful careers of any series character. Wolfe lives in a brownstone on Thirty-fifth Street in Manhattan, and solves most of his cases without ever leaving his home. Wolfe is attached to his residence because he is (1) enormous; (2) indolent; (3) a gourmet, and prefers to eat the elegant meals prepared by his chef, Fritz Brenner; (4) assisted by Archie GOODWIN, who does his legwork for him; and (5) a cultivator of orchids, 10,000 of which are housed on the top floor of his brownstone. He also enjoys compelling others to conform to his schedule, which includes two almost inviolable hours each morning and afternoon with his beloved plants.

Wolfe gives a blunt statement of his aims in *Too Many Cooks* (1938): "I entrap criminals, and find evidence to imprison them or kill them, for hire." This is meant literally; sometimes Wolfe persuades the murderer to commit suicide, as in *Booby Trap* (1944), in which the culprit blows himself to pieces in a park, or *Fer-de-Lance*, which involves an even more spectacular exit. In *Black Orchids* (1941), the killer is made to unwittingly gas himself.

One of the interesting things about Wolfe is that he is a tough guy—or at least a tough *mind*—swathed in layers of urbanity and fat. There is more than one echo of Conan DOYLE. Nero Wolfe looks very much like Sherlock HOLMES's brother, Mycroft, and has a similarly lazy disposition. Wolfe can also be pedantic, and is a strict grammarian. He refuses to accept the word "contact" as a verb, and rejects "ad" as an abbreviation. Wolfe even has his own MORIARTY, in the person of Arnold ZECK; their "Final Problem" is IN THE BEST FAMILIES (1950). Stout chose not to have his detective age during the course of the series; he said "I hope he lives forever." Like Holmes, Wolfe strikes many people as being a real person. He was the subject of a "biography" by BARING-GOULD.

Despite his air of complete rectitude and immunity to human passions (particularly of the sexual and political sort), Wolfe was sometimes maneuvered by Stout into pursuing the author's own extra-literary crusades. In *The Second Confession* (1949), Wolfe somewhat unbelievably undertakes to find evidence that a man who is involved with the daughter of a rich mining executive, James U. Sperling, is a communist. This mundane and sordid case eventually develops into a struggle against Arnold Zeck, but in it Wolfe hardly sparkles, and as though in protest against the plot, does very little himself. Archie Goodwin's performance is entertaining, however, especially when he is slipped a MICKEY FINN at the same time as he is trying to slip one to his pigeon.

How fat is Wolfe? Goodwin frequently mentions that Wolfe weighs a seventh of a ton, or 285 pounds, 11 ounces. But Wolfe presumably does not weigh that much in *Not Quite Dead Enough* (1942), in which he decides to enlist in the Army to help the war effort. He exercises four hours per day, gives up beer, bread, cream, and sugar. Archie, now a major, comes home and finds nothing but oranges, prunes, lettuce, tomatoes, and applesauce. (The book's only other noteworthy feature is its bloodthirsty talk about "killing Germans.") In *In the Best Families,* Wolfe has to go on the lam to avoid being killed, and loses 117 pounds as part of a disguise. This would bring him down to an inconceivable 168 pounds; no wonder Archie says the skin is hanging off him in folds. THE BLACK MOUNTAIN (1954) includes improbably vigorous activities in Yugoslavia that Wolfe somehow performs without having a heart attack, having hardly moved in the twenty years since his first appearance. In *The Rubber Band* (1936), Wolfe initiates an exercise program by taking up darts. The reason behind his quite intentional obesity is that Wolfe was once almost starved to death and, like Scarlet O'Hara, vowed never to be hungry again.

The real substance of the Wolfe novels is the by-play between Wolfe and Archie Goodwin, supplemented by Wolfe's arguments with the long-suffering Inspector CRAMER, lengthy interviews with suspects and clients, and Goodwin's reporting of his own investigations and those of regular legmen Orrie Cather, Fred Durkin, and Saul Panzer—the latter a completely unobtrusive and nondescript man who is called the best operative in New York. In some novels, particularly the later ones, the plots are quite thin and the wisecracking has grown old. On the other hand, the series includes one acknowledged masterpiece, THE LEAGUE OF FRIGHTENED MEN (1935). Other good books in the series are: SOME BURIED CAESAR (1939), AND BE A VILLAIN (1948; British title *More Deaths Than One*), MURDER BY THE BOOK (1951), and A RIGHT TO DIE (1964; sequel to *Too Many Cooks,* 1938).

In addition to the novels, Rex Stout wrote many collections of novellas or novelettes. These short pieces are never as successful as the novels, though some are ingenious. The last volume of novelettes was published in the early sixties, but *Corsage* (1977) anthologized for the first time the novelette *Bitter End,* a Wolfe novelette based on the Tecumseh FOX novel *Bad for Business.* This piece was reprinted in *Death Times Three* (1985) along with other novelettes. See also BASEBALL.

BIBLIOGRAPHY Novels: *The Red Box* (1937), *Over My Dead Body* (1940), *The Silent Speaker* (1946), *Too Many Women* (1947), *Prisoner's Base* (1952), *The Golden Spiders* (1953), *Before Midnight* (1955), *Might As Well Be Dead* (1956), *If Death Ever Slept* (1957), *Champagne for One* (1958), *Plot It Yourself* (1959; British title *Murder in Style*), *Too Many Clients* (1960), *The Final Deduction* (1961), *Gambit* (1962), *The Mother Hunt* (1963), *The Doorbell Rang* (1965), *Death of a Doxy* (1966), *The Father Hunt* (1968), *Death of a Dude* (1969), *Please Pass the Guilt* (1973), *A Family Affair* (1975).

Novelettes: *Black Orchids* (1942), *Trouble in Triplicate* (1949), *Three Doors to Death* (1950), *Curtains for Three* (1950), *Triple Jeopardy* (1952), *Three Men Out* (1954), *Three Witnesses* (1956), *And Four to Go* (1958; British title *Crime and Again*), *Three for the Chair* (1957), *Three at Wolfe's Door* (1960), *Homicide Trinity* (1962), *Trio for Blunt Instruments* (1963).

WOMAN IN WHITE, THE (1860) A novel by Wilkie COLLINS, considered by some to be superior to THE MOONSTONE (1868). It uses one of the most popular themes of the Victorian novel, the inheritance, and one of its favorite villains, the weak debtor who is drawn to crime in order to solve his financial problems. Laura Fairlie stands to inherit a large fortune. Her father, Frederick Fairlie, a rich hypochondriac, engages a tutor, the artist Walter Hartright, for her and her half-sister Marian. Although she is in love with Hartright, Laura is married to Sir Percival Glyde, who is plagued by debts. Glyde's friend, the evil Count FOSCO, convinces him to fake Laura's death in order to get hold of the estate. Meanwhile, a woman named Anne Catherick is languishing in an insane asylum; because she looks like Laura, the plan is to substitute Laura for her when Anne dies. Thus, Anne is duly buried in a grave as "Laura Fairlie," and Laura is held captive as Anne. The real Laura then has no proof of her own existence; she, her half-sister, and her lover struggle to defeat her corrupt husband and the devious count.

The Woman in White was serialized in DICKENS's magazine *All the Year Round,* and was an instant success. Collins partly based the story on a French case of the previous century, and also on his own experience: it is often noted that the scene in which a woman in white accosts Hartright mirrors the way in which Collins first met his lover and companion of many years, Caroline Graves.

WOMEN A "boom" in stories about female detectives is usually dated to the late 1970s and early 1980s, when writers such as Sue GRAFTON, Marcia MULLER, and Sara PARETSKY became prominent in the mystery field. Patricia CORNWELL was a later but even more successful entrant in the subgenre. All of these authors write about female series protagonists; although they worked in feminist themes, they adhered more or less closely to the conventions of the HARD-BOILED or PROCEDURAL style. A new wave of authors who write about female sleuths, including

Margaret MARON, Laurie R. KING, and Barbara NEELY, signal a shift in women's mystery writing toward the "alternative" mystery that foregrounds race, class, and sexuality.

But the proportion of female mystery writers, as opposed to characters, has always been large, and women might even be said to have dominated the genre. During the GOLDEN AGE of detective writing, the leading British mystery writers were women (Agatha CHRISTIE, Ngaio MARSH, Margery ALLINGHAM, and Dorothy L. SAYERS), though only one of them wrote about a female detective (Miss Jane MARPLE). These writers continue to be popular and never go out of print, while some of their male counterparts who were giants in their day, particularly John RHODE, are unknown to many mystery readers.

The creation of a successful twentieth-century female sleuth was long in coming (for nineteenth-century female detectives, see below). Mary Roberts RINEHART tried and failed to make a compelling character of the nurse Hilda ADAMS; she succeeded better with TISH, but neither was as successful as her non-series work. Mignon G. EBERHART, on the other hand, became famous for her well-received mysteries about nurse Sarah KEATE.

During the Golden Age, male writers had less success writing about female sleuths (with the exception of Erle Stanley Gardner's Bertha COOL) than female writers did writing about men—as the continuing appeal of Lord Peter WIMSEY, Hercule POIROT, Inspector ALLEYN, and Alan GRANT would show. One of the few men who tried to create a female detective, Rex STOUT, wrote only one mystery with Doll BONNER as protagonist. Edgar WALLACE wrote an amusing series about a female thief, FOUR SQUARE JANE.

Although Kay SCARPETTA, Kinsey MILLHONE, and other female detectives are now among the most popular in the genre, they are by no means pioneers. The female detective has existed as a viable character since the mid-nineteenth century. The first collection of stories about a female detective—called, simply, *The Female Detective* (1864)—was published by a man, Andrew FORRESTER, Jr. In the same year, another Englishman, William S. Hayward, published *Revelations of a Lady Detective.* In the last quarter of the nineteenth century, female detectives became common, constituting a new subgenre. Among the most famous of these sleuths was Loveday BROOKE, the most important nineteenth-century female detective to be created by a woman (C. L. PIRKIS). L. T. MEADE also wrote about female protagonists, both detectives and villains.

Ellery QUEEN's anthology of stories about women detectives, *The Female of the Species* (1943; British title *Ladies in Crime*) was for long the definitive collection of the subgenre. A sampling of early stories featuring female detectives from the Victorian era to the forties is also given in *Crime on Her Mind* (1975), edited by Michele B. Slung. The editor includes a catalogue of 100 women detectives, covering the period 1861–1974. Historical revisionism has provided further mysteries set in this period, including the adventures of Victorian Egyptologist Amelia PEABODY, and Gillian Linstock's HISTORICAL MYSTERIES. New anthologies of stories about women detectives abound. A primary source book and bibliographical reference devoted to female mystery writers and their sleuths is *Detecting Women* (1994), which lists 450 series detectives created by women, but does not cover the nineteenth century.

As far as attitudes toward women in mystery fiction are concerned, distrust of women and misogyny are unfortunately features of many mystery and detective stories. Like all popular literature, the genre reflects the tastes and prejudices of the times, which may not make the views any less offensive. Several characters, however, *consciously* express their negative judgement of women as a philosophical position. Of these, the primary example is Sherlock HOLMES, who says that "Women are never to be entirely trusted—not the best of them." The most famous misogynist detective is Nero WOLFE, who dislikes even having women in his house. His respect for them is purely Darwinian; he states that they are "astounding and successful animals." (Of course, the fact that a character expresses misogynistic attitudes does not mean that the author holds the same views). Mike HAMMER and some other HARD-BOILED private eyes had a sexist approach to women that was actually violent.

W.O.O.C.(P). The most secret and smallest branch of British Intelligence in Len DEIGHTON's THE IPCRESS FILE (1962), to which Harry PALMER is seconded. The name satirizes the intelligence services' love of acronyms.

WOOD, MRS. HENRY (born Ellen Price, 1814–1887) The English writer who published as Mrs. Henry Wood has been described as a "crude" and "sensational" writer, but in her time she was immensely popular because of her novel *East Lynne* (1861). Melodramatic she undoubtedly was, but perhaps no more so than melodramatic writers of today. In the novel, Lady Isabel Vane runs away from her husband with another man; later, she returns disguised as a nurse in order to care for her own children. This tear-jerking plot was adapted for the stage and was if anything even more successful in that form.

Ellen Price was the daughter of a Worcester glove maker. Born with a deformed spine, her activity was restricted and she was a reader and writer from an early age. Henry Wood was a banker; after her marriage in 1836, Mrs. Wood lived much of the time in France. She contributed to various magazines, and in 1867 bought *The Argosy,* in which most of her work was serialized.

Although her romantic novels are no longer taken seriously or widely read, Mrs. Wood wrote a number of books involving mystery and detection, including *The Channings* (1862), *Trevlyn Hold* (1864), *Within the Maze* (1872), and *The Master of Graylands* (1873). One of her other novels, published anonymously, was so reactionary and anti-worker that it caused a riot.

Like many of her contemporaries, Wood may have done her best work in the short story form. In *The Argosy,* she published a series of short stories about Johnny Ludlow, a boy attached to the family of Squire Todhetley, a good-hearted but credulous Worcestershire landowner. These stories were collected in *Johnny Ludlow, First Series* (1874) and other volumes. They are well written, and Mrs. Wood's forbearance in the area of romance is rewarded with sometimes vivid scenes of Victorian life. "Going through the Tunnel" concerns imposture and a con game aboard a TRAIN. The etiquette of the railway, still a fairly recent invention, works to the disadvantage of the gentlemen, and the behavior between the sexes and classes is remarkable. "The Ebony Box," singled out by Dorothy SAYERS, is a long story that shows how suspicion builds when a box filled with gold guineas disappears—not once, but twice—and how public opinion and small-town small-mindedness leads to the persecution of a young lawyer thought to have taken it.

WOODS, SARA (pen name of Sara Bowen-Judd, 1922–1985) Sara Woods was forty before she wrote her first book, *Bloody Instructions* (1962), but from then until the end of her life she was prolific and successful. Her barrister sleuth Antony MAITLAND appears in forty-eight novels. Although it is implausible that he gets embroiled in so many mysteries before they become cases, the trial scenes are realistic and believable. Like Perry MASON, Maitland is a defender rather than a prosecutor (except in *Cry Guilty,* 1981). The titles of the books are all Shakespearean quotations.

Woods's legal background came from her work in the office of her brother, a London solicitor. Woods was married to an engineer and moved to Nova Scotia in 1957; all of her books were written there, so she has been adopted as a Canadian writer.

WOOLRICH, CORNELL (1903–1968) Cornell Woolrich was one of the strangest writers in a genre with more than its share of eccentrics. Born in New York City, Woolrich went to Mexico when he was three with his father, a mining engineer whose business took him all over South America. These youthful experiences are visible in such works as THE BLACK PATH OF FEAR (1944), partly set in Havana, and *Black Alibi* (1942), a story about a publicity stunt gone awry (it was filmed in 1943 as *The Leopard Man*). Late in life, Woolrich became a recluse and lived in a hotel with his mother. A chronic alcoholic, he let a foot infection fester and had to have his leg amputated. He died shortly thereafter.

Despite the grimness of his end—and of much of his fiction—Woolrich started out his career as something of a golden boy. Woolrich attended Columbia University for three years but dropped out; he had already begun writing his first novel while still a student. Entitled *Children of the Ritz,* it won a $10,000 prize. Woolrich's early books were heavily indebted to F. Scott FITZGERALD (who had published "A Diamond as Big as the Ritz" in 1922). Woolrich now had money to go with his Fitzgerald image. He wrote several more derivative novels before he came up with his first crime novel, THE BRIDE WORE BLACK (1940). Although badly written, the story had the originality and power of Woolrich's best work, using the themes of obsession and revenge that were steady undercurrents in his crime stories. Woolrich was also preoccupied by madness, AMNESIA, guilt, and terror. He invented a kind of urban GOTHIC in which the city is one vast House of Usher, populated with sick people, like the emasculated veteran in his last book, INTO THE NIGHT (1987), who is so tortured by his unfulfillable desires that he handcuffs himself to a steam pipe in his dismal room. The terrible anonymity and loneliness of modern industrial society are a source of equally terrible, sometimes blackly humorous ironies: in I MARRIED A DEAD MAN (1948), a fatal train accident allows a woman to slip into the identity of a dead woman. *Waltz Into Darkness* (1947) explores the possibilities of the mail-order bride scenario (unlike most Woolrich novels, this one is set in the past, the year 1880). In the story "Postmortem," a woman learns that her late husband held a winning lottery ticket, and that it was in the pocket of the suit he wore in his casket. In "Three O'Clock," a husband sets a bomb to kill his wife and then is set upon by burglars who leave him tied up in the basement. Although Woolrich was not very concerned with believability, he invented some of the most ingenious plots in mystery and suspense fiction. Perhaps his most famous story is "Rear Window," in which a man laid up in his apartment by a broken leg witnesses what seems to be a murder in the apartment across the way. It was made into a film by Alfred HITCHCOCK. Many of Woolrich's books were filmed, and he himself worked briefly in Hollywood.

Although Woolrich was married and divorced, Francis M. NEVINS establishes in *Cornell Woolrich: First You Dream, Then You Die* (1988) that Woolrich was gay. Woolrich gave conflicting information about his life, and no doubt a psychoanalytic reading of his work would find corollaries in his life for the guilt and fear of his characters. In actual fact, Woolrich's tales are so much the product of wild ingenuity and imagination that his biography is largely irrelevant to an appreciation of his work.

WORMOLD, JIM The mild-tempered vacuum cleaner salesman in Graham Greene's OUR MAN IN HAVANA (1958) who allows himself to be recruited as a spy by the British government in order to raise money to support the whims of his endearing but flighty daughter, Milly. Pressed to produce some "intelligence," Wormold draws pictures of vacuum cleaner parts, exaggerates the scale and claims they are mysterious weapons. The story is farcical, but Wormold's discovery of reservoirs of belief and strength in the face of danger is not. The anti–Cold War message is somewhat belabored in the end.

WRECKER, THE (1892) An adventure story by Robert Louis STEVENSON and Lloyd Osborne, sometimes classed as a mystery. The narrator, Loudon Dodd, joins his friend Jim Pinkerton in buying a wreck at auction in San Francisco. They pay an outrageous fifty thousand dollars for the *Flying Scud,* which lies wrecked on Midway Island, based on a rumor that the ship contains opium. The crew, rescued by a British warship from Midway, suddenly disappear. A chase ensues to get to the wreck and solve the mystery. A number of clues are discovered on the wreck, but the key to the mystery is a shadowy REMITTANCE MAN.

WRECK OF THE MARY DEARE, THE (1956) A novel by Hammond INNES that combines the sea story, suspense, and mystery. It is also very believable (not always the case with suspense, or with Innes), and the characters fully realized. The narrator, John Sands, has left his insurance job at Lloyds after putting aside money to buy a boat. He and his friend Mike work at salvaging until they are able to buy the *Sea Witch,* a two-masted 40-tonner. While crossing the English Channel with the boat to Southampton for a refit, they are nearly run down in heavy weather by a ship, the *Mary Deare;* apparently there is no one aboard, and the ship is going full speed ahead. The ship presents a mystery similar to that of the MARY CELESTE, and the salvage man Sands cannot resist going aboard what would be a major windfall for his fledgling company. During his search, Sands finds scraps of information about the disappeared crew, and evidence that the ship had been through a severe gale, an explosion, and a fire. Just as Sands discovers that he is not alone after all, the storm outside becomes more violent, and in his attempt to escape he is nearly torn from the side of the ship. Thus marooned on the *Mary Deare,* Sands continues to pick up pieces of the story of the unlucky derelict. Told with relentless suspense, *The Wreck of the Mary Deare* describes the horror and fatigue of the battle against the sea, but it is more than a sailing yarn. The story has a dark center, presenting a grim picture of human turpitude. Innes remains true to his subject, and instead of a routine victory over all odds, ends on a note of despair. The story's hardness and fatalism as much as its subject show the influence of CONRAD.

WREN, M. K. (pseudonym of Martha Kay Renfroe, 1938–) Martha Kay Renfroe has hit upon three subgenres of mystery fiction at the same time. Her series about bookstore-owning private detective Conan FLAGG is part of the regional boom (the books are set in Oregon), the bibliophile subgenre (see BOOKS), and even has a CAT in it. With this amount of overkill, the books are not only COZY but cutesy. Wren has written SCIENCE FICTION in addition to her mysteries.

WRIGHT, L[AURALI] R[OSE] (1939–) The Canadian author L. R. Wright began her series of novels about Royal Canadian Mounted Police Sergeant Karl Alberg in 1985 with *The Suspect,* which won an EDGAR award. A former reporter in Ontario, Wright sets the stories in British Columbia. Alberg is a middle-aged divorced man. The novels focus on the relationships between people and issues like loneliness, love, and personal loss. Crime (not necessarily murder) is one cause of loss—and sometimes of need. In *A Touch of Panic* (1994), a sadist and killer is searching for what he thinks will be his one true love. Unfortunately, he fastens on Cassandra, Alberg's girlfriend, as his candidate. One subplot involves a quirky older woman who drives a cab and another woman (thrown out of the house by her husband) who moves in with her. Wright's approach to her characters is similar to that of Ruth RENDELL in the Barbara Vine books, or to Margaret Atwood. In addition to several other Alberg mysteries, Wright produced several non-series books before writing *The Suspect.*

WRIGHT, WILLARD HUNTINGTON See VAN DINE, S. S.

WRIGHTSVILLE A small town, the setting for several of the Ellery QUEEN novels. Wrightsville has the feeling of an Upstate New York town, and is so described in *The Murderer is a Fox* (1945), though elsewhere it is placed in New England.

WRITE WHAT YOU KNOW This familiar author's axiom applies to a number of mystery authors: Dashiell HAMMETT was a Pinkerton operative; Joseph WAMBAUGH was in the Los Angeles Police Department; William LEQUEUX was a spy; Cyril Coles and Adelaide Manning (Manning COLES) both worked in British intelligence, as did John LE CARRÉ, Graham GREENE, Valentine WILLIAMS, and others; Erskine CHILDERS was a diplomat who ran guns with his yacht and was shot during the Irish Civil War; Charles MCCARRY worked for the CIA; Dorothy UHNAK was in the New York City Transit Police for fourteen years, and Ed DEE was a policeman in the same city; Janwillem VAN DE WETERING worked for the police in Amsterdam; Joe GORES was for a dozen years a private detective; Geoffrey HOMES also worked for a time as a private dick; John WAINWRIGHT was a Yorkshire policeman; and Parnell HALL was a private eye. The policemen in the above list often wrote in the PROCEDURAL format, and have been praised for the accuracy of their depictions of routine. Some of the espionage veterans, like LeQueux, wrote stories full of fantasy, glamour, and adventure, while others like Le Carré depicted spying as nasty and ignoble. Perhaps the earliest secret agent who became a writer was Daniel DEFOE.

On the other side of the law are writers like Chester HIMES, who did time for robbery. These writers have attracted attention for their particularly realistic, unromantic, scary, and often very disturbing works written from the inside, literally. Among them are Edward BUNKER, who spent half his life in jail.

"WRONG HAND, THE" (1918) Although one can see the ending coming from miles away, Melville Davisson Post's "The Wrong Hand" is one of the most spectacular of the Uncle ABNER stories. Abner goes to visit Gaul, the hunchback, whose brother Enoch has slashed his own throat with a razor. Gaul has inherited everything, leaving Enoch's children dispossessed. Sleet is falling, and the scene inside is like a picture by the brothers Grimm: a burning apple tree stuck in the great fireplace, the hunchback on his threadbare throne, with his blue coat and a cane with a gold piece in it. Gaul is tough as a knotted, stunted oak, and Abner is "like a man of stone"—two such immovable objects must collide. As in a fairy tale, Abner's nephew is wrapped up in his giant uncle's greatcoat and watches the scene through a buttonhole. The battle is a philosophical one, with Gaul flinging out that "it was Abner's God" who made him a twisted thing; he calls God a "scarecrow," a fake whom he has found out. It can be no coincidence that Gaul and *gall* are homophones. Abner is magnificently controlled, bending Gaul to his will, putting flesh on the "scarecrow," and eliciting the truth.

"WRONG HOUSE, THE" One of the most famous RAFFLES stories, collected in THE BLACK MASK (1901). Fog interferes with Raffle's plan to burglarize a stockbroker's house. Raffles refers to the caper as "the Apotheosis of the Bunny" because of the way in which his accomplice Bunny Manders saves the day. Bunny does pull one dumb play, however; when they go to escape on their bicycles he takes the route leading uphill, not down.

WYCLIFFE, CHARLES Detective Chief Superintendent Charles Wycliffe is a large, taciturn presence in the novels of W. J. BURLEY. Reserved and essentially kindly, Wycliffe investigates crimes mostly in the West of England. Although fiftyish and well up in the hierarchy, Wycliffe mostly does his own legwork, like Jules MAIGRET.

Despite his rank and profession, Wycliffe is intuitive rather than PROCEDURAL in his investigations, which necessitates his stooping to involve himself in cases that interest him, much like an amateur sleuth. Wycliffe seems to be drawn particularly to cases that involve sex. In *To Kill a Cat* (1970), the victim is a prostitute and striptease artist who is strangled and mutilated in a hotel. *Death in Stanley Street* (1974) also involves the murder of a prostitute. *Three-Toed Pussy* (1968) has a sexually attractive and available woman found murdered in her cottage in Wales. Women are also victims in *Guilt Edged* (1971) and *Death in a Salubrious Place* (1973). Whatever it says about Wycliffe's preoccupations, the narrowness of subject matter leads to some repetition and also a suspicion that shock value has been used as a crutch.

In the later books, however, Burley goes further afield for plots. *Wycliffe and the Scapegoat* (1978) concerns an old Cornish ritual in which a human effigy is affixed to a wheel and rolled flaming off a cliff into the sea to bring the community good luck. Naturally, a substitution is mysteriously made. In keeping with the ancient background of the story, the victim is named Riddle, who, comically, happens to be an undertaker as well as a local tycoon.

BIBLIOGRAPHY Novels: *Wycliffe and the Pea-Green Boat* (1975), *Wycliffe and the Schoolgirls* (1976), *The Schoolmaster* (1977), *Wycliffe in Paul's Court* (1980), *Wycliffe's Wild Goose Chase* (1982), *Wycliffe and the Beales* (1983), *Wycliffe and the Four Jacks* (1985), *Wycliffe and the Quiet Virgin* (1986), *Wycliffe and the Windsor Blue* (1987), *Wycliffe and the Tangled Web* (1988),

Wycliffe and the Cycle of Death (1990), *Wycliffe and the Redhead* (1997).

WYLDER'S HAND (1864) A novel by Sheridan LE FANU. Mark Wylder is a former naval lieutenant who is about to marry the heiress Dorcas Brandon, a "grave and listless beauty," to settle the feud of the intertwined (and interbred) Wylder and Brandon families. The narrator, Charles de Cresseron, is an acquaintance of Wylder's, and tells the story from the perspective of old age.

While the company are passing the time waiting for the wedding, Stanley Lake arrives. Stanley is the brother of the blonde-haired Rachel Lake, a more natural and healthy beauty than Dorcas and with a strong streak of integrity. Her brother, however, is a bad hat, though Wylder is no paragon himself—"little better than a sailor ashore, and not a good specimen of that class of monster." Stanley Lake and Mark Wylder are on a collision course; then Mark abruptly leaves for London on sudden business, and after sending a series of curt letters, goes to the Continent and continues to write from France and Italy. His reappearance long after is a stunning, horrifying moment.

The narration by Cresseron is far more fluid than that in UNCLE SILAS (1864), enlivened by his humorous observations of others ("Captain Lake was a gentleman and an officer, and of course an honorable man; but somehow I should not have liked to buy a horse from him") and his startling encounters with the ghostly figure of Uncle Lorne. Stanley Lake's selfish manipulations and self-justifications are outrageous and so believable that he is sickeningly human. Although the outcome is not hard to guess, the other characters have interesting personalities and even more interesting secrets.

WYLIE, PHILIP [GORDON] (1902–1971) Philip Wylie was a prolific writer of mysteries, SCIENCE FICTION, and crime stories. He collaborated with Edwin BALMER and published under several pseudonyms. Wylie was born in Massachusetts and educated at Princeton University. He worked for *The New Yorker* and also wrote screenplays. Wylie was a competent writer who often seems to have worked in a hurry, leaving a spare, plain prose in which story is all. His novels and novelettes are now unread and difficult to find. Wylie spent a lot of time in Florida and set many stories there. In "Murder at Galleon Key" (1935), a storm traps a group of people on an island where Douglas Lee, a ruthless mining magnate, has been harpooned to death. Everyone has a motive—the man he ruined, a cast-off woman from decades before, her jealous husband, and most of all the narrator, who was banished for wanting to marry Lee's daughter. The MODUS OPERANDI is interesting and calls for the assistance of a shark. *Experiment in Crime* (1948) is the story of a sheltered college professor in Miami who is sucked into the underworld, with which he is comically unfamiliar.

WYLLIE, JOHN (1914–) Canadian author of mysteries set in Africa. Wyllie flew with the Royal Air Force during World War II, and afterward, along with his wife, worked for many years with organizations in West Africa, among them the British Red Cross. The Wyllies helped to establish maternity and child welfare clinics and worked with other development projects. Wyllie was over sixty when he wrote his first mystery story.

Unlike other Europeans and North Americans who chose to write African mysteries, such as Elspeth HUXLEY, Wyllie decided to make his detective an African rather than a white man. His name is Samuel QUARSHIE, and he is a "Big Man" in the West African nation of Akhana. The first book in the series was *Skull Still Bone* (1975). In addition to making the hero a black man, Wyllie introduced in an almost allegorical way a lot of information about the turmoil of contemporary Africa. In fact, at times it seems that the series is a vehicle for shedding light on African problems, politics, beliefs, and the legacy of colonialism. Quarshie is often victimized by petty, unscrupulous, and sometimes barbarous government officials. Wyllie cannot be accused of using the setting as "local color," or making it appear exotic. Whether Quarshie is investigating a snake cult, invoking the community's ancestors, or dealing with grotesque poverty and conditions, nothing he encounters is considered strange from his viewpoint—except the behavior of whites, and the ambitious Africans who have adopted their materialism and disrespect for the environment and the people who live in it. Other books in the series are *The Butterfly Flood* (1975) and *The Killer Breath* (1979). While Quarshie's debates with the other characters over comparative religion (indigenous polytheism versus Christian monotheism) and economics (pan-Africanism and free trade) are extraneous to the plots, they reveal the author's deep experience and prevent the investigations from being merely a variety of safari.

WYNNE, ANTHONY See HAILEY, DR. EUSTACE.

X, MR. Another name by which Arnold ZECK is known.

YACHTING See MURDER AFLOAT.

YAFFE, JAMES (1927–) Born in Chicago and raised in New York City, James Yaffe wrote his first story for *Ellery Queen's Mystery Magazine* while he was still in high school. He went on to win several prizes in the magazine's contests for his "Mom" stories. Mom is the mother of a New York City police detective and solves cases for her son without ever leaving her house in the Bronx. Yaffe's other works include *Nothing but the Night* (1957), which was based on the LEOPOLD AND LOEB case.

YAP Apart from the meaning "mouth," *yap* began as a slang term for "farmer." Like RUBE, it subsequently developed the meaning of sucker or dupe. In the thirties, it was used to mean a small-time or novice criminal.

YEGG Dating from the latter part of the nineteenth century, the term *yegg* originated in San Francisco and referred to a beggar or tramp. Later it came to mean thief, a safe blower especially. The word is said to have come from a corruption of a Chinese word ("yekk") that was used by the residents of Chinatown to tell beggars to get lost.

"YELLOW FACE, THE" See DOYLE, SIR ARTHUR CONAN.

YELLOW ROOM, THE (1945) A late novel by Mary Roberts RINEHART, set at the end of World War II and full of returning servicemen. It follows what Rinehart referred to as her usual format: a "surface" plot, a "hidden" plot underneath it, and a romance. It also takes place among the wealthy New York–Bar Harbor set, of which Rinehart herself was a member. Carol Spenser is on her way to Maine with her aged mother to open up their house, Crestview, so that Carol's brother Greg can stay there while on leave from the Army. On the way, Carol stops to leave her mother with Carol's older sister, Elinor; Elinor seems very distracted and disappears for long periods of time. Things become more suspicious when Carol arrives in Maine. The door of Crestview is open, but there is no sign of preparations for their arrival, and the house is permeated by a burning odor. A charred body of a woman dressed in fragments of a negligée and a fur jacket is found in an upstairs closet. Rinehart plays up the haunted house element—one of her trademarks. Lucy Norton, who was supposed to prepare the house, is in the hospital, having been scared by a hand reaching out of the closet and grabbing her.

The detective element and the love interest are supplied by Major Jerry Dane, who is in town recuperating from a war wound. There is some intrigue about Dane because no one can find a mention of him in directories of the armed services. Whoever he is, he is able to see through the mistakes of the local cop, Floyd, and eventually identifies the woman who had stayed in the yellow room at Crestview. His efforts to establish the woman's connections with the various families are punctuated by further mysterious acts of violence. Elinor's arrival on the scene to clear herself from suspicion is also a catalyst for more action. *The Yellow Room* is a familiar type of Rinehart story, but with greater complexity.

YELLOW ROOM CONSPIRACY, THE (1994) A novel by Peter DICKINSON. The story begins with two elderly people, Paul Ackerley and Lucy Vereker (Lady Seddons), remembering the murder of Gerry Grantworth shortly before the Suez Crisis in 1956. The only remaining survivors of this political and sexual scandal, Paul and Lucy, longtime lovers, discover that each had suspected that the other was the killer. What follows is a fascinating family saga going back to the eve of World War II and showing the complex relationships that led up to the killing. The center of the action is Blatchards, a sprawling old country house where the five Vereker sisters are raised under the benevolent eye of Lord Vereker and his dizzy wife. It is also where Paul first falls in love with Lucy, and she with—Gerry. He is the most enigmatic of them all, a golden boy who seems to be good at everything, works heroically with Yugoslav partisans during the war, and then somehow loses his way in life. One of Lucy's sisters marries Michael Allwegg, a hirsute, brutal, ambitious, and cruel man. His shady dealings, as well as the Verekers' own attachment to the insular world of Blatchards (where they stage an annual cricket match, "Blatchard v. The World"), help bring about spectacular ruin. The death of Gerry itself is a LOCKED ROOM mystery that is only unraveled at the very end, but it is almost incidental. The real interest of the novel is Dickinson's vivid evocation of a class, a time, and a world that is gone. What is most believable and human about his characters is that, when the chance comes, they reach out desperately but also courageously to heal themselves through the satisfaction of thwarted passions, despite a variety of risks and often with the knowledge that the happiness gained is most forbidden because it is evanescent.

YELLOWTHREAD MYSTERIES A series of novels by William MARSHALL, set in Hong Kong. Yellowthread is the name of the street where the police precinct house is located. The chief character is Harry Feiffer, who presides over a group of Anglo and Asian detectives. One of them is Senior Detective Inspector Christopher Kwan O'Yee, a sarcastic WATSON who taunts Feiffer. Dawson Baume is a pathologist who plays postal chess with Russian Grand Masters. Philip Auden is a dim-witted arch-Brit who longs for the days of colonial ascendancy and subservience by the natives.

Despite the cast, the series is not PROCEDURAL as much as bizarre. The novels have involved AXE murder (*The Hatchet Man,* 1977), flame throwers (*Sci Fi,* 1981), and other outlandish murder methods, motives, and plots. In *Skullduggery* (1979), an identity puzzle, a corpse on a raft floats into the harbor and appears to be a man missing for twenty years, although the false teeth do not match the corpse. Subplots concern a deaf bandit and an elevator robber. The complicated plot involves trips to Macao, secret societies, offshore banking, and a clue provided by an allergy to fur. The story has some resemblances to Michael Innes's THE GAY PHOENIX (1976), published a few years before. In *Out of Nowhere* (1988), one occupant of a van shoots another to death moments before all four passengers are killed in a head-on collision with a truck on a Hong Kong freeway.

Marshall seemed to abandon the Yellowthread series when he began his Manila Bay books, but in 1994 he returned to Yellowthread Street after a six-year hiatus with *Inches.* The series continues to focus on the surreal and the impossible. Detective O'Yee is assigned to a pointless duty by the mysterious police boss known only as RTG-68; O'Yee wanders around town posing as a homeless man and writing the word "Eternity" on the sidewalk. *Nightmare Syndrome* (1997) was the next book in the revived series.

BIBLIOGRAPHY Novels: *Yellowthread Street* (1975), *Gelignite* (1976), *Thin Air* (1977), *Perfect End* (1981), *War Machine* (1982), *The Far Away Man* (1984), *Frogmouth* (1987), *Head First* (1986).

YET SHE MUST DIE (1974) A novel by Sara WOODS. The barrister Antony MAITLAND convinces his uncle to defend a detective story writer, Jeremy Skelton, accused of killing his wife in a manner copied from the famous Julia WALLACE case in Liverpool. Unfortunately for Skelton, his wife had a few days before her murder announced loudly at a party that he had asked her for a divorce and that she had refused. To further complicate matters, Skelton admits in one of the prison interviews that he has been writing a book based on the Wallace case, in which a fake phone call was used to decoy the husband away from the house. Although Skelton appears not to be totally candid, Maitland investigates; the case ends theatrically with the classic courtroom confession of guilt.

YORKE, MARGARET (1924–) Except for one excursion into the detective series, the English author Margaret Yorke has written novels about relationships with murder in them. Yorke was a librarian at Oxford University in the late fifties and early sixties; her one series character, Patrick Grant, is an Oxford professor of English. His first case was *Dead in the Morning* (1970). Grant excited little comment, being one of the bland detectives of the seventies, like Henry TIBBETT. He appeared in four more cases: *Silent Witness* (1972), *Grave Matters* (1973), *Mortal Remains* (1974), and *Cast for Death* (1976).

Although she has been patronized as a "women's writer," Yorke is not a romanticist and does not shy away from ugly subjects. She has dealt with the issue of rape several times, as in *The Hand of Death* (1981). In *Almost the Truth* (1994), a man is blamed for his daughter's rape by a burglar (he urged her not to resist). After the crime, his daughter leaves home, and his already shaky marriage disintegrates. His life ruined, the husband hunts down the criminal, who has already served time in prison.

"YOU SEE, BUT YOU DO NOT OBSERVE" One of the most famous lines in the Sherlock HOLMES stories, it occurs in A SCANDAL IN BOHEMIA (1891).

Z

Z (1966; tr 1968) A novel by the Greek author Vassilis VASSILIKOS. This masterfully written book takes a literary approach to its story of political assassination. Vassilikos based the novel on the murder of Gregory Lambrakis, who was a doctor, a pacifist, and an important figure in protests against Greece's military dictatorship. After his assassination, "Z" became a ubiquitous graffito—signifying *zei,* or "he lives."

The first part of the novel is told from the perspective of witnesses to Z's murder; beginning with the killing, Vassilikos then slowly unravels the plot against Z and the organization of the attack by the police. Then the narrator changes, becoming the soul of Z, flying above the train that is bringing his body back to Athens from Salonika. In a strange and lyrical monologue, he talks to himself, explaining his feelings and the events. This monologue continues to the end of the book, interspersed with other pieces, including the investigation instituted by a courageous prosecutor, stories in the press, and the trial. In his idiosyncratic style, so unlike the usual manner of the THRILLER genre, Vassilikos produces a deep analysis of personality and a profound sense of a living person. The cinematic and poetic techniques used by Vassilikos were perfectly suited (in some ways, perhaps better suited) to film. COSTA-GAVRAS's 1969 adaptation was considered as much of a masterpiece as the original novel.

ZADIG (1747) This novel by Voltaire is considered as an important PROTOMYSTERY, even though the detection occurs in only one chapter. It is actually a case of tracking: Zadig interprets marks left by the queen's dog and the king's horse, deducing obvious features, such as how the horse is shod, and difficult ones, including the fact that the dog recently had a litter. The rest of the story has nothing to do with crime or detection.

ZALESKY, PRINCE A detective created by M. P. SHIEL, Zalesky is a Russian nobleman. The first of the stories to feature Zalesky appeared in 1895, and the last in 1945. The setting is lush, and the prose often purple: Zalesky is "victim of a too importunate, too unfortunate love, which the fulgor of the throne itself could not abash," and when he is excited, in his eye "flitted the wonted falchion flash of the whetted, two-edged intellect." Prince Zalesky, however, rarely stirs from his room in his mansion with its "bat-haunted vaults," a castle as lavishly decorated as a pharaoh's tomb (it includes a sarcophagus and mummy). He is waited on by Ham, his devoted black servant, and only stirs when the narrator, Shiel, brings him a problem. Like Sherlock HOLMES, Zalesky is an addict, but in his case the drug is cannabis.

Zalesky behaves—and thinks—eccentrically to say the least. In "The S.S." (1895), the narrator comes to speak to the great man about the European suicide epidemic, but Zalesky is absorbed in "co-ordinating to one of the calculi certain new properties he had discovered in the parabola," and refuses to talk to him for the first two days. The number of suicides reaches 8,000, and Zalesky becomes preoccupied with the papyrus scrolls found in their mouths. He displays a great deal of learning and facility for ciphers in arriving at the solution, as well as a startling sympathy with the social Darwinism of the time.

The stories were first collected in *Prince* Zalesky (1895). Prince *Zalesky and Cummings King Mark* (1977) includes "The Return of Prince Zalesky," a story that was lost in the mail decades before.

ZANGWILL, ISRAEL (1864–1926) The English journalist Israel Zangwill gave far more of his life to political causes than to the writing of fiction, but he has a secure place in the history of the detective story because he was the first to write a novel-length LOCKED ROOM MYSTERY. This book, THE BIG BOW MYSTERY (1891), was first serialized in the *London Star* and made Zangwill famous as a fiction writer (he had already achieved a degree of notoriety for his Zionism).

Zangwill's father was a peddler from Latvia who had emigrated to England, and his mother was from Poland. The father was often away from home on trips to the West Country, and the family was very poor; the experience of poverty forged the author's political commitments and colored his writings, including his otherwise half-serious mystery novel. Zangwill's father was very devout, and later emigrated to Palestine. Israel Zangwill himself married a Christian, but became an assistant to the Zionist leader Theodor Herzl and was a major figure in the movement in his own right.

After graduating from the University of London, Zangwill wrote articles and short stories for various newspapers and journals (the press is a prominent element in *The Big Bow Mystery*). An essay on Judaism brought Zangwill to the attention of the Jewish Publication Society of America, which sponsored the first of a series of novels about urban Jewish life, *Children of the*

Ghetto (1892). *Ghetto Tragedies* (1893), *The King of Shnorrers* (1894) and other works followed. Zangwill met Herzl in 1895 and became his closest assistant in the effort to found a Jewish national home.

To all of these political activities, *The Big Bow Mystery* was no more than an aside. In a later preface, Zangwill said that he wrote the book in a fortnight in response to a "sudden demand" from the *Star,* for which he was then writing. The preface also stipulates Zangwill's requirements of the ideal mystery, many of which prefigure the tenets of FAIR PLAY conceived decades later. The author also felt in retrospect that he had taken the element of humor too far. Indeed, at times *The Big Bow Mystery* reads like a PARODY, though by the final trial scenes and the surprise ending it has become a suspense novel. The background of the story reflects Zangwill's political commitments, and much of the humor is really social satire against the rich, capitalists, and those proponents of trade unionism more interested in their own glory than in the plight of the worker. Both the victim who is found in the room with his throat cut and the main suspect are trade unionists.

The Big Bow Mystery was first published in book form in 1892. It was short enough to be collected in Zangwill's *The Grey Wig* (1903), a volume of stories, and has been anthologized many times since, for example in *Three Victorian Detective Novels* (1977). Among those writers who were influenced by Zangwill's novel (or novella, or novelette, or long short story) was Gaston LEROUX.

ZECK, ARNOLD The NAPOLEON OF CRIME whom Nero WOLFE runs afoul of in several mysteries, most notably in IN THE BEST FAMILIES (1950). Zeck runs his operations from his command post in Westchester county—a mansion on top of a hill with underground chambers. Zeck has shark-like eyes, thinning hair, and a dome-like forehead, making him not unlike MORIARTY.

ZEN, AURELIO An Italian police detective in a series of novels by Michael DIBDIN. Zen is hardly a sympathetic character, but the series has been highly praised for the author's recreation of the Italian atmosphere and culture, which some have even said is flawless. Whether or not it is the author's intention to show that important police figures are human, Zen is an incredible egotist who is not as smart as he thinks he is. His mind is unsubtle and prejudiced, his grasp of psychology unimpressive; some of his dumb moves cause pain, suffering, and death to others. The first novel, *Ratking* (1988), has Zen investigating the kidnapping of a wealthy businessman in Perugia, where Dibdin had lived for several years. In *Vendetta* (1990), Zen is in Sardinia to investigate the murder of an architect. At the time of *Dead Lagoon* (1994), Zen is a Vice Questore with Criminelpol, a high rank in the most powerful branch of the Italian police. When an ex-lover, an American woman, asks him to investigate a case for a very high fee, he takes a vacation and becomes in effect a private eye working undercover. A rich American has disappeared and the family needs a body in order to inherit, but the case has been closed by higher-ups and to Zen the matter reeks of politics and corruption. The Venetian atmosphere throws an eerie and fantastic light over the case.

In *Così Fan Tutti* (1996), Dibdin uses the famous opera as a palimpsest upon which Zen's most ridiculous adventure is written. Zen has been disgraced and moved to the lowly position of commander of the harbor police in Naples. He does as little as possible, while a gang of garbage men assassinate prominent Neapolitans. The comic-operatic subplot has Zen, posing as "Dottor Zembla," trying to entrap two hoods into being unfaithful to their lovers—the daughters of his landlady. The final sex-comedy ending ties up the tatters of the very loose plot and also has Zen chastised for his total incompetence.

BIBLIOGRAPHY Novels: *Cabal* (1992), *A Long Finish* (1998).

ZENCEY, ERIC See CELEBRITY MYSTERIES.

ZIMMERMAN, BRUCE See GOLF MYSTERIES.

ZINBERG, LEN See LACY, ED.

ZONDI, BANTU DETECTIVE SERGEANT MICKEY Character featured in novels by James MCCLURE. Sergeant Zondi assists Lieutenant Tromp KRAMER in his investigations, and often comes out appearing to be a better investigator. Zondi is a Zulu, and though he has a responsible job and carries a gun, he lives in a segregated neighborhood in a house with a dirt floor. He is married to a Zulu woman, Miriam, and they have five children. Zondi has to retain a submissive attitude toward his white superiors, but McClure is able to communicate the strength, courage, and cunning of the man within. While Kramer talks, Zondi thinks.

ZORAK A character in *No Happy Ending* (1981), by Paco Ignacio TAIBO II, whose story forms a little parable of Mexico. Zorak tries to escape from his past as Arturo Vallespino González, a Durango milkman and gym teacher, disappearing for a month and then reappearing as "Zorak," in a turban, blue Mao jacket, and gold cape.

He does death-defying feats until one of them actually kills him. The story of Zorak's disappearance and attempt to remake his identity is an echo of the story of Flitcraft in THE MALTESE FALCON (1929). The past, Taibo seems to say, cannot simply be shed like dead skin.

ZUBRO, MARK RICHARD See GAY MYSTERIES.